THE LAST HOUR of GANN

This book is dedicated to Joey, Christie, Dawn, Pearl, Melissa, Stacy, Rachel and all the other fine, patient people at Bordertown who watched me write it.

Purplhouse@gmail.com

BOOK I

AMBER

The eviction notice was hanging on the door when they got back from the hospital. The time stamp said 1:27 am, six minutes after Mary Shelley Bierce's official time of death, an hour and twenty-eight minutes before her two daughters sitting in the waiting room had even been informed.

Amber sent Nicci in to bed while she stood out in the hall and read. The eviction gave them thirty days to either vacate or sign under the terms of the new lease, a copy of which was attached. Amber read them. Then she folded up the notice and slipped it into her pocket. She made herself a pot of coffee and sipped at it while watching the news. She thought. She said hello when Nicci woke up and that was all. She went to work.

The funeral was held three days later, a Tuesday. The insurance company covered the cost, which meant it was a group job, and although it was scheduled 'between the hours of eight and eleven,' the other funerals apparently dragged long and then there was lunch and so it was nearly two in the afternoon before Mary's name was called and the cardboard case with her label pasted on the side slid by on the belt and disappeared into the oven. Nicci cried a little. Amber put her arm around her. They got a lot of dirty looks from the other mourners, even though it had only been sixteen years since Measure 34 had passed—Zero Population Growth, Zero Tolerance—and they had both been born by then.

Amber was used to getting dirty looks when she went out with Nicci. Sometimes siblings could pass themselves off as cousins or, even better, as just friends, but not the Bierce girls. Even with different fathers, they were each their mother in miniature and the three years between them had an oddly plastic quality: in the right light, they could be mistaken for twins; in the wrong light, Amber had occasionally been addressed as Nicci's mother. Part of that was the size difference—Nicci was, as their mother used to be, fine-boned and willowy below that round, cherubic face, while Amber was pretty much round all over—but not all of it. "You were just born old, little girl," as her mom used to say. "You were born to take care of things."

She tried to take it as a compliment. The only part of Mary Bierce that knew how to be a mother had been cut out years ago and tossed in a baggie with a biohazard stamp on the side. The parts that were left after that didn't give a damn about homework or lunches or scrubbing out the toilet once in a while. Someone had to be the responsible one and if Amber wasn't actually born knowing that, she sure learned it in hurry.

* * *

There could have been a lot more than two children at the funeral if it hadn't been for Measure 34. Mary Bierce (known to her clients as Bo Peep for her curly blonde hair, big blue eyes and child-sweet face, a name she was quick to capitalize on with frilly panties and ribbons and the intermittent plush sheep) had never been the careful sort. Amber had been putting out cigarettes, sweeping up broken bottles, and making sure the door was locked since she was six; she knew damned well that her mom wasn't going to lose a good tip by insisting her clients wore a condom when she was working. Bo Peep had been to the aborters three times that Amber knew of and there had probably been others, but that all ended with the Zeros and Measure 34. One day, she went off for her regular monthly shots and came staggering home three hours later wearing a diaper. She sort of collapsed onto the sofa, sprawled out like she was drunk, only she wasn't loud and laughing the way she ought to be. Her mouth had hung open slightly and there was some kind of gooey paste caked at the corners of her lips. All her makeup had been wiped away and none too gently; she looked haggard and sick and dead. Nicci—easily frightened under normal circumstances and utterly terrified by this slack-faced stranger who looked like their mom—started crying, and once she did, Mary Bierce burst out into huge, wet sobs also. She lay spread out over the sofa with her legs wide open and that plastic diaper showing under her skirt while her daughters hugged each other and stared, but all she seemed capable of saying was one nonsensical word.

"Spayed!" their mother wept, over and over, until she was screaming it. Screaming and digging at her stomach so hard that one of her bubblegum-pink fingernails broke right off. "Spayed me! *Those motherfuckers spayed me*!"

At last, in a kind of desperation to quiet everybody down before one of the neighbors had them written up again, Amber climbed up on the kitchen counter and brought down a bottle of her mom's black label. She poured a juice glass for Mary and, after a moment's uneasy deliberation, a sippy-cup for Nicci and made them both drink. Within an hour, they were both asleep, but her mom kept crying even then, in a breathy, wailing way she couldn't quite wake up for, and all she could say was that word.

Spayed.

Later, of course, she had plenty to say—about Measure 34 and the Zero-Pop zealots who passed it, about the insurance company and their fine print policies, and about men. It always came back to the men.

"They'll spay the hookers, sure they will," she'd sneer at some point. "But do they ever talk about neutering the fucking johns? Oh no! No, they're still selling Viagra on the fucking TV, that's what they're doing! Let me tell you something, babies, what I do is the most honest work in the world because all women are whores! That's how men see it and if that's how they see it, little girl, that's how it *is*!"

And Amber would nod, because sometimes if you agreed enough early on, the real shouting never got started, but privately she had her doubts. Privately she thought, even then at the age of eight and especially as she got older and Bo Peep Bierce grew more and more embittered, that it didn't prove a whole lot to say that men thought all women were whores when the only men you saw in a day were the ones...well, buying a whore. If you want to hang with a better class of man, Amber would think as she nodded along with her mother's rants, quit whoring.

Not that you could quit these days. But it had still been her choice to start.

And these probably weren't the most respectful thoughts to be having at your mother's funeral. Amber gave Nicci's shaking shoulders a few more pats and tried to think of good things, happy memories, but there weren't many. Her mind got to wandering back toward the eviction and the Manifestors. It had better be today, she decided, listening to Nicci cry.

After the funeral. But today.

* * *

She didn't say anything until they got back to the apartment. Then Amber sat her baby sister at the kitchen table and put two short stacks of papers in front of her. One was the eviction notice, the new lease, and a copy of their mother's insurance policy. The other was an information packet with the words *Manifest Destiny* printed in starry black and white letters on the first page.

"Please," said Nicci, trying to squirm away. "Not right now, okay?"

"Right now," said Amber. She sat down on the other side of the table, then had to reach out and catch her sister's hand to keep her from escaping. It was not a gentle grip, but Amber kept it in spite of Nicci's wince and teary, reproachful look. Sometimes, the bad stuff needed to be said. That was the one thing Mary Bierce used to say that Amber did believe.

"We're going to lose this place," Amber said bluntly. "No matter what we do—"

"Don't say that!"

"—we're going to lose it."

"I can get another job!" Nicci insisted.

"Yeah, you can. So can I. And they'll be two more full-time shifts at minimum wage under that fucking salary cap because we dropped out of school. And that means that the most—the absolute most, Nicci—that we can make between us will be not quite half what we'd need for the new rent."

"What...? N-no..." Nicci fumbled at the papers on the table, staring without comprehension at the neat, lawyerly print on the new lease. "They...They can't do that!"

"Yes, they can. They did. Maybe they couldn't raise Mama's rent, but they can sure do it to us."

"How do they expect us to pay this much every month?"

"They don't. They expect to evict us. They want to get a better class of person in here," she added with a trace of wry humor, "and I can't say I blame them."

"But...But where are we supposed to go?"

"They don't care," said Amber, shrugging. "And they don't have to care. We do. And we've only got about four weeks to figure it out, so you really need to—" She broke it off there and made herself take a few breaths, because *stop whining* wasn't going to move the situation anywhere but from bad to worse. "We need to think," she finished, "about what we can do to help ourselves."

Nicci gave her a wet, blank stare and moved the papers around some more. "I don't...Where...What do you want to do?"

Amber picked up the brochure and moved it a little closer to her sister's trembling hands. "I went to see the Manifestors."

Nicci stared at her. "No," she said. Not in a tough way, maybe, but not as feebly as she'd been saying things either. "Amber, no!"

"Then we're going to have to go on the state." She had a pamphlet for that option, too. She tossed it on the table in front of Nicci with a loud, ugly slap of sound. More a booklet than a pamphlet, really, with none of the pretty fonts and colorful pictures the Manifestors put in their own brochure. "Read it."

"No!"

"Okay. I'll just run down the bullet points for you. To begin with, it'll take six to eight weeks before we're accepted, *if* we're accepted, so we'll still lose this place. However, once we're homeless, there shouldn't be any trouble getting a priority stamp on our application to move into a state-run housing dorm, so there's that."

Nicci put both hands to her face and sobbed harder. Amber's own eyes tried to sting, but she wouldn't let them. Crying was a pointless little-girl thing to do and it hadn't fixed one goddamn thing since it had been invented by the very first pointless little girl. Problems only got solved when you did something about them.

"We'll only be allowed to take one standard-size carry-case each," said Amber evenly, watching her baby sister cry, "and we can't afford a storage pod, so most of this stuff will have to be sold or left behind."

"Stop it! Please, just stop!"

"And we probably won't be able to live together. Not in the same dorm room, maybe not even in the same complex."

"I can't be alone!"

"You won't be alone, Nicci. You'll be rooming with up to seven other women, they'll just be strangers."

"No!"

"We'll lose our jobs and have to work a state-job as partial payment for those dorms, where our salary cap will be half what it is now, so once we move into those dorms, we are never getting out."

"*No*!"

"*Yes*, dammit!" Amber snapped. "These are the facts, Nicci! We can't stay here and nothing we do can change that. This place is all over. Maybe if we had enough time, we could find another place we could afford on just what we're making now, but you know goddamned well that we'd end up on a first-served list and we could be there for years! Where are we going to live in the meantime, huh?"

"You could get more time!" Nicci snatched at the lease, tearing it in her haste. "Did you even ask? There has to be a number that...that you could call and they'll give us more time if they know we're...on a list or..."

"We can file for a four-week extension. That's what we can do, and only if we can prove we can pay the lease at the end of those four weeks. That's all they care about and that's all they have to care about. Everything else is on us."

"Then I'll do like Mama did! I'm not leaving!"

"You mean you want to be a whore."

Nicci flinched. Amber did not.

"You want to do like Mama did," said Amber, ruthless and calm as her stomach churned. "You want to be a whore."

"I..."

"How are you going to fuck men—"

That flinch again.

"—for money—"

Nicci broke, tried to get up. Amber caught her by the wrist again and held on in spite of her sister's squirming efforts to tug free. She hated this, hated herself, but she kept on talking and her voice never shook. Sometimes you had to say the bad stuff, right, Mama? Right.

"—if you can't even admit you'll be a whore?"

"I can do it," whispered Nicci, but she wouldn't look at Amber.

"Maybe you could, but you couldn't do it here, and you had better be sure that's the way you want to go because they don't let you stop anymore once you start. You'll have to get the barcode and you'll be subject to scans at any time. They'll cancel your insurance—look at me, Nicci—and garnish your wages to pay for the state insurance and all your monthly tests, plus the initial registration and the operation where they spay you, and you know it took Mama five years to pay all that off. And in the meantime, where will you be living? Because you won't be able to pay the new lease on a state-paid whore's salary and this place will still be just as gone."

"Stop it!" Nicci shouted. "Stop bullying me! I'm not leaving!"

Amber pressed her lips together and folded her hands. She told herself she wasn't a bully. "What are you going to do, Nicci? Where are you going to go?"

"Shut up!" Nicci beat her palms on the table loud enough that old Mrs. Simon in the next apartment banged her cane on the wall. "I'm *not* leaving! You can't make me *leave*, Amber! You can't make me leave the *planet*!"

"I'm not making you do anything," said Amber, knowing damned well it was a lie. "I'm just telling you that I'm going, with or without you."

Nicci stared, her mouth working in silent horror.

"There is no other place for us to go," said Amber.

And she waited, but Nicci still couldn't find anything to say, so she picked up the brochure and started to flip through it.

"So I went to see the Manifestors," she said. She sounded, to her own ears, a lot like the pinch-faced old man at the orientation seminar, trying to be professional while still getting through something deeply unpleasant and perhaps contagious as quickly as possible. Everyone knew about the Manifest Destiny Society and their ship; she said it anyway. "They've still got room. I guess they're having some trouble filling their quota for young women, so we're actually guaranteed a contract if we apply."

"They're having trouble because it's never been tested!"

"Sure it has. They've Tunneled out to all the other planets."

"Oh what? To Neptune? Saturn?" Nicci uttered a shrill, fearful laugh and shook her head. "They've never taken it to this other place! This...This..."

"Plymouth," supplied Amber, not without rolling her eyes a little. The Director of the Manifest Destiny Society was simply full of the pioneering spirit. "They're calling the planet Plymouth."

"I don't care what they're calling it! I don't want to go!"

"You don't have to. But I am," said Amber again, and watched her baby sister start to cry. "The trip's going to take about three years, they said, but we'll be in Sleepers the whole time. That's kind of like in the movies, when they freeze you, only we won't actually be frozen. We won't feel anything and we won't age, although the guy said sometimes the umbilical...the place where they plug you in leaves a pretty gnarly scar. Those weren't his exact words—"

"Amber!" Nicci wailed.

She waited, but that was apparently the sum and substance of Nicci's argument, so after a moment, she just went on.

"When we get there, the ship lands and becomes like the staging area for the colony. We'll be building the colony up around it—farms and stuff, I guess—but civilians like me won't be responsible for much. I guess it'll be pretty hard work, but it's only supposed to be a six-hour shift, which is less than I'm working now. I got one of their silver civilian contracts, which means five years—Earth years, that is, and it doesn't include the transport time. They're going to pay me twenty thousand dollars a year, plus five thousand just for being a fertile female of childbearing age."

Nicci looked up, her tears hitching to a brief stop in her throat. "W-what?"

"Plus another ten thousand for every kid I have while I'm there, but I'm not having any. I told them that, and they said that was my decision, but I still have to take my implant out before I go. They won't pay for that, but they do pay for a full medical exam and I'll get all my shots so I'm clean to go. By a doctor," she added. "Not some insurance company's medico. Plus, I'll get the Vaccine."

Not *a* vaccine. The *Vaccine*. And even Nicci, who obviously tried so hard to understand as little as she possibly could, knew what that was. Because before the Director had been the leader of a bunch of space-happy freaks, he'd been a doctor, and much as he would like to say that his greatest contribution to humanity was the ship that would carry the first colonists to another world (and he said that a lot), he would probably always be known best for the Vaccine, which worked itself all the way down into your DNA and made it so you could never get sick again. Here on Earth, people paid hundreds of thousands of dollars to endure the agonizing year-long process while the Vaccine was introduced, but the Director was just giving them all away to his happy little colonists, who'd get them painlessly in their Sleepers, which was the perfect application process, according to the brochure. No more worrying about that niggling little 14% failure rate or the greatly exaggerated reports of the birth defects caused by genetic drift. They'd just wake up, secure in the knowledge that now they were cured for life of every possible virus—of the flu, of HIV, of whatever alien illness might be crawling around on Plymouth. Of everything.

Amber could see this sweeping, silent argument hammering away at Nicci's defenses. Ever since the Ebola attack at the UN summit, there had been a dramatic end to the prohibitions on biological warfare. These days, it was fight fire with fire, and now it seemed every country was bragging about the bugs they could grow. Super-polio, rabies-13, dengue, hanta, yellowpox and God only knew what else. They lived in the city. They were a target. It could happen any day.

"Well..." Nicci ran her wet eyes over the papers on the table without seeming to really see any of them. "Can't we go on the next ship? When we know it's safe?"

"No."

"There's going to be more!" She reached tentatively for the Manifestor's pamphlet, but withdrew her hand without touching it. "We can take the next one, okay?"

"No, Nicci. They only pay people to be colonists for the first ship, *because* it's the first and everyone wants to wait and see what happens. After it gets there safe and sound, the Manifestors stop paying and start charging."

"You don't know that!"

"I do know that, actually, because I was there and I talked to them. I also know that the next three ships are already booked, so it's this or nothing. Well," she amended ruthlessly, "it's this *or* go on the state *or* start whoring. I guess we do have options."

Nicci sniffled and rubbed at her face.

Amber picked up the brochure on the ship and made herself read it. It took a lot of time and when she was done, she could not remember a thing she'd just read. She'd hoped it would settle her twisting stomach some, but if anything, the wait and the silence and the sound of Nicci sniffling made her feel even sicker. She folded up the brochure and put it down, talking like she'd never stopped, like she didn't care, like she was sure. "The best part is, the five years I spend on the planet counts as improved education when I get back. Not as much as a degree would, but some. My salary cap will be raised and I'll even be eligible for college credit, just like if I'd been in the army."

She waited. Nicci kept sniffing and wiping.

"Fine," said Amber, sweeping the papers together in a single stack. "You stay here and have fun with the whoring. I'll miss you."

Nicci didn't call her back as Amber walked down the narrow hall to the room that the sisters had shared since Mary brought baby Nichole home from the insurance company's birth clinic. Amber put the papers in the drawer with her shirts and socks, then changed out of her funeral clothes and into her work uniform. She went into the bathroom and threw up in the sink. She tried to be as quiet about that as possible and she didn't feel a lot better when it was done. In the other room, she could hear her baby sister crying again. She looked at herself in the bathroom mirror and saw a big (*fat*) unsmiling (*mean-eyed*) stranger (*bitch*) who'd bullied her only living relative on the day of their mother's funeral.

"It had to be said," whispered Amber. She rinsed her mouth and washed her face and put her hair up. “Sometimes you just have to say the bad stuff.”

She went on out past weeping Nicci and off to work like it didn’t matter. In a way, it didn’t. They simply didn’t have any choice.

2

They called the ship the *Pioneer*, of course. The launch had originally been scheduled for August 3rd, but it had been pushed back three times and now was set for January 22nd, and, barring another sanction from the United Nations, set in stone. That gave the Bierces a little more than twelve weeks to prepare for the flight, but they only had Bo Peep's apartment for four. The Manifestors provided housing, but required a signed contract before approval, which in turn required a certificate of medical clearance. They got their exams the third day after requesting one and Nicci passed hers easily. Amber hit an old, familiar snag.

Her tests were all negative, the medico assured her, as though Amber needed assurances. She did not. Her job at the factory took the weekly drug-and-disability tests allowed by law and Amber had seen too many people dismissed, often with a hefty fine for 'misrepresentation of faculties,' to ever be tempted by her mother's stash. No, the problem was what the problem usually was: Her weight.

She wasn't huge. She had more than one chin and she lost her breath easy when she had to take the stairs, but she got her clothes at the same store Nicci did, just on the lower shelves. So this was a setback, but it wasn't unexpected and it couldn't be insurmountable. She just wasn't that big.

"How much would I have to lose?" Amber asked bluntly, interrupting the medico's careful dance around the three-letter F-word.

"It isn't a matter of, well, weight."

"It isn't?" she asked, surprised. "Is something wrong with me?"

"Not necessarily. Your blood pressure is, well, on the high end, but normal, and although you show some pre-diabetic conditions, your glucose levels are just fine."

"How do you have a pre-diabetic condition? Isn't every healthy person a pre-sick one?"

The medico's lips pursed slightly.

Amber made herself shut up. She glanced at the nicely-tiled ceiling and then at the pleasant wall-mounted light meant to mimic a curtained window, since the actual view of rundown buildings and garbage-strewn alleys was so deplorable. "I'm sorry," she said. "I'm not trying to be a bitch, I just really want to go."

The medico softened slightly, even smiled. No doubt she saw before her an excited, if fat, young pioneeress on the threshold of a lifelong wish and she alone had the power to grant it. Amber let her think whatever she wanted. This was the last hurdle and if she could just get her fat ass over it, she and Nicci would be on their way.

"I have to do this," said Amber. "So just tell me how much I have to lose."

"I'm really not sure. The problem isn't just a matter of weight, as I said. It's a matter of risk. You have to realize that even though your tests all fall within the normal range right now, you'll be contracted to the colony for five years as, well, as a potential mother. Obesity creates an increased risk for all pregnancies."

They thought she was obese? Amber rubbed her stomach and scowled. "Okay. I'll be back," she said, and went out to the clinic's waiting area to collect Nicci. She made herself a second appointment for the end of the month, the same day the apartment's lease expired. She went home, saw a nervous Nicci out the door and on her way to work, then took half the money out of her bank account and got back on the bus.

* * *

Amber knew where he lived, but she went to 61st Street anyway because when Bo Peep moonlighted, which was almost every night these past few years, she did it on 61st and the Six-Ones might be feeling territorial. Sure enough, after standing out in the grey rain for a good half-hour, a kid sidled up and asked who she wanted. She asked for the Candyman. He had a lot of names, and Amber even knew a few, thanks to his long working relationship with her mother, but that was the one that could always find him. The kid went away and another ten minutes passed. Permission came in the form of a low, black car with tinted windows that rolled down just enough for some other kid to tell her where to find him.

The Candyman wasn't much to look at—a scrawny, toothless man of indeterminate age and race, with a propensity for cheap suits and a swishy way of talking that should have made him a target on these streets. Instead, he was perhaps the one man who could walk freely from 14 East all the way up to Brewer Drive and get nothing but nods from the people he passed. It wasn't just the drugs. Just what it was, Amber didn't know, but the drugs made an easy sideline and he was good with them. He rarely met with anyone apart from his own crew and the leisure girls who did the things he liked in exchange for the glow only he could give them. But he met with Amber, perhaps just because he'd seen her before, hanging on Mama's hand and wishing she was someplace else while Bo Peep begged in her pretty way for the sweet stuff, trying to pretend Mama really meant candy, like the lollipop he gave little Amber on the way out his door.

He admitted her past ten or twelve of his heavily-armed good friends to the squalor of his apartment as if to a royal audience, which she supposed it might be, in a way. He said a few solemn words on the passing of her mother, which was nice of him. And then he got down to business.

"Are you going on the state?" he asked in his mushy, sing-song way. "Candyman can talk around, you bet, find you a prime place to strut. No charge, even. Out of respect. Would you like a soda? Nickels, get Bo Peep's little girl a soda."

"No, thank you. I need to lose a lot of weight in the next four weeks," said Amber. "A lot. And I need to pass a drug-and-disability at the end of it."

"Mmm-hm." Candyman leaned back in his chair and steepled his hands. "That does limit our options. Let me think."

He thought. And then he went into his dingy kitchen, rattled around, and came out with a crinkled paper lunchbag, well-used, but strong enough still to hold whatever it held. He folded the top down three times and pinched the crease sharp with his knobby, stained fingers. "You take one of these in the morning, sweets, when you get up. One twelve hours later, no more and no less. It make you hum around some, you bet," he said, and tittered. "You say four weeks, uh-huh, you take this three weeks and let the last week go. If you like to tip the bottle, you best be setting it aside for a while or you find you lose all the weight, all at once, and go slithering off in just your soul."

"How much do I owe you?"

"I like this girl. She all business," Candyman remarked to one of his good friends and the good friend grunted. "Well, Miss Business, out of respect for your dear departed mama, I'ma give you this for just twenty a shot, mmm-hm. That's twenty-one days, two shots a day...help me with the higher mathematics here, Snaps."

"Eight-forty," rumbled one of his men.

"Just so." Candyman held out the bag.

Amber didn't take it. Eight hundred and forty dollars was more than she had on her, but not more than she had. On the other hand, she still had twelve weeks to get through and she didn't like spending so much of it at the beginning without knowing how it was all going to end. But then again, if she passed her medical exam, she'd be in the Manifestors' care for most of that time, and after that, it didn't matter. She meant to put whatever she hadn't spent in one of the colonist's accounts, so whatever she had when she left could sit in the Director's bank growing by half a percent a quarter until she got back. Maybe by then it'd be up to four digits. And when she did come back with her colonist's pay, eight hundred and forty dollars was going to be pretty small change.

"Give me a little time to put that together." Amber turned around.

"Ooo, now I really like her. She don't haggle, she don't beg, she don't cozy up other arrangements. She just gets things done," said Candyman, and he must have gestured because two of his good friends stepped sideways in front of the door. Amber studied them, aware that this might be very bad, as behind her, the Candyman considered.

"How much you got in your pocket?" he asked at last.

Dumb question to answer in a room full of men with guns.

"Five hundred."

"Mm-hm. Tell you what I'm going to do, because you're Bo Peep's little girl and because I like you, I'm going to take that five hundred right now and you gonna give me the rest plus another one-sixty—another even five, you hear me?—the day you take your last shot. You do this like an honest businessman, yeah? And we got no problems."

She looked at him. "Is there a catch?"

"I do like her," said Candyman to Snaps. And to Amber again, "Just another business arrangement, nothing bad. Good business. Repeat business, if you understand me, anytime you find yourself in the market. You just let Candyman take care of you, we gonna get along just fine."

"I can agree to that," said Amber, who had no intention of either buying his products or selling her body. She doubted he'd follow her offworld to complain about it.

Candyman smiled at her, but his eyes turned cold and somehow older—the eyes of a crocodile, half-sunk in swamp and too damned close to shore. "Whether or not you *can* is not what I'm waiting to hear, Miss Business."

"Sorry," said Amber, and unlike the nurse, the apology did not soften up the Candyman in the slightest. "I mean I will." And she put out her hand for him to shake.

He looked at it. His friends looked at it. They all looked at each other. Some of them laughed, but it was good, honest laughter.

"Business all the way," marveled Candyman. He shook with her. His hand was soft and bony at the same time, with too much skin for its little size, and abrasive calluses on the fingerpads. He did not release her right away. "You gonna find I'm a man of my word, despite what you might be thinking, and that can be good or bad depending on how you want to play this out."

"I came to you for help," said Amber. "That's how I'm playing it."

"Mm-hm." He opened his hand and let hers go. "I knew your mama," he said, giving her the lunchbag. "I knew her about as well as she let anyone know her, if you feel me, and if you don't mind my saying, you not a whole lot like her."

She knew. And she knew it probably wasn't a compliment, but she took it as one.

* * *

She took her lunchbag home and put it in Mama's room without looking at it. Then she cleaned house. Ice cream, frozen pizzas, peanut butter, all the nuke-and-eat dinners in the freezer and the just-add-hamburger boxes from the cupboard—opened or unopened, it all went into a garbage bag and straight out to the dump-bin behind the building. If it wasn't here, she wouldn't think about it; if it was, she'd probably eat it all, just to have something to do. It wasn't until much later that night, after Nicci was in bed and Amber sat alone in Mama's room that she opened up the thin, stained paper and had her first look at forty-one pre-loaded needles. She tried not to think about how many times they'd been used when she pushed the first one in.

She didn't even have enough time to wonder when it was going to hit before it hit. She didn't sleep that night. She didn't sleep much at all for the next twenty-one days, but she hummed all right. Sometimes her heart raced hard enough that she made herself sit down with the telephone on her lap and her finger on the emergency-response button, just waiting for the last reason to push it, but she got through it.

She lost her job, but not for the shots. She wasn't sure how they found out about Manifest Destiny, but they must have, because in spite of her 'recent increase in enthusiasm and productivity' at work, they felt that, regrettably, she had ceased to envision a future with the company. They didn't offer to send her last paycheck and she didn't ask. She considered herself lucky they hadn't taken her to court for breach of occupational contract.

Jobless, she counted days by the mornings when she shot up and nights the same way. Otherwise, there was no time, no sense of its passage, no sense of change in herself, only sleepless nights and blurry days and gradually loosening clothes.

She paid the Candyman his money the morning of her last injection. He told her she looked good, reminded her of their future business arrangements, said he'd see her around. She did, once or twice, but only at a distance.

She made her appointment at the clinic on time after sleeping nearly two days straight through. She looked and felt like home-brewed shit in her opinion, but she didn't have the same medico and the new one didn't remark on her appearance beyond voicing some concern that if the records were accurate, Amber appeared to have lost fifty-seven pounds since the last examination.

"Mistakes happen," said Amber. "Do I pass?"

The medico took some measurements. He flipped through some papers. Then he excused himself. Amber waited for a few seconds, then eased the door latch silently down and opened it just a crack. She could hear her medico down at the nurses' station, conferring with whoever else was there in low, urgent tones.

"—not sure what to tell her," he was saying.

"How old is she?"

"Twenty-four, but she's a big girl. I don't think the—"

"She clean?"

"What? Yeah, she's fine other than the—"

"Pass her."

"Are you sure she's going even going to fit in the Sleeper? They don't exactly make those things in plus sizes."

"Did you look at her home address? She's asking for her clearance this early, it's because she wants to move into the housing those nuts are offering. And she is not getting any bigger over there, I guarantee it."

"I don't know..."

"Seriously, I have to spell this out for you? The Director has God knows how many investors convinced that this deep-space disaster of his is a five-year swinger's party. If they show up with their money and find a fucking weiner roast, they're going to make him very unhappy and he will make his underlings unhappy and that shit will roll downhill until it hits us. Who cares how big she is? Someone will be into that. Pass her."

Amber got her health clearance. She took it to the local branch of Manifest Destiny and got a room for her and Nicci to share at the compound for thirty dollars a week and a thumbprint. It took just a few hours to load up their things and sign out of the apartment. She left all the big stuff behind for the super to steal and got on the shuttle that took them to the busport that took them to their new, temporary home. It was a nine-hour drive with seventeen other hopeful colonists and nobody did much talking. That night, in their new beds and their old sheets, Nicci cried. Amber slept.

* * *

Time came back.

She had eight weeks to kill with nothing to do. She went to all the seminars the Manifestors offered. She took a class in agrarian infrastructure, and another in canning, figuring they'd be useful skills to have on the new planet. She went to the gym every day, but gained back five pounds. She would have gone back to the Candyman for another thirty pounds' worth of needles if she had the money, but she didn't, so fuck it. Once the ship took off, it would be too late for the Director to hang out his No Fat Chicks sign.

Finally, their boarding orders. They were boarding the corporates first, the gold class second, and the families third, in alphabetical order, so Amber and Nicci were scheduled for eight in the morning on January 17th. There was an orientation lecture on boarding procedure. Amber went. Nicci stayed home and cried.

On the last day, Amber packed. They were allowed to bring whatever they wanted for free, provided it fit in one of the standard Fleet-issued duffel bags. Anything other than that, they charged for. Amber put in the three spare colonist's uniforms first, leaving only the one she'd be wearing for boarding. Then she rolled up a few sweaters, some jeans, socks, underwear, her favorite tee and, with what little space she had left, the most useful study material from the seminars, and two coffee cups. She stared at it for a while. She packed Nicci's duffel for her, rummaging through the apartment stuff for more than two hours to find the shoebox with their photos. She removed the pictures where Bo Peep was too obviously strung out and put the rest in Nicci's duffel bag. Then she cried, but she did it quietly in the bathroom. It was almost morning, almost time.

It was almost over.

"Here we go," muttered Amber. She dried her eyes and switched out the light, saying, with absolutely no sense of premonition, "Plymouth or bust."

3

That day, Amber learned early that standing around in an skyport was pretty much exactly like standing around in an airport. This was probably because, regardless of the Director's many efforts to make it look futurific and exciting, it *was* an airport, only with a space shuttle behind it instead of a bunch of planes. The actual ship, the *Pioneer*, was already in space, where it and the rest of the Director's fleet had been built.

As 'strongly advised' in the seminar, she and Nicci took the transport two hours in advance of their boarding time, only to discover that the line was already stretched out of the maze-like queue and wrapped three-quarters of the way around the terminal. It was not the best weather for standing in line. The Manifestors, or maybe just the airport people, had set up several canopies, but the rain got in anyway, splashing in fat, random splats against her arm, her neck, her eye. Outside of the canopies, the rain quickly plastered her official Manifest Destiny flightsuit to her body, and since it was white, it exposed not only each and every unsightly bulge of fat, but also the pebbly bumps of her nipples and the hem of her panties and God alone knew what else.

The conditions were bad enough; the company was worse. All around them were young couples hiss-fighting their way through the nerves, bickering teenagers, screaming babies, and every shade of human misery in-between. Adding to the fun was Nicci, who kept insisting it wasn't too late yet, they could still go back and maybe talk to the super, just talk to him, Amber, and maybe get their old apartment back and they could make it work, they really could. By the time she reached the terminal doors and bared her face to the gust of heated air blowing down from the overhead fans, Amber was ready to tell her to go wherever the hell she wanted to as long as she shut up when she did it. And that made her feel sick all over, because she knew her sister's fear wasn't only genuine, it was normal. They were doing something that had never been done, had never even been tested in any real practical way. Fear was a perfectly reasonable reaction, but it still didn't change the fact that they were homeless, jobless and alone. Whining about it was not going to change anything.

They made their way back and forth through the ropes of the queue holding hands. Manifestors walked happily up and down beside them, offering hot coffee and smiles and sedatives for those who needed them. A young mother not far from Amber abruptly ducked out of line with her small son, only to be met by three Manifestors who politely but firmly reminded her of the contract she had signed, the amenities she had already accepted, and the criminal charges awaiting her if she left. The mother began to cry, the son joined in, and both were ushered swiftly away. Not out the door, Amber noticed, but deeper into the terminal. They did not come back. Maybe Nicci was watching too; she stopped asking to go home, but the hand that gripped Amber's trembled the closer they got to the head of the line.

Halfway there, they were met by a registrar—not one of the skyport's, a Manifestor—pushing a cart loaded with baskets of flat and featureless metal bracelets. She was accompanied by an honest-to-God Fleetman. Seeing him in his plain military uniform was, even more than the queue or the rain or the space shuttle itself on the launching platform out the window, the slapping hand of reality for Amber. The registrar had to repeat herself before she could bring herself back from that.

"I'm sorry?" she stammered, wrenching her eyes off the Fleetman.

"I need your print, please?" The registrar lifted her scanner higher.

Amber offered her thumb. The scanning plate was warm and a little slippery. Quite a few sweaty hands in the line ahead of her, she supposed.

"Amber Katherine Bierce, do you accept the terms of the contract you have signed with the entity identified as the Manifest Destiny Society and revoke all other rights save those guaranteed you in the aforementioned contract until such time as the contract has elapsed?"

"Yes."

"Do you understand that by agreeing to these terms, you have become a member of the Manifest Destiny Society and a civilian of the planet identified as Plymouth, subject to all laws of that entity and that planet, both existing and to be determined, until such time as your contract has elapsed?"

"Yes."

"Do you understand that when this document is finalized, you will not be permitted to renege on its terms and any attempt to renege on its terms will be prosecuted on three felony charges of theft, fraud and conspiracy to defraud, carrying no less a sentence than fifteen years in prison and a fine of no less than two million dollars, and that failure to pay that fine may carry its own liability?"

Nicci trembled.

"Yes," said Amber.

"Great!" The registrar turned to let the Fleetman, who was apparently doing the witnessing, tap at the scanning screen. The registrar played with it some more, then printed out a plastine label. She applied this to one of the bracelets on her cart and fit it onto Amber's wrist, pinching it to make it tight. "There you go! Enjoy your flight! May I take your print, please?" she chirped, turning her sunny, Manifestor's smile on Nicci.

Amber watched the Fleetman run his restless, military stare out over the crowd of would-be colonists. He looked bored. When his eyes met hers, she said, "Are you coming with us to Plymouth?"

"Hell, no," he replied. "They had to pay me double just to do this much."

That earned him as dirty a look as the registrar seemed capable of manufacturing on her perky, young face. He shrugged one shoulder in something like an apology, tipped Amber a wink when the registrar resumed the legal stuff, and went back to crowd-watching. Nicci got her bracelet. The trudge through the queue continued.

Not just 'no', but 'hell, no'...

The next time the line took them close enough to a registrar, Amber reached out and waved for the accompanying Fleetman's attention and asked if he was boarding.

"No, ma'am," he replied firmly, which was not as unsettling as 'hell, no,' but was still pretty negative.

"I was told there was going to be a Fleet presence on Plymouth. I mean, the flight crew are all Fleet, right? They're not...um..." *...a bunch of Director-worshipping space-zealots*?

The Fleetman smiled. "There will be a full military flight crew, ma'am. Six hundred and forty proud men and women of the first United States Deep-Space Fleet."

"Is that all?"

"This isn't a military operation," the registrar inserted with a disapproving frown. He was a lot better at that than the last registrar.

The Fleetman gave him a knowing sort of glance and asked Amber if she had any other questions. She did not and the line was moving, so she shuffled on ahead and let them get started on the next colonist.

Six hundred and forty. Didn't seem like a lot of crew for a ship the size of a football stadium, let alone the police force for fifty thousand people.

'We'll be way too busy colonizing to need policing anyway,' Amber told herself, but couldn't make herself believe it. She didn't think it mattered how tiring life on the farm was going to be. People were always going to need policing, especially when things were new and scary and people were apt to be at their worst.

Nicci was looking at her, all wide eyes and apprehension. Amber smiled and squeezed her hand, disguising her misgivings with an ease born of many long years of practice. Worrying was useless now; the bracelet on her wrist was as good as handcuffs.

'I'm not scared,' thought Amber, stepping up to the head of the line at last. 'I'm the tough one. I'm the strong one. I'm the one Nicci's going to lean on for the next five years, so suck it up, little girl.'

They ran them and their duffel bags through the usual set of scanners, checked their thumbprints against their bracelets, gave them each a smile and the opportunity to opt out and be arrested—Nicci opened her mouth, but Amber squeezed her hand and she closed it again, shivering—and then they were sent down the tunnel and onto the shuttle, which was, in spite of its size and the cool lights and the seatbelts that locked them in and had no release button, just a big airplane. It smelled like one, especially when all the other people got squeezed in around them; it sounded like one, once the pilot droned out the weather conditions and how it affected their launch time; it felt like one when they taxied away from the terminal and turned onto the runway.

"Here we go," said the pilot, sounding comfortingly bored.

No one else made a sound.

The shuttle began to move, slowly at first, but picking up speed fast until Amber could feel the funny tugs of lift under its wings. She squeezed Nicci's hand again, but her sister did not respond—not with a word, not with a shiver, not even with tears. The shuttle bumped up once, twice, and then lurched into the sky and stayed there. Amber tried to look, but the nearest window was six nervous people away and it mostly showed her the wing anyway.

The shuttle was tipping as it flew, leaning everyone further and further back in their chairs. "Just a little jump now," said the pilot, and almost exactly on the word 'jump,' there was a tremendous roar behind him and a mighty lurch straight up.

People screamed in the reedy, I-know-I'm-being-silly-but-Jesus-Christ-not-cool way they sometimes did if the elevator they were on suddenly quit working or some yappy dog on a leash took an unprovoked lunge at them. Some of them laughed a little afterwards as the shuttle ripped them out of Earth's sky. Some cried instead. Amber squeezed Nicci's hand and watched the stars come out through the nearest window.

The roaring noise gradually died away. The shuttle didn't slow down or right itself, but with nothing but space through the windows to orient themselves around, it seemed to do both. Quite a few people threw up in the courtesy bags provided for that purpose. 'Spacesick,' Amber thought, watching everyone's hair drift.

Now the shuttle slowed, firing its engines in little lurching bursts while the real ship rolled in and out of view through the windows, impossibly huge. The pilot came on to tell them they had permission to dock and that they'd feel a little bump when the clutch made contact. These words were followed within a few minutes by a loud scraping noise and a thump that made everyone rock sideways in their seats. The lights flickered. People screamed again, laughed, cried, threw up. 'We sound like crazy people,' thought Amber, frowning, and she put her arm around her sister and hugged her.

They waited for what felt like a very long time without anything happening until someone at the window suddenly announced they were going in. Everyone tried to lean over everyone else and look. Amber hugged Nicci and watched the lights dim and glow, dim and shiver.

According to the pilot, they docked. The clamps engaged. The stabilizers were initiated. Atmosphere was restored—she could see that one for herself when everyone's hair came down—and the engines were cut. The pilot reminded them not to forget their bags and wished them all Godspeed and a great adventure. The shuttle doors opened. Their safety restraints unlocked.

No one moved.

Another perky Manifestor stuck her head inside and smiled at them. "Let's get going, shall we? Just follow the white line to the boarding hub and an usher will be waiting to direct you to your room! So exciting! Single-file, just like back in school!"

"My school used the buddy system," someone said, sounding worried.

The Manifestor looked at him. So did a lot of people, but her smile was nicer.

"Then I'll be your buddy," she said and held out her hand.

And just like that, it turned back into an airplane. People started getting up, looking for their bags, muttering and laughing and getting tangled up in their seat belts, and everything was fine again. Shouldering her duffel bag, Amber waited for a break in the stream of disembarking people and then joined it, holding her sister's hand firmly in her own. 'Just like an airport,' she thought, stepping onto the painted line. 'Nothing to worry about. Keep walking. Stay calm. It's almost over.'

The queue moved faster than the one back at the skyport. They were already in space; she supposed there was really no point in anyone dragging their feet anymore. The halls they walked through were clean and well-lit and carpeted, not at all like the grim, utilitarian ships you saw in sci-fi movies. More like a hotel, except for all the shiny metal trimming. There were no windows, nothing to remind them that they were in space. There were a few pictures on the walls in the boarding hub, but they were all of the Director—walking with various dignitaries, frowning seriously at important documents, gazing pensively into the sky, clasping hands with his loving cultists, and just generally being inspiring. Supposedly, he was putting in a lot of public appearances these days, but she hadn't seen him anywhere around the compound.

She found herself wondering if he was even coming to Plymouth with them.

"Welcome aboard!" said the square-jawed young usher waiting for her at the end of the line. He even fired off an honest-to-goodness salute which, in addition to raising Amber's eyebrows, brought out a gust of laughter from the actual Fleet soldiers lounging around a little further down the corridor from the Manifestors. "I'm Crewman Everly Scott of the *Pioneer*! And you are...?"

"Amber Bierce," said Amber. "Space Adventurer."

The Fleetmen down the hall laughed again and this time some of the Manifestors joined in. Crewman Scott's enthusiasm visibly iced over. He lowered his saluting hand and looked at her, not smiling.

'Great,' thought Amber. 'Now he thinks I was making fun of him.'

Weren't you? some small part of her wanted to know. It sounded a lot like her mother.

"Sorry," Amber said, setting her duffel bag down. "I didn't mean anything by that. Just nervous, you know. It's my first time going to another planet."

This prompted another good-natured rumble of humor down the hall, but did not appear to thaw Crewman Scott much. His professional smile went no further than his clenched jaw as he scanned their thumbprints again, checked whatever came up on his little screen against their papers, then against their wristbands, and finally gave them both an official nod of approval. "Bierce, Amber K.," he said. "You've been assigned to bed FH-0419. Follow the green line to the family housing bay, take the elevator marked H to the fourth floor, turn right, and bed 19 is down the first hall on your right, okay?"

"H, four, right, right. I got it."

"Bierce, Nichole S., you've been assigned to bed FW-1866," Crewman Scott continued.

"What?"

"Follow the green line to the family housing bay and take the elevator marked W to the—"

"Hang on," interrupted Amber, giving Nicci's startled, clutching hand a distracted pat. "We're supposed to be together."

"—to the eighteenth floor—"

"I was told that we'd be together," said Amber again, a little bit louder.

"—turn left and you'll find your bed on the third hall on your right," Crewman Scott concluded, holding out a helpful printed map of the ship. "Enjoy your flight, ladies."

Amber did not take the map. "Are you finished?" she asked coolly.

"Enjoy your flight, ladies."

"We were told we'd be stationed together."

"Enjoy your flight, Miss Bierce."

"I hope you can say that all day, because I'm not moving until I get this cleared up and seeing as I'm standing in the boarding hub of the friggin' *Pioneer*, I think you can safely assume I've got nowhere else to be."

Crewman Scott continued to hold out the map.

Amber folded her arms across her chest and waited.

The other uniformed people in the hall were still watching them.

"I'm sorry," Scott said with a polite smile. This time, it made it to his eyes, but not in a very polite way. "I don't have anything to do with the bed assignments. Please follow the green line. There are other people waiting for assistance."

"I want to speak to your supervisor."

"This is a starship, Miss Bierce, not a Starbucks. I don't have a supervisor, I have commanding officers. You can speak to one by going to the family housing bay and picking up any courtesy phone. If you'll please follow the green line—" he suggested, reaching past her to scan the next man in line.

Amber took the scanner out of his hand and set it down firmly on the desk. "I'll let you know when we're done here, pal."

"Miss Bierce—"

"Everly," she countered. "Get your goddamn supervisor."

Nicci shuffled off to one side, looking slightly relieved now that the situation was being handled by a person and in a manner she was accustomed to. The people behind them in line gave them a little space. Crewman Scott stared at her, his mouth shut tight and his ears brick-red, then turned around and walked stiffly up the hall to the place where the other red-suited Manifestors were standing. They listened to whatever he had to say and soon one of them came for Amber.

"Good morning," he said pleasantly. "I'm Steven Fisch, the docking coordinator. How can I help?"

"She doesn't like her assigned—"

"I'm handling it, Scott," said Fisch, still pleasantly and without looking at him. "What seems to be the trouble?"

"My sister and I signed up for a five-year contract," said Amber, presenting her thumb for him to scan, which he did. "And I was told we'd be stationed together for the flight and at the colony."

"Mm-hm. And it looks like you've both been assigned to beds in the family housing unit."

"Right, on different floors and different, um, letters. That's not acceptable to me," said Amber as Nicci sidled up closer to her. "I'm not looking for trouble, but I was told we'd be together and I kind of want what I was promised."

"I understand."

"We don't have anything to do with the bed assign—"

"I'm handling it, Scott," said Fisch again, not quite as pleasantly as before. He pushed a few buttons on his digireader. "It looks like you waited for the last minute before signing on with us, Miss Bierce. And Miss Bierce," he added, with a nod to Nicci, who nodded nervously back at him. "I'm afraid the group units in family housing filled up months ago. There's nothing left except singles and frankly, I'm a little surprised you got beds there at all. It's just like any big event, Miss Bierce. These are the best seats in the house and after a certain date, you just don't find two of them together. I'm sure the recruiters made you all kinds of promises to get you, but they don't have anything to do with you once you're on board and they shouldn't have made you any promises at all."

"I realize this seems like a petty problem to you," Amber began.

Crewman Scott uttered one of those huffy little breaths that snotty people liked to use when they didn't quite dare to laugh out loud. Amber was willing to overlook it this time, but Fisch's face went cold.

"Excuse us for just a moment, please," he said, and took Scott aside.

Amber couldn't hear anything that was said and couldn't hazard any guesses to judge by Fisch's broad and rather bland face, but she waited and watched Scott's ears turn red with a faint sense of satisfaction. In less than a minute, Fisch was back, smiling again.

"I apologize for the interruption, please go on. A petty problem...?"

"We'll both be in Sleep," said Amber. "I get it. We won't be conscious, we won't be lying there missing each other for years, we won't miss anything at all. But we've been checking in for three hours already. I've got no reason to expect to check out in less time. And yeah, it may only be a few hours, but it'll be a few hours on another planet, for God's sake, and I want my sister with me."

"Please," said Nicci.

Fisch glanced at her and his eyes lingered. When he looked back at Amber, he seemed somewhat less politely pleasant and more sincerely thoughtful.

"Isn't there anything you can do?" asked Amber. "We don't have to be in family housing. We just want to stay together."

He hmmmed again and checked with his digireader, tapping the stylus through several screens before frowning at her. "I think we could find a way to accommodate you, Miss Bierce, but you need to understand that once you're confirmed to a bed, those may be your living quarters for quite a long time after we arrive."

"We know."

"The family units are much larger and, honestly, far superior in terms of comfort and entertainment purposes. The general housing mods are pretty much your beds, some public showers and a cafeteria. There's no comparison to family housing. To prison, maybe, but not to family housing. And signing you off on a corporate mod or a suite or anything like that is simply out of the question, so if that's what you were hoping..."

"General housing works just fine if we're together."

Fisch tapped his stylus against the top of his reader and glanced at Nicci. "Miss Bierce?"

Nicci stepped back, holding her case in front of her like a shield against his attention. "I...I guess. I don't know. Amber?"

"Please," she said.

"All right," said Fisch, in that rising, sighing, I-wash-my-hands-of-this way that people use when they think you're making, if not the biggest mistake of your life, at least the one people will be bringing up for the next ten years to embarrass you. "Scott, come over here, please. Gen-Pop hasn't been boarded yet, so we're just going to take two beds in the women's dorm and bump them up to family housing, then put the Bierces in their place. See how I did that?"

"Yes, sir."

Fisch sighed. "Scott, for God's sake, relax. Mr. Fisch will do just fine. Did you see what I did?"

"Yes, um...yeah."

"Okay, it's probably not going to be the last time, so do the best you can with it and try to remember that these people are not the enemy."

Scott's ears pinked. "Yes, sir. Mr. Fisch."

"Good. I'll take over here for a bit. Why don't you help these ladies with their cases and get them settled in their beds?"

Pink deepened into red. "Um...sure. I could do that. I don't mind." He turned stiffly to Amber, hesitated, and then turned away and took Nicci's things.

She could have let it go. She should have let it go.

Amber cleared her throat and held out her duffel bag.

Scott did his best to stare her down, but Fisch was standing right there and now he was watching pretty closely too. He took the strap out of Amber's outstretched hand and slung it over his shoulder with as much dignity as such a menial task allowed. He started walking, his boots clicking firmly along the grey stripe on the floor like it was a tightrope over lava.

"He looks mad," whispered Nicci, following close behind Amber as they moved out of the intake line, away from the rumbling, stuffy excitement of a thousand nervous families and into the largely empty corridor leading to the general housing mods. "I don't think he likes you very much."

"He doesn't have to like me," Amber told her, talking low but making no real effort to be inaudible. She didn't care if Crewman Everly Scott heard this or not. "There's going to be fifty thousand people and an alien planet to entertain us where we're going. We're never going to see each other again."

Scott did not reply or give any indication that he'd even heard them. He brought them into the empty, echoing, half-lit elevator bay and over to the lift marked with an A. Between the gunmetal-grey paint and the stark stenciled lettering, everything looked very much like a military operation. Cold. Authoritative. Menacing.

The lift was big enough for fifty people, according to the capacity rating posted above its utilitarian doors. The sound of three people breathing was very loud. They went up just one level and Nicci was clinging before the doors dinged open.

The first two doors on the first left-hand hall were theirs. WA-0001 and WA-0003. They opened at a swipe of their keycards on what indeed appeared to be a broom closet: narrow enough to touch both walls at once while keeping her elbows bent, just deep enough to accommodate the Sleeper, with a door she had to duck through and a ceiling that did not allow for jump rope.

Crewman Scott dropped Amber's duffel and went inside to secure Nicci's to the wall. He opened up her Sleeper and moved back as far as the dimensions of the room allowed. He waited.

Nicci looked at Amber. "Do I...just get in?"

"Yeah, that's what they said at the seminar."

"I don't...I mean...Do I take my shoes off?"

"You can if you want," said Amber, and Scott said, "No, you can't. No loose articles in the cabin."

"She can put them in her bag," Amber told him.

"I already secured her bag."

"You can unsecure it and secure it again with her shoes inside!"

"I'll just wear them," said Nicci, looking and sounding right on the edge of tears.

"Okay?"

Amber looked at her, feeling her temper at full throb right behind her eyes, and then turned that look on Crewman Everly Scott. "Listen, Space-Scout."

"Amber, please!"

"You got a problem, you take it up with me, you don't take it out on my sister."

Scott gave her a cold look and a wide smile and said, "Just lie down, Miss Bierce, and we'll get you all tucked in!" in a voice like preschooler's poison.

Nicci slunk past Amber, her head bent and lips trembling. She sat on the edge of the Sleeper, kneading at its hard sides as she looked one last time from Amber to Scott and back to Amber. "Please," she said, but whether it was *please say we don't really have to do this* or *please don't fight*, she didn't know. Scott put his hand on the Sleeper's lid and Nicci lay obediently down, even as she gasped out the first hoarse sob. The lid shut, snapped, hissed, and the single panicked, silent cry that Amber saw her sister make faded into sleep. Or into Sleep, she guessed.

The snake-like cable of the umbilicus slipped out of its port inside the tube and slithered under Nicci's shirt. She watched it tunnel across her sister's unmoving body until it reached her navel. The stiff fabric of her clean, white, colonist's shirt bulged and then slowly deflated. In almost the same instant, the panel above the Sleeper lit up, all its many systems diligently engaged. Amber could look at that panel and see that her baby sister's heart was no longer beating, her lungs were no longer working, her brain was no longer thinking, and all this, according to the Sleeper, was perfectly normal.

She looked dead.

"Any time," said Scott, waiting in the hall.

Amber backed up until the door hissed shut on the sight of Nicci in her (*coffin*) tube. She told herself they had nowhere to go, no one to take them in. This was the only way out. It was the only choice.

'I just killed my sister,' she thought.

"Your turn," said Scott, printing out a nameplate on his scanner and inserting into the protective sleeve on door WA-0003. He did not pick up her duffel bag. He opened up her Sleeper and stood back against the wall.

This was really it. She was going to close her eyes and it would be over and either she'd wake up on Plymouth and she'd be fine, or...or she wouldn't. And that would also be fine, she supposed. At least, it'd be just as over.

Amber slid her duffel bag into the rubbery, vaguely unpleasant-feeling net and gave it a pull to make it retract, just like in orientation. She got into the Sleeper, wriggling over as far as she could and very much aware of Scott's contemptuous stare as he watched her try not to overfill the narrow mat. Just watching.

"You waiting for a tip?" she asked, knowing she was blushing and hating him for seeing it.

"Your shirt's pulled up," he told her flatly.

Amber reached down, her face in flames and her chest in knots, to tug the stiff fabric down over the exposed swell of her stomach. There was no one to reprimand him for his huffy little laugh now; he made sure she heard it.

"Yeah, they must have been desperate, all right," he said, dropping the lid on her. She never had the chance to say anything back. She heard the snapping sound of the lid's locking mechanism, but not the hiss of the gas.

She was asleep when Scott held his middle finger up to the glass plate before her face and called her a bitch. She was asleep when her tube wormed its umbilicus under her tight shirt, asleep when it punctured her navel and began the painful process of rendering her dormant for the flight. She slept through the next four days as the rest of the colonists were processed and the ship steadily filled. She slept through the historic speech of Manifest Destiny's charismatic leader as the *Pioneer*'s mighty engines fired up behind him on the video screen in the press room where he was still standing, very much on Earth. She slept through thirteen routine medical scans and six hundred thirty-three automatic maintenance cycles before she slept through the asteroid field that pierced the hull and pulled the active crew out into space through approximately seven thousand coin-sized holes. She slept through two hundred sixty-six years of Tunneling as the speakers above her bed blatted a polite, unheard alarm. She slept through the crash. In the last eleven minutes, as her umbilicus began to retract its countless filaments and her Sleeper gently reanimated her long-static cells, Amber dreamed of the beach and her mother was there, smoking one of her endless cigarettes, and they stood hand in hand together to watch the sun set so red over the ocean, and all the gulls were screaming...

4

Amber woke up on her side, which she knew only because she could sort of feel the hard mat under her cheek and the cold, curved glass panel of the Sleeper's lid pressing on her nose and forehead. She tried to roll over, but couldn't. Her limbs were dead; she was beginning to register the discomfort of her arms crossed and crushed against the Sleeper's wall, but she still couldn't do anything about it. God, how annoying.

She had always been a light sleeper and was used to coming up and alert at a moment's provocation, but she couldn't do it this time. The Sleeper's computer had complete control and seemed far more concerned with talking about the process of waking her up than actually doing it. She could hear it through the speakers in its pleasantly androgynous, vaguely British-sounding voice: "—is estimated to complete in...five minutes seventeen seconds. Please remain calm. Your movements have been inhibited during Sleep. This condition is temporary and will be restored upon removal of the umbilicus."

Right. She remembered now. The orientation seminar had explained all this. Although she couldn't move, she could feel herself twitching as the computer systematically tested her muscles. She could also feel it where the vent was gently blowing on her ear. Why the hell was she on her side, anyway? The seminar had assured all of them that Sleep wasn't really sleep and there wouldn't be any dreams, but she'd had a real whopper. She didn't understand how she could have thrashed around when she was supposed to have been paralyzed, but maybe that was just for the landing, not the whole flight.

And what had the big nightmare been? Why, a trip to the beach with her mother. Bizarre. Bo Peep Bierce did not take her babies on outings. Oh, they'd gone to the courthouse a couple of times, and when they were very young, they used to walk down to the childcare place together until Bo Peep failed a drug test and got kicked out of all the state programs. Other than that, Amber couldn't think of a single trip they'd taken together, unless it was to get drugs.

'Maybe that's why you dream about it,' she thought to herself, and would have rolled her eyes except that they were still kept shut and paralyzed.

It had been such a vivid dream, though. So vivid that she could still imagine the smell of her mom's cigarettes. So vivid that she could still hear...

What...What was she hearing? Was that...people?

She was on her side...but she wasn't really on her side, was she? The vent was blowing on her ear and the glass partition of the lid was right up against her face and her arms with all her weight behind it. She wasn't on her side; the Sleeper was.

Amber could feel the fear leap into her, but she couldn't move, couldn't speak, couldn't even open her eyes. The computer kept stubbornly monitoring and testing, untroubled by the smoke it gently breathed in at her along with the oxygen and the screams she could hear behind the walls. It didn't sound like a couple panicking colonists getting cold feet on their new planet. There were so many people screaming that they had formed a single, endless, ululating voice. That didn't take just a lot of people. That took hundreds. Maybe thousands. Maybe...all of them.

Amber tried again to break the paralytic hold of the Sleeper on her body, but the only result of all her invisible efforts was a mild musical tone before the pleasant voice interrupted itself to say, "Heart-rate elevated. Please remain calm. Your reactivation is proceeding normally and will complete in...three minutes eleven seconds. You are not paralyzed. Your movements will be restored when the umbilicus is withdrawn. Please remain calm."

Three minutes? Something was burning. People were screaming. How much worse could this get in three whole minutes?

Again, she fought to take back possession of her body, but focusing all the willpower in the world couldn't even open her eyes.

"Please remain calm," said the voice after another censuring chime in her ear. "Your reactivation is proceeding normally and will complete in...one minute fifty-seven seconds. You are in no physical danger. If a medico must be dispatched to attend you, you will be liable for the cost of any restraining measures. Please remain calm."

The fact that she could smell the smoke at all—and now feel it itching at her nose and throat—meant that the fire was somewhere in the ventilating system. Or, even worse, that the Sleeper wasn't airtight the way it was supposed to be, and if it wasn't, what else wasn't working right? Where were they? Dear God, was the ship burning in space? No, no surely not. The false gravity the ship used during flight pulled everything straight toward the floors, no matter how the ship itself was tipped. She was on her side, so there had to be real gravity, meaning that they'd landed.

Only she was on her side. So they hadn't landed. They'd crashed.

"A medico has been notified of your distress," the voice informed her. "Your reactivation is proceeding normally and will complete in...one minute eleven seconds." A short pause and that musical tone again. "The umbilicus is about to be withdrawn. You may feel some discomfort."

She didn't or perhaps simply couldn't notice against the prospect of the ship burning all around her, but she could hear the whispering sound as the cable slithered out of her clothes and back into its port.

"The umbilicus has been successfully withdrawn," the computer said. "You will shortly begin to recover mobility—"

Amber's hands twitched. Then her lips, although she couldn't manage to shape the word she wanted, which was just as well since it was nothing but a swear and no one was there to hear it anyway.

"—will not open immediately. Please remain calm. Your Sleeper is in perfect working order and will unlock as soon as its final maintenance scan has been completed."

Amber's eyes opened at last, but showed her only the glass plate against her face, fogged over by her own breath. She saw no smoke, except the thin ribbons sneaking in through the vent. She was able to see only by the light of the monitoring bar as it finished its sweep down by her feet; the overhead lights had not come on the way the seminar had said they would. Her room remained perfectly black.

She rolled over, her numb arms falling limply across her stomach, slow to respond after being crushed up between her and the Sleeper's wall. The computer was still talking, telling her that she should report to the recreational area of her housing unit as soon as she was released by a member of the crew. The disembarking stations had been alerted and someone would be here shortly to release her. Did she want directions to the recreational area now?

"No," croaked Amber. She got her arm up, groping clumsily at the underside of the Sleeper's lid until she hit the medico alert switch. "Hello?" she said and coughed. The air coming in through the vents suddenly seemed smokier. And hotter. "Hello? This is Amber Bierce in room...um...three. In the women's dorms. Mod A. Or WA, I guess. I'm okay, but there's something wrong with my Sleeper. I can smell...smoke...hello?"

No answer. If she held her breath to listen, she could hear the faint hum of empty air in the speakers, so they were probably working. But no one was answering. Of course, they might all be away from the alert station, if every screaming person Amber could hear had their own medico dispatch, but Amber really didn't think so. There weren't enough medicos on the ship to answer all those screamers.

"Hello?" Amber pushed the switch again, and again, and then really leaned her thumb on it and kept it there, but no one buzzed through and told her to get off and quit being a bitch. No one told her she was on the list of panicky people to deal with and she'd be charged a fee or even arrested for making a nuisance of herself on her first day awake. No one told her anything. Because no one was there.

"Bullshit," said Amber, badly frightened. But she stopped playing with the alert switch at once and started hunting for the latch.

It opened without incident, dispersing the fear that she would be burnt to death right here in the tube, but it didn't go far. She could still be burnt to death in this room. She rolled out and onto her feet, but kept her hands on the Sleeper to help keep her balance until her head was together. The floor was definitely slanted, but not as much as she'd thought inside the tube. Maybe it was a little steeper than the average incline on, say, a wheelchair access ramp, but not much more. She could walk just fine.

Amber let go of the Sleeper and moved to the wall, unlocking her duffel bag from its restraints without any thought in her head at all except for how much she needed to hurry up and get out. Getting her luggage was Step Two of that process, right after exiting the tube and right before opening the door, so she did it. She didn't think she was in shock. She knew she was scared, but she thought she was handling it rather well, all things considered.

"Please remain in your room until you are released by a crewman. Failure to remain in your room may result in loss of privileges or reduction of earnings."

"Fucking bill me," said Amber and opened her door.

The smoke came sweeping in, eddying around her in gusts and streams, sometimes thick enough to choke, but not often. The wind was blowing the other way. The wind...

Amber looked out through her open doorway at what should be the central hall of Mod A and saw an ugly overcast sky instead. The hallway broke open just a few meters outside her door, leaving nothing but a handful of odd-numbered rooms before those too were just...gone. Out of the entire mod, there were only five doors—

nicci

Amber lunged for her sister's door, catching at its frame to anchor her on the metal ledge that used to be a hallway. Nicci's door opened as easily as her own had done. Nicci's Sleeper was still shut. Nicci was on her side, both hands pressed to her face, crying. She screamed when Amber opened the Sleeper, slapping and kicking and trying to pull the lid shut again until Amber got her by the arms and gave her a shake.

"I'm having a nightmare," sobbed Nicci, still struggling. Then her dazed eyes finally seemed to focus. She shrank back against the wall of her Sleeper, then let out a startling cawing cry and attacked.

To Amber's knowledge, Nicci had never hit anyone or anything in her life. It was the last thing she was expecting; she never thought to duck away but only stood gaping as her baby sister slapped her in the forehead, the ear, the chin and the nose. Then Nicci burst into fresh tears and lunged in to hug her, howling, "You promised there wouldn't be dreams! I want to wake up now! Right now!"

Amber brought up her arms and hugged her back. If it wasn't for the mild throbbing of her nose—Nicci was no better at hitting than Amber at dodging—she'd wonder if it had really happened at all. Nicci didn't hit people and Nicci would never hit *her*. They were sisters. They were all either of them had left.

'She's in shock,' Amber decided. 'People in shock do weird things.' "Come on,

Nicci," she said out loud. "Get your bag."

"I don't want it."

"Get it anyway. We have to go."

Nicci allowed herself to be pulled from the Sleeper and put on her feet, but she made no effort to do more than that. Amber had to pull down her duffel bag and put it in Nicci's arms, and then had to take her sister by the hand and physically lead her through the door. Nicci moaned when she saw what was waiting outside and refused to step out onto the broken ledge, but Amber didn't try to force her yet. She didn't know where to go either. Following the green line back through the ship to the boarding bay was the only thing she could think of; it seemed that the ship had broken cleanly off at the perimeter wall of Mod A, suggesting that the rest of the ship was still there. That it might be a very bad idea to go any deeper into the burning ship did not yet occur to her. She let go of Nicci, who promptly began to cry harder, and eased carefully out along the ledge until she could reach the keypad beside the sealed door that separated the women's dorms from the rest of the ship. The ship was slanted so that gravity pulled her into the wall, which was lucky because she was not the most coordinated person under the best of conditions. When the door didn't open at her touch, Amber turned around and put her back to it, utterly lost. Where was she supposed to go now?

Down.

She looked down through shifting walls of smoke and saw Mod A and the rest of the *Pioneer* about five meters below her, all three levels—*crew civilian and ship's functions thank god for all those informative seminars i learned so much*—pancaked together in a rumpled ruin, like a burnt blanket someone had tossed on the floor. Beyond it, the blackened scar of the ship's landing reached out for miles, lifeless.

But someone was alive. The screaming/sobbing/hysteria had never stopped, never even slackened. People were alive and they weren't in Mod A, that was for sure.

Amber crept back along the wall to Nicci. "We have to get down from here," she said firmly. She felt better, having a goal, a plan. "So we're going to drop down—"

"No! No, we can't! We'll fall!"

"It's not that far, Nicci. We can do this."

"We have to stay here, okay? Someone will come and get us, okay?"

"Maybe," said Amber, looking doubtfully back at the sealed door that led deeper into the ship and where she knew (in the shocky state she didn't realize she was in) the crew and the Fleet were mobilizing to meet this emergency. "But it could be a long time before they get to us and the ship is on fire. I'm not waiting. We're going down."

Nicci shook her head frantically, even as her tears subsided. She had to be tugged out onto the ledge, but after that she moved on her own. Giving orders made Amber feel better; taking them had the same effect on Nicci.

"Right there." Amber pointed to the little jut that was left in front of the mod door. "That'll be the shortest drop. Send your bag down first and try to land on it."

"You go first, okay?"

Amber shook her head. "I've got to check the other rooms."

"No! Don't leave me! You can't leave me!"

"I'm not leaving, I'm just—"

"No!"

"Damn it, Nicci, just do it!" Amber shouted. "This is serious, so stop acting like a fucking baby and go!"

Nicci stared at her, tears sliding sideways on her face in the wind.

Amber stared back, as stunned or more than she'd been after Nicci's attack. She and Nicci fought now and then, but she didn't think she'd ever raised her voice before. At Mama, sure...but not at Nicci. She wondered if the crash had made her go crazy, the way that things sometimes did in the movies. "I'll be right behind you," she said.

"Okay?"

Nicci nodded, silent. She looked down, hugging her duffel bag to her chest, then slowly got to her knees. Her lips moved, but the wind took away her words.

"You can do it," said Amber, backing away. "I'll be right back."

Nicci did not react. She might not have heard, the way Amber hadn't heard whatever she'd said. It was the wind...and the screaming.

Amber turned around, groping her way along the wall past Nicci's room and her own to the next room, WA-0005. The door opened when she slapped the pad and the woman pacing inside immediately turned on her in the kind of calm, accusatory fury that meant she was probably on the verge of some pretty impressive hysterics. "It's about goddamn time! What the hell is going on? Who are you? Are you one of the crew?"

"No, I'm from next door. We crashed. Get your things."

"Figures. This is all the military's fault," she spat, yanking ineffectively at her duffel bag until Amber came over and opened the restraints. "The Director had billions and billions of dollars, but oh no, he had to let the military take over and what did they do? They contracted out to the lowest bidder. Over eighty percent of this ship was built in Uruguay, do you believe that?"

"Uh..."

"It's a fact," the woman insisted, shrugging the duffel onto her shoulder. "You can look it up. Or at least, you can look it up when we get back to Earth and you better believe that's where I'm going right now. Right now! And if they don't have a lifeboat on this goddamn thing that can get me there..." She faltered, some of the fire in her eyes fading behind a shine of watery panic, but only for a moment. She shored herself up, her shaking hands clenching into fists around her duffel bag's strap. "Where are we going?"

Amber moved aside. The woman's eyes flicked past her to the smoky sky where the other half of the hallway should have been. Her brows knit. She took one step forward and looked down, at the top of the *Pioneer*. Her lips parted, then pressed firmly together.

"I am going to sue their precious little Director to death," she announced. "I'm going to start a class-action suit and just...just kill him with it. Where do we go?"

Amber pointed down the ledge to the place where Nicci still huddled, hugging her duffel bag. "Drop down from there. Make sure she gets down too, okay?"

The woman nodded and went, keeping one hand on the wall and the other in a firm grip on her duffel's strap. Amber watched until she saw the woman talking and Nicci listening, or at least looking up, and then worked her way back to room WA-0007, but when the door opened, it showed her only half a room. The hallway wall might continue on for two more doors, but the ship itself stopped here. There was no Sleeper, no angry occupant ranting about lawsuits and Uruguay, no floor. There was only smoke, broken framework, spitting cables, and the ruin of the ship below her. Of the four thousand people who shared this mod of the women's dorms, she'd saved everyone there was to save.

All three of them.

The shock she hadn't known she was in suddenly welled huge inside her and popped, soundless, like a soap bubble. Amber staggered back, feeling the slant in the floor and the distance between her and the ground for the first time to real, disorienting effect. Smoke filled the gasping breath she took; she bent, coughing, and saw the world darken around her.

'If you faint up here, you'll fall and die,' she thought, but she wasn't fainting. The world really was darker. The clouds overhead were thickening; the heavy wind didn't seem to be blowing them away, but rather pulling them down. She'd never seen clouds do that before. It wasn't even raining.

But it was cold. It was cold and the wind was brutal and the only shelter Amber could see was a burning ship.

She didn't know what to do.

5

She stood there for an undeterminable stretch of truly awful minutes, locked in a kind of mindless, paralyzed panic, aware that time was passing but utterly incapable of doing anything about it. It was bad, and she often thought back on that moment later with the idea that that had to be at least some of what Hell was like, if there was a Hell worse than this, but eventually Amber looked down and saw Nicci below her, huddled small against a twisted flap of metal in the torn hull. Smoke poured through this wound so thickly it formed a solid wall behind her, but Nicci just sat there. Like it was a safe place. The other woman had left already but Nicci was waiting for her. Nicci needed her, just like always. She had to be there.

"Okay," whispered Amber, and started back down the ledge. "Time to suck it up, little girl. Let's do this."

She dropped her duffel bag over the side and tried to dangle herself over it, but her arms gave out before she even had both legs free of the ledge. She fell with a yelp and landed mostly on her back, missing her stupid duffel bag entirely. She lay there for a second or two, dazed and breathless, needing Nicci to come tug at her arm before she could pull herself together enough to try and stand.

"Are you okay?" she managed, rubbing at her back.

"No."

Amber looked her up and down. "You're fine," she said, and picked up Nicci's duffel bag, shoving it once more into her sister's arms. "Where'd the other lady go?"

Nicci looked helplessly around. "I-I don't know..."

"Nicci, we have to stay together," Amber said firmly. "I know you're scared, but we'll get through this. Now I need you to pull it together. Which way did she go?"

Mutely, Nicci pointed across the smoky wreckage.

"Okay," said Amber. She shrugged to feel the weight of her duffel bag more securely against her shoulder. She took her sister's hand and squeezed it. She was fine. They were both fine. She started walking.

When they reached the edge of the hull, there was another drop, but the buckling of the *Pioneer's* metal skin when Mod A had broken off made for a fairly easy descent. Not as easy as walking down a set of stairs, but there weren't any more painful landings and when they reached the bottom, they were standing on the ground. True, the ground had melted and cooled again into a mass just as rigid and uneven as the crumpled hull had been, but it *was* the ground and that made her feel better. She was off the ship and she'd gotten Nicci off the ship. Now she just had to find the others.

They walked, hand in hand, around the side of the *Pioneer* and as soon as they'd navigated the corner and were out of the smoke and most of the wind, there they all were. And at first, she thought it wasn't that bad. People were screaming, crying, and hysterical, sure, but there were a lot of them. They'd survived. That had to count for something, right?

Her relief at seeing so many survivors was a kind of second shock, and its bolstering effects wore off much more quickly. Even as she was taking that first reassuring look at the crowds, her vision seemed to double, and suddenly the hundreds of people before her shrank back into the miniscule fraction of fifty thousand colonists and crewmen that it really was. She staggered on her feet a little and then turned slowly around and looked at the ship.

This time, she really saw it.

The *Pioneer* had scraped over the skin of this alien world for miles, sharpening itself like a knife; family housing and the rest of the forward compartments were gone, rubbed away, and the pointed tip of what was left had ultimately struck something unyielding in the ground and stabbed itself in. This was what had created the steep angle of the ship's final position, which had in turn created the awful weight that had caused not just Mod A but also Mods B and C to break away and fall. All the women's dorms were gone. The men's mods were still there, jutting crazily into the sky and spewing fire from every opening. Virtually everyone was dead.

The world got oddly lighter. This time, it wasn't the clouds. Amber realized with a start that she was trying to faint and so she sat down and leaned forward to put her head between her knees as far as her bodily dimensions made possible. She really didn't want to faint. Whatever was going to happen next, she wanted to be awake when it happened. Bo Peep's little girl was not about to die with her eyes closed.

The warmth and soft press of a body beside her told her Nicci had sat down too. Amber raised her head a little and looked at the *Pioneer* some more. This was what she'd spent six days bullying her baby sister into. This was what she'd lost her apartment, her job, and sixty pounds for. This was it.

She leaned forward again and opened her mouth, but apart from a groggy belch, nothing came out. She hadn't had anything in her stomach for years, after all. Maybe a lot of years. Like...hundreds.

That made her want to throw up again, but since that was just futility, Amber made herself look around some more instead. She could see a cluster of uniforms standing apart from the rest, close to the biggest gash in the smoking side of the ship, and a little ways from them stood just two—one crimson and gold Manifestor and one military grey Fleetman, close together, deep in conversation.

She stood up.

Nicci caught at once at her hand. "Where are you going?"

The last thing Amber wanted was to start a mob. She bent over to speak softly against Nicci's ear. "To see if I can't find out what's going to happen next."

"Next?" Nicci's hand tightened painfully. She didn't seem aware of it. Her eyes were huge, glazed, pleading. "We're...Someone's going to come, right? Someone's going to come from Earth and rescue us? We're going home now, right?"

A few people looked their way. Amber made a point of patting Nicci's hand, trying to look as if she were comforting someone. She wasn't sure if people really patted other people's hands for comfort or if that was just in books, but no one paid them too much attention, so she guessed that was all right.

"Keep your voice down," she said, once she was fairly confident they had privacy again. "And don't freak yourself out. Panicking can't help anyone."

"Amber..." Nicci's staring eyes became a wondering, glassy gape. "Amber, the ship crashed! We crashed here! People are dead!"

"I mean it, Nicci, calm down."

But Nicci either wouldn't or couldn't obey. Her voice kept rising, sending shards of panic through every quavery word. "We crashed here! Half the ship is gone! Amber, the ship is broken! We have to be rescued! *We have to be rescued right now*!"

Amber grabbed a fistful of Nicci's shirt and yanked her to her feet, thrusting her face right up close. She hissed, "Shut up or I'll slap the shit out of you and I guaran-goddamn-tee I'll be better at that than you are! Shut! Up!"

Nicci did, trembling. She blinked and tears came bubbling out of her, but they were silent tears for now. Her lips pressed together, turned downwards in a clownish exaggeration of sorrow.

"If you panic, other people are going to panic and once that starts, we are not going to be able to stop it, so you take deep breaths or do whatever you have to do, but you keep quiet, do you hear me?"

Nicci nodded. The action tipped a few more tears out of her. They trickled sideways across her cheeks, blown off-kilter by the wind, and fell into her hair. "I'm scared," she said. Little Nicci, like she was all of six years old again.

"Go ahead and be scared all you want," said Amber, releasing her. "Just do it quietly." She looked back at the uniforms. They were still talking. She took Nicci's hand (*cold jesus how cold is it going to get when the sun goes down i don't see any animals no birds not even bugs maybe it gets like a hundred below and nothing can live here*) and started walking, trying to look aimless so she wouldn't get too much attention, but movement has a way of attracting the eye and people were staring.

Halfway there, Nicci started bawling. That helped. There was enough misery around here that no one wanted to see any more of it. The people who had been dully watching her found other places to send their thousand-yard stare.

Nicci...

Amber dropped back a little and put her arm around her sister's shoulders. Nicci hugged on her like a child wanting to be carried and cried the same way, loud and graceless, soaking heat and wetness into Amber's shirt.

"It's okay," she heard herself say inanely. She rubbed at Nicci's shaking back and watched smoke fly away in wind-blown stripes from the ship. So much smoke. "It's okay, we'll be okay."

"I didn't want to be here!" Nicci brayed. "I didn't want to do this!"

Guilt knotted at her heart and sank all the way down into her stomach. "I know."

"You made me! Why did you *make* me?"

"Nicci...please, it'll be okay."

"I want to go home!"

"I'm sorry, Nicci. I am. Come on."

The two men who seemed to be doing the deep talking stopped as Amber approached them. She recognized the Manifestor up close—Crewman Everly Scott, who she'd made such a great impression on at boarding—but not the Fleetman he was with. If she knew how to read pips, she'd know his rank at least, but all Amber could see was an older black man of distinctly military bearing, with a worried face and smudges of soot along the left side of his mostly-hairless head. "Can I help you, ma'am?" he asked, once it must have been obvious that she was really coming to talk to them.

"I can't think of how," Amber replied honestly enough. She rubbed Nicci's back some more, trying to quiet her so that they could talk without shouting too hard. The wind made that difficult enough. "I'm not trying to put you on the spot or anything, but if you guys are talking about plans, I'd like to hear them."

"Go sit down," said Scott firmly. "As soon as we've debriefed ourselves on proper procedure—"

"No offense," Amber said, looking at him. "But I don't believe for a second you actually have a procedure that covers something like this. I am all for postponing the main panic, but we all need to know what happens next."

"Go find a seat," Scott began again, but the soldier stopped him there.

"At this point, ma'am," he said, "all we're doing is talking out the situation."

"But we're going to get rescued, right?" Nicci reached out to grab at his uniform. He gave her hand a pat. He did it a lot better than Amber had, using the gesture not only to pry her off, but also to sit her down on the ground.

"If you've got any ideas," the soldier went on, taking off his jacket to drape around Nicci's shaking shoulders, "I'm willing to hear you out. But if I can be as blunt with you as you've been with us, if you haven't got something to say, you need to move on and let us try to do our job."

"You can tell us how you're going to sue us later," Scott added derisively.

Amber shot him an angry glance, then redirected herself to the other man. "I feel like I need to get the stupid questions out first, just so we're all on one page, okay?"

"Fair enough."

"Do you know what happened?"

"More or less. We were hit by some sort of unmapped interstellar traffic...an asteroid field or maybe we passed through the tail of a comet or something. The shields are supposed to be able to repel collision, but...the hull was penetrated in a number of places...a lot of systems took heavy damage. There was massive explosive decompression. None of the active crew appear to have survived it."

"Is this...all of us?"

"I don't know." The Fleetman's gaze skewed away to stare at the ship, at the men's dorms in particular, burning so hard they could actually hear it, even over the wind. "The military mods survived the crash more or less, but the asteroids...or whatever they were..." He trailed off, then shook his head and looked at her. "Most of the Sleepers I saw in my unit looked like Swiss cheese, ma'am. So did the people inside them. People I knew."

"I...I'm sorry." The smallness of that sympathy could not stand against the present horror. Amber groped for something better, then gave up and simply said, "So we're it?"

"There could be others. I just don't know. The mods sealed themselves as part of the emergency lockdown. None of the communication stations appear to be working. I have no idea what the situation is...underground. For all I know, parts of the ship could still be intact, but it's...not likely. I've got some men trying to organize a search and rescue operation, but it's been...slow starting."

Amber nodded. "How long have we been flying blind?"

"I don't know how long, but we can't have been entirely blind or we wouldn't be breathing this atmosphere, we'd be melting in it." He broke off there, ran one hand over the side of his smooth head and started again, more calmly. "The ship has several emergency failsafes in place. Locating an Earth-class planet and landing was one of them, but...I don't even know off the top of my head how many others had to fail for that one to engage. In the event of any major incident, the ship was supposed to take us home."

"Do you know where we are?"

"No, although the guidance system itself has to be functioning or we never would have made it here. This planet is very Earth-like. And before you ask me which world it is, understand that there are over seven thousand Earth-like planets in the Fleet's database, and we've mapped less than one percent of one percent of this galaxy. Without a working guidance system's interface, we have no way of discovering where we are."

"Can anyone repair it?"

He spread his hands, his expression pained. "With what?"

"All right. I have to ask. Is there an emergency beacon or any way to send a transmission of any kind back home?"

The Fleetman nodded back in the direction of the fractured ship while still holding her eyes. "At the very best, we have lost thirty percent of the ship's structure, including the entire command center, and the primary and tertiary lifeboat launching bays. That number could be as high as seventy-five percent if none of the structure below the surface has survived impact. Even if the halls have collapsed, the skeleton could be intact. Right now, I have to hope that it is, because only if we can tunnel our way in to certain engineering portals do we have any hope of making the necessary repairs to the guidance system."

"You said the primary and the tertiary bays were out. What about the secondary lifeboats?" Amber asked. "Is there a beacon or anything with them?"

"There is. And that—" The Fleetman pointed up at the extreme tip of the blazing men's dorm. "—is the bay where it is located. It looks like it might be intact and if it's locked down like the rest of the compartment doors, it might not even be burning. Getting to it is going to be a process, but I have to tell you, ma'am—"

"Amber. Amber Bierce."

"Amber." His brows furrowed slightly. "Jonah Lamarc, Lieutenant Junior-Grade."

That was a lot further down the authority ladder than she'd been hoping to hear, and by the look on his face, he knew it. But he struck her as a thoughtful man and definitely not prone to panic. She put out her hand impulsively.

He shook it while Crewman Scott watched.

"It's going to be a process?" Amber prompted.

"But I believe it can be done, once the fire burns itself out," he finished, and then gave his head a grim shake. "Miss Bierce, I don't think I'd say this to anyone else out there, but you seem to have a level head and I want to be honest with you."

"Go on then. I'm braced."

"I'm not sure we can launch a beacon from this location—planet-side, I mean—but assuming that it is possible, we first have to get guidance repaired, online and talking to the beacon so that it can orient itself to Earth. After that..." He paused again, looking down at Nicci, who had drawn up her knees and was now resting her head atop them and lightly rocking. He looked back at Amber, his expression drawn and greyed with strain. "I haven't talked around much yet, but I served my second shift before the incident, so I know it's been at least two years, plus however long the ship was flying blind to get to this planet after it was hit. But even if we magically crashed the instant after I went back in Sleep, we'd still have been Tunneling for two years before that. We can't be less than five hundred light-years from Earth," Lamarc said softly, slowly. His eyes communicated far more than his careful words. "And that is way more than we have mapped out along our pre-arranged route. Even if we were only knocked a little bit off-course, which I'm guessing—" He looked pointedly around, taking in the whole planet at a glance. "—may be overly optimistic, our guidance system might not be able to find Earth."

Nicci moaned and began to sob again.

"Okay," said Amber. "Now what's the real problem?"

He shared her lackluster smile. "Believe it or not, there is a real problem."

"Oh for God's sake. Okay. What is it?"'

"The beacon doesn't have tunnel-drive. It was never meant to travel at anything close to that speed, not even at light-speed. So even if we are only five hundred light-years away, and even if we can reach the beacon, repair it, program it, and launch it tomorrow through this planet's atmosphere and onward straight to Earth, it will take more than six thousand years for the damned thing to get there."

"So there's no point in looking for it," said Amber. After a moment, she hammered the reality home with a nod. "All right. So we're here."

He frowned at Nicci, then at her. "I didn't say that and I wouldn't, if I were you. For a while, that hope of rescue is all that is going to keep some of these people alive."

"So what are you planning?"

"We haven't decided," said Scott.

Lamarc glanced at him, still frowning. "We're discussing our options."

"What have you come up with so far?"

"I believe our best hope of survival lies with the ship," said Lamarc, and did not react when Scott heaved a short, hard sigh at him. "It was built to be a ready-made city.

It provides shelter and security against the elements here and, most importantly, familiarity. We have food, moisture evaporators and purifiers, medical facilities, and general supplies to last easily a hundred years. Comfort is going to be our most precious resource for the immediate future and it should not be underestimated."

Amber looked at the ship and said nothing. She could hear the logic in his words, but she could also see the smoke funneling out of dozens, if not hundreds, of wounds. And where there was smoke...

At last, just to demonstrate that she wasn't a complete bitch and he shouldn't feel the need to be a complete bastard, Amber looked at Scott. "What do you think?"

Even if she was a civilian and therefore an unnecessary component to this conversation, Scott seemed pleased to be asked. "I think the first thing we need to do is re-establish a chain of command. And maybe we shouldn't be so quick to blindly adopt the ranks we held before. It's clear that the disaster has taken a mental toll on certain members of the Fleet and I would be hesitant to put any of them in a position of authority. And we could even bring some civilians in," he added, including Amber in a magnanimous sweep of his arm and completely overlooking the fact that, snappy uniform or no, the Manifest Destiny badge on the sleeve of his jacket did not put him on the same level as an officer in the Fleet, or in any other army, or even in the Cub Scouts. "Some of them, anyway. But the main thing is, if we're going to establish any kind of a future here, we have to know who's in charge."

She had a feeling he had a name in mind. "Okay. Let's pretend it's you. What's your plan, Commander?"

Scott threw Lamarc a fierce smile, the sort that could make even a handsome man like him look schoolyard-small and mean. "Like he said, we have enough supplies to last us for a long time, so nothing is more important than knowing what we're up against. We need to organize units to scout out the terrain and establish a perimeter. We need to organize defenses. We need to arm ourselves."

"And I told you, the munitions bay is gone," said Lamarc flatly. He turned to Amber. "What about you? Do you have any suggestions?"

She scowled, her eye going back to the ship and the smoke pouring out of it. "Lieutenant Lamarc—"

"Jonah," he said quietly.

Scott frowned.

"Jonah, that ship is on fire. And there aren't enough words in the world to fully express just how bad a feeling I have about hanging around a burning ship where the extent of the damage is completely unknown."

He nodded once, acknowledging without comment, waiting.

"I agree with what you said about shelter and security, but I'm sorry, until those fires are out, I think we'd ought to make camp somewhere else."

"Which means we need to start scouting now," said Scott. "Before we lose the light."

"I haven't made a count yet," said Jonah. "But at a guess, I believe I'm looking at close to two thousand badly frightened people, some of them with missing loved ones, and all of them in shock. Present company most definitely included." He rubbed at the side of his head again. "Moving that many people overland on an alien world away from the ship they rode in on would be disastrous to morale, not to mention devastating to the terrain itself. If it rains, which is damned likely looking at that sky, two thousand pairs of feet are only going to need a few seconds to turn this ground into quick-mud. Also, we might be able to carry enough food with us for a few days, but not water. We have evaporators and we have purifiers, but we have no actual water. And, I'm sorry, but where are we going to go to the bathroom? I can see you think that's a pretty trivial point, but I guarantee it won't seem as trivial when two thousand people have dysentery."

"We're going to have all those problems no matter where we are."

"Yes, eventually. But here at the ship, we can postpone them. Amber, if we don't give those people some kind of familiar routine, something safe to cling to, we're going to lose them. People this lost, this desperate...don't need a lot of help to die."

"Okay," interrupted Scott as Amber gazed out at the sea of survivors, "I think these are all valid points, but you've brought us right back to the issue of who's in charge. You can't develop a routine without someone giving orders."

Amber shook her head and looked back at Jonah. "I admit it's been a while since my last babysitting gig, but I'm pretty sure that making sure the babies don't catch fire is higher up on the priority list than making sure they don't have nightmares. Jonah, staying here is a bad idea!"

"I know it looks bad, but each compartment of the ship is designed to seal itself specifically so that fires don't spread."

"Yeah, and the ship is designed to turn itself around and go back to Earth if it gets hit by an asteroid. And who knows what else has been damaged? Things can be leaking and melting and overheating as we speak! We can't afford blind faith, Jonah! We can only trust what we can see and I can see the smoke!"

"Can you see the people?" he asked quietly. "Can you see their faces? Can you see yourself marching them away when the wind is blowing this hard and this cold and no one knows what night will bring? And what about the people we can't see? What about the people who may still be trapped behind those sealed doors, just praying that someone up here at least *tries* to find them? Amber—" He took her hand between both of his; she looked down at her small wrist being swallowed by his giant grip and thought of him patting Nicci as he guided her to the ground. He was awfully good at the comforting stuff. "Amber, if we don't give these people some time to come to grips with what has happened to them, some of them never will. You may be thinking of them as two thousand survivors and I know Crewman Scott sees them as two thousand colonists, but they are neither. Right now, as of this moment, they are two thousand *victims* and they need to be taken care of. Please."

Scott paced a few meters away and came back, looking profoundly annoyed with both of them.

"I want to take them in out of the wind for just two or three weeks. Let them dig for that beacon and fix a few broken doors. God willing, let them save a life, just one, to remind them that life is precious and hope can be rewarded. Put them back in control and then talk to them about survival. What can it hurt to give them just two or three weeks to learn how to cope? I want your support on this," said Jonah. "Please."

Amber looked at the ship. She tried not to see the smoke. She tried to look through the emergency doors at the hold and imagine two thousand people sleeping there tonight. She threw in a snowstorm to help weigh down the vision and a couple generic howling-monster sounds. She pictured Jonah with his jacket off the next day, arranging teams to work in shifts clearing the halls, repairing machinery, sorting supplies, and later, building gardens and houses and latrines. She saw him taking charge and it was an easy thing to see. She saw the ship turning into a colony after all, and maybe it would only be the shell of one at first, but as she pulled back the camera of her mind, she could see the ship in a better time, in the summer maybe, with crop-fields and canals in orbit around it, a thriving hub of life and hope and—

—or it could all blow up in an hour, she thought, in a voice so clear it might as well be someone speaking directly in her ear. And she saw that pretty damned clearly too: the wind, just like it was now, whipping the giant fireball of its belching destruction into an orange tornado for maybe two or three seconds before blowing it all away. Nothing would be left but the crater where they landed, the twisted skeleton of the hull, and a Rorschach scorch-mark burned into the stone, maybe in the shape of a butterfly.

"I can't stay here," Amber heard herself say.

Nicci raised her head and looked at her.

"Not tonight," she amended. "I think...I think maybe Scott's got a point about the perimeter thing. Maybe it would help these people start coping faster if we took some of the mystery out of where we are."

Scott looked surprised for a second and then smiled.

"So here's what I think. I think we should make a camp..." She looked around and pointed. "On that ridge. Call it a lookout post. We'll organize a team and take whatever supplies we need to set up, you know, some latrines and supply tents. If nothing else, it'll give people something to do who don't know how to fix doors or program emergency beacons. And who knows? We might look down from that ridge and see...I don't know, a lake or whatever they have for cows or someplace easier to live than this."

Jonah shook his head, not in denial, but in mute helplessness. He looked out at the survivors and then down at her. "Can you give me until morning to work with them? Please. We can take a head-count, get some kind of inventory for our supplies...If nothing else, give me that time to see if anyone is trapped in there."

That wasn't unreasonable, she thought, and said instead, unexpectedly, "No. I'm sorry, but if anyone is trapped in there, they're already dead. The ship is on fire. It is not a safe place. We have got to get away from it tonight."

His gaze was troubled; his hands, warm. "They won't be moved tonight."

"Then move as many as you can. We..." *can't save everybody*, trembled unspoken on her lips. She swallowed them, wondering where in the hell this was all coming from. She didn't feel panicked, but maybe panicking was like being crazy or having a fever, where you couldn't tell just by feeling at yourself. "We can't stay," she finished.

Jonah looked at the people again, watching them the way another man might watch the tides. His eyes went back and forth, tracking motion no one else saw.

"I think a lookout post is a great idea," Scott announced. "I'll start putting a team together."

"I can't leave them," said Jonah quietly.

"I said I'd do it," said Scott, frowning again. "I want to be in charge. Of the lookout team. You can be in charge of these people."

"I wish you'd come with us," Amber said. The words felt heavy, too much like a confession.

"Yeah, well...I wish you'd stay." Jonah uttered an oddly thin laugh for such a big man. "When the lights go out, things are going to get a lot worse. I was really starting to hope you'd stick around because I'm going to need someone to roll around with if I'm going to get any sleep tonight." He rubbed at his head, shook it, rubbed some more. "That was offensive. I'm sorry. I'm just..."

Scared. And fear does weird things to people.

"Jesus, man!" Scott was staring. "I can't believe you just said that!"

Amber gave Jonah a lopsided smile and squeezed his slack hand. "I'll help you sleep plenty at the lookout post, Lieutenant Lamarc. Just come with us."

Scott gaped at both of them now.

"Another time, Miss Bierce." Jonah pulled in a breath and let it out as a military man. "I can think of a few men who you might want along. I'll talk to them."

"I'll come back," said Amber. "As soon as the smoke stops, I swear."

He nodded, started to walk away, and then stopped. When he came back, she thought for one dizzying, unreal moment that he meant to kiss her and she'd already made up her mind to allow it (*total stranger old enough to be my father for god's sake and what he'd want in a chubby little white girl like me i don't know he probably doesn't either but fear now fear does weird things oh yeah play it again sam fear can really fuck you up*), but instead, he put out his hand.

They shook.

"Take care of things," said Amber.

"I will," he replied. "Come back safe."

"I wlll."

They walked away then, and as things turned out, those were the last words they said to one another and they both lied.

6

Crewman Scott put himself in command. This initially made for some tense moments when he was trying to recruit for what he was calling 'reconnaissance and establishment of a forward operations base,' particularly from the Fleetmen, who certainly seemed open to doing something but were visibly hostile to the idea of taking orders from a Manifestor in a make-believe uniform. No punches were thrown, but Scott quickly moved his efforts to the cluster of sobbing, shock-eyed civilians.

Amber left him to it without much hope and distracted her jangling nerves as much as she was able by venturing into whatever exposed areas of the ship she could reach, picking through the wreckage for anything they could use. Since the supplies had been evenly distributed among each mod throughout the ship, there was plenty to find, even if it was all mashed together in the aftermath of the crash. Unfortunately, the crates were all marked with such baffling examples of Fleet-speak that she had to bust them open to find out what the hell was inside. This was a lot of work with little reward; none of the really useful things were portable and most of the small stuff was ridiculous. Thumbtacks. Baby bottles. Yarmulkes. Replacement sponge-heads for the oscillating arm on a model Dynamo-3Z cleanerbot. Swimming goggles, for Christ's sake, perfect for lounging around the colony pool on Plymouth.

The frustrating search ultimately turned up a stash of duffel bags (each one proudly screaming out the Manifest Destiny logo), which she started stuffing with the one useful item she had dug out of the wreckage: some Fleet-issue ration bars packed like bricks in a khaki-colored crate where the available flavors were listed as Choc, Van and Other. These were Other. Nowhere on the individual bars did it indicate what Other was, but she guessed as long as it wasn't worm, booger or bubblegum, she was fine.

"Ma'am?"

She looked up without stopping, taking stock of the four Fleetmen coming toward her—three boys and an older man—and making up her mind right then that if they pulled some bullshit military rule out of their asses to stop her from taking this stuff, she'd kick it right back up there.

But, "Lieutenant Lamarc said you were looking for a few good men," said one of them, putting out his hand. "Eric Lassiter. Engineer Second Class."

"Engineer?" she said uncertainly. "Did Jonah, um, Lieutenant Lamarc tell you what I wanted was to get away from the ship?"

"Yes, ma'am. We're here to help."

"Are you sure? Wouldn't you rather stay here with, you know, the other engineers?"

He was already shaking his head. "Enlisted engineer," he said, putting the stress on the first word. "That's construction. Well, that's the grunt work for the construction units, but I'm pretty sure I can help you throw together your forward operations outpost or whatever that idiot out there wants. This is Crandall."

"Brian," said the next guy, also shaking her hand. "Electronics tech. And before you ask, I've already given this tin bitch my professional attention and concluded that she's fucked. So I figured I could at least carry shit around."

"Same," said the third man. "Gunnarson, Dagwood D. Call me Dag." He nodded at the duffel bag she was filling. "I was the main supply clerk in Corporate Mod G, so I know where everything was. I know it all got tossed around pretty good, but if nothing else, I can read the codes on the labels." He gave the haphazardly-opened crates around her a meaningful glance. "Maybe focus on finding stuff we really need, like tents."

"And medical supplies," said the last of them. He was the older one, although it was tough to say just how much older. He was Asian and his face was creased but ageless. He had no accent, unless it was a trace of some southern state, but he bent his head to her instead of taking the hand she extended. "Yao. Lucas, I should say, circumstances being what they are, but I prefer Mr. Yao."

"He's a doctor," Eric supplied, pointing at the little frills sewn onto Mr. Yao's sleeve which apparently proved it.

"I am not a doctor of medicine." The older man did not look around. "And I'd just as soon be Mr. Yao from now on. My service contract appears to have expired."

There was a short, ugly silence while the five of them stood there, avoiding one another's eyes.

"I'm Amber," she said belatedly, just to get them talking again.

It worked.

"So you are the right girl," said Eric, glancing once at Mr. Yao, who wandered off, righting crates and checking labels as he went. "Great. Lamarc said you were heading out with that other guy. Thought you might like a hand."

"If we can ever get going. How's he doing out there? Scott, I mean."

"He's bringing 'em around, shockingly enough." Dag shrugged, rolling his eyes as he did it. "He's got all the enthusiasm of a bulldog with none of the brains—and those are some dumb dogs, lady—but give the man his credit, he can talk a great line."

"Of bullshit," snorted Crandall, checking the contents of the packed duffels. "Lady, you need to disperse some of this stuff. No normal person's gonna be able to carry a hundred pounds of MREs."

And after that, it was all unpacking and re-packing and shouting questions or advice at each other across the dark, cluttered bay. It kept Amber's mind nicely occupied until they were done and emerged into the cold, smoky light to find that Scott was still talking, although he was at least winding down.

Amber sat down on a bundle of tents to watch as he marched himself importantly among the masses, trying to win them over with talk of setbacks and the necessity of moving forward in the footsteps of their pioneer forefathers, who had also suffered unspeakable tragedy in the fulfillment of their goals, also undertaken in the name of Manifest Destiny. And because it was manifest, because it was true, because it was a goal set in their hearts by that higher power that all men, regardless of creed, aspired to, it was still a goal worth seeking.

"At any cost!" Scott thundered in conclusion, smacking his fist into the palm of his hand. "But never think that makes us unmindful of the cost. The cost will be counted, just as we remember and honor those who perished in the crossing of the ocean, who were buried alongside the ruts carved by covered wagons, and whose wooden markers were paved under by the rising streets of San Francisco! The people we have lost today are our fallen heroes, but *we* are the heroes who go on!"

To Amber's mild astonishment, that actually worked. Not on everyone, of course, but he got some applause for that flowery heap of horseshit even while Scott was still pumping it out.

"What'd I tell you?" said Eric beside her, shaking his head. "I guess it's true what my grandma says. God gives even the biggest fool one real talent."

"What's yours?" asked Amber, watching people line up to shake Scott's hand.

"Hoops."

"You wish, whitebread," said Dag, who was just as white as a man named Dag Gunnarson ought to be.

Scott shook hands, patted shoulders, began to put people in a group.

"I'm ambidextrous," Crandall announced suddenly.

"Oh yeah?"

"Selectively. Eating, smoking and jerking off." He started to mime, re-discovered Amber in their midst and stopped, looking flustered.

"I ain't blushing," she said dryly and wasn't. She'd heard worse—seen worse—in the stairwell back home.

Scott finally headed their way, with Nicci walking close at his side although she was quick to do her huddling next to Amber once she got there.

"We're ready," he said, giving the Fleetmen a stiff, soldierly sort of nod. "I haven't done an official head-count, but there must be a couple hundred of them."

"Yeah..." said Eric, eyeing the crowd. He shook his head. "They might all be willing to come live in the tents once they're up, but I bet we don't even get half that when it comes to carrying this stuff up that hill tonight."

"So let's hurry and get them set up," said Amber, slinging her duffel over one arm and snatching up a bundled tent in the other.

"Just relax for a bit, Miss Bierce," said Scott, also frowning back at the crowd now. "Let me talk to them some more and—"

"Do what you got to do, Everly," said Amber, walking. "You can meet me there."

She didn't mean it any way but exactly what she'd said—do all the talking he wanted, get more people on board, meet her on the ridge—but he took it for a challenge and an ugly one at that. She heard him clapping his hands and shouting people into order and within a few minutes he was shouldering his way roughly past her to take the lead.

She thought about saying something *(ah hey i didn't mean it like that be cool you're still the commanding space scout here so grow the fuck up and quit shoving),* but in the end it was enough that they were moving. Amber reached out to catch Nicci's hand and give it a reassuring little squeeze. They were moving and as bad as things were, that made her feel just a little bit better.

* * *

Much later, in the waning light of the alien, cloud-covered sunset, Amber finally took that head count. She couldn't do anything else at the moment, not after that hike, except sit on the ground with her aching, rubbery legs splayed out before her, trying to gasp her lungs into working again.

She'd been the last to come into camp, except that wasn't right, was it? 'Coming in last' implied there had been a line and she'd been at the end of it. Well, there had been a line, and she'd come in about three and a half hours after it, breathing so hard she could barely see and dragging her duffel by its strap. Nicci had been carrying the tent by that time, and Nicci was setting it up with the help of Mr. Yao and thank God for that, because Amber had spent the last hour of the hike thinking she was going to faint and now that she was here, if she had to stand up and move again, she damn well knew she would.

So she counted people, just in case no one had done that yet, trying to fool herself into thinking that was contributing in some way. Altogether, herself and Nicci included, there were forty-eight of them, a sad fraction of the hundreds Scott thought he'd won over with his inspiring speeches (although, to give him his due, it had seemed like a lot more than that when they were passing her, one by one, all the fucking way across the burned scar of the ship's final landing). Of that number, only eleven were women. There were no atheists in foxholes, it was said, and she guessed when it came to lugging crates uphill in the freezing wind on an alien planet, there were no feminists either. Maybe there'd be more tomorrow. Maybe spending the night in a burning ship would make more people feel better about coming out to the ridge.

Or maybe spending the night in a tent would make all of Scott's people want to go back to the ship. And if that did happen, if they all left, would she go with them? Was it worse to do something she thought was stupid, like make herself at home in a burning ship, or something she already knew was stupid, like sit alone in the wilderness on an alien planet?

'Wait for it,' she told herself. 'There are enough real problems here, little girl. Start making plans for those and stop worrying about what may not happen.'

"Amber?" That was Nicci, coming to fret over her. Probably wondering if she was having a heart attack or something. There'd been times on that hike that Amber had wondered herself. Even the Candyman's humming little shots hadn't made her feel like this. "Are you okay?"

"I'm getting there." She smiled to show how much she meant it. Nicci flinched a little. Amber stopped smiling. "I'll be stiff as hell tomorrow, but if they all go back to get more supplies and people and stuff, I'll just stay here and...I don't know. Guard the camp. From what, I don't know, but..." Amber trailed off with a frown and looked around—at the ridge, at the scarred plains with the ship burning in the middle of it, at the sky. "Do we know yet if there's any animals on this planet?"

"Mr. Yao was just talking about that," said Nicci, sitting gingerly in the grass beside her. "And he says there's plants, so we should expect there to be animals who eat them."

Sensible. Although by that logic, if there were animals who ate plants here, there were probably animals who ate meat, too. Forty-eight unarmed humans made an awful lot of meat.

"But no one's seen any?" Amber pressed, already thinking that even if there weren't animals, that was a whole new kind of trouble, because those MREs wouldn't last forever and she wasn't exactly seeing fields of wild corn and apple trees out there in all that grassy nothing. "Not even bugs?"

"Well, yeah, bugs. The ground kind. And Mr. Yao says there's a lake on the other side of the ridge."

"So there might be fish?"

"I guess, but Mr. Yao says if there are animals, we might see their footprints and stuff down by the water."

"Oh. Yeah, right. Makes sense." Amber knew nothing about animals except the little she'd seen on television and in most of those programs, they wore clothes and talked. Times like this made a girl wish she'd paid attention in Biology to something besides Trevor Macavee in the second row.

Nicci drew up her knees and hugged them, shivering a little. They watched people mill around in the camp, opening packs, eating ration bars, lighting fires. Nobody seemed to be talking much, but no one was crying and no one was wearing that empty survivor's stare. The outlook was just as bleak as it had ever been, but at least they had something to do.

That made her think of Jonah and so she turned listlessly that way, seeing nothing but the ship like a guttering torch in the growing dark. She wondered if he'd organized all the people Scott had only half-convinced into being his search and rescue team. She wondered if they'd found anyone alive to save. She wondered who he'd roll around with tonight to help him sleep.

She wondered if she was doing the right thing.

"Commander Scott wants to send you back," said Nicci suddenly, softly.

Amber rolled her eyes, once more firmly in this moment, on this hill. "Crewman Scott can kiss my pudgy white ass."

"He says there's no room for stubbornness out here. He says if someone can't do something to help, they need to get out of the way."

"I was miles behind everyone else most of this damn day. I couldn't have been more out of his way."

But it bothered her. Because he talked a great line and people listened. And applauded.

"What does everyone else say?" she asked finally.

"Nothing much. Except Mr. Lassiter said that Mr. Lamarc told them to go with you, not him, and Ms. Alverez said she didn't see him pulling people out of the ship when we were first waking up so he should just shut up, pretty much."

"I didn't pull anyone out of the ship either," said Amber, startled.

"Yeah, that one lady. From the room next door."

"Oh. Yeah. Lawsuit-Lady."

"That was Ms. Alverez."

"Oh!" Amber looked at the camp again. "Which one is she?"

Nicci stared at her.

"I don't remember what she looked like." Amber hesitated, then admitted, "I don't think I looked, you know? I was kind of...out of it."

Nicci frowned, but pointed. Scott, not quite at the end of her arm, immediately noticed and looked their way. Nicci put her hands back around her knees.

Amber glanced at her and uttered a huffy, humorless laugh. "What, are you afraid he's going to write you up for creating dissension in the ranks?"

"He's in charge."

"No, he's not."

"He says he is. No one says he isn't." Nicci chewed at her lower lip for a moment, then lowered her voice to say, urgently, "And he really doesn't like you."

"He can suck it up. We've got real problems to worry about. I am not in the mood to compete in his personality contest."

"Well, Sabrina says—"

"Who the hell is Sabrina now?"

Nicci looked surprised. She raised her hand to discreetly point, lowering her voice to a whisper. "Over there, with Lani and Rachel, see?"

Amber looked, but saw only a loose knot of people—Manifestors, indiscriminate to her eyes—sitting on the concrete bags to keep off the wet ground. "Which one? The redhead?"

"No, the..." Nicci hunched and whispered, "The black lady," before nervously looking to see if she'd been overheard.

"I think she knows she's black by now, don't you?" Amber asked, smiling.

Far from returning it, Nicci recoiled with a look of embarrassed horror. And what had she expected, really? Neither of them had much of a sense of humor, at least not around each other. They were sisters; they loved each other, and nothing made Amber feel better than to know she was taking care of her sister, just as nothing made her feel worse when she couldn't. Amber had fed her little sister breakfasts and dinners, washed her clothes, walked her to school, but they didn't talk very much and they didn't joke around even when they did.

"Okay, so who else am I looking at?" Amber asked, pretending to care as she looked back at the other people where 'Sabrina' sat with 'Lani' and 'Rachel'. "Do you know them all?"

"I think so." Nicci hesitated a few glances that way, her eyes darting from face to face. "There aren't that many."

"I guess not." But there was no guessing about it. Forty-eight people was nothing. It was less people than had shared a classroom with her in school, less than half of the number that worked with her at the factory, less than a quarter of those who had lived at the apartment complex. There was nothing amazing in Nicci's knowing everyone's name; it was, come to think of it, a little disturbing that Amber didn't.

The wind blew. Nicci sat and rocked beside her, hugging herself and rubbing at her sleeves. The ship burned.

"Do you think they found anybody?" Nicci asked. "You know...alive?"

"I don't know." Amber's gaze drifted up to the men's dorm mods, still burning high and hot. "I kind of hope not. We may not have a doctor or a medico or anyone like that, so if someone's hurt...and they'd have to be hurt...what could anyone do about it?"

Nicci ducked her head and rubbed her arms some more. "What's going to happen to us?"

"I don't know."

"Do you think they'll find the beacons?"

Amber glanced at the burning ship and away again. The sky was now completely black, but the *Pioneer* gave them more than enough light to see each other by, even at this distance. If there were animals, either they'd stay well away or they'd probably go investigate there instead of here. She wondered if Jonah was prepared for that. She thought he probably was.

"Amber?"

"Nicci, you were sitting right there when Jonah and I talked about this. You know what I think."

Nicci's arm bumped hers. She'd started crying again, quietly this time. Amber watched Scott move around the camp—inspecting his troops, improving morale, being a dick—amazed that her sister could still have any tears left after all the crying she'd already done. They said catastrophe stripped away the masks. A person could be almost anything with enough time to prepare for the part, but it took a disaster to show the world who you really were. Maybe even to find out for yourself. And she sure didn't need the ship to crash to know Nicci was a crybaby.

'And I'm a bitch,' she thought disgustedly, and held out her arm in a silent invitation for Nicci to come in under it. "We're going to be okay," she said as they huddled together in the grass. "I don't know what's going to happen, but we'll be fine. I'll take care of you, you know that."

"I don't believe you!" Nicci sobbed.

"Oh come on," said Amber, smiling to hide how deeply those surely thoughtless words had hit her. "When have I ever let you down?"

"When you brought me *here*!" Nicci shouted, turning heads all around the camp. "When you pushed me around and made me come here! I *hate* you sometimes, Amber! I hate you!"

And with that, she shoved herself back and out of Amber's stunned embrace, stumbling back to the group. Amber tried to follow, but her legs collapsed under her, all the hurt in the world not enough to undo that hellacious uphill hike. She had to sit and watch as the people at the fire took Nicci in, patting at her back and rubbing at her arms and closing in around her until she was lost to sight.

Scott looked over at her across the tops of all their bent, consoling heads. She couldn't tell if he was giving her a commander's frown of censure or just an asshole-smirk.

She turned her back on him, on Nicci, on all of them. She watched the ship burn.

* * *

Nicci came back, of course. And there had even been a mumble of apology and lots of hugging, but the hugging felt forced and when it came time to make their beds, they made them well apart, even though sharing heat would have made more sense. The tent Amber had half-killed herself lugging up here had been given to Mr. Yao, partly because Mr. Yao had carried the much-heavier packs of rations and had already agreed to do it again in the morning, and partly because Scott decided he had the authority to pass out tents and was being a dick about it.

If it had been anyone else...but it was Mr. Yao, who had apparently been told during the many hours it took Amber to catch up that it was his tent all along, and so even though taking it clearly made him uncomfortable and even though he offered to let the sisters share it with him, Nicci and Amber slept outside in the grass under the thin silver sheets of the laughably inadequate emergency blankets. Amber kept waiting for it to rain, since that would have perfectly frosted the shit-cake and some part of her was still tensely waiting for the other boot to drop, but it never did. If anything, the storm eased up a little and the night would have been quiet, except for the constant rattle of the wind shaking the tents and all those emergency blankets. Between that noise, the burning ship (and the smell that came with it, that horrible sneaky smell that was like burnt hair and batteries but was probably charbroiled people), and the aching of her overused muscles, Amber didn't think it was possible to sleep.

But she did.

And in the middle of that first night, when she had been so sure that nothing could get any worse, Amber woke up to the most godawful howling roar she had ever heard or could have imagined. She was on her feet in an instant, aching muscles or not, and so, it seemed, was everyone else. Half a dozen filmy silver sheets went flying as the people who had been wrapped in them scrambled free to stand, helpless, and listen.

It roared again, this time in quick, forceful bursts, as if God Himself were bent close to the ground and shouting, "Ha ha ha!" at them in an especially vindictive fashion. Then, quiet. They all looked at each other, waiting for the noise to be repeated, but the minutes dragged on and nothing happened.

"What the fuck was that?" Crandall asked at last.

"Sounded like a moose," said a woman. Amber couldn't see which one, but it didn't sound like Lawsuit—like Ms. Alverez.

"It sounded like a fucking dinosaur!" Crandall corrected with a shaky laugh. "Jesus, all night long, I been thinking, 'What next?' Now I'm gonna be eaten by a fucking dinosaur. Why the *hell* did I join the Fleet?"

"The wind could be carrying the sound, right?" someone said. "From miles away, maybe."

"It didn't come from upwind," said Eric. "It came from downwind. I don't think sound carries against the current."

A flashlight came on and there was Scott, standing at the lip of the ridge and shining it down at whatever was on the other side.

"Are you crazy?" Crandall hissed, jumping to snatch the flashlight away.

Scott simply pointed back at the *Pioneer*, which was no longer going like a Roman candle but still glowed out strong like the dying ember she supposed it was.

"They can see us," said Scott. "Furthermore, the wind is blowing right across us and down this hill, so they can smell us too. As long as they can already see us and smell us, I'd just as soon see what's out there, especially if it's thinking about coming up here."

He put out his hand. After a second or two, Crandall gave him his flashlight. Scott switched it on and aimed it back down the ridge.

Amber couldn't help herself. She limped over and looked with him.

"Go sit down, Miss Bierce," he told her, sweeping the light back and forth over the dark water that was down there—the lake Nicci had mentioned—either looking for whales or having trouble remembering where the shoreline was. Although honestly, one was as sensible as the other. There was no law saying alien whales couldn't roar and she sure as hell didn't know where the shoreline was.

She needed to start making peace with this idiot.

"What do you think we should do?" she asked.

He gave her a long, narrow stare that faded out at the end into uncertainty before making a few more passes over the lake. He finally found the bank, but between them and it, the grassy slope seemed entirely empty. "I...I don't know. What do you think?"

"Whatever it was, it seems to have moved on. But if there's mud down there—"

"Yeah, there is. We checked it out earlier. I almost lost my boot."

"Then it might have left footprints. They won't tell us much, but we can at least get an idea of size."

"Good point." He gave the grass one more sweep with the flashlight and then nodded—a firm, commanding nod. "Okay, Bierce. You're back on the team."

She opened her mouth to point out that, as far as she was concerned, she'd never been off the team, but mutely closed it again. Just like when Nicci had come shuffling back with her half-hearted, "I didn't mean it, Amber. You know that," Amber just nodded and kept her fat mouth shut.

"Listen up!" Scott was saying, now oblivious to her and her status on the 'team'. "We're going to go down and check it out. Now we're not going to go look for it," he said as people began to rumble out their first startled mob-protests. "We just want to look at the mud and see if it left any footprints."

The rumbling died down.

"I'm not saying everyone has to come along," Scott continued. "But if there are prints, I think we'd all probably feel better for knowing exactly what they look like. And if there aren't, I'd personally feel better knowing that you all saw there was nothing instead of me just saying it and you all thinking I'm covering something up."

"Don't be paranoid, man," said Dag, patting his shoulder.

"I'm not, I'm just being careful."

"Plus, I'd really like it if we all stayed together," said Eric, switching on his own flashlight and coming to stand at Scott's side. "So let's do this smart, people. Stay calm, get your boots on, find yourself a buddy and stick close to someone with a light."

And the Fleetmen were the ones with the lights. The four Fleetmen...and Scott, of course. His own little army. And she had to remind herself all over again to be nice.

She limped back to her blanket, which was weighted down at one end by her duffel bag and at the other by her boots but was still flapping and crinkling like crazy in the middle. She rolled it up, packed it away, put on her boots, and then, for no real reason, picked up her duffel bag and slung it over her shoulder.

"What are you doing?" asked Nicci, alarmed, as if the idea to carry all her shit around with her at all times were a direct order she'd been caught disobeying.

"I just don't want it to get lost," said Amber. She knew that was a stupid answer, but mumbling 'I don't know' and putting her duffel down again seemed stupider and people were watching.

Nicci tied her boots nervously and packed up her own blanket. When she too picked up her duffel bag, some of the other people around them did the same thing.

The Fleetman whose light they were sharing, Dag, watched them with a puzzled smile and finally aimed his flashlight at Amber. "You know, we're coming right back."

"I don't want to lose anything."

"Like what?"

An emergency blanket blew suddenly and noisily between them before being yanked up into the sky and lost.

"You were saying?" Amber prompted.

"Smart ass." But Dag cupped his mouth and shouted, "Remember to pack up your blankets if you don't have a tent, people! Keep your stuff together! Let's go!"

They made their way down to the water in the dark. And it was dark, much darker than it had been up on the apex of the ridge, where the sullen red glow of the smoldering ship had been their nightlight. It was a lot steeper on this side as well, so they went slow. It seemed like hours before they actually reached the water's edge and saw with their own eyes that the many tracks left in its muddy bank were all made by their own boots. Even after they spread out and searched, just exactly the way Scott had assured them they would not do, they found nothing.

"Well, we might see something in the morning," Eric began as he and Dag slogged their groups over to join with Scott's. He said something else after that—Amber could see his lips moving—but he made no sound.

All thc sound was gone. Even, for that split-second, the wind. But that was all the warning she got. And then she was in the water.

She thought she'd been pushed—the name Everly Scott leapt to the top of a short list of suspects—and while that thought certainly brought out a lot of anger, outrage and confusion, it didn't come with fear. She didn't gasp or try to scream; she knew she was underwater, even as she was curiously unable to process that the water had lit up brilliantly orange and churned out of all visibility.

Then something struck her in the back of the thigh and she realized that she wasn't the only one in the water. She arched instinctively, trying to surface, and instead bumped painfully into a rock. Her world spun; she was upside-down, absent all sense of gravity and perspective. She twisted clumsily and got her feet against the ground, knowing that the water couldn't be very deep this close to shore, that she should be able to just stand up, but although her legs straightened out, she remained submerged.

It was then that several revelations came to Amber: the slight ache of her lungs as they began to make their first complaints for air, the orange murk that had been perfectly normal water just an instant ago, the shadowy figures of other people struggling in the pond around her—any one of whom might be Nicci—and over all things, the terrible roar that was not merely the sound of water in her ears after all, but something else, something bigger.

Something burning.

Underwater, she had no idea how deeply, Amber jumped. Her feet left the ground, but her reaching hands did not break into the air. She'd never learned to swim, never had the opportunity and never really felt the lack, but now here she was and she had the rest of her life to learn. Amber kicked upwards, directly into the path of a flailing arm that punched into her stomach. Bubbles spilled out of her mouth in a watery cry, but there was no new air to pull in. Panic flared, hot and tight inside her aching chest. She lost her last hold on calm and began to thrash, clawing at the water above her without any sense of rising, right up until her face broke out into the wind.

The hot, glowing, smoke-thick wind.

Amber gasped in new breath, but it burned in her lungs. Her second was mostly water. She sank briefly, came up fighting again and was driven under a third time by some screaming lady trying to use her as a float. She didn't want to hurt whoever it was holding her down, but she was underwater, where restraint meant drowning. She broke free with several clumsy punches and grappled her way to the surface once more.

Only now did she see that she had not merely fallen into the lake, she had somehow been thrown in and thrown pretty damned far. She oriented herself to the shore through a screaming mass of splashing limbs, but managed only a few clumsy strokes before she stopped again and this time, turned around.

The light. The smoke. The roaring.

The ridge they had crossed over was burning. The flames blew sideways in the wind, flapping like party streamers, beautiful. The sky—the whole sky, as much as she could see in the treeless expanse of the hilly plains—was on fire. Heat blasted at her face, chapping her lips and searing at her eyes even as she choked on water.

Like the moment between standing on the shore and finding herself submerged, the next little space of time just seemed to melt away. Amber was not aware of swimming, but she must have done so because she had been ten meters or more out into the lake when she breached and at her next dim moment of awareness, she was only knee-deep and sloshing her way onto the bank. She grabbed the first duffel bag she saw and then two more before she found the one that was probably hers, but she didn't let any of them go. Their weight and the wind made her stagger at every step, but she fell only once and landed with her face in some kind of rough, smelly hole. Pushing herself awkwardly up in the mud, she could see dozens of short, pipe-like openings all around her that she was pretty sure hadn't been there before.

They were boots, she realized. Everyone's boots, stuck in the mud. Her own boots included. They had all been blown out of their boots.

Her first steps were toward the ridge, but she made herself stop. There would be nothing left to see, not if the whole fucking sky was on fire. There would be nothing left to see and she knew it.

She knew it because there was nothing to hear beyond the ridge except the roaring of the fire. No screams. No cries for help. No coughing. Just the fire.

In the crowd, in the panic, she heard Nicci scream her name. Even when she could make out no other single sound, she heard that. Hearing it pushed all the rest of the world out of focus and into it at the same time. She turned her back on the burning sky and fought her way through the tangle of wet, panicked people, shoving them into the water or into the mud until she could catch at her baby sister's arms and pull her protectively close, just as if her arms were some shield against the heat that had already dried her hair and her clothes and wouldn't need more than a few minutes to boil away the water in the lake and burn the skin off all their bodies.

But she held Nicci anyway, bellowing into her ear that it was all right and she was there and to close her eyes and keep them closed. She knew it was all over, but she wasn't scared. There wasn't time. The same numbness that kept her from understanding how she'd gotten into the water or how she'd gotten out kept her nicely cloaked against the horror of being burnt alive. She could only hope it wouldn't take long.

But the wind changed. Suddenly and forcefully, it blew back against the ridge, pushing both the heat and the smoke entirely away and replacing it with choking cold.

Amber staggered in the wake of this new wind, trying to clear her lungs of the sediment made by water, smoke and heat. She didn't feel very successful and the effort left her throat, chest and, oddly, her eyes feeling scraped and bruised. Cold, clear air cut at her lungs, making her cough even harder.

"What happened?" Nicci's hands dug painfully at her neck, but Amber didn't push her off. If anything, she pulled her sister closer, so that Nicci's next frantic shout rang out painfully right in her ear: "What happened? Oh God, what is this?"

"It's the ship," Amber croaked, even though she knew Nicci couldn't hear her through her own panic just yet. There wasn't much point in talking, but Amber said it all anyway, just to hear it out loud and know that it was real. The waiting was over; the worst had happened. "The ship blew up."

BOOK II

MEORAQ

In the city of Xheoth, in the state of Yroq, in the world and the hour of Gann, a pillar of fire rose up in the east, reaching like a desperate hand to heaven. It was a cool night, but not a cold one, and rainless although the wind was strong over the city, and so there were many who saw this miraculous sight. Uyane Meoraq, Sword of Sheul and well-honored in His sight, was one of them.

He supposed that was a smallish sort of miracle in itself. He spent enough time under the open sky that, given his leisure, he preferred a closed hall for his evening meditations. But the hall was engaged this night for the young initiates of Xi'Xheoth to take their oaths of ascension and so Meoraq took himself to the rooftop courtyard instead. He saw the fire that he might otherwise have never seen and therefore, there must have been some significance to the vision meant only for him. He meditated upon that as he watched it burn.

The sky had been filled with omens for many years, they said, but this was the first Meoraq himself had seen and he was a Sheulek—God's Striding Foot—who had spent most of the past twelve years in the wildlands. And this, this was far more impressive a sign than the occasional glimpses of light or colors that some claimed to have seen behind the ever-present clouds. For hours, that blazing arm strained upwards and its many fingers grasped at salvation, but though it fell with each strong gust of wind, it always rose again.

Behind the low walls that separated the temple's courtyard from those of the city's ruling Houses, Meoraq could see smaller flames spark to life as braziers were lit, until it seemed all Xheoth had come out to see. As a man who often went many days without seeing another living man or hearing any dumaq voice but his own, sights such as these still had power over Meoraq. He admired the city as he admired the fire in the sky. Walls a quarter-span thick, now alive with lights, formed a perfect ring around the protected fields where cattlemen and farmers labored. In the daylight, from this same vantage, he would be able to see the lush colors of living crop against the dead wastes of the world outside the city walls. But at night, on this night, the fires of so many braziers seemed a wondrous proof of life, a miracle in itself, and as precious as any burning pillar Sheul had sent to be seen.

Meoraq bore it a reverent witness, keeping his own company as the rooftop over the temple-district filled with on-lookers. Although they kept a respectful distance, every backwards glance showed Meoraq more priestly robes: acolytes, monks, scribes, oracles and even the young candle-wards came to stare until it seemed there could not be a man left in the rooms beneath his feet.

Hours passed, each one marked by the tolling of bells throughout the city, not quite in sync with one another. It began to rain, dampening not only the fields below—the sweet, green smell of freshly-wetted manure billowed up at once and Meoraq breathed it in, still thinking of fields, of farms, of life—but the enthusiasm of many of those watching. Braziers all across the city roof began to gutter and die, breaking the perfection of the ring they had so briefly formed, but some stayed regardless of the discomfort. Meoraq was one of these. There would always be rain and he would always have days when he had to walk through it and nights when he had to sleep in it, but this fiery arm might never come again and he still had not determined its meaning.

As he meditated, one of the acolytes was jostled suddenly forward by the crowd, stumbling hard against Meoraq's back. Meoraq spared his immediate bows and apologies a distracted grunt, but the damage was done. With a few shouts and clapped hands, the courtyard was cleared of all but the highest members of the priestly caste. The next man who drew near to speak apology was the abbot, whose name escaped Meoraq for the moment, but who seemed an amiable sort, for one of his caste.

They watched the fire together in comfortable silence. The rain and the wind both grew stronger, making the gesticulations of the flame wilder and more desperate even as it began to die down.

"It seems to be beckoning," the abbot remarked.

Meoraq acknowledged him with a grunt, but his interest intensified. It did look like a beckoning arm now, less like the clutching one he had first imagined it to be.

"How far away would you say the fire burns?" asked the abbot.

It was a fair question. Meoraq was one of perhaps a hundred men in Xheoth this night who had ever been beyond the city's walls. To speak in measurements of distance had only the most abstract meaning to most citizens, but this man had surely made pilgrimages in the past to be in a position of such authority now and so Meoraq considered the question fairly.

"The shadow of the Stepped Rise stands before it," he said at last. "And is not illuminated by it. It could not be less than thirty spans."

The other man grunted thoughtfully. "To see a flame at thirty spans...What city lies in that direction?"

"Tothax," Meoraq replied at once. He knew every city that fell within his circuit well, and quite a few others that did not. Tothax, he knew better than most. He had received an urgent summons to that city half a year back, a summons not merely for a Sheulek but for Meoraq himself, and refusing to name the charges. This had so annoyed him that Meoraq deliberately made Tothax his last stop upon his circuit and he made certain the courts of Tothax knew it. Indeed, upon his arrival in Xheoth, he had found another summons waiting for him, even more tersely worded than the last. And if there was a reason why he had perhaps overstayed himself in this city many days after the last dispute had been heard and the last trial judged, there it stood. He was a Sword of Sheul, greatest of the warrior's caste, a Sheulek. He took orders from his father and from God and no one else. He would move on in his own time, and he fully intended to make himself obnoxious in the House of whoever wanted him so damned badly right up until the last lick of autumn.

Ah, but then it would be home, home to Xeqor and House Uyane. Familiar faces. A bed more myth than reality. His father's company in the evenings, and perhaps his brothers' as well, if they were home from their own duties. Well...Salkith would be there; he was a governor's guard and entitled to a room in their barracks, but he preferred to sleep at home where he could punish those who joked about his infamously slippery brain instead of force himself to laugh along. Nduman was a Sheulek with his own circuit and his visits were infrequent enough, but he was also keeping a low-born woman and several children in Vuluth, outside of conquest and without formal marriage, although he thought it a great secret. Thus far, their father had seemed strangely inclined to tolerate this, but Rasozul was lord of Uyane and steward of the bloodline and could not ignore the scandal forever. As for Meoraq himself, he was what he was: the eldest son of a legendary man, the heir to a glorious name and a proud House of Oracle Uyane's own lineage, a servant in the favor of great Sheul, and a man who was perhaps not as humble as he ought to be. He was working on that.

"Tothax," the abbot mused, bringing him roughly back to himself.

"If somewhat to the north."

"So it is not Tothax that burns."

"No." Regrettably. "There is nothing there that should burn for so long."

"Without moving," agreed the abbot, tapping the back of one hand broodingly with his fingertips. "A plains-fire would move in this wind."

"And swiftly die in this rain," added Meoraq. His clothing was now plastered unpleasantly to his scales. "And no plains-fire would ever burn so tall."

"Yet still it burns. And beckons."

Meoraq grunted.

"It is a true sign of Sheul, then."

"So it would seem."

They watched. Another hour was tolled and the fire waved, feebly but still with some life, as it slipped lower and lower.

"He has set a mighty banner," the abbot remarked. "But for whose eyes, I wonder?"

Meoraq flattened his spines. The elderly priest gazed benignly straight ahead and did not acknowledge his narrow glance.

"I should have journeyed on to Tothax many days ago," Meoraq admitted at length.

The abbot bent his head at a polite angle, flexing his spines forward with interest. "Perhaps the message is meant for you."

"Perhaps." But now he felt certain it was. Meoraq had trained a lifetime to hear Sheul's voice and feel His touch. Now he saw His waving arm. It would be a foolish thing to pretend he did not know what it meant.

Or what he had to do.

"I leave for Tothax immediately," he said. And naturally, it was raining. "I require provisions for the journey."

"Name them and be met, honored one," said the abbot mildly. "Shall you take a bed until the morning?"

"No." Meoraq turned away as the burning arm, its work done, finally slipped behind the horizon and returned the night to uninterrupted black. "Sheul has lit His lamp for me at this hour. I can only trust it is the hour He wishes me to follow. It would seem I have lingered too long already."

"We shall pray for you," said the abbot, bowing. The other priests remaining on the rooftop bowed as well. "Go in the sight of Sheul and serve Him well."

* * *

Meoraq descended the stair and beckoned indiscriminately to the crowd of youths and low-born priests still clustered in the upper halls hoping for a glimpse of the miraculous fires. Several came forward at once. He took the first to reach him for his usher, made his few demands to the others, and allowed himself to be led back to the room he had been given for his own upon his first night's arrival. He did not have many preparations to make, but it was the polite thing to give the temple's provisioner time to arrange his supplies so that they would be at the temple gate when he did leave. Rushing out at once only to wait around where all could see him would only embarrass Xi'Xheoth and those who lived there. Meoraq knew he was not always as patient as he ought to be, but he tried not to be rude. Sometimes he tried.

The boy bowed in ahead of him and lit the lamp, then waited, his small head pressed to the floor and back stiff with pride at being made usher for so prestigious a guest. Meoraq dismissed him with a silent tap to the shoulder and, knowing that little eyes would be on him and little ears listening, kept his back to the door until he heard it shut and catch.

He was alone.

"Fuck," said Meoraq, and gave the cupboard where he ought to be sleeping even now a solid kick. He hit the supporting framework rather than the lower door as he'd intended, so that instead of a resounding thump as his boot struck home, he damned near broke a toe. He swore again, limping over to the simple chair provided for his simple needs.

It was raining. It would be raining. Thirty days he'd passed in Xheoth and it had not rained once in all that time. Thirty days, but now he was leaving and the water poured out of the sky as from a cattleman's pump.

He sat there in his soaked leather breeches and the city-soft tunic the priests had given him while his own was laundered, dripping puddles on the floor, and cursed the rain, which did no good. He had dry clothing in his pack, but could see no point in donning it only to have it drenched ten steps out of the city gate. The rain fell and he would just have to walk in it as just punishment for staying so long in Xheoth.

"A refinement to my sense of humility, I suppose," muttered Meoraq, glancing heavenward. "And I thank You for it, O my Father. It is so comforting to know that You take so personal an interest in the improvement of my character."

Sheul did not reply. Not here, at any rate, although it might be raining even harder outside.

Meoraq tightened his bootstraps and loin-plate and finally glared at the table where his weapons awaited him. The abbot had requested, as all of them did, that he not go armed within Sheul's House. Meoraq's usual reply to this was that all the world was Sheul's House and he went where directed ever-ready to do Sheul's work, but having the right to be an arrogant ass whenever the whim took him did not make it an obligation and this abbot was a better man than most.

He put his travel-harness on over his wet tunic and clipped the great hook of his beast-killing kzung at his hip. Its weight was an immediate comfort to him. Next came the long, wide samr, sheathed and slung across his back to be drawn against those whose crimes either did not merit or could not wait for trial. Last of all, his honor-knives, the slender sabks, buckled high on his arms. They were meant only for the arena in the sight of Sheul, but were frequently used in the wildlands for all manner of menial work. If his years of service had taught Meoraq nothing else, it had taught him that one could not skin a saoq with a blade as long as one's arm. If Sheul saw it as disgrace, He had never let Meoraq know.

A soft knock upon his door. A familiar sound these past many nights. Not a priest.

"Enter," Meoraq called without turning. "And stand."

She had already taken her first steps toward him. Now they faltered to a stop. Her voice was as hesitant as her footsteps. "Sir?"

"Sheul calls and I go to answer. You have done well in your service to me," he added, damned generously. "Go in my favor."

She retreated one step, but only one. Her hands clasped, trembling, at one another. "Have I offended you, sir?"

She had not. Nor had she gone to any great effort to please him. Indeed, she had done little to make any impression on him whatsoever. She hadn't even told him her name.

Nor should she, in all honesty. She was not a friend to him, only one of the many women who came to the temple after being turned away by their husbands for want of children. They haunted the halls of the temples in every city, veiled shadows in the shape of women, offering themselves in solemn rituals in the hopes that Sheul's sons would heal their wombs. She did not come to him for pleasure and he should not expect to find any in her.

She was neither young nor beautiful, but Meoraq had been compelled to have her all the same when he had passed her in the hall, returning from his first judgment in this city. As Sheulek, he had the right to any woman he was given to desire, but it was this one who lit the spark in him that night and every other night that she came to him. The marks of many Sheulek before him scarred her from neck to mid-arm, but she had not burned for Meoraq and his own did not stand among them.

He had not decided yet how this made him feel. His masculine pride was, in truth, somewhat insulted, although he knew it was Sheul who had the ultimate judgment over each mortal coupling and therefore His will that she not conceive of him, but only receive Meoraq's fires. If that was enough to heal her barren womb, so be it. If not, well, Meoraq didn't particularly want her haunting the halls at House Uyane anyway. Sheul had blessed him at each coupling, sometimes twice, but the sex itself had been as unpleasant as sex could be. Her way of bending silent and motionless beneath him disturbed him. He had given her permission to move, to speak, even to struggle, but she did nothing except to whisper her prayers and drift away when it was over.

Now she seemed dismayed at his leaving, as if it were some failing of hers that drove him out from the city in the dark hours of night. That if she had been more winsome, or if her worn flesh had just been fresher, he might stay and give her the children Sheul had thus far denied her. That she had displeased him, shamed herself, failed God.

Meoraq understood the situation well, but he knew no better how to extract himself from it than he ever had. He finished securing his travel-pack and slung it onto his back, then turned to face her at last.

She bent her neck at once, hiding her eyes from him as a proper woman learns early to do, but her hands grasped anxiously at one another, never entirely still.

Meoraq started walking, but stopped at the door. He sighed, rubbed once at his brow-ridges, then came back to her. He stood awkwardly before her while she cowered, then reached out and brushed the back of his hand gently across her well-scarred shoulder. Her short spines only flattened further, uncomforted.

"I thought surely it would be you," she whispered.

"Mine is the same clay as any other's. Look to no living man for your restoration."

"He has forsaken me."

Meoraq gave the door a glance, wishing it would be miraculously filled by a priest who would know better how to handle this. It remained shut. The woman before him continued to stare at the floor between her bare feet, even as silent tears welled in her eyes. He was Sheulek, a true son of Sheul, and he had felt His touch and heard His voice all his life, but for the sake of that same life, he could not think of a thing to say to her.

"We are all tested in our time," he said at last and immediately regretted it. It was precisely the sort of lame and obvious non-answer that priests liked to give and which Meoraq himself had always found simply infuriating.

But she only brushed at her eyes and made a quiet sound of wordless acceptance. Living here, no doubt she'd heard such answers too many times to be moved by them any longer.

"Forgive me, honored one," she said, sinking to her knees. "I have delayed you with a foolish woman's unhappiness. Go your way in the sight of Sheul, I pray, and good journey to you."

All spoken as heavy as the eternally overcast skies. He found himself wishing she would look at him, as wildly inappropriate as that would be, to show him her naked eyes and let him see some glimmer of a future in them.

But the burning arm beckoned. A Sheulek answered to God above his brothers, his teachers, even his own father. He could not spurn Him to linger with this woman, particularly since he could be of no comfort to her.

He touched her again, actually gripping her shoulder this time in a more direct farewell than he had given anyone else in Xheoth, but she cringed beneath his hand, understandably confused and dismayed by this intimacy. He left her, shutting the door behind him to give the first of her soft, broken tears some privacy.

* * *

His usher was waiting in the hall to lead him to the temple's gate, trying—and failing—to disguise his curiosity at the sexual mysteries he knew to be unfolding behind the door once the woman entered. He seemed very surprised to see Meoraq so soon emerged and it took him some little time to remember the proper genuflections. Meoraq, brooding, waited out about half of them and then set off without him.

He regretted it within a few moments, knowing it was only the difficult scene with the woman and the prospect of walking in the dark and the rain that fanned the impatience in him, and knowing also that the boy would suffer the kind of poisonous insinuations that only one's young peers are capable of making for his perceived failure to perform this very simple task. He'd been a boy once. He'd heard those insinuations. Hell, he'd made them.

When he reached the gate and the cluster of priests waiting to see him off with the right chants and prayers, Meoraq made a point of tapping the boy on the shoulder. "I have left my bedroll. You may have it, if you like." And to the smiling abbot, ignoring the boy's immediate outcry, "I leave Xi'Xheoth to you."

"We thank you for your service, honored one, and pray we shall not soon require your return."

His provisions were presented, exactly as he had demanded: Two waterskins sized for long travel, bread enough to see him to Tothax and cuuvash enough to see him right through and on to Xeqor, a fresh bedroll, and a good thick blanket to hold back the growing chill at night. Of his own will, the provisioner had added a candle-brick and a small pot of honey, doubtless from the temple's own waxbeetles. Meoraq would not have asked for these things. He was entitled to whatever he was moved to demand, but Xheoth's usual prosperity had been hard-tested this past year and he was loathe to take away even its most frivolous resources. Besides, he had every intention of making outrageous demands when he reached Tothax and the House of whoever dared to summon him without giving cause. Oh yes. Then, he meant to replace his tent, his travel-packs, his boots, his harnesses—both travel and battle—all his buckles, his various tools for skinning and scaling, and he thought he might even be up to feeling a strong need to acquire a mending kit with metal needles and every grade of stitch from sinew to fine thread. And a tea box. A nice one, not just another clay pot with pouches. He wanted to see some inlay after half a year of summons.

The abbot began to pray as Meoraq made himself ready, and since it was the custom for the prayers to continue for so long as the honored visitor was there to hear them, he did it quickly and moved on before the elderly man's voice could tire.

Beyond the temple gates, the city moved and breathed. At this hour, on any other night, the inner passageways of the city would have been empty, save for the watchmen on their patrols and the beacons with their lumbering carts, measuring out dippers of oil to keep the lamps lit.

Now the walkways were choked with people and most of the food-stalls in sight were opened as merchants took advantage of the crowds. Looking around at all this activity, anyone would think it was full day outside.

A shifting beside him. The temple had sent for watchmen to escort him out of the city and they waited nervously for his acknowledgement, looking at him with eyes that said they knew as well as he did for whom the message in the sky had been written.

Meoraq beckoned and started walking for Southgate. He was recognized—in his battle harness, with blades hanging off every side of him, he was damned hard to miss—and hailed in many voices all at once. Each had a different turn of phrase, but it all came to the same question: What was the meaning of the fire?

As if any man could know the mind of Sheul. The fire had been for him, and even Meoraq did not know what it meant.

He kept moving. The temple watchmen fell in close beside him, warning back the crowd when they pressed too close, lest some overenthusiastic fool catch at Meoraq's arm and earn himself a cut across the face from a Sheulek's samr, or worse, catch at the samr itself and earn himself a cut across the throat. Such things happened far more often than Meoraq ever would have imagined in the days before his ascension. Fools forgot themselves easily. And thus there would always be a need for Sheulek.

It was a long walk to Southgate. Meoraq's clothes were nearly dry when he arrived, having just reached that damp, clinging stage where they pulled at every scale. The doorkeeper was expecting him and, by the flat-spined sour-faced look of him, sorely offended by this upset to his routine.

"On your way," he said, indicating the watchmen at Meoraq's flanks with two fat fingers in a lofty wave. "To your work and leave me mine. Go on, I say! What are you waiting for?"

"My word of release," said Meoraq.

The doorkeeper stood back, his head twitching downward with flustered ill-humor he tried to hide, and waited.

So did Meoraq.

One of the watchmen shifted, but only once.

In the stretching silence, the doorkeeper's discomfort grew until it finally burst out of him in a grumbling, "Do you wait on something, honored one?"

"I do. I wait on your salute."

For the second time, the doorkeeper gave ground, this time enough to bump his backside against the heavy door he guarded. His neck bent. He made a surly genuflection, and another, more formally, when Meoraq continued to wait. Then and only then did Meoraq dismiss his escorts. He didn't look to see if they saluted before they went. He was not a man who cared about salutes; he cared about being pointed at by some unwashed doorkeeper as if he were a servant.

'Patience,' he thought, watching the doorkeeper work his keys in the impressive lock of Southgate. 'Sheul, O my Father, give me patience, if not enough to get me through this life, at least enough to get me out of Xheoth without disgracing the name I carry.'

"Fire in the sky, they tell me," grunted the doorkeeper.

Meoraq did not reply. Doorkeepers were born of the warrior's caste, like watchmen and the slightly higher-ranked sentries and, for that matter, butchers and smiths and fleshers and even the lowly handlers whose job it was to stand watch in the kitchens and see that no man took up the bladed weapon in defiance of Sheul's law, but instead used only those poor tools built for them. Yes, this man had been born in God's favor, and Meoraq supposed they must have at one time stood some of the same training, but he was not a warrior, he was not a brother, and he was not a friend.

'I am in a truly piss-licking mood tonight,' Meoraq thought in a faintly wondering way.

They walked together down the long, damp passage through the wall of the city, feeling its colossal weight and age bearing down from every side. The doorkeeper, well accustomed to this walk and perhaps annoyed at Meoraq's silence, lit no lamp. They walked in darkness until Meoraq could feel the cool air of the outside world blowing against his eyes and hear the rain above their own echoing footsteps.

The doorkeeper stopped. So did Meoraq, and he heard a low, irritated sound escape the man beside him, cheated of the peevish pleasure of hearing the high-born Sheulek walk into a gate. Meoraq smiled to himself in the dark.

Keys rattled. The scrape of metal in a lock. The heavy creaking of weathered hinges. "Stands open, sir," said the doorkeeper sourly. "Watch your footing."

Meoraq opened his mouth to demand a parting salute that he wouldn't even be able to see, but made himself bite it back. A truly piss-licking mood. He deserved a long walk in the rain in which to meditate upon the Prophet's many sermons on the subject of emotional restraint.

There was silence behind him as he went on ahead, out of the last length of the tunnel and into the full storm Sheul had waiting for him.

"Who walks there?" someone called. One of the sentries, huddled against the wall to wait out the last hours of his patrol.

"Uyane Meoraq of Xeqor," he said, making a final adjustment to the many straps of his packs. "A Sword of Sheul. Challenge me or cry surrender."

"I cry," the watchman said, wiping rain from his face, and, the last formalities dealt with, added, "First rain of the season is treacherous enough without flying thunder and fiery towers. So good journey to you, honored one, but mind your footing as you go. A man can see a thousand miraculous things in his life and still be washed away by one bad turn on a stretch of bad road."

Good advice. Meoraq raised him a brother's hand in farewell and walked on as the gate of Xheoth slammed behind him and all the empty world of Gann waited in darkness for the dawn.

2

It stopped raining a quarter-span outside of Tothax, with the city walls looming black and tall before him and his clothing as heavy as another damned man riding about on his back. Meoraq cast a surly word of gratitude upwards, accepted the final mutter of far-away thunder for the rebuke it surely was, and walked the last length of road ankle-deep in mud. At least, it seemed mostly to be mud, although Meoraq knew the road could not possibly be so softened, even by days of rain, unless some prospering cattleman had driven his herd out to graze beyond the walls very, very recently.

"Perhaps I will demand my boots cleaned once I have answered my summons, eh?" Meoraq said to himself, spines twitching in a grim, self-indulgent sort of humor. "And once I am satisfied that they are clean enough for a Sheulek's feet, by Gann, I'll demand them replaced. I never much cared for these boots anyway."

"Hail and stand fast!"

Meoraq halted and raised one hand in acknowledgement. He had been aware of the sentry circling him for quite some time and suspected he was being hailed now only because the man had finally met up with reinforcements. Tothax was hardly a city teetering on the undefendable frontier, but every city raised out of Gann's flesh knew violence. Meoraq stood with his arms raised and hands empty, waiting for the sentries—and yes, now there were three of them—to nerve themselves for a cautious approach.

"I see Uyane, a Sword of Sheul," said one of the sentries, bending his neck in swift apology.

The face was familiar, but Meoraq couldn't scratch up a name, so he merely grunted and tapped at the man's shoulder in what he hoped came across as casual and forgiving as well as wet and entirely out of patience. "Uyane Meoraq stands before you. I come to take Tothax. Challenge me or cry surrender."

"We cry to you, conqueror." The sentry raised his head, frowning. "Exarch Ylsathoc requests your audience immediately."

A name at last. And an exarch, no less. Highest of the governing caste, they followed circuits of their own, moving from city to city to oversee the legal affairs of the most eminent Houses. This one was probably here about some oversight in the records of one of his recent trials, and wasn't that just like one of the governing caste to sit around half a year sending summons just to have a handful of questions answered? Meoraq grunted again, less politely, and walked on toward the gate.

Behind him, the sentries conferred in uneasy mutters. The one who had called him by name now called out again, saying, "Have you a message for me to carry, honored one?"

"I do not ask my brothers under the Blade to carry my messages," Meoraq replied, still walking.

It was a rare thing for a sentry to hear himself addressed as brother by a Sheulek and it gave these three pause enough that Meoraq had nearly reached the outer gate before they tried again.

"When shall I tell Exarch Ylsathoc you will see him?"

"Name any hour that pleases you," said Meoraq, drawing his kzung to strike against the gate. "But any lie is a lie before God and you must answer for it. If I choose to see this man you speak of at all, it will be in my own time."

"I mark you, sir. "The sentry sighed, rubbing at the bony ridges over his brows in a dejected manner. "I only give the message I am given."

The sentries retreated and Meoraq was given a few moments in the relatively dry pass-way to kick the worst of the mud from his boots while the gatekeeper finished locking them in and turned around. He made an offensively cursory salute, which Meoraq immediately forgave since he also offered both a flask of twice-brewed nai and to carry Meoraq's pack. The drink was hot and strong and good—Sheul's love in a swallow, as his father often said—and it was difficult to bear in mind that he would have as much nai as he wished once he was settled, but this flask would be all the gatekeeper could claim until the end of his shift. A Sheulek had the right to seize whatever goods he desired of any man he wished, but Meoraq did try not to be an ass.

"Suppose I should ask your name," grunted the gatekeeper, striking a lamp. "See your bands and the seal of your blades and all the rest of that ribbony shit, but I've had that over-groomed slaveson bleating in my face six times today alone and if you aren't the Uyane he wants, by God and Gann, you're still the man he'll get."

Meoraq grunted, flexing his spines forward to show some degree of acknowledgement, but he had no intention of seeing anyone until he'd had a bath and a hot meal.

The rest of the walk through the pass-way was comfortably quiet. The gatekeeper made a mutter when the urge came on him, but like Meoraq's own mutterings were so often apt to be, they were not made in expectation of answers. The flask passed back and forth between them freely, and Meoraq never refused it, although he did limit himself to sparing sips. By the time they had reached the inner gate, it was down to the dregs and bitter with coarse, smoky grounds.

"Keep it," grunted the gatekeeper when Meoraq tried to return it. "I see you've not got one and that's a hard lack when the weather turns."

"I do not ask the gate to make provision when the temple summons me," said Meoraq, and firmly held out the flask.

The gatekeeper snorted humor as he brought out his keys. "Ask for a flask from that crowd and they'll bring you the finest jeweled *cup* your eyes will ever clap to. Priests. They think worth is in riches, not use. Hear me and mark well," he went on, just as if he were a training master and Meoraq a boy on his field. "A thing is not what it looks like, but what it *does*. Finest priestliest cup in the world won't keep nai hot in its belly on a long walk in the rain."

"I mark," said Meoraq, amused.

The gatekeeper grunted again, swinging the door wide open. He bellowed for an usher then turned in the same breath to give the proper formal farewell, since little ears were around to hear them: "Tothax is yours, honored one. Show mercy to us."

Meoraq raised the flask as he would raise his sabk in the arena, then slung its strap around his neck and walked on, smiling.

* * *

One city was very much like another, each one being made after Oracle Mykrm's design at the Prophet's direction. It had been half a year since Meoraq had last been in Tothax, but he did not need the boy to guide him. He knew the way to the temple district in every city of his circuit and took himself easily down to the busy streets of the inner ring with his usher hurrying to keep ahead of him.

This was the living body of any city: the inner ring, where farmers and cattlemen met abbots and oracles, where merchants ruled over lords and the taxman ruled over all. Voices struck out on every side—hailing friends, hawking wares, protesting price—until they all came together in a great cursing, laughing, chanting wave of chaos. After so many days alone with nothing to see but the rain and the empty road, the thousand sights and sounds and smells of the city were both welcome and abrasive. They were close enough to the terrace that the grey shine of true light could be seen if Meoraq looked to his left down the long rows of shopfronts, but if he looked to his right, orderly rows of hanging lamps burned a far brighter path deeper into the protected city and that was how he turned as soon as he reached the wide archway that led to Xi'Tothax—heart of Tothax—the Temple district.

Gradually, the crowds loosened and the clamor faded. The many noisy bodies became a few strolling priests and even fewer scampering boys. Meoraq slowed his long strides to let his particular boy take a proper place before him.

The Temple gates were closing as he neared them, but the watchmen posted there gave the sabks riding at Meoraq's arms a glance and opened them right up again.

"Exarch Ylsathoc—" one of them began, bowing, but shut his mouth at Meoraq's upraised hand. He basked in the warmth of their uncomfortable silence as his usher exchanged himself for one of the temple's own boys and then he walked on.

"I will meet with the abbot," he said to his new boy, making certain the watchmen at the gates could hear. "And him alone."

The usher, oblivious to everything but the naked blades adorning Meoraq's harness, gave breathless obedience and set off.

Meoraq followed, thinking pleasantly vindictive thoughts of the faceless Exarch Ylsathoc pacing himself into a frothing fury in some priestly corner of the temple, and it was some time before he realized he was not being led to the cloister, but to the stronghold. He started to say something about it being the custom to show a Sheulek to his chambers before all else, but turned the half-formed sound to a wordless grunt instead. He had said he would meet with the abbot, so the boy was by-Gann taking him to the abbot and if he went there tired and wet and muddy as a cattleman, he had only his own peevishness to blame for it.

'Life is filled with small lessons,' thought Meoraq, casting a dour eye up at the soot-black ceiling and through it, to Sheul's ever-watchful gaze. 'I hear You, O my Father, and I am humble at Your instruction, but just once I would like to indulge a mortal failing without having to learn from it.'

Sheul did not reply.

The boy brought him into the hold as far as the doors to the Halls of Judgment and there delivered him with great importance to an amused council guard. They waited, showing each other the proper motions of dominance and submission with one eye on the boy until he was entirely gone. Immediately after the closing of the door, the guard dropped his arm mid-genuflection and gave Meoraq a slap to the chest.

"Ssh, you're wet!" he said, shaking out his hand.

"It's raining. Or has been. Ten days and nights. Here." Meoraq thrust his damp, muddy pack maliciously into the other man's arms. "You can carry that."

"You are a low man, Raq."

"The man who walks in the sight of Sheul walks the high path at every hour," Meoraq replied piously and walked around the low wall separating them to help himself to the guard's cup. Also nai, but quite cold. Meoraq drank it anyway, fingering thoughtfully at his new flask. "How are you, Nkosa?"

"Walking, working and getting dipped. Guess that means I can't complain." Nkosa folded his arms and watched as Meoraq forced the last bitter swallow down and turned the empty cup over on the wall.

They were somewhat related, Nkosa's mother having been a servant in a house where Meoraq's father had once stayed on a circuit. She claimed him for the sire, and even though she carried no scars to prove it, when the baby opened up male, Rasozul had paid for the boy's placement at a training hall (or whatever passed for one in a city like Tothax). Of course, the woman had been swiftly married to one of her own caste, the man whose name Nkosa carried. Meoraq had known nothing of this until their first meeting, when Nkosa rather shyly asked if he was by chance related to Rasozul and the whole story had come out. Meoraq had seen no reason to query his father for confirmation. The Uyanes were Sheulek all the way back to the founding of the House; it was inevitable that he should find blood-kin. Really, it was a wonder he didn't find more of them.

"You're late," Nkosa said now, cocking his head to a censuring angle.

"Impossible."

"You come through twice a year, early sowing and second reaping, regular as a cattleman bathes or an abbot shits. Last harvest was a quarter-brace ago. You're late."

"A Sheulek moves at God's hour."

"Mm. Was it a woman?" Nkosa asked, with just a hint of wistfulness. During their infrequent and much-enjoyed chats together, he had confided that he had stood twelve years of the seventeen required of a Sheulek's training before he had been culled, but he was still a bastard, even if he was one of Rasozul's, and there never was much hope of him being called higher than he stood now. "It was my mother's doing," he liked to sigh at the end of this confession. "If only she'd been presented to him as a daughter of the House instead of some linen-girl who helped him rumple up the sheets before she changed them, I'd be wearing a set of my own blades." Such things were not supposed to factor in a Sheulek's selection, but of course they did. Politics had no place in Sheul's sight, but this was Gann's world.

"There was no woman," said Meoraq. He did not consider it a lie. The woman who had given herself to him for healing during his long stay at Xheoth was no pleasure but a compulsion of Sheul's granting and never entered his mind.

"Was it two women?"

"No."

"Ten?"

"No," said Meoraq, grinning. "Although I appreciate your high opinion of me."

"I would trade all the teeth out of my head to be you for one night," sighed Nkosa, and turned his empty cup right-side up again.

"And it would be a fine night, I suppose, if you abused it right," said Meoraq, flicking his spines dismissively, "but you would be toothless the rest of your life and I think you would remember that best."

"I will eat soft bread and think of all the shoulders I have bitten." Nkosa shivered elaborately, then sighed again and gave the wall a careful kick. "I suppose you heard I married."

"No. It was only rumor when I was here last."

"Omen, you mean. The ill-boding shadow of my inescapable future. I think her father owed my father some cattle or something," he said vaguely, meaning, of course, the man his mother had married and not Rasozul. "It's been a bad year for cattle, so we got the girl instead."

Meoraq frowned.

Nkosa noticed and snorted. "It's not like that, they tell me. The debt still stands, it's just that her father has longer to pay us at a more forgiving price because, you see, we're kin now. Her name is Serra. Serra! What kind of a name is that?"

Meoraq knew better than to ask if she was pretty, since that would have been the first thing his old friend would have mentioned, if true. Instead, he said merely, "How does she suit you?"

"Eh. She stays in the other side of the house most of the time, with my father's wife and the servants. I hardly know her."

"Your women share rooms with the servants?"

"We don't all have Houses, Raq," said Nkosa with a snort. "Some of us just have homes. But she's all right, I suppose. I just wish I knew what to do with her."

"Your father really should have explained that to you years ago," Meoraq said with a concerned frown. He gave Nkosa a comradely tap and said, "Sometimes, when a man sees a woman, Sheul will give him certain urges—"

"You are such an idiot," snapped Nkosa, shoving at him, and naturally that was what he was saying and doing when the door opened.

The man who had walked haplessly through that door frowned around at once, saw Meoraq, saw the honor-knives at his arms, and dropped the cup he had been idly stirring. It shattered on the tiles. Nai splashed over his feet, staining the hem of his neat, clerkish breeches, but it wasn't hot enough to steam. "*What* did you say?"

Nkosa opened his mouth, but the other man gave him no time to answer.

"How could you—? Inexcusable! Representing this hall—!" Words briefly failed him. He floundered, then drew himself up and pointed two shaking fingers at Nkosa, saying, "This man will be punished, honored one, severely punished!"

Meoraq kept his hand on Nkosa's shoulder and clenched it, preventing a repentant bow. He said, quietly, "You are intruding on a private conversation. If it is in me to take offense, it is far more likely to be with you. Remove yourself."

He did, stammering apologies, but the mood was dead and there was no reviving it. Nkosa muttered something that might have been the other man's name and some slur on his parentage, but he kept his head bent. They were almost brothers by blood, almost brothers under the Blade, almost friends just by nature...but only almost. Sometimes that was enough to bridge the gap between them. Sometimes it just wasn't.

Meoraq released him. Nkosa went and started picking up shards of nai-damp clay. "I should tell someone you're here," he said, not looking up. "Some foreign official has been waiting on you for days."

"Exarch Ylsathoc." Meoraq flicked his spines dismissively. "So I hear. Do you know why?"

"You have to be better than a front-room watchman before they tell you things like that. I only see his name and yours on my duty sheet. It might be nice if someone here thought I could do my job," he added at a mutter. "But if you want to hide from him, there's a petition in the hall right now."

"A Sheulek doesn't have to hide from anyone," said Meoraq. And frowned. "A dispute at this hour?"

"They've been here half the day. They brought their champion, so it must be serious. I didn't hear the charges."

Nor was there any reason he should. His sole responsibility was to this one gate in this one room. And assuming it was not ingloriously stripped from him for one moment's thoughtless joking, it would be the most responsibility he ever had in all his service as a man of the warrior's caste.

"I suppose I should put my name in," said Meoraq, heading for the door. "It was good to see you, 'Kosa."

"Think of me tonight when you're making free with all your conquered virgins," Nkosa said morosely.

"I sincerely hope not. But think of me while you get dipped with your wife."

"I always do."

They both laughed, but it wasn't quite the same laughter as it might have been.

The clerk, or whoever he was, was in the hall just outside, gesticulating wildly as he hissed to a whole crowd of solemn-faced men, some of them robed as judges. Civil judges, perhaps, but a very bad thing to see. They all looked at Meoraq.

Nothing he did now could possibly be the right thing to do. If he said nothing, Nkosa was sure to be punished, which could mean anything from the loss of his post to a public whipping. If they waited to bring their charge against him until Meoraq was gone and another Sheulek heard that he had put his naked hand on Meoraq, Nkosa could easily be exiled to the wildlands or even executed. But if Meoraq did speak in Nkosa's defense, he would make a public issue out of what still might be a private one, humiliating not only his friend, but the man whose name he carried. The taint could reach as far as his household's master, the steward-lord of House Kanko, who might take the view that House Uyane had dishonored him personally. For that matter, the governor of this piss-miserable little city might raise formal charges against the governor of Xeqor, since House Uyane was that city's championing House.

The only reasonable response was silence.

Meoraq twitched his spines...then flattened them and strode purposefully over to the watchful crowd. "Twice a year," he said over their bowing heads, "I have the pleasure to see my cousin." It wasn't entirely untrue. They were blood-kin, anyway. "We have precious few moments together and you—" He leaned close, staring furiously into the top of the clerk's bent head. "—have robbed me of three of them. One for the interruption I might have forgiven. Two for the threat you had no right to make. And three that I find you so soon smearing the tale out into the hall. How say you, man?"

The man could not seem to say anything. Meoraq was not entirely certain he was breathing, although he did appear to be trembling very slightly.

Meoraq gave him a quick count of six to feel the weight of all these staring eyes and then he straightened up and drew his samr.

Everyone took a long step away, save the clerk, who dropped with a wheeze of terror to his knees. He stared up at him, his eyes in the lamp-light like daubs of jelly, like something already dead that only glistened.

"Uyane Meoraq stands before you," spat Meoraq. He was calm, quite calm despite the venom in his tone and the shine of his naked blade. "And with the right to carry this weapon comes the right to use it however I will. You offend me."

From the kneeling man's motionless, open mouth came a series of soft, dry clicking sounds. After a moment, Meoraq decided he was trying to say, 'I cry,' but managing only the first glottal before his strength failed. His bladder, Meoraq noticed, already had. A twinge of disgust flexed through his spines, seeing that. He did not expect every man to face death as a warrior, but he should at least face it as a man.

"I have not decided to forgive you," he said, sheathing his samr and stepping away before he got piss on his muddy boots. "But I will think about it and let my judgment be known when I return in the sowing season."

He left unspoken but very clear the understanding that if he returned to news that Nkosa had been punished, his judgment would be severe.

"Thank you, honored one," breathed the man on the floor, still without moving.

Meoraq turned his eyes on the best-dressed of the men still clustered to witness all this nonsense. "Where shall I find the abbot?"

"I don't...In the quorum?"

"He might be in sequester," another man offered. "I think there was a vote tonight."

"A sequestered vote?" asked the first, clearly surprised.

"One of the oracles died."

"Orved," said a third, timidly nodding in Meoraq's direction to excuse himself for speaking. "He was on the roof when the fire went up and he fell down the stairs."

"Oh. I heard about that but I didn't know it was Orved."

"Where do you think he's been all this time?"

"The Halls of Judgment don't exactly drip oracles," said the first crossly. "I don't see any number of people for days on end, but I don't assume they're all dead!"

Meoraq folded his arms and gripped his biceps very close to the hilts of his sabks, waiting.

He had their attention again at once.

"If he is not sequestered, honored one, then he should be in the quorum. There is a dispute in session...ah...Are you here for the dispute?"

Meoraq turned away without feeling any strong urge to answer, although he did spare a last glance down at the floor where the kneeling man still knelt. He had recovered only enough to close his eyes and that was just as recovered as Meoraq wanted to see him. There was a great rustling behind him as men made their salutes and bows, but Meoraq didn't stay to witness them. He knew where the quorum was. It abutted the arena.

* * *

There was a man posted outside the quorum doors, swordless, with a brutal-looking hammer at his side. Not one of the warrior's caste. A bailiff, then, and not one Meoraq knew or at least not one he remembered. He gave his name and went into the arena hold to wait. It was his right to hear any dispute where he might be called to challenge or champion, but he wasn't in any kind of mood to hear the bickering that invariably accompanied legal disputes.

He was not alone in that, it would seem. There was a man in the arena hold already, sitting on the altar and leaned back against the wall, by all appearances asleep, except that no sleeping man's breath was so precisely even. He wore nothing but a battle harness and a loin-plate, cinched tight over a ridiculously young and unscarred body. His sabks were metal and shiny, as young or even younger than he was. He rested one finger lightly on the hilt of each.

Unwilling to interrupt a brother's meditations, Meoraq gave no greeting. He set his pack down and opened it, working quietly through his supplies until he came to his spare clothes, which were not much cleaner and not much drier, but some of each and worth changing into. He began to undress.

"I had a bath brought," the other man said without opening his eyes. "Water's cooled, but not too murky."

Meoraq located the basin in an unlit corner of the hold and went to use it, grunting appreciatively. The other man acknowledged this with a grunt of his own, but that was all.

The water was indeed cool where it lay in the basin, but there was more in a closed pail and that warmed it some. It made for rather a deep bath, but Meoraq didn't mind sloshing over. He didn't have to clean the floors. There was soap in a sachet and several grades of brush and the bath was quite pleasant even if he had to do it himself. Oh, he could have sent for a servant, and really preferred to use one, but they always sent women and that was too distracting before a trial. A Sheulek was supposed to be the master of his clay and impervious to all temptation, but Meoraq had found that having a woman rub oil into his naked body had a tendency to arouse him regardless of how inappropriate the place or time might be. He was working on that.

Bathed and dried, Meoraq briskly oiled up and made ready for trial, if it came to trial. The other man finally slid his eyes open toward the end and watched as he whetted his sabks. Meoraq let him watch. They were good knives, made in the age before the Fall of the black, stone-like substance called qil, which no man could now duplicate. The knives had served his bloodline since the founding of his House and he never drew or sheathed them without this hot, fierce leap of pride, remembering how it had felt to take their weight for the first time and feel his father's hands binding them to his arms. In all his lifetime, including his years of service as Sheulek, Meoraq had never seen a more intimidating set of honor-blades.

The other man hardly cowered at the sight, but he did tip his head and flare his spines forward in respectful admiration. "Ni'ichok Shuiv stands before you," he said, and glanced down at himself, still very much seated on the altar. "Metaphorically. Sheulteb in service of House Arug."

Ah, Sheulteb. If a Sheulek was the Striding Foot, then the Sheulteb were God when He stood. Only one short year of training and one degree of rank separated them, and they shared many of the same duties, save that Meoraq served every city on his circuit and the Sheulteb were called to only one House, to act as champion if it had no lord born to the warrior's caste. There were more of those every year, it seemed. Even Uyane's line in other cities had Sheulteb now. The Age of the Warrior was ending, men said, and perhaps it was true. Too many of the old blades were broken.

Meoraq sheathed his sabks and went over for a brother's tap—his open palm to Shuiv's chest, Shuiv's open palm on his own. Their hearts were already in sync.

"I do not recall the privilege of meeting one of Ni'ichok's sons, but I know House Arug well," said Meoraq when it was done. "He has had more than his share of troubles in recent years. What curse has he brought upon himself?"

"A curse of daughters," said Shuiv, wryly smiling. "And neither wealth nor name enough to sell them all off."

"Sell them?"

"Not so boldly as to be criminal." Shuiv flicked his spines forward carelessly, then leaned back against the wall again and closed his eyes. "But I had one waiting in my chambers the day I took oath for him, before any blade had been drawn on his behalf. And as soon as I had made her belly round, I found another."

Meoraq recoiled with a disgusted hiss.

"My samr and I explained together to her father the laws defining incest." Shuiv flared his mouth briefly, showing the tips of his teeth in idle expression of meditative contempt. "But he has had one catastrophe after another ever since, it seems, and he tries to solve every one of them with the offering of marriage."

"A foolish way to empty one's House."

"Oh, he's emptied it," said Shuiv with a snort. "The mediators have cited him for frivolous intent eight times this season alone, and each fault doubles his fine. He's sold two fields already to pay them, not to mention his sovereignty over two hundred households, and low though it may be to repeat rumor, I could not help but notice that two of his creditors forgave his debts after a speedy marriage to his daughters. But he has a legitimate complaint this time," Shuiv admitted, opening his eyes.

After so many years of judgment, Meoraq rarely bothered to hear complaints. They had a way of prejudicing a man's mind and when he stood in the arena as an instrument of Sheul, his own will could only prove a distraction. Besides, the grand trials that pitted righteous but wronged men against corrupt and cunning powers that he had read about in his boyhood were just that: stories told by priests to impress and excite young minds. Men did not need reasons to indulge in acts of evil, just as they did not need evil enacted against them to send them crying to the courts for justice. Still, Meoraq tipped his head to an inviting angle, showing interest he did not particularly feel, and the young man before him sat up a little straighter.

"Arug's debts have been such this year that he sought to squeeze in an extra harvest between riak's reap and sweet-pod's sowing. He couldn't afford to compensate his farmers with coin, so he promised those who met his demands that they would have one-half the final crop of the year rather than the customary quarter. For a surprise, he held to his word. But one of the farming households under his sovereignty went out to find that most of his share of the field's crop had already been harvested. He suspects a certain farmer, a man who had suspiciously great yield in his own rows, but there is no proof. Both men claim to be wronged, one by theft and one by slander."

"And as Arug is lord over both, he cannot find for either man without appearing to show favor," finished Meoraq. He glanced heavenward through the ceiling and sighed.

"Glamorous, I know." Shuiv gave his spines a rueful flick. "He brought them both here so that they could see how assiduously he serves the interests of his protected, but really, he wants the mediators to make a ruling for him that neither man can hold against him. And probably offer them each a daughter in commiseration, ha. I know he's brought a few."

Meoraq grunted his disapproval, but felt his belly warm.

"They've made him sit all day in the antechamber while they heard every other dispute in the logs," Shuiv went on, "but he's refused to leave and now that you are here, the mediators will surely take it for proof that Sheul has a will in this matter and send the whole stupid thing to trial."

"Surely. Yet trials have been called over smaller disputes."

"Not a spear of grass grows save by His design, so my training master told me. And even Arug must serve Him in some way, I suppose. Yet I wonder if I see no more omen in you than a Sheulek coming in out of the rain." Shuiv settled back against the wall once more, letting his eyes slide shut. "What did bring you, brother?"

"I received a summons. Many summons, to be precise. Commanding me by name. May I be safe in assuming they do not come from House Arug?"

"I shouldn't think so. If secrets were teeth, Arug still could not keep them in his mouth and I would remember if I heard him utter your name." A sly peek beneath heavy lids. "It is rather a well-known name."

"It is not the sword, but the hand that wields it," Meoraq replied, just as if he were not flattered. "I have been half a year ignoring these summons and so Sheul sent me one of His own."

Shuiv did not ask his meaning, but studied him with new interest. "I was in meditation that night. I never saw it. They said it filled the sky."

"I would not say so, but it was tall enough at its first rising to touch the clouds, to pierce them."

"And you think it was set for you? Truth?"

"I think it was set by Sheul. I think it was tall enough that there might be a thousand men who saw it and believed it for their eyes alone."

Shuiv waited, faintly smiling.

"It was mine," said Meoraq.

Shuiv grunted, closed his eyes, and quite some time later said, "The man who has been summoned by Sheul's own torch must have further to go than Tothax."

"Then there will be some other sign to lead me on, if it was indeed for my eye. All things indeed serve Sheul, but I can't think how the squabbles of two farmers and a few rows of riak could be dire enough to warrant a tower of fire on a rainy night."

"It was gruu, actually."

"Ah, well that makes all the difference then. For gruu, I should be surprised there wasn't a hammer of ice to go with it."

Shuiv snorted.

"I hear," mused Meoraq, "there is also an exarch who wishes my audience."

"An exarch in Tothax is rare enough that word has even reached lowly House Arug," Shuiv replied, eyes shut. "But as he only arrived twenty days and some ago, I can't think how he could have been sending summons half the year, as you say. As for the exarch himself, I hear nothing save that he has a scandalously gilded taste for drink and a free hand with the abbot's coin, but there may be more envy in that than truth."

Meoraq grunted, inviting the conversation to continue if it was the other man's wish, although the politics of priests and farmers and the eternal rift between them were of no interest to him. Perhaps it would be different if he were a Sheulteb, shut up every day of the year in that common House with its common problems and common tongues forever flapping, but he was not.

"I used to wish for exciting trials when I was young and stupid," Shuiv said after a companionable silence. "Well, younger. And less stupid. Then I had my first trial..." Shuiv hesitated a glance at him, seeking censure, but Meoraq merely waved at him to speak on. "And as proud as I was to burn with Him, I found myself wishing afterwards for a long, boring post. Which was given to me. And on the way here for—I don't even know anymore—the sixth time? The tenth? I wished again that something real would happen, something meaningful. And here you are." There was quiet between them and then Shuiv laughed a little. "It does not bode well for me in the trial to come. May I ask you a brother's consideration?"

Meoraq tipped his head, knowing what was coming.

"My woman bore my child near the freshening of the year. If it opens a son, will you see him taken to my father? Knowing Arug, he'll have married its mother off again before my bones are even black and I don't think I can die completely if I have to worry over another man raising my son. Especially the sorts of men Arug's been hawking daughters to."

"My oath is yours, brother. If I stand in Sheul's favor, I shall pass through Tothax in the early spring."

"It should be proved by then. My thanks."

The door opened. Not the door to the hall, through which Meoraq had come, but the door to the arena. The bailiff entered, bowing low. "Honored ones, the court of Tothax under High Judge Sen'sui requests your judgment at trial."

Shuiv pushed himself off the wall, his smile broad and guileless, eager as only a young man could be. He offered his arm and they clasped shoulders, then left the hold. The bailiff lowered the stair for them. Meoraq descended first—the Swords were equal in the eyes of Sheul, but he reasoned that he had more years of service and if he didn't take the initiative, they risked standing in the doorway saluting each other like idiots while everyone watched—and Shuiv came after, but they went together to the center of the ring and bent their necks.

It was not a large room, really. They never were. A man could count off fifty paces if he crossed at its widest point, but only if he was sparing with his stride. The corners were rounded; the floor was bare stone, sloping toward its center where the drain was set, to make cleaning easier; the mediators and witnesses had no access to this level, but watched from behind a screen from the floor above. There were no furnishings, no banners, no embellishments. The one indication of this room's singular importance was the window set high in the ceiling, round as an open eye and stained with colors. In the right hours of day, the light that fell through that window seemed to pour fire itself over the arena floor, but it was growing late now and the arena was mostly dark.

One panel of the enclosing screen slid open, revealing the witnesses' box. Meoraq knew Arug by his garish clothing and the frantic way he was hissing at his manservant, who then left at a run. He could guess the reason easily enough, but did not dwell on it. What happened after the trial was not important. All his mind and body now belonged to God.

The high judge raised both hands, although there was only solemn silence around him to begin with, and said, "The trial of Ezethu, a man of House Arug, against Mihuun, a man of House Arug, is hereby brought to light before Sheul."

The men were not identified, but Meoraq knew them for their staring faces, where horror painted itself as thick as awe. Simple farmers with a petty squabble, neither man could have possibly foreseen this dispute going to trial and both clearly feared the consequences—a sure sign that both carried some measure of guilt.

The bailiff came while the high judge read the formal charges, to paint the sign of the Sword in white upon Shuiv's chest. Somewhere behind the high half-wall, one of the farmers was marked in the same fashion, just as the other would be wearing the hammer now being painted in red over Meoraq's own heart. He acknowledged the bailiff's murmur of apology for taking such liberties, but scarcely felt the touch. His muscles were tightening, anticipating. He had fought three hundred battles and more; they were all the first and only one.

"—and submit ourselves before You, great Father. We await Your judgment. Do the Swords of Sheul stand ready?"

Meoraq saluted. Beside him, Shuiv did the same.

The bailiff retracted the stair and shut the door to the arena hold. The high judge brought his hammer down against the top of the half-wall with a flat, unimportant rapport and closed the screen. He could see shadows moving as Arug and his farmers drew slightly back, unsure what to expect, and hear the stern rumble of a judge's voice warning them to be still. He closed his eyes as Meoraq the man to clear his mind of these distractions and opened them again as Meoraq the Sword.

As the ranking warrior between them, Meoraq began, drawing his sabks. "I do not spill my brother's blood," he said, facing Shuiv. "I do not bare my blades for men. I am not Uyane Meoraq within this ring."

"I am not Ni'ichok Shuiv." Shuiv smiled as he drew his new, shining knives. There was already color coming in at his throat. "I have no heart and no will in this hour," he said, now in unison with Meoraq. "I know no fear and no vengeance. I am no more than a sword in Your hand, O my Father. Let them behold me, drawn. And let Your will be done."

Shuiv began with the same ritual movements they had been taught as children, stylized expressions of balance more than battle whose familiarity helped to focus and center him. Meoraq's body knew just how to meet him; his mind drifted, counting breaths while he watched his hands work. Their blades clashed and scraped, clashed and fell, clashed and whirled. He knew no urgency, no fear, nothing but the heat rising in his throat and belly, and the simple pleasure that could always be had from indulging in something fine after a long and difficult day.

How long that first, formal stage of battle lasted, he could not say. Shuiv's movements became steadily more ragged as the color at his throat grew stronger. Meoraq could hear his breaths falling roughly out of rhythm, see the fires burning high in his eyes. He knew the moment that Shuiv let go and became the sword in Sheul's hand, but he did not soon follow. So perhaps it was not for him after all, he mused, parrying the younger man's increasingly savage lunges and thinking of the tower of fire. Or if it had been, strange that it should have been all to bring him this far to Tothax only to end him in the arena over a few rows of gruu and some bitter words. Perhaps it was Shuiv who was meant to go on. For a young Sheulteb to take victory over a veteran Sheulek of so grand a House as Uyane was certainly the start of a damned good story.

But his own breaths were coarsening now, his thoughts becoming more difficult to grasp even as they slipped through his mind. He was aware, vaguely, of that curious blankness stealing in while he pondered Shuiv and whatever fate awaited him, replacing words he knew with timeless stretches of empty heat. He stood against it for as long as he could, because the struggle was as glorious as the burning, but his world became a blackness.

He burned.

Fire. He felt it every time, but this time, disturbingly, he saw it. It spilled upwards from the heart of the black, filling his vision and searing at his soul's flesh, brighter than it had been that night on the rooftop of Xheoth. Not beckoning. *Demanding*. And in that endless moment between Meoraq the man and Meoraq the Sword, there was only stillness and his heart beating and that tower of fire burning his eyes, and he said or heard or perhaps only imagined the word, "sukaga."

It caught in him like a fishing hook, almost familiar...

And then the blackness slipped away again. Weight and substance fell back onto his bones; he staggered, catching blindly at a man's shoulder to steady him until he could see Shuiv's face through the flames that still coursed through him. He looked down, confused, and saw the black blade of one sabk deep in the younger man's chest. He had no idea where the other one was.

The high judge's hammer struck twice, invisible. Meoraq leapt back with a mindless hiss, slashing at the empty air before he could master himself. The fire rose again, but this time, he closed his eyes and made himself breathe until it cooled. Shuiv was dead and Sheul's judgment, known to all. He was Uyane Meoraq once again; the Sword of Sheul was sheathed.

He closed his eyes, counting his breaths the way every boy born to his caste was taught, with the primary verse for the Six. A slow count, they called that. Slow and calm and even. A Sheulek must be the master of his clay and so, 'One for the Prophet, the wide open eye...Two for his brunt and the sign of the fist...'

He couldn't believe he was standing here. His palms ached, but apart from that slight pain, he didn't think he'd even been scratched, although he felt worn enough that surely the battle had been a long one. Shuiv had started to burn so quickly...but not for the honest man, it seemed. And now House Arug had his widow to care for, at least until her infant had opened and Meoraq could judge it for a son or daughter and see it placed accordingly.

'Three for Uyane, the unclad sword...Four for Mykrm, the hammer of his law...Five for Oyan of the ash-stained leaf...'

Ashes...Fire...Like the tower he had seen from Xheoth and followed to Tothax. Like the tower he had seen in the blackness of his burning, where he had never seen anything before. And the word, sukaga...a name, perhaps, but not one he immediately knew. Why was it now so maddeningly familiar?

'Six for Thaliszar and the healing hand...'

It went on from there, but Meoraq started over at one (they only named the low castes to fill out the numbers from seven to ten; the Six were the only verses that mattered) and let his mind wander. By his third slow-count through, he was completely cool and lucid enough to really wonder what he'd done with his other sabk. He cast about for it on the floor while the high judge finished the trial's closing prayers, then went to see if he'd left it buried in the body anywhere odd. He was careful with his brother's body as he turned it. Shuiv's blood was slow, his life gone, but he would not truly be dead until his funeral pyre had been consumed. While he could still feel, he deserved no less than the highest respect.

"Honored one."

Meoraq looked up to see that the bailiff had lowered the stair and now stood before him, offering his sabk. Bloodied.

Meoraq took it and pinched the blade to clean it. "Where was this?" he asked curiously.

The bailiff bowed. "By Sheul's judgment, through the throat of Mihuun."

Meoraq looked up, startled, and saw that the screen wall above him had indeed been battered open. A great deal of blood stained what he could see of the narrow chamber beyond. He looked at his hand, turned it upwards, slowly flexed his fingers. Splinters.

"Having seen that, I think...Ezethu?...will not be quick to bring future disputes to his lord's attention," he remarked, sheathing his sabk to pick them out.

The bailiff bowed again. "Ezethu was first to fall beneath Sheul's judgment, honored one." He paused, clearly wondering if his next words were in bad taste, then lowered his voice and said, "But I think we have finally seen the last of Lord Arug."

Pity it took a man's life to stop a greedy lord from abusing the law, but he was so seldom called to court for good reasons.

Meoraq glanced back, then went and knelt by Shuiv again. He pressed his palm against the still chest and bent his neck in a warrior's bow. "I will envy you, my brother, when you behold our Father's face tonight," he said, and looked up through the high, colored window to the heavens. "Take him, O my Father, and receive him well. He is a good man."

The bailiff grunted approvingly. Not every victor of the arena gave respect to a fallen Sword, but Meoraq did not do it just because it was the custom. Not this time, anyway. He often felt strange in his own skin after a judgment, but this was different. The vision of the burning tower; the word, sukaga; and Shuiv, falling into God's fires right in front of him—everything seemed braided, bound to him, impossibly heavy.

He felt a sudden restlessness, an urge to call for his pack and just leave. Never mind the exarch and never mind whoever it was that had been summoning him half the year. He knew what awaited him in the next room and there was a time when he would have been eager to go to it, but not tonight. Sheul was calling him. Meoraq wanted nothing in this world more than to answer.

But he could not answer from the arena and men were surely waiting to bear Shuiv away for his final rites, so Meoraq finished his respects. He found Shuiv's shining sabks and broke the blades, placing the hilted halves carefully at his feet. He said the Prayer For the Fallen and the first three verses from the Book of the Sword. Then he let the bailiff lead him back into the arena hold.

3

They had cleaned away the bath and his pack, but the room was far from empty. The high judge was there, of course, with another bailiff, the court scribe, and two lesser mediators. At their center stood Lord Arug in his grossly inappropriate finery and baubles, along with the servant he had sent running from the court at the trial's beginning. And behind them all, bowing, motionless, scarcely visible in the shadows, was a woman.

'A girl,' Meoraq thought, trying to be severe, to be scornful even. Not a woman at all, but hardly more than a child, to judge by the narrowness of her build and the grey tint to her immature scales. One of the many curses laid upon House Arug. Nothing but that. Nothing worth noticing at all.

And as restless as he was to be gone, he could not stop staring at her.

"My daughter, honored one," said Arug, bowing almost as low as the girl. "Tem."

Meoraq flared his mouth in annoyance, but could not quite pull his gaze from the curve of her bent back. His heart, raised in combat, did not slow. A second pulse began in his belly, building to urgent harmony where his cock was contained. She wasn't pretty, wasn't the sort who would ever catch his eye if it were his own will, but there must be something in her that appealed to Sheul, because the fires burned in Meoraq and the urge to take her became as violent and undeniable as the urge to burn in the arena.

"Leave us," he said, drawing a sabk.

Lord Arug and the mediators made their salutes and withdrew. Tem, well-coached, did not.

She bent lower, her hands trembling on the tiles, as Meoraq came toward her and did not move until he stood over her with blade in hand. "This is the blade of conquest."

"I am a virgin of my father's House," she replied.

He stared at her, frowning.

In a moment, she'd realized her mistake. Her eyes flashed wide and she fumbled at her wrist, stammering out breathy apologies. Soon, she had her wristlet off—a shiny thing of woven metal wires, perhaps purchased earlier this day for just this moment—and held it out to him in a shaking hand.

He took it, feeling his spines flex and flatten outside of his control. 'Breathe,' he told himself, stabbing his sabk through the delicate band at the nearest exposed wooden beam in the wall. 'She's young. She's nervous. She's probably fragile. Just breathe.'

He turned around, already reaching to unhook the fastens of his loin-plate. "I am Uyane Meoraq," he said as he swept his belt away and his cock came thrusting furiously past his armor. "House Arug stands in the shadow of my blade. I am a Sword of Sheul and I demand the right of conquest."

Tem started to bow again, of all things, only to straighten up fast with both hands raised in frantic supplication. "No, I—Wait! I was meant to run!"

Meoraq managed not to hiss at her, but it was a near thing. Yes, she was nervous, but he was Sheulek and the fires were upon him. He had little patience for these female rituals under the best of circumstances and now that patience was all but gone.

"Run, then," he said tersely. His toes flexed, ready for the chase, and he had to remind himself that she was no true opponent, only a girl, and easily hurt. He must be the master of his flesh even now, with his cock aching in the open air and every thought his mind could make coated in Sheul's flame, and he must not harm her.

She rose, sending anxious glances in all directions, as if the empty arena hold were a thicket filled with obstacles that needed navigation. Her roving eye came to him, touching his cock with the weight of a living hand, and she seemed to shrink within herself. She did not run. She did not even appear to be breathing.

So be it. Meoraq strode forward and caught her by the girdle.

She screamed in his face, then clapped both hands over her snout and looked properly appalled with herself. "F-Forgive!"

He was beyond forgiving, beyond offense, beyond caring. Meoraq swung her around and put her firmly against the wall beside the beam where his sabk impaled her wristlet.

"I am a virgin of my father's House!" she babbled, clutching at the bricks.

"You are permitted to fight me," he told her, raising her skirt in a fist-hold and pinning it at her back.

She didn't, either because she feared another insult to the ritual or because she didn't know how. It made no difference in the end. Conquest, such as it was, was over.

Meoraq wedged her legs apart and fit himself to her opening. She was sealed fear-tight, but arousal made him slick and he pierced her as easily as his sabk had pierced Shuiv.

She screamed again, this time with pain. She did not struggle, but her body, his enemy, tightened at once, working to push him out. He knew by many conquests that speed was the key now, or this muscular sleeve would clench too tightly to penetrate at all without tearing her. Meoraq put a steadying hand on her belly, rocked onto the balls of his feet, and thrust hard.

The girl's cry swept up into a shriek and then broke into sobbing, incoherent pleas that were only partly directed at him. The rest, as so often was the case, were hysterical cries for her mother. But he was in, his oiled shaft fighting past the constriction of her sleeve until he pushed free into her soft well. There, the grip of her body became a seal at his narrowed base, holding him in even tighter with every futile effort to expel him.

Now that the initial difficulty of sex had been overcome, Meoraq made some deference to the girl, slowing to give the hurts of this first invasion time to ease. She was struggling now, but she was trapped and as he continued to move inside her, the ferocious grip of her body was made to relax by the slow knead of his. Her tears became sniffles and then soft panting. Soon she bent her neck to press her sloping brow to the bricks, arching her back in such innocently lascivious pleasure that he almost forgot himself, that just for a moment, it was almost fun.

Meoraq savored it as long as he dared, then reluctantly brought his mind to focus and began his prayers: "Sheul, O great Father, make this woman worthy."

The girl interrupted with a moan, her hips bucking back in unskilled, spastic motions. He was briefly overcome by his clay's carnality, and lost several minutes to mindless, fiery fucking before he regained a hold on his conscious thoughts. Somewhat dazed, he forced himself to a stop, which was not easy to do with the girl thrashing back at him. She was fully open now, and each movement of her hips made the sleeve of her female sex slide along his full length as she rocked back and forth—still a squeeze, but certainly not an unpleasant one—begging him in a largely incoherent way for more. Her hand reached back to catch at his hip; his first instinctive response to this fetching gesture was a fighting hiss, but he shook out of it almost at once. He knew where he was now, and he began again with strong, purposeful thrusts.

"Let her soul be pierced and made open. Let her womb be warmed to receive my spirit and Yours." His head swam. He closed his eyes to concentrate. Through the fires of Sheul, each word seemed alive with significance and nuance, like the girl herself. He could feel her hands pulling at him, lost in her own fires, and his heart swelled with sudden affection for her. "If it be Your will, raise her up with Your blessing and give her the gift of new life," said Meoraq, and found that he meant it, which he very rarely did these days, a subject of much meditation when he was at his prayers.

Sheul heard, and perhaps His mortal son's sincerity pleased him, for He blessed her. She flung her head back in a silent, eerily graceful arc, the top of her head slapping home against his chest and pressing hard, outwardly motionless in the grip of Sheul's blessing while her small body bloomed with exquisite heat. Meoraq cupped her jaw and breathed into her gasping mouth just as his own fires overwhelmed him. He came, offering his seed and spirit for Sheul to do as He willed.

The moment could not last, and when it ended, Meoraq nuzzled her head aside and made his mark upon her. She flinched, which made the bite quite a bit deeper than he otherwise would have wanted, but the marks of his teeth were distinct and that was what mattered.

"Now you are mine," said Meoraq formally and licked the wound to stop its bleeding.

Her answer was a wordless mewl—the sort of soft, feminine sound that girls are coached early to make when their man requires no special reply, and which Meoraq had always found personally to be repulsive, a cringing animal sound that did not belong in any person's mouth, much less the mouth of a person he had just been joined to sexually.

Meoraq resheathed himself and stepped back, holding her arm until she steadied and seeing to it that her skirts fell properly. He'd had more than one conquest wander out into the hall with her skirts tucked into her girdle and her freshly-opened slit exposed and glistening for all the world and her own father to see.

"Thank you, honored one," said the girl, bowing. "May the House of Arug be strengthened by the blood of conquest."

'That is a flat head,' thought Meoraq, studying it with a weary eye as he dressed. A churlish thought, unworthy of a Sheulek. Oh, she was polite and earnest—not that earnestness was a particularly desirable trait in a woman—and pretty enough from the brows down. If she struck him as a bit vapid, that could be just her youth and the sheltered life of any high-born girl (and if not, well, most men found a streak of stupidity a charming quality in a woman. Many women actually feigned it whenever circumstance forced them into a man's company, often to such a degree that Meoraq couldn't stand to be around them at all).

They were waiting in the hall and all made the appropriate sounds of subdued respect to see the mark upon the girl's shoulder. Her father took her back with pride and perhaps even a gleam of avarice, and why not? If she did nothing else in her life, still she had received Sheul's fires and her womb would be strengthened immeasurably. In fact, it was not impossible that she might conceive of Meoraq, even from just this one encounter. And if the child opened up male and Meoraq had no wife, Arug had every reason to expect his daughter to be taken in, flat head and all, and installed in House Uyane where she would give glorious birth to the sons of one who would be that bloodline's steward in his own time. If the father of such a woman were the doting sort, he certainly had the right to visit her in her husband's House...where he could expect rooms and servants and other such amenities...for however long he chose to stay...for years, if the lord of the House were not so vulgar as to throw him out.

Meoraq was not a vulgar man, but he did have every intention of dying long before he was made to assume his father's place. Ha. Let Arug call on his House all he pleased. Rasozul would throw him out on his snout without a moment's regret.

"House Arug thanks you for your service, honored one. Let me extend the humblest and most sincere invitation of hospitality. Please, come to my House tonight," said the steward, actually patting at his daughter's bent back as he made the offer. Meoraq thought it very likely that if he accepted, he would find Tem tucked away in his cupboard like a spare cushion. Perhaps she had been a virgin—maidenly panic could be contrived and he was experienced enough in the ways of women to know that he had surely been deceived before—but her virginity had served its purpose and now it seemed Lord Arug was eager to see it well and truly rubbed away.

"I understand Ni'ichok Shuiv leaves his woman and a child to your House," Meoraq said bluntly. "You will keep them."

Arug hesitated, his smile fading before he forced it broadly back. "House Arug is honored to care for the mother of her champion's son."

"I will return to see the child placed at the appropriate time." Meoraq inclined his head toward heaven. "If Sheul wills that I should return. If not, I suppose I must trust you." His gaze shifted to the bailiff. "I require a witness."

The bailiff bent his neck briefly and produced a tablet and stylus.

"I want the woman's rooms inspected," said Meoraq, his eyes back on Arug. "Regularly. She is owed the respect of a Sheulteb's wife. She is also owed a widow's stipend. See that it is not misplaced into her father's coffers."

Lord Arug kept smiling, but his spines were very low, visibly shaking with the effort not to flatten them completely. "She shall be kept as one of my greatest treasures," he said. "You may see her chambers for yourself, if you like."

"I prefer to stay in the Temple," he said. Which was true enough, and also more tactful then commenting aloud on the man's perceived willingness to turn his daughter into a common dip for the first Sheulek who came along.

Arug bowed to conceal his obvious disappointment—*that's rather a flat head as well*—and withdrew with Tem. She looked back once, shyly seeking his eye until her father hissed and yanked her hood down. Then they were gone.

"You may show me to my room," said Meoraq, prodding at his wound. The edges had sealed beneath his scales, but it still ached abysmally and would probably swell and bleed again by morning if it were not properly cleaned and tended. He was tempted to neglect it. Shuiv had seemed a good man and a brave warrior; Meoraq was not ashamed to wear his last scar.

The bailiff merely bowed, rather than walking ahead of him down the hall. "Forgive me, honored one, there is a dispute awaiting your judgment."

Of course there was. Tothax was not the most remote city in the world, but it was easily the most remote on Meoraq's circuit. On his last visit, there had been four disputes awaiting his judgment, one of them half a year old and so entirely irrelevant by the day of Meoraq's arrival that he had been divinely compelled to slap both parties across their petty-minded faces before walking into the arena. But however many disputes there might be awaiting him, it was customary to separate them over the course of many days. To judge two trials in a single night, so soon after his long journey, bordered on insult.

His temper flared, but six breaths brought him reason. Just because the first of their disputes had been a paltry one did not mean they were all so. And besides that, Meoraq's blood was still warmed by battle and a second fight had its appeal (as well as the promise of a second conquest once the fight was done, perhaps even with a pretty woman, or at least one who had a properly-shaped head). In either case, he was Sheulek, and it was his duty and his privilege to serve Sheul, no matter the hour or the inconvenience to his mortal clay.

"Then I will hear it," he told the waiting bailiff, but he took six more slow breaths before he followed. He loved God and would never question His commands, but there were times he wished he was not quite so often in His eye.

* * *

Back they went to the mediation chamber, which was again filled with spectators disguising themselves as witnesses. One of the galleys was curiously empty, he saw. The other was occupied by another man dressed as a warlord and the kneeling figure of yet another woman. The man was only vaguely familiar, although Meoraq noted that his lordly garb was, unlike that of Arug, functional rather than ceremonial, and he carried several admirable scars prominently across his powerful body. The woman, however, he recognized at once despite her bent back and ducked head.

Meoraq glanced again at the empty galley and snorted. He folded his arms, resting his hands close to the hilts of his sabks. "Where is the baby?" he asked, interrupting the high judge mid-prayer.

"If you had come when I first sent word to you, you could have seen it born," the lord said, also interrupting the judge, who was attempting to both apologize and reprimand Meoraq at the same time.

"Why would I want to?"

"Honored one, please!" snapped the high judge. "This is a formal matter!"

"I am not in the mood for formalities," said Meoraq.

"So be it." The lord stepped forward, beckoning behind him to one of his many men. "I am House Saluuk," he said, for the benefit of the court's scribe. "Once Saluuk Tzugul and a Sword of Sheul. This is my daughter."

"I remember," said Meoraq. And he did, although the fires had burned hot in him that day. He remembered her not because she was pretty, which she was, rather, but also because she had been particularly tiresome in conquest—breaking the ritual after only a few stammered lines and then trying to flee the arena hold. He'd been forced to pursue and to hold her down, neither of which he minded much in the burn of Sheul's fires, but she'd also screamed all the way through the sex, and afterwards, just lay there in a heap, sobbing. A bad night, and one that had a way of slipping back into his thoughts when he was alone and his mind unquiet. A Sword of Sheul knew no remorse for the things he did in the grip of holy fire, and yet...she had been so small beneath him, so small as she lay weeping on the floor...

And now there she knelt, and there indeed was the infant, carried in a servant's arms to be displayed before the court. It was the right size; he wondered whether she had been corrupted after his conquest or before.

To think he'd lain awake so many nights, haunted by her tears.

"I remember," Meoraq said again, coldly. "And I remember that Sheul's blessing was for myself alone. I do not acknowledge that child. Its blood is the blood of Gann."

Shocked gasps met this accusation and then whispers flew. Lord Saluuk's throat began to pale in streaks of color, but he betrayed no other sign of emotion as he reached down, took a fist-hold of his daughter's wrap and yanked it open, revealing her scarred shoulder as she twisted her face away.

Meoraq had been many years a Sheulek and knew it had made him cynical. He was used to expecting the worst of people, but this, he never anticipated.

"Lies!" he roared, at once full in the grip of Sheul's killing fires. It was his training alone that kept his blades in their sheaths; every bone of him wanted to draw and paint every damned wall of this room with blood.

Breathe. A Sheulek is a master of every impulse.

"Lies," he said again, hissing but at least not shouting. "She may have been virgin—I will not say otherwise—but she did *not* burn and that is *not* my mark!"

"I stand before you, judges, in the sight of Sheul." The steward released his daughter to her huddle and faced the tribunal. "Every servant of my household is present and able to swear that this woman has been in proper confinement every hour of her life, save that when she was last in this arena." He swung to stab at Meoraq with his stare, saying, "Or do you say House Saluuk allows its daughters to rut wild in the alleys?"

"I do not," said Meoraq, just as coldly. "Whether she goes out or her bulls sneak in should concern House Saluuk, but it is no matter to me."

"You come very near to making a personal insult, honored one," one of the judges said with a respectful nod.

"I do not come near," snapped Meoraq. "I make it boldly! Your daughter has gone to Gann and that is not my mark upon her."

Before Lord Saluuk could make his snarling reply, the woman flung out her bare hands and cried, "I have been with no man but you!"

The whole of the tribunal stared at her.

Her father was first to recover. In two swift strides, he had returned to her side and slapped her to the ground.

"Oh yes, she knows her place well," another judge remarked, but Meoraq killed what little humor that stirred up with a glance. The woman's tears as she knelt at Lord Saluuk's feet were too much as they had been a year ago when she had been huddling at his own feet. The sound woke the infant, who added its own wails until the servant holding it was ordered to take it into the hall. Meoraq found himself scowling suddenly into its little face as it was carried past him; it flinched away as from Gann Himself, clutching at the servant and renewing its cries, now with terror.

As soon as it was gone and the door shut against its noise, the high judge rose and raised his hand. "Stand the girl up."

Lord Saluuk obeyed, and none too gently. The girl sent a wet-eyed, imploring gaze at Meoraq, who folded his arms against her and refused to look away. She was a good one for heart-stirring looks, it seemed.

"Steward, it is your duty to make those of your House aware that what is said before this tribunal is said in the sight of Sheul. A lie spoken to Him is a wound to one's very soul."

"She knows," said Saluuk, giving his daughter a glance as hard as a second slap.

"So be it. Girl." The high judge leaned sternly over the tribune wall, addressing himself to her directly while the lesser judges struggled not to react. "Before Sheul, who do you name as the father of that child?"

"Before Sheul, I swear that I have been with no man but Sheulek Uyane."

Meoraq flared his spines, but that was all. One embarrassing outburst was enough for this tribunal and it would be hers.

"Before Sheul," the high judge went on, narrowing his eyes, "who put that mark of conquest upon your flesh?"

Meoraq's spines flared again as his hands drew into fists upon his biceps in anticipation of the lie he must endure...but the lie never came.

The girl bent her neck and did not answer.

The high judge leaned back in his chair and stroked at his throat.

"Why do you waste our time interrogating a woman?" Lord Saluuk demanded. He unsheathed his sabks in a swift hiss. "If this man will not acknowledge his seed as the Word itself demands, I will challenge him and let Sheul be our judge!"

"This man," said Meoraq with contempt, "will meet you, steward, and Sheul will end your lying bloodline."

"Enough! How dare you draw a bladed weapon in this hall!" The high judge struck his hammer on the tribune wall, and again, until Lord Saluuk grudgingly resheathed. "There is no need for bloodshed! You! Fetch a wax tablet from the archivist's stores! If the honored one will make his mark, a simple comparison shall be enough to determine the truth here."

Meoraq grunted approval, eyeing Lord Saluuk, whose expression had taken on a narrow, calculating stare. The servant was dispatched to the stores, but he had been gone only a moment when the steward suddenly turned and caught his daughter by the throat.

"Will the marks match?" he demanded. "Answer, girl!"

His grip made any verbal reply impossible, but her choked wails held such hopeless despair that no words were necessary. Lord Saluuk released her with a shove and said, "I have been deceived and so wasted this tribunal's time. I shall pay whatever fine you deem appropriate."

"I have been with no man but you!" the girl blurted. "Please, you must believe me! I did not burn, I admit that, but even without His fires, I was blessed! Oh, hear me, honored one, will you not hear me? This is your child!"

Spectators exclaimed amongst themselves in gleeful shock at this blasphemy. The high judge struck his hammer upon the wall, but silence was not forthcoming, and though Lord Saluuk seized hold of his daughter's arm, she did not go quietly but instead increased her struggles, actually reaching out to try and catch at Meoraq's arm.

"Everything you say is truth!" she cried. "My only lie was the mark that—"

Lord Saluuk's arm swung and ended whatever she meant to say next, a slap no longer but a fist that broke the delicate upper bone of her narrow snout and sent her crashing to the floor. "Bridle her!" he roared, and no less than six of his servants leapt to obey. "I will hear no more lies spoken through that poison tongue! Remove her!"

Meoraq's disapproving hiss earned him half a pulled knife before Lord Saluuk shoved it back into its sheath.

"Go on with you, sprat!" he spat. "Go back to Xeqor! I knew your father and don't you *just* fill his fucking shadow! He's bred his House nothing but lack-wits and bastard-makers since he took the blade! Be damned to him for pissing you out and be damned to you—"

The hand of Sheul touched his heart; Meoraq's own flew out and caught Lord Saluuk by the wrist. In a moment, the warlord was on his knees with his face mashed against tiles still wet with his own daughter's tears and Meoraq was on him, trying to think through the haze of Sheul's fire and unsure, for an eternity of moments, whether it were an enemy beneath him or a woman.

The pounding of the judgment hammer cleared his head some. He shook himself, focused on the body twisting and hissing in his grip, then pulled his hooked kzung—a hunting blade, and still more than this particular animal deserved—and put it to Lord Saluuk's vibrant throat.

"Hold, honored one." The high judge struck his hammer a final, deliberate time. "This tribunal has not been concluded. If you have offense, you have the right to seek redress, but only at the proper hour."

Truth. Meoraq closed his eyes, breathed himself calm in the cooling grip of Sheul, and then released Saluuk with a contemptuous shove and stood away.

"How do you speak, lord?"

The steward of House Saluuk fought himself to his feet and turned a perfectly murderous glare on Meoraq. After several deep breaths of his own, he pressed his empty hands together and bent his stiff back in a bow. "I have offended," he hissed. "My accusation stands false in the sight of Sheul. I will make whatever reparation this tribunal demands for bringing her lies to this hall. My daughter—" His flat spines made a dry, scraping sound as they tried to flatten further against his skull. "—has gone to Gann. Uyane Meoraq stands acquitted of her and her bastard."

The judge raised his hammer, but Meoraq halted him with a raised hand. He cocked his head meaningfully, waiting.

Lord Saluuk glared at him, color throbbing in his throat. One moment became many, but it finally came: “Forgive me, honored one. I have offended you and your House.”

Meoraq’s head canted further. “And the father who pissed me out?” he prompted blackly.

Lord Saluuk’s spines ticced. Breathing hard, all but stinking of hate, Lord Saluuk knelt. One knee first, then both, and then he bent to touch his head to the floor and turn his naked palm up beside Meoraq’s boot. “Forgive.” He managed this time to say it without hissing, although the effort clearly came at a high price. “It is Saluuk Tzugul before you, son of Ulhathev, son of Shagoth, son of all my fathers before him. I am my House and the bloodline of my fathers and I have offended. I bend before you, Uyane. Forgive me.”

Meoraq grunted and stepped back. He did not make an answer, but then, the law demanded that pardon be asked of him, not that he give it.

“You are perhaps too quick to remove evidence from this tribunal, Lord Saluuk,” said one of the judges after a moment. “An impression could yet be made of the girl’s scar and compared to those men of your household whom you suspect—”

“She’s gone to Gann,” the steward spat, already back on his feet and just as furious as he had been before his showing of humility, if not more so. “Why should I care who sired her bastard?”

“Forgive, lord, but it is the matter of who put a Sheulek’s mark upon her that concerns me.”

Saluuk continued to glare at Meoraq for a breath or two, but then slid his cold stare up at the tribune wall.

“The girl’s corruption may be a sin,” said the judge, “but the forging of that mark is a crime. If these witnesses you bring before us can truly account for every hour of the girl’s life, then one of them surely aided in her deceit. She did not bite her own shoulder.”

The other tribune judges grunted solemn agreement. The spectators eyed one another and whispered.

“I will hold interrogations,” Saluuk said at last, visibly struggling with his temper. “I will find the man responsible and send him over the wall with his lying poke.”

Meoraq frowned. It was customary to exile those who had been corrupted beyond redeeming—giving to Gann those who had given themselves to him—and only after they had served a certain time of imprisonment under the Temple’s watch. Only when the priests had declared her unforgiveable would she be sent out to wander in the wildlands until Gann took her into darkness. She would never be burnt, never truly die, and Meoraq supposed she would come to this fate whether she walked out the Temple gate or fell from her father’s rooftop, but still it troubled him.

And he was not alone, for one of the lesser judges hesitantly said, “Would it not be better to place the girl in Temple custody until her guilt is proved?”

“Her *guilt*,” Saluuk hissed, “is biting at her teat! I will *not* be dishonored in my own House!”

As all the judges bowed, Meoraq said, “You have been too long within walls if you can think to preserve the honor of your bloodline only by exterminating it.”

Saluuk’s neck stiffened, the marks of his anger visibly throbbing in time with his heart. “If she cannot behave herself as a proper woman of my House, better she be dead. Her and her bastard both.”

“Honored one,” said the high judge reprovingly. “Your opinion is not asked. You stand acquitted and your part in this tribunal is done.”

Truth, and if he could not get clear of Lord Saluuk’s presence, he knew it would end in violence regardless of all the training in the world. Meoraq bent his neck briefly and received the bows and salutes of all those who shared the hall with him. The high judge beckoned to an usher and Meoraq left, feeling Saluuk Tzugul's eyes burning on his back all the way out into the hall.

* * *

The Halls of Judgment were empty enough to echo beneath Meoraq's feet. The sound worked on him like the hammers of a headache, adding to his black mood instead of easing it. A bad business, Saluuk, and he could have handled it better but it should have waited until the morning. He had always been too eager to see blood spilled after a battle and he knew it.

'I thank You, Father, for Your temperance and restraining hand,' Meoraq thought sourly. 'Without which, I would surely have slaughtered a man with much disgrace and deep satisfaction.'

Sheul did not receive his prayer.

"I do thank You," Meoraq said again, aloud this time, and with the proper gravity. The usher did not look around; a Sheulek speaking to God could hardly be a singular occurrence. "O my Father, I am ashamed that I require Your hand upon my heart to hold me from brawling, even with so low a man as the steward of Saluuk. Gann's touch stains more than the daughter, I think," he added with a scowl. "It would not shock to me to learn he put the scar on her himself."

It would shock him, actually, but it was also disturbingly easy to visualize. Lord Saluuk learning of his daughter's pregnancy and, knowing Gann's taint would soon be visible to all, making certain she carried an honorable scar. He had been a Sheulek once, and doubtless knew how the women of a Sheulek's many conquests melted together over time. Perhaps another Sheulek would have accepted his responsibilities without contest, and who knew? If the girl had not been so memorable in her tears, Meoraq might have been fooled. She was so very skilled an actress (*I have known no other man but you*) that a part of him was tempted (those pleading, tear-filled eyes) to believe her even now.

There were men in the world who actually envied a Sheulek the liberty to take whatever woman Sheul moved him to take, not realizing that so many of those women were sired by men like Arug or Saluuk, that the women themselves were largely forgettable, and that years of exposure to all of Gann's carnality and deceit made a man see it everywhere. In everyone.

Meoraq walked, lost in brooding thoughts of conniving fathers and flat-headed babies, as the usher escorted him to the outer courtyard of the shrine. The priest waiting to admit him offered prayers, which Meoraq, in his black mood, felt strongly compelled to accept. His meditations were lengthy and fruitless, scored through by disruptive visions of Saluuk's Gann-lost girl and her baby, and he did not end them so much as abandon them for another night. He did not notice that they were not taking the right way to the garrison until he followed the usher through a door and found himself in the holy forge at the shrine's heart.

A white-cowled priest stood before the eternal fires, his hood pulled low over his eyes. His robes were richly trimmed, the hem weighted with gold plates and cut to glide just above the floor rather than pick up even a trace of dirt. Each finger was armored to the tip with delicate bands of fine metal. His collar was so heavily crusted with jewels, it was a wonder he could breathe. He did not bother to acknowledge Meoraq, although he had surely heard him enter.

"You wished to speak with me?" said Meoraq after a few calming breaths. He would have liked to demand that he be shown a Sheulek's proper respect and damn well be left alone, but he'd indulged in enough shameful behavior for one night. He would show his divine Father repentance with patience and respect, even if it was a damned inconvenience.

The priest turned, pushing back his hood to get a better look at him. "Sheulek," he said, eyeing his sabks. "You are Uyane Meoraq of Xeqor?"

Obviously. How many other Sheuleks do you have in your damned city tonight?

'Forgive me, O my Father, and give me patience,' Meoraq thought. He said, politely, "I am."

"I am Exarch Ylsathoc Hirut."

Meoraq waited.

The exarch frowned, clearly annoyed that he did not fall back cowering at the name. "Surely you were told that I wished to speak with you as soon as you arrived, as I was told the moment that you passed the gates of this city. But that was more than an hour ago. And here I have been. Waiting."

I am a Sheulek and I go where I fucking well will.

'Forgive me, O my Father, and give me patience.' "It is my duty to attend Sheul's judgments before attending to my own personal audiences," Meoraq said.

"I see. So be it. At least you are here now. I had begun to think you had forgotten this stop upon your circuit, although I can easily see why you would. Sheul the All-Father surely knows that it is only my love for Him that holds me in this pisspot, but then, I was born in Gedai and know better how a city ought to be. You, now..." The exarch cast a disapproving look back at him over his shoulder. "Where have you been?"

Engaged in the duties I am sworn to and the privileges I am owed, one of which may include putting a knife in that eye if you roll it at me again.

'Forgive me, O my Father, and give me patience.' "I was detained at Xheoth."

Ylsathoc grunted, then turned all the way around. He held out a long, pale object which Meoraq actually needed in his hands before he recognized it as a thigh bone.

Its meaning stabbed into him like a knife's blade. And twisted.

"Your father is dead," said the exarch without further preamble. "Sheul has named you steward of House Uyane. Xeqor awaits her champion."

4

The exarch wanted to read him the oaths immediately, but Meoraq refused to hear them. He was given the use of the temple's finest room for his bedchamber that night, but he didn't use it save as a place to store his pack. He went instead to the innermost cloister and there knelt at a firelit shrine with the knife of his fathers heavy over his heart.

The holy smiths of Xi'Tothax executed their craft well; his father's thigh bone had been expertly cut and carved to make the hilt which the reforged blade so perfectly fit. It was not quite the knife he remembered hanging from his father's neck, but he was proud to carry it, as proud as he was reticent to claim it.

His feelings had no bearing on the matter. In accordance with the law, it was his own, and unless it passed to the hand of one of his brothers before the turning of the year, it would be his forever. Or at least until his death, when it would be broken, the hilted half burnt with him upon his pyre and the edge sent onward to his future son. This was House Uyane, ever-changing and eternal as this knife, and he should be honored to take his place in that endless line.

He should be.

And yet...

Meoraq knelt, sleepless, for all the hours of the night as priests and other residents of the temple district came and went. He made all the appropriate prayers, but he didn't feel the bereavement he felt he ought to and the psalms tasted of lies in his mouth. Eventually, he gave them up and fell silent, although he remained bent before the fires, brooding.

He wondered if it marked him for a bad son for thinking more of the House he was doomed to inherit rather than the man he had inherited it from, but he couldn't help that. He'd loved his father, in the same way and at much the same distance as he loved Sheul, but he didn't know him well. Why shouldn't the legal problems of the House weigh on him in his first hours of mourning? He knew the law better than he'd known Uyane Rasozul.

He had left home at the age of three to begin his training, like all sons born under the sign of the Blade, and although he had wintered each year at home in Xeqor, he had seen little of its lord. Since taking his oaths, it seemed Meoraq had even less time at Uyane, although he stopped in whenever his circuit brought him near enough to make such a diversion possible. Rasozul always made time to receive him if he was in, but he was much withdrawn since the death of Meoraq's mother and there weren't many pleasant times to recall now.

Here in Xi'Tothax, many days distant from Xeqor and the House he must assume, Meoraq brooded. He was proud of his father, proud to wear this knife and touch the smooth, solid bone of its hilt, but all his pride seemed to spring from other people's memories. Meoraq didn't know the hero of Kuaq, who had climbed the walls when raiders held that city's gates and cut through a hundred and eleven men alone, one of them the Raider-Lord Szadt, the most evil man ever gone to Gann. He didn't know the Sheulek who had, in the course of his service, emerged the honest victor of more than one thousand battles, better than twice the account most Sheulek could expect. He had never seen the man his training masters remembered, never knew the reasons men invariably paused when they heard Meoraq's name and came back to say, "Uyane of Xeqor? A son of Rasozul?"

No. Meoraq knew no hero, but only the man who sat in his rooftop garden in the evenings, preferring to sit on the tiles with his back propped against his chair as he read. He knew no warrior, but only the father who sometimes tapped at Meoraq's door if he saw a light beneath it, bringing hot tea on cold nights and trading tales of roads they had both traveled, each in his own time. He knew no Rasozul, but the husband who showed altogether too much attention to the woman who wived him and who had mourned her with embarrassing steadfastness for seven years now. And that was still a good man, surely, but no man to inspire a full night's worth of prayer. He prayed anyway...yet his mind wandered, and eventually he cried surrender and let it.

He still thought of his father some—vague impressions at the very fringes of far more trivial memories—but when his mind finally seemed to settle, it did not bring him to House Uyane at all, but to Tilev, where he had stood his training. He could see its halls in his mind as clearly as the cloister of Xi'Tothax would be now if he only opened his eyes, and this unexpected clarity so surprised him that he did open them.

The fires burned low in the holy forge before him. It would need its keeper to fuel it soon. Sheul's forges must never be allowed to grow dark.

Glancing aside, Meoraq counted three priests among the few men come at this early hour to make their prayers. None of them seemed in the least otherworldly. As he watched, one of them stole a hand into the side-pocket of his robe and scratched at his groin. Hardly the act of some divine vision. No, he was awake and his mind, though far from quiet, did not ring with the voice of Sheul as He lent a needful son His guidance.

Well, he was done here, wasn't he? He'd run out of prayers long ago, even after repeating several of them. He hadn't paid an ear to the ringing of the hours, but judging by the people around him, he would put it at three. Nearly dawn. If he left now, he could catch almost a full hour's sleep before the meal was called at four and be on the road again right after.

The road home. To Xeqor. To renounce his oaths as Sheulek and take up the stewardship of his bloodline.

Meoraq shuddered, then hissed annoyance because he had shuddered, and finally bent and pressed his brow to the cold tiles because he had startled several people around him with the hiss. A Sheulek must be his own master at all times, over his flesh and over his emotions. He breathed deeply. He found calm. He closed his eyes.

And was again in the halls of Tilev. Vaguely at first, but soon with the same surprising clarity as before, until he felt almost as though he could reach out his hand and touch the door that stood ajar before him in his imaginings.

It was a door he knew, a memory he had often revisited, and he was comfortable watching it all play out again in the quiet of his meditations. Gradually, the sounds of praying worshippers and groin-scratching priests faded out until this memory became a kind of reality. Between one slow breath and another, Meoraq slipped away from his true self and became the boy he had been at fifteen, his considerably smaller body drawn tense with apprehension as he stood outside Master Tsazr's door.

* * *

He'd been Master Tsazr's brunt that year. A boy of fifteen and a brunt. Not the youngest ever to hold that rank, but two full years younger than most. Then again, Meoraq was the son of a Sheulek, and more, a son of House Uyane, the championing House of all Xeqor. So it did not wholly surprise him to receive a brunt's tabard on his return to school, and it would not surprise him three years later to hear that Nduman had received his, or six years after that, when even Salkith had one (although he recalled that it did surprise Salkith). They were the sons of House Uyane and, for good or ill, there were expectations.

Perhaps because of this, Meoraq had been assigned to serve Tsazr Dyuun, the weapons master, who was notorious for his physical approach to discipline when it came to dealing with high-born students...and their fathers, when necessary. It was true that Meoraq had received many slaps as Tsazr's brunt, but not undeservedly and never for trying to hide behind the shield of his father's reputation. And Tsazr had never sought to provoke him on the subject, or even indicated that he knew Meoraq's father, although Meoraq knew he and Rasozul had shared the same circuit in their years of judgment. He was a hard man, Tsazr, and he had a hard hand, but Meoraq had served him half a year and could say honestly that he was much improved for it and hoped to be brunt to him again the following year (if he was called, he supposed he should say, although there was no real doubt. His were not the highest marks, but there were few boys of his age who knew the Word better and none at all who could best him in the ring).

The brunts enjoyed a fair amount of celebrity among the other students for the very few privileges afforded them along with innumerable additional responsibilities. The position was, of course, in reference to Prophet Lashraq's own brunt, who had set the highest possible standard for devotion and piety while in service to another, but who had not (as was often bitterly remarked at the brunts' table) been asked to make top marks in school at the same time. Meoraq's duties were possibly even more strenuous than the others, with Master Tsazr to judge them, but they had been greatly diminished in the sixty-some days prior to the moment when he stood before this open door. Master Tsazr had been away, and not just away, but away on a pilgrimage. As his brunt, Meoraq had harbored secret hopes that he might journey along with his master, and he yet remembered the acid disappointment with which he had watched Tsazr walk away through the gate, leaving him behind with little to do but run errands for the watchmen and bully his younger brothers around in front of their age-mates. Still, to have a master away on a pilgrimage was a point of pride to any brunt, and this pilgrimage even more than any other because Master Tsazr had gone to Xi'Matezh.

Xi'Matezh. Spoken one way, it meant Forge of the Soul; with raised inflection, it became All-Beginnings; solemnly and with proper pitch, it was The One Heart. All names were truth.

Xi'Matezh had stood since the Fall of the Ancients, and although it had done so well beyond the reach of any city and without a steward of any kind to care for it, it had not fallen into ruins. Nor would it ever, it was said, for Sheul dwelled there as tangibly as any mortal man. It was well known that the doors of Xi'Matezh's inner sanctum stayed fast against the vast majority of those who sought entry there, but the doors did open for some. And while rumor made many claims after that, upon one point all tales agreed: those judged worthy to enter heard the voice of Sheul. Not in prayer, not in dreams, not in the quiet reaches of their conscience, but the true voice of the living God.

So it was to Xi'Matezh that Master Tsazr traveled in the first year of Meoraq's service to him and it was from Xi'Matezh that he had returned. That was the word awaiting him when Meoraq emerged from lessons and so he had raced across the whole of Tilev and up three flights of stairs to find that indeed his master's door stood open.

All of this ran once more through Meoraq's meditations, bringing fresh color to old memory until it was nearly with the same sense of excitement that Meoraq the Sheulek watched the brunt that he had been raise his hand and push his master's open door further open. And it was new all over again—to see the man who had been so long absent sitting on the ledge of his window as though he had never left. Just sitting there, motionless, watching the wind blow clouds across the sky.

Meoraq's first thought was that he didn't look as if he'd been gone sixty days, even sixty days walking across the wildlands. He looked older. Not just tired or travel-worn, but older. By *years.*

Master Tsazr had not seemed to notice him yet. That didn't necessarily mean he hadn't, but Meoraq knew he ought to leave. Being Tsazr's brunt did not give him the right to come so far into his master's private chambers and he knew it. Still he lingered, not quite daring to intrude but hesitant to retreat.

There was mud on Tsazr's boots. Wet, black mud on the soles, fresh from the world just without the walls of Xeqor. Black mud, yes, but under that, caked high on the leg and staining the laces, was older mud, as red as rusted iron and proof of a far larger world...a world that only the Sheulek could wholly claim.

When Meoraq raised his eyes from this enticing sight, he found Tsazr gazing back at him. He managed not to flinch, but it was a clumsy salute he finally gave and an even clumsier excuse for his presence: "I've come to clean your boots, sir."

Tsazr's spines flared. He shifted his legs slightly apart and leaned forward to look down at his feet. He seemed to stare for quite some time. When he looked up again, he was frowning. "I know you. You're one of Razi's sprats. Nduman, is it?"

That cut at him. Yes, it had been sixty days and some, but he had been in service to Tsazr half the year before that. "Meoraq," he said, as neutrally as possible. "Your brunt."

"Ah yes. So I recall. Well, I knew it wasn't Salkith, so I think I can count that half a stroke in my favor." Tsazr rubbed at the side of his snout, studying Meoraq's face intently. "You look very much like your father. Have you ever been told?"

"Yes, sir."

"You'll only hear it more as you get older. Striking man, your father." Tsazr leaned back again into the curve of the window and looked out. "The stuff of bad poetry. Handsome as hell, but a hard-cut face and a stare like the edge of a knife." He glanced idly back at Meoraq and grunted, then returned his gaze to the sky. "Pity there's not a mark of your mother on you, boy. At least Salkith got her eyes."

He didn't know how to answer that, so he said nothing. Whatever first spark of pleasure there had been in receiving so direct a conversation from his normally-taciturn master was now entirely turned to ash. Even the compliment of this comparison to his father (even if it was only to his looks) added to Meoraq's growing unease.

"I saw your mother once," Tsazr was saying now. "Pretty eyes. They don't do much for your brother, but you can't blame Yecedi for that. The finest windows in the world can't improve the view and Salkith's brains are no stronger than his bones. I know what you want to ask me," Tsazr said without pausing or changing his mild, musing tone.

"Sir?"

"And it ought to be something along the cut of, 'Where the hell did you see my mother?' but it isn't." Tsazr glanced back again, but his eyes stayed far away. "So cough it up. You've got me in a rare mood, boy, but I don't mean to make it easy for you to take advantage of me."

Meoraq's breath caught in his throat, so that he very nearly did cough. His feet took him forward, however unwisely, until he was not merely intruding upon his master's private room, he was actually in reach of him and the slap he probably deserved for this outrageous impropriety. Even knowing that, he couldn't stop himself. "Did you reach the temple, sir? Did you stand at Xi'Matezh?"

Tsazr's head tipped past humor to sarcasm, but his eyes stayed sharp. "If I choose to answer only one question tonight, is that really the one you want to ask? If I reached it? If I stood?"

"Did the doors open?" Meoraq asked. Demanded, almost. A part of him remained lucid enough to be appalled at the tone he took, but all the rest of him was lost to fever. A Sheulek must be the master of his impulses, but Meoraq was not Sheulek yet. "Did you enter?"

Tsazr gazed at him a long time without moving, without even blinking. "Yes," he said at last and looked back out the window.

Meoraq's hand twitched, but he kept them both at his sides. "Did you hear Him?" he asked hoarsely. "Did Sheul speak to you?"

Tsazr was quiet, but his eyes moved constantly, shifting from cloud to cloud as the skies rolled endlessly onward. When he finally spoke, it was not in answer. Or at least, not in any answer that made sense.

"There used to be lights in the sky at night."

Meoraq drew back, slapped somewhat from the curiosity that had gripped him, although not so much that he made his proper apologies and left. "Sir?"

Tsazr gestured upwards. "Long before my time, of course, but it is truth. You can read it in books. You can even see pictures if you know where to look. They had a name, but I don't remember what it is. You can't see them anymore, but I suppose they're still there. The only lights we have left...Here, what would you call that?" he asked suddenly, pointing out at the sky.

Meoraq looked, hesitated, and ventured, "The sun, sir."

"Would you indeed?" Tsazr snorted, then laughed boldly. "Lies."

The thought of retreat finally raised itself in Meoraq's baffled mind. One foot even eased backwards, but that was all. Tsazr had never been a talkative man before this night and might never be again. "What is it then?" he asked uncertainly.

"It is the *light*," said Tsazr, with startling force and venom, "of the sun. And you might think they are one and the same, but you'd be wrong, Uyane. It may be proof that the sun stands behind it, but it is *not* the sun and it is neither honest nor right to let others say that it is, and even less so to let them believe it when you know better. Having said that..." Tsazr paused and rubbed at his snout again, rubbed hard enough that Meoraq could actually hear the tendons in his master's hands creaking. It had to hurt, but if anything, Tsazr only rubbed harder. "Having said that," he said again, quietly but with the same force. "I must also tell you that the doors of Xi'Matezh did open and I did go inside and yes, Uyane, Sheul spoke to me. Why not? The light is not the sun, but it is proof undeniable that the sun stands behind it and so I say I heard the voice of Sheul. His words were not a comfort to me. Do you say truth or lie?"

Meoraq's mouth dropped open for possibly the first time in his life, aghast at the notion of daring to pass judgment on his master at all.

Tsazr took his hand away from his face. "I said, what say you?" he hissed. "Don't you stand there and gape at me like your idiot brother or I'll knock the teeth right out of your head! Answer!"

"Truth!" he blurted.

Tsazr snorted again, but it was an angry sound and not a laughing one at all. "And why is that, brunt? Because I am Master Tsazr, once Tsazr Dyuun in the sight of Sheul, or because you suddenly realize you are in the easy striking reach of a madman?"

Meoraq answered without thinking, which was never a clever way to answer a training master, but all his training seemed to have left him. "You are not a madman, sir."

"Ha! You sound pretty damned sure of yourself."

"Yes, sir."

Tsazr continued to glare at him for a time, but it ended with another snort of humor. He looked back at the sun. "I used to be pretty damned sure of myself once, too."

That was all Tsazr seemed inclined to say and it would have been a good time to leave, but Meoraq stayed and eventually Tsazr heaved a sigh and looked at him again.

He wanted to ask. He even opened his mouth a few times, but he couldn't quite dare to speak, not with the man looking at him this way. He wasn't a madman, Meoraq was sure of that (however unreasonably), but he was still a dangerous one and Meoraq had done enough this night to earn six sound beatings. At last, in defeat, Meoraq bent his neck and made a salute.

"Fuck it," Tsazr said, under his breath but quite distinctly. "Do you want to know what I heard in Xi'Matezh, boy?"

Meoraq shut his eyes. "Yes, sir."

"Why? What could it possibly mean to you?"

"I don't know," Meoraq admitted.

"You want to come up with a better answer than that, Uyane. My patience is right at the last grains."

"I have never heard His voice," said Meoraq, again without thinking. A very bad way to answer, but so too would be any hesitation to think up something good. "I know only what I have read in the Word."

"Isn't that enough for you?" Tsazr asked, with surprising acid.

Meoraq resigned himself to the sure knowledge that he was not getting out of this room without a slap and there was no point in prolonging it. "Was it enough for you?"

Tsazr snapped himself to his feet so fast that Meoraq flinched, even though it had been better than three years since the last time he'd shied away from a punishing hand. But although Tsazr loomed over him with the yellow coming out strong on his throat—and he'd never seen that, not on Master Tsazr—the slap never came. Ultimately, Tsazr's scales faded back to black and several minutes after, he uttered a low, sour grunt.

"You had the juice to ask," Tsazr said, reseating himself in the window. "I suppose I should have the juice to answer. It was enough...until about eighteen years ago. My last circuit as Sheulek, in fact. Something happened that made me think I could actually open the doors at Xi'Matezh if I ever went. It's been itching at me ever since, the idea that there could be something more than the Word...something just for me. And there was. And it was terrible to hear. Do you still want to know what He said, boy?"

Meoraq opened his mouth and made himself close it. He thought long enough that Tsazr turned away from the clouds and the light of the sun that shone through them to look at him.

"Yes," said Meoraq slowly.

"Why?"

"Because...Because they were His words."

Tsazr's expression shifted somehow, but in a way difficult to define. "So?"

"In school, they taught us—"

"If you give me a schoolroom answer, I'll crack your bones for you, sprat," Tsazr said. "I don't care who your father is and in this moment, I don't even care what it will do to your mother. I will snap something fresh for every word you are about to utter and make you count them off when I do."

Meoraq hesitated, then plunged on ahead with a kind of despairing courage. "In school, they taught us that truth is only truth when everything is heard. Every word of the Word changes all the rest of them. So whatever He told you...it changes the truth in the Word." He paused, but Tsazr only watched him, frowning. "And I want to know how," he finished lamely.

Tsazr just looked at him as Meoraq's heart hammered against his as-yet-unbroken ribs.

"Not so much a schoolroom answer," Tsazr murmured at last. "You did all right by this one, Razi. At least you gave him all the brains you scooped out of Salkith."

Meoraq waited, not entirely confident that he had escaped.

"Truth," said Tsazr after another minute or two.

"Sir?"

"You want to know the truth."

"Yes, sir."

"Of course you do. That's your blood-right talking to you, boy. Your history. Your destiny. Because that is what we do, Uyane."

"We, sir?"

"You'll be Sheulek at the end of all this," Tsazr said with a cross, dismissive wave. "We all know it, so shut your mouth and mark me, because this is important. The other boys here, they think being Sheulek is about glorious battles and walking freely through any gate they please. To them, the call to carry the honor-blades is nothing but a writ of privilege over any man they meet. Or any woman." Tsazr snorted and looked out the window. "Is that about what you think, Uyane?"

Meoraq stifled a premonitory cringe and said, "All these things are the right of a Sheulek, sir."

"Not your best answer tonight," Tsazr said wryly. "I'll let you try again out of respect for your father before I knock you down. Is that what you think being a Sheulek is? What it means?"

"What something is and what it means aren't always the same."

Tsazr looked at him sharply, his spines flat. "Example?" he inquired in a low, dangerous voice.

"Being a brunt," said Meoraq.

His master stared, his expression growing slowly more thoughtful as his spines came forward. "Truth," he said after a very long time. "You really are doing very well tonight. So let me tell you about women, brunt. I have had more of them than I can count. I mean just what I say. More than I can count. But I remember only three...and one of them is your mother and I never laid a hand on her. What does that tell you?"

It told him that sex probably wasn't very memorable and if that was the truth, Meoraq wasn't sure he wanted to hear it. He wasn't a child; the last of his scales had turned black before he'd received his brunt's tabard and the incident that had led to the metal loin-plate he was now wearing (and would wear for the rest of his life) had been dimming in the back of his mind for two years now. No, there were no women in Tilev and none at home, excepting servants glimpsed as they went swiftly and silently about their business, but there *would* be women someday and after two years wrestling with Gann's temptations, he'd hoped the wait would be worth it. Now his master was staring him down, so Meoraq groped for an honest answer and finally managed, "I know nothing about women, sir."

Tsazr heaved a short, impatient sigh and cut his hand through the air. "Fine. We'll have to talk again someday, but for right now, we'll stick to truth. That is the true work of a Sheulek. Never mind what they tell you in school about law and government or even about the Word itself. When we step into that arena, it is not for glory, not for women, not even for God, but for only truth. We accept that we may die and we embrace that death if it means the truth is exposed. Do you hear me, Uyane?"

"Yes, sir."

Tsazr grunted and eyed him for a moment before looking back out the window. "And do you understand me?"

Meoraq braced himself once more for that slap. "No, sir."

But Tsazr pointed two fingers at him and said, "Truth. I don't know if you mean it, but that doesn't matter. You spoke and I judge your *words* to be true ones, regardless of your motives. That's my whole point, boy. *Why* does not matter to us.

Only truth." He fell quiet for a time, then said, "And truth does not care if it comforts you."

Out in the greater hall, the bells rang for the mid-day meal. Tsazr stirred himself, glanced at Meoraq and then swept a hand over his snout.

"So here it is," he said. "The truth that changes everything. Prepare yourself."

Meoraq bent his neck and took several deep breaths, forcing his muscles to unlock and his heart to beat slow. Nothing he was about to hear could be a good thing, but he meant to meet it fairly. At last he looked up, calm. "I mark you, Master."

"The truth," said Tsazr, "is that if you want to know what I heard in Xi'Matezh, go there."

Meoraq's breath fell out of him in a disorienting rush that was part relief and part disappointment, and for the life of him, he couldn't have said which was the larger part. "Sir?"

"I can read the Word *to* you, Uyane. I can't read it *for* you. Go on." He rubbed at his snout some more. "Get out of my room. I'll put my boots in the hall for you when I'm damned good and ready."

Meoraq turned around at once, but paused after only a few steps. He told himself he was not defying a direct order as he had every intention of obeying it...right after he asked one thing. "Sir?"

"I ordered you out, brunt."

"Yes, sir." But his feet wouldn't move.

"I give you a choice, Uyane, because I'm in that sort of mood, although not for much longer. Here it is. You can walk out of here right now without getting hurt, or you can stay and say what you want to say. I'll let you and I may even answer, but I absolutely will beat you down for it."

"What happened that made you think the doors at Xi'Matezh would open?"

Silence. It grew at his back until he was forced to turn around and face the slap.

This time, Tsazr gave it to him. Hard. But as Meoraq unsteadily straightened himself, Tsazr said, with singular bitterness, "Nuu Sukaga."

And after everything he'd heard, that was still bizarre enough to make Meoraq forget the immediate pain throbbing through his snout. "Sir?"

"Nuu Sukaga. I waited eighteen years to say it and you are exactly right, Uyane. Those two words changed all the others. Now get out," Tsazr said, sitting back down in the window. "Or you'll be cleaning my boots from the infirmary."

Meoraq went and since nothing more happened that day (it remained the longest and strangest conversation he was ever to have with Master Tsazr, who never mentioned it, or the name, if it was a name, of Nuu Sukaga, again), he let the memory go and brought himself gradually back to the present to think about what it meant.

Because each word did change the truth in all the others, and this memory did present an entirely new alternative to his present situation. Surely that was why Sheul had brought it to his attention so vividly.

"Honored one?"

Meoraq stirred and opened his eyes. He gazed into the light of the holy forge (which had been renewed at some point during his meditations, he saw), before turning an expectant eye upon the nervous usher who bowed beside him. "What is it?" he asked.

"The abbot sends his apologies for this intrusion on your prayers, honored one, but requests that you send your demands to the provisioner as soon as possible."

"A reasonable request," said Meoraq after a moment. "Have you the means to make a list?"

"Yes, sir." The usher produced a wax tablet and stylus from the inner fold of his robe.

“Very good. Write small,” he advised. “And see to it my demands are sent specifically to Exarch Ylsathoc, for I know it was he and not the abbot who sent you to me, although I believe it is only the abbot who apologizes for it.”

The boy’s first mark in the soft wax was a meaningless gash of guilt. “Sir?”

“Foremost, I require a tea box,” Meoraq began in a musing way. “A nice one...”

5

Meoraq woke at the sound of voices while they were still in the hall. He raised his head without opening his eyes, listened until he had identified one in particular, and settled back into his bedding.

His door crashed open. "I don't care if I wake him up!" Exarch Ylsathoc Hirut shrieked to someone in the hall. "I *want* to wake him up! I want him to explain himself and this...this insult!"

Meoraq smiled sleepily into his cushion.

Expensive-sounding slippers slapped rapidly across the room. A soft fist struck the mantle above his cupboard in the fearless manner of a man who has never challenged a Sheulek. "Insult, I call it! Do you hear me, you...you..."

"Honored Sword of Sheul?" Meoraq suggested, still smiling.

"You get out here this instant!" the exarch screamed. "I demand to know the meaning of this...this...extortion! A new samr and kzung! I can see your old ones right there! There is nothing wrong with them! What is this? Boots! Buckles! A new tent! A quilted mat! Blankets, cushions, a new pack...and a full mending kit! What could you possibly need to mend when everything is new?"

"I like to be prepared for every eventuality."

"Is that a *joke*? Are you *joking* at me? No, no, *this* must be the joke! An inlaid *tea box*?!"

"I trust you also received my list of favorite teas."

"This is an outrageous abuse of power and I will not honor it! I refuse! You will have a brick of cuuvash and a change of clothes and nothing more from me! I am a son of Ylsathoc!"

Meoraq slapped his palm flat against the cupboard door and shoved it open. He leaned out, no longer smiling, and yanked the exarch down by the neck of his fine white robes until their eyes were on level. "And I am a son of Sheul," he said quietly.

The exarch glared, breathing hard and fast, the color strong at his scrawny throat, but he said nothing.

"Honored one..." Unnoticed in the doorway, the abbot of Xi'Tothax now came into the room and bowed again, both arms open. "Please, the temple is proud to make provision for you."

"But I do not ask the temple." Meoraq released Ylsathoc with a shove and swung himself out of the cupboard to stand in the exarch's place, naked and damned glad he was naked, just to see Ylsathoc flinch. "I ask the man who gave my name at the gate—what did I hear, six times?—and who ordered the sentries of my conquered city to carry me in to him as if I were his errant cattle! Do not speak to me of insult, priest. You will meet my demands and you will thank Sheul at every one that I ask only your material goods and not your fucking hand!"

He made himself stop there and take a slow count of six breaths before he really lost his temper. He'd had too little sleep...which was a poor excuse and he knew it. A Sheulek was supposed to be the master of his emotions at all times, even when dealing with insolent, self-important bureaucrats. If he had to wake up to someone this early, why couldn't it be a woman?

'And now I want a woman,' he thought, striding to the table to reclaim his clothing. He didn't mind being naked in front of another man as long as he looked intimidating while he did it. He minded very much being extruded and undignified.

"If the temple wishes to show its obedience, it can bring me hot nai and a meal," Meoraq said, strapping on his loin-plate and cinching it biting-tight. "The exarch here shall see to my rations for travel, but he had best be quick about it. I mean to be on my way by fifth-hour."

The abbot gave his assurances and bowed his way out. Ylsathoc watched him go and then watched Meoraq dress. His spines were stiff enough to quiver slightly with his pulse. The scales at his throat were still striped with yellow as bold and bright as paint.

"Have you something more to say?" Meoraq asked.

"Forgive me," said the exarch, sounding anything but apologetic. "But how does the honored one expect me to meet his demands before fifth-hour? I did not come to Tothax with a tea box."

"Inlaid," Meoraq reminded him. "And I expect you to purchase whatever you do not have, the same as any other man must do when a Sword of Sheul takes his conqueror's privilege. If I learn that you have turned my list into your own and demanded it as gifts from this city, I will see you judged for theft."

The exarch was quiet for a time, although Meoraq could see the yellow patches at his throat moving with unformed words. At last, in a voice as edged as any blade Meoraq carried, Ylsathoc said, "I will have to purchase several things on credit to meet your demands."

"So?"

More silence. More hard, hoarse breathing. More yellow.

Meoraq put his boots on and pretended not to notice or care. He waited, grimly enjoying himself and reminding himself to meditate on the cause of that enjoyment because it really was a terrible sign of his true character.

"My father will have to pay those notes."

Meoraq finished buckling the last strap on his boot, then straightened up and looked the exarch directly in the eye. "You have your orders. Leave me."

Ylsathoc managed half a stiff bow and then burst out, "This is spitefulness and nothing else! What did I do but my given duty in informing you of your House's need?"

"You did not inform me," said Meoraq. "You summoned me. And then you stood me in your borrowed chamber and dared to interrogate me, much as you are daring to protest to me now."

"I am an exarch over all the eastern lands! My father's House stands as champion over Chalh, the city that champions all Gedai! I had every right to—"

"I do not care if you are the high chancellor over all the city-states of Gann," said Meoraq, folding his arms. "All men bend before the honor-blade."

Ylsathoc looked at those blades now and at Meoraq's hands so close to them. He lowered his voice before he used it again, although he still spoke with an indignant hiss. "You cannot need half these ridiculous things for your journey!"

"You sound very sure." Meoraq leaned forward, holding the other man's stare. "Where is it you think I am going?"

"Why, to—" Exarch Ylsathoc frowned. The yellow stripes at his throat finally began to fade, just a little. "To Xeqor," he said after a long, puzzled pause to search Meoraq's eyes. "Your House requires a steward."

"And if that is Sheul's will, it will be me," Meoraq agreed. "But first I will know that it is Sheul's will."

"I don't understand."

"It is not necessary that you do. Your role in this is ended, or will be as soon as you have met my demands."

"But..." Ylsathoc retreated a step, then appeared to suddenly notice the tablet still in his hand. He looked at it as if reading it for the first time. "But all these things...Where are you going?"

Meoraq smiled faintly. "Xi'Matezh."

The exarch rocked back and stared at him with such astonishment that Meoraq could not resist twisting the knife. He leaned in even closer, close enough to be threat as much as insult, and smiled. "Seen in that light, I haven't asked for too damned much at all, have I?"

"That will take...days!" Ylsathoc sputtered, backing away again. "A brace of days! Two braces at the least!"

"Three is far more likely."

"Winter is all but at the gate! The cold season—"

"I know about cold."

"You will never make it there and back across the mountains before the snows!"

"I do not expect to."

"You cannot mean to leave your House empty so long!" Ylsathoc grappled visibly with the humility he had been warned to demonstrate, but outrage soon defeated him. "It is the founding House of Uyane's bloodline, the line of that great oracle's descent! Its steward champions all Xeqor, who champions all Yroq, who sits at the very heart of all that is left of this land! Where is your sense of duty?"

"I have a duty to more than one father," Meoraq replied. "He who sired my clay would surely understand that I serve He who hammered my soul first. Sheul has called me to a pilgrimage. Have my things waiting at Eastgate by fifth-hour and if you dare to protest just once more, I swear to you here in the sight of Sheul that your father will receive a note for the cost of your funeral along with the rest of your expenses."

Ylsathoc looked down at the list and up again. He opened his mouth.

Meoraq waited, ready to draw. He was well aware of his own propensity to be impatient, particularly with those of the lesser castes, and he would even admit to the spitefulness Ylsathoc had alleged (although never to the other man's face), but in spite of his divine right and his frequent threats, he had never killed anyone just for rudeness. Scarred a few, though. And he'd by-Gann be scarring this one if he said one more word.

But Ylsathoc only sighed and shut his mouth again. He bent his neck in a sullen sort of bow and swept out past the returning abbot, reading his list and muttering about impropriety to himself in much-offended and very soft tones.

The abbot waited in the doorway while the boy he'd brought labored his food-laden tray over to Meoraq at the table and poured the nai. Then he said, without reproach, "It is a mark of great favor to be born under the sign of the Blade, honored one."

Meoraq grunted and broke open his bread. It had been stuffed with gruu, fried in fat to a crunchy paste and should have been very good, but Meoraq could not eat without thinking of the previous night's trial and how a few rows of gruu, more or less, had killed a Sheulteb. All things served God and Meoraq knew he'd done His work well, but still it made the bread bitter this morning.

"Fewer yet are called to be Sheulek," the abbot continued.

"No one feels that privilege more deeply than I, priest."

"But do you feel the privilege, honored one, that He continues to show you? Not one Sheulek in sixty will ever stand as steward of his bloodline or Lord of his House. You are the Sword He raises highest."

"No," said Meoraq, tossing his inedible bread down on the tray. "I am the Sword He has sheathed! And if that is His will, I accept it, but before I submit to that end, I will hear it in His own voice."

The abbot's boy gaped at him. The abbot himself merely bowed.

Meoraq looked at his untouched food, then drank off his nai and banged the cup down empty. "I am done with this," he said brusquely. "I am taking the rooftop. See that I am not disturbed."

"Yes, honored one."

"I want to wash first," said Meoraq, which was not the truth. He did not want the bath; he wanted the woman whose task it would be to bathe him and he didn't care who knew it.

The abbot bowed again, silent in his assent. He gestured to his boy, who took up the tray. They left, shutting the door softly behind them.

Meoraq sat alone, staring at the ceiling and counting his breaths.

"Fuck," he said, and went to the roof without his bath. He still wanted the woman, but he suspected he needed to pray.

* * *

Somewhere between the third hour and the fourth, the rooftop door scraped open.

Stretched out on a bench to watch the clouds roll by, Meoraq raised the samr he had been idly tapping against his boot and called, "I do not wish to be disturbed."

"I know."

Meoraq sat up and sheathed his sword. "Nkosa," he said, surprised.

"I shouldn't be here," his blood-kin admitted, still lingering by the stair. "And if you don't want to see me—"

Meoraq gestured at the bench beside him, his spines forward in invitation. "How did you get up here?"

"I relieved the guard below," said Nkosa, settling himself uncomfortably on the very edge of the bench. "And as soon as his real relief shows up, he or I or all three of us are probably going to be whipped. I just...I heard about Rasozul."

Meoraq grunted and looked inanely at the rooftop wall, which had nothing at all to show him. "I envy him," he said. "He sees our true Father's face tonight."

"Well...I'm sorry anyway. I know you were looking forward to seeing him at home."

Meoraq glanced at him and frowned at the wall some more. "I will see him in the Halls of Sheul."

"Until then," said Nkosa quietly, "I'm sorry."

The wind blew.

Meoraq's stiff spines lowered some. "Thank you," he said. He wasn't sure that was the thing to say, but he didn't know what was. He'd killed many men in his time of service, but he had never had to suffer a loss of his own.

Nkosa tapped at Meoraq's knee with the backs of his knuckles, awkwardly proving his sympathies, then took his hand back. "Everyone's talking this morning. They said that exarch was here to appoint you steward?"

"Yes."

"And you didn't let him?"

"I had to pray."

"About what?"

Meoraq flicked his spines and stared at the wall.

"Now they're saying you're leaving for Xi'Matezh?"

"Yes."

"Xi'*Matezh*?"

"Yes."

Nkosa waited, his head tipped to encourage further explanations that never came. At last, he blew out a rude breath and said, "Forgive me for pointing out the obvious, O mighty Sword of God, but if you want to kill yourself, you can just jump off the wall."

Meoraq tried and failed to catch the laugh that coughed out of him. He eyed his cousin, rubbed his snout, and sighed.

"Marriage isn't all bad," said Nkosa.

"That would depend on who you get," Meoraq muttered.

"At least you'll have a choice."

"For all it matters." Meoraq sat up straighter and looked at his blood-kin. "I don't want a choice, 'Kosa. In fact, you could say that I am going to Xi'Matezh so that the choice is made for me."

"I could." Nkosa flicked his spines in polite incomprehension. "And why in Gann's grey hell would I say that?"

"Sheul lit that fire in the sky for me," Meoraq said, stating it as plainly as such a statement could be made. "I thought it was to bring me here, but even when I first saw it, I knew it didn't lie directly in the line of Tothax. It was further east."

Nkosa frowned, uneasy. "In the line of Xi'Matezh, you mean."

"Yes."

"But you can't possibly know that. You can't sit on the roof in Xheoth and know where Xi'Matezh is."

"I know," Meoraq insisted.

"Fine, then point to it."

Meoraq looked out at the wildlands, his spines low, scowling. "I can find it."

Nkosa snorted. "So could I. East to the mountains and over into Gedai, then east to the Ruined Reach and up along the end of the world until you trip over the shrine. That's the thing about legends, everyone knows how they go. But don't sit there and tell me the burning tower was pointing the way to Xi'Matezh because you can't know that."

"It was."

Nkosa slapped a hand over the end of his snout and rubbed it, hard. "I really hate talking to you when you're like this."

"Like what?"

"A fucking Sheulek." He dropped his hand. "You've been a good friend to me and I'm proud to hear you call me cousin like it was truth, but 'Raq, are you sure you aren't looking for reasons to do something you already want to do?"

"Why would I *want* to walk across the whole damned wildlands this close to winter?" Meoraq asked reasonably. "Why would anyone?"

Nkosa shrugged his spines, still looking troubled.

"For twelve years, Sheul has spoken through me," said Meoraq. "Now He is finally calling me to Him. I have to go. My father's...My House will wait."

"What are you going to do when you get there and He tells you to go home and get married?"

"If that is what He has called me to Xi'Matezh to hear," said Meoraq with confidence, "then I am sure He has a particular woman in mind."

Nkosa looked at him for a long time before saying, quite matter-of-factly, "That sounds like you expect God to provide you the woman."

Meoraq thought about it, then shrugged his spines.

"That is the closest thing to true blasphemy I think I've ever heard anyone say."

"'Kosa, he summoned me out of Xheoth with a pillar of fire. Does that sound like He wants me to go home and take the first woman I see?"

"How many women do you expect to see in Xi'Matezh, you idiot?"

"One," said Meoraq. "The one He means me to marry, *if* He means me to marry."

Nkosa rubbed at his brow ridges, plainly choosing his next words with great care.

He settled on: “I hope this isn’t what you told the exarch.”

“I don’t have to tell him anything,” said Meoraq, dropping back against the bench with a dismissive wave. “I have a whole year before Uyane has to present a steward. I could crawl to the Reaches and back in that time.”

They sat, Meoraq watching the clouds and Nkosa watching him.

“You’re going to make me say it,” Nkosa said finally.

“Say what?”

“Sheul is not going to give you a woman.”

“So,” said Meoraq, untroubled. “That will be a sign of something too, won’t it?”

“Did you sleep through the lesson the day they were supposed to teach you about sophistry?” Nkosa demanded, still trying to laugh as if this would all turn into a joke if he just believed in it hard enough. “What makes you think you’re even going to get through the doors?”

“Nuu Sukaga.”

Nkosa leaned back, his spines flaring all the way forward. “What’s that mean?”

“I have no idea,” said Meoraq and smiled.

Nkosa stared at him some more, then grunted and heaved himself up on his feet. “All right, please yourself. Give me a tap, crazy person,” he ordered, palm out.

Meoraq smiled. Ignoring Nkosa’s outstretched arm, he rose and put his hand against his blood-kin’s heart like a brother, then pulled him close in a rough embrace. It didn’t last long and wasn’t entirely comfortable, but he was glad he did it, if only the once.

“Come back before the year is up, if you can,” said Nkosa, slow to back away. “I know you won’t be able to after you take your House and I’m going to want to see the man who walked all the way to the ends of the world just to get dipped.”

“I’ll be back in the spring,” promised Meoraq. “I’ll even stay with you and do you the honor of sharing your wife.”

“Ha. Only if you share yours.”

“Done. Now get out of here,” he said gently. “I can’t stop them from whipping you every day, you know.”

“Well, in that case don’t bother coming back at all.” Nkosa raised his hand, hesitated, and then curled it into a fist and touched his heart in a real salute. He turned his back at once and went quickly to the door, checking the stair with a look of resignation, then slipped through and was gone.

Meoraq stretched back out on the bench and clasped his hands behind his head. The clouds above him blew eternally onward. To the east, he noted. Toward Xi’Matezh.

His destiny.

BOOK III

LOST AND FOUND

In retrospect, the trouble with Scott started immediately, but it took a few days before Amber caught on to just how bad it was. She knew she was as guilty as everyone else of letting him take over. She also knew that she didn't want to be the one in charge when the whole human race was just forty-eight people on an alien world with a handful of supplies camping in spitting distance of the melted remains of a ship that could very well be radiating cancer into every living thing for miles around. Oh no. Fuck that. Scott could be in charge of that mess all he wanted.

And if there was one thing Scott was good at, it was putting himself in charge. Before the sun came up over the remains of the *Pioneer*, he'd made two trips to the top of the ridge and compiled a complete inventory of what they had left, which wasn't much but was still more than they should have had.

Tents, for example. All the tents that had been up on the ridge had been incinerated in the *Pioneer's* explosion. Not just burned. Erased. There was nothing left up there to prove there'd ever been a camp at all except a melted heap of glass and metal that had probably been one of the solar generators. But as bad as that was, it could have worse.

Not knowing how to set up an outpost, Scott had apparently just dumped the supplies in piles wherever he thought he might like to put a building someday. Most of those piles had been up on the ridge, but he did have a number of tents down by the lakeshore, marking the proposed site of the colony's pump house and filtration station, to hold the necessary equipment and materials until he'd decided exactly when and where to begin construction.

"Tents?" Maria interrupted immediately upon hearing this. In her firm, furious tone, Amber heard again her threat to sue the Manifestors and their Director right down to the ground. "You said there weren't enough tents! I was in a sleeping bag and you had more tents the whole time?"

"They're for keeping the equipment dry," Scott answered. "They aren't for personal use."

"Well they are now, bucko. It's pouring! Where are they?"

"I haven't decided how to assign them," said Scott, and whenever Amber thought about it, she always came back to that as the only moment when someone might have been able to put a stop to things. But you can't take out the guy in charge without replacing him. And she did not want that job.

So when people started arguing and those angry voices started climbing and Scott was holding up his hands in an ineffectual bid for silence, Amber said, "That was smart, Scott."

He swung around to glare at her, holding up one hand against the storm—the miraculous storm which had probably saved their lives but which showed no sign of blowing off any time soon.

"I'm not being sarcastic," she told him. "That was smart. If you hadn't set that stuff aside, we wouldn't have anything right now. How many did you save?"

And that was the word that did it. Save. Like he'd planned it. Like he'd pulled them out of the fire with his bare hands and carried them to his desperate people.

Scott squared his shoulders and gave his crewman's jacket a brisk tug. "Six. Two command units and four bivies."

"What the heck is a bivy?" Maria wanted to know.

"How big are they?" Amber asked.

"Not very," someone else answered. Eric Lassiter, one of the soldiers Jonah had sent her. "What he's calling a command unit is just your typical one-room dome tent. Allegedly, it could hold eight people."

"If they were greased up," Crandall added dubiously. "And drunk."

"And a bivy is pretty much a sleeping tube."

"More like a body-condom," inserted Crandall.

"Two people could share one if they were really, *really* cozy, but even if you packed them all full, most of us are going to be out in the weather."

"Well, that's bullshit!" said Maria, doubtless ready to add a few new names to her list of impending lawsuits for her brother to receive back on Earth.

"No," said Amber, as quietly as the driving wind and rain allowed. "That's just the way it is. Getting mad won't help."

There were mutters, but that was all, and even Maria didn't protest when Scot kept one of the command units for himself, because he was in command. He gave the bivies to the Fleetmen—Eric, Dag, Crandall and Mr. Yao. The last tent, he gave to the women at the end of a chivalrous and deeply concerned speech in which he referred to those women, not just once or twice but at least a dozen times, as resources. And Amber let him. So it was her fault too.

She didn't even get a space in the tent. Despite Eric's assertion that eight people could fit, only six of them actually did and there were eleven women. Amber didn't try to bully her way in, because she knew she was fat and didn't need to hear it again.

As for the rest of the equipment Scott had set aside, they had another solar generator, but nothing that really needed running except the water purifier, which was useless because they didn't have any intake hoses. They also had six crates of irrigation pipes so they could run purified water all through the camp, but none of the joints or valves. They had everything they needed for the pump, except, of course, the motor and belts. They had a power mixer without a battery and enough bags of concrete to pour the floor for the pump house, currently being stored in all those one-man tents so the rain couldn't turn them into sixty-pound bricks. The rest of their provisions were comprised of 1500 other-flavored ration bars packed together with emergency blankets, flashlights and fire-strikers in about thirty duffel bags in assorted neon colors with the Manifest Destiny logo on the side. And one medikit.

The medikit belonged to Mr. Yao and during the next morning's debriefing, which Amber was not invited to but attended anyway, he opened it up and read out its contents: Six rolls of sterile gauze, one box of medium grade self-sticking bandages, a tube of burn relief gel, a tube of antibacterial ointment, a bottle of low-dose aspirin, a bottle of extra-strength aspirin, and a dermispray pen with twelve doses of nalfentypine.

"What's that?" Scott wanted to know.

"A synthetic opiate used for pain management."

"That's part of the kit?" Eric asked, not quite smiling.

"Of course not," said Mr. Yao. "It came with the surgical supplies you brought, but they were lost on the ridge. This was with my personal effects."

"And how did that happen?"

Mr. Yao looked at him without emotion. "In my medical opinion, I required sedation."

Eric held up his hands in surrender.

"I require sedation," Crandall said hopefully.

Mr. Yao ignored him and looked instead at Scott. "I want you to know that I have this, and I want you all to know where to find it and how to use it, because this is now the only source of anything like anesthetic we possess. But I think it would be best not to let everyone know of its existence, because it would also make an extremely effective form of suicide."

"So does that lake," said Amber, the first remark she'd made at that meeting.

"Miss Bierce, if you're going to eavesdrop, at least do it quietly. We're trying to have a debriefing."

Mr. Yao ignored Scott and turned to her. "Drowning oneself, like hanging oneself with one's shirtsleeve or cutting one's wrists with broken glass or any number of options presently available to us, requires a great deal more courage and determination than putting a dermisprayer against one's arm and pressing a button. I would rather save it for our first broken leg than make it available to those seeking a quick, painless way out of our present circumstance."

"Good point." And because he was glaring at her, Amber looked at Scott and said, "I guess it should stay here, huh?"

They were all in Scott's tent at the time, the command unit, the only place they could all squeeze together out of the drumming rain and wind. Scott blinked around all the same, as if he expected a bank vault to open up behind him. "Why here?" he asked.

"Shouldn't the really important stuff be with the guy in charge?"

Mr. Yao waited, holding the medikit on his lap.

"Well, I...guess I have more room," said Scott cautiously.

Mr. Yao passed it over.

"So...So I guess I'm in charge of the food and stuff too?"

That was a lot more unsettling than letting the man babysit the first aid supplies.

"Someone ought to be," Amber said, hoping her hesitation hadn't been too obvious. "And the rations do need to be kept dry."

"And away from hoarders," said Eric. "Because there will be hoarders."

Amber started to nod her agreement, then noticed they were all looking at her. "You know, every now and then, I manage to go two, sometimes three whole minutes without eating," she snapped, and they all looked away again. "I know the food is finite. I also think we need to start thinking now about what we're going to eat when it's gone."

Scott frowned at her, but the severity of this effort only made him look younger and more uncertain. "You mean..." He eyed the other men in the tent and lowered his voice a little. "...people?"

Amber rocked back. "What?"

"We don't have to talk about this until someone actually dies," said Eric.

"Oh my God," Amber said, staring at both of them. "No, I meant looking for fish or rabbits or whatever freak moose thing was shouting up the place last night! People? You thought I wanted to eat *people*?!"

"We'll get to the native flora and fauna as soon as we're able to arrange teams for reconnaissance and study," Scott told her, blushing. "And we were already looking into that, so please be quiet, Miss Bierce. I know you think you're contributing, but you're a civilian here and you're distracting us from the real problems under discussion."

She could have pressed the matter. None of the Fleetmen seemed eager to jump in, and other than making sure the public was kept under control, Scott himself seemed to have run out of steam. So she could have easily forced them all to face the food issue head-on. Instead, she sat back and let the whole thing drop.

Scott opened the medikit and studied the contents, then closed it again and looked around at them. "Then I guess the only other thing we need to talk about is the *Pioneer's* salvage prospects. Do I have a volunteer to head that team?"

"Salvage?" Amber checked the others, but they seemed as stunned as she. "Are you serious?"

"The escape bays were designed to survive catastrophic failure of the ship. The beacons may still be recoverable."

Amber stared at him, utterly unable to make those words make any kind of sense, given the situation. "Mr. Scott," she said at last, making a real effort to speak softly, reasonably. "How far are we from the ship?"

"What does that have to do with anything?"

"Mr. Lassiter, then? Mr. Crandall? What are we, about five miles?"

"Three, maybe," said Eric, and Crandall shrugged and nodded.

"Okay. Three miles." Amber pointed through the tent wall in the direction of the ridge, which was at that time just lighting up with the grey promise of another day through one hell of a roaring rainstorm. "We were three miles away from the explosion last night, Mr. Scott, and you said our solar generator melted."

His jaw tightened. "The escape bays are heat-proof up to, I don't know, thousands of degrees. The beacons are our only hope of rescue, Miss Bierce, and they could be all right."

"Okay," she said, although she personally thought this was horseshit. "Say the escape bays are intact. It could happen. But they're going to be intact at the center of the melted pile of slag that used to be the rest of the ship. How are we going to get to them?"

The other men looked at Scott. He flushed and glared back at her.

"Jonah...Lieutenant Lamarc said that even if the beacons could be launched, they'd need the guidance system on the *Pioneer* to find Earth," said Amber. "And we don't have that anymore. Mr. Scott, I'm sorry, but I think we can cross rescue completely off the list."

"I'm not prepared to do that, Miss Bierce," Scott said stiffly.

"And then there's the little matter of all this rain."

"That you want to go hiking in," Scott interrupted.

"Yes, I do. Before it floods the lake we're camping next to." Amber hesitated, unsure whether she really wanted to bring out the big guns yet, but in the end, she just couldn't not say it. "And before all the toxic seepage from the *Pioneer* washes into the water we're drinking. And before you ask, no, I don't know for a fact there's anything seeping out of it, but it seems like a pretty goddamn good bet this morning, doesn't it?"

"I don't need to hear the swearing," said Scott.

"It could be happening, though." Eric unfolded himself and stood up as straight as the tent allowed. "Okay, Bierce. If there's a vote involved here, you just got mine. But we can't just pack up and go, we've got to have a plan." He paused, then glanced at Scott and said, "Right?" in the same careful way that Amber told him he could keep the food.

Scott scowled. "Sure, as far as that goes, which is why we need to prioritize our efforts. Organize teams. Investigate our options."

Amber pressed a hand over her eyes and tried very hard not to either sigh out loud or shake her head. "We don't have time for that."

"I'd rather take a little extra time than charge stupidly out into the wilderness without any kind of plan."

"And thanks to you," Eric inserted gently, "we have at least the beginnings of that plan."

Scott's frown went crooked, distracted. "What? We do?"

"When we scouted this place out yesterday, we found several watersheds that emptied into the lake here," Eric explained, gesturing vaguely over his shoulder at the tent wall. "I suggest we follow the biggest of them upstream and get to high ground."

"I am not willing to abandon the ship," said Scott, also standing up.

"It's not going anywhere," Eric argued. "But for the moment, it's probably still burning on the inside and still very much a threat to us. I think we'd all feel better if we got some distance and got out of the imminent flood zone, but I agree that it's important that we don't go so far that we lose our water source, because I was looking yesterday, and the water we're camping next to was the only water I could see."

He turned to Amber, directing his next words only to her. "I know it must make you nervous to be here. I know you must be thinking of pretty much everything that might happen. I know. But if we get too far away from the water, we're going to die. Not might. Will. We have a purifier—"

"But we don't have water," said Amber, thinking of Jonah, who had said the same thing. She nodded, sighed, and then shook her head, her shoulders slumping. "So just sit around and talk, is that all we're going to do?"

"And this is why I didn't want you in here," Scott remarked.

"Just be patient," said Eric. "Let us figure a few things out. I know you want to do something, but the day after we've all seen our ship blow up is the wrong time to expect everyone out there to pull it together and start marching in line."

"I get it. I don't like it, but I get it."

"You don't have to like it," said Scott. "And I'll tell you right now that I'd better not hear you running off your mouth out there about toxic seepage and floods, trying to scare people into doing what you want them to do."

"Running my mouth?" Amber shook her head and then just had to laugh before she got pissed. "You're in charge, for Christ's sake! Want me to go out there and build a rooftop so I can shout it?"

The soldiers all looked at each other. Crandall snickered.

"I'll let you know when I've made my decision," said Scott, moving to unzip the tent for them. "This meeting is over and Miss Bierce?"

"I know, Everly," she sighed, heaving herself up. "Don't let the flap hit me in the ass on my way out. Let me tell you something."

"Bierce," said Eric warningly, but Crandall, grinning, said, "Let her talk, man."

"Sooner or later, you are going to have to say something that people won't want to hear," Amber said. "And if you can't handle that, you shouldn't be in charge."

Scott tried to stare her down, but she refused to look away. Eric watched them for a while and then heaved a loud sigh and said, "Don't we have enough real problems here? Come on, you two, lighten up." He pushed his way between them and walked out. The other Fleetmen followed. Soon, Amber and Scott were alone and for just a few seconds, she had the chance to either apologize and try to put things right between them or run after Eric and try to form some kind of future that didn't include 'Commander' Everly Scott.

She did neither. She left. So if there was blame, and she knew there was, she shared it.

2

It rained for days. Amber lost track of how many. They had no computers anymore, no digireaders, no handhelds, not even wristwatches. They talked about hours or minutes, but in truth there was no time on this world—just one endless day cycling between grey and black, filled with wind and rain.

The lake started rising, and on the day the water first climbed over the mudbank and reached the grass, Scott did two things. He gave the order to pack up the camp and move upstream, and he cut Amber's rations from two bars to one. This, when she knew that everyone else was getting three.

"What the hell did I do?" she demanded.

"This isn't personal, Miss Bierce," he'd said, handing Nicci a ration.

"The hell it isn't! What, it rains for six days so I go to bed without supper? What the fuck is that about?"

"I don't need to hear the swearing, Miss Bierce."

In spite of everything, Amber had managed to keep a pretty good grip on herself. She had neither turned into a shell-shocked sleepwalker nor a senseless hysteric. For days, she had slept without complaint in a raging downpour with nothing but a piece of tinfoil to wrap herself in. She'd made a point of supporting the man who was incapable of wiping his ass without calling a meeting or holding a meeting without calling it a debriefing, and now he was punishing her because she'd dared to suggest that rain could cause flooding.

She lost her temper. Not a lot, not at first, but just like the rain, once it started pouring out, there was no end in sight.

"Don't you fucking walk away from me, Space-Scout," she snapped. "I'll tell you when we're done talking."

Scott stopped in his tracks and turned around. Nicci shuffled back, her eyes huge, clutching her ration so tightly that she'd pinched it in half through the wrapper.

"You don't get to take away my food just because I was right about needing to get out of this valley."

"First of all, moving this camp has always been under discussion. You had nothing to do with it." Scott zipped up his duffel bag and slung it decisively over his shoulder. "And secondly, I'm not cutting your rations because of your attempts to sabotage my authority here, I'm cutting them—"

"Sabotage your authority?"

"I'm cutting them because—"

"You were supposed to hold the rations because you were hogging the biggest tent, that's all! You were supposed to keep them dry, not use them as your own personal gold-star stickers for all the people who kiss your ass!"

Nicci took another step back. She looked as if she might be on the verge of tears. "Please don't fight!"

"No one's fighting, Nichole," Scott assured her, then turned his best in-charge frown on Amber. "Miss Bierce, you are grossly overweight."

"Grossly?" she echoed. She looked down at herself and up at him again, as derailed as she'd been when the medico back on Earth had called her obese. The next argument that wanted to come out of her wasn't even about him, but just that she'd lost sixty pounds, goddammit, and how overweight could she possibly still be? *Grossly*?!

Scott seized the opportunity of her angry silence to make another speech, half-turning away from her to include all the other people watching them as he said, "It wasn't all that long ago that you decided you had to lecture me on how a leader should be willing to sacrifice his popularity when he makes a command decision. Well, we all have to make sacrifices, Miss Bierce. We have limited rations and frankly, you can live off your reserves for a while."

"I'm fat, so I don't need to eat ever again, is that what you're saying?"

"Hey." Eric stepped up between them, both hands raised and empty. "Both of you. Calm down."

"I'm not upset," said Scott. "There's nothing to get upset about. The facts are these: A human being can survive without food for at least three weeks, provided he or she has plenty of water, which we have."

"Now wait a minute," said Mr. Yao.

"And judging from the looks of you, you could probably go twice that, easy. Now we've got a long hike ahead of us, Miss Bierce, so why don't you stop complaining and get ready to go."

Nicci grabbed at her arm. "Please!"

Amber shook her off. "These aren't command decisions, damn it! This is just you being a dick!"

Scott did not immediately reply. Instead, he reached out to touch Nicci's shoulder, his brow furrowed with concern. "Are you all right, Nichole?"

Nicci blinked at him. So did Amber.

"I didn't hit her, for Christ's sake!" she sputtered. "Why wouldn't she be?"

"Mr. Gunnarson, can you take Nichole and see if you can't find her some tents or something to carry?"

Dag glanced at Amber. "Sure," he said, beckoning to Nicci. "Come on, people. Show's over and we got a lot of shit to shift."

Scott waited, watching while the crowd loosened up and milled away. Amber waited too, watching only him. When they were mostly alone, except for the other Fleetmen, he finally turned back and faced her again.

"I'm warning you," said Amber. "This is not the way you want to play this."

"Miss Bierce, I'm willing to continue to take care of you, but I'm not going to stand here and entertain your selfish little temper tantrums. This is still a colony—"

"It's a what?"

"—and now more than ever it is absolutely essential that we support one another in the spirit of that colony. You do not have the right to ask the rest of us to suffer the consequences of your choice to be obese."

There was that word again. Amber sent a single furiously baffled glance down at herself—*this is not obese damn it i fit in the sleeper i fit in your stupid clothes this is not obese this is just plush*—and when she looked up again, Scott was walking away.

"Let him go."

Amber swung around, ready to throw all her embarrassment and anger right in Eric's face. "And thank you so much for standing up for me!"

"Come on, this isn't personal."

"That," she snarled, pointing at Scott's retreating back, "was personal! If the food is so limited and we've all got three weeks before we start starving, why am I the only one losing my rations?"

"I'll talk to him about that," said Mr. Yao.

"What did you expect?" asked Eric, looking pained. "You've been out here convincing people the whole valley's going to flood out when we told you how important it was to keep people calm."

"What? I have not!"

"We've had, like, six people bring that up in the last two days," Crandall said.

"Because it's *raining*, you idiots!" she exploded. "We're in a goddamn valley taking in all the goddamn runoff that's pouring over the goddamn fucking hills! I don't have to say a fucking word! Everyone can see the water rising!"

The Fleetmen exchanged frowning glances.

"I'll talk to him," said Mr. Yao again and this time, he headed after Scott.

"So don't tell me it wasn't personal!" snapped Amber. "You just admitted he thinks I'm plotting against him!"

"No, at the moment he only thinks your bitching is bad for morale," Crandall said. "If he thought you were really plotting, he'd toss you out on your butt."

"He can't do that!"

They looked at her. Crandall laughed a little. After a moment, Eric swiped rain out of his face, sighed, then looked her in the eye. "Have you ever been popular in your life?"

She blinked again. "What?"

"Popular. Have you ever been. In your whole life."

"No," she admitted, puzzled. "But I'm still standing."

"Yeah, yeah. Stick to yes or no, Bierce. Have you ever been popular?"

"No."

"Have you ever had any reason to think that being popular doesn't matter in social situations?"

Her eyes narrowed.

He waited.

"No," she said.

"Is this a social situation?" he asked patiently.

"It's a fucking survival situation!"

"Aside from that."

She glared over her shoulder at the camp, which was already coming down and being crated up. Dag was still with Nicci, trying to teach her how to bundle up a tent when all she seemed willing to do was hold one.

"Making friends here matters," said Eric, coming up beside her. "Making friends with Scott matters. You're a smart girl, Bierce. Surely you've got to see that."

"I'm smart enough to see that he doesn't know what he's doing. Why the hell aren't you the one giving orders? You were trained for this!"

Crandall laughed again.

Eric looked at her for a long time as the rain drilled their hair flat against their heads. Then he said, without expression, "Yeah, I was Fleet. And when I enlisted, they taught me how to shoot guns we don't have, run computers we don't have, pilot vehicles we don't have, and keep the peace on a ship we don't have. I'm not the hero here, Bierce. I don't want those people down there to look at me like I am. When it goes bad here, the guy in charge is probably going to get strung up from the nearest tree."

"We are one more disaster away from a mob as we speak," Crandall agreed, crookedly smiling. "I think the space-scout is finally starting to wise up to that and that's bad for you, sweets. He's going to need someone else to blame when the shit hits."

"Keep your head down and your mouth shut," Eric warned. "For what it's worth, I actually think you've got your head on pretty straight, but I'm not putting my ass on the line to cover yours. Regardless of what that loudmouth says, this isn't a colony. This is a whole new world, Bierce, and it's every man for himself."

3

They hiked for days in the rain, moving the camp piece by heavy piece, following a storm-swelled fall of water up the eastern slope and away from the *Pioneer*. It shouldn't have taken as long as it did, but Scott refused to leave anything behind. The purifier, the generator, even the stupid bags of concrete—everything was the property of Manifest Destiny, everything was necessary to the settlement of a self-sustaining colony, and everything came with them.

Amber did not object. She carried her concrete all day and slept in the rain all night and took the single ration she was allotted and did not so much as mutter under her breath. Now and then, Scott came out of his tent long enough to say inspiring things about the indomitable spirit of exploration or the human will to thrive and survive, and it bothered her to see so many people not only listening but smiling and nodding and sometimes clapping their hands, but she didn't say anything.

The rain began to wind down the same day that they actually made it over the top and started down the other side. The view was pretty much what it had been on the other side of the valley, except that there wasn't an enormous skid-mark slashed through the middle of it or a pile of melted wreckage entombing fifty thousand human beings. It was just grass. Brown grass and tangles of trees stretching out for God knew how many miles beneath the low, rolling clouds, uninterrupted by even the most ambiguous sign of civilization.

But there was life. The total lack of cities, roads or any other distraction made the small groups of animals grazing on the plains impossible to miss. To Amber, whose personal experience with animals could be almost entirely summed up by dogs, cats, rats and roaches, they didn't look too scary. Long-necked bodies and four thin legs made them look more or less like deer, except that they also had long tails. Instead of antlers, they had a set of back-sweeping horns, in addition to which they also had two huge jutting tusks. Their shiny, scale-covered skin was brownish on top and black underneath, with a white stripe on their bellies that only showed if they stood up on their hind legs, which two of them kept doing, gronking and clawing at each other with their hoofless, taloned feet.

People began to murmur in an uneasy way.

"They're not going to bother us tonight," said Scott firmly. "Let's establish our camp and secure a perimeter. Over there."

He pointed at a hilltop not too steep or too far off, with a few trees around it, but not so many that they had grown into impassable thorny walls. It wasn't right up by the stream anymore, but maybe that was a good thing, if the native animals decided to wander over in the middle of the night for a drink.

That first night wasn't bad. The wind never let up, but no one complained; it felt good just to dry out a little. There was enough deadwood lying around to start a couple fires and Scott pulled out a pocketknife, of all things, so that people could take turns cutting grass and dried thorns to keep burning. Dag roasted his ration on a stick, so a couple other people did too. Amber didn't have another ration. She sat next to Nicci, watching her sister try to heat bites of concentrated protein supplement on a stick, and listened to the scaly deer-things bawl and gash at each other.

When it got dark and the talk died down and Nicci wrapped herself inside her laughably ineffective emergency blanket and fell asleep, Amber picked up one of the roasting sticks and fingered thoughtfully at its heat-hardened point.

* * *

Early the following morning, Scott crept out of his tent and gathered the Fleetmen for his usual meeting. Amber woke up as they filed quietly out of the sleeping area and over to the crates and things, stacked at one end of camp to form Scott's idea of a windbreak. It hadn't worked.

She drowsed for a few minutes to let them have their male-bonding time during the morning pee, and when she heard their low voices begin to pick up again under the wind, she got up. She rolled up her blanket, stuffed it in her duffel, picked up Nicci's roasting stick, and headed over to join them.

"—unless we can provide them with some kind of future," Scott was saying, but he stopped when the others looked at her and turned to see her for himself.

He blushed, which was a weird reaction. "This is a debriefing, Miss Bierce. Please go sit down somewhere. I'll pass out the MREs when we're done."

There were so many things she wanted to say about the democratic process he kept insisting they still had in this so-called colony, but instead, she forced on a smile, held up her hands, and said, "Truce, okay?"

They all looked at the stick she was holding.

"I'm aware that you haven't sorted out the priorities yet," began Amber, picking her way very carefully toward her goal in her most diplomatic tone, "but when you get around to wanting a closer look at those animals, I think it would be a good idea if the people in your scouting party had something like this with them. Just in case, you know?"

Eric reached out and plucked at the tip of the stick.

"You're not anywhere on my list of people to go on that scouting mission, Miss Bierce," said Scott bluntly. "So get it out of your head right now. I need people in peak physical condition for that."

"No fat chicks, I get it." Amber made herself stop there, then pinned up that smile again and started over. "Even if I can't do the running around that's involved, I can at least help with the preparations. If I could borrow your knife, I—"

"Not a chance."

"—could spend the whole day making grown-up versions of this," Amber said stubbornly, but softly. "So when you get a team organized—"

"That is not where my priorities are right now, Miss Bierce."

"Then let me do it. I'll ask for volunteers, I'll make the spears—"

Scott stepped forward so fast and so unexpectedly that she jumped back, banged the back of her knees into a crate of pipes, and went down hard on her ass. He leaned over her, absolutely furious, but barely speaking above a whisper, careful not to wake anyone in the camp beyond them. "Before you start re-enacting *The Lord of the Flies* around here, you might want to remember what happened to Piggy. You're not the only one who ever thought of sharpening sticks."

Before Amber could decide how to respond to these bizarre but unmistakably hostile statements, Scott turned around and stalked off.

Baffled, Amber looked over at Eric and Dag. "What the hell was that about?"

Eric shook his head, looking away in a vague manner, frowning.

"It's from a book they made everyone read in school," said Crandall. "About some gay Brit kids who get stranded on some island."

"Did he just call me a pig?"

"There was one in the book."

Amber eyed him narrowly. "What happened to it?"

"I think the kids fucked it or killed it or both." Crandall shrugged. "Yeah, it didn't make a lot of sense in the book either, but I had to write a whole page on how incredibly fucking profound it was, I remember that."

"So..." Amber sent a searching gaze across the camp, but Scott had gone inside his tent. She tried to laugh the whole thing off, but no one joined her in it and the sound she made was clearly an angry one. "So what the hell kind of threat was that?"

"You just need to back off a little," said Eric quietly. "That's all."

"Back off *what*? All I want to do is think about hunting! I didn't say it had to be today! I just want him to plan for it! How is that so wrong?"

Eric and Dag exchanged another set of glances. She followed their gaze afterwards to the stick in her hand.

"What?" she said, tightening her grip.

"It just doesn't look good," said Eric. "Arming yourself. Calm down. It's nothing serious."

She turned to him fast and hissed, "He! Doesn't! *Feed* me! That feels pretty fucking serious to me!"

They shuffled a little and avoided her eyes.

"I asked for his permission! I gave him every opportunity to go back and pretend like it was his idea! Does he think those stupid rations are going to last forever? What does he think we're going to eat when they're gone?"

Eric shrugged, still not meeting her eyes. "He'll come around. Just let him figure it out on his own. Let him decide when it's time."

Amber threw up her empty hand and slapped it loudly down on the top of the crate. "Wait until the food runs out, is that it? Look, we don't have guns here. We don't even have bows. We have Scott's pocketknife and a whole lot of stupid sticks."

"I know, I know—"

"No, I don't think you do. I don't think you get it yet that when it comes to hunting, we're going to have to chase things around and stab them! How many meals do you think we'll have to skip before that becomes impossible?"

"Okay, calm down."

"I don't want to calm down, I want *you* to get pissed! Scott can talk all he wants about how a human being can live three weeks without food, but I guarantee you, two days after we eat the last of those crappy ration bars, no one is going to be able to run down one of these fucking deer!"

Eric and Dag went for Round Three of the meaningful looks. At the end of it, Eric sighed and raked his hand through his hair. "Yeah, I know," he said, and sat down on a stack of cement bags.

"Then why aren't you helping me?" Amber demanded. "If we all talked to him together, we could make him do something!"

"Oh, he'd do something, all right." Crandall snorted and kicked a crate. "Look, Bierce, you've got balls, no one's saying you don't, but it's obvious you didn't do too well in school."

"What, because I never heard of the Lord of the Pigs? Who the hell cares about that now?"

"Flies," Crandall corrected. "And also because you suck at basic math. So let me help you with your homework, honey. The four of us, and maybe Yao, plus alien critters we know nothing about, minus guns, plus pointed sticks, equals somebody getting hurt. Guaranteed."

"But we can't just—"

"Shut up a sec, I'm not done. So far we've been really lucky and so far people have stayed pretty calm—that's some more math, see if you can figure it out yourself—but when we come back from our first big hunt carrying some bloody, screaming mess that used to be you, people are going to freak and they might not stop."

"Used to be me, huh?"

"And when it happens," Eric said quietly, "Scott is going to be right there telling everybody how sharks can smell blood from ten miles away and who knows what could be out there tracking you down. You'll be gone, Bierce."

"He can't throw me out," she scoffed, "He can call himself Captain or Commander or King of the fucking Fly-People for all I care, but he can't make me leave if I don't want to."

Crandall gave her a crooked, scornful smile. "There's this other book they made us read in school called *Animal Farm*. Bet you never read that one either, huh?"

Amber rolled her eyes. "No. Is there a pig in it?"

"Yeah, as a matter of fact, there's two. One's a real smart pig who wants to help all the dumb sheep and dogs and chickens on the farm, you know, live a better life. The other one's pretty much a talker. Guess which pig takes over and which one disappears?"

"What happened to the sheep?" asked Amber.

Crandall quit smiling.

"Come on, Bierce, we're on your side," said Eric, with a warning glance at Crandall. "All he's saying is, Scott wouldn't have to do anything to you but what he already does, and that's talk."

"Is that what you're scared of?" Amber demanded. "That he'll talk at you?"

"Not at us," said Eric, with just a hint of disdain in his expression even though his tone remained even. "Against us."

"I'm shaking."

"You should be."

"Basic math," said Crandall again. "Even if you got the three of us to stand up for you—and I'll tell you right now, I wouldn't—and maybe Yao and, sure why not, that whiny little bitch of yours, he'll get all the rest of them."

"He's got most of them already," Dag commented. "Just because they're Manifestors like him."

"He's out there every day and night telling people they don't have to worry, this is all temporary and no one will ever get hurt. And what are you saying?" Eric asked, now blatantly contemptuous. "That we have to kill aliens to survive."

"We do!" Amber exploded. "For God's sake, I'm not sending anyone out after giant bugs or dinosaurs or those...those fucking black-banana-headed things! They're *deer*! They eat *grass*! They're *tiny*!"

"They're almost as tall as we are, they have horns and tusks, and they fight each other constantly!" Eric shot back. "That's exactly the kind of bullshit that makes it easy for him to talk people onto his side, because you act like this is no big deal and it fucking well is!"

She'd never heard him swear before and it rattled her. Amber looked at her spear, picking strips of bark away from the unfinished point, still angry but unsure how to argue.

"We need to figure things out. I admit that, Bierce. I agree. I'm on your damn side! But you have got to back off and let Scott come around in his own time!"

"We'll talk to him," said Dag. He put out his hand.

She looked at it, at her stick, then at him again. "What?"

Dag sighed and Eric said, "Give it up, Bierce. You'll get it back, I promise."

"No."

"Okay," said Crandall, smiling. "Give it up or I'll knock you down and take it."

Eric murmured something too low for Amber to catch.

"The hell I won't, man. I show up with that thing in one hand and Bierce with a black eye in the other and that prancing little prick will probably give me a medal.

Nothing personal, sweets, but then again, you are starting to piss me off."

Dag looked at Amber again. He sighed and held his hand out further.

She gave him the stick. "This is wrong and you know it."

"Yeah, but it doesn't change the way things are and *you* know it." He put the stick on his shoulder like a rifle and walked away, heading for Scott's tent.

Eric followed. Crandall stayed.

"You know what your problem is?" he asked, not without a careless sort of sympathy.

"Pretty sure I'm looking at it."

"Ha ha, but only sort of. Your problem, Bierce, is that you expect us all to be survivalists just because we've survived something. The fact is, those people you're pinning all our future hopes on are Manifestors. That means they were sheep before the ship crashed, so why the hell you think they're not going to be sheep now is beyond me."

"Because our lives are at stake, goddammit." She kicked at the ground and glared at him. "And some of those sheep are supposed to be soldiers."

"Soldiers?" He laughed at her. "Lady, I ain't even old enough to drink. Nine weeks of basic training, twelve weeks of so-called deep space training, and I'm in the Fleet. You call that a soldier? I call it a forty thousand dollar check I'll never get to cash." He leaned out to look back toward camp, where more and more people were waking up, then settled back and just studied her for a while. "You gonna live?"

"Are any of us?"

"Little Miss Sunshine." He glanced over his shoulder at the nearest stand of trees and looked at her again. "Want to fuck?"

"Excuse me?"

"I didn't stutter. And you ain't blushing, remember?" He ran an eye over her shirt-front in an interested way, but somehow without leering. "We probably got a few minutes before people really start to get underfoot. I'll settle for a blowjob."

"You'll settle for jerking off."

"Suit yourself, but this is opportunity knocking here. You ought to know that Scott's already talking about taking you off the MREs completely."

"What? He can't do that!"

Crandall shrugged. "See, this is what happens when you don't play ball nice. The biggest boy picks it up and goes home."

"I don't need you to take care of me." Amber stood up and pushed past him while he smirked at her. "But you go right ahead and tell Scott I don't need his rations. If that's the way he wants to play it, I can make a spear without his stupid knife."

"Sure you can."

"And just for shits and giggles, let's imagine that I actually come back with something, shall we? How many sheep do you think that'll get me?" She swung around and glared at him. His smile was gone. "If he wants to line everybody up and make them choose sides, that's what we'll do. And while all you big boys are off playing with your balls, I'll be having a barbeque with all my new friends. How does that sound?"

"Like a real nice fantasy, Bierce. You hold on to that. It'll get you through some cold, rainy nights."

"Amber?"

Crandall's gaze shifted past her. He smiled. "Hey, Nicci."

"Um, hi. Commander Scott wants me to start the fire and I can't get it to stay lit."

"I'll be right there. Go on."

Nicci turned around, but looked back when Crandall called her name. Smiling, he dipped into his back pocket and came out with a wrapped ration bar.

"Don't even fucking think it!" Amber snarled, violently enough that Nicci fled.

Crandall grinned and tossed the ration to the crate beside her. "Give it to Babycakes if you want, no strings. But think about it."

"Fuck you." She didn't touch the ration, didn't even look at it.

"That's the idea. Listen, Bierce. Seriously. You're a tough little cookie, but you are in no condition to take care of yourself. I can. I'm not such a bad guy." He shrugged, ducking his head in a sheepish sort of smile without ever taking his eyes off her. The combination was unsettling. "I'm not looking for a girlfriend. I just want someone who can keep her mouth shut when I want it shut and open when I want it open."

"Charming."

"I ain't a charming guy. I ain't pretending to be. But I can take care of you. Come on, you're smart enough to know that you're not going to have a choice forever."

The wind didn't blow any harder, but it got colder.

"What are you talking about now?" Amber asked. She tried to say it hard, like a tough woman right at the end of her patience with little boys and their bullshit, but it didn't come out that way and she knew it.

"Basic math." He still wasn't leering. "There's eleven of you girls and thirty-seven of us guys."

"So?"

He rolled his eyes. "Okay, whatever. Play dumb, get mad, do whatever you have to do. When you're done, I'll be waiting for that blowjob. Be discreet," he said, heading back to camp. "I don't want anybody thinking I'm a chubby-chaser."

Amber snatched up the ration from the crate beside her and threw it. It whipped through the air, missed him entirely, and landed in the wet grass. He picked it up, laughing. Then he was gone and she was left shaking in the wind and trying to tell herself it was because she was angry.

Just angry.

4

Although the right to move freely between the cities of Gann had been a favorite dream as a boy, Meoraq the man did not enjoy travel. He didn't hate it; travel was an inevitability of being Sheulek, which was so great a sign of his divine Father's favor that he could hate nothing that came of it. But the distance between the cities of his circuit was vast and the land that separated them, gone ugly with the coming winter. The wind was always blowing—frequently in his face—and at this time of year, the steady rain necessitated the choice of walking on the road and miring himself in mud or cutting across the wildlands and soaking himself to the hips in wet brush. Meoraq had only one comfort as he walked and it was the knowledge that he was not going home to take possession of House Uyane. The extraordinary honor of entering Xi'Matezh and hearing the voice of God was shamefully secondary, but he was praying about that.

So he was deep in the wildlands and wet to the hips, comfortably numbed within his own mind but keeping an idle eye out for danger, alone and expecting nothing but to stay alone for all the days of his journey, when Meoraq saw what was probably the strangest thing he'd ever seen.

His circuit of service was a wide one, encompassing twenty-three of the fifty-one cities in Yroq, and he had been predisposed to wander in his first years of service. He had explored many ruins and seen many forbidden relics, but after close inspection of this new thing, Meoraq decided it wasn't old. Many of the machines the Ancients left behind them still functioned, maintaining themselves with surprising success even after all this time, but all of them showed their age. No matter how clean a thing was or how often repaired, age got in. The air itself could corrode a thing, given enough time, but this looked new.

Of course, men did fall from Sheul's laws. Those who lived in wretchedness and sin outside the city walls did occasionally try to remake the machines. Some even succeeded to a small degree. But this was no machine. He didn't know what it was, but it was no machine.

What it looked like was a bedsheet, blown into a hsul tree where it had been so hopelessly tangled in its thorny branches that the wind could not carry it out again. It was not a bedsheet, however. It was metal. At least, it looked like metal, the shiny grey-white of purest silver, save that it was as pliant as fine cloth and thinner even than a sheet of paper. Although the thorns of the hsul had pierced it and the wind torn its unbound edge to streamers, Meoraq suspected it had begun as a single squarish piece.

He had no idea what it was supposed to be, but clearly he had been meant to find it. Meoraq made his camp there and sat in the open mouth of his tent most of the afternoon, watching the silvery ribbons of the windblown thing snap and flash. When he slept, he dreamed of the tower of fire rising in the night, beckoning.

The silver sheet remained unfathomable by morning's light and so Meoraq left it. He considered cutting a piece to carry with him, but ultimately decided against it. The thing could not be a relic of the Ancients or the construct of men; therefore, it was a sign from Sheul and as such, it was probably a sin to cut it. It made him uneasy to think that there was nothing in the Word about such manifestations and whether it was safe to touch them, but this was a pilgrimage and tests were to be expected.

His journey continued. The land resumed its customary view of nothing, but his mind at least was occupied. He meditated as he walked, wondering what the silver sheet had been meant to represent to him and feeling more and more like he'd failed in his first ordeal, but he was not so distracted that he failed to see the footprints when he came to fill his travel-flasks at a stream.

So. The wildlands might appear lifeless, the same way they appeared barren, but even as the rolling sameness of the landscape was made up of grass and trees and beasts and a thousand living things, every shadowed dip or stand of trees could hide a raiding party. No, it was not curiosity that made Meoraq crouch down to read the marks better, but the alarm that came from seeing, not a ragged band of six or twelve or even twenty, but a well-shoed troop with numbers great enough to trample down the stream-bank four body-lengths to one side.

He thought of Szadt, the only raider he'd ever heard of that had commanded numbers such as these. He knew Szadt was dead and buried deep in Gann's cold grip—another brick to add to Uyane Rasozul's wall of legend—but the thought bit at him all the same. Sheul's Word said that each generation was given one great plague, one scourge, and one blessing. Szadt had been the scourge of his father; perhaps this one was Meoraq's own.

He filled only one flask, keeping his burden light, and followed the tracks upstream. He made no camp that night, set no fires. He ate bites of cuuvash when he required them and drank only what his body needed. He found the ash-pits of their many fires, the flattened fields of their many messy encampments, the rain-soaked and half-hidden piles of their stinking dung, and before the sun had reached its highest point on that next day, he had found them.

Soon after, Meoraq lay on his belly in the brush beneath a small stand of prairie trees, trusting to the tall grass to hide him as he watched them. He did not count them; he could see at a glance there were more than he could fight. He saw no sentries, which he did not trust given the size of this band, and so did not dare to approach closer than this ridge, but even at this distance he could see that there was something wrong with them.

They could not have been long in this camp, he decided. There were no hides hanging from the trees, no bone-midden, no sign of any shelter apart from a handful of flimsy, silvery tents. He could see crates, presumably for trade (for there would always be men wicked enough to develop that evil hunger for phesok and strong drink), but no sleds or carts. The mystery of the curious depth of the tracks he had followed seemed to be solved, but the mystery of why they were carrying their goods in arms only deepened. He supposed some of those he saw might be slaves, but all the prints he'd seen were those of very well-made boots and what raider would shoe a slave?

Then there was the matter of their dress. They did not wear hides, nor could he make out the lines of any belt or harness cut across their colorful clothing. He could see no weapons strapped to any back or slung in a communal heap for the easy reach of all. In fact, many of them appeared to be gloved and hooded, because what he could see of their hands and faces looked pale. Not merely grey, as with youth or bad diet, but really *pale*. He couldn't imagine how they could be covering their faces like that and still see.

Then one of them got up and turned to the side and Meoraq realized they had not covered their faces after all.

They had none.

5

At the center of camp, unaware of the new eyes watching them from the shadows, the survivors of the crash of the *Pioneer* prepared for their first Stone Age hunt. Amber was right in the thick of them, heating up the tips of the spears she'd helped cut earlier that morning. Scott had deigned to give her his approval, and she knew she ought to be wired up with the thrill of that victory if nothing else, but she wasn't. She wouldn't leave camp at all today if it weren't for the fact that she knew Scott expected her to chicken out when it came time to actually get out there and stab a scaly deer. He probably already had some kind of speech prepared to the effect that she was a whiny little bitch and if she didn't like the way he did the leading around here, she could leave.

She didn't need Scott's help to feel like shit today, anyway. That had started last night, when the skies ripped open and dumped what felt like a bucket of water directly over her head. The rain hadn't lasted long, but it had been just exactly like standing in the shower while it was happening. Or lying in the shower, rather. Covered in an emergency blanket that couldn't keep the wet out no matter how she wrapped herself in it, so tired that she didn't even care that she was lying in rainwater, Amber had thought she felt as bad as it was humanly possible to feel.

And then she'd heard Eric, jogging back from a brief midnight trip to the bushes, pause beside Maria's blanket. "You sure you don't want to get cozy?" he'd asked. He'd had to shout it, really. So much rain. "Two people can fit if they're cozy."

Amber raised her head to watch, expecting a tirade that might actually end in some kind of fair tent rotation since it wasn't coming from Amber herself. Instead, Maria threw back her blanket almost at once, snarling, "I am *so* ready to get cozy. Let's go."

If Eric was surprised by the speed and ease of this capitulation, he hid it well. He helped her up, grabbed her pack, and the two of them splashed through the soggy grass to his bivy. It bucked and rolled for a few minutes as they worked their way in and then the flap zipped shut.

Amber put her head back down and listened to their two voices, unintelligible beneath the rain. In the dark, she could make out only the faintest outline of the bivy. When it started moving, she closed her eyes. She pulled her emergency blanket over her ears so the rain could hammer out the identity of the women who went to the other bivies. She just put her arm around Nicci to make sure she couldn't be one of them. She pretended not to know why when Nicci started crying.

And she slept, eventually, because she was just so damned tired.

She woke up before dawn, soaked to the pruny skin, and hobbled into the bushes to pee. She thought the low ache in her belly was hunger right up until she got her pants down and saw the blood.

Terror woke her all the way up before she realized what she was looking at. Of course. Her implant was gone and the stupid umbilicus in the Sleeper had been giving her works a tune-up and oil all the way here, wherever here was. She wasn't dying; she'd gotten her period. Her very first period. Wearing a pair of white pants.

Motherfuck.

"Suck it up, little girl," she hissed at herself, absolutely disgusted. "Grow a goddamn sense of proportion. This shouldn't even make your *list* of problems."

So she went back for her duffel bag and took it a little deeper into the trees. She pulled some grass and wadded it into a pad of sorts and stuffed that in her panties. Off came the white pants with the red badge of womanhood stamped across the crotch and on went her only pair of jeans. As for the evidence, she stuffed it under the exposed roots of one of the trees, scraping up handfuls of wet earth to push into the hole until it was good and buried. She felt guilty doing it since they were perfectly good pants, but she was never going to get that blood out and if she had to listen to just one joke, she was going to have to kill someone. After washing the (*blood*) mud off her hands at the stream, she'd gone back to camp, walking right past Scott and his loyal lieutenants at their morning debriefing so she could curl up in her blanket and pretend nothing had happened.

She lay there while the sun crawled higher behind the clouds, wondering if it was supposed to feel like this. She'd had the implant since she was ten—God bless Measure 34 and Zero Tolerance—and at the moment, she felt like she could cheerfully give up anything, even her place on a lifeboat back to Earth, to get the stupid thing back. Second-grade sex-ed was a long time ago; she couldn't remember how long this was supposed to last, only that it would happen again about once a month for the rest of her miserable fucking life. Was it normal to hurt like this? How much blood was she going to lose? Was there something she should be doing besides just packing her panties with grass and waiting for it to be over? She'd gone to so many stupid seminars preparing her for life in a colony that were about as useful now as that solar generator they were lugging around, and she'd never even thought about reading up on what was going to happen to her own damn *body*!

Naturally, it had been later that morning, when she could not have cared less, that Scott gave the speech Amber had been waiting for—the ration bars were almost gone and it was time to learn how to catch dinner. "Miss Bierce has volunteered to make spears," he'd said at the end of it, and there she sat, hugging her cramping stomach in one arm and Nicci in the other, wishing he'd take that pocketknife he was holding out to her so gallantly and pound it right up his ass.

She made the spears. It wasn't as easy as she'd thought it would be. The first set of sticks she was able to break off the trees were way too small once they'd had their points cut. The next set—deadfall branches she'd picked off the ground—seemed okay as she did the carving and heating, but every one of them broke when Scott sauntered over to give them a practice throw, and as much as she'd wanted to sock him for doing that, even she had to admit he was right when he pointed out that if they'd break that easy, they'd be no good as a weapon. But three seemed to be the charm and the day was only half-over. The deer drifted back and forth across the plains as they had for days now, but never went far. It was almost like they were waiting for them.

"How are we doing on those spears, Miss Bierce?"

"I'm doing fine, Everly," said Amber, testing the point of a hot spear before setting it aside in the Finished pile with the other six. "How many have you made?"

It didn't seem to embarrass him. If anything, his officious little smirk widened. "You asked for this job, remember? You practically begged for it."

"I remember. That was the day you called me a pig."

"I did not." But he looked to see if anyone else was close enough to hear. When he saw a few frowns pointed their way, he blushed. "Miss Bierce, if you can't do what you promised to do, that's all right. I'll understand if your physical limitations—"

"Godammit, I am not too fat to make spears!"

"I never said that either, Miss Bierce, but you are clearly having difficulty. Instead of getting angry with me, why don't you tell me what the problem is?"

'At the moment, it's the jackass breathing down my neck,' Amber thought. Aloud, she said, "I'm just trying to finish this. What are you trying to do?"

"Have a civil conversation with someone who is determined to cause trouble in this colony." Scott heaved a sigh. "There is absolutely no reason for this, you know."

"For what?"

"This." Scott waved irritably at the sky, as if her question were a distracting fly. "I get it, okay? I understand."

Amber felt her eyes narrowing. "You understand what?"

"Why you're like this."

Had he found her pants? Amber made herself pick up another spear, even as she told herself that this was probably not a good time to fill her hands with weapons. Fat jokes she could handle, if not entirely with good grace. If he pulled out a period joke, she was clubbing him.

"I understand that you feel like you have to be a bitch because you think that people will take you more seriously if they think you're strong."

She let out a laugh before she could help herself. He hadn't found her pants. He was just being his usual dicky self. "I think we're done with this conversation."

"No, we're not. This is something we should have said a long time ago. Amber." He came and put his hand on her shoulder, did it like he was knighting her. His expression was that of a bold and rugged space adventurer comforting his distressed damsel—noble and determined, with just the right degree of pity. "We're going to take care of you, Amber. You and all the other girls. You're our most precious resource."

"What?" she said flatly.

"This is still a colony," said Scott. His hand was still on her shoulder. "Only we're not in it for the five-year contract anymore and you are one of only eleven wombs. We've been talking about this."

"Wombs."

"And we've made some difficult decisions regarding our duty here." Scott ran his commanding eyes across his gallant colonists. "It may be our immediate goal to persevere, but our ultimate goal hasn't changed from the day we boarded the *Pioneer*. It's not just about living, surviving. It's about preserving our lives, yes, and our *way* of life, our very future. Yes, Miss Bierce, we have a duty...and we're going to have to be mature about this."

"Says the man about to order people to fuck," said Amber, and quite a few people flinched, just like that wasn't where that little speech was going. "Were you planning to pass us out like the tents or let everyone draw straws? Let me guess: Your lieutenants get the first pick?"

Maria looked at Eric. He did not look back at her.

"You're right, Scott," Amber said, removing his hand from her shoulder. "This is a conversation we should have had before now. Because it seems that someone actually has to point out to you that eleven wombs plus one or two hundred years equals so much inbreeding that it ain't even funny. This is not a colony."

"And what is it, then? What is it you expect all these people—" A sweep of his arm included the whole camp, quite a few of whom stood quietly up and moved a little closer to him. Taking sides. "—to do, Miss Bierce? Just stand around waiting to die?"

"No, *Everly*, I expect us to stop standing around and start finding a way to live! Picking out who to screw ought to be dead last on our list of priorities, right after building a goddamn musical theater and casting for *The King and I*! Clean water! Food! Shelter from this constant cold, windy piss we're stuck in! That ought to be where your head is at, not in my pants!"

"Oh believe me, nobody here is looking forward to getting in your pants." Scott gave that a dramatic pause, then added, "Although God knows there's room for two or three in there once you're out of them."

"Another fat joke," said Amber, rolling her eyes. "If you can't quit the name-calling, can you at least pick a new name?"

Several female voices called agreement and a few of the men standing behind Scott slunk off and sat down again.

Scott noticed. He glanced around, flustered and trying not to show it.

"You're losing your crew, Commander," said Amber.

"No one ever taught you when to shut up, did they?" He looked at her again, almost but not quite sneering, and dropped his voice until it was just for the two of them. "You want to call this a win, you go right ahead. But there is no future in all your self-righteous talk about what we eat and where we sleep. There's a future in fucking. So you give it a week. Give it two. And then you get ready to spread that butter because things are going to change."

He waited, just in case she wanted to get the punches started, but she turned her back on him instead, since that had always been the best way to chap Nicci's ass when they fought. They both walked away, but it sure didn't feel over.

"All right, people." Commander Everly Scott, in charge once more, clapped his hands to get people's attention just like the argument itself hadn't done that. "Volunteer hunters, front and center. Miss Bierce will be in charge—"

So it could be all her fault when it failed.

"Dick," Amber muttered, picking up her last spear and throwing it down again on top of the Finished pile without bothering to test it.

Nicci came and sat down beside her, but she was looking back at Scott. "What are you going to do?"

"Get a deer." Amber clapped a hand to her cramping belly and rubbed hard, giving herself something painful to feel to try and avoid throwing up out of sheer, messy misery. "Or die trying."

* * *

Amber had made twelve spears altogether. Of these, Scott judged eight acceptable; the other four, he said, were good for nothing but firewood and he proved it by tossing them on the fire. Then he picked out the hunters, in spite of the fact that this was allegedly her hunt. It was impossible not to notice that he did not permit any of the Fleetmen, all of whom had volunteered, to join them. If he could have smeared her with fresh blood and honey and tied her hands behind her back too, he probably would have.

Still, Amber managed not to instigate another argument she couldn't possibly win. She took what little she was given and limited all the outrage seething in her stomach to one small stabbing: She invited Scott to come along.

She did it solely to keep him from stealing any time alone with Nicci and she really didn't think it would work. She'd been ready to bully Nicci into coming with her once Scott brushed her off, but to her surprise, her, "And of course, you'll be hiding way back here," really seemed to get to him. He'd replaced one of his Manifestors on the spot, although he was just as quick to declare he was only there in a supervisory position. The success of the hunt (or more accurately, she was sure, its failure) rested squarely with her.

They finally set off sometime in the early afternoon, which Scott just had to point out was probably the worst time to go hunting. Deer came out at dawn and at dusk.

"Yeah, well, I couldn't exactly pull these spears out of my ass at dawn this morning," Amber told him. "I had to make them. If you'll recall, I asked for your permission to do that days ago and you called me a pig."

"Miss Bierce, it is deeply troubling to me that you perceive every attempt to educate you as a personal attack."

She wanted to go on, maybe give him a real personal attack so he'd know the difference the next time they got to talking, but his Manifestor friends were listening and ready to repeat whatever they heard back at camp. She wasn't afraid to speak her mind, but she was beginning to realize she'd better have more on her mind when she did than 'fuck you'. So she kept quiet and focused on not letting her cramps or the fact that she hadn't eaten since the previous morning keep her from walking at the front of the line and not the end. Her failure on this hunt might be unavoidable, but she wasn't going to give Scott any help burning her at the stake.

The herd had been drifting further from camp all morning, but now that they were finally on the hunt, the scaly deer-things abruptly wandered out into the open plains and drew together into a beautifully obvious target. Watching them, Amber hesitated, knowing this was her chance but unsure how to begin. The spear that had seemed so crucial and so solid upon its making now seemed woefully inadequate, a splinter in her hands. Could she really hope to use this thing? And not just use it, but actually stab it into something alive and moving and do enough damage to kill it?

And what if the deer-things fought back? They fought all the time. A handful of them were fighting even now, balanced on their long hind legs so they could slash and butt away at their rival. These blows did not appear to be very effective against their scaly hides, but Amber was pretty sure they could tear through human skin just fine.

Scott was smart enough to recognize a golden opportunity when he saw it. She could almost see the gears of his mind turning as he realized that bringing home the first kill after Amber had not only failed to hunt but actually failed to act was immeasurably better than just letting her fall on her face. He stepped up.

"I've got this, Scott," she said tightly.

"You don't seem too sure about that. Okay, people, why don't you two go around that way—"

"I said, I've got this! Come on!"

They started forward, spread out and low to the ground, with no specific idea of what to do or which animal to target. The scaly deer-things kicked sullenly at each other and gored the ground for roots, as oblivious to the humans creeping clumsily toward them as the humans themselves were to the dumaq prowling unseen in their own wake. They were close—close enough to see the golden rings of color around their huge dark eyes, close enough to count all three craggy claws at the end of each delicate foot—when Scott whispered, "Should we do it now?"

"No, get closer. We have to get—"

"Now!" Scott shouted, and all six of the Manifestors in the party jumped up with ridiculous cries of attack and threw their spears while they were still at least twenty-five meters away.

"No, dammit!" Amber shouted, running forward, but it was too late.

The deer quit fighting for one miraculous, motionless instant to gape at the aliens who had just popped up beside them and then the solid mass of the herd exploded into a hundred running animals, all going in different directions. One of them came right at Amber and she, thrown into a thought-free mode of adrenaline and panic, swung her spear like a baseball bat. Naturally, it jumped, but she still managed not to miss it completely. If she had, it would have sprinted away and left her staring after it, defeated.

But no. She swung. It leaped. Her spear connected, not with its fragile-looking deer-like head, but with its bounding hindquarters.

And that changed everything.

It landed and fell, dragging its body behind its kicking forelegs for a few stunning seconds while Amber gaped at her good luck. Then it was up and running again (but limping) and Amber lunged after it with a scream that was only half-defeated and the chase began.

They tumbled through the grass together—wounded animal and winded human—the distance between them heaving long and staggering short. Twice, she got close enough to swing her spear again, but missed both times. The only other chance she had to hit it came when it unexpectedly doubled back on its trail and when it did, she forgot the spear entirely and grabbed at it instead. She caught it (*and if you'd used the spear you dumb bitch you'd have hit it lamed it up some more or even killed it what's* wrong *with you*) and was dragged along for a few violent seconds only before it kicked her off. She fell, lungs on fire and head spinning, and thought it ran off without her, but when she finally got up, there it was, not even five meters away, head down, gasping.

It saw her about the same time as she saw it. With a high, bleating cry, it threw itself at her. She swung her spear, missing it completely and throwing herself so far off balance that she fell on her face in the thorny grass. It fled right over the top of her, its clawed feet trampling at her back and butt. She kicked in a blind panic, connecting only once but connecting solidly with its other hind leg, so that it fell all the way over and lay on its side for one glorious second.

Then it bolted, bawling over and over, aiming for a thicket. She took off after it, lurching more than running at this point and scarcely able to see past the pulse pounding in her head, and knowing the only thing worse than missing your only chance at dinner at the very start of the hunt was following it all this way...and losing it at the end.

It bounded through the outer ring of stiff, dead vines and thickening thorns, leaving Amber further behind as she fought to follow after, and when it reached a thick copse of wind-twisted trees and broad-leafed bushes, it staggered. And stopped.

And there it stayed, while Amber fought and failed to get any closer. There was no walking through the tangle of underbrush it had passed so effortlessly, and the harder she tried, the more damage she did to herself. Her clothes tore and her boots got caught and she cut the living hell out of her arms and hands and face, but she didn't gain a fucking step on it and finally, in a fit of frustration that was nearly orgasmic in its entirety, she let out a howl and threw her spear from the impossible distance of four or five measly meters away.

It leapt aside and was swiftly lost in the deeper shadows of the thicket.

It leapt aside...and something else was there.

She never saw it until it moved, and it had to move or her spear would have gone right into its scaly chest. It whipped aside, pivoting at the hips, and suddenly her spear was suspended and quivering at both ends with its fist wrapped around it in the middle.

It looked at the spear.

And then it looked at her.

* * *

The creature let out an exhausted whoop that probably could have been a scream if it had more air and then fell over. It was not the faint Meoraq thought it was at first, because it was struggling almost at once. Its boots were tangled in dried thorns. More thorns snagged on its clothes, pulling its top-wrap half off and scratching up its pale skin with terrible ease. It fought to free itself, but it was trapped and, by the look in its eerie eyes, it knew it.

It would have been a simple thing to kill the creature. It certainly seemed like the most prudent thing to do, particularly since allowing it to live would alert all the others to his presence. And yet, Meoraq found himself strangely disinclined to strike.

There never should have been a reason for this encounter. The thicket where he had settled in to watch the creatures hunt was well out of the way, and yet the injured saoq had aimed itself directly at him. The will of Sheul could make itself known in many things, perhaps even this.

So then, what was Sheul's will? Meoraq looked at the creature's weapon again. Weapon, ha. A young tree, its branches torn away, made sharp at one end and tempered over a campfire. And what had the creature done with its fine pointed weapon? What, but swing at the saoq as if it held instead a club.

Meoraq had indeed watched the hunt, from its disastrous commencement to this unforeseen ending. It would have been easy to laugh at what he saw, except that, no matter how stupidly played out, it was still a coordinated attack. But as the hunt limped on, Meoraq's derisive humor faded. It was trying. And no matter that it hadn't a hope of success, it kept right on trying, until Meoraq actually thought it might take the saoq after all. He had, in fact, been sorely tempted while the saoq stood gasping before him in the thicket to put an end to the chase himself. One swift cut across the right tendon...it wouldn't even bleed that much...the creature might think it had done it all itself.

But he never had the chance. The spear was thrown. The saoq fled. And now here he stood with the creature's eyes wide open and full upon him.

"Sheul, my Father, I feel Your hand," mused Meoraq, studying the burnt point of the creature's weapon. "But I do not hear Your voice. Speak, I pray, and tell me what I am to do."

The creature spoke.

Meoraq looked at it. It was watching him closely, its hand still clutched around the torn edges of its caught clothing, yet it had ceased its attempts to free itself. Its eyes, so curiously like that of a dumaq, shone with intelligence in its flat, ugly face.

More than animal intelligence, perhaps.

Meoraq regarded it with growing unease as it became inescapably clear that he was not merely being seen by this creature, he was being measured.

The thought of killing it came back, stronger than before. Meoraq's hand tightened on the creature's spear—

'If it is a man,' thought Meoraq suddenly, 'that would be murder.'

Ridiculous. A Sheulek, by very definition, could not commit a murder. A Sheulek was the Sword of God and the arbiter of His true Word. He could kill anyone or anything he wanted and he did not necessarily need a reason.

But he really ought to have one. Meoraq hissed, annoyed (the creature immediately renewed its struggles to escape the thorns), and looked again at the spear. Just a pointed stick, without an open blade to stand in defiance of Sheul's laws.

Never mind, there had to be some other law it had broken.

There was a fine thought for a Sheulek to have. Just kill it; everyone is guilty of something. If that was what his years of service had done, perhaps it was time he retired.

Scowling, Meoraq picked his way forward out of the thicket. With every step, the creature fought the brambles harder, tearing its hands and arms and even its face, until Meoraq drew a sabk and knelt beside it.

Then, shockingly, it lunged and caught his wrist.

And Meoraq found himself trapped, not by its grip, which was a flimsy shackle indeed, but by its eyes. They were frightened but not wild, and in them was all the strength and fire its feeble hand could not possess.

'This is a person,' thought Meoraq, motionless as a man in thrall to phesok smoke. 'This is a person with a soul hammered at Sheul's forge just the same as mine.'

"Easy," he heard himself say—speaking to it!—just before he did something even more incomprehensible.

He gave it its spear.

It looked at it, then released Meoraq's arm to take it, but it did not raise it again as a weapon. It merely held the thing limply in its grasp, now staring at him with its queasily soft-looking fur-striped brows drawn together. It made sounds at him. Words.

"I do not know Your will, my Father," said Meoraq, cutting the thorns that held the creature. "But as it seems You have gone to some effort to put us in one another's path, I will walk with them awhile and see if I can learn what You wish for me to know."

Freed, the creature gained its feet and immediately adjusted its torn clothing, as if Meoraq had any inclination to ogle its repulsive body. But it looked at him...studying him...and so, almost against his will, Meoraq examined it in return.

Being this close to one of them made him somehow stop seeing all the obvious differences there were between their kinds and see instead the very few similarities: not just its eyes (which were the green of new leaves), but the basic lines of its body, the shape of its slender arms and legs, and every subtle thing that marked it as a child of Sheul's design. He had no idea what horrific sin of its bloodline could have bred such malformation into its face, its skin, its very bones, but when he stood this close and saw it looking back at him with such eyes, he could not be repulsed.

Like a man in a dream, Meoraq watched his hand rise and brush the backs of his curled fingers across its high, smooth brow. The creature flinched, tearing its eyes off his boots (which it had been staring at so raptly, one wouldn't ever imagine the thing was wearing a pair of its own) to look at him. And Meoraq, who could hardly believe he'd done that much, now found himself stroking his fingertips along the flat plane of the creature's cheek. The thing's skin dimpled even at the lightest touch, like drawing his hand across water. Meoraq followed the curve of its face down its jaw to its pointed chin, and then, as if he hadn't done enough, moved to touch the ridiculous nub of a nose it wore above its flat mouth.

Its brow furrowed, but it let him touch. And then it raised its own hand and touched his face in return.

Meoraq stiffened and withdrew his hand as a fist, fighting the urge to knock the creature back into the brambles only with the aid of many long years' training. A Sheulek is the master of his impulses, always.

Truth, but then, no man may freely touch a Sheulek. If Meoraq sought just cause to cut his blades across the soft throat offered to him, there it was.

Meoraq did nothing. He stood, tense and oversensitive to the slight feel of weight and warmth as the creature rubbed its fingerpads along his snout, up to his brow-ridges and right to the base of his first spine (he felt it twitch, not slapping flatter to his skull but actually relaxing outward, pressing into the creature's touch), before slipping down over the side of his face toward his neck.

That was too much. Meoraq swiftly stepped back, catching the creature by the wrist before it could touch the sensitive scales over his throat. He should have pushed it away; he should have, but instead he turned its hand over. His thumb moved, tracing a circle against its palm. He looked up and saw its eyes fixed on his hand and its own, joined.

Joined.

A bolt of something hot and bright and not as deeply unpleasant as it probably ought to be struck Meoraq right in the soul. He released the creature and took a step back for good measure.

"I know Your ways are many and mysterious," said Meoraq to Sheul, his heart racing, "but that cannot be what You intended."

Sheul gave him no answer.

But the creature did.

It spoke, waggling its mouthparts to make its sounds. Then it waited, watching him, and said the same sounds again, this time patting itself on the chest. Mmbr. Mmbrrrbrs.

It had a name.

Meoraq recoiled, but the creature was adamant. It came a half-step closer, canting its head to an angle Meoraq could not help but see as intrigued and tinged with humor, saying its sounds over again, but with such impossible variation that he could not begin to imitate them.

Instead, and not without a faint sense of surrender, he gave his chest a half-hearted knock and said his own name in return. Not the whole thing, of course. He may or may not be killing the creature later; he wasn't getting too formal with it now. "Uyane Meoraq."

The creature's mouthparts flattened and opened around jaws tightly clenched, exposing its teeth, which were small and white and largely blunt, and which filled its mouth with no space at all between them. Yet it wasn't snapping or growling or anything beast-like.

He thought it was smiling.

"Uyane Meoraq," it said, or rather, those were the sounds it chewed up and regurgitated in ways that rendered the name itself only just discernible and deeply insulting. Oo'yanee, with no effort at all made to match the honorifics in pitch or tone. No, it was just Oo'yanee, meaningless sound, and Mee'orrak, which was actually worse because the creature put all the stress on the first syllable and bit off the rest in such a way that it came uncomfortably close to making his name a derivative of male genitalia. He hadn't heard his name spoken quite that way since he'd been twelve.

"Meoraq," he said clearly, and knocked his chest again.

"Mee'orrak," it babbled back. This time, it put the stress on the last syllable.

He tried a third time, leaning forward to put his eyes on a level with its own, as if his stare alone could help the fool thing understand him: "Meoraq."

"Mee'orrak!"

It had to be *trying* to mangle his name. How else could it manage to such a spectacular degree?

It was knocking its own chest again: "Mmbr! Thtzmi. Ef'uqantok yu'af t'bi'ablt'sa minam. Mmbrrr!"

"I do not mark," said Meoraq, openly showing the thing his confusion with the flexing of his spines, even though he had no reason to think the spineless creature would know the gesture's meaning. "Do you mark me at all? Eh? Do you know speech?"

"Mbr. Imambr! Dam'mt donjst'sterritmi sa'a somthn! Mmbrr!"

"Gtdon!"

Meoraq recoiled for a second time, looking past Mmbr to the second creature who had come boldly across the prairie without him noticing. This creature also had a stick, which it held as if it were nerving itself up to point it at someone and just hadn't decided yet whether it should be Meoraq or Mmbr.

"Gtdon," it said again, waving one arm. "Imgnna killit."

"R'rufukkn ntz?" Mmbr demanded and after that, the words between them were too many and too heated to sort out.

Meoraq's eyes darted from one to the other, but otherwise he did not move. He knew that he could kill two creatures as easily as one—for that matter, he knew that he could kill all of them, especially now that he had seen the way the creatures hunted—but something stayed his hand, something more than he could fathom. Sheul spoke into his heart...but like Mmbr's words, it was sound without meaning. He knew only that his fate was tied to them.

The creatures were still barking at each other, neither one bending its neck to the other, and eventually the second creature abandoned words entirely. It shoved Mmbr aside, still barking, and raised its spear—not pointing it, but only wanting to make sure Meoraq saw it.

So Meoraq let him know he'd seen it by plucking it out of the creature's pink little hand and snapping it over his knee. The creature let out a shrill sort of shout and leapt back, tangling its boots in the same thorns that had caught Mmbr, and fell over.

"Wut'thfuk," said Mmbr, raising its arms to heaven and dropping them with a slap to its sides. "Skt wut'thfukz rong wth'u?"

The second creature pointed a shaking hand at Meoraq. "Tht'theng trid t'kilmi!"

Mmbr snorted. It was a perfectly recognizable sound, so much so that Meoraq had to look around and see the humor in its eyes for himself. And it was there, by Sheul, of a contemptuous sort, but there.

"F'thatwertru uudbi'ded," said Mmbr. It looked up at Meoraq and its mouthparts curled, grotesquely pliant. It put its hand on his arm and took a step backwards, into the prairie. "Cm'n Meoraq. Donlzzn to'm. Eezadik."

It wanted him to follow it, he realized.

And out of nowhere, for no reason whatsoever, thought, 'She. *She* wants me to follow *her*.'

He looked from one creature to the other, stunned and not a little disgusted, and saw that Mmbr's face indeed had more delicate features and although its clothes obscured much, its body as a whole was both smaller and rounder. Its chest in particular was as full as a milking mother's, which it could very well be.

'So then,' he told himself brusquely. 'It's female. What of it?'

Her hand upon his arm felt warmer.

She grimaced at him, then turned around and started walking, picking her way back through the brambles past her sullen companion, trusting Meoraq to follow.

And he did.

6

Amber was never able to put into words just why she brought the lizard back to camp. When asked (and they asked, many times, for days afterwards), she was always able to come up with something plausible-sounding about how useful he might be, but that first impulse remained indefinable. She only knew that she wanted him with them.

So now he was here and he was staring at her. And that was okay, because honestly, she was staring back at him.

She should have been prepared to see something like this. An alien, that was. From the moment she'd first seen the scaly deer if not sooner. But there was a big difference between knowing intellectually that there were forms of animal life on this world and seeing a six-foot tall lizardman come at you out of the bushes with a knife in his hand.

Lizardman was perhaps a derogatory term. It was also the only one that fit. There was nothing wholly recognizable about his features, nothing she could point at and say with authority that looked like a crocodile or a komodo dragon or an iguana, but lizard summed it all up nicely. It was the 'man' bit that bothered her.

She was pretty sure he was a man, anyway, or at least a male. Masculinity was a stamp over the whole of his body: his lean and muscular build, the craggy scars cut into his scales, even the predatory way he had of crouching down and holding perfectly still while he stared at her—none of it was any guarantee of gender on an alien, but all of it screamed male to Amber's eye.

So he—if he was a he—was a biped and essentially humanoid, with two legs and two arms and no tail. His was a gladiator's body: a long, V-shaped chest, heavily scarred and ridiculously muscle-wrapped, that tapered into a flat stomach and narrow hips. His skin was the smooth, scaled hide of a snake rather that the rough one of an alligator, but however you looked at them, they were scales, black and shiny. But his hands had only three fingers, and they *were* fingers, not claws. His legs looked like normal legs, and although he had a habit of walking forward on the balls of his feet, they weren't all bent backwards and bestial. He was even wearing boots.

The fact that he wore clothes had a way of wanting to boggle in Amber's mind, as if the toughness of his scales rendered further covering superfluous and never mind the man's modesty. He had pants stitched out of dun-brown hides with a wide leather belt to hold it on, and a harness over his largely-naked chest that seemed to serve mostly as an anchor for his hammered metal shoulder-guards. Apart from that, and the boots, he wore only weapons: a pair of short knives strapped to his bulging biceps, a hook-shaped sword clipped to his belt so it hung over one equally-bulging thigh, one broad, highly-polished sword carried in a sheath across his back, and a leather cord around his neck from which hung yet another knife, a small one this time, with an ivory handle. It appeared to be his favorite; his hand had a way of straying there when he muttered to himself. He did a lot of that, although he didn't look crazy when he did it.

Not that she would know crazy when she saw it on a lizard, she supposed, but she was convinced there was a quietness to his expression. Not a calm, maybe, but a quietness. And she would be the first to admit that this was an unreasonable assumption because there was next to nothing that was readable about his face. He had two eyes aimed forward just like hers (except for being too big and for the color, which was a deep red, flecked with gold), under a heavy brow-ridge lined with pebbly scales that became a tight double-row of flexible spines that swept over the top of his skull to about halfway down his neck. His nose and mouth were combined into a dragonish snout, which was broad, lipless, and immoveable except at the corners; she could see the point of his thick, rigid tongue when he opened his mouth to speak, but couldn't figure how he was shaping his words at all. Like a parrot, he just spilled out sound, then closed his mouth again and looked at her. It was easy to imagine she saw frustration mounting in those reptilian eyes as she tried to repeat him, and eventually he quit talking at all.

He just stared at her.

"I'm telling you for the last time, that thing is not sleeping in this camp tonight," Scott announced.

The lizard's eyes shifted to him.

"Good," said Amber. "If it's the last time, maybe now you'll shut up about it."

The lizard's eyes came back to her.

"Miss Bierce—"

Back to Scott.

"—that thing is carrying a dozen weapons. It's dangerous."

"Wow," drawled Amber. "Good eye, Commander. I can only count five myself. Where are the rest?"

The lizard's eyes stayed on Scott. That was weird enough that she glanced around, too.

Scott was glaring at her. She was getting that look out of him a lot these days.

"You may not care what happens to these people, Miss Bierce—"

The lizard reached back and pulled that long, shiny sword out of his back-sheath. He didn't do it fast, but he did it so smoothly and silently that it still looked like magic (and at the same time, he managed to make it clear that he could have done it fast if he'd wanted to).

"Here's a thought," said Amber. "If you're really all that concerned about how dangerous the lizardman is, why don't you stop antagonizing him?"

Scott walked away.

The lizard's eyes tracked him. The sword stayed in his hand.

Scott came back.

"I want you both out of this camp right now," he announced.

Amber's eyes went automatically to her sister, seeking support or at least surprise, but Nicci didn't protest. She didn't even stand up. Nicci just looked back at her with that same lost and unhappy vagueness she'd pretty much worn since the crash.

And for the first time since that day, Amber had to fight—really fight—the urge to slap that vacant stare right off her.

Instead, she made herself turn back to Scott, and with all the disgust she could not unleash on her baby sister, she said, "I have a reality check for you, Everly. You are not Commander-in-Chief of the entire planet or even this miserable little piece of it. You don't get to say who stays and who goes."

He muttered something, flushed and glaring.

"What did you just say?" she demanded, knowing damn well she'd heard him. "Oh no. No no. If you're so goddamned sure of yourself, you say it right out loud!"

She didn't think he would, and for a moment or two, she could see him waver, wanting to back down, find his supporters, regroup. Then, without warning, he changed his mind and stepped up.

"I said, things have changed. And whether you like it or not, I am in charge. And while I'm in charge, you better watch your fat fucking mouth or else."

"Hey." Eric stood up, his hands open and raised. "Everybody calm down."

Scott took a step forward.

Amber hopped up to meet him and bumped into the lizard's back. He really could be fast when he wanted to be; he'd been behind her just a second ago. She had to move around him to see why everyone else had suddenly gone so quiet.

For the moment, Scott's head was still firmly attached to his neck. For the moment. The edge of the lizardman's sword hovered motionless in the air just beyond the throbbing vein in Scott's neck and the lizardman seemed content to leave it there. All day.

"Call him off," Eric said.

Amber looked around, thunderstruck, and sure enough, he was talking to her. More astounding, everyone else was looking at her. "Hey, this is not my trained alligator!" she said crossly. "If he wants the sword out of his face, he needs to stop acting so fucking hostile!"

The alien punctuated this with a low, menacing hiss.

"You're not helping," Amber snapped. She started to take his wrist, but thought better of it and snapped her fingers a few times instead. "Hey! Meoraq!"

He looked at her. The sword stayed where it was.

"You're not helping," she said again, and just said it this time. "Ease up on him. We're all friends here. Sit down. But while I have your attention," she went on as the lizard grudgingly lowered his arm and hunkered down again, "I would like to point out that this is the only guy in camp who knows where the next nearest waterhole is. He might also know which plants are poisonous and which ones aren't. Judging from his outfit, there's even a good chance he knows how to take down some of those stupid deer-things and he maybe even could help us turn a few of them into clothes of our own. This is a godsend and you'd know that if you weren't so worried about who's in charge!"

"She's right," said Dag, looking at Scott. "If nothing else, we're going to need to know what we're up against, right? I mean...if there's one, there must be more."

"And I don't believe for a second they're all going to be happy to see us," declared Scott. "Miss Bierce can believe what she wants—as loudly as she wants—but that doesn't change the fact that, historically speaking, natives don't take it too well when strangers show up."

"Particularly when the strangers start acting like dicks!" Amber interjected.

"No," said Eric, also moving around to Scott's side. "I'm sorry, Bierce, but you are dead wrong on this one. Unfortunately," he added, looking at a smirking Scott, "that's the best reason I've heard yet to let the lizard stay. I'd rather have him where I can see him than let him go who knows where and say God knows what to who, you know?"

"Well," said Scott after a moment, "I guess we could kill him."

"Oh my God, seriously?" Amber stepped aside and flung both her hands at the lizard's battle-scarred chest. "I want to see you try it," she said as the lizard cocked his head at her. "Right now. Whip out your little knife, Space-Scout, and see what he does with his."

The three of them stood close together and eyed the lizard with caution until the lizard glanced their way. Then Dag and Eric backed away and Scott turned pink and angrily said, "Have you even thought about the germs that thing could be carrying?"

"We all got the Vaccine," she argued, but she didn't like the way it came out, almost as a question.

"The Vaccine isn't magic, Miss Bierce. We are all very much vulnerable to bacterial infection and other forms of contamination which I'm sure never occurred to you. No," Scott said, frowning very seriously at the lizard, who stared expressionlessly right back at him. "Bringing that thing into our camp without consulting anyone was a stupid and reckless thing to do and we are all at risk because of it. He may turn out to be friendly, I don't know, but his intentions aren't the only things potentially endangering us. You're on probation, Miss Bierce."

"Oh for Christ's sake."

Scott stared her down with unbelievably effective dignity. "You may not think this a colony. But it is a community and that community cannot afford to have members who don't care about the consequences of their actions."

She was not going to win this one, not with an alien sitting in their camp, dripping with swords, scars and bacteria. Amber turned her back on Scott and stared at Meoraq instead. After a few minutes, he noticed and shifted his red eyes from Scott to her. He frowned; the corners of his mouth were the only flexible parts of his whole face, but they were turning down.

"How can he possibly help us?" Scott demanded, coming up behind her. "He can't even talk."

"Yes, he can. He just doesn't know English yet." Amber hesitated, and then eased a little closer to the lizardman and sat down, facing him. His spines came all the way forward. Otherwise, he was perfectly still. "But we can teach him."

"Sure you can. This I've got to see."

"Meoraq," said Amber, reaching a hand toward the lizardman's chest.

His hand snapped out and caught her wrist. He held her for only a second or two, which was plenty long enough for her to feel how easily he could be breaking her bones, and then slowly opened his fist.

"You're going to get hurt," said Scott. "Or you're going to be responsible for hurting other people who don't deserve it. And sad to say, that will probably be the only way you will ever admit you were wrong to bring him here in the first place."

The lizardman glanced at him, then looked at Amber some more. He raised his own hand and tapped a knuckle to his chest. "Meoraq."

"And I'm Amber." She patted herself. "Amber."

He watched her hand while it was moving, but made no effort to repeat her.

"This would be funny if it weren't so sad."

"Shut the hell up already, Scott!" Amber snapped. "You made your point. Now you're just acting like an asshole."

"Leave her alone," Eric said. "You know how she gets."

"I know I'm getting more than a little tired of how she gets," Scott announced, but he moved away. Everyone just stood around, staring like they expected her to do something. The lizard kept looking at her and she had no idea what he was thinking.

"Amber," she said again, feeling foolish and a little desperate.

He uttered a curt grunting sound without opening his mouth and reached out to thump her on the chest with one knuckle. He still didn't try to say her name.

But he knew it was her name. That was something.

"So...okay. We—" Amber waved around at the whole camp to include everyone; the lizardman's eyes never left hers. "We're humans. We're from another planet. Called Earth. Um...Earth? Humans? Feel free to make an effort here, Meoraq."

His spines twitched. "Meoraq."

"We're humans. Um...what are your people called?"

Nothing. No reaction. Not one word. Not even another grunt.

This wasn't working. She didn't even know what she was doing wrong. Amber started to get up, then sighed and sat back down. She rubbed her face, then looked at her hand and raised it up like she was making a shadow-duck.

The lizardman's eyes moved to it and narrowed.

"We came here from Earth," she said, sweeping her hand through the space between them and down to thump on ground. "And we crashed."

The lizardman frowned, watching her turn her hand over into a limp, dead palm. With her other hand, she made walking fingers to step out of her palm into the grass.

"Then the ship blew up." She tried to show him by flexing her fingers and making what she hoped was a fiery whooshing sound.

The lizardman's spines ticced. He looked up—not at her, but at the sky. He said something, then frowned at her again.

"I guess you saw that, huh?" This time, when she waved at the camp, he looked at the people instead of her hand. "We're the only ones left and we can't get home."

"You don't know that," Scott interrupted.

Amber simply looked at him, then shook her head and looked back at the lizardman. "We need your help. I wish I knew how to make you understand. We need your help, Meoraq."

He looked at her, unmoving and unmoved. Then he leaned back slightly and muttered to himself for some time, frowning and rubbing at the side of his snout. At last, he stood up and shrugged out of his backpack.

"What's he doing?" Scott asked.

The lizardman unrolled a huge bundle of leathery something to lay on the ground, but it was not until he also began to assemble some short threaded lengths of metal rods into flexible poles that Amber had an answer.

"He's...putting up a tent," she said, a little dumbfounded that aliens even had something as banal as a tent.

"Why is that thing putting up a tent in the middle of my camp?"

His lieutenants exchanged glances.

"To sleep in," said Amber. "Just a guess, but—"

"I said I'd think about it! I never gave you permission to let that thing stay!"

Amber watched the lizardman hammer his poles into place and raise the tent up. It was bigger than Scott's, and a part of her could not help but wonder if that was the man's biggest objection to it. "He's not asking for permission."

"He'd better," said Scott, marching himself over. "This is my camp and if—"

The lizard turned around and extended his arm with a sword magically at the end of it, so suddenly that Scott almost walked right into the point.

"Amber," said Eric quietly, after it became obvious that Scott had rooted himself to the spot and the lizardman's arm wasn't going to get tired anytime soon.

"Jesus, you people. What do you want me to say to him? Meoraq!"

"Meoraq," the lizardman said without looking at her. He said something else too, and then said, "Meoraq," again.

"Please stop poking swords at Scott! Being a dick is not a capital offense where we're from. See? He doesn't—"

The lizardman sheathed his sword and went back to assembling his tent.

Scott swung around and glared at her. "You call me that again, you dumb bitch, and I'll kick your fat ass for you! See if I don't!"

"Calm down," said Eric before Amber could say anything. "You're being kind of...aggressive."

Scott looked at him, then past him to the lizardman, who was still making himself at home. His jaw ticced. After several cooling minutes of silent thought, he looked back at Amber. "You really think you can teach it to talk?"

"He already talks. It's just a matter of teaching him English."

"Fine." He gave his jacket a few curt tugs and ran a hand through his hair. "Then do it. But the rest of you—" He swung to face the watching crowd of Manifestors and they obediently shuffled back a few steps. "—keep a prudent distance. Until the full ramifications of Miss Bierce's decision are known, I'd just as soon not risk any more lives."

They obeyed, huddling up at the far end of camp to watch the lizardman, and Amber, with equal parts awe and suspicion.

"Make sure they stay back," Scott told the Fleetmen. He glanced once at Meoraq, who gave the front of his tent a last adjustment and then went inside it with his backpack. "And keep an eye on that thing. I want someone watching it at all times."

Dag snorted. "What the hell are we supposed to do if—"

"We'll figure something out," Eric interrupted, giving Scott a nod. "Come on. Let's...Let's get all the tents moved back."

Amber watched as the Fleetmen left, knowing that a few more choice words were coming and that now that the witnesses were all gone, no one would ever believe he'd started it, so no matter what happened next, she'd have to shut up and take it. "We got something more to talk about?" she asked, as calmly as she could.

Scott waited until they were good and alone before he bothered to turn around and look at her. "Just this. I'm letting this happen because I can see the slimmest chance of it working and I know there's some benefit to having one of the natives as a member of this colony."

That word again. Amber rolled her eyes.

"You're making it happen," Scott continued, "because you're a stupid bitch who's trying to make trouble for me. But okay. Fine. Have it your way. If you can actually teach it to talk and we can get it working for us, I may even re-evaluate your position here, but I'm warning you right now, Bierce, the first thing you'd better teach it is some goddamn respect for authority, because if I don't start seeing it from it and you, I'll bounce you both right out of here. Dare me if you don't think I can do it."

Amber clenched her jaws shut and said nothing.

Scott nodded once and stepped back. "I'll let you get on with it then. This debriefing is over."

She watched him walk away. Then she went across the camp—her jaws hurt, but she couldn't seem to unclench them—to find her duffel bag. No one said anything to her, not even Nicci, although she could feel stares on every side of her and hear their whispers under the wind. She got her things and her spear and came stalking back to throw them down next to the lizardman's tent.

The lizardman lifted the flap and looked at her.

"Repeat after me," she said tightly. "Scott is a dick-headed motherfucker."

The lizardman grunted, now looking at all the other people looking back at him. He let the flap drop.

Amber clapped a hand to her face and rubbed until her wind-chapped skin had warmed some and her aching muscles began to relax. Then she said, "Meoraq."

The rustling noises inside the tent paused. After a long moment, the flap lifted again. He looked at her, the double-row of spines on his head and neck twitching first higher, then flatter.

She didn't know what to say to him. He couldn't understand anything anyway. Amber stared at him, feeling hot and angry and cold and useless all at the same time. At last, she reached out and patted the ground in front of her. "Please."

He looked at the ground, then at her. He frowned.

She patted it again, trying to smile, although the effort felt ghastly and she couldn't imagine it looked very convincing.

He dropped the flap. Amber's shoulders sagged in defeat, but almost in the same instant, the tent opened and Meoraq came out. Ignoring her, he cleared a small area, gathered up enough rocks to form a ring, piled up some deadwood, and took a burning stick from one of the other fires to start his own, close to his tent and to her. When it was going strong, he broke down some fairly long branches and lashed them into a tripod-shape, then set this close to the fire and hung a smallish leather pouch from it. He filled it with water he poured from a huge leather flask almost as long as Amber's arm, then ducked back into his tent, emerging with a few round, polished stones which he placed in the hottest part of the fire. Back he went into the tent, this time for his swords, which he stabbed into the ground after deliberately pacing off six long strides, kicking two stray duffel bags and a pair of boots ahead of him. When he came back, Amber was on her feet with her bag and her spear, ready to move on, but he plucked them both out of her hands and set them down again more or less where she'd already had them. Then he finally sat down.

Looking at her, he knocked on the ground in front of him like it was a door.

Amber stood there.

The lizard knocked again, this time with a few words and a flick of his spines.

She sat down where he wanted her.

He grunted and looked away, watching all the people who were watching them. He muttered under his breath, glanced skyward, scratched his throat. If he had a reason for calling her over, he was in no hurry to tell her what it was.

"Meoraq," said Amber.

He grunted, still without looking at her. Scott was at the head of the crowd now, just beyond the invisible boundary marked by the lizardman's swords, listening to the complaints of the people who'd had their bags kicked.

"Meoraq," said Amber again, reaching for his arm.

He caught her before she could touch him, but he looked at her.

Now what?

"Hand," said Amber, feeling stupid and a little desperate. She pointed at her own, caught in his unbelievably strong, scaly grip. "Fingers." She wiggled them.

Meoraq released her, frowning, and watched as she brought her arm up between them.

"Fingers. Look! One, two, three, four, five. Hand," she said, now pointing at her other one. "And fingers. One, two, three, four, five."

He said nothing.

"Head," said Amber, pointing at herself. "Hair. Ear, see it? And this one. Ear. Two ears. Eyes. One, two. Two eyes. Nose. One nose. Mouth. All of it together? This is my *face*. My *face* is the front of my *head*. It...Damn it, will you *say* something?"

He did not, but after a long, frustrating silence, he slowly raised his hand.

"Hand," said Amber, rubbing her eyes.

He splayed it.

She straightened up a little. "Fingers."

He made a fist and brought them up one at a time, listening as she counted them off. He began to point—at the fire, his tent, the trees, the grass, the sky—stopping only once, when one of the Manifestors broke the boundary-line of his camp. Other than that warning hiss, he never made a sound. He made no attempt to repeat the words she said for him.

But this was progress. This could work. She would make it work.

Amber talked, breaking things down into smaller and smaller words, talking until her throat went dry. Meoraq watched, listened, and was silent.

7

The longer he listened, the more certain Meoraq became that the strange chatter of the creatures who called themselves humans was indeed a true language, entirely separate from his own. This troubled him. The Prophet's Word is the only Word. This was the first law of Sheul, repeated no less than twenty-three times throughout the book of His Word, and apart from the obvious, it had been interpreted to mean that there must be a single language so that all men might hear and understand the wisdoms of Sheul. Where once there had been countless tongues spoken over Gann, there was now only one: Dumaqi, the speech of men.

So. That the humans neither spoke nor even seemed to understand dumaqi was therefore an ominous sign of their true nature, but Meoraq had to admit that he had not emerged from his mother's womb speaking it either. He would have to meditate on the matter. In the meantime, this left him struggling to make sense of a creature who thought all she had to do to talk was move her mouthparts around. And really, what else could they do? A human's flat face had no snout, which meant no resonance chamber, and Sheul alone knew how hard it must be to make those wriggly little mouthparts shape the sounds those deformed tongues could not. Given their limitations, their absurdly simplistic language was no more than sounds strung together, entirely lacking the subtle nuance and precision of dumaqi. By the end of that first day, Meoraq was already beginning to glean some understanding from the creatures' jabber. Not much. A word here. A sound there. A name.

Amber. Her name was Amber.

She sat with him throughout the grey hours of the day when all the other creatures came, stared awhile, then left again. Her hands moved as she spoke, gesturing here or there to add emphasis to her simple sounds, often returning to indicate just her, just him. Her gaze remained disturbingly direct; her eyes were so damned green.

When darkness fell, they lit more fires—heaps of wood that gave out more smoke than heat—and sat around them to mutter and stare. They had no meat after their one failed hunt, but the one called Scott eventually brought out a satchel of something in small, wrapped portions for his people to eat. Meoraq was himself overlooked, but as the stuff appeared quite disgusting, he was happy to make do with cuuvash. And since Amber was sitting with him and had not been offered anything, he snapped her off a square too.

She took it. Not immediately and not without a glance back at her people, but she took it. And after watching him bite into his, she gnawed off a piece of hers and sat, frowning with her entire malleable face, chewing it like cattle.

Scott came back over, also frowning. He spoke at some short length, gesturing. Amber answered. Scott spoke again, louder. Amber took another bite of cuuvash and appeared to ignore him. Scott aimed his next roll of gibberish at Meoraq. Now Amber said something, but Meoraq pointed two fingers at her and she quieted. "No one speaks for a Sheulek," he told her. To Scott, he said, "Go away," making shooing sweeps of his arm so that his meaning could not be misinterpreted.

Scott talked, not louder but much, much longer, before finally pointing aggressively at Meoraq's cuuvash.

"Get your own," said Meoraq, contentedly grinding his cuuvash against the roof of his mouth until it was soft enough to swallow.

Scott waited, moving his angry eyes back and forth between him and Amber, but eventually walked away. Meoraq watched him at the largest fire, speaking tirelessly and looking like nothing so much as a city governor holding court. He could see that Amber was listening, although she did not watch, and she did not appear easy with what she heard. She looked at the remaining portion of cuuvash in her hand and, after only one small bite, tried to give it back to him.

Meoraq turned his head to watch the clouds roll over the moon and pretended not to see. Eventually, she put the cuuvash in a fold of her clothes and he looked at her again. That freakish little nub of a nose. Those fat, purplish folds around her mouth. The rounded shells of her ears.

And her eyes. The living green fire of her eyes.

"No one man can ever comprehend all the wonders of Sheul's making," he said, speaking to himself more than to her. "So it says in the Word and I always thought that I believed it. But how could I believe it when I never truly understood until now how much further the wonders of His making could surpass a man's comprehension?"

"Mee'orakk," she replied and reached to touch his chest.

This time, he allowed it, frowning down at her hand where it pressed on his bare flesh. "No man could have imagined a hand like that," he mused. "Five fingers and those round, flat, useless little claws. Scaleless. Hairless. Soft. And yet what have you done with that hand but touch a Sheulek?"

"Amber." She patted herself just above the twinned swellings of her chest.

"I hear you," he said, studying them. "Are those really teats or do I just think so because I suspect you to be female and am looking for proof? If they are teats, where is the baby? It would have to be a suckling to swell you so. Or babies, I suppose; you have two teats, you must bear two babies."

Amber said her name. Meoraq replied with his. He watched her slap her hands to her face and hide behind them, rubbing just as though she had brow-ridges to rub.

That was kind of cute.

"I have to pray," Meoraq told her, told them both, really. He retreated to his tent to do it and meditated there for some time, fruitlessly, before commending himself to his Father's divine hands, here in the camp of these creatures, and lying down upon his mat to sleep. He did not undress. He kept his kzung drawn beside him. He feared no creature-assassins but was ready for them. He breathed the way he had been taught, counting six steps over and over, and stopping to listen each time the creatures approached his tent.

As he waited for Sheul's peace to overtake his restless mind, he found himself wondering what the young of these creatures might look like. He could almost imagine them—twin monsters in miniature—small hands and greedy mouths at work at the fullness of their mother's teats (Amber's, for no other reason than that she was the human he'd been sitting with all day), perhaps one at each.

Outside, the wind gusted, moaning like a woman lost to fire. Scott's voice briefly overtook it and Amber answered, her tone as fearless as her hand had been upon his body. Meoraq listened, smiling, then rolled onto his side and closed his eyes to sleep.

* * *

He dreamt.

Dreams, by their very nature, frequently touched at strangeness and he was not a man who attached much importance to them, even when he recalled them upon waking, which was not often. But this...

When he became aware of it (he could not say 'at its beginning' for, like so many dreams, it seemed to have much more history than he could recall upon waking), he found himself seated in the lessons room at the training hall in Tilev. Many others were with him, paying rapt attention to Master Tsazr at the head of the hall, who was going on in his terse, impatient way about something. None of this yet seemed odd. It had been twelve years and some since his ascension, but Meoraq still dreamed of his training days upon occasion. At least he was wearing clothes in this one.

But when he turned his head, he saw that half the students around him were humans. Amber sat at his side, a lessons slate in her lap and a stylus in her five-fingered hand, scratching out notes in alien markings. At his other side sat a dumaq, a stranger, wearing the garments of an exarch with the hood pulled so low over his face that Meoraq could see nothing but his painted snout. His was rather a plain robe, sparsely trimmed and not entirely clean, nothing at all like the fine dress of Exarch Ylsathoc.

Without looking at him, this stranger said, "What is it you seek in Xi'Matezh?"

Wasn't that just like an exarch, to involve himself in someone else's personal business?

But Meoraq found himself answering, and answering with both honesty and respect: "I seek communion with Sheul."

"A man need not travel to the end of the world to seek what can be found upon his knees in his own courtyard. Your House is empty," the hooded figure said before Meoraq could reply, not that any reply came to his dreaming mind. "Should not a son see to the continuance of his physical father's honor rather than undergoing lengthy journeys in his spiritual Father's name?"

Meoraq rarely felt emotion in dreams, but shame stung at him now. Shame, oddly, and not annoyance at the presumption of this stranger. "I never said that I would not take stewardship of Uyane!"

"You certainly seem eager to postpone it."

"No!"

"No? Then why—" The exarch's head cocked, still revealing nothing but paint and shadow and now the pinpoint gleam of one eye. "—do you seek Xi'Matezh? What would you ask of Sheul that requires so arduous a journey?"

And rather than tell this man his prayers were for Sheul alone, Meoraq said, "If it is Sheul's will that I am retired to Uyane, so I will serve Him."

The exarch dipped his head once, acknowledging, expectant.

"But I do not wish to spend all the years of my remaining life bound to stewardship if it is not His will!"

"Is the House so hateful?"

"The House?" Meoraq looked over his shoulder where, as only seemed right and natural, the lessons room had opened into the rooftop courtyard at the fore of House Uyane. He could see the stone couch his father favored beneath the drooping branches of a ribbonleaf tree, and the wide steps where he himself used to sit when he was at lessons (or when he was hoping to steal a glance at the servant girl who scrubbed the courtyard tiles). "No," he said now, puzzled. "It is my father's House and has all my love."

"Not all, it would seem, if you would travel to the end of the very world to escape it."

"It is not the House I wish to escape."

"No?"

Meoraq looked again, but now the courtyard had become his father's innermost chamber, as seen through the eyes of the young boy he had been on the only occasion he had seen it. And just why he had gone to such a forbidden room, he could not recall, but he could perfectly remember how it had been: the light of lamps behind the screen casting shadows on every wall, the scent of some flowery incense heavy in the air, and the cupboard of his father's bed standing open so that he could see the broad, scarred field of his father's back as it bunched and heaved and arched.

Meoraq averted his eyes fast, but the sounds persisted. His father's deep, steady breaths. His mother's feeble, mewling cries. The stealthy rasp of scales moving together. The wet pull and suck of sex in its second round.

The stranger was watching, his long hands steepled beneath his chin. "This embarrassed you."

Meoraq did not reply and did not look again.

"Is it not a lord's responsibility to preserve his bloodline? To sire sons of his loyal woman?"

His loyal woman. Meoraq's jaws clenched.

"Surely you do not question Yecedi's loyalty?"

"I am sure she was ever faithful to my father," Meoraq said curtly. And he was. Yecedi had passed directly from her father's own House to Rasozul's and did not leave it until the day she died.

"She was a good woman."

"I suppose so." Meoraq shrugged his spines, wishing the sounds of sex would stop or at least that his mother's urgent moaning would. "She was a perfect high-born wife, obedient and invisible and able to produce three strong sons upon command."

The exarch looked at him. "Do you think your father gave it as his command?"

The sounds died away suddenly, swallowed up by the lessons room wall. Meoraq glanced that way, saw dark stone and students, and shrugged again.

"Of course, when you bore that night your reluctant witness, your father had already done his siring," the exarch mused. "What embarrasses you most, I wonder? That you saw your father in Sheul's fires, or that you saw him with your pregnant mother instead of some pretty young servant?"

"My father had no business taking her to his bed!" Meoraq burst out.

"Is it not the duty of a loyal woman to answer all her man's desires?" said the exarch with the faintest hint of sarcasm.

"No, it is the duty of a loyal woman to sit in her damned room and grow her son! What was she even doing in that part of the house that he saw her?"

"Perhaps she was invited," the exarch murmured, steepling his fingers again.

"He could not have passed fewer than three other women if he went to fetch her out. Any one of whom would have been honored to receive his fires!"

"Do you think so?"

"But, no! He had to have gone all the way to her room and back and for what? Sheul does not give a man sexual urges so that he can spend them with a woman already carrying his child!"

"The bond between man and woman is sacred even in the eye of Sheul. Nothing they took as their pleasure together offended Him."

Meoraq snorted.

"When you take up the stewardship of House Uyane, will you not want a woman such as Yecedi?"

Meoraq tried to snort again but it came out as a hiss. He rubbed at his snout, then his brow-ridges, and finally his throat, where he could feel anger throbbing.

"A good woman. A loyal woman."

A mewling little breed-pot, forever shackled to Meoraq's wrist. He would have to live with her each and every day, unless he were away defending his House or his city's honor, and he would not be permitted to send her out until after he had at least two grown sons to guarantee his continuance. Or unless she were barren, in which case he would have to replace her immediately with an entirely new mewling little breed-pot.

"Is it so impossible to imagine you could be happy with a woman?"

"I am frequently happy with women," Meoraq snapped.

"With one woman."

He rubbed his brow-ridges. "If that is Sheul's will."

"And so you travel to Xi'Matezh."

"Yes."

"To pray for Sheul's guidance."

"Yes."

"That He may lead you to a good woman to take into your House."

Meoraq hissed again and shook his head. "Yes."

"Perhaps you could find one here."

"Here?" Meoraq looked around the lessons room, at dumaqs and humans side at side, all the way to Master Tsazr, indiscriminately lecturing all. "There are no women allowed in the training halls!"

It was a dream, and his voice, which had gone unnoticed all this time, suddenly rang out like tribunal bells. Every head turned.

"Uyane!"

He snapped to his feet at once, dream or no dream, and Master Tsazr came swiftly forward to slap him deservedly across his snout. It did not hurt in the dream, but it still staggered him some. Master Tsazr had a wicked hand.

"No women in the training halls, eh? Have you come to work your mind?" Tsazr inquired caustically. "Or your clay?"

"My mind, sir."

"I have my doubts. Amber." The human name fell perfectly from Tsazr's mouth.

"Yes, sir." The dumaqi words came perfectly from Amber's.

"What is the day's lesson? Remind Uyane."

"We speak of the Ancients, sir."

"Tell Uyane your lesson."

Amber turned her soft, flat face toward him. The bad light of the lessons room made her pale skin seem wholly white, her dun-colored hair seem grey as ashes, and her nondescript training garments as black as the Abyss, but her eyes were still green as new leaves and deep as wells. She said, "Our numbers swelled until our cities covered all the earth. When we had no more land to cover, we built our cities on top of themselves and milled in them all together, like yifu. We took the holy gifts of medicine and science and used them in frivolous and dangerous ways. We made machines to give us comfort and used them until we poisoned all our earth and water and air. We made trade of sex and suffering and war. We mocked Sheul and we corrupted Gann."

"The Ancients corrupted Gann," agreed Master Tsazr, striding along the rows of silent students and pausing often to run a speculative (and largely dismissive) eye over each face. "And Gann in turn corrupted them. The Ancients turned from Sheul, devastating the land to fuel their wickedness and making constant war upon themselves until at last Sheul rose up and smote them with His judgment. Uyane!"

"Yes, sir!"

"Name the three acts of the Fall of the Ancients."

Thank Sheul in His heaven for an easy question. "The first act was the punishment of wrath, when every man was consumed by rage and war enveloped all of Gann."

"For how long?"

Meoraq stared for a moment, utterly thrown. Back came Master Tsazr's hand, but it could not knock answers into him when there were none.

"Amber," said Tsazr, turning around. "How long did the act of wrath last?"

"It is still among us," she replied, which was the most nonsensical thing she could have said here, in Sheul's world of peace.

But Master Tsazr grunted approvingly and walked away. "Speak on, Uyane. What was the second act?"

"The curse of blight," he said at once, "when the land failed and the skies were filled with storms. The cities of the Ancients fell and famine and disease preyed upon the landless people."

"For how long?" asked Tsazr, casting a cold eye back at Meoraq.

He looked at Amber, but she was bent over her slate, making human letters. In another moment, Meoraq was reeling from the dream-like painlessness of Master Tsazr's blow. Amber's voice drifted up from his side, the dumaqi words made haunting in her human mouth: "It is still among us."

"Uyane."

Meoraq straightened up and put his arms to his side, only to find that Master Tsazr had somehow been replaced by the strange exarch with the low hood.

"What was the third act of the Fall of the Ancients?" this figure asked in Tsazr's voice.

He knew this one, thankfully. "It was the return of Sheul and the hope of His forgiveness. And it is still among us," he added, anticipating the next question.

The stranger did not reply, but the silence that swept the lessons room proved more disconcerting than his hooded stare. Meoraq looked away and saw the prairie all around him; he looked back and there was Amber before him and they were sitting, face to face, in the dark of the humans' camp.

"We built a ship," said Amber. She raised her hand to make a wedged shape and passed it between them. "And it flew through the sky, beyond the clouds that covered our world, into the lights that shine forever." Her arm arced up, graceful as the neck of a thuoch. Her eyes never left his and they were green, so green. "But the ship was hurt and it fell here, out of the storm. It broke open over Gann. It died and many died with it." Her hand fell to earth and opened, her fingers flaring out and curling slowly back toward her palm. Her second hand lit upon this imagined carnage, made walking fingers, and stepped out onto the grass. "But some of us survived and now we're here. We're here and there's no way home." She looked back over her shoulder and let out a shaky breath, then turned back and caught his hand in both of hers. Her hands were soft and warm; her eyes were terrible in their beauty. "I need you."

Something in him shivered right down to the core of his soul. He tried to say her name, but the magic of the dream ended, it seemed, with his mouth. "Mmbr," he said, just as he always had, and shook his head with disgust. His next attempt was nothing but a hiss and a choke of meaningless sound.

"Please, Meoraq," she said. "I need your help. And you need mine."

He did not remember getting up, but they were standing suddenly, the two of them together before a dark structure he somehow knew was Xi'Matezh. They were standing, yes, and his arms were going around her just as if that were not a perfectly appalling thing to do. He could feel her heat against his body and her horrible face was right before him and her name, ah, her name was like wine in his mouth. "Mmbr," he said, bending close. "Mm—"

* * *

"...mbr," he mumbled, and the sound of his own voice jolted him awake.

Meoraq opened his eyes and was, for one disorienting moment, shocked to see that Amber's own were not before him. He found his lamp and lit it, but saw only the interior of his shelter.

What did he expect? Meoraq clapped a hand to his head and rubbed roughly at his scales, then rolled over and sat up. His cock was out, he noticed, pinched between his belly and his loin-plate and still dully throbbing with Gann's lusts. He retracted it with great distaste and pressed a hand over his slit to hold it in while he tightened his belt, meditating on the dream. Already, it was so tangled in his mind that he could not say what the message had been.

Dreams. Only fools and priests believed they had messages.

He put on his breeches and opened his tent.

The creatures slept in heaps all around him, cocooned in more of those silvery bedsheets. They looked like fat, metal maggots. A deeply disturbing sight.

And there was Amber.

He could see the twin lump of herself and the other human that clung at her, together in the grass at the very edge of his camp. At the edge of Scott's camp as well, far from any fire. The sight of her sleeping in the open air like an animal did something unpleasant to his emotions and gave him back disturbing fragments of his dream...particularly there at the end, when he'd been holding her.

Dream-nonsense, he told himself brutally. If he hadn't awakened when he had, he probably would have bitten her or something.

The image his mind sent out at that thought was not that of a monstrous dumaq devouring Amber neck-first, however, but of a mark of conquest upon her naked shoulder. His cock, safely constrained behind his loin-plate, throbbed with Gann's senseless need.

Meoraq shuddered, started to retreat within his tent, and then rose resolutely and tromped over to where Amber lay. She roused at the noise, pushing back her damp cover and squinting up at him through sleep-dazed eyes. "Get up," he said, and beckoned, knowing she would not understand him. "To your feet, soft-skinned creature."

More humans stirred. "Wzzee wnt?" someone called, and Amber answered, "Elleff'ai'no," in a puzzled fashion, but she got up.

"I dreamed of you." Meoraq led her to his firepit and pushed on her shoulder until she sat. He crouched to knuckle through the ash until he found a bit of branch only half-burnt, then woke the embers to a flame bright enough to see by. "And while dreams are largely foolish things, Sheul often hides some shard of insight there. So do I recall one thing I think to be His wisdom. Take this."

She let him thrust the charred branch into her hands. She frowned at it, and then her brows raised and she gave him a startled sort of look. She dropped to her knees at once before him, intent and eager as she patted her hand across the ash to flatten it.

And she began to draw. Not the strange markings she had made across her lessons slate in his dream, but an image of some rounded shape (*we built a ship*), amplified by sweeping motions of her arm, which she made fall by drawing a line just beneath it (*it broke open over Gann*). She started drawing line-men to spill out of it, chattering explanations, and Meoraq leaned back on his heels to listen. He did not try to mimic her words, but he did interrupt now and then with questions of his own, raised with gestures and drawings in the ash.

The story he was able to glean through this crude communication was a confusing one. She seemed to be trying to tell him that the creatures he saw before him now were all there were, not just here, but in all of Gann. He tried many times to get her to tell him where the ship had sailed from and how they had come inland so far without being seen, but kept getting the same baffling response: The ship did not move on water, but through the sky. She seemed to want him to believe they had not come from Gann at all, but from some other world. She illustrated this by drawing two circles in the ash and the rounded shape of the ship between them, sketching the line of their travel over and over and jabbing at the sky above them with her stick.

She must think he was an idiot. That a ship had sailed, Meoraq did not doubt, and perhaps it had even come across the sky if it were some relic from the time of the

Ancients or a machine made after that fashion. That it had come to some disaster seemed equally plausible. That they were all there were in the world, as helpless as newborns and meaning no harm to anyone, was patently absurd.

And yet...

And yet, there was Amber, grimacing at him happily as she told her tale. He liked to think that his years in service to Sheul had given him some power to see lies when they were told to his face, and even though hers was a strange one, it could still be read. When he gazed on Amber, when he looked past the cold and hunger and other hardships of travel in the wildlands, he saw no evil. He saw sorrow and he saw loss. He saw anger sometimes and sometimes guilt. He saw strength and determination and so much tenacity that he often questioned his odd certainty that she was female, but he had never seen deceit in her. Not when she looked at him. Not when she looked at anyone. There were things she did not say, perhaps, but what she said was honest.

We built a ship...and it flew through the sky...

Meoraq took the stick from her hands and swept the ash flat. He looked at her, frowned, then looked past her to the other creatures, all of whom had gathered by now and were watching him with unreadable emotion across their grotesque faces. He thought of the dream, but it was a glancing tap at best; dreams were of no value in the waking world. He was not easy about what he was about to propose, but he felt Sheul's hand upon his shoulder and, although His ultimate plan was not clear, His immediate will seemed obvious.

Meoraq sketched out a few creatures—round heads atop line-bodies; he was not a great artist—and then, not without a moment's misgiving, drew himself among them. He tapped the image, saying, "Sheul has put you in my path for a reason. I will stay until I know what it is."

"Wutz'i sa'en?" Scott asked.

"Do'ispeeklzzrd?" Amber replied, tossing the words crossly over her shoulder before reaching out to try and take the stick from Meoraq.

He wasn't done with it. He took her wrist with a stern look and moved her hand back to her knee. He captured his drawings within a circle, making it clear they were bound together, and then leaned out to sketch the shrine at Xi'Matezh. He'd never seen it, but he'd seen enough of them to know they all pretty much looked alike: a round, walled courtyard and tall, central tower. "But I see no reason to interrupt my journey," he went on, tapping first the ash-creatures and then the ash-shrine. "So we will go together."

"Wutztht?"

"Stldntno, Scott. Stldntspeeklzzrd." Amber leaned forward, reaching across him to point at the ash-shrine. "Wutzthz Mee'orrak?"

"Meoraq," he corrected, and then shook that away irritably. She was never going to say his name properly and it didn't matter at the moment. He touched the ash-shrine and said, "This is Xi'Matezh, the holiest shrine remaining from the age of the Ancients. We will go there—" He emphasized this with several lines between ash-creatures and ash-shrine. "—and I will ask Sheul what is to be done with you."

"Ithnkeewntz t'tak'uzther." Frowning, Amber patted her chest with one hand, gesturing at the other creatures as she did so, then pointed at Meoraq and made wiggling, walking movements with her fingers. "Wergo'in t'gthr? Yutu?"

"We all go together," he told her, pointing at his drawings. "If His will is not made known to me upon the journey, Sheul shall surely tell me what to do in Xi'Matezh when I stand before Him."

"Wut izthtpls?" Scott asked.

Amber threw up her hands, slapped her thighs, and swung around. "Frfkz'sk Scott i'dntno! I'dntspeek fkknlzzrd!"

Meoraq hissed at the creatures to silence them, then poked Amber irritably with his stick to take back her attention. When he had it, he swiftly made some sketched animals to fill the empty space between the ash-creatures and the ash-shrine. "The journey is long and dangerous. The prairie is filled with wild beasts and godless men and we are very near to winter. I will protect you—" Ash-Meoraq received a few ash-knives and the very badly-drawn ash-tachuqi nearest him was rubbed out. "—at least until I know whether or not I am meant to kill you. That you are to be a test of my faith is clear to me," he mused, once more gazing into Amber's unsettling eyes. "But I am Sheulek and my faith is as enduring as the wind. I shall not fail my Father."

Amber's pliant little brow-ridges drew together as she listened. Her eyes were green and she had felt warm and soft and disturbingly real in his dream when he held her.

"But if it is His will that I stand with you," Meoraq said, now speaking just to Amber, "I shall not fail you either."

"Wutz'i sa'en?" Scott wanted to know.

This time, Amber answered without taking her eyes from Meoraq's. Her mouthparts curved upwards. She said, softly, "Eezcm'mn wthuz. Eezgnna hlpuz."

And she held out her empty hand, just held it out, open in the air. After a moment, Meoraq put down his stick and held his out the same way. She huffed and moved to take his hand in hers. Joined.

Behind his loin-plate, some hot urge of Gann flared and throbbed. Meoraq willed it back. He released Amber and stood up. "Enjoy these last hours," he told her. "When the sun rises, you and all your kind belong to me."

"Meeor'ak," she said.

"Just so," he agreed, and gave her a tap on the top of her freakish, furry head.

8

And just like that, the lizardman apparently considered the matter settled. He rose from the fire, said a few words while pointing sternly at the tents, and then walked away into the tall grass without looking back.

"Grab it!" Scott shouted, backing out of Meoraq's path.

No one moved.

Meoraq kept walking and was soon swallowed up by darkness.

"You let it get away," said Scott, and for a change, the accusation wasn't aimed at Amber.

"We're not set up to take prisoners," Eric told him. He pointed back at the lizardman's teepee. "He'll be back. He left his stuff."

There just wasn't a whole lot to do at that point. Scott hustled the Fleetmen into his tent for an emergency debriefing (all but Mr. Yao, who went back to his bivy in spite of Scott's threats to consider that insubordinate behavior). Everyone else drew off at first to sit and talk in low worried voices about if and how this changed things, but it was early and not entirely dry, and one by one, people drifted back to bed. Amber sat up until the fire died and even dared to interrupt the debriefing to ask for a flashlight, but Scott said no and it was just too dark to move around without one. She paced around the edge of camp for a while, banging into crates and tripping over bags of concrete while she strained her eyes trying to see shapes in the black. There was nothing, only the endless wind and a few icy pellets of rain, so in the end even she gave up.

Nicci was already sleeping soundly. Amber pulled out her blanket and wrapped up to stay dry. She lay down, but only to huddle close to her sister and share as much warmth as she could. She was way too wired to sleep now, couldn't even if she'd wanted to. She was only keeping Nicci warm while she waited for the lizardman to come back.

The next thing she heard was a heavy, squishy, thumping sound, like someone falling over in the mud close by. Amber pushed her blanket back and dragged her head up into the light of late morning.

"I fell asleep," she croaked and dropped back to the ground, slapping both hands to her face.

A low grunt answered her. The lizardman walked around the scaly deer he had just deposited on the ground in front of her and hunkered down to investigate his firepit. His little leather stewing pouch was slung over one shoulder like a ladies purse, bulging and heavy-looking, which had to have some connection to the dead deer, which was slit wide open and was all shiny and pink and empty inside.

'Gross,' thought Amber sleepily, trying to rub her face awake. Then she thought, 'Food,' but that wasn't quite right, was it? No, it was *Meoraq's* food and that was a very different thing.

She looked back into Scott's side of the camp and saw dozens of people watching, looking like nothing so much as a horde of hungry prairie dogs, motionless and staring. At their center, Scott slowly stood up, towering over the rest of them for a few seconds before Eric and Dag popped up too.

She started to say something to Meoraq—just what, she didn't know, especially since he wouldn't understand it anyway—but then saw that he was making a fire. Amber sat all the way up, trying to pay attention to how he did it, but there wasn't time. He just cleared the ground, laid out some branches and a few bundles of grass, put something from his pack up next to the kindling and then there was fire.

"Nicci, look at this," said Amber, reaching out to pat her sister's hip. "Look what he's doing."

Nicci rolled away from her. "Is he building a starship?" she mumbled.

"No, but—"

"Then I don't care. Leave me alone. I'm sleeping."

"Oh come on!" There was now a roaring fire where nothing but ash and mud had been less than a minute ago. Amber found Nicci through the crinkly blanket and shook her. "Look at this!"

Nicci heaved a sigh and raised her head just as the lizardman pulled the long sword off his belt and hacked the head off the deer. It rolled over, tongue lolling and sightless eyes staring. Meoraq picked it up and set it over the fire, carefully balanced on rocks to keep it out of the forming coals. The deer's scaly lips shrank back, steaming, into a dead, idiot leer.

Nicci looked at this, then at Amber, open-mouthed.

"That's not what I wanted you to see," Amber said.

Meoraq grabbed both sides of the dead deer's ribs and broke them well apart, forming a meaty platter where he upended his stewing pouch. Lots of shiny organs came tumbling out—heart, liver, kidneys...other things—along with a small splash of blood.

Amber slapped her hands over her face again.

"Thanks so much for sharing that!" Nicci punched her blanket into her duffel bag and stormed off through the mud to the other fire, where just about everyone else was already up and sitting together. They let her in, listened to whatever she had to say to accompany those angry arm gestures. A few of them looked at Amber.

Damn it.

Meoraq watched Nicci go without obvious interest as he cut up his assortment of organs and impaled them on sticks. He put these gut-kabobs over the fire, licked his fingers, then started cutting the deer out of its scaly hide.

"Looks like it's going to be another great day," she muttered, taking Nicci's blanket back out and rolling it up neater. "Thanks for coming back, Meoraq."

He covered his eyes with the back of his least bloody hand and muttered, "Meoraq," under his breath. His spines twitched up and down as he thought. Then he pointed the tip of his knife at the half-butchered animal and said something.

"Meat," she said. He hadn't needed any help to catch it, either. He hadn't even needed a spear. "And I, on the other hand," sighed Amber, turning back to watch Nicci at the other fire," never tried so hard to do something in my whole life as I tried to run that goddamn limping thing down. Take a note, lizardman: That was the best I could do. Amber Bierce's very best was a miserable fucking failure."

He caught her by the chin and pinched, not hard enough to hurt (although it was impossible not to feel the tremendous strength in that grip), but enough to shut her up. He pointed his knife down at the dead thing. He spoke again, just one word.

Did he want her to repeat him? Amber tried. "Soo—"

He pinched harder. Spoke.

"Saw...ow. Ak. Saw-owk."

"Saoq," he corrected, but released her. With the tip of his finger, he quickly drew a deer-shape in the wet dirt. "Saoq," he said again, and stabbed his knife into its muddy heart. He said something else, pointed at the dead animal and said it again.

"What does that mean?" Amber asked. "Is it 'dead' or 'meat' or 'hunt' or—"

He caught her chin and pinched. He said his word.

"You know, I realize we're the aliens here, but Scott wants you to learn English, not for us to learn lizardish."

Pinch. He leaned close. He spoke once.

She repeated him, then crossly added, "Meat. *Meat.*"

He grunted, released her, and went back to butchering the animal...the saoq. He cut away a chunk of meat and held it up. He said a word.

"You should also know that I took Spanish from the second grade on up to the seventh and I flunked every single year."

Meoraq cocked his head. He reached for her chin.

She pulled back out of his reach and said the stupid word.

The corners of his hard mouth turned up. He grunted, pulled the meat off the blade of his knife and skewered it on a thin bit of branch instead. He propped that over the fire beside him and said a new word, pointing at it.

Cook? Fire? Whatever it was, she parroted it back obediently.

His mouth opened in a hissing grimace. He took one of the gut-kabobs off the fire and held it up, steaming and dripping juices down its skewer, still partly raw and a little black around the edges, but enough to flood Amber's mouth with eager water. He gestured at it, his spines flaring in what she could only hope was an encouraging manner.

She said the word she thought meant meat and then strung it all together into what she hoped was almost a real sentence: "Meoraq cook saoq meat."

He winced. Sighed. Put the kabob back over the fire and looked at her.

"If you don't like it, learn English. At least I'm making an effort here. Listen!" She reached out to pat the corpse. "Meat—oh yuck, it's still warm. Oh God, and sticky!" She started to wipe her hand off on her pants, then changed her mind and dragged it over the ground instead. She only had so many clothes. "Meat! Say it with me! Meat!"

He frowned at her, silent.

"Any progress, Miss Bierce?"

Meoraq's gaze shifted past her to watch Scott join them. His spines flattened. He bent over the saoq, ripping it out of the rest of its hide and muttering under his breath.

"What do you want?" Amber asked.

"Nothing. I'm just not comfortable leaving the heavily-armed alien unsupervised."

"I'm here."

"Also unsupervised."

Scott probably had more to say, but whatever scathing insult he was cooking up turned into a gagging cry as Meoraq shoved a skinless, disemboweled, dead deer against his chest. He tried to back away, but Meoraq only shoved harder, more or less forcing Scott to embrace the corpse.

"What does he want?" Scott demanded shrilly.

Meoraq spat out some suggestions, then looked at Amber and cocked his head.

She replayed his words and realized there were a few in there she knew. "He wants you to eat it."

Meoraq gave the corpse a last push and pointed firmly back at the other fire. He hissed through his teeth, his flat spines scraping at the top of his scaly head.

"And he wants us to leave him alone," Amber translated. She started to get up.

Meoraq's hand slammed down on her shoulder and seated her with a squishy thump back on the ground. He hissed at her next, exactly the same way. On his throat, faint lines of yellow color were coming into his scales. He pivoted at the hip and pointed at the other fire, spitting out lizard-words faster than she could follow. The message, however, was clear: Go back to your side of the camp and stay there.

Scott backed up, holding the carcass clumsily before him like a shield. "If that thing attacks me again, I'm holding you responsible," he warned.

"He's not attacking you, he's feeding you," said Amber, rubbing her shoulder.

"Am I responsible for that? Seriously, Meoraq, that hurt."

"Meoraq!" spat the lizardman, still glaring at Scott. But then he leaned back on his heels and cupped the end of his snout, taking deep breaths and muttering to himself, and when he looked at her again, the scales on his throat were all black once more. "Meoraq," he said, and gestured toward her, grudgingly inviting her own name.

"Meat," she said, using his word and rubbing her shoulder some more.

He flung up his hands, took one stomping step toward the fire and the gut-kabobs roasting there, then pulled himself up with a jerk and really stared at her.

"Yeah. Amber-meat. And if you make some joke about bacon—" she began, rounding on Scott, but he had taken advantage of Meoraq's distraction to retreat. She could see him at the other fire already, surrounded by worshipful Manifestors, rewarding their loyalty with someone else's food. And they loved him for it.

Something nudged her arm. Meoraq, impatiently trying to get her attention. He had another gut-kabob in his hand, this one a bit overcooked, and as soon as she was watching him, he plucked the chunk of liver off the top end of the skewer, said a word, and popped it into his mouth. He didn't chew, but she could see the underside of his jaw moving as he worked his rigid tongue back and forth against the roof of his mouth. He swallowed, said the word again, and pointed at her with two fingers.

Her stomach growled. She clapped a hand over it stupidly, but it was too late. Meoraq looked at it and then at her, frowning.

"Meat," she said in lizardish, stubbornly adding, "Meoraq's meat," just to let him know that she had no expectations.

His frown became a glare, so she knew she'd said it wrong, but he understood enough to pluck a second kabob off the coals and put it in her hand.

"You don't get it. I don't want you to take care of me," she told him, trying to push it back at him. "I want you to show me how to take care of myself. Okay? Because I can't be..." Her eyes wandered, seeking and finding the wisps of blonde hair flying above the crowd that could only be Nicci's. "I have to take care of myself," she said at last. "I have to take care of her."

Meoraq rolled his eyes and scratched at the side of his snout, scowling at her. He started to speak, and then suddenly leaned out and caught her by the chin again. The scaly pads of his fingers dug in and forced her to face him. Red eyes that could never even pretend to be human stared her down while he talked at her. The word for 'eat' was in there. He hissed at the end of it, just a little, like putting an extra-hard dot on an i, then let her go and pointed at her kabob.

She ate it. It was tough as hell and overchewing it brought out all the wrong elements of its flavor, which was vaguely like beef, but darker, earthier, almost bitter with minerals. She was all too aware of how she looked as she struggled with it—the fat chick stuffing her face—but the first bite turned into the last one embarrassingly fast. When she looked up, sucking grease from her empty fingers, Meoraq was still holding on to most of his, his head slightly canted, watching her. So was the saoq's head in the fire. Both of them with nearly the same expression.

"Thanks," mumbled Amber, rubbing her mouth.

Meoraq grunted back at her. He took a piece of what might be kidney off his skewer, then paused, his gaze shifting beyond her, and popped it into his own mouth.

She looked back, already knowing she was going to see Scott, and there he was, marching toward them. He wasn't alone. Since the saoq was cooking and staring at it couldn't help it roast faster, quite a few Manifestors were trickling over to Meoraq's small fire, hungrily eyeing his gut-kabobs, his roasting severed head, even the bloody heap of hide. The lizardman watched them circle without expression, but the hand that did not keep an easy hold on his saoq-kebob drifted down to the hilt of one of his swords.

"You might want to give him some space," Amber remarked.

Scott took a step back at once, then pinked and glanced behind him at the watching Manifestors. "I can't believe you say that thing isn't dangerous. It's a textbook example of a hostile alien predator. Textbook. Even if we could disarm it, he could still bite someone's hand off."

"He's not hostile and he doesn't bite."

Meoraq naturally chose that moment to take a huge bite of liver. His relatively few yet large and apparently very sharp teeth sheared through the tough meat so easily that they snapped audibly when his jaws met. He eyed Scott, contentedly eating in his lizardish way, and drew his hooked sword to tap against the toe of his boot.

"Really?" said Amber, looking at him.

His spines flicked.

"The only reason for anything to have a mouth like that is for biting," Scott announced in a knockout imitation of a man who knew what he was talking about.

"Olfaction," said Mr. Yao.

They all looked at him—Amber, Scott, and the lizard.

Mr. Yao rolled one shoulder in a shrug (Meoraq's spines swept forward; he rolled one of his shoulders too, just a little bit, as if testing its range of motion). "I'm not a doctor of medicine," he said. "I'm an evolutionary biologist."

A short silence followed this statement. Mr. Yao seemed to be expecting it.

"Okay," said Amber at last. "I have no idea what that means."

"It means that I have studied the way animals evolve. I was assigned to this mission to assess whatever forms of life we might have encountered on Plymouth. There was always a chance, you see, that it might be inhabited, even though the probes never detected any higher signs of intelligent life."

"Higher signs like what?" Amber asked as Scott said, "This is probably classified and you shouldn't be discussing it with civilians."

Mr. Yao chose to answer Amber. "Signs such as city lights, roadways, radio or satellite transmissions. Anything, in other words, that could be detected by a probe. They never found anything, but Plymouth was an Earth-class planet with a wide range of eco-systems. There were plants, it stood to reason there would be animals, and while they would surely be of some alien design, those designs must still serve some logical purpose, such as—" He glanced at Scott. "—the reason why certain animals have a snout-like mouth. Not to hold teeth, but to hold scent receptors."

"Okay, that's a great theory," Scott said dismissively, already waving one hand to try and cut Mr. Yao off. Meoraq's head tipped; his eyes tracked each movement of that hand. "But you can't possibly prove it. This is an alien."

"Nature follows necessity," said Mr. Yao. "Generally speaking, the more pronounced the nasal area is, the more advanced the animal's olfactory ability should be. Since our friend does not have many teeth, it can be assumed he uses that space for some other purpose, such as scent reception. In fact, if you look at him closely—"

They all did. Meoraq returned their stares without obvious concern, except that the sword he was playing with lifted ever so slightly.

"—you will see several pit-like pores around his mouth, separate from his nasal openings. Certain animals—particularly reptiles—have two distinct olfactory systems, one of them used mainly to detect pheromones. If I were to hypothesize further—"

"There's nothing to be gained by discussing any of this," Scott interrupted. "Regardless of *Mr.* Yao's ideas on alien physiology, just the fact that the lizard is armed to his extremely sharp teeth proves that it has the potential to be dangerous."

"He also has the potential to bring us food," Amber pointed out. "And I noticed you took it before you started all this bullshit about how dangerous he is. Look, if he'd wanted to sneak out and come back with an army of raging lizardmen, he could have done that. If he'd wanted to slit our throats in the night, he could have done that too. Instead, he brought us breakfast and you're bitching about it."

"Thankfully, it's not your job to concern yourself with the safety of others, Miss Bierce, because you appear to be as bad at that as you are at teaching English. I, on the other hand, can be objective about the benefits and detriments our native friend brings to the colony. So why don't I do my job and you can try to do yours and everybody will be much happier?"

"Fuck you, Scott."

Scott nodded as if this were exactly the answer he'd expected. If he'd reached out to pat her on the head as his smirking expression indicated he might, she might have lost it, but he didn't, so she didn't. He walked away, taking his Manifestors with him and instructing these to gather wood and those to build more fires so they could all see how commanding he was.

Amber watched them go, confused and pissed off and mostly tired and cold and still hungry. She had always been very good at dealing with life's little shit-heaps, but she honestly couldn't see any way out of this one. She could see it getting worse almost by the minute, but she couldn't see how to stop it. All she could do was get the lizard talking as quickly as possible and hope that once the others saw that someone was with them who actually knew what he was doing, all this Commander crap would just...blow over.

'Never happen,' she told herself in the voice of her dead mother. 'If it all goes right, the lizardman will be Commander Scott's friendly native guide. If it all turns to shit, he'll be the mistake you brought into camp. Either way, Commander Scott is here to stay, so you can suck it up, little girl...'

"Or you can blow it out," Amber finished, then sighed and looked at Meoraq. When he looked back at her, she made herself smile. "We're going to do this," she told him. "We just have to start simple, right?"

He frowned.

"Right." Amber patted herself on the chest. "Human. Say it with me. *Human*."

Meoraq's gaze dropped to her hand. He grunted and handed her what was left of his gut-kebob. He told her to eat it, then got up and went into his tent, leaving her alone with the saoq's slowly roasting head and its silent, judgmental stare.

9

The first days among the creatures who called themselves humans were a true test of Meoraq's discipline. Oh, they weren't wild, or at least, they weren't aggressive. Although they remained cautious and their leader in particular did a lot of barking from a short distance, they accepted him into their pack without challenge. It was what they did afterwards that wore on a man.

In spite of their clothing, their shelters, and their primitive attempt at language, Meoraq often found himself questioning his conviction that these were intelligent creatures—people—and not constructs of Sheul's devising made just before their first meeting. They showed no ability or even any interest in taking care of themselves. Except Amber, who made herself positively obnoxious every morning when he set out for the day's hunt.

Meoraq had no experience with either cattle or children and had to rely upon prayer and his own instincts where the bulk of their care was concerned. At times, he marveled that he had not lost one yet, especially since it seemed that the instant his attention wandered, they were squabbling or wandering out into the plains or falling asleep with their fires unbanked. Some days it seemed his prayers were evenly split between asking Sheul for guidance in keeping them from killing themselves and begging Him to let Meoraq do it himself. And perhaps the humans sensed it, because although they ate what he fed them, none of them dared to come too near.

Well...one of them dared. The fearless little spear-hunter. Amber. She spent more time with him than with her own kind, and far from shooing her off, he shamelessly encouraged her by feeding her and allowing her and her friend, Nicci, to sleep by his fire. But if he showed a certain proprietary interest in her, it at least served a greater purpose. After all, nothing could be accomplished until they could talk to one another.

Amber had not flagged in her determination to teach him the crude speech of her people, although she seemed amenable to learn dumaqi as well, inasmuch as her physical defects allowed. As the days passed and she continued to mangle the simple words he gave her, he could see her frustration mounting, but he refused to resort to humani. The Prophet's Word is the only Word; his many meditations on the First Law had brought him no clear answers, only the same vague feeling that these were people, and if so, then Sheul had deliberately made them in this mold, with the deformities that made dumaqi impossible for them to speak, and if *that* were true, how could he, Meoraq, born of clay, judge them for being as God made them? Nevertheless, it remained true that he must hold to the admonitions of the Prophet and speak only Man's tongue. He could see that Amber understood his words far less than he did hers, but she had made some progress already and could only make more. With Amber, Meoraq found he could be at least a little patient. With the others...

Yet for all the aggravation of tending them, it was not so terrible an ordeal. He'd never kept a pet before and keeping close to fifty of them all at once in the wildlands was not how any man ought to begin, but he seemed to be having some success at it and he had to admit, he liked having someone to talk to, even if she couldn't talk back.

Funny. He'd never thought of himself as a personable sort. He spent the greatest share of his life alone. Travel along the empty roads between the cities of his circuit took the bulk of his time and what was left over was rarely passed among company. It was not considered fitting for a Sheulek to socialize with others of his caste. Even the thought felt scandalous and slightly sinful—God's Striding Foot at the garrison's recreation hall with common watchmen and gatekeepers. He might pass a few moments before a trial with a man like himself, as he had passed them with Sheulteb Ni'ichok Shuiv in Tothax, but these moments, while pleasant, were few. Home was the one place where he might be allowed to relax in the company of other men, to trade stories, share nai, tell low-humored jokes and laugh at them without embarrassment, but only once a year, only for the cold season, and only with the most immediate members of his family. It was something of a curiosity to discover that he liked looking into Amber's ugly face and listening to her earnest gibberish. He liked telling her—over and over and over—to put her spear down and go back to sleep and see her sulk as she obeyed him. He liked coming into camp and seeing her stand to greet him, even if it was just because he fed her so often. He liked her company and he supposed it must mean the rest of them had some redeeming quality as well.

But they did test a man and every now and then, it was either walk away from them and their constant neediness or slap them until either his hand or their heads fell off.

So it was that the end of a very long and trying evening found Uyane Meoraq, twelve years a Sheulek in God's service and honest victor of hundreds of trials, outside the vague boundary of the humans' camp, hiding in a tree.

He knew he was hiding. He could even see the humor in it, in a sour sort of way. A Sheulek was the master of his clay. He knew no fear and no hesitation when he stood in the arena in the sight of Sheul, and yet here he was. Not so far away that he could not leap down and defend them if the humans drew some danger into their midst, but hopefully out of sight. The coming winter had caused most of the leaves to brown and a few to drop, so he was not as invisible as he would have liked, but corrokis couldn't look up and perhaps neither could humans.

It was surprisingly pleasant up here. Meoraq was not a man fond of heights under most circumstances, but today he found the scope of the view soothing to his eye. The evening air was cool but dry for the moment, and there was enough light yet that he could see small herds of saoq moving in the prairie, and the larger dark dots of corrokis grazing among them.

He supposed he had time enough for a short hunt before the sun was gone, but he had brought one meal into this camp already today and that would just have to be enough for the greedy bellies of his humans. He himself had most of two bricks of cuuvash yet and he didn't mind eating some in front of them. For now, he was content just to feel the edge of his appetite as he meditated with his eyes open, clearing his mind of all thought but open to the will of Sheul on the slim chance that He should speak, and just watching the world while he still had it to himself.

It was peaceful.

But it didn't last.

It began with one human, the one called Scott, trudging noisily through the trees and yawning against its hand with no apparent purpose to its wanderings until it leaned itself up against the very tree in which Meoraq sought refuge and opened its breeches.

Meoraq had no intention of watching the human undress, but before he could avert his eyes, the human reached into its clothing and drew out a short, thick tube of discolored flesh. The human held this limp and repulsive appendage in its hand as it scratched sleepily at its hair, and after a moment or two, out arced a steaming sluice of bright yellow fluid.

It was pissing. Standing up.

But through what? It hung, finger-length and flopping, beneath a short thatch of dark hair, much darker and curlier than that which grew on Scott's head, and above a second distended lump of flesh Meoraq presumed to be its bladder, externalized by some quirk of human design. The appendage itself seemed to be boneless and had no real distinguishing characteristics that Meoraq could see at this height, apart from its loose outer skin which could not quite cover the dark, bulbous tip from which its urine endlessly poured. That stream, as well as the coincidental placement of the appendage between the human's legs, made it seem uncannily like...

By Gann, it was its penis.

It was *pissing* out of it.

It was pissing out of its soft, blotchy, malformed *cock*.

Two more humans were coming. The one called Scott glanced in the direction of their noisy approach as his stream slackened, then actually waggled the flabby spout of his organ to shake free the last drops of urine before folding itself back into his breeches. The humans met and grunted greetings. Scott retreated; the other two opened their clothing, muttering to one another, and drew out two more floppy cocks to piss through. They differed somewhat in size and color, but that was all.

So they were uncontestably males. Which meant that there were also females. Amber would be a female. He had suspected that from the first and he felt absolutely nothing at having his suspicions confirmed because it did not matter to him if a human were male or female any more than it mattered if, oh, if a saoq were male or female. Animals were animals, and in a purely animal sense, the only question worth pondering was whether some or all of those human females might at this moment be breeding.

Meoraq forced himself to look down, to study the limp things the human males had and ponder the breeding of humans. He had no experience with the husbandry of animals; if there was a way to look at these creatures and know how quickly it made young or how many it could drop in a litter, Meoraq did not know what it was. He thought he ought to know too, because whether or not they were breeding at the moment, if they had opposing gender, there would be offspring eventually. If the swollen teats of their women were anything to measure by, those offspring might already have been recently birthed, but they were not in evidence now, which could mean the females would soon be ready to conceive again.

He had to think of Amber then, much as he had been fighting it. Amber and her silly spear. Amber, who spent so much time sitting at his fire and taking the little bites he fed her (right from his hand) and trying with such spectacular unsuccess to mouth his words. And yes, Amber, who was female, not that this mattered, and who might be breeding (he caught at his snout to stop the hiss that shot insensibly out of him) as she damned well should be (Meoraq swung himself down and out of the tree's fork, moving fast from branch to branch until he dropped with a curse to the ground) instead of running over the wildlands with pointed sticks!

"Although You have made no law against this," Meoraq acknowledged, glancing heavenward as he aimed himself for the humans and their camp. "And I admit I like better to see her at her foolish hunt than to see her N'ki doing nothing but waiting to be fed in proper female fashion."

Nicci did everything in proper female fashion, come to think of it. She sat quietly, kept herself largely invisible and showed obedience to male command, since now he knew Scott to be male. Amber did none of these things, really. She talked almost constantly when she was with him, even reaching out to touch him if she did not think she had enough of his attention, and she let her frustrations show plainly on her ugly face. She kept apart from the rest of her kind, but was quick enough to argue with them if she thought they gave her cause. As for obedience, ha! He tried to imagine Amber as a proper female, to picture her in her father's House (it greatly resembled his own in Xeqor) kneeling meekly, her neck bent and hands turned to heaven...

He couldn't do it. Perhaps she had been feminine once, but no longer.

He liked her better like this anyway.

There had to be something wrong with him.

It was not far into the evening, and yet the humans were bedding themselves down in broad rings around the fires when he returned. Amber was still sitting up, wrapped in the shiny skin of her blanket, watching the other humans gnaw on saoq bones and talk at each other while she sat alone. She did not look at him until he had been standing over her for quite some time and she did not smile when she finally did.

She. So he had been thinking of her all this time, but he wanted to be sure. He needed to be sure. Just why he needed to be sure this instant, he didn't know and did not explore. He simply hunkered down and started drawing in the dirt.

She watched listlessly until he had made two images, featureless blobs with arms and legs and hairy heads. She knew they were human and said so, tapping at them without enthusiasm even as her attention wandered back to the fire.

He caught her chin and made her look at the drawings as he, not without an internal wince, carefully added twin curves to one image and a short line to the other.

She studied the pictures in silence, her mouthparts slowly turning up at the corners. "Yeh. I ges we ki'indaskipt tht'biht. Man," she said, pointing at the male figure. And at the female: "Woman." And then she patted herself on the chest, right above the swellings of her—yes, her—teats. "Woman."

'If they are people, it is not a sin,' he thought vaguely, and his belly warmed at once. 'If they are people, she is a woman in your camp, under your protection, and she owes you every obedience.'

Even so, it would still be one of the unforgiveable sins and he knew it. The Word forbade all men, even Sheulek, to lie with a girl not yet in her woman's years, or with any woman in her sickbed, or with a milking mother, unless she was his wife. Amber may indeed be female, but the proof of it was as good as a warning.

He made himself the master of his clay and put aside sexual thoughts—mostly—to add a third drawing to the first two. He wasn't happy with it. He'd made it very small, armless and legless, as if wrapped in a blanket, but the effect was disturbingly grub-like instead. He scowled, started to rub it out and try again, then just looked at her and gestured around the camp. "Where are your children?" he asked boldly.

She tapped the grub. "Ba'bee. Orkid I ges. Ch'iild. You no litelpursen."

"Where are they?" he asked again, determined to keep her focused. "Where is your child?"

She actually seemed to understand some of that, enough to draw back and crease up her brows at him. "Mine? Dijju'just say werz my ba'bee?"

He started to point at her teats, then changed his mind and pointed at those of the dirt-woman instead.

"Oh." She chuffed and looked down at her chest anyway. "Yeh. Theh'alwez luklyk'thss. D'ssnt alwez meen therza ba'bee. We don't hev enee ba'bees heer'rytnow."

It took some time to break that apart and bring it together in a way that made sense and once he had, he did not quite trust the meaning he took away. Hesitantly, he tapped the dirt-woman directly on one of the teats, then tapped the dirt-child.

"Nope," said Amber, a clear and definitive negation. "Jsst big'buubs."

He leaned back, trying very hard not to stare at them. It was grotesque to think her teats were always swollen, but if there was no suckling, then there was no sin in mating with her.

And that was where his mind went, yet again. Right there. Like a lodestone clamping on to steel. There was something really wrong with him.

As he grappled with this, one of the figures at the fire rose and came back to join them. Amber's friend, Nicci. She sat—he knew it was a she by the teats—and gave Meoraq a wary nod.

"Wutz he duun'eer?" Nicci asked, eyeing the pictures in the dirt as if she thought they might be poisonous.

"Nuthnn," said Amber, showing her teeth in a smile. "Litel'lengwij lessn thatzal. Sex'ehd lzzrdstyl."

Nicci frowned, slowly drawing up her knees and hugging them to put the barrier of her skinny arms and legs between them. This act pulled the fabric of her breeches very tight across her loins, forming folds that made it appear as if she had a slit. Meoraq looked at the sky.

"Itz nuthnn," Amber said again, no longer smiling. "Luk itwuz bountoo cummup."

"Why? Wutz he wantwthuz?" Nicci whispered, her eyes still fixed on Meoraq.

"Nothing! Fr'Cryzzakes, eeza lzzrd! Eez jst nevrseen buubz b'for!"

"Thn wutabout tht?"

Silence. Meoraq risked a glance to see why and found the two of them studying the diminutive dirt-penis on his dirt-man.

"Peepel tokabout yutu," said Nicci.

"O fuktht!" Amber spat with startling venom. "Thziz my j'b Nicci! You wanna givmeeshit about'ow I doit, doit yorgod dam slf!"

She threw off her shiny blanket, punched it down into her pack, and stomped away.

Meoraq watched her go, frowning. He'd embarrassed her—and he could hardly claim innocence after drawing a penis and showing it to her—but he himself felt no shame. In truth, he felt nothing as she fled him except a simmer of resentment at this Nicci, who had turned an awkward but promising conversation into a big puddle of piss.

They sat there, and after a time, he went ahead and looked at her.

She flinched and ducked her head, so exactly like a dumaq woman that he expected her to mewl at him. Gann's unreasoning lust both leapt and curdled to nauseating effect. He got up at once and stalked away to his tent.

Safely shut away from human eyes, he tore off his tunic and boots, threw himself on his mat and gave the loin-plate girding him a vicious slap. It stung his palm a little. It hurt his stubbornly extruding cock a lot, but he doubted that would teach it any lasting lessons. Even now, in this storm of furious reproach, he knew that if it had been Amber who bent her neck to him, he would be on her, in her, right this instant.

Six breaths, Uyane. A slow-count of six. One for the Prophet, two for his brunt, and onward, as many times as it takes to remember that you are the master of your clay.

Six breaths. Six more. Six again.

Of course, Amber never would bend her neck.

Six breaths. Lashraq. His brunt. Uyane, father of his own line. Mykrm. Oyan. Thaliszr. And back to the Prophet.

Unless she were looking at her boots. Then she might, but then she wouldn't care what he thought about seeing the back of her neck. And she certainly would never make that sound. She didn't know anything about how to be a real woman, and that more than anything bothered him, because what did it say about him that he still wanted to have sex with her?

This was part of the ordeal. It had to be. Sheul had made the humans to test his resolve, his patience and his resourcefulness, and He had made Amber specifically to test his self-control. He needed to stare that down, own it, conquer it, and get on with his damned life.

Six breaths, like rising stairs. Meoraq climbed them over and over, determined to find peace at the top. He had almost done so—almost—when out of the pure black nothing, he suddenly thought, 'You don't like her in spite of the way she acts, you know. You like her because of it.'

'I don't like her at all,' he thought back defiantly. At once he felt the Sheulek in him judge that for the lie it was. He may hate the feelings he had—they felt dangerous and deviant, even when they were not wholly anchored to his loins—but he couldn't pretend he didn't have them.

And sometimes...he wasn't even sure he hated them.

10

And that was how the time passed for Amber. Days that had seemed hellishly interminable when there was nothing to fill them but wind and rain, hunger and cold, now flew by. Even when Meoraq wasn't there to give her his blank, silent stares as she pleaded with him to say her name, say hello, say fuck off, say *anything*, the time slipped away from her. If it wasn't for Scott's regular reminders that she'd wasted six days trying to teach a lizard how to talk...ten days...twelve...she would have lost track of them completely.

Which wasn't to say that they hadn't made any progress. Meoraq still had not said one word of English, but he responded to it. Of course, his responses were all in lizardish, which stubbornly resisted all of Amber's attempts to decipher. Oh, she thought she was picking some up. She thought that every day until she actually tried to talk and inevitably insulted him. She didn't even know how half the time. She'd just be there, clumsily coughing up lizard-words, and suddenly he'd stiffen and glare at her. If he felt like giving her another chance at that point, he might correct her (invariably with the same exact word she'd just said). More often, he just told her to be quiet and went on with what he was saying. Sometimes, he got up and left, muttering to himself and to his god on high, which was an open invitation for Scott to come over and illustrate all the ways in which she was a failure.

She tried not to let it worry her. Whether or not Meoraq ever learned to talk, Amber didn't really think Scott would throw him out (and only partly because she didn't think he could). She hadn't seen a ration bar since Meoraq had started feeding them; she thought the last of them had probably been eaten in a celebratory binge during an extra-long, extra-quiet debriefing several days ago. Scott may not like the lizard, but he had no trouble recognizing the benefits of having him around.

He was off hunting at the moment, Meoraq. She'd heard him leave a little before dawn and even though the sun was now well up over the horizon, he might be gone for hours yet. Regular meals had done wonders for the morale here at camp, but steady predation had definitely made the saoqs skittish. They were nowhere to be seen anymore, not even from the top of the ridge. Meoraq never came back without one, but whatever secret tracking technique he used to find them, he kept it to himself.

And that bothered her. A lot. Amber knew her first hunt hadn't exactly been the sort of thing to inspire confidence, but she sure wasn't going to get any better at it without practice. She couldn't understand how everyone could just sit around, day after day, waiting for Meoraq to come back and feed them, and sometimes even bitching to each other about how much time he took to do it, like he was a waiter slow-poking himself out of a tip.

And Meoraq, who should have been the first person to insist on some effort, was no help at all. The first time Amber had snatched up her spear and tried to go with him on his morning hunt, he'd actually laughed at her (she was pretty sure that gargling hiss was a laugh). Now he just said no, or occasionally, "No, damn it! Sit down!"

She refused to quit trying to go with him, though. Which was probably why he snuck out today before dawn. Big scaly jerk.

"How are those English lessons coming, Miss Bierce?" Scott called as Amber and Nicci came back from the bushes to join the others.

"Fine," she said curtly and sat down. She didn't want to sit down. She didn't want anything to do with these people, but the alternative was just to sit by herself wrapped up in her blanket and wait for Meoraq alone. She still might do that, but Nicci wanted to be with people, so she sat.

"That's good. When do you think you could arrange a formal debriefing?"

"It could take a while. I don't think he has a tux," said Amber, which was about as witty as she got first thing in the morning.

A few people laughed. Scott wasn't one of them.

"Is that your way of saying a debriefing would be...premature?"

"Look, I'm working on it, okay?"

"No," said Scott. "No, it's not okay. Do you realize it's been two weeks already? Two weeks. Now I think that I've been very patient with you, Miss Bierce, but it's obvious that there's a problem on someone's end. Is it with him or with you?"

"Maybe it's with the person who thinks two weeks is enough time to learn a new language."

"I wasn't expecting him to be fluent. A simple yes or no would be enough to answer most of my questions. Do you think he can manage that?"

Amber went back to rubbing her face.

Scott nodded as if that were the answer he'd expected. "I can't help but think that any cognizant being would have managed some kind of communication by now."

"We communicate."

"You mean it grunts and hisses and you imagine you hear words."

"I dare you to say that to his face. I fucking dare you."

"Be cool," Eric said.

"I don't need to hear the profanity," Scott agreed, smiling. "And you don't need to be so sensitive. I admit that the idea had some merit, but communication is never going to be possible without a certain level of intelligence." He paused, then added, "I mean the lizard's intelligence, of course."

Some of the Manifestors laughed.

"What exactly are you saying?" Amber asked. "That he's not smart enough to talk? He talks all the time!"

"It vocalizes," Scott agreed. "But an animal vocalizing is not the same as a person talking. I'm beginning to wonder if you know the difference."

"Yeah? I'm beginning to wonder how Meoraq's going to feel about bringing you food every goddamn day if he hears you saying he's not a fucking person."

Scott quit smiling. "I'm not going to tell you again about the profanity."

"Oh what now? You going to wash my mouth out with soap?"

"Be cool, Bierce," Eric said again. "We're just trying to figure things out."

"It is amazing to me," Scott added, "that you are the only one who seems to think that you don't need to make any effort to get along with the rest of us."

"Just you, Scott. Just you."

In the crowd, Dag leaned over and whispered something in Eric's ear. Eric nodded and ran a hand through his hair. "Take a walk, Bierce. Cool off."

She blinked at him. "What?"

He raised his head to look at her. His gaze was steady. "I said, take a walk."

She stared at him and then at Maria, sitting next to him, and at Dag and Nicci and all of them, but the only one who would look back at her was Scott.

"Fine." She shoved herself up, went to where her duffel bag was parked and grabbed her spear up from beside it.

"Amber, wait!" Nicci called, but she didn't get up, just hugged herself and looked unhappy. It was Crandall who came after her, content to jog behind her and call her name two or three times before he finally caught her sleeve. When she shook him off, he gave her a slap to the ass which made her briefly see red, but only briefly. It wasn't him she was mad at.

"Let me ask you something," she said, just said.

Crandall shrugged and fell into easy step beside her. "Shoot."

"Is he going to be content with humiliating me or should I be afraid for my life?" God, she was proud of how calm she sounded. Pissed, but calm.

"I don't know," Crandall said.

"Would you tell me if you did?"

"Yeah, probably." He glanced over his shoulder at the now-distant camp and caught at her sleeve again, this time pulling her to a stop. "Look, you want some free advice? Take a dive."

"What?"

"You and Scott have been throwing punches from Day One. Time to hit the mat, little girl. Let the man win."

"Is this a sports metaphor?" she asked, baffled. "Do I look like I know the first fucking thing about sports?"

He rolled his eyes. "Okay, whatever. When you go out there today, don't do anything stupid. Stay where you can see the smoke from our fire, give it five or ten minutes, and then come back and apolo—"

"The hell I will!"

"Oh come on, Bierce," he said, actually rolling his eyes, actually *laughing* a little. "My feet are getting wet. Unbunch your panties and be a good girl for one day. I promise, it won't kill you."

Amber started walking again. This time, when he caught at her arm, she shook him off. "You're still not getting that blowjob out of me," she spat. "But you seem to prefer kissing Scott's ass anyway."

He quit laughing. When his smile came back, it was thin and hard and ugly. "Have fun getting killed out there, bitch," he said and went back to camp without her.

* * *

The problem was, Amber had always been too practical. And looking at it from a practical point of view, Amber knew that she couldn't stay mad all day. It was exhausting and it upset her stomach, but more to the point, it didn't accomplish anything. Scott was an idiot, but just saying so wasn't changing anyone's high opinion of him. The way she saw it, she had only two choices: Unbunch her panties and let Scott be in charge, or find some way to convince people that the armed alien lizard in their midst was a better candidate for the job. It was obvious to her (although she didn't know how happy Meoraq would be when he found out he'd been nominated); she just had to figure out how to prove it.

The answer, she was certain, was food. Scott had successfully taken command with nothing but a duffel bag filled with Fleet-issue rations. Meoraq hadn't been able to shake anyone's confidence yet, even with a freshly-delivered dead animal every morning, but he had the significant handicap of being an alien, and the only one of them with weapons, which he did not share and which he did frequently point at people if they got too close. What Amber needed to make them understand was that in addition to taking care of them, he could also teach them to take care of themselves.

She'd already stormed out of camp in a huff, pretty much exactly the way that Scott had wanted her to do, and she couldn't help that now, but maybe she could salvage something if she came home with her own dead deer. She had her spear and enough regular meals to make her feel more confident about running down the next saoq that put her in that position. She'd go hunting. She'd catch something. And she'd show everyone what Scott and his everything-will-be-all-right bullshit was really worth. For that matter, she'd show Meoraq that they weren't all just a bunch of starving alley cats waiting for someone else's handouts. And maybe the next time she picked up this spear and walked out of Scott's camp, she wouldn't go alone.

It wasn't the noblest motive, but it was an invigorating one. With renewed purpose, Amber set off again. An exhausting march over the thorn-covered hills and marshy ravines didn't bring her to any saoqs, but after God knew how many hours stubbornly struggling along, she found something. A whole herd of somethings, in fact.

Like the saoqs that she kept trying to see as deer, when Amber first realized she was looking at animals and not boulders, her brain tried to force them into a shape it already knew. So they were armadillos at first glance. Armadillos the same size and general shape as those bubble-top cars that Volkswagen tried to bring back for their centennial anniversary. Armadillos with massive cloven hooves and shovel-shaped tusks. Armadillos that periodically sidled up and bashed at one another with the huge, bone-studded clubs of their tails. Armadillos that did not appear to be terrifically light on their feet, but that surely wouldn't hesitate to trample her fat ass to death if they could catch it. And they probably could.

Watching them, Amber slowly realized that no one knew where she was.

No one would be able to hear her when she screamed.

No one would ever find her body.

And while Amber huddled in the grass, trying to decide the best way to get the hell out of there without being seen, Meoraq's scaly hand slipped over her mouth.

She screamed into his palm, even knowing it was him. He yanked her back against his chest long enough to hiss something in her ear—blah blah blah something about God blah blah you idiot—and then he was dragging her rapidly and none too gently backwards through the grass.

After he had put a little distance and the slope of a hill between them and the giant armadillos, Meoraq stopped. He stood her up, swung her around, and snapped back the hand that had been over her mouth for one mother of a roundhouse slap.

She flinched, but only because she was stupid that way. Standing here with her heart still pounding from the adrenaline of knowing she was about to be tail-whipped and trampled to death by a herd of for-God's-sake armadillos, she knew she deserved a lot worse than a smack in the face. She kept her arms at her sides, her spear low in her hand. She didn't try to defend herself, even with words. She just wished he'd get it over with.

His arm hovered. His fingers flexed and curled in the air. His chest heaved in silence. The black scales of his throat were striped with yellow as bright as a school bus. Then he just turned around and started walking, moving fast and with unnatural silence through the grass. She trudged after him, her spear trailing in the grass behind her, but not for long. He came back, seizing her by the front of her shirt like a man grabbing the collar of an errant dog, and pulled her along with him at his swift, angry stride.

In spite of that, it seemed like a long walk back, made even longer with nothing but the wind to listen to. Meoraq seethed beside her, his hand still knotted in her shirt. If she stumbled over a hidden stone, he kept going, dragging her until she found her feet. He didn't need to stop and check his bearings, never lost his breath or caught his boots in the thorns, but still the morning was over and the afternoon getting long when they got back to camp.

"Welcome back, Miss Bierce," Scott called when they finally arrived, making sure everyone stopped what they were doing and looked at her. "We were all starting to get worried. What were you trying to prove, wandering off like that?"

Meoraq snarled something before Amber had a chance to reply, but she couldn't make it out. He dragged her over to the fire, where the saoq he had brought back had already been eaten down to the bones. He made her sit down, smacked her in the back of the head when she tried to get up, then stalked off to his tent, muttering.

"You seem upset," Scott remarked with a smile.

"Should I take another walk, asshole?"

His jaw tightened. "Watch the profanity, Miss Bierce, or you will."

Meoraq swept out of his tent and stalked back to the fire. He crouched down at Amber's side, took her wrist again and slapped a square of his jerky-stuff into her palm hard enough to sting.

"I don't want it," she said, pushing it back at him.

He looked up at the sky, rubbing the jerky between his fingers while the scales at his throat faded between yellow and black, yellow and black. He began to talk then, but not to her. He started out calmly enough, but in less than a minute, he was on his feet, his voice steadily rising as he paced back and forth, pointing at Amber and bellowing into the clouds.

Several people eased quietly away.

"What's he saying?" Eric asked finally.

"He's praying," said Amber.

"That's a prayer?"

Meoraq swung around and shouted directly at her for a while, then threw himself down very suddenly in his thinking position—crouched low and bent forward, one hand open on the ground and the other resting on one knee, head bent, eyes shut. He breathed, silent.

"Now what is he doing?" Eric asked.

"Praying harder."

Meoraq muttered under his breath, rubbed at his brow-ridges, inhaled, exhaled, and was still.

Everyone watched except Amber, who poked at the saoq bones in the fire and wished she had something to eat, and Scott, who was watching her.

"I would like to ask a question," said Scott presently. "Could you, Miss Bierce, translate one so-called word of that *prayer*? Because I'm very curious about this lizard-god. What's he called? O Great and Scaly One?"

Meoraq's eyes opened.

"Do you know what I think?" Scott pressed, oblivious to the narrow, red stare now boring into him. "I think you're making it up. I don't think you have the first clue what that thing is saying. I think you're just too stubborn to admit it's not saying anything at all."

"Dude," murmured Dag, watching Meoraq's head slowly tip to one side. "You might want to drop this."

"No, I think it's long past time we had this out." Scott came briskly back to the fireside and stood over Meoraq with his arms folded in his most commanding posture. "Say something," he ordered. "Say anything. Talk. Pray. Heck, sing some dirty limericks. Come on, Meoraq. Let's hear it."

Heads turned all around the camp as people waited for Meoraq to speak.

Meoraq kept his narrow stare on Scott and did not say one word.

People began to whisper.

Scott threw up both hands in a gesture that was at once victory and surrender. "Miss Bierce, you justified the tremendous danger of bringing that thing into my camp by insisting that it could act as our guide once we had achieved some form of communication. Now I think I've been more than patient with you—"

"Bullshit you have!" Amber sputtered.

"—but all I've gotten out of the endeavor so far is a lot of argument and profanity," Scott concluded. He didn't shout. It was actually worse that way. If he'd shouted, she could have jumped up and shouted back, but as it was, he just talked, sounding disappointed but so damned reasonable. "All you had to do was teach that thing enough English to tell us, oh, anything! What his people are called! What planet this is! Yes, no, *anything*!"

"I tried!"

"She tried!" Nicci came out of the crowd of Manifestors, past a suddenly-flustered Scott, to stand at Amber's side. "She tried every single day. For hours. No one can *make* someone else speak English."

"Yeah, come on." And that was Maria, miraculously enough. Lawsuit Lady herself, ignoring Eric's whispers to stand up and take a challenging step forward. "What was she supposed to do? Hold hot irons to his feet?"

Meoraq's head tipped back. He looked at Amber.

"He can talk," Maria declared. "Even I can understand him a little, and so could you if you weren't too busy campaigning to listen."

Scott gazed at her for a moment or two while Eric raked his hands through his hair. "And what was he saying, Miss Alverez?"

Maria hesitated, looking at Meoraq, who kept his eyes on Amber. "I couldn't quite...He was talking pretty fast."

"In other words, you don't know."

"I—"

"And yet you're convinced it was a prayer. How do his prayers usually go?"

Maria sat down again and put her hand on Eric's knee almost defensively. Eric wouldn't look at her.

"So, in point of fact," Scott continued, "you didn't understand any of it."

Maria opened her mouth. Eric murmured something. She glared at him, but pressed her lips together, silent.

"I can appreciate that you're trying to help, Miss Alverez," said Scott, dismissing her with a wave, "but Miss Bierce needs to answer for her own failures."

"My failures?" Amber echoed. "It's complicated, goddammit!"

"And if you have something to say, Miss Bierce, find a way to say it without turning it into a personal attack."

Meoraq glanced at him and snorted. It was nice to know that someone else saw the irony in that, since it seemed that most of the people watching them did not.

"It's complicated," Amber said again, struggling to keep her voice down and sound as reasonable as he did. To her own ears, she sounded weak and sullen—a child making excuses for skipped homework. "Everything he says can change just by how he says it! Like...gann."

"Guns?" All of a sudden, Scott was interested again. "Those things have guns?"

"If you're going to interrupt, pay attention," she snapped. "*Gann*. One sound, but I've heard him say it different ways to mean different things. Like, um, gann—"

Meoraq glanced over at her.

"Which I think is the name of this world. And gann," Amber continued, dragging the word up into a higher pitch and watching his spines slowly flare forward. "Which could mean a person, or at least a person's body. I'm not sure. Or gann. That's just dirt. And then there's gann, and I don't know what that one means, except that it's a swear of some sort. There's others, and I can hear the differences when he says them, but I can't...I can't do it right."

"Well, I still don't hear words in there at all," Scott announced loftily. "I'm not convinced that Miss Bierce isn't confusing some animal vocalizations with—"

"Oh for Christ's sake, how stupid are you?" Amber exploded. "Look at him! He's wearing clothes!"

"Yeah, and my Aunt Harriet used to put hats on her terriers all the time, but that didn't make them people."

"He's wearing boots and pants and everything but a fucking top hat and a pair of spats, not to mention all the knives! I mean, what are you really suggesting here? That someone dressed him up and turned him loose? Can Aunt Harriet's terriers put up a tent? Start a fire? Whose food are you eating *right now,* you fucking moron?"

"I'm not going to tell you again to stop with the profanities. And all I'm suggesting is that the things you like to call proof of intelligence look to me like nothing more than proof that some as-yet unknown master race has trained a considerably lesser one to perform certain menial tasks. Look at it logically," he said, turning back to the Manifestors. "As Miss Bierce herself acknowledges, he's starting *our* fires, providing *our* food, patrolling around *our* camp...tasks he took on literally the moment he met us!"

Meoraq's head tipped a little further. The fading yellow stripes on his throat grew a little brighter. He said nothing, did not move.

"But has he tried to learn our language? No. In fact, does he make any effort to speak with anyone who doesn't speak to him first? No. Does he show the slightest curiosity about where we come from? No!" Scott began to pace back and forth in front of the murmuring crowd, gesturing now and then to punctuate his points. His color was high; his step, light. He was a man in his element and, ragged uniform and scruffy beard-stubble aside, he looked good when he was there. "When native tribes are first discovered by a civilized society, they *react*, ladies and gentlemen. They show awe. Curiosity. Excitement. They're people who recognize foreign people for the first time and it's an amazing, fantastic moment for them! But has this...Meoraq ever showed even a smidgeon of interest in...in our clothes, for example? Has he ever tried to touch someone's hair? Indicated that he even noticed we have more fingers? Different features? Different bodies? No! Obviously, there is some higher life on this planet somewhere," Scott concluded. "But after observing this particular specimen, I am more convinced than ever that we haven't found it yet. What we have here is..."

He paused dramatically to think, and in that pause, Amber suddenly realized that she had been struck speechless for the first time in her life. It was a terrifying thought; maybe it had been outrage that silenced her, but she'd been just as silent all the same. Mesmerized. Not just letting him say it, but letting him say it in front of Meoraq.

She opened her mouth.

Meoraq put his hand on her shoulder without looking at her and squeezed hard.

She closed her mouth, fuming.

"Okay," said Scott, holding up both hands as if to quiet all the people who weren't talking anyway. "What we appear to be dealing with is a kind of dog. And before you all get offended on its behalf—"

No one appeared to be offended. Amber opened her mouth again and this time got a squeeze and a silencing point. He still didn't look at her.

"—dogs can be highly specialized animals," Scott concluded. "We have bomb dogs, don't we? Drug dogs. Seeing eyes and hearing ears. And of course, attack dogs. My point is, no matter how well-trained the dog is, no one would ever confuse it for a sentient life form, would they? And why not? Because even when the dog can do what it does better than anyone else around it, it still can't *think*."

"Just because he can't speak English doesn't mean he can't think!" Amber insisted, shrugging off Meoraq's hand. "He—He drew pictures, for crying out loud! He gestures! He—"

"So do monkeys," said Scott.

"But if he's so intelligent," said Dag, and immediately backed off when Meoraq looked his way, "and I'm not saying you aren't, man. But if he is, how come he can manage twenty different ways to say gann, but not human? How hard is that?"

Everyone looked at Meoraq, Amber among them. Meoraq eyed them all and then just looked at Amber. His spines were flat again.

"I don't know," she said slowly. "Maybe we're thinking of it too...one-dimensionally. Like sound is all there is. But for him, the *way* you say it matters as much as the sounds it makes. I don't know."

"That's such a ludicrous answer," muttered Scott, and made a point of walking away a few steps just so he could shake his head and come back. "Just admit it, you're as clueless as the rest of us."

"I did admit it," she said tightly. "That's what *I don't know* means."

"And for those people who are trying to learn a non-inflected language like English when their own is more tonal," interrupted Yao, "it can be very difficult. There are five different ways to say *ma* in Mandarin. It can mean anything from mother to horse. Language is not a science, Mr. Scott. It is far more abstract than most people realize, and to this I would add that the physical structure of our speech may be impossible for him to emulate."

"Yeah, that's another thing," said Amber. "His mouth. He doesn't have lips, you know? And his tongue is all weird."

Crandall made a loud, derisively suggestive sound that earned him all of Meoraq's attention.

"You're a dick," Amber snapped. And to everyone else, said, "I mean it's different from a normal tongue. A human tongue," she amended, catching a narrow glance from the lizard. "I don't think it moves much. He pretty much only uses it to chew, so however he's making the sounds he makes, he's not doing it the way we do."

"As usual," Scott sighed, "you don't know what you're talking about."

"But I do." Mr. Yao stood up and faced himself off squarely against Scott. "If your Aunt Harriet had parrots instead of terriers, you might know what Miss Bierce is trying to tell you. Our friend appears to have bifurcated trachea—a split flap at the back of his throat which produces all his sounds. The shape of his mouth could easily account for some sort of resonance cavity which allows him precise control over sounds our ears may not even be capable of hearing."

"You said that was for pheromones," Scott said with a meaningful glance back at his Manifestors. Some of them obediently laughed or rolled their eyes.

Mr. Yao's lips thinned. "One does not supersede the other, Mr. Scott. I cannot advise you strongly enough to learn that particular lesson. One does not supersede the other, and if I can be blunt, I would observe that his ability to speak our language has nothing to do with his ability to understand it."

"Which he does," Amber insisted. "And sooner or later, he's going to stop being polite and you're going to get your proof about whether or not he knows what we're saying in the form of a sword up your ass!"

The slap didn't hurt. Not really. She staggered back a few steps, but she wasn't in any danger of falling down, and if she'd known the slap was coming, she probably wouldn't have even staggered. But that was the thing; she didn't see it coming. Scott was able to pull back his arm and smack her right across the mouth and she never...never really saw it coming.

She stared at him, one hand cupped over her stinging lips, unable to quite believe she'd just been hit. There wasn't any blood on her fingers, although she could taste it, coppery, on her throbbing lips. She looked around, blinking in a kind of numb bewilderment, and saw people she knew just looking back at her. Some of them were frowning, but whether at her for swearing or Scott for slapping, she couldn't tell. Some of them dropped back in the crowd, or picked at their fingernails, or found something else to look at, as if she'd done something embarrassing and vaguely disturbing, like wet her pants. She looked at Nicci, but Nicci wouldn't meet her eyes. She looked at Meoraq, but he was looking at Scott. So she looked at Scott.

He tipped his chin up, giving her a grim sort of nod. "I've given you all the last chances you're going to get, Miss Bierce. It's time you learned to start watching your mouth when you speak to m—"

He didn't see the slap coming either. Whap, right across his cheek. It hurt her wrist quite a bit. All the ladies in the movies acted like slapping a man's face was about as difficult as swatting a fly, but faces were pretty hard surfaces, really.

Scott staggered back, tripped over his boots and fell on his ass, which was satisfying to see even though she knew it was mostly luck.

"You ever lay a fucking hand on me again and I'll knock your fucking teeth out!" she shouted. "You don't get to tell me how to run my fucking mouth!"

"Okay, calm down." Eric eased himself forward a step, his hands once more raised and placating. "Take it easy."

"Tell him to calm down!" She brushed at her mouth again, but it still wasn't bleeding on her. Her hand was shaking. She could not believe how angry she was.

Or how close to tears.

No one told Scott to calm down. Dag was helping him up. People were whispering. Looking at her. Saying things that made Scott nod in his tight, angry way as he brushed grass off his clothes.

'I don't care if they like me!' she thought furiously.

"Okay," said Scott. He straightened his sleeves, his collar, his shirt-front. His cheek was a little red where she'd hit him, but only a little, like her lips that felt so swollen and tasted so coppery but stubbornly refused to bleed. He said, "I'm not doing this tonight. If you want to freak out and start hitting people—"

"*You hit me first*!"

Scott threw up his hands, a see-what-I-have-to-deal-with gesture straight to God. People murmured, commiserating. Amber could feel herself blushing, feel her breath growing hotter in her chest. "I'm done with you. *Done*. You show me some respect or the next time you take a walk, I won't send the lizard after you."

Meoraq had not moved more than his eyes or his spines in all this time, but at that, he suddenly stood up. He took two steps, unhurried, and slapped Scott right out of the air even as he was leaping away. He caught him before he hit the ground, pulled him close, then said quietly, "Lizard?"

He said it strangely, softening the z and rattling on the r, but he said it and it was easy to hear because no one else made a sound.

Meoraq tipped his head to the side in that way he seemed to think was threatening and said, once more in lizardish, that no one sent him anywhere and if *S'kot* or any other *human* (he said that oddly as well, drawing out the ooo-sound and hammering a hard T on the end) thought otherwise, he would...something. The word he used was not a familiar one and in this context could have meant anything. Whatever he said, he sounded like he meant it. And then he tipped his head even further on its side and asked if S'kot understood him.

"Yes," said Scott at once, his eyes huge.

Meoraq asked if he was sure. S'kot apparently heard nothing but *hisses* and *grunts* (he exaggerated the animal quality of these sounds; Scott flinched hard both times) of a *lizard* when Meoraq spoke.

"I..." Scott rolled his eyes wildly back at Amber, waxen-faced. "Say something, for God's sake! What does he want?"

"What does he want?" Amber huffed out an angry, humorless laugh and rubbed a final time at her unwounded mouth. "He wants a fucking apology, *Commander*."

Scott's mouth worked as his face slowly filled up with color. He made a few half-hearted shrugging gestures, looking for help in the crowd while Manifestors averted their eyes and his loyal lieutenants just looked at each other. "I'm...responsible for these people," he said at last. "I wasn't trying to be rude, I just...need to be sure what we're dealing with. That's all."

Meoraq's eyes narrowed. His head tipped. He waited.

"That's as close as he's going to get," said Amber. "You might as well let him go."

Meoraq hauled back one hand and slapped Scott again. The sound was a shocking thing, loud as a gunshot. People jumped, Amber among them, but Meoraq kept slapping. His spines were flat, but his throat was dark; his arm raised and swung five more times as Scott thrashed in his grip, and he was calm the whole time. At the end, he just stopped and waited while Scott brayed, "I'm sorry! I'm sorry! *Get him off me*!"

Meoraq released Scott with a shove and turned around. He went back to his place at the fire and crouched down. He picked up a stick and stirred coals.

Scott looked at Amber, wild-eyed and shock-white everywhere that Meoraq hadn't slapped him purple, his clothes still bunched up around his neck. His mouth worked a few times, but his eyes kept cutting at Meoraq. Finally, he spat, "You just remember to watch *your* mouth, Bierce," then spun around, grabbing at Eric and Crandall, and staggered away.

Amber sat down and waited while people cleared rapidly away. She could hear Scott across the camp, loudly holding court, but she couldn't make out exactly what he was saying. She didn't have to. She could guess.

Meoraq was watching her. After a while, she looked back at him.

He pointed at her and said something stern about never speaking for him again. He was a...foot?...and when he wanted something said, he'd say it.

She started to get up (*but not in a huff she could be pissed off without going off in a huff like a stupid girl*), but he caught her shoulder and shoved her back down. He said something she was too angry to catch, squeezed her shoulder extra-hard, then let go of her to pat her once on the head. He told her he didn't need...something. Defending? But that he acknowledged her obedience and he forgave her for wandering off.

Forgave her. Like she'd done something wrong. Big scaly son of a bitch.

"I'm sorry," she muttered, looking back at the fire.

"Eh?"

"For calling you a lizard all those times. I guess it is pretty rude."

He snorted, then tapped at her knee with his knuckles. He told her he knew she didn't mean it as an insult.

"Sometimes I do," she admitted. "Let me ask you something. Honestly."

He rolled his hand through the air in a bring-it-on gesture that translated perfectly.

"Is there any point to this? To you and me, I mean. Talking. I don't know." She rubbed at her face. "It doesn't feel like anything's changing. Unless it's getting worse. I don't mean just me and Scott, although God knows that's about as bad as it can get."

Meoraq grunted in what she was coming to think of as his affirming way. His stare was unnervingly direct.

'He's getting this,' she found herself thinking. 'And if he's not getting every word, it's at least nine out of every ten.'

"Is it just me?" she asked, and immediately wished she sounded more frustrated and less...whiny. "I always thought I was pretty good at coping with things, but I've got to tell you, Meoraq, I suck at this marooned-on-an-alien-planet crap."

His hand rolled again, inviting examples.

"We have to start working together. We have to start planning for our future, you know? Otherwise, he's right, all we're doing is killing time while we wait to die. And I realize that I could maybe be better..."

She gave him a chance to comment, but he merely looked at her, wonderfully inexpressive as only a lizard could be.

"But damn it," she sighed, combing restlessly at her hair, "if the future means getting along with that son of a bitch, I'd almost rather see it all end here."

His head cocked the other way. He leaned forward, the tip of his snout in kissing distance of her face. He spoke. You blah blah blah, something about God...blah blah and stop whining.

"Easy for you to say. If Scott gets bitchy at you, you can slap him around and leave. I have to live with these people!"

Meoraq scowled and scratched at the side of his snout. After a moment, he asked what kind of help she wanted.

"Oh hell, I don't know." She rubbed at another chunk of headache. "But I feel like I'm the only one who's actually trying to find a way to live here! And everyone else is trying to find a way to live back on Earth. I want to go home too! I want clean sheets and a cheeseburger and a hot shower and everything else they want, but it's not happening! We have to be here! We have to kill things if we're going to eat and pick grass out of the water we drink! We don't get soap and we don't get toilet paper and if we can't figure out what we *do* get in one hell of a hurry, we're all going to die here!"

He looked briefly heavenward and then rubbed at the bony ridges over his eyes. He muttered something about his God sending him to them.

"Yeah, and I can see you're thrilled to be a part of that—"

He snorted.

"—but I'm glad you're here, because we're all going to die without you." That sounded a lot more true than she liked. She tried to hide it with a smile, but it wouldn't stick. "Everything is so hard. I'm tired. I can't...do this forever."

He said something she mostly understood without guessing: "Things will get easier when we can speak more freely."

"Easier is a relative term, lizardman."

"Truth," he agreed in lizardish. "But then, life is in the journey. If you cannot have an easy journey, have an interesting story."

"That needs to be a fortune cookie," said Amber. "I don't know how my story can possibly be more interesting than it already is without...well, I was going to say alien invasion or a giant lizard, but we appear to have those bases covered."

He grunted and gazed into the fire.

After several minutes—she had all but forgotten he was there, lost in her own relentless playback of the whole rotten day—he nudged at her arm. When she glanced his way, he was holding up that square of jerky and staring straight ahead into the fire.

She took it. "Thanks. What is this stuff, by the way?"

"Cuuvash." He clasped his empty hands and watched the embers.

She repeated him, pretending not to see the way he rolled his eyes at her pronunciation, and gnawed off a piece of the dried meat. Her jaws were still sore from the last time he'd shared this stuff, but it was still pretty good. Like jerky, only not as salty, with a richer flavor and a weird undertaste almost like cheap wine. She ate, eyeing him suspiciously. "You're not having any."

He said no again, but in a different way. Not yet, maybe. Then he stirred, rubbing at his brow-ridges, and looked at her. "It's time to go," he told her.

An icy stone dropped into her belly. The jerky...the cuuvash got stuck in her throat. She swallowed hard, coughed, and managed, "You're leaving?"

He told her yes in some complicated way, said something about the weather and something about mountains, and that he'd only waited this long so that they could learn to talk. "Tomorrow, we leave," he said at the end of it. It was not a question.

"We?" Part of the knot in her throat relaxed a little, but her stomach stayed tight and sickly-cold. "You mean all of us?"

"Yes." He sent a black glance over his shoulder and cupped the end of his snout, muttering something with Scott's name in it. He told her it would be a long journey.

"And an interesting story," Amber guessed, rubbing at her stomach to try and ease up the rest of that rock before she had to puke it out.

His gaze shifted to watch her hand. He frowned and looked away, feeling idly at the buckle of his belt as if mimicking her movements. "You will tell S'kot to have his humans ready to travel tomorrow."

"Sure, why not. And I'll be ready, too."

The corners of his mouth flicked up in a smile before his usual fierce frown replaced it. He leaned toward her, aggressively close, the way he'd been before the slaps started flying. He said something about Scott and the others...no, he said, "When you are S'kot's human, you may disobey him all you like. When you are mine, you do as I say."

He waited, but apparently took her lengthy efforts to translate as a sign of submissive assent. He grunted again, but in a pleased way, even though his scowl stayed fixed to his face. He leaned even closer, filling her field of vision with nothing but his scowling, scaly face. "And when you are mine, if you ever leave my camp to—" Something...and probably not flattering. "—I will—" Again, she had no idea precisely what the threat was, but, "—you may never walk again," gave her the gist of it. He paused and frowned a little. "Did you mark that?"

"Most of it."

"Then I have your obedience."

"I didn't exactly plan to go anywhere this morning," she told him testily. "But I wasn't lost. I was just hunting. And I wasn't in trouble."

"Human, you are not yet *out* of trouble." But he leaned away from her and looked up at the sky. He said something she couldn't catch in an inquiring tone, then gave her a rap to the knee with his knuckles. "God sees us both and we can both show Him improvement. Tomorrow."

"Right." Amber popped the last of the cuuvash in her mouth and went to work on it, poking at the coals so the fire wouldn't die. She woke a few flames up. They crawled along the saoq bones, releasing a great smudge of black, foul-smelling smoke directly into her eyes and then went out.

Perfect.

Amber tossed down her coal-stirring stick. "God sees us, huh?"

"Yes."

"Right now?"

He seemed puzzled by the question. "Now and always."

Amber looked at the clouds. "Could you possibly make this day any worse?" she demanded.

A drop of rain hit her in the eye. Then another. And then the skies opened up and began to pour, killing the last coals in just a few steam-hissing seconds and drenching her to the skin.

Meoraq threw back his head and roared with curiously hoarse and chuffing laughter. His hand slapped at her back once, nearly knocking her cuuvash out of her mouth, and he got up, still grinning, and walked away into the grass. She could hear him talking to God as he went, but she couldn't hear what he said over the rain, or for that matter, over the cries of fifty Manifestors scrambling to get out of it. Amber herself stayed stubbornly where she was, already as wet, cold and miserable as she could get, determined to wait it out and start the fire again when it was over.

"And I'm still an atheist!" she shouted, swiping water from her face.

So there.

BOOK IV

PIONEERS

Meoraq was a warrior and had been all his life. He had been born under the Blade, raised in the training halls of Tilev, called to serve as Sheul's own Sword in judgment. These were the ways he knew—to cut, to grapple, to conquer—and every man who ever spoke a word in his presence spoke it with respect and by his leave.

He was Uyane Meoraq, son of Rasozul, who was son of Ta'sed, son of Kuuri, and forty-three names more, every man of them a Sheulek in his own time, all the way back to Uyane Xaima, who had walked with Prophet Lashraq himself. He was the veteran of better than three hundred judgments and if Sheul willed it, he would either go on to three hundred more or retire to stand as champion of Xeqor. He was a warrior. He was not a cattle-drover.

The humans said they were ready to follow him. Yes, they said this, even on the night before, when they bedded themselves down free of sentries and of care, trusting him to keep all danger from their little camp. They said this when it pleased them to wake the following morning, most of them not only after dawn, but well after. Those with tents made no effort to strike them. Those nearest the fire were setting it alight. They all assured him they were ready and then they just sat there!

Meoraq worked his way through four humans, dragging them bodily onto their feet and setting them in a line, but when he reached for a fifth and noticed all four of his humans had drawn off into a cluster, he had to cry surrender. He bellowed it, in fact. And then he stormed off in search of Amber.

She was sitting on a crate at the edge of camp with her Nicci. Both had their packs on their laps. Amber stood when she saw him, although he noted she put her pack down, rather than shoulder the strap for travel.

"What are they waiting for?" he demanded. "Did you not tell them dawn? Where is that chattering cattle's ass who calls himself your abbot?"

Amber's green eyes rolled heavenward, just as any dumaq's eyes might do if one were entertaining thoughts best not spoken aloud to a Sheulek. "Oh Scott!" she called in a curious, lilting way. "Meoraq would like a word with you."

"A word? I'd like my hand upside his snout, if only he had one! Half the morning is gone! S'kot!" Meoraq grabbed Amber by the arm and dragged her with him as he strode ahead to meet the human hesitating toward him. "I wanted these people ready to march at dawn! Where is your obedience?"

Scott looked at Amber.

"He's not happy about the delay," she said.

"What delay?" asked Scott.

Meoraq drew back. "Is he serious?" he asked dangerously.

"Yes," she sighed. "Look, Scott, he wanted us on the road first thing this morning.

First thing. Like, the sun comes up and we get going."

Scot heard this without apparent concern, certainly without apology. "Well if that's what he wanted, he should have been ready."

"What in Gann's grey hell does he mean by that?" Meoraq demanded.

"I don't know. What are you talking about?" she asked Scott. "He's been ready for hours. His teepee's packed. He's got his good, um, belts on. Or whatever he's wearing...Are those suspenders?"

"This is a travel harness!" Meoraq snapped, clutching at one of its buckles. "And it's a damned expensive one! I would have to sell three of you as cattle to make the cost of this harness and I can hardly see the sin of that since you have made no effort to obey me as men must do! Get your damned humans on their feet and make them ready!"

"And what was that?" Scott asked after a wary moment.

"Your guess is as good as mine, but it's a safe bet that it's got something to do with all this standing around."

"Fine." Scott turned boldly away from Meoraq and addressed Amber alone, folding his arms as though he wore a pair of blades upon them. "Tell him that if he wanted us to start early, he should have had our food ready on time."

"I should have what?" Meoraq hissed.

"Are you high?" Amber asked, and while it was impossible to read either her malleable face or her tone, both were clearly touched by some sort of emotion. "He's not running a hotel here, he doesn't owe you a continental breakfast!"

"He does if he wants us to follow him anywhere. I like this camp exactly where it is, Miss Bierce. We have the high ground here, we're in easy reach of water, we have the herds—"

"This is not your decision, human!" Meoraq snapped. He could feel his throat warming in pulses. His color was coming in. He made an effort to take deep breaths.

"What herds?" Amber asked. "The saoqs are hours away these days and you have no guarantee that they're coming back."

"Deer don't migrate, Miss Bierce."

"These aren't deer, you dumb dick! Stop acting like this is Earth!"

Meoraq terminated her further words with a silencing grip on her shoulder. "Enough. Speak my words, human. Do not speak for me. I am Sheulek."

She shut her mouth and waited, glaring at Scott who made a point of gazing loftily back at all his lounging people as he said, "If you want to go, go. No one's stopping you. But you are going to have to give me some incentive before I uproot these people a second time. We have everything we need right here in *my* camp. I'm not leaving just because you say so."

"So be it," said Meoraq, once he was himself quite calm. "Sheul has put you in my path and until I know the reason, I accept that I must care for you. So I will make a hunt for you. But if you want to share in it, you will have to be at *my* camp."

Amber relayed this, more or less, while Meoraq stood behind her and punctuated the words with hisses where necessary. "Now here's a little something from me," she said at the end of it. "In all this time, you haven't done a goddamn thing except hold meetings and tell us everything is going to be okay. When Meoraq walks away, you don't get to say that anymore. Instead, you get to tell them to pick up a spear and figure out how to use it before they starve to death. You think anyone is going to care how far they have to walk as long as they don't have to do that?"

Scott said nothing. His face had turned a deep purplish-red color, like shadesweet fruits left too long on the vine and gone to poison. "I'll think about it."

"Think as long as you like," Meoraq told him and turned to Amber, "Gather your things and whichever of your people—"

"You do and you're out of here!" Scott shouted, grabbing at Amber's shirt. "Don't you dare say one word to anyone, Bierce! This is my camp! Mine!"

Meoraq had never lost his temper so entirely or so quickly in all his life. Shoving Amber aside, he seized Scott by his soft, pink throat and lifted him right off the ground. "No one interrupts a Sword of Sheul!" he bellowed. "Not abbots, not judges, not governors, and not you, you freakish little gutter-bastard! Give me your obedience or I'll send you back to the clay that shat you out!"

Scott strangled and battered futilely at Meoraq's arm.

"Obedience, I say! Show me your fucking fist! Tell him—" he roared, turning, but Amber was nowhere to be found. Meoraq blinked, breathing hard, looking left and right and finally down, where Amber sprawled across the wet ground, clapping one hand to her head and staring dazedly at the sky. Blood, red as those shadesweet fruits in their fullest, dappled her fingers and streaked her hair.

And his first thought, unwelcome as a cold draft blowing across a dark and empty room, was not that she was injured, but only that she was a woman lying at his feet upon her back. He saw that and somehow forgot his anger even as it continued to throb in his throat, just as he forgot the human gasping for air at the end of his fist.

But thankfully, that moment ended.

Meoraq turned all the way to her and let Scott go. He didn't mean to throw him, but he wasn't careful either, and Scott crashed into a wooden crate and slid gasping to the ground. Meoraq was on one knee in the next instant, chasing her hand away to probe through the springy, matted mass of her hair.

The damage he found was little more than a scrape, neither deep nor wide. It bled, as head wounds were apt to do, but Amber did not give any kind of cry when he nudged at it. She pulled irritably out of his reach instead, saying, "I'm fine, damn it! You pushed me in the mud, not off a cliff! Christ, these pants were clean just, uh...I guess it was a week ago, but still! Damn it, Meoraq!"

"You're bleeding."

"I'm what?" She noticed the red smears on her fingertips and stared at them without comprehension, then touched at her head and studied the fresh daubs of blood she took away. "I didn't hit a rock or anything," she said, seeming puzzled but only a little troubled. "It must have been you."

He drew back, his spines flaring forward.

"You have rough hands," she told him. "Your...you know, your scales."

He stared at her for a long time before slowly looking down at the faint sign of her blood, like red frost, on the side of his hand.

"There he goes," said Amber, climbing to her feet. She was watching Scott, who had already retreated across the whole of the camp to gather his lieutenants and hiss at them. "It doesn't look like he's telling people to pack up and get ready, either."

"I do not care," said Meoraq distantly. He clenched his hand to a fist and opened it again, watching the blood shine where it was still wet and crack where it had already dried. "If it is to be Sheul's lesson that I learn to herd cattle, so be it. I shall tether them up in a line and whip their flanks, but they will walk, by Gann."

He heard a dry, fleshy, smacking sound. Amber had clapped both hands to her face and was holding them there. "You can't talk to them like that," she said, sighing in the same breath that she spoke, which was a clever human trick.

"Of course I can. I am Sheulek."

"I don't know what that means."

"It means I am owed all obedience."

She sighed again. "Listen. This is...This is a social situation, okay?"

"What does that mean?"

"It means...You have to make friends with these people."

"Eh?"

"Friends." She cast about with her eyes, then shrugged her arms out in futility. "Friends, you know? You need them to *like* you."

She said it, as she said most things, with sincerity even though he knew it for a lie. Friendship could be pleasant, but it could also be a dangerous distraction. A boy born under the sign of the Blade did not play with the other boys of his caste, but competed against them, brawled with them, beat and were beaten by them. The masters at Tilev allowed no leisure hours in company, only study, meals and sleep, where every stolen whisper risked a slap across the snout. The brunts at least had some leeway to chat amongst themselves, but were set against each other so often and so brutally as part of their training that even then attachments were few. After his ascension, his duties as a Sheulek kept him moving from city to city, and what company he might share with a man like Nkosa was kept brief. A Sword of Sheul must always be honed and ready to strike, and personal feelings could only complicate things.

"Do you like any of these people?" he asked, gesturing toward the camp where a few humans were reluctantly gathering up their gear.

She dropped her eyes as if it were a reprimand before glancing shamefacedly at her people. "I should."

"Why?"

"Because...Christ, I don't know." She covered her face again, baring her teeth as if she wanted to bite something. "Okay, so I'm a horrible hypocrite and the last person who should be trying to explain this to anyone, but that doesn't make it any less true. People need people." She grimaced even as she said it, not in a smiling way. "What would you do if Scott convinced them you were some kind of...of raging, man-eating, bloodthirsty lizardman?"

"Kill him," Meoraq said with a snort.

She stared at him for a moment before asking, in some exasperation, "Wouldn't that just prove him right?"

"I might as well, since he's already convinced them in your scenario. At least he wouldn't be around to gloat afterwards." He watched Scott as he moved among his people, touching them, bobbing his head, speaking lengthy and serious words, and motioning quite often back at Meoraq with the whole of his Gann-damned hand. He found himself toying idly with the thought of killing the man, then more than idly, and then he let it go and looked at Amber instead. She was also watching Scott. The blood in her hair had dried, forming a short series of stiff, brown spines, which stuck straight up as if she were in a state of great surprise, comically at odds with the solemn expression on her face. He looked back at Scott and said, "I did not intend to strike you."

"Yeah, I know. I'm fine."

He grunted, then pointed brusquely out at Scott (with the whole of his own hand, ha). "How long is this likely to take?"

"I don't know. Longer than it has to, I'm pretty sure."

"Are you prepared to travel?"

"Me?" She looked around at the crates where she had left her pack and her Nicci. "Yeah, I'm good to go."

"Then let's see if we can hurry them along." He shrugged his own pack higher on his back in a meaningful way and started walking. A great outcry rose up from those humans who noticed, and it had not fully settled before Amber was hurrying to collect not only her pack and her pet human, but one of the heavy, sealed sacks her people usually used to sit upon. Its weight gave her obvious difficulty, but she heaved it up and managed a loping run back to his side. Soon all the humans were finally scraping themselves together, shouting out for him to stop, to wait, to give them a damned minute, just as if he had not given them all morning.

Meoraq listened, at once annoyed and grimly pleased with the commotion he had caused, and unthinkingly gave Amber a two-knuckle tap to the shoulder in a far more intimate welcome than he ever should have given one of her kind, much less a woman of any kind. Luckily, she took it for a command, looking back over that shoulder in a puzzled way at the humans who were struggling to follow in his wake.

"Yeah, they're coming," she said. And looked up at him with half a smile, half a frown. "But I don't think you made any friends."

"In the Book of First Hours, it is written, 'If every hand of every man reached out to you in friendship, so it would yet remain they reached from Gann. A true son of Sheul is never tempted, but seeks always to clasp the one hand that reaches down from heaven.'"

"I got...practically none of that."

"It means I am Sheulek," he replied, patting her companionably but safely on the unfeeling swell of her pack. "And I don't need friends."

* * *

Which was just as well, since he made none that day.

Meoraq knew it was no easy thing he asked of them. He had waded through the hip-deep bog of reeking water that the lowlands became in the rainy season, crossed the middle plains under the sweltering wet heat of summertime, and climbed the highland steppes when the icestorms raged so violently that his clothes were frozen to his body. He had walked both by day and by dark of night, upon whole roads and fallen roads and no roads at all, and he had done all these things with no company apart from the ravening beasts of the wild and the equally ravening men who had gone to Gann. He had suffered and survived the consequences of his ignorance, recklessness and, yes, outright stupidity, and knowing the humans were strangers to this land and its hardships, he was resolved to forgive much.

In forming this resolution, Meoraq had perhaps failed to recognize that he was not the most forgiving of men.

No matter how many times he ordered them to stay together and be quiet, they soon drifted apart, shouting back and forth whenever they had something they wanted to say. When his words were not enough to bring them under control, Meoraq dealt out a few cuffs. Mindful of human fragility, they had been the most glancing of blows, hardly more than two-knuckle taps, and yet they yelped (and occasionally bled) and whined about it so much that he soon cried surrender and let them do what they wanted.

Before the first hour was ended, they had stretched themselves out so thinly, half of them were no longer in sight. The ones with the least to carry left the rest so entirely behind that when they came to an obstacle—which was often in this roadless wilderness—they had time to set up their camp so they could whine at each other in comfort while they waited for the others to catch up.

The whining! Great Sheul grant him patience against their constant whining! It was muddy. It was cold. They were hungry. They were tired. The only thing worse than having to hear it was knowing that tomorrow, he'd also have to hear them whine about how sore they were.

And they were going to be sore, judging from the difficulty they were having carrying their supplies. Meoraq had no sympathy. If they'd had the resources to construct crates, they should have made carts as well, but no, they built these enormous, ungainly casings and then heaved them up by their edges, since they didn't even have grips or pole-holds or anything. Most of the day—not even half but *most*—

was therefore spent either waiting for the crates, arguing over whose turn it was to carry them, or struggling to move them out of the mud, through the thorns, or up over some tumbled stone ridge.

And what could he do about it? Not a Gann-damned thing. The humans couldn't mark half of what Meoraq told them and wouldn't listen to the other half. He worked with them until his patience was gone—scouting ahead for the least arduous route while they rested, sharing out his water, even striking fires for them during their many lengthy rests—and told himself it would all be worth it when he stood in Xi'Matezh.

If he ever got there.

"Meoraq!" Scott called from the bottom of a steep rise which was giving considerable trouble to the exhausted men trying to carry a crate up it. "Come here!"

Meoraq, who had been waiting at the top of that rise for some time now, lowered his spines and did not move.

Scott was not deterred. He pointed imperiously at the crate and said, "Come get under this end."

"Fuck your fist," Meoraq replied, making sure to speak clearly and evenly.

"Right here," said Scott, patting the crate-top. "Come on, you haven't helped out once all day. Meoraq? I'm saying that right, aren't I? Why is he just staring at me?"

And he whistled, like a cattleman after calves, with his soft little mouthparts puckered up like an anus. He was farting out of his face. Meoraq was rarely one for that sort of crude humor, but he laughed.

Scott threw up his hand and slapped it down on the crate-top, turning to his men. "I never know what the hell he's thinking. Where's Bierce?"

"Look, man." This was Eric, who was not as objectionable as Scott, but as one of his servants, was still never going to be one of Meoraq's favorite humans. "I keep telling you, it doesn't matter how many people get under it."

"He's stronger than we are," Scott said indifferently, trying once again to lure Meoraq down from the top of the rise. "He could probably carry this end by himself if he ever gets it through his thick head that's what he's supposed to do."

Supposed to, no less.

"The ground is way too loose," Eric argued. "We'd have to build some kind of support—"

Meoraq clapped a hand to the end of his snout and rubbed. Building anything to lift that crate to the top of this rise would take at least to the end of the day, if they knew what they were doing as they built it, which was doubtful, and if they bothered themselves to do anything about it today, which was even less likely.

"—and we don't have a hammer or rope or even duct tape!" Eric finished. "We're going to have to find another way up."

Scott considered this, then turned back to Meoraq. "Do you have any rope?"

"Yes," said Meoraq, thinking himself wonderfully patient. "However, there are no trees up here to act as anchor."

"What?"

"Trees, idiot." Meoraq mimed the tying of a knot, then opened his arms in a broad gesture of futility. "Rope does you no good without something to tie it to."

Scott patted the crate even louder. "We're going to tie it to this," he explained, and rolled his eyes at his generals. "Not the sharpest pencil on the planet, is he?"

Meoraq started to speak, then abruptly flexed his spines forward and shrugged off his pack. He opened it up, dug out the coil of strong braid he kept at the bottom, and tossed it down to them. He watched while Scott instructed his servants in how to bind up the crate (it both amused and disgusted him to see that Eric followed the man's directions only until Scott moved on, then quickly untied it and did it right), then moved aside so that they could ascend to the crown of the rise and see for themselves there was nothing to tie it to. Undaunted, Scott ordered his men in a line, like boys playing Heave-To with the crate acting as the opposing team.

Meoraq glanced at the tumble of rock at the bottom of the rise and moved a little further back. He waited.

"Everybody pull together!" Scott called, coming over to stand next to Meoraq. "One! Two! Pull!"

They obeyed. Grunting, straining, with Scott calling officious encouragement at them, the humans dragged the crate out of the mud and onto the slope, where they managed to drag it about halfway up before the first man's feet slid a little too close to the edge. The ground gave, not much, but enough to throw a start into the heaving humans. Men tumbled over each other with cries of alarm and the one man who did not let go of the rope let himself be yanked painfully down the slope to land head-first against the crate, once more resting in the mud at the bottom.

Meoraq leaned out and watched until he saw enough movement to satisfy him that there were no real injuries, then turned and looked at Scott. "I want my rope back. And I want it cleaned before it's coiled."

Scott glared at him with color in his face and complete incomprehension in his eyes. He turned to his men. "We're going to try that again," he announced.

Meoraq bent his neck for a few deep breaths, rubbing at his brow-ridges.

"But first we're going to get some branches or something to use as poles. Some people can stand at the bottom and push with the poles—"

"I cry," Meoraq said.

Scott looked at him. "What?"

Meoraq dropped his hand and shrugged his tight spines. "I cry," he said again, simply and without anger. "I have stood for truth in three hundred trials and surely struck down two hundred more of Gann's corrupted in my time, and I have faced and defeated every wild beast left to this land from a denning she-ghet to a rutting bull corroki, but Uyane Meoraq, son of Rasozul and Sword of Sheul, cries surrender to you and your fucking crate. We stop here for the night."

"What the hell is he saying?" Scott asked, puckering up his flat, ugly face in an expression of annoyance. "Where's Bierce?"

"You had best find her," Meoraq ordered, pointing right into Scott's face with the whole of his hand. "Because I have a few thoughts and if I cannot express them in words, I mean to do it with the beating of your miserable, misshapen life."

Scott moved unhurriedly back, saying, "I don't know what the hell he's saying. Go ahead and let's make camp. We're done for the day. Someone find Bierce before I forget how useful this thing can occasionally be."

Meoraq grunted and went to gather up his emptied flasks, reminding himself at every step that this was a pilgrimage, there were supposed to be ordeals, and they were called ordeals because they were not endured easily.

Even without a sandglass or bells rung at every hour, Meoraq had always had a good sense of time. A man who spent so much of his life with nothing to look at except the sun (or the light of the sun, according to Master Tsazr), learned to read it almost unawares. Meoraq knew that they had left the fast-flowing stream behind perhaps two hours ago, and although he also knew it would not take nearly so long to reach it again, he was not prepared to find himself standing at its edge as quickly as he did.

Two hours...and here was the stream.

Meoraq did not fill his flasks. He shouldered them instead and, in a fouler mood than ten days' rain outside of Tothax had been able to inspire in him, kept walking. He marked the sun as he went. By his judgment, he reached his destination and returned in just a little more than an hour, stopping only once to fill his flasks at last.

He came back into the humans' camp, ignoring those brave few who dared to express their disappointment that he had no meat with him. He set his water down beside his pack—calmly, a Sheulek was the master of his impulses—but kept the one object he had taken from his walk tight in his fist and went in search of Amber.

He found her sprawled on her back on a heap of the wrapped cushions, which, judging from her flushed face and rough breath, she had only just finished hauling up to the top of the rise where Scott had put this camp—the first show of common sense the man had demonstrated. Her clothes lay over her in damp, rumpled folds that emphasized, rather than hid, the wasted hills and valleys of her exhausted body. Her eyes were shut; the flesh around them, dark and hollow-looking, like sockets in an empty skull. There was still a stain of blood in her hair.

Anger he had struggled all day long to contain faded somewhat. He opened his mouth, grappled with and was defeated by the sinful nonsense of her name, and turned instead to Nicci, who sat on the cushions close by, wrapped in one of their metal blankets, watching him.

He gestured uncomfortably at Amber. "Is she sleeping?"

Nicci spared the prone human beside her a glance. "Looks like it."

Meoraq grunted and beckoned to her. "Leave her. You mark me well enough. I require my words carried to your abbot. Come."

Nicci reached out to nudge at Amber. "Wake up."

Amber's eyes opened, but the impossible green of them was dulled into something greyish. Dead. She looked at Nicci, who was wrapping herself up again, then at Meoraq, who was battling the urge to slap Nicci right out of her shiny metal blanket.

"Hey," Amber muttered. She visibly gathered her strength, then rolled onto her side before pushing herself into a seated position. Her arm trembled as she raised it to rub at her face. "I can't believe I actually crashed like that."

Crashed. Not a word he'd ever heard for rest, but one almost painfully apt. She had not been sleeping, not lying that way under the open sky with rain pooling over her eyes. She had crashed, like the ship she claimed had carried her here.

He wished briefly and with singular bitterness that he really had gone hunting after all. She looked terrible and what did he have to offer her but—

She saw the object in his hand and her brows pinched together. "What's that?"

He looked at it himself, just as if he had not been the one to pick it up and carry it here. His anger returned, an ugly shadow of the good, clarifying fire it had been, but just as undeniable.

"I need you," he said and curtly added, "To speak."

"Yeah, okay."

And she took his arm.

Reached right up and took it.

Meoraq held very still as she used him to climb to her feet, unsure where he should be looking. He was excruciatingly aware of everything around him: the wind whispering through the grass, the piercing warble of laughing humans, the smell of wet leaves and earth, Nicci's silent staring eyes, and above everything, the warm press of all five thin fingers that gripped him.

No woman in all his life had ever...*ever* touched him like that. In other ways, yes. He tended to be permissive with his women, particularly if they, like the woman in Xheoth, came to his room more than once. Those he took in conquest after trial, like the flat-headed girl in Tothax, were permitted to struggle, but they rarely did and even they did not touch him like that—flesh to flesh, uninvited and unrepentant for it.

Then she let go and moved away, taking the short, limping steps of an old woman. "Oh Scott!" she called in that musical way.

At some short distance, surrounded by his generals, Scott turned around. "Miss Bierce," he said without welcome.

Amber smiled. "Everly."

Meoraq stepped between them.

"Do you know what this is?" he demanded, thrusting the object he had collected on his solitary walk—a plain stone, charred along one side—out before him.

Scott looked at it. So did Amber, although she had to come around the side of him to see.

"What did he say?" Scott asked in a tight, impatient way.

"He...wants to know what that is."

Scott looked at her. She rolled her shoulders and shook her head. He frowned.

Meoraq waited.

"It's a rock," said Scott.

"And do you know where I got it?" Meoraq inquired.

Amber asked.

Scott's brows puckered. "How the hell should I...? This better be what he's really saying, Bierce, because if you're just trying to make me look stupid—"

"You don't need my help to look stupid."

Meoraq gave the rock a terse shake. "Answer!"

Amber rolled her shoulders again, adding, "I hope to God you don't want us to walk back and look because I'm done in, lizardman."

"I took it from your fire-pit!" Meoraq bellowed, so suddenly that both of them—and quite a few of those around them—jumped. "We have been walking all day and for what? We are still in easy distance of your first camp's fires! I could walk further on two broken legs!"

"What's he saying?" Scott asked.

Amber ignored him, beginning to scowl up at Meoraq in her fearless, senseless way. "Hey, I think we're doing pretty goddamn good here!"

"We have not gone half a span, human! Not even half of half! Do you know what a day's shamefully idle distance is for me?"

"Do I care?"

"Five!"

She looked at him, then down at herself, and up at him again. "Look at me!" she said angrily. "Do I look like I can go any further than I did today? Do any of us?"

"I could," said a human.

"Shut the fuck up, Crandall!"

"Well, I could. Hey, realistically, we did, what? Two miles?"

"It had to be more than that," said Scott, looking alarmed.

"Uphill, loose terrain, bad weather, and of course, lugging the heavy stuff. It took us forever to get going and every time we took a break, we'd end up sitting around like two hours. I wasn't going to say anything," he added, rolling his shoulders. "I mean, I realize you guys aren't soldiers."

"But we could have done a lot better," Eric said quietly.

"Well, you just tell him we need this equipment," said Scott, turning back to Amber. "And while you're at it, you might find a nice way of suggesting that he pull the stick out of his scaly ass or someone just might have to kick it for him."

"How many times do I have to tell you? He understands English just fine!"

Scott frowned at her, then looked at Meoraq.

Meoraq slapped him.

"And we're not slowing you up for the fun of it," Amber told him as Scott staggered back. "This stuff is heavy."

"Then leave it behind! I have never seen you so much as open those crates! How can they be so essential?"

"What is he saying now?" asked Scott, cradling his jaw just as though Meoraq had broken it.

"He wants to know if what we're dragging around is important," said Amber.

"What we're dragging around is none of his business. His only job is to act as our guide."

"No, human," said Meoraq, darkly amused by the man's audacity in spite of himself. "My only true task is to serve Sheul as his Sword and his Striding Foot, and in that pursuit, I am given all liberty. All, S'kot. To defy me is to defy Him, and the cost of that defiance is death."

Scott continued to glare, although his brows creased above his snapping eyes with a human expression of confusion. "What did he call me?"

"He didn't call you anything," Amber replied. "He just said he doesn't work for you. And...something about God, I'm not sure what. And I think that bit at the end was him telling you to quit arguing with him."

"I'm not arguing with him! He's arguing with me! Look, Meoraq," he said, turning briskly to face him even as he edged out of easy striking reach. "I can appreciate your concern and I share it. If it was within my power to expedite our progress, I would."

"You could carry something," Amber remarked in a dry tone.

"Your input is not requested, Miss Bierce," said Scott without looking at her. "If you can't act as an interpreter without inserting your uninformed opinions, I will end this discussion right now."

She opened her mouth.

Meoraq put his hand on her shoulder in warning and squeezed it. Miraculously, she silenced herself, even if she had to roll her eyes first. "I am prepared to hear you, human," he told Scott. "But so far, I have heard only your insolence and a lot of human whining. I will not carry you all the way to Xi'Matezh!"

"It isn't his decision, Miss Bierce!" Scott said loudly once Amber had repeated this in their own rumbling tongue. "It's mine! And you can tell him that we aren't going to be walking forever! Someday, we're going to have to make a permanent home with a permanent infrastructure! These things are essential to our ultimate goal and, regardless of how he thinks this inconveniences him in the short-term, we're keeping them!"

Meoraq cocked his head. "He has a tendency to use longer and stranger words when he thinks he's losing an argument, have you noticed?"

"Oh boy, have I noticed."

"Don't talk to him!" Scott snapped, glaring from one to the other of them, his face coloring up high in the cheek. "You're just the translator!"

Meoraq acknowledged this with a grunt and did his best to address Scot without sarcasm. "If the things you insist on carrying are vital to your settlement, I will allow you to hold them for now, but the weather *is* turning and I will *not* be caught by it."

"How bad is it going to get?" Amber asked, frowning.

"If this day is anything to measure by, the mountains will be hip-high in ice before we come to cross them," he told her, then gave her a hard rap on the brow with one knuckle. "Speak my words. And tell him that he must prove these things to be truly needful before I allow them to anchor us further."

"It's all necessary!" Scott barked before she had hardly begun to obey. "Every single item is absolutely imperative to our survival in the new colony—"

"Oh Christ, not this again," sighed Amber, rubbing at her eyes.

"—except you!" Scott finished, rounding on her.

"I'm the translator," she told him. "And the translator would like to know what fantasy you're living in where half a filter pump and fifteen bags of concrete is useful."

Meoraq put his hand on her shoulder in warning. "My words, human. Give this fool my words now and have your own arguments later."

"What did he just call me?" Scott demanded. "Did he just call me an idiot?"

"Oh, that you understand, eh? Then understand this." Meoraq moved Amber aside and pointed at Scott with the whole of his hand in undisguised contempt. "I do not ask your will. I declare mine. Open the crates and I will judge them for myself."

Scott looked at Amber.

"He wants to see what we're carrying," she said.

Scott's face filled with color. "No!"

Meoraq's spines slapped flat. He folded his arms, lay his first fingers along the hilts of his sabks, and calmly said, "I would be very clear, human. Do you answer her or are you defying me?"

"It would be pointless!" Scott insisted, backing away. "He couldn't possibly understand anything we showed him!"

Meoraq drew his samr and looked at Amber. "Did he just call me a fool?"

"Oh come on!" Scott was now retreating rapidly, trying to shield himself among his people except that they kept moving out of his way. "Look at him! How am I supposed to explain a solar generator to a...a..."

"*Lizard*?" Meoraq hissed, advancing.

Scott bumped his back end into a crate and scuttled around it at once. "It's highly sophisticated technology and you...that is, your species...You're not very advanced!"

"So now we are *all* fools!"

"Meoraq."

He looked back at Amber, catching at Scott's clothing to keep him close. His samr remained in his hand, raised and ready to use. He grunted an inquiry, but kept his spines flat, a silent warning that he was not of a mood to entertain foolishness.

"I know this is going to be hard to believe," she said, "but he's not insulting you on purpose. We really do have stuff in there that...that you probably won't understand."

He eyed her while the human in his grip held very still, and at last, not without some reluctance, the truth she spoke found resonance in him. He was not Sheul, after all. It was not for Uyane Meoraq, born of clay, to know the infinite workings of the world and all things in it. So it may well be that the land which had vomited out such creatures as these humans had also allowed for the making of many equally unknowable things.

Meoraq raised his spines with some effort. He let go of Scott's shirt-front. He prepared himself to abide by another's judgment and gestured roughly at the crates around him with his samr. "Do you say these things are necessary then?"

"Yes," said Scott.

Meoraq turned all the way around and stared at him until Scott backed away, tugging at his clothing and turning various shades of red. Meoraq looked at Amber again. "We have a long way to go and the weather has already begun to turn. We will never make the crossing into Gedai at a quarter-span's travel each day. You must understand this. If the things you carry are indeed so vital as this cattle's ass insists, you will have them, but if they are not, you must give them up. I will carry tools, human. I will carry shelters. I will carry any instrument of your profession that will help to settle you at our journey's end. I will not carry sentiment."

She sighed and rubbed at her face.

"What's he saying?" Scott pressed.

She looked at him and then rubbed her face some more. "Scott, we have to leave some of this stuff behind."

"Out of the question!" Scott turned an extremely unwise sneer on Meoraq. "This discussion is over!"

"Is it now?" he hissed, raising his samr.

"I don't want to fight," said Amber. "I've been hauling a sixty-pound bag of frigging concrete around just so I wouldn't start a fight, but for God's sake, enough is enough. Maybe it used to be the cutting edge of colonizing technology once upon a time, but it's all junk now, Scott! The only really useful things are the crates themselves and only if we empty them out and use them as shelters!"

"I don't know whether you're really this stupid or just short-sighted, but in either case, if you can't see the big picture, it is not my job to draw you a new one, Miss Bierce. I'm done talking to you," Scott declared, turning around. "Both of you."

Meoraq had been right on the verge of sheathing his samr until he heard that. And although he managed not to run the pompous little piss-licker through the middle when he did hear it, he had reached the end of his patience with these negotiations. He stormed over to the nearest of the crates, jammed his samr into the topmost seam, and pried the thing open to look for himself.

He didn't know what he expected to see. A Sheulek did not involve himself in the menial task of guarding those infrequent caravans that traveled between the cities and he had not the smallest notion of what was involved when households moved themselves. He supposed he had anticipated furniture—Scott's furniture, no doubt, which he would recognize by its overwrought and garish making—and he had even the sour tickle of a notion that he might find rich food or wine or something of that sort too luxurious to share out with the likes of those who served him. It might have been works of art or chests filled with official robes or coffers of coin or anything at all.

Anything but this.

Meoraq ripped his samr free and leapt clear of the thing in the crate. It did not move. The light of the fading day gleamed dully off its metal hide, showing him a square body, armless, faceless, motionless.

"Meoraq, it's okay," Amber said.

He swung on her, pointing back at the crate with an arm that actually shook. "You knew about this?" he demanded. "*You?*"

She wrinkled her soft brows at him.

"Where did you..." His samr trembled again. He shook his head to clear it and aimed his blade with force at Scott instead. "Where did you get this?"

"Okay, well, he's obviously decided to freak out," Scott began, rolling his eyes. "So as soon as you figure out what he's saying, come and get—"

"*Stand and be judged!*" Meoraq roared. "I am not Uyane Meoraq but the Sword in His hand and I will cut you down if you do not answer just as if you answered for Gann! Did you build the fucking machine?"

"Meoraq, what's wrong?"

Her voice, so timid that it might have been Nicci's instead, somehow fell on him as a hammer, knocking the wind from his lungs and the bones from his body. He dropped his arm limp at his side and stared at her, his thoughts in such storms that even he didn't know what he was thinking.

Perhaps they had only stolen it. They weren't using it, after all. It had been crated all this time. He'd never even seen anyone near it, except to sit on it. A man could pass through the old ruins without offending Sheul, open those doors, fill flasks at those pumps. He had himself read by the light of those ancient lamps without a twinge of conscience. The only unforgiveable sin...

"Did you build it?" he asked her. "Say truth."

"No, but why?"

"Why? How can you..." He backed away from her, shaking his head harder and harder. "How can you ask? How can you pretend not to know?" He fought with words and his temper, then lost both and shouted, "How can you bring that...*thing* into my camp? How dare you stand against the Word of God *in a Sheulek's camp*!"

"This is exactly what I was afraid he'd do," Scott said from the distance he had taken during this distraction. "He doesn't know what he's seeing so he...he thinks it's a demon or—"

"I think it's a *machine*!" hissed Meoraq, never taking his eyes from Amber's. His chest hurt. He wished he'd killed her the day she'd first dropped gasping at his feet in the thornbreak than come to this moment, this betrayal. How could she dare to look at him like this, as if she did not know what he was saying? "And you must tell me the truth. Is it one of the Ancients' making or your own?"

"It's ours," she said. "But no one here made it, if that's what you keep asking. It was made clear back on Earth. That's kind of my whole point," she added, directing herself to Scott. "It's broken and no one here knows how to fix it, so why are we still hauling it around?"

He seized on those words. "It cannot be restored?"

"No, and before you say one stupid word, Scott, look at it! What, are you going to chisel a solar panel out of stone? Make wire out of grass? It's dead. The only reason we're dragging it around with us is because it came from Earth."

"From...your homeland? You carry it...as a keepsake?"

"Something like that. But if you honestly expect us to start putting the miles behind us, we are going to have to drop the dead weight."

"I can think of some weight we can drop," said Scott.

"Quiet, all of you. I must pray." Meoraq bent his head and closed his eyes, shutting away the immediate whispers of the humans around him. The Second Law forbade the children of Sheul from seeking to remake the machines or to master them as the Ancients had done. In the Word, it was written that the man or woman who removed those devices from the ruins to be restored or put to use had broken faith with Sheul and could not be redeemed. He could think of no passage that forbade the keeping of a dead machine, but he certainly was not easy with the idea of carrying it about in a closed litter like an unholy relic.

Meoraq opened his eyes and there were Amber's, impossibly green, unafraid. They showed him no guilt, no stain of sin. They were the very eyes of innocence.

But even a child could touch a naked blade in innocence and go to Gann for it. The machine was here, dead or not, and Scott at least spoke as if restoring it for use were part of his ultimate goal, this thing he called colony. Amber did not seem to think that possible, but still the humans were carrying it, revering it, and if it was not a working machine, what did that make it but an idol to Gann?

"Get your things," he told her. And turned around. "I share no camp with the trophies of Gann's age of dominion. We move on, humans."

"We are not leaving our—" Scott began, and for a wonder, Meoraq did not have to say a word. One of his own men reached out and caught his arm. Meoraq could not hear what was said, but Scott looked hard at his samr when it was done and made his face change colors. He had no more objections.

"How far do you want us to go?" Amber asked. She had gone only as many steps as were necessary to take her Nicci by one hand and the strap of her pack in the other, but both dragged behind her. "Because I know you don't think we were trying very hard, but...but I just don't have a whole lot more left in me."

Some of the other humans agreed, softly at first, but adding more and more voices until it seemed they were all whining at once. They were hungry. They were tired. They had walked all day. Their feet hurt and their backs and their shoulders and every other part of their malformed bodies—a growing litany of complaint that scraped and scraped at him until it finally stabbed itself in.

"Damn it, why can't just *one* of you do what you're told without whining at me?" he exploded, and turned on Amber. "You tell these bawling calves that I am slapping the very next mouth that opens!"

The furry stripes above her eyes rose in arches. "Wouldn't I have to open my mouth to do that?"

He tipped his head back and took a deep breath, letting it out very slowly.

"What did he say?" Scott asked after a moment.

"And why would he want her to open her mouth?" asked Crandall.

Amber started to turn toward them. Meoraq caught her chin and made her look at him instead. "I am a Sword of Sheul and I honor Him always. Always. To see His laws broken and do nothing is to break them myself. Do you mark me?"

"I think so."

"If the land of your birth makes such machines, then your land is lost to Gann. But you have left it, and that, at least, may be some sign that you can be redeemed. Perhaps this is why you were set in my path. Tonight, I choose to believe so. But not even for one hour will I tolerate Gann's corruption among us now that I know of it. Do you mark me?"

She stared at him for a long time while her people whispered at each other behind her. "Are you telling me the Devil built our solar generator?" she asked at last. "Because I'm all for leaving it behind, but that's just stupid."

"What I tell you is that I honor Sheul. And if you honor Him also, you will not require me to enforce His laws. You will obey because it is His word and you love Him."

"Because I what?" Her face puckered as if in pain, although she huffed out a laugh at him. "Meoraq, I don't even believe in my own God, much less yours."

"Jesus, Bierce, don't tell him that," said Crandall, more amused than alarmed.

"Well, I don't. So please don't ask me to haul my tired ass another two miles or even two meters because God hates our broken solar generator, because I won't do it. I'll stay here and take my chances with the smiting."

"I ought to let you," Meoraq said, releasing her. "That would teach you a very brief, very profound lesson. But I won't. If you will not go for Sheul's sake, go at my command and I will honor Him for both of us. Nevertheless, we are leaving."

"The hell you say."

"I do say." And despite the seriousness of the situation and the insult he surely would have taken had it been anyone else who stood against him in this way, he felt the stiff set of his body ease and heard his voice quiet. "And you will not defy me," he told her, only her, "even though you are sore and weary, because you know I would not give that order without cause. Get your people ready."

She pressed her hands to her face and shook her head several times, but at last she sighed. "Yeah. Yeah, okay."

This was all that Scott could stand. "Goddammit, Bierce, you are not in charge! You don't have people here and you don't give orders to any of mine!"

Meoraq caught Amber by the shoulder as she began an answer and moved her firmly aside. He advanced, and kept on advancing as Scott retreated, until he'd backed the human up right against the machine's shining carcass. He put his hand on the hilt of his samr and leaned over, face to ugly human face. "What are your orders, S'kot? Do you walk with me or go to Gann?"

Scott glared at him, deeply colored in parts of his face and very pale in others. A paradox, like his mouthparts, which were tightly pressed together and yet trembled. "Someone, say something."

"You're a dick," said Amber, somewhat less than obediently.

Meoraq snorted, stirring the hair on the human's head, and tapped his samr. "If I draw this again tonight, it will be to strike the head from your skinny neck. Mark me, human, or do not mark me. My patience is gone."

He did not see much of understanding in the sullen face that stared back at him, but when Scott spoke again, it was to command his people to gather their things. The few tents and small packs they carried did not take long to set in order and soon the whole grumbling herd was following in Meoraq's wake. Whenever they found air enough to whine at one another, Meoraq quickened his pace until at last they were quiet. He meditated as he drove them, thinking this was the first ordeal of his pilgrimage that he truly felt as though he'd conquered, and even if the humans were angry (or even if he cared if the humans were angry), it was still a far easier walk than it had been all the rest of that day. Tomorrow, they might even thank him, but even if they didn't, they would walk. He was Sheulek; they were *his*, and it was long past time they knew it.

2

Once upon a time, Amber Bierce lived in a two-bedroom apartment. She shared a closet with her sister and had a shelf and two drawers for her other clothes. She had four pairs of shoes, two coats, a scarf she never wore, a new pair of gloves every year because she could never find the old ones, and socks. Once upon a time, Amber Bierce had her own bed, a mattress and boxsprings both, sheets and blankets and pillows that had to be just right or she couldn't get to sleep. Once upon a time, food was nothing but a phone call or at the most, an extra stop on the bus ride home, and she could curl up on the couch and eat as much as she wanted even if she wasn't hungry, just because it tasted good, and maybe even drink a beer or two before she took her shower...washed her hair...brushed her teeth...went to bed.

Once upon a time.

Now and then, as Amber lay on the rocky ground with the cold rain trickling in under the emergency blanket to warm against her reeking body, that apartment and that life seemed as hazy and unreal as the fairy tale words she used to invoke them. It was occurring to her more and more often these days that life wasn't going to get any better. Easier, sure. Already, it was easier. They still hadn't managed to walk far enough in one day to make Meoraq happy, but they were making a hell of a lot better distance without the concrete and crates. They ate almost every day, not a lot, but enough. No one was sick, no one had tripped over a rock and broke his head open, no one had found a thick limb on a short tree and hung himself. Perhaps even more impressively, no one had pissed Meoraq off to the point where he left. Bad enough when he stomped around, hissing and hitting people, and praying as loudly as he could for patience; it was so much worse when he got quiet and just watched them.

Watched her.

She could never tell what he was thinking on those nights, but she was often gripped with the fear that those were the nights he thought the hardest about leaving, and if he did, it would be her fault.

Because they weren't friends. She wanted to be, tried to be, but she'd never been good at making friends and now that her life actually depended on it, she had no idea how. He was gone in the mornings when she woke up and he didn't walk with anyone on the daily hike, just kept moving around them, ever vigilant and increasingly pissed off. By the time camp was struck, he was rarely in the mood to be bothered by anyone, let alone her, but sometimes he sat with her when the time came to feed his whining humans and sometimes he stayed to talk while everyone else went to bed. On the nights he didn't, she sat up alone. She had no friends and when she was stupid and girly enough to feel bad about that, she just told herself that Amber Bierce didn't care what other people felt about her. Once upon a time, it had been true. Once upon a time and far, far away.

"Are you sorry you found us?" she asked one night, one of the good nights, when she'd been able to pretend that she wasn't just some pest he had to take care of.

And he said no, said it without even seeming to think about it first. But he also didn't seem surprised by the question or her (not quite) teasing expectation that he might say yes.

"You think you'll be sorry when it's over?"

"That would depend on how it ends, but I doubt it." The blunt bony spines on the top and back of his head flared forward and relaxed back in that shrugging way he had.

"Right now, it's too easy to imagine that it will never end."

"Will you miss us when we're gone?" she asked, grinning and expecting a resounding lizardish version of 'Hell, no,' but to her surprise, he took the question seriously.

"There are qualities I'll miss," he said after a considering pause, adding with a glance toward Scott, "If the company were better, I imagine I'd miss it more."

She waited, but he seemed content to stare into the coals all night, so she said it for him: "Aren't you going to ask if I'm going to miss you?"

He looked at her for a very long time, then told her to go to sleep.

She did. She dreamed about the ship again, the night it blew up, filling the whole sky with that tower of howling fire. This time, everyone got away okay, and they were all there, thousands of them, even Jonah, but Scott was there too, telling everyone in his soothing, determined way that they could leave as soon as they were all on board and so they were walking, all of them, in a neat, orderly line right back into the fire. Eric and Maria went together, holding hands. Jonah followed, the bloody sweat on the side of his bald head already turning to steam. Then Nicci, shaking off Amber's clutching hands and crying. Amber tried to chase after her, but the heat pressed her back, and still they all kept walking until there was no one left but her and Scott.

"Your room is ready, Miss Bierce," he told her, savagely triumphant in the firelight. "All you have to do is say you're sorry and I'll let you come too."

She woke up too damn close to the fire, with Meoraq on the other side of it, just watching her. The dream died at once, tangling itself up as it receded until she was left with only few vague images and an upset stomach. And a staring lizardman.

"I don't talk in my sleep, do I?" she asked, trying to smile.

He didn't smile back.

Her stomach flipped slowly over and curled into a hot knot. "What did I say?"

"You said you were sorry."

She stared at him in horror. He looked back at her without expression.

"Well, I'm not!" she blurted.

"Should you be?"

"No!"

"It was a dream," Meoraq said, getting up. "Dreams don't mean anything." He came over to her side of the fire and pulled her blanket back. His body was cool and rough and heavy on top of her, and it felt good in ways that sort of thing never had back on Earth. He caught her chin in a pinch, made her look at him when he entered her. "Dreams are only dreams," he told her seriously. "This is real."

She came hard, kicking and thrashing, and suddenly found herself alone in the mess of her blanket with rain falling into her stupidly gaping face and Meoraq once more on his side of the fire, watching her.

He didn't speak, didn't move, certainly didn't come over and have sex with her.

"I don't talk in my sleep," Amber whispered shakily. She didn't try to smile this time. "Do I?"

His spines twitched forward. "No."

"You're talking in my sleep," Nicci muttered, curling up tighter.

Amber pulled her blanket up and rolled onto her side, away from Meoraq. Her thighs clenched on the useless heat of an empty place that still stubbornly insisted it was having sex. She wanted to cry so bad it hurt as much as her stupid dreaming womanparts, but Amber Bierce was not a crier. Or at least, she never used to be, once upon a time.

Everything was different now. She didn't know what she was anymore.

She closed her eyes and although she didn't think she slept, it seemed that she only floated in that black pool of misery a few minutes before she heard the heavy leather flap of Meoraq's tent slap open. She sat up, raising one hand to shield herself from the grey light of morning. He thumped her on the shoulder with a knuckle as he went by, but didn't look at her. His spines were already pretty flat. It was going to be one of those days.

She felt awful. She was stiff and crampy and sore all over, and her feet started screaming the second she stood up on them, but the worst was her head, which felt swollen and throbby and almost hung over. Dehydration, she guessed, but what the hell was she supposed to do about that? They filled Meoraq's huge waterskins every chance they got, but there were fifty people drinking from them and there wasn't always enough. And her stomach hurt. She couldn't possibly be getting her stupid period again this soon; she thought this was plain old hunger and there was nothing she could do about that either.

She wanted more than anything to go back to sleep, but she could hear Meoraq stomping around, rattling poles while he took down his tent and making conversation with God on the subject of all the lazy humans he'd been saddled with, so Amber rolled up her blanket and put it in her duffel bag. Even that hurt and it only hurt worse when she picked it all the way up and hung it on her shoulder.

'I don't think I can do this again today,' she thought, just like she had a choice.

Where were they going? Meoraq had a name for it, but he'd never bothered to tell them what the name meant and no one had asked. He could be taking them to the human-zoo or home to meet his parents or to the world's tallest cliff so he could pitch them off. No one knew. No one cared, as long as they had someplace to go and some way to pass the time until they were all dead.

'It's not that bad,' thought Amber, and it probably wasn't.

Not yet.

Meoraq was making more noise, deliberately she was sure, and when he ran out of patience for being passive-aggressive, he'd swing into aggressive-aggressive and expect her to translate while he told everyone off. Like people didn't hate her enough already.

Amber bent down to give Nicci's shoulder a shake. Nicci moaned and pulled her blanket over her head.

"Come on, don't do this. We have to get ready to go before the lizard blows a gasket."

"You smell."

"Everyone smells," said Amber, but she backed up and put her arms down at her sides. "We've all been wearing the same clothes for, like, six weeks. You're no bed of roses yourself."

"I'm rosier than you are," Nicci muttered under the blanket.

"What do you want me to say?" Amber asked, blushing dully. "I'm fat and I sweat a lot. Feel better? You have to get up now."

"Why?"

"Meoraq wants to get moving soon."

Nicci rolled over.

"Come on." She gave her sister's shoulder another shake and was again shrugged off. "We'll get washed up before we have to go, okay?"

"How?'

"What do you mean 'how'? Down at the stream."

"You go."

"Come with me."

"No. It's freezing."

"Please, Nicci."

"You're the sweaty one, you go." But she rolled back over and peeled her blanket down. "I'll be ready when you get back, okay? I just need a few more minutes."

"Come on, please? I...I don't want to go by myself."

"I didn't want to come here at all." Nicci pulled the blanket back up over her head. "But you didn't care then and I don't care now. Leave me alone."

Amber waited, but her sister ignored her...and she did smell. She looked around, but although she could hear Maria talking to Eric inside their tent, none of the other women were up and she sure didn't want to ask a guy to come with her.

It didn't matter, she decided as she started for the tangled clot of trees that grew around the stream. She'd be close enough to shout if something did happen and nothing was going to happen. She didn't want anyone to see her naked anyway. She didn't even like to see that.

The walk felt a lot longer than it was. Her feet crunched over dead thorns in the grass and stumbled over rocks. The wind blew her hair in her eyes and her hair stank. She felt awful, but she couldn't decide if it was feeling sick or hurt or just ugly. She took her boots off down by the water and walked out into the cold mud and looked down at her reflection in the slow-moving stream. She couldn't see herself at first, just Bo Peep after a bad night.

She got undressed and didn't look at herself again.

The water was very cold, but it wasn't freezing. She lost the feeling in her feet pretty quick, which was something of a relief, but the cold water and the wind started her shivering, and once she started, she couldn't stop. She couldn't bear to wade in any deeper, so she splashed and rubbed as best she could, wishing she had soap, knowing it wasn't enough. Crouching awkwardly over the stream, she dunked her hair and rinsed until it stopped smelling like smoke and sweat, and smelled like smoke and sweat and wet hair instead. Eventually she gave up and waded out to get dressed. She still stank, but she'd done her best, so okay, what came next?

She dipped her old shirt in the stream and started to wring it out, then gave up and just tossed it on the bank on top of her pants. There was no point in cleaning them...or pretending to clean them, seeing as she had no soap. She wasn't going to drag her dirty laundry around with her if she didn't have to. She put on a clean pair of underwear. The elastic was going; she hitched it up over her hips twice, but it kept sagging. Nothing she could do about it. Nothing lasted forever.

"So suck it up," she told herself. "Amber Bierce, fearless Space Adventurer, can live with loose underwear."

Which was great, because sooner or later, she was going to have to live without it, too.

Never mind. Don't think about it. Worry about today. Worry about walking a million miles in the rain gasping like a beached whale. Worry about Meoraq being too disgusted at the end of the day to look at you. Worry about Nicci.

Amber opened her duffel bag and pulled out her last fresh pair of pants. She put them on, at first only seeing how blindingly white they were, and then noticing with a start that they were big on her. Not quite to the falling-off stage, but not just loose either. She was actually going to need a belt soon and where the hell was she going to find one?

Uneasily, she put on her shirt. It was the same size as the one that had been so stiff and tight over her belly the day she'd gone into the Sleeper, she knew it was. And it was still stiff; the excess fabric stuck out on either side of her like wings, flapping loudly in the wind.

"Big deal," said Amber, pulling at the front to make the reassuring roundness of her stomach stand out. "It's not like you didn't have it to lose, little girl. If it comes to that, you could stand to lose some more."

But not a lot more.

"Everybody's losing weight," she reminded herself.

But not like this.

"You're not starving, for God's sake!" she snapped. "*Nobody* is starving!"

And this was true, thanks to Meoraq. So far, he'd put a dead saoq on Scott's fire practically every single day, not that Amber had ever been invited to share it. Her meals came from Meoraq's own portion and although she tried to be grateful, it was all the grossest bits: gut-kebobs, or worse, gut-stew, made from liver, heart, lungs, and who knew what else, along with whatever scraps she could peel off a roasted head. She tried not to be presumptive about it and she'd never asked for it right out loud, but when that head went over the coals, Amber Bierce knew she'd be chewing on a tongue in a few hours while Scott and his happy Manifestors got all the good parts. But she wasn't starving, nobody was starving, and if she was showing it more than the others, it was only because she had more to lose.

Never mind. She didn't need to worry about how her clothes fit or how much weight she (or Nicci) was going to lose before they figured out how to feed themselves. She had to think about today and how the hell she was going to survive that fucking hike. Meoraq was right; she needed to stop holding on to the stuff that couldn't save her life.

Amber dragged her duffel bag over to a rock and sat down to rummage through it. The first book she pulled out was the one on gardening. It wasn't the heaviest, and she knew that if Scott knew she had it—or any of these books, for that matter—he'd turn her wanting to leave it behind as an act of colonial treason. She didn't really want to leave it either, but she also knew that just being from Earth didn't make it holy. It wasn't any good for gardening, not here. All the advice it had for her was about testing the pH balance of the soil or how to use the power tillers and set up the irrigation network. What was the point of knowing the optimum climate and humidity range for growing tomatoes or that planting cucumbers with radishes made them both grow healthier when she was never going to see tomatoes, radishes or cucumbers ever again?

So she tossed it and after that, it was easy to toss the rest of them: *Canning Made Easy, Fundamental Agriculture, A Beginner's Sewing Pattern Book*, the Manifestor's five-year planner and their even less-informative guidebook to planet Plymouth. Once she'd tossed them into the bushes and kicked some leaves over them, she'd halved the weight of her duffel bag, easy. And she could stop there if she wanted. She didn't have to give up anything else. Maybe they couldn't save her life, but they weren't heavy. She could keep them.

"Oh suck it up," said Amber, but she didn't sound tough at all. She sounded like a fat chick in flappy clothes, hugging on to a pair of fucking coffee cups.

She brought them out and held them, staring until rainbows and kittens and sunflowers and letters all blurred together. They were just things, like the books. They couldn't help her. They weren't sacred. They were just things.

The only things she had left from that whole life. Two lousy coffee cups.

* * *

Meoraq counted them three times before he convinced himself that, yes, he'd lost a human. The very morning after he'd told them all to be ready to move out at sunrise, one of them had wandered off. Well, the sun was up, and he'd had time enough to wake every still-sleeping human and make them take their camp down and herd them all together and then count them three damned times, and he was of a mind to leave anyway and let that be a lesson to the rest of them. But he counted a fourth time, just to be sure, and on that fourth count, he realized just who was missing.

Meoraq stopped mid-stride and rubbed hard at his brow-ridges, counting his breaths. A slow-count of six and then another, and when he was calm, he opened his eyes and walked back to Scott, standing close to Nicci. "If you sent her out of my camp again, I'll kill you."

Scott's flat face showed him no obvious alarm. "Miss Bierce?" he called. "Can someone find Miss Bierce? I have no idea what this th...what he's saying."

"He's looking for Amber," said Nicci. "She'll be back soon."

"Back? Where did she go?" Meoraq demanded. A thought struck him. "Did she take her spear? O my Father, restrain my hand. If she's gone hunting—"

"She hasn't."

"No one interrupts a Sheulek!" Meoraq snapped, then paused and looked down at Nicci again. "You know where she is?"

Nicci cowered and Scott stepped forward to take her against his side. The man started to speak; Meoraq shoved him away and took Nicci by the chin, leaning in aggressively close.

"Answer me at once," he ordered. "Where is she?"

"Down by the water, I think," she whispered, trembling in his grip. "I don't know. She...She left without me."

He released her with a grunt of disgust and started away, snapping, "Stay here and be ready to travel on my return," over his shoulder as he went.

"Hey!"

Meoraq stopped and looked up at the sky. "Why?" he said, conversationally.

"Because I want to talk to you!" Scott answered, coming to face off against him.

"I was not speaking to you." Meoraq rubbed at his brow-ridges again, then folded his arms in a warning any dumaq would understand. "But since you're here, what do you want?"

"I want you to understand that in my camp, it is not acceptable for you to get physical with us."

Meoraq felt his spines shifting slowly forward and back again. "Go on."

"I am in charge of these people," said Scott, oblivious. "I'm responsible for their safety. And while I appreciate your efforts in acting as our guide—"

Meoraq tipped back his head and began another slow-count of six.

"—I am not going to tolerate all this hostility!"

Meoraq opened his eyes and leaned close. "I am going to give you the opportunity to amend those words," he said mildly. "Because I think even you know that I have not yet been nearly as hostile as I could be."

"Um..." Scott's fur-striped forehead wrinkled with something that might have been uncertainty. He glanced behind him at his watching people. "Did, ah, did anyone catch that? Nichole?"

Meoraq gripped his brow-ridges again and this time hissed a little. "Father, I beg You to let me kill just one of them," he said, then dropped his hand and bellowed, "*Stay here*!" right in the human's flat, ugly face.

Scott let out a reedy shriek and threw himself backward, tripping over his own boots and falling on his backside.

"And be quiet!" spat Meoraq and stalked off. This time, he was not followed.

By the water, Nicci had said, and the humans had left a trail broad enough to lead him there even after only a single night. He had almost reached the greenbelt when Amber came out of it, carrying her pack over her shoulder. She'd changed her clothes; her clean ones were so white and loose they made her look like a candle-ward, which almost made him smile even as annoyed as he was. And if she had looked even the least bit repentant, he might have let her apologize and come back with him and have it all over and forgotten. Instead, she saw him and scowled.

So be it.

"Where have you been?" he demanded, advancing on her with two fingers pointed right at her throat. "I told you when I wanted to leave and you run off alone? No, do not dare open that mouth! I gave you an order and unlike the rest of your idiot kind, you understood it! You..." His spines flicked upright. His pointing hand lowered somewhat. "What's wrong with your eyes?"

She swiped her sleeve across them at once and pushed past him on her way up the trail. "Nothing!"

He caught her by the arm and swung her around, peering closely at her face. Her eyes were indeed swollen and red, as if she'd been sitting in smoke.

"Are you hurt?" he asked, concerned.

"I took a bath!" she snapped, yanking against his grip. "Is that all right with you? Jesus!"

"A bath," he said, keeping an easy hold on her despite her struggles. "This is the second time you have forced me to chase you down and you know how pressing time is! A *bath*? Where do you think you are, human?"

"I stank."

"I don't care! I care that you disobeyed my spoken will and ran off on your own when all the rest of your herd is waiting on my word to move on! You—"

"I'm hungry, Meoraq!" she shouted. "I'm cold! I'm tired and I'm hurt and I'm...scared..." Some of the fire faded from her eyes. She rubbed at them and backed away, keeping her gaze averted and her arm stiff in his grip. "And I stank. And I thought I could do something about the smell. But I still stink. So...So do what you're going to do and then leave me alone."

The wind gusted, sweeping dead leaves out of the trees and over their feet. Meoraq watched them blow away in eddies. He did not release her.

"You are not to leave my camp alone," he said at last. "Take N'ki with you if you must go. And tell me when you do. I want to know where you are."

She laughed—a shrill, humorless sound. "*I* don't even know where I am."

"Damn it, stop arguing with me! If you don't give me your obedience right now, you'll never bathe again!"

She put her free hand up and covered her eyes. Her body was very stiff. Her breaths were short and shallow...and shook.

She was crying.

'Oh, well done, Uyane,' he thought, and looked up at the sky. He let go of her. "Go," he said gruffly. "I am going to fill my flasks and once I have done that, we are moving whether your people are prepared or not."

She turned her back on him at once and walked away, her head bent and both hands gripping the strap of her shoulder-pack. Meoraq watched her pick her way through the trees until he couldn't see her anymore. He scratched at the side of his snout, sighed, and started walking down to the water. The first thing he saw coming out of the bracken was the damp heap of her old clothing lying on the bank. Strange that she hadn't bothered to keep them. They were filthy and not new, but they still had some good days of wear left in them to his eye.

'Perhaps she didn't think she had time to wash them,' he thought to himself, hunkering down to prod at them. 'And seeing as you came down to whip her back to camp like wandering cattle, perhaps she was right to think so.'

If they weren't lying in the mud like this, he could take them himself, but he didn't have a spare satchel to put them in and didn't want to get everything he owned wet and dirty. He felt a little sorry that Amber had managed to get her feelings bruised, but she could have taken her bath last night and washed her clothes then so they'd be dry and she ready to march this morning. She had instead made the choice to wait and he refused to help her feel like more of a victim because of it. She had other clothes, clearly.

He straightened up, turned around, gave the two colorful objects perched atop the stone an idle glance, started walking, and then halted and looked back at them. Amber's bootprints, the only ones fresh enough to hold a little water at the heels, made a clear trail from the water to the stone and onward to the trail. She had to have been sitting there, right where the objects now sat, which meant she'd put them there. She hadn't dropped them by the bank, as with her discarded clothing, and she hadn't thrown them into the bushes. She'd set them down carefully. And she'd left crying.

Meoraq rubbed at his brow-ridges and scratched the side of his snout. He glanced at the trail, which was still clear for now, and then turned away from it with a sigh and went to see what the hell he'd bullied her into giving up.

He realized what they were after just a few steps. It startled him at first, although he didn't know why it should, really. They wore boots and slept in tents; why shouldn't they drink from cups?

"Fuck," muttered Meoraq, picking one up. Two cups, each with single handles sized for human hands and narrow bowls to accommodate human mouths. They were made of fired clay, or something similar, garishly painted and glazed to a high shine, and as ugly as they were, to judge by their symmetry and the craftsmanship of their nonsensical coloring, they had to be tremendously expensive. He had never seen her drinking from them. She'd been saving them. Perhaps treasuring them. And now she was leaving them.

Meoraq sighed, then unbuckled his travel-harness and slid out from under his pack. "This is not my doing," he announced. "If she wants to crawl off and run water out of her eyes over a pair of cups, that is entirely her decision. I would have let her bring the damned things."

I will not carry sentiment.

"She didn't even ask me."

Why can't just one of you do what you're told without whining at me?

"Fuck," Meoraq said again, wrapping the cups, one in his spare tunic and the other in his spare breeches, and shoving them down deep in his pack. He felt thoroughly disgusted—with himself, with Amber, with the whole of Gann. Cocking an eye at the rolling face of Sheul's heavens, he said, "Tell me just one thing, my Father, I beg. Is there ever a right answer?"

Sheul listened, but said nothing.

Meoraq filled his damned flasks and sat down on the stone, kicking dourly at Amber's bootprints until he'd rubbed out all he could reach. He did not hurry back to start the day's march. When Amber looked back to see if she was clear of him and free to do the rest of her crying, he wanted her to think she was alone. He wasn't completely insensitive.

3

So followed several days of travel and, with compromise on both sides (Meoraq took a savage pleasure in this, that he was able to compromise with these creatures rather than beat them into obedience, and if that wasn't proof of his humility and therefore his worthiness to enter Xi'Matezh, nothing was), they forged a tolerable routine. Meoraq allowed the humans to wake in their own time and to eat whatever was left of the previous night's meal. Then they walked, scattered widely after their habit while Meoraq prowled around them, trying to take point, foot and both flanks along their careless line. They made frequent stops for resting, but managed, he thought, at least three spans each day and that was acceptable. Toward evening, they made their camp and Meoraq hunted. Thus far, Sheul had rewarded his efforts at herding human cattle with fair game and sweet water, gifts he acknowledged each night in his meditations and which the humans seemed to think was only their due.

After three days, they finally came out of the muddy lowlands and began the long, slow trek across the stony fields of middle Yroq. Tempting as it might have been to find a road and lead the humans across it as far east as could be managed, Meoraq forged his own path. There weren't many roads and there were always eyes upon them; worse than the risk of encountering messengers or merchants or even a Sheulek about his circuit, a caravan of near fifty moving bodies would certainly attract whatever raiders were about. Better by far to keep to the wildlands, keep moving, and keep quiet.

But the first day in the plains was even slower than it had been when the humans insisted on carrying their machines with them. The ground was marginally more level, but riddled with broken rock and thorny overgrowth that made passage difficult even for an experienced Sheulek. The humans tripped and staggered like children just learning to walk, tearing their soft flesh and bruising their soft bodies with shocking ease. When he finally called for camp and took inspection of them, he found himself amazed only that no one had managed to break a bone yet. How he was going to get them over the mountains into Gedai loomed in his mind, more and more of an impossibility the longer he pondered it, but he would just have to trust that Sheul would provide the means when the time came. There were problems enough for him to solve right now.

His hunt that night turned up no meat, but plenty of good wild gruu. He gathered up an armload and took it back to soften in the coals, and once he'd taught the humans how to get it out of its leathery peel, they seemed to find the taste agreeable enough to squabble over. They ate like animals, barking and chuffing through mouthfuls of food, reaching across one another, picking at their teeth with the flimsy claw-like protrusions that tipped their fingers. From what he could see, they didn't even wash their hands—not before falling on their meal and not afterwards. He left them to fight over the peels and made a lengthy patrol, stopping once to fill his flasks and bathe at a small ground-spring, and once again at a stony ridge to watch the sun set through the clouds and pray.

He did not return to camp until well after dark and he returned troubled. He had heard the calls of tachuqis behind the wind and seen the blood-stained and trampled grass that marked the site of one of their recent kills. He could only hope it was recent enough that they would not be actively hunting tonight, because a pack of ungainly, unarmed humans would be a damned easy hunt indeed and Meoraq needed to sleep.

Most of the humans were huddled around the fire he had set for them—at least they hadn't let it go out this time—and the rest had bedded down already. A few nodded to him, their bobbing heads an unpleasant reminder of the tachuqis who were perhaps nearby, and Scott rather grudgingly raised his hand in some sort of human salute, but that was all. His time with them had taught him well not to expect better tribute than that.

"And why should they pay it?" he muttered, unbinding his tent and assembling the first of his poles. "Who am I but the man who protects and provides for them in their most desperate days? Lazy, useless, machine-worshipping pests." Meoraq snorted, sending a scathing glance back over his shoulder, only to find Amber almost immediately behind him.

"Hey," she said and offered him a somewhat mangled-looking hunk of gruu.

He looked at it, then at the starved and half-chilled human who had saved it out for him. The hand of Sheul was heavy upon his shoulder. He grunted and began to put another pole together. "Eat it."

Her hand slowly lowered, melting out of the air like the grimace melting off her malleable face. She turned around.

Damn it.

"Sit down." Meoraq kicked the rumpled roll of his tent into a kind of mat and took his own offer, indicating a place beside him and realizing only afterwards that he'd done it with the back of his hand—an intimate gesture—and not the two-finger point that would have been proper for a Sheulek dealing with subordinates, civilians, cattle, and surely humans.

She hesitated, frowning over her shoulder at him.

He said it again, speaking slowly in case it was his language and not his complete lack of tact that held her at bay, gruffly adding, "Eat with me."

"You don't have anything."

He grunted and dug into his pack for his cuuvash, showing it to her before snapping off a square and putting it away again.

She sat down. The tent was still folded and not quite long enough to accommodate them both, especially as he'd dropped himself in the middle of it. Her shoulder bumped his as she settled; he heard the faint slap of her hair on his scales whenever the wind caught it; he felt the warmth emanating from her body all along his side. He thought he should probably move over and give her more room. He didn't.

"See anything out there tonight?" she asked.

"There is always something to see." He tore off the first bite of cuuvash and softened it, watching her jaws work as she ate her roasted root. The thought that he had provided the gruu that fed her did not annoy him the way it did to think of feeding the other humans. Instead, it made him wish he'd brought more. He brooded on this, his spines low, while he ate.

"I heard some weird sounds," said Amber.

He grunted, inviting elaboration.

"A kind of...ooo-*wah* ooo-*wah*!"

He was more fascinated by the cupping of her hands around her mouth than the noise she made by doing so. It took a moment or two to regain focus, another moment to make sense of the clumsy human sounds, and yet another few moments to think about what it meant. "When was this?"

She hesitated again, then took an obvious guess at his meaning. "Not right here, but pretty close. I went out to look, but I didn't see anything."

"Not where—" he began, and stopped to frown at her. "You went out to look? Alone?"

She only looked at him.

He poked her. "You," he said and made walking fingers. "Went out." He moved that hand away from his body. "Alone." And glared at her. "Against my command."

Her brows dropped in an infuriating human scowl. "I had my spear!"

"Would you like to be burned with it, you senseless little calf?"

"Would I what?"

"You stay here!" he told her, thumping two fingers down (on his tent, but he would not notice this until later). "You do not leave the sight of this camp for any reason and you do not go even one pace away alone! Swear it to me!"

She frowned, but it was not incomprehension that made her do so, only stubborn human defiance. "Why?"

"Because I said so!" he snapped.

"I can take care of myself."

His spines slapped flat. He stood. "Get up."

She took that for an order to leave him and started angrily away, so that he was forced to catch her arm and pull her bodily back to him. He turned her around, held her firmly until she stopped trying to shake him off, then released her and said, "I am a tachuqi. A lone tachuqi. One only man-height, with no beak or talons, ha! I am just such a lamed and feeble enemy and you have come this close to me. Take up your spear."

She looked around, as if thinking it would present itself, then closed her hands hesitantly around empty air and bent her knees in a clumsy warrior's stance. She eyed him with suspicion and uncertainty in equal parts and then lunged for him.

He kicked as a tachuqi kicks, leaping up and driving his leg outward, even sweeping his foot downward in the slashing motion that would disembowel if he had the beast's killing talon. She tried to dodge—she also finished her lunge, stabbing her imaginary spear into his side as her dying act in a move that he knew his training masters would roar with delight to see even as they beat her for her suicidal stupidity—but his boot caught her fully on the chest and knocked her hard to the ground. He bent, his hand hooked to make a tachuqi beak, and gripped her firmly by the throat. "You are dead," he told her. "Get up."

She did, but wary now. Her hands flexed upon a new nonexistent spear. She braced herself, mud on her chest in the shape of his boot-print, and lunged again.

He leapt back as a tachuqi leaps, arms spread in imitation of their defensive posture, and kicked her in the back as she went by. She staggered, swinging as she fell so that her spear again found its target, and ended on the ground with his hand on her throat. "You are dead," he said again, letting go. "Get up."

She did, breathing hard—too hard, she was too new to this, too underfed, too small and weak, too human—as she pulled a spear from the air and readied it against him.

This time, she charged, dropping to her knees and stabbing upwards in a move that was, however ultimately futile, worthy of an admiring grunt as he, the tachuqi, darted nimbly aside and tore out the back of her neck in a single bite. "You are dead," he told her, pinning her face briefly against the ground. "Get up."

She didn't, not right away, but when she finally got her arms up and her feet under her, she was arming herself invisibly yet again.

"Survival in the wildlands is not a matter of persistence," he said, ignoring her to sit down again on his mat. "Only knowledge, strength and skill. You have none of these things. Stay within your camp, human. I am with you and Sheul's eye is upon us both." He picked up his cuuvash and broke off another bite, pretending not to watch her.

She glared at him, weaving slightly on her feet with her empty hands still locked around an invisible spear. She was tired enough, bruised enough, muddied enough, that he thought she might give in despite the look in her eyes.

But this was Amber.

She dove at him.

He was not a tachuqi any longer. He caught her up upon the heel of his hand, her feet flying out before her with the force of her aborted momentum, and down she went upon her back much more gently than she would have gone were he an honest enemy. He held her there, waiting as she gasped herself calm, aware that every human in the camp was awake and watching them. A little water collected at the corner of one eye, just one, and it did not replenish itself once it fell. She did not cry surrender.

Meoraq moved his hand from her breastbone to her elbow and helped her to sit up. She wouldn't look him in the eye, but she took a piece of cuuvash when he offered it and put it in her mouth. She chewed, staring fixedly at the ground.

Gradually, the other humans settled themselves, although some continued to watch them. Scott was one of these. Nicci, he noticed, was not.

"Can you teach me that?" Amber asked at last, still avoiding his eye.

Meoraq snorted. "Yes. Come to me as soon as you can present the signet of your father's House, proving you are a son born to the warrior's caste and we shall begin the seventeen years of training. Don't talk at me like an idiot. We don't have time to waste in foolishness."

Her mouthparts pressed together into a flat, pale line. Her lower jaw trembled.

He waited until he was certain she had accepted her defeat and then said, firmly, "You will stay in sight of this camp always. You will not go even one step beyond its borders alone. Give me your obedience."

She looked up and directly at him with eyes that were too bright and too green. "No."

He stared at her, knowing his spines were fully extended and surprise etched in every scale of him for all the world to see. "What did you just say?"

"I said, no."

"You did not!" he said inanely.

"Want to hear it again, lizardman? No. And you don't get to argue with me about it."

"*You* forbid *me*?" That was a killing offense, and yet he was not in the least angry. Stunned, yes, but the first emotion that bled in when shock finally faded was still not anger, only amusement. "If you have something else to say before I bind and muzzle you, I suggest you come to it quickly."

"That's exactly what you're going to have to do," she told him. "Look, you're already sick to death of us. You aren't going to stick around one minute longer than you have to. When we get to wherever it is you're taking us, you'll leave."

He opened his mouth to tell her this was not necessarily so, but closed it again with that unspoken because the alternatives so obviously included killing them and he would rather not have that possibility between them just yet. And it would be a lie in any event to say that leaving the humans behind was not a pleasant thought. She surely knew it and he would not insult her by pretending otherwise.

"Life sure as hell isn't going to get easier," she was saying. "Right now, the only thing standing between us and a horrible death is you. And you're leaving. So, no. No, I am not going to stand around all damn day waiting for you to come home in one of your pissy moods because you're doing it all yourself. If you don't want me with you, that's fine, I'll figure things out by myself, but you don't get to tell me to stay home and just...just wait to die."

And she'd done it again. She forbade him to give her orders. Unbelievable.

"I am tending to you, human," he said, trying very hard to sound reasonable. "It is not an easy task and requires my full attention. Do you think you can just stride out into the wildlands at my side and be anything *but* a hindrance? Your intentions may be good, but I can't afford to indulge them and if you truly believe it is not an indulgence, that only proves you don't understand how desperate your circumstances are."

"I think you're the one who isn't getting it, lizardman." She paused and raked a hand through the mess of her hair, snagging all four fingers before she had even reached her ear. She swore, disentangling herself, but the distraction quieted her some. "Listen," she said, frowning. "Just listen, okay?"

Meoraq rubbed his brow-ridges and gestured for her to speak.

But she didn't, not right away. She searched his face, her human mouth opening and closing, and finally she said, "There were these stray cats that lived under the building where I lived, and the lady three doors down would feed them, you know?"

Meoraq leaned back with a frown. What was she saying now? Was the argument over? Had he won or lost?

"The super kept threatening to evict her for it, so what would happen is, she'd sneak out in the middle of the night every few days and dump this bag of food out on the ground, and if you looked out the window, you could see them all together and purring as they shared it. It must have made her feel real good, like she was saving them." She paused to frown at him uncertainly. "Are you...Are you getting any of this?"

"I mark enough. Go on."

"Well, she wasn't saving them. She was just feeding them. And eventually, she disappeared. I don't know, maybe she died. My point is, she was gone and do you think the cats started catching all the rats and roaches that were absolutely infesting that building? Do you think they started taking care of themselves just because they *had* to?"

Meoraq glanced over at the other humans. They looked curiously back at him as they ate the food he had provided and warmed themselves at the fire he had built.

"No, they stood outside where the old lady used to feed them and yowled all day and all night, because *that* was what they knew how to do. And when they got hungry enough and desperate enough, what they started eating was each other. Every time you looked out there, you could see them, all those cats, with their bones showing and their fur falling out and blood all over them like...like zombie-cats, still yowling and fucking...and eating. Finally the super put out some poison. He was picking up dead cats for weeks and the moral of this story is, feeding someone isn't saving them. You want to talk to me some more about luxuries now, lizardman?"

The hand of Sheul was heavy on his shoulder.

"I need to pray about this," he said at last.

Her glare deepened. She folded her arms like a warrior, gripping at her slender biceps where a Sheulek's honor-knives should be. "I'll wait."

He grunted and closed his eyes, finding stillness with just a few breaths. 'Sheul, O my Father, guide me, I pray,' he began silently, but then stopped and just sat quiet. He was not ready to know Sheul's mind just yet. His own knew too much unrest.

There was nothing in Sheul's Word to specifically forbid a woman from carrying a spear or standing a watch. The goodly virtues of a woman—to be invisible and chaste while in her father's House, to show her husband meek obedience and loyalty, to be fruitful and to raise her children in the sight of Sheul—did not seem to apply to Amber's present situation. If it dishonored her father that she was wandering the prairie in the company of so many human males, it was no concern of his. It was disgraceful behavior, perhaps, but not criminal.

You're already sick to death of us...feeding someone isn't saving them...

He'd felt something when she said that. He felt it again now, clarified in the quiet. He didn't like to call it hurt...an itch, perhaps. He had fantasized many times, in much detail, during each day's walk and each evening's patrol about the end of this interminable journey. He had imagined walking across the courtyard of Xi'Matezh with the humans at his back and seeing the doors that had stood fast against so many travelers open wide for him. He had imagined kneeling before the holy forge at which Prophet Lashraq and the rest of the Six had met with Sheul Himself and hearing His voice spoken aloud and perhaps, just perhaps, feeling His hand with warmth and living weight upon his shoulder, looking up and seeing the very face of God looking down at him.

Ah yes.

But afterwards? If Sheul gave him no command regarding the humans who presently plagued him, what would he do with them? He could not leave them at Xi'Matezh to desecrate that holy place. Surely God would lead him to some other place. Some secluded valley, perhaps, with a slip of a stream and a few trees. He would help them build a smokehouse and fleshing pit and then he would go and let their fate fall into their own hands.

His mind conjured the fleeting impression of Amber alone with her spear in her hand, receding as with distance. He pushed it away, but now found himself thinking...If Sheul led him to that gentle valley, of course he would leave the humans there as Sheul willed. But if Sheul instead gave him his own will in the matter...what would he do then? With her?

Timeless stretches of unquiet passed and left him with no answers.

'Well, it is very simple,' he told himself abruptly. 'Will you kill them?'

No. Not all of them, anyway. Scott had a way of getting under his scales, but the rest of them were only minor annoyances in a large group and once they were behind him, he thought he would forget easily enough. He didn't need to kill them to have peace.

'Then you will abandon them to the wilds and let them find death at the hour Sheul decides. It is not your responsibility to hold watch over all the people of the world. Besides, if they are still unable to provide for themselves after you have carried them all the way to Xi'Matezh, it can only be because they are meant to die.'

Then he would leave them to their fate, but he would take Amber with him.

'Why?'

Why not? He would not be the only one ever to take mementos home from his pilgrimage.

'Most people settle for bits of broken temple bricks.'

It would be as long a journey home as it was to reach the shrine and Amber made better company than a broken brick.

'Only sometimes. She's far more often a profound annoyance. And she's ugly.'

He was uncomfortable with that, however true it was. Surely her flat face, furry patches, and clay-soft body would be gruesome aberrations to any dumaq, but she was human. And for a human, she was...agreeable.

'And what will you do with your agreeable human and her agreeable pet? Because even if you convinced her to leave the rest behind—unlikely—Amber would pull the heart from her breast before she left her Nicci. Will you wander the wildlands for the rest of your days tending the two of them?'

No. With Amber, that was at least only a foolish thought. Add Nicci and it became lunacy. He would have to take up stewardship of House Uyane just to give them a place to safely stay. Even in the depths of his meditations, he could feel himself wanting to laugh at that, but before he could, the image abruptly fell on him of how it would really be to bring Amber into his House. If humans were people, then she was a woman. He would be bringing a woman into his House. *His* woman. And he, the steward of his bloodline.

'At least until your brothers challenge you on the grounds that you have bound yourself to a monster.'

He'd best them.

'You sound very sure.'

He *was* very sure. Even if he could be persuaded to abandon his woman and bastard children, Nduman fought with favor to his left arm ever since the judgment at Riqar and Salkith was an idiot. A well-trained idiot, but still an idiot and no match for a true Sheulek. He'd best them easily, both together if necessary, and then he'd put Nicci away in his mother's old rooms and give her a servant or something so he wouldn't ever have to deal with her. He could spend the rest of his life waiting to defend Xeqor and all the households of Uyane's protection, a portrait of domesticity to do his father's memory great honor.

'And what will you do with Amber?'

This was disturbing for one or two short moments, and the most disturbing thing about it was the apparent ease with which his imagination was able to provide him with suggestions for how the two of them might sexually combine. Too many of his thoughts were turning in that direction lately. He accepted that for the distraction that it was, embraced it, owned it, and finally fought it down to a place where it could be ignored. Sex was not the issue. Amber was, in herself, not the issue. What was to come of the humans once he was away from them was not the issue, although it was bordering. The issue was and remained whether it was permissible or wise to set a human female at watch while he slept.

But he found he trusted Amber.

'You don't trust her, you just want to fuck her,' he told himself cruelly, but the thought, although unsettling, did not sound like truth. Amber was weak and she was ignorant. She would not know every danger if she saw it. But if she did know it, by Sheul, she would defend him.

Meoraq opened his eyes on Amber, watching him with predictable exasperation and impatience. It really was the most amazingly ugly face, if one stopped to think about it. Strange, how often he simply didn't see it.

'She would never be boring,' he thought, and snorted.

"That better not mean what I think it means," she said, scowling at him with mud on her face and grass in her hair. Pinned to Gann four times, and not defeated yet.

His hand went out without his will to brush at her flat, smooth, pallid and generally disgusting brow—the second time he had done so. They both recoiled a little.

He recovered first, frowning. "So be it," he said briskly. "We will hold watches between us at night and I will take you to hunt with me whenever possible."

"Tomorrow?"

He hesitated, then shrugged his spines. "I could spare an hour in the morning if you rise early, although the only thing we're likely to spear is more gruu."

"At least it won't run far," she said with a crooked smile. "Maybe I can actually catch a limping potato."

He grunted, then pointed sternly at her face. "But when I am not with you, you will stay within my camp. You go nowhere alone, do you mark me?"

"Okay, okay," said Amber, rolling her eyes. "In the spirit of compromise, I promise to buddy up when I go to the bathroom."

"Uyane hears your vow. You have the first watch tonight. Wake me when you begin to tire."

"Got it." She pushed herself onto her feet, but stayed bent awhile, brushing at dried mud and grass. This gave Meoraq the unlooked-for and not entirely unwelcome opportunity to watch her odd body in motion, so that when she finally straightened up and asked if he was going to sleep right away, the only honest answer was, "No. I think I have to pray."

"Oh. Well...good night." She backed up, then walked away across the camp, raising her hand as she went without bothering to look at him.

Meoraq watched her go until she took up her spear and a sentry's position at the boundary of the camp, then resumed the assembly of his tent, trying to ignore the undeniable fact that he was profoundly, even painfully aroused. "Father," he murmured, stabbing poles into the ground with more force than was usual. "See Your son in his ordeal and grant him the strength to endure it, because without Your hand upon me, O great Sheul, I do not know how I am going to survive this."

Footsteps.

Meoraq glanced around, but it was Scott coming toward him, not Amber. He grunted dismissively and flattened the spines which had been flaring forward in greeting. "What do you want?"

"What were you two talking about?" the human asked, making a very poor effort to sound merely curious.

"If you wished to know, you should have come closer and joined us."

A lengthy pause led Meoraq to silently congratulate himself on a scathingly civil retort, right up until Scott's hesitant, "What?"

Meoraq sighed. He gave the tent-fasten under his hand a particularly vicious yank as he tied it to the pole and turned around. "I told her," he said, speaking slowly, "to stand a watch."

Scott stared at him and, after Meoraq had ample time to prepare a defense of this admittedly outrageous order, said, "What?"

"Go away!" snapped Meoraq and stomped past him to fetch up his pack and bedroll. "Why do you throw questions around when you cannot catch the answers? Swaggering idiot," he muttered, ducking into his tent. "Sheul, my Father, grant me Your divine patience, and if You cannot grant me that, grant me the strength to knock his head off with one blow so that I don't have to listen to him squeal."

"What did he say?" called Scott, retreating.

Meoraq tied his tent shut and spread out his mat. He had the liberty to undress now, if he wished; if he opened his loin-plate the smallest degree, he would be out of it. He took his boots off, but left his clothes on and lay down. Eventually, Scott went away. The night was quiet. The wind was low. Amber was close and impossibly fierce with her pointed stick in her little hand. Meoraq prayed drowsily, indulged a few lustful thoughts of Gann's devising, prayed some more, and slept.

* * *

He woke in his father's room and did not, for some reason, think this was at all strange. He could smell breakfast in the making—bread baking, nai brewing, and something being fried in salty fat—which made the notion of going back to sleep considerably less attractive than it ordinarily might. His father's cupboard-bed abutted the interior window, so he could see even without flicking the curtain aside that it was still early, not yet dawn.

He rolled over, rubbing the sleep out of his scales, and nudged the door open with his foot. The daughter of House Saluuk was there, her slender body broken into strange new alignment, but this was not strange to him either. She was pouring him a bath and she did it well, despite holding her silent, bloodied baby in one arm. Meoraq dismissed her with a wave and she went without speaking.

After washing, Meoraq opened his bedroom door and brought the first servant he saw to him. It was Shuiv, Sheulteb to House Arug in Tothax, dressed now in livery rather than a warrior's harness, immaculate save for the small stain over his heart where his mortal wound yet bled. Meoraq gave the order for his morning meal to be brought and closed the door again, taking his father's private stair to the roof.

His father was there already, seated on the ground with his back propped on a bench and a book balanced on one bent knee, reading. They raised hands to one another in the distracted, comfortable way they always had, but Meoraq kept walking. There were lamps lit behind the latticed wall that separated his father's personal garden from that of his mother, and the sound of humming on the other side. Meoraq opened the connecting door without any sense of impropriety and went on in.

His mother was painting. He'd never seen her do that. She gave him an embarrassed sort of smile when he came to get a better look, turning the board so he could see the garden she had painted—a garden at night, mere suggestions of growth and blossom rendered in midnight shades of blue and black and silver, with three columns of brilliant orange fire rising at varying distance behind it. "I call it *Blooms*," she said shyly.

Someone was watching him. Meoraq glanced around, not particularly troubled, to find a hooded man standing in the corner of the garden. He was dressed at first glance as an exarch, but his white robes were plainly made and worn about the hems. A priest of some sort, though. A familiar stranger.

"Do I know you?" Meoraq asked after a moment.

"I know you."

The voice was also familiar, but only a little, as if he'd heard it in a dream.

"Where have we met?"

"We haven't."

"You're in my house," Meoraq said, but did not, oddly, draw a blade and cut him down for the invasion.

The stranger's hood bulged as the exarch shrugged his spines beneath it. "You're in mine. Am I not welcome?"

"I suppose so." Meoraq returned his gaze to his mother's painting. She was adding tiny points of white light to the dark sky there. "I think I'm dreaming."

"Do you?" The stranger's head tipped, curious. "Why?"

Meoraq looked down at his mother, then at the unnamed exarch. "My mother is dead," he explained.

"So?"

"So she couldn't really be here. This—" Meoraq waved at the garden. A few leaves fell. "—isn't really my father's House."

"No," the stranger agreed. "It is yours. Each man builds his own House and it will always be haunted."

Most of that was nonsense, of course, but one thing did stab in deep enough to raise Meoraq from his mother's paint-board. "Uyane is mine?" he asked, looking back at the stranger in surprise. "Am I back? Am I married?"

"Would you like to be?"

Behind him, footsteps, absurdly soft and light against the stone tiles. Meoraq straightened and turned as Amber came into his mother's garden with Nicci trailing in her shadow. Surprised, he raised a hand in welcome. Amber smiled back at him, that grotesque human smile, and took her wristlet off. She held it out to him, saying, "I am a virgin of my father's House."

Nicci offered hers as well, silent, unsmiling.

Meoraq started to reach, then dropped his arm and looked back, scowling, at the exarch. "Must it be both of them?"

"It is her House also," the exarch replied, a little sadly he thought. "And she brings her own ghosts."

Meoraq took the wristlets, drew a sabk, pinned them both together to the flowering ribbonleaf tree that overhung his mother's bench. A little blood welled up from the bark, trickled down the blade, let just one pregnant drop fall from the shivering hook of Amber's wristlet onto Nicci's.

"Now you are mine," Meoraq told her—well, told both of them, but it was Amber he reached for.

She came, putting her hands on him in that fearless way, and there was no pretending he took her in his arms this time to bite her in some insane dream-way. He wanted exactly what he did and he wanted it with all the heat and surety that was in Amber's bold embrace as well. Then they were naked—with his mother and Nicci and the white-robed exarch right there—and Meoraq leaned her up against the tree beneath the blade of conquest and he supposed he was inside her, although that didn't seem important. They were face to face, and he could feel well enough her arms around him and her twinned teats pressed flat to his chest, but if there was sex going on below that, it happened without him. It was enough for him to just be with her, to see her, feel her, to need her and be needed by her, and everything that should have been wrong about that feeling—not the least of which was indulging it in this fashion while his mother sat right there on her bench and painted—was instead so overwhelmingly right that it broke the whole of the dream in two and woke him back into the world.

He lay with his heart pounding in his chest, staring without comprehension at the top of his tent until he had calmed down enough to realize two things: First, that the reason he could see the top of his tent was because he had overslept and it was a good hour after dawn, and second, his belly was wet.

Cursing, Meoraq yanked his blanket back, fought his belt open, ripped away his loin-plate, and stared in disbelief at the thin veneer of semen glistening over his scales.

He hadn't done that in years.

He hadn't done that in years and he'd just done it with his loin-plate on. Who *did* that? Who came in his sleep, fully constrained, dreaming of a...of a fucking *creature*?

What was wrong *with him*?

Meoraq fumbled angrily with his pack until he found his flask, using what little water it still held to wipe himself off. His slit felt very tender.

Outside, footsteps. The humans were awake, some of them at least, and Amber was surely among them. If he listened (he did not want to listen), he would no doubt be able to hear her particular voice among those rumbles and barks that made up the crude human speech. If he looked out, he would see her.

Meoraq buckled his belt back on, cinching it biting-tight, and dressed in furious silence. He strapped his blades on, all of them, like a Sheulek. He untied the tent's fastens, threw back the flap, and stepped boldly out among the humans who were his trial upon this pilgrimage, and not a damned thing more.

Amber was there. She saw him. Smiled.

He felt again what he had never felt—the warm crush of her body naked against his—and felt with it some ghost of that lying emotion that was nothing but a part of this ordeal.

"Hey," said Amber, picking up her spear as she climbed to her feet. She came toward him, smiling. "Are you ready?"

He froze, just for an instant, and suddenly remembered their talk of the previous night. Hunting. She thought he was going to teach her the ways of hunting.

He put his back to her. It helped, but not much. He started walking. "Not today. Stay here."

"Oh come on. I promise I'll be quiet."

"I said, no." He walked faster. "You were supposed to wake me."

"I wasn't tired." She followed him. "I'm totally ready to do this."

"You are tired, whether you admit it or not. You are useless to me now. Stay."

"I'm fine, for Christ's sake. Come on, I won't even do anything if you don't want me to. Please, Meoraq, I just need to see how—"

She caught at his arm and nothing else she said mattered. There was no time, only a dark place between one beat of his heart and the next in which he had time to think, completely, that he could be alone with her. Just the two of them in the wildlands, with a tree, perhaps even a ribbonleaf tree, to lean her up against...

"*Get away from me*!" he roared, and swung around to shout it right in her face. Her *ugly* face. "Don't you ever put your hand on me again!"

She drew back and stopped smiling, both so suddenly that he might have reached out and slapped the look right off her face. Around them, human heads turned and human eyes watched. Meoraq's heart knotted; he gave it a strike with the haft of his hunting blade and snapped, "I told you to wake me and you ignored me! I told you to stay here and you argue with me! So now I see how you obey my orders! Why would you think I would want you with me after that? I don't *like* you! We're not *friends*! Stop pawing at me and go sit down!"

Someone—Scott, by the smirking look of him—uttered a fluttery sound through his closed mouth. Amber heard it, too. She shot a fiery glance that way, her face darkening either with embarrassment or anger, and then turned all the way around and started to walk away from him. Not deeper into camp. Into the wildlands.

Without him.

She'd be killed.

Meoraq lunged after her and snatched the spear out of her hands.

"Give it back!"

"*Stay here*, I said!" he roared at her.

"I don't need your permission! I can go if I want to! Give it back, that's mi—"

Meoraq snapped it over his knee and threw the pieces at the ground.

Scott let out a, "Whoa!" of happy surprise and laughed again.

Amber stared at the halves of her hunting toy. Her mouth was a thin line, pressed pale, shaking at its edges.

"I shouldn't have to spend every hour of every damned day looking after you," said Meoraq brusquely, pushing past her. He felt heavy, as if the hand of Sheul Himself were pressing down on him, body and soul, but the words kept coming, spitting out of him as bitter as bile. "Stay here and stay out of my way."

A scraping sound.

Meoraq looked, his hand tightening on the hilt of his kzung, knowing she had picked up half of her spear and was coming to knock it against his head.

Only she wasn't.

She was taking it into the prairie to hunt.

"Go on, then!" he spat after her. "If there's anything left of you for me to find, I'll find it when my hunt is done and not before!"

She kept walking.

"O Sheul, my Father, she is Yours," Meoraq said loudly. "And if feeding the beasts of the wildlands is as much use as she can be to You, so be it!"

Sheul's answer was a darkening across his heart, a terrible weight of censure in his very soul. Meoraq found he could not hold his eyes to Amber's stiff back; they went instead to the dull half of her broken spear, and his blood crawled with shame.

'She smiled when she saw me coming,' he thought. 'She had come to greet me.'

He had once seen his mother come to the outer courtyard to greet his father just that way after the battle at Kuaq. Meoraq remembered well his embarrassment that she had let herself be seen so publicly and with such effluence of emotion. And he remembered how Rasozul had reached out his arm to clasp her shoulder in passing, a gentle touch shared just between them in that one moment they had, and how she had bent her neck to brush at the back of his hand with her cheek, as if the touch were all she craved in the world.

Amber was a dark stripe in the distance—a foolish female with half a spear and no strength in the arm that carried it. None of the other humans moved to follow. Not even her Nicci.

Someone came to stand beside him. Scott, of all people. Scott, wholly ignorant of how deeply Meoraq wished to bury his blade in his smirking face, saying, "You better go after her."

Meoraq looked at him, his spines flat and his pulse surely flashing yellow in his throat. "I do not like you either," he said quietly.

The human's happy grimace quickly wiped itself away as Scott retreated.

Meoraq looked again into the prairie, but Amber could no longer be seen. 'Idiot,' he thought, and felt the word echoed back at him.

He should go after her.

All the humans were watching.

Meoraq turned around and walked in the opposite direction. Her temper and the pride that fueled it would cool. She would return and he would take the higher path and allow her to ask his forgiveness for her fit of human petulance.

The wind blew. The morning air was still clear and dry, but not so fresh as it had seemed. The sun had risen higher behind the rolling clouds, yet the world seemed no brighter. Meoraq walked in darkness and he walked alone.

4

Meoraq's heart may not have been in the hunt, but his heart was not necessary. His body made an easy kill of two panicked saoqs drinking at a distant ground-spring, which he could have taken at once back to camp for his hungry humans. Instead, he butchered them alone in the plains and he made thorough work of it, not merely fleshing and skinning. There was dried dung enough for a thousand fires, so he built one and sat beside it as he worked. There was bowel to clean, long bones full of precious marrow, and time, plenty of time, to think.

He thought of the spear he had broken. The clumsy, crooked, childish spear which Amber had probably made herself. Over and over, he saw himself breaking it. Over and over, he saw her walking away into the wildlands with the splintered tip he'd left her.

He prayed.

At last, Meoraq buried the meat and moved his fire atop it. He threw the most of the emptied bones into the coals to burn, trusting the foul smoke to ward away any beasts who might otherwise be drawn in by the smell of blood. He bundled his marrow and all the clean fat he'd scraped off to render down if he had the time. Into the last carrying pouch of his possession, he set the edible offal, wrapped in grass to soak in the blood. Then he left it all in Sheul's hands and walked half a span across the plains to the nearest stand of zuol trees.

Making the spear took all the rest of that day, which was fine, because the saoq had to roast anyway. He hadn't made one, even for idle amusement, since his boyhood days, but it was one of the lessons Master Takktha had taught and what the body has had beaten into it by Master Takktha, it does not soon forget. This spear might never have had the honor of hanging on the wall in the training yard, but Meoraq was certain it would have earned a turn in Takktha's hand at least. He'd cut six zuol saplings before he'd found the balance he'd desired in a haft; he did not consider this a waste, since there were ten thousand uses for the fine, straight poles of young zuol and the humans were entirely without them. He then spent easily two hours peeling bark, trimming branches, and smoothing its length with the rough side of a stone—far more work than was strictly necessary, but it did look damned nice when it was done. There was plenty of xuseth around, all gone to seed this late in the year, but he dug up a few roots and split them to rub its oily fibers into the green wood. After some meditation, he took the flared wings of the saoq's hip-bones (which he had tossed to the coals earlier, but which had fallen aside by Sheul's grace and gone unburned, though heat-cured and hard as rock) and carved along their outer edges. Then he carefully split the green wood of the spear's tip—a difficult task made infinitely easier by the xuseth oil—and worked the shards of bone beneath so that they protruded in flaring points along four sides. By this time, the fire had died down to perfect coals and he spent the rest of the day alternately baking the spear over them and applying more xuseth until the spear was as strong as stone. He made a few practice throws just to satisfy his vanity, then swiftly bound his spare poles into a sled and loaded the meat for travel.

It was dark when he finally left, but the shine of the moon behind the clouds was enough to guide him until he could make out the many fires of the humans in his camp. He was surprised to see meat in several hands as he pulled his sled through their slow-moving bodies, and he saw that they were almost as surprised to see him at all. So. They thought he had abandoned them, and this had been all the motivation they required to see to their own survival. He was now of half a mind to abandon them again tomorrow.

He could not see Amber at a casual glance, so Meoraq turned himself and his sled toward the sound of Scott's voice, because Scott sounded angry and that usually meant he was talking at Amber. Soon, he saw the man himself at the fore of a loose ring of other humans, all together around a fire where the smell of roasting meat and burning bones was strongest, and yes, Scott stopped his angry words at the first sight of Meoraq and said instead, "He's back. Get up right now and apologize," so Amber had to be there somewhere.

Meoraq hissed and humans moved aside for him, revealing her on her knees with the fire turning her hair to red and her back full to him, but she was starting to turn and there was a grudging sort of curl on her mouthparts as she raised her hand to greet—

The poles of the sled fell out of his grip and the world itself seemed to drop away with it.

There was a knife in her hand.

"O my Father, no," he heard himself say.

She scowled, deciding to be angry. "What the hell is it now?"

He threw the spear down—the spear he'd spent all damned day making—and turned away from her with both hands digging at his scales. He closed his eyes, not daring yet to speak, not daring even to think.

"Meoraq?"

The law was clear.

"What's wrong with him?" someone asked and Scott said, "If you two are going to fight again, do it somewhere else."

Was that it? Because he'd shouted at her? 'Please,' he prayed. 'I didn't mean it.'

His will was nothing. The Word of the Prophet must be upheld.

'She's human. She didn't know.'

But the law was Sheul's. If the humans were His children, they were subject to His rule and to the judgment of His Swords.

And after all, some evil voice observed, *you don't even like her.*

"So this is Your lesson," he said in the dark. His voice, no louder than a whisper, caught at his ears like hooks.

"Well, Jesus Christ, lizardman, what the hell did I do n—"

He pulled a knife as if it were a bone he pulled from his own body. He used the knife of his fathers. He could do that much. He opened his eyes and looked at her.

"Amber!" Nicci cringed back even as she cried out, but no one else moved. "Someone do something! He's going to kill her!"

"No, he's not," said Amber, frowning uncertainly at the knife he held.

It hurt.

"Do you wish to pray?" he asked hoarsely. "Please. Do not make me send you from this world into darkness."

There followed a terrible stillness. Amber looked past the gleam of ancient metal to search his face and for a long time, it was only that and the watchful eye of Sheul upon them both.

"Are you really going to kill me?" she asked at last. Her voice trembled, but only once.

"I am a Sword and a true son of Sheul. I am the arbiter of His law, which you have broken. I have no choice in this matter." And then he said, not thinking, what he had never said with a blade of judgment in his hand. "I'm sorry."

"Someone stop him!" Nicci begged.

"We can't interfere with their customs."

Amber's baffled stare turned briefly molten. She swung around, snarling, "Fuck you, Scott! Nicci—" Her voice trembled again, then turned harsh. "Don't look. Someone get her out of here. Dag...or someone...Don't let her see this."

Nicci began to wail, but she walked away, she was not carried. Many other humans faded back with her. Scott stayed. Scott meant to watch. His eyes were bright in the firelight.

Amber turned her back on them all. She lifted her chin with a defiance belied by her too-bright eyes. "Do it, if you're going to do it. I don't care."

"Will you not pray?"

"I had nothing to say to God before. I've got nothing to say to him now." Her jaw clenched, biting on the shiver in her words.

"So be it. Human, you have broken the Third Law and taken up a bladed weapon—"

"Wait a minute, what?" Amber looked down at the knife in her hand and then back at Scott.

All the remaining humans were looking at Scott, whose skin had gone a curious greyish color. And as Amber opened her mouth to speak, he lurched forward and shouted, "She's a fucking liar!"

The temper broke in Meoraq and suddenly his kzung was in his other hand—not his father's knife, not for this human—and he shouted, "I do His will now, but I will be free to do my own when it is over, so do not provoke me!"

Scott put up his open hands, but his eyes stayed on Amber, hissing, "There's nothing anyone can do about this and you know it, so don't you even think about getting anyone else in trouble!"

"You fucking yellow bastard." Amber put her hands on the knife, folding the blade into its own haft, then threw it to the ground between Scott's feet. "It was my knife," she said loudly. And turned to face Meoraq. "But I didn't know that was your law."

"It is Sheul's law and not mine to forgive." Meoraq took resolute hold of her shoulder and put the blade against her neck. "I will be quick."

"Wait, just...What is the law exactly?" she asked. "The actual words."

He frowned.

"Humor me," she said. "As my final request."

He could feel the heat of her shoulder through his hand. Living warmth. He could feel the tremble of her mortal fear, but she stood and she faced him.

"No man may raise his judgment higher than the true Word of Sheul," he said, reminding himself as much as her. "I am Sheulek. I have no mercy to show you."

But he did not make the killing cut and after another long moment, he eased the edge of his blade away from her thin skin. Red blood, red as dye-berries, welled up where it had rested.

"'And the third law writ was this,'" he said in something like surrender. "'Let no man who is not born of the warrior's caste and raised under its sign take up the bladed weapon, for the age of the Ancients is ended and wrath belongs to Sheul alone. For he who is born under the Blade, all liberty is given, but for all other men of this world, this sin shall be unforgiveable.'" The last word fell like a hammer on his heart, briefly silencing him. "No allowance can be made," he told her, as soon as he felt he could. "The Prophet writes plainly that whatever man touches the bladed weapon, even if he has taken it up in defense of his life or that of his son or even of his abbot, if he is not born to that caste, he must be judged unforgiveable. He...*You* must die."

Amber's eyes had narrowed. "Are these laws open to any interpretation?"

"None."

"Not even from you?"

"I would spare you if I could." He raised the knife. "But I am Sheulek and His law is mine. I will be quick."

"You said no man can hold a knife," she said, and reached up to catch the bone-hilt of his. "But I'm a woman."

The world dropped away for a second time.

"Is there a law against women holding knives?" Amber asked. Her eyes were intent. Elsewhere, at some unknown distance, human voices began to whisper.

Meoraq bent his head. He breathed.

The First Law: Sheul is master over all His children. There is no mortal being or beast born of clay who does not bend before Him and none whose judgment can be raised higher than His sacred Word.

The Second Law: The Age of the Ancients is ended. Let their cities fall to ruins. Let their time pass out of memory. Let no one seek to master or remake the machines with which they poisoned Gann, lest they be corrupted in return.

The Third Law: Let no man take up the bladed weapon...no *man*...

Meoraq opened his eyes and found them already gazing into Amber's. He sheathed his father's knife. Then he bent, as a man in a fever, without conscious thought or plan, and licked the blood from her neck. It tasted coppery and bitter and he drank it in like wine and pressed his brow to her warm shoulder.

"I take it that's a no," said Amber. Her air fell out of her in a shaky rush. "You scared the *piss* out of me, lizardman."

"Sheul instructs with a burning hand," he replied, still somewhat light-headed. "I have to pray." He turned around, but caught her arm as she first moved away, no doubt to find her weeping Nicci.

She waited, tense, while he tried to puzzle out his reason for stopping her. He only knew that he wanted to say something, but whatever it was would have to be witnessed by all these damned staring humans.

Nicci was coming. He could hear her sobbing through the crowd, as hysterical with joy as she'd been with grief. Amber's gaze wavered; she looked behind her.

Meoraq released his hold and stepped back. "I have meat," he said, and rather unnecessarily plucked up his travel-pack to thrust into Amber's arms. "See that your people are fed."

Then Nicci was there and Meoraq retreated so he wouldn't have to watch them embrace and feel...whatever the hell he was feeling.

* * *

Meoraq was sleeping when Amber finally nerved herself up to try and talk to him, or at least, he was lying down with his eyes closed and his arms tucked beneath his head. He was outside though, and fully dressed, boots and all, so Amber waffled for a second or two, and maybe he could feel her stare, because he said, without opening his eyes, "What do you want?"

"Nothing. I brought your, uh, entrails. Thanks for the food. Go back to sleep." Amber set the leather pack down by his mat, trying to get in and out of his space fast to disturb him as little as possible, but he was faster.

His scaly hand locked around her arm. He sat up, frowning at her, then beyond her, and then let go. He grunted, pointed at the ground and picked up his pack.

"I don't want to keep you awa—"

"Sit down."

She sat.

He rummaged through the organs, pulling out this or that disgusting lump of bloody grossness and occasionally grunting to himself. One of them he set on the ground, hesitated, then picked it up and gave it to her.

"What is it?" she asked dubiously, eyeing the pile of blood-streaked yellow mush and hoping it was not edible.

It was marrow, as he eventually managed to explain, and he wanted her to eat it.

"How do I cook it?" she asked.

He looked at her, "I have roasted it already. Eat."

"I'll just save it for later," she hedged, easing it toward the ground behind her.

"Eat it!" he snapped.

She scooped a jiggly blob of it up in two fingers and sucked it squeamishly down. It tasted pretty much just like bland, vaguely blood-flavored jelly, which made it easily the most disgusting thing she'd ever had in her mouth and that included the time Bobby Wykes up the street knocked her down and made her eat a slug.

Meoraq reached over and helped himself to a heaping palmful, licked his fingers, then went back to untangling intestines.

"I saw the spear," said Amber after a while. "It's nice."

He grunted. "It belongs to you."

"I figured." And, inanely: "I'm glad you didn't have to kill me."

"So am I." He glanced at her. "Where did you get the knife?"

It wasn't an unexpected question. "I'm not going to answer that."

"So be it." He took more marrow. "He would be well-advised to be rid of it. If I see it in his hand or the fold of his clothes, I will kill him. That is not a threat, mark me. That is the vow of Uyane Meoraq and God hears me. I will kill him and I will not burn his body. It can lie there and rot. And I hope ghets scatter his fucking bones."

"Hypothetically speaking, if someone did give me the knife, he wouldn't have done it to get me killed."

"Only because he didn't know the law. If he had, he would have urged the knife on you the first day of our meeting because he is an evil little clay-born smear of shit." He said this without inflection or any sign of interest, yet long patches of scales on either side of Meoraq's throat were turning yellow. He was doing that a lot lately.

The yellowing intrigued her, especially as it seemed to go hand in hand with high emotion. Maybe she'd been wrong about the 'he' thing this whole time. Maybe he really was a girl, and he was PMS-ing. It was something hormonal, plainly.

"Can I ask you a question?"

He grunted, put his empty pack aside and pulled out one of his many knives.

The knife gave her some pause, but now she felt more or less obligated to finish. "You are a man, right?"

He stared at her. Then the double-row of spines on his head kind of flicked forward and he looked at the knife in his hand. "Ah," he said. And looked at her again. "I am a man. I am also Sheulek, born of the warrior's caste to serve God as his Sword and his Striding Foot. Blades are not forbidden to me."

"Oh." Amber waited, choking down marrow and watching the yellow patches on his throat fade back to black as he sliced the saoq's intestines into long strips. She didn't say anything until he was done, but once he had, she said, "So...what did I do to piss you off this morning?"

He frowned, glanced at her, and kept working.

"I thought we had an agreement and yeah, okay, I didn't wake you up, but is that really a good enough reason to go at me like that?"

He ignored her.

Amber picked at the marrow, then put it aside. "Do I bother you?" she asked bluntly.

He made a few half-hearted passes at the stripped bowel, then leaned the blade of his knife against his boot and rubbed at his brow-ridges. He didn't answer.

"That's a yes," said Amber. She made an effort to sound cheerful, or at least, the sarcasm-laden sort of cheer she usually dished out when she was in a good mood and her feelings weren't hurt. "It's okay, Meoraq. Believe it or not, I understand."

"No," he said quietly, still rubbing. "You do not."

"Yeah, I do. I wouldn't want to be stuck with us either. For what it's worth, I appreciate everything you've done for us. I'll try to give you your space. I know I'm in the way and I'm not the easiest person to live with even when I haven't been stranded on an alien planet, that's for damn s—"

"Enough." He moved his hand and looked at her with eyes that pierced but were impossible to read. His voice had not risen, but there was something new about it that she did not imagine because she could see people looking their way and wearing pretty much the same expressions they'd worn when they'd thought he was about to cut her head off.

It bothered her even more now that no one was doing anything to interrupt than it had then.

Meoraq tipped his head back and looked at the sky. He stayed that way as Amber picked at her bootlaces and rubbed traces of marrow off on her pants. She'd never been good at social stuff. She got the feeling he wasn't, either. The silence sat between them like a cancer, squeezing everything else out as it grew.

"I don't—" he said, and then just sat there, watching the clouds roll by.

There were too many ways that sentence could end to walk away from it.

"You don't what?"

Silence. And just when she'd decided he wasn't going to answer, he said, quietly and without a shred of emotion either in his voice or anywhere on his body, "I don't know what to do with you."

"I thought...I thought you were taking us to this temple place."

He grunted. It could have meant anything. Then he finally looked directly at her, if only for a second. It seemed to her that he flinched a little before he went back to staring at the sky. "I know you want to learn things. It may even be that this is God's will as well. But I don't...I don't think I can teach you. You...upset me."

Her heart sank. She could actually feel it sinking.

"Meoraq, I know I haven't given you a lot of reasons to believe me, but I swear I'm not as dumb as you think I am. I've just been in the city all my life. I can figure this out. Please, just give me a chance."

"You do not mark me," he said, but he didn't say how and after another long stretch of cloud-watching, he abruptly changed the subject. "Did you kill the saoq I saw you roasting?"

She huffed out a little laughter. "Yeah. With my broken spear. Like the stubborn bitch that I am. And then I had to drag it all the way home. I was trying to be careful, but it still looked like I'd rolled it off a cliff by the time I got it back. Plus, it tasted like shit because all the blood was clotted inside. Some of the guys told me I should have drained it, but how the hell was I supposed to do that?"

He frowned, but didn't answer.

"Then you show up with two of them, already skinned and roasted, on a friggin' sled..." She tried to smile, but the bitterness in her tone made the effort somewhat wasted and Meoraq was just looking at her, so she let it drop. "And I felt like a fool."

He stared into the sky.

"For about three seconds. And then I felt like a walking dead woman. You are one scary son of a bitch when you want to be."

"I know."

He wasn't in the mood to talk, clearly, and she was all out of things to say, except for the stuff she'd had seething through her head all day—*you made me run out of here like a fucking little girl you yelled at me for no good goddamn reason you broke my spear you made me cry no one's begging you to stick around and I don't like you either so there*—and the stuff she'd never say even if he stuck another knife to her throat—*I thought we were friends*—so she guessed they were done. Amber managed another wan smile for the road and started to get up again.

"Take the marrow."

She hunted around for a tactful way to say what came next, then just said it. "It's gross, Meoraq."

"I don't care what you think of it, human. Eat it." He rubbed at his brow-ridges, scowling, then crossly added, "Share it out with your N'ki if you must, but eat it."

"Well okay, but she's going to think it's gross too." She bent over to get it.

He reached up and brushed the back of his knuckles across her forehead.

It was the third time he'd done something like that and she never seemed to see it coming. She looked up, startled.

He looked back at her, frowning, silent.

She straightened up haltingly, fussing with the marrow until she had it folded again in the wide square of leather he'd used for its wrapping. 'That was a weird touch,' she thought, tossing the words out defiantly into the recesses of her brain just like it was all there was.

And the thought came back, like some distorted echo: 'He's going to ask me to sleep with him.'

Her stomach flipped over, but not in a scared and pukey way. She wrapped up the marrow some more, thinking (*no he's not don't be stupid that's just his half-assed way of saying he's sorry for picking a fight this morning or even heck trying to kill you tonight except that was more of his god stuff and he probably doesn't feel sorry about it but whatever he doesn't want to sleep with you he's a* lizard) nothing in particular.

"I'll do what I can with you," he said finally. "For as long as I can stand it."

"You won't be sorry."

He grunted in a way that suggested he already was, and rubbed at his knobby forehead again. "Go. Now. I...I need to pray."

She backed away, clutching the leather with its jiggly blobs of marrow to her churning stomach and watching as he bent over and put his hands flat against the ground. His eyes closed. His breathing evened out.

He did not ask her to sleep with him.

'Jesus Christ, you really are a fool,' she thought disgustedly and picked her way back to Nicci, peppering herself with silent and scathing recriminations until she excused herself on the pretext of visiting the bushes, where she threw up and had a record-breaking second crying jag in one day and then went back and fell miserably asleep.

5

Things changed after that, but Amber found it difficult to say whether they were good changes or not. They should have been good. Sitting up for a few extra hours at night didn't win her any prizes with Scott and his loyal Manifestors (although sometimes the Fleetmen might come over to sit with her for a while if they were awake. Crandall, mostly, whose profanity-thick banter was surprisingly welcome provided he kept his hands to himself, or Mr. Yao, who rarely said or did anything at all, but was still oddly good company), but she seemed to have come back from her near-execution with a smidgeon more of Meoraq's respect.

He still hadn't taken her hunting with him, but every morning, as soon as dawn and his footsteps woke her, he took her out into the world beyond their camp and tried to do something with her. Finding water always came first, because "water is life in the wildlands." He could spend hours hunkered down over a mudbank, trying to make her see animal tracks in what her city-bred eyes stubbornly kept telling her was just a tore-up mess. If it was dry, which wasn't often, he might attempt to teach her to crawl, which she would never have thought was a skill anyone over the age of two would need to have. Belly-down in the grass, she kicked and elbowed her way through thornbreaks and over rocks, while Meoraq snaked silently over the ground beside her to prove it could be done, hissing at her when she got too noisy or smacking her butt whenever it popped up too high. If it rained, crawling lessons were cancelled and he instead stood over her and made her throw the spear and fetch it back several billion times, so that she inevitably started the day's hike exhausted. He never gave her so much as a "Nice try," not even on those rare occasions when she thought she'd actually done pretty good, and on the really bad days, he wouldn't even look at her when he grunted out his commands. Those were the days she was likeliest to find herself trudging back to camp just a few minutes after leaving it, with nothing to do except wonder what she'd done wrong until Meoraq came back and ordered everyone to start walking.

And then he ignored her. Throughout the day, he circled them, freely doling out cuffs and hisses if he thought people were talking too loud or straying too far from the group, but he never so much as glanced her way when he chanced to stalk by and wouldn't offer even a grunt in return if she spoke. The only time he ever interacted with her was to use her to yell at Scott and those moments were mercifully few. He kept his distance, and the miserable planet they'd crashed on made sure there was plenty of cold whistling wind to fill it.

Once he gave up for the day and let them set up camp, she seemed to be worth noticing again, but only to work. The very first night after he'd put a knife to her throat, before she'd even had the chance to dig the rocks out of her boots, he was standing over her with his empty and almost-empty flasks. "Fill these," he'd said, dumping them unceremoniously in her lap. "And start a fire."

And off he'd gone to hunt.

She'd filled them, although it meant another meandering hike back and forth between promising greenbelts before she found an actual creek, but there weren't more than a handful of trees around her, and all the dead branches she'd been able to drag back to camp burned up in less than an hour. There she'd sat, beside a clumsy ring of stones and a heap of cold ash, until Meoraq returned with an enormous, crab-mouthed eel-thing and nothing to cook it over. He let her get just three words into her excuse—"There's no wood"—and then threw down his eel, grabbed her by the scruff of her shirt and dragged her out into the plains with him.

According to Meoraq, wood was an extravagance. The real fuel of the wildlands was dried poop.

Saoq poop was common and burned well when bundled with dried grass, but corroki poop was the best, he told her, if the beasts themselves were not around. If they were, she was not to approach. They had poor sight and hearing and were very aggressive when they believed themselves surprised. When he described them further, she quickly realized that corrokis were the giant armadillos she'd stumbled across the day Scott made her take her walk.

"I don't see any corrokis around here," she said, scanning the plains. "So why are you telling me all this?"

He sighed, gripping at his brow-ridges. Then he caught her head in both hands and aimed her eyes like a cannon. She stared, feeling hot and sick and frustrated, but saw nothing except grass, pale on the slopes and dark in the valleys. At last, hissing into the back of her hair, he let go and pointed.

But at what? Amber searched all the way to the horizon and back, wind stinging at her eyes (yeah right, the wind), but it was just...grass.

"Sheul, my Father, give me patience," he muttered, and gripped hard at the back of Amber's neck. "Tell me what you see, human."

"Grass."

"What color is the grass?"

"I don't...brown. Just brown!"

"All over?"

"Light brown, dark brown! It's all brown!"

"What makes it dark?" he asked, sounding very testy.

"How the hell should I know? It's a shadow!"

"A shadow?" He spun her around to stare at her directly. "Cast by what?"

She looked up at the cloud-shrouded sun and felt herself blushing. Of course it wasn't a shadow. "It's mud, then," she mumbled.

"It is mud," he agreed. "Made by?"

"Water?"

"Water would grow a greenbelt," he told her, and she blushed hotter because she knew that, damn it. He'd lectured her most of the morning about what water looked like. "What else makes a path of mud so wide and so long as to be seen at this distance?"

She looked back at it helplessly, but there were no magic clues hovering in the air above it.

"A herd," said Meoraq, biting off each word very clearly, "of corrokis. They have passed through. They have moved on. Go down and fetch dung."

She went. Fetched. It took six trips there and back, lugging armloads of dry, crumbling, shit-patties as high as her chin before he told her to stop and start the fire.

Back she went to Scott's side of the camp for the second time that evening to beg for his lighter. This time, grinning, he refused.

"Don't fuck with me tonight," she snapped. "You know you're going to want to eat, so just give me the stupid lighter and let me get started."

"I really don't think I want to eat anything you've touched tonight, Miss Bierce. Ask me sometime when you haven't been wallowing in manure for several hours first."

And back she had to go, empty-handed, to tell Meoraq she couldn't get a lighter.

He was not sympathetic.

"If I wanted you to use tools, human, I would have given you mine."

"Meoraq, for crying out loud, I can't start a fire without a lighter!"

His head cocked, not in the way that meant he was teasing, but on the side and a little forward—the annoyed way. "Fire is one of those things which mean life and death in the wildlands and by God and Gann, you are going to learn to make one. You won't always have strikers, will you? No. So stop whining at me and pay attention."

He wanted her to start with sticks, which meant walking all the way to the nearest tree to break a branch down so that she could hunch over on her aching knees trying to spin one stick between her hands fast enough into the notch of another stick to make a fire. She couldn't do it, and meanwhile the eel-thing was lying there, only getting deader, and the sun had finally stopped screwing around and was going down. She got a blister and a little smoke and a tiny red glint that went out as soon as she took the spinner away and that was it.

She stared into the fireless pit, breathing too hard and too fast, until she threw the sticks away in a swearing, furious fit. Scott and everyone else watching erupted in applause and laughter. Meoraq didn't look at them. He simply sat there and waited until the threat of tears had passed and she was back to feeling useless and exhausted. Then he stood up, recovered the sticks, knelt down, and built a fire almost as fast as she could have said, "He built a fire," and he did not say one word to her.

Amber left him cutting up the eel and staggered over to where she'd left her pack. She wrapped herself in her blanket, trapping the distinctly unlovely smells of sweat and animal shit in with her, hid her face in her aching arms, and cried herself to sleep as discreetly as possible. He'd left the eel's head, roasted and grinning, by the fire when he woke her for her watch; she ate what she could off it and threw the rest in the fire. She wanted to throw up just to feel better, but she was still so hungry and there were no guarantees she'd eat again tomorrow. So she sat, fighting her stomach until the urge to purge had passed, and held her watch.

That was the first night. The next day, it began all over. And the day after that. And the day after that. Lying under her blanket at night, she often found herself revisiting that moment right after he took the knife from her neck: the feel of his arm like iron as he gripped her waist and pulled her roughly to him, his weirdly hard tongue licking at her, and the weight of his head when it had rested, just for a moment, on her shoulder. How could that moment, with all of its implied emotion, possibly lead to this string of hellish days in which he punished her over and over and over?

On the fifth night, she actually got the fire lit before Meoraq came back from his hunting trip and had to do it himself. He did not remark, just cut his dead thing up and started roasting the strips, but the next day, he stood over her at each of their rest stops long enough to watch her spin out a fire. When evening rolled around and he called an end to the day, he dumped two new objects in her lap along with the flasks. His strikers.

"Set them on my pack when you've finished with them," he said, turning away.

"Wait!" She struggled to her feet, clutching the strikers in her fist. "I want to come with you!"

He kept walking and didn't look at her. "When I judge you ready."

"I'm ready!"

"But you are not the judge."

"Oh, come on!" She lunged out and caught his arm.

He stopped cold, but didn't look at her, not even at her hand. She let go, stepping in front of him instead. He tipped his head back to look stone-faced at the sky. People were watching, snickering.

"Damn it, Meoraq, there's supposed to be some give and take here!" she exploded. "Would it kill you to throw me a bone?"

Bad choice of words. Someone, Crandall by the sound of it, let out a whoop of delighted laughter and quite a few others joined in. Blushing, flustered, she retreated a step and Meoraq immediately started walking.

The last thread of her pride trembled...but didn't snap. She didn't run after him, didn't beg, didn't stand there and bawl. She was tougher than that, and regardless of what that scaly son of a bitch might think, she was plenty tough enough.

He didn't look back. Didn't slow down. Didn't care.

She would have given anything to have had a room she could have stormed off into or even just a door she could slam. Instead, she filled the flasks. Rolled saoq poop and grass into bundles for burning. Started a fire. And put herself defiantly to bed before he could come home and ignore her after she'd spent the whole day being his bitch.

Meoraq's boots tromping up beside her woke her that night well after dark. She ignored them, pretending to be asleep while he paced around her in a full circle and finally came to a stop in front of her head.

Sadistic goddamn alien lizard. He could stand there all night for all she cared.

He sat down.

She could actually feel his stare, like two fingers pressing down on her head. Her body began to ache in the joints from holding so still, especially her clenched jaw. Real sleeping people were never this quiet or this still, she thought. She could hear them all around her: snoring, muttering, rolling over.

All but Meoraq, motionless, silent. Waiting.

"Go away," she said, keeping her eyes stubbornly shut tight.

"I am the sword and the striding foot of God and I don't take orders from the refugees I allow to stay in my camp," he replied. "Come stand your watch."

"No."

After a very long pause, he said, quite calmly, "You did not just defy me."

"The hell I didn't." She rolled over, turning her back on him to prove it. "You want me to say I quit? Fine. I quit. I don't need to bust my ass for you all day so you can treat me like shit. I get enough of that from Scott."

She heard the low rasp of scales on scales as he rubbed either his knobby brows or his snout. "Please yourself," he said after another long pause. He got up and started to walk away.

Started to.

Then he stopped.

She'd been able to feel his stare. Now she could hear him think.

He came back. Then he said something so baffling she simply could not believe she'd heard it right.

She fought the urge as long as her confusion let her, and then she had to sit up and stare at him. "Did...Did you just ask...if I was ever a baby?"

"You mark. Now answer."

"Y-Yes...?"

He crouched down until their eyes were more or less on level. "Did you leap whole from your mother's belly and stride out into the world?"

She waited, but he seemed to be serious. Pissed off, but serious. "No."

"No," he agreed. "You learned to stand before you walked. You learned to crawl before you stood. You learned to roll onto your belly before you crawled. You learned which way was up before you rolled. So. You want to learn how to survive here, you say, but to teach you those things, I have to begin at the beginning. I am teaching you exactly how I was taught, with far, far less slapping than either I received or you deserve."

"It doesn't feel like you're teaching me anything. It just feels like you're mad at me." She rolled her eyes, hating herself for the stupid goddamn *girly* thing she was about to say, and said it anyway. "We never just talk anymore."

He didn't say anything at first, only frowned. Then he stood up, very suddenly, as if throwing his height like a wedge between them. "I can't."

"Why not?"

“Because I can’t. Don’t get up!” he snapped, and she settled back into her blanket and stared at the ground. “I’m not angry with you, damn it! I just...can’t have you around me all the time!”

A little ways off, Nicci rolled noisily over and mumbled, “Come on, it’s the middle of the night!” and a few other voices sleepily agreed.

Meoraq hissed at them and rubbed his snout. “Stand your watch,” he said finally, walking away.

He was gone. Amber got up, carrying her blanket with her, and trudged over to sit by what was left of the fire. There was a scrap of leather there, folded around an unappetizing lump of marrow and a few charred roots. She wrapped them up again and set them aside. Later, if her stomach settled, she’d have to try and eat them. She was going to need her strength for tomorrow. When she had to do it all again.

6

It was on a chill, gray morning, early enough that everyone was still in a line (a thick line, since people tended to group up on these walks), when it occurred to Amber to wonder if Scott just might be crazy. Not in the hearing-voices sense, or the kill-people-and-keep-body-parts-in-a-jelly-jar sense, but in some real and tangibly crazy way beyond the mere what-is-wrong-with-this-guy sense.

She didn't think she was wondering just because she was feeling bitchy, although she supposed she might be. She knew she didn't like him. It had been another cold, wet, miserable night and she wasn't in the best mood. And she also knew he really wasn't doing anything different today as opposed to every other day, so objectively, she had no reason to suddenly call his sanity into question.

But once that question popped out there, it couldn't be ignored. You couldn't put toothpaste back in the tube; once you'd seen Waldo, you might as well throw the book away. So if it couldn't be unseen, it had to be answered: Was she or was she not looking at a crazy man?

It started benignly enough, with everyone hiking up a rocky, thorn-covered hill in what was almost rain, and when Scott, who was in the lead just behind Meoraq, reached the top, he turned around and started his speech. She was used to that. He liked to begin every day with a speech, and since Meoraq wouldn't wait for him to make them at camp, he had to find the time and the breath to make them on the trail, and it was a rare day that he didn't make at least three of them in his constant effort to keep morale up. The fact that it actually did keep morale up instead of piss people off continued to surprise and annoy her, but it took his, "This is just like the westward expansion of the 1850s," to finally put the word 'crazy' in Amber's head, because for the first time it occurred to her that he might not just be talking them up. He might really believe it.

She understood that not everybody had a Bo Peep in their lives conditioning them since birth to suck it up or blow it out, and that was fine. She understood that not everyone could look at being marooned for life on an alien planet unless they had some kind of happy lie they could tell themselves (for example: I'll be fine once the lizard shows me what to do), and that was also fine. In the beginning, Scott's fixation with having authority and proving it with speeches had certainly seemed harmless enough. It made it easy for everyone else to avoid responsibility and he was actually pretty good at keeping the larger crowd calm in the face of overwhelming horror. But like a cheap pair of boots—such as the boots she wore now as she slogged through the mud that was made when fifty people walked ahead of her in the early morning drizzle—even the smallest defects got bigger with wear. In fact, if Scott's ability to bullshit his fellow Manifestors could be likened to the sole of her boot, the talent, like the tread, could stay more or less intact even as the glue behind it failed. Now, although it left a fairly solid-looking print behind in the mud and no one looking at that print would ever suspect the boot that made it of damage, it sure didn't keep the mud out, and every step that Amber took came with the slap-slap sound of a loose sole tearing itself further and further open.

What all this meant to Amber was that, even though Scott still sounded sane enough as he went enthusiastically on comparing the survivors of the *Pioneer* to the true pioneers, who had also gone on foot over the endless American wilderness with their savage (and not entirely trustworthy) native guides, and seemed to have no trouble convincing his fellow colonists that their trail, like that of the Oregon-bound pioneers of old, would end in the eventual comforts of home, all Amber could hear was that slap-slapping sound. Scott may not be foaming at the mouth and wearing panties on his head, but ultimately she decided that, yes, if he believed what was coming out of his mouth, he was a little bit crazy. Also, her boots were falling apart.

"Let me ask you something," she said, turning to Nicci. "Hypothetically. When somebody consistently refuses to accept reality, when does that stop being optimistic and start being dangerous?"

She thought that was vague enough, but Nicci gave her a look of immediate and undisguised horror, and the two ladies who'd been chatting with Nicci closed ranks and sped up like the conversation was catching.

"Nothing's wrong with him!" Nicci hissed. "Nothing!"

"He's still calling this a colony. We're his pioneers!"

"So? What's wrong with that? What do you want him to call us, his victims? Why do you have to think that if no one is freaking out and terrified all the time, we're not taking it seriously enough? God, this is so like you!"

That gave her a twinge. "Okay, okay. Whatever. Calm down."

"Stop telling me what to do! I don't have to listen to you anymore!"

"I said, okay," said Amber, more harshly than she meant to. People were watching and now they were whispering too. "Forget I said anything. Jesus, Nicci."

"He's right about everything he says about you," Nicci said. She sniffed and gave her head a little snap, tossing her hair just like their mom used to do when she'd drunk enough to get pouty, not quite enough to get mean. "You're trying to turn me against him."

That managed to be ludicrous and infuriating both at the same time.

"You know what?" said Amber. "Right at this moment, I don't give a rat's ass what either one of you think about me."

Nicci tossed her hair again, this time with their mother's mean little snigger. "He says you only say stuff like that because you already know nobody likes you. He says you have a psychological need to push people around because you don't have any self-esteem because you're fat."

"I bet he'd say lots of things to get in your pants," said Amber, but before she could add something even nastier (*not a bitch i'm not and i'm not even that fucking fat anymore so there*), another dried creeper hiding in the trampled mud caught in the toe of Amber's slap-slapping boot for the umpteenth time. She gave it the same little shake she always gave it to free herself, but when she tried to keep walking, she found that it hadn't let go. There was a swift ripping sound, a flare of pain across her toes and down the bottom of her foot, and then the monotony of another day-long hike in the rain abruptly interrupted itself by pitching her onto the ground in this world's first belly-flop. Without a pool, no less.

She landed boobs-first, which as painful as that was, probably was the best way to land, and her duffel bag came up behind her and whacked her solidly in the back of her head, slamming her face-down into the muddy footprints of everyone who'd walked up this hill ahead of her.

"Ha," sniffed Nicci, and kept right on walking.

There was a wet sucking sound when Amber pulled her head up—*shhhhlup*—followed by a brief flurry of giggles, the startled playground kind that weren't really mean as much as just surprised, and then Mr. Yao asked if she was okay. Just Mr. Yao. Nicci was already gone.

"Yeah." Dragging her sleeve across her face, she tried to get up, but her stupid foot was still caught. She rolled over instead.

Her first shocked thought when she saw her boot hanging backwards on the end of her leg was that she'd broken her ankle so spectacularly she hadn't even felt it. Then she saw her naked pink foot lying in the mud beneath her boot and realized she'd just torn the sole off. Not entirely. A few centimeters of rubber still connected the sagging tongue of the bottom of her boot to the rest of it, but it didn't put up much of a fight when she grabbed it and ripped it away.

"Motherfuck!" she snarled, and threw it into the grass.

No one giggled that time.

A second later, as she was struggling to untie her stupid laces so she could throw the rest of the fucking thing after the sole, the dark weight of a lizardman's bad mood dropped over her. Meoraq hunkered, moved her hands curtly out of his way, and looked at her foot sticking out of her boot. His spines, already pretty damn low, went flat.

'Oh sure, like I did it on purpose,' Amber thought, but didn't say. She wiped some more mud off her face and tried to ignore him.

He picked up her other foot and inspected the sole on that boot too, grunting to himself as he touched each of the cracks and holes he found. He put it down again. He clasped his hands. He looked at her.

"What?" she said, and hated herself because it was such a sulky sound.

"This was inevitable," he replied. "What have you done to prepare for it?"

Meoraq did not ask rhetorical questions and he didn't like it when she treated them that way. Amber tried to wait him out, but after just a few seconds of watching that piss him off, she gave up and looked away. "Nothing," she said. She tried to say it, anyway. It was more of a whisper. If she'd said it any louder, her stupid voice probably would have cracked. "I didn't know what to do."

He caught her hard by the chin and yanked her head back to face him. He leaned in close, red eyes burning. "I did. Why didn't you ask me?"

And without any warning at all, all the poison of this miserable day bloomed hot in her chest. Her stomach flipped over. She had a split-second when she thought she was going to throw up right on his boots, but what came out was even worse: "Because you hate me!" she shouted, and everybody shuffled back, except Meoraq of course. His eyes narrowed, but that was all. "Why the hell would I ask you for help when you've made it so fucking clear that all I do is whine at you? Leave me alone!"

He stared at her without blinking, without moving. Even his spines, the usual barometer of his lizardly emotions, were perfectly still. When he spoke, his voice was very quiet, very calm: "Please yourself."

Then he stood up.

"We are not stopping!" he snapped at the people who were sitting on their packs and waiting for them. "Move on, all of you!"

Amber finished taking her bottomless boot off and held it limply in her hands, watching them walk away. "What—" Damn it. Her voice did crack. She took a few breaths to toughen up and tried again. "What am I supposed to do?"

"Walk in one boot!" Meoraq snapped over his shoulder. "As that was your plan before this hour, I see no reason you should change it, but when you come to my camp tonight, *insufferable* human, perhaps you will be ready to ask my advice!"

That was all he said to her, although she could see him continuing the conversation with his god until he reached the top of the hill and passed from sight. No one else waited for her; she didn't really expect them to. Nicci did linger, and Amber almost called out to her, but then one of the other girls plucked at her arm and Nicci gave her hair that drunken Bo Peep toss and walked away. Just as well. Amber didn't feel like keeping anyone's company right now. She was fat and had low self-esteem.

Amber tossed her broken boot to the side of the muddy trail and started walking, but came back after just a few steps to collect it again. She really didn't want to have to make a whole other boot if all it needed was a new sole. And a few more awkward, lurching steps after that, she took her other boot off too. She tied the laces together, slung them over her shoulder, put her head down, and just walked.

* * *

It made for a very bad day, like the mud and the cold and the rain and the whole crashed-on-an-alien-planet thing weren't doing enough of that already. She tried to keep up, but her feet were cold and she just fell further and further behind. Soon, she couldn't see them at all anymore, just their footsteps in the muddy trail she was walking in.

Why hadn't shc said something about her boots? What had she been waiting for, really? Did she think she was going to cross over one of these hills and see a strip mall with a Shoe Outlet and a McDonald's all lit up and waiting for her? Talk about people who consistently refuse to accept reality. Amber Bierce did not ignore problems and hope they'd go away! She wasn't Scott and she sure as hell wasn't Nicci! She was different! She was tough!

Yeah. And now she was barefoot.

Stupid cheap Manifestors' boots. Weren't they the ones that were supposed to last for five whole years of colony work? But hell, the ship didn't work, why should she expect better out of the boots? The Director with his billions and billions of dollars probably outsourced that too. She hoped someone, somewhere, was suing the holy fuck out of him, just like Maria had threatened to do. Class-action lawsuit, you bet.

Everyone gets what they deserve.

The wind slackened off some. The rain fell harder. The trail got slippery, so Amber and her frozen feet moved off into the grass, stumbling now and then over dead vines and picking her way around thorns, but staying upright at least. The grey smudge in the sky began to sink about the same time as the rain finally stopped. She trudged over the top of yet another rolling hill and found the others at the top of the next one, setting up their tents under a half-dozen knobby-armed trees. It probably wasn't even another hour after that before she was there with them. No one said anything to her as she made her way to the fire and sat, pushing out her aching feet to warm them. She watched the mud dry and crack and drop off in little flakes.

She had no idea how long Meoraq had been sitting beside her. She only found out for herself when she turned to see if there was some water in easy reach that she could maybe wash up in, and there he was.

They looked at each other. His head wasn't tipped. His spines were relaxed, neither high nor low. He could have been thinking anything.

The fire spat and hissed around the wet braids of grass and dung it burned. The other people did the camping thing, watching them maybe, but keeping their distance. Amber waited, thinking that if he wanted an apology to go with her lonely barefoot hike in the rain, they were in for a long night.

His gaze shifted at last to her shoulder. He picked her boots up by their laces and looked at the broken one. He grunted. It was one of his good ones. She wouldn't go so far as to call it approving, but it was better than another 'insufferable human' comment.

He untied the laces and set the boots down, then turned to his other side and brought out some flattish pieces of bark. He drew a knife, pointing it absently toward one of the nearest trees. "Mganz," he said, setting her boot down on top of some bark and tracing around it with his knife. "Good for very few things, but this is one of them."

"I can do that."

"You will. For now, be quiet and learn something."

So she watched, silent, as he carved out the new sole from the inflexible chunk of bark, somewhat bigger than it needed to be. From his pack, he took a small wooden case and opened it, selecting a long metal spike from the various needles and skeins of cord it contained. Using the hilt of his knife and this awl, he bored holes all around the sole and then passed it all to her.

"Score the soft side," he ordered, rummaging through his pack some more. "To cushion it."

Using the tip of the awl, Amber scraped awkwardly at the wood and the torn fibers fluffed out a little. She scraped some more, trying to get it as plush as possible all over without digging too deeply through the wood, and just sort of hoped it didn't have bugs. If there was any way at all this day could get worse, it would be with a screaming case of boot-bugs.

Meoraq had found a thin roll of leather, just scraps apparently, and was waiting for her to finish. At her lackluster nod, he covered the sole and held out that small wooden case. "Find a strong needle and a thick thread," he said, or at least that was how she filled in the blanks.

She'd never sewed anything in her life. She didn't wear clothes with buttons and if she ripped a shirt, she threw it away.

She got one of the thickest needles and picked out some cord to thread it with. He took it from her once she had and began to stitch, pinching and tucking the leather as he worked around the sole to make a kind of crease. It looked pretty rustic, but at the same time, she knew hers was going to look like a total shit-cake, so she tried to pay attention to exactly how he was doing it.

"Keep it tight," he muttered, sewing. "Do not allow folds or pockets to form. If you discover one, take it out, regardless of the effort it requires. There is no hurry. Just keep a strong pull and take whatever time you need."

"Thanks."

He sewed, silent, until he had finished the sole. He handed it and her broken boot to her. "You will need to use the awl. Keep them at least a finger's width up from the edging. The holes needn't line up exactly. Keep the stitching even and tight. The seam will draw up this way, and form an overlap. Mend them both. I will have something to seal them in the morning."

She nodded and got to work.

He sat and watched her. Not her hands, not the boot, not the tools she was borrowing. Her.

She struggled with the awl and kept her head down, her eyes stubbornly on her work. She ignored him.

"Pride," said Meoraq, very quietly, "has no place in this camp."

The wind blasted its freezing breath into her face, and still she felt the blush heating up her cheeks. She kept her eyes fixed and her hands busy and did not answer.

"You have asked me for training. You have demanded it. I have agreed to give it, because you have shown me the necessity and I judge you fit enough to learn, but there is no place—" He caught her chin and made her look at him. "—for pride in this camp."

I know. I'm sorry. Please stop. Please.

His eyes shifted to a point beyond her. He stood up and walked off without another word. Shortly afterwards, Nicci crept up and sat down.

And for a second, Amber was disappointed. She hunched over her boot again, forcing the awl the rest of the way through the leather. "Hey."

"I'm sorry," said Nicci. "I really am, Amber. I'm sorry we fought."

"I know. I'm sorry too."

So that was okay. Almost.

Nicci turned her head to watch Meoraq move around the camp. "He went back a few times. To check on you, I guess."

"Yeah." She hadn't seen him, but she hadn't done much looking at anything but the trail in front of her. And in all honesty, Meoraq probably could have been in arm's reach of her the whole way and if he didn't want to be seen, she wouldn't have seen him.

"I'd have gone back too," said Nicci after a moment.

"I know."

"I just thought it was best if we were all together."

Amber looked at her and although she was okay and she really wasn't even angry, it was right on the tip of her tongue to say that she'd have never left Nicci behind like that, never. But her sister's eyes were the same anxious, lost and pleading eyes that they'd been pretty much since they got here and Amber couldn't stand to see them wet again, not after the day she'd just had.

"I'm fine," she said. She even smiled a little, for Nicci. "It was nothing. I was acting like a bitch and I got a little spanking, that's all. I'm fine."

Nicci nodded and picked at her laces. "Can you do my boots for me? They've got, um, holes."

Amber kept smiling. "Yeah, sure."

Nicci took her boots off and got up. One of the ladies sitting around the fire outside the women's tent called her name, waving, then saw Amber and hesitated. Nicci waved back and stood there, looking awkward.

"Go on," she said.

"Are you sure?"

"Beats sitting around and watching me do this all night. Go on," Amber said again, just like she didn't even care. "Have fun."

Nicci left and sat down with the other women, disappearing into their laughing, talking circle. Amber sewed.

The sun went down, and as the grey light dimmed rapidly to black, people began to shake out their blankets and clump up around the fires to sleep. As it got later and more people went down, Nicci finally wandered back. Amber set her boots aside, but Nicci just put herself to bed. And that was okay. They were all tired.

Meoraq's scaly knuckle tapped at her shoulder. He crouched down and gestured vaguely at her duffel bag while staring over his shoulder at nothing. "Sleep."

"I'm not done yet."

"Finish in the morning."

"I'll finish now. I always have the first watch, don't I?"

He kept his head turned, his eyes moving as if he could see some hungry thing pacing back and forth beyond the edge of camp. And for all she knew, he could. At length, and without further argument, he simply stood up and walked away.

Amber resumed boring holes through her boots, but had managed only one more stitch before he was tapping at her shoulder again. He gave her a piece of cuuvash, acknowledged her thanks with a grunt, and moved to the other side of the fire where he crouched and watched people. The firelight threw orange stripes over his scales, broken by scars. They shifted as he breathed, as mesmerizing as the embers themselves could be. He did not respond at all to her stares, perhaps didn't even notice them.

The awl was starting to hurt her hand. She put it down and ate her cuuvash, taking small bites, making it last. Eric and Maria passed close by on their way to his tent. Amber raised a hand and said good night. Eric nodded at her or maybe at Meoraq, it was hard to tell. Then they were gone.

She ran out of cuuvash and had to pick up the awl again. Her hand still hurt. Meoraq watched her make one hole and then went back to staring at nothing. Everyone else was in bed. They were alone.

"Are you still mad at me?" she asked finally.

He thought about it. "No."

"I wish you'd talk to me."

He ran his red eyes over the camp, over every blanket-wrapped lump, every tent and bivy, every person. Except her.

"Say something, then," he said suddenly. He was frowning.

"About what?"

"I don't care. Talk to me."

Amber opened her mouth without any idea of what she was going to say and out popped, "My mom had to go to rehab when I was six and I had to go to state-care. They had a yard with a big hill that had a few big trees and a chain fence at the bottom and the game all us kids used to play was to climb up that hill and roll down it with your eyes closed. There were trees and broken bricks and stuff. You mostly didn't hit them, but you could have. That was part of the game. I only did it once. Because I loved it so much. If it had been scary, I'd have done it every day."

He said nothing. What the hell was there to say to that even if he knew what she was saying? God, she was an idiot.

"It's your turn," she said, thinking he wouldn't say anything.

And he didn't, at first. She had enough time to punch the last hole through her boot and stitch the new sole on, making it whole again, and then he said, "In my ninth year at Tilev, I had trouble with one of the brunts. I had trouble with most of the brunts until I became one. That's what brunts do. But it was my first year in the middle classes and I wasn't used to it. I tried fighting back and he beat me. I tried avoiding him and he hunted me down and beat me. So one night, I threw a blanket over him from behind as he came back from the pisser and I went at him with a practice sword. I beat him until I broke, oh, seventeen bones all together, I think they said."

She looked up from her work, frowning. "Good God, Meoraq."

He grunted and rubbed at his throat, then at his knobby brows. "I didn't know how badly I'd hurt him at the time. I just hit him until he quit moving and moaning and I ran back to the billets. I didn't even take the blanket off him. They found him in the morning on the way to watch, but by then there wasn't much they could do. He slept six days and died."

"Jesus!"

"The masters called us to assembly and commanded the guilty boy to come forward. I did. They had a trial and God moved for me, so that was all right, but I still think about it sometimes. I shouldn't, but I do."

"God moved...? You didn't get in trouble?"

"No."

"Not at all? Not even detention?"

He shrugged his spines.

"Jesus," she said again, because there was just nothing else to say. She knew Meoraq had killed people, in the same indisputable yet off-screen way she knew her mom had fucked men for money, but this was different. "How many—" she began, but faltered to a stop. She didn't really want to know, just like she didn't want to know how many men there had been.

"Three hundred and some. I don't keep an exact count anymore." He was quiet for a while, staring straight ahead and thinking his own thoughts. When he spoke again, it was in a low, almost halting manner utterly unlike him. "The Word tells us that there is no sin in the lives we take as Sheulek, but I was not Sheulek for that one and I think about it. God moved for me when it came to trial, but in my heart I know He was not proud of me. Not then." He paused, his spines flexing and flattening. "And not today."

She dropped her eyes back to her boot and resumed sewing. "I was fine."

"You walked in our Father's sight."

"Nicci said I walked in yours too."

He glanced at her and away into the night. "You are determined to stand a watch?"

"Yeah, why wouldn't I?"

"You look tired."

"You hear me whining about it, lizardman? I'm not falling-over tired. I'm fine."

"Please yourself," he said, almost exactly the same way he'd said it before he left her out in the plains. He reached into his belt and took out a small, cloth-wrapped bundle. He peeled it partway open to show her a grayish, thoroughly unpleasant-looking blob she naturally assumed was some sort of food until he said, "If you want to bathe."

Soap? She stared at it and him, the awl poked halfway through the side of her new sole, in the kind of astonishment that she had only ever known as a child, when Bo Peep might occasionally announce a trip out for ice cream. Half the time (more than half, to be honest), it was really just an excuse to pick up her fucking drugs and little Amber would end up sitting on one side of a booth, watching her mom nod off and finally just shoveling melted ice cream into her mouth as fast as she could so they could go home. But sometimes she really meant it, so there was always that first cautious swoop of hope that something good might really happen.

He covered up the lump again and set it down in front of her. "Return it to me," he told her. "And don't allow S'kot to claim it for his own." He stood up and went to his tent, resting his hand briefly on the top of her head as he passed her.

Alone again. Amber picked up the awl and the first of Nicci's boots, then put them down again. She'd told Nicci she'd fix her boots and she would, but having honest-to-God soap in front of her made thinking about anything else impossible. Hearing about some kid getting beaten to death by the man sleeping in the tent just a few meters away should have ranked a little higher, but it didn't. For the moment, the only thing that mattered was that everyone else appeared to be asleep, so if she wanted to clean up at all beyond just changing her clothes, this was the perfect opportunity. On the other hand, no matter how quietly she tried to go about it, taking a bath in a bag was easily awkward enough to wake someone up and it wasn't like she had a wall to put between her and anyone else.

She pretended to debate the matter, but pretending was all it was. Even as she weighed risk against reward in her mind, her hands were busy building up the fire around Meoraq's heat-stones. While they got hot, she found the leather sack he used for cooking, still with a little cold tea in it. She drank it off—bitter as it was, she hated to waste it—then filled it with fresh water from one of his big flasks and hung it from its tripod.

All of this moving back and forth was bound to catch some attention and it did, but only Nicci roused herself enough to actually lift her head and look at her.

"Go back to sleep," Amber told her.

"But what are you doing? It's the middle of the night."

"Just...Just thought I'd try and do some laundry, that's all."

"Oh." Nicci pushed her pack out from under her head. "Can you do mine?" she mumbled, already rolling over and wiggling herself comfortable.

Amber went and got her sister's clothes. It was no big deal. She really didn't mind. It was kind of wasteful to wash just her own stuff anyway.

Heating up the water felt like it took forever, which meant in reality it probably took about twenty minutes. She kept her hands busy when she wasn't trading hot stones for wet ones and vice versa by making grass bundles for fuel. When she had enough, she took them behind Meoraq's tent and lit another fire, not so much to keep the water warm (although she brought the heating rocks with her) as to see by. She was careful to keep the fire small, as careful as she was to keep Meoraq's tent between her and the rest of the camp. It wasn't much cover, but it was all she had and she wanted to make the most of it. She took it on faith that she had privacy as she undressed, and she did for the most part. While several people woke up during Amber's bath, the wind covered her furtive splashing and the intermittent chattering of her teeth, and Meoraq's tent blocked both her and her little fire from sight. The only one who saw her was Meoraq himself.

One word was all it took to catch his attention. One word, her hissy little "Shit!" when she thought she'd put her live coal out, just before it caught and grew into the fire that splashed her shadow onto the wall of his tent. There was no reason to watch her once he'd identified what she was doing...but he did. He watched, first from the corner of his drowsing eye, then brazenly rolling onto his side to face her.

Amber, believing herself entirely invisible but knowing that someone could come yawning into sight to take a piss any second now, stripped herself naked and got down to business. The hard lump of what Meoraq called soap did not lather when she rolled it between her wet hands, but its pungent aroma grew immediately strong enough to fight against the wind and sting her sinuses with its sharp, green smell. Rubbing at her arm was not quite as abrasive as attacking herself with one of those green kitchen scouring pads, but it wasn't too far from it. On the other hand, whether the dried mud got washed off or scraped off, at least it was off.

Amber started scrubbing at her face and worked her way down. The water was nice and warm at first, but it didn't stay that way. She felt each blush of warmth as she splashed hurried handfuls over her neck and breasts and shoulders, but the wind was always there, turning blessed heat to icy pins and needles in seconds. She wanted to stop almost as soon as she'd started, but she made herself keep going and didn't let herself half-ass it. Who knew when she'd get another chance at a bar of soap?

So she got it all, even the spots she'd never given much attention before: her belly, her hips, her thighs. It was like washing a stranger's body. Gone were the soft curves and smoothness of her old self. In its place, the new Amber's body was all rough-chapped skin, bony joints, hard muscle. She had lost all the weight she'd ever been teased for, but it hadn't made her thin and pretty the way she used to tell herself she didn't care if she ever was. It just made her uglier. Haggard. Hungry. She closed her eyes and refused to look.

In the tent, Meoraq watched her bend herself in half and bounce with the vigor of her scrubbing motions. Silently, he sat up, drew in his legs and rested his palms lightly on his knees, unthinkingly adopting the relaxed yet intent posture of any child at lectures. He studied every line of the silhouette she showed him and yes, he knew she was only cleaning herself, and no, there ought not to be anything remotely sensual in such a process, and yes, he supposed it said something about his character that there was this fire in his belly as he sat in the dark and watched her, but no, he felt no pressing urge to meditate until he had resolved it. Not yet.

When she reached her knees, Amber stopped. She was freezing, but that was only part of it. Half her hot water was gone and her fire was getting low. She straightened up to stretch her aching back, then bent over again to dip her hair clumsily in the stewing pouch. Rubbing the soap over her head did not appear to do anything except rough up the knots in her hair, but she rubbed anyway, then poured what was left of the hot water over the matted results in a slow trickle. Even if the soap wasn't doing anything for her, the hot water might loosen the grime enough to rinse...well...cleaner. Clean was probably one of those things, like pizza or television, that had made the eternal transition from reality to memory. But cleaner was better than nothing and when she was done, she thought the effort had been worth it, assuming she ever warmed up.

Shivering, Amber crouched down by her pack and rifled through it for almost an entire ass-freezing minute before she realized she didn't have any more clean colonists' pants, just her old blue jeans, the ones she still thought of as her 'skinny jeans'. It was darkly hilarious to think that they still weren't going to fit. They were her 'fat jeans' now.

The fire was only getting lower and colder and she doubted like hell the clothes fairy was coming tonight. Amber fished out some panties, put them on, straightened up to shake out her jeans...and her panties fell off. Somehow the prospect of being caught with her underwear around her ankles was more mortifying than being caught bare-naked. Amber yanked them up again, held them uselessly at her hip while she looked in vain for a WalMart lingerie department to spring up behind her on this alien planet, then gave up and tied them on with handfuls of her panties' own excess fabric. She stepped into her jeans fast, as if to hide evidence of a particularly ugly crime, but as she bent over to fish out a fresh shirt, those fell off too.

"Motherfuck!" Amber hissed, hugely embarrassed. She looked around again, this time for the women's wear section of that WalMart. What was she supposed to do now? She couldn't tie the jeans on, for Chrissakes!

'Suck it up, little girl,' she told herself in Bo Peep's dry, half-drunk voice. 'You've got bigger problems out here, so quit whining about your clothes and just put them on.'

"I am not whining," she whispered fiercely, and put a shirt on. It was another of the Manifestor-white ones, one of only two clean ones she had left, and there was no kidding herself that it was just loose. She couldn't walk around in this damn thing. She needed a belt.

Motherfuck.

Holding her jeans in one fist, Amber kicked the fire out and picked up her dirty clothes and her greatly depleted pack. She trudged around to the front of Meoraq's tent and half-knelt to work the flap open. "If you're awake, don't stab me," she whispered. "It's just me. Amber."

No response. She peeked inside. The light of the fire out where Nicci slept turned one wall of his tent a hazy orange, letting in just enough light to suggest Meoraq's body beneath his blanket.

"Are you still awake?" she whispered.

A lizardish grunt was her only answer. Hearing it, she felt her stomach knot inside her. She'd woken him up, obviously. She should have waited. She was going to get him for his turn at standing watch in a few hours anyway. What was she doing here?

"You're letting the wind in," he said without moving, not even raising his head.

"Sorry." She started to let the flap drop, then, not without a nervous glance over her shoulder, she crawled inside. He still didn't move, but she could feel his stare even if she couldn't see it. Fidgeting with her handful of denim, Amber awkwardly settled herself in the furthest corner from his mat and whispered, "Do you...Can I...Look, I'm sorry I woke you, but do you have an extra belt I can, um, borrow?"

Wordlessly, the dark lump of a lizardman propped itself up on one elbow to open the pillow of his own pack. Rustling sounds. The shape dropped back down. His arm reached out to her, holding the folded length of a leather strap.

She took it, her cheeks flaming. "Thanks."

He grunted.

"Sorry I woke you."

"You didn't." A pause. He shifted. "Tie the fastens, woman. You're letting the wind in."

“Sorry.” Belt in hand, she crawled back out into the freezing night and tied his tent down. Threading his wide belt through the loops of her jeans was not exactly effortless, and figuring out the buckle took several minutes, but as soon as it was on, she felt a lot better. She guessed she was ready to do the laundry.

The heating stones went back in the coals of the fire next to Nicci. Amber moved the cooking pouch and its tripod back and filled it. Meoraq probably wouldn't be thrilled to discover how much water she'd gone through in one night, but maybe she could get them filled again before he noticed. Unlikely. He noticed everything. But maybe. And as long as she was imagining things, why not imagine that he'd forget all about being woken up early for her wardrobe malfunction.

And speaking of clothes, how exactly was she supposed to do this? Amber was no stranger to the chore of laundry, but it had always involved pre-measured packets of detergent and a handful of tokens. She doubted rubbing a little soap over her clothes was going to do the job. Still, like her own bath-in-a-bag, it had to be better than nothing.

Amber gathered up all the shirts, pants and underwear she and Nicci owned and waited for the water to heat back up. It wasn't a very big pile, and for the first time since the crash, Amber made herself think about just what they were going to do for new clothes, because they were going to need some soon. Not in some hazy future sense, when these wore out completely (although that day probably wasn't as far in the future as she was pinning it), but soon, before it got so cold that people stopped just bitching about the weather and actually froze to death.

She'd have to ask Meoraq. Maybe he could teach her how to make new clothes, although it was difficult to imagine how he could turn the rough, scaly hide of the saoqs into anything like the supple leathers he wore. If it was as much of a process as she suspected, he might not want to take the time. For that matter, he might not know how. In spite of the fact that he dressed in leather, they weren't all ragged edges and rawhide ties. They were evenly stitched, trimmed and decorated, with metal buckles on his harness and belt. In other words, they were probably store-bought. She could hardly ask Meoraq to take them to the nearest LizardMart and buy everyone new outfits, but she did find herself uneasily wondering why he wasn't at least taking them to town. The fact that they hadn't so much as seen one on the horizon meant that he had to be deliberately keeping them away. In spite of how dangerous he insisted the wildlands were, he wanted to keep them here. Where no one else knew about them but him.

Amber thought about this as she did the washing—dunking each article of clothing, rubbing it all over with Meoraq's latherless soap, dunking it again, wringing and rubbing and dunking some more—and ultimately decided it didn't really matter. Scott was unlikely to let them go to any lizard-city anyway. It was one thing to pioneer their way east across the alien landscape with their native guide, but it would be something else entirely to be the ones who were outnumbered. To be the aliens, in other words.

And that only brought her around to the even more disquieting matter of just what they were going to do once Meoraq was gone. Not just for food, but for boot repair and heating-stones and stewing bags to dunk their dirty clothes in. Scott could kid himself all he wanted about how this was a colony, but once Meoraq was gone, she had a feeling things were going to fall apart in one hell of a hurry.

She didn't doubt for a moment that Meoraq would leave them at the end of the road. The only question was whether or not he'd leave them even sooner. She would if she were him, especially after tonight. God, what had she been thinking? Just barge right in, little girl, and as if that wasn't bad enough, by all means, sit around until he actually has to tell you to get out.

'He didn't,' the half-drunk voice of her mother remarked.

"Didn't what?" Amber muttered, wringing what looked like pure hot cocoa out of one of Nicci's shirts. She really ought to dump out what was left in the bag and start over with fresh water.

'He didn't tell you to get out.'

"Well, no, not in so many—"

'He told you to close the door.'

Amber froze, her mouth slightly agape, her arms jutting out stiffly before her with murky water dripping from the rat-tail of Nicci's shirt, because there was a difference, wasn't there?

"Bullshit," she whispered, but she looked furtively back over her shoulder at the leathery peak of Meoraq's tent.

Tie the fastens, woman. You're letting the wind in. Not even 'human,' but 'woman.' *Tie the fastens,* woman.

And just why the hell was that running circles in her head instead of *I beat him until I broke seventeen bones* or *He slept six days and died*? But now the thought was there and her brain ruthlessly showed her how it could have been if she'd done it...if she'd closed herself in and then crawled over to the half-glimpsed shape of him and then what, for God's sake?

Her hands were freezing. She was still holding that stupid shirt and her wet knuckles were actually throbbing with cold. Quickly, Amber dunked the shirt into the warm water and wrung it out again. She was doing the laundry, damn it, and that was it. He didn't even like her.

'You don't have to like someone to fuck them,' observed Bo Peep's sly, smirking voice, and she ought to know. 'Besides, it was nice in there, wasn't it? Out of the wind. He had a real blanket, too. And he's warm.'

"Shut up."

'You thought so even way back then, when he took the knife away and licked you. He's not cold at all, like reptiles are supposed to be. He was so warm.'

She was not going to stand here and argue out loud with her dead mother's disembodied, imaginary voice. Tight-lipped, Amber gathered up the chilly armload of dripping laundry and carried it over to the nearest tree. She began to tie things to the lowest branches. Double-knots. Extra secure. She wasn't thinking about it. For God's sake, he was a *lizard*!

'He's a man. And men are all the same. Go on and tell me you've never caught him looking at you when it's just the two of you up at night and Eric and Maria are shaking the walls of that pissant little tent.'

Sure, she had. She'd seen those looks and, let's face it, she'd seen them because she'd been looking for it, hadn't she? Yeah, he was a lizard. Yeah, okay, no getting around that, but he was the lizard who, although he clearly didn't like her, wouldn't walk with her, and avoided even looking at her these days, he was the lizard who *had* touched her. Three times, in fact, his hand had stroked across her forehead in what could only be called a caress, and who could forget that endless moment after he'd decided not to execute her after all, when he'd put his arm around her waist and yanked her hard against him and licked her neck and pressed his scaly forehead against her shoulder?

"It isn't like that!" she hissed, tying up the last pair of pants with a particularly savage twist. She knew she was talking to herself and she hated herself for doing it, but she had to say it out loud because the silence felt too much like shame-faced agreement.

And it wasn't like that! It wasn't! She'd had no trouble at all telling Crandall off when he'd tried to buy a blowjob with a lousy Fleet ration, and she'd done it a few times since on those nights when he decided that the privilege of his company was worth a kiss and a quick cop under her shirt. She had no pangs of conscience when it came to putting herself between Scott and her sister, or speaking up over his persistent efforts to convince everyone that a loyal pioneeress served her colony's best interests by making babies. She knew some and maybe all of the other women were creeping off with certain guys from time to time and she didn't blame them, exactly, but she was different. She was tough. Things were bad right now, but she was learning and she wouldn't need to be taken care of forever. She wasn't...God damn it, she wasn't a little girl!

The wind flapping through the wet clothes sounded to her ears like slow, sarcastic applause. Her mother used to do that when she was feeling witty. Amber turned her back on it and went back to the fire, where the stewing bag was waiting to be washed out. After she'd done that, she could cut some more grass and bundle it up for fuel. Then as long as nothing snuck in and ate someone, Meoraq would wake up and think she was doing a good job. And maybe he'd tell her so and maybe he'd even give her one of those friendly knuckle-taps and maybe he'd never put his arm around her that way again, but that was just fine. Amber Bierce did not need a fucking hug and even if he were to open his tent this instant and order her inside, she—

...she...

...she'd go.

Amber sat in the grass with the stewing bag and the bar of soap stupidly clutched to her chest. She pulled her knees up, put her head down, and wept without sound until she thought she was going to pass out. Then she dried her eyes, finished washing out the bag, hung it up on its tripod, and got back to work on Nicci's boot.

7

After being wakened for his watch, Meoraq brought out the fires, meditated until dawn, then went out and found a saoq to kill. There were no herds nearby, nor was he likely to find any more save by Sheul's grace, but the young rogues who had been defeated and driven out were still in plentiful number in the plains. His kill was a finer specimen than most, but it had been gored deeply across the face and the infection which made it easy for Meoraq to find and kill had also swelled half its head with poison. Perhaps not all the meat was bad, but it wasn't worth the risk. Meoraq left the head and the bowels steaming over the cold, dead earth and came back to feed his many whining mouths.

He made certain to walk past Amber on his way through camp, and a short time later, as he was pulling the saoq out of its hide, she came yawning up behind him with her clean, white clothes blown wide around her. She didn't look like a candle-ward anymore. Neither did she look like a tent or a windmill or any of the other humorous comparisons that might have at one time occurred to him. In the grey light of dawn, she looked like nothing but what she was: a sallow-faced, sunken-eyed starving person.

He frowned and continued to butcher his kill.

"Morning," she said.

He glanced up at the sky. "So it is."

"Yeah, so...thanks again." She lifted the lower edge of her gusting sail of a shirt to show him the top of her breeches and his belt threaded through its loops, but only for an instant. Her smile seemed nervous. "Sorry I woke you up last night. I should have just waited until it was time for your watch."

"I wasn't sleeping." He did not, however, elaborate on just what he had been doing. It did not bother him much to receive an idle glance or three while washing up for a trial—waiting around in the arena hold was boring—but if he had ever found himself the subject of such a stare as he had given Amber's silhouette, he thought it very likely a knife would be drawn over it. And what had he seen, even? Her human body was just as much a mystery as it had ever been in all save the broadest sense, that of its shape beneath the oversized things she wore.

"So...about last night..."

Meoraq grunted and continued hacking the saoq into manageable pieces, setting meat aside for the hateful human Scott and tossing the bones into the fire, waiting for her to say something. It seemed a long time in coming, but the kind of stench raised by burning bones could make any silence thicker.

"I...I just wanted to say that I...shouldn't have let myself in like that."

"You have," he pointed out. "Twice."

"And I should have left as soon as I had the belt. You know. Before you had to tell me to leave."

'I didn't,' thought Meoraq disgustedly, and cut the last stubborn fiber holding the saoq's heart to its body. Aloud, he said nothing.

"It won't happen again," said Amber.

She seemed to be waiting for something and Meoraq had no idea what she wanted to hear. He savaged at the carcass some more, preserving the tastier organs, but burning the majority. It occupied his hands the way that counting breaths occupied his mind, but it was not peace.

"Are we good?" she asked finally, in what seemed for her a rather weak voice.

"I do not mark you."

"Are we..." She faltered to a short, helpless silence, looking back over her shoulder at the sleeping people of his camp, and when she faced him again at the end of it, it was with obvious strain. "I know what you said about not needing friends and I...I know how you feel about me—"

He frowned.

"—but I need someone around that I can still talk to," she finished in a shaky rush. "And if I fucked that up last night, I'm sorry. I wasn't thinking. I just need to know that we're still...the same."

Meoraq started to rub at his brow-ridges, saw the blood on his hands, and settled instead for stabbing his knife into the shoulder of the saoq. He looked up at her, making an effort not to look ferocious. "I don't talk to people, human. I never learned how and I think I must not be any good at it. If there's something you expect me to say back at you, you are just going to have to tell me what it is."

"Are you mad at me?"

His spines flared. "No. Why would you think so?"

"Because I barged in on you and woke you up for a stupid reason."

"How many times—" Meoraq stopped there with a snort and unbuckled the belt he wore. He stripped it off, looped it over so it hung even, and held it up to her.

Her hand reached out and drew back again. "What's that one for?"

"So you can whip yourself and be done with it."

She stepped away at once, actually hiding her hands behind her back for an instant like a child.

"No? You're certain? Then shut the door, human, it's done." He put his belt back on. "I wasn't sleeping and it wasn't a foolish request. As for your, ha, invasion of my tent, I forgive you for it. Enough, eh? Enough."

She opened her mouth, closed it, opened it again, then said, "Can I do anything to help with that?"

Meoraq followed her nervous gaze to the saoq before him and studied it as if it were new. "What would you do, if you could?"

"I guess I could make some skewers."

"Well then?"

She wandered off toward a tree. He heard wood crack as she fought a few thin branches down. He heard some of her people protesting the noise as well, although no one seemed to be protesting the thought of roasted saoq when it pleased them to wake up.

Amber returned to sit at his side, mangling meat onto her harvested sticks with considerable difficulty. The bark of the mganz was the hardest thing about it; its wood was soft and wet enough to be useless either for burning or tool-making. He took the opportunity of her distraction as she fought with it to run a critical eye over her boots. Not a bad effort, for her first. Nothing that would earn her any prizes, but not bad. They still needed to be sealed, however.

He got up, gesturing to the rest of the saoq so that she could keep herself occupied, and returned to his tent. The hide flap's stays were not tied in the knot he'd used on leaving this morning. Just within and to one side, out of danger of some errant stride, his mending kit and his wrapped brick of soap rested together atop his greatly diminished supply of leathers.

She'd come right into his tent. Right inside. He could smell the soap on her skin and the wet smoky smell of her hair and she had been right here.

Enough. Close the door, wasn't that what he'd just told her? Good advice. It was over. Close the door. He hunted out his bottle of proofing resin, and returned to the fire to find that Amber had finished skewering the meat. She had also taken it upon herself to put the meatier bones into his stewing pouch with his heating stones and just enough water to cover them. She wasted nothing...except the heart, liver, kidney, and bitteret, all of which she had seen him set aside.

She saw him looking and hesitated, holding her skewers of meat awkwardly between her fists and as far away from her clean clothes as possible. That cause was lost, of course. She had already smudged herself with soot, dirt and several good smears of blood. White showed everything, which was why they made the brunts wear white tabards at Tilev. It didn't stop them from brawling out of the training ring, but it usually made them think before they did it, at least long enough to take their tabards off.

He'd actually told her about that brunt in his middle years. He'd never told anyone—not his father (although Rasozul had surely been informed), not his brothers, not even Nkosa. But he'd told Amber...and she had still come to sit with him this morning.

"Am I doing something wrong?" Amber asked.

Kneeling that way, half his height and draped in too much overshirt, he suddenly found it easier to picture her as a human child on the hilltop she'd spoken of. He could see the crowd of children around her, chanting and jeering the way that children do when injury is imminent, but she would not have hesitated. Fearless Amber. Stubborn Amber. He saw her tumbling, her thin arms hugged close to her chest and eyes squeezed shut, flying blindly past trees and bone-cracking stones until she came to a dizzied stop. Just the once and never again. Just the once, because she had loved it.

"Meoraq?"

He wanted to tell her that he understood. He had spent a lifetime learning it—in Tilev, where he had lived out every year from age three to twenty, never home for more than a two-brace and that during the coldest days of the season; in House Uyane, where his own father was more a name than a man even to his son; on the road that Sheul had set before him, where every journey began and ended in battle and the almost-friend you looked forward to seeing after half a year's absence could be whipped or worse just for slapping you once on the chest. He knew that joy can be a terrible thing to feel, when you know you can't have it every day. He wanted to tell her...but the other humans were stirring, and so instead he said, "Give those to S'kot."

She hesitated again. "All of them?"

"Yes." Meoraq opened the bottle of resin and set it where it could warm.

"Um...I hate to admit this, but they're not going to save you one."

He snorted. "You think I need you to tell me this? Go on."

She went. He watched her go, and when she was bent (*her shadow black against the firelit leather as she bent and stretched and then came crawling in to him*) and at work in the coals, he turned his knife back on all that was left of the saoq. Choice meats, they called this in the cities. The food of governors and lords. He remembered without warning being a child at Rasozul's table—a rare privilege—being served cattle's heart, and how terribly grown-up it had made him feel. These days, it was just an extra-tough cut of meat and he ate it as little as he could. But that would change when he went home, he supposed. If he was made steward of House Uyane, he would be eating heart nearly every day. Farm-raised, young cattle's heart, minced with herbs and simmered slow or fried quick and served with roasted riak.

But today, he was still Sheulek, and he was eating wildland stew.

Amber returned. He could hear her bare feet padding over the crushed grass, and he could hear them slow as she saw him drop bits of saoq heart, black and dripping with blood, into the water. Meoraq tipped his head at her and nicked the end of the bitteret so he could squeeze out the crumbling mass of its protected organ, along with the tangy fluid that it floated in.

Amber put the back of her hand against her mouth and watched solemnly as it all went into the stewing pouch. She said, "I don't even know what that thing was."

Meoraq glanced at the dangling tube of the empty bitteret before tossing it into the fire. He told her the word, then flexed his spines and said, "It has something to do with digestion, they tell me."

"Do you have one?"

"Of course not. Only grass-eaters, like saoq and cattle."

"What does it taste like?"

"It tastes," said Meoraq, now cutting up the liver, "like the food we are fortunate enough to have."

"Which means it's gross."

"I don't ask you to enjoy it." He added the kidney and wiped his knife clean before sheathing it. "But I warn you, I've been pressed to eat far worse things in my time than stewed bitteret."

She laughed, stirring once at the contents of the pouch. "So have I, if it comes to that. Thanks for helping me with my boots, by the way. I know you don't believe me, but I swear I'm not trying to make things even more difficult."

He grunted, nudged at the still-warming bottle of glue, and then leaned back and looked at her. "Do you see those trees?"

"Huh?"

"The mganz trees. Do you see them?"

Amber looked over her shoulder at the trees. "Um...yeah?"

"Do you see any others?"

She looked at him again, frowning, but sat up a little taller and searched the plains around their hilltop camp. There were thickets here and there and, in the distance, shadows of what might be zuol copses, but no other trees in sight. "No."

"Sheul set them in my path."

She rolled her eyes and settled back down. "Of course he did."

"Yes. As easily as He set you for me to find." Meoraq leaned close, lowering his spines. "But even He cannot make you ask for help when you need it."

Color rose pink in her cheeks. She looked down, picked at the unsealed seams of her boots, said nothing.

He could have said more, perhaps a word comparing a fall in the mud of the prairie to a fall in the mountains they would eventually have to cross, but couldn't think how to phrase it and it was very distracting to be this close to her. He leaned away instead, letting the matter go, to lift the cap of the sealing glue and show her the brush affixed to it. "This is ready. Just paint a thin skin along the edges where the sole joins the body of the boot. Take care to make a full seal."

"Okay." She started to get up. "Guess that means I'd better go get Nicci's."

His spines came forward in surprise and then flattened. He waited and true enough, Amber returned to him with a second pair of boots, newly resoled.

"You taught her well," said Meoraq darkly.

She sat down with the boots in her lap and just looked at him.

Meoraq traded out stones. The bloody water in the stewing pouch was beginning to simmer, sending out tiny bubbles like beads to slide along the lumps of largely unidentifiable chunks of meat. It gave him something to look at while he mastered his rising temper and counted breaths. At last he said, "My mending supplies exist to be used. I do not begrudge their loss if they teach a useful lesson."

"I think I did okay."

"Yes. You learned to use a needle and an awl to mend your boots. N'ki learned to use you." He slammed a wet stone down in the embers and glared at her.

Amber applied resin to a boot. Nicci's boot. "She's doing the best she can."

He had to look at her twice to be certain this absurd statement was not meant as some human joke, but she appeared to be serious. So he snorted at her, and if that were not enough to let her know what he thought, he added, "Sheul provides the raw stuff of our souls, human. The polish is left entirely to us."

"I didn't catch much of that."

"It means we are responsible for our own character. N'ki is helpless because she wants to be helpless, and if that is what she wants, that is what she deserves to be."

"Lighten up, lizardman. It's not easy to hike through the damn wilderness when you're not used to it. If I can make it a little easier for her, why shouldn't I?"

"What a stupid thing to say!" he said disgustedly. "Do you think it helps your N'ki to be coddled like that? Do you think it helps any of your people, who must all work that much harder to care for her?"

"I'm taking care of her. You don't get to judge me for that."

Meoraq leaned in aggressively close to say, quietly but with feeling, "I am Sheulek, human, and I get to judge everyone." Straightening up, he added, "You were the one to tell me that feeding is not the same as saving, and it is just as true for N'ki as it is for you."

"She shouldn't be here," said Amber, and immediately coughed out a sour laugh. "None of us should, but she really shouldn't. She didn't want to. I made her come with me. I made her come here."

"If you can do that, making her fetch water once in a while should be easy."

But she didn't smile and her stiff-backed silence as she sat proofing her Nicci's boots made the echoes of his own words seem fanged, which of course they had been. Meoraq hissed almost soundlessly through his teeth, rubbed crossly at the end of his snout, and changed out the heating stones. The wet stone hissed; the hot one spat.

"Who is she, then?" he demanded suddenly. "What is she to you?"

"My sister." Her mouthparts faintly turned up even though anger was still in every hard line of her. "You honestly can't tell?"

"Are you saying you're kin?"

"We're family. You know. Sisters." She touched her hand to her chest and moved it rapidly out and back again, tracing an invisible line between hearts.

"You come of the same father?" he guessed, and swiftly sketched two badly-drawn humans in the ash around the fire, on their knees in female fashion. After a moment's thought, he added the swoop of human hair above them, then drew in the governing figure of a father. "You were sired of one man?"

Her smooth brows knitted. She hesitated, then shook her head. "Our mother," she said, and leaned forward to draw curves on the father-shape—not head-hair, but an embarrassingly accurate suggestion of twinned teats. He did not look at her when she was done. "But we had different fathers," she said, indicating them vaguely, one to either side of the mother. "Different men."

He twitched his spines to show he understood, and if he had successfully translated her words, a great many things had just become clear.

When a Sheulek came to the House of conquest and the steward had no daughters to offer for his fires, the accepted alternative was to give one's wife. Any sons who came of this union were for the Sheulek to raise, but if a man's wife bore a daughter, what harm could come of raising it in its mother's household with the other children of her marriage? So it seemed cbvious that Amber was one of these—sired of Sheulek, or whoever took that role in their human cities—while Nicci came of their mother's wedded man. They were not true sisters, only blood-kin, like he and Nkosa. Blood-kin through the maternal line, but blood-kin all the same.

"Who was he?" Meoraq asked. "Your father."

"I don't know. I never knew him."

"Your mother's man, then. What man did she marry?"

"What did she...what?"

"Marry." Meoraq held up his hands and clasped them. "How was she bound?"

"I'm not...sure I'm getting you, but if you're asking who she lived with, she lived alone. Well, with us, but not with a man."

"How is that possible?"

"What do you mean?" Her mouthparts were curling up again, as if she found his suspicion humorous. "Why would she have to?"

"Who raised her children?"

Amber's human smile faded. She went back to work on Nicci's other boot. "I guess the polite answer is, she did."

"Say truth. Who raised her children?"

"She did. It was her house. In her name, paid for with her money, filled with her things. Hers. Women don't have to get married where I'm from if they don't want to."

Meoraq leaned back, staring at her. He tried to picture the land she described, a land of milling humans, like yifu in some great undiscovered nest, but the images his mind presented were those of the ancient ruins, and the people he saw inhabiting them, his own. It had been that way for dumaqs once, before the Fall. Men and women, living together, walking freely about in the streets, open to any man's eyes; it remained a shocking prospect. Meoraq flexed his spines, then shook that off and frowned at her. "What did she do? Your mother?"

Amber's thin smile broke and she refocused her attention on Nicci's boots, although they were entirely sealed. "She died. I don't want to talk about that, okay?"

Meoraq watched her fuss with the boots. Eventually, she realized she was done with them and set them aside. She took up her own and finally got to work on them.

"Were you married?" he asked, and when she gave him that puzzled frown again, clasped his hands together. "Were you bound to a man?"

Understanding smoothed out her clay-soft features, but she didn't answer right away. She only looked at him, her thoughts moving like stormclouds behind her eyes. "Why do you want to know?"

Why *did* he want to know? He scratched irritably at his throat, but his scales still felt cool. "I'm trying to understand you," he said. That much was truth. He wanted very much to understand this creature who crawled into his tent uninvited and left without dismissal, and more than that, he wanted to understand which of the many males in her pack had a claim over her. Because...?

Meoraq hissed suddenly through his teeth and snapped, "I don't need a reason!" which Amber not-surprisingly believed to be directed at her.

"No," she said. Her head bent. She dipped out proofing resin and painted her boots. "I was never married."

"Did you..." He wasn't even certain how to ask this. "Did you keep your own household?"

"No. We lived with our mother."

She did not look at him when she answered. Her voice was tight and the silence that followed it, even tighter.

"Did you take labors?" he asked at last.

"Yeah, of course I did. Me and Nicci both."

"What did you do?"

She slid him a glance and laughed without much humor. "I built machines."

He recoiled.

"Well, I didn't build them. I stood next to the machines that built the other machines and made sure they ran smoothly. I couldn't even fix them if they broke. Just a button-pusher, really."

He wasn't sure if that was better or not.

"N'ki did this also?"

"Oh hell no. Nicci was a waitress." Amber glanced at him, read the confused slant of his head perfectly and said, "Do you have places where people go just to eat?"

"Yes, of course." Surprised, he sat up straighter. "N'ki kept such a place? She never cooks!"

"No, I know. She showed people where to sit when they came and they'd tell her what they wanted to eat and she'd bring it." She set her boots down, capped the resin, and held the bottle out.

"Is that all?" He pointed at the ground, away from the fire. "She carried food?"

"Yeah." Without the business of sealing her boots to occupy herself, Amber returned her attention to the stew. It was bubbling constantly at the sides now, but it would need an hour at least before it stopped looking like chopped offal in water and became food instead, and it did not require constant tending in the meantime.

"For coin?" Meoraq pressed.

"Yeah."

"Someone gave her coin just to carry food?"

"Not a lot, but yeah."

Meoraq leaned back to think about that. When he visited a public kitchen, which was often, the cook passed him his meals directly. He could not comprehend why anyone would pay a woman just to touch it for him, and he could tell by the small smile on Amber's pliant face that his confusion was very evident.

"And I built machines," she reminded him. Her smile faded. "Do you have to kill me now?"

He thought about it, concerned, but ultimately determined that he did not. "The Word forbids us to master or seek to remake the machines of the Ancients. Your machines were those of humans and not the Ancients. You offend none of His laws. Besides, you are here now."

"Yeah." She raised her head, searching the empty plains that surrounded them. "My machine-making days are definitely over."

"But you must not seek to master the machines you may encounter here or you will be subject to my judgment."

She stirred the stew and didn't look at him. "I'll try to control myself. Making you kill me after you've gone through all the trouble of teaching me to light a fire would be pretty ungrateful."

"It hasn't been so much trouble," he said, showing her a careless flick of his spines to hide his irritation. He picked up the nearest of her boots to prove it, inspecting the seal and grunting his approval. "You learn very quickly." And before he knew it, certainly without planning, he said, "I like teaching you."

"The hell you say. You can barely stand to look at me."

"I know." He shook his head with disgust and stood. "Come, human. Let's go have a look at this land while your boots dry."

"What, in my bare feet?"

"Don't whine at me. We won't go far and you won't be walking much once we're out in the open," he added with a certain evil humor. "You'll be crawling."

She looked down at herself, at her mostly clean clothes and fresh-washed skin. "Great. You're sure I don't need to stay here and cook?"

Meoraq glanced over to the far fire where the skewers of saoq roasted, the first of which were already brown and spitting merrily. The scent of food had drawn a handful of humans from their nests. He raised his arm and when one of them raised an arm back at him, he beckoned it over. "Tend to those," he ordered, pointing at the meat. "How do you mark me?"

The human gave Amber an uncomfortable glance. "Where are you going?"

"With him, apparently."

"For how long?"

"I don't know."

The human's eyes narrowed, which gave it a distinctly suspicious look. "Why?"

Amber's brows puckered, first in confusion, then in irritation. "I'm going hunting! Why the hell do you think?"

Meoraq raised his hand to catch the other human's attention, then pointed down to his stewing pouch. "Keep it hot," he ordered. "And don't put it over the fire! I only have one water-tight pouch."

"Then how am I supposed to—"

"Change out the stones," said Amber, pointing at the one heating in the coals. "Just fish out the old one, drop in the hot one and try not to get too much ash in there."

"Why can't you do it?"

The question was directed at Amber, but Meoraq did not allow her to answer it. He snapped his spines flat and leaned in close enough to smell the unwashed, male stink of the human now trying to back away, and hissed, "Because it is not the task I set her. It is the task I set you!"

"Is there a problem over here?"

Meoraq leaned back, rubbing at his warming throat and allowing the human to escape so Scott could take his place. He was calm. A Sheulek is always calm.

"It's not worth it," Amber murmured behind him. "I'll stay."

"Get your spear and fill the flasks. I'll find you at the water."

"Meoraq—"

"Go."

She went.

Meoraq folded his arms, resting the lengths of his first fingers along the hilts of his sabks, even though if it came to killing, he would never use an honor-blade on the throat of the hateful human Scott.

Scott smiled at him. Like all his smiles, it was a lie. "I'm glad we have this opportunity to speak privately."

"So it seems," said Meoraq after a moment's judgment. "I will hear you then."

"You've been a tremendous help to us in these first difficult days."

Meoraq snorted. A 'help'.

"And I appreciate it. We all appreciate it. However..." Scott's face shaped itself into an expression of grotesque concern. "We are all increasingly uncomfortable with your attempts to assert control over us."

Meoraq thought that over and took slow breaths and decided he'd better be sure he'd heard that before he lost his temper. "I do not mark you."

"Control," Scott said again. "Command might be a better word. Telling people what to do. And trying to intimidate us when you do it."

"Ah. Go on."

"I just don't want there to be any confusion over who's really in charge here. Now, I'm happy to assign someone to take care of the cooking detail this morning," Scott said magnanimously. "And I'll see to it that your...uh...whatever that is, is kept hot while you and Miss Bierce are..." Scott's eyes rolled and his smile took on a crude sort of slant. "...doing whatever it is that you do, but I don't want there to be any further incidents. In the future, if you have requests to make, you bring them to me and I'll see what I can do about meeting them, but you need to stop just barking orders and slapping my people around."

"I see." Meoraq's throat was very hot and tight-feeling now, but he made no attempt to hide its color or breathe it away. He did not draw; he remained calm. "Is that all you have to say?"

Scott considered. Meoraq's throat throbbed painfully.

"I guess that's it. But I do want you to know that I don't hold you responsible. Miss Bierce has always been a disruptive element. I realize now it was a mistake to let her act as my intermediary during our initial contact and I apologize for that."

"I forgive you."

The subtlety of dumaqi sarcasm was entirely lost on humans.

"Okay, then." Scott clapped his hands noisily together and rubbed them. "I'm glad we got that sorted out. Is there anything you'd like to share?"

"Oh yes."

The answer seemed to catch Scott by surprise. His smile slipped; the one that replaced it had teeth. "Go ahead. I'm listening."

"Good. Because I am only going to say this once. I don't know who you were in your homeland or what you think gives you the right to talk at me like an equal—"

"Now wait a minute—"

"Do not interrupt me," said Meoraq, quietly and distinctly. "This is not your camp and these are not your people. Everything you think you had became mine the moment I set my tent among you and will remain mine until I choose to release you. I am not asking your obedience. I demand it. I have forgiven much and will forgive more, I am certain, but the one thing I will never do is make myself your servant in the camp I have conquered. So here we stand, human, and either you will do as I command and cook the fucking gift of food—" Oh, calmly now. Breathe. A Sheulek is the master of his clay and his emotions, always. "—that I have brought you, or you can let it burn, but you will have no more from me until I see the obedience I am owed."

Scott looked back over his shoulder at the far fire where the saoq roasted. More of his people had wakened and gathered there, but they stayed close to the food. These words were still private.

When Scott turned back to Meoraq, he was not smiling. "I think there's a lot of people over there who would object to being thought of as your property."

"Is that a threat?" Meoraq demanded, more incredulous than angry, although he was very, very angry. "You and all your piss-licking people together couldn't take me if I were tethered to a tree!"

"It's not a threat," Scott mumbled, but his face had gone dark and even uglier.

Meoraq clapped a cooling hand to his throat and rubbed, rubbed. It didn't help much. He closed his eyes, tried to breathe, and for no reason at all, the memory of Amber crawling into his tent in the dark watches of the night leapt full to the front of his brain. Hissing, he opened his eyes and there was Scott, brazenly scowling at him.

Something in him tore. It did not break, maybe, but it tore and it tore deep. Meoraq's vision briefly clouded, as it sometimes did in the arena, before the fires took him. His flesh became a stranger's, throbbing everywhere, every nerve and vein and scale. His thoughts were black.

With all that was left of Uyane Meoraq, he said, "Raise your hand right now and show me your fucking fist, or I swear here in the sight of Sheul that I will end you."

Scott said nothing, did nothing. Sheul, whose name had been invoked to bear a witness, let neither His voice be heard nor His hand felt. The wind blew at the mganz trees, moving their soft branches in odd gusts, as if it were breathing; six breaths, deep and slow.

'Amber is waiting,' Meoraq thought, his first real thought in quite some time. He opened his hands—they ached—and let go his sword. "If you don't want to tend the food I bring, I'll stop bringing it."

Scott mumbled at him, flushed and frowning.

"I did not mark that."

"I said we'll do it. I never said we wouldn't, you know," he added churlishly. "I was just—"

"I know what you said."

They stood together, silent. The words they had spoken sat and soured. The words they did not say screamed between them. Meoraq watched the mganz branches blow. Scott watched the fire.

Meoraq said, "We will not walk today." Amber's boots—and Nicci's—would need to dry. It should only take a few hours, but the damp in the air would slow the process and he wanted a good, strong seal.

Scott muttered some kind of acknowledgement Meoraq did not ask him to repeat.

"I am glad we had this talk," he said instead and he thought he said it sincerely. Something he'd learned from his early days at Tilev and its public toilets: It was always better to open the doors and let the stink out than to try and close it in. "But you would be wise not to approach me again unless the need is very strong."

"No, but I'm sure you'll have plenty to talk about with Bierce, won't you?" Scott snatched up the pair of sticks Amber used to manipulate his heating stones and began to fish savagely through the stew for the stone there. "I bet you just talk each other's brains out, don't you? All night, every night."

There was an insult somewhere in those words, but the more Meoraq tried to puzzle it out, the more he found himself distracted by Amber's tracks in the wet grass. She would have found the water by now, he knew, having found it himself the previous night. He could see her in his mind's eye, sitting on the bank with her bare feet tucked up beneath her to keep warm, waiting for him.

"And as far as I'm concerned," Scott was saying, now struggling to pick up the stone in the coals and move it into the stew, "you can have her."

"I don't need your permission," said Meoraq, thinking of Amber sitting on that bank, Amber tumbling down a hill, Amber crawling into his tent in the dark and whispering his name. "I am Sheulek here and what I want, I take."

And with that, he turned his back on Scott and the rest of his humans and went to find her.

BOOK V

SCOTT AND THE SHIP

It was raining the day that they came to the ruins, which was nothing really new. It had been raining off and on for several days, but this was a whole new kind of rain. Dawn came, nearly as dark as dusk, and the wind that came with it was almost a warm one. The rain alternated between tiny pellets as harsh as hail and fat blobs of icewater that plastered Amber's hair to her scalp and wormed freezing trickles underneath her clothes.

Walking in the rain was bad enough, but on this day, there were also hills to contend with. Not tall ones, but very steep and rocky as hell beneath the tangle of creepers and thorns that covered them. All day long, they trudged up and down, hunched against the weather, stumbling and swearing but otherwise not speaking. Throughout the morning, the clouds pressed claustrophobically close, smothering them with wet slaps of wind to make their already uneven footing even more treacherous, but when the dim smudge of the sun reached its highest point, the clouds suddenly lifted, as if Meoraq's God had chosen to maliciously swoop back a curtain and show them their options.

Door Number One was the southwest, the direction of the odd, warm wind and its icy rain, where they could all see the real storm not just growing on the horizon, but filling it, overfilling it, seemingly motionless but as solid a thing as the land it crawled upon. In the east, Door Number Two opened half a dozen needle-thin rays of light over a crumbling sprawl of what her eyes tried to see first as stones, then as giant trees, before finally showing her buildings.

The city had been huge in its day, straddling both sides of what might be a picturesque river, if all the rain hadn't turned it into this swollen, frothing nightmare. Most of the bridges that had joined the city together had fallen in, but at least two appeared to be all right, from this distance anyway. As for the city itself, it too had mostly fallen in. Grass grew right over the crumbled remains, forming hundreds more of those steep hills they'd been climbing all day. Toward the middle of the ruins, these hills grew taller, sprouting eroded chunks of masonry and metal, and occasionally whole walls held together by the small prairie trees that had rooted themselves in windows and along broken ledges. And here and there among the centermost section of the ruins were pockets of shocking normalcy where the roads were not only cleared and the buildings sound, but the lights were on.

Bluish lights.

Electric lights.

Amber had stopped walking when these two tableaus revealed themselves, and she had been staring back and forth between them for some time before she realized that everyone else had stopped too. On every face, she saw the same bewildered apprehension, as if both choices were equally disturbing.

Even Meoraq had stopped, she saw. He stood motionless ahead of everyone else, his spines forward and one hand toying at the hilt of the knife that hung around his neck while his gaze moved from east to west and back again. One by one, all heads turned to watch him. They waited, some drawing up into familiar groups, to hold their own low conversations until he came to a decision.

At length, he raised his hand, beckoning without bothering to look at them, and started walking again. From that first step, it was obvious he had no intention of taking them to the ruins. He was instead turning them south, not quite straight at the storm but certainly not away from it.

The murmurs gusted at once into a wave of alarmed babble. Nicci clasped onto Amber's hand. Scott gestured for everyone to stand still even though no one—not even Amber herself—had made any attempt to follow, and quickly caught up with Meoraq. Amber couldn't hear what was said, but it didn't appear to go the way either one of them wanted. When Meoraq started moving again—south—Scott turned around.

"Okay, people, listen up!" he shouted, clapping his hands a few times. "We're going down into that town there."

Meoraq stopped and looked back at him, his head cocked in what Amber was coming to understand more and more was never a gesture of curiosity on a lizardman. Sometimes there was amusement in that look and sometimes irritation, but regardless of what emotion accompanied it, it was always a warning, always the way he silently said, 'Stop and think about what you're doing,' usually with some variation of 'you insufferable human' at the end. Amber gave Nicci's hand a squeeze and got a little closer.

"We've got plenty of time before the storm gets here," Scott was calling, oblivious to the stare at his back. "Everybody relax. Let's just stay close and keep moving. The storm will be over before we know it, but there's no reason—" He paused and amended, "No *good* reason we can't wait it out where it's dry. Let's go."

People murmured in a relieved way, not without a few nervous glances at the distant storm, and drew themselves back into their sprawling approximation of a marching line.

"He doesn't look happy," Nicci whispered.

Meoraq had moved exactly one muscle: the one it took to lower his spines.

Scott waved at him gallantly. Lead on, O faithful native guide.

Meoraq's head took on a distinctly deeper tilt. "God's own Word forbids His children from dwelling again within the cities of the Ancients."

"We're not going to live there," Scott said, rolling his eyes back at the others and letting everyone know how patient he was being. "We're just going to hike through—"

"No."

"—and wait out this storm where it's dry—"

"You will obey the Word as it was given."

"—and then we'll use one of those perfectly good bridges—"

"You will obey me."

"—to safely cross the river instead of swim it, which is what you apparently have in mind."

"Watch your next words to me, S'kot, or I will show you exactly what I have in mind at this moment."

Scott's broad smile faltered. Meoraq's stare did not.

Behind them, a low grumble of thunder reminded everyone of the storm slumping inevitably toward them. Scott took advantage of the distraction and deliberately started walking toward the ruins. A few people followed. Then a few more, breaking away in larger and larger groups until they were all trailing in Scott's commanding wake. Nicci tugged at Amber's hand once, then let go and walked quickly away to join the other women. Meoraq watched them go the way another man might watch a parade, but if Amber thought for even a moment that he was annoyed by this defection, that ended when he looked at her.

He was furious.

With a sigh, Amber trudged over to him. He took her arm and turned around, but that was as far as she was going and when he felt it, he stopped too.

He didn't look at her again, didn't speak, didn't take his hand off her. She stood quietly behind him and watched the yellow come in on the side of his throat and fade slowly out again.

She said, "If it was you or Scott, you know it'd be you. You know that."

His head turned, not enough to look at her.

"But you're asking me to choose between you and my sister. And that's not a choice."

His head turned the other way, turned fully, staring after Nicci.

"Please don't leave us here," said Amber.

His hand on her arm tightened minutely, then let go. He started after Scott and the others, taking long strides but hardly moving, so that he seemed almost to be gliding through the grass like a hunting cat. She could not help tensing when he came up behind Scott, but he simply moved on ahead and took the lead.

Scott smirk was obvious even in his voice. "Glad you decided to join us."

"Don't talk to me," said Meoraq curtly.

"You need to work on this attitude of yours. There's no reason we—"

Meoraq swung around and slapped Scott clear off his feet, sending him crashing into Dag and Crandall. Then he drew his hooked sword. Without a word, he turned back around and kept walking.

After that, no one said anything. It made the mood, already low, that much worse, which in turn made the landscape around them seem even bleaker than it was. To Amber, the fallen towers looked like tombstones in some forgotten cemetery, and why shouldn't they? She knew now that they had been walking across the burial mounds of this city all morning. For hours. And a city that size didn't just curl up and die on its own. Something had killed it.

An unnecessarily theatrical turn of phrase, perhaps, especially considering the already bleak landscape, but no sooner had it taken its crawl through Amber's brain than it was underlined by the first hint of rot in the air.

She wasn't sure at first. No one else seemed to have noticed, or at least, no one else had reacted. The wind was at their backs (and pushing the storm steadily toward them) and the smell came and went with the force of its gusts. But the closer they got to the ruins, the stronger that smell became, until Amber finally turned to her sister in some desperation and asked if she could smell it too.

"It's nothing," said Nicci. And in a sudden, angry rush, "Stop trying to make trouble all the time! You always do this!"

Startled, Amber stopped walking. Nicci did not. If anything, she went faster. Even after Amber started moving again, the distance between them kept growing, until Nicci was up with the women from the Resource Tent and Amber was alone.

'So let it go,' she thought, watching some sympathetic Manifestor respond to whatever Nicci was saying with a sidelong, walking hug. 'Let it go and she'll come back. She always does.'

But something stank. Something was dead and rotting. Something big.

"Doesn't anyone else smell that?" Amber called.

Immediately, half a dozen Manifestors groaned at her to shut up, but Maria turned around and called back, "God, yes! I feel like I'm going to puke!"

"It's nothing," said Scott.

Meoraq, his sword still drawn, threw a flat, unforgiving glance back at him.

Scott moved over to put a few more people between them. "Probably a dead deer," he told Maria. "It won't be as bad once we get into town."

If Maria had a reply apart from the scornful look she gave him, Amber couldn't hear it, but no one else said anything.

The grass began to thin. There was pavement beneath, so weathered that it looked more like gravel poured out and glued in place, but obviously pavement. A street. The hills to either side got steeper and lumpier as the grass receded, until suddenly they weren't hills at all, but heaps of broken concrete, metal, glass, and all the wreckage one might reasonably expect to see when a city block has been demolished.

Except that the streets had been cleared. Had to have been. Buildings did not fall straight down and pile themselves up like that, leaving the weathered pavement beyond the curb largely uncluttered. And as they traveled deeper into the ruins, the streets not only got wider and cleaner, they also began to show signs of repair. Likewise, the devastation lining the streets gradually changed from piles of debris to hollow shells, missing one, two, or even three walls, but upright and recognizable buildings. And then even those were behind them, and they were there in one of those lamplit pockets which had looked so much like it might still be inhabited when viewed from a distance.

Scott stopped, so everyone stopped, bunching up there at the first intersection where things had gone from knocked down but cleaned up to empty but sort of functional. Meoraq alone moved on, a sword in each hand and eyes in constant motion, to check each of the crossing streets and peer through each broken window. He had almost made it back to them when Scott suddenly cupped his hands around his mouth and hollered out a hello. The wind, greatly deflected by the buildings now surrounding them, ate the echoes after one or two bounces, but that was enough.

No one came out to greet them and although the fine hairs on the back of Amber's neck were standing straight up and prickling almost painfully, she got no real sense of being watched. There was movement—furry things scurried in the shadows, considerably smaller and less threatening than the rats Amber had grown up with—but no life. The city was dead; the last of its concrete bones, rotting; and whatever was keeping the power on and the streets swept probably did not want its rest disturbed.

Meoraq was staring at Scott, his head cocked, his throat striped with bright, bright yellow, silent.

"I think maybe we should move on." Scott looked back at his loyal lieutenants. "What do you think?"

"I think it's creepy as fuck," Crandall replied with half a shrug, "but creepy won't kill us."

Eric seconded that with a firm nod. "That storm is going to hit us before we even get near one of those bridges, much less check it out and see if it's safe to cross. Any salvage you expected to find here is long gone, but even if shelter is the only thing we get out of this place, that's good enough for me. Having said that—" He glanced up, up, and up at the nearest tower. "—I am not comfortable bedding down right here."

"Plus, it stinks," Maria announced.

"Miss Alverez, this is an official debriefing, so please be quiet," Scott told her, and to the rest of them, announced, "For now, we're going to keep heading for the bridges, but we'll be keeping our eyes open for a good spot to take cover. Don't worry, people. We'll all stay dry tonight."

Exclamations of relief met this rather lofty promise, but looking around, Amber could see doubt for the first time in a number of faces as they eyed the height of the broken towers enveloping them and perhaps reflected on the fact that rain was not necessarily the worst thing that could fall on a person's head.

But Scott had decided and there was no point in arguing. He chose a street and headed out. Eric followed him and Maria followed Eric, and that started the first group, which started the next one, and pretty soon they were all walking. Even Amber, so what did that say?

* * *

After so many days struggling through hip-high grass, wading streams and climbing rocky slopes, a little stroll down the street should have been an easy feat. Distance, like time, could be subjective without a mechanical means of assessing it, but Amber knew they couldn't be much more than a mile from the first of the bridges and it was taking all day to get there. The ground still rose and fell, but gently, in city-hills that had been smoothed and paved and was unquestionably easier on Amber's feet than Meoraq's wildlands. It wasn't what they were walking on that slowed them now, but what they were walking through.

It wasn't quite silent. Passing too close to the dark shops made the windows sputter and light up, playing out the corroded remains of advertisements for whatever products had once been on display, but few of those recordings played for more than a few seconds before dying out and one of the windows shattered from the effort. On another street, the remains of what had obviously been a restaurant groaned out some of the daily specials and wheezed its door open at them, showing anyone who looked in the desiccated carcass of a saoq who had apparently wandered in and been unable to get out. Several furry heads poked curiously out of the nest that had been built in its dried belly.

When the whole crowd of them stopped at an empty intersection so that Scott could 'get his bearings,' the remnants of some ancient public address system fired up and blatted out noise. What little she could make out through all the audial corrosion were mostly unknown words, peppered with odd, random-seeming numbers or verbs. The longer she had to stand there and listen to its tortured, droning gibberish, the easier it became to imagine how the blanks could be filled: *system pressure rising* warning warning *severe storm watch in effect until nine hours and three* error *trafficeye six reports all lanes open on Cinoq Bridge please drive safely* error *trafficeye seven reports* error error error *no lanes visible on Jaavi Bridge please drive with caution the current time is three hours and sixteen contagion risk seven percent* error error *threat level high but stable tune to* error error error *for news and updates—*

"This way," Scott decided, and set off.

Amber lingered as the group moved on, reaching out to touch the cracked, dead window of a kiosk on the curb. It flickered and came on, spilling writing and static across its face until the whole window was filled and then going black again after voicing the grim message, "No response. No arrival," in a dead, metallic voice. She shivered and moved around to the next window, reaching.

Meoraq caught her wrist. "Don't."

"What happened to this place?" she asked as they went together after Scott and the others.

He shrugged his spines, but they snapped pretty flat when he was done. He looked okay and he sounded okay, but he was still pissed, clearly.

"Do you even know where we are?"

"It was a city once, is that what you need to hear? No longer. The Ancients fell and all of their works fell with them. There is nothing to find here."

"That smell is getting worse!" Maria called, trying to cover her face in her sleeve. "Can't we just leave?"

"We are leaving!" Scott said irritably. "We're just...taking a shortcut!"

"How can this be a shortcut when you don't know where we're going?"

"I know it's shorter to go through something than to go around." Scott gave Eric something of a dirty look and turned up another street, seemingly at random. It took them to the bottom of a long hill lined on both sides with clean, burned-out buildings.

"Oh my God, really? Uphill?"

Eric put his arm around Maria's shoulder. "Ease up, baby. We'll be out of here in just a sec."

"You've been saying that forever. God, what *is* that *smell*?!"

Amber tried to exchange glances with Meoraq, but he was looking down another street. "We're not going to see a huge pile of bodies over that hill, are we?"

"I don't know. I've never been here before."

"But is that what a huge pile of bodies smells like?"

"It would depend on what they died of," he said, sounding distracted and a little annoyed with her, but not particularly bothered by the idea.

"You don't believe in ghosts on this planet, do you?" said Amber, only half-kidding. At his puzzled glance, she added, "Dead people...walking around after they've died? Ghosts?"

"Ah." He glanced down another side-street. "Yes, we do."

"You do?"

He grunted.

They walked.

"Do you think this place is haunted?" Amber asked, just as a soft, cool hand slipped into hers.

She didn't scream, but what she did was bad enough: grabbing at Meoraq's arm, who already had a sword in his other hand and aimed over her shoulder at what turned out to be just Nicci.

His head cocked. His sword did not immediately lower.

"You scared the ever-loving *Christ* out of me!" Amber snapped.

"I was just...I only..." Tears, the big, slow kind, dribbled down her baby sister's pale cheeks one at a time and dropped off her chin. "I don't like this place," she whispered. "Can't I please come walk with you?"

Amber took her hand at once, pulling her into an awkward hug as Meoraq slowly let his sword-arm drop. "Yeah, of course you can, you know you can."

"You're always yelling at me!" Nicci wept.

Meoraq flared his mouth open at Nicci's shaking back and exhaled soundlessly through his teeth.

"I don't mean it," said Amber, glaring at him. "You know I don't mean it. We're sisters, Nicci. I love you. You're all I've got."

Thunder clapped and rolled, not on top of them yet, but close enough to echo in the empty streets. Nicci jumped in her arms and wailed even louder.

"And now it's going to rain," groaned Maria, somewhere at the head of the crowd. "Perfect."

"Baby, please. You know I love you, but please."

At the top of the hill, Scott suddenly stopped walking.

Maria threw up her hands. "Fine, I'm shutting up!"

Scott didn't answer. He didn't even turn around right away and when he did, he looked greyish. He looked at his people, and then he looked past all of them at Meoraq. He didn't say anything.

"Stay here," Meoraq said and ran, jostling people roughly aside and reaching the top in maybe half a minute. He saw what there was on the other side. His spines came forward. He slowed to a walk, sheathing his sword.

So it couldn't be that bad. Amber gave Nicci a squeeze and let go of her. "Stay here. I'll be right back."

By the time she got to the top of the hill, a crowd had formed, thick enough to shield whatever they were looking at from view, but loose enough that she could slip through it without pushing too many people. She heard Scott (who sounded just as grey as he'd looked) asking if this was bad, if they were in trouble. Then she saw it for herself.

It wasn't a pile of bodies after all.

It was a pit of them.

It looked like it was miles across, although it probably wasn't. It was just the shock of seeing something so big thrown down in the middle of the city which had followed such neat, orderly lines. It was perfectly round in shape, with a raised lip of broken pavement all the way around it. The sides appeared smooth but uneven, melted. It had partially-filled with water—if it could be assumed that black foulness had started out as water—and although that might smell bad enough on its own, there could not have been less than a hundred bloated corpses mushed together along the sloping sides.

Somehow worse than what was in the pit was what was around it: small triangular flags had been set around the lip, outlining the whole thing in a hundred shades of fluttering yellow. Whatever had caused this crater had happened long ago and the animals might be falling in on their own, but someone had planted those flags.

Staring at them, trying to estimate how many hundreds or even thousands of flags she might be looking at, it dawned on Amber that the only reason she was able to see the pit at all was because virtually everything between it and the top of this hill had been flattened. There were no more buildings down there, no kiosks, no lamps—only the grey crazyquilt of their foundations and the nice, clean streets that ran between them. It was not perfectly flat; the ground buckled at regular intervals, forming concentric rings around the pit, almost like ripples in a pond after someone has dropped a rock in it.

'Or a bomb,' thought Amber, creeping forward in sick fascination.

Meoraq pulled her back, started to push her toward the crowd, then yanked her around and gaped at her, all his spines up and quivering for a split-second before they slapped loudly flat. "I told you to stay where you were!"

"I, uh, thought you were talking to Nicci."

He thrust a finger in her face, leaning close enough that she could feel his breath against her skin. "That is a lie and it had better be the only one you ever tell me!"

Amber looked back over her shoulder at the pit...the crater...and felt Meoraq blow a fuming snort against her throat. "What killed them?" she asked, eyeing the bodies. From here, she couldn't be sure, but she thought they were all animals. She just didn't know yet if that made her feel better or not. "Did they...Did they just fall in?"

"I don't know."

"Shouldn't we go check it out?"

A flash of far-off lightning made his red eyes spark. "Why?"

"I want to make sure the animals fell in and then died instead of, you know, the other way around." She gave the pit another backwards glance, as if to make sure it wasn't creeping any closer. "And I want to make sure they're all animals. And not people. Especially if it was the other way around."

"I'll go with her," said Crandall, stepping forward.

Meoraq immediately swung her around and behind him, as if Crandall had been offering to cut her throat instead of walk with her down to the crater, but when the thunder caught up to the lightning, he seemed to shake out of it some. He didn't let go of her, but he grunted and raised his other hand to rub at the yellow patches on his throat. “No one is going anywhere.”

“Meoraq—” she began.

“Insufferable human, I said no! Mark me, if there are men who feed that place of death, they are men to stay well away from. If it is a trap of Gann’s making, so too should you stay clear. And if it still holds the poison made at the time of the Fall, we are too damned close already!”

“Okay! Jesus, okay! Now will you please let go of me?”

“No!” he shouted.

Thunder groaned.

“Okay,” said Scott. He still looked a little grey, but he sounded more like himself. He turned around, raising his hands to get everyone’s attention. “Okay, I’ve made my decision—”

Meoraq hissed, then clapped his free hand to his throat and started rubbing again. Amber could hear him muttering under his breath as Scott listed all the reasons why everyone was still perfectly safe but they should all get the hell out of here as quickly as possible. Meoraq muttering at himself was hardly a new phenomenon, but he didn’t seem to be praying this time. He was counting.

“Are you okay?” Amber whispered.

He looked at her and for a second—a very long second—there was absolutely no recognition in his eyes. Then there was, but it wasn’t a better moment. His head tipped slightly; his spines flicked forward; his hand stayed knotted in her shirt and even clenched a little tighter.

“Am I in trouble?” she asked, trying to laugh.

He didn’t smile.

“You look like you’re going to bite me.”

His gaze shifted to her shoulder, lingered, and came slowly back to her face.

Another flashpop of lightning distracted him before Amber could make the leap from concerned to nervous. He looked up as the thunder rolled, a whole lot closer than it had been, and closed his eyes while the wind blew over him. He took a deep breath. He took another one. He let her go.

The urge to run was extremely strong in those first few seconds.

“All right.” Having consoled the masses, Scott was back and at his most in-charge. “I think we should go around this, um...new development and keep our distance as much as we can.”

Meoraq grunted. His eyes were still shut.

“So what we’re going to do is, we’re going to turn around and go that way for a bit, see if we can’t find a building that’s more or less intact and hole up for the night.”

“What, here?” asked Amber.

Meoraq began to count again, very softly.

“Do you see that storm blowing this way, Miss Bierce?”

She looked. Lightning obediently forked.

“That’s going to catch us before we’re out of this place. No one’s going to want to walk in that.”

“Want to...” Meoraq murmured. He took a very deep breath, held it, let it out, and began to count again.

“So we need to find some shelter, preferably before it starts dumping directly on our heads. All I want from you, Meoraq, is a little help finding our way out of here without accidentally getting any closer to that, um...thing.”

The yellow patches on Meoraq’s throat brightened fast and slowly faded. “Accidentally...” he breathed.

“Why can’t we just go back the way we came?” Amber asked. “There were lots of buildings back there that were still standing.”

"Because I don't want to lose ground, Miss Bierce, and I'm not going to stand here and argue with you. All I want right now is for the liz...Meoraq here to do his job."

Amber cast a cautious glance up at Meoraq to see how he was taking the news that he was now in Scott's employment. Meoraq did not appear to have reacted in any way. He breathed, counted slowly to six and started over again. The yellow stripes on his throat fluxed, but seemed to be dimming overall.

Scott waited, growing first an impatient frown and then a puzzled one and finally the worried one that Amber had been working on for some time. "Is he okay?" he asked in a low voice.

"I don't know."

The storm crawled steadily closer. The smell of the crater stayed pretty much the same. The people watching them began to whisper at each other.

"Okay," said Scott at last. "You stay here with him and I'll take the others—"

Meoraq tipped his head forward and opened his eyes. He looked at Scott with a solemn, vaguely curious expression as the rain came down harder and the lightning worked its way closer. He said, "I really don't like you," in the way of a man who has suspected this for some time but only recently found it to be true and perhaps worthy of some response.

Scott took a step back. So did Amber.

Meoraq started walking back down the hill. He didn't tell them to follow, didn't look to see if they needed to be told. He showed no sign that he even saw the humans shuffling out of his path, just marched himself through them and onward.

"What's his problem?" Scott demanded, but he made sure to ask it well out of earshot.

"We are," said Amber, her heart sinking.

"Can't you talk to him?"

"And tell him what?" she asked. "That he's not doing his job?"

"I didn't mean it like that. Besides, you pissed him off before I even opened my mouth."

"Yeah. I know."

They started walking together, well behind all the rest of them, side by side and silent. The rain came—fat, infrequent drops that became a pouring downfall in seconds, plastering her hair to her skull and her clothes to her body—and the thunder got louder and longer. Lightning came in spears and sheets and sometimes just going off in crazed sky-broad flashes deep behind the clouds. It was going to be a bad one, all right, and she guessed it was silly to camp in it when there were all these empty buildings lying around.

"Truce," Scott said, angrily enough to make the offer a lie at its inception. "Truce, okay? Look, Bierce, I have got to know...Is this guy safe to have around?"

"Yes."

"You didn't even think about it."

"It doesn't do a whole lot of good to ask when you don't trust me."

"Why should I? I know you and I know what the two of you are doing," he added in a petulant sneer. "I don't know why I thought that you might actually put the safety of your own kind—"

"What the hell do you mean, you know what we're doing?"

"Don't even try to deny it, Bierce. He doesn't. The only thing that matters is whether we can trust him to look out for us or not, because the last few days, all I've seen is an armed, dangerous alien getting increasingly hostile and unbalanced."

'You mean he's not putting up with your bullshit,' Amber thought, but didn't say it. She also thought, 'And while we're on the subject of people becoming increasingly unbalanced,' but didn't say that either. What she did say, as mildly as possible, was, "I trust him. I don't think he's crazy. He's just not a people-person."

"People-lizard," Scott muttered. "Look, just tell me how I'm supposed to get through to him. How do I make him listen to me?"

She had to laugh. "Sure, like he listens to me."

"I'm serious, damn it! I can't afford to have all this...confusion! People need to see him respecting me!"

"Yeah, well, I think marching us off into the middle of Plaguesville today has pretty much shot that dream to shit, but maybe the next time he tries to 'do his job' and guide us safely around a place like this, you ought to let him."

Scott didn't answer, just walked and fumed and glared at Meoraq's back as the city receded. The wind picked up as streets narrowed and the buildings shrank, although everything was still clean and well-maintained. The rain fell harder, throwing sheets of water up from the pavement directly in their faces. The first of the really big clouds reached them, bringing on the dark too early and making up for it with near-constant waves of high, flickering lightning, like a visual metaphor for Scott's bad mood.

The street ended at a neat square of disturbingly well-manicured greenery. On the other side of this little park were more buildings—great, grey cubes with smaller blocks butting up against them, all of them connected by second-floor corridors, fanning outward from the only building that made any effort to look nice. Warehouses, then, or some sort of shipping company. It seemed they'd come out of the downtown area into the industrial district. Here, Meoraq stopped and looked back, counting heads as they all came out of the street to stand in the grass. He saw her alone with Scott, away from everyone else, and even at this distance, she saw his spines go flat.

But Scott didn't notice. He was looking at the buildings beyond the little park. One of the cube-shaped warehouses had a hugely gaping wound in one wall where a tree had fallen. Scott jogged away through the rain to get Eric and investigate, leaving Amber to trudge over to Nicci under Meoraq's baleful stare.

"You okay?" she asked, and was distantly dismayed to realize she didn't care how Nicci answered.

"I'm soaked," said Nicci, shivering. "And my feet are killing me. Can you carry my bag?"

Amber took it wordlessly. In the next instant, a scaly hand snatched it out of her grip. Meoraq slung the pack onto his shoulder, not looking at either of them. His spines were still flat.

"Yeah, but admit it. You're going to miss me when I'm gone," said Amber.

He gave her a scathing sidelong glance and did not reply.

"This is perfect, Meoraq!" Scott called.

Meoraq opened his mouth and hissed quietly through his teeth. Scott, busy climbing the fallen tree that had bashed through the wall of the warehouse or whatever this place was, did not notice. He checked whatever lay inside, made some gestures to Eric and then climbed down and came running back to them.

"Perfect!" he said again, giving Meoraq a clap to the shoulder.

Meoraq stiffened and looked at his shoulder. Yellow flared on his throat and began to fade again almost immediately. "Don't do that again," he said in a distracted, indifferent way that Amber felt sure hid a deep desire to snap someone's fingers off.

Oblivious to danger, perhaps thinking that he was showing his faithful Indian guide some appreciation in the hopes that respect would soon be reciprocated, Scott moved off and started herding people across the park.

Amber followed, holding Nicci's hand but looking sideways at Meoraq. "Are you all right?"

"You keep asking that."

"You keep scaring me."

He grunted—one of his sarcastic grunts—and said, "You're not scared enough, human, or you would not be here."

"Oh come on, look at that!" Amber waved her hand toward the approaching storm, which threw out a strobing flare of lightning that lasted several seconds without stopping, almost as if it were waving back.

Meoraq gave it an incurious glance. "So?"

"So we can't walk in that!"

His flat spines shifted against the top of his head, trying to flatten even more. "A man can walk anywhere in God's favor."

"Yeah, well, maybe God wants us to sleep here tonight, did you ever think of that? If he can put trees and people in your path, why not this place?"

"Do not be blasphemous," Meoraq said curtly. "His Word commands His children to let the ruins and all the trappings of the Ancients fall to dust. This is not shelter. It is nothing but a grave."

Ahead of them, Scott was busy directing people into a queue. Dag boosted them up onto the sloping trunk of the tree, while Crandall waited on the wall to help them over. Eric was nowhere to be seen; presumably he was inside, helping people down. Amber watched people climb, crawl, and drop in this orderly procession, with the black wall of the storm howling ever closer in the background. She could understand Meoraq's hesitance, given his beliefs (his stupid beliefs, if he really thought strolling through a thunderstorm was somehow more righteous than sleeping in an empty building), but she didn't see any alternatives.

"For what it's worth," she said finally, "I'm sorry we didn't listen to you earlier. But we're here now. I don't know how bad this storm is going to get—"

She stopped there, frowning at the tree. Then she looked at the ground, turning in a slow circle so that she could see the whole park stretching out behind them.

"What's the matter?" Nicci asked, watching the line move on without them.

"The tree," said Amber, beginning to be alarmed. She turned around again, this time looking beyond the park and in all directions, her hands cupped against the weather. At one side, Nicci fidgeted, hugging herself and casting longing looks at the promise of shelter. At the other side stood Meoraq, unmoved by the wind or rain, watching only her. And on the tree itself, waiting impatiently for Nicci to notice him and need the hand he kept holding out to help her up, was Scott.

"For Christ's sake, Bierce!" he shouted finally. He had to shout, and even that was scarcely perceptible over the howl of the storm. "What are you looking for?"

"Trees!" she shouted back. Amber pointed at the massive thing under his feet. "Where did that come from?"

Scott raised himself up cautiously against the wind and looked around, then dropped down again to clutch at the trunk of the broken tree. "Who cares?" He twisted around to say something to someone on the inside, then came back around to shout, "Right! Maybe they grew it here! You never heard of landscaping? Get in here!"

"There's no hole!"

"What?"

"Amber, come *on*!" Nicci moaned. "It's raining!"

"There's no hole!" Amber pointed at the root ball of the broken tree, where huge clods of disturbingly fresh dirt still clung, then at the unbroken ground.

"So it fell a long time ago!" Scott shouted. "I repeat, Bierce, who gives a damn?"

"No, it didn't!" Amber insisted. "The wood is too fresh!"

"Oh for...What, you think it fell out of the sky?"

Amber looked around again, past Nicci and her imploring, wind-burned face, past Meoraq and his thoughtful stare, past the empty waste of the ghost-city, to the distant clumps of prairie trees, which were all of the small, whippy-limbed variety. She looked back at Scott. "Yes!"

He glared at her, then shook his head again and started to work his way down the tree and into the building. "Fine! Stay out here and freeze!"

"Wait!" cried Nicci. She took a step, looked back at Amber.

She waved her sister on ahead, but moved closer to Meoraq. "Where did it come from?"

He glanced at the tree without much interest, then pointed out into the nothing.

She looked, but could still see no large trees. "How can you tell?"

"By the angle of impact," he told her.

"But how did it get here?"

He cocked his head at her, then bent over and plucked a blade of brown grass. He held it up for her inspection, then opened his fingers and let the wind rip it away.

Amber looked at the tree—thicker than she stood tall, a broken stub still fifteen meters long at least—and tried to picture the storm that could uproot it, much less bring it hurtling through the air from who knew how far away to land here.

Meoraq's hand closed around her upper arm. He propelled her forward a few steps, then released her and looked away, frowning, back at the city.

"Are you sure you want us in there?" Amber asked uncertainly.

"I am sure I don't, but I want you together. If it has to be together in that building, so be it. Go."

She let him push her toward the tree, but didn't start climbing. "Aren't you coming with us?"

"Soon. I need to make a patrol."

"I'll come with—"

"No. Stay here and keep your people together." He walked away into the storm.

Amber struggled up into the tree, which was not as easy as even Nicci made it look. Her hands, numbed by freezing rain, couldn't seem to hold their grip; her technique consisted of lunging and sliding until she could climb onto the broken wall itself. There was a large heap of debris directly beneath her, so she wiggled over as far as she safely could before dropping down. Her boots hit the ground with a painful shock that went straight to her knees, which buckled and pitched her directly into the pile of concrete chunks and tree bark she'd been so careful to avoid falling on. It wasn't a bad fall; she scraped her palms, thumped her elbow, bunched up her shirt and scratched her side, but that was all. She was fine.

"Nice dismount," said Crandall, and a few people laughed.

"You okay?" asked Nicci.

"Yeah." Amber swiped away the pain-tears that stung at her eyes and rolled off the worst of the debris. Mr. Yao was there to help her up and he kept his hands on her until her eyes adjusted to the considerable dark of the ruined building.

What she saw struck her briefly speechless.

This wasn't a warehouse. She didn't know what it was, but it wasn't a warehouse. Dominating the first floor of the cube they had invaded was some sort of inner chamber with perfectly round, perfectly seamless, transparent walls. It reached all the way up to the ceiling and through it, up through the next floor and however many floors were between them and the top of this building, where it let in plenty of grey stormlight, enough that she could clearly see the spiders and the web.

They weren't really spiders, only three wiry legs around a shiny, metallic ball, but that was all she could think to call them. There didn't seem to be many of them, but since they were all exactly alike and moved so fast, it was impossible to say just how many there were. They swarmed back and forth, effortlessly leaping, climbing and sliding along the thousands of filaments that filled their chamber. When Amber reached the inner wall (she had not been aware of walking toward it) and craned her neck to see up past the dark ceiling, she could see the entire web, with something like a spider's egg sac the size of a man suspended in the very center. On this side of the spider-chamber, a bank of perfectly recognizable, if alien, computer stations formed a tight ring right up against the glass. Evenly-spaced between monitors were clear tubes that made Amber think of hamster cages. Now and then, a spider would slip through one of these tubes and extrude a proboscis of some sort from its stomach into the back of a computer, insert whatever it thought it was inserting into the entirely dead system, and then scuttle back out and onto the web.

"What is it?" Amber asked, dimly aware of what a stupid question that was. No one here could possibly know the answer.

"Besides creepy?" asked Maria.

Beside her, Eric turned back to give the spiders a speculative looking over. "If I had to guess, I'd say either some sort of power generator or maybe a data storage and retrieval system. But yeah, all it is now is creepy."

Scott brought out his flashlight and clicked it on, painting the glass with a sudden pool of white radiance. The spiders scuttled on, oblivious. Scott watched them for a second or two, his face flexing uncertainly between wonder and revulsion, before a sudden gust of howling wind reminded him he was supposed to be saving the day. He swung the light around and almost immediately illuminated a door.

Everyone looked at it, at each other, at the door. Scott took a tentative step forward, then abruptly changed his mind and went to examine one of the computer panels instead.

There were chairs, Amber saw. Most of them were still neatly tucked in under their matching desks, as if the workers monitoring this station had only just stepped away for lunch and turned out all the lights behind them. There was a coffee cup at one of the desks, or whatever kind of cup they called it when they didn't drink coffee. It had writing on the side, almost aged entirely away but still just perceptible in the fading light. 'Gann's Best Dad,' maybe, or 'Techies Do It With Tools'.

"Where's the lizard?" asked Scott suddenly.

"He wanted a look around," said Amber, still staring sickly at the cup.

"But he's coming?"

"That's what he told me."

Somewhere, Crandall snickered, whispered, and got a few more people to laugh.

"Why is it so clean in here?" Nicci asked suddenly.

Amber, once more blushing, looked back at her baby sister and then around at the room. It was clean, she realized. The glass she'd been staring through for who knew how long now was damned near spotless. There was no stain of long-emptied drink on the inside of the coffee cup. The dead eyes of the many monitors were dust-free. The rain had brought in a spreading slick of water, but there was no sign of previous flooding. Amber had fallen on a good-sized heap of debris caused by the tree crashing through the wall...but 'heap' was definitely the operative word, and it was a clean, well-managed little heap at that.

"Someone's living here," said Dag. "Someone's living here *right now*."

And the door opened.

Amber jumped along with everyone else. A few people screamed. She didn't, but only because Nicci slammed up against her and knocked the scream out of her throat.

Scott's flashlight beam came swinging wildly around, shining a spotlight over the open door, the blank wall, the ceiling, and then finally at the floor where the little robot came whirring in.

The second group-scream was almost as loud as the first, but the thing reacted to the sound no more than the spiders reacted to light. Short, squat, and rounded—a metallic blister with many panels and a black scanning plate that ran around its middle, it looked so completely like one of the cleanerbot models that you sometimes saw advertised in tech catalogues or (if you didn't mind a plastine model) on TV late at night that no one screamed again even when it came at them.

It rolled inside, sending a thin bead of light ahead of it, indifferent to the rapid retreat of the many humans before it. When it reached the glass wall, it hesitated, then opened a small panel and sent out a thin, metallic tendril, like the questing arm of a squid, to tap and test at the surface it found. It clicked at itself under the anxious weight of fifty alien stares, then withdrew its tendril and opened a second panel. It sprayed out two careful bursts of some kind of greyish foam, paused as if undecided, then added a third. It turned away, leaving the 'soap' to bubble and gradually start to slide *up* the glass, picking up speed as it climbed.

"It's a cleanerbot," said Scott. He sounded utterly astonished. "The lizards have *cleanerbots*! Just like ours!"

Amber leaned a little closer to the glass in spite of Nicci's tugging hands and saw a thin, spreading mass of tiny beads. Metallic, like the spiders, and like the spiders, lifeless as they went about their work. "Not quite like ours."

The bot had moved on, rolling slowly through the shuffling feet that surrounded it until it reached the first puddle of rainwater. There it stopped, testing, tapping. It began to roll from side to side, trying to map out its dimensions, and, finding that it reached from wall to wall, retreated a short distance to think.

"Is it okay?" Nicci asked nervously.

Amber shook her head.

The bot sat immobile, 'arms' retracted, 'face' dark. Every so often, that bead of light would dart out and flicker off the water. Twice it opened a panel, half-extended some unidentifiable tool, hesitated, and retracted it again. It hummed now and then, audibly and for no reason that Amber could determine, as if it were talking to itself.

"Oh my God, I have got to get out of here," Maria whispered.

"It's okay, baby," said Eric, watching the bot with a queasy expression.

"It's not okay, it's a fucking zombie!"

The bot slid out its tendril again. It felt at the water, then opened a third panel, reached in decisively and brought out a small triangular flag. It planted this firmly in the puddle and turned around. It moved on.

"We're not really staying here, are we?" Maria asked. She was trying to laugh, but it was the kind of gape-faced laughter that sounded more like someone working herself up to a scream and no one joined in. "Come on, people! We're not...We're not really going to *sleep* here?"

Outside, a crash of thunder answered in unequivocal terms.

The bot came to the pile of broken concrete and bark. It felt at it, paused, and felt at it some more. It made another soft, electronic sound—a sound that struck Amber as one that was almost distressed. *Someone's been sleeping in my bed*, she thought, a nonsensical accusation gleaned from some forgotten fairytale back in those bygone days of state-care. *Someone's been sleeping in my bed, oh dear, oh dear. Someone's been sleeping in my bed and she's...still...HERE*!

It ran out a second tendril to join the first and slowly, methodically, began to stack the debris back into a neat heap, talking to itself in its worried way.

"No," said Maria, backing rapidly away as it went about its fussy work. "Seriously. I will sleep in the rain. I don't care. Get me away from this place."

The bot retracted one of its tendrils and ran out a brush, cleaning the concrete chunks. It began to hum.

Without warning, Eric picked up a basketball-sized chunk of concrete and brought it smashing down on the bot's head. The bot caved in on itself without resistance, smooth sides bursting to spew out guts of wire and jelly. One fat, blue spark spat out from its core, leaving a plume of greenish smoke and some ungodly, hot stink in the air behind it. There was no last metallic cry, no dying grope of its tendrils, no planting of a final caution flag to warn people not to slip in its spilled oils. It was dead.

"Thank you, baby," said Maria.

Eric checked the mess under the chunk of concrete and then brought it down again, giving it a little twist and shove this time. He wiped his hands unnecessarily on his shirtfront; the concrete had been quite clean.

"I don't see why we have to wait around in here," announced Scott, striding forward to stand in front of Eric. "It's out of the wind, but it's just as cold and not a lot drier."

"And it's creepy," muttered Maria, eyeing the bot's leaking, smoking corpse. Eric put an arm around her, watching the spiders instead. Amber found herself watching the 'soap' as it made its way doggedly across the glass wall. And when it reached the end, she wondered, what would it do? Would it just cluster up and wait to be collected? Or would it come trickling across the floor to crawl back inside the broken husk of the bot and sit there forever?

"I'm going in." Scott waited, either for protests or applause, but there was nothing and his awkward hesitation looked so much like the bot's that Amber actually shuddered.

He noticed. He blushed. He gripped the flashlight like a weapon and marched over to the door, which slid itself open as obediently as any automated door back on Earth. Scott walked through. The door slid shut.

Dag followed. Then Eric and Maria. Crandall. Mr. Yao. And then all of them, shuffling along in a subdued line past the spiders and out of the rain.

It was cold out here. And wet. "Come on, Nicci," Amber said, following.

"Shouldn't we wait for Meoraq?"

Amber spared the (murdered) bot a final glance, unsure just why it bothered her so much. It had been a creepy little thing and a part of her was very glad to know it would not be rolling up next to her in the middle of the night to clean her while she slept. "He'll know we were here."

They went through the door.

And like some magic door in a fairytale, they came out in Earth. Or so it seemed to Amber, as she found herself confronted with an ancient alien civilization that was none of it ancient or alien *enough*. Whoever the lizardmen of yore were, they kept keepsakes on their desks. The decorative pot for some sort of plant still stood in the corner of one office, its occupant long turned to dust and swept away. There were pictures on the walls, but after so many years exposed to light, their images had faded entirely out to white. There were trophies in a glass case in the hallway, monuments to the office Lizardball league. There were no aliens here; there were only people, and they were all gone.

She knew that she was being left behind as she lingered in the halls, but *someone* had to look at it, someone had to *witness*. She drifted from room to room in silence, until she came to a door, just another door. Recessed lights in the ceiling came on with a drill-bit whine when she opened it. On the other side, she found a bathroom.

And that was the end for her. That was where it all swelled up and shut down. Seeing the sinks and the stalls and the corroded mirrors, recognizing them in spite of the little differences because no matter the minutiae of design, the function was still the same. Aliens gotta pee, after all. Lizardmen were going to want to wash their hands before they put them back on their keyboards. Lizardladies were going to want to touch up their cosmetics and adjust the lie of their lizardish clothes.

Skyscrapers and bridges, offices and bathrooms, desks and chairs and coffee cups—none of it was the product of uniquely human invention. They weren't special. Forget the vastness of the universe and the infinite potential of its diversity, they weren't even significant right here in this room. The lizards had built all this—plumbed their pipes and wired the lights and programmed the cleanerbots and even fired off the bomb that had ended it—without any human help at all. If there was some great cosmic entity floating out in space, puking up planets and scraping people together out of mud, He was doing just fine without them.

"Hey, Bierce!" Crandall was coming for her, his flashlight bobbing as he jogged up the hall. "You die back there?"

'Yes,' Amber thought, still staring into the bathroom. There was a dead bot next to the sink; it had been cleaned so often and so thoroughly that its hull had been worn away entirely in several places. 'We're all dead. This place is haunted and we're the ghosts.'

"Hey." Crandall glanced into the bathroom without much interest and thumbed back the way he'd come. "Space-Scout says to stay together."

So had Meoraq. Amber backed up and let the bathroom door slide shut. She stood there for a few seconds, then opened it again. The lights, which had been dimming, whined back to life. One of them popped, throwing one of the stalls into darkness and puffing out a little plume of bluish smoke. Shards of whatever the bulb was made of tinkled down over the floor. She wondered if there were any cleanerbots left to come sweep it up.

Crandall was still there, watching her with half a puzzled smile. "You okay?"

"Yeah. I don't know. This place..."

"It's fucked up," he agreed at once. "Come on."

She let him take her away, past a dozen other doors to the T-section at the end of the hall. There, instead of a directory or a motivational poster, was a door, with what was probably a bot's charging pad pulled out into the middle of the floor in front of it. Crandall just stepped over it, turned right and moved on, but Amber stopped. After a lengthy internal debate, she opened the door to find a maintenance closet. As with the bathroom, it was easily recognizable. Here were the shelves for cleaning supplies, there were the various tools too large or specialized to come standard on a cleanerbot, and there, where the bot's charging pad used to be, there were sixteen bodies' worth of bones.

The skulls were lined up in four rows, easy to count. All the other bones were organized just as well—arm bones here, ribs there, vertebrae strung together and hanging where there might have been coats once. There were two columns of pelvises (not eight and eight, but four and twelve; male and female maybe) stacked one inside the other like bowls in a kitchen cupboard. The smaller bones were all in boxes with printed and precisely-centered labels, and while Amber supposed those labels might say Paperclips or Discs or anything at all, she thought it much more likely they said Fingers, Toes...Teeth.

"Jesus, look at that." Crandall reached in and picked up a skull, working the jaws in snapping motions. "Can't you just see that crazy thing cleaning all the bodies every day until it had bones to pick up?"

She could, actually.

"There's other bots. We've found three of them so far, but none of them are working...Hey, check it out." He put the skull down and picked up an arm bone, turning it to show Amber the evenly-spaced cuts on one end. "This was no boating accident," he said solemnly.

"Huh?"

"Doesn't matter. Just saying, looks like the commander was right. They really can bite someone's hand off if they want to. Come on." He tossed the bones back into the closet, upsetting the bot's neat stack, and took her hand.

"I'm fine," said Amber, and pulled away from him.

"Would you relax? You look a little freaked out so I'm trying to be a nice guy here. You don't have to be a bitch about it."

"I don't need my hand held so I'm a bitch?"

"Whatever, Bierce." He threw up his hands, headed back out into the hall. "So what do you think happened here? You're pretty tight with the lizard. He ever talk about this stuff?"

Amber shook her head. "I do most of the talking."

"Maybe you ought to bring it up. If we're going to be puking up our intestines from radiation poisoning tomorrow morning, I want to know about it tonight." He threw her a grin. "Make my last night worth living, you know? Over here."

The door he indicated opened on some sort of inner reception area or waiting room, and probably a very comfortable one in its time. It had no windows, but a few of the lights overhead were working, however noisily. Everyone else was already here, milling around the cushioned seats and many low tables stacked with flat panels of some synthetic material, not plastine or even plastic, but something colorful and fake. Scott tried to pick one up, but it broke in his hand, brittle as junkyard cellophane. He tried to catch it, but it collapsed, the greater part of it falling back onto the stack, which also shattered, and then the table under it, until the whole thing was a dusty heap with no bot left to clean it up. One of the Manifestors was dumb enough to try and sit on a chair, which predictably tore and spilled her into its frame, and while just about everybody was involving themselves in extracting her, Amber wandered out through the opposite door into the lobby alone.

The floor here was tiled and her footsteps echoed, overloud and lonely. There was a round, sunken space along the back where two walls met in a curved corner—a dried-up fountain, perhaps. The walls themselves boasted a grand, room-length mosaic, which must have been something to see when the full sunlight used to stream through the slanting front windows. Now, in the stormlight, it was just another part of what made this place so creepy: rolling fields and golden pastures dotted with fanciful wildlife far distant from either the scaly deer or monstrous armadillos she'd seen so far; forests hung with flowering vines as colorful as Chinese lanterns; cozy farmhouses along winding roads that led to a city of oddly organic-looking towers and arches; and overlooking it all from a grassy ridge, a happy lizard couple with their lizard child between them, hand in hand in hand. Alien markings in a complicated chain of base characters and accentuation formed a double row of words at the center of the jewel-green sky, dotted by wispy suggestions of clouds and a single shiny wedge of an upwards-arching aircraft.

She didn't know how long she stood staring at it, but she knew it was the ship she saw most clearly, the ship and the cut-tile shapes of the lizardmen who probably never dreamed that one day there would be a crater in the middle of their ruined city and a neat stack of skulls in the closet where a slightly psychotic but well-intentioned cleanerbot used to sleep.

The door whispered open and shut again. She knew who it was by the sound of boots on the tiles. "See anything out there?" she asked, not turning.

Meoraq's low grunt rolled through the whole room. "There is always something to see. I told you I wanted you to stay together."

She pointed at the lettering in the mosaic's sky. "Can you read that?"

The boots finished their walk and halted next to her. She still didn't look at him, but she could feel him, dark and extremely solid at her side, even though he didn't touch her. "Some," Meoraq said after a moment's consideration.

"What does it say?"

"The first bar is senseless sound and I will not give it voice. Below reads: Then. Now. Forever." He said it without any trace of irony that Amber could detect, but spared the front windows a glance afterwards, as though measuring the fact of forever against the rosy picture put forth in the mosaic. He grunted.

She echoed the sound without thinking, her eyes lingering on the ship. Airship? Or starship? Were the tiny tile-people riding inside it bound for lands across the world? Or across the universe?

And what did it matter now, really? Any ship back then would be no better than this place now—empty, dark and dead. With effort, she made herself look away, at Meoraq. He had tracked the line of her gaze and now he was looking at the ship. She could read nothing in his face. She seldom could, but she thought he was actually trying to be inscrutable now.

"What do you see?" she asked.

His spines twitched in some tell-tale gesture he wasn't quite quick enough to stop entirely. "Nothing," he said blackly, looking right at the ship.

"There's always something to see," she reminded him.

He slowly turned and fixed her with a stare as good as a smack to the side of the head, then went back to looking at the mosaic. His spines were flat against his scales.

'I got a real talent for pissing people off,' thought Amber. It was not a new thought and it frequently came with an underlining of secret pride, as if some part of her were trying to convince the rest of her that it didn't matter if the world thought she was a bitch as long as she was good at it. But the world was one thing. Meoraq was another.

"What," he said suddenly, angrily, "do you see?"

She looked at the ship again. Airship or starship, it was just a painted piece of tile in a room no one walked through anymore. "Do you want the truth?"

He was quiet for so long, she thought she'd finally made him angry enough that he was ignoring her. That made her feel a little sick to her stomach. She was on the verge of leaving when he said, "Yes."

"I see us."

He frowned, his eyes moving restlessly back and forth across the few tiled shards of the ship as if reading them.

"Not you and me. Me and...the rest of us. It's not a good feeling."

He glanced at her and stared at the ship some more.

"It's everything we lost, too," she said, wondering why she was still talking.

He didn't answer, but she felt the rough slide of his scales as he brushed the back of his hand against the back of hers. Just once. Probably not deliberately. He stepped away.

"I told you I wanted you all together," he said curtly. "I should not have to repeat myself. Go."

She went, but he didn't follow right away. When she reached the door and looked back, he was still standing there, once more glaring at the mosaic. His spines were flat again. His eyes were fixed on the ship.

2

The storm continued throughout the day, growing in strength with each unmarked hour that took them into night. It was difficult to resign himself to so foolhardy a thing as making camp in these ruins, but long before the darkness made further travel impossible, Meoraq knew he would never coax the humans out into the storm. They believed themselves safe here and since convincing them of the truth would only make them more nervous, Meoraq cried surrender and let them settle in.

He was not happy with the situation and as the night stormed on, his tension only increased. He put it to use with long patrols—pacing restlessly from the foreroom where he could watch the striking of Sheul's hammer behind the clouds, along every empty hall and through every dark door, to the rearmost chamber that lay open to the weather and all those who might be seeking an escape from it.

Because they were out there. He had seen nothing living on his first patrol, except those few machines whose eternal task it was to tend the empty city, but there were signs these ruins had been used in the past to shelter travelers—the charred ring of a bygone fire, butchered bones, a discarded boot with a sizeable gash across the heel, the clay shards of several broken bowls or pots—but it was difficult to say just how recently these travelers may have passed.

The boot troubled him. It was city-made, embossed at the cuff and toe, and worn right through its heel by the travel it had seen. A careful search of the surrounding area had not turned up the boot's mate either. He saw no toothmarks to suggest the boot had been carried off by some four-legged scavenger, but that remained far more likely to his mind than the thought of any man wealthy enough to buy this boot throwing out one but continuing to wear the other. That kind of thrift usually meant a man who did not buy boots at all, but acquired them only as the opportunity presented itself.

Or, to say a different way, a man who stole them.

Easy shelter and far more readily defended than any tent-camp, ruins such as these made powerful lures for the raiders who dwelled in the wildlands outside of Sheul's grace. During the fair season, the migrations of the few travelers they preyed upon and the pursuit of Sheulek who preyed on them kept them moving, but when the weather turned cold, raiders, like all creeping beasts born of Gann, denned down.

So Meoraq was cautious and, as usual, he was the only one. The humans tried all night to sprawl themselves out where he could not keep an easy eye on them in direct defiance of his orders to stay together. Even Amber slipped away more than once to stand by herself in the foreroom, in full sight of the glass wall where any scouting eye might see her, staring at the tilework. She stopped once Scott found her there, but only because Scott then saw the tiles and began an infuriating campaign to call the others in to see it.

Meoraq knew what they were looking at and it was not the fertile land or sunbright skies that made up the Ancients' world before the Fall. It was just five shards of metal, pressed together to make a single shape smaller than Meoraq's hand. He did not know what the Ancients meant it to be, but he knew what the humans saw.

A ship. A ship that sailed through the sky. Like the ship they claimed had brought them to this world from some other. Meoraq stood alone before that shape for a long time himself, hating it.

He did not believe in the thing called Earth. Sheul's Word spoke of all things and never mentioned it, and therefore even to consider that such a thing may exist seemed vaguely blasphemous to his mind. There were no ships that flew above the storm and there were no worlds beyond Gann.

Meoraq had seen many lies told to his face. The humans were not always honest in the things they said, but when it came to talk of their Earth, he could not see those lies. It bothered him. Most of the time, he was able to close his mind to this conflict, since the humans had little energy during their travels for Earth-talk and even less inclination to spend their resting hours in his company, but here in these ruins, with this damned image inescapably pressed into the wall, there was no avoiding it.

Either the humans had come in a ship from another world never mentioned in Sheul's Word or they were lying to him. All of them. Even Amber. And he did not believe that, either.

The door hissed softly open.

"Get out," said Meoraq without taking his eyes from the tiled wall.

Retreat.

He was going to be chasing them out of here all damned night, he just knew it. Because of the ship. He thought he could chip it free of the mortar that held it, but decided the satisfaction couldn't be worth the damage to his blades and they'd all seen it already anyway. Nevertheless, the temptation remained.

The door hissed a second time. The light of a human's lamp-machine fell in a pool across his back, throwing his shadow as tall as Sheul's own across the mosaic. There, the ship was a blade aimed at his heart.

"O my Father," said Meoraq loudly. "Give me Your arm, I pray, that I might beat this human so severely, none other will dare to defy me."

"Bring it, lizardman," said Amber.

He grunted and moved away from the tiles at once, before she could come any closer. Useless gesture. She had seen the ship, but he didn't want her looking at it again. "And now it is you," he said, advancing on her. She did not so much as lower her eyes, not even when he stood toe-at-toe with her. "I do not want anyone in this room. How is it that I am still not understood after all this time?"

"I understand you just fine." She rolled her eyes a little. "Scott sent me to find out why not."

Some hot, red emotion stabbed him, too deeply to be identified, too bright to be ignored. "And you do his bidding now, do you?" he snapped. "Even you?"

"I can't justify being a bitch all night, every night, for no good reason. Unlike some lizards I could mention. What's your problem?"

"I don't want you in here! How many times do you need to be told?"

"I'm going to need a better reason than just because you said so," she fired back, "or my answer is going to be a big fat I'll go wherever I want to. And if you think you're man enough to stop me—"

There, a spear of stormlight struck down, illuminating the whole of the room with its silvery flash and cutting Amber's words away as neatly as if it had struck her dead. She shone her human lamp past him at the window.

"If I am *man* enough?" Meoraq echoed, but Amber did not re-engage him. Thunder broke and boomed across the plains, making her flinch back. The lightning came in sheets overhead, filling the night with a constant, flickering illumination that periodically let out a flash of white brilliance. It wasn't enough to read the Word by, perhaps, but it was more than enough to see Amber's round, staring eyes.

"Go back to the others," Meoraq told her, once it became obvious she was content to stand there all night.

She stirred, like one waking from a sleep, and shone her light on the glass again. "You don't have tornados here, do you?"

He took her wrist and forced the light down. "Mind where you aim that damned thing! Go, I say. Obey me!"

"Quit grabbing at me. I want to see—" And there she stopped, not for the storm this time, but to give him a sudden, startled look. "Oh shit. It's not the ship, it's the window."

"Eh?"

"I thought you were just being a dick about—" She started to shine her light at the tilework on the wall, then stopped and forced the beam down. She looked at him, her brows creased in alarm. "We're not alone out here, are we?"

Meoraq flexed his spines a few times (If he was man enough, she said. If.) and finally forced them to relax. "I haven't seen anyone, but that is no reason to set a beacon at every window."

She tipped the lamp upwards, so that it shone its light briefly across the underside of her face, then switched it off. The storm continued, pouring light in sheets across the churning skies, more than enough to let him see the furrow of a frown on Amber's troubled face. "Maybe we shouldn't stay here tonight."

"Now?" he asked irritably. "You have to say that *now*? Human, it is hours too late to move on, even if your accursed people would condescend to be moved."

"I would much rather get rained on than murdered in my sleep," said Amber, but she jumped at the next clap of thunder all the same.

"You are under my watch. No one is going to murder you, except perhaps me if you insist on ignoring my commands. Go back to the other room and stay with your people."

She did not react to the threat. Indeed, she gave no sign she'd even heard him. She was staring at the window again, clutching her human lamp, now dark and lifeless, in both hands. Both shaking hands.

"Calm yourself," said Meoraq gruffly. "It's only a storm."

"I'm calm," she said, but in a strained and distracted way. "Do you see me freaking out? No. I'm totally calm. I just...don't feel very safe."

"There is nothing to be gained by worrying over the weather. We are in Sheul's care tonight."

"I know you think that's comforting, but it's not."

"So be it. Console yourself instead with the knowledge that you aren't sleeping in the rain. And treasure it, human, because I promise you, that *is* a luxury."

"But we're completely boxed in. If anyone bad comes, the only way out—"

Meoraq unclipped his kzung and showed her the shine of its blade in the stormlight. "—is through them," he finished, and flared his mouth to bare all his teeth. "Is that man enough for you?"

The flicker of the storm made it difficult to tell, but he thought she smiled. And then she screamed as lightning struck the ground directly outside the window, sending shards of stone into the glass. The thunder that followed shattered what the stones had cracked; the window blew inward and smashed itself across the floor. Meoraq turned his head away from the wall of freezing wind that blasted in at them and was nearly knocked from his feet when Amber slammed up against him.

Like a little fork of lightning inside his mind, Meoraq's thoughts washed out to white. He could not hear the storm, feel the wind. For a moment—the very briefest moment, the very longest—he was aware of nothing but the press of her body to the whole of his, her hands digging at his back, the warmth that was her breath blowing against his heart. He could not feel himself at all, except where he was defined by her touch.

Her embrace.

Meoraq returned his sword to his belt and awkwardly hovered that arm over her, lowering it by hesitant degrees until his hand just touched her shoulder.

Amber pushed herself away quickly and no sooner had she done so than the door hissed open and they were joined by Scott and several of his men. In near-perfect synchrony, they threw up their arms against the driving rain that had found its way indoors, but Scott had enough voice to shout, "What the hell happened in here?"

"Out!" Meoraq ordered. He caught Amber by the wrist and headed through the door, pushing Scott and his men before him and towing Amber after.

"What did you do?" Scott demanded on the other side, and without waiting for an answer, thrust his arm at Amber and said, "She broke the window!"

"I did not!"

A crash of thunder like Sheul's own hammer turned the rest of her words to a scream he could not hear. She ducked down, her hands at the sides of her head to cover her human ears, and she stayed that way even after the thunder rolled away.

And she wasn't the only one, Meoraq saw. Many other humans had assumed protective positions or had at least cleaved on to some other human. Some of the females were actually crying.

"Okay," said Scott, and said it several times in his attempt to restore order. "Okay, just calm down. It's only wind."

"Yeah, so is a tornado," said Crandall, looking nervously up at the ceiling. "I'm from Kansas. I see this shit all the time. Hey, lizardman, is this place safe?"

"How do you mean?"

"I mean—"

Thunder. Screams. Meoraq waited.

"I mean, this is an old building, right?"

"Yes."

"So is the roof going to fall in on us? It's not, is it?"

Meoraq flicked his spines forward and back dismissively. "It might."

Some of the humans screamed some more, but this time, there was no thunder to frighten them. Scott hastened to settle them with complicated hand gestures and soothing words, but the face he turned at last on Meoraq was pale and strained. "That's not funny."

Anger flared and his hand snapped up, but he caught the slap before he threw it. "I am not in a joking mood, *S'kot*," he hissed. "The ruins are old. The wind is strong. The walls could fall. I advise you all to pray tonight, for it will be Sheul's will alone if this place still stands at the end of the storm."

Thunder again, shaking the very foundations of the building beneath their feet. Humans screamed, males and females together now. One of them groped at Meoraq's own arm and he was compelled to slap the thing away. Immediately after he'd done it, the thought came to him that he had not slapped Amber away and she'd had both her arms around him. It did not make him feel badly for the human he'd struck, but it did make him look for Amber among her people.

He found her clinging to Nicci, the two of them huddled so tightly together that he could not quite be certain whose arm belonged to who or whose head was buried in whose hair. A spark of thought—*Must it be both of them*?—lit and faded in his mind, as bright and brief as lightning. He frowned and turned deliberately away. "We have more shelter here than out upon the open plains," he said loudly, determined to cut through their chatter if he could not quell it. "That is what you wanted most, isn't it? So. This will be our camp. Remove these things," he ordered, pointing at the chairs.

"And put them where?" Eric asked.

Meoraq pointed again, at the foreroom. "With the rest of the trash," he said. "After which, none of you are to enter that room. Mark me, all of you. If you need to use the necessary, exit through the room you entered by, but you are to be swift about it and return here immediately."

The humans eyed one another as the rain drummed down and the thunder shook at the walls. At last, Eric uttered a grating sort of sound in the back of his throat and began, "That sounds like a lot of work. I mean, there's a lot of empty rooms. I don't see any reason why we can't spread out."

"Because I said so!" Meoraq hissed and grabbed onto his brow-ridges as if to hold them to his head. "I don't have to give you reasons! I give commands! Where is your obedience?"

"Okay, okay!" Eric raised both hands and patted the air. "Here is good. Be cool. Bierce, you want to come deal with this?"

"Do we get a fire at least?" asked Maria, standing close to her man's side. "Or do we have to be cool in the literal sense as well?"

Eric dropped his hands and looked at her, his face puckering as with pain. "Baby, you're not helping."

"Excuse me for being cold!"

Meoraq took two swift steps forward and put his face close to Maria's even as she tried to hide behind her man. "Stop," he said, very quietly. "Whining. At me."

Maria did not answer. She clutched her Eric's shirt and did not move.

Meoraq straightened up and gave Eric a dark stare, then turned around to address Scott. "This is not a discussion. I am giving you my orders. Clear the room, settle your nests, go to sleep. No fires," he added, glancing back at Maria. "Most of these old buildings have fire dampening devices. Some of them still work. No fires. And no lights anywhere—*anywhere*—where they can be seen outside. How do you mark me?"

They didn't answer, but they marked him well enough. Eric took his Maria firmly in grip and they began to move furniture into the foreroom, Eric hauling the larger pieces and Maria picking up the inevitable debris that broke off. Some others followed their example, but most just huddled up to mutter at each other and eye the ceiling whenever the storm hammered on it. Meoraq paced as far away from the lot of them as the dimensions of the room would allow before setting out the components of his tent. It was a shameful extravagance, and he knew he could be comfortable enough with just his mat, but the lights were going to burn for as long as the room sensed occupants and if he had to look at humans all night, he was going to kill one of them. This was no longer a facetious thought. Not tonight and not in this place.

"Meoraq?"

Amber.

"Leave me," he ordered, looking at the pole he was assembling and not at her.

She stood there a moment more while the color throbbed in his throat, and then knelt down next to him. She picked up two pole-quarters and threaded them together. "I know you're upset," she said in a low voice. "I'm sorry."

"Are you?"

She recoiled a little. "Yes!"

And she probably was, but he didn't feel like forgiving her. He was, as she said, upset. He supposed he had been angrier than this several times in his life, but he didn't think he'd ever been so angry for so long, and it was wearing on him. He needed to pray, but here in the ruins, surrounded by humans, that peace was well out of his reach. Even Amber (whose arms had been around him, wholly around him) put an itch under his scales—the kind that could not be unfelt once you were aware of it, the kind that just grew and grew until even the sanest, calmest man alive wanted to take a knife and cut it *out*.

Cursing under his breath, Meoraq put his hand to his throat and rubbed, trying to cool the hot throb there or at least cover the color he knew he was showing. A Sheulek must be the master of his clay, always.

Amber was watching, no longer even pretending to fuss with his tent-poles. "Are you okay?"

He didn't answer.

He didn't know.

He didn't really care much.

That itch...

Meoraq leapt up and backed away from her, still glaring, still rubbing. "Assemble this," he ordered curtly. "I need to make a patrol."

"Are you crazy? No, Meoraq, it's too da—"

He snapped his pointing finger around in front of her face; she recoiled as if she thought it were a knife. "You do not give me orders," he said, and even though he said it quietly, all human chatter ceased at once. Amber's eyes were huge and green and baffled; seeing them should have made him feel something other than this black itch, but it didn't. It made it worse.

"You are in my camp," he told her. He should have been telling all of them, but it was only her. She was, in that moment, the only thing in the world he was aware of. "You belong to me. You give me your obedience and you do not argue with me."

Thunder crashed and groaned. She looked up fearfully until the reverberations faded, but as soon as Meoraq turned to go, she was on her feet and clutching at his arm with her naked hands.

"Please, don't go! I know you're pissed at all of us and I wouldn't blame you for leaving, but please don't, not tonight!"

He found himself staring at her hand—her soft, pink hand—where it lay in stripes across his black scales. His mind was moving. He could feel it move, even though he could not quite catch his own thoughts. His mind was moving, but he couldn't hear it. Like the hand that touched him, the hand he could see but not...quite...feel.

Meoraq closed his eyes and took a breath. Just one, for now. One for the Prophet, the wide open eye.

"Please," she was saying, still touching him. "Okay?"

He opened his eyes and studied her from the quiet of his moving, uncatchable thoughts. He leaned forward slightly and took another breath—two for his brunt—and held it. She smelled like smoke and unwashed skin. She smelled like mud and dead grass and the animal dung she bundled for burning. She smelled of Gann and those were good smells, but they were all on the surface. Beneath all that was something different, something shiny and strange, like tiles pressed into a wall, like lights in the sky at night.

'I have to get away from you,' he thought, and it was not until he saw her immediate flinch that he realized he'd said it out loud.

She let go of him and stepped away, anger rising up fast in her ugly face. "Fine. You do what you want to do, but let me tell you something, lizardman. You may think God will protect you out there, but when you jump off a cliff, God doesn't catch you. His divine protection ends when people insist on doing stupid things they know better than to do!"

"Where was this insight when you followed S'kot into this place, eh?" he asked acidly. "Or do you think he will catch you when you all leap from his wall?"

"Hey!" said Scott.

Meoraq swung on him. Scott vanished behind his people like smoke in the wind and all at once came the urge to go after him, to hack his way through the whole, monstrous mess of them until the screaming had stopped...but the thought was wrapped in some unfathomable way with the memory of Amber's body slapping up against his and her arms going around him. He began to feel distinctly indistinct...the way he felt in the arena...just before the blackness of Sheul took him.

He pulled himself away, turned his clay toward the door and started walking.

"Then I'm going with you," Amber declared.

He swung back, but she was already leaving his unmade tent to collect her spear.

"You are not!" he said loudly.

"Give me a flashlight," she told Scott.

"You are not leaving this room!"

"If you go, I go," she said. "Fine, be a dick. Someone, give me a flashlight."

Yao provided one. She thanked him. Everyone else was watching Meoraq.

"I have given you an order, human! You stay here!"

"I'm going with you," she insisted, and struck the butt of her spear onto the floor for emphasis. "Someone has to be there to run for help after a building falls on you!"

He cocked his head, his spines flat to his skull, but she would not bend her neck. She trembled, but she stood and stared him down.

"So," he said at last, when he was calm. Truly calm, as opposed to the burning, thoughtless unquiet which had been as close as he could come to it most of this miserable day. He even smiled. "Give me your hand," he said, offering his.

She eyed it, the stubborn set of her human jaws easing, then slowly moved her spear from right to left and took it.

He had her spun, disarmed, and on her knees with both arms behind her before the first wail was out of her mouth. He unbuckled his belt one-handed, whipped it free of his waist, and bound her wrists together. He seized her spear—every human in the room took a long step back, but none interfered—stabbed it low into the nearest wall at a steep angle, then picked her up and threaded her over the pole, accepting her kicks in grim good humor. He thumped her down, gave her a tap for farewell, and left her there, screaming curses at his back.

* * *

Amber thought she knew storms. They were the occasional nuisances that knocked out the phones and TV for a few hours, made a little noise, and got the garbage wet. She had never lived through one like this, didn't know they could be lived through: Thunder you could feel; lightning you could smell; rain that made the floor you slept on vibrate like an idling car. The thought that the roof might drop on top of them was not a fear, but an inescapable fact.

So she waited for it, leaning up against the wall with Nicci's head in her lap, stroking her as she would an anxious cat, watching people sleep. That part was easy enough; the overhead lights were still burning. Lots of people had looked for a switch, but no one had found one yet, so either the lights were programmed to stay on as long as there were people in the room or only the bots could turn them on and off. A few people complained, but in the end, it didn't stop anyone from sleeping. Amber understood that perfectly. She was exhausted, in spite of the lights and the thunder and the general creep-factor of the ruins, but she couldn't sleep. She wished Meoraq was here, or failing that, that he'd let her go with him when he went out on his insane patrol, and failing *that*, that he hadn't tied her up and hung her on her own spear before he'd left, thus subjecting her to a roomful of humiliation and snickering before Crandall and Mr. Yao finally dared the lizard's wrath and set her loose.

She'd considered going after him even then, but two things stopped her. First and most sensibly, she knew she'd never find him. The quintessential dark and stormy night was raging on just outside and even though the lightning was coming in sheets, so was the rain, which made visibility a big fat zero. And secondly, more personally, she was afraid that he'd come back and find her gone, then have to go out and get her, and yell at her some more when he found her. So she'd stayed in. She'd finished setting his tent up, even put his pack inside *without* first opening it and flinging crap around at random.

It wasn't really her he was mad at and she knew it. He just didn't want to be here. She didn't doubt that he'd search the area thoroughly for bandits or animals or whatever he was looking for, but mostly she thought Meoraq just wanted to be alone.

It was time to come to terms with the fact that he was not going to stay much longer. He may believe that God had given him this babysitting job, but she also knew that if he started looking for divine signs to quit, they were one funny-shaped cloud away from losing him. And when that happened, they were dead.

Another clap of thunder banged down on the roof, the first to do more than grumble in quite a long time. Immediately afterward, the muted falling-nails sound of the rain picked up and up until it drowned out all the sleeping sounds that nearly fifty people could make in one big, empty room. Nicci shifted beside her, then rolled over, shrugging off Amber's hand. Amber let her. Nicci was putting her leg to sleep anyway.

She decided to take a walk. Not outside, but just around the building. Meoraq wouldn't like it, but Meoraq wasn't here, so there. She'd stay away from the windows, but she needed to stretch her legs.

Nicci raised her head when Amber stood up, but she didn't say anything and after a few bleary-eyed seconds, she just lay back down. It gave her a twinge—not the usual feeling of helpless guilt as she watched over her baby sister, but something low and ugly and resentful. She swallowed it quickly, told herself she'd never felt it at all, and bent down to touch Nicci's shoulder so she'd know that Amber was there and loved her. Nicci did not respond, but that was okay. She was sleeping.

The hall outside was dark and quiet. Only half the lights came on when Amber went through the doors, and most of those were slow and sputtery. She wandered from shadow to shadow, listening to the thunder, stopping to inspect each picture on the wall, each empty pot that used to hold a plant, each award for excellence in whatever the hell field this used to be. She wasn't going anywhere in particular, so of course, she ended up at the closet full of bones. She didn't want to open it, but she did. She didn't need to look at it, but she did that too.

She had no idea how long she stood there, just staring into the closet. It was not until lights that had been dying further back in the hall suddenly struggled back to life that she really woke out of whatever hypnotic hold the sight of the bones had on her.

"Hey," said Crandall, walking up behind her.

"Hey." She closed the closet door.

"Can't sleep?" he guessed, sympathetic.

Thunder boomed. She heard the muffled clatter as bones tumbled out of place.

"You'll get used to it," said Crandall. "Tell you the truth, this shit makes me feel more homesick than anything else."

She didn't want to talk, not at all and not with Crandall in any case, but she supposed she ought to make an effort. He'd already called her a bitch once tonight.

"You must get a lot of this in, um..."

"Kansas. Yeah. Where are you from?"

"Earth."

She'd meant it as a joke, but it came out flat and unfunny. Amber looked at the nearest framed piece of time-whitened nothing, wishing he'd go away.

"You worried about the lizard?"

"He can take care of himself."

"You still pissed at him?"

"No. I don't really want to talk about him right now, okay?"

"Yeah, sure. Come on, I want to show you something."

"What is it?"

"Nothing huge, just something cool." He gave her his aw-shucks smile, the one she trusted least, and walked off.

Probably another dead bot, or maybe some other sample of ancient lizard technology like the spiders in back. Maybe even another closet full of bones. Amber couldn't think of anything she might find in this place that she'd actually want to look at, but God knew she had nothing else to do.

She followed him.

He led her around a few corners, down a few halls, and opened one of the office doors. She stopped at once, but he went on in without her, so what was she going to do, stand out in the hall alone? She wasn't really a bitch, despite what everyone thought. She went in after him, determined to see whatever stupid little man-toy he thought was so cool and get out again before Meoraq came home and found her disobeying his direct order not to wander in the halls.

The overhead lights in the office were dead, but she could still see Crandall over by the window and he could see her. He waved a little. "Come and see this."

"I can see it from here," Amber told him queasily, and she could. The sky was alive; lightning rolled through behind the clouds so often, it actually seemed to be breathing. Now and then, white lines popped in and out of sight, hot enough to leave colorful burns hanging in the sky wherever she looked, but the worst things, the horrible things, were the smudgy greenish blobs that hovered around the high towers of the city, sometimes arcing one to another, flaring bright or winking out and occasionally splitting the difference in an explosion of showy sparks.

Meoraq was out walking around in that.

"Pretty cool, huh?"

"Yeah," breathed Amber, but she barely heard herself. Meoraq was outside in that, and maybe it was because he really believed God was looking out for him or maybe it was just preferable to babysitting a bunch of humans one more night, but he was outside in that. And he had been gone a long time.

"Come here. You can see the bridges. It's wild."

Did she want to see the bridges? Did she want to see the bridges Scott was going to make them cross over all lit up with green fire and throbbing? No, she didn't, but she moved to the window and looked out anyway.

A constant thread of lightning danced and spun at the highest arch of the nearest bridge, making it seem as though it alone were holding it up. More lightning spat and crawled along the sides, spilling down almost in slow motion to drip from the bottom into the water just like a fountain. It was wild, all right. She supposed it was even beautiful. Mostly, though, it was terrifying.

Just then, something huge hit the roof with a bang and bounced off, sending Amber leaping into Crandall's side with a hoarse, unflattering caw of terror. He laughed and put his arm around her, saying, "Relax, Bierce," in his aw-shucks way.

"I'm fine," she mumbled, backing up. "Cool bridge, but I'm going back now. I've got to get some sleep."

"What's your hurry? Come on, Bierce, what do you want from me? Roses and violins? Why do you have to be such a bitch every time I try to get friendly?" he asked, still smiling, but sounding a little irritated with her, just as if he had every right to be. "I ain't asking for your damn hand in marriage. Nothing else you've got going on has to change. I don't kiss and tell."

"Of course not," said Amber, still trying to get out from under his persistent arm. "Then everyone would know you were a chubby-chaser."

Crandall ran an appraising eye down her body. "No one can accuse me of that anymore. Naw, I'm just not a bragger, that's all. I may not be a class act, but I'm not a total dick either. Come on."

"And I'm not interested! How the hell more obvious do I have to be?"

He put the other arm around her. "Yeah, yeah. Big, tough Bierce don't need a man. I get it. That's fine. Look, no one has to know. The lizard'll probably be gone all night, so why don't you take the chip off your shoulder and just relax? I promise I won't tell anyone that you're really a girl."

"Fuck you," she snapped, pushing harder.

"Aw, come on. Don't be mad. I'm just playing." He bent down to kiss her.

"I'm not!" She gave him a real shove now, jerking her head away. "Get the fuck off me!"

He stopped chasing her mouth and looked at her without smiling and without letting go. Lightning strobed across his face, making it a stranger's, an alien's.

"I'm getting real sick of this, Crandall," she said, just like her heart wasn't pounding and her guts weren't in knots.

The stranger in the stormlight looked thoughtful. "You know what? So am I."

Without warning, he seized her by the collar of her shirt and shoved her hard against the wall. Before she could make a sound, he had a hand over her mouth and his thigh between her legs, wedging them apart and making that Hollywood staple of a man-dropping kick to the jewels impossible. She heard the purring sound of fabric tearing as he forced his other hand under her shirt, and although she struggled, he grabbed onto her naked boob and squeezed until she whinnied in pain and panic.

But that was all he did. His body crushed up hard against her, but his expression remained fixed in that annoyed/impatient way. He waited for her to stop struggling and when she did, he gave her boob another crude honk and said, "Anytime I wanted, Bierce. Any fucking time. But I didn't. I ain't that kind of guy. But the lizard isn't going to be around forever and when he leaves, you might want to wise up to the fact that not everyone here is going to want to get with his sloppy seconds. So maybe you ought to stop acting like a fucking priss when a guy wants to be friendly, because this is going to be one lonely fucking world when you're in it by yourself."

One more twisting squeeze and he shoved himself off her, turning his back and walking away without another word. Amber stayed up against the wall, breathing hard and hugging her breast until the hurt was gone and only the shock remained, but the shock was plenty. She wanted to throw up, but she didn't want to make a mess now that the cleanerbot wasn't there to clean it up, so she waited it out and took deep breaths. She was fine, after all. He hadn't really done anything.

"He's not that kind of guy," Amber whispered and laughed, a little hysterically.

But no, she was fine. A little roughed up, maybe. Her shirt was torn at the neck, deep enough to expose her left breast all the way to the nipple, but she could...she could tie it closed for now and...and she still had one more shirt and her sweaters and...and the bridge was still standing, right? Lightning struck...and struck and struck...but the bridge was still standing and Amber Bierce was fine.

* * *

Meoraq did make a patrol that night, all the way around the edge of the building to the front door, where he ducked beneath a sort of awning that had formed when whatever decorative steeple had once crowned this atrium had caved in. Here, mostly out of the weather and entirely alone, he knelt, slapped his hand to the ground with force enough to sting, and shut his eyes. "I am the clay upon Your wheel, my Father," he said. Hissed, really. He hoped God could forgive that, because after the day he'd had, he didn't think he could help it. A Sheulek was supposed to be the master of his emotions at all times, but it was all Meoraq could manage just to be master enough of his clay that he didn't kill anyone.

But no...no. Feel the anger, Uyane. Acknowledge it. Own it. And set it aside. Even here, in the city of the Fallen Ancients, he was in his Father's House.

"I am the new-poured sword beneath Your hammer," Meoraq said, calmly this time. The calm was not honest yet, but it was closer than it had been. "I am the lamp You raise in the darkness. Shape me. Forge me. Illuminate me."

He prayed for hours, unmoving, reciting the Word in the silence of his mind, beginning with the Book of Wrath, which seemed appropriate, and taking great comfort from the Prophet's tales of his own wanderings in that first age after the Fall, and from the proof that he had found of Sheul's dominion even over that shattered land. He meditated. He breathed. He was Uyane Meoraq in the House of his soul's Father, and at last, his Father let him in.

By that hour, the storm had moved on. The lights still sparked in the distance and the grumble of thunder still sounded, but dully now and not often. "God's wrath fell over every city," Meoraq murmured. "And lo, towers did fall and walls did crumble, and the crying of all men in terror and despair did rise as flames to heaven, but even His wrath is not everlasting. Nothing there shall be in all His House that is everlasting save His judgment and His love. There is no night, however dark and filled with woe, that is not followed by dawn."

Truth. And he would get through this, even this, somehow.

With regret, Meoraq rose off his aching knees and moved back around the side of the building to the hole that had been cut in its side. He entered past the killed machine and started down the long maze of halls that led to the foreroom, where he would make a count and where he fully expected to find that several had wandered off in direct defiance of him. He wasn't going to lose his temper when he saw it, either. They wouldn't have left the building, not in this weather. They had only wandered as far as necessary to annoy him because that was the ordeal which he had accepted in taking this pilgrimage. He would be calm. A Sheulek is the master of his clay and his emotions.

And no sooner had this resolution hammered itself into form in his mind than he heard the unmistakable sound of a muffled human moan behind a sealed door.

Meoraq stopped where he stood. His hands closed into fists. His head tipped back. He studied the ceiling and listened to the noises and thought a few black words to himself until he had more or less convinced himself not to be an insensitive brunt. They were probably mating and since they were people, their men had every right to use their wives when the urge took them. He had often wished they would be more careful in concealing themselves when they did so (it was a rare night that Meoraq did not have to suddenly alter the path of his patrol to avoid walking right out on top of a pair of mating humans), but tonight, keeping them under his eye was more important than their privacy.

Whoever was inside moaned again, more breathily than before. The tone was not urgent and he could hear no other sounds, no grunting, no chatter. Good. Either he had stumbled on them before they'd truly gotten started or they were right at the end.

Meoraq struck his fist on the door.

The sounds ceased at once.

"Get back to your bed," he said bluntly.

There was no argument, no apology, no reply of any kind.

"Show me your obedience at once and I will forgive you this defiance," he announced. "It is late. I am tired. I am in no mood for foolishness."

The humans ignored him.

Meoraq hissed at the door, then slapped at the sealing pad and opened it.

The function of the room within was a mystery he did not care to explore at the moment, but he took idle note of its design anyway, since the humans were in no hurry to reveal themselves. It was a small chamber, not wide but rather long, separated into many walled spaces rather like stalls in a stable. Opposite them, before many mirrored panels, grew a pillar of sorts, with several fluted openings arranged over several cupped basins. The pipework and drains set in this structure made it obvious it was some kind of fountain, and it had been non-functional a very long time; one of the Ancients' machines had died nearby, its metal face aimed at the pipework and its many arms extended in a final death-pose of silent frustration.

And of course, the humans were here. They weren't sprawling out in the open for a change, but the lamps made by the Ancients would betray any living body no matter how well it hid from him. The humans breathed in soft, shallow breaths, believing themselves undetectable, yet their grubby little handprints were on the mirrors, on the fountain, even on the dead machine. The smell of smoke and an unwashed body was strong, very strong, but there was no sex-smell yet.

"I know you are here," he said. "Put yourselves in order and get out."

No response.

His patience slipped. He made no effort to regrip it.

"It would seem the room is empty," he hissed. "I think I'll just lock the door so that no other human wanders in."

"Leave me alone."

That was Amber's voice. Meoraq took a step back, inexplicably embarrassed, and then lunged forward in an equally inexplicable fury. "Who the hell is with you?" he demanded, managing not to shout only by the aid of Sheul and half a night's meditation.

"Nobody. Go away."

Nobody? Meoraq took another look at the handprints marking up the mirrored walls and saw they were all the same size. But the moaning, the ragged breaths...?

"I told you to stay together," he said at last, because he had to say something.

"You said to stay away from the windows. See any windows in here, lizardman? Go away!"

He did not see windows, only the smudgy image of himself in the ancient mirrors. His reflection—distorted by time in spite of, or because of, the ages of meticulous cleaning it had received—glowered back at him. It rendered his face unrecognizable as his own; the body, hulking and malformed.

Without warning, it occurred to him to wonder if the humans thought him ugly. If his face seemed lumpish and horrible compared to their smooth, flat ones. If he was, in fact, monstrous.

He looked at the closed doors of the many stalls. Behind one of them, Amber hid from him.

'I hung her up like a cut of meat in a butcher's window,' he thought suddenly. And he'd done it in front of all her people. He'd done it with a smile. Meoraq scratched at the side of his snout, which did not itch. "What are you doing in there?"

"Nothing."

And before he knew it, out came his father's: "You can do that anywhere. Come out where I can see you."

"No."

He showed his teeth to the stalls and then rubbed hard at his brow-ridges. He had no experience with this sort of thing and, he suspected, no talent. "Is something wrong?"

She laughed, which was encouraging right up until she also said, "Why no! What the hell could possibly be wrong? Go away! I don't want to talk! I put your stupid tent up, so go lie in it."

Meoraq went to the first of the stalls and opened it. Apart from whatever incomprehensible device of the Ancients occupied it, it stood empty.

"I'm warning you!"

"Are you indeed?" he snorted, opening the next stall. Also empty. "It should be interesting to see how that plays out." The next stall opened, and the one after that, but the fifth did not give to the pressure of his hand. "Because I rather suspect it will not go in your favor." He tapped two fingers meaningfully on the lock-plate. "You have until the count of six," he told her, "and then I knock this door in."

"Just go away!" Her voice cracked on the last word. She was quiet a short time, and then calmly said, "I'll be out in a few minutes."

"One," countered Meoraq.

"Just give me a few minutes, for God's sake!"

"Two."

"Goddamn alien prick!"

"Three, four, five—"

The door came open with a wheeze, its design preventing the violent bang she intended. Her first efforts to shove past him proved futile and somewhat laughable, so there she stood, furiously trying to meet his eyes while her own were wet. "What do you want?"

"Tell me what you are doing here."

She snorted right to his face. "You couldn't possibly understand, so no. You wanted me to go back to bed? Fine. Get out of my way and let me do it."

"You have until the count of six—" he began.

"Oh for—I ripped my shirt! There, are you happy?"

He knew he'd heard her and yet that made no sense at all. She'd slunk off to cry over a tear in her clothes? He didn't believe it. Maybe if it were Nicci, but not Amber.

He tipped his head to a cautious angle of inquiry. "I did not mark you."

"I ripped my shirt," she said again, her angry voice cracking a second time. "Now I've got this huge hole that I can't fix."

"You have no other shirts?"

"They all reek," she said, refusing to look at him. "And they're all full of holes too. I only have one new shirt left, but it's the last one and if..." She pressed her shaking lips together and did not speak for a long time. "It got to me, okay? You can think it's stupid all you want. I agree. You're right. It's stupid. Now leave me alone."

Meoraq hunted for something to say while Amber stared at the wall beside his shoulder and kept her too-bright eyes dry. "You knew I have a mending kit," he said finally. "You might ask to borrow it."

Her mouth pressed tighter together. She did not reply.

Her clothing was worn thin. He'd marked it before this night. Long before. And the weather was only coming in colder. He couldn't see the tear she spoke of, but by the stiff way she stood, hugging her arms to her chest, he could guess where it was. And he'd probably done it himself, binding her to her own spear. He tried to think back, but couldn't truthfully say one way or another. It was likely, though.

He really was an insensitive brunt. Her clothes were falling off her. They hadn't been designed for hard travel in the first place, much less this endless wear. He could order his replaced at the next city he passed by, but hers...hers were all she had.

Meoraq exhaled an uncomfortable hiss and made a half-gesture behind him at the door. "I have a spare tunic."

Her eyes snapped to him and away, blazing. "I don't want it."

"Eh?"

"I said, no! Stop giving me things! Just stop! What do you think people are going to say when they see me wearing your shirt tomorrow?"

"What do you want from me then?" he exploded.

"I wanted you to leave me alone!"

"Well, you don't get what you want!" he shouted, very dimly aware that what had begun as a poor imitation of a calm conversation had shattered beyond repair into splendidly irrational bickering. "*I* get what *I* want and I want you to shut up and wear my fucking tunic!"

She burst into tears.

"And if I tell you to wear the harness and the breeches that go with it," Meoraq raged on, "that is what you'll do! I'll dress every Gann-damned sliver of you if it pleases me to do so and I will not hear another word about it!"

"You can't make me, you scaly son of a bitch!"

"Ha!" And yes, he was entirely senseless now. "I don't even know what that means so I can't be offended by it!"

"It means your mother was a bitch!" she screamed at him.

"She could have been!" he roared back. "But my father was Uyane Rasozul in the sight of Sheul, twenty-six years a Sheulek, steward of his bloodline, lord over his House, and champion to all Xeqor, and it is *his* son who stands before you now! You see *Meoraq*, ha, here before God and Gann! Tell me again what I can and cannot make you do and just see what happens!"

He had to stop there for a breath, and it was there that Scott's voice rang out with brilliant clarity: "Do you mind? Some of us are trying to sleep!"

Meoraq and Amber both stared at the door. He honestly wasn't sure which of them moved first after that, but in another moment they were both storming back into the sleeping room, side at side, like an army of two.

Meoraq went straight to Scott, who sat up fast and scooted foolishly backwards while still wrapped in his bedding until he hit another human and had to stop.

"I have been listening to you talk all night!" Meoraq spat. "If you look into my face and tell me you were sleeping, I will stand you up and have judgment for the lie!"

"I wasn't!" Scott said at once. "But other people were and—"

Meoraq swung around and raked his eyes over the whole of them. "Who *dares* order me to silence?"

"I do," said Amber. "Shut up."

"Oh my God," said Eric, very quietly, almost respectfully.

Those were the words that hooked at him, not Amber's. Which was not to say that Amber's passed serenely through him, but it was Eric under his burning stare next. Meoraq could feel himself sway, as if his metaphorical precipice of control had caused him to physically teeter, but when he fell, it was on the side of seventeen years of training. Because God indeed was with him and His eyes were always open.

Meoraq closed his eyes. He took a breath, held it, then let it slowly out again. He looked at Amber and said, "Come here."

Human heads turned all through the room. Human eyes watched, solemn and staring, as Amber stood alone among them.

She did not move for a long time.

But when she did move, she came toward him.

Meoraq waited. She came within his easy reach and tipped her head back just a little, a combatant no longer but only an exhausted and unhappy human in torn clothes waiting to be struck so she could go to bed.

Meoraq left her standing there and went to his tent. He found the mending kit and brought it back, taking her firmly by the wrist and slapping the case with force into her limp hand. "When you are ready to apologize," he said, releasing her, "I may be ready to forgive you. Until then, mend your shirt and keep your mouth shut."

Her chin trembled, but in the end, she did not answer, only took the kit and left again. Back to her stall, perhaps, and this was just as well. He was willing to take the higher path, but he wasn't ready to forgive, not quite yet.

The humans were watching, wary. He hissed at them and went into his tent as they scattered. He lay down, tight and angry and itching beneath his skin. He thought of Amber sitting alone in that empty room, mending that worn-out shirt just so it wouldn't be the last one she had in the world. He thought of her calling him a son of a bitch too, but he tried not to let that be the master of him.

3

Morning came, but daylight did not lessen the storm that blew without the walls any better than sleep had eased the storm of Meoraq's mood. He kept to himself in a foul humor, hiding in his tent until the humans woke and began to mill about, talking about the rain, talking about food, talking about the building itself and the Ancients who built it...and talking about the ship they imagined they saw in the tilework. As galling as the thought of that ship was, he was glad when Scott took the lot of them away to the other room to look at it, even if it was against his expressed order, because at least it gave him the opportunity to slip out without having to deal with any of them.

But when he opened the fastens and stepped out, there was Amber, leaned up against the wall in her useless human blanket, waiting for him.

He didn't want to talk to her yet. He wasn't sure he wanted to talk to her at all. He gave her a grunt of acknowledgement and left her.

Halfway down the first long hall that led to the rear of the building and the hole in the wall, Meoraq stopped and turned around. He folded his arms, hands flexing close to his honor knives, and waited. He wasn't going to run away from a woman, by hell. If she wanted to thrash this out, they'd thrash. Ha! And she'd know how it felt to thrash with a Sheulek by the end of it.

Time, measured out by his own even breaths and the drumming of rain against the outer windows.

Meoraq waited. Waited. And finally let out a curse and stalked back up the hall and into the sleeping room.

Amber, still leaning against the wall, turned her head and looked at him.

Now he was really annoyed.

Perhaps she could tell. She looked away, fixing her eyes on her own knees without change to her expression. This act bent her neck, making her look very much like a dumaq woman, which did not mollify him in the slightest but was instead somehow grotesque. He felt himself cooling and had to stop and remind himself that she had started all the fighting and it wasn't over until he said it was.

"I am not angry with you," he announced, hoping to provoke her.

"Lies," she muttered, but she looked at him. Glared at him. And that was better.

"A Sheulek is the master of his emotions," he told her. "I have every right to be angry with you. I choose the higher path. I forgive you and we will say no more about it. Give me my mending kit."

She reached it out from beneath her pack, but only held it for a while. "I should have thanked you for this last night," she said finally. "I don't know how it is with your people, lizardman, but when it comes to humans, you don't interrupt a girl's crying jag and then expect her to be grateful."

He could not believe this.

"Are you criticizing *my* behavior?" he asked incredulously.

Her shoulders fell. "Sure sounds that way, doesn't it? Damn it. Here."

He did not move to take the kit and, after a few awkward moments, she let her offering arm drop again.

They looked at each other.

She said, without heat and without warning, "I've never needed anyone before. Never in my life. I hate that I need you."

Meoraq cooled a little more and this time, let those fires burn out. He went over and took his mending kit from her. "I am not your enemy."

She snorted without much humor. Without much feeling of any kind, it seemed. "No, you're my babysitter. Or, what was it you called me? Your runaway sheep?"

"Something of the sort," he mumbled, scratching at the side of his snout. He bared his teeth briefly, then irritably said, "You ran off, didn't you?"

"Yeah, I did. So that I could have my useless goddamn girly moment in private. You were the last person I wanted to see that."

The kit in his hands seemed suddenly to weigh ten times what it should. He looked at it foolishly, picked at a loose thread in its side-seam (it ought to be repaired and that was nearly ironic—to mend a mending kit), and put it away. "Why?"

She was quiet for a long time, long enough that he thought she did not intend to answer at all, and he was debating how to handle that when she suddenly, listlessly said, "Because I'm supposed to be the tough one. I'm supposed to be different. And I'm not."

"You are." He snorted and came over to give her a forgiving tap. "Hear the words of Uyane. You are without equal in the realm of the very different. I handle it...badly."

"Maybe I wasn't at my best last night. But you were pissed off all day—"

He grunted acknowledgement and did not point out that he had every reason to be angry when some cattle's ass tried to take command of his camp, let alone when the one human he found tolerable turned her back on him and followed said ass into a city of the Fall against the will of Sheul and Meoraq both. He was being very patient.

"—and then you disappear all night, during the worst storm I've ever seen—"

"And what exactly did you expect me to do about the weather, woman?"

"Nothing! Just...and while we're on the subject, what have you been telling Scott about me?"

His spines flared. "This is the subject?"

"It relates," she said defensively.

"Apart from the usual death threats which he ignores, I try not to speak to S'kot at all. When circumstance forces me to do so, it certainly isn't man-chat about you."

She looked down at her empty lap and said nothing. It was not a look of relief. More of a flinch, if anything.

He studied her frowning face, seeing thoughts there he could not read. "Why? What does he claim I say?"

"I don't know."

He clapped one hand to his snout and physically pinched it shut, determined to be tactful. Then, because towering over her like this wasn't helping even if it was entirely appropriate, he hunkered down and tapped her on the knee. "S'kot can't open his mouth without piss falling out of it. If his people choose to believe his lies, that is their foolishness. It doesn't have to be yours."

"Meoraq, he's telling them—"

He pinched her chin, silencing her. "I don't care if he's telling them he is Sheul Himself in human form. You know better. You know truth. How do you mark me?"

She stared at him in silence, at last waggling her head up and down in human acknowledgement.

He grunted and released her, looking broodingly around the empty room where the Fall of the Ancients went on and on in some other plane. "This land is poison. I allowed it to infect me last night, Soft-Skin, as perhaps it infected all of us. I should not have been so harsh with you. Will you take my spare tunic?"

"No."

"Please yourself. I will not command it today. If you come to any sense, you know that I have it." He stood. "Gather your things and pack my tent. I need to scout our path out of this God-accursed place and I want S'kot and his cattle to be ready to leave the very instant that I return for them. Tell him."

"Okay."

The door to the foreroom opened, drawing both their eyes. There stood Scott himself, chattering back over his shoulder at all the humans who had followed him into that room in defiance of Meoraq's command.

He gripped his brow-ridges. He was not going to shout. He was going to be patient. He was.

"Oh good, you're up," said Scott. "I want to talk to you, Meoraq."

"Sheul, O my Father, be with Your son."

"Not a good time, Scott," said Amber.

"Miss Bierce, this is none of your business. Be quiet. Meoraq." Scott's soft face became what he probably thought was very stern. "What can you tell us about the people who used to live here?"

"They're all dead. What else do you need to know?"

Scott paused to roll his eyes at his watching people. When he continued, it was in the slow, smiling way that usually meant he thought he was talking to a fool. "Let's start with this place. Where are we?"

"Eh? This very building?" Meoraq glanced at Amber, but she did not correct him. He flicked his spines. "I don't know."

"The room in back, the one with all the little metal creatures—"

"The machines," said Meoraq, folding his arms. "What about them?"

"What are they doing?"

"I don't know."

"Why?" asked Amber.

"Miss Bierce, this doesn't concern you. Now, Meoraq, can you find out what the bots are doing? The lights are working," he said, pointing up even though more than half of the lights in this particular room were dark. "And the doors have power, so maybe you could fire up one of the computers in the back and—"

"And what, S'kot?" Meoraq interrupted, snapping his spines audibly flat. "What would you have me do in defiance of Sheul's holy law? What, when all men who are His children know it goes against the Word to take mastery over the machines of the Fallen Age or to dwell again in the cities of the Ancients? Speak your mind plainly to one who is the Sword of His judgment. What?"

Scott puckered his soft lips so that he appeared in every way to be the ass he was. After a long pause, he said, "Do you at least know how long this place has been empty?"

"In years?" Meoraq asked, baffled. "I have no idea. It comes from the age of the Ancients."

"Now we're getting somewhere. But you can't tell us how long ago that was?"

"Since the Fall? No one can."

"You don't keep track of time on this planet?"

"It's Year 33 of Advocate Y'zhare Selthut's stewardship under Sheul."

"So it's been thirty-three years since...since whatever happened?"

"Eh?" Meoraq checked with Amber again, but she was only listening. "No, it's been thirty-three years since the death of Advocate Falhiri. He held the advocacy, I think, seventeen years. Before that...I don't remember, but if you want me to recite them all the way back, it won't happen, human. I couldn't even do that for my true training master."

"So, what, they reset the calendar every time they elect a president?" Scott frowned over that a short while, then shook his head. "It doesn't matter, I guess. How about this: What can you tell me about what happened here?"

"What do you mean?" asked Meoraq, and immediately cut his hand across those words, severing them. "There is no time for this nonsense. Gather your things."

"Do you know what happened?"

That was Amber. Meoraq hesitated, looking down at her. "The Ancients turned from Sheul. They gave themselves over to Gann and were punished for their sins."

"Right," she said, still frowning. "But what killed them all?"

"Sheul's wrath."

"Was it a war?"

Meoraq sighed and rubbed at his brow-ridges. "It was Sheul's wrath."

"That doesn't mean anything to us," Amber said, but before he could reply, she added, "Will you tell me about it?"

Meoraq shot her a black glance, but there was no trace of the sarcasm with which she so often responded to his mention of Sheul. Instead, she seemed almost over-serious. Perhaps even apprehensive. Did she fear that Sheul's wrath would fall again, simply for that they'd stayed one night within these crumbling walls? His arm twitched—a comforting tap, quickly suppressed. He said, "Mastery is more than the need of the moment. So long as we do not take the machines out of the city or seek to remake them, we do not threaten the Second Law."

"It's not that. I'm more worried about what happened here...and what happened in that pit outside. How did...How did everybody die? And are they..." Her troubled gaze broke from his as she looked back at her people. None of them spoke. It took several false starts before she could finish. "And are they still dying?"

The memory of a dream slipped like a phantom hand across his brow, chilling him. *It is still among us...*

He threw it off with a flick of his spines and smiled at her. "No, Soft-Skin. It was a long time ago. If you wish to hear the story of the Fall, I'll tell you, but you needn't fear it. The Hour of Wrath is ended."

"Tell us all," ordered Scott, gesturing to his people, all of whom gathered close in a broad ring around him.

Meoraq felt his spines flatten, but now it seemed he had been penned in. It would no longer be possible to extricate himself from their company without shoving one or more of them bodily out of his way.

And Amber was waiting, a kind of apology in her eyes for trapping him in the role of storyteller, but still listening, still wanting to hear. And he found he wanted to tell her, even if it wasn't just the two of them anymore.

"Sit then, all of you," said Meoraq, defeated. He hunkered down among them as they obeyed. "I will tell you a child's lesson, in the manner that I was first taught, which is to say that if I am interrupted, I will slap you across the snout," he finished with a glare at Scott.

Scott showed him empty hands. "We're all listening."

And they all proved it by agreeing and murmuring assent and generally raising the kind of noise that would have sent every one of them to the ground with their hands clapped to their stinging faces if he were a true training master. Meoraq rubbed at his brow-ridges some more and gradually, they quieted. When he looked up again, he looked only at Amber.

"We are all born of two fathers," he told her. "The father of our mortal bodies, who joined with our mothers and set the features of our clay. And our true Father, great Sheul, who gives us life forever through the forging of our eternal souls."

"Great," said Crandall, crawling up to sit with Scott. "I fly clear across the galaxy to get stuck in bible camp again."

Meoraq swung, the flat of his palm landing lightly but with a satisfying clap of sound across the human's soft face. Crandall fell into Scott, who fell on the floor, and Meoraq waited, disguising the deep pleasure it gave him to watch the two of them untangle themselves. Judging from the faint curl at the corner of Amber's mouth when he met her eyes again, it wasn't as much of a disguise as he'd hoped for.

"These are the two natures of all men," said Meoraq, continuing on as Crandall righted himself and rubbed his blunt human snout. "One part the clay of Gann and one part the fire of Sheul. And so we are meant to be in balance. You do not seem surprised to hear this," he added.

Amber rolled her shoulders. "I've heard it before. Sort of."

"Good. So then. The Ancients grew to believe themselves greater than God. They gave themselves to the comforts of their clay and then to its pleasures and finally to its excesses. They grew in greed and lust and violence until all the world groaned under the weight of their sin. These were the Ancients," said Meoraq, glancing around the ruined room, "and Sheul's wrath fell upon them."

Amber lifted one hand and just held it there, in the air. Meoraq stopped and studied it for a moment, puzzled, then flared his spines at her. "Eh?"

She let her arm drop. "What were their sins, specifically? Do you know?"

"Now hit her," said Crandall.

Scott leaned out of the way a spare instant before Meoraq slapped his servant down a second time. Then he also raised his hand in the air.

It must be a human thing.

"You may speak when I am finished," Meoraq told him. And to Amber: "The exact deeds of the Ancients are not recorded. It is said only that they corrupted Gann, that they poisoned the world and their own bodies, and that they made trade of flesh."

Amber frowned. "Made...? You mean they...they were selling people or—oh, I'm sorry," she said, sitting up a little straighter. She indicated her face. "Go ahead."

Inviting a blow, he realized after a confused moment. For interrupting him.

He snorted and slapped her, just a tap really, hardly enough to turn her head and they both knew it. "They made trade in every way that profit could be had," he said while she rubbed at her cheek. "They engaged in sexual depravities for coin. They made wars just to sell weapons. They built machines to do all their labor, so that every man could have the pleasure of possessing slaves to his will. Sheul made them stewards of His House," he said, "and they destroyed it."

The humans looked at one another, every one of them showing some degree of discomfort.

"Sheul's wrath fell over them," said Meoraq. "The land they had poisoned became blighted, and a curse of barrenness fell over every womb. The waters turned to bile and the heavens to storms. In the first days, the fires that burned for the dead so filled the skies that it was impossible to know whether it was day or night, and blood ran so thick over the land that the trees put forth red-stained leaves and bled red sap when cut. War covered the land as skin covers a man, and for many years that followed, there was only death and rot and sickness. Then came the Prophet. But you don't want to hear that," he said. "You asked for the story of the Fall. So. You have heard it."

"Who was he?" asked Amber. "The...whatever that word was. The holy man."

"Was his name Jesus?" someone asked, and someone else laughed and said, "Wouldn't that be hilarious if it was?"

"His name was Lashraq. He and his oracles served Sheul after the Fall, performing acts of penance for the sake of the dead and the dying."

"He and his what?" asked Amber.

"Apostles, I think," Scott answered with a crooked smile. "This is kind of funny, isn't it? Where there twelve of them?"

"They were six altogether," said Meoraq, knowing he was being baited in some way but unable to understand exactly how. "Prophet Lashraq and his brunt, and the four first oracles: Thaliszr, Oyan, Mykrm and Uyane."

The furry stripes over Amber's eyes rose. "Isn't that your name?"

He smiled, his spines flaring with pride. "Yes. My House is the House Oracle Uyane founded in Xeqor, where my fathers have stood ever since as champions to all Yroq. There are names and Houses as great," he admitted, "but none greater."

"Wow."

"But this is not my story. It is the tale of the Prophet in the first hour of the Fall. Such was his faith and humility that Sheul at last called the Six to Him."

"What, he killed them?" Amber asked, and smacked herself in the forehead. "I did it again. I'm sorry." She thrust her chin out for him.

"I forgive you this once. Sit quietly. And no. When I say Sheul called him, I mean only that. Lashraq heard the voice of God, which no man then living had heard, and it called him to the holy shrine of Xi'Matezh."

"Fucking lizard's pet," muttered Crandall.

Meoraq looked at him.

"Dude, you just do not learn," Eric remarked.

Meoraq pulled his arm back, but Amber caught it.

"Forget him. Please, I really want to hear this. Xi'Matezh...I know I'm saying that wrong, but that's where you're taking us, isn't it?"

Meoraq looked at her hand. She let go of him at once, but he completely ruined the severity of the moment by reaching out to tap at the back of her hand in forgiveness. "Xi'Matezh," he agreed. "The shrine that stands at the ruined reaches of Gedai, at the very edge of Gann. When all the world fell, Xi'Matezh stood and stands yet. Lashraq brought his oracles across the wildlands, just as I am bringing you, until he arrived at the shrine. There, the doors opened and Sheul Himself received them."

Her furry brows rose again into arches. "For real?"

"Yes."

"They actually met him?"

"Manifest as flesh," said Meoraq.

"No way."

"Truth. They heard His words and, at His command, wrote them into laws that could be carried to all men. These are the written teachings known as the Word."

"Oh," said Amber. Her brows lowered. "I get it. Okay."

"Xi'Matezh is the holiest of the surviving shrines from the Age of the Ancients."

"I'll bet."

"Because all who enter," said Meoraq calmly, "hear the voice of Sheul."

That made her look at him in a whole new way. Meoraq smiled.

"You mean that metaphorically, right?"

"I don't know that word. I mean precisely what I say."

"Everyone hears God?"

"All who enter. The doors of Xi'Matezh do not open for everyone."

That knowing look came over her again. "Ah."

"But they do open. They will open for me," he added.

Her eyes narrowed. She leaned forward slightly. "Have you ever personally met anyone who'd been inside?"

Meoraq snorted and leaned forward to meet her. "Yes."

Her brows rose yet again. Their pliancy was truly astounding to behold. "You have not!"

He took her chin in his hand and gave it a squeeze. "Do not question the word of a Sheulek. We are truth incarnate."

"You really have?"

"Yes. One of my training masters."

"What did God tell him?"

"That, he would not speak of." Meoraq flexed his spines, then lowered them. "But he was changed by it. Changed to the very heart of him."

Amber frowned, searching his eyes while her own remained troubled. Her flesh in his hand was very soft...very warm...

"I can't believe that," she said at last. It seemed to take her some effort. "I'm sorry. I just can't."

Meoraq smiled and released her.

"Now he's going to hit her," Crandall remarked, and quite a few humans leaned away from her.

"I don't think you're lying to me," Amber went on, unafraid of him or his punishing hand. "And I don't think your teacher was lying to you, exactly. I'm just saying—"

"That you do not believe in Sheul. And therefore, He cannot be truth because all the truth in the world is known to you."

Amber cut her eyes away in a wince, but did not protest that. Instead, after several false starts to gather her nerve, she said, "I'm just saying that there's a lot things your teacher could have seen or heard that maybe...you know...he didn't understand."

Meoraq's spines twitched. Smiling, he gestured for her to continue.

She winced again, seeing his amusement but perhaps not knowing how to read it. Yet she did resume her argument, however uncomfortable it clearly made her. "People tend to find what they look for, Meoraq. That's my point. And if your teacher went looking for God, he might have been willing to...to see God. In a lot of things. Especially things..." Her gaze wandered restlessly behind her, tapping at this device or that one as they sat surrounded by the trappings of the Ancients. "...that were unfamiliar to him."

He waited, and when he was certain that she had no more to say, Meoraq leaned forward and gently said, "Do I really strike you as so superstitious a man?"

She started to protest, but this time, he interrupted.

"Do you see me cowering in fear beneath these 'magical glowing crystals' or cringing away from the 'metal creatures' that litter these ruins?"

Amber's soft brow creased. She looked up at the lights and then away, at the door, and finally back at him.

"I know what machines are," he said. "I know how they were used. And I know many of them yet function in some small, dying manner. I have seen the moving images left by the Ancients and heard the echoes of their words and never once been tempted to mistake it for the voice of my eternal Father. The idea is absurd."

He could see that argument at war with the thoughts inside her and he saw the exact moment that it was defeated.

"Maybe it was someone else," said Amber.

Meoraq huffed out a breath of exasperation. "A man, you mean."

"Pretending to be God."

"So you acknowledge I would not be fooled by a disembodied voice, but instead fall down in worship of a mere man. Your lack of faith in Sheul does not disturb me half as much as your lack of faith in me."

Again, she failed to read his teasing tone. Dismay filled her ugly face and all the humans around them drew back to give him room to swing. He reached out to give her a playful tap—just the tip of his fingers to her forehead—and said, "Sheul does not require me to prove His existence. You and I will stand together in Xi'Matezh. You will hear His voice when He speaks to me. Perhaps He will even speak to you."

She continued to gaze at him in the same searching way. "What if the doors don't open?"

"They will."

"What if..." A small crease appeared between her troubled brows. "What will you do if he's not there?"

"A far better question is this." He leaned forward very close. "What will *you* do if He is?"

She drew back, frowning.

Meoraq spared Scott a glance and his smile slipped. "Speak now, if you must."

Scott leaned in at once, intent, to ask the most incongruous question Meoraq had heard out of him yet: "What does the temple look like?"

"Eh?"

"Is there a tower, maybe?"

Meoraq looked at Amber, only to see her looking at Scott, her human face puckered in confusion. "I've never seen the temple," he admitted. "I don't know."

"But it's old, right? Like this place. It's from before your big war."

"Dude," said Dag. "What difference does it make if there's a tower or not?"

"It makes a big difference, depending on whether it's a bell tower, say..." Scott paused to eye his people with thinly restrained and completely inexplicable excitement. "Or a transmission tower."

The words meant nothing to Meoraq, but the effect they had on the humans was clear enough to see. Most merely continued to show puzzlement, but some immediately captured and reflected Scott's own excitement while others, like Amber, seemed stunned.

"Think about it," Scott was saying. "The doors don't open for everyone—there's some sort of security system. People hear voices—a communications relay. Their Jesus guy called it God because that's what he wanted to think, maybe what he needed to think after most of the world gets wiped out, but what if their temple is really a skyport?"

"A skyport?" Amber echoed. "Why the hell would you go there? Why not a radio station or a...a regular airport? No, you go straight to skyport?"

"Didn't you see the picture?" Scott demanded. He climbed to his feet, standing over his people as color began to come into his face. "They had ships! Maybe starships!"

"What does it matter what they had a hundred or two hundred..." Amber trailed off, looking around the room with a strange, despairing sort of look. "...or a thousand years ago? It doesn't mean anything to us now."

"If this place he's taking us to is a skyport, then they don't just have any old transmission tower out there, it could be a deep-space relay! We could be saved!"

And then all the humans were talking at once, it seemed. Some to each other, some catching at Scott's sleeve, but all together, louder and louder, using human words that could not be fathomed and making arguments that only grew more violent.

"Enough!" Meoraq shouted, and most of them drew back and quieted at once.

Most of them.

"You don't know what's out there!" Scott insisted. "They had the technology! They built all this, they had to have had some kind of global media system!"

"That's not the goddamn point!" Amber shouted.

Meoraq got a hold on her and one on him and thrust them both back. "I said, enough!"

Amber leaned out around him to stab eyes at Scott, undaunted. "What are you doing? Why are you working people up like this? You wouldn't know how to use anything we found anyway!"

"Don't tell me what I know!"

Meoraq hissed and gave them each a crisp shake.

"It all makes perfect sense!" Scott insisted. "They hear voices, Bierce! From people who aren't there! That's a transmission tower and if it's still working, we can use it! We can—"

"We can what? Phone home? We don't know where we are!"

"It's still a chance!"

"No it isn't, God damn it! *This* is our chance, right here!" Amber shouted. "*This* is where we are and *this* is where we have to live!"

"Not necessarily!"

Meoraq surrendered the effort to quiet them, released his holds, and slapped them both—first Scott, then Amber, and then Scott again, because he was the most irritating. He hissed, "Are you children?"

Scott and Amber flushed together. He said nothing. She said, sullenly, "No."

"Enough then," he said curtly. "You have had your story. Now we are moving on. Gather your things."

"We're going to talk about this later," Scott said.

It was not clear whether he were warning Amber or Meoraq, but in the event that it was him, Meoraq answered. "There will be time enough, I am certain, but if you cannot manage your words without lowing at one another like animals, I will drive you out into the wildlands where animals belong."

Scott started to speak, but then obviously thought better of it. He shut his mouth and turned away.

The circle of humans began to break apart, withdrawing to their sleeping spaces to mutter amongst themselves as they packed. He could hear his name (or as close as they could manage to speak it) and he doubted it was spoken with favor or respect, but he would not be baited by that. He had promised Sheul patience and even now, when holding his temper felt so much like holding a knife in his chest and twisting, twisting, he would let his soul's Father judge him honest.

Beside him, Amber was noisily punching her shiny blanket into her pack, the mark of his hand standing out brightly on her cheek, scraped raw and beaded on one edge with blood. He watched her for a time, wishing he had never begun the tale that had brought them to this moment, because although she certainly deserved a sounder cuffing than he'd given her for her outburst, it had utterly undone all the difficult mending of their first quiet talk this morning. He wanted that moment back, as clumsy as it had been.

He half-raised his hand twice, very much aware of the other humans, even though Amber herself did not appear to see them, or him for that matter, but in the end, he reached out and nudged at her with two knuckles.

She looked at him. In spite of her obvious anger, she kept her mouthparts pressed tight together, waiting on his word. So maybe it hadn't all been undone.

"I forgive you," he said.

She just looked at him for a while without any apparent change to her expression. Then her eyes shifted past him so that she could watch Scott.

"I don't find you at fault," he said after a moment. "This place is nothing but Gann's poison. When we are away, things will be better."

"Well, I'm glad you think so, lizardman," Amber said, sounding anything but glad. "But I don't. In fact, I'm pretty sure things are only going to get worse from now on. A fucking *skyport*."

* * *

The walk out of the city went much quicker than the walk in. They no longer stopped each time a window lit up or a kiosk spoke to them. If a door opened, most of them passed it without even a curious glance at what might be inside. At one of the intersections, an insectoid bot replaced lamps that had been broken in the storm, and they all just strolled by like they'd seen giant metal centipedes doing linework all their lives.

It could have been because the ruins had lost the gothic oppressiveness they'd had in an impending thunderstorm. It could have been because they were hungry and wanted to be back in the prairie so Meoraq could hunt. It could have been because several towers had collapsed during the night and seeing them instilled everyone with a natural drive to get the hell out from under the rest of them. It could have been a lot of things, but Amber knew the real reason was Scott. Scott and the ship.

One night in a crumbling old ruin with a couple shiny tiles stuck to the wall had completely reinvented his sense of purpose. They were no longer pioneers fording their way across a desolate, alien landscape; now they were also castaways orchestrating their own rescue. Street after echoing street, it was Scott's string of outrageous skyport promises and not Meoraq's grim-faced guidance that kept them moving.

All the way down to the river, Scott talked. Each groaning, error-thick recording to issue from a corroded kiosk brought on a fresh promise of a working deep-space transmission tower. Every intact window or undamaged wall was greater evidence of a surviving skyport than all the rest of the broken ones. They passed a massive junklot where some unseen bot had towed thousands upon thousands of derelict vehicles, stacked into a single rusted brick filling the back of the lot end to end and easily a hundred meters high; the few vehicles which the tow-bot had missed remained where they had died in the street, most strip-salvaged and weathered away to nothing but a ring of rust and a few unusable parts, yet it was the bot who did it which Scott chose to point out as undeniable proof that a starship would still be able to launch itself and fly them home.

Amber heard all this and worse from her usual place at the tail of the marching line, and not just from Scott himself. He had shot the idea of a return to Earth into them like a drug and now they were all laughing and talking what-ifs and planning the first thing they were going to eat, the first place they were going to go, the first person they were going to sue. Humming, as the Candyman would say. Amber remembered what that felt like and she knew it wouldn't last, although Scott managed to keep them going strong all the way through town and down to the river.

The waterfront district of the ruins was just like the waterfront district in any big city. The few surviving windows of the narrow storefronts they walked along promised all the same sleaze that Amber had seen peddled on her own street back home: Cheap rooms, knock-off brands, no-questions loans and quick cash for whatever you wanted to sell, booze and drugs and sex. Even worse were the commercial bots; unlike the maintenance units which were happy to ignore and be ignored by the aliens in their empty city, the commercial bots were drawn to them like missiles. They dragged themselves behind Scott and his group, croaking advertisements and error messages and occasionally sparking out or banging into debris. The most stubborn of these limped behind Amber for six blocks, plucking at her sleeve with a damaged tendril and offering up enticements such as, "Young ones, boy- and girl-meat. Be their first, safe and clean! We catch and release. They cry!"

At last, Amber swung on it and raised her spear, but either the bot recognized the threatening gesture or it had reached the end of its territory. Either way, it turned back and crawled away, its horrible litany of services and showtimes receding as the sound of water grew louder.

They crossed at one of the bridges soon afterward—the bridge that had been vomiting lightning all night long, in fact—and not only did Meoraq not try to stop them, he gave the order that marched them across.

"Please be kidding," Amber had said, horrified. "Nicci, stay off that thing! What, was it some other lizardman telling us that these buildings could fall down any second and God alone was keeping them up?"

He threw her an impatient, annoyed glance as he pointed people onto the bridge. They went, not without hesitation, but they went. "God will hold the bridge if it is His will we move on," he told her. "As I believe it is His will."

"Well, I can't say that's the craziest thing I've heard today," she countered, looking hard at Scott. "But only because I've heard so much crazy."

Wasted. The only one close enough to hear her was Meoraq himself. Even Nicci was already heading out across the derelict suspension bridge of unknown age, spanning the freezing, storm-swollen river.

"This is such a bad idea," said Amber, following.

Meoraq fell into step beside her. "We walk in God's sight, Soft-Skin."

"Yeah? Seems like he's been doing a lot of blinking lately."

"Do not be blasphemous."

They walked. The sound of a hundred tromping boots on an otherwise empty bridge made an ugly sound that neither the perpetual wind nor the rushing water below could drown out. She imagined she could feel the bridge swaying in time with their steps, but she was not imagining the groaning, twanging, snapping sound above them as the ancient suspension cables had to carry them. Amber didn't realize just how much she expected a collapse until she stepped off the bridge onto solid ground on the other side and felt, not relief, but the unmistakable rush of surprise.

She turned around to stare for a while, but the bridge stubbornly refused to fall down, even now at the most blackly appropriate time.

At length, Meoraq tapped at her shoulder. "We are not stopping here."

"It's not fair."

He frowned, rubbing at the side of his scaly snout for a few seconds before gruffly saying, "We will rest a short time then."

"That's not what I meant. I don't want to rest here. I don't want to spend another damn minute here."

"And yet here you stand."

She threw him a scowl and started walking. Scott and the others were well ahead of her, beyond all hearing. She knew he was talking by the way he moved, gesturing at the windows as they lit up and at the commercial bots that came skulking in from the alleys. In his exuberance, he turned all the way around to make some point or another, walking backwards and pounding his fist into his open palm. She saw him see her, pause...and then wave her way and say something that made all the others look back.

"Deep breaths, Soft-Skin," said Meoraq. "A count of six, deep and slow."

"Don't you even care what he's telling them?"

His spines shrugged. "No."

"It matters, you know."

"Not to me."

She didn't argue the point, but she didn't bother to hide her annoyance either and after several amused sidelong glances as she walked and fumed, Meoraq finally thumped her on the shoulder with two knuckles. "Hold a moment."

"No. We're not stopping until we're out of the city, that's what you said."

He caught her by the wrist and stopped them both. Big scaly jerk. Far down the street, Scott apparently saw something interesting and led everyone around a corner and out of sight. All at once, they were alone—the last two people on the planet.

Meoraq too was watching as Scott and the others disappeared. Now he grunted, although he continued to gaze in that direction. "S'kot lies. Do you need me to tell you this?"

"No, of course not! But you've got this crazy idea that just because everyone knows that Scott talks out his ass, no one believes him!"

A snort of lizardish laughter. "Talks through his ass," Meoraq murmured. "And farts from his face."

"Focus, Meoraq. Our track record for disbelieving things just because they might seem stupid or dangerous is piss-poor. The only reason any of us are here is because we got on an untested ship and let them put us to sleep and shoot us into space."

"No, you are here because it is where God willed you to be."

The effort not to roll her eyes made her hand fly up and slap over her face. She rubbed her eyes wearily. "You're killing me with that crap."

"Truth does not care if it comforts you, Soft-Skin."

They walked.

"Honestly," said Amber. "It doesn't bother you at all when Scott says your God's voice is just a two-way radio?"

"Everything S'kot says annoys me," Meoraq replied with a flick of his spines. "If he wished me fair weather and a warm bed, still it would be all my will to hold from slapping him to the ground."

"He says there's machines in Xi'Matezh," said Amber, petty as that was.

If it was bait—and it was—Meoraq wouldn't bite at it. "There may well be," was his mild reply. "And if S'kot seeks to make himself their master, I will judge him for it. Until then, he can pour piss out of his flapping mouth all he pleases."

"And you don't even care who else he hurts with it."

Meoraq glanced at her, then put his hand on her arm and stopped them again. "I don't know humans, but I know fools. And I know the surest way to encourage fools to follow a wicked man is to tell them not to."

Amber couldn't argue.

"It is a long walk yet to Xi'Matezh," said Meoraq, patting her on the head. "For now, his talk may be exciting, but it will pale with time. He will repeat himself and embellish on his lies, and doubts will grow. When we reach the temple and they see no reward for their wrong-placed faith, yes, it will be difficult, but they will come away stronger, for even the unkindest truth strengthens a man more than the prettiest lie."

'Says the man who thinks he's going to find God there,' thought Amber, but she couldn't bring herself to say it, no matter how rotten she felt. He was trying to comfort her. It wasn't his fault he was terrible at it. What she said, as neutrally as possible, was, "I think you're seriously underestimating how pretty this lie is."

"He can't promise you anything better than God."

"Of course he can. None of us have ever met God before and we're just fine with that. We are!" she snapped when he rolled his eyes. "And for that matter, so are you! So you may *want* to see God when you get there, but you don't *need* to. You can live without it if you have to."

"Live without God?" he said with a lizardish smirk.

"Live without meeting God. Look, all I'm saying is, it's impossible to miss what you've never had."

"I'll have to meditate on that, but in this moment, I do not agree. I know a man," Meoraq mused. "Blood-kin of mine...a friend...who misses very much, or believes he misses, the birth-right that should have belonged to both of us, but which only I achieved. He stood some of the same training. He has at least some understanding of the struggle and pains which I endure, but he misses it anyway. Because it seems so much easier to him, I suppose."

"I think you're confusing missing something with wanting it."

"Perhaps. So. Do you miss your old land—" He looked at her, head cocked, unsmiling. "—or do you just want it?"

To her profound irritation, she had no idea how to answer that.

Meoraq grunted and flicked his spines. "It doesn't matter anyway. A man may want, or miss, many things in his life, but in the end, we all serve God."

"Go ahead, lizardman. Pound it in with a hammer."

"Eh?"

She was saved from having to explain that admittedly snotty remark by the sudden reappearance of Nicci, running down the street toward them, alone. Adrenaline filled her mouth with the taste of metal and she would have bolted forward to meet her except that Meoraq had better reflexes. He caught Amber at her first twitch forward and thrust her behind him, his hooked sword already in his other fist.

Nicci scraped to a stop immediately, her mouth open in a round hole of alarm, both hands flying up in a helpless gesture of surrender.

"What's wrong?" Amber demanded, ducking under Meoraq's sword-arm where he couldn't snatch her back so easily. In theory. "Where is everyone? What happened?"

"Nothing," Nicci stammered, still staring at the sword in the lizardman's grip. "We found something, that's all. Commander Scott wants you to see it."

"I give no obedience to S'kot!" Meoraq hissed, advancing. "Before you carry his commands to me, you had best ask yourself if you are willing to stand in his place for my answer!"

Nicci backed up fast, stumbling over the broken curb and falling against the wall of a shop whose steadfast commercial bot immediately moved to open the door for her.

Amber gave Meoraq a sharp swat to the bicep, which had to have hurt her a lot more than him, but he actually staggered like she'd hit him with a truck. He turned all the way around to look at her, his spines fully forward and quivering, but she refused to be intimidated. "What's the matter with you?" she snapped. "Don't you threaten my sister!"

To her great surprise, Nicci chimed right in alongside her. "Why do you always have to push us around?"

Meoraq kept his eyes on Amber for as long as it took the insistent commercial bot to gronk politely for their attention three times. When he finally broke that stare, it was with a pensive upwards glance and a private word with his god. Then and only then, did he lean back and clip his sword back onto his belt. "So. We will see this machine you have found, but you can tell that cattle's ass who pretends to lead you that we are not carrying it out of these ruins."

"We couldn't even if we wanted to," Nicci said, her brows pinching together in a look of lofty scorn that Amber hadn't seen to quite that degree since her teen years. "Why do you always have to be so negative about everything Commander Scott does? And after everything he does for you?"

Meoraq's spines rose—not flicking forward, but coming up slow until they stood at full extension. "What a remarkable thing to say," he said in a dangerously mild and distracted way.

"He found something amazing!" Nicci insisted, now openly glaring. "Something that he knew you were going to want to see most of all! And here you are, jumping to conclusions and...and...stabbing him in the back!"

Meoraq smiled. It was not an edgy, tooth-filled, predatory smile at all, but almost a dreamy one. His eyes unfocused briefly. The smile broadened.

"We're coming," said Amber.

Meoraq's hand dropped over her shoulder and squeezed. "In a moment," he told Nicci. "Leave us."

"You don't have to leave," said Amber, but Nicci was already moving rapidly down the street.

Meoraq watched until she was good and gone, keeping his hand comfortably locked on her shoulder despite her efforts to shrug it off. It took several minutes, and each one stretched out thinner and longer, until the small greyish blob that was Nicci turned a corner and vanished. Immediately, Amber went on the defensive. "I'm sorry she said that, but what do you expect?"

"Cattle will bellow and beetles will bite," he said scornfully. "S'kot will talk out of his ass and his fool people will repeat him. I don't concern myself with N'ki's behavior. I concern myself with yours. So." Suddenly his scaly face was right in front of hers. "What am I about to say to you?"

Her mind went wonderfully blank. "How many guesses do I get?"

His face got even closer, as improbable as that was. "You," he said, "hit me."

She blinked and looked at her hand, which was still pink and stinging a little. "Are you going to tell me it hurt?" she asked incredulously.

His red eyes narrowed. "I did not mark that. And before you repeat yourself, know this: It is the law of all the city-states under Sheul that no man may lay naked hands upon a Sheulek, save at invitation, for his is the flesh of the Father and the punishment for such presumption is death. So. What did you say?"

"I'm not a man. I'm a woman."

His head cocked. "I did not mark that either. What did you say?"

"Uh, I said I'm sorry and I won't do it again?"

Meoraq straightened up with a grunt and resumed walking.

As she followed, Amber studied his raised spines, his black throat, and what few other minutia existed to help her gauge his mood, decided it was safe to be a little catty, and added, "I also said you were being kind of a baby for making a big deal out of it."

He coughed up a dry laugh. "Did you indeed? You ought to know that it is as much a crime to insult one of God's Swords as it is to lay naked hands upon one. If we were at home, you would be publically whipped for what you have just 'said', and I don't believe I could stop it."

Her feet rooted at once. "You're not going to...I mean...Nicci...?"

He shrugged his spines. "I suppose I could make the effort to feel offense, but you would only insist on bearing her punishment."

Would she? The doubt pricked at her just once before she crushed it in a kind of horror. Of course she would. They were family. They were all each other had. Amber would always stand up for Nicci, and Nicci...would always stand up for her.

"Have you ever seen it happen?" Amber asked. Blurted, really. Anything to keep from thinking.

"Eh? Of course."

"I mean to you. Or over you, I guess I should say. Have you ever got someone hurt because they called you a...a scaly son of a bitch or gave you one of these?" She slapped lightly at his bicep.

He glanced at his arm where her hand had struck, smiling with his mouth even as his head cocked—not quite enough to really be a threat. "Yes."

"Really?"

"Many times. I wasn't always offended, to say truth," he said in his careless I-have-people-whipped-every-day way. "But law is law. When I am at home in Xeqor, I have the authority to forgive, but when I travel, such forgiveness reflects poorly upon the leaders of that city. They must show mastery, especially in conquest."

"Even if they were just kidding?" Images from old movies spun through her head—pilgrim ladies set in stocks in the town square, sailor guys tied to the mast while the bosun whipped his back bloody—but it wasn't all the movies, was it? There were always stories in the news about some rich jackass partying a little too hard in some foreign country getting his ass caned and turning it into an international incident. She'd never had much sympathy for those people before, and yet the idea that she personally could be dragged away and beaten in front of a jeering crowd just because she'd called Meoraq a baby and swatted him on the arm boggled her mind.

"Intent is of no consequence to the law. Sheul's Swords may suffer no abuse from lesser men. Only another Sheulek or a Sheulteb has the right to confront me. All others, even if born under the Blade, can be severely punished for a thoughtless word or an idle blow." His spines twitched. His gaze grew distant. "Even...if they are kin."

"And you're okay with that?"

No answer, not even a grunt. They walked half a block in silence.

"I'm not trying to be rude," said Amber finally.

He roused himself from wherever he had gone to give her a friendly nudge. "No one is here to see us, Soft-Skin. Say what you like. I'll let you know if I'm offended. You won't stop," he added with a wry tilt to his head. "But I'll let you know."

Another half-block passed, with crippled bots making the only conversation. This time, the silence was Amber's.

"I'm a bitch, aren't I?" she said. It just fell out, landing heavily and dragging along behind her like one of those iron balls you saw chained to a prisoner's ankle in the old-time cartoons.

"I don't know what that means."

She didn't know how to explain and didn't entirely want to, knowing that she'd called his mother one just last night. Instead, she nerved herself up for an honest answer and asked, "Do you think I'm hard to live with?"

"Eh." He flicked his spines in a careless manner, not even bothering to shrug them all the way. "I'm the wrong man to ask. I've never had to live with anyone so long as I've lived with you humans. Even the Prophet himself would likely be in under my scales by now."

"In other words, yes." She tried to smile like it was a joke, but it wasn't and she couldn't, quite.

"No one speaks for a Sheulek. My words are my own. There are no others. You should—" But just then, they rounded the corner and saw the others, and whatever else Meoraq had been about to say ended seamlessly with, "Fuck Gann."

It got a laugh out of her, the first real laugh since they'd stumbled into this god-awful place, the first laugh in what felt like lifetimes. "I should what?"

He glanced at her, still scowling over Scott, but a little sheepish, she thought. "That isn't what I meant to say."

"I thought God's feet only told the truth. Your words are your own. There are no others."

"Insufferable human," he said. "Come. I need to see what this cattle's ass is about now, and if God be merciful to me, it will end badly."

The wind, which had been blowing more or less non-stop since Amber first crawled out of the wreck of the *Pioneer* and which had long ago become a kind of white-noise sensation she scarcely noticed, suddenly threw an extra-cold breeze their way, sending an honest-to-God chill up Amber's spine. At the same time, the lit window they were standing beside flickered and died. She tried to laugh over that (*sheesh all we need is some ominous music duh-duh-duh-DUMMMM the omen is officially here*) but it wasn't really funny. It was Scott. Of course it was going to end badly.

Scott and the others were standing in the middle of the street two blocks down, but even from here, Amber could see what they were looking at. It was another kiosk, but one of enormous size, planted in the middle of the intersection so that each side faced out into traffic. Centered in each wall of the kiosk was a video screen, and judging from the way everyone had ringed around it, all of them were working. Bands of static cut across the image, but the lizardman speaking there was still perfectly discernible, if muted. Amber had to be right up next to the group before she could hear anything at all. Only one of the speakers seemed to be working and the audio feed was in terrible condition, but a few words had survived.

"...won't help anymore," was the first phrase to fall out of hissing static into recognition. "It's everywhere. It's in everything. You can't..." And back to static.

"What is this?" Amber asked, and was violently hushed by a dozen people.

The audio came back with "...still alive. I have to believe that," the lizardman said, and no amount of static could dampen the feverish intensity with which he said it. "I have to. I do."

Static.

"Just wait. It's coming up next," said Nicci, slipping into the small space between Amber and Meoraq. Amber thought she heard a hiss, but when she glanced over, Meoraq was walking away, looking down empty streets in his usual restless way.

Amber waited, and after a long stretch of damaged tape and gibberish without any context to draw from, a single word leapt out: "Matezh."

She jumped a little, but there wasn't time to look for reactions in anyone else. The lizardman on the feed was still talking, but the sound was terrible, requiring all her concentration and a lot of guesswork to translate.

"...look for lights...careful, because the roads are...locked, but I..."

And then something else, something Amber couldn't begin to figure out, but which made Meoraq stop and look sharply around—two words: "Nuu Sukaga."

"What does that mean?" she asked, once the feed had collapsed again into static.

"I don't know," Meoraq told her, but the kiosk had all his attention now.

"It will ask for your mnabed—"

Amber touched Meoraq's arm and he said, frowning, "A key...I think. The base of the word is the same, but I've never heard this variation."

"—but just say it again. Nuu Suk—" A sudden storm of static obscured the rest of it. The lizardman on the screen kept talking, just a ghost behind waves of distortion and TV snow. The sound was nothing but electronic pops and scratches for several minutes, but there had to be more coming because several people were fidgety, anxious.

And then it came. The tape clearly hit the end of its recording, blipped to black, and then came back, relatively clear. The lizardman tapped at something at a console out of sight, looked directly up into whatever camera was recording this, and said, "If you can hear this, you're not alone. But if you're still in the cities, you have to leave. I know the emergency channels are still transmitting orders to stay in your homes, but that isn't safe. And as far as I can see, the aid stations have all been overrun. But listen, I'm sending this from my base in Matezh. It's got plenty of food, plenty of water, and it's absolutely impenetrable. It's also got probably the best communications system in the world," he added with a shaky smile. Or maybe it was just the recording that shook; it was getting hard to tell. "So I know you can hear me. And you need to know—" The tape blipped and rolled back a bit, the color skewed. "—need to know that as long as any one of us is left alive, there's still hope. But we have to come together. We have to—" Static and squeals filled the speakers for a few seconds and came back at deafening volume with, "—come to Matezh," before snapping back into normal range. "This is no world to be in alone," the lizardman said on the monitors. "It's not too late. I know it seems that way, but it's really not. I'm still here and so are you. We can still—"

He kept talking, but the audio was gone, and the next thing that came in clearly was, "...won't help anymore," so she knew it had gone the full loop.

"So," said Meoraq. He looked around, not as if hunting out dangers this time, but just looking. Seeing the ruins, perhaps for the first time. "This is what he heard."

"Huh?"

"Master Tsazr. The man I knew who entered Xi'Matezh." His eyes finished their slow crawl over the dead city and came back to her. "He was here."

"Maybe." Amber spared the kiosk a distracted glance. "He says he's transmitting across every bandwidth, or at least, I'm guessing that's what he's saying. So your teacher might not have been here, exactly—"

"You've always got to poke holes, don't you?" interrupted Scott.

"—but this is probably something he heard if spent any time in one of these cities where the TV was on," Amber finished, ignoring him. "I'm a little surprised you'd never heard it before. I guess you've never been in any ruins, huh?"

"Many times." Meoraq tapped at the kiosk wall—the monitor nearest to his hand flickered—and shrugged his spines. "I've never listened to the things I've heard there before. Ha. I might have heard this a hundred times." He paused and looked back over his shoulder at Scott. "I admit, you make me curious," he said, and cocked his head (not, Amber recalled, a gesture of curiosity). "Why did you stop to listen? What is it that you believe it means?"

"Well, isn't it obvious?" Scott waited until Meoraq deliberately flattened his spines before declaring, "It's proof."

Amber gave the lizard a few torturous seconds to jump on that, but he seemed content to just stand there and study Scott, so in the end, she broke. "Of what?"

Scott looked at her, smiling. "It's a transmission, Miss Bierce. It's coming from Matezh. And since you appear to be incapable or unwilling to add two and two, I'll do it for you: There is a transmission tower at Matezh *and*," he went on, raising his voice and one finger as Amber opened her mouth. "*And* it's still working!"

Again Amber tried to talk, but this time it was Nicci who stopped her. Her color was high, but the shine in her eyes was too bright and brittle to be only excitement. It was a Bo Peep look, when the high was gone and she was trying to cozy just one more hit out of someone until tomorrow, just one more hit and everything was golden, just one more and it was all love.

"Listen," Nicci pleaded in their mother's voice, wearing their mother's face. "Just listen to him, okay? He makes sense!"

Sense? Amber shook her head, looking back and forth from her baby sister/dead mother to the lunatic in a damned usher's uniform, but it was Meoraq she kept coming back to. Meoraq, who merely watched it all play out with his head tipped up like that and his arms calmly folded.

"I'm aware of our situation here and I'm aware that we may all be living it with different goals," Scott was saying, addressing all of them now. He talked fast and loud, making eye contact with everyone as he paced in front of the kiosk, and the choir was already clapping and swaying along. "I want to find a transmission tower at the end of this road. Hell, I want to find a skyport! Is that fantastic? Yes! But how fantastic, really? Meoraq—" He swung to point and Meoraq's spines slapped flat. "—wants to find a temple where he can talk to God," finished Scott, backing away. "And Amber Bierce wants us to find *this*!"

His voice bounced off the walls and down the lifeless street, making people look uneasily around them, reminded of the emptiness all over again.

"What are you doing, Scott?" Amber asked. She didn't like the sound of her voice following those echoes. "How can you stand there and talk about skyports like it represents some sort of real chance?"

"Why not? Look around! All their stuff is still here! It still works!"

"Yeah, right. We don't know what it's doing, but it works. At least, the stuff that hasn't crumbled literally to dust still works."

"That was just the synthetic stuff."

"And God knows there won't be any of that on a *starship*!" Amber flung out her hands in a kind of furious surrender. "Okay, you know what? Fine. Let's go to the magical land of Make Believe and pretend there is a ship somewhere in Xi'Matezh. What makes you think you could actually fly it? Piloting a starship isn't something you just hope to figure out *on the way*. Do I seriously even have to point out that it'll be an alien ship? With alien technology?"

"Technology follows logical rules, no matter who makes it," Scott declared. "Look around you, Miss Bierce. The lights look like lights. The doors open like doors. Heck, even the bathrooms look like bathrooms."

"And the giant fucking spiderweb in back of the building last night? What did that look like, genius?"

"I'm not going to continue this discussion if you can't be reasonable."

"I'm the only reasonable one *in* this discussion! We will not be able to fly an alien ship! Even if we found a manual, we couldn't read it! This is craziness!"

They booed her. They actually booed her. She thought Crandall started it, maybe as a joke, but there couldn't have been less than a dozen others who joined in. In the echoing street, it sounded like more. A lot more.

"See, that's the difference between you and me," Scott told her in his lofty Commander-on-Deck voice. "I don't need to scare people to feel better about myself. I'm not afraid to give people hope."

Amber stared at him, at all of them, speechless. Then, the explosion. She never felt it coming. One second, she was fine, if dumbstruck; the next, she was shouting up the whole world. "There is no fucking ship, you lying son of a bitch! We are *never* going home! This is it! This is what's real! *There is no fucking hope*!"

Meoraq's hand closed over her shoulder. Hard.

"You see? This is her reality," Scott told the rest of the crowd while Amber tried unsuccessfully to shrug herself free. "The one where everything is pointless and we might as well give up and jump off the first cliff we come to."

"No, *Everly*, it's the reality where we're starving to death on a fucking alien planet instead of making people think we don't have to try anymore because we'll all be saved by a magic ship! *That's* giving up, jackass! *That's*—Get your goddamn hand off me, Meoraq!"

"Hush," he said.

"But—"

He looked down at her, his head cocked and red eyes burning.

She shut her mouth, breathing hard, fighting not to cry.

"Thank you, Meoraq," Scott said, turning back to his Manifestors. "I never said we don't have to try, now have I? The difference is, what I think we need to try to do is survive until we can find our way home, while Miss Bierce seems to think we need to survive until we die. *She* says there's no future. *She* says there's no hope." He paused to send her a scornful glance. "I think we're all pretty lucky you're not in charge."

"This isn't about who's in charge!" she insisted, and just as suddenly realized that, where that was concerned at least, she was dead wrong. Flustered, she looked around and saw a hundred accusing, angry eyes aimed back at her. Even Nicci's. And she guessed that shouldn't really surprise her, since Nicci had better reasons than anyone else here to think Amber was a bitch and a bully, but it still hurt. "You can't...Come on," she said, not shouting anymore but only trying to make them understand, to make Nicci understand at least. "Think what you want about me, but just...be sensible. Nothing we find out there could possibly be in better condition than this place, and just look at this place! It's falling apart!"

"Stuff still works," said Eric after a moment. "The doors open. Some of the lights come on. The bots look okay."

"Okay?" Amber pointed accusingly at the straggling commercial units that had followed them—all spitting out damaged audio feed and error messages, their dented hulls and cracked face-plates showing countless years of erosion no matter how well they'd tried to maintain themselves. "That's what you call okay? That's what you're using to prove we can power a ship up? Launch it? Navigate our way back to Earth?"

Meoraq's hand on her shoulder tightened briefly, making her realize how her voice was climbing...and quavering. Again, she quieted without conscious effort, but her attempts to catch his eye were futile. He watched Scott, only Scott, with his head still on the tilt and now his mouth very slightly open to show the glinting tips of a few teeth, but he wasn't saying anything. Why wasn't he saying anything?!

"A ship would be in a hangar," Eric said after an uneasy glance at the bots. "It'd be protected. Like the spider-things from last night. They were all okay, not even a little bit wonky. Even the bot that lived there was doing just fine."

"One of them! All the others were dead! You can't just ignore that! You can't..." She trailed off, seeing nothing in Eric's face but a flat disdain that she simply couldn't understand. He wasn't some crazy Manifestor, he was a Fleetman who'd called Scott an idiot a hundred times behind his back. He knew better than what he was saying. He knew better! "Look," she said, abandoning Eric to try and appeal to the others. "I want to go home as bad as the rest of you—"

Scott laughed loudly and several others joined in with scorn.

"—but this isn't going to happen," Amber insisted. "It's just not! It's...It's silly!"

"You're right, Bierce," Scott said, actually smiling at her. She was down, surely he had to see that, but he just couldn't resist a parting kick. "Thinking we might find a starship is just silly. Why don't you look Meoraq here in the face and tell him we're on our way to meet God? Why don't you ask Him to send us home? Hell, let's ask Him for a brain and a heart and some courage while we're at it, what do you say?"

Amber never had a chance to answer. The hand that gripped her shoulder with such strength now abruptly shoved her to one side so that Meoraq could stride furiously forward. Scott jumped back, but he wasn't quick enough. In fairness, Amber really didn't think anyone was quick enough. Meoraq snagged him by the shirtfront and yanked him close, holding him easily upright even when Scott's feet went right out from under him.

And then he tipped his head back, studying the sky with a calm and thoughtful air while Scott struggled at the end of his arm. "I do not require your belief," he said at length. "Not yours. Not hers. Not anyone's. Sheul needs no standard carried before him into battle. His will permeates all things, human. All things. So. I do not require your belief," he concluded, still speaking softly as he raised Scott up just a little higher, just a little closer to his furious dragon-like face. "But I will not tolerate your mockery. Perhaps it does not offend Sheul, but it fucking well offends me."

"I didn't mean it like that," Scott said hurriedly. "I was just trying to make a p—"

"Regardless of what you think you will find when we reach Xi'Matezh, that is where I am taking you. It is not a matter for discussion and it is certainly not a matter for you to argue over. 'But the Second Law writ was this: Lo, the Age of the Ancients is ended. Let their cities fall to ruins. Let their time pass out of memory. Let no one seek to master or remake the machines with which they poisoned Gann, lest they be corrupted in return, for such corruption shall be deemed unforgiveable.' So did God speak and so did the Prophet record and so am I, Uyane Meoraq, bound to enforce. Hear me and mark me well, *S'kot*, Xi'Matezh is the oldest of the shrines built at the hour of the Fall and there may well be machines even in that holy place, but if you seek to make yourself their master—" Meoraq brought Scott right up to his scaly face, lifting him until nothing but the very tips of his scrabbling toes touched the ground and doing it with just one hand and no suggestion of effort. "—I will draw His blade and cut you down and leave you to rot where you lie. How do you mark me?"

"Meoraq, you can't arbitrarily—"

"How do you mark me?"

"How is it a sin to use a starship if God Himself put it there for us to—"

Meoraq drew his long sword and raised it slightly, just slightly. "How do you mark me?" he asked, no louder and with no greater menace. He didn't really need it.

"I understand," said Scott.

"Do I have your obedience?"

"You've always had my full support, Meoraq. You're an invaluable resource and I'm confident we can come to some mutually respectful compromise before we reach your temple. In the meantime, you can rely upon me to direct my people to provide you with any assistance you feel you require in the course of your efforts."

Amber could see that Meoraq knew that none of that had been an enthusiastic, 'Yes, sir!' He let that be fairly obvious; he probably wanted Scott to see it, too. But there were subtler signs that suggested Scott's usual tactic of using big words in complicated ways had been once again successful and Meoraq had no clear idea of just what Scott had said at all. Amber waited tensely for the slap that precedent suggested was coming, the slap that would lead to the bellowing and apologizing, which would lead to the whispering and the dirty looks and everything that was bad already would only get worse and worse and why couldn't Meoraq *see* that?

But maybe he did, because in the end, he grunted and set Scott on the ground. "So. I consider the matter closed, and I will hear no more about it," he warned, sheathing his sword. "I will not allow you to preach at me all the way to Gedai. If I am present, you are silent."

Scott straightened out his jacket (too briskly; one of the sleeves tore a bit up at the shoulder when he tugged at the cuff, exposing the slightly deeper crimson of the other jacket he wore beneath it) and nodded once, in a commanding way. "I have to admit that I am disappointed."

"I am present," Meoraq said curtly. "You are silent. And we are leaving."

He proved it, walking away up the street without even a backwards glance to see if people obeyed them. They did, drawing off in little groups to whisper and giving him plenty of distance, but they did. Amber lingered, wanting to run after him, to walk beside him and soak in his confidence until she could wear it like a coat and let all these ugly stares just bounce off. She thought he might let her, even if he wasn't too happy about it, but she also knew how it would look. Not just like she was running off to hide under Meoraq's skirts after he'd gone waving his sword around again, but like she'd put him up to it in the first place. They might already think so—and if they didn't, Scott would have them thinking it before long—but she wasn't going to show them they were right.

"Come on, Nicci," said Amber, reaching out her hand. "The sooner we get out of here, the better things will—"

"Leave me alone," Nicci said, anger thinning her voice into a caricature of their mother's. "Just leave me alone. I'll talk to you later, but right now, I'm so sick of you that I can't even look at you!"

"Nicci—"

"I'll take care of you, Nicci!" Nicci spat, screwing up her face in a horrible sing-song sneer. "We don't have a choice, Nicci! I know what I'm doing, Nicci!" Each name was another bullet and when the chamber was empty, Nicci threw the gun. "I wish Mama was here instead of you."

And as Amber stood there, stupidly gaping, her baby sister deliberately raised her arm and slapped her in the face. The blow mostly caught her on the cheek, a little on the nose. Heat flooded her wind-chilled face. Amber didn't move.

Nicci turned around and left her. She ran to catch up with Scott (*i was going to do that wasn't i but it was meoraq i wanted meoraq i want now O god to catch his arm the way she does and have someone to walk with*) and they all walked away.

"She didn't mean it," said Amber, alone in the street. "She always comes back and we'll say we're sorry and it'll be fine."

"I have to believe that," the recording in the kiosk hissed. "I have to. I do."

Amber looked at him. The lizardman in the screen looked back at her through a haze of static. Then the image blipped once, hard, and the whole kiosk went black and silent. A thin plume of smoke rose out of the speakers and the wind took it away.

She started walking.

4

Meoraq viewed the time spent in the ruins as time lost and it took some hard driving over the next few days to make it up. Without the distraction of the ruins to stop and stare at, they moved themselves along much faster, faster even than they had moved before they had ever seen the damned place. Scott used his lies as a cattleman used a bait-stick and the humans were just as happy to trot in pursuit as any mindless beast. Truth, as long as it kept them moving at this pace and he didn't have to listen to it himself, Meoraq was content to let Scott make all the promises he liked, although he knew it upset Amber.

As it should upset him. "To let a lie stand is to speak it with your own throat." That was in the very first verse of the very first chapter in the Book of Admonitions. Meoraq could remember learning to make his letters by that self-same verse, and how his hand had cramped in the practice because he could not make them perfectly at first undertaking. And now he stood, twelve years gone in the service of Sheul, willing to close his eyes to the sin in his own camp for the false peace that masked it.

Meoraq meditated on this—once they were well-gone from the ruins and he had some leisure to do so—but an hour's prayer at his fireside with all the humans milling nearby in their clumsy, complaining way proved too much a distraction. His thoughts kept turning from the failings of his character to places he had no desire to explore: the image of the ship set in tiles on the wall; House Uyane and whether Nduman had been called home from his own circuit (or from the woman and bastard children he covertly kept) to manage its households while Meoraq took this pilgrimage; Amber throwing herself against him, frightened by the storm.

That was the image that hooked on him and he found himself opening his eyes to study her where she sat now. He thought she looked thinner. He couldn't be certain of it, but he thought so. He hadn't really paid that much attention to her body until the night she'd bathed beside his tent and cast her shadow over it...and crawled in to him afterwards...and he knew that filthy, ragged clothing such as she wore had a way of making the body beneath seem smaller, but he didn't think she looked right.

She'd had a pot of tea with him this morning before their travels, and a largish share of his cut of the gruu he'd found last night, but his share had been a spare one to begin with. Before that, there had been only bites of cuuvash for him and her both. The last real meal she'd taken had been days before coming across the ruins.

So. He would meditate later. His obligations came first.

Meoraq found his feet and beckoned to Amber. She looked at him, but did not move from her place at his fire. "Keep your people close until I return," he ordered.

She didn't ask where he was going. Neither did she take up her spear and try to join him. He wouldn't have allowed it in any case, but she didn't even try. She only bobbed her head in silence. She was watching Scott's fire, so he watched it too, but saw nothing unusual about the throng of humans that surrounded it.

A thought struck.

"Where is your N'ki?" he asked.

"Over there, somewhere." Amber turned away to prod listlessly at Meoraq's fire with a bit of burnt stick. "She's still mad at me."

He couldn't think of anything to say to that. Well, that wasn't strictly truth: He could have easily told her that Nicci was a mewling little pest whose opinion ought to matter about as much as the mud on which Amber sat, but he knew it wouldn't help.

He often found it incomprehensible that the same Amber who dared to strike him with her naked hand and shout insult into his face could be so beaten down by a single scornful glance from the wretched sack of flesh that was her blood-kin. He didn't say that either.

"Stay here," he said instead and was further troubled when she gave that same silent acquiescence, enough to say against all wisdom: "Or come with me, if you wish."

She glanced toward her spear, but touched it only with her eyes. Her head turned side to side, a human refusal, wordless. Spiritless. "I don't want to leave her."

"I'm not running you on into Gedai, just out for a short hunt. I thought you wanted to learn how," he added, trying to prick at her.

"I do, but..." She looked up at him and away. "When she comes looking for me, I need to be here."

He snorted.

She did not respond.

'She's dying,' he thought suddenly, and was alarmed to find how swiftly and completely he believed it. The flesh was not the only part of a man that could die. The soul was eternal, not immortal. Whatever circumstance had brought her here (even if that circumstance was not a flying ship from another world, which was still flatly impossible) had left deep wounds in Amber. Now Nicci was carving more, and over what?

Scott. Scott and his talk of ships in Xi'Matezh.

He could do nothing for her (although the thought of dragging Nicci out of her nest of mewling friends and slapping some respect into her was appealing on some base level) except leave without pressing her further, so he did.

The wind was strong and sharp with the first of winter's teeth. He could see rain on the horizon, but not moving this way, not yet. Still, there was a heaviness in the air that said the season's storms were in the brewing and he was not surprised the game was in hiding. Night was coming on and unless he wanted to lose himself in the open plains after dark, he needed to find something quickly. Even another patch of gruu, bitter as it had been, would be welcome. His eyes were always open, tracking without conscious direction every small sign of life the wildlands gave up, but his mind wandered. Amber. It should have been all of them—Amber wasn't the only one who hadn't had a full belly in days—but no matter how often he set the aim of his inner thoughts, they always came back to Amber.

"Sheul, O my Father, hear Your son," he muttered, his voice no louder than the wind that stirred the dead grass. Yes, he wanted God to hear him, but not the game, if there was any. "Raise up Your lamp and show me what I am meant to do. You have given me the charge of these humans and I have labored mightily in that appointment, O Father, but it is not enough. They are growing weak in my care, great Sheul. Weak in flesh and weak in spirit. Grant me Your wisdom, I pray, that I may strengthen them in turn and do Your will by them, whatever that will may be."

Sheul walked with him, he was sure, but was silent.

Meoraq kept moving, pausing often to inspect each patch of spoor, but found nothing fresh enough to follow. There might be a few rogue males about for another brace of days, too weak or too unwelcome to join their herds in their seasonal migration, but after that came the true test. After that, he must either hunt tachuqis or corrokis—one, a vicious sword-footed predator; the other, an armor-plated club-tailed behemoth. Neither were likely to be solitary at this time of year. Both were dangerous even to seasoned warriors, invariably lethal to the inexperienced. If he could just get by until he reached the mountains, there would be other game—woolly xauts and burrows filled with mimuts, just right for two to share. Even the thuochs who preyed on them were said by some to be tasty. And once over the mountains...well, Meoraq had no idea what there might be for hunting in Gedai, but it had to be better than this. It would be warming up again by the day of his return, when the herds would come back, and it would be an easy road to Xeqor, if that was how Sheul directed him. In the meantime, he was here with all his humans and they were hungry. Amber was hungry.

"Father, I've no resistance to sharing out my cuuvash," he said, crouching to investigate the long-dried track of a ghet—many ghets—in the thin layer of mud that had washed over this slice of earth in the last storm. Ghets, too, would be plentiful in the plains during the cold season. They would also be poison, in their meat and in their mouths, so if there were any nearby, he wanted to know it. "I will even share it out with all of them, although it would cost me all I have left, damn their greedy mouths, and they will be crying at me again tomorrow."

But not Amber. Her mind was so full of Scott's poison and Nicci's pettiness that she might not even feel hunger anymore. He wanted to do something for her. A full belly would be a fine start, but it ought to be more than that. He fed all the humans, regardless of personal feeling. He wanted to set Amber apart in a way that she could see, to show her that he did believe she was 'different,' that they were still 'good.'

Now if only he had some idea how to do that.

"It is a silly thing for one of Yours to trouble over, my Father," admitted Meoraq aloud. "But what strengthens the heart, strengthens the whole. So if You have no other will in this small matter, I pray You inspire me, because I haven't the dimmest spark of an idea how to make a human happy."

The wind sighed. The sense of a watching eye, a listening ear, had never been stronger outside of the arena. Meoraq grew still, straining with all his soul to receive his Father's word, but there was nothing.

So never mind humans. What did women like? Amber was a woman.

His mother had been fond of sweets, not that she'd ever said so in Meoraq's hearing, but Rasozul had almost always brought her a little pot of honey or a tin of fancies if he left the house, and she'd always received it with embarrassing enthusiasm. Meoraq still had most of the honey he'd been given in Xheoth and he didn't mind making a present of it, but it seemed wrong somehow to just hand over something he already had and wouldn't much miss. He didn't know what to do, but he wanted it to show some effort. Besides, Amber would only feed the honey to her blood-kin anyway.

If he had a better idea of where he was, he might make a run to the nearest city and find something there. More tea and cuuvash—that was only practical—and something special just for Amber. Pretty clothes? But no, she'd give them all to her Nicci and go on wearing hers to rags. What else did women like? A new wristlet, maybe; hers was rather plain.

But it was a long way to go and a great risk to take over something she couldn't really use. What he wanted was something *she* wanted. Something that would make her happy. Something...

The wind gusted again. Meoraq turned his head, just to get the sting of it out of his eyes, and there before him saw a clean saoq track in the only patch of ground nearby soft enough to take one.

He smiled. "Yes, my Father," he said. "I hear You. Necessity before desire."

He readied his kzung, put the thoughts of wristlets and fancies from his mind, and returned himself to hunting.

The tracks led him to a small pile of saoq droppings, still warm. Shortly afterwards, Meoraq had the beasts themselves in his sight, a small herd of males banded together against the coming winter. He killed two of them and they landed in their death-throes atop a cluster of lhichu...

Lhichu! The stalks of the plant were strong and supple enough to let him truss the saoqs together, but it was the roots he thought of, the roots he had been meant to see.

Sheul's hand rested briefly on Meoraq's shoulder and took itself away, but not far. Never far. Meoraq prayed his thanks and knelt to gather in his blessings.

Amber came to help when he returned with the saoqs, carrying Scott's share over to his fires and keeping the rest of the humans out of his way until Meoraq was done with the butchery. When she came back, he gave her a sabk and the offal and put her to work making the skewers that would be their own meal, and while she was busy with that, he set the two saoq heads down on a sturdy patch of ground and cracked their heads open. Then the heads went on the fire—not without some regret; the meat wouldn't be near as tender with the skull open and empty—and Meoraq put the brains in his stewing pouch with water, hot stones, and the chopped lhichu root. He mixed this into a thick paste with his hands, shook them clean, more or less, and then turned to her and said, "Take off your clothes."

Several of the nearer humans twisted around to stare at them. The one called Crandall let out a loud whooping sound and began to laugh.

"No," said Amber, plainly startled.

"Just your breeches then, at least." He unfastened his own harness and shrugged out of his tunic.

"The hell I will!"

"Please yourself," said Meoraq with a shrug of his spines. He took Amber's shoulder and shoved her firmly to the ground, then picked up one of the saoq hides and dropped it in her lap.

She let out a startled cry, trying unsuccessfully to scoot out from under it.

"Be quiet and learn something." He removed his breeches and sat down facing her wearing nothing but his loin-plate, which, being metal, was easily washed. He handed her one of the scrapers from his pack, pulled the second hide over his folded legs, and went to work. "You will find it tempting to stroke along the grain, but it is far more effective to cut against it," he told her. "Start at the neck, like this, and work your way down. Let the weight of the unfinished hide pull against your grip and keep it as taut as possible. If we had trees, I would show you how to build a frame, but that will have to wait for a future lesson. How do you mark me?"

"I'm covered in blood! Damn it, lizardman, I'll never wash this shit out!"

"I told you to take your clothes off."

She scowled at him, then picked up her scraper and hunted out the neck of the saoq's hide. Her first clumsy pass only smeared the bloody fat across the membrane, but before he could correct her, she leaned over to see what he was doing and copied it with a fair amount of success. As he'd hoped, having something to do had brought her back to life. Having something to prove would liven her even more.

"Just throw it in the fire," he said when she had her first handful of scrapings. "Try not to get blood on the cleaned area."

"You're kidding, right?"

He showed her his work. "This is what it should look like."

"How the hell are you...? Okay." She bent, yanking at the hide to try and keep it taut, and scraped harder. "Like this?"

"Keep your wrist straight and the pressure of your hand even as you stroke. Go slowly until you know how the tool wants to move in your grip."

"That sounds so dirty and you don't even realize it. You've done the whole neck already," she said, eyeing it with hot disbelief. "How are you doing that so fast?"

"Practice. This is not a contest. Mind your own work." He took a moment to roll some of his excess cleaned hide, noting as he did so that the other humans were still watching them. No one looked particularly interested in the work itself. They appeared to just be watching him and Amber...and some of them were smiling.

"You understand these people," he said crossly. "What are they staring at?"

"The guy who told me to take my clothes off."

"What does that have to do with—" He broke off and looked her, then at himself in his loin-plate only, and then at her again. Bizarrely, the first words that came from his throat were no heated denial, but merely, "What, here in front of them?"

She rolled one shoulder. "Dinner and a show."

"Is that what you thought?"

"No." Firelight could be deceptive, but her face seemed pinker than it was. "I don't know...No!"

Meoraq's spines twitched. "How can you not know what you were thinking?"

"The same way you can not know what it looks like when you start stripping and tell a girl to take her clothes off," she replied. "Nice panties, by the way."

It was a joke, although its meaning eluded him. "And when I began to cook the brains?" he inquired, pointing back at the satchel with his scraper.

"Soup."

"You thought I meant to feed you *brains*?"

"How is that more disgusting than what you always feed me?"

"Example!" he demanded, laughing through his incredulity.

"How about all the heads?" she shot back, pointing at the two in the fire.

"The head is the best part," he replied. "I save it for myself and allow you to share it."

"Okay, marrow. Marrow is horrible."

"The food of lords and abbots," he countered. "Delicious."

"Liver."

"Ah, well. Liver is good for you."

She finally gave him a smile, even if it was a pale effort. "So yeah, brain soup. Mmm-mmm, good."

He gave her a teasing hiss and went back to work on his hide. "The Book of Oyan forbids men to eat either brain or bowel, so you need never fear that particular dish be set before you. Besides which, I've put lhichu in that, which is probably poisonous."

"Put what in it?"

"Lhichu root. To preserve the hide and soften it some. These will never be quality leathers, of course, but they would be utterly unworkable without lhichu."

"Yours will be okay," she told him, tossing another handful of scrapings on the fire and taking a moment to change out the stone in the simmering brains for a hotter one.

"You don't mark me. I mean that we are merely curing these, not tanning them."

"Why not?" she asked and immediately rolled her eyes and answered, "Takes too long."

"I would not begrudge the time if you learned something from it, certainly not something as useful as tanning, but we don't have a fleshing pit. A brain-cure and smoke will be sufficient for our needs until Sheul provides the means for better."

"I didn't catch that one word. We don't have a what?"

"A fleshing pit. A lined hole or even just a basin where we would soak the raw hides in rending matter so that they could be more easily defleshed. If we tried to take the scales off without one, we would tear the hide to pieces."

"Oh, I get it." She started to scrape again, then paused and looked sharply up. "Wait, soak them in what?"

"Rending matter," he repeated patiently. "Stale urine, mostly. And various other ingredients to bate and soften skins. The hides would soak several days, depending on whether the beast has scales or hair—"

And then he realized why she'd stopped him. 'Rending matter,' he'd said, using the single dumaqi word which loosely summed up all the unpleasant materials used in the process, and that word, of course, was s'kot.

He glanced around at the other humans, but watching hides being cleaned was tedious work and they had returned to their own side of camp to watch the saoqs cook. Scott was there, too far away to hear his name in Meoraq's mouth and learn its meaning (the low part of him that heard Gann's whispers felt a short pang of disappointment), but Amber heard, Amber understood. He raised his eyes to her, braced for the eruption.

She was smiling. "You know, I always wondered why you said it like that, with that little hitch in the skuh-part."

"It seemed fitting."

"Extremely. What does human mean?"

"Eh?"

"Don't play dumb. Human. You say it weird. Like yooo-mont. What is it?"

"It refers to a kind of beetle."

"A good kind?"

"Not...particularly." And because he knew the question was inevitable, he added, "This is n'ki," as he drew a careless loop in the air with his scraper. "The form of it, you mark? The...eh...the roundness."

Her brows creased. "I don't get it. Nicci's not fat."

"I didn't need a word with true meaning. I just needed a word."

She watched him work. Her brows stayed wrinkled. "Why?"

"It is one of the laws of Sheul. The Prophet's Word is the only Word and your name cannot be spoken in dumaqi."

"Seriously? It's a sin to speak another language?"

"Not one of the unforgiveable sins," he admitted. "But even the smallest flecks of shit will eventually flavor the stew."

"Gross, Meoraq."

"Mud, then. My point is, even the smallest sins can weigh heavy with repetition." He hesitated, his hands slowing, and said, "Did you never wonder why I have never called you by your name?"

"Well...yeah." She rolled her shoulders, keeping her attention on her hide. "I figured it was just your way of telling me to keep my distance. Like when Scott calls me Miss Bierce and I call him Everly, you know?"

"No. I have never understood why either of you did that." He glanced at her, then glared fixedly at his hands and pretended to care what they were doing to the hide. "I assumed they were human endearments."

"What? No! My God, man, why would you even think that?"

Taken aback, he could only gesture with his scraper toward the other humans, attracting some attention, but only some. Scott's sermon had spread to include a larger crowd. "I thought that was what you people did."

"Why, because of Eric and Maria and all their kissy-baby talk?"

"They aren't the only ones who do that and it always seems affectionate."

"Trust me, when it's Scott, it's not us being cute. We genuinely hate each other."

Meoraq grunted, unaccountably pleased, and then looked up again. "You think I don't use your name because I hate you? I don't hate you."

"Yeah, yeah. You don't hate me." Even though she was smiling, the words struck at his Sheulek's ears as a lie. He saw her again, sprawled in the mud with her bare foot thrust through the torn bottom of her boot, shouting that he hated her, that she was nothing to him but a nuisance, or words equal to that meaning. She might smile now, but there was something in her that believed it, something he knew he was to blame for, because he didn't know what else to do but push her away...or bring her in closer.

"I don't hate you," he said.

"Okay, whatever. We can drop it now."

He should. All the good feeling that had nested in him since receiving the lhichu had dimmed to coals and he could see the shadow creeping in again over Amber. He could shut the door, find something new to talk about, and maybe it would feel the same...but he didn't think so.

"Look at me," he ordered.

She did, with exasperation and defiance, and that was so damned incredible and she was so damned ugly, it seemed to go right around the wheel of funny and turn into something heart-breaking instead.

"It is Uyane Meoraq before you," he said. "Son of Rasozul, who was son of Ta'sed, who was son of Kuuri, who was the forty-third son of the line descended of the Prophet's Uyane Xaima. I am my House, that which champions the city of Xeqor in the state of Yroq, in the hour and the land of Gann. I am the Sword and the Striding Foot of Sheul. I am all these things and I say to you, I do not hate you."

She met this declaration with a huffing breath and went back to scraping at her hide with considerably more force and less precision than before.

"You don't believe me," Meoraq realized.

"Actions speak louder than words, lizardman. Especially the ones you don't say."

"That ought to be my argument," he shot back. "Who am I sitting with right now? Who am I teaching to cure a hide? What does a name matter? And if it bothers you, why haven't you said anything until now?"

"Because I thought it was all of us!" She yanked the hide, half-done, further over her knee and went to work on the bloodier side, her arm jerking and slashing. "And then when you started saying people's names, I figured I'd be next eventually. But now I know that, thanks to your stupid God, I get to be 'Hey, you,' for the rest of my life and you don't even think there's anything wrong with that!"

"Mind your work. If it upsets you this much, I'll give you a dumaqi name." The offer was bitter in his mouth. Naming was the work of a father; he didn't always know exactly what he felt about Amber, but he knew none of those feelings were fatherly.

"I don't want a new name! I have a perfectly good name! I want you to use it!"

"It is not a word," he replied, stubbornly scraping at his hide and refusing to look at her. "It cannot be spoken."

"I speak it just fine! Amber! Say it with me, lizardman!"

"No. Mind your work."

"I am!" she snapped, but she put her glaring eyes back on the hide. "You have the most ass-backwards religion I've ever heard of. You're perfectly okay with killing people but *my name* is some huge sin. *My name* sends you straight to Hell. *That's* where you draw the line."

"The line is not for me to draw."

"Well, that's just stupid."

"There is no Word but the Prophet's Word and I am done with this discussion. Mind your work!" he snapped, pointing, but it was too late.

The scraper slipped in Amber's careless hands, narrowly missing her fingers, but cutting a gash right through the hide. Embarrassment lent new fuel to anger and she let out easily the most vulgar variation on a timeless epithet he had ever heard in all the years of his warrior's life.

"That had better not have been addressed to me," he said blackly. "My mother was a virtuous woman."

"It had nothing to do with you," she snapped, inspecting the damage to the hide with deep disgust. "I'm just a foul-mouthed bitch. Damn it, it's ruined!"

"Hardly," he said, taking it from her before she could finish shoving it off onto the ground. He arranged the hide across his own lap, going back over the places she had too hurriedly finished. "You should have stopped if you weren't going to give it your full attention. It is better to do half a hide well than all of it poorly and teach yourself habits you will have to unlearn."

She started to stand, flush-faced and tight-lipped.

He caught her by her bloody wrist and seated her again, perhaps with more force than was necessary. He did not release her right away, at first because he could see that she was just going to get up again, then because he was busy counting off six breaths, and finally because he could look at her calmly and see that beneath her senseless anger was embarrassment and unhappiness and exhaustion and everything else he had been hoping the gift of his hide-making lesson might soothe away for just one night.

He opened his mouth to tell her she was acting like a child and heard himself say instead, softly, "Do you think I would not call you by your name if I could?"

She looked at him and away, trying to pretend she was not attached to the arm that ended in his grip. "I guess you think it doesn't matter. I guess you figure as long as I still answer to 'insufferable human,' it's fine."

"It's honest, at least." He sighed, opened his hand and rubbed at his brow ridges instead. "There are three words I could call you that come close to the sound of your name. Taambret, a disease we have that causes festering sores of the mouth."

She blinked, her brows puckering.

"Mb'z, a vulgar term for one weak of mind," he continued. "Amyr, the name of a kind of swimming creature that lives and feeds in the mud. And I will not call you by these names."

"You said...You said it didn't matter what the word meant as long as—"

"Not for you."

She looked at the fire.

Meoraq picked up the scraper and continued cleaning her hide. "Take this one I have finished and make ready with the brains," he ordered. "Pour half of them out—like that, yes, in a line—and let them cool."

She obeyed, silent.

"Now use your hands to rub them in. This is why it is so essential that the hide be completely cleaned. Any fat or blood left behind will prevent the cure from absorbing well. I despise S'kot and I don't care what I call N'ki," he said, still scraping. "I will not offend God, but I will not insult you either, whether or not you know it is an insult. Any pieces of lhichu that have not softened can be disposed of now."

She picked up the chunk she had been trying to press into the hide and dropped it into the fire. She still did not look at him as she went to work, but he could see her thinking. After a few false starts, she braced herself and said, "I'm sorry I yelled at you."

The apology was as embarrassing to hear as it had plainly been to say. Meoraq acknowledged it with an uncomfortable grunt and waved vaguely at the hide under her rubbing hands.

They worked in silence, he scraping and cleaning, she rocking back and forth while her hands made endless spirals over the wet and slippery surface of the hide. He did not watch her.

"Now fold it over. Flesh to flesh," he told her, and was annoyed to feel a coiling warmth in his loins at those artless words. "By which I mean, the wet sides should press together to form a kind of seal to itself."

"Okay," she said, kneeling on the folded hide to pat it down. "Like this?"

"Fair enough. Tonight, you sleep on them. The weight and warmth of a living body helps the cure to absorb. Tomorrow, we scrape away whatever did not. We should smoke them too, but we will need good green wood for that so we will do without. Here."

She took the second finished hide and laid it out on the ground, pouring the rest of the warm brains over it without being told. "What are we making out of them?"

"I haven't decided yet."

"Oh." Her eyes tapped at his and fell away. He could see her shoulders stiffening, armoring herself as if against a blow. "I...I don't suppose maybe I could get a jacket or...you know...something?"

"Not without a fleshing pit and not with saoq in any case, but there will surely be better hides in the mountains. And when we find them, you will already know what to do. You can make your own clothes."

All of Amber's face wrinkled around in ways that meant surprise, except for her smile, which was nothing like a dumaq woman's smile and yet reminded him with great force and satisfaction of his mother receiving that little pot of jam or tin of candied blossoms and how she had looked at his father. If Meoraq had draped Amber head to foot in jewelry, he doubted he would get half the smile she gave him now for being told she could do a smelly, messy, body-breaking chore. He glanced up to send his Father another silent thanks and noticed the heavy skies all over again. "I want you to sleep in my tent tonight," he said, frowning at them.

She looked up, brains dripping down her raised arms. "What? You what?"

"It means to rain. The hides should be kept dry."

"Oh. Put them in your tent. Right." She laughed a little. "I thought you told me to sleep in there."

"I did," he said, puzzled. "If you can't mark my words, tell me so that I can repeat them. You need to sleep on the hides so that your weight and warmth—"

"In your tent?" Her face was very pink. Drops of brains fell lightly on her blood-stained thighs. "With you?"

Some great invisible hammer came clubbing down on the whole of his body, leaving him to stare foolishly back at her as if asking a woman to share his bedchamber, even if it was just a tent, had no special significance at all. How could he even say that without realizing how it could be perceived? If he'd said this to a dumaq woman—any dumaq woman—she would be bowing herself there right this moment to receive his fires.

And with this unplanned thought, the warmth in his loins became flame.

'I only want her out of the damn rain so the hides won't get wet,' he thought stubbornly. He wanted the hides to stay dry while they cured and he would admit to nothing more, but when Sheul wanted him to make leathers, He provided lhichu, and when He wanted His chosen to breed, He gave them women.

'And she is a woman, no matter what else she is,' he thought. 'A stubborn woman, an insufferable woman, a *human* woman, but a woman and when I order a woman to my room, by God and Gann, she goes!'

His head tipped warningly. "Do you not mark me?"

"I understand you just fine."

"Then you will sleep in my tent."

"Why?"

"What? Why do you think?"

She did not answer and the silence gradually stole both the edge from his voice and the urgency from his constrained member. He leaned back, scratching once, needlessly, at the side of his snout.

"Why *do* you think?" he asked finally, quietly.

"I think," she said, not meeting his eyes, "you know you can sleep on these things without me."

He looked at her without really seeing her. His mind was like the clouds, heavy without weight, in constant motion but unchanging. He did not think, exactly, but after a certain span of time, he said, "Come to my tent tonight."

She stilled, but only for an instant. "No," she said, and backed away to fold the hide over.

So. He'd not only ordered her to his tent, she had refused to go. Meoraq rubbed at the side of his snout several times, until it began to hurt. "Why not?"

She closed her eyes and just breathed. Meoraq found himself counting her breaths; a slow-count of six. She opened her eyes and raised her head just enough to look at him. "Because if it was just to get me out of the rain, you'd ask for me and Nicci."

He did not amend his offer, which was vaguely disturbing to him in the part of his mind which was still thinking.

She seemed to be waiting, and when he only sat there and said nothing more, she slowly leaned back and gathered up the saoq hide to hold loosely in her arms. "What do you want from me?" she whispered, color dull and dark in her cheeks.

"I don't know," he told her and it had to be truth, however much it felt like a lie.

"Is it..." She clapped one brain- and blood-smeared hand to her face and pushed at her eyes, then shook her head and looked right at him. "Is it sex?"

"No," he said, troubled.

The color in her cheeks deepened to an alarming shade and she looked away. "Okay." She stood up, eyes averted and too bright. "I'm going to put these in your tent."

Meoraq reached out and caught at her leg before she could flee. He rubbed his brow-ridges, cursing himself and all the words he could not make, because there was no way to tell her that it wasn't sex, it wasn't either that fierce eruptive will of Sheul or the shameful temptation of Gann, but *this*...this nameless *thing* that was neither fire nor clay but as constant as the wind, sometimes a storm and sometimes only a breeze, was *always* with him. No, it was not sex, but it had to be something that made him look for reasons to sit with her, to speak with her, even to fight with her if that was all there was, because even the most tedious and foul chore of curing a damned animal hide could become something to look forward to if he was with her. And it wasn't sex, but he wished it was; it wasn't sex, but if it had been, even that could be good, could even be *glorious*, just because it was with her.

He released her and said nothing as she carried the hides away. The wind gusted, throwing smoke into his eyes. He closed them and began silently to pray.

5

He slept on the hides alone that night. When Amber woke him for his watch, he offered her his tent again, but she refused and he did not insist. The rain came and went, rattling noisily off the metal blankets of those humans unlucky enough to have no tent, then blowing away. By dawn, the wind had mostly dried things out and there was plenty of cold saoq to pass around, but it was a cold morning and it only grew colder as the day went on.

They walked into the biting wind, moving fast to keep warm. The extra effort exhausted the humans quickly, which meant longer rest periods than usual. Amber lit a fire at each stopping place and Meoraq was generous with his reserves of tea, but still it was Scott they all clustered around—Scott with his endless talk of the ship awaiting them at Xi'Matezh and their lost Earth, as good as found once more.

They made their camp that night beside a thick copse of trees that gave them at least some shelter from the wind and enough wood to set several good fires. Meoraq's evening hunt proved fruitless, but Scott and his people still had a few bones to gnaw and Meoraq had cuuvash for himself and Amber. Afterwards, he took her to the open plains to continue her spear-training. She didn't want to, but she didn't fight back when he pulled her bodily away with him, and after a few light cuffs, she stopped trying to stare off at her Nicci and paid attention to him.

When it grew too dark to see, Amber took the first watch and set off to make her noisy patrol around the camp with renewed and entirely undeserved confidence. Meoraq occupied himself as best he could in the hopes that she would tire soon and come back to keep him company, but eventually he ran out of things to do. Alone and restless, he retreated to the edge of camp and tried to meditate, but Amber's face intruded in the stillness of his mind and her words kept creeping back: *Is it sex?*

He'd told her it was not and he thought he still believed it, but he didn't know what else to call the persistent distraction that took him every time he heard her, saw her, thought of her. It wasn't sex, or at least it wasn't the way sex had always been in his life, but it was something hot and deep and urgent beneath his skin, something he could not conquer no matter how often or how fervently he prayed. He could not in truth pretend surprise at this; a prayer must be sincerely offered to earn Sheul's ear and he could not swear that he truly wished to be free of these feelings. The Word told him there was no sin in temptation, only in surrender, but that wasn't much comfort to him as he fought night after day after night to find peace from his clay's carnality.

A boy of the warrior's caste learned the Word long before he felt any urgings of his clay, but learning a thing does not always prepare one to encounter it. Meoraq had known of sex from books, from lectures, from the whispered speculations of older boys, and of course, from that night that he had seen his pregnant mother with his father, but he had been well into his thirteenth year before he ever felt the burn in his own belly.

There had been no cause for it that first time. No woman had ever set foot in Tilev. Boys did all the work normally done by servants. Even those females who met the fires of the training masters did so in the antechambers between Tilev and the eastern garrison. So there had been no spark, only a sparring match no different from hundreds of others he had fought without incident. But this one brought out the fires in him—which had itself been happening more and more frequently that year—and they didn't go away when the match was won. And it must have been a bad win at that, because Meoraq remembered very vaguely being pulled from the beaten boy and held in half a choke by Master Takktha when it was over. Had there been a certain watchfulness in the old man's eye as he watched Meoraq struggle his way back to calm? He hadn't noticed then, but he thought so now. Once released, he had retreated from the ring to lean against the wall, still fighting those fires while they burned and flared needlessly inside him. He knew the Word, yes, and the lectures and the lessons and all of it, but sex was the furthest thing from his mind in that moment. If he'd wanted anything at all, it was to get back in the sparring ring and beat on someone until these fires either went away...or swallowed him. And so it was thinking that and kneading through his breeches at his slit, which had ached worse than a broken tooth but still somehow wanted to be touched, that Meoraq felt himself extrude for the first time.

He remembered screaming, even though he must have known intellectually what was happening to him. He screamed because of the alien thing pushing out of his own body and he screamed because it hurt to touch his breeches or even the swollen edges of his slit, but mostly he screamed because it wasn't him at all, it was Gann inside of him, and after all his years of training and all his top marks and awards, he was utterly powerless in Gann's grip.

Master Takktha cleared the arena at once. As Meoraq fell to his knees in mingled shame and shock and that first awful, baffling need, he remembered feeling the training master's hands on his shoulders and hearing that voice calm in his ear: "Breathe, Uyane. Put your hands on the ground and give me your breathing. A slow count to six, son, deep and even."

And he'd managed, somehow. His hands had been bruised for days from beating against the tiles to keep from gripping at himself, but gradually Master Takktha's voice steadied him and he began to count. By his fourth recitation, he could feel himself slowly retracting, but it had been all Meoraq could do in that time not to take that terrible thing in his fist, right there in front of Takktha and Sheul and all the world.

Of the rest of the day, he remembered little, except that he had been released from lessons to pray, and he'd had to get a real metal loin-plate from the commercer before he went back to the barracks. As he'd been undressing in the dark, the weight of his new loin-plate like a stone tied to his belly, some brunt acting as dorm-warden laughingly called out to him, asking if he'd been locked in the closet where he'd run off to rub his cock. Meoraq spent the rest of that night in a holding cell with shackles binding his aching hands. The brunt spent that night and the one following in the infirmary.

Cock-rubber. It was the worst name to call a boy, the worst thing a boy could do. Every other carnal sin spoken of in the Word could be shut out behind the walls of Tilev, but every boy was alone with his clay and the temptation of 'Gann's grip'. Some succumbed. More than half the whippings administered in Tilev were in answer to that crime. Meoraq personally knew of three boys who had been locked into their loin-plates and one who had actually been branded and exiled after exhausting all forgiveness.

Endure the flesh, said the Prophet, *do not indulge it*. What pleasure came with the act of physical union was never to be sought for its own sake, but only as a sincere exaltation of life and as Sheul's own blessing. To that end, there were no less than forty-four carnal laws written in the Word by which men could be judged, although it could not be said that all men were judged as equals. Most men were permitted none but their wife's embrace during their lifetime, but the steward of every great House had a husband's right over every woman who owed him obedience, and all those born under the Blade had liberty when Sheul gave them the fire.

Of course, one still had to see a woman to know His fires, and most of those in the warrior's caste were men like his cousin Nkosa, who might have a servant now and then to add variety to the drudgery of siring sons on his wife, but who surely could not expect to bend more than six backs beneath him in a lifetime. Meoraq might have that many in a day, if he wanted them, and have each one twice at each encounter without breaking faith.

He had been with many women in his twelve years of Striding (as Master Tsazr had said on that long-ago day, more than he could count), but what of that? He had also gone cheerfully without, not merely for days but for days by the *brace*. And while there were a few times that he could recall being aware of the lack, for the most part, he seldom thought of women at all if he were not exposed to them. He had felt Gann's lusts on occasion when traveling but never, *never* suffered from them. Then again, he had never felt them this way before—dawn to dusk to dawn again, every hour almost unceasing. It was more than temptation; it was torture.

The endless wind dropped to no more than a breeze, catching some human's low moan in its sudden silence. Maria, he thought, stubbornly refusing to open his eyes and see. Maria and her man, her Eric, shut away in their silly little tube of a tent. Doing whatever it was that humans did when they were mating. He was not listening. He did not care. Someday, long years hence, when he was in some distant city after conquest or (just perhaps) home in Xeqor as steward to his House, he might think of this moment as he gripped at the bent back of a true woman, a normal woman, one obedient and respectful in her manner, who knew to bend her neck to a Sheulek's whim and show some damned appreciation for it. A pretty woman, while he was at it, or at least not one with flesh like warm putty and hair sprouting everywhere and a face that looked like she'd been using it to beat her way through a brick wall. A proper woman who would never raise her eyes to him, much less her voice. A mewling, bowing, milk-veined woman...but it was Amber he wanted tonight.

Meoraq hissed to himself, stubbornly ignoring the ache and throb behind his loin-plate. He tried to meditate, counting breaths in the dark.

Never mind. Regardless of the wife he would be given when and if he returned from Xi'Matezh, he was Sheulek now. He was the master of his clay at every hour and in every temptation. He was Uyane Meoraq, a Sword and a true son of Sheul, and no slave to the lure of any female. He was his own man, and even if one were to drop this instant at his feet—

A heavy body struck up against his back and, with a sharp cry and a failed grasping hand, Amber tumbled over his shoulder and landed heavily half in and half out of his lap. Her knee knocked him in the snout as she thrashed to right herself. He swore, grabbing at her with one hand and his injured face with the other, and heaved her off onto the ground. "Mind where you put your feet, damn it!"

"Don't yell at me! What the hell are you doing, sitting in the middle of...of..."

"Of the *ground*?" he suggested. "Where else should I be sitting, eh? In the sky? What are you doing walking about in the dark anyway?"

"I couldn't see you," she grumbled, righting herself and rubbing at her knee.

"Then carry a lamp. Where are you going?"

"Scott has all the flashlights and he never lets me have one. And I still say you should be in your tent and not lurking around where people can trip over you. Aren't you supposed to be lying on those hides anyway? Tell me I didn't carry one all day so you could ignore it."

"If it bothers you, go to my tent and lie on them," he countered, and felt with bitter triumph the immediate throbbing of his slit. "A Sheulek goes where he will, asks what he will, and sits where he will. Now, and for the third time, where are you going at Gann's hour, insufferable human?"

"I'm on watch! I was watching things!" She stopped there, perhaps in deference to the few raised voices protesting this interruption to their sleep, then heaved a sigh at him and punched her hands onto her hips. "I thought I heard something, that's all. I wasn't going anywhere."

Meoraq's frustration sharpened itself at once to a ready point. He put a hand on his kzung and stood up fast, peering into the dark in all directions.

"Relax," said Amber. "It turned out to be nothing but a bad mood with a lizardman attached. Go to bed, Meoraq. I'm getting you up in a few hours."

She stomped away without his word of release, muttering to herself and leaving Meoraq to count his breaths and silently beseech his soul's divine Father to give him either some measure of mastery over the lust that was once again throbbing behind his loin-plate, or mastery over the temper he was forever losing to these fits of human incivility. Where did she get the nerve to speak to him like that in the first place? To give him orders?! He was Sheulek, damn it, and she was...she was...

She was a woman, was what she was. She was a woman in his camp and beholden to him for the protection he provided, just as any woman of any city he had entered as conqueror. She owed him her respectful obedience and if he ordered her to bend her back, she—

Her neck, he amended in some distraction. Bend her neck. This was a matter of disrespect and whatever else he wanted (*Is it sex?* she asked, the first time he had ever heard the word spoken aloud by any woman. *Is it sex?* and she'd been looking right at him) was nothing but an ordeal of this pilgrimage to be endured and defeated. Until then, Amber—along with all the rest of her people—would bend her neck and give obedience to the master of this camp and that was all, *all*, he wanted from her.

He was Sheulek. Truth was his bloodright. He knew a lie when he heard one spoken. He knew a lie when he spoke it himself.

Cursing, Meoraq got up and stalked into his tent. He fastened it against the wind and against the soft sound of Amber's footsteps as she made her clumsy patrol. Then he lay down on the damned hides, fully dressed and aching behind his loin-plate, and pressed both hands to his brows. "O Sheul my Father, look down and see Your son in suffering," he muttered. "As clay is made hard by the fires, so do I ask that my weak flesh be tempered and made fast against the wickedness of Gann. I cannot stand alone against sin, my Father, no more than clay may hold its form unfired."

Fire, fire, and fire again. Where was his mind? Meoraq hissed through his teeth at the top of his tent and began again, the Supplication this time.

"Great Sheul, O my Father, behold Your son in the hour of Gann. I am the unformed clay upon Your wheel. I am the untempered sword at Your forge. I am the unlit lamp without Your fire at my heart. Shape me, temper me, illuminate me."

It was not immediate, but as the ache in his loins subsided, peace overtook his troubled mind at last. He lost himself gradually in meditation, slipping in and out of memory, undisturbed now by the soft sounds that sometimes escaped the tent where humans lay together in what little privacy they had and vaguely proud of how undisturbed he was.

'I wouldn't be, if it was Amber in one of those tents,' he thought suddenly, and that was all it took to break his peace.

It was a long night and a bitterly cold one, and Uyane Meoraq knew no rest.

* * *

Amber woke up cold. That was nothing new, but this time, it wasn't because it was raining and the water had leaked in or her blanket had come loose. No, she was dry and tightly wrapped, just cold. And odds were good it was only going to get colder.

'Should have slept in Meoraq's tent,' she thought drowsily. She'd certainly done herself no good by sleeping out here. Nicci had come back to her usual place at Amber's side, but her only response to Amber's attempts at talk had been, "Unless you're ready to apologize, I'm not interested," to which there might have been a thousand diplomatic replies, but Amber had gone with, "Okay, I'm sorry you're such an idiot that you believe Scott can pull a starship out of his ass," and they'd both gone to bed angry.

Nicci was probably awake right now, thought Amber as she stared at the unmoving tuft of blonde hair that protruded from Nicci's blanket, but if so, she was pretending to be asleep so she wouldn't have to talk. And Amber was fine with that. Maybe later, she'd try again to patch things up, but the world didn't care if Nicci's feelings got hurt over a non-existent skyport and right now, neither did Amber.

She got up, scrunching her blanket down into her duffel and pulling out a fresher shirt to put on over the top of the two she was already wearing. That cut the chill to a tolerable level, but it left her duffel bag with nothing in it except her blanket and the one untouched Manifestor's shirt she had left. The practical part of her knew it was just stupid not to wear it when it was cold like this—the damn thing wouldn't fit right anyway—but stupid or not, as long as it sat folded up and brilliantly white in the bottom of her duffel bag, she felt like she had something in reserve. Once she was wearing it, she had nothing.

So today, like every day, Amber zipped it up where it would stay clean and neat, and told herself it wasn't that cold yet and she'd be fine for one more day. Today, she could also tell herself that when they reached the mountains, there would be another lesson in how to make hides, and maybe clothes. They'd look like shit, she was sure, but even the worst-looking leathers were going to feel wonderfully warm. Maybe the animals in the mountains would even be furry. If nothing else, she could make a blanket.

Meoraq was hunched by his fire when she looked for him, working on something. He grunted a greeting as she approached, and gestured at the ground beside him. When she sat down, he lifted a leathery mass out of his lap and dropped it into hers. "You can finish this," he said, heaving himself onto his feet for a bone-creaking stretch.

'This' was a pack, smaller than her duffel bag and designed after his own back-pack. He had done all the necessary cutting and stitching already, and was mid-way through sealing the seams with the same smelly gunk she'd used on her boots. Amber found the jar and picked up where he'd left off, trying very hard not to feel cheated.

"I wish you'd waited until I could watch you do this," she said finally.

"So that you could make your own," he agreed, watching her work. "But this one is yours and it should last several years, so there seemed no reason to teach you."

"Mine?" It wasn't entirely unexpected, but she wasn't comfortable accepting it either. As a kind of compromise, halfway between thanks and protests, she said, "My bag's still all right."

He wasn't fooled. "Did I ask if you wanted it? I said it was yours. Insufferable human. Hold." He stretched again, then ducked into his tent. He came out with what appeared to be an armload of grass bundles. Each one was roughly the length and thickness of her arm; lashed together, with the second saoq hide stretched over the top, they formed a mat that Meoraq unrolled to an impressive length.

"Good God, you were busy," she said, capping the resin-seal to touch the mat. "What did you use to wrap them together like this?"

"Lhichu stalks, split and soaked."

"Really? And that'll hold for...?"

"Eh." His spines shrugged. "Travel and hard use will wear them down in a brace or two. Fortunately, there's plenty of grass in Gann's world, and the hide itself will last you for years, once you're done preparing it. Take this."

She reached for the small pouch he held out to her, but drew back with a start as she realized what he'd said. "Hang on, last me for years? You can't give this to me too!"

"You sound very sure."

With a growing sense of unease—because unease sounded so much prettier than panic—Amber looked around. People were waking up and the sight of a bed, even a little roll-up job like this one, had everyone's attention. "Meoraq," she said softly, urgently, while she still had a chance of saying anything privately. "This has to be yours, okay?"

He continued to hold the pouch out. "I have one."

"This is going to make all kinds of trouble, you have no idea."

He bent down and slapped the pouch into her hand. "It was inconvenient for me to wait until you were awake to assemble your pack, so I proofed it myself, but it is for you to prepare your mat. Yours, I say. I have no interest in arguing with you, so we will pretend that you fought bitterly against it until I forced your obedience. Now pay attention."

She gave up, picking unhappily at the simple drawstrings to open the pouch. "Okay," she said, shaking out the hard, oily block it contained. "What is it and what am I doing with it?"

"Proofing wax, and you are going to rub it over the surface of your mat—"

"I really wish you wouldn't call it that."

He thumped her hard on the head. "Don't interrupt me. The proof has no color. If it leaves a residue, you are using too much. Use your hand to thin it out if that happens. How do you mark me?"

"It goes on clear." She gave the bottom corner a rub and frowned at the nothing it left on the saoq's scales. "How will I know I got the whole thing if I can't see it?"

"It has a shine."

"Oh." She rubbed a little more. "Okay, I see it now."

"Two layers," he warned her. "Don't rush. Give it a chance to rest between layers." He glanced behind him. "Take my tent down and fill the flasks while you wait."

"And what will you be doing?"

"Watching you take down my tent and fill the flasks."

"I see."

"Finish sealing your pack first. The mat can rest as we walk, but your pack needs to dry before we move on. There's tea in the pot if you want to finish it. If not, rinse it and my cup and pack them away. Will you wear my spare tunic?"

"No."

"So be it. I will not make it my order yet. What do you want?"

Amber looked up and there was Nicci, with a small crowd of Manifestors watching from a resentful distance. Her stomach tightened. She put the wax down on the mat—on her mat—and started painting sealant onto her pack's stitches again.

"Nothing," said Nicci. "I'm just talking to my sister."

Meoraq looked at her, then at Amber. He grunted and began to fuss with his many belts, making entirely unnecessary adjustments and glaring at both of them.

"Hey," said Nicci. She sat down on the mat. "Wow."

Amber's stomach clenched tighter, but she made her mouth smile. She didn't feel it and doubted she looked it, but she had to give Nicci the benefit of the doubt. They were sisters. "That nice, huh?"

"It's amazing how much difference it makes." Nicci ran her hands over the hide, making a twin rasping sound. She smiled. "Remember our old beds?"

"Yeah."

"You were always so uptight about having pillow cases on the pillows and clean sheets every week. Yours and mine. Always taking care of things." Nicci thought about it and shook her head. "I remember once you woke me up and made me change the sheets at, like, two in the morning."

"I did?"

Nicci nodded, still stroking the mat.

"I don't remember that."

"It was a long time ago. In the Holland Mills apartment. We were still sleeping with Mama."

Holland Mills...She couldn't have been more than eight. "Are you sure I wasn't changing the bed because she puked in it?"

"I guess she could have. I don't remember that part, just you waking me up and making me move. You could be a bitch sometimes, even then." Nicci ducked her head and gave her a crooked smile through a curtain of dirty hair. Her cute smile. Bo Peep's smile. "I guess it's been my turn lately, huh?"

Meoraq, boldly watching all this, said, "Yes."

Nicci's back stiffened. She threw him another of Bo Peep's looks—the haughty fuck-you one—and wiggled around on the mat so that her back was fully to him.

Amber said nothing, just painted more resin on the seams of her pack.

"I know you've been trying to make up. I'm really sorry I've been so snotty."

'I'll bet,' thought Amber, and wished she believed she'd still be hearing this even if Nicci wasn't sitting on that fucking mat. "It's okay."

"So we're good?"

Meoraq opened his mouth and hissed silently at the back of Nicci's head.

"We're good," said Amber, glaring at him. "Don't you have some hunting to do or something?"

"No."

"Can you at least go lurk somewhere else?"

"No."

"This is really nice." Nicci petted the mat's scaly top a few more times, all her attention on her hands. It looked even less natural and casual than before. "Maybe we can share it. We could take turns. Like, you could have it every other night."

Amber turned the pack and continued painting, feeling Meoraq's eyes like honest-to-God coals on her face.

"Or you know what? Since I always go to bed earlier than you, maybe I could get it for the first part of every night and you could wake me up."

This, not even five minutes after telling her how Amber had woken her up in the middle of the night when she'd been, what? Four? Three? But she'd remembered it all these years so that she could use it now as proof that Amber had always been a bitch. Still, she hesitated, and in that hesitation, Meoraq slapped a fuel-bundle down into the fire hard enough to blow out sparks and ash, and stood up.

"No," he said, advancing on Nicci with his head so far on one side that it looked like he'd gone and hung himself in the night. "It belongs to *me* and if she will not have it, I will take it back!"

Nicci shrank down a little, but only a little. She hadn't scooted back off the mat. She hadn't even stopped petting it. She just waited, avoiding his eyes and pretending the touch of saoq scales was the most fascinating and hypnotic touch in the whole world.

"I know how to make them," said Amber. "Meoraq can get some more of the roots before we leave today and the next time we get a saoq, I'll help you make your own, okay?"

Meoraq spat at the fire and kicked one of the burning bundles of grass.

Nicci petted the mat.

"Okay?" Amber said again. "I don't know where they are, Meoraq, or even what they look like! Please?"

"You can make another one," said Nicci. "And I can use this one, okay?"

Meoraq glared at her.

Nicci ignored him, but at least looked up at Amber. Her eyes were big and her smile, small and fragile. "Okay?"

'Little girl,' said the ghost of Bo Peep, laughing her drunk ass off in the back of Amber's mind, 'you are being played.'

Yeah, so what else was new? They were making up, and however it happened, that was a good thing, right?

'You call this making up?' Bo Peep inquired, smirking. 'Do you really? Because I admit things have gotten a bit fuzzy since I died, but I'm pretty sure that's usually called being bent over and fucked.'

No. They were sisters. Nicci loved her.

'I loved people too. When they paid me. You selling, little girl?'

"No," she said.

Meoraq's head tipped slightly back and his spines twitched forward.

Nicci looked at him—a flustered, accusing stare, which he shrugged back at her with a singularly spiteful grimace—and then at Amber. "W-What?"

"No," Amber said again, to Nicci this time. "You can make your own. I'll help you, but I'm not doing it for you."

"How is that fair?" Nicci demanded shrilly. "You're a total hypocrite, you know that? You didn't make that! He gave it to you! And everyone knows why!"

"Oh?" Meoraq's spines rose a bit higher. "Why?"

Nicci looked at him, hesitated, then swung back on Amber. "Why do you always have to be such a bitch? All I'm asking you to do is share!"

"Yeah, share. You sleep in it and I carry it. Is that about right?"

Nicci burst into noisy tears and clapped her hands over her eyes. Her dry eyes, whispered Bo Peep. "You said you'd take care of me!"

"I am," said Amber. Her stomach cramped and rolled, but she made herself pick up the resin and go on sealing seams like nothing was wrong. "But it's time for you to start meeting me halfway, Nicci."

"You owe me! This is all your fault!"

"Lies," said Meoraq, folding his arms.

"You stay out of this!"

"It is a lie," Amber said. "And I'm getting awfully goddamned tired of hearing it. Maybe I did put you on the ship, but I didn't crash it. If you want to be a victim for the rest of your life, you go right ahead, but I'm done taking your blame. I'll teach you how to make a mat like this if you want, but you better be sure you really want it, because I'm not carrying it for you."

"I hate you!" Nicci shouted, scrambling to her feet.

"Grow up," said Amber, painting resin onto the last bit of stitching.

Nicci stood over her, silent except for her harsh, angry breaths, and when Amber finished her pack and picked up the pouch with Meoraq's little brick of proofing wax, Nicci abruptly turned on Meoraq. "You made her say that!"

"I would love to think it true," he replied evenly, and left.

Nicci stumbled after him, her mouth working, and finally screamed, "Lizard!" at his retreating back.

He stopped walking. His head cocked. He thought about it.

When he turned around, Nicci tripped over Amber's mat backing up and fell sprawling. Amber reached for her hand, but Scott somehow got the other one, catching her between them like a tug-O-war rope. A sudden pop from the fire (*O god her arm i pulled her arm off*) made Amber let go, and Nicci spilled onto Scott's leg and hugged on tight, babbling apologies that even Amber couldn't fully understand.

Meoraq went past her without a word and into his tent. A moment later, he was out again, hanging his little metal flask around his neck.

"This is my third gift to you in a single day," he said without looking at her. "A pack, a bed, and a reprieve for your blood-kin's beating."

'And everyone knows why.'

"Thank you," she whispered. "Will you...Will you please...?"

"I'll gather the lhichu. But I won't give it to you. She'll have it when she asks my forgiveness and if that means she never has it, so be it."

Nicci could probably hear him, but she did not react, except with sniffling. Scott helped her stand up, patting her shoulder and murmuring. She looked so wounded as she stood there under his arm, so little and bruised, and so goddamn much like their mother that Amber wanted to throw up. Fighting that urge meant squeezing the bar of proofing wax hard enough to leave finger-shaped impressions along the edge.

Their eyes met—Amber's and Nicci's—with half a camp and whole worlds between them. This time, Amber supposed she was the one who looked like their mother, the Bo Peep who wasn't playing for sympathy, the Bo Peep who had none. "You better say you're sorry when he gets back. And you better act like it too, at least as well as you act like a fucking baby."

"Hey now," someone said in a startled voice, and someone else, one of the ladies, said, "Hey nothing. We need him. She's lucky *I* didn't smack her."

"Amber!"

"Go somewhere else for a while." Amber made her first savage swipe of wax across the mat. It took a surprising amount of force, but the violence struck a satisfying resonance down in the Bo Peep part of her. "I love you, Nicci, but I don't want to talk to you right now."

Beneath the wind and the rasp of wax scraping over scales, she could hear Scott telling Nicci that she didn't have to grovel for Meoraq's amusement, that if their guide insisted on an unfair dispensation of resources, she could always come stay in his tent, and furthermore, if Amber was going to insist on fomenting a hostile environment within the confines of his camp, she might just find out that she wasn't welcome on the ship when they reached the skyport.

"Why don't I just fly a pig home?" Amber snapped, shoving harder. The wax left whitish smears across the top of the hide and she had to stop and wipe them away. "I declare there will be a pen full of flying space-pigs. You're right, Scott. That's so much easier than facing reality."

Scott's jaw tightened, but it was Nicci who balled up her fists.

Amber stopped waxing and glared up at her through the hanging tangle of her hair. "You don't want to mess with me right now," she said flatly.

Nicci faltered to a stop, hesitated, and then clapped her hands over her eyes and cried, "I wish you'd just let me stay home!"

"So do I," said Amber. "Shut up, Nicci. I mean it. Unless you're really crying, you shut the fuck up."

Nicci stared at her, pale and silent. Her eyes were dry and open wide. She shivered. Amber didn't. The wind was cold. Amber, it seemed, was colder.

Slowly, Nicci turned around and stumbled away, either back to Scott or back to her friends from the Resource Tent. Amber didn't really care at the moment. She bent her neck and went back to work. Her arms began to hurt. She worked harder. She worked until that was all she could feel.

6

Days. Nights. Wind and rain and walking. They left even the shadow of the ruins on the horizon to make their way through a dense, swampy thicket. Three days later, they left that behind to climb a steep, stony incline onto a crumbling stretch of what Meoraq called a road. They followed that another three days before Meoraq herded them off it and east again, back into the plains, which were growing increasingly hillier.

The only animals they saw in all that time was a single group of corrokis lumbering south, which Meoraq had led them cautiously around, downwind and at such a distance that the car-sized monsters blurred into an uncountable blob. There were no more saoqs, although Amber occasionally glimpsed old spoor that proved they had passed through. The streams, swollen by all the rain, held no eel-things, only frothy, storm-clotted water. When he went hunting, he brought back only bitter leaves and tough roots to eat, and he had a tendency to slap the people who complained about it.

She could understand his frustration, even though she wished he could find another way to express it. But he shouldn't have to do everything himself. Once she felt confident enough about identifying these edible, if unappetizing, food sources, Amber began to forage for them as they walked. Meoraq did not comment, except to drop back now and then to point out some new kind of plant as they passed it. Even with his coaching, she didn't manage to fill her pack very often, and what she had didn't go far, but she made sure Nicci had something every night even if no one else did.

And Nicci thanked her, sometimes. They had both said some sorries in the last few days, but sorry was a piss-poor bandage for the other things they'd said, and the things they still weren't saying. It wasn't the same as it had been and probably never would be, but at least they were talking again. They walked together during the daytime, unless Scott was giving one of his inspirational skyport-themed speeches or the ladies from the Resource Tent were having a gossip-fest. After they stopped for the day and Amber got done filling flasks, lighting fires and putting up Meoraq's tent (her chores, she thought of them now, and Meoraq probably thought of them the same way because he didn't bother telling her to do them anymore), Nicci would come and keep her company, at least until the food was gone. And every night, as Amber took the first watch, Nicci used the mat. Amber didn't always wake her when her shift was over, but she usually did. Sometimes Nicci cried a little when she had to move off onto the cold, rocky ground, but not if Meoraq was close enough to hear her. He was still carrying the lhichu root he'd gathered; Nicci had not apologized, had not said one word to him, refused to even look at him when he was talking. So it was better...but it was still pretty bad.

Meoraq was unfamiliar with the silent treatment and day by day, his tolerance for it thinned. He spent a lot of time now just staring at Nicci with his spines flat when he thought no one was watching and then staring at Amber the same way. She didn't know what to tell him, but "Go ahead and hit her," was what she thought the most often, which only made her feel worse.

It couldn't go on like this. Scott, Nicci, Meoraq, Amber herself—everything and everyone was a thread away from snapping.

But for right now, she didn't have to worry about that. Right now, it was the middle of the night in the middle of nowhere and Amber was alone, standing her watch.

Tonight, she was standing her watch while sitting down, sacrificing her ass to the damp that was always in the ground these days so that she could huddle up over her folded arms and folded legs and conserve what little heat her body was putting out these days. She'd tried sitting on a rock for a while, but discovered that cold rocks never warmed up no matter how long you sat there and were full of jagged bumps and corners besides. Nicci was using the mat, so Amber moved to the grass off on the edge of camp, which was wet, but at least provided some padding between her and the hard earth. It had been years since she'd last been able to fold herself Indian-style on the floor, but she didn't think of that yet. All she thought about was how cold it was getting, how wet her ass was, and how both her feet had gone to sleep some time ago and were going to wake up with that pins-and-needles thing. Meoraq would not approve of sitting, she was sure, but Meoraq did not appear to feel the cold as much as she did and he was asleep anyway, so the hell with his approval.

It was a dark night. Now and then, the clouds thinned enough for her to see a faint grey glow where this world's moon hung, but it didn't put out enough light even then for her to see anything. It would be a crescent of a moon, she thought. A mere sliver. And then that was all she could think of for a while: Earth's moon, as curved and slender as a drawn bow in the night sky. They couldn't ever see many stars in the city where they grew up, but the moon was still there. More yellowish-red than white, but that was the city's fault, not the moon's.

She was never going to see that moon again.

She may never see *any* moon again.

Amber brushed at her eyes and sure enough, they were wet. What a pussy she was turning into. Whatever happened to the old Amber, the tough Amber, the Amber who never let anything in? Who was this pathetic little orphan huddled in the wet grass crying over the memory of a friggin' moon?

The wind changed course and gusted suddenly right in her face. She shut her eyes and bent her neck and leaned into it, dimly aware that Meoraq wouldn't approve of standing her watch with her eyes closed either, but who could keep them open? It wasn't like air at all when it got this cold, it was more like whips. Frozen whips. It was actually cutting into people now. When she looked at the faces around her during the day, she saw cracked lips and purple-red roses scraped into every nose and every cheek. She knew she looked the same; when she touched her face, she could actually feel the chapped rash the wind was growing on her.

She unfolded her legs, grimacing as blood rushed into her sleeping feet and woke them up. The lie of thick warmth that had cloaked them until now melted out and the pins took its place. Agony. Amber kept her jaws clenched tight and did not make a sound. Tough Amber. As Meoraq was so fond of saying, she was a master over her clay.

The pins and needles had their way, but when they were finally reduced to sullen stabs and that weak, watery feeling, she rolled herself onto her knees and up, using her spear for a crutch. There, she had to stand, waiting for the last of the weakness to pass before she started walking. At least she could turn her back on the wind.

And look at their camp. God. She knew they had almost fifty people, but couldn't count more than a dozen between the dark sky and the low coals of their fire. And the ones she could count were just lumps sprawled out on the ground like corpses. Oh, and Commander Scott, of course, hidden away in his tent where the wind could blow all it wanted and never touch him. A living blueprint for how to build an asshole, as her own mother used to say. Pearls of wisdom from Bo Peep Bierce.

The second suckerpunch of homesickness hit her and this time, she pressed the heel of her hand into her eyes, first one and then the other, not wiping at her tears as much as shoving them back in. The real Amber would never go blubbering all over herself over her mother, who, she reminded herself brutally, she'd had to pick up off the floor and carry to bed damn near every night for the last three years, with Bo Peep puking up cheap booze and drunken rants the whole way.

Amber started walking, using her spear as both a probe and a cane to navigate around the stony ground as she circled the camp. Patrolling. She made it about halfway before she discovered that walking around after sitting down for long periods of time had an inevitable effect on one's bladder, so she veered away from camp and went out into the plains.

'And here I am,' she thought disgustedly as she crouched down in the dead grass about fifty paces away. 'Amber Bierce, Space Adventurer. I would sell Scott's immortal soul for a single roll of toilet paper.'

The wind shook whatever unseen trees were close by extra hard and then finally died away a little. Amber pulled her pants up, tucking her spear between her shoulder and her chin like an oversized phone so she could tie her excess underwear off and tighten Meoraq's belt around her waist...and then paused and looked around.

Sounded like the trees were still shaking. Not a lot. Not at all anymore in fact. But it had definitely lasted longer than the wind.

Come to think of it...what trees? They'd made their fire tonight out of dead grass and dried corroki dung. She knew because she remembered so vividly the colorful comments of those who'd watched her carry the stiff patties into camp. The nearest trees had been dark smudges in the distance.

But if it wasn't wind in the trees...what was it?

Grass whispered on her left, and sure, that could be the wind, but there was something about the way it was whispering that raised the fine hairs on her arms to prickles. It wasn't one long whoooooosh but more of a wa-whoosh wa-whoosh.

Like footsteps.

Amber got her spear in her hand and backed up, promptly kicking her heel into a protruding stone and nearly going down on her butt. She recovered, but heard quite clearly a low and oddly bony-sounding clicking or tapping sound, this time on her right.

'Don't run,' she thought, even as her body tensed to do just that. 'You don't hear them very well. They might not hear you very well. They might not see you any better than you see them either. If you run, that's all over.'

Good advice. She had the best fucking advice at the worst possible times.

She walked, forcing herself to test her footing and cringing at each damp slap of grass hitting her legs. Her spear felt at once huge and weightless where she gripped it; she had a feeling that would change if she ever actually had to use it. The wind gusted again, once more right in her face. The sound of it roaring in her ears overwhelmed any little noise the...the whatever-they-were made in their pursuit. If they pursued. If they were walking this way at all.

But why wouldn't they, for Christ's sake? There was the fire! And as tiny as it was, it was still the only fire out here! The only light of any kind! She was following it, why wouldn't they?

She ran—yes, now a run, and if she hooked her foot on one of these rocks, she had no one to blame when she tripped and broke her head open—and slapped at the taut wall of Meoraq's teepee in what she hoped did not sound like the panic it sure felt like.

"I need you," she said loudly. Over her shoulder, even louder: "Nicci, get up."

Nicci squirmed under her blanket, but she raised her head, along with several other people. "Hunh? Why?"

Before Amber could answer, the flap of Meoraq's tent twitched once and was thrown open. An entirely naked lizardman burst out of it with his breeches in one hand

and his hooked sword in the other. “What is it?”

“I heard something,” Amber stammered, trying without success not to look at the featureless mound between his legs. Entirely naked. “I didn’t see anything, but—”

“Where?” he asked crisply, managing not only to step into his breeches and pull them up while walking, but also not letting go of his sword while he did it.

She pointed, saying, “I thought there were footsteps, too. I could have been mistaken about those, but I’m sure about the clicks.”

He cinched his belt and buckled it, tipping his head at her in that way that rather urgently demanded more information as opposed to just wanting it.

She clicked her tongue at him a little, and then shook her head because it was all wrong. “Like that, but not really. It was...I don’t know, bigger. Harder.”

One of the many people coming over to listen suddenly laughed and said, “What?” as several others sniggered.

“Oh grow up!” she snapped, and Meoraq reached out and caught her chin, jerking her firmly back to face him. “It was...I don’t know how to describe it. It was harder. Like...Like rock or maybe wood. It sounded...hollow.”

He released her at once and drew the other sword. “Stay here,” he told her curtly. “Get your people up and move them together. Build up the fire. Go.”

Barefoot, he ran agile as a deer over mud and around rocks and was gone.

“All right, you heard the man,” said Amber, wondering just what in hell she was feeling. It was relief, she decided. Relief that she’d done her job and now someone else knew what to do and was doing it. It had nothing to do with seeing the lizardman naked. “Everybody better wake up.”

“We’re not your people,” said Crandall, glaring at her even as he moved closer to the fire. “So fuck you, scale-bait.”

“What’s going on?” someone called. Maria, maybe, because it was Eric’s voice that answered, muttering, “Bierce is stirring things up again. It’s nothing, just come on over here for a few minutes.”

“Did she see something?”

“No,” Crandall answered loudly. “Someone saw her coming out of the lizard’s tent, so she’s acting like she was going to get him or something.”

“What were you doing in his tent?” Nicci asked.

“I wasn’t in his tent!”

“And he was bare-scaly-ass naked,” Crandall inserted meaningfully, tossing a few grass-bundles onto the fire. Burning ash puffed out and fresh flames caught, turning his smirk into a red-tinted leer. “So draw your own conclusions.”

Nicci’s puzzled frown became a gape.

“Oh for Christ’s—That’s not what we were doing!”

“What were you doing?” Nicci asked in a low voice.

“We weren’t doing anything!” Amber shouted.

Nicci’s dubious expression did not change.

“Get up,” Amber ordered, coming over to catch her little sister’s arm. “Go over by the—”

A beam of light hit Amber in the eyes. A moment later, Scott’s most commandingly pompous voice rolled out: “Is this your idea of a joke, Miss Bierce?”

She’d raised a hand against the glare of the flashlight. Now she lowered it, clenching it into a fist. She looked at him and then beyond him to all of them, so angry she couldn’t seem to pull a single face into focus. They were just a crowd. A staring, smirking, hostile crowd.

“Okay, everybody calm down,” Scott was saying. “Just go back to bed. We’ll sort this out in the—”

Something just out of sight in the plains let out a piercing shriek. Meoraq roared back, almost completely unheard beneath the commotion of people leaping up, scrambling back, grabbing each other and screaming.

"Stand together!" Amber shouted over the top of it. "Whatever you do, don't panic! Make the fire bigger! Burn everything! Give me that," she finished, snatching the flashlight out of Scott's hand. The sound of something big thrashing and shrieking was dead ahead of her, but Meoraq clearly had that one. In the plains, she'd heard two.

"I didn't say you could have that!" Scott said shrilly as she moved out into the plains. He backed up toward the fire, looked around to see everyone else already there and watching him, and then came after her. "Give it back! That's stealing!"

She ignored him and ran as fast as she dared in the dark, completely unaware that he was running after her until she stopped to shine the light around and he snatched it out of her hand.

"There is no place in this colony for thievery!" he announced as she gaped at him. "Or for selfish, small-minded people who have hysterics to get attention!"

"This is not the time for this, goddammit!" she hissed. "How stupid are you to pick a fucking fight right now? Give me that and go back to the others!"

She made a grab for the flashlight.

He hit her with it.

She didn't see it coming until it was too late. Even when he drew back his arm, she thought he was just being his usual snotty self and playing a grossly mistimed game of keep-away when in fact he was winding up for his swing. Impact came as a sensation of amazing heat all down the left side of her face and a ringing in her head. Through that, she heard a cracking sound—*my skull O god he broke my skull open*—and felt an insignificant little burn across her ear.

She went down with a caw, arms and legs outflung in shock, executing a near-perfect belly flop right on the ground. Rocks caught her at the hip, thigh, left arm, and the mother of them all in the stomach. She rolled onto her side, choking and grabbing at her middle with one arm, clutching at the side of her head with the other, terrified that she would feel the hot jelly of her own brains squeezing up through her fingers. But there was nothing, nothing but hair.

Scott was looking into the broken head of the flashlight. It was still shining, but the face-cap had cracked and the lens was missing, which made the light dimmer as it underlit Scott's frowning face. "You broke it," he said accusingly, as something huge slipped out of the blackness behind him and into the beam of that weak, yellow light.

She wanted to call it an ostrich, because that was the only frame of reference her stunned brain had to give her, but it bore no more true resemblance to one than a saoq to a deer or a corroki to an armadillo. She wasn't even sure she could call it a bird. What her eyes wanted to perceive as feathers clearly weren't; what it had were flat, wedge-shaped plates thrust out from its body, rattling like wind in dry branches when it saw them. It walked on two muscular legs and had five toes each, the middle toe twice as long as the others and bent backwards so as to rest the massive length of its scythe-like talon on its ankle. Its arms were long and ridiculously skinny, terminating not in a hand but only a single blunt claw, with thousands of those plates—long and thin and tapered to points—sprouting from it to make wings. Its neck was long, but very thick and the head that sat atop it was huge and blocky, with a wide, hooked beak that opened now for a deafening, extremely unfunny, goose-like honk.

Scott jumped and turned around. He screamed as Amber heaved herself onto her feet with her spear in both hands. It was a perfectly glorious B-movie scream and the only reason Amber didn't join him in it was because her stomach and head hurt so fucking much.

The bird opened its wings and shook them, stalking forward with its head low and canted on its side. Amber swung her spear, making just one slapdash attempt to scare it off, but she knew it wouldn't be scared and it wasn't.

It lowered its head and charged.

"Run!" Amber rasped, lunging to meet it.

Scott stood there and screamed again.

The bird jumped, both legs folding up and two middle toes slicing out. Amber grabbed Scott's shirt and pulled as hard as she could while throwing herself forward.

Scott's scream yelped itself off when he hit the ground, a split-second before Amber drove the point of her spear into the bird's breast. She heard fabric tear, felt a pulling sensation, and even though she could *see* it had snagged her shirt and nothing more, she still thought, 'That's it, I've just been disemboweled,' and actually heard Meoraq telling her she was dead. Then she was wrenched violently to one side by the spear going crazy in her hands. She lost her footing, but held onto the spear, and was dragged painfully in a wide arc as the bird spun, trying to free itself.

Then it saw her at the end of the spear.

'You know,' Amber told herself in a remarkably mild inner voice. 'It's never quick when a person goes out this way. You're always alive when they eat you.'

It lunged, shoving her ahead of it, and its beak clopped shut on empty air where she had been. It tried again, this time with a short running start that pushed Amber through the mud and grass until her butt hit a rock and the unexpected leverage combined with the bird's momentum pushed the spear in further.

It shrieked, staggering and kicking at her. She fell back but never lost her grip, keeping the spear between them as its talon slashed through her shirt. In seconds, she was wearing nothing but two sleeves, three buttons and some shreds.

It couldn't reach her. But only just.

Amber burst out laughing. It was sort of a hysterical sound, but honestly, it was funny. If she let go of the spear, the bird would kill her. If she stuck the spear in any deeper, the bird would kill her. Damned if you do, little girl, and damned if you don't.

The bird let out another of those ear-splitting shrieks, which was easily identifiable, now that it was happening at arm's reach and not off in the dark somewhere, as the sound of a very pissed off bird and not a mortally wounded one. It didn't even seem to care that it had a spear stuck in it, only that the tasty bag of meat dangling off the end of it remained just out of reach. The bird lunged at her in a beak-snapping frenzy and Amber felt the spear go in a little deeper and catch again. The bird recoiled, thrashing and kicking and beating at her with its wings, which felt a lot like getting horse-whipped with a bag of broken glass. Her arms went numb before she could even process the pain; the spear slipped out of her hands and she spun through the air and fell on her face.

Well, motherfuck.

Amber flung herself on her back in the perfectly ludicrous hope of fending off the monstrous beak that probably would not kill her right away, and got hit in the face with about a quart of hot blood.

'Mine?' she had time to think dizzily and then the bird's head and about two-thirds of its neck fell to the ground next to her. Some disgusting little tubey bit lapped up against her cheek like an overenthusiastic puppy's tongue.

And Meoraq's hand came down to grab her by the remains of her shirt and haul her to her feet.

"You idiot," he said.

Amber let out a whooping cry of relief so violent it was nearly orgasmic and threw her arms around him.

He recoiled, his already hard-feeling body turning at once to stiff-backed stone, but then clumsily raised a hand and patted her twice on the back. Just twice. There-there.

His obvious discomfort did more than any word of reassurance could have to clarify her mind. Amber let go of him and backed away. Scott's flashlight was lying on the ground. She picked it up and fussed with it, feeling stupid. "Sorry," she mumbled.

Meoraq grunted, avoiding her eyes, and moved past her to pull her spear out of the bird's breast. It wouldn't come easily, even for him. She heard bones snap as he wrenched the haft and finally got it out. Those little scalloped tips he'd put on it...They'd gotten stuck in the bird's breastbones somehow.

"If I'd been using my old spear, I'd have been killed," Amber realized, unaware she spoke aloud.

"All things follow God's ultimate plan," said Meoraq, inspecting the tip. He gave it back to her. "He must have known you were fool enough to do this."

Her blush deepened. "Were there only these two?"

"Three. A mated pair and this, their young one."

"Their young...? This is a *chick*?"

He looked at her, at it, at her again. "Half a year. Near its fullest weight, but inexperienced. Its parents were the hunters here. It came stupidly in where it was not prepared to be," he added, aiming a scowl at her. "And now it is dead."

That stung. "I'm okay."

His scowl deepened. "A more experienced tachuqi would have bitten through your spear in one moment and had your belly opened in the next." He started to gesture at her stomach, then executed a lizardly double-take as he saw it for himself.

"I'm okay," said Amber again. She clutched at the hanging tatters of the lower part of her shirt and pulled them aside to show him her unscratched stomach. "It only got my shirt. See, it never actually touched—"

His head cocked. He sheathed his sword, took the flashlight, and aimed it at her stomach. Yellow flared to life in the black of his throat. "Who did this?" he asked quietly.

Amber looked down. She'd fallen on the mother of all rocks; now she had the mother of all bruises coming in to prove it. "Oh," she said. "I fell on a rock."

He looked at her.

"A big one," she said lamely and tried to cover herself.

Meoraq caught a fistful of shirt-strips and yanked them aside, tearing them even more.

"Is everyone okay?" she asked.

He grunted in the affirmative, now running the flashlight slowly up her body.

"Even Scott?" she asked, looking around. They appeared to be alone.

"Lamentably." The light was on her face now. "How did this happen?"

"I fell down," Amber said again. "Are you sure? Where is he?"

"At the fire with the others. Hold still." His fingers probed at the side of her head and came away with a small shard of plastic. He studied it in the dim beam of the flashlight, scowling. "So far as I know, you were the only one fool enough to try to chase down a tachuqi in the dark. What is this?"

"Did you actually see him there or is that just where he ought to be?"

"Why do you care where S'kot is?"

"I just want to make sure he got back okay. He was here," she said reluctantly as his head tipped to a curious but menacing angle. "He was with me when the bird attacked us, but I kind of...lost track of him."

Meoraq's head slowly straightened. He stared at her for a long time as yellow began to lighten up his throat again. Then he looked down at the piece of plastic he'd taken from her hair. Slowly, very slowly, he turned the flashlight over and looked at the broken lens.

"It's not what you're thinking," Amber said hastily, but of course it was.

He didn't bother arguing with her. Without a word, he turned around and walked back to camp.

Walked fast. His weight was forward, balanced on his toes like a predator, and halfway there, he threw the flashlight violently away and yanked his sword off his back.

"Oh God," said Amber, following him, and began to run.

He got there before she did and stopped, sweeping his head left and right as he searched the camp for his prey. "S'kot!" he bellowed. "Stand and be judged or die on the ground like the animal you are!"

Amber grabbed at his arm, even as some part of her remarked that this was a very stupid thing to do to a lizard this angry. He didn't shake her off, but it didn't slow him down either; he dragged her along without any acknowledgement of her presence whatsoever as Scott darted around to the far side of the fire, shouting, "Whatever she told you, she's lying! I never touched her!"

"Jesus, Bierce," said Crandall, staring at her. "What did you do now?"

"You dare to call yourself the leader of these people?" Meoraq started left around the fire, then right as Scott continued to evade him, then noticed Amber. He plucked her off him with a hiss, and then leapt right through the fire to grab Scott by his shirt. "You looked me in the face and swore you did not know where she was!"

"I didn't!"

"*You were with her*!" Meoraq gave him a shake that made Scott's feet lose contact with the ground. "*You abandoned her*!"

"It was dark! I didn't see which way I came!"

Meoraq loomed over him, his sword high and poised to fall. His breath steamed out of him against Scott's face like smoke from a dragon's mouth. Scott himself did not appear to be breathing at all.

Meoraq's sword rose higher—

People made all the same gasping/screaming sounds they make watching racecars crash or kids fall out of Ferris wheels, and Amber lunged forward yet again, even knowing she was too late, but shouting for him to stop anyway.

—and sheathed it.

"She asked for you," Meoraq said, shoving Scott away with a look of contempt. "She wanted to know if *you* were safe."

He walked away. Still prowling. Still furious.

"Where are you going?" Amber asked weakly.

"To get the meat!" he spat, not looking at her. His neck was bright, bright yellow. "Stay here, all of you!"

Then he was gone. And everyone was looking at her.

"Are you okay?" Nicci asked finally.

"So that's how it is!" Scott shrilled out before anyone else could speak. He slapped at his shirt to straighten it, his face wild and eyes glassy. "That's you, huh?"

"Me?" Amber looked at him disbelievingly. "What the hell are you pissed off about? I didn't do anyth—"

"You stole my flashlight! Huh? How about that?"

"What?"

"You stole it and you go running off! You endanger all of us!"

She tried to say another *what*? but could only mouth it, so great was her astonishment at this attack.

"I have to go chasing after you! I have to try to bring you back when you knew, *you knew*, we were all supposed to stay together!"

"I—"

"And you call that bird-thing!"

"*What*?!"

"Okay, easy," said Eric, raising his hands. "No one called it, that's just crazy."

"She *called* it!" Scott insisted, pointing at her hard enough to make his arm quake as violently as his voice. "She called it by tromping around out in the grass where she knew she wasn't supposed to be! She admitted it! She made herself a target and then she brought them all back here!"

"They were already coming here!" Amber told them. "They saw the fi—"

"And she pushed me down!" Scott shouted. "Yeah! Huh? How's that for heroic? When it jumped out at us, you pushed me in front of it!"

"I pulled you out of the way, you liar!"

"Nuh-uh! No, you didn't! You pushed me, see?"

And he held out a pair of scraped palms to prove it, while she stood there bruised from head to fucking toe, so dumbfounded by the enormity of this lie that she could not even breathe.

"Okay, everybody. Calm down." Eric gripped Scott's shoulder and turned a stern eye on Amber. "I think maybe you'd better apologize."

She gaped at him. "For *what*?!"

He nodded as if that were the reaction he'd expected and, while disappointing, it was not unmanageable. He said, "Then I think you'd better take a walk right now. I think maybe the rest of us need to talk."

Amber opened her mouth, but it was Maria, of all people, who suddenly said, "Oh my God, enough already!"

Eric flushed. The mob-mutters that had been rising now subsided. People shuffled back, some looking very vaguely ashamed, but most still glaring.

Maria was glaring, too, but at Eric. "I don't like her either," she was saying, "but don't you stand there acting like you believe his playground pushed-me bullshit story!"

Amber stared at them, dimly aware that her mouth was still open, and saw only mob-faces staring back at her.

"Okay, let's not go making this any worse," Eric murmured, taking Maria's arm.

"Baby, I love you, but grow some balls. Maybe we couldn't see him, but for Christ's sake, look at her! We all know who got pushed down!"

Her chest hurt. She realized she was holding her breath and made herself start again. The first few came out too rough and too ragged. Too close to tears. She looked down at herself in a torpor of confusion and saw the bright magenta color of her bruise through the shreds of her shirt. She had blisters on her hands coming in from trying to hold on to her spear when it was stuck in the bird. The fight itself felt bizarrely like it had never happened and never stopped at the same time.

"She had it coming," Scott mumbled, trying to finger-comb his hair into place. "She stole my flashlight. And she broke it."

"On what, her face?" Maria demanded, advancing on him. "Hey, you know what? She's a bitch and it's okay to hate her, but you are a lying, cowardly little coil of dogshit and you are not doing yourself any favors tonight."

Scott shut his mouth tight and shifted his sullen stare to Eric.

"All right, baby, that's enough," said Eric. This time, when he took Maria's arm, she sniffed but let it stay. "Everybody's emotions are running high. You're not helping. The lizard wants to cook, so let's...let's just give him some space and everybody try to settle down and get some sleep."

The mob began to thin out, muttering and throwing mistrustful glances over many shoulders as it left Amber behind.

'What about *my* apology?' Amber wanted to say, wanted to scream. She didn't.

'I don't care,' she told herself, but the tears were still there, stinging at her eyes.

...it's okay to hate her.

'But she used to like me,' she thought, staring into the fire. 'She used to say I saved her. She used to say I pulled her from the ship when it was burning. She used to...'

"Amber?"

"Bring your blanket over here somewhere, Nicci," she said, and was proud of how level and unaffected her voice sounded. "Nothing else is going to happen tonight, but just for my peace of mind, you know?"

"Well...I think I'm going to go sleep in the tent with Lani and Sabrina and, you know, the other girls. Is that okay?"

Amber looked up. "You're going to the Resource Tent? Why?"

"It's not...you know, what they were saying. It's just..." Nicci looked away and then fiddled with the hem of her shirt a little and looked back at her. "I don't want to be alone right now, okay?"

"Yeah, I understand. Of course it's okay. You don't need to ask permission," she added, even managing a little laugh. She felt like throwing up, as much as she knew that would hurt her already aching guts. "Sleep wherever you want, just as long as you get some rest, okay?"

"Okay."

The wind gusted, covering the little sound of Nicci walking away. A short time later, another fire was struck out past Scott's tent. She could see people moving around it, some bedding down, others standing close and talking. Looking at her.

Amber moved over to the fire and numbly rearranged it for roasting. Smoke got in her eyes. The tears came streaming out. She tried not to be too conspicuous about it. She didn't care if they hated her, but she didn't want them to see her cry.

* * *

All things served Sheul. Meoraq had often mentioned his increasing difficulty keeping the many lazy humans fed when at his prayers, and so came meat, directly into his camp. That it came in the form of hunting tachuqis was surely a divine comment of another kind, and one which Meoraq humbly acknowledged as he butchered them and gave his thanks.

He did not try to glean every strip of meat on the beasts' bones. Tachuqis, particularly those with young, were aggressively territorial and he could not imagine there could be others close enough to be a threat to him, but the blood on the wind was sure to bring ghets eventually. Meoraq stripped the first corpse of its breast, flank, and tail meat, took the legs for meat and marrow, and hacked the spines away to get at the tender strip of dense, salty fat it carried. For organs, he took only hearts, kidneys and livers, and left the rest behind for the inevitable scavengers.

When he returned to camp with the first load, he was not surprised to see that the humans had withdrawn themselves beyond the borders of labor, and that Amber tended the roasting coals alone. She took the meat without asking instruction and he moved rapidly on to the next animal, annoyed with her for no reason whatsoever.

But no, he had reasons. She'd stood her watch, had carried back a timely warning, and had acted swiftly and well to preserve the lives of her people. All fair and good. And then she'd run off alone into the dark with her spear and stabbed it blindly into a damned tachuqi.

Except that she hadn't been alone, truly. She'd begun, at least, with Scott.

And that made him...so angry.

That she had gone with Scott out after the tachuqi was bad enough, but he thought he could forgive it in time. What he could not—would never—forgive was the blood in Amber's hair, the broken end of the human's lamp, and Scott himself safely back at the fire telling him he did not know where Amber was. Even these thoughts in Meoraq's mind put such heat in his throat that he could not swallow; he was actually drooling through his bared teeth like an animal. Again and again, he tried to count his breaths, but thoughts of Scott and blood broke every scrap of peace he found. The butchery of the tachuqi gave him only pale gratification, but at least it occupied his hands.

He brought the second beast's bounty to the fire. Again, Amber took it without comment. The first tachuqi was roasting well, save for the salt-back, which she didn't seem to know what to do with, and the marrow-rich bones, which she'd set aside as trash.

"Save those," grunted Meoraq, pointing. He'd show her how to cook them when he was done with the butchering.

She nodded, silent.

He went to deal with the last tachuqi, musing as he went on her uncharacteristic quiet. Women should be quiet, of course. A good woman should be all but invisible in her man's House. Or her father's, rather. Then her man's. It was unnerving to see Amber as well-behaved.

Then again, she had just faced down a hunting tachuqi. Courage and stupidity may have helped her wield the spear, but perhaps now that it was done, she was reflecting on her actions and how badly things might have gone.

Her shirt was torn. Had the spear been a hand's width shorter...

"Idiot," grumbled Meoraq, and began to cut the dead tachuqi out of its skin.

Midway through this difficult process, it occurred to him that he had called her an idiot to her face. She'd embraced him anyway (he was not going to think about that) but she still might have heard it. Perhaps he'd bruised her feelings.

Bruised. The image of Amber's stomach behind the tatters of her shirt intruded, scratching across his mind and raising that fighting urge once more. It was light enough yet, but by dawn, her colors would be in as dark as thunderclouds. Fell on a rock, she said. Running in the dark after her tachuqi. And blissfully forgetful of all the fragile human organs she carried in that soft belly that could be split as easily as they could be bruised. She might have been seriously injured. She might have been killed.

Or she might not. He had to remind himself that a wound was not the same from human to dumaq. No creature he knew of showed injury so vibrantly or so easily as humans. Dumaqs bruised when they were young, before their skin thickened and scales grew in dark and hard. Meoraq could remember carrying the colors of his warriors' training as proudly as if they were priestly medals, at least up to his fifteenth year and the beginning of his last growth. He'd come to it no earlier than the other boys in Tilev, but he'd had time since then to see boys outside the warrior's caste. The sons of farmers and cattle-hands, the sons of craftsmen, the sons of priests—they were still grey and thin-scaled well into their seventeenth, even their twentieth years...

He thought about that in a distracted, brooding way as his hands went about their work uninterrupted, waking back to himself to find that he'd cut the tachuqi's middle talon from its foot. He studied it there in his hand, his head cocked, curious and amused. He was still in his boyhood mind. Hunt-Master Takktha had taken his best students out into the wildlands occasionally to hunt tachuqi. If anyone managed to take one, it was his habit to award the boy the talon for a prize. It was not bladed and so stood fair in the sight of Sheul, but made a good knife for a boy, and a damned good story in the envious eyes of those who had to stay in Tilev. On the shelf below his sleeping cupboard at home, Meoraq probably still had the three talons awarded him over the years.

And was this Amber's? Here she was behaving properly for the first time in all the days he'd known her, and he was making her a boy's knife to go with her spear.

"I am a terrible influence," Meoraq declared, tucking the talon through his belt. He could make her a hilt if they ever found decent wood to craft one from.

He went back to the humans' camp in much smoother spirits than he had set out from it, hauling the last of the meat behind him and thinking ahead to the hilt he would make and the trick of sizing it for a human's hand. Amber was still at the fire, alone. There were the tracks of tears on her face, although her eyes were presently dry. She did not seem to see his approach, although he made no secret of it. She saw him only when he flung his load of meat onto the heap, and it was with a start that she turned away to poke at the fire and the roasts and covertly rub at her cheeks.

He probably should not have called her an idiot.

'Well, it was an idiotic thing to do!' he thought defensively, and went over to have a better look at her. "Stand up."

"Why?"

"Because I told you to."

She huffed a breath out through her nose, not loudly enough to be a true snort, and looked away.

Meoraq caught her up by one arm and hauled her to her feet. She let out a hoarse cry and slapped at him, but he chose to overlook the blow and frowned instead at her flat, ugly face, which was now flat, ugly and horribly bruised. There was a scraped place along the plane of her left cheek, and a short gash at the tip of her ear which had bled enough to raise a few crusty spikes in her hair, but in spite of the swelling and the impressive color, he didn't think the wounds were serious. Meoraq moved the shreds of her shirt (over her hissing and embarrassed protests) enough to see the bruise he remembered on her belly. It was huge, beginning just under the curve of her ribs and continuing on under the ties of her breeches, but it did not look swollen. He prodded at it cautiously and she smacked his hand. "Does this hurt?"

"Of course it hurts! Let go of me!"

He did, but he was frowning. "I want to see you urinate," he told her.

She huffed again and sat down, returning her attention to the fire. "I wanted to see Midnight Eclipse when they played Madison Square, lizardman. Life is full of things we want and are never going to get."

"Truth," he muttered and rubbed hard at his brow-ridges. He was no surgeon, after all. If she had done herself an injury, Sheul alone could cure her.

The thought gave him surprisingly little comfort.

"These need to be cooked," Meoraq said gruffly and hunkered down to make room on the coals for the fat and bones.

"I wasn't sure that was food," said Amber, not rude any longer, but only...dim.

He shouldn't have called her an idiot.

'Admitted, but I still would have thought of her as one,' he thought. Aloud, he said, "When I bring it as food, you may be assured it is food."

"Even the bones?"

"The bones especially."

Her brow creased for a moment, then smoothed out in dismay. "Oh, is it more of that gross bone jelly stuff?"

"Yes. And stop making that face," he added. "You need the marrow more than meat in these days."

"I'm not having any."

He snorted. "Yes. You are."

"I don't want it, Meoraq."

"I don't want to feed S'kot. Life is full of things we do not want to do and must do anyway." He turned the strips of tachuqi fat, which were browning up nicely already. "Meat may keep the life in your body a little longer, but no one stays healthy on meat alone. The season for green leaves and grain is done. My cuuvash is spent. Marrow is what I have to give you and you will eat it."

"I don't see you forcing it on anyone else."

"I don't care about anyone else."

It took a moment for him to realize what he'd just said.

Sheul brought His hammer down on Meoraq's chest just once. He straightened up sharply to disguise his flinch and glared at her, thinking, 'I said that. Why did I say that?' and thinking fractured thoughts of her bruised stomach under her torn shirt, the clean streaks of tears under her dry eyes, and the little sound it had made—that muted, soft sound—when her body slapped up against his and she threw her arms around him.

She was staring back at him, but he didn't know what she was thinking. Her eyes were too wide, too bright in the firelight. There was still blood on her cheek and in her hair; the urge to wet a cloth and wipe her face had barely formed before it had melted into the much less clear desire just to touch her. Not sexually (not at first), but just to touch. To feel her flesh, warm with life. To put his arm around her shoulders as he so often saw humans do with one another. To hold her and feel her holding him.

'There is something wrong with me,' he thought, and took the fat off the coals. He pulled his samr and served half the delicacy warrior-style, across the blade. She took it eventually and set it on her knees, staring at it instead of him. She shivered once.

"Eat it," he grunted, and ate his off his kzung. It crackled open and melted in his mouth like a good custard, and he scarcely noticed. The rich, salty taste was a luxury in this world, prized by priests and lords and rarely savored even by Sheulek, but he could not enjoy it. He wished he knew what to say to take the heaviness out of the air.

Amber stirred herself at last and touched a fingertip to the roasted fat. It broke and oozed invitingly. "If I say something, are you going to call it whining?"

What a curious question. "I can't answer that until I hear what you have to say."

She rolled her eyes back and rubbed briefly at her face, then looked at him. "Fine. If I whine, will you shut up about it and just let me do it for once?"

"Probably not," he admitted. "I have very little patience with whining, particularly when one is whining about the food." He pointed.

She gave the fat a lackluster glance, but dipped her finger in the steaming inner jelly and put that in her mouth. Her mouthparts twisted into a grimace, not one of her smiling ones. "Why is everything you eat so damned gross?"

"Because these are the wildlands and here we eat for survival, not pleasure. Is this what you want to whine about? The food? When you should be thanking Sheul for His mercy that you are alive to eat at all?"

"No." She took another taste of the fat and finally nerved herself to scoop up a quivering mouthful and eat it properly. Her eyes scrunched shut and stayed that way even after she'd swallowed. "This is indescribable."

"Good, eh?" He took another salty bite of his own share. "Men pay high coin in the cities to eat salt-back roasted on real coals just this way. I prefer mine cooked with riak and czaa, when I have the chance. You might like yours better that way."

"If it came baked in a bar of gold, I don't think I could ever like this. It stings my mouth."

He looked up sharply. "Are your teeth loose?"

"No, I'm just cut up some from when..." She didn't finish. She looked away at the other fire, where humans huddled together to sleep or exchange low words. She watched them in silence for a long time and then rubbed at her face in a terrible, broken way. "I really screwed up with these people, Meoraq."

That was a new turn of phrase and he wasn't wholly certain of her meaning, so he said nothing.

"The worst part is, I don't really know how. I don't deserve this—I don't think I do—but I don't think I can stop it either. It's not because I think I'm right all the time and it's not because Scott's a dick...or maybe it is. All I know is, I could walk over there right now with a spaceship in my arms and they'd probably club me to death with it before they thanked me for it."

Meoraq leaned back in some surprise. "Do you want thanks?"

Now she looked at him, her brows furrowing. "Don't you?"

"No. A Sheulek requires no man's favor when he stands in God's sight."

"Oh come on. Don't you think you deserve a 'thank you' after herding us across the wilderness and giving us food and water and then patrolling half the night to keep the man-eating chickens out of our camp while we sleep? Don't you want just once for someone to *appreciate* it?"

He shrugged his spines. "Sometimes. I'm still a man and men can be petty, but I try to take the high path. Sheul may yet reward me for my efforts here; your people never will, I think. That cattle's ass, S'kot, likes to keep them afraid of me." He pointed yet again at her tachuqi fat and studied her face while she picked at it. "Did you think I hadn't noticed?"

"He's been pretty obvious, but you don't act like you see it."

"Because I don't care. The world is filled with fools like S'kot, and worse, with the fools who let them act as wardens over them. They deserve each other. I don't care what they think of me and neither should you." He pointed at her tachuqi fat. She rolled her eyes again, but began at last to really eat it, and after she had taken several bites and he'd had time to think, he said, "I am Sheulek. Have I told you what that means?"

"It means you're a foot." She glanced at him. "A wandering soldier or something, right?"

"A Sheulek is more than a warrior. We are the instruments of God's judgment."

"I don't think I got that."

"Sheul's will is not always manifest to those of us who dwell on Gann. When conflicts arise that cannot be settled by men, we Sheulek are called to mediate. Most of these matters can be settled with words," he added, taking back his samr to clean and sheathe it. "If you have conflict with S'kot, call him forth and I will mediate."

"I don't think that will go over too well."

"How do you mean?"

"I mean, court will be in session all of three minutes before you bang the gavel down on Scott's fat head. Admit it," she said, giving him half a smile that did not much touch her eyes. "You'd love the excuse to take him out."

"You think I have had no excuses before this?" He took a bite of his salt-back, swallowed, and added, "I don't need one anyway. One of the privileges of carrying these blades is that I can use them against whoever I want. Yet for now, this moment, I must believe Sheul put him in my path for a reason."

She snorted. "Maybe it's to kill him."

"Father, hear Your son's desire, but in the meantime, I don't require his good opinion of me," said Meoraq with a dismissive flex of his spines. "It wouldn't mean much, coming from him."

"Easy for you to say. You don't have to live with these people."

"Neither do you."

Her eyes rolled. She looked at the fire and moved roasts around.

"If you want his approval," said Meoraq bluntly, hating even the taste of the words, "give him yours. Lay your open hand at his boot for all your people to see and his favor will fall like rain."

"No. He's an idiot. And I know you think I'm an idiot too—"

He never should have said that.

"—but if I just smile and let him do whatever he wants, he'll kill us."

"Do you believe that?"

"Yes!" She stopped and frowned into nothing for a few moments. "Yes," she said again, with less heat but more feeling.

"So. Do what is right. Stop pursuing the gratitude of your pathologically ungrateful people." Meoraq put a hand on her bent knee and leaned forward until his face and hers were a breath apart. "And stop whining."

It seemed the right thing to say, for a change. She smiled a little anyway, and when she smiled, it was as though a cold hand reached directly through his flesh and squeezed at his stomach.

He had nearly lost her this night. A thumb's width of bone at the end of her stupid spear had been all that made the difference between his Amber sitting at this fire...or burning on it.

Meoraq gave her a tap and stood up, looking away. "Mind the meat," he said unnecessarily. Of course she'd mind it. "I need to do something with the carcasses before the ghets come." He hesitated, then looked down—not directly at her, but close—and said, "You were very brave tonight."

"And stupid."

"But brave." He reached...but closed his hand into a fist and walked away without touching her. He wanted to. And that was why he just didn't dare.

7

Amber fell asleep while cooking, which, if someone had told her it had happened to them, she wouldn't have believed was possible. In the aftermath of the taohuqi attack, she had thought she would be awake all night and so she'd busied herself with chores while the others gradually went back to sleep, ultimately ending up behind Meoraq's tent with a small fire and the stewing pouch, washing up and crying some more. The next time she checked on the meat, Meoraq's mending kit had been set out in a conspicuous spot, so she went back behind his tent to see what she could do with her shirt. The hanging shreds were beyond help; she ripped them off, then went ahead and ripped the whole shirt up to the neck and started sewing. The new seam was as ugly as a surgery scar, but the shirt fit a lot better, so she did them all the same way, even her sweaters from home, leaving only her last new Manifestor's shirt still folded and untouched in the bottom of her pack.

She didn't think she was tired, the same way she didn't think she was too badly hurt, but with her adrenaline burned out and her emotions pulled thin, a full stomach and a dark night, it happened. One moment, she was leaning over a half-sewn shirt to turn slabs of meat on live coals, and in the next, it was day and Meoraq was shouting the place up: "I said, get *back*! That is for smoking, not for eating! You have had all that I mean to give you today!"

She woke up, but not fast. Her head felt cottony, thick with hurt, but her head wasn't even half the problem. She'd never hurt so much in her life. Her stomach was a furnace of so much sick heat that it felt almost like a separate entity—a pregnancy of pain—with a weight and a pulse all its own. She had to touch it, thinking with half-asleep logic that she could measure the extent of her internal injuries by how much swelling she found, but decided she must still be dreaming once she had. 'I am not this flat tummy,' she thought decisively, and was comforted. She left her hand on the stranger's stomach, though. It hurt to bear her hand's weight, but it felt good to be cradled, and after she'd had a few minutes to brace herself, she sat up.

It wasn't easy and it wasn't quick, but she made it happen. Cold air hit her as gravity took her blanket away, forcing her to pull it back up. While it would have been exaggeration to say that the blanket felt like it weighed a hundred pounds, she could honestly say it felt like ten, and that was ten too many for the arms that had kept a giant man-eating ostrich at spear's length the night before.

All these thoughts had time to pour themselves, thick as syrup, redly throbbing, through her head before Amber noticed it wasn't her blanket. Her Fleet-issue sheet of tinfoil was nowhere to be seen. In its place was a real blanket made of some heavy woven material, dark red in color, wonderfully warm. After that sank in came the real shock: she was in Meoraq's tent, lying on his bedroll, which had her grass-bundle-and-waxed-saoq-hide one, great as it was, beat all to hell.

While she was staring at this in a stupefied kind of horror, a lizardman's shadow grew suddenly huge and dark on the wall. "Be quiet!" Meoraq hissed. "If you say one more word, S'kot, even to beg my forgiveness, I will split you down to the ground! Great Sheul, O my Father," he continued under his breath, "see Your son in his hour of trial and give me the strength to keep from killing that ass-headed fool just one more day."

With that pious thought hanging in the air, the mouth of the tent rippled, bulged and finally opened. He stuck his head inside, moving carefully and making no sound, only to see her already sitting up.

His spines slapped flat. "Fuck," he said, and withdrew. His silhouette twisted, his long head turning in profile, sparking some vague storybook memory—a dragon, a cave, a damsel in distress—before he shattered it by shouting, "Get back, you pack of ghets! You! If I see you reach your hand toward my fire again, I'll cut it off! Back!" Then he looked in at her again.

"Hey," she said.

He glowered and came all the way inside, flinging the flap shut behind him like it was a door he could slam. Muttering savagely under his breath, he dropped to one knee and began rummaging through his pack. His spines were still flat. Those yellow stripes were out and glaringly bright on his black throat. Amber re-thought her 'What the hell am I doing in here, lizardman,' approach and said instead, "I didn't mean to fall asleep."

He grunted, pulled a rolled-up mass of something from his pack, and tossed it at her. It fell open on impact and dropped into her lap. Some kind of leather shirt, long-sleeved, nicely-tailored. His spare tunic.

She hurriedly pushed his blanket down, exposing her mended shirt with the new black stitching staggering its way from neck to hem. It was still a little big on her and the cloth puckered and bunched all along the ugly seam, but it covered her. "I don't need that. I fixed my shirts."

"I decide what you need. Put it on."

"Meoraq—"

"Put it on."

"I can't!"

"Don't whine at me. Put it on." He leaned back on his heels and looked at her, rubbed his throat, checked his belt buckle, and suddenly spat, "How do you feel?"

Amber plucked listlessly at one sleeve of the tunic. "About this?"

"I don't care how you feel about that!" he snapped. "How badly are you hurt?"

She dropped her eyes to keep from looking at his, which were blazing, bright as fresh blood, furious. He wanted to get moving, of course. She'd slept half the day away already, and yeah, she hurt, there wasn't a square inch on her that wasn't reliving last night—worst of all her stomach, which felt like she'd swallowed a hot, jagged rock—but she for damn sure wasn't going to whine at him about it.

"I'm okay," she mumbled, looking at the tunic. His tunic. The tunic everyone was going to see her wearing.

Silence. He was staring at her. She could feel him staring, even though she didn't dare look.

Outside the tent, people were talking, moving around. She found herself wondering who'd started the morning fire, who'd topped off the flasks. Her stomach hurt.

"I'll be out in a minute, okay?" she said finally, desperately. "Just let me get myself together and I'll be ready to go."

"Take all the minutes you want," he replied. "You're not going anywhere today. Tell me where it hurts."

"I'm fine."

"You may not go anywhere tomorrow either," said Meoraq, just as if she hadn't said anything, as if she weren't even there. His scaly fingers closed on her chin, forcing her head back. He glared at the side of her face, then pulled her chin down almost to her chest so he could see the top of her head. When he was satisfied with that, he nudged her shielding arm aside and pulled her shirt up to expose the plum-colored skin of her stomach. She sat there, clutching his tunic and waiting for it to be over.

"You're very quiet," he remarked, prodding inevitably right where it hurt the worst.

"Does anything I say matter?"

"What would you say if it did?"

"We have to keep moving."

"Then, no, it does not." He dropped her shirt and pinched her chin again, having another look at the side of her face. "We leave at my command, and I wait upon our Father's. No more arguments."

Amber shut her eyes and waited until he was done thumbing through her hair.

"I have tea and a little stew I want you to take," he said at last, releasing her. "And then I want you to rest."

The thought of having to eat anything put another hot, jagged rock in her stomach. They ground together, breaking off points that stabbed their way into her heart, her throat, her eyes.

Amber nodded.

He grunted and left, letting in a great gust of frigid air before the flap fell shut behind him.

Amber pushed his blanket back and moved off of his bedroll. She put his tunic on over her shirt so she wouldn't have to feel it touching her skin. It was soft and warm and a bit stiff. It smelled faintly of smoke, but mostly of new shoes; it had never been worn. She cried a little, but only a little. Then she scrubbed her eyes dry on her sleeve, put her boots on, and crawled out of his tent.

The sun was even higher than she'd thought, almost directly overhead. Everyone was up, milling restlessly through the camp with nothing to do, nowhere to go. She saw Nicci first, because Nicci was there on Amber's mat where she could dimly remember leaving it, although the memory felt days old, unreliable. Amber limped over, holding her stomach in the cradle of one arm, and bent laboriously to collect her spear.

Nicci watched solemnly until Amber had straightened herself out. Then she huddled up tighter under her blanket—hers and Amber's both—and said, "Are you all right?"

All her life, no matter how she'd actually felt at the time, the answer to that question had been yes, usually in the kind of scornful, impatient tone that was meant to make the other person sorry they'd ever asked. Now, although she still could not bring herself to admit to the truth out loud, Amber shook her head.

"You look pretty bad. Amber, I...about last night, I mean..." Nicci looked away, shivering under her blankets, toward Scott's fire. Toward Scott himself, standing by his tent and watching them. She dropped her eyes, not looking at either of them anymore, but said, "Do you need help? To...you know...go?"

Amber considered it, which was depressing enough, but in the end, she knew that no matter how uncomfortable the short walk to the boulder designated as the bathroom might be, it wouldn't hurt any less to hang off Nicci's arm. She shook her head again and limped off alone.

By the time she managed to shift her clothes, squat without falling over, pee out the shrieking leaden hell in her guts, and put herself right again, she had begun to feel dizzy as well as tired and hurt. Feverish. Gripping her spear, she sat on the rock that had hidden her bathroom activities from camp and bent forward as much as her stomach would let her, letting her swimming head dangle over her knees.

"Here you are! And by Gann's closed hand, here you are *alone*!"

She raised her head just enough to see Meoraq's boots stomping toward her through the grass. "I had to pee," she said dully. "I don't do that in front of an audience."

He kept coming, which she expected, and when he reached her, he took her by the chin and forced her to sit up straight. She more or less expected that, too. But the hand that wasn't iron at her jaw was gentle as he stroked her hair back and peered into her eyes, and the yellow stripes at his throat had faded almost entirely to black. He was still glaring, but it was hard for lizards not to glare.

'He said he liked me,' she thought suddenly, which was not exactly true. What he'd said was, 'I don't care about anyone else,' but the implication was there. He'd said that and then he put her in his tent to sleep and gave her his tunic in the morning and where was she supposed to go from there? She found herself wondering...if she put her arms around him right now, would he give her another of those stilted pats? Or would he hold her?

"I would be very clear now," he murmured, rubbing his thumb lightly back and forth beneath her left eye. It hurt a little, like it had bruised up. She didn't think she'd even been hit in the eye, just the ear. "You are not to leave my camp. Not alone. Not in company. Not at all. How do you mark me?"

"I'm still in camp. This counts as camp." She watched his red eyes move, reading all the pain the old Amber could have kept hidden, thinking how easy it would be to just let go of her spear and hold on to him instead. "It isn't your camp anyway."

He snorted, but even that was gentle. "Whose then?"

"It belongs to all of us."

"Ah." He stepped back, gesturing for her to stand, which she eventually was able to do. He watched, spines forward, intent, as she took her first steps, then joined her at her side. He said, "I took a talon on my first tachuqi hunt."

"Oh yeah?" She had no idea what that meant.

"Truth. And on my second, I took its foot to my chest. Why I wasn't killed, only God could say. As it was, I was thrown some distance and briefly lost my reason, but I was able to walk back to the city and I slept in my own bed in the billets that night."

"Wow," said Amber, because she felt like she ought to be in the conversation. She hoped her noticeable lack of enthusiasm didn't make it seem like she was being sarcastic, but she just hurt too much to care.

"I remember thinking that night how blessed I had been. A few shallow scratches, a knock on the head—hardly worth the mention." His spines flicked. He glanced at her, smiling in that severe, lizardish way. "Come the morning bell, I felt as if I'd been nailed into a crate and thrown down the stairs."

That was such an apt description of what she feeling that Amber managed a thin, strained smile.

"But the following day was tolerable, if not pleasant, and the day following that, I decided I would live after all. Every day, Soft-Skin." He tapped her companionably on the shoulder. "A little better."

"In the meantime, I'm making things worse." She stopped walking while they still had some privacy, leaning heavily and with shaking hands on her spear. "Look at me. I'm not going anywhere today."

"No."

"You don't get it." Amber looked into camp, where more than a few faces were turned toward them, watching. "We've used up all our screwing-around time and they all know it. Now they all know I'm going to slow us down even more. Acting like it doesn't matter doesn't make me feel any better."

"It matters," he said mildly. "But if Sheul wills that we are on this side of the mountains when the snows come, so be it. Xi'Matezh will wait for us."

"We'll starve to death if that happens."

He thumped her lightly on the forehead with one knuckle. "You forget that I have wintered in the wildlands before."

"With fifty people to feed?"

His expression did not change in any way that she could see, but it became more thoughtful all the same. It was not, however, a good-gracious-I-hadn't-thought-of-that kind of thoughtful, but more of a how-can-I-dumb-this-down-any-further? "God has set me on this road," he told her. "And God will see me reach its end."

"I'm sure he will," said Amber, rubbing at her eyes. "But God has made it pretty fucking clear that he doesn't care if the rest of us die."

"Do not be blasphemous."

"Don't be a zealot," she snapped back, and rubbed her eyes some more.

"Come." Meoraq tapped at her carefully with his knuckles. "I have tea for you."

"I don't want it."

"I know. Come anyway."

Amber raised her head. One of the women was pointing at her, saying something unheard to the rest of them while they all stood outside the Resource Tent and shivered in their worn-out Manifestors' uniforms. One of the others shrugged and, looking Amber right in the eye, made a crude circle of one fist and rammed her finger into it a few times. A riot of *ewwws* and *Oh Gods* drifted toward her on the wind as they laughed.

Nicci was with them. She didn't laugh, but she didn't walk away either.

Meoraq put his hand on her back and gave her a little nudge.

She looked at him, wishing she was the old Amber, the tough Amber, the Amber who could just walk away. She dropped her eyes back to the toes of her resoled boots and let him take her to his fire.

* * *

After his own encounter with the tachuqi that had kicked him to the ground, a young Meoraq had been on light detail a total of fourteen days. He wished he could give Amber the same, but he simply couldn't.

On his frequent patrols, taking careful note of each fresh ghet-track and gnawed tachuqi bone, Meoraq found himself thinking of the road they had crossed outside of the ruins. The Gelsik road, he thought, although the particulars didn't matter. It would lead to a city where Meoraq could declare conquest and demand enough cuuvash from its provisioners to make the rest of his pilgrimage without worry. He would have to demand a cart and a young bull to pull it, and since it seemed wasteful to haul two or three hundred bricks of cuuvash in an otherwise empty cart, he would demand enough tents and blankets to keep all the humans out of the weather. Warm clothes for Amber...and maybe even a new wristlet.

But as tempting as the thought was, he knew he would never do it. If pressed to give reasons, he could have said that this was a holy test set before him by Sheul Himself, and if the only way he could come through it was to cheat, he had already failed. That was a good reason, one that left unsaid the far more honest facts that if he took the humans with him to a city, his pilgrimage might well end there, and if he went alone, Scott would leave Amber to her own care, which was no care at all.

So Meoraq thinned the tachuqi meat as much as possible by stewing it with all the edible roots and leaves he could forage, and on the morning of the third day following the attack, when the last bitter drop was taken (given to Amber, fed to Nicci), he gave the order to strike camp and move on.

They walked, and if Meoraq had wagered his own left foot against the making of three spans distance in the course of that day, he would yet be walking. Even the humans complained it was not enough—there had to be some black joke in that—and Amber's name was in all their mutterings.

She had begun well enough but soon flagged, dropping further and further behind until she and her Nicci were only two dark points on the very edge of the world. At first she carried her spear, then dragged it behind her, and finally began to lean on it. Meoraq spent much of the day looking back from some ridge or another, watching her struggle, thinking of himself limping along just that way, and the fourteen days he had been given for healing. But that was fourteen days within the walls of great Xeqor and this was the wildlands. He knew she was driving her exhausted body to the very edge of collapse so that she would not be a burden to them. He knew also that she was a burden anyway.

Meoraq had been the tool of Sheul's judgment all his adult life. The unfairness gnawed at him.

That evening, after his camp was made (if it could be called evening while the sun was only half-fallen from its highest point), Meoraq went alone into the plains on the pretext of hunting. There, he removed his harness and his tunic, and bent his neck before Sheul. He prayed, reciting the Deliverance through all twelve invocations, and meditating until his heart was clear and all his clay was numb with cold.

When this was done, Meoraq bent yet further, gathering a palmful of wet earth to daub over his mortal heart. The wind dried it to a gritty shell against his bare skin in moments. He bowed low, shivering, to press his hands flat to Gann. His prayers were not ended, but only begun.

"O my Father," he said, "hear Your son. I cry out to You from the darkness where I am in desperate need of succor. Great Father, the cold season is almost upon me and I can see no way for all the humans You have given me to survive such a wintering. I know that the lives of these few humans are a small measure of the hundreds of families who would depend upon me if I am called to be steward of Uyane's line in Xeqor and I am ashamed to show my face to You and admit that even so, the burden is too great. I must cry out to You, merciful Sheul, for shelter in the wild places, for food in the hour of famine, and for strength in the bodies of the weak."

Meoraq paused to reapply humility in the form of mud on his exposed chest. He could not feel it anymore. His shivering had become a constant tremor throughout his limbs. It took great effort to bend back to the ground without sprawling across it—effort that made him think of Amber fighting one foot down in front of the other, where his thoughts had been since this prayer began. Now he must come to it.

"Great Sheul, O my Father, You have called me to this pilgrimage and given me the honor of this ordeal. My heart is sick with shame that I cannot steward these humans without Your intervention, but I must be shamed, O Sheul, or I must see them die. We have been too long in the wildlands and with this new attack upon my camp, we will be there longer still. A woman was injured..." Meoraq trailed off, painted more mud onto his numb and aching chest, and said, "A good woman was injured, but by Your mercy, she lives. Now I bend on her behalf."

Hearing those words spoken aloud, even before Sheul who surely knew all things, made Meoraq profoundly uncomfortable. He hesitated, then said the words which were soon to haunt him: "Her wounds slow us all and I cannot tend these humans in the wildlands indefinitely." This was truth, but even truth could be molded into many shapes. "I ask You as Your true son who has served and loved You all my life, relieve her of her pains and so relieve me of this burden."

Dead grass rattled in a slow gust of wind. Meoraq raised his head, but the plains were empty and the skies above were growing dark.

"I leave myself in Your hands, O my Father," he said finally, decisively, "as You have left them in mine. Be with and watch over Your son as I tend them, and bring us safely to Xi'Matezh. I am ever grateful for Your blessings, for every breath is Yours, O Father, and I thank You humbly for each pain that I am alive to feel."

He bent one last time, touching his brow to the muddy grass and holding it there while he took a slow count for the Six and spoke their names. Then he dressed again and went on his hunt while he still had light enough to see the ground.

He found a dead corroki calf lying close to a trampled tachuqi in the muddy path of its herd with an obvious story to tell: A tachuqi attack and a vengeful cow whose herd rallied around her. The tachuqis retreated when one of their half-grown chicks was killed, moving on after easier prey (Meoraq thought it very likely these were the self-same tachuqis who had come upon his own camp, now three days behind him). The corrokis lingered, waiting for their cow's animal grief to dim, and finally traveled on this morning. The tachuqi's carcass was too mangled to serve him, but the calf, well-preserved in the cold, would feed his hungry humans for many days.

Meoraq began cutting the calf out of its armored plates, grateful now that he had made his camp in the middle of the day. All things served according to Sheul's design. He heard all prayers and answered.

That thought too would haunt him.

As the sun sank low behind the clouds, Meoraq returned to camp, dragging the first load of meat on a crude litter fashioned primarily from the calf's own back-plate. He dropped it by the fire, heaved a great stack of human packs off the sled he had made, oh, a brace of days ago, then beckoned to Scott and his servants and went to cut some poles so he could make a second.

Eric alone came to him, but he listened to Meoraq's commands and put together a fairly competent sled with a minimum of instruction. Meoraq, in a generous mood, gave him a tap on the shoulder and even refrained from pointing out the areas that could have used improvement. "It isn't far," he said, taking up the tether of his old sled while Eric manned the new. "But it will take more than one journey and I want to run if you can manage it."

"Where do you think you're going?"

Meoraq stopped and looked at the sky. 'I am grateful,' he thought. 'For every pain that I am alive to feel, O my merciful Father, I am grateful.'

He turned around, but he was not the one under attack. Scott and his remaining two servants, Dag and Crandall, were on their feet before the fire (before the slab of meat Meoraq had brought them also, he noted), staring Eric down.

"I need my people here," said Scott, furiously pointing at the ground beneath his boots. "If Meoraq wants help, he can use Bierce."

"She's hurt," said Eric.

"I'm fine!" Amber called, struggling to rise from her mat.

"Sit down," Meoraq said.

"But I can—"

"Sit." He glanced at her, lowering his spines warningly, and she sat. When he turned back to Scott, the cattle's ass was right in front of him.

"Stop giving my people orders," said Scott. "If you want something, you respect the chain of command. You ask me and I'll consider whatever it is, but stop giving my people orders."

And while Meoraq was still reminding himself that he was the master of his clay and it would upset everyone if he cut Scott's head off in front of them, however deservedly, Eric—of all people—suddenly said, "You gonna stand there with him and bitch about the chain of command or you wanna come pick up some food?"

It was unclear to Meoraq just which of them he addressed, but Dag and Crandall both pinked up in the face and dropped their eyes. After some uncomfortable moments, they shuffled away from Scott to stand with Eric. And it was Eric who looked his furious abbot in the face and said, quietly, "You need to get over this, man. You need to. Because this planet is not fucking around anymore. It's going to kill us."

"When we get to the skyport—"

"If there is one," said Eric. "If."

They locked eyes. All around them, watchful humans fidgeted and whispered. It was very strange to be one of the watchers instead of the one fending off Scott's challenge, to feel none of the hot pleasure in seeing Scott skulk away, but only a growing unease. The storm had not passed, but was only darkening.

Like the sky, he thought with another upwards glance. What was coming with Scott...it would just have to come. Until then, he had work to do.

It took four trips and two sleds to strip the calf of all usable meat, and by the time they were finished, night was full upon them. The humans led the way with the light from their lamp-machines until they could see the fires that Amber had built. She was roasting the meat, stewing the organs, and hammering away at the marrow-bones with a rock when Meoraq came up beside her.

"This stupid fucking disgusting glop is not worth the effort it takes to get at it," she snapped by way of greeting.

He grunted and handed her his samr, moving on with Scott's servants to unload the sled. He listened to the chopping sounds as she broke into the bones, and since they didn't come with shrieks as she dismembered herself, he allowed himself to become absorbed in portioning out the meat. For Eric in particular, he gave the tender neck flesh. With humans, as with any half-domesticated animal, good behavior should always be rewarded if one wished to see it repeated.

It was not until the sled was empty that Meoraq straightened up to discover that Eric had gone no further than Meoraq's own fire. His Maria was there with him, not cooking, but only sitting and chatting with Nicci. Scott's other servants, Dag and Crandall, seemed to be in no hurry to wander off either.

He looked at Amber, who was trading out heat-stones in the stew and sitting watch over the marrow. She looked at him, her mouthparts crooked up at one corner.

The words, "Get away from my fire," rose to his throat, but no further. Amber wanted to be liked by these idiots. It cost him nothing to welcome them for one night.

Well...not welcome, but he could tolerate them.

So he simply walked over, set the last of the meat over the coals, and gave Crandall a hard rap on the top of his hairy head. Crandall scooted away from Amber and Meoraq hunkered down in his place. Amber was eating marrow, he saw. On the flat of his samr, warrior-fashion. "Do you like it any better than saoq or tachuqi?" he asked, gesturing at it.

"I can't taste the difference," she told him. "It's all gross."

"I can't taste the difference either," he confessed, taking some. "But they tell me there is one."

Crandall was staring at him. After a while, Meoraq stopped politely ignoring him and stared back. Crandall got up and went to Scott's fire instead. The few humans sitting up there made room for him and listened to whatever words went with his angry arm gestures. Some of them laughed. Scott himself was nowhere to be seen, which was odd. This was the time of night when he was usually pacing around the camp, hearing the many complaints of his people as they bedded down and telling them lies.

He watched for a time, making certain Scott was really gone and not just keeping himself uncharacteristically quiet and still. At last, he reached out and gave Eric a tap. "Where is your abbot?"

"In his tent," Eric replied, and his woman added, "Sulking."

"He'll get over it," said Dag, stealing a bit of heart-meat out of the stewing pouch.

Meoraq's hand twitched, but he managed not to slap. Barely. "Get over what?"

Nicci rolled her eyes and made a chuffing noise.

"Same shit, different day," said Amber. "You're undermining his authority."

"Would it kill you to be nice once in a while?" Nicci demanded, glaring at her. "He has so much to worry about right now and you just...you just push him around!"

"Scott does his share of the pushing." Amber stirred the stew as all the humans found something else to look at.

Meoraq turned back toward Eric. "Does your abbot truly believe he will find a ship in Xi'Matezh capable of sailing him into the sky?"

"I don't know," said Eric after a moment. "Sometimes I think he does."

Beside him, his Maria snorted. "If he didn't, he couldn't convince anyone else. He needs that too much, so yes, he believes it. And he'll go on believing it until we get there and don't find anything."

"We might," said Nicci, glaring at Eric's woman, who snorted again.

"Meoraq..." Amber's nerve appeared to fail her. She fussed with the heat-stones unnecessarily, and just when he thought she would wait until someone else changed the subject for her, she looked up again and said, "Why are you going to Xi'Matezh? Yeah, yeah, I know," she said quickly, waving her hand. "You want to talk to God. But you talk to God all the time and I'm sure you think he answers—"

Meoraq sighed and patted her knee.

"—so why would you walk across the whole world to do it now? I mean, you're tough, but this place could kill you."

He acknowledged that with a flick of his spines. "I was called to find you. You were placed in my path."

"Okay, whatever, but you were already on the road, is my point. Why?"

"The road..." mused Meoraq. He thought about it, beginning to smile. "So. I am on a sort of road. At one end, I am Sheulek, as I have been since my ascension. At the other, I am steward of my bloodline. House Uyane is the last of the great Houses in Xeqor to hold a direct line of descent. Whoever stands as steward stands in the sight of all men. Yet a Sheulek stands in the sight of God. It is too great a decision for a man to make."

Maria leaned forward slightly to look at Amber. "What, is he the lizard-king?"

"Baby, be cool."

"I'm just asking."

"No," said Amber, sounding annoyed. And to Meoraq, "Is it really worth all this walking just to ask God if you should quit your job?"

"It is a serious matter. I serve as His Sword and the tool of His judgment."

"Can't you serve him at home?"

"Of course," Meoraq said uncomfortably.

"Just not the same way?"

Discomfort grew. Now it was Meoraq who leaned out to check on the stew. "In many of the same ways, actually. A steward must mediate conflicts in the households under him and may even be called to trial if one of those households falls under accusation."

"But you have to stay home?" Amber guessed.

He looked at her.

Her arms raised, putting all the world on display. "Where you miss all this."

"Ease off, Bierce," Dag murmured.

"Don't speak for me," Meoraq told him irritably.

"Look, I'm sorry," said Amber. "It's your life. And I guess I can understand that running around out here is more exciting than staying home. The point is having an interesting story, right?"

Meoraq was startled into laughing out loud. "I don't know any stories about Sheulek. Boys may think this life is exciting, but one city is the same as any other, walking means nothing but boredom and bad weather, and you can't even remember the trials. No. The best stories, the legends, are told of stewards. They do the things that men see, after all."

"Tell us one," said Maria.

They all looked at her.

Eric leaned over to whisper, but she shook him off. "It has to be better than the bedtime stories the Commander tells. Come on, Meoraq, let's hear it."

It was right in the back of his throat to tell this woman that Uyane Meoraq, whether Sheulek or lord-steward, would never wallow so low as to put himself in competition with Scott for the favor of the fools who served him...but Amber was watching. These were her people and this was the first time he had ever seen them share her company at his fireside.

So he swallowed his first response and after some consideration, Meoraq said, "My father is...was steward of the bloodline and lord of House Uyane, which is the championing seat of Xeqor. As such, he was subject to be summoned to the city's defense and his battles on those rare occasions earned him as much fame as honor. He was very well known, not only in Xeqor, but across all the world. Or as much of the world as is left under Sheul," he amended. "Many years ago, when I was...six, I think. I suppose I could have been as much as seven, but I am certain it was winter because I was at home to see it. But however long ago it was, it happened that a band of raiders led by a man called Szadt attacked the neighboring city of Kuaq and took one of its gates.

"Here," said Meoraq, waving them closer. He took up a burnt bit of stick from the fire and sketched in the soil as he spoke. "Here are our cities, entirely enclosed within walls, with our cattle-lands and fields protected at the open heart, you see?"

"Like a doughnut," said Amber.

Nicci rolled her eyes. "The Commander's right," she muttered. "It's always food with you."

"Okay, it's like a tire," Amber said crossly. "Is that better?"

"There are four great gates at the cardinal points and often others in the various districts around the city, for ease of trade and the summering of cattle, but whether civil or private, each gate-house is fashioned with but one tunnelway that opens to the outside at one end and to the inward terrace here. No other door opens to the outside and no other door opens to the city. The many watchmen appointed at the gate-house are garrisoned along either side of a central stair with the private homes of the officers and their families above, arranged to rank, with the warden's home topmost, encompassing the entire floor so as to be the only home with access to the roof. So it is," Meoraq concluded, eyeing his poor drawing for faults, "that there are only three access points to the gate-house: the outer gate, the inner gate, and the rooftop stair. All three points were easily held by Szadt and his men. The gates were built to stand and Szadt had the whole of that armory at his disposal. Apart from that, he had somehow acquired certain machines—either from the stores of the Ancients or built after their fashion, I do not know—which could be tossed out through the inward windows. These burst and burned to terrible effect, capable of killing twenty men or more in an instant."

The humans looked at each other, but didn't seem much amazed.

"They still worked?" Nicci asked. "The grenades or whatever they were?"

"He said they were built by this other guy," Amber said before Meoraq could answer. She was scowling.

"He said *maybe* they were. And maybe the other guy just found them."

"Can you two fight about this later please?" asked Maria, ignoring the censuring mutters of Eric. "I want to hear the story. Go on, Meoraq."

He paused, not to let Amber and her blood-kin settle, but to think about whether or not he really wanted to give the human Maria the idea that she could give him orders. In the end, he continued, but only because it was a good story and he liked telling it.

"Kuaq rallied its defenses immediately, of course, and if Szadt had advanced out into the streets, surely he and his men would have been taken, but instead Szadt sealed himself within the gate-house to plunder it at his leisure. All attempts to break through the inner gate met with burning death. So too ended the efforts to send warriors around the outer wall to that gate. And so ended the disastrous assault upon the rooftop, when two whole legions of warriors were dismembered alive by more of the Raider-Lord's infernal machines. And in the lull that followed each onslaught, Szadt provided those encamped without the gate-house with the terrible sounds of his entertainments as he tortured those watchmen he had taken prisoner. At one point, he offered to release the families for certain goods, but when another attempt was made to break the gates, Szadt ended all negotiations. For hours, the cries of the women and children were heard as the Raider-Lord shared them out among his men and then threw them screaming over the inward wall at each tolling of the hour."

"Jesus," said Maria, and shivered. "Okay, you two can fight now. I don't want to hear any more."

"Kuaq fought tirelessly to remove the invaders, but in vain. Eventually, it was decided that they should send their plea for reinforcements to Xeqor. Our governors at once dispatched two forces: one, a legion of warriors capable of making the march to Kuaq in just six days, and the other, my father, who went alone and was there in three.

"He waited, hidden in the prairie, until night fell. And then he scaled the wall, here." Meoraq tapped the burnt tip of his stick against his sketch. "Not to the rooftop, but to one of the outer wind-ways which Szadt had not thought to guard, it being set the height of ten men in a sheer wall and sized for the children whose task it was to keep them clear. How my father made that crawl must have been its own story, but he made it and once inside, my father hunted down every last raider of Szadt's band and killed them all. One hundred and eleven men at final count," Meoraq said proudly.

"No way," said Eric, his brows rising. "That's seriously bad ass, lizardman."

Meoraq grunted, deciding to take that as praise, and went on. "My father's attack must have begun soon after dark and was swiftly discovered. All of Kuaq saw the erupting fires of Szadt's machines and heard the cries of battle, although the gates remained impervious to assault. At the striking of dawn's hour, the Raider-Lord's headless body fell from the rooftop where he had thrown so many others to their deaths. The fighting continued, but the core of Szadt's band had broken and by nightfall, it was silent.

"The governors prudently waited some time to be certain of my father's victory before they hailed the gate-house, but received no answer. No answer, but no killing machines from Szadt's raiders, either. And as time passed and the silence continued, it was decided that my father had received some mortal wound and succumbed to it. Attempts were made to break the gates, but they held. A locksman was brought, but he hadn't yet managed to craft a new key when the legion from Xeqor finally arrived and my father let them in."

"Why didn't he open the inner door?" Amber asked. "There had to have been enough noise...I mean, he had to know someone was out there."

Meoraq shrugged his spines. "Perhaps he was at prayers. In any case, he opened the outer gate, gave the keeping of the gate-house to the legion's commander and came home."

Amber's eyes narrowed slightly. Her head tipped, but he knew better than to think that meant the degree of sarcasm which it would mean on a dumaq. "He just left? He never opened the other door?"

"My father had little enough patience when dealing with the governors of his own city. As it was, the legion who'd had nothing to do with the retaking of the gate-house were detained three days by a grateful council. After killing a hundred men and bearing a witness to the remains of the women Szadt had given to his band, I doubt he was in any mood to celebrate."

"The remains," she echoed, frowning.

"My father never spoke of any of these things," said Meoraq. "But I have heard from many of those who were part of the legion that went to Kuaq and saw the gatehouse in those first hours. It has been supposed that Szadt meant to return to the wildlands that same night, as he had assembled certain supplies and bound what few of the women and children he had not already murdered for travel. But when he knew that it was over for him, it is said that he butchered them, even as they were tied and helpless at his feet. He left no survivors."

He did not tell them all of what he had been told—that even with his men being cut down in the rooms above him, in the madness of his great evil, Szadt had not only hacked his bound victims to death, but had also engaged some of them sexually. Some before their murders and some clearly after. Bootmarks in blood proved that Rasozul had gone in and out of this room many times, and Meoraq knew that was where his father had been during those days that the governors of Kuaq had been bashing away on the inner-city gate, preparing the bodies for their pyres or searching in vain for life among the dead or perhaps only bearing that terrible scene his witness for however long he could manage. He'd asked once, years later, when he was Sheulek himself and his father had seemed in an open sort of mood, but Rasozul's face had closed before the question had even come fully from his mouth. "I've told all there is in that tale once to your mother," he'd said. "And I'll tell it again to Sheul, but not to you, son. Not to anyone."

"My father returned to Xeqor a hero. His name is known in every city I have ever passed through. His name is known," he repeated meaningfully. "Mine is not."

"Then why don't you want to go home?" Amber asked.

"I go where Sheul sends me," he said. "That is enough talk for tonight. Finish eating and bank the fire. I'm going on patrol."

Amber stopped with her hand half-raised, a lump of marrow quivering on her fingertips. Her mouth opened.

"No," said Meoraq.

Dag laughed. Waving off Amber's glare, he excused himself, heading back across camp toward his little tent. No one hailed him. It was early as the bells would have rung it, but night in the wildlands kept its own hours. All the other humans were sleeping.

"You didn't even let me say anything," Amber said.

"You were going to ask if you could come with me." Meoraq stood up, stretching the stiffness out of his limbs. "And the answer is no. You rest."

"I've rested all frigging day!"

"You could barely walk a few hours ago," Eric remarked, grinning.

His woman looked at him, at Amber, and then took his sleeve and towed him to his feet. They left, whispering and laughing.

"I get the first watch," Amber insisted, reaching for her spear. "I always—"

She stopped there. Meoraq was smiling and holding out his open hand.

She looked at it while her blood-kin heaved a noisy sigh and tromped away, muttering something about being back in a few minutes to untie her. Amber closed her eyes and rubbed them, then crooked up the corner of her mouth and put her hand in his.

He pulled her to her feet and released her. "I found a dead tachuqi where I found our meat."

Her gaze sharpened at once. "More of those things that attacked us?"

"Not more, but the same group, or so I believe. We are still in easy distance of our previous camp."

She dropped her eyes. He waited until she dragged them up again.

"But if I am wrong, there are tachuqis very close to us tonight. If you come with me, if we find them, can you stand with me and fight?"

She did not answer.

"Rest," he said. "Sleep, if you can. I'll wake you for your watch."

She looked away again, staring hard into the fire at their feet. She nodded once.

He gave her a pat on the shoulder and left her there, passing Nicci on his way out of camp. She tossed her hair at him and sniffed in answer to his (admittedly terse) grunt of acknowledgement, but that was fine. He'd rather she give him a brief rudeness and move on than stand around and chirp at him as she did with her human friends.

But there was another light ahead of him, which meant another human wandering in the wildlands. Scott, he soon saw, slouching by himself on a jut of stone beside the stream. He didn't have time to slip away unnoticed; Scott shone his lamp right at him.

There was no one else around to see them, no one to intimidate or impress. Alone, they eyed one another with undisguised mutual dislike. Meoraq was first to speak. "What are you doing out of camp?"

He was so proud of his self-restraint.

"Thinking," said Scott. "When you're in charge, you have a lot to think about."

There was a challenge in his words, naked as a sword's edge.

"Truth," said Meoraq. Such self-restraint. Surely Sheul was with him. "Now go back to your den. I want you all together."

"Where are you going?"

"Patrolling. There is tachuqi-sign nearby." Sheul's hand slipped; Gann's gripped him. "Join me, S'kot. We'll hunt them down together."

The human's eyes narrowed. His smile was a cold gash across his face.

"No? Ah well. I suppose you are too important to your people to risk."

"They need someone to be able to make decisions without waiting for a sign from God first."

Meoraq laughed scornfully. "And you do that very well. In fact, I think that's about all you do. But I note that even you don't call them good decisions."

And he walked on, taking a low pleasure in imagining the look on Scott's ugly face as he was left behind to steep in hate. As he circled his camp, he warmed himself with thoughts of Scott sulking on his rock, maybe for an hour, maybe even all night. He supposed he ought to ask Sheul to heal him of his spite, which was a poison and a shameful thing to live in the heart of a Sheulek...but he'd already asked Sheul for so much tonight.

In reality, Everly Scott left right after Meoraq did, and while he did sit in his tent for about twenty minutes, he wasn't sulking. He was thinking. And when he was decided, when everyone was sleeping, he slipped out again.

Amber was a light sleeper, but she didn't hear him. It was the cold that woke her—the cold that blew down her back as a careful hand pulled her blanket away from her neck. Even then, there was no prescient leap of fear, only a sleepy annoyance. "I'm up, I'm up," she mumbled, rolling over. "Back off, liz—"

She saw the medikit, oddly. Just the kit, which she had last seen the day Mr. Yao placed it in Scott's hands. The medikit, open, and a blurry field of dirty crimson behind it that she never had time to recognize as the uniform jacket of a crewman for the *Pioneer*.

Then there was a hand in her hair, shoving her head back so that all she saw was night sky and a few sparks from the fire riding smoke out on the wind. She took a breath and something bit her on the neck. It was her last conscious thought: Snakebite. She heard it hissing again and again, hissing as it bit and bit, and she tried to scream, but her lungs were full of lead and the black got so much blacker and there wasn't time to think Nicci's name even once and that was it for Amber.

Elsewhere, not far, Meoraq walked, a bit too spiteful in his Sheulek's heart, but ever vigilant against the beasts that hunt by night.

8

There were no tachuqis. Meoraq knew it before that first hour was out, but he made himself stand a full watch. When the night was half-gone, Meoraq returned to wake Amber so that he could have a few hours' rest before moving on. He ought to meditate before he slept—he had indulged plenty of flaws to meditate over tonight—but he wasn't used to staying up this late anymore and he was tired.

The fires had been banked, giving him little light, but the humans' blankets caught all there was and reflected it back like mirrors. He picked his way carefully through them, searching for Amber and trying not to step on anyone. Ever since waking up in his tent, she had been fairly obnoxious about not bedding down too near him. No, it was always right in the thick of her people, where she was all but invisible, and he could do nothing but creep along and peer at each protruding head while praying for patience.

Patience had become little more than a word in prayer to him these days and it troubled him. Neither the late hour nor the cold wind was Amber's fault, but she had made herself damned difficult to find tonight. Usually she slept as light as any true warrior, rousing at the slightest disturbance, and until this night, his tromping boots had always been enough to at least provoke a shift or a murmur. Ah, there. Two pale tufts of hair, like summer-thick fronds of hillgrass, sprouting out of two silvery lumps on the ground—Amber and her Nicci.

Meoraq stomped loudly over. Nicci slept on, as usual. So did Amber, which was not. Her sleeping breaths were equally uncharacteristic—wet and heavy, as if labored. He circled her uncertainly until he saw the pale stripe of her arm lying over the edge of her mat onto the trampled grass. It was surely Amber's arm; that was her saoq-hide pack close to her hand, with his spare tunic stubbornly folded up inside so she could pretend she didn't have to wear it in the morning.

"Up," Meoraq said. "It is half-past late enough and well on to later still. Come stand your watch."

Amber did not stir.

He'd started to walk away, so much did he expect her grumbling obedience, but at this...this nothing...he paused. She'd done this before, when they were at cross-wills, but they weren't fighting tonight, or at least he didn't know they were. Cautiously, he turned back. "Soft-skin? I say waken."

Nicci muttered something and lifted her head out of her bedding, giving him a bleary and blameful look before shifting her eyes to Amber. "Get up," she mumbled, prodding at the bulk of her blood-kin's form.

Amber rocked without waking. Her wet breaths made a brief bubbling noise as she rolled onto her face and back again, but otherwise she made no sound. Her fingers twitched, but her hand wasn't moving.

She...wasn't moving.

Meoraq's spines flexed forward and slapped back hard and fast enough to hurt. He was at her side in one step and ripping away the silver nothing-skin to expose her in a splay that might well have been only sleep...save that she did not waken. Her mouth yawned when he rolled her over (and oh great Father, it was like moving meat. Only her upper body twisted toward him until he pulled on her thigh as well) emitting the same laboring sucks and gusts of air as strings of drool hung from her slack lips. She'd been lying in a great pool of her own salivations, so that one half of her face was pink and wrinkled. The eye on that side had swelled and was partially opened, so bloodshot and so dilated that it seemed a black slick upon a red sea. She had urinated on herself some time ago; the stain covered her entire left side from the sleeve of her arm to the cuff of her breeches.

"What happened?" Nicci asked shrilly. She grabbed at him and he shook her off without thought, pressing his palm to Amber's chest, first atop her shirt and then beneath it in an effort to catch the echoes of her life's pulse. If she lived.

"My God!" said Scott, appearing out of the dark as white and welcome as a strike of lightning. "She's dead!"

A great storm of shock followed as humans bolted out of their beds to either crowd around him or hover away.

"Be quiet!" Meoraq roared, and while they did not obey precisely, they quieted enough that he could detect Amber's heart beating at last. The feel of it brought him no relief, only more dread. Too heavy and too slow. Far too slow. He tried to make a count between beats, but there was no rhythm, only torpid shudders and infrequent slams, as inconsistent as the kicking leg of a dying saoq.

He told himself the freezing hand that gripped his own chest was premature. Her heart might beat this way all the time. How would he know?

His eye flicked to Nicci. He lunged out and caught her, dragged her squealing to him, and put his hand roughly between her swelled teats. Her heart hammered, rapid and strong, until she yanked herself away. He let her go, searching again for Amber's life-beat and finding it exactly as he'd left it, indisputably *wrong*.

"What happened?" someone asked.

"Is she dead?" Nicci cried, already in tears. She stumbled away and Scott took her in, clutching Nicci against his chest.

"It's going to be all right, Miss Bierce," he declared. "We'll all miss Amber. She had so much of the pioneering spirit and I know we will never forget her."

Meoraq gaped, then hissed at him with such violence that it was nearly a shriek.

"Back off, man," Dag said in a low voice. "There goes his neck."

"I think she's breathing," said another human. "I mean, she's looking really bad, but she's not dead yet."

"When did this happen?" Meoraq demanded.

They all looked at each other. "She looked all right when she went to bed," Eric said at length. "Maybe this is some kind of, I don't know, infection or something. From when she got...uh, hurt."

Scott flushed and glared at him.

Yao came to kneel beside Amber and Meoraq reluctantly gave her up to his inspection. The first thing he did was to take her wrist and just hold it for a short time, frowning. Then he pulled up Amber's shirt and felt at her soft belly. The bruise, now several days old, had lost its glossy purple-black color, gained some greenish smudges, and separated into three distinct marks rather than one massive one. "I see no inflammation...no sign of internal bleeding...pulse is weak and thready...she's extremely hypothermic. It could be sepsis, but she's shown no symptoms until now and her breathing is very slow and arrhythmic. This looks pharmacological to me," said Yao, prying open one of Amber's slack, glazed eyes.

"It's not drugs!" Scott interrupted. "Where would she get drugs?"

"I didn't say..." Yao paused, his narrow eyes narrowing further as he gazed into nothing. "Drugs," he murmured. He looked at Amber. "It could well be. Bring me the medical kit."

Scott stared for a moment and then suddenly, forcefully said, "I lost it. Back when we had to leave our infrastructure behind to avoid upsetting God. What does it matter? You can't fix this with aspirin and bandages! And you're not a real doctor anyway! You don't know anything!"

Yao merely nodded, unaffected by these insults. "Then it must be something else," he said, looking around at the dark plains. "She might have exposed herself to any number of toxic plants."

"You are a surgeon?" Meoraq asked, following what he could of this exchange. "You can heal her?"

Yao looked at him calmly. "As I see it, there are three possibilities. If this is sepsis, a worsening of her internal injuries, she will almost certainly die. If she's exposed herself somehow to an alien toxin against which she has no immunity, she will likely die. If she's ill—"

A wave of murmured alarm swept outward through the humans.

"—then she might pull through, but her injuries and this environment have surely weakened her body's defenses. Her chances are not good," Yao finished. "We can keep her warm and comfortable and hope for the best, but I must tell you, I see nothing hopeful about her condition."

Meoraq looked from face to flat, ugly face, but no one else had anything more to say. He gathered Amber up and stood, resting the thin skin of his neck briefly over her brow to test for fever. That, he knew how to cure, although it was by no means a certainty that he would find the necessary herbs. In any case, she was not hot with fever, but cold, as cold as if her life were already lost.

"Take her to the fire and build it up," he ordered, holding her out. His mind was racing ahead already, battering from one point of useless healing lore to another, trying to remember if he had seen anything, anything, on his watch that might help her. There was little enough to look at in the wildlands and medicinal herbs were so precious that his eye had a way of marking them whether he had immediate need of them or not. He knew he had seen no teaberries, no healershand, not even the dangerous comfort of phesok. There might have been gift-of-God and feverleaf by the bushel were this a warmer season, but the coming winter had turned it all to hidden roots. His memory showed him nothing but grass in all directions, dead thorns, and barren trees twisted out of shape by past storms. The only leaf he recalled with any medicine at all was deathweed, down by the stream, and if that was a sign from Sheul, Meoraq chose to ignore it. He...

He was still holding Amber.

No one had come to take her. By the looks of them, no one meant to.

Meoraq's confusion erupted in an instant to rage. "What the hell is wrong with you people?" he roared. "She could be dying!"

They shuffled back, looking at their feet or their fellows or their leader, and did not answer him. Scott, who was always first to be the voice of his people in every situation, whether it warranted a voice or not, now patted sobbing Nicci and was himself very pale and silent.

"Yeah," ventured Crandall when it became clear their appointed leader would not step forward this time. "But, I'm sorry, that's just a really good reason to keep her away from us. Whatever this is, it's bad."

And Meoraq's first impulse, self-defeating as it was, was to throw Amber down and hit him. Throw her.

Like meat.

Amber made a sudden weak gurgling noise. With her head tipped back in his arms, she was choking on her own saliva. Meoraq hurriedly shrugged her forward and drool spilled out in a fall over her lip and onto her chest. She did not seem to be able to close her mouth. A fool's gape...or a corpse's.

"Gross," someone whispered.

His throat too tight for speech, Meoraq turned his back on all the shuffling, staring humans and carried Amber to his tent. She did not resist him when he propped her up on his knee to strip away her soiled garments. Apart from the intermittent twitching of her fingers, she did not move at all as he lay her down on his mat.

So limp. So cold. Pale as snow everywhere that lying in her own urine had not burnt her to a vivid shade of pink, everywhere she wasn't bruised. So many bruises...

He passed his hand over them, gingerly probing for some sign of a greater injury, but her belly was cool and flat. Too flat. Sheul forgive His errant son, he could see the slats of her ribs and the nubs of her pelvic girdle. But no, he could not look at that now. Whatever this was that worked in her, it was not starvation any more than it was a belly-wound. But what was it? He could see a perfectly round inflammation at her throat, shot through with numerous tiny red dots, but he did not know what to make of it. He had never seen such a bite before, but human hide was thin, as Amber's many bruises proved. It was entirely plausible that a beetle with jaws far too weak to penetrate dumaqi scales had bitten her. Could beetles be poisonous? Twelve years walking in Gann's land and he simply did not know.

Meoraq lay down beside her, wrapped them both in his blanket and held her close, willing the warmth of his body into hers. She did not try to speak or move. She gave no sign that she knew who was with her or that anyone was at all. "Great Sheul, O my Father," he whispered, searching her slack face for life. "Hear Your son's prayer. You have passed these humans into my care for a reason and surely my ungrateful complaints have made this lesson necessary, but I am humble before You now. Only you can know the cause of this terrible sickness. Therefore, I place myself in Your hands, O Father. Show me the way to heal the woman."

He shut his eyes and listened, but Sheul did not speak, or if He did, Amber's wet breaths were louder. And if Sheul never spoke? If He left her life in mortal hands, as He so often did, what then? He needed a surgeon and never mind that no dumaq would have the slimmest idea how to heal a human. He could follow his backtrail to the road as soon as there was light enough to see by, and while he didn't know exactly where he was along its track, he knew he would find Gelsik to the north and Fol Dzanya to the south, but there were ten days running between them, plus three each way to run between road and camp, and it would take twice as long with the humans dragging at his heels, even longer since Amber would have to be carried. He would have to leave the humans here, leave Amber in their care, and run...knowing she would surely be dead by the hour of his return.

Truth, but against all the truth in the world lay Amber and she needed him.

So. He needed the sun to find the road. And he would have to sleep until then, so that he could make his journey at a run. The knowledge that he might well wake holding a corpse sat in him like frozen clay, but he could do nothing for her here. He had to find a city. He would not bring Amber with him. He would simply describe her symptoms, demand medicines, and return as swiftly as he was able. He would have to trust the other humans to tend her until then, and oh but that thought was as chill in his heart as Amber's limp body against his breast.

"Father, please," he whispered, but said no more than that. He didn't know what else to say. His earlier prayers hammered at him, *hammered,* with a weight and an impact that left a physical pain inside him: *The burden is too great. Her wounds slow us all. Relieve her of her pains.*

Relieve me of this burden.

He touched the back of his hand to her smooth brow. Amber did not know he was there.

Meoraq rose and left the tent. He would speak slowly, he decided. He would not be hostile. He would draw no blade. He would say only that he had done much for their (*miserable worthless wretched cowardly*) lives and he would ask one of them to tend to Amber in his absence. And if they refused, he would politely and without drawing weapons, observe that he could not look after them while tending to a sick woman himself. And if that failed to sway them—

Nicci's tearful voice cut across his thoughts, bleeding meaning before he consciously translated the words: "We can't just leave her!"

Meoraq stopped walking. His head cocked. He had not heard that, he decided. Or if he had, it held some other meaning.

Their backs were to him, black shapes in the night, flames making night-terrors of all their ugly faces, making them all strangers. All but Scott. Scott he knew at once.

"The fact that she's sick at all, in spite of the Vaccine, means we can't just assume what she's got isn't catching," he was saying in that calm, urgent way he thought hid his mind so well.

"Then why aren't we all sick?" someone asked. "If the Vaccine doesn't work—"

"No one's saying it doesn't work," Scott said quickly. "I'm just suggesting that maybe it only works up to a point. If someone keeps putting themselves in contact with a potential contagion..." Scott paused to let those words work on his murmuring people, then gravely said, "She spends a lot of time with the lizard."

Meoraq's head tipped further. He felt his spines flattening.

"Talking to him. Sharing his food. Touching him. Whether or not they're doing anything...intimate," said Scott, as his people's low whispers grew louder, "my point is, they're always together. Who knows what kind of germs he could be carrying? If she's caught something from him and it jumps to the rest of us..." Scott paused yet again to survey the effect of his words. He liked what he saw enough to let his thought go unfinished. Instead, he said, "The safety of the colony matters more than any one individual. Miss Bierce and I may have had our differences, but I know she'd say the same thing no matter who was in her place."

Nicci put her hands over her face and cried harder. She did not protest, not even when Scott came and put his arm around her shaking shoulders.

"I can't agree to this," said Dag suddenly.

Meoraq looked at him, curiously unrelieved, waiting.

Dag said, troubled, "How are we going to find this temple-place without the lizard? We need him."

"We can keep the lizard," Scott assured them as his humans murmured. "We just need to be more careful about coming into direct contact with him."

"Hey, I'm all for that," said Eric, shrugging his arm up around his woman's shoulders. "Particularly when he gets into one of his slappy moods. But you need to consider the possibility that he might not want to keep tagging along after Amber dies."

And that was too much.

"After?" said Meoraq with a furious hiss. "Not even if, but after?"

They turned with satisfying leaps and cries. Scott took his arm off wailing Nicci and put more of the fire between them. He was a coward, but not a fool. "This isn't personal. Everyone here appreciates what you've done, uh, Meoraq."

His spines flattened with a slapping sound. "I do not like the way you say my name," he said. He did not raise his voice. He did not draw a weapon. He was a Sword of Sheul and he was his own master. "I don't like much of anything I hear you saying."

"How is she?" Scott asked, backing up again.

His spines began to hurt. His throat was already throbbing. "She rests in Sheul's sight tonight. Tomorrow, I go to find a surgeon in the city."

Surprise in every human face and then unease. "Is there one around here?" Dag asked.

"No," Meoraq admitted. "I will be away many days. Twelve at the least. Perhaps more." And as alarmed noise began to whisper through their mouths, he said, "You must tend the woman while I am gone. I will have your word on this!"

"Twelve days? You can't leave us for twelve days!"

"Anything could happen!"

"What about those monsters? What if they come back?"

"She's not going to make it anyway!"

Meoraq whipped around to aim his hand like a knife at that one, the female Maria, hissing, "You shut your poison mouth!"

She did, shrinking back while her man shielded her, and all the humans quieted for a time. Again the hateful Scott gauged his people's mood. Then, with all apparent concern, he said, "Do you really think she's going to last another twelve days? Really?"

"I think she'll die if no one cares for her. Or is that your intent?" he hissed.

Scott's ears pinked and his mouth tightened, but not for long. "Are you calling me a murderer?" he demanded in a very loud, fast, oddly-pitched way.

"Ease up, man," said Eric, catching at his leader's arm. "I'm sure he didn't mean that the way it sounded."

"Do not tell me what my meaning is, human!" he snapped. "If she dies in spite of your care, that is Sheul's will and I honor it, but if she ails and you *let* her die, *that* I call murder and I will see every Gann-damned one of you judged for it!"

"Easy," said Eric, his eyes huge and orange in the firelight. "Easy, Meor—"

"*Stop saying my fucking name like that*!"

Humans scattered back all around him, some with their hands held up and empty, some darting behind others, all staring at him. Meoraq clapped his hands to his face and breathed, battling the killing rage that wanted so badly to take command of him. A Sword of Sheul is a master over his emotions. Six breaths, just as he had trained from boyhood, six breaths deep and slow, like winding steps to peace. Always, he had envisioned Sheul at the last riser, His arms outstretched in welcome. Now, he saw Amber, lying still as death at his feet.

He lowered his arms to his side, calm again, and looked at them. 'I hate you all,' he thought, but he thought it calmly.

Scott waited, letting the silence stir at fears, then said, "You're right. Whatever happens to Amber is God's will. None of us can change that. But regardless of what happens, the rest of us need to take care of ourselves. Sentimentality has no place in this decision. You knew that when you saw her holding that knife and you have to know it now. I know you don't like me—"

Meoraq passed a hand over his eyes again, trying to shut out the human's voice, to seek Sheul's behind it.

"—but you must know I'm right. Say you do go off to the nearest doctor. Are we really supposed to just stay here and wait for you? We don't have the resources to wait twelve days without you."

"There is water at the stream and, if you are sparing, enough meat to last until my return."

Scott glanced towards the sleds, where slabs of corrokis meat had been wrapped in some of the humans' packs and stacked in anticipation of the next day's journey. "I'm sure it would be, if we were moving. But if we're just sitting here, that much meat in one place is nothing but an invitation to all this planet's hungry animals to come get an easy meal. How are we supposed to defend ourselves?"

Several watching humans voiced uneasy agreement.

Scott nodded at them in encouragement before turning gravely back to Meoraq. "I have to weigh the risks here and the fact is, Amber Bierce is just one person. It's difficult to admit this, of course." He paused and, although his expression remained as grimly serious as ever, something about him smiled anyway, invisibly and fanged. "But a leader has to make difficult decisions."

"You will not take her in," Meoraq said. It was not a question. He could feel the color throbbing in his throat, but his thoughts were calm. Black, but calm. "You would let her die to stab at me."

"She's not dying!" Nicci shouted before Scott could answer. "Don't you even say that, you...you...She'll be fine in the morning! She's always fine!"

"Will you look after her then?" Meoraq asked her.

Nicci fell at once to a sniffling silence.

Scott patted her shoulder. "If you were offering any kind of real solution, that would be one thing. But to be brutally honest, I'm not sure how we *could* take care of her for twelve days. She was choking on her own spit a few minutes ago. How are we supposed to give her food and water? I'm sorry, Nichole, I know this is difficult for you. It's difficult for all of us, but I really think it would be best to let nature take its course. Or let God's will be done, if you like that better."

Meoraq's hand came back to his brow-ridges, rubbing hard enough to hurt. Six breaths, he told himself, and counted them off with his eyes shut. Six breaths, deep and slow, six breaths to Amber.

"I'm not enjoying this—"

"Lies! You'd *fuck* this moment if you could!" he spat, and took several stabilizing breaths while Scott stood very quiet. At last, Meoraq raised his head and faced them. "I will meditate upon your words and give you my answer in the morning. I don't want to see any of you until then."

No one had any reply to that, which was just as well.

Meoraq turned around and went back to his tent, where Amber lay on her side on his mat, just as he had left her. He undressed, placing his clothing in a thin layer atop the blanket before joining her beneath it and pulling her unresisting body against his to warm.

"Father, this world itself moves as You command it," Meoraq said, pressing his palm gently to her brow. The words were bitter in his mouth, bitter as the bile on Amber's wet breath. "And whether You choose to heal her or take her into Your halls, I will thank You and love You no less. Only hear the prayer of Your son, I beg, and let Your will be done swiftly, whatever it must be. The hateful little Gann-bastard is right."

* * *

It was a terrible night that followed. Amber lay silent and cold beside him through every endless hour. He was afraid to give her water, afraid to drown her right there in his arms, but as the day dawned, in a kind of desperation, he did attempt it. She only drooled it out. He tried to imitate the cattle-hands he had seen, who sometimes gave their livestock medicines by stroking their throats to make them swallow. Amber only lay there choking under the weight of his hand. Twice, he brought out the knife of his fathers and held it over her. Twice, he sheathed it again, but he didn't know if that was the right thing to do. He had dealt deaths beyond counting in his life, but he had never had to wait this way, had never borne the silent struggles of some fragile life his witness and felt so damned helpless and useless and alone as he did now.

He prayed, because that he could do. He said the Healing Chant until the words became as mechanical as any construct of the Ancients. He said the Prayer of Appeal and all forty-three verses of the Bridge of Men. Mostly, he prayed in the words he might use with his father, speaking as thoughts came over him. Sheul might have heard him; Amber never did. He knew long before the dawn showed him her slack face that there would be no surgeon, no medicine, no run to the city. She did not have twelve days to wait for him. She would be dead in three, if she could not rouse to drink. The hope that she might awaken and be miraculously whole had brought him through the night, but when he could see her again and see what those long hours had done to her, he felt even that stubborn hope strain.

The sun rose and Meoraq did not stir. He watched Amber's clay struggle to hold life within it and listened as the humans outside gathered their goods and made ready for the day's journey. If they were quieter than usual as they went about these tasks, this was the only sign of their concern. It was as if she were already dead to them—dead and burnt, her memory so far distant that grief was just another word, if they had ever known it at all.

He could not be angry with them, although he wanted to be. Grief, like so many things, was a luxury in the wildlands. And as the first hour of the new day stretched into the second, Meoraq's heart began to understand what his head had been telling him all night: It may be within his power to prolong Amber's life, but he could not prevent her death. The longer he tried, the more she—and all the rest of her people—would suffer for it. Between the hated living and the beloved dead, said the Prophet, look to the living, for the dead have done their service and rejoice in Him, but the living may have long roads yet. How many loved ones had Lashraq burnt and left behind him before he came at last to Xi'Matezh and saw his Father's face?

It was surprisingly little comfort to him, but still Meoraq knew what he had to do. "Take her then," he said, stroking the smooth curve of Amber's brow. "Take her, O Father, and receive her well. She is a good woman."

Then he left her and went out into the bitter cold of Gann's world.

The humans were waiting for him, all of them clustered around Scott's fire to share its warmth and whatever was left of the previous night's meal. They'd struck their tents and taken up their beds, filled the flasks and were even now loading their packs onto the sleds. Scott came to meet him, as he had known he would. "How is she?" he asked, pretending deep concern.

Meoraq looked past him to Nicci, standing small and pale at Scott's side. "Do you wish to speak to her?"

"Is she talking?" Scott asked, looking so surprised as to seem alarmed.

"No. But perhaps she will hear you."

"I..." Nicci looked at Scott. He put his arm around her. She bent her head and trembled. She did not go to Amber's side.

So be it.

Meoraq drew the knife of his fathers from the sheath over his heart. It was the best he could offer her. "Gather fuel. As much as can be carried. The fire will have to burn all day."

"What are you going to do with that?" Nicci asked, staring at his father's knife.

He looked at her, knowing that even she couldn't really be so ignorant as to ask that. And she was crying already, so yes, she knew. "It will be quick," he promised. And, as much as he detested her, his heart thawed a little, enough to give her an honest tap at her smooth brow with the hand that did not hold a killing blade. "Don't grieve. She will see her true Father's face soon and I believe His arms will be open to her."

"Don't let him do it!" Nicci begged, clutching at Scott's arm. Water ran out of her eyes in fresh streams. "Please, make him stop!"

Scott nodded, patting at her back. "You're not going to kill her," he told Meoraq.

The words should have carried some hope to him, but Scott's look of somber joy never faltered. "I don't mark you," Meoraq said, sheathing his father's knife.

"We've discussed it." Scott put Nicci aside and, as she sought out another chest to support her, put his hand on Meoraq's arm and led him a short distance from the others. A very short distance. He still wanted to be seen. He still meant to be heard. "We've decided to leave her here with a few supplies...some water...maybe a blanket...In case she wakes up."

"I don't..." Meoraq stared for several breaths, uncounted, then shook his head clear and tried again. "I don't mark you, human."

"She could still pull out of this," Scott said, and actually patted Meoraq on the arm as if he were a damned child in need of comfort. "I wish we could wait for her, I truly do, but she could be contagious. I have to think of the greater good."

"The good? How...How can it be good to leave her to die?"

"We don't have a choice," Scott said. "It's not just about her slowing us down, although she would. Right now, the way she is, she's a health hazard. You may not understand that, but you have to accept it."

"I accept that I can do nothing for her but to send her to our Father gently and give her a decent funeral." The terrible truth in that sank into him until it found something even more terrible and without thinking, he suddenly spat, "Isn't that enough for you, S'kot? Can't you just be happy she's dead? Do you have to see her damned before you feel like you've won?"

His flat, ugly face first paled, then flushed a dull red. "This has nothing to do with me. This has to do with common human decency, something you clearly can't comprehend. Because she is a person, like you said, she's one of *my* people and I am not going to let you murder her when there's a chance, however slim, that she could recover from whatever this is and rejoin us. No," he said, turning his back on Meoraq to address the pack of animals that had made him their abbot, "we can't afford to sit around and wait for her to die. I wish we could. I wish we had doctors and a hospital or even just a safe, dry place to hold our vigil over her, but the fact is that she's sick and she's potentially contagious. Nobody wants to leave her, but this is our reality."

"Piss on your reality!" Meoraq said, loudly enough that many humans looked uncomfortable, but still none of them spoke. "I won't expose her on the fucking plains like a...a runty calf! This is a person! This is one of *your* people! How can you even speak of leaving her body to...to rot like an animal's! To be scavenged and...and lost to the grey hells of Gann? That is worse than murder! That is obscene!"

"If she wakes up, she can rejoin us and be perfectly welcome. If not, at least we'll know we did our best by her, right?" Scott nodded at his people expectantly and they nodded back at him, even as they shuffled on their feet and cast Meoraq uncomfortable glances. Scott turned back to him and took Nicci again under his arm. "So we'll leave her some supplies. A blanket, some food...I'm sure she'd appreciate it if you left one of your water flasks."

"I want no part of this murder."

"No, the murder you want is the one where you slit her throat. Or the one where you hold us here until we all become infected with whatever she's got. I understand your feelings, Meoraq, but what it comes down to is, you can't put her life above all of ours."

The urge to stab him right through his profaning, poison-dripping mouth was strong, but on the slim chance that it came more from Meoraq's clay than from his higher spirit, he restrained himself. He bent his head. He breathed. He cleared his mind of all emotion. He looked up and said, "I have seen many deaths, human. I can imagine none worse than to be torn open, alive and helpless, by wild beasts. I will pretend to believe you when you say you do not wish for her to suffer," he added acidly, and Scott's pink face flushed a darker red. "So I will give her an easy death and I will see her soul to Sheul's halls with an honorable funeral. You need not witness it if you do not wish to show respect we all know you do not feel."

"I have plenty of respect for her," said Scott, staring him down. "Too much to stab her in her sleep and call it kindness. You talk like a religious man. Now act like one. If you really believed in God, you wouldn't hesitate to leave her in His hands."

Many humans had gathered by now. Meoraq looked at them, these people, these children of Sheul. He gave each face the weight of his stare. He watched each eye drop away from his. He gave each mouth a chance to speak. He listened to each silence. Last of all, he turned his head and looked at the sleds, stacked deep with the humans' provisions. Amber's distinctive saoq-hide pack was there, along with her bedroll and her spear.

"You will leave water," Meoraq said, studying the sleds. All of his flasks were there, excepting only the small metal flask given to him by the gatekeeper of Tothax, which hung around his neck.

"Yes, of course."

"And provisions."

"Yes."

Now Meoraq looked at Scott, although he had to clench his hands into fists to keep them from his swords. "Show them to me."

Scott half-raised a hand to gesture vaguely at the empty ground around the ashes of Meoraq's fire, where Amber had last been sleeping. His gaze wavered toward the sleds, but did not quite reach them. The pink tentacle of his tongue peeked out to slick his lips, but he said nothing.

"Tell me your name," said Meoraq quietly, "and the name of your father."

Scott blinked several times, glancing around at the others, but his people defended him no more than they defended Amber. "Uh...Everly Scott? My father's name was Richard? Why?"

Meoraq closed his eyes and counted six breaths. He was calm. A Sheulek is always calm. He said, in the darkness, "Var'li S'kot, son of Var'li Reshar, you are a liar and a thief."

"Hey!"

Meoraq opened his eyes, swung his arm and slapped Scott as hard as he could. As Scott sprawled in the mud with blood beading up over the side of his staring face, Meoraq walked through the silent crowd to the sled he had himself built and took back one of his flasks. Just the one. He slung it over his shoulder and moved to the other sled, where he tossed packs roughly aside until he had uncovered Amber's things.

"Xi'Matezh lies to the east," said Meoraq as he claimed them. "Hold to the path of the sun until you reach the mountains. Cross through and hold your course. You will come to the end of all the world. Go north along the Ruined Reach and you will find the temple. Go now and go with God, if He will have you. I will not."

Now they protested, these creatures who would not even give her a gentle death but who would leave her to be savaged alive in this strange, cold fever by tachuqis, by ghets, by *beetles*! And when it was done, what next for her but to be left lying in the mud, screaming for all eternity unheard as she rotted back into the clay. Her own kind would do this, her own blood-kin!

"You can't do this!" Nicci pushed through the crowd to catch at his arm. He slapped before he could stop himself, but she only fell at his feet and clutched his boot instead. "You promised to take us to the skyport! You can't leave us here!"

"Take your hand off me, you clay-fucking *monster*! I am done with you! All of you! Go! And especially you!" He shook Nicci off his boot, but managed with Sheul's aid not to raise Amber's spear in his hand and drive it through her hateful, ice-filled heart. "Wailing, useless...she-bastard! You do not deserve her! *And she did not deserve you*!"

"Go ahead and kill her," said Scott, scrambling to his feet and out of Meoraq's easy reach. "I mean, if it's that important to you. Shut up, Nichole. Go on. We'll wait."

"Start walking, human."

"But you can kill her now!"

"Get out of my camp."

Scott backed away, hands up, licking at his mouthparts. "Okay, but you're going to catch up with us after she dies, right? We...Come on, you can't do this! She's already dying! If you leave us, you're killing us!" He looked wildly around, his eyes coming at last to the tent where Amber lay, and Meoraq saw the very moment that Gann whispered. "At least pray about it first," Scott said suddenly, pointing a shaking hand out into the wildlands. "You go pray and we'll wait here and we'll...we'll just let God decide what to do."

Meoraq studied him as the humans around them offered their own promises, bargains and pleas. Their voices meant nothing to him. There was a blackness inside him and he thought that if he closed his eyes and let it out, he might open them again to find an hour gone and every human dead, and that was, in this moment, a very fine thought. Instead, he took six breaths with his eyes open and Scott as full in his sight as Meoraq himself was in the sight of Sheul, and then said, calmly, "I should have killed you long before this."

Scott said nothing. What was there to say?

"I'll pray," said Meoraq. "And so should you. Hear Uyane: If Sheul tells me to end her, I will build the pyre and see her to His eternal embrace."

Scott nodded once, his face straining with the effort of showing so much concern.

"And then I will kill you," Meoraq concluded thoughtfully, "and leave you to lie on the open ground with your blood rotting in your veins. But I will take your people on to Xi'Matezh. For her sake."

Scott's mouth worked, but no sound came out.

"However, if Sheul allows me the hope of her life, I will give you yours and let you lead your people out of my camp. And if she dies, so be it. I will not follow you. I will take no more vengeance. I will go to Xi'Matezh alone and if I see you there, I will not even draw this blade—" He patted the hilt of his beast-killing kzung. "—and gut you like the ghet you are. So. I will pray."

He turned around and immediately Scott retreated, hissing at his people to get away from here before the crazy lizard started killing them. Some obeyed. Some protested. Some even followed Meoraq away, but he ignored them all. He entered his tent and knelt in the darkness there and picked up Amber's limp, heavy hand. He shut his eyes on the sight of her white, waxen face. He counted off six breaths listening to the thick, laboring sound of her own. He prayed.

Between the hated living and the beloved dead...

But she wasn't dead. She wasn't dead!

Meoraq rubbed at his brow-ridges, but they hurt, so he stopped. He looked at Amber and then he reached down and pulled her up onto his knee, holding her to his chest and forward some, so that she couldn't choke on her saliva. He fit his hand to the flat place between her soft, swollen teats and just stared at the top of his tent for a while, feeling her heart struggle at its work.

Amber needed him, of course she did, but so did all the rest of them, and while it was true that Amber might recover with his care, it was also true that the chance to spare one life did not and never could balance the risk to forty-seven other lives. If he did this solely because it was Amber, then he would carry every death of every other human as if it were murder. He would be Sheulek no longer. He would be damned in the eyes of God.

I do not want to leave her, Father.

He might have said it aloud. He might have only thought it. Sheul heard all prayers, no matter how they were spoken, and this was the most fervent prayer of all his life. He asked for nothing, sought nothing. He was scarcely aware of thought at all, but Sheul burned in his mind and Amber burned brightest of all against his heart. He sat and stared and held her and might have remained so for hours had not the flap of his tent lifted.

There stood Eric, with his woman cringing against his side. Seeing shame in their ugly faces did nothing at all to cool the fires charring at Meoraq's heart.

"The thing is," said Eric after a long silence, just as if he were continuing an argument and not beginning one, "this is it for us. We're all there is. We need this stuff and she...doesn't. So you can hate us if you want to, man...I kind of hate us too...but what else are we supposed to do?"

"You are supposed to be people!" snapped Meoraq. "How dare you crawl in here and whine at me because I will not allow you to pick carrion from one who isn't even dead! Get out! Get out and go back to your murdering master!"

His woman retreated. Eric lingered.

"It's nothing personal," he said finally.

Meoraq was on his feet and face to ugly face with the man in an instant. "It should be!" he hissed. "It should be very fucking personal when you leave someone to be torn apart by wild beasts...her bones...scattered!" Rage briefly blinded him. He fought it back, but his color was up and throbbing in his throat, and he knew the blackness would take him if he couldn't calm down. "You don't even have your own hate to spur you to murder her! You use *his*!"

"She started it," said Eric.

Meoraq leaned back on his heels and just stared at him.

"She's the one that made us pick sides. She's the one who wouldn't just let anything go!" Eric backed up a step, his neck bent and his eyes in constant motion, looking anywhere but at Meoraq. "She was always on us about how we had to do this and we had to learn that...It's her own fault no one wants to be around her."

"She wanted you to *live*," spat Meoraq. "And you let him punish her for it, you bastard son of Gann. Damn you and damn all of you."

Eric's face darkened. He mumbled something more, but Meoraq could hear no words in the sound. Perhaps there were none. The human let the tent-flap drop between them and Meoraq returned to the watch he kept over Amber and her terrible sleep. She gasped when he brushed at her brow, but lay still as clay even when he lay down beside her and tried in vain to press his living warmth into her. Only the fluttery feel of her failing heart, throbbing from her flesh to his, told him she lived at all.

They were leaving now. He could hear their many feet drumming on the wet earth, moving away into the east. It was not too late. He could make it quick and easy. She would never waken. He could build the pyre, pray while she burned, and catch the rest of them before nightfall.

"Are you with me, Soft-Skin?" he murmured, stroking at her cold, damp brow. "Open your eyes. See me."

They did open, and Meoraq let out an unmanning shout of relief, but they only rolled back and shut again. She had not seen him, did not know him.

But she had opened her eyes.

"Uyane Meoraq is with you," he told her, and put his hand over her heart. "Hear me where you are and follow. Sheul, our Father, has set you in my path. So did you come to me and so you belong to me. Do you hear me, woman? You are mine! I found you, I *own* you, and I forbid you to die!"

His voice, risen to a shout, was a thunder in the tent, a whisper in the world. She did not answer. The heart that beat beneath his hand beat no stronger.

"I won't leave you," he said softly. "Please don't leave me."

Nothing. She did nothing.

Meoraq curled around her as close as his separate clay could press and closed his eyes. "O my Father, I cry out to You. You gave her to me and if I have not been as grateful as a son should be, I am sorry. But You gave her to me. Now...please...give her back."

BOOK VI

GANN

Thunder, falling like a hammer into her brain, knocking her out of her nice, safe sleep and into reality. She heard screaming, her own, and then felt hands, not her own. She fought them, but the hands were thunder, inescapable, pressing her down and holding her fast in this world of cold and fear and hunger.

It hurt. Amber tried to scream, but she couldn't find her voice and didn't have much breath anyway. She managed a hoarse groaning sound, utterly swallowed by the pound and roll of the thunder, and after that had to just lie there under the hands and feel her heart racing in terror because she didn't know where she was or why or even who.

Flapping. The world was made of leather walls close around her and those walls were flapping. The wind had its jaws around the world and was shaking them, shaking them. The thunder was its voice and its fists. At each new crash and roar, she screamed and struggled, but the hands owned her. They pushed her down, they held her, and the thunder opened its throat and breathed her back inside it.

* * *

The second time Amber opened her eyes, it was calmer, both inside the tent, where the wind still steadily shook the walls, and in her mind, where the storm had mostly ended. She rolled and kicked her way onto her side, then lay weakly panting, wondering where in the hell she was.

She could see. The air in the tent was an unhealthy, mottled yellow—the color of daylight filtered first by clouds and then by skins—but she could see, and by an exhausting process of elimination, she eventually realized that the only reason she could possibly see Meoraq's leather tent on every side of her was if she was in it. Why was she in the lizard's tent again? Why did everything hurt? And why was she so dry?

The dryness was worse than the hurt, actually. Her tongue felt swollen and sandpapery and stung when she tried to lick moisture out of her mouth. Her lips were unfeeling things, cracked and scaled—Meoraq's mouth. Even her eyes felt dry. All of that, and yet she was soaked in wetness. The leather mat she lay on squished at her every feeble movement; she could feel beads of moisture tickling over her belly, her breasts, the hollow of her throat, her thighs. Her hair was plastered against her cheeks and neck, ugly to feel and probably pretty damn rank. Rain? Sweat? Did it matter?

Amber found a gripping place on the itchy blanket lying like lead over her body and fought it off. It was not a fight of just one battle. This was ridiculous. She had not been that damn sick. No one could be that damn sick!

She sat up. Her head swam and then hit something. The mat. She'd fallen over? Yes, she had. She sat up again.

Light. She warded it off with one raised hand, then promptly hit her head on the ground again because she apparently needed both hands to hold herself up. Two sudden dives to the mat in as many minutes was too much for her; she dragged her fists up under her chin and lay shivering, wishing the light would go away.

It did, but suddenly Meoraq's huge black body was coming at her, and even though she knew it was him, *knew* it, panic still rolled its own thunder over her and she wheezed out a little scream. That was stupid. She frowned, gasping in the aftershocks of that pointless terror, as Meoraq's scaly hands dipped impersonally beneath her armpits and hauled her up.

She couldn't remember ever being carried before. Ever. Not even as a little girl. It was an odd feeling. Her legs dragged bonelessly across the mat until he got an arm under her and she flopped against the plates of his chest and then she was up. Carried.

"Too heavy," she mumbled, embarrassed. "Don't."

He grunted in the space above her head and shouldered the tent-flap open. Out they went into the unbelievably cold air, air so fresh and clear it seemed to cut her brain when she breathed it in. The light was blinding. She slapped some of it off and then just rested with her hands over her face, rocking limply back and forth as Meoraq walked, wishing he'd put her down. She didn't want anyone to see her being carried like this. She especially didn't want anyone to see it when Meoraq dropped her fat ass on the ground.

But no one was saying anything. It was pretty windy, but she still ought to be able to hear them murmuring and snickering at each other. If nothing else, Crandall should be making a few comments. Especially since...oh for Christ's sake, she was completely naked.

"Put me back!" Amber wailed, pressing her hands even harder against her face because now it made perfect sense that no one was talking and if she had to see them struck speechless by the sight of her naked body, she was going to die right on the spot. "Damn it, lizardman, put me down!"

He did. She felt herself swoop downwards, bump up against his bent knee, and then finish out the slow fall in a heap over the hard, frozen ground. She curled miserably around herself, knowing she couldn't cover everything, and finally made herself face the horror head-on.

Only no one was there.

She kept stupidly staring, right on over nothing, nothing, and more nothing all the way to the horizon. She could see the blackened rings where the campfires had been. She could certainly see the wide path where all their tromping feet had flattened the prairie grass. But the places where the bivies and tents should be poking up out of the ground were empty.

Meoraq's leather teepee was the only one left.

Anywhere.

Something nudged her arm. She blinked around at the mouth of a small, shiny flask, then followed it up Meoraq's arm to his face.

"What happened?" she croaked. "Where is everyone?"

He took her wrist, put the flask in her hand, and made her take it to her mouth. She needed his help to hold it while she drank. The warm water cut her mouth all to hell. She choked and he let her choke, but after she was done, he made her drink again. She had maybe half a dozen swallows before her stomach cramped, and then had just enough instinct to shove the flask back and bend forward before puking it up.

It came out as smooth and tasteless as it had gone in. That made her want to throw up again, but a froggy belch was all she could manage. She groaned and started to cup protectively at her stomach, but Meoraq took her wrist and put the flask back in her hand.

"I can't," she said, trying to push it away.

His spines flattened.

So she drank and even though he made her take twice as much, it stayed miraculously down. Her mouth, wet, throbbed with hurt, but she could feel the rest of her sucking the moisture in, and at the end of his third silent urging, the flask was dry.

He took it back with a grunt of satisfaction, then got up and left her there. She looked after him as he went back inside his tent, and kept right on looking because it was still the only one around.

Meoraq came back with his blanket and draped it around her shoulders, tying the corners together so the wind couldn't blow it off. It was warm, but so heavy. So ridiculously heavy.

"I'm not supposed to get sick," she told him. "I got the Vaccine. We all got it. I can't get sick anymore, they said so. They promised. What happened to me?"

"What do you remember?"

"Everything!"

"Tell me." He hesitated, then gestured toward her stomach. "Had you...been having pains? Were you hurting...all that time?"

"Huh? No, I was fine. We were talking. We..." She thought about it, reaching up to rub at her thick head as if she could comb out a clearer memory with her fingers. It seemed to help, actually. "You told that horrible story about your father."

He drew back a little. "Horrible?"

"And then...and then I was banking the fires and packing the food. I don't...I don't remember going to bed. I don't..." Something tugged at her, just a flutter of sound, an impression more than a real thought: Snakebite. "I think something bit me."

He seemed to relax, just a little. "There was a mark," he said, and looked away.

He watched the clouds roll by. She watched the empty camp. There was no time.

"Where's my stuff?" she asked.

"In my tent. Do not trouble yourself for any of it now."

Amber nodded and pulled the blanket closer around her body. "Where are my clothes?"

"Washed and in your pack. For now, you do not require them."

Which was a nice way of saying he wanted to wait until he was sure she wouldn't piss in them. As was only sensible.

She nodded again, rubbed at her mouth, sat there.

A few seconds passed.

"Where is my sister?"

Meoraq did not answer. He didn't even look at her, just turned his eyes up in his restless way and watched the clouds churn by.

"How long have they been gone?"

"Five days."

"Five days?" She brought her hand up, but didn't touch her eyes. After a while, she just dropped it again. "Where...I mean, did they go someplace...to wait for us?"

He did not answer.

"They wouldn't just leave us," she argued, trying to stare him down, but he kept watching the sky. "They wouldn't do that."

No reply.

"Oh come on! My sister? Nicci? She wouldn't..."

He watched the clouds.

She wanted to keep talking. God knew, there were arguments she could be making. It was absurd to think that they'd actually packed up and left her and no, she wasn't the easiest person in the world to get along with and sure, Everly Scott hated her guts, but no sane person would ever go along with leaving someone behind like that. Just because they didn't like her didn't mean they didn't need her. And if they needed her for nothing else, she was still one of Scott's precious wombs, wasn't she? He wouldn't walk away from that. And no one would walk away from Meoraq, that was just insane! He was the only one who knew where to find this temple they all wanted so desperately to find, so obviously, they were waiting for them.

Just up ahead.

They'd left her.

Amber touched her fingertips to her lips, but they weren't trembling. She felt at the thin skin beneath her eyes, but it was dry. Her heart felt cold, but it kept right on beating. She realized, impossible as it seemed, that this wasn't going to kill her.

Meoraq hadn't moved. He looked perfectly comfortable as he hunkered there against the wind and seemed content to read whatever epic novels were being printed for his viewing pleasure across the sky, and if he cared at all that he had been abandoned by Commander Scott and his brave pioneers, he showed no sign of it.

"Five days isn't very long," said Amber, and looked at the sky. "We could catch up."

Meoraq grunted.

"When are we leaving?"

He rubbed at the ridges over his eyes. Then he looked at her, only this time, she was the one who didn't look back. He hissed under his breath and looked back at the sky.

The way the clouds moved really was pretty hypnotic. She could understand why he did this so often.

"We will go when you can walk," he said at last.

"Then we're leaving tomorrow. I don't care if we only make it to the top of that ridge," she said, pointing. "But we're going. They need to be able to look back and...and see us trying to catch up."

He turned his head and spat, letting the wind take that little comment and carry it off. "So be it."

"And we're going to catch up."

"If it is God's will."

"God has nothing to do with it. Nicci is waiting for me."

That, he didn't answer. Instead, he picked her up again and started walking. She put her arm around his neck in the hopes of better distributing her weight but thought she felt him stiffen, so she took her arm back and just hugged unhappily at herself until she was back inside the tent (*which reeked humiliatingly of sweat and bile and oh what's that gentle fragrance boys and girls that's piss is what that is*) and out of the wind. He set her on the mat (she turned her head so she wouldn't have to see how badly she'd stained it), covered her over with the blanket and the leaden fur besides, and stood up again.

Just stood there. After a moment, he backed up. After a few moments more, he opened the tent-flap and put one foot outside, but he didn't leave, he just looked at her. Or maybe he was only pretending to look at her while he aired the tent out. It needed it. How many times had she pissed the bed, *his* bed? How many times had she *shit* in it? And how could she even care about that when she knew that all the rest of them were out there right now, that some of them might even die because she'd made Meoraq choose her over the others? And would Nicci be one of them?

Her eyes stung; she was too dry to make tears, but her vision blurred anyway. She watched through this tearless haze as Meoraq let the hide-flap fall with him still on the inside. She scratched her eyes shut and turned her face away, but soon felt his scaly fingers on her chin. His strong hand stroked once across her matted hair and down to cup the back of her neck. He pulled her close and pressed his cool, unfeeling brow to hers. She could feel his bony ridges digging at her skull, feel each hot puff of breath against her throat. "Rest in His sight. He sees you well, Soft-Skin. He sees us both."

"Tell him to watch out for Nicci. Because I'm not there, Meoraq. And neither are you." She wiped at her eyes—still dry, still hurting—and pushed him away. "And until she's back, don't you dare tell me this is God's will. If your god sent my baby sister out there to die, then I hate your fucking god. I hate him and I'll tell him so to his face. I'll tell him..."

She lost her breath and then the train of her thoughts and finally had to let him lay her gently down and cover her up again beneath the crushing weight of the blanket. "Tell her she can have the mat," Amber whispered. She no longer knew precisely who she was talking to or why, but the words seemed very important. "Tell her I'm sorry and she can have it now. I'm so..." Her thoughts slipped again and she forgot how to end. Sorry? Thirsty? "Tired," she finished.

She slept.

2

Meoraq sat up all night, watching Amber sleep by lamplight (and often resting his hand between her teats to feel the breaths he could plainly hear and see). Through every long hour, Gann rode his back and whispered in his ear that this was the last rally of a dying soul and that dawn would find her cold beneath his hand, but Sheul's mercy prevailed. She lived. She drank—water at first, then tea, and finally broth made of boiled cuuvash. She mumbled in her restless dreams at times, but when her eyes opened, she always knew him. She had come out of the very shadow of death and she would be well.

And she did make it to the top of the ridge the next day, but only because Meoraq carried her. Six steps. That was all she could manage on her own. Six steps, and they left her so drained that she fell asleep soon after he set her down. Meoraq built her a fire and started the stones heating for tea, then ran on ahead along the wide trampled path left by the humans' passage.

He didn't go far, just up to the next rise. He could see perhaps a quarter-span from this vantage, and Scott's trail cut through all of it, keeping steadily eastward until it vanished over the hills. He waited for some glimmer of the disappointment a righteous man would feel and felt none. If he'd found them, he would be honor-bound to go and fetch them back and he hated even the thought of that. He would do it if Sheul asked it of him, and for Amber's sake he would even do it in good humor, but if he never saw them again, he would lose no sleep over it.

The next day, Amber managed a little better distance, but still needed Meoraq's arm to lean on to get over the next rise, where she took one exhausted look at Scott's trail winding away into nothing and began to cry. Meoraq kept his eyes fixed on the trail and pretended not to notice. This was ludicrous enough when she was only weeping, but when she reached the end of her tears, she just as suddenly fell to shouting.

She said things. Meoraq tried not to listen. Grief had made her half-sick and weariness took her the rest of the way. Once she'd rested, she might not even remember this...remarkably creative string of profanities...so it behooved him to just let her vomit it all out.

He stood while Amber cupped her flat face and screamed Nicci's name until her voice roughened. He studied the rippling lines of shine in the wind-blown grass as Amber cursed Scott for a madman and a murderer. He watched the clouds when she turned on him, slapping and punching at his chest—the blows as weak as a child's—and ordered him to go after them, find them, bring them back.

At last, the tears returned. Meoraq helped her collapse without hurting herself. He left her moaning into her hands and went out into the plains for water. There was ice along the bank of the creek where he drew it. The first ice of the season, thin and white as paper...but it would grow.

She refused to speak to him that night. When he tried to put her mat in his tent, she pulled it out and sat rebelliously with the fire between them and her spear over her lap, just like she thought she could hold a watch.

Meoraq went to his tent and meditated. When he emerged, she was soundly sleeping, still sitting up. He put her to bed; the Amber he had always been able to wake just by walking past her did not stir even when he carried her into his tent and took her boots off.

She slept through the night, past dawn, and deep into the day. When she finally emerged, Meoraq had just finished the last of the hot tea. He grunted a greeting and began to brew more.

Amber sat down there in the mouth of his tent and watched him change stones and meditate. Neither spoke as the water heated. Meoraq could only hope that was a good sign, because she wasn't showing him any expression to gauge her mood by.

"When will you be ready to walk?" he asked finally.

She stared at him dully for a long time and then said, in a voice still rough from yesterday's screaming, "Two or three days, I guess."

Relief struck him like a slap—a short shock and a spreading glow. He grunted again and filled the steeper with some of the redsash leaves. She didn't want to be told that was the right decision. A brace or two ago, Meoraq had known nothing at all about women, but he already knew that much.

"Where did you get that?"

The lifeless question held no clues. Meoraq followed Amber's incurious gaze to the tea box in his hands. Odd...he'd never really looked at it before, beyond determining that it was sufficiently lavish to satisfy his spite. Now its inlay reminded him in an uncomfortable way of the mosaic on the wall in the ruins—a lost world, a flying ship.

He flicked his spines and tossed the steeper into the stewing pouch. "From a man in Tothax."

"A man?" She took the box back and inspected it more closely. "Hunh. It doesn't look like something a man would give."

"He didn't have a choice."

Amber opened and closed a few drawers, sniffing disinterestedly at the various blends. "I guess you like tea a lot, huh?"

"Better than I like boiled water."

"Please go after them." The hoarseness of her damaged voice robbed it of all passion. Her face showed no more emotion than her voice, but her eyes saw him, he was sure. She was very close to death (he would never admit it, but Meoraq had begun to wonder if she might be dead already, her unburnt clay going through the motions of life and no more), but she was not speaking from grief now. She thought she was calm, reasonable. She thought she could convince him.

"I swore I would not leave you," he said.

"I'm asking you to go."

"I didn't swear myself to you."

Amber put his tea box back in his pack and his pack back in his tent. "It's the same as killing them, you know." Her voice was still calm, still reasonable. "Scott can say anything he wants about his imaginary skyport, but if you know they'll die without you and you let them leave anyway, you killed them."

The Sheulek in him judged that uncomfortably close to truth, but not entirely so. "I gave them a choice," he told her, which was also not a whole truth.

"We aren't leaving tracks." Amber turned her head to look back the way they'd come, but there was nothing to show their passage. "Every day, the ground is getting harder and the wind is always blowing. When I woke up, we were five days behind them. Now we're seven, because I can't get myself together. And we'll be ten days or more before I can make a real effort here, and by then, their trail will be gone."

"They will go east," he reminded her. "They will go on to Xi'Matezh the same as we do. He thinks his ship is there."

"They'll starve."

"Starvation is not a quick death." He hated to give the thought, plausible as it was, any more validation, but it was only truth. "Their strength will flag long before they fail. They will den down and we will find them."

"Thirst, then. They don't know how to look for water."

"They won't have to look too hard after all this season's rains, and they have nearly all my flasks to help them carry it. Apart from which, even before I found you, S'kot had sense enough to make his camp by water."

"They'll freeze. Animals could eat them. The storms will come back. Another starship could crash on top of them! A thousand things could happen, damn it!"

"The tea is ready," said Meoraq, dipping his cup. "Come and have some."

She did not come, but she took the tea when he offered it. She drank, wiped her eyes, then drank the rest. He refilled the cup. She held it and stared at him.

"They made a choice," he said again. "So did I."

"And that's it, huh?" She shook her head side-to-side, started to drink, then breathed out a harsh sigh and put the cup aside. "Do you have a family, Meoraq?"

The question took him aback. He could not imagine what had prompted it and dreaded where it would lead. He felt his spines lower and had to force them up again in feigned nonchalance. "Two brothers. Some blood-kin in other cities. Why?"

"How would you feel if they were out here? How easy would it be for you to just sit back and say God will keep them safe?"

"Nduman is out here," he replied. "At least as often as I am. And Sheul keeps him safe. Salkith...You may have a point about Salkith, but I feel I ought to observe that not even he would be out here following S'kot."

"All right, so she made a mistake. You don't just give up on family!"

'She did,' Meoraq thought. To keep from saying it—and oh, but his whole heart and soul wanted to say it, even knowing how deeply it would stab her—he said instead, "Have you any other family but that...but N'ki?"

"No. It's just me and her." The words faltered as they left her mouth. She looked away. "I guess it's just me now."

"I am with you."

"Yeah." But she stayed quiet for a time, just staring into nothing. At last, while he struggled to find something to say to bring her back from wherever she had gone, she stirred and looked at him. "What about you? Where are your parents?"

"My mother died years ago. My father...very recently."

"I'm sorry," she said, just as N'kosa had done.

"Thank you." He still wasn't certain that was the right response. "He served well, died well, and dwells in our true Father's Halls now."

Her brows creased. "How do you have a good death?"

"He died in judgment and Sheul was with him."

"That makes a difference, huh?"

"Yes."

She fell into a silence, which should have been welcome enough, but oddly wasn't. At length, unable to think of what else to say and loathe to let the conversation die, he said, "Your mother is dead also?" and wanted to hit himself for saying it almost immediately. When was that ever good conversation?

Yet Amber merely said, "Yeah. But I don't think God was with her."

It was a startling thing to say on its own merit, and doubly so for the dry way in which she said it. "Why not?"

She did not answer, only stared into the fire and was silent. The light had a way of playing about her face, making her seem a stranger—too hard-worn for his Amber.

"How did she die?" he asked.

She sighed and rubbed at her face. "Christ, I don't even know how to answer that. I guess some people would say she was sick."

"What do you say?" he asked cautiously.

"I try not to say anything. How did your mother die?"

He frowned, but answered readily enough. "She was probably childsick. I remember she complained of feeling overtired for a few days and that she felt heavy. My father offered to send for a surgeon, but she said she was sure it would pass. Then one night, she just started screaming."

The walls of House Uyane were strong. It had not been Yecedi's screams but that of her dressing-maid running to Rasozul's chamber that woke Meoraq and his brothers in the room they shared when home from school. Too big to share a cupboard, too young to have earned a room of their own, they sat up in huddles on the floor, looking at each other in the light from the lamp that stupid Salkith couldn't sleep without and listened to the thunder of their father's feet racing to the other end of the house.

He was back again in mere moments, it seemed, bellowing for the carriage. Salkith, the only one of them senseless enough to act, opened the door just as Rasozul flew by with their mother thrashing and weeping in his arms. Salkith, naturally, dropped right there in the doorway and started crying, but their father hadn't even seemed to see him. All the rest of that night and deep into the next day, they waited. When Rasozul finally opened their door, he had seemed a different man, or a dead one—cold clay in the shape of their father—the air around him choked with the stink of smoke more foul than anything he'd ever smelled in his life. Salkith took one look and started bawling again. And their father, who seldom had much patience for Salkith's soft-headed moods, slid down the door's frame to the floor, pulled Salkith onto his lap, and began to weep with him.

"Meoraq?"

He stirred and focused on Amber, on whose strange face his eyes had been resting all this time while he sat silent. He grunted an acknowledgement at her to disguise his embarrassment at losing himself that way, but her creased brows only creased that much further.

"I guess you were close, huh?"

"No," he admitted. "I didn't...know her very well."

Now they were both quiet. Meoraq, determined not to fall back into that same pool of sucking mud, gazed into the fire instead and refused to think about Yecedi's pyre and the stink that had clung to his father's skin for days afterwards.

"My mother killed herself," said Amber.

He looked at her. She looked at the fire.

"I don't know if she meant to. I guess it could have been an accident. She was taking something that she thought would make her feel good, something she knew was poison. She took it anyway and she took too much. I came home and she was trashing the apartment, puking and pissing herself and smashing stuff on the walls. She was out of care credits, so they wouldn't send a medi-bus. I had to drive her to the hospital with her screaming in my ear and Nicci crying in the back and me yelling at both of them to just shut up." She was quiet for a moment. "Those were my last words to her. 'Shut the fuck up.'" Another short silence. Amber shrugged and looked at the fire. "And they let her die. You know how it is. High risk, low insurance. I guess I should be mad at them...but I'm not. I'm mad at her."

Meoraq looked lamely back into the fire. He wanted to say something, but he didn't know what. He did not know what poison the woman had taken, but suspected it was something like phesok, which fools often chewed in defiance of the Word, breaking faith with Sheul for a handful of dreams. What could he tell her now to comfort her? Amber's mother did not see their true Father's face; she had masked herself forever.

"When they told us she was dead, do you know the first thing I felt? I mean, the very first thing." Amber uttered a short flutter of humorless laughter. "I was relieved.

Nice daughter, huh? I'd just lost my mother, not to mention our home, our insurance and our whole damn life, but for that first moment, the weight fell off, not on, you know?"

He grunted, uncomfortable but listening.

"She wasn't a bad person, I guess." Amber glanced at him. "She didn't build machines or anything. And she had friends. Not many, but she had them. It was just me."

"You?"

"Who didn't like her." Her eyes flinched even when no other part of her did. She looked away. "I didn't like her," she said again. "My own mother. She was just so...bitter and angry and so fucking eager to stick poison in her veins and trade everything she had—including us—for more. And I know that's a pretty sick excuse, but I felt like I'd been watching her die for years. As bad as it was, having it over, finally *over*, felt good."

Her voice cracked. Meoraq frowned and watched the coals.

"I wish I was the kind of person who could just...miss her! But I don't. You have to understand, she was my mother and for the last three years of her life, all I wanted was to just grab Nicci and get away from her. And then she finally died and I don't even think I waited a whole day before I started planning how I was going to make Nicci get on the ship that brought her here!" She flung out her hands to show him all the empty world, then slapped them down again on her thighs. "I appreciate that you saved my life. I'm grateful. It may not sound like it, but I am. I don't want to die. But how *could* you? One person—and I don't care who that person is—one person is not worth the lives of fifty other people, especially when that one person is *me*!"

"You?"

"I'm not...I'm not nice, damn it! You put everyone else in danger to save a horrible human being!"

"You are as our Father made you, Soft-Skin." And as she slapped her hands over her face, he calmly went on, "He knew you would come here, where modesty and gentleness and womanly subservience could only get you killed. All things follow Sheul's great design."

"Bullshit. God has nothing to do with me."

"Do not be blasphemous." He reached out to gentle the chastisement with a tap to her knee, and another, for no real reason at all, to the soft blade of her cheek. "When you came upon your mother sick with poison, you tried to save her. You say you didn't like her, but you tried."

"Meoraq, you're not listening."

"And you forced Nicci on the ship, you say. I doubt you had her tied and dragging behind you, but even if so, you put her on the ship because you would not leave her behind. That is who you are, Soft-Skin. So say whatever you like about how evil you are and how poor a person and how small of worth, but even in the midst of all that, remember that you still took the time to thank me."

She stared at him, her soft brow furrowed.

He picked up the now-cold tea, poured it back into the stewing pouch and dipped her out a fresh cup. She took it when he held it out, but she was still frowning, still trying to think of the right words that would move him on without her.

"I am a Sword and a true son of Sheul," he told her. "I will not leave the one human He has returned to me to chase after those who have put their faith instead in S'kot. Make whatever argument you wish. Ask as often as pleases you. I will not go if it means leaving you behind."

He could see the thought that came into her eyes then. See it and read it, as easily as words written on a page.

"And you will not go," he said dryly, "if it means leaving me. Hear Uyane Meoraq and mark him well, human: Sheul has given me your life and I do not give it back to you. I have been lenient with your freedoms until now. No longer. Do not test me. I'm not very nice either."

She started to speak, then abruptly raised the cup and drank tea instead.

He relented and gave her a tap, letting the touch linger somewhat longer than was appropriate. "Yet they will go on to Xi'Matezh, eh? Whether by Sheul's guidance or by S'kot's, they will go. And we will follow. If God gives them back to me, I will take them in."

She shook her head again, up and down this time, but she didn't seem much comforted. He didn't know what else to tell her, and after the silence had stretched out long enough for her tea to cool again, he finally cried a mental surrender and said it: "What are you thinking?"

"Why?"

"Insufferable...This is my camp and I'll ask whatever questions I please."

She was already shaking her head, one hand back over her face. "No, I meant, that's what I was thinking. I was thinking why? What you just said..." She uncovered her face to look at him, frowning. "You're really not nice. Everyone knows it."

He shrugged that off.

"So why did you stay with me? Five days..." Her eyes grew distant. She huffed out a laugh without a smile. "You did things for me my own mother never did. What..."

More silence. Meoraq took the cup, renewed its contents, and drank it himself.

"Look, I'll just say it," she said suddenly. The color was high in her cheeks, very bright against her sickbed pallor. "What do you want from me? Because I realize I'm in no position to bargain, but I need to know."

He studied the question, knowing it was trapped, but unable to see the trigger. Cautiously, he said, "I want you to be well."

"And after that?"

He did not know how to answer that. There were answers—*I want things to be the way they were. I want to talk the way I talk when I'm with you. I want to stand at Xi'Matezh and see your face filled with wonder when our Father receives us. I want to take my pilgrimage and share it with you. I want you to want to share it with me*—but nothing in Meoraq's life had prepared him to speak any of them out loud. He hesitated, hunting for some true thing he knew how to say, and said, "I wait on Sheul's will."

She leaned slightly forward and searched his eyes while he held very still and kept them open for her. Wind shook the walls of the tent and carried smoke away. The tea, half-gone, cooled in his hand, but he didn't notice. Her eyes were so green and all he could think as he stared into them was that moment when she had opened them from the thick of her dying sleep and seen him.

Amber drew back, frowning. "Okay. But I'm sleeping out here from now on."

He grunted assent, still thinking of her eyes, then abruptly snapped his spines up in surprise. "Why?"

Her jaw clenched. "Because."

"That's a word, not a reason," he said mechanically and smacked a hand over his snout. "I can't listen to myself anymore. You're turning me into my father."

"Because I'm not your pack or your spare shirt or whatever it is that your god told you I was. I don't belong in your tent!"

"You're not two days yet out of a killing sleep, you lunatic! A strong rain would wash you away!"

"Wouldn't be the first time I've slept in the rain."

Meoraq rubbed his snout, his brow-ridges, his throat...but in the end, he had to laugh just a little. "I asked You to restore her," he admitted. And to Amber: "I'm not going to sit here and argue with a sick woman. Drink. I have meat if you think you can eat. Rest as much as you can—wherever you like," he added generously. "And we'll talk again when it rains."

He rose and took up his empty flask, already planning to turn the next pouch of heated water into a bath. They could both use one, although he already knew she wouldn't want to share. He wasn't sure he wanted to, either. Amber naked and white with fever at his side was one thing; Amber naked and rubbing soap into his scales was quite another.

Meoraq stopped at the edge of camp and looked back. Amber was still sitting in the mouth of his tent, holding his cup in both hands like a child. Her hair, like trampled grass, bent crazily in the wind. His shirt on her body was oversized, loose enough at the neck to show a dark, tapering line—like a guiding arrow, he thought vaguely—pointing down between her swelled teats to her belly.

The second thought that came to him was relief so profound as to be prayerful that she was here at all—awake, alive, and arguing with him. Weak yet, but with sleep and warmth and decent feeding, she would soon be strong, he was sure of it, and when he made his prayers tonight, he would make them upon his belly in humility before the merciful God who had lifted her out of the ashes and set her again in his hands.

But that was his second thought. His first made it plain that he was not ready to share her bath.

3

So she rested and even if it was the right thing to do, she still hated it. The days took forever with nothing to do except eat and sleep and watch Scott's trail fade away. The nights were even longer, lying alone next to the fire, often with Meoraq on the other side of it, staring at her. Two days. Three. Four, just to pace around the camp and work the stiffness out of her joints. And on the fifth, after she woke up to a few drops of rain tapping on her blanket, she rolled up her mat and packed her pack.

Meoraq, already awake and drinking his morning tea with his back to her, sighed and poured what was left into the flask he carried around his neck. He gestured at the waterskin, lying empty next to the fire. She took it away to fill it, knowing he was watching her and looking for the slightest weakness—if she stumbled, if she panted, if she shivered a little in the rain that was already coming down like pellets—any excuse to make her stay another day. She didn't give him one. He helped her take down his tent without speaking and they were on their way.

It rained all morning and they walked in it. Amber kept her head down, holding onto Meoraq's pack like a baby elephant to its mama's tail. She didn't think. The cold had numbed her brain as much as her body, but her eyes were open and as long as she could see the trampled path left by Scott and his pioneers under her feet (only trampled, the panicky part of her would cry, not muddy or tore-up, but only *trampled*), she felt okay. The rain finally stopped, but the wind kept blowing, chapping her face and stinging her eyes, but drying her clothes, so that was all right. Meoraq kept trying to make her rest and she didn't argue with him, but she made sure she was always the first one back on her feet again and when he started in with his passive-aggressive observations on where she thought would be a good place to make camp, she managed to put him off three times with a casual, "Let's try over the next hill."

The fourth time she said it, however, he stopped, turned her roughly around, took her pack and her spear, and dropped them both on the ground.

"I can keep going," she said.

"Stubborn idiot!" he snapped, throwing his pack on top of hers. "This is not a contest to see who can go further!"

"Meoraq—"

"No! You will go over that hill and over the next and over the next until you can't walk and can't think and then the tachuqis will come or the ghets or a pack of raiders because there is *always* something to watch for, damn it! These are the wildlands and surviving here means stopping before you exhaust yourself!"

"Maybe you're right, but—"

"*Maybe*?!"

"But we have to catch up!" she insisted. "We're just getting further behind!"

"We will find them in God's time, not yours. Now, you rest."

"But—"

"Rest, I say! No one but you would argue with that!"

Amber bit at her lip and followed the trail the only way she could, with her eyes, through the plains and eastward out of sight. "Maybe—"

"No."

"I didn't even say anything!"

"And I am not going to hear anything! You are resting!"

"Maybe you should go without me."

He threw down a half-assembled tent pole and leapt up.

"I'll rest right here and you can go find them!" she said, trying very hard to sound reasonable while speaking loud and fast to stave off his inevitable interruption. "I'm just slowing you down and we both know it!"

"And we both know my answer, so stop asking!"

"You can find them and bring them b—"

He thumped her hard on the forehead with one knuckle and pointed severely at her trembling mouth to make her shut it. Those yellow stripes were coming out on his throat. "I am not leaving you," he said, not shouting, not even hissing. Somehow, that was worse. "I am *never* leaving you. If it is our Father's will that we take the hateful S'kot and his hateful servants back into my camp, so be it, I serve Him in faith. For now, it is *my* will, human, and I will have your obedience. How do you mark me?"

"My sister is out there," she whispered.

He broke the hold his hot, red eyes had on hers and stared over her left shoulder for a long time. Then he stepped back, rubbing at his throat until it cooled to black again, and went back to assembling poles without speaking.

She stayed quiet and out of his way, knowing she could fight all night if she wanted and never change his mind. "Can I help?" she asked finally, defeated.

"No."

She looked around at the wind-blown plains, but saw no game and no sign that anything had passed through recently. There were no streams, no green swath of promise where water might be hiding, not even a swampy piece of lowland, just more dead hills rolling away on every side of them. The closest tree was easily fifty meters away and all alone—a huge, cancerous-looking thing with a squat, lumpy body trailing parasitical vines like hair from its few remaining branches.

"I'll get a fire going," Amber offered, heading toward the tree. It had clearly been dead for some time, which she hoped meant she'd find some branches around the bottom. She could see some kind of spiky bush at the dead tree's base, so if nothing else, she could always burn that.

"We don't need one yet. Just rest."

"You rest. I'm fine," she said, still walking.

"Insufferable human."

"Scaly son of a bitch."

He grunted without looking at her and went on putting his tent together.

The gully was deeper than it looked. The grass was hip-high and hard to walk through, with plenty of creepers wound through to try and trip her up. Amber went slow, muttering and swearing, keeping her eyes on her feet and determined to go one day, just one, without falling on her stupid face and giving Meoraq yet another reason to think—

"Stop!" he shouted behind her. "Stop now! Here to me!"

Amber rolled her eyes and turned around to see him running down into the gully after her. "I feel fine, damn it, would you relax?"

Meoraq yanked the hooked sword from his belt and no matter how pissed off he was, he would never pull a sword on her.

'Don't turn around,' Amber thought with such clarity and in such a reasonable inner voice that she nodded along in agreement. 'If you don't turn around, nothing will be there.'

Very true. Very good advice.

Amber turned around and watched the spiky bush at the base of the dead tree raise its head and turn magically into an enormous, quill-covered monster, oh, about a meter and a half away.

It saw Meoraq first. Its sleepy eyes squinted, assessing this danger, as it raised one massive, claw-tipped paw—it had no fingers or toes that she could see, just a leathery pad for a palm and four huge hooked claws—to scratch at its neck. The quills that covered its entire body turned to fine hair over its flat face and chin, but kept growing along its jawline in a dead-on evolutionary imitation of a muttonchop beard. That, combined with its severe frown as it watched the sword-swinging lizardman tear across the plains toward it, made it look hilariously like President Martin Van Buren. There had been a row of presidential portraits all around the tops of the walls in her seventh-grade world-history class. She had not realized until this moment that she knew any of them and that was kind of hilarious too.

"Ha," said Amber. She didn't mean to. It just came burping out of her.

The creature's head swung left and right, then down. It saw her. It had eyebrows, of a sort. It raised them. Now he was a surprised Martin Van Buren. *Mr. President, it appears William Harrison has just won the election. Pack up your shit and leave.*

"Ha ha," burped Amber.

The creature thumped its paw into the ground and stood up. And up. And up.

Even as a bush, it had been a pretty big bush, the kind that might burn maybe an hour. She had thought, following its magical transformation into an animal, that it was the size of a bear, because even though she'd never been to a zoo or seen a bear close-up, she'd seen them on TV and figured she knew how big they were, and yeah, big had a way of being subjective the closer a person came to a real live bear, but whatever this thing was, it was no more a bear than it had been a bush. It stood up on all fours and its ass was already taller than Amber, and then it stood up on its hind legs, doubling its height in a slow-motion second. It drew back its arm with a severe, presidential frown and swung.

Something hit her. It wasn't Mr. President the Porcu-bear because she was looking at him. It wasn't a car either because they had none on this planet, or at least, none that worked anymore. It felt a little like a car, though. She'd been hit once when she was little. Mama had gone running across the road so little Amber went running after and the cars had mostly stopped, but one of them hadn't quite and although Amber didn't remember it hurting, she remembered that whole-body double-WHUMP of the car hitting her and then her hitting the pavement. Then, she'd gotten herself a scraped elbow and maybe a bloody lip, she couldn't recall exactly. Now, she tumbled over the grass and thorns and looked up dazedly to see grey skies and rolling clouds and Meoraq hacking at Mr. President's neck. The porcu-bear turned away from Amber at once and slapped with his other paw, aiming at Meoraq this time.

It must have connected, because it seemed from Amber's vantage that Meoraq flew back, but he landed and pivoted and lunged again with such effortless and brutal grace that it might have been choreographed. The sword went in, not bouncing off the quills this time but stabbing through them, slashing deep into the porcu-bear's neck. It bellowed and dropped to all fours, shaking its head and slapping Meoraq away. Again, Meoraq rebounded, pulling his other sword from his back even before he hit the ground. His boots kicked a clod of grassy dirt onto Amber's chest. She tried to pick it up, but it broke apart in her hand.

The porcu-bear stood up again, fanning its fingerless claws with both hands and bobbing its head as it roared, which made it sound a lot like Martin Van Buren during some fairly intense coitus, but when Meoraq came at it again, it dropped and tried to run.

It managed surprising speed for the first dozen steps and staggered for a dozen more before collapsing carefully onto its knees. Glaring at Amber, who it clearly blamed for its predicament, the porcu-bear rolled onto its side and lay panting.

"I didn't see it," someone said. It sounded like her, but she hadn't felt her lips move. Her eyes were still fixed on the dying animal, and even though she could see it lying there, it was as if she could also see it rising up in front of her too—just rising and rising, a mountain of quills and hot breath and muscle—ready to kill. She hadn't seen it? Really? How could anyone miss it?

"It was lying down," someone explained in her voice. Even Amber thought it was a weak excuse. "I thought it was a bush."

Meoraq grunted and stomped into view. The porcu-bear took a swipe at him which he easily stepped over. He planted one boot on the animal's side, gripped the hilt of the sword jutting from Mr. President's neck, and shoved. There was no last kick, no grunt, no slump, but Amber knew the difference immediately. It had been alive; now it was dead. That was how quick it could happen.

Meoraq yanked twice and finally got his sword back. Drops of blood fell like beads from a broken necklace, scattering prettily over the animal's stiff quills and rolling out of sight. Meoraq wiped it off and hung it back on his belt. "Kipwe already. We must be nearer to the mountains than I—Are you all right?"

"You could have been killed."

His spines flared and flattened. "By a kipwe?" he demanded, sounding pissed. He knelt down to carve some meat out of the quill-covered carcass, and maybe he was talking to her while he did it, but she couldn't hear him. His back was to her and on his back was a ragged tear in his tunic with the wet gleam of blood beneath.

"Oh my God, you're hurt!" she blurted.

"I realize that," Meoraq said testily, prodding at another tear, this one on his side. And there was another on his arm. His stomach. His thigh.

"You're bleeding everywhere!"

"Calm yourself. You see here—" He opened the neck of his tunic for her, showing off a smattering of dark, wet smears over his chest. "—only scratches."

"These are not just scratches!" Amber seized his tunic and pulled it out from his body, exposing an uneven line of dashes across his side where the monster had slapped him. There was very little blood, but there were several jagged nubs sticking out through his scaly skin: the splintered tips of the creature's spines, broken off and buried in Meoraq's flesh.

He had not resisted her grip, but stood silent and very, very tense as she stared in dismay at the many points protruding from his chest, hip, back and thigh, and it wasn't until she raised her eyes to ask how bad it was that she noticed he was looking at her and not the wounds at all. His head tipped slowly to one side. He stared at her some more, this time with his spines forward and a frown on his face. "Are you all right?"

The question made no sense to her. None. The words danced around in her head, distracting and unintelligible, and flew away again. She looked back at his chest, because that still mattered, that still made sense, that was still everything.

"You're bleeding," she said. "There's blood everywhere."

His frown deepened. He looked at the gory hunk of meat in his hand, then tossed it into the grass next to the dead porcu-bear and sheathed his knife. He took her firmly by the chin and tipped her head this way and that, checked her hair, turned her around, and finally took her arm and started walking back to camp.

"I'm sorry," she said.

He grunted.

"I didn't see it."

"I know."

"You're bleeding."

"I want you to stop saying that."

"It almost killed you."

"I really want you to stop saying *that.*"

He brought her over to her pack and sat her down, checked her hair one more time, and walked away again. She sort of lost track of him for a while, as impossible as that should have been. He came in and out of her awareness and somewhere along the way, he must have gone back down to the gully because when she finally noticed the fire, there was a piece of Mr. President cooking on it.

Meoraq was on the other side of the fire, heating water in his stewing bag, watching her. "Are you here now?" he asked when their eyes met.

"You've still got blood all over you."

"It isn't serious." He put a wet rock in the fire and a hot one in the bag. "You looked much, much worse than this the night you threw yourself at a tachuqi."

"No, I didn't."

"No one argues with a Sheulek, human."

"I had a few bruises. You're covered in blood. It almost k—"

He cut his hand through the air and pointed it at her. "If you say that one more time, I'm going to muzzle you. No son of Uyane's line has *ever* been killed by a kipwe."

The porcu-bear sizzled enticingly while Amber's stomach churned. Meoraq watched her and heated his water. The wind kept blowing and the world kept turning.

"Come here," Meoraq said suddenly and stood up.

"Why?"

"Because I tell you to."

She got up, not sure what to expect, and he began to unbuckle his harness. "It scarcely tapped me, Soft-Skin," he grumbled. "I'm not hurt. But if it will bring you back from wherever you've gone, tonight you will be my woman and tend to me."

"How?"

He shrugged out of his tunic, tossed it and his harness together to the ground and gestured vaguely at himself. "Find a wound and clean it. I may have overlooked some quills. If you find one, take it out."

Ignoring the arm he offered, Amber immediately moved around behind him to what she considered the worst of the injuries, or least, the one that had bled most profusely. High on his back, from just under the blade of his left shoulder to the deep valley of his spine, were at least two dozen stuttering dashes where the porcu-bear had slapped him. One of its quills remained, its broken stump as thick as her pinky-finger, stuck at the end of the bloody groove it had carved. She put her hand beside it, stupidly splayed so as to catch it if it tried to dart away.

She realized only after she'd done it that it was the first time she'd touched him, really touched him. Not his sleeve or even his wrist, but the real, solid, flesh-and-bone *him*. The feel of his scaly skin was thick and abrasive—much more so than it looked even—yet flexible over the swells of his muscular body, the way she imagined a crocodile might feel, or a dragon. And he was warm, the way she remembered from that day when he'd taken the knife away from her throat and pulled her roughly against his body. So warm.

"Now what?" she stammered.

Silence.

"Meoraq?" Hesitantly, she touched the tip of one finger to the rough edge of the protruding quill. "Do I...Do I just pull it out?"

His neck turned, not quite enough to let him actually look at her. "As opposed to what?" he asked. "Hammering it further in?"

She pinched at it nervously and let go again almost at once. It felt very solidly caught. What if it was lodged in his bone? Or his lung? What if she made it worse by pulling it out? What if he started bleeding and she couldn't stop it?

"Take firm hold," he prompted. "And pull in the direction it points. They aren't barbed. It should come out cleanly."

Amber pinched at the quill again and this time, tugged it free. She was horrified by its size: not quite as long as her thumb, which did not seem impressive until she saw it coming out of a living body. Meoraq's blood rolled down its sides onto her thumb. Warm blood. She dropped the quill, fighting the urge to stomp on it too, and wiped her hand on her shirt half a dozen times, succeeding only in smearing the blood around.

"How does it look?" Meoraq asked. He didn't sound very concerned. "Is it still flowing?"

Amber tore her eyes off the stain on her shirt and looked at his back. His scales, wedged aside when the quill had pierced him, had merely slipped back into place, sealing the wound almost bloodlessly, but the scrape preceding it, and all the other lesser ones, were so smeared by blood that it was impossible to tell if they were still leaking or not.

"A little. Should I...What do I use for a bandage?"

"Bandage? Stop trying to paint it out worse than it is! Just lick it."

"What?"

"Lick it. To help it heal cleanly."

"That may work with you lizard-people, but I'm pretty sure I remember hearing that human mouths are dirty. Here, wait." She dashed over to her pack for her last Manifestor's shirt. It took a little effort to get it going, but she soon tore one of the sleeves off and came running back to him.

"That was your good shirt," he said, watching her dunk it in the hot water.

"It's the only thing I have that I'm sure is clean," she told him. "Turn around."

He didn't, just stood there, so she went behind him and dabbed at the blood on his back.

He didn't move, didn't speak.

"God, there's another one." Amber pulled a second quill, buried so deeply that it had snagged her wash-rag before she'd seen it, and immediately began searching for a third by sweeping her bare hand back and forth across his skin.

He stiffened so dramatically that it was like feeling a man turn to stone, just like a troll in those story-books she could so vaguely recall from her state-care days. When she'd been six. She'd been six and Nicci was being taken care of in the baby-wing upstairs and Mama was gone. She'd been six and she got three meals every day plus snacks and the sheets were always clean and the dishes were always done and life was story-books and juice boxes and the hill in the yard that she rolled down just one time, just the once, tumbling fast and screaming and laughing and free past all the trees and broken bricks and trash that could have hit her but didn't until she lay there at the bottom on her back thinking life was good, life was great, and it could never get any better. And it hadn't. She'd been six.

Amber burst out crying, puking out tears fast and hard and very loud for the few mortifying seconds it took to swallow them down again. She took her hand off Meoraq's unmoving back and stumbled away, swiping at her face.

The wind blew over them, stirring the grass and pushing smoke in a hot curtain between them. Meoraq's eyes on her were unblinking, hot as live coals. She couldn't look at them, had to look at his dark blood on the sleeve of her last clean shirt instead.

"I'm so sorry."

He did not reply.

"I should have seen it."

Still no answer.

"Please..." *don't leave me.* Amber bit down on that until her lips stopped shaking, but as soon as she unlocked her jaws, it found another way out as a trembling, "Please don't be mad at me."

He broke his gaze at last, turning his terrible eyes and whatever furious emotion was in them on the sky. "I'm not."

"I didn't see that thing or I never would have gotten so close."

"I know." He glanced at her, scowled, and rubbed at his brow-ridges. "A sleeping kipwe is well-hidden in the wildlands. I didn't see it either. And you..."

She waited, twisting her wet, bloody sleeve between her fingers.

Meoraq hissed something under his breath impossible to catch. He rubbed at his brows again, then at his throat, then dropped his hand to his side and yanked a quill out. He glared it down, tossed it away in the grass, and looked at her again.

Without speaking, he unbuckled his sword-belt. It and the hooked sword he carried landed on the discarded heap of his tunic.

"What are you doing?" Amber asked, and hated the little whisper in which she asked it.

"I, nothing," he said brusquely, sitting down in the grass to unfasten his boots. "You are tending my wounds. And you can bathe me while you're about it."

"Oh."

"Such wounds," he grumbled. "There will be songs sung of it one day, surely. Meoraq and the Kipwe." He lay down and bucked his hips up (Amber felt a blush like a physical slap to both cheeks) to push his breeches down. He kicked them off indifferently, still muttering, and unbuckled his metal panty-panel.

Then he was naked. Completely naked. Wearing nothing but his scaly skin and his favorite knife on a cord around his neck, he stood up again and beckoned her to him.

"I've never...bathed anyone before," she stammered.

He stared at her like he thought she was kidding. "Well," he said finally. "I think as long as you don't use mud, you'll make a good effort of it."

She hesitated forward a step and he turned around, raising his arms like a scarecrow, muttering under his breath about the absurdity of a land where women got paid to carry food but didn't know how to bathe a man.

Amber dipped the rag in warm water and dabbed at his back, just under the scored place where the porcu-bear had scratched him. "What was it? The thing you killed. You called it something."

"Kipwe. They come over the mountains every year to winter in the plains. We must be close."

"I didn't do anything."

"Eh?"

"I just stood there." Amber looked at the torn scales under her hand and then at the dark blood staining her rag. "I just stood there and watched you get hurt."

"I'm beginning to take that personally," Meoraq said, tilting his head to a dangerous angle.

"What do you call it when you get stabbed with hundreds of bony spikes?"

"Shameless exaggeration."

"So, what? You're going to stand there and tell me that thing wasn't dangerous?"

"Anything can be dangerous under the right conditions." Meoraq held up his hand to stop the bath and went to move the roasting kipwe off the hottest part of the coals. When he came back, it was to lie down in the grass at her feet. He gestured vaguely at himself and tucked his arms up behind his head, closing his eyes. "You seem to think yourself a coward for not leaping at the thing with your naked hands. Whereas I would think you a fool if you had." He snorted, then added, "For all the rest of your life."

Slowly, Amber knelt down beside him and began to clean around one of the fresh scratches on his arm. Her fingers made a rasping sound as she moved over his scales, a sound that made the gooseflesh pop out on her arms and her stomach want to shiver.

"Does this hurt?" she blurted. "When I touch you?"

He was quiet for so long, she thought he'd dozed off, but then he said, without opening his eyes, "My flesh is not fragile. A Sheulek feels no pain even when he is broken. When he is not, he feels nothing."

He had more quills stuck in him. She could see two of them now, tucked up under his armpit—just two nubs, scarcely discernible against his uneven skin. They had been lodged deeper than the last one and both took some work to worry loose, but Meoraq neither moved nor made a sound when she told him they were out. She looked at him, but he ignored her, lying splayed and by all appearances asleep, and after a while, she put her hands on him again and began to sweep them in small circles over his body, washing with one hand while the other quested ahead for more lost quills. The *shush-shush* sound this action produced summoned a tangle of images too dim to grasp, but she didn't try to alter her rhythm. Her hands kept moving—her hands on his body—over his shoulders, over his chest, up along his throat and down again.

The quiet was crushing her, filled with nothing but that sound and the reality of his flesh under hers. How could she be thinking like this? Now, of all times! Looking at him stretched over the ground so silent and still was like seeing him dead and it could have happened, regardless of what he thought, it could have happened just like that and then she'd be out here alone, which she deserved to be, because she just stood there and didn't do *anything*.

A sob rose in her throat and she had to cough it out, but she swallowed the rest of them. She squeezed her eyes shut and tried to breathe herself calm the way she'd seen him do so often, but it didn't work for her. When she opened her eyes again, all she could see was Meoraq, sleeping.

There was another spine between two of the long plates of his abdomen, so tightly lodged that she had to bend over (*please stop thinking please stop not here not now not me*) and bite it out. His blood tasted bitter on her tongue and had a smell curiously like cloves. She had to fight not to bend down again, fight not to press her lips against those scales that couldn't feel her anyway, fight not to lick the way he'd licked at her neck once. She wanted him to put his arms around her. She wanted to be all right, dammit, and to know she was all right just once more, just *once*!

"You saved my life," she heard her voice say. It broke on the last word. "Again. I keep...making you...*save* me."

She stopped, gulping air to keep herself from openly crying, but he did not reply. His breathing was deep and even; his body beneath her hand, perfectly relaxed.

"Are you asleep?" she asked, now in the plaintive, scratchy, sing-song way that said tears were coming no matter how hard she tried to breathe them back in. "Meoraq?"

Nothing.

She patted his stomach timidly, found a quill and pulled it out, then looked at the bloody sliver pinched between her fingers and that was it. Her mouth cramped. Her eyes swam. Her head began to pound and her chest began to heave. She folded over, choking on breaths that wanted to be sobs, until she was curled against Meoraq's warm side in a small, shaking ball. She had become an expert in the fine art of quiet crying; the only sounds she made beyond a hoarse *huh-huh-haaaaah* were intermittent mousy squeaks and they weren't enough to wake Meoraq.

At length, the storm passed, but she huddled there for some time anyway. Her eyes were open, but unfocused, processing nothing beyond light and shadow, grass and sky. When she finally raised her head and looked, Meoraq was still asleep.

Amber picked the cloth out of the grass and washed her face. It was cold. She dunked it in the stewing pouch, now the bathing pouch, and tried again, but the wind took away the heat before her skin had time to really feel it. She dabbed at Meoraq's bloody scales some more; he couldn't feel her or the wind or the cold.

She finished cleaning him up, then made one last pass for quills, not so much because she expected to find them, but just so she could keep touching him. The tough old Amber who didn't need anybody was dead and buried; the weepy, useless Amber who was left needed to be touched tonight, even if all he did was wake up and grab her wrist and tell her to keep her hands to herself.

But she found one last quill buried in his hip. His blood had blackened it to the same color as his scales and it had broken off right at the surface of his skin, making it easy to miss and hard to get out. She spent several minutes trying unsuccessfully to pinch it between her fingernails before she had to give up. "I think I need to borrow your knife," she said.

No answer. His chest rose and fell slowly. His eyes stayed shut.

"Meoraq?" She patted hesitantly at his stomach.

He did not respond.

Amber hesitated, then closed her hand around the bone-hilt of his favorite knife and pulled it from the sheath slung across his chest. He did not move. The tip slid in under the quill, slicing easily through even his tough scales. She sucked in a whispered curse, but Meoraq never flinched. Fresh blood welled up and trickled out around the quill; she eyed it and him uncertainly, then cut the wound a little wider, just enough to get her fingernails on it. She had to twist at it a long time before she had enough to bite, but she did eventually get it out and he slept through the whole thing.

Amber dabbed unnecessarily at the wound, which had already sealed itself. His blood was hot on her fingers, but cooled fast, darkening to black in the open air. The scent of cloves wafted up. Meoraq slept.

She watched him. After a while, she put her hands on him again, stained now with his blood and hers, and ran them gently back and forth as she stared into his face. She wondered if she would be able to tell him from other lizardmen, if she ever met one. She wondered if he were handsome, for a lizard. She looked at him, at her hands on his stomach, and then at the smooth place between his thighs.

Which was not entirely smooth.

She waited to feel something, some flare of guilt or shock or something, but didn't, not even when she saw her hand travel down to the slight swell of his groin. She cupped him there, rolled her palm in just one gentle pass, then lightly squeezed. 'Now his eyes will be open,' she thought, and looked, but they weren't. He slept.

She should have felt relief. She didn't. If anything, she felt worse. Small and scared and lonely and...and human. The last human. The one human, and a weak, ridiculous one at that.

'I'm useless,' she thought. 'I am a scared, weak, little human. I am a scared, weak, little *girl*.'

Tears stung. Of course. Girls were crybabies. Had she ever really thought she was tough? She would give anything, *anything*, to be held tonight.

Amber's fingers flexed, kneading at his groin as if it were a woman's breast, and discerning as she did so the solid press of something inside him. She could fathom little of its shape beneath his thick skin, only that it bulged out into a hard knot at one end. She moved her hand beneath this, exploring its dimensions, and when she squeezed him there, the scales of his groin suddenly split and extruded the blunt head of an organ.

She opened her hand. It slipped back inside him, leaving the wet shine of some clear, viscous, clove-smelling oil to show her where the opening had been. She looked at his eyes. They were shut.

You could press the mid-pad of a cat's paw, she thought, and squeeze out its claws just like that. But he couldn't feel it, not any of it. She rubbed low underneath that half-felt lump, then kneaded at him boldly in the same rhythm as her spike-finding caresses earlier until, with a heave, the whole of it came thrusting out.

It looked only just enough like a penis that she was sure that was what it was. Only just, and no more. It was scaled, like the rest of him, but the scales there were so fine that she could see the veins throbbing just below its thin surface and did not dare to touch it. At the base, just where the edges of his slit wrapped around it, she could see part of the hard lump she'd probably been squeezing: a thick knob of flesh, swollen to a high shine and covered in dozens of small, blunt barbs, all of them oozing more of that spicy-scented oil. The shaft that sprouted from this dubious bulb was not smooth, particularly along the underside, where it formed pronounced ridges, the very sight of which made her shiver. At the head of his cock, a short, stiff nub curled slightly back toward his body, and even seeing it for the first time, some instinctive animal part of her knew just where it would strike inside her and how it would feel.

Her hand, firmly gripping at his groin, shook. She stared into the slick eye of Meoraq's cock and saw herself, how it would be to shift her clothes and straddle him, right here. She'd put that alien cock inside her and maybe it would fill everything that was empty and not just the useless woman-part. It probably wouldn't take long. He might sleep through the whole thing.

Her hand opened. His cock jutted stubbornly another few seconds, and then his body took it grudgingly back again. Amber wiped at the streak of oil left on his scales, then stood up, away from him. Eyes burning, she staggered over to his tent and crawled inside, unrolling her bedroll and pulling his blanket over her head. Something big howled, not far from camp. Never far.

She began to cry without noise, without moving, like Meoraq when he slept. She slipped her hand down her pants and into urgent moisture. 'Fear-sweat,' she thought, rubbing. She came. She cried. She slept.

* * *

Meoraq waited until Amber was quiet before he sat up. He pulled in his legs, rested his elbows atop his knees, and stared at the tent. His flesh was not fragile; neither was it stone.

He was not fool enough to throw down his guard and sleep so soon, not with a dead kipwe in easy distance of his camp and hungry ghets prowling nearby, and he was genuinely surprised that Amber believed he would. She, who had seen death snap at her so many times, had seen it snap at him and it had made her...well, a woman. He had hoped giving her a domestic chore like bathing him would calm her down, but it hadn't. Feigning sleep had seemed the polite thing to do, in part because it let her tears have some privacy, and in part because being bathed by a woman had a tendency to arouse him and those were Amber's hands moving over his naked body and he was a horribly insensitive brunt who absolutely was not going to have sexual stirrings while Amber cried herself calm. So he'd shut his eyes and slowed his breath and meditated, trying to unhear her sobs with some success and unfeel her hands with somewhat less success, and he had just begun to wonder when he ought to 'waken' and maybe brew some tea when she put her hand boldly between his legs.

Of all the things she might do, that had never occurred to him. Not even in his darkest fantasies, on nights when Gann had given him a thousand burning thoughts, had he ever imagined she would put her hand on him. But she did and it was no accident. She wasn't bathing him; she wasn't searching for injury; she was cupping him just below his slit and gently kneading—so shocking an act that he could not at first move...and then did not want to. A Sheulek must be a master of his flesh in every situation, but her hand moved and moved and Sheul Himself could not have unfelt that. He felt himself extrude and still he did not open his eyes. He only breathed, waiting in a kind of paralytic fever for what came next.

'It's not a sin,' he'd reasoned, if one could call that shiver-white throb of heat in his brain a reasoning thought. 'It's only a sin if I do it. There's nothing in the Word that says she can't do it for me.'

So he'd waited, but she hadn't. He could hear her breathing above him, feel the tremble in her hand, and then, by all the names of God and Gann, she took her hand away. She'd left him there, stabbing foolishly out into nothing, and put herself to bed and the only thing that had stopped him from leaping on her like a raging beast had been the sound of her soft tears. That, and the thin hope that she might come back if he only lay still enough long enough.

But no. She fell asleep. She'd put her hand on him and brought out his cock and *breathed* on it and gone to sleep.

And she'd left his father's knife uncovered in the dirt. Meoraq glared at it, but did not recover it, much as it infuriated him to see it neglected there. She might wake and remember it, and if so, she must see only what she had left behind her. A naked blade. A sleeping man. Both primed to enter flesh and abandoned.

He lay back down and shut his eyes, frustration like a forge in his belly.

Perhaps she didn't know, he thought suddenly. Perhaps she did not recognize his cock because it was not limp and loose and generally disgusting. He supposed that humans did not mate as dumaqs, did not penetrate at all but only...what? By all the movement he had glimpsed on past encounters, he knew they had to be mashing themselves together somehow, but as horrible as that image was, Amber surely would think it just as wrong to have a dumaqi member stabbed into her.

And yet...

He'd seen her naked many times during the terrible days of her illness and so he couldn't help but notice the slit at her loins. It meant nothing to him at the time, which was a better testament to his character than it was now, when he could think of nothing else. Regardless of how their males were formed, he knew that human females were similar to normal women, at least on the surface. He may not be able to sheathe himself entirely, but there was *something* and he could pierce it.

In a burst of determination, Meoraq flipped onto his feet and took two long strides toward the tent. He was done. He'd been patient. He'd tolerated every unintended offense and quite a few intended ones and, by Sheul, he was ready to be the man that proved she was a woman! If it meant getting creative about the method, so be it, Amber's hand had put him in a damned creative mood, but he was waking her up right now!

The wind turned abruptly, stirring the grass with whispers in which Meoraq heard the ghost of his father's voice: A Sheulek is the master of his clay, always.

Meoraq cursed silently, blasting his own thought-space with profanities he never would have dared to utter to the true ghost of his father. A Sheulek was a master of his emotions as well, but he would just have to work on that.

He went back to the fire and lay down beside his disgraced knife. He glared at the tent where the human slept on, oblivious to him. He closed his eyes, measured out his breath—

She'd put her damned hand right on him.

—and began to pray.

4

In another few days, Meoraq saw the mountains. They were just a smudge on the horizon now, a broken blue line he could see only from the highest point of one of the many steep hills they had to climb, but they were in sight. The borders of holy Gedal, birthplace of the Prophet and of the Word, a land Meoraq had heard of all his life but never expected to see, and now the mountains were before him. They had ceased to be a part of the myth of Xi'Matezh and had instead become inevitable.

He pointed them out to Amber with a broad smile, but regretted it immediately when she dropped her pack and lunged ahead. "Where are they?" she gasped, searching the empty wilds. "I don't...I don't see them."

He could see it in her soft face, how she tried to be a little happy when he told her about the mountains, but she didn't care. He had meant to show her how much closer they were to God's true House, but without intending to, he had instead shown her Scott's people, her people, and then removed them all over again. She said it didn't matter. She kept walking. And she cried that night, when she thought he couldn't hear her.

He wanted to give her back her people, as much as he hated the thought of having them back. He wanted to prove they were all dead so her grief would finally end, but he couldn't do it without killing her blood-kin, her damned Nicci. He wanted Amber, the whole Amber, and he wanted her to want him the way she thought she wanted the cowardly, treacherous cattle who had left her in the grass to die. He wanted all these things, all at the same time, and the conflict left him in such a constant state of resentment and self-disgust and sympathy that he could hardly speak to her at all.

Sheul would make His will known in time. Meoraq believed that, even if Amber didn't. Sheul would make His will known and until then, they walked.

The hills grew steeper, more compact and more orderly. Meoraq knew what that meant and he could have led Amber around easily enough—she had a tendency to fall into her own mind when she tired and she tired very easily these days—but he didn't. Scott would have come this way, walking between the hills where it was relatively flat, as slopes gradually gave way to rubble and the rubble to ruins.

"I knew it," said Amber behind him.

He grunted, his eyes moving restlessly from tower to archway to raised loop of road—all destroyed, all decayed, all fallen. Little remained that the land had not at least begun to swallow, and Meoraq could see several structures that would not be standing at all but for the years of dead thorns enwrapping them. No sane and reasonable man would ever get closer to those cracked towers than Meoraq stood now.

"Do you think they went in?" Amber asked.

"Yes," said Meoraq. They were poor ruins, even as ruins could be reckoned, but Scott would have insisted on walking through them if he'd seen them.

And Meoraq thought he'd probably seen them. There was little left of the humans' trail these past few days, but there was enough yet to catch a trained eye. Boot prints amid the animal tracks in the frozen mud at an icy stream. A tattered jacket, blown into a thorn break after its owner had no more use for it. The ash-heaps of their fires wherever they'd stopped to camp. No, they weren't close, but the last sure sign of their passing had been only a quarter-span back, so they had seen these ruins.

Meoraq shrugged off his pack and handed it to Amber. "I'll go. You rest."

There wasn't even time to take one step before his pack struck his back and her challenging, "You rest! I'm fine!" rang out.

He sighed and rubbed at his brow-ridges, reminding himself that he had begged for her restoration. "Must we do this every day?"

"Stop saying that like I'm the one doing it."

"Put out your hand."

"No! You'll tie me up!"

"I'm tempted," he admitted, "but no. Never again. Now put it out, Soft-Skin."

She glared at him, her mouthparts pressed together into a hard, pale line, and then suddenly thrust out her arm like a spear.

He waited, watching her hand tremble until it became too heavy to hold and she dropped it back to her side. "I'll go," he said, turning around. "You rest."

"Jerk."

"Pest."

"Be careful, then."

"And you."

He went alone into the ruins with his kzung in his hand, but he knew already that they were empty. No lights burned in these broken windows; no voices called out from the speaking-boxes. Scott had surely stopped to indulge his fascination with the machines that dwelled here and perhaps to shelter out some little fall of rain, but the ruins were no place to sustain a man. Eventually, Scott would want a fire, clean water, a chance at hunting. Meoraq would find nothing here worth stopping for and he knew it, but he would find whatever there was and he would make some report of it to Amber, easing her mind just enough to let her sleep tonight, and that alone made this inconvenience tolerable to him.

Meoraq's eye wandered at that thought, drifting up over the broken walls where rooftops should be to look at the sky. High clouds, thin cover, fairly pale. He'd hoped for rain. He shouldn't, as far as travel was concerned, but nights that it rained were the only nights Amber joined him in his tent. There was enough room for both their beds (with half an arm's length between them, unless Meoraq arranged his bedroll just right, which he was very careful to do every night, just in case), and his blanket was wide enough to share, but she was being stubborn. Each night that the rains forced her inside, she'd perch on the very edge of her mat, wrapped in her silvery sheet, curled up small until sleep loosened her limbs. If she dreamed badly, she'd move around on her mat until some part of her found some part of him, and then the rest of her would creep in and cling.

So far, Amber's hands (her freezing hands) had not slipped down over his belly to knead at him again, but they might. He told himself he had not decided how to handle it when that happened, but on rainy nights, Meoraq had taken to sleeping naked.

But he didn't think it would rain tonight. He still had perhaps three hours of daylight left, and the weather could do almost anything in three hours' time, but he thought tonight Amber would be out on her mat by the fire, stubbornly trying to hold a watch even though he'd told her not to bother anymore. They were in Sheul's sight, just as he had been during all the years he had camped in the wildlands alone, and must trust to His watch. She did not agree.

Three hours until dark...

He supposed he could waste enough time here that they would have to camp nearby (not within the ruins, he would not allow that even for Amber's ease of mind), but he didn't see the need. Amber might not want to go, but if he phrased it right—*We should stop here so that you can have a half-day's rest*—he was confident that she'd march herself on. They could put another span behind them in that time, even if she had to stop again.

So then. Meoraq returned his beast-killing blade to his belt and, just to be able to say honestly that he'd done all possible, cupped his hands around the end of his snout and bellowed Scott's name. The call bounced away down the streets, unheard. Meoraq listened, waited, watched a machine wheeze out of one alley and into another, then cupped his snout and hollered again: "Humans! Come!"

A thin, metallic finger tapped at his leg. A machine coughed out some unintelligible inquiry, prying at its front panel.

"Get away," Meoraq told it absently, and it coughed again and moved on. "Humans! Give cry if you hear me! It is Uyane!"

Still nothing. Meoraq allowed himself a smile, but only a short one. He turned around and headed back to Amber, his eyes sweeping from wall to broken wall only because that was how he'd been trained when traveling in the wildlands. He saw nothing, just stone and metal husks digesting in the open air. Time and raiders had picked the place over down to its rusted old bones, leaving nothing but wreckage and decaying relics for the machines to tend until their last spark of perverse life was spent and they died.

Or were killed.

Meoraq stopped walking and looked back over his shoulder at the dead machine that had inspired the last piece of this rambling (and somewhat smug) line of thought. A machine. A bot, as Amber would call it. It stood just inside a rather small, plain structure, whose only notable feature was that its roof had only partly fallen in. Through the broken wall, Meoraq could see it lying like a protective shield over what few furnishings had survived the years of exposure and salvage. Just a big, empty room and a dead machine...which had been smashed to death by a piece of stone broken off the wall. He had seen a machine killed that way once before.

Meoraq put his hand on the hilt of his kzung again, but didn't unclip it from his belt. Amber was waiting. He could go. One dead machine meant nothing worth investigating further and there were only three hours, maybe less, before nightfall.

"Fuck," said Meoraq. He climbed through the wall.

Past the worst of the debris, beneath the overhang of the surviving section of roof, he saw the char of their fire. The little that remained told him they'd burnt their sleds, and while Eric had built one of them, the other Meoraq considered his even after Scott stole it, and he was annoyed.

"Humans!" he called. "Come out, if you hear me! Uyane Meoraq stands before you! Come!"

Silence. The wind outside gusted, making a moaning sound as it blew through open windows and over roofless towers. Here, nothing stirred.

Two sleds could not have burned long, but the humans had stayed by their fire long after it had gone out. When they'd moved on, some had walked through the ashes. Smudgy bootprints led Meoraq out of this dubious shelter into an adjoining room, one with a window. There, the tracks suggested the humans had gathered, shifting aimlessly as humans did when Scott was speaking.

Meoraq frowned, looking through the window to try and see what Scott had seen, what Scott had wanted everyone to see.

He wished Amber were here. She'd see whatever it was at once, he was sure. All Meoraq saw was the wreckage of a city he shouldn't even be in.

Had it been a machine? Decaying vehicles and other unwieldy devices littered the streets and infested the innards of the broken buildings. Any one of them might have inspired Scott to some new sermon, but he thought not. Maybe if one of them were working, but not these. Even the living machines, the bots, were so decrepit that they could only undermine Scott's effort to convince them of a viable flying ship in Xi'Matezh. So what, then? What else was there?

Roads, walls, scrap, sky. He couldn't even see the mountains from here because the window faced north. No, it was nothing but ruin as far as he could see, cut into slices by cross-streets, fallen poles, a canal, until the plains took it all away. Nothing.

And yet, when Scott had led his people onward, he had chosen to lead them out through this broken window.

Meoraq followed, his spines flat to his skull. The tracks quickly faded and were lost. He had to stop and search every alleyway, every open door and broken window, every small space a human might have squeezed through, but found no sign of them.

He ended at the canal, which was not a true canal after all, but some sort of stormway, collecting the rain as it ran off the roads and whisking it away through a tunnel. Stormways like these were used in modern cities to irrigate farmland or water cattle while reducing damage caused by seasonal floods. Perhaps the Ancients used them the same way. In any case, there were some machines alive to tend them, because the stormway had not filled in with the unavoidable detritus that even abandoned cities excreted in hard rains. There were some cracks in the wall, and the grate that had discouraged foolhardy children of the Ancients from exploring the tunnels had fallen, but otherwise, it seemed well-kept. The canal was quite wide and easily twice Meoraq's height in depth, but there was only a little water in the bottom, standing clear on top of a thick layer of greenish-black sediment.

Clear enough for Scott to want to fill his stolen flasks here? Meoraq hunkered down on the edge of the canal and thought about that, trying to be objective.

He couldn't see it. The first person who got sick drinking this piss would end Scott's power over the rest of them.

Meoraq straightened up, scanning the ruins on the far side of the stormway, but he didn't see anything and he saw no reason to keep looking. The slope of the canal's sides were shallow enough that he ought to be able to simply walk across, but he hated to get his boots mucky and he could just imagine what that sediment smelled like when it was kicked up. Yes, Scott had been here, but even he'd had the sense to move on.

Meoraq turned away from the canal...and slowly turned back.

The storm grate lay in the bottom of the canal's eastern end, staining the sludge around it rust-orange. The tunnel's mouth yawned above it at roughly knee-height, tall enough for a machine to walk comfortably within if maintenance were called for. Or a man. Or many men, walking in a line.

His eyes shifted from the perfect black of the tunnel's mouth to the sloping wall of the canal. The stormways were being maintained, but they weren't scrubbed down often enough to prevent a thin veneer of scum from forming where water regularly flowed. A greenish-brown film skinned the lower half of both walls...but it had been scraped down on this side. Not cleanly, as a machine would do, but in clumsy stripes. Like skidding feet. Like boots, to be specific.

Meoraq walked along the edge of the stormway until he stood right above that scraped place. He hunkered down, peering into the tunnel as far as he could see. His arm could have reached further than his eyes, but his eyes reached far enough to show him all the scum-black tracks left by their human boots. All aimed inward.

"I am not going in there," said Meoraq.

No one answered him.

"I say no. I say, in fact, fuck the fist of that very idea. I would not follow the Prophet himself into that hole and I for damned sure will not follow S'kot."

Still no answer.

So. Decided, Meoraq stood and marched back up the narrow street, past the ruined building where Scott and his people had sheltered, and out into the broad travel lanes of this city. There he stopped and stood for some time, his head bent, meditating.

His prayers ended with a muttered curse. Then he raised his head and loudly said,

"I require assistance."

Three machines nosed out of their dens and crawled toward him. They all spoke, but only one of them was capable of making itself understood. "How may I direct you?" it croaked, opening its chest to display a glowing window where tiny images appeared in a neat row. "Error. Directory assistance not found. Error. Public communications channel not found. Error. Community calendar schedule not found. Error—"

"Come with me," Meoraq said curtly. His meditations had left him with the strong conviction that mastery was more than the command of a moment's need, but he knew he stood upon the very edge of breaking the Second Law. For now, Sheul was with him, but if he found Scott in that tunnel, he was going to kill him there.

"How may I direct you?" the bot asked, struggling along after him. It kept asking every few seconds all the way back to the stormway, where it tried to rattle out some complicated machine-reason why it couldn't go any further. It made some equally obscure threats when Meoraq picked the fucking thing up and carried it with him to the bottom of the canal. His boots were swallowed at once in a shallow pool of stagnant slime, and it stank just as bad as he'd thought. Meoraq thumped the bot down in the mouth of the tunnel and stepped up onto the storm grate, doing his best to scrape his boots off.

"There has been an incident," the machine observed, probing one of its feelers into the scum that covered the tunnel's floor. "Maintenance has been notified. Error error. Channel not found. Error. No response, no arrival. How may I direct you?"

Meoraq aimed its glowing chest into the tunnel, where it shone every bit as bright as one of Scott's human lamps. He could see now fifty paces, maybe more, but there was still nothing to see apart from their tracks. He listened. Deep in the darkness, water dripped onto wet stone. There were no breaths but his, no footsteps, no life. The smell was that of cold, moldering stone and black water—the very breath of Gann.

He was not going in there. It was madness to do even this much. And Scott was hardly the sort of man who would strike off boldly down an unlit, unmapped, unmaintained tunnel. That took more than just idiocy. That took a certain degree of idiotic courage as well.

"S'kot!" Meoraq called.

"How may I direct you? Error. Directory assistance—"

"What is this place?" Meoraq asked.

"Error. Directory assistance not found. Updates requested. Error error. Channel not—"

"Stop. These tunnels...Where do they lead?"

"Welcome to Citymap! Please wait. Error. Signal not found. Updates requested—"

"Stop! Enough. Let me think."

So. Meoraq's sense of direction was, like his sense of time, fairly well-tuned after a lifetime of travel. Although the tunnels might turn any number of ways after boring off into the blackness, right here, the stormway ran west to east. It could be fairly assumed that the tunnels stretched as far as the city, and if so, they might go on forever. The cities of the Ancients were the very flesh of this world in their age. A man could dig down anywhere and find their relics.

Did Scott really think he could travel through to Gedai in this tunnel, crossing not over the mountains, but under them? Or had he only intended to explore them a short way and lost himself? The human lamps were neither infinite nor infallible. They might well be just ahead, just outside of hearing, camped in blackness, waiting for rescue.

"You'd better be here," Meoraq muttered, climbing up onto the tunnel's lip. His first handhold broke off in his hand. Not an encouraging omen. And not the only missing handhold, he saw. Who could possibly pull a piece of the tunnel out and keep going?

"S'kot!" he shouted, and the tunnel shouted it onward for him.

"How may I—"

"Just follow me." Meoraq started walking, his gaze shifting between the bot-lit black of the seemingly endless tunnel ahead of him and their tracks on the floor. He thought of rain while he walked—the rain that sent Amber crawling in to share his tent, the rain that had not quite fallen enough to spill into this tunnel and wash these tracks away. The rain could be fickle.

The sound of water dripping grew closer. The bot's light caught the surface of a wide puddle ahead, casting water-shine over the walls and ceiling. Thinking of rain, Meoraq walked right through it.

His boots squelched down into what might as well have been a puddle of black oil and went wildly out from under him. Meoraq's right hand flew out to anchor himself to the wall (his left slapped down over his groin in a futile effort to relieve some of the strain of having his legs skid out in opposite directions), but there was nothing to grip and he dropped smack on his ass in the same stuff. He felt the shock all the way up his spine. And then he felt the icy sludge seeping into his breeches.

"Why am I doing this?" he muttered.

"I'm sorry. Please rephrase your question."

"Can you not shut up for one fucking minute?!"

"Would you like to contact an usher support technician? Error error. Channel not found. I'm sorry I could not assist you today." The light glowing from the machine's chest snapped off. "Goodbye."

Meoraq clapped both hands to his face, then threw back his head and howled, "I require assistance!"

Light obediently bloomed. "How may I—"

"Just stand there and stay quiet!"

"Standing by."

"Great Sheul, O my Father, I thank You for every pain I am alive to feel," he spat, pulling himself out of the muck with a wet sucking sound that would have been hilarious under circumstances that did not include him. He got up carefully, straddling the puddle in an awkward crouch, and ventured deeper, feeling his way along the wall. "Humans, come! Give cry if you hear—"

He slipped again, just one boot this time, which had the effect of throwing him hard against the tunnel wall. He hit snout-first, which was bad enough, and then the wall collapsed, pitching him painfully through the rotten stone and into a series of equally rotten pipes. They burst, spraying out stormwater like needles in his eyes and breaking away even more of the crumbling wall. The flow quickly slackened, but the wall kept falling, opening a wider and wider gap below and above him until pieces of the tunnel's ceiling were breaking off.

Meoraq scrambled back, his limbs skidding wildly through that damned puddle until he finally thrashed free of it. The bot pivoted to watch him go, lighting his graceless retreat until a crunch and a shower of sparks threw him into darkness. Meoraq bolted back up the tunnel, smashing from one wall to the other until he leapt out into open air.

He landed hard, skidded what felt like half a span, then hit a crack under the sediment and went right over on his belly in the bottom of the canal. Cold sludge sluiced up over his snout and poured itself in under his clothes, swallowing him in stink.

He lay there, dazed. He didn't think he'd ever been dazed before. He could feel his brain still careening through its own black tunnel, seeking some gripping place, and what it eventually hooked onto was, 'Salkith must feel like this all the time.'

He laughed, spewing bubbles up through the watery muck, then pushed himself out of it. Behind him, the tunnel was quiet. The mouth stayed open, round and innocent, silently asking if he'd like to try again.

Meoraq gained his feet, wiping compulsively at the end of his snout even though he knew he was only rubbing the taste deeper into his scent-cavities. He took a breath, coughed it out, took another, and decided he was all right. Bruised, reeking, and without a damned thing to show for it, but all right.

He started to pray his thanks, stopped to climb out of the stormway, finished his prayer, and headed back to Amber.

She hadn't put his tent together—it was still too early for that, in spite of the eons he'd spent in the tunnel—but she had lit a fire and was heating something in the stewing pouch while she waited for him. He had plenty of time to watch her watch his approach. Her face was as good as a mirror, but he didn't need it. He couldn't possibly look worse than he smelled.

"What the hell happened to you?" she asked as soon as he was close enough.

There were many things he could have told her, things she deserved to know, but he couldn't think how to do it.

"I fell down," he said. That was true enough.

"That's tea," she warned, watching him reach for the stewing pouch.

"As far as I care, human, it is now oddly-scented bathwater." He splashed a little over his face, rinsed his mouth, then began to undress.

She pulled his pack over and found his soap, started to hold it out and then drew it back when he put out his hand. "Am I supposed to...? You want me to help?"

He laughed curtly. To have Amber bathe him again had been pressed into his imagination, his fantasies, ever since that night...but now, with this stink in his scales, he could not be less aroused. Sheul heard and answered every prayer. Ha.

"Yes," he said, raising his arms.

She obeyed, wetting the bar and rubbing it between her hands before she gave it to him. While he attempted to clean his mouth, nose, and especially his scent-cavities, she moved behind him and started scrubbing at his back.

"See anything down there?"

He didn't know what to tell her.

"There's always something, Soft-Skin."

"But no sign of them, huh?"

She thought she knew what he would say, and yet there was a hopeful tremor in her voice. She had contented herself all these days with footprints, with ashes, with dung. She could follow their shadow all the way to Xi'Matezh as long as she knew something was casting it. Take that away...

Uyane Meoraq, twelve years a Sword in Sheul's service, with conscious thought and in full sight of God and Gann both, lied.

"None."

Her hands on his flesh stilled. He felt, in exquisite detail, the fingers of one hand open and lie flat just under his shoulder. Her breath sighed onto his back, first warm from her body, then cold in the wind. "I thought...I was so sure..."

Meoraq said nothing.

She sighed again, but resumed bathing him. "Thanks for looking, anyway."

'Father, forgive me,' he thought, staring into the sky where the light of the sun stared back at him behind the clouds. 'Truth does not care if it comforts her. But I do.'

5

It started raining immediately after Amber tied up the last piece of laundry to dry. As if she needed more proof that this whole planet hated her.

"Meoraq?" she called. "What should I do? Take it down or leave it up?"

No answer. She leaned out around the tree that was serving as her laundry line, but he was still sitting there on the flattest and most hospitable rock in camp, naked, just staring into space.

He'd been very distant lately, ever since the ruins. He wouldn't talk about it, not to her at least, but he sure prayed a lot, even for him. And when he did talk to her...

"Are we still going the right way?" she'd asked this morning, not whining or anything, just asking.

He'd rounded on her at once, flinging out one arm and shoving his face right in hers. "Do you see the mountains?"

"Yeah, but I haven't seen any sign of Nicci and the others for—"

"And you think I have?"

"Maybe!" And because that did sound like whining, she added defensively, "If you stopped to tell me everything you saw, you'd be talking all the time! You haven't said two words all morning, does that mean you haven't seen anything?"

"I've said more than two words," he'd said disgustedly and stomped off.

Some days, it wasn't even worth trying. "Have you seen anything or not!" she exploded. "Jesus!"

"I see what God gives me to see."

She'd stopped there before she started a real fight, but after she'd fumed long enough to make him happy, he'd said, without looking at her, "No."

"See? That was all you had to say."

Another long stretch of nothing but wind and the marching of their boots.

"The doors of Xi'Matezh may not open," Meoraq had said suddenly. "I will have to live with that...if it happens."

"I don't think I want to hear where you're going with this."

"We may never find—"

"Shut up, lizardman."

He did, and that was pretty much it for chit-chat until they set up camp for the night. They'd talked a little then—him at his end, bathing out of the stewing pouch, and her by the fire, trying to stretch out the saoq they had left with roasted roots. Although neither one had commented on the day's chilly silence, his bad mood was never further than arm's length and she'd left him alone after his bath.

And now he was getting another one, it seemed. Look at him. Just sitting there. In training all his life to be God's foot and he still didn't know to get out of the rain.

"Meoraq?" Tucking her hands under her arms to warm them, she headed over. How in the hell he could sit there without a stitch on in this weather (or any weather) amazed her. "Meoraq, wake up."

His spines twitched. He looked up, looked down, looked at her. "It's raining."

"I hadn't noticed," she said, shivering. "I just got your clothes hung up, too."

He shrugged his spines. "Leave them. They could use a soak."

Right. He insisted they still smelled, even though she'd been washing them every night since they left the ruins.

Meoraq stood up and collected the clothes he hadn't bothered to put on. He still didn't bother. He pointed at her mat and went on into his tent without speaking.

It was going to be another fun night.

Amber dug their dinner out of the ashes before it completely turned to hot mud, packed it into her pack, rolled up her mat, and joined him.

He'd put on his panties at least and lit his lamp. He watched in his serious, distracted way as she arranged her bed, but closed his eyes when she asked so she could change into drier clothes. Rattier ones, but drier.

"I think I've reached the point where mending this is only going to make it worse," she remarked, carefully shrugging into one of her old shirts.

He grunted.

"But I guess nothing lasts forever."

"God's will is infinite, His love, eternal."

"Okay, but nothing real lasts forever."

His eyes opened.

"Nothing physical," she amended, holding up her hands in surrender.

He glanced at them, then ran his gaze thoughtfully across her well-worn shirt down to her bare thighs. He frowned and looked away. "Put your clothes on."

She rolled her eyes, but found a huge pair of jeans to step into. Her skinny jeans. "Like you haven't been sitting around bare-ass for hours. Like you're not—" She eyed him. "—ninety-eight percent naked right now."

He grunted.

And did it bother her? She wasn't sure. She told herself it didn't, but she told herself a lot of things these days—*we'll find them they're fine they're looking for us too*—she didn't entirely believe. It was his tent and the man had every right to sleep in the nude if he wanted to. Besides which, he was so perfectly casual about his body that she felt it might be...she wasn't sure...*impolite* to say anything.

But it *was* his body and on nights like this one, when he made her sleep beside him under his blanket, bother didn't even come close to what he did to her. She knew he knew it; he had to know it; there was no way she could look at him or not look at him or touch him or not touch him that didn't scream everything that had happened that night, and everything she'd wanted to happen.

But he just fell asleep.

Amber spread out her wet things so they had a chance to dry and sat down. "I hope these are done," she said, pulling dinner out of her pack.

Meoraq watched her unwrap the mixed mess of fatty saoq and sooty roots, but didn't reach for any. She couldn't blame him, but she took a big bite anyway.

"Well," she said, after she simply couldn't chew any longer and had to swallow it. "They're cooked enough. But I wouldn't call it a success."

He did not comment.

"I was hoping the fat would help flavor these godawful roots," she explained.

"Gruu."

"This godawful gruu. But instead, the gruu made the saoq taste bitter. Now they're both incredibly nasty. Have some."

He pinched off part of one softened, fat-smeared root and ate it.

"It's horrible, huh?"

"I thank You, O my Father, for food in the wildlands to sustain me when the world dies for winter."

She rolled her eyes and took another bitter bite.

So did he. "And I thank You for the human who prepared it," he said. "And for the life which sustains her also. Even here, in the very shadow of Gann, O Father, You have set our table and filled our cup."

"Rub-a-dub-dub. Thanks for the grub. Yay, God."

He looked at her.

"You pray in your way, I pray in mine."

They ate, but not much. Prayer did not make the stuff taste any better and Meoraq's heavy mood would have made even cheeseburgers and fries difficult to eat. Soon Amber was wrapping the remains back up in the hopes it would magically disappear before morning.

It wasn't very late, but the rain made things darker, so Amber went ahead and put herself to bed. The sound of her blanket crinkling as she wound herself into it was all there was for several minutes. He waited until she was settled before dropping half his blanket over her. He didn't offer first, he just did it. Like he always did.

And then he just sat there and watched her.

Well, okay. Might as well light it up, as Bo Peep would say, and see who inhaled.

"Something on your mind?" she asked.

"Yes."

"Want to talk about it?"

"No."

"Why not?"

He scowled and looked at the wall. "I know what you'll say."

Flat spines and a narrow stare warned her not to ask, unless she wanted to see his neck light up too. Amber rolled onto her stomach, idly flapping a shadow-bat across the tent wall with the help of the lamp. Meoraq had never seen shadow-puppets before; the last two times it had rained, she'd done dogs and ducks. She didn't have a lot more to show him, but she was saving the elephant for a finale.

He watched for a while, but not with the same interest as he had on other nights. She wasn't surprised at his abrupt, imperious, "Say something."

"About what?" she asked, letting her hands drop.

"I don't care. Talk to me."

Amber had never been a social person, but she knew instinctively that 'What the hell is going on with you lately?' would have been the wrong way to begin. She said, "Is this the furthest you've ever been from home?"

The tense set of his shoulders relaxed slightly. His spines came up, just a little. "Yes. By far."

"You ever think about what's going on at home without you?"

"Sometimes." He scratched at his snout. "I'm sure they've sent for my brother by now, but he might not attend until after the cold season. My father's ministers can manage the House until I return and Nduman has...somewhere else he wants to be."

"So if you go home—" The if was important. Home was a touchy subject for him. "—what's the first thing you're going to do?"

"Pray."

"Well, duh. I meant after that."

"Mm." He leaned back to think about it. Slowly, his brooding scowl became a smile. "In the steward's private chambers, there's a full bath...You won't know what that is, but it's like a deep basin, twice the size of this tent, that can be filled with water and kept heated."

"Imagine that."

"My first meal will be held in the festival hall, or in the lord's garden if the weather is fair. They'll hang the lamps. My father's ministers as well as the heads of the more important households will be there to give me their oaths, so I'll be expected to provide entertainment. There will be music and singing and some sort of dramatics...I'll have to find out whether or not Uyane has performers on staff, although I can't really imagine that we don't. I'll have to attend as long as the guests do and they'll be trying to impress me with their loyalty, which means we'll all be there all night." He thought about it, quietly laughed. "It's going to be hell."

"What will you eat?"

His smile became a smirk. "Calf's head and marrow, probably."

"Gross."

"A feast for lords."

"It's still gross."

"I'll send down to the kitchen for something else later if you like."

"What makes you think I'll be there, lizardman?"

"You belong to me."

"Think so, huh?" Her voice didn't rise. Her smile wasn't strained. They'd had this exchange often enough that she didn't even consider it a fight anymore.

Amber rolled onto her back and brought out the shadow-bat again. His head turned to track its movements. On impulse, she made a tusked fist with a broad, cud-chewing thumb: a corroki.

"You want to know what I think is funny?" she asked, lumbering it across the tent wall. "You've never asked what it's like where I'm from. Never once."

He watched the corroki and said nothing.

"Don't you think that's odd?"

His spines flexed and flattened a few times.

She killed the shadow-corroki and sat up. "Really? You're not even a little curious?"

Nothing from the lizardman. He kept staring at the wall as if it were still covered in shadow-puppets. His face had lost that easy smile and gone as grim as he could make it, which was pretty damned grim.

"Well," she said, trying to pretend nothing was wrong, that this was still a cheerful way to pass a rainy night. "The sky is different. I mean, I'm from the city, so I never saw much but smog anyway, but it's still different."

Silence.

"How is it different, you ask? Well, to begin with, it's—"

"No one speaks for a Sheulek."

"I wouldn't have to if you'd talk to me."

He grunted, glaring at the wall above her head.

The rain pattered down.

Unexpectedly, almost angrily, he said, "Were there lights?"

"Sure, all the time."

He gestured curtly upwards. "Were there lights in the sky at night?"

She started to answer, thinking in a confused way that he meant city lights, and realized all at once what he really meant. "Stars? Yeah, we had stars. But you couldn't see them in the city even when the smog was down. The other lights were just too bright. I never saw them myself, except on TV. But they were there. Haven't..." She hesitated, but he was finally looking at her, so she went ahead and asked. "Haven't you ever seen the sky? The real sky, I mean."

"The Age of the Ancients ended," he said by way of answer. "For His wrath was great. And the blight covered every land, and poison bled into every cup, and madness into every heart, until the shadow of His wrath gloved all the world."

Amber sighed and rubbed at her face. "That's a direct quote, isn't it? I asked you a question and you're quoting your Bible at me."

"The Age of the Warrior awakened, which the Prophet called the Hour of Gann's Dominion, but there is nothing eternal, save His love and the promise of His forgiveness."

"What a remarkably roundabout way of not answering me."

"When God's faith in His children is renewed at last, the Hour of Gann will end, and with it, the shadow of His wrath. We are in the last days, Soft-Skin."

"Uh huh. And you know this because...?"

"Other men have seen the storms clearing."

"But have you?"

"It was not my time to see."

"Oh for Christ's sake."

He watched her rub her face (with both hands now; some nights he drove her crazy). His own expression was a lot like hers had to be: resigned and frustrated and amused all together.

"I have never seen the sun," he said, "but I have seen its light. Is that what you want to hear?"

"Be nice if I could hear it without listening to Gospel Hour for Lizardfolk first," Amber muttered.

"I didn't mark that."

"I'm not repeating it."

"Ah." Meoraq's head cocked. "Tell me about your human god."

Amber looked up, startled, to meet red eyes glinting with challenge. "Why?"

He snorted, as if his point had been made. "I have often thought that you argue with me solely because you enjoy argument. Now I know it."

"I do not!"

"I have been twelve years in God's service. I have been His Sword in hundreds of trials and felt His hand upon my shoulder a thousand times more. Before that, I studied His laws and read His true Word and in every possible manner learned to see His mark where He left one. I have been my entire life in His sight, and even before, when He chose to have me born under the sign of the Blade. And yet you argue with me each time His name is invoked, when you know nothing."

"What were you hoping for?" she asked. "What, if I tell you about my god and you tell me about yours, they'd pop up and fight it out?"

"Don't be blasphemous." He thought about it and snorted. "Sheul would win."

"Your god could beat up my god. Seriously?"

"You have no confidence in him," said Meoraq with a derisive flick of his spines, making sure she could hear his lower-case h. "Why should I?"

"I bet if I looked, I could find plenty of people on this planet who don't care as much about your god as you do," she countered. "Besides, it doesn't matter how much you believe in something. Believing doesn't make something true."

Meoraq snorted again.

"Scott believes there's a skyport at Xi'Matezh," she snapped, and he frowned. "He got fifty other people to believe it with him. They all believe they're going to hop on and fly home and, I don't know, eat star farts and Hershey bars the whole way there. Nothing you ever said after twelve years as God's foot made a damn bit of difference to any of them. That's what belief does to people, Meoraq. Blind faith has got nothing to do with truth."

He just sat there, frowning.

"I decided a long time ago that all religions are pretty much the same horseshit and I didn't need it to feel better, so if you call that a win, you won." She rolled over, yanking her blanket up around her ears.

The wind lapped at the side of the tent. Somewhere in the world, a lone corroki let out one of those moose-like bellows, but only one and it was very far away. Inside, it was quiet.

Amber took it for a long, long time. Then she peeked back over her shoulder.

Meoraq was still sitting there, frowning exactly the same way.

She pushed herself up on her elbows. "Why do you want me to talk about God?"

"I want to see if you can."

She sat all the way up. "Or if I'll what? Burst into flames?"

His red eyes narrowed. "I want to see if you can talk about your god in the rational way you claim I do not, or if you'll just call it shit and stop talking for the night."

"Okay," she said. "There is no God."

"*Ha*!" He thrust his hand at her, grimacing hugely in lizardish triumph. "And you can't do it!"

"You can't get more rational than that!"

"I asked you to tell me about your god," he shot back. "And you gave me your opinion. And if that's all you can do, I fail to see how that is so much more sensible than what you call my 'blind' faith."

He had a point. Scaly son of a bitch.

"I can't quote the Bible at you," she said finally. "But I could maybe tell a story."

"Do so."

"Not a true story, just the sort of thing people say to make a point."

"I will judge whether it is true or not," he declared.

"Yeah, right." She took another moment to collect her thoughts and began, "So...There once was a very religious man who considered himself very devoted to God and faithful and righteous and all that."

"All that *nonsense*, you mean," Meoraq muttered.

"You want to tell the story?"

He grunted and gestured for her to continue.

"One day, it began to storm really hard and someone came to this man's house and warned him to leave because it was going to flood. But the man refused to leave his home, saying he had served God faithfully and felt certain God would protect him now. Kind of like saying that he walked in God's sight so storms don't matter," she added.

"Is that part of the story?" asked Meoraq. "Or is it just your opinion?"

"It rained and rained and suddenly the river overflowed and the whole valley flooded, including this man's yard. So he was inside praying and watching his basement fill up with water when another man came by in a boat and shouted for the man to come with him to high ground. But the man refused, saying God would save him."

Meoraq snorted disdainfully, but that was all.

"And it rained and rained and finally the man was forced to climb up on his roof. But he wasn't there long before a third man came by in a helicopter and shouted for him to climb aboard and he'd take him to the rescue station. But the man refused, saying he had chosen the righteous path all his life and now God would surely save him. And it rained and rained and the water came up over the roof and washed the man into the raging floodwaters. He knew he was going to die and with his last breath, he cried out to God, saying, 'All these years I have served you! Why did you do nothing to save me?' And God said—"

For the first time, the sneer left Meoraq's face. "He spoke?"

"Yeah, in the story. Anyway, God said, 'What do you mean I did nothing? I sent a warning, a boat and a helicopter! Why didn't you listen?"

Meoraq leaned back, frowning.

"That's it," said Amber. "That's the whole story. It isn't true."

"Perhaps not," he said slowly. "But I will not be certain until I have meditated on its meaning."

"Oh for...I can tell you right now that it never happened. Isn't that enough?"

He focused sharply in on her, his spines flaring forward in surprise. "Just because a man saw the story in his mind instead of on the street doesn't necessarily make it less true."

"Um...yes, it does. In fact, seeing a story in your head instead of in real life makes it *entirely* less true. In further fact," she said, trying to match his expression of severe gravity and failing with a short laugh, "it makes it a bald-faced lie."

"If a blind man tells you the sky is grey, is it less true because he can't see it for himself? And if someone told him the sky was some other color, some ridiculous color..."

"Blue," Amber suggested dryly.

He pointed at her. "Blue," he agreed. "And he tells you it is grey, is it still the lie he believes it to be? Truth is not always what someone says, Soft-Skin. Truth is what something *is*, what it *means*."

"You can make a story mean anything, Meoraq. But that's the thing with you religious people, isn't it? God is this glorious intangibility, so *no* proof *becomes* proof just by how you spin it."

His head tipped by degrees, like the ticking hand of a stopwatch, until it was all the way in humor and he could openly laugh at her. At *her*. Honestly. "You are going to have to tell me," he said in that laughing way, as he swung out one arm to put the whole world on display for her, "what you see that constitutes *no proof* of God."

She started to answer, but then just sighed. "I could point out that you've just made my case for me, but I doubt you'd see it that way. Why don't we just agree to respect each other's crazy ideas out loud, mock each other in private, and go to sleep?"

"That would be a lie, wouldn't it?"

"Little white lies make the world go 'round, Meoraq."

"Your world, perhaps. Mine spins by its weight and magnetism, they tell me."

"How shockingly scientific of you. I thought you'd tell me God spun it Himself."

"Who do you think gave the world weight? Comfort yourself with your lack of faith if it pleases you," he added, putting one hand on the floor of the tent and bending in his attitude of prayer, still smiling. "God does not require your permission to exist."

"I don't require His, either," she countered, tucking herself in under the blanket. "Good night, lizardman."

"Rest easy, Soft-Skin." Meoraq's mouth gaped in a brief grimace of fine-edged humor. "We are in His sight."

She rolled her eyes, then closed them.

* * *

In the midst of that night, Meoraq spoke to God.

Amber's tale of the human god had been, like the wind upon the prairie, an ever-present whisper in his mind throughout his meditations. It seemed to him that there was truth within it, truth far greater than the message it carried plain upon its face. He spoke it to himself as Amber slept, turning human speech into his own as much as words like *helicopter* allowed, but changing tongues did not remake the tale nor clarify the questioning itch that had lodged itself in his brain. So he meditated while Amber slept beside him and the wind blew endlessly across the empty plains.

He had never fallen asleep during meditations before. Therefore, he surely did not do so now.

The thought-space he inhabited did change, though, becoming a dreaming place he recognized as the antechamber of the temple of Xi'Tothax. As before, he stood before the holy forge, but the forge was lit now, melting the air around it with its heat and power, and the man who stood before him with the thigh-bone of Rasozul in his hands was not Exarch Ylsathoc. He kept his face deep in the shadows of his cowl.

"Your father is dead," this man told him. "The House of Uyane stands without a lord. Will you come now to take up the stewardship of your bloodline?"

Meoraq could not speak, save for the words he had already spoken. They left his mouth in the way of dreams, separate of his will and emotion. "I have loyalty to more than one father. I cannot make this decision without knowing the will of Sheul."

Eyes gleamed in the depths of the exarch's hood, lit with accusation. He looked into Meoraq's soul and saw the truth: not pious supplication before God's will, but an unwillingness to be fettered to one woman, and worse, the sort of meek, milk-veined woman who would be no more than a breeding vessel with legs for all the sons he would be expected to sire and all the daughters he must raise in meek, milk-veined imitation of their mother.

He could not have said this to Ylsathoc and he could not say it now to a stranger. Ashamed, Meoraq turned away, from the exarch and his oaths of office, from his own father's bone, and in that small movement somehow left the temple and arrived in the plains on a bright morning. He could see the humans walking away from him. He could see Amber lying at his feet, her face white and still.

Now he could speak, feel, act. He ran after the humans and caught furiously at Scott, shouting, "Damn you for a coward and a murderer! How can you leave her?"

But the man who turned to face him, human though He appeared to be, was not Scott. Meoraq stumbled back. He had never known fear, true fear, the kind that froze the fire in one's veins. Therefore, he did not know it now. He was uncertain.

"Fathers, take caution of the women you wive, for they will raise the daughters who wear your name," said the man wearing Scott's form. He spoke in dumaqi, quoting the first line of the Admonition of Womanly Virtues, which was so unexpected that Meoraq backed away again. "See that every woman of your household is brought forth as a proper woman in the sight of Sheul, Father of us all. A woman wears modesty around her neck and keeps low her eyes when her man speaks. A woman's trust lies below her man's boot, as her open hand also, to take in with graciousness all that he places before her. In all ways does she acknowledge him as steward over her, nursing no bitterness in her throat to be brought forth as slight and slander. A woman keeps herself covered and away from all eyes, save when her man alone has will of her, and receives him gladly at his every command. A woman speaks not against her man's ear, nor walks before him, nor shows her eyes, but in three things forever seeks: To obey his word, to lessen his burden, and above all, to bear his sons."

Nicci, wet-eyed at Scott's side, expressionlessly opened her mouth and emitted a ghastly mewling cry, like a chorus of hundreds of faceless women all at once.

Meoraq did not step back this time; he leapt back. And when he looked at Scott again, Lord Saluuk of Tothax stood in his place. He bent, pulling Amber up from the ground, which became the very edge of the high wall of the city in a moment. "If she will not behave herself as a proper woman," he spat, "better she be dead."

Meoraq snarled and lunged forward, but again, between one running step and another, he was suddenly in Master Tsazr's room at Tilev. He staggered to a stop, then checked his body to see if he had become a brunt, but the hands he held before him were a man's hands and the chest he saw below his chin was the scarred playing field of a Sheulek. He looked up again just in time to meet Master Tsazr's hand slapping hard against his snout.

"I expected better of you," he heard as he lay dazed on the floor. Master Tsazr's mud-caked boots tromped around him and away to the window-ledge. "I knew for eighteen years that the doors of Xi'Matezh would open for me. For eighteen years, I prayed for a reason worthy enough to let me go. But you, ha! You make a holy pilgrimage just to avoid your responsibilities at home!"

Meoraq braced his hands on the floor and slowly pushed himself up. He kept his throbbing head bent, feeling his former master's stare like coals on his scales.

"You stood here in this room and pretended to listen when I told you that being Sheulek meant more than seeing the world and fucking a different woman in every city." Tsazr snorted contemptuously. "And here you are. Walking all the way to the end of the world and back so you can have just a little more time to do it."

"No," said Meoraq, but he could not raise his eyes.

"Lies! Go on then! Ask! If I choose to answer only one question, what will you make it? What have you been rehearsing for the day when you stand in the temple at the Heart of Gann? What will you ask when you have God's own ear? Say it!"

He would have given every coin he had in the world to be the master of his own mouth in that moment, but the vision took his tongue and the words came out: "If I am to be the steward of my bloodline, where is the woman worthy to be bound to me? Set her down before me, O Father, or let it be Your will that I sire my sons as Sheulek."

Tsazr let a full silence fall before he breathed out his sneering hiss. "And you are *such* a prize."

Whatever had hold of him let go. Meoraq shoved himself to his feet. "It wasn't supposed to sound like that!"

"How was it meant to sound? 'O great Father, if You want the benefit of my superior seed, I command You to provide me a woman no more than twenty-two years in age, with black eyes and all her teeth, very pretty, who can cook, sing, dance, write poetry, and stay virgin-tight for all her life, or You can settle for those I sire by conquest'? How dare you make demands of Sheul! He is not some servant in your House, Uyane, *you are a servant in His*!"

"I can have any woman I want!" Meoraq shouted. "Do you think I don't know that? Do you think I don't know there will be sixty of them waiting at my door when I get home? And every one of them, the same fucking woman!"

Tsazr's eyes sparked. He leaned back, his arms folding under his sabks.

"I don't want a pretty, black-eyed, cooking, singing, dancing, *simpering*, mewling, whining, empty-headed *idiot*!" he finished, now in full throat-throbbing rage. "Give the fucking House to Nduman! Give it to *Salkith*! I would rather die a Sheulek tomorrow than live fifty years with a wife like that!"

"A wife like what?" asked a new voice, one that severed his fury as easily as the stroke of a sword severs flesh.

In turning, Tsazr's room at Tilev became his father's House at Xeqor, and there stood Rasozul, beyond his prime but still powerful, showing his son only his broad, scarred back as he donned his armor.

Meoraq betrayed himself with a step backwards. "Father?"

The old warrior glanced around. "Are you ashamed of me?" he asked, in that same calm, reverberant voice Meoraq remembered of his father.

He recoiled, stricken to the very heart of him. "No! Never!"

"No? Not even in the disgrace of my retirement? Did I not accept the defeat of a woman bound to my bloodline? Is this not the fate that drove you out into the wildlands?"

Meoraq felt his soul wither. He knelt, palms open upon the tiles, but no hand came to him in a forgiving clasp. His father continued to gird himself—endless armored plates and sharpened edges went on, only to vanish into his skin, leaving nothing but another scar and a place to put another piece of armor, another weapon.

"Your mother was a responsibility of the office I accepted when I came to this House as its steward," said Rasozul. "I did not want her. I chose her wristlet from a barrel of such trinkets and wed the woman to whom it belonged, so little did the matter mean to me. But when her breeding years were done and I had my sons by her, I did not turn her away. I did not begin nor end any day that I passed within these walls without sharing at least a warm drink and a private word in her company. My fires burned for her alone, all our years together. I gave her memory the only tears I shed in my life. This is the fate you despise, to have earned the true affection of a good and faithful woman. This was the woman you despised, who never heard a word from her eldest son that was not spoken with contempt. You were ashamed of her, my son. And it made me ashamed of you."

Meoraq bent his back yet further, bent until his faithless head touched the floor, but no touch of forgiveness came and no more words. When he dared at last to look up, he was in his father's House no longer.

He was nowhere at all.

But he was not alone.

Before him, his neck bent and palm to Gann, Meoraq saw Meoraq.

"No more of this, I beg you," he said hoarsely.

The other Meoraq meditated and did not reply.

He staggered to his feet and saw blackness in all directions, devoid of life or light. His copy remained motionless, tranquil, as Meoraq ran first one way and another, exhausting his body only to find himself exactly where he had first stood. At last, he swung to face himself, shouting, "What do you want of me?"

"What," the other Meoraq mused, "do you want of me?"

"Why am I here?"

"Why did you come?"

"Why do you torment me?"

"Why do you perceive it as torment?"

Meoraq managed not to swear, but could not stop the snarl. He stalked in a futile circle that led nowhere and turned back to find himself now standing and gazing at him with alien eyes, just waiting.

"I do not know what you want me to do," Meoraq said at last. The words tore at him, a confession of the worst kind of failure.

"I want you to *know* what to do," his copy replied, in the very faintest tones of exasperation. "How hard does it have to rain?"

Meoraq drew back, baffled.

His copy waited.

"I know who You are," said Meoraq, and much as he fought to be master of himself, his voice shook.

His copy's spines flexed in an amused fashion. Otherwise, he did not respond.

Meoraq gathered his nerve and took a step forward. "Why did You set the humans in my path? Was I meant to take them to Xi'Matezh? What else could I have done with them?"

"I sent you a warning," his copy replied.

"What warning? I saw none!"

No reply. His copy stared him down.

"Why did You strike the woman ill and allow her people to abandon her? Where are they now? Is it Your will that I find them again?"

"And a boat."

"A what?"

"And a helicopter."

"What are You telling me?" Meoraq cried out in frustration.

His copy threw out his arms and cried back, "Why don't you *listen*?"

And then the blackness shattered and Meoraq lay in his tent. After several stunned, stabilizing breaths, he found his lamp in the dark and struck a light. He could see Amber sleeping, curled small under her thin wrap, and at once the vision (no dream; a Sheulek does not fall asleep during meditation) coursed through his veins in a second, fiery pulse, growing hotter as he stared at her.

He knew. All at once, he knew.

Sheul's fires burned in his belly, but that was nothing to the fire burning in his mind, taking away all thought and all but one: He had begun this journey to ask Sheul to guide him to a worthy woman. Well, here she was and if she did not have a dumaq woman's looks, neither did she have one's mewling mannerisms. She was not the woman he'd expected, but she was a good woman and God Himself had given her to him.

The light from the lamp had finally succeeded in rousing her from her sleep. Amber rolled toward him, holding up one hand to shade her blinking eyes. "What's wrong?"

"Nothing."

"Is it morning?"

"No."

She got her elbows under her and pushed herself halfway up. "What do you want?" she asked crossly.

He knew what he wanted. The only question remaining was how to go about it and in the waking heat of his vision, there was only one answer. He drew his ancestral knife and showed it to her. "This is the knife of my fathers, the blade of conquest."

She looked at it and then at him.

He waited.

So did she.

"This is the knife of my fathers," he said again, a touch testily. "This is the blade of conquest."

"Uh huh, I heard. And this is my mother's honey-blonde hair," she said, pointing at her head. "What do you want, lizardman?"

Her hair? He'd been expecting her wristlet, as dumaq women were themselves wont to offer. The intimacy of her choice briefly staggered him. He shook that off too, then gathered up a fistful of her mane as she began her formal protests, and cut it off. "You are permitted to fight," he told her, but she was already slapping at him, so their mating rituals must not be too dissimilar.

"What the hell are you doing?"

Meoraq stabbed the blade deep into the ground, still piercing the hair—to hell with the tent; he could get another tent—and swept back the blanket. His belly was hot and every nerve felt new and alive in a way he had never known. He had never been so aware of his own body or of a woman's. And she was still struggling, still pretending not to understand, but when he slipped his hand through her tangled hair and behind her head, her shouting, swearing protests stopped and she grew very quiet as he leaned close to scrape his chin along her throat, filling his senses with the fullness of her scent.

"What are you doing?" she whispered.

His throat was too tight to answer, but hers was soft. He nuzzled his way up to the underside of her jaw and scraped his chin slowly down again, breathing her in. The heat in his belly had become pain, a second pulse like a hammer from within. His hand dropped, feeling along the front of her shirt and plucking once at the alien fastens he found there. "Take this off," he murmured. "I don't want to rip it."

Obedience was not immediate—it never was with Amber—but at last he felt her shift and heard the rustle of fabric as she opened her clothing. At once he put his bare hand between her breasts and, as he tasted his way from her throat to her naked shoulder, he moved that hand slowly up and down, up and down, a little further on each gentle stroke, until he had slipped beneath the loose waist of her breeches.

She grabbed at his wrist, her skin smacking audibly against his scales. The next sound he heard was the soft thump of her back hitting her bedroll and she was flat beneath him and he was above her and his hand was there, stroking hard up and down through the small patch of coarse hair that grew above her opening. Her shoulder was soft and warm and tasted of smoke and rain and Amber as he gently bit, not piercing, not yet, but wanting to, needing to. Was she fighting again? It was hard to tell. One of her hands was on his chest, pushing; the other, at his back with her blunt claws prying at his scales. When he looked at her, her eyes were shut and her neck irresistibly arched, so he bit it and then scraped his chin hard where he had bitten, until he could taste her in every breath.

He didn't want to wait anymore and neither did she. The edges of her slit were oddly plump and human-soft, but already open to his lightest touch; she was *very* aroused. Careful exploration with his fingers (she clutched at his wrist again, but did not move him and did not really appear to be trying) proved she was deep and pliant and that was all he needed to know. He burrowed his free arm beneath her, pulling her up off the mat, and yanked her breeches down until they tangled with her boots. He unfastened his loin-plate eagerly and then, with the last of his reason, he paused and leaned back so that she could see him.

His cock had flexed free the instant it had liberty to do so and now stood primed and ready before him. Amber froze, as he had suspected she might, to stare at it. Her expression was strange, difficult to read.

"Don't be afraid," said Meoraq awkwardly. He hated to break the mood, but some surprises were pleasant while mating and some were not. Human males were small and limp and fleshy. This had to be a shock. Far better to break the mood than to stab her with what she might perceive as a weapon.

"This is my masculine member," he explained, and pointed. "It will go here." When she did not correct him, he gripped her thigh and said, "Open to me."

She stiffened, staring intently and in tight-lipped silence into his eyes, but then she obeyed without allowing him even a token show of force, submitting as one already in his possession.

He resisted the urge that swept him then, instead touching the soft skin below her brilliant eyes. "You are mine," he said. It was early for these words. They were meant to come after, when conquest was done, but conquest, it seemed, already was.

She put her hand on his cock—a hesitant touch at first, one that grew firm as she closed him in her fist. She looked down, watching with a faintly furrowed brow as her fingers moved over him, growing slick with the oils she brought from him so easily.

Few women had ever done this for him and no woman had ever looked as she did now, neither angry nor afraid but still fierce when she met his eyes. No woman had ever said the words she said next, in a voice like the prairie wind, that shook but still blew strong, "I want you."

She frowned when she said it, as if confused by her own meaning. He understood very well how that could be. Sheul's voice had not been clear to him in all this time, and he had been trained to hear it.

"I want you," he told her. These words had no place in the ritual at all, but they felt right in the air. He said it again as she lay down before him and again as he rose over her. He entered with those words and the proof came at once with the first rush of Sheul's blessing, filling her womb before a single stroke had been made.

He'd never mated this way before—lying down and belly-to-belly—but it felt new and exciting and perhaps just a bit deviant. Covering her in this fashion, he was all that she must feel. His flesh, his weight, were all her sensations. Looking down, he saw her looking up and knew he was all that she could see. This was the conquest all others had been imitating.

Hers was not a dumaq body. There was no resistance, no clenched sleeve of muscle to battle through, but only a soft, tight well that gripped the whole of his length at once. He was free to withdraw and stab again, thrusting with the whole of his body and crushing her possessively beneath him as he made himself drunk on this strange, enthralling sensation. He was vigorous in his passion, perhaps too much so, his weight driving her back and forth across the ground, but she did not protest. Indeed, she fell back, relinquishing all control to him with a hoarse, human cry. Her little claws gripped at his back, their points prying at his scales as she bucked up at him. Not so fragile, then.

"Sheul, O great Father, make this woman worthy," he groaned. "Let her soul be pierced and made open. Let her womb be warmed to receive my spirit—" And never mind it would be for the second time. The important thing was that he'd remembered to say it at all. "—and Yours. If it be Your will, raise her up with Your blessing and give her the gift of new life."

She cried out suddenly, and at the same time, he felt her body seize on him in the grip of her own blessing. In the next moment, he shared it.

The second explosion was greater, which was so seldom the case. He felt it pour out of him, unbearably bright and alive. He could not pray aloud in its grip, but the name of Sheul and all his ancestral fathers burned in his mind until it was done and he slumped heavily atop her. He felt he could keep going—he wanted to try, anyway—but three was the sacred number of creation and belonged to Sheul alone. He would not sour this gift with blasphemous lust.

"Now you have become completely mine," he said. "Let Sheul who has made you for me witness as I take you from your father's House and give you the headship of my own. I take you in, Soft-Skin, to be Uyane under me for all the days that remain to you. Hear me and know that you are mine."

She spoke no word of submission, shyly or joyfully or any way at all, still lost in her own fires. He nuzzled at her, scraping the end of his snout hard across her skin to fill his senses with her scent and taste, and, every nerve alive with Amber, bit deeply into her shoulder. She yelped and struck him fetchingly as he drowsed, licking at the wound to stop it bleeding and thinking of what a fine scar it would make.

At last, Meoraq rose and retrieved his knife, careful to keep the hairs it pierced together. It wasn't easy. After a moment's thought, he held it out to her. "Plait this into a cord," he ordered, "and I shall wear it."

She looked at him for a long time before she took it. Perhaps among her people, a trophy of first conquest was burnt or buried.

Well, her people had turned her out. Now she belonged to him. He licked her shoulder once more and went, smiling broadly to himself, back to his mat and slept.

6

Dawn woke her, but he was already gone. His pack and hers were already bundled and good to go. A little more than half of last night's horrible dinner had been tucked up beside her head next to his flask. Apart from the aching, scabby bite, a brand-new breeze on her ear and some dry threads of grass itching around inside her pants, she could almost believe she'd dreamed the whole thing.

She ate. Drank. Packed up the tent. Reached into her pocket and brought out what been covering most of the left half of her head the previous day. Her hair. He wanted to keep it. Like a trophy.

She honestly did not know how to feel about that. He'd taken her by surprise (so to speak), but in the cold light of day, she knew she hadn't tried very hard to fight him off. Hell, if he'd chosen to wake her up with his hand between her legs instead of hacking at her hair, she probably wouldn't have fought him at all. It had all happened so fast and felt so inevitable that she'd just...given in.

All the same, this didn't feel like her usual morning-after regrets. Part of her wanted to braid this hair and see him wearing it; it brought to mind those story-book pictures—Amber as the damsel bestowing her favor and Meoraq playing a dual role of knight and dragon. But that was only part of her. The rest of her remembered only too well looking up through a haze of cramping pleasure to see him working at her in unhurried rhythm with his eyes fixed on the wall above her head and no expression on his face. Yes, he said he wanted her and yes, he told her to make his little keepsake, but all the rest of the pillow-talk had been between him and God. She was just "this woman" in that little chat, like it didn't even matter if it was Amber, like any warm squeeze would do. And after the bite that had branded her, he'd put out the light and gone to sleep, leaving her to pull her pants up and button her shirt in the dark. She'd had to lie awake a long time while the ghost of her drunken mother talked to her about men and whores. She didn't believe it, not really, but it was hard not to listen.

Amber braided the hair.

It wasn't easy. She'd worn her hair in braids as a very little kid, but only when her mom did the braiding. Messing around with hair was a girly thing to do, a Nicci-thing, the sort of thing Amber rolled her eyes at with lofty disdain. Who'd have ever thought that was going to come bite her in the ass on an alien planet?

She had managed to produce a mangled-looking snake of snarls and was working to tie off the end when Meoraq came prowling back with the big waterskin. He grunted at her as he passed by. It sure didn't sound like a good-morning-radiant-woman-of-my-fantasies greeting. He checked the weight of the wrappings containing last night's leftovers, gave her a disapproving glance, then noticed the clumsy braid in her hands. He grunted again and beckoned to her. "Come. You may tie it around—" He eyed the length critically. "—my arm."

Amber frowned up at him for a moment, then got to her feet and went to him. He offered his arm. His bicep bulged. She could still remember the strength in those arms as he grappled with her, the power evident even in his gentlest touch. And there had been a few of those too, even though he was not a gentle man.

She tied the braid on just under his shoulder, where the bulk of his muscle would keep it from slipping down around his wrist. It stood out surprisingly bright against his dark scales. Every loose strand and ugly knot showed clearly, but he seemed pleased with it. Proud of it, like the look in his eye when he shifted his gaze to the bite on her shoulder. He even gave her a deeply unsettling yet probably playful lizardish grimace before moving past her to collect their things.

"Aren't you going to say anything?"

He straightened up, gave that some obvious thought, then cautiously said, "Good...morning?"

"Not that. About last night!"

His spines snapped irritably flat. "What am I supposed to say?"

"Why don't you start with why, after all this time, when you've never so much as crossed your eyes at me, you suddenly decided we had to have sex?"

"I had a vision," he replied. "A true vision of God."

It was not a shocker, as revelations went. Amber covered her eyes with both hands solely to keep them from turning into fists. In the dark behind her palms, she said, "God told you to have sex with me? Seriously? That's what you're going with?"

"Yes." He shrugged into his pack and secured the straps. "We need to get moving. I see a hard rain coming and I want to put the spans behind us before it reaches us. No more arguments, woman. Let's go."

There was that word again. All of a sudden, the whole issue with her hair seemed a lot less important as making love took an ugly turn into fucking. "Did you just call me 'woman'?!"

He shouldered the filled waterskin and gestured at her pack. "Yes."

Absurdly, her first impulse was to snatch her hair back from him. She restrained it. "And just what in the hell makes you think you get to do that?" she demanded.

He looked at her, his expression tipping back and forth between annoyed and confused. "Why wouldn't I?"

"Because it's rude! I don't call you man!"

"Yes, you do. Lizardman, even," he added with a glare.

"Not all the time. Only when we're fighting."

He threw out his arms, his head cocked hard and eyes snapping. "We appear to be fighting," he told her, then pointed at her pack. "Get your things, *woman*, and let's go."

Her stomach clenched. "Stop calling me that."

"You're my woman now, I'll call you whatever I want."

"The hell you say! I'm not 'your' anything. Just because I slept with you once doesn't mean I belong to you."

"You slept in my camp. That means you belong to me. You have been mine from the day—" He stopped there, then rolled his eyes and heaved a hard sigh. "Fine. How many times do humans mate before the woman considers herself conquered?"

She stared at him for a long time before she was finally able to say, "That's not how it works with us," biting off each word and spitting it like a bullet.

"More pity for you," he said with a careless shrug of his spines, "because that's how it works with us. No more talk. We're leaving."

She put her pack on, snatched up her spear and started walking, too angry to even look at him anymore. "Well, clearly last night was a huge mistake."

On the horizon, thunder muttered, attracting his immediate attention. "You don't mean that," he said, frowning back over his shoulder at the sky.

"Don't tell me what I mean. I don't care what God told you, I don't belong to you."

"Yes, you do," he said, not in a romantic way, but just another argument in his favor. "You are mine as much as my own skin. God Himself has married you to me."

"No, he didn't," she snapped, slapping at her forehead.

"Yes. He did."

His matter-of-fact tone finally pierced all the way in and made everything else she was feeling fade to an uneasy black. She looked at him, feeling her brows draw in.

"Yeah, but we're not really married."

His head tipped, as if he were very, very slightly puzzled. He caught her by the sleeve to make her stop walking, leaned close, and said, clearly and distinctly, "Married."

"What, just because we had sex? That's ridiculous!"

"It would be, if that were the only reason. We are bound by God's will, Soft-Skin, and what He has joined, no force on Gann may sunder. You are mine. My woman." He raised his hands and clasped them together with a sound of impressive finality. "My wife."

The wind blew between them.

"You don't mean that," Amber said, but her voice rose at the end, making it almost a question.

"Don't tell me what I mean." But his spines lowered and he brushed his knuckles across her brow, then along the shorn half of her head. "How can you say you're not mine when you gave everything you had to me? Everything you are..." His fingers scraped lightly down her cheek, along her throat and under the neck of her shirt, peeling it back from her skin so that he exposed her bitten shoulder.

And did she roll her eyes? Shrug off his hand? Take even one step back out of his reach? No. She just stood there with her mouth slightly open and her girly heart fluttering and a hot glow way down deep in her belly and let him do it.

"God gave you to me," he murmured, nuzzling under her jaw. "Even when I did not know how to ask. He found you anyway and put you in my path. You are the woman I was born into this world to find."

"To own," Amber whispered.

"Do I own my skin? My bones? I possess them." He moved to the other side of her neck and roughly nuzzled her some more. "It's not the same, when you think about it."

"I don't want to think about it."

"Please yourself. Fortunately—" He straightened with an air of reluctance, checking the fit of his belt before adjusting her shirt and covering her up again. "—you don't have to. We'll walk now. We'll talk later, if you still want to. All right?"

She looked at the sky, which dropped a blob of rain in her eye, then gave up and nodded. He turned around and started walking. She leaned on her spear for a moment, thumping her head on it until the urge to run after him and hold his stupid hand was gone. Then she shrugged her pack up higher, put her head down and followed.

* * *

They walked all day, like any other normal day. They stopped twice—once to ford a rain-swollen ravine and fill their flasks, and once just to stop—and they were normal rests. They made camp in the late afternoon on the top of a stony bluff next to a patch of champagne-colored berries which smelled light and sweet, but tasted so fantastically bitter that Meoraq had to threaten her in his normal way to eat them. He put up his tent, had a nice normal argument with her when she picked up her spear, then took her hunting. They killed a saoq together, and he stood over her with a critical but approving eye while she butchered it, and then they went back to his camp and cooked it up. They ate a normal dinner, having normal conversation, and when he'd finished wrapping up the leftover meat for tomorrow's hike, he unbuckled all his buckles, shrugged out of his harness and zzzzzupped off his belt, tossed his metal panty-panel carelessly to one side, and said, "Do you want to lie on your belly or your back?" in a perfectly normal tone of voice.

"Uh...my back," was her somewhat dumbfounded answer (but only somewhat), and with an approving grunt and a playful nip to her shoulder, he pushed her down and climbed on top of her.

The sex was much as she'd remembered it from the confusion of the previous night's battle and as before, she could not summon any defense against that spined, hooked, alien weapon that he fought with. He stabbed her once and it might as well have been over.

There was no petting, no caresses, no pillow-talk. He stared straight ahead while she thrashed and clawed at his back, his neck arched so that all she could see when she tried to look at him was the yellow stripes glowing out from the black scales on his throat. He moved nothing but his hips the whole time, kept breathing in the same slow rhythm, and ignored every effort she made to pull him closer. Amber had never had the kind of flowery romantic sex that people had in movies, but it still bothered her. Even so she came first and came again and came until she was actually screaming with pleasure for the first time in her life, something she'd always thought only happened in the made-up letters in men's magazines. By the time he trotted out the, "Make this woman worthy," part of his prayer and came to his own hissing climax, she had begun to feel dangerously close to losing consciousness.

If he noticed, he didn't think it necessary to remark. He merely licked again at his bite-mark on her shoulder and got off her. While she struggled to recover, he adjusted himself to let his penis retract, scooped up his harness and his panty-plate, and said, "I will have the first watch. You will sleep in my tent. Rest well." And off he went. Just another normal night.

He was giving her permission to use his tent? Where the hell else did he think she was going to sleep after all that sex, curled up at his feet? And rest well? What the hell did that mean?

She put her clothes back—not back on, they'd never been all the way off, just back to where they were supposed to be—snatched her blanket out of her pack and her own bedroll, scooted over to a less sexed-up patch of grass, and shut her eyes in a haze of defiance and misery.

Footsteps woke her in the middle of the night. She raised her head and watched Meoraq drop an armload of grass-and-dung bundles by the fire. He simply tapped a knuckle to his brow when he saw that she was awake and went on in to his tent.

It was a long night. She ate a few more of the bitter berries, made herself some tea, and entertained herself by tying the bundles together into little lizardman shapes and burning them. She didn't mean to stay up, but her stupid brain wouldn't shut up and the more she listened to it, the more upset her stomach got, and before she knew it, the sky was turning grey.

She was still staring at it in the first blush of astonishment when Meoraq's tent flaps jerked and opened. He emerged with a skyward glance and a scowl, his tunic hanging open and his half-fastened harness dangling at his knees, and stomped off into the underbrush.

Christ, she'd pulled an all-nighter. And now she had to walk all day and she was already exhausted. She could ask him for a little time to sleep before they set out, but she was pretty sure she'd just get another of his 'let this be a lesson to you, insufferable human' lectures instead. Or worse, he'd agree and be pissed off about it, and she'd know he was pissed off and be too upset to actually sleep, so she'd be even more tired when they finally left and they'd have to stop early as well as leave late.

He came back as Amber was sitting and rubbing her churning stomach, buckling the last buckle on his harness and muttering to himself. "Is there tea?" he asked.

"A little. It's probably gone cold. I didn't think it was this close to morning."

He grunted and glanced at her. "Is that an apology or an excuse? I can't tell."

She'd been trying for an apology, but if that was how he was going to be...

"Neither, it's just me whining at you again, you jerk. I can stay up as long as I want."

He didn't rise for the bait, just took the stewing pouch off its tripod and dumped out the cold tea. "You look tired."

Oh, he was good at fighting.

"I'm fine," Amber said tightly.

He moved off into the berry bushes. "We could pass another day here."

Amber scrambled to her feet, dismayed. "The whole day? Come on, can't you just slap me?"

"This is not a punishment."

"The hell it isn't! We've got to catch up, Meoraq! I can walk!"

He eyed her as he steadily filled the pouch with berries. He didn't say anything.

"You do what you want, then," she told him, rolling up her blanket and stuffing it into her pack. "But I'm going, with or without you."

He snorted, but put the last handful of berries in the pouch and came out of the bushes. "This is my camp, woman, and I decide when we leave it."

"Have fun bossing yourself around all day, lizardman." 'And screwing yourself all night,' she thought, but couldn't bring herself to say that.

"I can't deal with you before I've had something to drink," Meoraq said, kneeling by the fire. "And there are days, woman, when tea is not enough. Go to sleep before I—"

He stopped. His spines flared all the way forward and slowly lowered again, not quite all the way flat. He put the berries down and picked up a dung-and-grass lizardman.

Amber smacked her palm into her face. She thought she'd burned them all.

He stared at it, very still, for a long time. Then he looked at her and while she was hunting for a way to simultaneously apologize and explain that she hadn't really meant anything by it and not to get his metal panties in a bunch, he got up.

"Meoraq—" she began, holding her hands up in surrender.

He took them, pulled her to her feet, and put his arms around her.

"We will walk, Soft-Skin," he said in an oddly-subdued voice. His hand moved from her back to cup her head, then her shoulder, then back to her head, as if he wasn't sure what to touch. "Sleep a short time. I will wake you and we will walk."

"I don't need to sleep! I can go now, damn it! I'm fine!"

He drew back, frowning as he searched her eyes. He opened his mouth several times as if he wanted to argue, but in the end, he set the grass-and-dung lizardman gently in her hands. "Then we will go now."

Amber stared at him while he started taking his tent down, then at the doll which had given her such an easy and baffling win. Not knowing what else to do with it, she put it on the fire. When she straightened up, Meoraq was watching her, his hands still gripping at the tent-poles but motionless. His eyes met hers briefly, troubled, and then he went back to dismantling his tent.

She supposed she could just ask him what he thought the stupid little doll meant, but it would inevitably lead to her telling him why she'd really made it and she couldn't see how any conversation that included the words, "I was burning you in effigy all night," could end well. And she didn't want to fight.

Well, she kind of did. But she shouldn't and she could admit that much at least.

Amber poked at the burning doll, breaking it back into the three bundles it had been before she'd tied them together. Flames leapt up at once and she watched them instead of Meoraq, knowing he'd be ready in just a few minutes more and then they'd be on the move again. And that was great.

The fire burned, strands of grass turning black and curling, one by one, before falling apart into white powder.

She wished she'd at least let him finish making his tea first.

* * *

They walked in silence most of the morning. Meoraq couldn't be certain of Amber's thoughts; whenever he glanced back at her, she always seemed to be wholly fixed on just not falling over. He wished she would say something, even if it was to call him an insensitive brunt (or more likely, a scaly son of a bitch), because his own thoughts were a torment. He carried them like stones in his belly, each one with the name and face of a human he had been ready to forget, and the largest and heaviest belonged to Nicci.

He hated Nicci. He'd hated her when he'd been forced to feed and tend her and he hated her ghost once she was gone, but no fire burns without fuel, and in her absence, hate had cooled to coals. In truth, he hadn't spared her even an idle thought in days.

But she had never left Amber. She was there still, silent, invisible, clinging on to Amber's hand and doubtless streaming water out of her empty eyes. Amber, who still spoke of 'catching' the others, just as though there were anything left of them to reach out and hold in her hand.

Because they were dead. He knew it and had known it ever since he had seen their broad trail end at a crumbling canal and realized that they had chosen to walk inside it. Why? Because it would be covered against the rain. Because it would be flat and easily traveled. Because no one was there to tell them not to walk in a storm canal in the rainy season and those idiots would need to be told. No, Meoraq could see it clearly: Scott had led them into the tunnel and some hours hence, some ancient reservoir had overfilled, prompting some unthinking machine to open a ventway and empty a few hundred thousand meti-weights of water into Scott's safe, dry, level road. They were dead.

But even in death, their souls would never be freed from their clay unless they were burnt. Meoraq knew that. He knew it, but he'd never once thought of them and the hell their undying clay must be now enduring. If he felt anything at all, it was only a grim satisfaction that he would never have to see them again. He had his Amber, now his wife, without the thorn of her annoying kind and especially her whining little blood-kin, and he had been content.

And Amber had said nothing, because she, as his obedient wife, must be content also. Content with nothing to burn but dolls in the shape of the one she loved enough to call 'sister'.

Self-disgust reached a sudden, jarring pinnacle throughout his mind and body, like Gann's own orgasm. Meoraq halted—Amber bumped up hard against his back—and began yanking at his harness-fastens. "We are stopping," he spat, throwing his tent to the ground. "I have to pray."

Amber made a sound of spiritless assent and staggered a few steps away, dropping her pack and collapsing on top of it. Seeing that made him feel even worse, but it had been her insistence that they travel. He would have been happy to give her a day's rest this morning if she had not been—

If she had not been burning Nicci.

Now he looked at her, even though he should be on his knees, palms to clay and deep in prayer. He looked at the woman Sheul had given him, married to him, and realized with a sinking belly that the dual burden of grief and illness were simply too much for even his stubborn Amber to carry.

He began to clear the earth and gather what tinder there was for a fire. She did not move to help him. A second glance showed him she was lost in sleep already, mired in it, despite the pain that yet twisted her soft features. He tried not to wake her, but she startled when he struck the fire, moaned, and finally dragged her eyes open. She stared without recognition at the growing flames for several seconds before her eyes went wide and filled with dismay.

She tried to sit up, fell, and tried again even as she protested, pleading with him not to make her stay, she could walk, she was fine.

He put his heat-stones in the fire and filled the stewing pouch with water.

She caught at his arm, cursing and apologizing, vowing that she would never stay up all night again, only please please not to do this. They had to catch up. They had to keep going.

He opened his pack and brought out his fine inlaid tea box. He put all he had left of the dawnslight blend in the steeper and dropped it in the water. He put away the tea box and brought out some of yesterday's saoq, tepid and greasy in its wrappings. He held it out to her.

She glared at him, lightly trembling, then snatched up her spear. She had to climb it as a crutch to gain her feet, but once gained, she set off into the prairie, limping and swearing at him. She fought when he brought her bodily back, but she was too tired to fight for long. She collapsed again on top of her pack, weeping furiously behind her hands, and fell asleep as soon as the storm lagged, tears still wet on her skin.

Meoraq sat and watched his tea heat. He did not pray, exactly. Certainly, he did not pray as he probably should have done, back bent and with all the ritual words in place, but any man's heart can be an altar if it is open and any man's words can reach God's ear if they are sincerely spoken.

"Father," said Meoraq at last, and knew that he was heard. He looked up into the sky, not to see Sheul's face among the rolling clouds but to show Him his own, naked and troubled, here on Gann. "Father, I cry out to You from the darkness. Lift up Your lamp and show me how to find them. Let me give them their last prayers and release them to Your judgment."

Sheul listened, but did not speak.

"I do not ask for myself," Meoraq admitted. "I should. They are Your children also and deserve the care all children of Sheul may expect in passing from this mortal life. I should love them, as the Word tells me to do, and seek them for myself, but I don't. I can't. Were it not for my woman's pain, I know I would not be calling to You now. Forgive Your son his failings," he said, touching his palm to Gann and taking away small daubs of mud to rub over his mortal heart. "But do not punish his wife because of them. I beseech You, Father, set me on their last path and let me find where they lie so I can give them true death."

Sheul's hand was heavy upon his shoulder, but His great voice still remained silent and Meoraq knew why. Finding where Scott and his humans had washed up would mean turning around. It would mean five days of walking back to the canal and who knew how many days more to search. The bodies might be spans and spans away; if he were lucky, the canal might have fallen in at some point, allowing the bodies to be vomited out on the street where they were visible, but if not, they had surely finished up in some ancient cistern. Or several cisterns, spans apart. Either way, a search could easily eat up the rest of the season, with no guarantee of ever finding even one body. And any body he did find...after so many days soaking in the stormways, he would never know which of them it had been.

Meoraq knew very little about women and even less about humans, but as much as he wished to make some grand romantic gesture to his grieving wife, the reality was that the other humans were gone. The clay of their flesh would crumble; the spark that had once warmed it, lost forever. This was truth, and as Master Tsazr had once said, truth does not care if it comforts you.

The fire was failing already. He would have to go find real fuel or let it die. The tea was not very dark yet, but drinkable and hot. Lost in his own brooding thoughts, torn between the realities of this camp and the intangibilities that lay beyond it, Meoraq reached into his pack and felt about for his cup.

His fingers touched something cup-like wrapped in his spare breeches, but with an odd protrusion he couldn't quite—

Oh. Oh no.

But yes, and soon he was holding them—one garish human cup in each hand—and asking himself how by Gann's wicked whim he had managed to forget the stupid things so completely? Damn him, all this time, Amber had thought them lost forever. All this time, he'd made her come to him in her embarrassed way to beg for his cup when he was done with it, and there were days when he had made damned sure she knew she was inconveniencing him. All this time, but like the humans themselves, as soon as they were out of sight, he'd simply never given them another thought.

"Great Sheul, take Your hand from my shoulder," he groaned, dipping out some tea, "and send it against my stupid snout. Wake up, Soft-Skin. Come, wife. Wake and hear me."

She muttered thickly and curled closer around herself, rolling away from him when he nudged the cup against her shoulder. "No. We're fighting. That means I don't have to deal with you if I don't want to. Leave me alone."

Sheul's hand stayed gentle where it rested on him. Meoraq simply leaned further over and set the cup down in front of her.

She made him wait a very long time before she opened her eyes, but he knew when she'd done it by the stiffening of her turned back. After several shaking breaths, she pushed herself up and looked at him.

There were many things he wanted to say, and some he did not want to say but knew he had to, but when her green eyes came to him, it all fell away.

"We are done walking for the day," he told her.

She picked up the cup and held it loosely between her hands, staring at the tea.

"Tomorrow, we will walk again, but we stop when I give that command and you will not defy me."

She stirred at the tea with her finger, but did not drink.

"All things are possible with Sheul, but I cannot promise you that we will ever find them."

Her eyes closed. "I know."

"I will not allow you to kill yourself searching."

"Meoraq—"

"No," he said forcefully. "It is not your life to give. It is mine."

She said nothing. A single tear welled beneath the tightly-shut lid of her left eye, but it never grew fat enough to fall.

He hoped the matter was settled now because he really did not know what else to say. He took up her second human cup, filled it, and arranged himself beside her. After a moment, determined to prove that he was not a scaly son of a bitch, or at least, not always, he put his arm around her.

"I'm tired," she said.

"I know. As soon as I have the tent together, I want you inside it. From now on, that is where you sleep." He put the hammer to that with an authoritative grunt and drank some tea. It was cold and overwatered. He drank it anyway.

"Then what?"

"Eh?"

"What happens next?"

"We travel on to Xi'Matezh," he said, surprised that she felt this had somehow changed.

"No, I meant tonight."

"Tonight?" His mind, wonderfully blank, suddenly lit with Sheul's own exasperated slap of illumination. He uttered a little laugh, surprised as much by her coyness as by this unexpected drift in the conversation. "You don't have to wait up for me, Soft-Skin. If the fires come, I'll wake you."

Her brows drew together. Her eyes flicked in a bewildered way toward the coals where his tea had warmed.

"Sheul's fires," he amplified.

Her confusion did not appear to clear. A troubling thought occurred to him. "How much do you know about sex?"

She snorted. "I know God doesn't have anything to do with it."

"So you...don't know anything." He thought about that, a little stymied by the enormity of the task now before him, and decided that, just like trying to teach something new to his brother Salkith, it would be best to start with gentle compliments. He reached out to pat her thigh. "You did very well during first conquest."

Her furry brows rose in peaks and then crashed thunderously down. "What the hell is that supposed to mean?"

It didn't always work with Salkith either.

"I enjoyed your struggles. I would permit you to fight again, if you like."

"Oh believe me, lizardman, I will."

He smiled. "It pleases me that you want to be my well-mannered woman," he said, peeling back the neck of her shirt. Ignoring her playful slaps, he licked at the mark he'd left in her soft skin. "But I would rather have the insufferable she-warrior I was given. So if you want me, put your hands on me and tell me so."

"What if I don't want you?"

"Ah, my wife, is that what's bothering you?" He licked her again, slowly this time, tasting the strange, rich bitters of her blood, and felt it when she shivered. "We have only been married two days. Surely that is too early for you to start worrying that I might set you aside, especially since you have burned for me so readily thus far."

"It wasn't like that!" she said, fetchingly embarrassed, as women often were, by this public acknowledgement of her pleasure. "I was lonely and...and scared! That's all!"

He could guess how much it cost his proud woman to make such an admission. He tipped his head to run the side of his snout gently along the curve of her shoulder, following it up to her slender neck in spite of her efforts to shrug him off. "And you needed me."

She stiffened.

"You wanted me," he murmured, and felt that same soul-deep thrill as when he had heard her say it.

"I didn't mean it," she whispered.

"Lies."

"It was just sex. You didn't even like it!" she said suddenly, renewing her shrugging shoves. "You acted like you were doing your damn taxes the whole time!"

He didn't know every word she used, but he thought he caught her meaning. He grinned and nipped at her. "A Sheulek is the master of his clay, Soft-Skin, but mine wanted very much to finish too soon. Be reassured, I liked it." He reached for his belt, nuzzling at her throat with long, slow strokes of his snout. Her scent filled his senses, became a taste, became a throb in his very heart. "Shall I prove it?"

"No," she said, but she didn't duck demurely away. She held onto her cup of tea as the color rose in her flat face and tried to pretend there was no hand kneading at her hip, no snout rubbing up and down the length of her throat. She even tried to drink.

"Your hand is shaking," he observed, and moved his own under her shirt to lie upon her bare belly.

She thumped down her cup and tried to scoot away, but she didn't have the leverage and fell back instead. He dropped comfortably atop her at once, nipping at her jaw and purring while he eased her stubborn legs slowly open around his. And they did open, but not without a lot of kneading and nibbling.

"Damn it!" she shouted, smacking her fist against his shoulder even as her thighs parted. "I asked you what you wanted, I asked you, and you said it wasn't sex!"

"It wasn't," he grunted, bracing himself on one arm so that he could sweep his belt off and let his cock extrude in an immediate and insistent rush. "It was marriage. The sex would just be sex without it. Not that there's anything wrong with the sex," he added, now struggling with the loin-plate, which had caught in his straining breeches. "If you're worried that you don't please me, you can be easy, Soft-Skin. Your body was made to pleasure mine."

"What a huge relief," said Amber in a curiously flat voice, each word carved and set separate from the others.

She really had been worried. He paused to stroke his snout along her throat again, then resumed the battle with his loin-plate and won. "I will burn with you, my wife. And you will burn with me."

"You're driving me crazy," she said, arching her hips to help him tug her breeches down. "You know we're not really married."

He stopped. It wasn't easy. His man's shaft pulsed in his fist where he gripped it for the guidance it needed to find its way inside her in this bizarre position, but he was the master of his clay and he ignored its urgings. "I didn't mark that," he said, a bit breathlessly, but with admirable self-control. "What did you say?"

She looked up at him, her brows furrowed, and bit at her lower lip with her small, blunt teeth. She was also breathless and flushed as well, and she looked down the hills and valleys of her body at the cock in his fist with an expression that was at once profoundly annoyed and entirely defeated.

"We'll fight about it later," she promised, reaching between them to take what he offered and guide him home.

A true master of his clay would have firmly removed himself and thrashed this out. Human speech did not change from one tone to another; he knew what she'd said and he knew he should not allow it to lie spoken.

But her body took him in, hot and wet and gently squeezing at the whole of his length in ways miraculous to feel, and he was no Sheulek then, only a man willing to trade every future argument in all the world just to stay right here right now. So he let it go, and whatever twinge of conscience he may have felt in that release was swiftly forgotten in the pursuit of the one that eventually followed. It was not his proudest moment, but he would just have to pray about that. Later.

7

Maybe it was true. Maybe they really were married. Amber had never actually befriended a married couple and didn't have much personal experience with the married lifestyle, but Meoraq certainly seemed to fit the stereotype, even though he'd never been to the movies. He grunted when she talked to him, insisted he knew where they were going even after admitting he'd never been here before, coddled her unnecessarily when he decided her poor little girl-body couldn't keep up, and then ignored her on the one occasion she asked to stop.

She asked for two reasons. First, the rain that had been drumming down on their heads for the better part of three days had undergone a series of disturbing changes in a short stretch of time. This morning, although drizzly, the wind had been relatively warm; next, it had stopped raining for maybe an hour, but gone very dark and very cold; about an hour ago, the sky had taken on a vaguely grainy appearance, almost like she was seeing an old movie, and it had started raining again, the drops like nails falling, not on her head, but straight into her face. Since then, it had been getting darker almost by the minute, even though she knew they had hours to go before nightfall. The lightning, which to be fair had never really stopped, picked up in frequency and intensity, until it began to feel like they were filming that grainy old movie in front of a huge crowd of paparazzi. And now there was thunder—not the low rolls and grumbles that had been following them for days from the distance, but the kind that she could feel shivering in her bones.

The second reason, the selling point as it were, was that quite unexpectedly, they were presented with a place to go. The hill they'd been climbing hadn't been the latest in a series of suspiciously regular, short, steep hills. It was just a hill, like any of a number of hills that had been growing the closer they came to the mountains. It wasn't particularly steep, but it was very slick and muddy, thanks to days of rain and the wind blowing directly in her eyes. The rocks that jutted out of its thorny, mud-slick sides weren't the squarish chunks of eroded walls that had fallen in and been covered over; they were obviously just rocks. There had been, in short, no clues whatsoever that this was waiting on the other side.

They didn't look like ruins. There were no skyscrapers, no buildings at all more than a few stories tall, just a few metal towers like antennae around the perimeter, and they were still standing. The roads were all flat—no overpasses pancaked to the ground—and they were all extremely well-lit. It didn't appear to be the protruding tip of an overgrown metropolis, but something small and complete, built to fill exactly the place it occupied. From here, so far away, any damage that time and neglect had invariably caused was hidden. The rain gave the illusion of movement to the lights that burned in every building and along every street. The wind could have easily been the sound of all the traffic Amber couldn't see. And looking at it, Amber suddenly understood how people could believe in Scott's starship. Looking at it, even Amber had a moment, however dim and fleeting, when she wondered if one of their old ships might really be able to fly after all.

Of course, she didn't say that. All she said was, "Let's go down there and look around until this blows over, what do you say?" and he said, "No."

And wasn't that what marriage was all about? Communication and compromise. Jerk.

"Hey," she said, and then had to shout it because of the wind and the fact that he was still walking. "Hey!"

She knew he heard her because his spines flattened, but he kept going.

"Hey!" That wasn't working. Amber gave in and ran after him. "Can we please stop?"

"No," said Meoraq.

The sky grew noticeably darker.

"Nicci and the others might be down there!"

"They aren't."

"You don't know that!" She grabbed at his pack, since she knew he'd just shake her off his sleeve, with far more success than she'd expected. He skidded, arms flailing, but quickly recovered his balance and before Amber could think to let go of his pack, he'd shrugged out of it and swung around. Lightning snapped across the sky, throwing her shadow in stark relief over his chest.

"Woman!" he bellowed. "Don't paw at me!"

"Then don't walk away from me when I'm talking to you!"

He snatched his pack out of her hands and glared right back at her. "This is not a discussion. We do not stop until I give that order!"

"So what I want doesn't matter?"

"Not in this instance."

"That's not fair!"

"Don't whine at me. Start walking."

Amber had often heard it said that after a while, married people achieved such a state of togetherness that they could finish one another's sentences. Apparently, there was an intermediary step in which one could see how the sentence was supposed to go without actually finding it necessary to fill in the blanks.

"I haven't asked for a damn thing in—"

"That doesn't buy my assent for—"

"Give me one good reason why we shouldn't—"

"God Himself commands—"

"I said a *good* reason, not more of your Bible-thumping bullshit! Why can't you just admit—"

"Why can't you?!"

They stopped as if by some prearranged signal to allow thunder to smash overhead and roll away behind them.

"You don't want to go down there because you don't want to find them," Amber said at the end of it. She was shouting, she supposed, but only because the storm made it impossible to be heard any other way. The thunder was still rolling, no louder but no softer, like a distant train that just kept roaring by.

His eyes narrowed, sparking white with reflected lightning. "You don't want to look for them down there," he countered, also shouting. "You just want to hide from a little winter storm!"

"Little winter storm? Look at that!" She pointed back the way they'd come, and because she was pointing, she looked that way too.

The last time she'd seen it, the storm had stretched from one end of the horizon to the other, all churning wind and the flashpop of lightning, black as a solid wall above the barest stripe of sky that could be seen beneath it. Now it was a lot closer and Amber saw for the first time thin tendrils of black, dangling down from the storm above and groping at the ground below if it were pulling itself along in some lurching, predatory fashion.

Thin tendrils...dozens and dozens of them...

A wall of tornados, as far as the eye could see.

"Oh my God," she said, except she might have only mouthed it. She couldn't hear herself speak, couldn't hear anything at all but the sudden pounding of her heart and the howling of the storm. Her pointing arm dropped slowly; her other arm came up like a counterweight to clutch at her throat, which had tightened painfully. All at once, she couldn't catch her breath. "Oh my God," she said again and she heard it this time, just barely. "Meoraq, look at that!"

He looked, but his annoyed expression never changed.

"We have to get inside!" she said (not shouting, not yet, or if she was, it was just because the wind and rain were so loud. She wasn't panicking. Amber Bierce had never had one moment of panic in her whole life). "Right now!"

"Not here."

"We're going to die!"

He rolled his eyes, then took her arm and pointed to a rocky outcropping in the middle of the empty plains, so far distant that she could see nothing beyond its general shape and some shadows around its base that might be crevasses or maybe only dark brush. "Do you see the caves? We'll weather down there."

"We'll never reach it! There's shelter right here! Damn it, Meoraq, we have to get out of this *now*!"

As if God Himself agreed, lightning slammed into the ground not half a mile away—which still seemed like a long ways off, until it was lightning hitting there—shattering the skeletal finger of a lone tree down to the ground. The storm-monster in the sky picked up its splinters, tasting them as it scoured the earth and tossing away the bits it didn't like.

Meoraq looked at that, too, but his expression hadn't changed. "There is no shelter here," he told her, raising his voice to a bellow in order to be heard, and turned around.

Amber stood with her mouth hanging dumbly open and the rain sluicing in, watching him walk away. Then she looked at the storm and the storm looked back at her. Never mind how that sounded, even in the privacy of her head, it looked and it *saw*. It hovered for a moment, drawing up all of its little grasping fingers, seeing her, seeing *Amber* alone and helpless, and then it opened the roaring funnel of its mouth and came right for her.

She panicked and ran.

Her boots skidded in the wet grass; twice, she tripped over juts of stone and went tumbling, but she was always up again at the end of it and if there was pain, she didn't feel it. When something snagged at the back of her tunic, she tore it off without stopping, and ran half-naked in the bruising rain until she hit the wall that surrounded the ruins. The towers that were arranged at points around it lit up all kinds of yellow when she climbed over, but nothing shot her down. As soon as she fell into the street—the flat, solid street—she was off and running again.

She didn't think about where she was going. The dumb animal directing her flight kept her going past this building or that one, dismissing them without explaining its reasons. *Notsafe* was the closest she came to a real thought. Those three long structures so much like airplane hangars, open at both ends and filled with half-glimpsed hunks of machinery, *notsafe*. That tall, three-story building with the windows all around it, mostly broken into jagged-glass smiles, *notsafe*. Those rows of solid-looking boxes at the other end of the ruins, they were all right, but the all the empty streets and slowing fences standing between her and them, *notsafe*.

But she had to go somewhere. She had to go somewhere or die here in the empty street. Amber staggered to a halt, gasping for breath and spitting out rainwater, but behind her eyelids, the world suddenly lit up red. Through the storm's roar, she heard a popping sound, followed by an almighty crash of thunder that sent her screaming forward again. There was a light ahead of her, burning calmly above a door, and in the split-second before she crashed up against it in a panicked attempt to beat it down, the door just opened.

She hurtled over the top of the bot standing in the doorway, hit the polished floor boobs-first and went spinning wild across the room until she crashed into an extremely solid object.

"Please present—" the bot began, and then there was a *shunk*, a hot-smelling pop, and Meoraq kicking the husk out into the rain.

She opened her eyes and saw him with the storm howling at his back. He dropped her pack on the floor, then her spear (she couldn't even remember losing them), and finally tossed her tunic—his tunic, really—down on top of them. He looked wet and muddy and pissed.

Things kind of greyed out for a moment, or perhaps she only thought they did because of the suddenly silencing effect when the door shut again. Amber tried to get up and fell uselessly onto her face. Nothing seemed to be broken, but the run, the rain and her disastrously comical fall had taken all the breath out of her. She listened numbly to Meoraq's footsteps striding swift and heavy toward her (he didn't slip; life was full of unfairness) without moving.

"Light," he said, picking her up and thumping her unceremoniously on her feet.

A light came on overhead. It did not happen quickly, as of someone flipping a switch, but slowly, sickly, accompanied by an insectile whine of effort that grew until, just before Amber clapped her hands over her ears, it died away entirely and left the lights brightly burning.

Meoraq glared at her until her eyes started stinging and then he turned his back on her. She saw his hands draw into fists and slowly uncurl. He took six breaths and said, "I cry. We'll stay here until the storm passes. Put your clothes on."

She limped over to their packs and picked up his tunic.

"Put *dry* clothes on," he snapped.

She dressed. Thunder rolled out in the plains, making the metal hum beneath Amber's feet.

"Is there a basement?" she asked. "Something below this? Something...safe?"

"How is it safer to be buried under a fallen building than to simply be crushed by it?"

"Please, Meoraq!"

"There is no place safer than within the sight of Sheul, woman. It doesn't matter how deep you burrow—"

"Can't I hide my atheistic ass just *once* without a sermon?"

Meoraq hissed at her and stomped away, shoving at what little blockish furniture had survived the ages and slapping at the walls until he found a panel that opened into the next room. "Stay here," he snarled when she started to limp after him, so she leaned carefully against the wall, rubbing at her aching hip, and waited for him.

The storm raged. She'd heard the cliché used before, had even believed she'd heard storms raging in the past, but never knew it could be like this. The walls had to be at least half a meter thick, all metal and concrete—or whatever they used for concrete on this planet—and the wind still shook it. She was alone with that, alone with the muted thunder and howl of a tornado that might be even now passing directly overhead, alone without even Meoraq's high-handed religious fervor to comfort her. The lights blurred; she looked up fearfully, thinking they were going out and she'd be trapped in the dark, then realized she was crying. And once she realized that, it was as though something broke inside her and suddenly she was sobbing so hard, she could barely breathe.

Something huge hit the wall with a deafening bang. Amber screamed helplessly and sank down the wall, sobbing because she'd banged her hip at some point in her wild spin across the floor and now it hurt to stand and it hurt to kneel and it hurt worst of all to sit. She couldn't remember the last time nothing had hurt; she didn't think she was ever going to feel that way again. This was it. She was never going to feel better and she was going to die huddled in a corner and crying.

She didn't know Meoraq had come back until his hands slipped under her arms and pulled her back up onto her feet. He didn't let go of her right away.

She kept her hands over her face, trying to shut her stupid self up and be the person she'd been all her stupid life without any effort at all, but the tears kept coming. He didn't say anything. She didn't want to look at him, didn't want to see him trying to think of something to say to this ridiculous, fretful, useless alien he'd been saddled with. She wanted to die.

Thunder savaged the walls. Amber wailed and then Meoraq's arms were closed fast around her, locking her against his broad, scaly chest. She wished she were the old Amber, the Amber who would have smacked him away and been tough and just fine, the Amber who wouldn't have been crying at all. Instead, she clung to him, weeping blindly, and grateful for every cautious touch as he kneaded her back.

"Come," he said after a moment. "The storm will pass. We will wait below."

She nodded, still weeping hard, painfully aware of tears and snot and even drool streaming down her damn face. Humans were disgusting.

He took her with him, his arm close around her, through a series of doors to a wide stairwell. He led her down several flights, leaving the sound of the storm behind them until all was silent except for her sniveling.

"I'm sorry," she said at last. Her voice, weak as it was, echoed.

Meoraq stopped to muscle a door open. He must have done it before, because the lights were on in the hall beyond and he'd known to throw his weight at it from the start, but it still took a great deal of effort and his only answer was a grunt.

She knew she should keep quiet, but no sooner had Meoraq finally managed to shove the door-panels apart than it came bleating out of her again: "Please don't be mad at me."

He'd started to walk on through the doors, but just as suddenly stopped (she bumped hard into his back and had to stagger to catch herself). He stood there for a second or two, not moving, then swung around and hissed, "I am not S'kot, damn it! I won't leave you!"

The words and the vehemence with which they were spoken might have each been sufficient on their own to take her aback. Together, they entirely overwhelmed her.

He resumed his prowling, pissed-off stride, leaving her there in the stairway to stay or to follow as she wanted.

She followed, but slowly, not daring yet to speak. The hallway they entered was wide but not tall, with a rounded ceiling and featureless metal walls that made it seem a lot like walking through a pipe. Here and there, other corridors intersected, but there were few doors and Meoraq did not stop to test any of them.

"They left you," he was saying. "They left you and I have tried and *tried* for your sake to be sorry, but I'm not. You say I don't want to find them and you say truth. I would go so far as to say I *dread* finding them, but I will take them back if I do. For God, yes, and for you, because you think you need them and you think it would make you happy if they liked you, but they never will!"

She flinched, surprised by how much it hurt to hear that out loud, even though it was hardly something she hadn't thought herself. "I don't care if they like me," she mumbled. It used to be true.

"If they were right here in this room—" His fist lashed out and thumped a panel on the wall as he stormed by. The door beside it wheezed halfway open, showing her an empty room, small and stark as a prison cell, before groaning shut again. "—you would take them back. Not just your N'ki, but *all* of them! And you would be glad you found them, glad to take them in and let them piss on you all over again!"

"What do you want me to say?" she asked dully.

He stopped and swung on her again. The stripes were out on his throat and brilliantly yellow. "I want you to tell me why you want them back! I want you to tell me why I—" He smacked himself on the chest hard enough to make her jump. "—am not enough for you! I want you to tell me why you can't just let S'kot go and be glad he's gone!"

"Because everyone else is dead."

He stared at her, breathing hard as the color on his neck faded. When it was almost gone, he looked away, then turned around and started walking again. She followed. Their footsteps echoed, making it seem like more than just the two of them, like Scott and all the others were walking invisibly right behind them.

"Say it," Meoraq said abruptly, disgustedly.

"Say what?"

"What you always say when I act like this."

She frowned, bewildered, and suddenly got it. "Scaly son of a bitch."

"That's it. I'm sorry," he said, in the impatient manner of a man unused to making apologies. "I should not be so harsh with you. This place—and all places like it—just put poison in my mouth."

"It's all right." Amber followed him around a corner, only to stop in her tracks almost immediately.

There was a corpse in the hallway.

Meoraq kept walking, talking back at her just as if he weren't also stepping over the blackened, mummified arm of a lizardman as he went. "No, it isn't. I don't want to be here, but I know you only want to come in from the storm and look for your people, and you should not be ashamed to want either."

"There's a dead body here," said Amber.

Meoraq looked at it, then at her. "Yes," he said. He did not say, 'And your point is...?' but she heard it just the same.

"Is this place safe?"

Meoraq looked at the corpse again, a little longer this time, and at her, a little harder. "What exactly do you expect dead men to do to you?"

She had no ready answer for that, so she asked instead, "Do you know what this building used to be?"

Meoraq backed up into the room behind him and looked around at whatever there was in there to see. "It somewhat resembles a niyowah." He glanced at her. "A place of display, such as one might exhibit trophies of battle or holy relics. Except that these were people," he added as Amber moved past him to see.

A niyowah, he'd called it, which she'd taken to mean a museum or something. But the word that leapt at once to her shocked mind was laboratory.

It was a great round room, the surfaces all neutral and utilitarian in appearance and architecture. The door they had come through appeared to be the only exit. The rest of the outer wall was paneled in glass, or this world's equivalent, and it would not surprise Amber to find it was one-way glass. On the other side were seven cells, each holding a small number of desiccated bodies gnarled together in a violent heap. At the center of these viewing chambers stood the room's control center—a raised dais sporting a horseshoe-shaped console whose video screens were attempting to come on in spite of several cracked monitors. From that vantage, the scientists or guards assigned to watch the prisoners or patients could see into every cell. And as impossible as that seemed, they must have just stood there and watched as the inhabitants of those cells slaughtered each other.

Each chamber was its own vignette of horror and no one had died peacefully. In the first, setting the tone for all of them, one mummy lay with its belly ripped open and another sprawling face-down in the cavity, as a third and fourth (stained black from chin to chest, as if they had been...feeding) remained where they had fallen, hands still locked around one another's throats. Not all the violence was reserved for murder alone; the male mummies were easily identified by the dried cobs of their genitalia, fully extruded at the time of their terrible deaths, and several had expired either in the act or as the victim of violent sodomy.

She didn't want to look at any of it, but was powerless to look away. Amber moved slowly from cell to cell around the steadily rising walkway, oblivious to the rest of her surroundings until she stepped on something that crunched underfoot. She looked down, already knowing what she was going to see.

She'd stepped on someone's toes, but of course, the someone was hundreds or even thousands of years beyond caring. He lay face-up and snarling against the console, his arms and legs sprawled as awkwardly as those of a rag doll carelessly thrown, his withered penis laying crookedly across one thigh, stained to his belly with old blood. Beside him, perhaps six other bodies knotted together. The body at the bottom was that of a woman, still pinned in place by three cocks that Amber could count—one in her vagina, one in her mouth (her snouted jaws snapped wide open so that her throat could be speared), and the last stabbed in just under her right rib—although it appeared that she had been dead for some time before the rest of her attackers expired. They had killed each other without bothering to stop the rape. Two were being themselves sodomized as they fucked her. The corpse crowning the heap, the last survivor one might assume, was fucking a hole in the back of someone's skull, nearly castrating himself in the process. It may have been what killed him.

"What..." Amber's whisper scraped across the dead air like a match. She tried to lick her lips, but had no moisture. "What happened here?"

"I don't know." And didn't care, his tone said.

Amber's hip shook; she put out her hand to steady herself and caught the console. As if drawing strength from her life-force, the monitor nearest her flashed an urgent yellow and played a few silent seconds of some lizardman's face. His mouth opened and closed as if he were talking, but there was no sound, only a low hiss. It was perhaps even the same transmission she had first seen and heard in the ruins where Scott got the idea of a skyport, but the picture spat and died without ever quite coming into focus and she couldn't be sure.

"What really happened?" Amber asked again, wrenching her gaze away to Meoraq. "What *was* the Fall? What the hell did God *do* to you people?"

"I don't know," he said again. But, with an air that suggested he was humoring her, he came to the console (nudging the rag-doll mummy aside with his foot), and examined each of the sputtering monitors in turn. "The Ancients used our letters, but made many senseless words. Something to do with safety," he read. "And with locks. Report to your...I do not know that word. Your abbot, I suppose. Doors will unlock...I do not know those words. It is a warning, clearly," he said, straightening. "The exact nature of the threat eludes me. I don't know what they used to do here."

"We call it biological warfare," Amber said, looking past him at the cells.

"Eh? I don't mark you."

"They made weapons. Very small ones." And it got out. Fear flared, but died away. Judging by the corpses, death may not have been immediate, but the bloodlust that had led to murder had been. If the germs were still alive and kicking, surely Meoraq would be raping her to death at the moment.

She eyed him warily.

He noticed and his head cocked. He was definitely annoyed, but certainly not consumed with murderous rage. He wasn't even annoyed enough to tell her there was nothing worth looking at in this room.

And yet she kept staring, curiously frozen, not just in her body, but her mind also. Because there was something about him, something obvious. Like lyrics to a song she'd heard a hundred times and couldn't quite sing along with; like getting the right word on the tip of her tongue, but no further; like those detective shows where the clues were right in front of her, but she never the saw the end coming until the TV-cop put it all together for her.

God's wrath. She'd asked him what the Fall was and he'd called it God's wrath, when the trees had bled red in the springtime because of all the blood soaked into the ground. War covered the world, he said, like skin covers a man.

She looked at the bodies on the floor again, the heap of them locked in dried-out death, and tried to imagine how it must have been, not just here in this room with the people you'd worked with for years, but everywhere. She could imagine the sound—alarms blaring, fire roaring, and everyone screaming—because she'd heard it once before, as she'd stumbled out of the wreck of the *Pioneer*, but even that was just one ship, just a few thousand people. This had been everywhere, everyone.

Meoraq's head was creeping over a little deeper into that pissed-off angle. She was still staring at him. Something was still wrong, but all she could think when she tried to figure it out was those two words: everywhere, everyone.

It had gone on for years, he'd said. The war and the blight and the storms—*years*—until the Prophet came and started tossing Bibles around. Heck, if you wanted to look at it that way, the storms hadn't even ended yet. It wasn't always as bad as it was tonight, but the wind was always blowing and the sun was never more than a shiny smudge behind the clouds on even the best of days. In fact, if you really wanted to be bitchy, you could argue that the land still looked pretty damn blighted. Nothing but grass and thorns and the toe-catching rocks, which were themselves mostly the eroded rubble of collapsed buildings.

Because they fell. All of them. All over the world. And nothing was left except ruins like these, like the little patches of trees that you could sometimes find out in the wasteland of the plains. The cities fell, and whether it was the dust of their falling or the ashes from all the funeral fires, the wind buried them and the grass covered them up, and it was starting to grow up again, starting to, but not really, because—

Amber felt it start in her stomach, of all places, like a menstrual cramp more than anything else, or even like an orgasm, if an orgasm could be cold and awful.

—because nothing could start over until whatever happened first had ended—

She felt it crawling up her spine in prickles, catching the breath in her lungs and biting her nipples into painful points.

—and nothing had ended yet.

She stared at Meoraq, caught and held in the terrible grip of a moment no larger than a pinpoint, a silence with three words like a billion voices screaming together: *He's still sick.*

Impossible. Viruses didn't live that long, did they? It hadn't just been years, but hundreds of years, maybe a thousand, and the whole planet couldn't still be sick!

But...

She thought of Meoraq and the way his eyes glazed over whenever those yellow stripes started showing up on his throat, that hot/dead stare he got, and how his hand had a way of drifting down to tug at his belt. She thought of that story he'd told the night she'd gotten bit, how his father had single-handedly slaughtered over a hundred well-armed men and then not answered the door for a day or two. How he'd just left...just left. And all the women and children that the bad guys had tied up to take away with them, he'd left them too, left them butchered behind him, and maybe it really had been the raiders who did it like Meoraq said, but maybe—

"How do you feel?" she asked.

"About what?"

"Just...in general."

"In my flesh, you mean?" He looked at the nearest withered corpse and rolled his eyes. "Well," he said, enunciating in that testy way he had. "I feel very well."

"Are you mad?"

He lost the irritated angle of his head almost at once, averting his eyes and scratching at the side of his snout. "I'm not angry, Soft-Skin. I only wish that you would understand that these ruins are meant as reminders of God's wrath, not as shelter."

"That isn't what I meant. You don't want to...I don't know...shove me into a wall and have scary sex with me, do you?"

He leaned back and just looked at her for a moment, then twitched his spines cautiously forward. "Is that a request?"

"No, I just..." Her gaze strayed down to a dead man's blood-stained dick, still half-sunk into that poor woman's side. "Should we do something for them?"

"No."

"But—"

"Let them lie."

"How can this not bother you?"

He looked down at the mummies tangled around the console, then around at the cells. "Their punishment is well-earned and it is not for you or I to end it."

"Can we at least go to another room?"

"This is the lowest level. Safest."

"Yeah, and if God wants us, he'll have us even if we're ten miles underground. I believe you now. Please, Meoraq. I don't want to stay here."

He sighed, but led her back through the maze of corridors to the stairwell and up. He didn't bother opening the doors on any other landing—marks in the dust indicated he had already done so once, so his unwillingness to do so now probably meant more bodies on the other side—and instead took her back up to the lobby on the ground floor. The storm was still roaring around them, but after the scene below ground, it was almost welcome.

"Define scary," Meoraq said suddenly, watching her pace a small circle around the room.

"What?"

"As you seem to think it will frighten you to be leaned against the wall for sex, would you prefer to lie down?"

She stared at him and finally heard a short, humorless laugh puff out of her. "You don't mean it."

His spines flicked. "I find it curious that you always manage to sound so certain about the things *I* mean."

"You can't actually *want* sex after seeing all that."

"They have been dead for ages," he pointed out. "How long would you deem a respectful time of mourning for them?"

"Would it mean anything to you at all if I said I wasn't in the mood?"

"It might. Would it be true?"

Her mouth opened and closed a few times. It seemed a straightforward enough answer. Baffled by her inability to give it some voice, Amber turned and paced away.

When she turned back, he was right behind her.

"You are an aggravating woman," he told her, his hand slipping around to the small of her back. "You make me feel things there are no words for. You make me want to do things I do not know how to do. You also make me very angry. How fortunate that these are the times I most desire you."

Cold fingers clenched in her stomach. She tried to back up out of his grip, but he flexed his hand once and brought her hard against him. Smiling. He was smiling. She tried to feel better about that...but the basement was full of bodies. She backed up again.

This time, he let her go, exposing his teeth in a playful grimace that suggested he was not much put off by the idea of chasing her down. For the moment, however, he just watched her retreat and pace around the room. "You want to be my woman. Do not pretend otherwise. I make you feel safe."

She had no idea what she was going to say until her mouth opened and she heard it shiver out: "Nothing makes me feel safe anymore."

"Lies." He caught her by the belt and unfastened it. She didn't stop him. "I am your shelter, and never more than when I do this." He shucked her out of her breeches in two tugs, picked her up in the same movement, carried her two steps forward as he pulled her thighs around him, and shoved her hard into the wall. She gasped at the impact, but she bucked into him anyway. He nodded once, as if accepting an accolade. "Never more than when I do this," he said again, loosening his loin-plate just enough to let his cock free. It pushed up between them, a brand against her belly for only a moment before he pulled it away and thrust it inside her.

Climax was immediate, unwanted, eruptive. Amber shook, digging her fingernails into his shoulders even as she tried to hide her face against his chest, but he wasn't through making his point. He kept his hands kneading at her thighs, his hips scarcely moving at all, so that their joining was little more than the crush of his weight against her chest, the throb of his pulse in her womb.

"Look at me," he commanded, scraping his scales lightly against her shoulder where his mark scarred her. "No, not so. Put your hands upon me. I am with you. Show me that you see me."

Her hands rose, trembling, to cup his strange face between them. She looked at him and saw him looking back at her. Just Meoraq, who could be a scary son of a bitch when he wanted to be, but who, for the moment, just wanted to be with her. He was fine. Amber felt herself smile a little, relieved right to the edge of stupid, girly tears.

He showed his teeth, approximating a smile for her, pleased. "Are you frightened?"

"No," she whispered.

"Not even here." Thunder crashed; he did not flinch. "Not even now. You are for me, Soft-Skin, and I am with you. Let go to me, my wife. Let go."

Amber dropped her brow to his shoulder, sobbed once, and did.

8

It was the last great storm of the season and even before he had pried the door open and seen the world for himself, Meoraq knew that winter had come. The previous day's rain was still wet on the ground, but his breath misted in the air and when he looked beyond the ruins to the mountains, he saw a fine dusting of fresh snow on their tips.

"Oh wow."

Amber crept out behind him, her soft hand catching at his. He squeezed absently, then released her and started walking, stepping over the remains of a metal tower, twisted together with a few trees and dropped here. Most of the ruins were gone, crushed into a single substance and spread over the streets like jelly over bread. Their shelter alone stood whole, although parts of several others protruded from the wreckage here and there. On the windward side of the remaining walls, debris sloped up like snowdrifts—omens of the weather to come.

"Why didn't this place break apart too?" Amber asked in a small, shaky voice.

"Because we were in it." He glanced behind him, only to see her still standing in the doorway. He sighed and reached out his hand. "We have never left His sight, Soft-Skin. We walk there still."

She didn't move.

"The under-levels are filled with dead people," he reminded her.

She eased out half a step.

"And now the doors are broken open and they're going to get wet."

Her whole face puckered and she finished her approach in a clumsy leap. "I'm not scared of dead people!" she snapped, clutching at the back of his belt.

"I never said you were."

"You implied it."

"I did."

They didn't talk until they were out of the ruins, unless one counted Amber's harried expletives as speech whenever her footing slipped on the loose rubble, but it was a comfortable quiet, comfortable cursing. Once back in the relative stability of the open plains, he had to stop and let her look back, which she seemed perfectly content to do all day. His pointed sighs had no effect on her. In the end, he just started walking and let her decide whether or not to follow. Of course she did, if not quietly. He could hear her back there, muttering in ways that suggested she wanted him to hear at least some of the unladylike things she said, but she didn't let go of his belt. His Amber, fearless once more in the morning light.

"Do you think they're okay?"

His smile slipped. He was glad she was behind him, where she couldn't see it. "I think we survived the storm," he said. "And so it follows that others could as well."

"That isn't exactly what I asked."

"What you asked, only God could answer."

"But if you had to answer—"

"If I could give them back to you, I would," he said, honestly enough. If he could have cut them from her heart forever, he would have done that too, but he kept that to himself.

She let go of the back of his belt, which seemed bad until she took hold of his hand. When he looked at her, she stretched up and pressed her mouthparts briefly to the side of his snout.

"What does that mean?" he asked curiously.

"Just a human thing."

"All right, hold a moment." He leaned in and returned the gesture, taking the precaution of holding her face firmly between his hands. He had very little sensation around his mouth.

"Your first kiss?" she asked when he started walking again. "What did you think?"

"You smell nice."

"Ooo, lies."

"Under that," he said with a flick of his spines. "The you-part smells nice."

"Wow. You charmer, you." She nudged her elbow into his side. Deliberately, to judge by her broad smile. "You need better compliments than that if you're going to get lucky tonight."

"No, I don't."

"Now you really do."

"No," he said with a snort. "I still don't. I am Sheulek and all things within my camp are mine. Besides, you're my wife and it is your divinely-ordained duty to serve my needs, whatever they may be. Besides that, you want me."

"Not at the moment."

"Always," he said, but he stole a covert glance to make sure she didn't mean it. She didn't. He grinned and thumped a knuckle playfully on her scarred shoulder, saying, "I must be among the very best of men, eh? To possess so fine a wife."

"Yeah, thanks, but we're not really married."

She was still smiling, but it wasn't a joke. Meoraq thought about it, then stopped walking and turned on her. "That's not the first time you've said that," he said, then thrust his face very close to hers. "Why do you keep saying that?"

She seemed startled at first, inclined to laugh at him, but her eyes darted up to take in his low spines and she decided to become defensive instead. "Because we're not! You can't just say something and make it true!"

"Yes, I can."

"No, you can't!" she snapped. "Anyway, there weren't any witnesses or anything to prove you even said it."

He rocked back onto his heels and stared at her. "A witness?" he asked incredulously. "Woman, I will do many things to humor your human whims, but inviting in an audience while I am having sex will never be one of them!" He paused, then leaned in again. "You were there. Why didn't you protest at the time if you had such objection?"

Pink color touched at her cheeks. "I wasn't exactly paying attention to what you were saying at that point."

He smiled.

"Oh shut up," she snapped, ducking around him to keep walking. "We're not married and I'm not arguing about it anymore. We're just not."

He snorted, but came after her, falling into step at her side instead of taking the lead. "This is not an argument," he informed her. "There would have to be a dispute in order for there to be an argument and it is not possible to dispute the facts. But now I am curious. How do humans make a marriage bond?"

"With vows, I guess, but there has to be a priest there, or at the very least, a judge."

Meoraq peered at her, then struck himself on the chest and flung both arms out, putting his whole body on display.

"Not you!" she yelled. The color in her cheeks was very bright now, a bold red that painted her all the way up to her eyes. "You don't count! It has to be *another* priest or *another* judge!"

He flicked his spines, still grinning. "When we return to Xeqor, I will have our bond formally witnessed by the abbot and the high judge both if you like. Does that satisfy you?"

Amber walked a little faster. "You didn't even ask me if I wanted to marry you."

"Why would I do that?" he asked, amused. He didn't have any trouble keeping pace at her side.

"Because you can't marry someone against their will!"

"Yes, I can."

"You can be a real prick sometimes."

Meoraq snorted. "That is the sort of thing you say when you can't think of anything else. If this is an argument, I think I have just won it."

She threw him a glare and tried to walk even faster. He had only to wait. Eventually, his same even strides were enough to bring him up beside her. She glared straight ahead, her back stiff and her mouthparts pressed together.

"Well?" she said, after a few minutes of what had been for him a fairly comfortable silence. "Aren't you going to tell me I'm beautiful when I'm angry?"

That was a trap if he'd ever heard one.

"No," he said. But took the risk and bent in swiftly to sweep his scent-cavities along the side of her throat. "But you do smell nice."

He gave that a moment more to settle, then put out his hand.

Her mouthparts twisted, but she took it.

* * *

The journey resumed. With the wind at their backs and the ground drying out and chilling hard beneath their feet, their speed greatly improved. The plains rose and became the foothills. Dead grass thinned over the stony soil. The earth took on the strange greenish-grey tint unique to the border between Yroq and Gedai. They made six spans that day at his estimate, six spans and still it was light when he called camp. And yet he lay awake that night with Amber tucked up against his side in a bed warmed by his fires, thinking.

Meoraq knew of no roads through the mountains, which was not to say there were none. From the moment the mountains were in sight, he had been looking for evidence of a pass. The relatively low peaks and shallow grades of this particular slope had brought him here, where he found the remnants of a road, but nothing that had been cleared or remade in years. Carving out a road, even in the plains of Yroq, was no casual undertaking and they were not abandoned on a whim. The inescapable conclusion was that there might be something wrong with this one and furthermore, that there must be a better crossing somewhere else, but he didn't know where, didn't even know whether to search for it north of their position or south.

In the morning, the mountains looked whiter. Meoraq prayed while Amber sat on a rock and pretended to be patient with him, but when he raised his head at the end of it, he still saw only the mountains...and the snow creeping down from its heights.

"Well?" said Amber, shouldering her pack and taking up her spear.

"This is where we cross," he decided, but he was not at ease with the decision.

They began to climb, making their way steadily over the loose rock and deadfall that littered the base of the mountains. There was no sense of progress made. They seemed to struggle over the same hill again and again while the mountains themselves stayed just beyond it. Meoraq had to look back and see the plains below them—a rumpled brown blanket with patches of trees and the short, ugly scar left by the storm days ago—to feel for certain they were moving at all. Their distance halved and then halved again as the snowline began to drop.

It began as a few flakes, which Amber tried to tell him were just blowing down from the mountains. He didn't bother to argue with her. In another hour, arguments were unnecessary. Their tracks were holes in dust at first, then depressions, then craters, and finally twin lines. By the time he called camp that night, they were in the white up to their knees and the snowline was lower than it had been even two days ago.

Amber held his pace without complaint, walking where he walked and taking no foolish chances over rough terrain. She learned quickly how to see softslides forming and where to put her feet on broken slopes, but he heard her fight for breath the higher they climbed. He felt the sharp tug of her hand on the back of his belt each time her footing slipped. He saw her cup shake when she drank her first swallows each time they stopped to rest. He felt the weakness in her arms when she put them around him at night.

The foothills could not go on forever. Already, the landscape was changing. The true mountains loomed over them: rock and ice and death in every misplaced step. The time was coming to make a decision. Meoraq put it off as long as he could, until at last, Sheul made it for him.

* * *

Meoraq crested a hill and when he saw what lay before him in the last valley before the mountains, he halted. Amber, bent nearly double to keep the stinging wind out of her fragile human face, promptly walked into him. She stumbled, her hunting spear at once tangled in his legs and hers, and probably would have fallen over if he hadn't caught her by the arm.

"What is it?" she asked, squinting through the falling snow.

It was a cave, and if a cave had been all it was, it would not have drawn his eye for more than a moment. But it was a cave with a mouth large enough to allow a grown man to walk through and small enough for said man to easily craft a hide door to cover it. It was a cave positioned midway up a gentle slope, neither on the valley's floor nor dangling unreachably over a sheer drop. The valley itself was wooded and well-traveled by mountain game, with a visible source of water and no evidence of past slides. Short of a second pillar of flame rising to heaven, the message could not have been more clear.

"Why are we just standing here?" Amber asked.

"We are done for now," he told her as his gaze moved over her. She did not look well. Her skin had turned a bright pink wherever it was exposed to the air, all but her mouthparts and the thin flesh surrounding her sunken eyes, which had taken on a deep, bruised color. Part of it was surely the cold, which her human body could not seem to combat, but the endless days of walking had taken a heavy price as well. If she was not at her limits already, they were well within her sights.

"It's hours until dark!" she argued, even as she weaved upon her feet.

"We are done."

"The mountains are right there!"

"We are done."

"Damn it, lizardman!"

"We—" He bent down to put their eyes directly on level, his face so near that he could taste her breath when he spoke. "—are done."

"You don't think I can do it, is that it?" she demanded.

Meoraq neither answered nor straightened up.

She swiped snow out of her face. "Fine. We'll take a break, but—"

"That cave shall be our camp," Meoraq said, pointing.

"That what?" She tracked the aim of his arm and scowled at the gift Sheul had given them. "A cave? I don't want to stop for the whole night!"

"We will not stop for one night, woman," he replied. "We stop for all of them."

"What do you mean?"

"Sheul has provided our winter's camp."

She stared at him, water welling and steaming in her eyes. Then she snatched her spear back from him and yanked her arm from his grip. "Have fun, lizardman. I'm not tired and I'm not stopping!"

He watched her go, struggling against the wind at every stubborn step. If this were any other woman, her foolishness might carry her another hour before she came meekly back to him, assuming there were any dumaq woman who would refuse him. If she were a man, her pride might take her well into the night before reason brought her slinking back to his camp. But she was Amber, and so Meoraq went after her.

She tried to shake him off when he first took her arm, saying something about this not being a matter for discussion, which was very true. Meoraq did not bother to answer, however, electing instead to sling her over his shoulder with his travel-pack. He picked up her spear, gave her a whack with it to stop her drumming her fists on his back, then turned back along the path of his tracks, loudly praying for patience. He did not stop until he had marched himself into the cave Sheul had given him and could have this fight out of the weather.

"Where will you go?" he demanded, setting her on her feet and giving her a shove when she immediately attempted to storm out again. "How is it you think you will find Xi'Matezh without me?"

"Maybe God will take me there," she said acidly.

"Sheul brought you *here*."

"I...I...I don't need to stop! I can keep going just fine!"

"Do you think I am making this camp for your sake?" he asked, incredulous. "I am a Sword and a true son of Sheul. I obey only His will. I do not ignore His direction for benefit of stubborn females without the sense to look after themselves. And if I did," he went on, his temper fraying, "I would have halted this march long before now as you are plainly, *plainly*, killing yourself to make it!"

"I am not!"

He ripped his samr from its sheath and seized her. She fought him with embarrassing effectiveness, but in moments, he had roughly turned her and thrust its polished blade unavoidably before her face. He shook her once to stop her swearing and again to make her look at it instead of at him and then there was quiet.

"Leave me alone," she said at last.

He snorted at the back of her stubborn head. "I am tempted to do just that altogether too often for a righteous man," he told her and released her, unbuckling his harness rather than re-sheathe his samr. He strove for patience, found some, and turned his attention to his surroundings, where it should have been from the start. The cave was not as roomy as he would have liked, but had a natural bend to it which protected it nicely against the worst of the wind and would make it easy to hang doors. It had clearly been used by men in the past, to judge by a stone-ringed ashpit and a number of pots and basins too heavy or ungainly to carry over the mountains, even a small smoker and drying rack. Far more recently, it had sheltered animals; there was a scattering of small bones to tell him that a thuoch had been and gone at some point, but now it was a kipwe's den. Perhaps even a mated pair of kipwe, to judge by the size of the nest of quills and shed fur before him. If they had not already descended to winter in the warmer climes of Yroq's plains, their two hides would make fine doors to seal off the mouth of the cave and their meat would make a fair start on their winter stores...

Amber had not moved.

Meoraq pondered her for a moment more in silence, then heaved a mental sigh. He may as well get the whole of the fight out of the way now, rather than portion it out over the next several days and impede all the other work they could be doing. He said, "All things happen in Sheul's time."

"Bullshit. *Lizard*-shit." She shot him a fierce, humiliated sort of stare and as quickly looked away. "Why don't you ever just come out and say what you mean?"

"Great Sheul, O my Father, give me patience. What do I mean?"

"You think I'm weak!"

Of all the things she could have said, this was the one he was least prepared to hear. "In what sense?" he asked guardedly.

"In the sense that you think I'm weak!" she yelled back at him. "There aren't a whole lot of different ways to say that, lizardman! You think I'm weak!"

"You are," he said, baffled by this outburst.

She stepped back with her spear so tightly clenched in her fists that it shook. Her mouthparts, as tightly pressed together, shook also.

"Your skin is soft," he told her, hardly able to believe he needed to make these arguments out loud. "It bruises at every touch. It tears. It can't hold its heat. In that sense, you are weak. In the sense that you can't carry the provisions you require to sustain you on this journey, you are also weak. You have suffered severe illness which makes you tire more easily. You may improve in that regard with rest and time, I don't know, but for now, you *do* tire easily, which makes you weak. You don't know how to survive in the wildlands. This is ignorance more than weakness," he added thoughtfully, "but it bears mentioning."

She turned around with curious difficulty, as if pulling against invisible hands.

"Your clay is much too frail," he went on, watching her walk clumsily to the mouth of the cave, "for the soul it must house."

She did not stop and he was obliged, not without a sigh, to follow after her for a second time.

"Sheul measures us all," he said, taking his place at her side and resisting mightily the urge to pick her up and carry her off again. "His greatest trials are reserved for those He takes greatest pride in. You must please Him, Soft-Skin."

"I don't believe in your stupid god."

He snorted. "It amazes me each time you say that, as if you truly believe it is necessary that you do."

She rolled her eyes in their bruised sockets and tried to walk faster, skidding now and then in the wet snow, but soon enough her step began to slow. She struggled on for a time, following the path they had made in her first senseless flight, but when she reached the mangled place where he had seized and carried her away, she went no further. She glared at the ground between her feet, not moving. Meoraq waited, watching the snow catch in her hair.

"They could be just up ahead," she said finally.

"All things are possible, but this is not likely." And in answer to her glance, explained, "If they passed through this valley, surely they would have seen that cave and slept within at least one night, and if they had, I would know it. You would know it."

Her shoulders fell. She stared at the mountains.

And because it needed saying, even as much as he hated to be the one saying it, he took grim hold of that spear and drove it all the way in. "I have not seen any sign of their passing in a long stretch of days."

"They're not dead. My sister—" She stabbed her eyes at him and looked away just as fiercely. "—is not dead. I'd know if she was."

"I'm not saying she is," said Meoraq, who nevertheless thought just that. "I say only that they have not come this way. Perhaps they crossed elsewhere. They may have made a camp to weather out the cold season or even abandoned their search for Xi'Matezh altogether. If it is Sheul's will, we will meet them again. But for us, for now, we are done."

Meoraq stood in the snow and let her think. She had begun to shiver by the time she was done, but he did not attempt to hurry her along.

Her breath heaved in and out of her. She turned around to face him. "If I go back with you tonight, I don't want to hear you tell me not one more word about how this is God's will."

He opened his mouth to tell her that, whether she liked admitting it or not, she was his wife and as such, sworn to obey him in all things, but the words would not come. Instead, awkwardly, he opened his arms. Glaring, wordless, she shuffled closer and let him hold her.

"I still have the lhichu," he said at last, for want of something intelligent and comforting to say. "We'll cure leathers and make clothes. The cold will pass. All things in...All things in time."

"Thank you," she mumbled.

They went together back to the cave as the snow fell and filled their bootprints.

BOOK VII

ZHUQA

The worst winter of Amber's life happened the year she turned five. These were among her earliest memories—freezing in the basement of the flophouse where Mama made them stay, hiding from the men with the big hands who stayed there too, Baby Nicci always crying and sometimes Amber crying with her because her stomach always hurt. The days of state-care with juice boxes and storybooks and all of life's cares erased in one wonderful tumble down a hill was months away, a fairy-tale Amber didn't even know to hope for.

The second-worst winter would probably have to be the one two years before her mother died. It had been Bo Peep's last real effort to kick the drugs, and even though everyone knew how it would end (except maybe Nicci), they all went through the same tired motions. Every night, Amber had to walk home from the bus stop with filthy snow seeping in through her shoes and her back aching from a full shift at the factory, not knowing whether she'd find Bo Peep passed out on the floor or fixing dinner. The bad nights made the good ones impossible to enjoy; the good nights made the bad ones worse. Hope and cynicism fought a constant, gut-wrenching war which finally ended on Christmas morning, when Amber came out of her room to find that all the presents beneath the tree (their first tree in years and how much fun it had been, flinging tinsel over plastic branches like a bunch of kids and laughing) gone, along with the TV, the rent money, and the microwave, of all things. Nothing left but wads of wrapping paper and Nicci's gift for their mom—a picture of the three of them together—tossed on the floor.

In fact, on the list of Bierce's Bad Winters, the one Amber spent in a cave with an alien didn't even make the Top Ten. If only she had enough good memories to make a Bierce's Best Winters list, it might actually be there instead. The cave was warm and a little homey. The food was monotonous but plentiful. Meoraq helped her keep busy (one way or another). Some days, it was more than just killing time. Some days, she was happy.

So why had she hiked all the way out here again, across the whole valley and up the south side of the mountain, skirting ledges no wider than her boots and climbing over icy chasms and fallen trees, just so she could stand here and look at the pass? It looked exactly the way it looked three days ago. And two days before that. And six days before that. The snow that filled the sharp V between the slopes was maybe a little more compact, but even she didn't try to kid herself that it was melting.

She couldn't understand that. It had to be melting somewhere. The little fall where they drew their water every day had tripled in size and sprouted a dozen brothers and sisters. The trees were warming up, or at least, they gave off a greenish sort of scent if she broke off a branch. And the animals were coming back after a long, scary absence.

Well...not so scary. In the first days of her imprisonment (he hated it when she called it that), Meoraq had announced that they were each going to get two full wardrobes, which meant that not only did he want the two of them to pee in a bucket and *keep* it, but he also killed pretty much every animal he saw. She called it wasteful and kill-happy and bitched about it right up until the time they got snowed in for thirty-three days straight. They still had two whole xauts and half a kipwe packed in snow, and yet, when she'd left the cave this morning, she'd told him she was going hunting and he didn't argue. He didn't believe her—he'd made that plain with a hard stare and flat spines—but he didn't argue.

They did a lot of not arguing these days, which was not the same as not arguing, but it wasn't arguing either, so that had to count for something. And arguing, she had discovered to her surprise, didn't have to be the same as fighting. They hadn't fought in forever, not even when they'd been snowed in for so long. This was due in large part to Secret Rule Number One: *No matter what ass-headed thing he's going on about, if his neck turns yellow, shut up and apologize*. It worked, mostly. Oh, there were nights when they managed not to touch even in that narrow bed, but they always woke up tangled together. She wasn't out here now because she was mad at him or felt like proving that he wasn't the boss of her or anything like that. She just...wanted to see the road.

And now she wanted to climb down and stand in it.

So she did, creeping along with pained care. The wind had blown all the loose snow around, hiding all the nooks and juts where she needed a handhold, hiding deadly pockets of ice as well. She'd had a couple of bad falls just walking the well-traveled trail between the cave and their waterfall; she wasn't getting stupid clear out here alone.

The snow at the bottom was hard and crusty on top, soft and slushy underneath. She balanced on its surface for only a second or two before punching through and sinking in past her knees. Undaunted, Amber pulled her snowshoes off her back and stepped into them. Now the snow held her.

She walked out a little ways, testing each and every step with her spear before she placed her snowshoe, but she didn't go far. Snowshoes had been her idea and even her first clumsy pair had worked great, but they tricky to walk in and hell on her ankles. Looking at the pass, she tried to imagine using them not just for an hour or two—difficult enough—but for days on end.

She could do it, physically. She hated using the fucking things and she probably wouldn't be able to stop bitching about them after the second day, but she could do it. What she wasn't sure about was what would happen if they got two or three days out and *then* the snow started melting. Snowshoes did not work in slush.

Lost in thought, Amber did not see the thuoch until it was nearly on top of her, which could have been very bad except that it hadn't seen her either. It trotted along the eastern slope in defiance of gravity, its long body rolling in its unnatural, humping gait. She watched it, admiring its effortless speed and slinky grace over the icy rock and snow.

When they'd first come to the mountains, the thuochs were still mostly brown, but now it was whiter than the old snow it walked on. Meoraq had killed two white thuochs for her, saving the pelts because he said he wanted to make her a 'good' coat. Better, presumably, than the overtunic she was wearing now, which she'd made from the kipwe hide. And which in all honesty looked like a total shit-cake after she'd scraped all the quills off, but it had been the first thing she'd ever made all by herself and she was proud of it, damn it. It didn't need replacing, not even with a pretty, soft, white thuoch-fur coat. Although she could probably make a much better one now that she'd had some practice. And it would almost certainly be warmer.

No more than ten meters away, the thuoch finally saw her. It froze and immediately assumed a posture of defense and threat, all its fur spiking out to make it appear double in size. At the same time, its lower jaw dislocated and dropped open in an unnatural gape that had creeped her out tremendously the first time she'd seen it.

The thuoch shook its fur and yowled at her, but Amber didn't move. She kept her spear in her hand and ready, in case the beast should decide to charge, but she didn't think it would. She could see the two tiny black beads tucked away behind the thuoch's bristling flank that were the eyes of its half-grown cub. Those eyes were the reason the thuoch wouldn't charge across the treacherous ice. They were also the reason Amber wouldn't take home her third winter-white thuoch pelt to finish her coat.

The two females stared each other down, but eventually the thuoch brought its jaws together. It slunk rapidly away to the western slope, snarling, keeping itself between Amber's spear and its cub until they were out of sight.

The wind blew stale snow into their footprints. Amber watched until all hope of tracking them down was gone. At last, with a final wistful glance at the road, she turned around and headed home.

Home. She'd have to stop thinking of it like that. She wasn't even sure when she'd started, but she had to admit that the little cave, with all its crude amenities, already felt more like home than her memories of any of the apartments she'd shared with Nicci and their mother. So far, she'd been able to stop herself from thinking too hard about what was going to be 'home' after this endless hike was over, but she could feel it creeping in a little more each day. Meoraq, of course, refused to speculate too wildly until God told him what He wanted them to do, but they'd had too many snowed-in days for her not to know about his home—his House—back in the west.

It unnerved her to think of it too deeply. Not just a city full of lizardmen, but just the house itself. The place he described...a wedge of the entire city from the outer wall to the inner ring, housing hundreds of families, thousands of people. There would be servants everywhere and so many rooms he couldn't count them for her. And as much as she did not want to be wandering in this rainy wasteland full of man-eating porcupines forever, the idea of living in a place like that didn't seem like much of an improvement. It was possible to avoid thinking about it for as long as they were stuck here, but once they were moving again...

Meoraq had admitted that he didn't know precisely where the temple was, but he seemed to think it wasn't far, once over the mountains. "Half a brace," he kept saying, which meant eighteen days, give or take. Half a brace, unless something else happened, and he could finally stand there in his empty temple and meditate until he felt good about going home. Then she'd have to think about all those rooms and servants and lizardpeople everywhere she looked, but until then, she could still pretend she had options.

Until then, she could pretend they were leaving to look for Nicci.

The sun was getting low behind the clouds and the light was leaving at its usual alarming speed. Nocturnal mimuts were emerging from their craggy burrows, like furry footballs bouncing over the ice. Amber speared a few, drained them of the gross stuff, and tied them into a brace (*half a brace and he'll hear what he's come to hear half a brace and i'll have to give up on her forever half a brace*) to carry them home.

Almost home.

Meoraq was by the fire when she came in, winding homemade sinew-thread onto a short length of stick. Restocking his mending kit, she was sure. Sometimes he went pretty far out of his way to keep busy, but this at least was something she could see the use of. Four sets of clothes made for a lot of sewing. There had been a good twenty-day stretch at the beginning when sewing, sex, and sleeping had been all they did. And fight, of course, but fighting had a way of turning into foreplay for Meoraq, which annoyed Amber no end if it was an argument she really cared about, so she'd learned to just let him be an arrogant ass...and he'd learned to let her be an unreasonable bitch, probably, but they made it work.

"Hey," she said now, shrugging out of her furry swaddle.

He grunted a greeting and wound up some more sinew. "See anything?"

"There's always something to see," she replied, setting her brace of mimuts down on the hearth beside him. "I went out to the road."

He grunted again, noncommittally. She knew he didn't approve, he knew she knew, no more was said. They'd had that fight already.

"There was a thuoch there."

"You should have brought it with you."

"It had a baby."

"Ah." He wound more sinew. He was almost at the end of it.

"It also had brown coming in on its face."

"It's warming. We'll have to finish your coat with turned fur." He flicked his spines at her knowingly. "How was the road?"

"Still filled in pretty good."

"Yes."

"But I think we could climb over it if we wanted to. With the snowshoes."

He nodded distractedly. Nodding was something he'd picked up from her over the winter and it still didn't look quite normal on him. He finished with his sinews and set the finished spools aside so he could pull the mimuts toward him.

She watched him skin them, as easily as if they were wearing little fur jackets. Then she watched him finish the butchering she'd started. She handed him a skewer when he reached for one. She brought the pot over so he could stew the organs he liked, and the smaller pot for the brains to make the hide-cure. Mimuts didn't have a lot of fur, but they'd be good to line her sleeves or something. She waited and he waited with her.

"You're going to make me ask, aren't you?" she said finally.

"Yes."

"Big scaly jerk."

He hissed through his teeth, but playfully. This wasn't an argument, not yet.

"When are we leaving, Meoraq?"

"When leaving will not kill us, Soft-Skin."

She sighed and sat down by the fire, pulling one of the fresh pelts over her knee so she could start scraping. Now it was his turn to watch her.

"Are you angry?" he asked after a few quiet minutes.

"Not really. But I'm not happy. Look," she said, shoving the half-scraped pelt away and facing him. "I know you've given up on my sister. I know you don't even consider her a factor when you think about us moving on. I can't do that yet."

He didn't argue, didn't say anything, just waited.

"I'm trying to trust you," she told him. "I am trying. But one of these days, I'm going to leave without you."

He took that well, although he couldn't quite prevent himself from rolling his eyes a little. When he'd more or less controlled himself, he nodded again and even gave her a two-knuckle nudge to the shoulder.

"I'll look at the road," he said. "But if I say it isn't safe, you will submit to my judgment. At least for a few days."

"How many is a few?"

"Six."

No surprise. It was his favorite number.

"All right," she said, and resumed scraping. "But if the road does look good, we have to be out of here the next day, okay?"

"If possible. I think you underestimate how much time it takes to ready supplies, now that we have them."

"I just don't want you running up unnecessary delays, that's all."

"Mm. I do that," he agreed mildly. "I'm always losing consciousness for days at a time and laming myself...or am I thinking of you?"

"I wasn't lamed! I just limped for a few days! I don't know if you've noticed, lizardman, but there's ice everywhere!"

"I'm not the one who wants to walk in it." He leaned toward her and rubbed his snout up and down along her throat, letting her know they could fight if she wanted to, but he was already winning.

"Maybe we should pack now so we're always ready," she suggested.

He glanced tolerantly around the cave. "Some things, I suppose. I'll see what I can do about making another sled."

"We can leave some stuff here, can't we? I mean, we'll have to come back this way, right?"

"I have not been curing hides all winter to leave them behind. Besides, the cold will last another brace of days at least in this corner of Gann's world and you can't hold your heat."

"Yeah, yeah. So what do you need me to do?"

He moved her hair and nipped suggestively at the scar he'd given her for a wedding present.

Amber heaved a sigh at him, but she was grinning. Every night with this guy. Twice, most nights. The only times he'd ever let her alone were when she was on the rag and he'd made it clear even then that he was humoring his silly wife by doing so. "Are we really going to do this now?"

"Yes."

"Okay, hang on."

At her gentle insistence, he released her and stood back while she moved the fresh hides and turned the roasting mimuts over. "But seriously," she said, untying her belt. "What can I do to speed things up?"

"Speed is not a virtue in this undertaking, Soft-Skin." He pulled his belt off, looped it playfully around the back of her neck and pulled her close for a quick nuzzle. Then it was all business—loosening ties, unbuckling bootstraps, peeling off outer layers, exposing inner ones. People in the movies made this part look so spontaneous, but it was actually something of a process when you were dressed for winter in the mountains. "It is not the snow that lies on the road that concerns me as much as the snow that still lies on the mountain."

"What about it?" asked Amber, hanging up his coat.

"Ice on the ground can melt from beneath," he explained, sitting down to work his boots off. "When that happens, the weight of the snow on top can cause it to break off in large packs and fall."

"Yeah, it's already happening some places. So what are you saying? We wait until the snow falls onto the road and then we walk out over the top?"

He sighed, then beckoned to her and took off his tunic and dropped it on the floor. "This is a mountain thaw," he told her, gesturing at it. "You see how it seems to lie flat, yet there are many folds and thin places over pockets of air that reach who knows how deep? Snow can smother a man quicker than you might think, or crush him, or cut him open."

"We're not waiting here until the snow completely melts, so forget it!"

"Calm yourself. What I propose," he said, gathering her against his bare body, "is that we climb out a little higher along the southern face, where the snow has already broken free, and travel on the cleared slope. It is not so safe a crossing as I would like, so I must limit the time we would spend in the open pass."

"Meaning?"

"Patience, Soft-Skin." He nuzzled at her shoulder again. "Patience is more than a word. It means that we will walk for every moment there is light, with little or no rest. It means we will not stop to hunt, but must have provisions to see us entirely through."

"We may also need to conserve our energy while we're traveling and not waste it frivolously having sex."

"We may," he said gravely, backing her toward the cave wall which Amber had privately dubbed 'Meoraq's screwin' place'. "We'll have to store up some of that, too. Do you want to show me your belly or your back?"

"You hopeless romantic, you."

"Back it is." He nipped her on the jaw and turned her around.

"Oh fine, but I get the next round in bed."

"I'll consider it."

"And take your panties all the way off this time. That thing is cold as hell on a lady's ass."

"Demanding creature." But his loin-plate clanked to the floor and then his arms were a warm girdle around her middle. He nuzzled thoroughly at her neck, breathing deeply and managing not to catch too much of her hair in his teeth until he deemed she'd had enough foreplay (the concept was still fairly strange to him). Without further ceremony, he tugged her hips into position and pierced her, slipping at once into that detached trance he claimed was a tribute to her overwhelming sensuality.

Amber closed her eyes against the sight of her hands splayed over the rough rock wall, letting the moan that wanted to happen just happen—a tribute to *his* overwhelming sensuality. Hearing it, the steady rhythm of his breaths broke in a dry laugh. "Try not to move."

"I won't."

"You always say that."

"I always start out meaning it."

But she tried. Taking a few stabilizing breaths of her own, she squared her shoulders and pushed her ass back at him, doing her best to pretend she was an inanimate object while he set her on fire one stroke at a time. She forgot all about the mountains and the road and Scott and Nicci and the mimuts on the fire and just fell deeper and deeper into that moment.

Concentrate. His breath tickling the fine hairs on the nape of her neck. The scour of his rough hands chafing steadily at her hips. The slow, insistent press of his flat stomach against her upturned buttocks. The cold rock under her hands and feet. She held onto these things as long as she could, because when they fell out of focus, it was over. Without these little discomforts, she was nothing but how he filled her, how he moved in her, how he made her part of him.

She could feel herself shivering with strain already, and much as she tried not to, the effort of holding so still and being so good was making her tighten up. Everywhere.

"Woman," he warned her hoarsely.

"Don't distract me, lizardman, I'm right on the edge."

He burst out laughing against her back, which did such unexpected things that she broke and began bucking wildly on his impaling shaft. This was usually his cue to hold still and let her finish or hurry up and finish himself so they could both wind down together. Tonight, in his playful, unpredictable mood, the sex became war.

Meoraq's fondness for rough play was no secret. It was one of those things—like sex standing up—that just felt more natural to him, but it wasn't without its risks. *Never let him fight when you can't see him*; that was Secret Rule Number Two, and

Amber wasn't so far gone that she didn't remember why the rules were so important.

But it felt so good...and she was so close...and he was always careful with her, always. He'd never really hurt her.

Amber grappled with it as he encouraged her with hisses and nips, but in the end, it wasn't a decision as much as surrender. She hissed back at him, scratching and slapping at his thighs in a sure signal that *no* in this case definitely meant *go faster*.

"Ha!" He seized her and the sex became fucking, driving her up onto her toes, crushing her against the wall, knocking her full-on into the orgasm she'd been a hair away from reaching anyway.

Amber rode it out, pushing at the wall, at him. He pinned her arms, battled her carefully to the floor (but not as carefully as he had the last time; she knocked her knee a pretty good one), and straddled her again, resuming his steady, forceful thrusts as she writhed and yowled like a common alley cat. Sometimes a little extra noise was enough to give him what he wanted without giving too much up herself.

Sometimes.

"Fight," he panted and, perhaps sensing her misgivings, gave her a playful head-butt between her shoulderblades. "Like you fought the first time. So I feel it when you surrender."

Climbing fast to her second climax was the very worst time to expect a girl to show some self-restraint. Amber managed a token hesitation and then gave up and fought. Bucking and thrashing, she broke free, forcing him to grapple her back into his embrace and under his control. She could hear him laughing as he struggled to hold her, but it *was* a struggle and she was proud of that. She knew she shouldn't be. Secret Rule Number Two...

The change was subtle, at first. His laughter faded gradually to hisses. His grip tightened. His love-bites at her neck and shoulder began to sting. Just when he broke his hard yet steady rhythm, she wasn't sure, but even through her body's frenetic sensory overload, she could tell that what had once been purely pleasure was now shot through with silvery threads of pain.

Her first instinct was the very worst response: She stopped play-fighting and tried to really stop him, then to get away from him. Whatever thin restraint he'd held onto all this time snapped at once. His roar blasted hot on her back as he shoved her down and pinned her under his weight. She knew it when he came by the hard, coughing sound he made, but something was wrong. This was where he usually stopped moving (in spite of the fact that she sometimes actually begged him not to), but tonight he kept at her. Like the bawdy punchline to a bad joke—harder, faster, deeper—and Amber couldn't do anything about it because she was cumming again. She managed only half his name before his powerful jaws clamped down on the back of her neck, actually shaking her like a dog with a doll to shut her up. He hissed into her hair like an animal and this was wrong, this was really, dangerously *wrong*.

Amber tensed, alarm putting real strength into her body, but that was the wrong way to win and she knew it. Every nerve was hot and alive, every sensation heightened. She used it as best she could—a moment's clarity, there at the razor's edge of yet another climax—and then she heaved herself, not backwards, but flat to the floor.

She lay limp and still, giving him nothing to fight against as she took deep breaths and tried to bring her racing heart under some kind of control. He'd never hurt her, no he never would, but he wasn't always *him*, was he?

Meoraq stopped, but he did not immediately back off. If anything, he leaned on her a little harder. She felt, with the perfect awareness of her tingling skin, the minute flexing of his fingers. He uttered a hard, snuffling grunt, but only one. She felt him rear back, shake himself. A second pause, longer than the first, and then he finally spoke: "Are you awake?"

His voice wasn't quite his own either. Breathless, which was to be expected, but also...thick. As if speech were something new to him and not particularly pleasant.

Amber waited, listening. 'Breathe,' she thought at him. 'Six breaths, Meoraq. Count them off.'

He did breathe, but only once. She felt it, hot on her back; he was hissing through his teeth in that silent, pissed-off way he had. Suddenly he let go of her aching wrists and put his hand between her shoulderblades, leaning over to pry unexpectedly at her eyelid. She flinched back, blinking, and he hiss/grunted. "You are awake," he said accusingly. "Why didn't you answer me?"

"I need to stop."

"Stop? Are you hurt?" he asked. It should have sounded concerned, but it didn't and he might have realized it because his next attempt was better. "Are you all right?"

"Please."

"Damn it, woman, I just..." He took a deep breath and let it out slowly. The hand resting on her back drummed once, then patted her. He was still hard; the sensation as he withdrew was enough to give her one final shivery, painful bloom, and then he was out. "A short rest," he warned her. "I'm not finished."

She rolled onto her side and put her hand behind her neck, feeling at the place where he'd bit her. Her fingers came away lightly smeared with blood. She glanced at him, watched him gaze at that blood with a shocking lack of expression, and said, carefully, "You were a little rough with me."

He grunted and stood up. "Your flesh tears too easily."

"I know you didn't mean to hurt me."

"If you know, why are you talking about it?" he snapped. His hand drifted down, paused, and rubbed in a brittle fashion at his stomach, which was clearly not what he wanted to rub. His cock still jutted, wet and urgent. This was the worst she'd ever seen him, the worst she'd ever let him get, but he *was* talking.

"I need a little time, okay?" Amber wiped her neck again—it had already stopped bleeding, but she made sure he saw the marks of his teeth there—and curled up a little, making herself look small. Helpless. Fragile. "Okay?"

Meoraq paced around the cave, watching her. He checked on dinner, picked up their discarded clothes, drank some of the lukewarm tea from the pot on the hearth, and finally went over to sit on the edge of their bed. "How much time do you need?"

"Feel free to start without me."

"You know I can't."

Right. Because it was a sin for a guy to masturbate on this planet, while sexing a woman into a coma was apparently just fine. "I need a little more time," she said.

He hissed at her, caught himself by the end of the snout, and then suddenly leapt up and came at her. "You do it," he ordered, beckoning tersely at her with one hand and himself with the other. It wasn't a sin if it was her hand, as he'd explained before. Ah, the fine points of Lizard Law. "Until you're ready, eh?"

She closed her eyes, pretending to be a woman on the edge of exhaustion, like her heart wasn't going like an engine and her stomach wasn't tying itself in knots. 'Breathe,' she thought at him, so hard she was giving herself a headache. 'Please, just start breathing.' Aloud, she said, "I need another min—"

"Now!"

She dragged her eyes back open to see how serious this was.

It looked pretty serious. Those patches on his throat were still out and brilliantly yellow, his spines were flat and his eyes were glazed and staring. It made her think (as she had thought so often this long winter closed in with him) of the mummies at the bottom of that old laboratory, and those three terrible little words—*he's still sick*—which had never quite left her mind.

She sat up and rubbed once more at her neck. His eyes tapped at her hand, lingered, and flicked away. He grimaced at her, badly disguising his impatience, and went back to sit on the bed. He fidgeted now and then, most often checking the tightness of a belt he wasn't even wearing, but at last those yellow stripes began to darken.

They watched each other.

"I'm not hurting you, am I?" he asked suddenly.

"No, you're fine." She got up, stiff from huddling on the floor, and joined him.

"Fine, eh?" He grimaced again, trying to be playful, but his jaws were a little too wide. Like the thuoch, it was a see-how-hard-I-can-bite look, whether he knew it or not.

"Better than fine," she amended, reaching up to rub briefly at his brow-ridges. He put his arm around her, pulling her onto his lap so he could scrape his chin along her neck. The danger appeared to be past, but she thought she'd better be sure.

"How are you feeling?" she asked.

"Ready," he replied at once, catching her hand and pulling it downwards.

She made a fist on the empty air before he had her where he wanted her. "Because I'm starving."

"Oh." He glanced over at the mimuts, which were nowhere near done cooking, then sighed and set her aside, reaching for his loin-plate. Putting himself away wasn't easy for him, clearly, but he did it and he didn't even look that upset anymore. His neck was black, his spines were up; he never had done his slow-count of six, but he seemed to be all the way back in his own head.

Relief hit her almost as hard as the fear she had refused to face all this while. She reached out impulsively and caught his wrist as he was tightening his belt. "Thank you," she said. For letting himself be put off or just for being himself again, she didn't know, but the gratitude was real.

He smiled and tapped his knuckles along her brow, then swept her hair away from the back of her neck and bent down to lick the place where he'd bit her. "I should have been gentler," he murmured, nuzzling her. "I lose myself sometimes."

She knew.

If he noticed the strain in her smile, he did not comment, but he did finish dressing. All the way. Right down to his boots.

"Are you going somewhere?" she asked tentatively, meaning, 'Are you mad?'

"Just a short walk."

It was a terrific way to get him completely cooled off, but it still unnerved her.

"Right now? It's getting dark."

"I'm restless." He fetched his coat and shrugged into it. "While I'm gone, you can start to pack. We leave tomorrow."

"Tomorrow?" She looked over at the fire, as if the Meoraq of ten minutes ago could still be found there, waiting to tell her how dangerous the road still was and how much safer it would be to hold off for a few more days, and then a few more and a few more. "Are you sure?"

"I'm very restless. Besides." He came back to the bed and pulled her up (roughly, far too roughly) for one of his clumsy, unfeeling lizard-kisses. "I want to get you home before the baby comes."

Of everything he'd said and done, ever, that was easily the most shocking.

"You what?" she stammered, following him stupidly to the mouth of the cave stone-naked. "The what?"

"It was different tonight," he mused, looking her over. And grinned again, with predatory suddenness and unmistakable pride. "Maybe I felt it happen, eh? I need to pray...but yes. I think I just gave you my first son."

He beamed while she gaped, incapable of speech, and then he was out through the flap and away.

* * *

It was a good night, dry and not too cold, with a smudge of moon to light his way and the scent of new growth in every breath—a perfect night for a man to be alone with thoughts of impending fatherhood.

He didn't think about it often, but after twelve years as Sheulek, Meoraq knew he had sired children. Certainly, he had been summoned to acknowledge several over the years, but with the exception of that bad business with Lord Saluuk in Tothax, it had only been the last step before marrying off their mothers. Oh, there were Houses whose lords might be keeping their daughters free in the hopes of the highest possible marriage—Lord Arug came immediately to mind—yet there probably weren't many. Proof of fertility was a far more valuable asset than pretty looks or even virginity, and there was never any guarantee that a Sheulek would live to retire and marry. With three Swords in active service (Salkith counted, even if he was only a Sheulteb), House Uyane might be supporting a hundred sons somewhere in the world, but if so, Rasozul had never deemed the matter important enough to mention. Meoraq had never put a bastard in the belly of some servant, which was more than Nduman could say (or Rasozul, come to think of it), so whatever children he'd sired, they were honorably got. If one of them were to come to his gate, Meoraq would welcome him as kin, but this was not the same as being a father.

Odd. He'd never given the idea of fatherhood much thought beyond the same vague sense of anchoring resentment that went with all a steward's responsibilities, but being married was certainly turning out much better than he'd ever thought possible. Maybe having children would be the same way.

Such were his thoughts as he traveled the well-worn path between the cave and the fall where they drew their water, diverting now and then when the urge took him. There, the pock-marked tree that bordered the edge of their training grounds; Amber's aim with the spear was as miserable as it had ever been, but she'd really taken to the sword. Here, the remains of the short wall she'd made, where she'd attempted to shield herself while pelting him with packed snow; she still insisted she'd won that battle. And there, the grass-cushioned patch where she'd coaxed him to lie with her on the first day after a long stretch snowed in. He lingered there, thinking how fresh and clean everything had smelled that day, how even the sounds seemed clearer, especially her ear-piercing yelp when that blot of snow slipped from the branches overhead and dropped down the back of her loosened britches.

He did not realize right away that what he was feeling was nostalgia. Strange feeling to have. But if he was nostalgic, that meant a part of him was already leaving and so he supposed it must be time, in spite of all his misgivings.

So be it. They could be in Xi'Matezh in half a brace and home by the turning of the year, and if he was right about putting his child in Amber's belly tonight, and if humans carried the same as dumaqs, it would be born around the Day of Redemption.

To be in Xeqor in the greening of the springtime...

His mother's rooftop garden would be in bloom. Amber could sit there, doing domestic things as she grew his son (he had only the vaguest notion of what these things might be). Some days, he would visit and prove he was not the mannerless brunt that life in the wildlands so often made him seem by reading with her or teaching her to play Towers or Crown-Me. And some days, he would visit and prove he was exactly that bruntish by having sex with her right there on the rooftop, spilling Crown-Me pieces simply everywhere.

It stabbed him, in some hot, unexpected way. Stabbed and twisted, not with lust, but with a kind of ferocious joy that lingered on in echoes after the vision itself faded away. Meoraq turned around and strode, not back along his wandering trail, but through stale snow and over iced rock directly to his cave. Amber tried to chat at him when he arrived, but the only thing Meoraq wanted to know was whether she'd eaten. As soon as he'd determined that she had, he took his wife to bed and it was there, after far too short a sleep, that Meoraq was awakened by Amber's hand firmly gripping his shoulder.

"Start without me," he mumbled.

"I think we need to talk."

Nothing good ever came of a conversation that began that way.

"I am agreed that we shall begin our preparations to leave," he told her, still not bothering to open his eyes. "But I am not doing anything more tonight."

"No, we need to talk about...um...babies."

"Oh." With effort, Meoraq woke himself all the way and rolled onto his back so he could at least attempt to look at her. "As near as any man can make a promise in Gann's land, I promise you we'll be home before you carry heavy. Eh?" He patted her thigh. "Now go to sleep."

"I really want to talk about this," she said quietly.

He caught the sigh before it could get him into trouble and rolled his hand at her invitingly. "I'm listening."

But she just lay there and frowned at him for several long moments. Meoraq waited her out in comfortable silence, moving his eyes sleepily over the mess of her hair and trying to imagine it in drapes over the cushions on the bed where he and his father and all the sons of Uyane were born.

"Do you..." she began at last, waking him from an open-eyed doze. "Do you really think...we're going to have a baby?"

"Is that a serious question?" he asked, smiling.

"Do I look like I'm kidding around?"

"You look—" He pulled her close enough for a nibble at her scarred shoulder. "—like a woman who has been burning hot with her man."

"Don't change the subject."

"I believe I just answered your question."

"We had sex. That doesn't mean we're having a baby."

Half-asleep and not thinking clearly, Meoraq was startled into laughter. He quickly cupped the end of his snout, but the damage was done.

"It. Doesn't," she said, with that icy enunciation that meant she was very annoyed with him. "I can't have your baby, Meoraq."

"Of course you can. Don't worry, Soft-Skin. I suppose it's the sort of thing women get nervous about the first time, but you'll do fine." He patted her thigh again.

"You're not listening. I can't be pregnant. You," she said with curious emphasis, "can't make me pregnant."

"God would seem to disagree."

She clapped her hands over her face and mumbled, "You're giving me a brain tumor," through them.

Watching her take deep, calming breaths, Meoraq decided it was just possible that, no matter how freely she said the word, she might not know what sex really meant. "Come, wife," he said, reaching out to catch her wrist until she allowed him to unmask her. "I don't pretend to understand what's upsetting you, but I'm willing to thrash it out if you are. Tell me plainly what you are thinking."

"You and I can't make a baby."

"All right." He took a moment to collect his thoughts and conquer his discomfort, and then said, speaking slowly, "Sex...is the mechanical means by which a baby is created."

Her mouth opened, just a little, but no sound came out.

Encouraged, he went on. "When Sheul wishes a man and woman to produce a child, He sets the spark of that life within the man's, ah, fluid, which is called 'semen'."

Amber clapped her hand over her eyes, then splayed it so as to stare at him through her fingers.

"This spark burns in his belly, causing him to desire sex. With Sheul's blessing, the man will release that spark with his, er, semen, and if the woman is also blessed, she will conceive by him. How do you mark me?"

She continued to stare, although she did drop her hand. "I know," she said at long, long last, "where babies come from. But you can't really think that's the only reason people have sex! We're just doing it because it's fun!"

"Each man's clay desires its own gratification," Meoraq admitted. "To eat beyond its fill, to take strong drink, to pollute the mind with poisons, and yes, to take the lustful pleasure that comes from Gann. That may take the form of sex, but it is no more than animal mating and it will corrupt beyond forgiveness if indulged. What we have, Soft-Skin, we have with God's blessing and with His holy fires comes the promise of new life."

She only looked at him, her thoughts in motion and her face unsmiling. "I can't have your babies, Meoraq," she said at last. "I can never have your babies."

"Why do you keep saying this?"

"We're two completely different species."

He waited, but that seemed to be all. "Are we not both children of Sheul?"

"That's like saying that since God made both tachuqis and saoqs, they should be able to have children too!"

"They could," he said, "if Sheul wished it."

She put a hand over her eyes hard enough to make a slapping sound.

"You're a good man," she said finally, without uncovering her eyes. "Strong. Brave. Noble, in a weird, hyperviolent kind of way. And I know you can be a smart man if you really, really tried."

He wasn't sure, but he thought there might be an insult hidden in all that praise.

She lowered her hand and looked at him. "I can talk myself blue in the face and never convince you, so just think about it. Think hard. Don't just throw it all up there in the name of God, look at the evidence. Think. Don't pray. *Think*."

"If it will put your mind at ease, I'll meditate upon your words."

"Meditate." She covered her eyes with another slapping sound. "I don't know why I bother. You see God in everything."

"Sheul is *in* everything." Meoraq sighed and rubbed at his brow-ridges. "You are so good at seeing evidence. How can you not see that?"

She dropped her hand to her thigh. That also made a slapping sound. "Because it's ridiculous. *People* happen, Meoraq. *People* make babies. People make the rules. And then people make up gods so they have someone else to blame when things don't go right."

"No," he said simply. "All things fall according to His ultimate plan."

"Oh for...Listen to yourself! Listen to what you're saying to me!"

"I hear it."

"Do you? Do you really? So, according to you, God wanted you and me together. With the infinite power at his disposal, he made a planet *clear across the fucking galaxy* and then he allowed it to get completely trashed so that we would have a reason to leave it, and then, oh yeah, he killed my mother just when the technology to leave the planet came along, all so he could put me on that ship and then lob a meteor at it, so it would break just enough to go careening out of control through space but still stay together long enough to land, killing all the apparently superfluous people—Do you know who those people were?" she demanded suddenly. "Do you know who your killer God chose to wipe off on the surface of your fucking planet like a booger on a bathroom wall? They were the *families*, Meoraq! They were the *children*! They were the pregnant women who supposedly conceived with his very fucking temporary blessing. There were also thousands of them, but hey, at least *I* got to walk away and meet you and then lose all the distracting other people God had no use for, including my sister, and all this, Meoraq, *all this* so that you and I could make a baby?"

"Yes," he said.

She stared at him for a moment and then flung out her arms, shouting, "There is no baby, lizardman! There's never going to *be* a baby! There's no baby and no God and the only reason we have sex—you might want to write this down—is because it *feels good* and *we like it*! You can call it God or Gann or the Great Gadzooks if you want to, but it's just two people *fucking*!"

She sat glaring at him in the bed, her breath as hard in her chest as if she had just run to him across two spans of rough road.

Meoraq studied her at great length, but she seemed perfectly sincere. "I don't understand you," he said. "You escaped the fall of your family's House by seeking passage on the first ship of its kind ever to sail in the sky...and this was not Sheul?"

She rolled her eyes. "No, it wasn't. It was just me making a bad decision."

"The ship was struck in the sky, yet sailed on...and this was not Sheul?"

She glared at him and got out of bed, snatching at her clothes as if she honestly meant to dress and go out at the mid-hour of night.

"The ship broke open over Gann, yet some survived its ruin...and this was not Sheul? At its ultimate burning, you and your fellows were yet spared and this—" He flipped onto his feet and caught her arm as she stalked past him for her boots. "This was not Sheul?"

"Let go of me!"

"What is it you think, woman, that all these things were an *accident*?"

"You're a zealot!"

"And you're a fool!" he countered, exasperated. "He has sent you a warning, a boat and a...a...I can't say it, but you know damned well what He sent you! And were that not enough, He sent you me!"

She drew back and stared at him.

"You may not know to see His hand upon the hammer, but I do. It is not for me to question His reasoning and neither is it for me to deny Him when I hear His voice in my heart!" Meoraq paused, inviting the will of Sheul. His will was immediate and undeniable. "And He says there shall be sons. Get back in that bed."

Her human brows descended fetchingly. "We're still fighting, Meoraq."

"No." He began to undress what little she had managed to don. "We are not."

She smacked at his hand. "*I'm* still fighting, with or without you!"

"I conquered you once." He drew the knife of his fathers, cast about briefly for a place to stab it, then settled for tossing it back onto the bed. "I can easily do it again."

She gave him a few token cuffs as he carried her to the furs, but by the time he lay her down, she was only glaring. When he nipped at her chin, she even put an arm around his neck, however grudgingly. "You really are a zealot," she sighed, wrapping his hips in the welcome weight of her legs.

"And you," he said, "truly are a fool." He swept the hair away from her shoulder and bit lightly at his mark. "Burn with me now, my fool."

"Your pillow-talk needs a lot of work," she told him, but she burned and when she finally slept, it was smiling with his hand over her belly where his new-sparked son surely grew.

2

The mountains were not wide. Meoraq assured her the crossing should only take four days, six at the absolute most. Then it would be back on the road, one with a beach at the end of it, no less. It was too much to hope that it would be a warm, sunny beach, but still, Amber had never been to one (*sleeper-dream of mama cigarette smoke screaming seagulls but o the sunset and the waves coming in*) and when she had it in her to hope for things, she did hold out a little hope for one nice day at the beach.

She'd thought she was prepared. No matter how sedentary her winter routine had become, her memories of the endless march across the plains were never far. She knew it would be tough. She knew she'd be cold and hungry and exhausted all the time, but she knew she could take it and keep moving. She was ready. Four days.

Except that Amber had quite naturally twisted her ankle on those fucking snowshoes within the first stupid hour of the first day after leaving the cave.

Except that on the second day, she'd also tumbled a good fifty meters down an icy slope into a slushbank when the ledge that had supported a hulking lizardman's weight and that of two sleds lashed together (Amber was no longer pulling hers because of her ankle) without any complaint whatsofreakingever gave way under her fat ass.

Except that on the third day, it had started snowing again that night for the first time in days and days and motherfucking days and now they were in it up to their knees again, which meant she was also back in the damn snowshoes.

Amber did not believe in God, but if ever there was some supernatural force trying to send a sign, Someone was screaming it. And Meoraq, who saw messages from God in plants, caves and even plops of animal poop, pretended to be oblivious. No matter what fresh slice of shit-cake got served, he just bandaged her up and kept going.

Amber could take all the punches the universe could throw, but waiting for the punch to hit was killing her. On the fourth day, the day they were supposed to be out and which found them camped in the middle of the same goddamn nowhere with the same goddamn ice storm crusting up the side of the tent, Amber gave up and said it for him: "You told me so."

Meoraq raised his head out of the pillow of his pack and rubbed sleepily at his face. "Eh? Was I talking?"

"You told me it wasn't time to leave and I made you."

He looked at her, spines flexed all the way forward, then laughed and dropped back into his arm.

Now that stung.

"I did!" she insisted.

He made a very bad effort at smothering another laugh. "I forgive you," he said gravely.

Amber took that for as long as she could and then she threw the blankets back and kicked free of them.

Meoraq groaned and rolled onto his side to watch her grab her mat and pull it to the other side of the tent in noisy heaves. "Please yourself. I don't forgive you. Shall I have you whipped, woman? Would that make you happy?"

She dug down through the layers of their bedding for the xaut fur in the middle and yanked it free.

"Where do you think you're going with that?" he asked, cocking his head.

"It's mine!" she said, wrapping herself furiously in its itchy warmth. "I made it and it's mine!"

He dropped onto his back and rubbed his brow-ridges. "Deep breaths, Uyane," she heard him mutter. "Deep and slow. So." He moved his hand and gestured to her. "What is it you want to say?"

"If you're mad at me, get mad at me!"

"If I'm not mad, can I just go to sleep?"

"Stop making fun of me!"

The slap/rasp of his hand rubbing back on his brow-ridges. The steady rise and fall of his broad chest as he breathed six times. Then he threw back his blanket and before she could untangle herself from the xaut fur and get out of his reach, he'd gripped the edge of her mat and yanked her against him. He stripped the fur away and made the bed again: blanket, xaut fur, blanket.

She stopped fighting halfway through and just let him tuck her in, her eyes burning with humiliation, staring at the top of the tent until it blurred into new colors. When he was finished, he lay back down and snugged an arm around her, grunting comfortably against her shoulder. He seemed to fall asleep.

The storm blew and blew. It never stopped here. Never.

"Shall I guess?" Meoraq murmured against her ear.

Amber pressed her teeth tight together and did not answer.

"I say..." His hand slipped up to rest between her breasts. It was his favorite place to touch her. God alone knew why. "It's just a little weather. And you say...it's weather that could kill us."

She shivered and tried to roll away from him. He waited until she was done and simply spooned up against her back. "And I say we rest in God's sight," he continued. "And you say, stop acting like it doesn't matter, *lizardman*."

She felt the breath catch in her throat almost like a laugh, and gritted her teeth even harder because it wasn't fucking funny, no matter how he said it.

"And I say, tell me what you want me to do about the weather. And you don't say anything at first, but you get that look. And so I say, tell me plainly what the matter is. And you say something inexpressibly foolish, such as how this is all your fault. And so I tell you how foolish it is to say that, which is a reasonable thing to say, and you become impossible to deal with. So." He nuzzled at the side of her neck. "I will say none of these things. It is absolutely no use trying to talk with women."

"Sexist son of a bitch."

"Ha." He snuggled closer under the blankets. "I win. So just say it, Soft-Skin, before you choke on it."

"We were supposed to be out of the mountains today."

"Shit happens." His language, her phrase. They were both doing a lot of that.

"And it is my fault. You can make all the smart-ass comments you want to."

"Lo," Meoraq intoned, "even his ass be wise."

"Jerk."

"Mm."

Wind blew, cracking the ice forming on the side of the tent.

"When I was a boy," Meoraq murmured, "and my training masters wished to give me the most severe punishments, they would set me to copying books. And the book that every boy most dreaded to see was Master Darr's book of maps, because every line had to be perfect, you see. Every hill, named. Every bend of every river, just so. I must have copied that book ten times, end to end."

Amber waited, gritting her teeth, but curiosity won out in the end. Meoraq could make the most random crap imaginable sound profound when he said it in that slow, meditative way. "And?" she said finally, surrendering.

"And when I first left Xeqor," he went on, "I thought I knew the land, because I knew those maps so well. I had no hesitation when I set off, for I knew where I would find the range of Aqcha and I knew where to find the city of Fol Ganis on the other side. It came as a hell of a shock when I climbed that first peak and saw more mountains."

"And the moral of this story is?" asked Amber, and immediately regretted it because it didn't sound tough and bored at all, just snotty.

"That everything looks small on paper," Meoraq replied. "But in Gann's world, shit happens."

The wind died down, making the relative quiet seem much louder and heavier than it should. Meoraq's body beside hers remained perfectly relaxed.

"I'm sorry for being such a bitch," Amber muttered finally.

He patted her breast companionably. "Forgiven."

"I mean it."

"I know."

She didn't feel much better. How the hell could he lie there so still? "Are you really this sleepy?"

"Yes. Wait." He raised his head. "Why?"

"Well, it's only the middle of the day."

"There's nothing else to do." He flicked his spines at her. "Is there?"

"Jesus Christ, really? How did you ever survive living with me as long as you did without having sex every other hour?"

"With God's aid alone," he said seriously. "It was a terrible time."

"Just talk to me, okay?"

"It is absolutely no use," he reminded her, but rolled onto his back and pulled her halfway onto his chest. "It hasn't been so bad, has it?"

She thought it was a joke and started to laugh at it, albeit in a bitchy way, but then got a better look at him and realized he was serious. "For you, maybe. I am a walking bruise, lizardman."

"You bruise too easily. But do you hurt?"

Of course she hurt! She opened her mouth...and thought about it, damn him.

"Not like before," she admitted. After all, she was just lying here, not sprawling in a gasping heap, half-conscious. If the weather wasn't so piss-awful, she'd still be walking. She ached a little on her hip where she'd done some serious splits on her way down the slope the other day, but unless she actually poked at a bruise, even those didn't bother her too much.

She didn't hurt. She wasn't tired. She wasn't even all that cold, thanks to Meoraq's tent, plenty of furs, and the clothes they'd spent all winter making. She hadn't been hungry in more days than she could count.

"No," she said, surprised. "I guess it's not that bad."

"And when it is over, it will be over forever. You will have a bed all the rest of your life, except on those nights when you have mine. You will have servants. You will sit at a table and eat from a plate."

"You say the most romantic things. You sure you want to risk letting other guys see me?" Amber asked. "Apparently, I have this overwhelming sensuality."

"Your servants will be women."

It took a few seconds for that to register all the way.

"Hang on." She pushed herself up a little so she could see his face. "I thought you said women didn't work on this planet."

"We don't pay them," he explained. "And most of them only care for their own households, so no one sees them. It's only if a man has too many daughters or a barren wife set aside that they end up working in House Uyane."

"What?"

"It's a big House. It needs a lot of tending and my father never had daughters. I don't think he even had sisters. It's the lord's responsibility to see that all those within his holdings are cared for, so why not put them to work? Besides, they're rarely out where we can see them. It's mostly the extra boys that do the running around and cleaning."

"Extra?"

He rolled one hand idly through the air. "Orphans and bastards and such. If they weren't born under the sign of the Blade, they're the responsibility of the lord-steward."

"What happens to them?"

"Farmers and cattlemen can always use more workers, but they have to be old enough to be useful. I've seen boys as young as six in the fields of other Houses, but my father waited until they were ten or so."

"Practically grown," said Amber sarcastically.

He grunted agreement. Several more minutes passed while Amber tried not to fidget as she thought about his place in Xeqor and whether or not she was supposed to help take care of all these extra kids. Meoraq just dozed. Suddenly, he tensed and roused himself, saying, "You will do no more work when we are home, woman. Swear your obedience!"

"Okay."

He eyed her mistrustfully and settled back down.

"So what kind of work are we talking about, since the kids do all the cleaning?"

"Eh." He yawned, rubbing at his eyes. "They cook and do the washing. In a House Uyane's size, that's a lot of work. I suppose they must do the heavy things a boy can't, like haul water. I don't know, really. Mostly, they stay below, out of sight."

"Why?"

"It's where the work is. Besides, if they come up, someone other than my father might see them."

"And?"

He raised his head up to look at her, as if he thought she might be joking. When he saw she wasn't, he laughed a little anyway, his spines flexed forward. "If a man saw them, he might want to have sex with them. Unless he were born under the Blade, that would be a crime. And even if he were, it's still trouble."

"But if your father saw them...?"

Meoraq shrugged and lay back down. "He was lord-steward."

Something dark and cold and incredibly heavy shifted in her stomach, not quite waking up all the way. "How is that fair?"

"Eh?"

"When women sleep around, they're possessed by the devil, but it's okay for men to get with the help? What kind of half-assed laws are these?"

"Not men," said Meoraq, in warning tones. "The lord-stewards, who are masters over all their households. And Uyane is not merely a House under the sign of the Blade, it *is* the Blade. Its stewards are highest in God's eyes. He wants them to breed."

'Even you?' She couldn't say it, since the answer was so stupidly obvious. Why wouldn't he sleep around with all the pretty little lizardladies that were sure to be cluttering up the house once they got back and she wasn't the only woman on the planet anymore? But she had to say something, because the two words she couldn't say were choking her, so instead, trying to pretend it was all still hypothetical, she said, "What about what the woman wants?"

"She is permitted to struggle," he said off-handedly. "There is no sin in conquest."

"Wow." It was all she could think of. It wasn't nearly enough. She said it again.

"Wow. That's easily the most sexist, pig-headed thing you've ever said, and I have to be honest, Meoraq, there's a lot of competition on that list."

He didn't answer.

Amber listened to the silence, torn between her strong desire to apologize for what was admittedly a bitchy comment and her equally strong desire to provoke him with another one. She knew he'd been with other women before (and like the men she knew he'd killed, she suspected the number to be not merely high, but actually beyond counting), but the thought that he might go on being with them had never occurred to her. Funny, how she could laugh at his insistence that they were married right up until the prospect of adultery came up.

'And this is how I deal with it,' she thought disgustedly, rolling her eyes at the tent wall. 'Calling him names. Yeah, that'll encourage him to stay home with the wife.' Aloud, she said, "Hey."

He grunted.

"They say we're not supposed to go to bed angry, so I'm sorry."

"Eh? I'm not angry." Meoraq shifted onto his back and tucked his arms behind his head. "I was thinking of my father."

"Why?" And in spite of her determination to let this go, out it came: "Did he have a lot of sex-slaves?"

"Servants," he said distractedly. "Yes, he did. But he never used them for sex."

"How scandalous."

"I wouldn't say *that*," he said after some reflection. He frequently had trouble telling when she was being sarcastic. "But it was odd enough that I noticed. There is nothing shameful in the fires given to a steward of the bloodline, and his bloodline is that of Uyane. The females of four hundred households bow under his protection and would be...would have been honored by his conquest."

"There's another one for that list..."

"But he reserved his fires for my mother. Even at inconvenience to himself." Meoraq lapsed into quiet, but tucked his arm around her shoulders. "I think he loved her."

"Oh. Well...that's sweet."

He didn't answer. That dark thing in her stomach shifted again, lifting its head.

"Isn't it?"

"There must have been a reason...something I never saw. Did she talk to him when they were alone together? Comfort him?" His fingers flexed lightly on her arm. "Argue with him?"

"Wouldn't that be a weird world?"

'Goddammit, Bierce, shut the fuck *up*.'

"She was special to him," said Meoraq. "I could never understand why."

"I'm sure she knew you loved her," said Amber after an uncomfortable silence.

"No, she didn't. Because it wouldn't have been true. I saw every private touch they shared, touches no less than these—" Meoraq squeezed her shoulder, his thumb running lightly over her scars. "—as a personal affront to the dignity of our House. It embarrassed me to see them together and it embarrassed me even more after she died to see my father mourn her. I feel..."

She waited, but in the end, he only blew out a rude snort and said, "I don't even know what I feel, Soft-Skin. It was his own House, and I made it impossible for my father to share an honest touch with his wife without fear of consequence. What an insufferable little prick I was."

"Okay, what's that mean?"

"What?"

"Prick. That wasn't your language, that was mine. What's it mean?"

"In dumaqi? Eh, it's the thing...the two things that fit together that make it possible for a door to swing open and closed. Why? What does it mean in your speech? I've never been able to puzzle that out, exactly. I only know that it's a curse."

"It's another word for this." She gave the smooth mound between his legs a pat.

"Another one? How many words do you need for that?"

"This from the man who can say gann eight different ways," Amber remarked, gently kneading.

"Twelve. You are amazing," he said seriously.

"Hey, I'm just getting started, lizardman." She rubbed her thumb along the moist edge of his slit, cupped the hard bulge she felt just below the surface, and squeezed. "But hold that thought, because I'll want to hear you shout it a few times."

Meoraq arched his neck and grunted. "Woman, I was just speaking of my father. This is hardly appropriate."

It wasn't, was it? But that thing was in her gut and if she didn't do something to get back to normal, it was going to eat its way out of her right through her mouth. "A woman should always be ready to receive her man's fires," she reminded him.

"To receive, yes, but not kindle them." He caught her wrist up and pinned it to the bed above her head, rolling atop her in the next moment to nuzzle aggressively at her neck. "And I'm not the one who does the shouting, am I?"

"You make your share of the noise."

He hissed at her, but the teasing light of his eyes suddenly died, replaced by an unnerving somberness. He frowned at her, his face very close to hers, all that she could see. After a few false starts, he suddenly said, "I love you, you know."

Her stomach clenched once, hard enough to hurt, and then slowly, finally, relaxed. She told herself it didn't matter, she wasn't one of those girls who needed to hear flowery shit like that, but...but he said it. He said it to her.

"I can't believe I'm saying that to a woman," he remarked, looking at the wall of the tent above her in an unfocused way, just like there was a window there to stare through. "But there it is, and it is the only word. I love you. Huh."

She gave him a few uncomfortable moments to come to terms with that, and when he only continued to lie there on top of her, staring at the wall and keeping her wrists pinned above her head, she finally put on her best state-paid counselor's voice and said, "And how do you feel about that?"

"Bitterly ashamed."

She stared.

His spines flicked as he gave her a sheepish sort of look. "Not of you. Of myself. It can be nothing less than a gift of God to know love...and I made my parents hide it. I would give anything..." He thought, frowning. "Almost anything," he amended, "to go back to just one day, one hour, and unmake the insufferable little prick that I was."

"Almost anything, huh?"

He met her smile with another of his terribly serious looks and brushed his knuckle across her brow. "I would not give you. My blood. My blades. Even my name, but not you, Soft-Skin. You are mine. I will give you up to our Father and no one else."

Amber sighed and patted the side of his snout. "Say that again, but try not to sound like such a stalker when you do it this time."

He leaned in to nuzzle her, scraping the end of his snout forcefully and deliberately up one side of her neck and down the other, inhaling slowly the whole time. He finished with a hard bite to her scarred shoulder, not quite hard enough to break the skin. "You belong to me," he murmured. "You will always be Soft-Skin under Uyane. In life, in death, and in the Halls where we reside after. You are mine."

She couldn't help smiling any more than she could help saying, "You don't know what a stalker is, clearly."

"You try so hard to convince me you are impossible to please, but I know better. Hold still." He pressed his rough mouth carefully against hers, then withdrew and flicked his spines playfully forward. "Do you want to have sex yet?"

"Oh boy, do I."

He grimaced and started undressing her.

"Wait. I..."

I what? I love you? Why? Just because he said it first? Sure, it seemed like the right thing to say, polite and expected and non-threatening, and who knew, maybe even a little bit true, although she refused to look at that too closely. Not right now. God, he was looking at her. Waiting, just like she'd asked him to. And she had no idea what she wanted to say, except that she knew it was still choking her out from the stomach on up.

And then she knew what she wanted to say, felt it whole and burning in her mind. It was just a question of whether she was too chickenshit to say it.

Amber Bierce had been a lot of things in her life. Chickenshit was never going to be one of them.

She reached up and caught Meoraq around his snout. He let her, although his spines came slowly all the way forward and just as slowly all the way back.

"When we get home," said Amber, "you keep your hands off the servants, you hear me?"

His head cocked. She kept her grip on his snout and even squeezed a little.

"I'm your woman. That makes you my man. You better not make me fight for you unless you're damn sure you want me fighting-mad."

Balancing easily on one hand, he closed the other over her wrist and freed his snout. He studied her as she lay beneath him for several long, expressionless seconds. "I do," he said at last. Then he grinned and dropped, rolling onto his back. He slapped his chest once. "You can even be on top."

3

So in the end, it took six days to cross over into Gedai, which was, as Meoraq made a point of reminding her, exactly what he'd said it would be at the outside margin. She did not appreciate the observation.

There wasn't much in the way of foothills on the other side, just a short series of long plateaus and steep slopes, almost like stairs. Meoraq took his time scouting each descent, which made them relatively painless once he'd finally settled on a path, although Amber still managed to go down two of the slopes on her ass. In spite of this (or maybe because of it), they went from the snowline to the ground in just one day.

When the sun came up the next morning, Amber and Meoraq were awake and watching from the top of the next hill over to see sunrise over Gedai for the first time. Holy Gedai, as Meoraq called it. Birthplace of the Prophet. The land where, in just a few more days, they would find the temple where Meoraq thought he was going to talk to God. Her first impression was that it looked a lot like the same brown grass, the same windy sky, the same open plains as they'd left on the other side of the mountain. Maybe a little more wooded, a little less flat, but that was all.

"What do you think?" she asked, studying Meoraq's inscrutable face in the thin morning light.

"Looks like your hair first thing in the morning," he replied. "Only it's everywhere instead of just in my face."

She didn't appreciate that observation either.

They started walking again, but even though they were out of the mountains at last, their speed did not improve. The ground under their feet was hard, frozen, stone-riddled grass, which while indeed much easier to walk on than boot-deep snow and slush, made pulling sleds absolutely hellish. Meoraq took the heavy one with all the meat and he still went faster than Amber and the hides. He didn't complain in so many words, but his spines got lower as the day wore on. When Amber inevitably hit the rock that tipped her sled and spilled all their gear to the bottom of the hill they'd spent easily twenty minutes climbing, he just patted her on the head and picked everything up.

"I think we'll camp early," was all he said, slipping back into his sled's harness.

"Oh come on! I hit one rock! I missed a billion others, didn't I?"

"I didn't say we were camping now," he countered. "I said it would be early."

"Yeah, but you meant now."

"I did not."

"When then?"

"When I judge it necessary."

"And why would it be necessary early?"

His glance was cool and uncompromising. "Because you're tired."

She couldn't argue, so she did what anyone would do. She switched targets. "You chew with your mouth open."

"I'm allowed to breathe when I eat," he replied, glaring. "And you growl in your sleep."

"It's called snoring and I do n—"

She hit another rock, tipped the sled, and spilled its contents down the other side of the hill. They stood together and watched until the last bundled hide had finished rolling. When she finally nerved herself up to look at him, he was already looking at her.

"In my defense," she said, lifting her chin, "there are a lot of rocks."

He sighed and untethered himself from his sled to start picking hers up. Again.

When he decided it was time to stop for the day (early) and set up camp, he left the actual setting-up for her. He needed to make a patrol, he said. A lengthy, far-reaching, thorough patrol. Alone.

She made a token protest, just to let him know she was tough enough to do it, but he pulled out his You'll-do-as-I-say-woman act and she let herself be bullied. Her feet hurt and she was hungry. If he wanted to crawl around for another mile or two after hiking up and down hills all day, he was perfectly welcome to do it. Still...

"And you expect me to just do all the work while you're taking it easy on your evening stroll?"

"It is a wife's duty and pleasure to lessen her husband's burdens."

"Says who, lizardman?"

"Prophet Lashraq, as written in Sheul's true Word."

"You mean a man wrote it."

"But God spoke it." He came to stroke at her forehead and she turned her face away. Undaunted, he nuzzled at her throat instead and patted her on the head. "Have food ready when I return. Use lots of meat. It's not as cold here as it was in the mountains."

"Okay. Put up the tent, gather poop, start a fire, make dinner. Anything else?"

He caught the sarcasm and paused long enough to pick up his pack and toss it to her. "Wash my clothes," he said and cocked his head, daring her to challenge him.

Amber cocked her head back at him. "How about I leave the laundry for tomorrow and wash you instead?"

He grunted smug assent and started walking. "I'll be back before dark. Be ready for me. And be rested."

"Yeah, yeah." She waited until he'd put a little more distance between them before adding, "Sexist scaly jerk," but she said it quietly. He didn't hear her, which was good. She didn't really mean it. Well, she sort of meant it, but not in a bitchy way. And she did like the idea of having the camp to herself while she took a bath. Privacy was something they'd had all too little of up in that cave.

So she put his tent together, started a fire and cut up some kipwe to warm on it, filled the flasks at the little stream nearby and put the heat-stones in the coals, then sat on the hide-cushioned sled to watch the clouds roll by while the water got hot. She had no itchy feeling between her shoulders or that prickly sensation at the back of her neck that people talked about when they said they 'felt watched.' And if she had, she would have only thought it was Meoraq, swinging by to look in on her before continuing on his patrol. After all this time, even hearing Meoraq talk of cities and other traveling Sheulek and even the various sinners who had been exiled to die in the wildlands, it simply never occurred to her think she was anything but alone.

She wasn't.

It really wasn't very windy today. The smoke from her fire made a strong, obvious arrow in the sky, pointing right at her camp. These raiders had come a long way from their usual route to investigate. There were only five of them now; the other six remained with the slaves they had acquired at the nearby city of Praxas, where they had traded bundles of dried phesok for the cast-off daughters of those who had them to spare. The raiders were certainly not above attacking Praxas (two of their number even now had been taken as young boys during such raids), but when trade was good, it behooved them all to use diplomatic measures.

Now they had spied a potential new target and so they came, crawling on their bellies as soon as they were near enough to see the lone silhouette at the glowing coals, blades out and ready. They had expected a warrior—it was always wisest to expect the worst, although far more common to find instead some fool youth who fancied himself a hunter or, ha, a raider—and they were ten body-lengths from the fire before they realized, almost in unison, that they had no idea what sat at camp before them.

They stopped, exchanging questioning glances in the silent way of pack predators. The man who was their leader considered for perhaps eight heartbeats. Then he gestured with his sword and the crawl resumed. The essential meat of the matter had not changed. Regardless of what form it took, this was prey. That it was also strange might or might not mean greater profit, but one could only know that once the prey was taken.

So they took it.

Amber didn't hear them; the light breeze hissing across the grass covered what nominal sound they made on their approach. She didn't see them; the fire before her occupied all her attention. She had no warning whatsoever...and yet, for no reason, she looked back over her shoulder.

Her eyes locked at once and without immediate comprehension on the eyes of the raider's leader. Her first thought, after the eternity of the split-second that followed, was that he had all Meoraq's same features and still really looked nothing like him.

Then she dove for her spear, snatched it and a handful of skin-slicing grass off the ground, and swung to face him.

Their need for stealth now moot, they rose and fanned out without speaking, flanking her, herding her from the fire so expertly that she didn't even know they were doing it until they had her away and closed in a ring around her.

'Woman, they're going to have you dead in about three seconds,' Amber thought, stunned and a little embarrassed by this development. She had to do something fast, something unpredictable.

She lunged forward with a howl, then spun around and blindly stabbed. Her first feint, she thought vaguely. A damned effective one. The raider before her—now behind her—had drawn up his arms and crossed his blades to block her strike; the raider behind her—now before her—had rushed right on to the point of her spear. A good thing, too. If it hadn't been for his strength and the power of his swift attack, she never could impaled him so deeply.

They stared at each other with what was left of the spear between them for what felt like hours and could not have been more than a single second. He said something in a tight, confused voice, but even though they were words she surely knew, Amber's shocked mind could make no sense of them. She twisted vainly on the spear to try and free it, but succeeded only in making him belch blood all down his chest and hers, so she snatched the short, hooked sword out of his hand instead and shoved him back.

He fell, but the others closed in even tighter, and she had been reduced to the reach of her own arm and the dying man's sword.

They eyed her as the man on the ground groaned and kicked, and Amber stood with the point of the curved blade jerking from one target to another.

"Ease off," one of them said, and that time her brain made the translation without effort. He sheathed his sword and unhooked a short length of cord from his belt, weighted at both ends with bell-shaped lumps of metal. He began to back up, swinging this fun new toy in tight circles at his side, watching her. "Weapons down. I want it alive. Aqizu, stay behind it."

She snatched a glance behind her, slashing at the lizardman's throat, but he was too fast for her.

"I think it heard you," one of them remarked.

"I think it understood you," another added, more meaningfully. "That's no animal."

"When was the last time you saw an animal in clothes?" their leader asked in his calm, intent way. Without taking his eyes off her, without even seeming to move, he suddenly interrupted the steady *shush-shush* of his weighted cord with a throw. Amber darted aside and back, slashing wildly, but she was not his target; the weighted bell on the cord's end crunched into the groaning man's forehead, leaving a sickeningly bloodless hollow where it had landed. He pulled the line back with a zip and a flick of his wrist, resuming its steady circles without any sign of effort or interest in the fate of the man he'd just killed. "Keep your guard up. Do *not* hurt it. Go, Vek."

She sensed more than saw the attack and swung around to meet it, slicing at the grasping hands and the face behind them indiscriminately. The blade of her sword skidded along his scales, then came down just right between his two middle fingers and sliced his hand in half all the way to his wrist. He let out a shriek right about the same instant the weighted cord wrapped itself around her arm.

Amber grabbed the sword from her trapped hand and let his zip-flick-tug take her right to him, but he was as fast as Meoraq and caught her wrist with a good six centimeters between the quivering tip of the short blade and his throat.

"Easy," he said, almost singing it, the way another man might try to calm a stray dog. One hand pushed her weapon aside; the other swiftly reeled in the slack on his weighted cord until the chance to break his hold was good and gone. "Easy, little one. No one here will hurt you."

"I mean to fucking hurt it!" Mr. Split-Hand snarled, bent double over his gushing arm. "I mean to hurt the damn thing plenty!"

"Quiet, Vek. Don't fight me, little one. Your tiny bones look easy to break. For the moment, I want you whole."

She struggled anyway, fighting a losing battle for just one chance to stab...but with the first flagging of her strength, he suddenly swept her arm around and pulled, letting her momentum carry her stumbling forward into the space he had just been, and then she was on her knees with him swiftly tying her wrists to her elbows behind her back. So she screamed, as pointless as that was, but wherever Meoraq was, he wasn't there to hear her.

Maybe they'd found him first.

"Fierce little thing," the leader grunted, planting his knee in the small of her back for the necessary leverage to catch and hold her legs together. She heard the *shu-u-up* as he pulled his belt off one-handed, a sound that had always meant Meoraq in an amorous mood, and Amber screamed again, uselessly.

"What are you going to do with it?" someone asked, nudging at her with his boot.

"There has always been coin for oddities. This is odder than most. Up, little one." He pulled; her shoulders creaked in their sockets and she arched instinctively backwards, helping him pull her to her bound feet. He bent, his grip firm and impersonal, and tipped her up and over his shoulder.

She bit him, her teeth grating over two or three scales before she found a gripping place and dug in, scissoring her jaws together with all the strength she had left in her. Hot blood gushed into her mouth. He barked and flung her forwards again, inadvertently helping her rip away a scale so that she could spit it defiantly at his knees when she landed at his feet.

"God's teeth," someone remarked.

"Sharp teeth, at any rate," the leader answered dryly. He checked the damage, which was nominal but bled heavily without any scales to help seal it, and as soon as he was finished shrugging off his harness and cinching it tight again with a bandage beneath it, he hunkered down before her and smiled. It was a gentle smile, disturbingly sincere, and it stayed that way as he showed Amber his open palm, drew it deliberately back and then slapped her hard across the mouth.

She hit the ground, sucking dirt up her nose and into her throat, so that all the involuntary brays of pain she made after that were choked. Now she could taste her blood, too, and feel the great, spreading heat of hurt where her lips had been mashed. But when his hand came down to cup her chin and turn her toward him, Amber exposed her bloody teeth at him and hissed through them, just like Meoraq did whenever he was good and pissed.

Several lizardmen stepped back.

The leader glanced tolerantly down at his chest where her defiant hiss had sprayed him with blood. He touched a few droplets, rubbed his fingers, then put out his hand. "Give me your belt, Vek."

Split-Hand glared at the leader, then at Amber, then stomped over to his dead friend and took that belt instead.

The leader accepted that (not without a dark and watchful stare), then made a loop of it, waited for Amber to stop coughing, then fit it over her tossing head. She clamped her teeth together. He pinched her nostrils shut. She bucked and flailed and finally had to breathe, whereupon he worked the belt between her screaming jaws and pulled it tight.

"Now we try this again, little one," he said conversationally, sweeping her up and over his shoulder. "But you ought to know that if I have to pull every fang out of your fierce little head to ensure your good behavior, that is exactly what I will do. Mind yourself. Let me see it, Vek."

Amber could see nothing beyond the leader's backside and the ground as Split-hand presumably presented his injury. She wriggled, chewing at the belt until her lips bled, and finally fell slack, gasping wetly around the leather. She was caught; she felt that she could keep fighting, at least for a few more minutes, but she knew she couldn't break free. She wasn't ready to give up yet, but she had to have a better goal than making him mad enough to kill her. She had to wait. Another chance to escape might come along, but until then, she just had to wait.

"No good," someone was saying. "It has to come off."

"I know it has to come off, cock-rubber! Fuck Gann!"

"Not here. I have no reason to think there is only one of these." The shoulder she rode jostled with a meaningful shrug. "Get what there is and get away."

The raiders got to work rifling through the packs around the fire. There wasn't enough to occupy all of them. One of them came strolling around to look at her instead, fingering at her hair.

"This is easily the most bizarre thing I have ever seen," he said.

The leader grunted—Meoraq's grunt, the one that meant he acknowledged the comment but didn't feel any strong need to converse.

"You mean to sell it?" the other man said once she was done. He was still touching her hair.

"Might."

"To who?"

"To me!" Vek snapped. "Hear me, Zhuqa, if you put that thing on the block without telling me, I will put a hook on the wrist where my fucking hand used to be and put the hook in your fucking head!"

"If I sell it, I'll give you due warning and a cut of credit besides. Now calm down and remember who you are speaking to."

"It's mine!" Vek spat, but he spat it without shouting. He came stomping around to the leader's back to glare at her, holding the bandaged lump of his ruined hand. He flared his open mouth threateningly, then dove forward and cracked his forehead into hers. She heard him stalk off muttering as she swayed near the grey area of unconsciousness, and finally, with a mental sigh of defeat, she fell on through.

* * *

Just as the raiders had not been able to tell human from dumaq at any great distance by the full light of the fire, so Meoraq could not tell dumaq from human by moonlight at the hour of his return.

He had been in a fair mood most of the evening, wandering far and observing the animals of Gedai that were ostensibly his reason for this patrol with only half an eye. He prayed as he walked, silently at first, then aloud, and soon was singing some of his favorite hymns at full voice. Amber wasn't there to mutter in her throat or heave her pained sighs or slap at her face. He loved his wife—more and more, that word felt true and right and real—but they had spent too many days this winter riding about in one another's pockets. He liked her company, but he missed his solitude and he meant to enjoy it as much as possible while he could.

At length, even as he saw the sun low to the mountains and knew his time was ending, he found a friendly jut of stone and sat himself to meditate, but his first moments in that welcome stillness were unquiet. He could do this back at camp, couldn't he? And truth, he supposed he could, albeit with Amber pacing restlessly somewhere at the outside edge of his perceptions. She'd want to talk at him or involve him in some way in the domestic things she did or maybe just pull him into the tent for sex. Meoraq was opposed to none of these things, but once in a while, a man just liked to meditate.

Still, that vague sense of unease persisted. A tickle of wind, the rough edge of the rock he sat on, the distant call of some unknown beast—every little distraction woke him wholly to his clay until he resorted to a child's trick, lying flat on his back with an arm crooked over his eyes, chanting the Prophet's Prayer over and over until meaning bled away and it was all just sound. Sound and blackness, yes, but still not peace. In its pursuit, he not only failed to truly meditate, but also entirely lost track of time. He believed that he spent perhaps an hour in that fruitless endeavor, but when he finally cried surrender and opened his eyes, it was full dark.

Amber must be terrified. No, strike that, she was furious. And in either case, she was just fool enough to come looking for him if she believed him lost or injured.

Cursing, he hurried back to camp, but 'hurry' was a relative term after dark. There was enough of a moon behind the clouds to show him his backtrail at first, but the wind which had been so calm all day now stirred itself up, soon erasing all sign of his passage until he followed nothing but a hope that this lesson in the cost of man's pride would end at his camp and not in a nest of ravening tachuqis.

But it had been his own camp in the end, although he glimpsed it from well to the east of where he'd thought it was, and he thought it was Amber sleeping there when he finally came to it. There was no tent and no fire and this he at first presumed with a mixture of resignation and annoyance was her way of telling him he was a scaly son of a bitch for leaving her so long, which was spiteful and childish, yet he would apologize because he was Sheulek and a Sheulek took the higher path.

Then the clouds above him thinned so that the little light from the crescent moon grew stronger and all at once, what had been Amber became a dead man. It seemed Sheul gave him hours outside of Time to see this, to feel it, and only when he fully understood did the weight of the world crash back into his clay.

His feet took him forward without conscious thought. He reached only to stab the corpse—he had drawn his kzung, it seemed, how curious—then staggered away, staring wildly in all directions for Amber—where was Amber?—and seeing nothing, only the night—why had he left her so long?—and the wind whipping at Gann's back.

He cupped his mouth and howled for her. Not with words, but just a cry, a dumb animal baying that he had never before imagined any dumaq could make. The wind alone answered, changing its course to drive him back. His boot struck the body. He looked at it and, with a sudden savagery he did not feel until it was upon him, he wrenched his kzung from the corpse and hacked at it again.

The head came free at his first blow. The chest cracked apart at his fourth. He took the left arm. Bisected the rib. The right arm. He struck until it was meat and bone and two legs. He struck until he had no wind and no moisture in his mouth but the clotted blood splashing up at him from the ground. He struck until he fell to his knees in splintery gore and leaned back, gasping.

He listened then, as he should have listened hours ago, but Sheul had nothing to say to him now.

Amber.

He dragged himself up, shaking on legs like water, and pulled his blade free of the mess on the ground. How long? The blood that touched his tongue had cooled, but was yet warm. The raiders might be close still. He looked and saw nothing, no sign but dumaq blood in spatters across the trampled grass. An hour ago, he would have seen their trail leading away, before the light failed and the wind grew strong.

An hour ago, he might have been here to stop it.

They had not left her body behind, only that of their companion. Perhaps she was alive still...or perhaps they had taken her corpse away as trophy. No, he must believe she lived! Lived and fought, as fiercely as the evidence here proclaimed, knowing he would follow.

"Sheul, O my Father, show me the way. Set me upon their path if she lives! Give me my right of vengeance if she does not!" He struggled with his fear and broke upon it, suddenly roaring, "*How could You have sent her to me just to take her from me now?*"

It was not for men to demand answers of God, no more than it was the recalcitrant son's right to demand forgiveness of his father. Meoraq knew this. He bent his back beneath the weight of guilt and silence, one hand splayed open in cooling blood, and knew—for the first time in all his life—no love for God.

The moment passed away eventually, but the Meoraq who rose from his knees at the end of that bad time would forever be changed from the man he had been and he knew it. He collected his weapons, cleaned and sheathed them. He gave what fuel remained to the fire so that he could count his remaining provisions by its light and make them ready for the next day's travel. Then he lay down and closed his eyes.

There was nothing he could do until morning.

4

Amber woke up to the sound of what she thought was an engine stuttering. In that moment, before she opened her eyes or even really had a chance to process sound or smell or anything lucid, she felt the overwhelming rush of relief that she had dreamed the whole damn thing. They'd said there would be no dreams in the Sleepers, but they'd been wrong, because she felt as though she'd been locked in that one for years. But she was awake now, which meant she was on Plymouth with Nicci right in the room beside her. There had been no crash. There were no lizardpeople. There was no Meoraq...

That hurt and it was the hurt that pierced her enough to drag her eyes open and see for herself what was real.

The first thing she saw was the wall. A leather wall, dyed black and stretched between some rough-cut poles, not so much to keep the weather out as to keep the light of their fire in. The crudity of this enclosure assured her at once that, for good or ill, she was still marooned on an alien planet with a race full of lizardmen.

Only after this fact sank in did she recognize that she was still bound—wrists to elbows, ankles to each other—and tethered to one of the poles holding the wall up. The belt that had gagged her had been loosened but not removed; it hung around her neck like a dog collar. The next thing she saw, what she probably should have seen first, was a small, slender lizardman—a lizardlady, maybe—hunched over with its wrists tied to a length of pole along with several other lizards, stuttering hoarsely without words.

Crying. All this time, she'd thought Meoraq had never seen anyone else cry but her. The sight of the lizard in a posture of such helpless, terrified surrender, coughing out its sobs as quietly as possible while the raiders (a lot more raiders, she noticed) talked around a campfire close by, pulled at Amber's heart in a way only Nicci's crying jags had ever been able to do before.

"Hey," she said before she stopped to think that nothing she said was going to make any kind of sense to these people. "Hey, don't cry. It's...well, it's not okay, but it will be. It might be."

The lizardlady (she was positive now that was what the captives were. They had smoother, more delicate features and, more to the point, they appeared to have a breast. Only one. It wasn't much—just a slight swelling in the center of each slender chest, more like a broad wedge than the round bubbles Amber had, but plainly a breast) gave her a fearful, shivering stare and began to stutter harder.

"What in the grip of God's loving arms did I just hear?" The leader rose from his place at the fire, silencing his men with a wave of one hand before aiming it at Amber like a gun. "Did you just talk?"

She clamped her bloody lips together and said nothing. Her jaws still ached and the taste of blood was still bitter in her mouth. She could be as defiant as she wanted in her heart, but the rest of her didn't want the gag again.

The raider's leader was not deterred. He crossed the small camp in just a few steps to hunker beside her and prodded at her shoulder with one blunt finger. "Say something."

"Fuck off," she said. Stupid thing to say. She could have wished him a Merry Christmas for all the good it did her.

"God blows blessings up my ass," someone else said, standing up. "It *can* talk!"

"You're both imagining things," said a third lizardman. "It's just making sounds, those aren't words."

"Those aren't dumaqi words," the leader corrected. He drew a knife—he wore a pair high on his arms, like Meoraq—and showed it to her. "I think it's time I had a better look at you, little one. Hold still and this won't hurt. Toss around and I guarantee nothing."

He did not untie her. He left her hands behind her back and her legs cinched together and simply cut along the seam of her tunic, severing each clumsy stitch she'd sewed on herself, until it just fell open. He grunted, flicking at strands of her hair with the tip of his knife, then stabbed it into the ground for safe-keeping and cupped her chin in his hand. He turned her head this way, then that, nudged at her lips, her ear, the ticklish flesh around some healing scratch on her cheek. Then he let go and dropped his gaze.

He touched her breast, then gripped it, kneaded it. His scales and the cold popped a nipple out for him; his thumb rolled over it thoughtfully, gave it a pluck, a careful pinch. He stopped when she winced, eyed her, then moved on to finger her bellybutton. He seemed to be trying to push his finger into it and when he finally decided that wasn't going to happen, he leaned back on his heels and just grunted again.

"Where do you suppose it came from?" someone asked.

"Washed in on some storm." He flexed the spines on the back of his head in a shrugging motion. "If you'd ever read the Prophet's Word, you'd know that the first years after the Fall brought all manner of new and terrible life out of Gann."

More than one raider cast his eyes skyward or hid them entirely behind a rubbing hand, but only the one called Vek, with a bandaged arm and a glazed look in his eye, was reckless enough to actually say, "Zhuqa, my missing hand is screaming at me in ways you can't imagine. I can't hear that piss-talk tonight and stay sane."

"You go north far enough, you will find monsters. Hairy beasts as tall as three men standing on each other's shoulders, swinging tails that can knock a man dead without even knowing he was there. Legless things in the rocky cracks that come up and bite, steal the feeling from a man's body, and while he lies there unable to move, they crawl up into his slit and make a den in his guts. Even the trees have teeth there and will eat a man if he stumbles too close. I have been to the northlands," he went on as his men murmured uneasily at each other. "I have seen all these things. This—" He gave Amber's breast another rough, almost petting squeeze. "—is new to my eyes, but if they have monsters in the north, they must have them elsewhere as well."

"This isn't a monster." Vek took a deep swallow from a small flask and came a little closer to them. "It's a person."

The leader grunted agreement.

"And I," Vek went on, bending over to blow a particularly pungent and strangely sweet cloud of breath at her, "am going to kill it."

"Ease off, Vek."

"I mean to take a few days doing it, too," he added, pointing at Amber. "I hope you understand me, you little smear of ghet-shit. I am going to cut off your hands and your feet and eat them in front of you."

The leader reached up and caught Vek's harness, gave him a small shake to make him look at him, and quietly said, "Ease off, I said. If I decide to sell it—*if*—I will give you the first offer. Until then, it belongs to me and you keep your distance. I'm feeling tenderly toward you at the moment, for the sake of all the years your two good arms have done me, but that doesn't mean I won't put you right into Gann's open mouth if you keep giving me reasons."

Vek moved off, grumbling and drinking, to collapse in a heap by the fire. He picked something up and looked at it—his hand, Amber realized—and threw it into the coals hard enough to send up a cloud of hot ash.

The leader picked up his knife again and resumed cutting. Her pants, as crudely made as her shirt, put up a little resistance at the waistband, and then he was able to put the knife away and just tear along the seams. Soon, she was lying there in her boots and the belts he'd used to tie her up and not a damn thing more. She tried to keep glaring, but the wind cut across her and the effect was completely spoiled by her sporadic shivers.

"What's it doing?" someone asked.

"She's cold," the leader said after a moment's silent contemplation.

All of them exchanged glances. It was some time before one of them said, "She? Are you sure?"

"No." He thumbed at her nipple again. "But I believe these are teats of some kind. And this—" He started to move toward her pussy; she yanked her bound legs up. He dropped his hand back to his knee with a look of tolerant amusement and finished, "—looks open to me. That means female."

"Oh that is disgusting," one of them said, almost exactly at the same time as another said, "That is so much money..."

The leader grunted. Then he leaned in a little and tapped at his forehead with two fingers. "Zhuqa," he said.

"What are you doing?"

"Say it," said the leader. He tapped his brow again. "Zhuqa."

Amber glared at him, shivering under her thuoch hide. She kept her mouth shut.

He flexed his spines again as he gently cupped her cheek. Then he lifted his hand, showed her his open palm, then slowly drew back his arm.

"Zhuqa," she spat.

All the lizards but one recoiled.

"She said it," one of them breathed.

"She tried." Their leader dropped his hand to her forehead and gave her one of Meoraq's friendly knuckle-taps. "Zhuqa means me. And Eshiqi...that means you. Say it."

She didn't think about it consciously, with words and arguments and a rational balance of pros and cons, but once again, that sense of helplessness welled up. It wasn't despair, only a ruthless acknowledgment of her new situation and the very few options before her: Fight and be overwhelmed (and probably killed), or play along and hope for something better a little further down the road.

All this had time to sink in before Zhuqa ever had the chance to show her his slapping hand.

"Eshiqi," said Amber.

"Good girl. Now look at me, Eshiqi. I want you to see this."

He untied her left hand, just the one. She watched as he took her gently by that arm, holding it not quite straight out from the shoulder. He smiled, cupped her elbow, then slid that hand in an unmistakable caress down to her wrist, down to the Manifestor's docking bracelet that she'd worn so long, she had forgotten it entirely.

"This," he said, prying the thin metal off with his eyes locked on hers, "is over."

He took it off, held it up briefly for his men to see, and then set it down. He drew a knife, the one he'd used to cut her clothes away, and as she struggled in vain to yank her hand out of his grip, suddenly stabbed it down. Into the bracelet.

Amber stopped fighting and looked at that. His men muttered and nudged each other. One of them rattled out a particularly nasty lizardish snicker. Zhuqa merely sheathed his knife again and tied her wrists back together, leaving the bracelet dead on the ground.

"Now you are mine," he told her, and lifted her back onto his shoulder. The moment ended. He gestured to his men and they started taking down the walls and kicking the fire out. "Water for the slaves and get them moving," he ordered, already walking. "I want to be home before dawn."

* * *

When the sun came up, Amber raised herself up as best she could as she swung over Zhuqa's back, searching for any dark speck that might be Meoraq, but she couldn't see anything. Not saoqs, not corrokis, not any living thing. Just hills and trees...and ruins. And where Meoraq avoided the fallen cities of the ancients, the raiders headed right for them.

Headed home.

The ground beneath Zhuqa's boots gave way to cracked pavement as the weathered framework and crumbling heaps of overgrown buildings slowly enclosed them. Ancient machines lay in rusty piles here and there along the streets, but their placement only seemed random at first glance. When she was behind them, looking out, Amber could see the sentries positioned behind them. One of them cupped his snout and let out a loud yodeling cry that Amber might have mistaken for a ghet's howl if she hadn't seen him do it. In the distance, someone else joined in and someone else beyond that, and then there were dozens of voices all raised together.

Soon, she could hear them coming, heavy boots tromping over the overgrown roads and speculative voices made indecipherable by the wind. The captives began to cry again, struggling in their bonds until the men walking at their sides were forced to cuff at them to keep them moving, but all Amber could do was hang there.

Trotting feet crunched up to them unseen and some new voice coughed out a laughing, "What is *that*?"

"The short answer is, 'Mine'." Zhuqa didn't even slow down. He passed a raider who fell into step behind him, his head cocked and gaze traveling freely over Amber. "You didn't want to come, remember, Iziz? All the way to Praxas, you said? In this cold? Fuck that, you said."

"Is it the first time I've ever been wrong?" the other asked. "What is it?"

"I call her Eshiqi."

"Her?" Iziz hooked a finger under Amber's chin and tipped her head up. "Gann's breath, that's eerie. It looks almost like a person."

Zhuqa laughed. "Almost," he agreed.

"You selling it?"

"You buying?"

"I might toss a bid out. Can you fuck it?" he inquired, looking more and more interested.

"It's got a slit in the right place. I haven't tried yet. She killed Godeshuq and took a hand off Vek."

Yet. He hadn't tried yet.

"And gave you a good bite, it looks like."

"Not half so good as she would have liked, eh, Eshiqi?" He shrugged to jostle her into a slightly different position as he ducked through a door into the ruined mouth of a building. More raiders lounged around in various stages of idleness, getting to their feet at the sight of her, only to be distracted by the captive lizardladies. Zhuqa showed no interest in any of them, only led the way through torchlit halls to a wide, echoing stair. He started down, bumping Amber hard against his shoulder on each step.

Iziz followed, toying with Amber's hair. "You never said if you were selling."

"If I do, I'll see that you know before the open bidding. Here." She felt him shift and saw a metal plate flicker as he tossed it over his shoulder for Iziz to catch. "Make yourself useful and take the new slaves to my pen. My men will want a wrestle; I ran them all night. Take one for yourself, since Godeshuq won't be needing her, but be polite. Take the one the others leave. And give Vek first choice. His feelings are bruised."

Iziz raised his fist and turned around to take charge of the slaves, herding them down another hall and out of Amber's sight. Soon she had nothing to look at but torchlight on the walls, another stairwell, another corridor, and then—

"Home," announced Zhuqa. bumping her in another good-natured shrug. She felt him shift again, heard the small scrape of a key turning in a lock, and then he took a few steps forward into darkness. "Not much, but better than wind and rain, even to fierce little snap-jaws like you. Did you note how many guards we passed on our journey to my chambers?"

Many. One at every landing. One or two at every crossways in the halls. Amber said nothing.

"I am going to put you down now and unbind you. Mark me, I don't have to unbind you, but I choose to. You may get the idea to run. If you do, I swear before God the All-Father I will let you. You won't get far and I will not come and get you for one full day and night because I will be rather cross with you. Do you hear me? Kick your legs twice if you do."

She kicked sullenly. Once. Twice. And stopped.

"Good girl."

He heaved her off and set her with a jarring thump on her feet, holding her at the waist until she steadied. Then he let go and moved away.

The door was open just behind her. She could see the red light of the torches in the hall. 'If my legs were only free, I could run,' she thought. Useless, suicidal thought, but it still had to take its tumble through her brain. Turn right at the second crossways, run to the end. Up one flight, run to the left. Up four more flights and out.

Stone scraped along metal. Sparks spat and caught on a narrow wick set in a mirrored bowl of oil. Zhuqa glanced over his shoulder at her, grunted, and walked away to light another lamp.

Amber didn't run. She looked instead at the room around her, a room which had perhaps been office space in the years before the Fall. She could see an open cupboard heaped with furs to serve as a bed, a scattering of mismatched armor and other clothing, a few small trunks and one very large one, a small table set with an empty plate and a cup, a chair crowned artistically with a tachuqi skull, and on the cracked walls, a few shelves and some hooks, one supporting a large and well-stained leather flask.

Her eyes came back to Zhuqa in the end. He was waiting for it, waiting for her to see him when he reached out to catch the door.

And pull it closed.

She glared at him. The glare was stupid, maybe, but she couldn't stop it from happening. She could stand there without running and she could keep her mouth shut, but she couldn't help glaring. It was too easy to imagine how it might be to snatch up that lamp and throw it, too easy to see him coated in oil, flailing, burning.

He saw it too. He glanced at the lamp beside him and, with insolent slowness, dipped his finger in the bowl and passed it over the flame. It didn't catch.

"Animal fat is far too valuable to burn," he told her. "We use xuseth oil here. It burns clean, as you see, but catches slow." He dipped his fingers again and rubbed the wick itself; the light guttered and nearly went out. "Learning to make wicks and seeing that I have enough light in my chambers will be part of your duties." He knelt to unbuckle the belt that held her ankles, the belt at her knees, the belt at her thighs...and there he stopped, gazing speculatively at the mound of her pubis.

"Easy now," he murmured, raising his hand.

Her thighs clenched, but she made that be all as he worked his finger between her folds. Well-oiled by xuseth, he moved back and forth along her opening several times before finally pushing up and inside her. Amber heard the angry sound catch in her throat and made it be the only one; felt her body tighten in a vain effort to force the invader out and made herself relax. It was going to happen no matter what she did, and the harder she fought before she lost, the more weapons she'd give him in all the fights to follow.

Zhuqa grunted pensively, questing deeper but with caution, until he withdrew and simply turned her around to unbind her arms.

"I keep my promises, Eshiqi, do you see?" he said, and straightened up to watch her rub painfully at her wealed skin as he coiled his weighted cord and set it aside. "I am told I'm not a hard man to serve. I won't hurt you unless you demand it of me." He studied her for a moment. "Say something. When I speak, you answer."

She rolled her eyes. "Four-score and seven years ago, our forefathers brought forth upon this continent a new nation, conceived in liberty. Fuck you." She turned away.

"I doubt very much any of that wished me well. Watch yourself, little one. The day I learn that tongue may well be the day you lose yours."

Amber licked her bloody lips and was quiet.

"The fact has not escaped me that you must have learned our words from someone. And the things we found at your fire were man-made. Where is he?"

If they were asking, they hadn't found him. Amber hesitated, then glanced back at him and drew her finger across her throat.

He grunted, eyeing her with a smile. "You are going to some lengths to convince me that you are a dangerous slave to hold, Eshiqi. I appreciate your efforts, but I do mean to hold you. So. Here we come to it, little one. I don't want to hurt you, but I will if that's the only way you'll have it."

He began to unfasten his harness.

Someone knocked.

Amber didn't bother to look around. It wasn't word of Meoraq, she knew that already. If her man were killing his way through the lot of them, no one would bother with this hesitant triple-tap. But somehow, the fact that they knocked at all came with its own vague feeling of offense, as if knocking were some fundamental human behavior they had usurped.

Zhuqa finished removing his harness before he answered it, letting his half-nakedness make a silent point to whoever stood beyond. He gave no word of greeting, not even a 'What do you want?' He held the door and waited.

"I interrupt you," said an unfamiliar voice, amused but not apologetic. "Shall I wait in the hall?"

"Do you have a report?"

"I have the seeming of one. The bones of it are: No change. How many did you—What is that?"

"That is what you are interrupting. Get on with it."

The raider in the doorway visibly wrestled with a remark, then apparently decided not to test his leader's good humor any further. "Our westward patrol encountered some of Ghelip's men the day after you left. They denied they were sent as an attack party at first—"

"Attack party? From Ghelip? How many were there?"

"Three, sir."

"And they were killed?"

"Yes, sir, after interrogation. Salahkthu will have their full confessions—"

"Three." Zhuqa gave his brow-ridges a knead. "Tell Salahkthu to resume normal patrols and to make his miserable skin available when I come up. Any other deaths to report?"

"No, sir."

"No?"

"Only slaves."

"How many?"

"I..."

"Make Hruuzk available as well." Zhuqa started to shut the door, then opened it wide again, catching the other lizardman just about to slink off. "Zru'itak."

It wasn't a word she knew and the answer was no clearer when the other lizard said, "Not yet."

Zhuqa grunted and shut the door. He stood, deep in thought, then strode past Amber to collect the waterskin from the hook on the wall. He uncapped it and drank, glanced at her, then held it out.

She shook her head.

He continued to hold it, now beginning to frown. "Come and take it, Eshiqi. You are for my comfort, not I for yours."

She started to shake her head again, but then just went over and put out her hand. She was thirsty. If that made her a coward or a traitor or a weak little girl, too bad.

She drank. It stung her lips badly enough to bring tears smarting to her eyes and tasted so fantastically bilious that her first swallow came retching explosively back out of her. She heard him cough out a curse as he snatched up the waterskin she'd dropped, but he didn't hit her and he even grabbed her by the arm when she staggered, supporting her until she knew she wouldn't fall over.

"Don't do that again," he said coldly. "This is difficult to come by and I punish those who waste it out of spite."

"I didn't want it in the first place!" Amber spat, wiping her mouth, but she didn't get in his face and shout it, and when he started to cap the neck, she reached out her hand again. She knew what was coming and as foul as the drink was, she sure wasn't going to face the rest of this night sober if she didn't have to.

Zhuqa studied her for a second or two before relinquishing his grip on the flask. She took three deep swallows, paused for a shudder and a grimace, and took one more. A smarter girl would start ingratiating herself now, thank him, maybe even flirt with him; Amber couldn't, not yet, but she wasn't going to fight him either.

Zhuqa hung the flask back up, then unfastened the ties of his breeches. Amber watched him undress without flinching, letting her head swim comfortably out of this moment, this room. Meoraq was coming for her.

"I'm not afraid of you," she said when he turned, naked, to face her. "I'm not afraid of this."

"Fierce little thing," he murmured, taking her chin in his hand. He stepped forward, pushing her before him until her back struck the wall. "There is not so much as a spark of fear in these eyes. I think you may have done this before. Ah, so you have." He released her to brush her hair back from her shoulder, revealing Meoraq's bite-scars. He traced them, then stroked his way over her smooth skin down to her wrist. He brought her hand between them to the slight swell of his loins. "Gently now," he murmured.

She closed her eyes and let her hand lie limp in his grip as he made her stroke at his scales. Once. Twice. The drink, whatever it had been, made it easy for her mind to drift out beyond these ruins. He could do what he wanted with her; Amber didn't have to be with him.

"You are determined not to make this easy on yourself," Zhuqa said, somewhere in the world. "So be it."

His hand became a fist around her wrist. Tendons creaked. Bones ground together. Amber let out a startled wail, her legs buckling instinctively. This time, he let her drop. Cold stone sent shockwaves of fresh agony up both knees, but all she could do was scratch at his restraining hand while he gazed coolly down at her.

She didn't know how long it lasted. Probably not long. A minute, maybe. Maybe only half that. When it finally stopped, the relief was enough that she sagged gasping against his thigh, actually clutching at it like a lifeline, her hate like shards of glass in her chest and pain like throbbing hell everywhere else.

He gave her a moment to recover. Then, the lightest of tugs. "Up, Eshiqi."

She got up, climbing his hip and then his chest, hating him.

He moved her hand back between his legs. "Gently now," he said again.

"I'm going to kill you," she whispered, cupping and kneading at the hard lump she felt beneath the cover of his scales.

His head cocked warningly even as his spines flexed in mild good humor. "Was that a threat, little one? I think it was. You're fortunate I'm feeling so forgiving, but if you want to keep me there, you'll have to make an effort. Find my slit. I'm ready for you, but I think you need the practice. There you are. I want to feel your hand through my belly-skin. Good. Now, carefully, get a good grip. Squeeze. Gently. Release. Now squeeze again. Steady. Like the beating of a sleeping heart."

"I'm going to put a knife through yours."

"Just so," he told her, color rising in the thin scales along his throat. "Keep your hand at work, but move your thumb up along my slit and when you feel moisture, push inside. It was easy, wasn't it? I could have been freed well before now, but then how would you know the way to do this? Someday, I will come home to you in Gann's own humor and you will be glad that you know how to do this, glad that all it takes is a skilled hand to coax me from a killing mood. Ah!" He closed his eyes, spines rigid and neck striped with brilliant gold, and in a strangled voice said, "What you feel beneath your thumb is my sa'ad. Stroke. Use small circles. Gently."

And before she'd made a single revolution over the prominent nub he meant, his cock shoved itself out in slick insistence.

"Enough lessons," he grunted, pulling one of her thighs up and around his hip. "You are easily the most deviant—" He broke off with a tight rattle as he penetrated and shuddering with pleasure when their hips finally met. "—thing I have ever done," he finished, and drew back his head to grimace at her. "How does that feel, Eshiqi?"

How did it feel? How else could it feel with his oils hot inside her and the blunt hook of his ridged cock rubbing insistently at the soft place just beyond her pubic bone? She bared her teeth at him like a dog, *hating* that she could feel him this way, hating that it didn't at least *hurt*. He grimaced back at her in good humor as he began to move, working in curt punching movements that drove her up along the rough side of the wall until her scrabbling toes lost contact with the floor entirely and it was either hang suspended on his stabbing cock or put her arms around him.

"Ah, that's good," he murmured, nuzzling at her while she twisted her face away. After that, there was no more speech, no more instruction, only his body like a spear inside her and hate, helpless hate, bleeding out into the wound it left.

* * *

As a child, Bo Peep Bierce's little girl discovered the elastic quality of Time. Until that golden summer of state-care, Time had always been a constant—precisely measured, easily predicted, immutable. Only after the lady in the flowery dress sent her and baby Nicci back to their mother did she understand that Time was more like a faucet, that it could run hot or cold, pour out fast or drip out slow, and that, if you knew the trick of it, you could put your hand on the knob and shut it off entirely.

Little Amber sat in non-Time in the closet at Holland Mills while her mother fucked men in the bed where she would have to sleep that night. Teenage Amber made it through two years of high school one non-Time class after another before giving up and getting a job. Grown Amber worked non-Time shifts at the factory, unaware of her aching back and feet and head until she had to walk to the bus station afterwards. And in Zhuqa's lair, Amber drifted in non-Time until he was done with her and tied her up again.

He left her on the floor and after he was gone, Time came creeping in again. The anger came with it and then the tears, which accomplished nothing except to make her head feel thick and heavy. Eventually she slept. It was not a restorative sleep. She woke when the door opened, feeling more exhausted than before, as well as sore and hung over and dried out. She raised her head and saw him in the doorway, holding a covered bowl in the crook of one arm, and suddenly she was hungry too.

Amber tried to sit up, wiggling worm-like in her bonds in an effort to get her back against the wall and lever herself up it. Zhuqa bumped the door shut, set the bowl down and came to help her. His hands were rough, but he was gentle. She hated him all over again, for what he'd done, for what he was going to do, and most of all for not being entirely hateful when he did it.

When she was sitting up, Zhuqa went back for the bowl, then came and knelt beside her. He lifted the cover, releasing a small billow of steam, but no smell. What at first glance appeared to be stew or cereal proved in the next to be a rag floating in water. He took it, squeezed it in his fist and began to wash her face.

Not soup. Just hot water. Tears stung at her eyes. She refused to let them fall.

"How long will you be angry with me, little one?" he asked tolerantly. His hands were gentle as they daubed her cheek, her brow. There was blood on the rag when he rinsed it, and soot and sweat and all kinds of scum she'd picked up in her travels. "A day? A year? You can be angry all you like, of course, as long as you're obedient, but you will find that hate is heavy. Too heavy, I think, for your little body to carry."

"I'll still give it the old college try, motherfucker."

"I have received seventeen offers for you, fierce one," he said, now wiping at her throat. Beads of water fell away, cutting an itchy path between her breasts to her belly. "More coin than I have ever been offered for any other prize. More coin, to say truth, than I knew some of these men even held. But for now, you remain my Eshiqi. So. What shall I do with you?" He swished the rag through the water, wrung it out, and put it between her thighs, gazing meditatively into her eyes as he scrubbed the raw well of hurt he'd used all morning. "Let us play a game."

Amber looked away, staring into the wall until her eyes hurt. Meoraq was coming. He couldn't be that far away now. He'd find her (*and never mind that he'd never found nicci never mind that at all this was different he was coming and he'd find her*) and all she had to do was live long enough for him to get her out of this. She could do anything for one day, right? Right. Suck it up, little girl.

She looked at him.

"I was not always the man I am now," he told her. His hands were gentle, always gentle. "There was a time I too stood in the sight of God, a time when I sought nothing greater than to serve in His name. A moment's doubt..." He withdrew, placed the rag in the bowl and the bowl to one side. "...and that life was ended. If it had not, I would be the steward of my father's House. I would have a woman who was my own alone. I often wonder what that would be like. So let us play a game."

He untied her ankles, turned her around and unfastened her wrists from her elbows. "We will play a game I like to call 'Zhuqa's House'," he said, helping her to rub feeling into her numb, cramping limbs. "I admit that I have played before and have some advantage over you, but I trust you will learn quickly and make as formidable an opponent as you did in battle. I will come home to you, my Eshiqi, and you will play that you are my happy woman."

She spat laughter at him, unwise as that might be. She wanted to live, she did, but her ability to suck it up had limits and that was well, *well* beyond them.

"The woman of my House, who kneels at my side in meek obedience, her outstretched hand open at my foot."

"You can make me be here, you son of a bitch, but you will never make me like it. Fuck you."

"Who opens herself to all the fires of lust Gann can give me and pretends a loyal woman's pleasure in her man's desire."

She shook her head, tight-lipped.

"Who drinks from my cup when we share our meals and unfastens the armor I don with solemn duty each day. It's a simple game," he said with a careless flick of his spines. "And in the playing of it, you may note my obedient woman does not require binding."

Amber turned her face away and stared into the far wall, ignoring him.

He waited.

So did she.

"It is not the only game I play," he said at last. "Merely that which I have most fondness for. The other game—" He rose and casually knotted a hand in her hair, yanking her forward onto her knees and dragging her toward the door with her first startled screams of pain just whooping out of her. "—I call 'Zhuqa the Warlord'. It, too, is a simple one. In it, I am master of a band of ruthless men, much like those above us even now." He opened the door and flung her out into the hall. She banged into the wall and fell, but couldn't right herself fast enough. He had her by her ankles next, pulling her over the filthy stone and speaking loudly, but still calm, always calm, to be heard over her howls. "In my game, I have a number of slaves who I provide to these men as whatever amusement they wish to take. For example." He heaved her around, swinging her completely off the ground (*used to do this with nicci didn't i airplane we called it do me airplane amber*) and letting go so that she crashed and slid into the first crossways, rolling and wailing to land at the feet of two curious guards.

"For example," said Zhuqa, striding down the dark hall toward them. He ignored their salutes and hunkered down to catch Amber's chin and force her eyes to his. "It might be the day in the game of Zhuqa the Warlord when I say, Uruul?"

"Sir," said one of the guards immediately.

"Get your cock out."

The second guard backed up a little, but whatever Uruul felt about this order did not make him hesitate. He shucked his breeches, slipped a finger into his slit and out came the dark thrust of his cock. He wasn't ready, was dry as sunbaked brick, but it was there and it was hard.

"And then I would say," said Zhuqa, not even looking to see if he had been obeyed, "Uruul?"

"Sir." The word was a grunt of some effort. His finger was still in his slit.

"I am going to count to six, and when I say the number six, you are going to put your cock in that hole and fuck it until you cum three times."

"Yes, sir."

"He'll be the first, Eshiqi, and once it starts, it will not stop. One," said Zhuqa quietly. "Two."

Amber rolled shakily onto her belly, choking on sobs that were still more shock than pain.

"Three. Four."

She put her hand next to his foot.

Zhuqa looked at it. "Palm to heaven."

She turned her wrist. Even that hurt.

Zhuqa grunted. He stood up. "Put your cock away, Uruul. Stand your watch."

"Yes, sir." Spoken with real relief. The second guard was staring at him with something like admiration as Uruul fastened his breeches.

"I'm a simple man," said Zhuqa, looking only at Amber as she struggled to right herself. "And those are really the only two games I know. Which one are you going to play, Eshiqi?"

Another woman would have spit on him. Another woman would have made him slap her in chains just so she could use them to throttle him. Another woman would never have needed someone like Meoraq to save her.

Amber got up and followed him back to his room. Zhuqa held the door until she'd limped through it. He did not slam it. He was not, she saw, angry.

"Zhuqa has come home," he said. "How do you greet me, woman?"

She wiped her face on her arms a few times, took a stabilizing breath, then faced him. Put her arms around him. Leaned her cheek against his chest.

"I can tell you have never played before, but you are trying and I appreciate your efforts. Tomorrow, I will put you to work with the other slaves so that you can see better how this game is played."

She nodded listlessly. Maybe Meoraq would be here by then.

"Still, it pleases a man to see his woman try. Come here, Eshiqi."

She went, not daring to look at him and not knowing whether it was to keep him from seeing the murder in her eyes...or the tears.

He took her hand, put it on his belt. He gave no orders.

"Grim as Gann Himself," he murmured, fingering her hair as she undressed him. "You will have to work at that. I don't mind if you hate me, as long as you hide it. Play the game, Eshiqi, and remember a woman's greatest happiness is to serve her man."

"I'll be happy when you're dead," she said. Her voice broke on every goddamned word.

He bent to graze his teeth along her shoulder when she began her kneading motions. It was the only time she faltered, thinking he meant to bite her, and it wasn't the pain she feared so much as the scar it would leave.

"Easy, little one," he murmured, his voice thick and strained. "I take no pleasure from your pain. You will carry no more scars while you stand in my favor. And when you do not, scars will be the least of your concerns." His next words became an inarticulate hiss as she found the slick nub of his clitoris-like sa'ad and they were his last effort at any kind of speech for a long time. He buried his brow against her shoulder, abandoning sight to only feel. He touched her when she touched him, his rough hands lightly scouring at her hip, her ribs, her thigh. He was gentle.

"I'm going to kill you," she told him, stroking his cock until his oils coated her hand and every flexing of her fingers made him shudder with the effort not to cum. "I don't know how yet, but I know I will. And someday, long after you're dead—" She turned around, her hands braced on the table on either side of the waterskin, fingernails digging curt furrows only for that first moment. Once he was in her, the oiled ridges of his cock rubbing heat into her mindless body (Gann's body, she thought, her godless clay), she was able to relax, separate from sensation, let it happen. "Long after you're dead," she went on calmly, her voice broken by his powerful thrusts and not by any of her own emotion, "I'm going to wake up in the night from a bad dream with your face in it, but I won't remember your name. And I'll go back to sleep. And I'll sleep just fine."

He groaned hoarsely against the nape of her neck, his hands digging painful grooves in her stomach. The first time never took him long, but that didn't mean it was ending. He wasn't human. He didn't have to stop until he wanted to.

"I won't remember you," whispered Amber, gazing at the wall as Time once again stretched out and stopped. "I won't."

5

At first light, Meoraq rose. He had not slept, but he had rested as best he was able within his unquiet mind and it was with clarity of sight and purpose that he looked upon his camp. The raiders had taken both sleds and all that they had carried. His pack and Amber's had been too worn to interest them, but their contents had been rummaged through and scattered. The clothes they had spent the winter making were gone, along with Meoraq's mending kit and tent. His bedroll was missing; Amber's remained. His tea box lay open on the ground, the more precious of its inlaid stones pried up and its many drawers knocked loose, spilling its remaining teas into the grass. Amber's cups were nearby, one of them in pieces.

He ignored the dead man for now. There was evidence there, he knew, but whatever he had not scattered in faithless rage would keep. He searched the ground for the things which had been hidden from him in the darkness, now brought to light.

He saw blood. More than could be accounted for by the dead man, even taking into measure Meoraq's fit of fury. Blood in a wide, dried pool, crushed into the grass by the trampling of many feet. Blood painting the tall stalks of wind-blown grasses. Blood that led into the plains.

Meoraq gazed into the north, the direction the blood had taken, then returned to the ashes of his fire and knelt to examine what was left of the body. The boots, worn and overlarge for the dead man's feet; not bought or made, but stolen. His companions had relieved him of any coin or weapons, but overlooked one bauble—a woman's wristlet, worn not upon his own wrist, but bent wide and hidden...treasured...around his ankle. He wore a battle harness of inexpensive make, patched with insignias taken from many different Houses—taken from those who had the birthright to wear them, no doubt—and breeches sewn of hides. He had little flesh left to inspect, but what there was had been heavily scarred, and the thicker scales along his back showed the buckling and discoloration of a diet with too much meat, too little crop. When he hunted out the head, he saw eyes yellowed by the overuse of phesok (smoked phesok, by the burnt pads of his fingers, once they were also located) and brown stumps of teeth that had never known cleaning.

Meoraq looked again at the metal-worked bit, turning it between his fingers until he found the jewelsmith's stamp on the backing. Ulhrug, it said. Ulhrug of Praxas. The city was not familiar to him, but he supposed the city didn't matter. This chain with its pretty ornament had likely come off the neck of some murdered traveler.

And yet...

He was well-fed, for a raider. Warmly dressed. He was a young man and not strongly-made; the burlier members of his pack should have stripped him of all his prizes and yet here he lay with his boots on and spoils intact. These were the wildlands at the very heel of winter. There were no travelling merchants to prey on and little enough game for an honest man to find, but he had certainly not suffered for their lack.

Whoever these raiders were...someone was trading with them.

Of course, it was both a crime against Man's law and a sin before the eyes of Sheul to have dealings of any kind with those who had gone to Gann, but men were weak. Raiders had phesok and strong drink; the cities had sweets, medicines and women. There would always be places where those on both sides of the walls were willing to sheathe their blades and offer goods instead. So it seemed this Praxas was such a place.

He tucked the dead man's trinket into his own boot and looked the body over one last time. He saw a hard life, begun and ended in violence outside the city walls. A boy born in the squalor of a raiding camp to become a man fallen from Sheul's grace. And that camp would be where they had taken his Amber.

He bent his head, closed his eyes and breathed. Six breaths. Six again. The Prophet. His brunt. Uyane. Mykrm. Oyan. Thaliszar. He was a warrior of his father's House. He was a Sword and a true son of Sheul. He was God's Striding Foot in the land and the hour of Gann. He was Uyane Meoraq.

Truth.

He listened to the wind brush across the plains, then opened his eyes.

On the blood-stained ground, he saw nothing new. In the blackened ring of his camp's firepit were only ashes. In the plains, nothing moved that breathed.

And in the sky, the forever-clouds of Sheul's storm lay open, showing a face of jewel-deep green and light in beams of gold pouring down all around it.

It closed and the wind blew on.

Meoraq passed a trembling hand briefly before his eyes, then closed it into a firm fist. He took up Amber's travel-pack and set her surviving cup within, cushioned by his own rolled-up pack. After a moment's dark non-thought, he bent and gathered the various pieces of his tea box, fit them back together and packed that away as well. As far as he cared (and he didn't know why he cared even that much), everything else could go to Gann.

He began to run.

* * *

Zhuqa didn't tie her up again. He didn't need to. He pulled the knife from the sheath he kept strapped high on his arm, showed it to her, then stabbed it into the door of his cupboard. That was almost intimidating enough all on its own, but he hadn't been trying to scare her with it. He just wanted a place to hang his bells.

He had to dig for them in a crate for some time before he found them, and the whole time he did that, Amber had to stand two running steps away from the cupboard and stare at the knife. They were jingle-bells, all wired together in a festive loop just like Christmas bells back on Earth, except they were made of some greenish metal. Not a minty Christmas-green either, but something ugly and snotty, the sort of color that made the whole thing look vaguely cancerous. He hung them over the hilt of his knife where the slightest movement of the door set them to shrill jingling, then put her in the cupboard to sleep with him, but he didn't try to touch her. No, he just put her closest to the wall with himself on the outer side, so that escape would mean climbing over the top of him and opening a jingling door...in other words, impossible.

He fell asleep almost immediately—two marathon bouts of sex in one day were too much for even mighty Zhuqa the Warlord—but Amber did not. She lay there for a very long time, doing nothing, thinking nothing, only staring into the black above her bed. She would have liked to have been planning something. Escape. Murder. Hell, dinner. But thought was like hate tonight, too heavy for her little body to carry.

She still believed Meoraq was coming. This was so obvious that it didn't even bear wondering about. He was coming and he'd find her. Meoraq could do anything. The question of whether he'd still want her after another man had been inside her had not yet occurred to her, but it would before morning. These were her last worry-free moments, but for now, no, she wasn't worried.

Someone knocked.

Zhuqa woke. Only he didn't just 'wake'. Between his sleeping inhalation and the swift snort of his waking exhale, he managed to flip into a crouch and draw his other knife. She knew about the crouch because she could hear the *pa-pad* of his bare feet hitting the hard mat they slept on. She knew about the knife because it was under her jaw.

"That wasn't me," said Amber.

Zhuqa eased up on the knife with a low grunt.

The knock came again, even louder.

"Someone better be dead," he called, and shoved the cupboard door open.

The bells were loud as sirens in the quiet, slow to leave the air. She heard his footsteps recede. A sliver of reddish light split the dark as he opened the door.

"Iziz," said Zhuqa. "In light of our many years of friendship, I will give you one word before I disembowel you."

"Zru'itak," said Iziz, seemingly unconcerned.

Zhuqa sheathed his knife and came back into the room. He left the door open, so she thought he was coming for his clothes, but while he did dress and strap on his weapons, modesty was clearly his secondary concern. "Up, Eshiqi," he called. "You are far too new to this game to be left to play alone."

He didn't offer her any clothes. Amber fumbled a blanket off the bed and wrapped herself in it as well as she could, running to make up what little time this cost.

He grunted, eyeing her as he cinched his belt tight, then gave the lizardman standing behind him a friendly slap to the stomach and said, "Say something to him."

"Gee," she said, in her most neutral voice. "I didn't have a speech prepared, but choke on piss and die."

Iziz snorted, his spines flaring in either amusement or surprise. "What the hell did that mean?"

"Nothing good, I should think." Zhuqa gave Amber's chin an affectionate pinch and went back out into the hall, trusting her to follow. Which she did. "Probably told you that your father was a ghet or a slave or a warm pile of shit."

"Could have been Gann himself for all anyone knows," Iziz said agreeably, walking backwards to watch Amber. "My mother isn't much for names. Those eyes...Does that thing really understand you or is it just doing tricks?"

"It understands every word."

"Eerie. Have you fucked it yet?"

"Yes."

"How is it?"

"Better than your mother."

"She could use some training up, couldn't she?" Iziz agreed and turned around just in time to avoid tumbling backwards onto the stairs. "You feeling proprietary?"

"For now. But stop a moment. Eshiqi, come here."

There on the stairs, with a guard on the lower landing looking up and two on the next floor looking down, Zhuqa beckoned.

She took a second or two to think about all the things he might want her to demonstrate with his friend and then she walked stiffly up to them and waited.

"Oh, that is snapping mad," Iziz remarked in an admiring tone.

Zhuqa moved Amber's hair to show off Meoraq's scar.

The effect on his friend was something of a surprise. He looked at it politely for a heartbeat or two, and then actually leapt back, banging into the stairwell rail and nearly going right over and down to wherever the bottom was in this place. Zhuqa's hand catching in his harness prevented that, but Iziz didn't even thank him.

"That's a fucking Sheulek bite!" he hissed, all his spines standing straight up.

"Yes."

"That thing belongs to a Sheulek?!"

"Used to." Zhuqa chucked Amber on the chin again and resumed climbing stairs. "She says she killed him."

"Then she's a fucking liar!" Iziz said, looking and sounding almost prissily outraged. "Where did you get that thing?"

"About three, maybe four spans off the old quarry road."

"Off the road? Where off the road? And when were you going to tell us to make fast against a fucking Sword of fucking *God*? Shouldn't that have been the first thing you did when you got back, instead of throwing a poke into *that* Gann-ugly thing for hours at a stretch?!"

"How long have we been here, Iziz? How many years?"

The second lizardman passed a hand over his eyes briefly and shook his head—not in negation, they didn't do that, but in the same way an irritated dog throws off water. "More than a few," he said, resigned. "Five? Six?"

"It is, in fact, eight. Eight years, settled. And wintering twelve years before that, under me or under Chuaan, and who knows how many years before that, for raiders *like* us if not this band exactly? These ruins have stood since the Fall and they may still be standing when men rise up to Fall again." He glanced back at Amber, his eyes glinting red in the torchlight. "No one is coming."

"You say that like no one ever has. I say to you, if little boys chasing after tachuqi talons can find this place, so can a Sheulek."

"Then I'll kill him."

Iziz snorted. "Before or after you catch lightning in your fist and squeeze it into wine?"

"I have killed six Sheulek in my time, Iziz. Seven, if you count a certain way." He gave Amber another glance, coughing amusement at what he saw in her face. "If he comes, he comes. And I will kill him and make a cup of his skull—" He reached back to pinch her chin. "—for my woman to hold for me when we share our meals."

She twisted out of his grip and rubbed the back of her hand across her chin, erasing the hated heat of his touch. It wasn't deliberate; she couldn't have stopped herself if she'd tried. It was all she could do not to bare her teeth at him like an animal.

"Fierce little thing," Zhuqa murmured and left the stairs for another hall.

There was more light here. And noise. Muted by distance and at least one other door, she could hear a lizardish screaming. Not high and frightened, not fresh. Whatever torture played out at the end of this hall, it had been some time in the act. Amber's step slowed as the last cry tapered to a moan and then came a terrible silence that stopped her entirely. Even when Zhuqa noticed, even when he came back for her, she couldn't move. She didn't want to see what he'd done to someone to make them make a sound like that.

Or to make them stop.

"These are my slave pens," Zhuqa said after a moment. "Zhuqa the Warlord has played many games in this hall I do not care to remember. Easy, my little one. This is not one of them. Come with me."

He turned around again. She followed.

They had not quite reached the door he wanted when it opened and a raider came out. She recognized him, although the name didn't come until she heard it in Zhuqa's mouth.

"Geozh." He folded his arms, an act that placed his hands very near to the sheathed blade strapped to his biceps. "You must be coming to fetch me."

"I was, actually." And, far from showing concern, Geozh gave his leader a clap to the shoulder. "You know what they say about the first one, but it's a tough little sprat."

He moved off down the hall, spines high but relaxed. Humming.

Amber frowned, watching him go. Zhuqa opened the door.

The clove-sweet smell of their blood struck her at once, followed by the gaspy rattle of someone's dry, labored breath. Amber stopped cold, but Zhuqa didn't wait.

He went to the cupboard where a few more raiders stood respectfully aside for him, and looked down at the lizardlady lying in the bed. She dragged her eyes open to look back at him, then turned her face away.

"Eshiqi, come here."

She went, pulling unwillingly away from Iziz as Zhuqa bent over and picked something out of the bedding. She knew what she was looking at—she thought she knew—but she still shied squeamishly back when he turned around and placed the wet, blood-streaked baby in her reluctant arms.

The lizardlady in the bed made a single unhappy sound. Not a word. Not even truly a complaint. Just a sound, scarcely louder than a sigh.

"And there we are," said Zhuqa. His eyes were on the baby, expressionless, watching its tiny hands and feet grip on to the blanket that wrapped Amber's shoulders. Its scales were white and slightly translucent, which gave it almost a pearly look beneath the gore of its birthing. It pressed the top of its weirdly flattened head to her breast and did nothing, made no sound. Its ribs bulged rapidly in and out. It was impossibly thin to her eye; no fat and happy human baby, but something skeletal and drowned.

Long minutes passed. No one spoke. The raiders sharing this moment stood very still, facing away, invisible in their own skin. There were, Amber saw, three other lizardladies a short distance away, keeping very quiet as they gathered stained cloth and other less-identifiable devices into baskets to take away. They didn't matter. Even Amber herself and the lady in the cupboard did not seem to truly manifest. This was all about Zhuqa and the baby. The silence stretched and stretched...and shattered with the scraping sound of a knife drawn from its sheath.

Amber flinched back with a wordless sound of her own, clutching the baby closer to her chest as if her arms were any shield against the killing blade.

Zhuqa paused, knife in hand, and gave her a long, thoughtful stare.

"Interesting response," Iziz remarked.

Zhuqa held the knife up in an elaborate display, turned it point-down, and pierced his forefinger. He sheathed the knife again as he pinched his knuckle to make blood well out past his scales, then closed what little distance Amber had put between them and drew a red-black line of his own blood down the baby's naked back.

"Welcome to Gann's world," he murmured. "Your blood is the blood of Zhuqa."

The baby did not move, did not squirm, did not make a sound beyond its rapid panting.

At last Zhuqa looked up, far deeper into Amber's eyes than she wanted to see him go. He read them without speaking. He did not step away. He said, "Zru'itak here was exiled from the city of Chalh for thievery. She would have died in the wildlands if my men had not found her. Is this not true?"

The lizardlady did not reply.

Zhuqa did not seem to expect her to. "They brought her to me and I gave her the gift of my protection. I fed her. I clothed her. I gave her every luxury this life allows. She was not grateful. I asked her to play a game with me. So. We played. I don't care if my woman hates me, but if she's going to play the game, she has to at least pretend. Zru'itak never had a kind word for her man, only insults."

He gave the lizardlady in the bed a pointed stare. After a moment, Amber looked that way, too. The lizardlady continued to face the wall until Zhuqa's hand moved calmly to his knife and then she finally turned. Her mouth opened.

The tongueless, empty hole of her mouth.

"After that, things became...strained," said Zhuqa. "I was willing to forgive, but she didn't want to play anymore. I am not a cruel man. I told her if she would stay one year, just one, I would let her go her way in Gann's world. For a time, she seemed content with that. Soon, I learned she was pregnant. I brought her out of my rooms and let her walk at my side. I made all the world our House and opened every door for her." He glanced back. The lizardlady looked at the wall. "And how did you show me obedience, faithless one? How did you serve the man who took you in? Who cared for you? Who put the fire of new life in your wretched womb?"

His voice never rose, never showed the slightest strain of emotion.

The lizardlady did not—could not—reply.

"She ran away," said Zhuqa. He gazed at Amber, his head cocked to show a faint degree of sarcasm. "She ran away, when all the *world* was my House, and she slapped my face when I went to fetch her back."

No one spoke. No one made a sound. No one met his stare but Amber.

Suddenly, he turned around, seized the blanket that covered the lizardlady, and ripped it entirely off the bed.

She saw. The baby in her arms uttered a chick-like peep; she'd squeezed it.

Zru'itak had no legs, no arms. He'd left her nothing, nothing but the delicate, polished bones of her toes and fingers, strung prettily together and hung around her neck.

"The year is out," said Zhuqa, dropping the blanket indifferently on the floor. "And I keep my promises. Take her back to where we found her. Let her go."

All the raiders but Iziz moved at once to pull the lizardlady from her bed. Her mouth opened for another of those terrible, quavering wails, but there were no words and no way to beg. Amber didn't know she was moving until her back hit the scaly wall of Iziz's chest. He caught her, but she didn't need catching. She might not be able to feel her legs at the moment, but they were holding her up just fine. She watched the raiders wrap the lady—*the moaning torso of the lady*—in the bloody sheets so that she made easier portage and then they took her away.

"So our game ended," Zhuqa said. He came to Amber, laid his hand upon the baby's back—eclipsing it almost entirely—but his touch was gentle. "And so you see the man you're playing with. Dkorm."

"Sir."

"Find Xzem and bring her here. My child will want feeding."

"Yes, sir."

Zhuqa's gaze shifted to the lizardman behind Amber. "See to it that everyone understands that while Xzem has the care of my child, no one is to use her. I don't care if Sheul Himself appears and puts His burning hand on your dick, no one touches Xzem."

Iziz let go of Amber and walked away. No sooner had the door shut behind him than it opened again, readmitting Dkorm with a lizardlady crouching nervously behind him, a much larger baby clutched to her chest. She looked at Zhuqa, visibly quailed, and then looked at the infant Amber held and staggered in horror to her knees.

Zhuqa turned away from Amber and reached down to Xzem. He didn't help her up. He plucked the baby out of her arms and held it over her head as she clasped both hands to her snout and shivered. He looked at it while it cried and kicked, then at its mother. "Do you love this child?"

"Please, I beg you! Please!"

"I take it you do. Then here is what I have to say to you. Mark me closely. If mine dies, so does yours. If mine lives out the next year, you and yours will go free."

She reached up tentatively. Zhuqa held the crying infant higher. Xzem hesitated, then cringed around him and held out her empty hands to Amber.

The baby's tiny fists twisted in the blanket. She could feel its pulse hammering at her even through the leather. It was still damp from its birthing and beginning to tremble in the draft.

Zhuqa looked back at her and looked for a long time. “Give it over, Eshiqi,” he said. “Unless you can give it suck, give it up.”

She didn’t want to. That was a disturbing thought. It was Zhuqa’s baby, for Christ’s sake! The man who’d spent the whole day raping her, not once or twice, but the whole damned *day*! The man who’d hacked the arms and legs of the baby’s mother and then thrown her out into the plains! *That* man’s baby! That man’s *spawn*!

Its head moved, prodding shakily until it found the valley between her soft breasts and there it rested. After a second or two, its heaving sides began to slow with sleep. It began to make a breathy rr-rr-rring sound on its exhales. Not snoring. Purring, maybe. Almost singing.

Xzem, increasingly nervous, finally reached up and took the baby, hissing frantically at Amber’s split-second resistance. The baby woke at once, let out a surprisingly loud yowl, and clung with considerable strength as Xzem broke its grip one hand and one foot at a time. It did not settle in its new mother’s arms, but struggled on, its head blindly tossing and all four limbs reaching out.

Zhuqa turned to the raider who’d brought her. “Welcome to the next year of your life, Dkorm,” he said, dropping Xzem’s baby into his hands.

The raider’s spines drooped. “Thank you, sir,” he said sourly, eyeing the squirming thing he held.

“Xzem lives with you now. See to it she has a mat and a few cushions to sleep with.” Zhuqa tickled at the crying baby’s chin. “You’ll be sleeping in your cupboard, of course, with this little one. You might want a crate or something to keep it in. It’ll leak.”

The raider closed his eyes, heaved in a short sigh, and did his best to keep the acid out of his voice when he said, “Yes, sir.”

“A comfortable crate. Have you named her, Xzem?” Zhuqa asked.

Xzem shivered and did not answer. Her eyes were glassy and dull at the same time—terrified and already resigned to terror—eyes that had seen the worst outcome play out so many times, she no longer expected to see anything else.

“Apparently not. So. You name it, Dkorm.” Zhuqa straightened up and looked expectant.

The raider stared at him, then down at the baby he was still dangling out at arm’s reach.

“We’ll wait,” said Zhuqa, and folded his arms.

“Sir, I—” The raider squeezed his eyes shut again, briefly flaring out his mouth to show his teeth. Color was starting to come in at his throat. “Rosek.”

Zhuqa echoed this thoughtfully. “Pretty. You must have had a sister. Rosek, it is. Now. Xzem may hold Rosek while she feeds her. Otherwise, Xzem does not touch her and you do not touch Xzem. My child needs all of her attention.”

“Understood, sir.”

Zhuqa glanced at the struggling baby still hanging in the raider’s impersonal grip. His spines flattened and his stare went cold. “Play with the fucking thing, Dkorm. It’s a baby.”

“Yes, sir.” The raider hastily jostled Rosek into the crook of his arm.

“Come, Eshiqi. It is late. Your man is weary.”

They walked together and in silence all the way to his dark room. He held the door for her, shut it behind them. He put her back in the cupboard closest to the wall and joined her in the bed. He didn’t bother to undress.

Quiet. His breath came in faint puffs against her shoulder. They didn’t touch.

He said, softly, “It pleases me to see you so protective of my child.”

“You’re a sick, murdering bastard.”

“During the days, as you learn the proper ways to serve me as a loyal woman, I will allow you time with it.”

"I'm going to kill you."

"You have said that often enough that I think I can guess what it means, little one. You ought to remember that Zru'itak was a fierce little thing once, too."

She had no reply to that.

He grunted, then rolled away from her and went back to sleep.

6

Meoraq lost and found the raiders' trail several times, but before the sun reached its highest point behind the clouds, he came to what had plainly been their camp. The scorched earth of their fire and a few holes where their walls had been told him it had been a lengthy stay. Amber's wristlet, discarded in the grass, hinted at the reason.

'But it is just her wristlet,' he told himself brutally. 'Not her body. Stop wasting time staring at it. Find her.'

Meoraq searched. They'd taken his sleds, but had carried them, rather than pull them over the ground and leave wounds for another man to follow. Nevertheless, the small band that had taken his camp had met with a larger one here and all those feet marching together left a path even Gann's wind could not wholly erase. Seeing it gave Meoraq hope (a lie; the savage flare that briefly took him had too much murder in it to be called hope), but every trail runs in two directions: One led into the wooded hills toward the mountains; one, into the open wilds of Gedai.

He tried to pray, to see this camp with Sheul's eyes, but he could not find his stillness. Amber needed him. Amber had been lost to him all night. For every breath he took seeking peace in this place, she might be screaming hers.

It had to be the mountains, didn't it? Having passed the winter quite comfortably in a cave, it was all too easy to imagine another, perhaps a network of many caves, enough to house even a pack this size. In the mountains, there was shelter, game, and plenty of distance from any Sheulek who might be traveling through the holy land of the Prophet's birth. It must be the mountains.

Yet he hesitated. How easy it would be to stand here and think of all the reasons why the wildlands might provide a better den. Who was to say they even had a den? They had walls, they had sleds, they had many men. They might be purely nomadic, making trade at whatever city would take them in, never in one camp longer than one night. Maybe they had burrowed down in the mountains for the winter, but winter was over.

'If I'd left the first day she asked me,' Meoraq thought, but the rest of the words would not come, even in the shelter of his own mind. It made no difference now. Nothing mattered but two trails in the grass and which one he meant to follow.

He had no time to meditate. He chose. He set himself on the path that led to the mountains and did not realize his mistake until hours later, when the woods he ran through thinned enough to show him the high wall of the city.

By that time, the sun was low, the winds were strong, and the clouds had thickened with the certainty of rain. He had been running the last hour without any trail at all to follow, only the faith that this was where the trail had been aimed and if there was a den, there would be proof eventually. And so there was, not of their den, but only their trading post.

Exhausted as he was, he found it in him to let out another of those wordless bays of rage, but he didn't stop. He couldn't. A full day's run weighed on his body—breath was a sword in his side and he was so badly dehydrated that even his scream of a moment ago was only a scrape across his throat—but that biting thing he called hope was still alive in him and he used it to keep running just a little further.

Because if this was their trading post, there was a chance that those who traded with them had some rumor of where they might be found. A pale chance, thin and fragile as a single hair from Amber's head, but he clung to it.

The wood that surrounded the city had been allowed to grow close, leaving only the most minimal border bared for defensive vantage. There were no roads that Meoraq saw from his hurried approach, and the city itself was in shockingly poor repair. Years of damage by fire, erosion and violence had been sloppily patched if at all. He could actually see places where the roof had cracked wide open, the exposed interiors sealed off and left to sprout. Although the light was failing, there were no braziers burning, no lamps lit at the gate. Neither did he see watchmen on the wall or sentries on patrol outside. No one hailed him. He crossed the open wilds at a run with a naked sword in his hand, aimed at a gate where he could clearly see three men watching him, and not one of them cried challenge.

"Open to Uyane Meoraq!" he called, as soon as he was near enough to be heard. "I am a Sword and the Striding Foot of Sheul. Open and submit to my conquest!"

Spines that had been flared forward in casual greeting quivered and slapped flat. Watchmen shifted, eyeing one another and fingering at their own blades. No one answered him.

None of this should have been unexpected from a city that he knew to be at least occasionally in league with raiders, but in that first moment that he faced it, Meoraq's temper took him. He took the last few strides at a sprint and bashed the sole of his boot explosively into the gate. "Get this fucking thing open now!" he bellowed.

One of the watchman bolted down the tunnel, escaping the grasping hand of one of his fellows by the barest margin. "Get Myselo!" this man shouted, and spun to grab the third man by the halter. "Get Myselo before that idiot brings back Onahi, now!" As the other watchman ran, he held up his open hands in a deferential salute, trying to smile and bow at the same time. "We're fetching a key, honored one, just one minute now."

Meoraq kicked the gate again and paced like a hungry ghet, back and forth, glowering in futility through the doors. Indeed, it could have been within one minute that he heard returning feet in the echoing tunnel, but his temper, if anything, tore further. He began to feel flame at the back of his skull and forced himself to stand still, to take deep breaths, to be the man who could save his Amber.

It was a young man that came to admit him, scarcely out of his ascension, unscarred, wearing no House's colors and no great name's standard, just a simple gatekeeper's uniform. He took a set of keyplates from his belt, but drew the blade from his back with his strong hand and came no closer than two arms' reach.

"Open at once," ordered Meoraq. "I am Sheulek. I claim this city. Where am I?"

"Praxas," said the gatekeeper.

So. Meoraq bent and retrieved the wristlet from his boot, thrusting it between the bars for the gatekeeper to see. "This Praxas?" he demanded.

The gatekeeper studied the trinket and the metalsmith's mark without reaching for it. "I know the shop. Does that satisfy you?"

"Then Praxas is mine. Submit and open to Uyane Meoraq of Xeqor. Give me your oath!"

"It is Chasa Onahi before you, sir," the gatekeeper said calmly. "And if you are who you claim to be, you will understand why I will not open without proof."

Meoraq spat, but raised his fist and turned it so the sign of House Uyane and the mark of Xeqor showed on his wristlet.

"This could be stolen," Onahi said, although he did draw a book of names from his sleeve and hold it up for comparison.

"I can give my lineage back to the Prophet's Uyane himself," Meoraq said. "Send for the steward of Uyane to hear it."

"There is no Uyane in Praxas."

If he had been told there was no air in Praxas, he could not have been more astounded. For a moment, even Amber was cut from his mind. "Impossible," he said.

"All of the great Houses are closed here. Even the governor is of House Rsstha."

The name was a stranger's. After ten years in service, fifty-three cities, hundreds of trials...he'd never heard of such a House. "What does that mean?" he asked.

"I do not say there is any meaning to it," Onahi replied. "I say only that there is no one here to hear you, sir."

"Then summon your governor and let him send a champion. God will give my proof. I am Uyane Meoraq and I will have this city. Open the fucking gate or I'll kill you through it."

Onahi, undisturbed, folded away his script. "If you are Sheulek, sir, my life is yours to take. However, the law of my caste allows me to pray." His eyes narrowed. "Perhaps you will pray with me?"

Meoraq struck the lock-plate with the side of his fist, then folded his arms and said, "Have you any particular prayer in mind?"

"The prayer of Eshiqi."

Meoraq's spines twitched, caught midway between amusement and offense. "That's a woman's prayer."

Onahi merely waited.

"Hear me, O Sheul, most loving Father, by whose eternal light we are all raised out of darkness. Breathe into me, for Your breath is life. Lay Your hand over me, for within Your open hands are found all shelter. Look down, O Father, and see me, for I am blessed in Your sight. Lo, You are the master at my husband's forge and I rejoice. Lo, You are the lamp my husband raises over me and I exalt in Your light. Lo, Yours is the hand that shapes all clay—"

"That will do." Onahi unlocked the gate and stood aside, saluting. "Praxas is yours, honored one."

'Be merciful,' was the customary way to end this exchange, but the gatekeeper, so meticulous in every other respect, did not say it. And by the look in his steady eye, the omission was deliberate. Another time, this would have been curious. Today, Meoraq had time for only one investigation.

"You will tell me everything you know of the raiders who trade with this city," he said.

"Raiders?" the other watchman echoed, attempting alarm.

"I am not permitted dealings with them," Onahi replied calmly. "I would guess that they were here four days ago, because I was then held from my usual shift."

"No one held you! Honored one, no one held him! They were changing mats in the barracks, is all! Hands were needed!"

"Suspicious work for a man out of his ascension," said Meoraq.

"There aren't enough boys!"

"Truth, so far as that goes." Onahi gestured in a general way at the city enclosing them. "Praxas had scarcely five thousand souls at last census, with perhaps three hundred under the sign of the Blade."

"That answers why I saw no one on your wall, why I met no sentries on patrol."

For the first time, Onahi's mask of cool civility slipped to show the real fury beneath. "*My* watchmen stand their posts. *My* sentries make their patrols."

"And where are they today?"

"Turning sheets," said Onahi, with only the slimmest trace of a hiss, "on all the new mats in the barracks."

This was not the man he wanted, Meoraq decided. He was too honest. Meoraq turned away from the gatekeeper and studied the watchman instead. He looked nervous. That was only to be expected under a Sheulek's hard stare, but what betrayed the man's anxiety the most were his eyes, in which the pupils had contracted to mere points.

It wasn't only nerves that did that.

"Show me your hands," he said.

The watchman blinked rapidly, his flat spines twitching in confusion. Hesitantly, he raised his fist in salute.

Meoraq caught the man's wrist, pried open his hand and examined the discoloration on the thin scales between his fingers. Fresh burns. And the thicker, misshapen scales where old burns had healed.

"Open your mouth," ordered Meoraq.

The watchman glanced back down the tunnel, where running boots could finally be heard, but if it was rescue, he knew it wasn't going to reach him in time. He cracked his mouth open, trying not to breathe.

His teeth were still good, if yellowed. Meoraq worked his hand in and forced the jaws open, waiting until the man's need for air gave him that first bitter exhale and the stink of phesok.

"So." Meoraq drew his samr.

"Sir, I don't know them! I swear I don't!"

"Not another word!" boomed a voice in the tunnel. "I'm the warden here and if you want to deal with that sniveling son of a slave, you'll deal with Myselo first!"

"He's Sheulek," said Onahi without emotion. "He holds Praxas in his shadow."

"Piss if he is! Piss if he does!" Myselo came into the light—a great belly of a man bulging out of suspiciously fine clothes for a warden's modest wages—and pulled a samr of his own. "Sheulek comes through mid-summer and this looks nothing like him!"

"It is Uyane Meoraq of Xeqor before you, a Sword and a true son of Sheul," said Meoraq coldly. "And it is Uyane Meoraq who will be cutting the head from your neck if you don't cover your blade."

And, by God and Gann, even here:

"Uyane of...?" Warden Myselo's spines flared as far as they were able. "Are you...any kin to...to Rasozul?"

"His son," said Meoraq, trying not to hiss.

Myselo's sword lowered. He looked at it in some alarm, as if it had only just now materialized in his hand. His spines flared again. He sheathed quickly and wiped both hands on his broad belly. "Eh...We're honored to welcome—You honor us, sir. I'll see you to, eh, to the governor's House to host you, if it please—"

"Who stood as warden to these gates four days ago?"

Myselo glanced at the watchman, who had pressed himself to the tunnel wall in an attempt to disappear within it, then at Onahi, and finally down at the sword still drawn and ready in Meoraq's hand. His spines lowered and shoulders fell. "I have the keeping of every gate in this city when its keeper is otherwise occupied, sir."

"Then you admitted the raiders who brought their phesok to trade."

"Admitted? No! No, most honored one, no. They weren't raiders as the word be reckoned. Exiles, I must acknowledge, but does not the Word say, eh...as every man has a need for air...no, wait...does not every man that breathes claim the right to air?"

"Book of Admonitions, verse thirty-five," Meoraq hissed. "Lo, a man's need for air is not a promise of breath, for every life may be cut that goes against the law of God."

Myselo struggled to take that in, then gave up. "It is not in me to see a man suffer!" he declared. "They come to trade, sir. Not phesok, I say, but only good game and hides, which this poor city has sore need of. Rsstha and his slit-licking merchants—"

"Then you admit you grow the phesok yourself?"

"I don't know what grows in the governor's fields, sir," said the warden after a moment's hard thought. "Nor what comes through the other gates when I'm away. I am just one man."

"A man who trades with raiders. If you deny that's what they are just once more, I'll split your lying mouth," he said as the warden began to speak. "They came to my camp last night. They took...everything...and I have spent this entire day chasing their trail in the wrong fucking direction. Now I will have lost it. So let me make this easy for you." Meoraq stepped forward and seized the warden by the folds of his throat, thrusting the point of his sword under Myselo's chin. "Tell me where they went."

"Sir, I don't know—"

"Do you wish to pray?" Meoraq interrupted. "If I can't have them, I'll have you, mark me. Tell me where they are or make your last prayer."

"I don't know!" the warden bayed. "They come and go! I don't know them! I don't—"

Meoraq gave the throat in his grip a calculated cut. It was hardly a mortal wound, but it bled. He was forced to deliver two restrained blows with the hilt of his sword to stop the warden's struggles, and then had to wait while his senses came back into order. At some point during this process, he was annoyed to discover that the watchman had fled. Onahi remained, and as the warden recovered himself, Meoraq spared the gatekeeper an assessing stare.

Onahi raised his fist, neither hurriedly nor fearfully. "I would tell you if I knew," he said without waiting for the question. "But I am certain someone here does know. Three days before the barracks 'changed out their mats,' trials were held for certain officers with accusations to make against their daughters. They have been awaiting exile in a holding cell beside this gate, but now they are gone."

Meoraq grunted and pulled the stirring warden in his grip onto his feet. "How do you contact them?"

There were no more denials, no excuses. Clutching his neck as if he were all that held it together, Warden Myselo whispered. "We send...the boy."

"Who?"

"Just some barracks-bastard. They took him...years ago. They take all the sprats they can find...when they raid...but this one, they brought back."

"I know him," said Onahi, already moving.

"He's the only one who knows..." The warden's rolling eye caught sight of his blood on the floor and his words broke. "Don't...Don't kill me, sir. I am...weak. Allow me the mercy to earn Sheul's forgiveness, for I sense I can be forgiven, sir, I do."

Meoraq spat and shoved him away. The warden fell into the wall and let it take him to the floor, babbling thanks and praise.

Ignoring him, Meoraq paced. It could not have been long before Onahi's return, although it felt endless enough with Warden Myselo moaning in his ears.

The boy that eventually came with Onahi into the light was older than he'd anticipated. He had a man's height, but was scrawny as a woman—as a girl—with a hunched, loping way of moving. He bowed when he saw Meoraq, raising not one but both fists in salute and peering through them at Myselo on the floor with a curious sort of frown.

"Do you know what I want of you?" Meoraq asked gruffly.

"To find Zhuqa's camp," said the boy.

"Zhuqa?"

"Their leader. He lets me pass to carry their messages. Before me, it was another boy." He looked up at Meoraq. "Are you going to kill me?"

Spoken without fear, only a very mild interest. It was not courage, not even of that foolhardy kind that came so naturally to boys his age.

"Not without cause," said Meoraq.

"Isn't it cause enough to have dealings with exiles?" asked the boy reasonably. "Sometimes they give me a few points for the message. Isn't that trade?"

"Words are not considered commerce by law and I would not judge it unforgivable to accept a gift of coin, no matter the source." Meoraq gestured impatiently at the gate.

"I've taken their drink sometimes too," said the boy. "When they offer a swallow. That's against the Word, isn't it? Strong drink?"

"*I don't care*!" Meoraq exploded. "I want what they took from me, Gann damn you! I forgive you all your past! All of it! I don't care if you rubbed your cock on the Prophet's burnt bones, take me to their fucking nest!"

"Now?"

"Now!"

"I'll ready supplies," said Onahi and left them.

Meoraq opened his mouth to shout after him, but forced himself to close it again. He needed supplies. He needed water, if nothing else. He could not save Amber if he collapsed in the wildlands and ended there.

"It's only an hour until dark," said the boy, watching as he began to pace again.

"We'll run through the night."

"Do I look like I can run through the night?" the boy asked, amused. "I couldn't run all the way down that tunnel. Hit me all you like," he added as Meoraq swung back his arm to do just that. "I'm not a runner and you can't make me one by beating on me. It's three days to travel. Four with weather."

Meoraq lowered his arm. It hurt. He turned his back on the boy with effort and began again to pace. Six breaths, he told himself. Six breaths, deep and slow. Six breaths, and think of Amber.

Amber.

* * *

She dreamed of Meoraq and the mountains, so that when she woke, the arm around her waist and the breath on the back of her neck felt safe and right and welcome. She had to wake up a little more before the bed she lay on had any meaning for her. It wasn't until then that it all came back.

She must have tensed. Perhaps she made some sound. She did something, anyway, because Zhuqa's sleep broke at once. He lifted his head, listening as she lay motionless, then grunted and pushed the cupboard door open.

"Hold still," he said, climbing out into the room. In another moment, he had a light struck and two lamps burning. He glanced her way, saw her staring back at him, and smiled. "Have you a kind word for your man this morning?"

Amber opened her mouth, closed it, took a few breaths (*six breaths just like meoraq always says six breaths and calm down*), then said simply, "Hi."

"No. Say, 'I see my man, my Zhuqa, first. I pray, let him see me.'"

"All that, huh?"

"Say it, Eshiqi. Use my words. Say it as best you can." Now he looked at her, just the shine from one eye. "To please me."

She tried. He did not correct her, although she knew she couldn't have possibly hit all the right tones and that every pause as she fought to fit her mouth around his stupid words changed its whole nuance. He let her wrestle it all out, and only after she was done did he look at her again.

He smiled. "I see you."

"I'm thrilled."

"Now come," he said, beckoning. "Do you remember how to show your man a proper respect?"

Amber got out of the cupboard. She went to him, fighting to keep her face a safe blank and hold all the hate on the inside where it couldn't kill her, but still, when the time came to kneel in front of him, she slapped the back of her open hand on the ground next to his bare foot and let that flat, brittle sound be her 'good morning.'

Zhuqa's smile became a tolerant laugh. He patted her on the head and moved away to put his boots on. "I'm going to leave you now. Just for a short while. I hope you are not tempted to do anything foolish while I'm away. I would hate to lose you so early in this game."

"Yeah, yeah." Amber got up off her knees and went back to sit in the cupboard.

Zhuqa grunted, shrugged into his harness and strolled over to the door. He looked at it, at her. He waited, buckling buckles, smiling.

"Oh, you son of a whore." Amber heaved herself up again and opened the door that kept her his prisoner. "I really, really hate you."

He nuzzled at her stiff neck before he went out. She shut the door...but she didn't slam it and she made sure she wouldn't catch him on the ass. She couldn't bring herself to be good, but she wasn't dumb enough to be as bitchy as it was in her to be.

She waited in the cupboard, for no other reason than because she was naked and it had blankets. She didn't know how long he was gone. Ten minutes or an hour felt like the same empty, elastic time. She tried to think of Meoraq, but it was hard to visualize him without seeing how big the world was. He was looking, she knew he was looking, but he'd been looking for Scott and Nicci and the others too. And never found them.

The door opened. Zhuqa let himself in. He did not have the breakfast with him that she'd hoped for, although he popped the last bite of something into his mouth as he entered. He caught the look on her face as he chewed, or perhaps he heard the sullen rumble of her stomach. His spines flicked forward. "Hungry?"

She looked away.

His smile broadened just slightly. "Not hungry enough, I see. Come here, Eshiqi. I have something for you."

"I'll bet," she muttered, but she went.

And it wasn't what she'd thought. The bundle of something half-glimpsed in the crook of his arm turned out to be a woven garment, shapeless as a hospital-gown, stained so often and by so many substances that it was impossible to tell just what its original color had been.

Amber took it, shook it out, turned it over in her hands. She could count her fingers through the threadbare fabric and when she rubbed a fold, her skin pinked up like she'd taken a scouring pad to it.

She couldn't help herself.

"Good enough," she said, speaking lizardish with extreme difficulty, "for Zhuqa's woman?"

His spines shrugged, amused. "At least I mean to dress you."

"In crap," she agreed, switching back to English. "And I happen to know you have plenty of good clothes, you thieving bastard."

"My Eshiqi isn't happy," mused Zhuqa, leaning back to study her. After some thought, he rolled the shift back into a bundle and tossed it aside.

And then he just stood there.

It took a long time, fighting not to squirm under that stare, not to anticipate too obviously the blow that he never threw, before she suddenly got it.

And he knew she got it, because no sooner had the thought hit her brain then his eyes narrowed and his chin raised. So there was no point in faking ignorance, only the question of whether or not she'd rather go naked.

And no, she'd really rather not.

So, biting down on all the dangerous things she wanted to say, Amber knelt and smacked the back of her hand onto the floor again.

"That was cute the first time you did it," Zhuqa remarked far above her. "Now do it right."

She took her hand back, calmed herself with a few deep breaths, and quietly bent to lay it palm-up beside his boot.

"Very good." Zhuqa tapped the top of her head and moved away to the cupboard. He opened a compartment above it, rummaged through its contents, then tossed her a new bundle.

She put it on—a simple pullover in a pale beige color that hung to her knees. It smelled musty, unused, but she could already see that it was nicer than the first one.

"I'll see if I can find better for you once the trade wagons start moving," said Zhuqa, watching her. "But for now, you are pleased."

It wasn't a question as much as a warning. Amber smoothed down the wrinkled front of her new shift and nodded. The gesture couldn't have meant much to him, but he accepted it.

"So today, you will make every effort to please me further," he said, crossing back to open the door. "I am going to take you to the workpit, where you will learn to keep my House. How say you?"

"Yippee."

He grunted and beckoned for her to follow him out into the hall.

She went.

The guards were positioned on the landings already, or maybe they were always there. Other men walked in the halls and passed them on the stair, more and more as they climbed toward the surface. Her clumsy estimate of their numbers kept stretching and stretching, until the word 'dozens' just wasn't enough.

There were a hundred men here. There might even be two. Like roaches, the ones she saw were only indicators of the ones that scurried around in the greater darkness. They might as well be infinite.

Meoraq was coming. And for the first time, that thought brought horror, because he couldn't possibly be prepared to find something like this, let alone fight it.

Zhuqa turned her aside while they were still two flights from the surface, leading her down a wide corridor past several sets of curious, disgusted, and fascinated eyes. Raiders were in constant movement here, hauling crates, waterskins and packs, while others just seemed to be lounging around, but all came to attention for Zhuqa and showed him their fists. He tapped a few, ignored most, and brought Amber without comment to a closed door at the far end of the hall.

"Do you know where you are?" he asked, bringing out his keys.

Startled, Amber looked back, wondering why he thought she should, and suddenly realized they were in what he'd called his slave quarters. They'd walked right past the door where Zru'itak had given birth.

"Do you know where you are?" he asked again, now with his hand on the open door and staring her down. He wasn't smiling. He wanted her to know this door before she walked through it. He wanted her to think about where she was while she waited for him and wondered if she was ever coming back out.

Amber knew she was a bitch a lot more often than was smart, but that didn't make her stupid. Where was she? Speaking lizardish, looking him straight in the eye, she said, "Zhuqa's House."

It wasn't the response he expected (and judging from the twitching of his spines, it took him a second or two to work it out), but it was definitely the right one. He smiled and reached out to stroke the back of his hand across her brow. Meoraq's touch. It was nauseating, but Amber would not allow herself to wipe this one away.

He opened the door on a huge room, maybe even several rooms, all connected. The stink was immediate: unwashed bodies and the green reek of compost. It was hot—she could see a huge fire burning in another room—but not stuffy. There were fans in the ceiling, big ones, locked away behind metal bars that either drew up the heated air and carried it away or blew cooler air down at them. It gave her a hell of a jolt to see that and to realize that, just like all the other ruins she'd seen, some parts of this one were still working. That maybe Zhuqa was even fixing it up. The metal bars that kept desperate slaves from trying to crawl out through the air ducts weren't that old.

Amber saw the fire and the fans because they were moving. The lizardladies that huddled around the walls, shelves and tables that cluttered these rooms were not. Her eye had taken them in only peripherally as lumps of laundry or stacked sacks right up until Zhuqa waved at them and they went back to work.

Now Amber flinched. Zhuqa gripped her shoulder, then patted it. "Easy, Eshiqi. Go on, then. You have work to do and so do I."

And with that, he left her there.

Amber waited for a few seconds, but the frenetic hush of all this work made it impossible to just stand there. She began to walk around, randomly at first, glancing back at the door every few steps, and then with more of an eye for what she was seeing.

None of it was work she knew how to do. After spending the whole winter in a cave doing one menial thing after another, that surprised her. Amber could put a pretty good cure on a hide, render fat into soap, draw sinews and turn them into strong cord, and countless other useful things, but she didn't know what half these women were doing.

Most of it was plant-related. Not cooking—that, at least, Amber could do—but other stuff. The plants in question were long, bulbous roots terminating in two wide, rubbery leaves with serrated edges as sharp as knives. Lizardladies with wrapped hands stripped these dangerous looking leaves; others split the stalks, pried them open, and scraped out the whitish meat; this was pounded into a flat, fibrous substance, which was in turn briskly combed out into fluff. Huge rough-woven bags of this fluff were positioned throughout the room, and when one got too full, someone took it into one of the adjoining chambers where more lizardladies and half a dozen pale-scaled children hip-high or smaller spun it into thick thread using nothing more than hooked sticks and spools. From there, the thread went on to be made into rope, cloth or who knew what in one of the other rooms.

It was a lot of work and should have made a lot of noise. Amber had worked line jobs of some kind or another all her adult life, and the eerie silence with which all these people went about their various tasks put an honest-to-God chill in her spine. She found herself thinking of Zru'itak's tongueless mouth more and more as she studied the faces around her, all of whom pointedly refused to study her in return. Only the children were at all animated—whispering and coughing quiet laughter, throwing fluff or spools at each other if they thought no one was looking, staring at Amber even as their little hands kept busy, and scuttling away if she got close enough for their courage to fail.

When Amber finally made her way back into the first room, Zhuqa was back, with a line of shivering, naked, dull-eyed lizardladies. His newest acquisitions. Standing beside them was another raider, a big one. Easily a head taller than even Zhuqa and built as solid as a coffin, with stocky limbs that bulged with so much muscle, he surpassed mere strength and seemed grotesque. He was missing two fingers on one hand, as well as an eye and most of the knobby ridges that should be above it. Several of his spines were either broken short or missing entirely and his snout had a wedge-shaped hole through it that looked like it had been on the wrong end of an axe years ago.

Zhuqa and the stranger exchanged a few low words as they looked over the women, then Zhuqa paused, noticing Amber's stare. He gave the broad, scarred chest a slap and said, "This is Hruuzk, my slave-master."

Hruuzk looked startled, then perplexed. He scanned the room as what remained of his spines flexed. "Who are you talking to?"

"Eshiqi. Come here and give your man a greeting."

Unsure how demonstrative he wanted her to be, she obeyed. Hruuzk grunted as he watched her ease up against Zhuqa's side. His gaze held nothing but the purest academic interest. "I heard about that. What is it?"

"Something new."

"Nothing new in Gann's land," the slave-master said. A philosopher. He bent his head in a distracted, deferential manner and held up his mutilated hand, scarred palm to heaven. When Zhuqa grunted approval, Hruuzk reached out and rubbed some of Amber's hair between his two remaining fingers. "Can you fuck it?"

"Yes. Shift your skirts, Eshiqi."

She looked at him, alarmed.

He brushed the back of his hand along her cheek, then gripped her chin and lightly squeezed. "You are Zhuqa's woman, never fear. Now shift your skirts."

As comfort went, it was a cold puddle of piss indeed, but it wasn't like she had any real choice. She lifted her dress up to her waist, shifting uneasily as Hruuzk hunkered down to get a better look at her pubis. He grunted, then raised his hand and gave Zhuqa a second inquiring nod.

Zhuqa's approval was a long time coming, but it came. "Hold still, Eshiqi."

But she couldn't, quite. Hruuzk's hand was huge and abrasive, repulsive in every touch no matter how impartially he prodded at her. She shuddered, twisting the fabric of her shift to keep from slapping him away, and shut her eyes as he wedged one thick finger inside her.

"She's open," Hruuzk said, amused.

"I'm beginning to think she's always open."

"Oh, that's a seller, if it's true."

"Isn't it."

Hruuzk got his finger up as deep as it would go, rubbing at her in a clinical fashion, then withdrew to clasp both hands between his bulging thighs and study her some more. "If you ever decide to sell that, I want it," he said at last.

"Vek has my promise of first refusal. She took his hand off."

"So I heard, but there's good coin in this thing. Let me have it for one year," he said, rising to his feet again. "Vek can have it back in just this condition and if I pour less than fifty thousand strips in your hand, you can have my other eye. Not points. Not rounds. Strips."

"Take it up with Vek, but for now, she's mine. Put your clothes right, Eshiqi."

Hruuzk grunted and shifted his gaze to the other lizardladies, the matter closed to him. While Amber adjusted her clothes, he moved out to get a better look, catching at their heads to examine their teeth or eyes, turning them around to pass a hand down their spines, and stopping at every one of them to pry their slits open and test at their insides.

"Weak batch," was his ultimate judgment. "Were you told these were virgins?"

"No," said Zhuqa, flexing his spines in a careless, shrugging gesture. "But they must be fresher than the ones we have, surely."

"Those two," he said, pointing, "are the pick of the lot. Virgin, or close enough, since I guess you let your runners go at them. If you put them up for bidding, they might go for as much as two hundred rounds each, maybe more. But with respect, sir, if you want me to stable them under you, I'll only send you back a quarter of their coin until I see for myself that they don't come with cargo." He gave the slave nearest him a pat on the belly. "They don't turn a dip this pretty out of Praxas on a whim."

"A point, but I'm bidding them all out. If there's cargo, it'll fall in the hands of the man who buys the cart."

"Please yourself." The slave-master turned his good eye back on the ladies. "This one's not as fresh, but she might go for as much as a hundred rounds. Slant-Eyes is the tightest of the lot, but she has a good case of the twist coming on—"

"Yes, I saw that on the run."

"—and Black-Stripe's mouth isn't right. Could just be bad feeding, coming from Praxas." Hruuzk shrugged again. "But I think it's the juun."

"Piss," said Zhuqa disgustedly, his spines going flat.

"Won't hurt for fucking."

"I am not selling a dip with the juun to my men." Zhuqa thought about it, stroking at his throat, where faint streaks of yellow were beginning to show. They faded while he pondered the matter, and at last he said, "Catch her up with Shu'ir and Ila, see if Ghelip wants to buy them. I don't mind cheating him."

"He might not be feeling very receptive. You know we killed three of his patrollers while you were gone."

"Throw Salahkthu in with them and call it an apology."

Hruuzk snorted laughter. "Done. The rest of them ought to go straight to the stables in my opinion, and if I see fifty points by year's end for the lot of them, I'll pay you back in rounds. They're worn loose already and two of them have been cut."

"The piss you say!" The color flared in Zhuqa's throat. "By my men?"

"No, they're good and scarred. Probably done when they were hip-high, so they could take an early poke. Bunch of perverts in Praxas," the slave-master remarked, his gaze once more straying to Amber. "But you may as well keep them because, as you say, they're fresher than the ones we have, and besides, we lost some while you were away."

"So I heard," Zhuqa said coolly.

The slave-master spread his huge hands. "What would you have me do, stand over them and help push?"

"It's a very simple thing, Hruuzk. If a man can't be trusted not to break the toy, he doesn't get to play with it. If you have to kill a few men to make that lesson clear, do it. I can always get more men. The dips are hard to come by. So." Zhuqa looked the new slaves over one last time. "Gather those three...no, those four and show them around to whoever's got coin to spend. How soon can you have them ready for the block?"

"How ready do you want them to be?"

"They'd ought to know their way around the workpit." Zhuqa glanced over at Amber. "My Eshiqi needs to know how to care for her man's House."

"Ah, you're doing this again," the slave-master remarked with a small smile. "All right. I'll start it on lamps for now. Does it talk?"

"Not much, but she understands you." Zhuqa pinched Amber's jaw again and put his face very close to hers. "And she's going to behave."

Hruuzk grunted and gestured for Amber to stand beside him, watching with undisguised amusement as she obeyed. "Ugly little thing, but I did like the grip of that cunt. How would you feel if I took a dip?"

"Murderous," Zhuqa replied mildly.

"All right," he said again, in much the same easy-going way. "Yllgami, come get the rest of the cattle and put them to work. Not you, Gold-Eyes. Stay right here and wait for me. We're going to take a walk. Come, Eshiqi." His huge hand dropped comfortably over her shoulder as he took her into the next room. "Let's get you started."

7

Amber's first jobs were plainly tests of her ability to understand and obey Hruuzk's orders: she wiped down tables, bagged fluff, hauled water around to each of the work stations, swept without a broom, washed without a sink, and did it all without a word. When Hruuzk was satisfied, he put her to work cutting lamp wicks and left her there while he took one of the slaves out on her 'walk'. Even this simple task was trickier than it seemed. They didn't have scissors, or maybe just didn't trust slaves with them. Amber had to feed the rope through a blocky guillotine-like device and smack a spring-loaded lever to make the cut. She'd worked a lot of monotonous factory jobs; she soon had the fiddly business of feed/measure/cut/pull/feed down to a comfortable routine.

When Hruuzk returned from showing 'Gold-Eyes' around to potential buyers, her table was piled high with dry wicks and he made her stop and soak them. While he took 'Shivers' out on her walk, Amber swished wicks around in a jar of xuseth oil, then hung them up on rods to dry. The oil ran down her arms each time she reached up to hang more wicks and soon the front of her shift was soaked and clinging to her like a second skin, exposing every line and shadow of the body beneath. Hruuzk's interest when he came back to drop off 'Shivers' and pick up 'Crook-Toe' was evident, but he kept his hands to himself.

"Good girl," he said, patting her head after she'd hung up the last wick and put the xuseth oil away. "Unless I tell you different, you start each day with wicks. This camp runs through about two, three hundred a day and they have to be fresh. You seem to be quick enough with those freakish little hands...you can make lamps."

Back he went to the door, to bellow at someone outside to bring him two blocks of clay. He waited, watching Amber clear off her table and fiddling absentmindedly with any slave who caught his eye, and soon after, a knock on the door heralded the arrival of the clay. Hruuzk inspected it as intently as any slave, judged it acceptable, and thumped both blocks down on the table in front of Amber.

A lamp began with a clay-snake, just like the kind she'd once made in state-care art class out of colored dough. The snake was coiled into a fat, shallow bowl with a bit of a lip for a mouth. Smooth down the sides, pinch the lip tight at one end to hold the wick (but not all the way closed), set it on a tray to be fired, and that was a lamp.

"Use it all," Hruuzk ordered, patting her on the head again. "Do a good job and I'll tell Zhuqa what a hard-working woman he has."

"Fuck you and him," Amber muttered, concentrating on smoothing her lamp without thinning out the side.

"Good girl. Crook-Toe, let's go."

So the next time she heard the door unlock, she thought it was Hruuzk again. She'd only made four lamps and she was a little relieved when it opened on the raider Dkorm instead, along with Xzem and two crying babies.

Dkorm looked around the workpit with an expression of profound disgust, kicked an empty bag out of his way, and stomped over to sit on a crate. The children who had been squabbling and playing through their work all morning withdrew very quietly to another room. The lizardladies bent their necks and focused even harder on whatever task was at hand. Dkorm pulled a heavy-looking sack of something over, punched it down in the middle, and put Rosek in the depression. She tried to climb out at once. He slapped her and thumped her down harder. Xzem flinched at the sound of the blow, but only bent her head at her child's howl of pain.

"Fucking sprat. Shut up and lie there. Xzem, I swear before God and Gann, if you don't quiet your little dip—"

"She's hungry," Xzem whispered.

"Then feed it! Do I have to tell you to do everything?"

Xzem crept over, hesitated, and held out the baby.

Dkorm folded his arms. "I don't want it. Put it down. Anywhere," he added as Xzem looked helplessly around. "Just put it—*shut the fuck up*!" he roared suddenly and Rosek, who had in fact been winding down now that her mother was beside her, went right back into screams.

Amber gave her lamp a vicious finishing pinch and stalked over to take Zhuqa's baby. It turned toward her at once, its small cries quieting. Xzem snatched up Rosek and retreated. Dkorm leaned back and laughed at both of them.

"Prick!" spat Amber, taking it with her to her table.

Dkorm laughed again, but in a puzzled way. "*What* was that?"

She remembered suddenly and with a sharp pang that 'prick' was also a dumaqi word and that she'd just called him a hingepin or something. It brought Meoraq right back to the surface of her thoughts, made her feel taken all over again.

Amber looked down at Zhuqa's baby and watched its tiny hand flail and punch until she gave it a finger to latch onto. Its grip was surprisingly strong. It squeezed once and then towed her finger up under its chin. It bit her, gumming harmlessly at her fingertip while she watched, transfixed by the working of its jaws, the minutia of its tiny fingers wrapping her giant one, the impossible detail of each individual scale. It was hypnotizing her and she wanted to be hypnotized, wanted to forget where she was and why and how long she was likely to stay because rescue was coming, sure it was, but it wasn't here yet.

"It'll piss all over you," Dkorm warned, watching her wrap the baby in the loose folds of her oversized shift.

She ignored him. The baby was singing, its chirring breaths gradually lengthening to fall into rhythm with the rise and fall of her breasts. It relaxed, arms and legs falling slowly open like a bud in the sunshine. Basking in her. Not her warmth or her scent or the sound of her voice. In *her*.

She lost herself in it. She never heard the door open, never knew anyone was behind her until she felt the weight of his hand on her shoulder.

Amber stiffened, her own hand cupping protectively over the baby's hot, wrinkled back, but that was all she did. She didn't try to shrug off Zhuqa's touch. And it was Zhuqa. She only had to look as far as the lizardladies bending their necks or Dkorm standing at attention next to Xzem to know who was behind her now.

The hand gave her a pat, then took itself away. Zhuqa stepped out from behind her and walked around the table, moving toward Xzem, whose breath quickened but who did not quite dare to cover her baby in the huddle of her own body. She crouched, rigid and in anguish, as Zhuqa peeled back Rosek's wrap and watched her nurse.

The silence was a hammer on Amber's ears. She could hear every wet sound as the baby sucked at her finger, every happy grumble and purr as it nestled close.

"Am I making you nervous?" Zhuqa asked mildly, still gazing at Xzem's baby.

"Isn't that what you're going for?" Amber countered.

"Not you, Eshiqi." Zhuqa's eyes shifted, shining lazily back at Dkorm. "Am I making you nervous, Dkorm?"

"No, sir."

"No?"

Dkorm fidgeted, checked himself, tried to stand taller. "I don't expect to see you in the workpit, is all."

"Ah." Zhuqa returned his easy stare to Rosek. "I thought you might be nervous."

"No, sir."

"It would not be an unreasonable feeling."

"Sir?"

"Particularly since the task of caring for whichever little sprat is not biting at Xzem's ample teat is supposed to be yours."

"Yes, sir."

"Yes?" Zhuqa allowed himself the posture of very mild surprise. "Then this was understood?"

"Yes, sir. Very well."

"*Very* well," Zhuqa mused. "So then. I confess to some confusion."

"Eshiqi wanted to hold it."

"Ah." Zhuqa reached down to stroke the nursing baby's cheek, and while he did this, Xzem did not breathe at all. "As it happens, I like to see Eshiqi hold it, but I believe my last word on the matter was that Eshiqi could see the baby, Dkorm." He straightened up and turned around. "*See* it. Not hold it."

Dkorm was frowning, flustered. "My apologies, sir."

"Well, yes." Zhuqa indulged himself in a small chuckle. "Apologies would certainly appear to be in order. You are passing my first-born around, Dkorm."

"I am very sorry, sir."

"To a slave, actually." Zhuqa began to walk back around the table.

Dkorm did not back away, but was quick to say, "Sir, I wouldn't have done it if it were not Eshiqi."

Zhuqa glanced back to rest his eyes on Amber and the baby in her arms. His spines were forward, relaxed. The scales at his throat remained black. "She does seem rather fond of it."

"Yes, sir."

"I confess to being fond of it myself," said Zhuqa. "Have I made any secret of that?"

"No, sir."

"No. I do not consider myself a sentimental man, but that is, as far as I know, my only living child. Do you have children, Dkorm?"

"I...I don't know, sir."

"Truth?"

"Sir."

"That is a howling shame. A man's legacy is in his loins. Once the soul is pissed out and the body goes to rot, there is nothing left in this life that endures, not the coin of his hoarding or the good word of his friends or any damned thing at all, save the name he has left to his children."

"I...Yes, sir."

"Look there—" Zhuqa dropped his arm around Dkorm's shoulders and gestured at the sleeping infant in Amber's arms. "—and you look upon my eternity."

"Yes, sir."

"Nestled in the arms of an unbroken slave."

Dkorm hesitated, but there was no safe answer and not a lot of give to the truth. "Yes, sir."

"Did you ever stop to think such a slave could, in a moment of defiance—" His fingers drummed once on Dkorm's shoulders. "—dash its helpless little brains out just to strike a scar on me?"

Amber's arms tightened on the baby.

Zhuqa waited, then looked down at Dkorm. "Did you?" he prompted.

"No, sir."

"Not even once?"

"No, sir."

"You disappoint me, Dkorm." Zhuqa studied the man standing rigid under his relaxed arm, then gave him another pat and stepped away. "I accept your apology. Let Eshiqi hold the baby if it makes her happy."

"Yes, sir," said Dkorm, only a little shakily.

Zhuqa came to the table and hunkered comfortably before Amber. He cocked his head, listening to the breathy rumble of its sleeping purrs. At length, he raised a hand to stroke at the side of its blunt snout, which caused it to curl up at once, mewing indignantly and turning into the swell of Amber's breast. Zhuqa grunted, his spines fanned all the way forward. He looked at Amber. "You could hurt me very easily if you chose to kill it," he said quietly. "But not so deeply or so well, I think, as I could hurt you by doing the very same thing."

He glanced back down to watch her arms tighten into a protective shell around the baby, then grunted, pleased, and rose to his feet. "Xzem, take it."

Xzem bent her head, then placed her squirming, complaining child in Dkorm's hands and came to take the infant from Amber's equally reluctant grip. The baby's mews, ignored, became howls. It fought the teat Xzem offered, twisting its head violently side to side and straining with all its fragile might to find its way back to Amber.

"Now, Dkorm, let me make my next order very clear to you: Nobody touches Rosek except you and Xzem...and Eshiqi, I suppose. If she wants to. Nobody else."

"Yes, sir."

"Xzem is to hold my child every moment that her own is not sucking at her."

"Yes, sir."

"During those times, Eshiqi can hold it. If she doesn't want it, you hold it. If anyone else touches either child—look at me, Dkorm—if God Himself lays on His benevolent hands in blessing, I will devote the next six days to killing you."

"Yes, sir," said Dkorm. His posture was exemplary. His hands on Xzem's wailing baby did not shake.

"Do you believe I can make it last six days?" Zhuqa inquired, chucking at Rosek's chin. She did not stop crying, but did give him a wet-eyed incredulous look.

"Yes, sir."

Zhuqa rubbed Rosek's small snout and smiled up at Dkorm. "I should have a certain reputation for honesty in this camp. I've worked hard to cultivate it."

"Yes, sir," said Dkorm after a puzzled moment, since Zhuqa seemed to be waiting.

"So I know that I am understood when I tell you that sitting in the workpit with slaves may not be how you want to pass your days, but it is a sign of my trust and my high regard. It is, in fact, an honor and I want to know that it is appreciated."

"It is, sir."

"Good. That eases my mind." Zhuqa headed for the door, then paused and turned back. "As an honest man," he said evenly, "I say if I have to tell you to play with this fucking thing one more time, I will make her a rattle-stick out of your own teeth."

Dkorm shrugged the baby up onto his shoulder and started rapidly patting her.

Zhuqa grunted and left, closing the door quietly behind him without another glance for Amber.

Dkorm immediately turned on Xzem, saying, "If there's a trick to shutting this thing up, you tell me right now or I'll muzzle it."

Xzem surged forward only to cringe back, her wide eyes filled with panic and pain in equal measure. The infant squirming at her teat renewed the full force of its waning screams immediately.

"Shut one of them up at least," snapped Dkorm, jostling the baby harder. And suddenly his spines smacked flat against his scales and he thrust Rosek out at arm's length, not quite fast enough to avoid the stream that came spraying out between her kicking legs.

Dkorm closed his eyes. He took a short breath between tightly-clenched jaws and sighed it out. His head bent. "I hate sprats," he muttered.

Amber eased warily onto her feet.

"Sit down!" Dkorm snapped, slapping at his leg. "Oh fuck Gann, it's in my boot! I'm going to be walking in your little poke's piss the whole rest of the day! Xzem!"

Xzem darted forward, pushing Zhuqa's screaming infant into Dkorm's hands and snatching her own away. Dkorm dropped with a mutter onto a bench, hooking the baby over his arm so that he could keep rubbing at the wet patches on his leathers. "Fucking sprat. I want you to know, Xzem, the very instant this thing dies, I'm pulling your little pisspot in half."

Xzem shivered, but made no sound.

"Baby," said Amber in lizardish, putting out her hands.

Dkorm glared at her. "What's the matter, Eshiqi?" he asked blackly. "Think I'm going to drop it? Think I'm going to bash its screaming little face into the floor and stomp on the fucking thing until it shuts the fuck up at last? Huh? It's fine. Leave it alone."

His neck was lighting up brighter and brighter with every breath.

Amber dropped her hands, looked around, then dashed into the other room to dunk a rag in wash-water and bring it back to Dkorm.

He eyed her with an ominous lack of expression, but then leaned back and gestured at his leg. Amber knelt beside him and scrubbed carefully at his breeches, feeling his stare like a physical thing on the back of her neck. The baby, inelegantly folded over his arm, squirmed and cried.

"Fuck Gann, but you're ugly," Dkorm remarked, fingering a few handfuls of hair. "I don't know why Zhuqa would want to dip it in you when he could have any other slave in this camp. Or all of them." His gaze dropped to the baby in his arm. He shrugged it roughly into a new position and gave it a few equally rough pats in an unsuccessful effort to quiet it. "I don't know why he wants this thing either. It doesn't do anything but eat, make noise and stink the place up."

"Why do you keep calling it 'it'?" Amber asked, and when he only squinted at her in confusion, she tried again, supplementing her terrible lizard-speech with pantomime. "Is it a girl?" she asked, pinching her thumb and forefinger together to form a tear-drop shaped opening. "Or a boy?" Blushing, she pushed a finger through from the underside so that it thrust out like a painfully true-to-life lizardman penis.

The yellow stripes on Dkorm's throat flashed a little brighter and began to fade. "You want to know the gender? Too soon to tell. Look." He caught hold of the baby's leg and moved it so that the baby's naked loins were broadly displayed (and the baby itself was almost upside down). The baby's slit was no more than a crease in its scales with a narrow hole at one end. Dkorm prodded this, saying, "It's just a pisser right now. It won't open for..." His spines snapped down and up again in a shrug. "...a year and some days. By dry season next, I should think. Some people say they can just tell, but some people piss out of their mouths."

She couldn't stand it anymore. She took the baby from him, righting it and drawing it in to lie against her breasts, where it quieted at once. He watched, folding his empty arms, in no hurry to take it back.

"Pointless," he said, watching the baby begin its shivering song of sleep. "The first one always dies. I suppose Zhuqa thinks he can save it with a better mother, but it won't work. Gann will have it. And once it's gone—and I split your little dip, Xzem, don't think I've forgotten—I'll finally get some sleep."

Xzem hunched a little further over Rosek as she wiped the baby clean.

"She was raider-got herself," Dkorm confided, running his eyes lazily over Xzem's huddled back. "How old were you when you had your first bastard?"

"I do not know," Xzem whispered.

"Young, then. We'll say too young and close the door. How many have you had?"

"I do not know."

"No, I suppose they all blur together after a time. Do any of them still live? No, you wouldn't know. She's been sold to so many camps, she's probably fucked half the sons she brought into this world. What say you, Xzem?" he asked, helping himself to a fresh cup of their foul drink. "They say a mother always knows her child, no matter the years or the distance. Have you ever wondered if those were your own eyes you saw in some stranger's face before he bent you over?"

Xzem cupped the back of the baby's head, nuzzling at it with her narrow snout, and stayed silent.

"She came to us so well-used, I was in her three shoves before I knew I was. Chuaan would never have paid for a woman like Xzem, but she had a sprat and Zhuqa's stupid about sprats." Dkorm rattled out a laugh and drank. "He actually wants one. Three of his play-women have squeezed one out for him, but they all died. And he burned them," he added derisively. "Last time, it was raining and he made us all stand out in the fucking rain and watch him burn that noisy little shit-machine like it *mattered*."

Dkorm punctuated this statement with a contemptuous glance at the baby in Amber's arms, but soon his gaze shifted to her body and took on a speculative gleam. He stood and came over to get a better look at her.

Amber moved to put the worktable between them. He followed as unhurriedly as she'd done it, watched her struggle to roll out some clay with the baby tucked up in the crook of her arm, and said, "You could do that better with both hands, I think."

Amber did not give him the baby.

He didn't come right out and ask for it either. She felt him lift up a sizeable hank of her hair and drop it again. Then she felt him pressing at her arm. When she glanced tensely back, she found him with his spines all the way forward, watching his fingers dimple into her flesh. "Soft," he said, almost to himself. "You soft like that all over, Eshiqi?"

She pulled out of his grip.

"Calm yourself. I don't drink from Zhuqa's cup," he snorted. "Besides, I'll find out soon enough. Zhuqa likes a little fighting spirit in his women, but only if he has the pleasure of breaking it quickly. When he decides you're too distracting, he'll put you up on the bidding block. Before long, you'll be like Xzem here, nothing but a catch-cock with a little meat attached to keep it warm."

She turned her back on him and went back to the lamps.

Immediately, his hand closed on her shoulder, yanking her roughly around before shoving her hard into the wall. The baby, jolted out of sleep, began to make its high, gaspy wails. Dkorm didn't even look at it. The color was out on his neck again and visibly pulsing. "Don't turn your back on me, you flat-faced dip," he spat.

All around the room, new slaves cringed back and old ones made themselves motionless and invisible.

"You don't show me your back unless I'm climbing it. I don't care who you fuck, you're still a slave in this camp. I can tell Zhuqa a thousand lies that will have that soft hide off you in strips." He held her gaze a moment longer, then dropped his eyes deliberately to the baby in her protective arms and looked up again. "Shut it up."

Amber moved warily over to Xzem, never taking her eyes from Dkorm, and passed the baby down. It refused the breast Xzem kept trying to coax on it, but did eventually exhaust itself into an unhappy sleep.

"Fucking sprats," Dkorm muttered, turning away. He eyed Rosek, sleeping on the floor against her mother's thigh, but moved on and found a crate against the far wall to sit on. In the other room, one of the children whispered; Dkorm's neck lit briefly and darkened again. "Fucking sprats," he said again, thicker. He dropped one hand to his groin and rubbed sullenly at himself, looking at all of them with a growing lack of emotion as his neck lit up brighter and brighter.

He wasn't going to take six breaths and calm down.

Amber found his cup and filled it. He watched her do it with ominously blank eyes as he kneaded at himself, but when she brought it to him, he took it. After a moment, he took a drink. After another moment, he leaned back into the wall and tucked the hand that had been between his legs behind his head instead. He looked Amber up and down one last time, then grunted and shut his eyes. "Get back to work, all of you. Quietly. You wake those things and I'll crack your bones."

There was an immediate rustle of sound as the lizardladies resumed work.

Amber turned around. Xzem at once dropped her eyes. She kept her head bent as Amber went back to the worktable and picked up her half-done lamp. Then Xzem reached out and tapped the back of her hand once on the top of Amber's bare foot. Just once—a touch so light and swift that if Amber hadn't seen her do it, she might not have noticed. Amber paused uncertainly, but Xzem did not look up and she was afraid of attracting Dkorm's attention. She went back to work in silence, like all the other slaves.

8

The sun rose in Gedai the same as in Yroq and Meoraq was awake to see it. They had made camp atop a high, narrow ridge, which gave him an impressive view in any direction. He could have watched the sun rise if he wanted. Instead, he sat with his back to the morning and watched the light crawl over the broken walls of distant Praxas.

He had hoped for a full hour of travel before darkness shackled him. He received perhaps half of that, not at a run, but at a torturous stride that seemed to hurl him back in time to that first day herding humans across the prairie.

The boy was not delicate. He did not run, but slipped through trees and thornbreaks as easily as any saoq, and had a knack for finding pathways far superior to Meoraq's own. Yet when the light was gone, the boy halted and would go no further. This was only common sense in the wildlands and Meoraq knew it. Still, he tried to coax the boy on and then order him and finally threaten.

The boy remained impervious, laughing as he invited Meoraq to beat him, "or whatever takes your pleasure, sir," but the day was done and so was he.

So they camped. The boy started a fire and brewed nai. There was bread and cuuvash in the pack of provisions Onahi had given them. There was no tent, but the boy was no stranger to sleeping wild. He lay down and was silent. Meoraq paced, drank hot nai, meditated, patrolled, drank cold nai, lay down, sat up, thought of Amber.

He did eventually sleep, but his sleep was thin and haunted. He woke uncounted times, only to stare in vain at the empty night, the faint coals, the boy.

A night's broken rest only further frayed his senses. Long before dawn, he was aware of paranoia, like grains of sand, itching under his scales. He heard things out in the forest, went out to search for the source, and then heard things at his camp. Worse, he did not hear things, which unnerved him even more, as ridiculous as he knew that to be. He felt tense and frustrated and always at the knife's edge of furious. He felt watched.

Now it was morning and as God raised His lamp over the world, Meoraq could feel clarity like a cooling hand once more in his heart and mind.

He reached over and shook the boy, who rolled muttering onto his belly and glowered at him through a shield of his crossed arms.

"You never sleep," said the boy.

Meoraq grunted and kicked dirt over the coals. "We're moving now. Get up."

"What did they take from you anyway?"

Meoraq caught the boy by the back of his ill-fitting tunic and hauled him to his feet. "We're moving," he said again. "Now."

"The Sheulek who comes in the summer makes the governor give him anything he wants. I thought that was the whole point of being Sheulek." The boy thought a moment, then shrugged and smiled. "That and getting dipped everywhere you go."

"There's a reason you were never meant to be one."

The boy's smile did not diminish, but even so, it grew a thinned, painted-on appearance. "I'm sure there's more than one." He picked up his pack and rolled his blanket away. When he straightened up again, his smile had broadened into a disturbing grimace of good cheer. "Luckily, I have you. Let's go."

They went. The boy didn't bother looking for a trail, but traveled vaguely eastward, veering toward landmarks as they came across them—this oddly shaped boulder, that great direthorn tree—and if reaching them meant wading a frigid stream or climbing a soft ravine, that was what they did. The sky took on the bruised color that came before a storm and within the hour, it had found them. The ground turned to clutching mud beneath their feet. The boy wasn't slowed in the slightest. Meoraq considered himself an expert at wildlands travel, but it was difficult to keep pace.

And why, by Gann? Because he'd had a few nights' bad sleep? Ran all the way to Praxas without food? Had to walk now in a little hard rain? In his first striding days, he'd run three days and nights straight through on nothing but water for no better reason than to get someplace with a hot bath. And a bather.

'I am not a young man anymore,' he thought, and felt a pang of dismay stab all the way through him. Not for the careless youth now behind him, but for the future he could only pray he hadn't lost. He would never be a young man again, but now, more than ever, he wanted to be an old one, in Xeqor, with his wife and children.

Lightning arced across the sky, close enough that he could smell it. Thunder came immediately after. The wind gusted, blowing stinging shards of rain directly into his eyes, so that for a moment, he seemed to be falling blindly forward.

"Hold!" ordered Meoraq, and threw down his pack. He hunkered beside it, breathing too hard, lost in thoughts of Amber, how she'd clung to him that night in the ruins...the little cries she made each time the thunder rolled.

"Are we stopping?" the boy asked, watching from a cautious distance.

"Resting." Meoraq tipped his head back, let his mouth fill with water, and swallowed. It tasted of the storm and strange, green leaves.

"I thought you Sheulek didn't need rest. I thought God moved you at His speed."

"Only at His direction. Mine is the same clay as any other's." Meoraq cupped his hands and splashed rainwater over his face. "You don't know much about Sheulek."

"True enough, I suppose. The one that comes in the summer only stays a few days. He stays with the governor." The boy moved from one tree to another, restlessly tapping at each trunk. "No one ever has a trial for him. He says Praxas is such a—"

Thunder cracked overhead, shaking the air over his scales and the bones in his breast as it rolled slowly away.

"—a peaceful place," the boy finished, now from behind him. "Why do you keep looking up? It's just rain."

"I know."

"You look nervous."

"I'm not."

But Amber...wherever she was...

'Sheul, my Father, be with her tonight,' he prayed, watching sparks sweep across the sky. 'She is so frightened of the weath—'

He had his head back, his snout raised, his arms at rest on his knees. The boy's looped belt dropped over his head and before Meoraq's eyes could identify the danger, it had cinched tight.

No air. A perfect choke. He had less than a minute to break it. Meoraq's sabks were already in his hands and stabbing backwards, but the boy skimmed around them with the same ease as he'd navigated thorns and gullies all day. Abandoning that, he slashed at the belt, but the boy wore a braid and the cheap leather was thick and stiff. He hadn't made a single good cut before the boy bashed the rock into his hand. Once. Twice. Then the other. Disarmed.

Through a haze of smothering grey, Meoraq heaved himself backwards, groping blindly for an arm, a throat, his tunic, anything. The boy leapt out of the way, heaving with him, and then Meoraq was on his back on the ground, staring at the world through shades of grey that shook with his own pulse. In his last seconds, he tried to pull the belt out of the boy's grip, but he had no leverage and no strength. He could feel the scratching of his scales on the taut leather vibrating through his skull, but even that felt distant, unimportant. He could see his mouth opening and closing; the world beyond was smoke and shadow and the white open eye of death.

Then, silence.

Rain fell into his open eyes. He could not blink. The boy's face loomed over him, colorless, indistinct. Was he dead? He couldn't move, not even when the boy shoved him over on his side. He could feel tugging, prodding—the boy, searching for treasure—and the final kick of frustration when he found none.

Stormlight flickered through the grey in a constant sheet. Meoraq could see the boy's boots circling to stand before him. He could see the black shape of his father's knife sprawled in the mud before his snout. He could see each dimpled knot in the cord of Amber's hair tied at his arm where it sprawled unfelt over him. He saw these things, only these things, and he thought that must be important.

More silence. It had become heavy, a weight on his ears. He could not hear his pulse anymore, but he thought he could still feel it, in his fingers of all places. The grey was fading slowly to black. His chest hurt.

"That was so much easier than I have been led to believe," the boy remarked. Even his voice was grey.

Meoraq's head was lifted, the belt loosened and then yanked away. He heard it go, felt it striping his throat with pain as scales caught in that cheap braid were torn loose.

The boy had killed him. That was bad enough, but he knew the boy would never burn him. He would never be wholly dead, never see the House of his true Father, never know the eternal peace that comes after. He must lie here and die forever. Would he feel it when he rotted? Would he feel it when the ghets came? Did they even have ghets in Gedai? He took a breath. He tried to cough and couldn't. Dead men couldn't cough.

His father's voice, pained: *Son, dead men don't breathe, either.*

...Truth.

The boy was unbuckling Meoraq's belt, replacing his own shoddy piece of leather.

'I take back my thought about your perfect choke,' he thought peevishly, and breathed again. 'I should be unconscious now.' He struggled to scrape up a better insult, but there was nothing in dumaqi good enough. 'You suck,' he thought finally, savagely. 'Lizard.'

"How long have you been a Sheulek?" asked the boy, buckling on Meoraq's belt. "I wish I'd asked...I've been doing this job for six years. Do you know what that means? Eh?" The boy's boot nudged at Meoraq's thigh, then drew back and slammed into his ribs. "It means they won't let me do it much longer," he said as Meoraq watched his fingers slowly grip the ground. "Too tall, they tell me. Too old. Soon it'll be another boy out here, and what the hell am I supposed to do? They say Zhuqa won't take me, not even to work their stupid crops or clear the canals. Zhuqa only takes real raiders." Another kick, harder than the first. "I could be a raider. I killed you, didn't I?"

In the midst of the grass before him, a single gray blade began to bleed in green. Color, coming back into the world. He breathed.

"I probably should have waited until we were closer," the boy mused, circling again. "Not sure how I'm going to move your body sixteen spans to the camp, but I probably don't need the whole thing. Nothing about the head proves you're Sheulek...and the arm doesn't prove you're dead..." The boy hunkered down to pick up one of Meoraq's sabks. He admired it in the stormlight, then struck it under Meoraq's chin and rocked his head back and forth. "What would you do if you were me?"

Meoraq took the knife and slammed it into the side of the boy's throat.

He and the boy stared at each other. He felt no need to speak. He had no questions, really.

The storm was moving on, lightning breaking into separate sparks, thunder growing distant. The rain fell even harder, but that was all right; the rain was cool on his scraped throat and bruised ribs.

Meoraq pushed himself awkwardly to his knees and then his feet, dragging the boy up with him. "The law," he rasped, and had to stop and cough into his palm. There was no blood on his fingers and the pain of the effort was minimal. It took strength to break a man's ribs, and everything this scrawny youth possessed had gone into the choke. Meoraq hurt, but he thought he was all right.

"The law requires me to ask," he said again, adjusting his grip on the knife's hilt. "Do you wish to pray?"

"This is not supposed to happen," the boy whispered.

Meoraq pulled the knife across his throat slowly, bringing blood in a fall and not a spray, guiding the boy to his knees while he made his little struggles, and then letting him fall where Gann willed when it was over. He found his other honor-blade, cleaned them both, sheathed them. He took his belt back. He found the pitted toy of a knife stowed away in the dead boy's boot and broke it. He stood and stared at the body until the rain had washed the blood away.

Sixteen spans. He didn't think the boy had been lying about that. They had been traveling east, and he didn't think the boy had been leading him false either. But crop? Canals? That was not a raider's camp. That was a settlement, one that could not possibly have gone unnoticed for as many years as the boy claimed to be visiting it.

The sky flashed; a final stroke of lightning, a final snap and growl of thunder. In the back of his mind, Meoraq heard the phantom crash of shattered glass and felt Amber slamming up against his back as she'd done that long-ago night in the ruins.

Ruins. For as long as Sheul had forbidden his children to enter the ruins, those who had gone to Gann had nested in them. Yes, they might hide their crop in the roofless husks where the Ancients had made their homes and yes, they might even have canals worth restoring, but so what? Sixteen spans, generally eastward, look for ruins? Was that hope? There were ruins everywhere!

But ruins stand, he thought suddenly. After so many days, he would never catch a moving pack, but ruins were a pin to hold his Amber in place. He could have her back.

If he could find her.

Meoraq looked wearily out across the world, his eyes sweeping dully across the whole of the horizon and up, up into heaven. The rain poured down his face and across his aching throat. "Mine is the same clay as any other's," he said. "I do not move at Your speed, Father, but at Your direction. I cry out to You from the darkness. I cry, Father. Please. I cry. Help me."

The wind changed, just a little. He turned his face to keep the rain in his eyes. To the east.

He started walking.

* * *

Amber's first full day as a slave passed because even the worst days do, hour by uncounted hour, undisturbed by rescue. There was no food in the workpit, only a barrel of stale water under a leaking faucet that served dually as drinking and wash-water. At some point, Hruuzk appeared and took the new slaves away. Dkorm left with Xzem and the babies soon afterwards. The work changed from doing things to cleaning up, so Amber rallied what was left her of her strength and cleaned alongside them, although she let them do the more vigorous sweeping and scrubbing while she put things away. After another stretch of time, Hruuzk returned and called the children to him in a noisy flock. He hunkered down to talk to them, tapping at this or that one to keep their attention, before he sent them out—chattering children in front, silent slave-women behind.

"Finish up," he called to her, pointing at the small lump of clay left on the table. "No sense running that all the way down when you can put another three lamps on the shelf and be done. Do it well, but do it quick." He pulled a piece of what sure appeared to be her last surviving Manifestor's shirt and used it to wipe out the socket of his missing eye. "Been a long day and I want a piss and a poke before it's over."

Amber rolled out coils of clay and made the last lamps with hands that ached like rotten teeth and barbed wire where her spine used to be. She found herself wishing dully that Zhuqa would hurry up and get here. All he'd want from her was sex and she could do that lying down.

When she finished and turned around, there was Zhuqa in the doorway with Hruuzk, as if she'd summoned him with the thought. She was not glad to see him, but she was relieved and that was bad enough. She started toward him.

Hruuzk stopped her with an upraised hand and pointed back at the table. "I said, finish. Wipe it down."

Amber looked at the slicks of wet and dried clay she'd been pressing into the rough planks all day, knowing there'd be no wiping that, it would have to be scrubbed. With her shoulders and her back. With her damned, aching hands.

She glanced at Zhuqa.

His spines came all the way forward; Hruuzk's slapped flat. In two long strides, Zhuqa's hulking slave-master was across the room with his huge hand on the back of Amber's neck, shoving her flat against the table. He yanked her shift up, exposing her all the way to the back of her head. The sound of his belt coming off lit up Amber's tired brain in every possible shade of panic, but before her fear had fully coalesced, it was dissipated with a crack like gunshot as he brought the belt down on her bare back.

She cawed, more from shock than pain, but the pain came with the second blow and then she was screaming. Amber had been slapped, shoved, punched, and hit with a car, but she had never been beaten like this. It wasn't even like he was hitting her, but more like he was cutting belt-sized strips into her flesh and ripping them away. Three, four, five, and after that, she could not count, could only kick and slap in futility against the table as the world lit up red and black with every swing of Hruuzk's arm.

Then he let go of her and she fell to the ground in a scrambling, sobbing heap. He picked her up by the hair, shook her until she found her feet, then smacked her on the underside of her chin with the folded loop of his belt to make her look at him. His neck was black. His eye was calm and alert. "In this room," said Hruuzk, not unkindly, "I am master. And no matter how badly you think you have it, I can always make things worse."

Amber nodded, trembling and slapping at the tears on her face. Her back was burning, as if she'd pressed it up against a hot furnace and just held it there. Every movement, even breathing, pulled the pain into new dimensions and blew it up hotter and hotter.

Hruuzk released his hold on her hair and patted her on the head. "Good girl. Go on then."

She staggered away from him into the other room and found a shallow basin. She had to lean over the barrel to fill it with water. She had to reach up to get a rag. Her fumbling hand dropped the coarse brush and she had to bend all the way down to pick it up. She poured out the water to soften the dried clay and scrubbed, screaming behind her clamped jaws as the coarse fabric of her shift scratched at her back. Hruuzk stood behind her the whole time with his belt looped comfortably around his fist; she made sure she got every trace of clay.

By the time she finished, her back felt as though it had been whipped with a leather belt, instead of flayed open and set on fire. She was all right. There were still tears leaking out of her eyes, like the hurt little cries leaking out of her throat, but her head was working again and she thought she was all right.

Hruuzk grunted when she limped past him for the second time to give the table a last rinse and finally put his belt back on. "You'd be best served to give her over to me for proper training if you really want to keep her. She's just clever enough to give you real trouble."

"Is that what I need to do, Eshiqi?" Zhuqa inquired.

"No," she said, tried to say, but there were so many variations of that word and she couldn't be sure which she'd used. To make it clearer, she limped over to him and knelt to put her hand beside his boot.

Hruuzk uttered a low, whistling grunt through the crack in his snout. "I want one," he muttered, eyeing her.

Zhuqa's hand came down to rest on her bent head. "I have men out looking for more of them, now that I've tendered up apologies to Ghelip and can trust him not to hunt us down."

"You can, eh?"

Amber's arms began to shake, but Zhuqa hadn't told her to stand or given her a tap or anything. She crouched lower, trying to take the strain off her shoulders only to put it on her knees, and all the while, her back was screaming. How long did he expect her to kneel here?

"Salahkthu's enthusiasm aside," Hruuzk was saying, "those three fools may not have been a raiding party, but it's my belief they *were* scouts. I think Ghelip spied you on your way to Praxas and sent his men slinking in to see how weakened we might be by your absence."

"I think you're right," Zhuqa said mildly.

"Do you? Then you've done Salahkthu a sorry turn, haven't you?"

"Sheul instructs with a burning hand, they say, but there is no greater honor than to be the instrument of His teachings," Zhuqa replied. "Today, Salahkthu teaches Ghelip the quality of my mercy and I am grateful to him for his service. If he had a son, I would honor him in his father's memory." He shrugged his spines, adding, "He doesn't, so you can have his dips and whatever else he left behind."

Hruuzk took the square key Zhuqa passed over with an expression of lizardish amusement. "Are you giving me gifts or ordering me to clean out his room?"

"The brightest light casts a shadow." Zhuqa finally reached down and tapped Amber's head, giving her permission to struggle to her feet. "God and Gann, Hruuzk. They come together out here. Hold, Eshiqi. Turn around and bend over."

She obeyed, biting on a groan as she braced herself on her thighs and tried to hold still. Zhuqa held her shift up. The air was cool on her burning back for a moment before his hand came down to rake dull coals into fresh flame in one light caress. She managed not to cry out, but she knew she flinched and both of them laughed at her for it.

"I wasn't half-swinging," she heard Hruuzk say.

"I know. Your Sheulek has been too tender with you," Zhuqa told her, letting the shift drop over her again. "There are children in this camp no higher than your hip who would have been embarrassed to make half the noise you made for that little whipping."

Damn him, she blushed.

He touched her cheek curiously, then pinched her chin and put his face close to hers. He was still smiling, but now his humor had teeth. "You looked to me for help. You looked to your man—" He gave her a shake to make her meet his eyes again after she tried to drop them. "—to take you away from the workpit and let you rest. Yes, you did."

"I was tired."

He acknowledged her human words with a grunt as he nuzzled under her jaw, scraping the tip of his snout lightly up and down along the full length of her throat before nipping at her shoulder. "If Hruuzk had not," he murmured, licking at her scars, "I would have whipped you for that devious little trick myself. And that would be a terrible hardship for us both to endure. In the future, you will do the work you are given and do it gladly, Eshiqi."

She raised her fist in the kind of salute she had seen the other raiders show him.

"Apologize to Master Hruuzk for disrupting his workpit."

Wanting nothing more than to just get out of here, Amber turned obediently to Hruuzk and said, "Sorry."

"You can do better than that," Zhuqa said.

"Sorry I made you whip the shit out of me for looking sideways at Zhuqa when I should have been scrubbing your table, you giant whore-mongering dick," she amended.

Hruuzk smiled at her. "I don't know the words in your mouth," he told her gently, "but I know the look in your eye. And if you were under my hand tonight, I'd whip you bloody from your neck to your knees."

"Once more," said Zhuqa.

She looked at him, then at Hruuzk. She couldn't begin to perform the necessary vocal aerobics to apologize in dumaqi. What the hell did they want from her? "I'm sorry," she said, feeling frustration in her stomach almost as hot as the throb and sting in her back. "Whatever you want me to say, I'll say it. Just let me get out of here, for God's sake. I'm sorry. I don't care anymore. I'm sorry. Let me *go*!"

Her voice cracked.

Hruuzk and Zhuqa exchanged a maddeningly knowing glance.

"Very good," Zhuqa said. He tapped her shoulder with two knuckles and turned around. "Come, Eshiqi. I'll take you home."

They walked back to his room together. He kept silent, acknowledging neither her presence at his side nor the salutes of the many guards they passed in their descent through the ruins. When he unlocked his door, she saw a lamp already burning on the table, which had acquired a plain metal cup and, more importantly, a wide-mouthed clay bowl generously heaped with roasted meat and charred roots.

The smell of the food struck her almost at the same instant as the sight of it. Her mouth flooded even as her back continued to throb and sting. She knew better than to take even one step toward it, but could not help staring.

Zhuqa followed the direction of her eyes as he unbuckled his harness. He did not remark, only smiled and undressed. When he was naked except for his loin-plate and the knives strapped to his biceps, he gestured at her.

She started to take her shift off, wincing as the coarse fabric pulled taut across her back, but he stopped her.

"In a moment. First, I want you to look there and see the plate I have set for us to share."

She looked. Her stomach growled.

"I know that you are very hungry," Zhuqa said behind her. "I see that you are tired. And hurt." His hand slipped like slow hell down her spine. "But Hruuzk tells me you have been obedient and hard-working...most of the day. And I am inclined to forgive your foolishness there at the end, because it so warmed me to see my Eshiqi seeking her man's aid. So. Are you hungry?"

"Yes," she said, and said it again as best she could in dumaqi.

"I'm glad." He took her arms and raised them over her head, taking the opportunity to nuzzle at her from behind. There, with his snout close to her ear and his hands like shackles around her wrists, he softly said, "Because if I find a weapon hidden on you, Eshiqi, I'm going to make you eat it."

She started to look at him. He released one hand to catch a fisthold in her hair and yank her head back, so that she suddenly found herself looking into his face. Viewed this way, upside-down and from below, his eyes caught the light in a strange new way, almost seeming to glow.

"If you took something out of the workpit, bring it out. I'll beat you," he said calmly, "but I won't kill you if you confess it now and beg my forgiveness."

"I don't have anything," she said, truthfully enough. It wasn't as if the thought had never crossed her mind, but the only knife she'd seen in the workpit had been strapped to the side of Dkorm's left boot and he'd been staring at her most of the day anyway.

"Please yourself. But remember that I gave you this chance." Zhuqa let go of her hair and pulled her shift off. He felt it out carefully, gave her a long appraising stare, then tossed it aside and resumed his impersonal search, this time on her body. He made thorough work of it: finger-combing through her hair, lifting her breasts, even thumbing at her belly-button. Unsatisfied, he then knelt to check between her toes, run his hands up her legs all the way to the crack of her ass, and once there of course, felt inside her pussy. "Take that look off your face, little liar," he remarked. "You've opened for me."

"Not open enough to hide a knife. Seriously, what are you thinking?"

He grunted and released her, his spines now flexed all the way forward, broadly smiling. "No weapons. Not even a splinter of wood to sharpen. Am I to believe my dangerous Eshiqi has been tamed?"

"Only long enough for Meoraq to get here."

His spines came forward at once. "Was that a name?"

Amber shut her stupid mouth.

"No answer? So be it. You're Zhuqa's woman now." He rose and walked over to seat himself at the table. "And Zhuqa feeds his loyal woman well."

She didn't let herself get carried away by relief at these words; he was altogether too pleased with himself. And sure enough, at her first cautious step forward, he patted his thigh.

She looked at his hand, then at his face.

He grimaced at her playfully (*first saw that look on meoraq yeah the morning after we first made love he probably has no idea how freaky it makes him look but at least he tries o god where is he*) and patted again. "I have only the one chair."

"I don't suppose sitting on the floor is an option."

"You will sit to eat—" Pat pat. "—or you will not eat tonight, Eshiqi."

She sat on his lap. He bumped his knee a few times, grimacing as she winced at the rough scour of his scales, then he pinched off a chunk of meat and held it up.

Her mouth snapped shut on a sudden river of saliva.

"This," said Zhuqa, placing the morsel against her lips without any further torment, "is for sitting so immediately and so well upon your man's knee."

And oh but it tasted good. Tachuqi meat, she knew that at once, but the best damn tachuqi in the world. They'd actually braised it in something; the taste was richer and more tangy than mere hunger's spicing. It was, in all honesty, the best thing she'd eaten since leaving Earth. Better than quite a few things she'd eaten *on* Earth.

He had a bite of his own while he enjoyed the sight of her trying (and failing) not to wolf it down in one swallow. Then it was gone and her hunger was fully awakened and clawing up her guts, and the real torture began.

"Put your hand on me, Eshiqi," he said. "You know the way."

Amber gave the bowl of food a pointed look and unbuckled his loin-plate. She cupped his groin impersonally and waited.

He tore off another chunk of meat. "That was neither immediate nor well done," he said and ate it himself.

"Sadist."

"Mm. It isn't bad for camp food, is it?" He licked his fingers.

"*Fucking* sadist!" Her eyes fixed infuriatingly on his mouth.

He took more meat and must have felt her hand on him tense in expectation because he glanced down before snorting laughter at her. "No, Eshiqi. One bite for you, one for me. That is how we share our meals. And you forfeited your last bite. This one is mine. But keep moving your hand. When I give you an order, I mean you to go until I tell you to stop."

She kneaded at him mechanically as he sucked the juice from the meat, pinched it off into smaller and smaller bites, and finally ate it. He started to reach for another, then paused, pretending not to notice her hungry stare, then held out his hand invitingly. "Taste?" he offered.

No way. No fucking way was she going to—

And then she grabbed his hand and sucked not just greedily, not just that...but gratefully.

Zhuqa rocked back hard, banging his head sharply against the back of his chair. Now his eyes were fixed and staring.

That's right. They didn't have lips. They could lick...they couldn't suck.

"Well, damn," mumbled Amber disgustedly, but she couldn't let go of his hand.

And as long as she was sucking on it, he was in no hurry to take it back. But the taste of meat was finite, and the taste of lizard could not provoke the same gusto. "Enough," he said, once her enthusiasm began to flag. He looked at his hand when she released it, flexing his wet fingers, and then at her.

"Yeah," she said. "We're going to be coming back to that, aren't we?"

He picked up one of the roots—not a piece, but the whole thing—and held it up where she had to look at it. "I want your hand on my cock."

His cock wasn't out. Amber stroked his slit, which, despite his obvious effort to keep it tight against her, was already oozing beadlets of oil.

"You are such a slut," said Amber, pushing her finger in to stroke his sa'ad. "Honest to God, that's what you are. Big, tough Zhuqa. You're just a dirty girl."

He hissed through clenched teeth, then groaned, then finally gave up with a hoarse laugh and let himself extrude. As soon as she closed her fist on his shaft, he gave her the root. "Remember, you obey until I tell you to stop. Keep your hand busy."

She did, although it wasn't easy to fight open the thick, burnt husk of the root with one hand while gently rubbing a man's dick with the other. Beneath the peel, the pulp of the root was grey and unappetizing, with a taste that was mostly that of the ashes it had been baked in. She ate it anyway, bolting it down in just a few half-chewed swallows, until she had nothing to do but work her fist and watch him slowly eat.

"You are good," he remarked between lazy bites. "Your Sheulek trained you well, but this is Zhuqa's House. Get up, Eshiqi. Put my cock inside you just how we are."

He looked so sly and serious about it, like sex in a chair with the woman on top was the absolute limit of unthinkable depravity, that she laughed at him. Then she got up, still shaking her head (very much aware of how closely he was watching her now) and straddled him. "Such a dirty girl," she said, milking at the base of his shaft until she'd worked the thick head of it inside her.

"Just so," he murmured, reaching up to stroke his thumb along her throat.

She bore down, rocking a little to let his oils make the entry easier, and then sat, eye to eye, waiting for further instructions.

"Make me cum," he said, not moving.

It took a few false starts; she didn't want to put her arms around him for balance and she *hated* having his face right in front of her while she bounced on his cock, having to watch him study the juddering of her breasts and smirking. So she leaned back, bracing her hands behind her on his knees and raising herself up on her toes to pump her hips at him while she looked at the ceiling instead. It put a lot of strain on her aching shoulders, but it wouldn't last long, she knew. It never did.

Or at least, it never had.

"It was a sick mind that taught you this," said Zhuqa in a mildly marveling tone. Apart from a minute clenching of his thighs now and then, he managed not to move at all. His breath remained slow and even. His hands stayed at his sides. His cock, ticking hard inside of her with the urgent hammer of his pulse, gave neither of them release.

Her shoulders couldn't take this much longer. "Hurry up and finish, motherfucker," Amber muttered, bucking faster.

He only chuckled. "Fierce little thing. A Sheulek is a master of his flesh. Just because I choose so often to revel does not mean I do not know restraint."

Which meant he was willing to go all night, for no other reason than to piss her off. Irritation became the spark of an idea. Amber caught his wrist, brought it to her mouth, and sucked at his finger, bobbing up and down its small length to the rhythm of her pumping hips.

"*Fuck Gann*!" he spat, yanking back his hand, but it was all over. His cock jerked; she felt the heat of his cum spitting over and over, like fireworks blooming in some internal sky, until he shuddered out the last of it.

He glared at her, close enough that she could feel the hot grunts of his breath puffing on her throat and stirring through her hair. His neck had lit up at some point during the sex, but the color wasn't fading now that it was done. If anything, it was getting brighter.

All sense of victory slowly died, leaving her nothing but Zhuqa's eyes burning into hers and the sting of the belt still crawling like coals over her back.

"That was stupid," said Zhuqa, scarcely audible even with his face right in front of hers.

Should she agree? Apologize? Stay quiet? Amber hesitated and lost the choice.

"You want me to finish with you, is that it? You have somewhere else to be tonight? Eh?"

"No," Amber said, tried to say.

"No! You don't decide when I'm done!" Zhuqa picked her up only to thump her down with ass-bruising force on the table and shove her flat. Her head hit the bowl, upending it. He swiped burnt roots and greasy meat out of his way, hauled her hips to the table's edge, and stabbed himself back inside her, snarling, "I'll fuck you until you bleed if that's my pleasure!" His empty hand splayed open and heavy across her chest, pinning her in place for his rapid, unfeeling thrusts. The table rubbing at her from behind might as well have been wrapped in razor wire. "I'll fuck you until we *both* bleed and you..." His back arched, bucking almost in convulsions, every cord of his throat pushing out through vibrant shades of black and yellow. "...and you...fuck..." His eyes were glazing even as he glared at her. "You," he said, but the rest was an animal hiss.

Amber didn't move.

Zhuqa closed his eyes. He began to breathe. "One," she heard him mutter. "One for the Prophet..."

Someone knocked at the door.

Zhuqa roared. Not like an angry man, or even an angry lizard. It was the roar of a dragon, wordless, tearing through the air and her bones together at decibels no mortal voice should even be capable of achieving. His hips pumped spastically, brutally, without seeming to be aware of her at all.

Amber did not fight him, did not cry out, did not even breathe.

Three more knocks, deliberate and loud.

Zhuqa stopped rock-rigid above her. His arms shook where he leaned on them, not (she was sure) from the strain and violence of his thrusts, as much as from the strain of not letting go to his killing rage. Amber, the only living thing in the room, held very still and watched him as he turned his head and looked at the door.

He breathed. Once. Twice.

"I," he said in a rasping, hellish hiss, "do not care if the *skies* have split open and are *shitting fire* all over my camp! *Move the fuck on*!" he roared, once more in that dragon's voice she felt even in her womb.

A moment's stillness. Zhuqa's heaving breath moved her minutely back and forth on the table. He didn't look at her.

Tok. Tok. Tok.

He shoved himself back and out of her, snarling curses as he gripped his cock and wrenched it with difficulty and obvious pain back into his body, cinching his loin-plate on to keep it there. Metal flashed; knives flew to his hands as he crossed the room, flung the door open—

And stood there.

Meoraq's name leapt like hope itself in her heart, but it died...because in that stillness, she heard what Zhuqa saw: the baby.

Amber sat up slowly, not daring yet to leave the table or even bring her legs together, but she had to at least look. Zhuqa's friend Iziz stood on the other side of the door, Xzem huddled small at his side, and the baby thrust out as if in sacrifice before Zhuqa's naked blades. She hadn't been able to hear it crying through the door. She could barely hear it now. Its cries, little more than an endless, rusty "*weh...weh...*" breathed through a throat scraped raw by screams.

"It hasn't eaten," said Iziz.

Zhuqa sheathed his knives. "Since?"

After a moment, and a light cuff to the back of her head from Iziz, Xzem stammered, "Since third-hour last, my lord."

"Since *third*-hour? You tell me this now?" Zhuqa looked at the baby, then at the woman who held it, incredulous. "Tell me why I should not go this instant and pull an arm off your shit-sired little poke!"

"Please, my lord! It is not my fault! It does not want me! I thought...it would suck when it became hungry enough, but...*oh mercy, my lord*!"

"Mercy?" Zhuqa snatched at the scruff of her filthy shift and yanked her off her knees. "I offered you mercy, woman! I offered you more than a used-up breed-pot like you deserves and you repay me by starving my child half the fucking day?!"

Xzem wailed.

"She says it quiets up in your creature's arms," Iziz put in. "She thought if the creature touched it..."

Zhuqa straightened up and glanced back at Amber. The yellow stripes at his throat throbbed, but they were fading. He released Xzem and stepped back.

Amber kicked down off the table and limped hurriedly over to take the baby from its weeping wetnurse. It hung against her breasts for perhaps half a minute more, and then suddenly brought both hands up to smack against her skin in a strong, pinching grip. It pulled in a deep, deep breath, and screamed it out—weak no longer, but full-lunged and furious. Fluid poured in an immediate, answering trickle from Xzem's flaccid teat, but it was Amber's breast it blindly gnawed, futile for them both.

The two men stood to one side while Amber and Xzem tried for several maddening minutes to fit the three of them together, offering no help and no encouragement. The baby cried louder, drawing strength from the touch it craved more than the milk it needed, until the flashings along its pale, scrawny throat began to turn yellow with rage.

Zhuqa and Iziz snorted in unison.

"It's a son," Iziz declared. "Only a boy could get that worked up over riding a woman."

"In fairness, it is one damned fine ride," Zhuqa replied.

"Better than a quick fuck into my mother?"

"Better than a slow fuck into God."

Iziz looked at him, startled and trying to smile. "That's a blasphemous lie."

"No," said Zhuqa seriously, watching Amber. "It isn't."

"You, sir, are a pervert. All that smooth skin. It must be like fucking a baby."

Zhuqa said something in reply, but Amber didn't hear. Smooth skin. Smooth and soft.

She looked around, then thrust the baby back into Xzem's arms and ran to the table. "Do you have anything else like this?" she asked in lizardish, holding up the wineskin. "To wrap it in?"

They looked at her, both of them frowning, as she mimed putting on a shawl.

Damn it. She slowed down, trying to work her mouth around the alien words: "I need something with smooth skin." Frustrated, she slapped her naked body a few times and then slapped the leather flask. "Like me!"

"What the hell is that thing barking on about?"

Zhuqa's spines flared. He looked at the baby and then at the wineskin. He came over to the table and took it from her.

"No, you idiot!" Amber said, exasperated into English. "I don't want a drink, I need—"

"I hear you, woman," said Zhuqa. He uncapped the neck, righted the bowl that had once held their scattered dinner, and carefully poured the contents of the wineskin out. As he shook the last drops free, he drew his knife.

"What are you doing? Oh Zhuqa, no. Please, that's a perfectly good—and there it is," Iziz sighed, rubbing at his brow-ridges as Zhuqa sliced the skin open down its lengthy middle. After a short silence and a few meditative breaths, Iziz turned a glare on Amber and snapped, "Do you know how hard it is to make a watertight vessel out in the fucking wildlands? No, of course you don't, you *are* a fucking watertight vessel!"

"Mind your manners," Zhuqa said distractedly.

"That was a perfectly good corroki bladder! What the fuck does she want with it?!"

"She wants to put the baby in it."

"Wants to...? Why by the names of Gann and God would she want to do that?"

"So it will think she's holding it, you fool. Quiet down." Zhuqa tossed the flap of the cut wineskin to Amber, who took it and folded the baby into its dry side until it was entirely cocooned but for its snouted face.

"Hush, baby," she said. "I'm here. Amber's here." And with that, she placed the damp, wine-stinking bundle back in Xzem's reluctant arms, its wailing mouth close to the leaking eye of Xzem's teat. At its first accidental bite, the small head turned, shoving itself up so that most of the lizardlady's single breast was swallowed into its stiff, lipless mouth. Its hungry cries turned at once to grunts of effort and then to soft, slurping sounds.

It drank.

"So," Iziz said after a moment. "It wanted a blanket. Shows what I know about sprats. My apologies for disturbing you, Zhuqa." He reached down to take Xzem's arm.

"Let it eat." Zhuqa sat down, picked up his cup and dunked it in the bowl. He gestured ruefully. "Have a drink. It'll be full of dust and dead yifu by the morning."

"Waste not the gifts of God," said Iziz piously, picking up the whole bowl for a series of deep swallows.

Zhuqa sipped at his cup, picked splinters off the nearest chunk of roast, and tossed that at Amber. "A good thought, Eshiqi. Eat."

She did, but without appetite, too much aware of Xzem's hungry stare.

Iziz helped himself to a baked root, unzipped its skin, and swished it through the wine a few times before popping it whole into his mouth. He studied Amber while he chewed and swallowed, then said, "You know I have to ask..."

"Go on then."

"What it is really like to dip it in that thing? Honestly."

Zhuqa grunted, looking Amber over, then flexed his spines in a shrugging gesture. "Perverse. More than you can imagine."

"With respect, sir, you have no idea the sorts of things I imagine."

"She's smooth, like baby-skin. Soft all over. Soft inside." He took another sip of his drink and chuckled. "She cums like a man."

"What do you mean?"

"She oils up when she cums. Like a man. She even has a little sa'ad."

"*What*?!"

"And she's so soft inside, softer than her outsides even. There's nothing to catch on, nothing to push against, nothing but this soft, wet squeeze."

Iziz drew back in a wince of queasily fascinated revulsion. "So it's like fucking a sack of hot shit. Your pardon, a hot sack of *male* shit. There's something wrong with you, Zhuqa."

"I don't describe it well. It's nothing like a real woman's sleeve. It's like...like skin. A second skin over your cock. Every time you move, you can feel it gripping and pulling at you, all over, all the time. Just moving in her feels amazing. The only thing that compares is my first fuck—well, my first with a woman—and only because it *was* my first and has that same sort of revelation. Otherwise, there is no comparison, no more than you can liken a bite of this shit—" He picked up a root and tossed it back on the table. "—to fried bread and fancies. She's hard to look at, but she's like fucking *God*."

Iziz studied him over the lip of the bowl. "Of all the sex you've had, you said. And then you said...with a *woman*."

Zhuqa looked at him, then at his cup. He put the cup down a little harder than he had to and gave it a short push away. "Strong drink weakens the mouth and the mind, says the Prophet," he muttered. "It was a long time ago, Iziz. The door is shut."

Iziz put the bowl down. "You weren't born out here, I know that much. You were a Sheulek!"

"In training."

"Still...who the hell got you on the ground long enough to get a poke at you?"

Zhuqa glanced at Amber. She looked at the baby. He snorted laughter and looked back at Iziz. "You are the fatherless son of a wildland exile and the nameless catch-cock who served the whole of his camp. What could you possibly understand about anything I could tell you of that life?"

"She has a name, I just don't remember what it is." Iziz drank. "Why are we talking about me? I want to hear the story of mighty Zhuqa getting plugged."

"That isn't what happened."

"It wasn't even a man, was it? I knew it. You were ravished by a wild kipwe."

"No."

"Before I came here, I ran with a camp that used to hold kipwe shows," recalled Iziz, his attention wandering to the bowl in his hands. "They'd strap a slave into a kind of harness. I don't know...the kipwe had to be trained special, I guess...and every time I saw it, I had to wonder...How the hell do you train a kipwe to fuck something? How do you even *start*?"

"Do you want to hear this story?"

"Yes." Iziz drank.

"In the cities, in the Houses, in the caste of the warrior, they take you away as soon as you can be trusted to walk without falling on your ass or piss without it running down your leg. They send you to a special place close to the innermost walls to train you. You live there with the other boys of your caste, all ages, all together, and you only go home for the cold season. You speak to no one but the men who train you and the boys who train beside you. You learn nothing but prayer and the laws of God." Zhuqa paused to fill his cup again from the bowl in his friend's hands.

"No women?" asked Iziz.

Zhuqa snorted. "The only time I ever saw women was when I was home for the cold season, and they were only servants. My mother had been turned out by then. I had no sisters. I think it's possible I went the first ten years of my life without knowing there was such a thing as women. Truth. No idea."

"Ten." Now Iziz snorted. "I was fucking them before that."

"It was a sheltered life."

"It was a wasted one. No wonder you were all cock-rubbers and boy-pokes."

"Never heard either word until I was sent out of the walls."

"Lies."

"God's own truth. God's and Gann's."

"Go on then. Your sick string of lies fascinates me."

"There was a man in the training grounds. Eight years my elder. High-born, low-bred. A rough."

"Used to crawl into other cupboards at night and poke the little boys," Iziz guessed.

"Wouldn't surprise me, but what he used to do to me was swagger around on the training field after the masters had left us to our targets and beat on whoever caught his eye. Just sneak up from behind with a practice staff and beat them down, calling out the techniques he used like he was a master at lessons, but really just beating on the boy. It wasn't the first time I'd played his game—"

"But this time," said Iziz dramatically, "you fought back."

"I fought back every time, boy. I was a Sheulek in training, not a camp-born cock-rubber like you."

They saluted one another, Iziz tapping his bowl respectfully at Zhuqa's raised cup, and both drank.

"But it had been a bad run of days for me," Zhuqa admitted after a swallow. "Angry days. Things I'd always been able to shake off were striking at me like lightning out of the sky, just—" Zhuqa brought his hands banging together, making Xzem jump and the baby let out one grunting wail before it resumed sucking. "—and I was burning," Zhuqa finished, glancing their way. His eye lingered on Amber. "And I had been all day on that training field with Master Naxuuk chewing off my hide one scale at a time, and it was all I could do not to just let that lightning burn me up when that staff came swinging out of the black and caught me right here." Zhuqa clapped a hand over his side, just below his ribs.

Iziz frowned. "God's Hammer, Zhuqa."

"Felt like it."

"How old was this man?"

"He was three years after his ascension, they said, so he must have been at least twenty and two."

"So you were *fourteen*?"

"Almost."

"Fuck Gann." Iziz put the bowl aside and eyed his leader with a disturbed expression. "What did you do?"

"You mean after I fell over pissing myself?" Zhuqa snorted. "He got in a few more good shots. I could hear him calling them out. Leaping Drop. Prayer Block. Radiant Twist. No matter what I covered up, there was something else for him to hit. And then he stepped back and let me get up. I could hear him talking, lecturing the other boys, and that lightning struck. And I went at him."

"Like piss you did."

Zhuqa drank, shrugging his spines. "He saw me coming and hit me again, ready with some technique or another. I don't remember what it was. I do remember that he hit me...but hitting didn't stop me. It was just more lightning. There must have been a time we were grappling because I remember climbing him...not on him, but *climbing* him, like a drop-stair. Then he went down and I began to beat on him the way I have never beaten anyone since. I have killed men, Iziz, and taken several days to do it that I did less damage. It wasn't enough. It could never be enough. I hit him until I broke every bone in my right hand and even that couldn't stop me hitting him. Have you ever been south as far as Kthuat?"

"Once or twice."

"They have stands of trees around there. Dead trees, mostly. Full of beetles—"

"Oh, Gann's fuck-stick, the yumont." Iziz shuddered. "I heard about those. Saw scars men said came from them. Thought it was a lie to scare us boys from wandering."

"They're real. They live in the meat of those dead trees where it's always warm and if a man should sleep up against one, they might come crawling out and bore in under his scales to live in his meat instead. Something in the bite keeps you from feeling it at first, but then they die. And they itch. If you're quick about it, you can pry up your scales and dig the body out, but they melt away pretty fast and if that happens, that itch clings around for days upon days and there's nothing anyone can do to help it. That's what it was like for me. Hitting him was like scratching over my scales at the itch I could never reach under them. And when it was over, he was lying there on the ground, trying to crawl away. My whole body was on fire wanting to get at that goddamned itch...and my cock came out. Look at her."

Iziz glanced around. Amber started to look at the baby, then gave up and looked back at them.

"Look at what? I can't read that face," Iziz said. "I don't even know how you can look at it while you're dipping in it."

"Just the eyes, then."

"I cry. What's she thinking?"

"I don't know," said Zhuqa. "But there's something in those eyes."

Iziz looked back and forth between the two of them for a few seconds, then snorted and gave Zhuqa a sock to the chest. "Forget her. You're just getting to the good part. Go on."

"The good part." Zhuqa checked his cup, but it was empty. He picked up a root and peeled it instead. "The only thing I knew about cocks at that time in my life was that I had one and I took that entirely on faith. Never seen it, mine or anyone else's. I knew nothing about sex, other than Sheul gives a man the fire so that he could pass it into a woman and she could grow a baby. Go on and laugh, I know you want to."

Iziz barked a few times, then rubbed at his eyes. "I was trying to hold it in."

"You were never any good at that. So it came out for the first time in all my sheltered life and I felt air on it and the air was fire. There was this swaggering little shit of a boy, crawling on the ground in a puddle of his own piss and blood, more than half-naked because I had somehow torn most of his clothes away beating on him. At no time did I think it would feel good or that it would serve the slaveson right. I didn't even hope it would hurt. I saw the pucker of Gann's pipe and then I was in it."

"Fourteen and didn't know about fucking," marveled Iziz. "How was it?"

"It didn't feel right."

"Noble Sheulek in training that you were."

"Piss on that. It felt great, just didn't feel *right*. It was that itch all over again, only six times worse. He was screaming and thrashing around worse than he'd done when I was beating on him, and all I could think was that this was close to whatever it was I needed and if I could just *get* there, everything would stop burning. Fucking helped, so fucking harder ought to help more, and that was what I did, without another thought in my head, until they pulled me off him. I don't even know who. I fought, but whoever it was got me in a choke and when I woke up, the itch was gone and I was in the cell."

"Cell? Did you kill him?"

"No. He was even at the tribunal, although he had to sit in a special litter and his face was mashed out of knowing."

"Tribunal?" Iziz laughed, but quizzically, as if he suspected Zhuqa were having him on. "For throwing a poke into some bullying sprat?"

"No, for throwing a poke into some *high-born* bullying sprat after I'd beaten him into paste. They had it posted on the gate before the hour was out and they were ringing it to order at sunset."

"Was that what you...?"

"No." Zhuqa finished off the root and beckoned Amber back to him. Once she was again uncomfortably straddling his thigh, he went on. "No, that wasn't what they had me for, although that might have been cause enough if they'd found anything in him. Fortunately, I hadn't cum yet, so in the end, they let me go. I took a public whipping the next morning and I never heard another word about it, except I know they must have sent a message to my father because when I went home for the cold season, I found the little poke my father kept to scrub the floors waiting in my room without a stitch sewn on her."

"Pretty?" asked Iziz, perking up.

"If you like the sort." Zhuqa's hand drifted over Amber's belly and lightly rubbed. "A little too grey yet for my taste and her eyes were sloped funny, but Gann knows I could sell her here for more coin than I could easily hold. She put her hand on my slit and out came my cock and before the hour turned, I knew indisputably that God looked down from His heaven and loved me."

"How many times?" asked Iziz. He was watching Zhuqa rub Amber's stomach with sleepy, slightly glazed eyes.

"Twice."

"Twice? You fucking waste of meat! Talk to me about God in His heaven when it's ten times a poke! I fucked my *mother* more than twice a night!"

"Three is the sacred number of creation and belongs to God alone, you ignorant heathen." Zhuqa's hand dropped, pushing two fingers along her folds once or twice before crooking up inside her. Iziz watched that, too. "Piss like that used to matter to me," he mused.

"Is that her making that sound?" Iziz asked abruptly. "Is she...oiling up at you?"

"No. I was in her once already tonight. Before you killed the mood and got me too drunk to care." Zhuqa glanced over at the baby, which now lay quiet and perhaps sleeping at Xzem's breast. "Got any teat-biters out there, Iziz?"

"Probably," he said without much interest. "You want the rest of this?"

Zhuqa waved the hand that wasn't working methodically at Amber's pussy.

Iziz picked up the cup and drank it off. "I want to fuck now. I'm taking one of your slaves for the night."

Zhuqa grunted and shut his eyes.

"Thought I'd mention. Manners are important to city-born scuff like you. Up, Xzem. Let Eshiqi give the sprat a tap and let's go."

Xzem crept forward and presented the wrapped baby from a servile crouch.

Amber looked at Zhuqa.

He grunted without opening his eyes or interrupting the rhythm of his fingers.

Amber reached out and brushed the back of her knuckles lightly across the baby's snout. It roused at once, sucking sleepily, but began to drift away again almost immediately.

"And that was all it wanted, all this time," said Iziz. "A smooth blanket."

"Doesn't care about the blanket." Zhuqa fanned his spines forward with deep, drunken pleasure. "Wanted his mother's touch. Something you would never understand."

"Piss on that. My mother touched me plenty!" Iziz declared and, giving Xzem a light smack to the back of the head, herded her out and shut the door behind them.

"I'm sure she did," Zhuqa murmured. "And I'm sure it felt like love. But you'll never touch my child like that, will you, Eshiqi? Because you love it. And you just may be the only other person in this camp who knows that when you love someone, sometimes you don't touch." He pulled in a deep breath and let it out slow, patting Amber's thigh. "Put yourself to bed," he told her, and gave her a nudge off his lap. He made no effort to follow, only sat there with his eyes closed and one hand resting on the table near his empty cup.

He looked like he was sleeping already, but she thought that would change in a hurry if she so much as touched one of the knives he kept strapped to his arms or took even one step toward the door. Amber went over and climbed into the cupboard. Sliding the door shut made the bells jingle; she looked out to see if they'd disturbed him and found him already gazing back at her through slitted, cat-content eyes.

"It's funny, isn't it?" he murmured. "The things you find to love in this life...so you don't hate yourself so much for living it."

She shut the door on him.

9

There was no real sense of time, but Amber thought three more days passed because she slept three times. Zhuqa fed her when they woke up—whatever they had left over from the night before, cold and greasy. He fed her when he brought her home from the workpit—mostly meat with baked roots, and once, some unknown animal's head with roasted marrow bones. He had a bath brought on the second night and let her bathe herself, after she'd bathed him, of course. He made her talk to him, sometimes in her language, sometimes in his. He had sex with her every night. For hours.

She worked. Busy hands make a light heart, as Hruuzk was fond of saying. She learned to make bowls, plates and pitchers as well as lamps. She mended shifts, shirts and breeches, using anything beyond repair as patches. She pounded thousands of xuseth stalks through a sieve with a heavy wooden mallet for hour after hour to get one lousy jar of oil. And of course, at the end of each back-breaking day, there was plenty of lifting, packing, sweeping and scrubbing.

Three days.

On the fourth, things changed.

It was subtle at first. Hruuzk had been coming at mid-morning to take the children and some of the older slaves off to work in the gardens, kitchens or canals, but not today. This was just unusual enough that Amber noticed, but she hadn't been there long enough to know what was routine and what wasn't, so she thought nothing of it except how much more crowded the workpit was. What she noticed next was activity out in the halls, not the crash and roar of a violent rescue, but merely a clamor of boots and voices that grew steadily louder and more raucous throughout the day—the sound of a stadium crowd...or a mob working up for a riot.

The veteran slaves simply kept their heads down and their hands busy, and if they were at all anxious about what was going on outside, they did not show it. Amber tried to follow their example, but when the unseen crowd began to clap, shout and stomp their feet in unison, she threw whatever wicks she'd cut in the oil to soak and retreated to the back room to sit with Xzem and hold the baby. They were making so much noise it was impossible to be sure, but she thought they were chanting, "Meat."

She didn't have long to wonder what it meant. The shouting came to a sudden swell of cheers and then Hruuzk opened the door. The children ran to him at once, infected by the unruly energy out in the halls, but he turned them back after just a few words and clapped his hands to stop work.

"The bidding is about to start," he called. "All my unstabled ladies, line up. Everyone else, keep working. No fussing," he added, pointing sternly at Shivers, who had begun to tear up. "Until I have coin in my hand, you all belong to me and my ladies do not what?"

"Piss out of their eyes," Shivers whispered.

"My ladies do not piss out of their eyes." He gave her a forgiving pat on the head, using the gesture to put her in the forming line. "Gold-Eyes, Crook-Toe, you go last. They want you, they'll have to pay for the rest of this lot first." He glanced through the open door, assessing something in the crowd outside, then beckoned to Amber. "Eshiqi, come."

She heard her name, saw him looking at her when he said it, and still it made no immediate sense to her. He couldn't sell her, she was Zhuqa's!

'Oh sure, *now* you're Zhuqa's,' the ghost of her dead mother said with a caustic laugh. 'If you wanted to hide behind his skirts, you should have played his game, little girl. You didn't, so suck it up.'

But Meoraq was coming. He was supposed to find her, kill Zhuqa and get her out of here.

'Well, he didn't,' Bo Peep said simply. 'And this is exactly what you deserve for sitting on your ass and waiting for someone else to save you.'

Hruuzk, making a last inspection of his ladies before they passed out of his keeping, finally noticed she was still sitting next to Xzem. His head cocked. He turned around to fully face her and hooked his thumb behind the buckle of his belt.

Amber's mind remained perfectly still, but her body did not want to be whipped before she was sold. She got up.

Watching her as he bounced Rosek roughly on his knee, Dkorm rattled out a laugh. "I believe that is surprise I see on that ugly face," he remarked. "I told you it would happen, didn't I? Although I confess I'm a bit surprised myself. Most of Zhuqa's toy cunts last at least a year."

"Did I hear my name?" Zhuqa asked, walking suddenly through the door with an expression of polite interest. "Was there something you wanted to say to me? Perhaps on the subject of my women?"

Dkorm snapped to attention, yanking Rosek into the crook of his arm and pinching her squalling snout shut with his hand. "No, sir! I was just...just..."

Zhuqa's gaze dropped to Rosek and hardened. "What the fuck are you doing?"

Dkorm let go and actually swept his hand behind his back like a kid trying to hide a forbidden candy bar. Rosek gasped in air and shrieked it out. Xzem held Zhuqa's baby and trembled. "Nothing, sir."

"Eshiqi," said Zhuqa. "Take Rosek."

"Sir—"

Amber lifted the struggling baby and stepped back. In the next instant, Zhuqa was across the room with his hand around Dkorm's snout, whose explanations became a choked wheeze.

"You," said Zhuqa, very calmly, "are making me regret giving you this assignment. Do you think—"

Dkorm began to struggle.

"—I would give the care of my child to anyone? Eh? Answer me."

Dkorm pitched himself back against the wall, slapping and scratching at Zhuqa's restraining arm.

"I'm beginning to think you don't want it in your care," said Zhuqa. "And I'm beginning to feel offended."

Amber could see Dkorm's chest heaving, bulging outward with each whistling effort at breath like an alien parasite was about to burst free.

And then Zhuqa's hand opened. With a howling gasp, Dkorm dropped flat over the crates, bags and barrels that had been his chair all day and just breathed for a while.

Zhuqa watched him until he'd lost the hoarse, shuddery quality on his inhales, and then he sat down beside him. "How are things with my child, Dkorm?"

"...fair...sir."

"Good to hear. Good appetite, I trust?"

"...better."

"Yes, it had some trouble early on." Zhuqa glanced at Amber. "But we seem to have solved it. Cry much?"

"...some."

"And Rosek, eh? Healthy?"

"...think so."

"Healthy lungs, it would seem." Zhuqa gave the baby in Amber's arms a tolerant smile. "She's quiet now, though. Do you know why she's quiet now?"

And before Dkorm could suck in enough of a tortured breath to answer, Zhuqa the Warlord had seized him by the throat and yanked him up. "Because someone is comforting her," he hissed. "Can you comfort a baby, Dkorm? Can you do that for me? Because babies cry, *all* babies cry, and when *my* baby cries, I want to know that the man I have honored with its care is not *pinching its fucking mouth shut*!" he roared, seizing Dkorm by the snout and shaking him hard.

Rosek, falling asleep in Amber's arms, jerked and let out a wail. Amber rocked her, rubbing her little back as Xzem whispered and together, they quieted her to sniffles.

"Do you see that?" Zhuqa demanded, pointing. "Do you see how she did that?"

"Yes, sir."

"There are a lot of restless men waiting for this sale," Hruuzk called.

"One thing at a time," Zhuqa told him, and put his face very close to Dkorm's. "My patience with you is right down to its last grains. So. Get up. Fetch little Rosek and if she cries and you can't comfort her, I'm going to kill you. Do you mark me?"

"Yes, sir."

"Go." Zhuqa released him and unclipped the hooked sword from his belt.

Dkorm stood up, understandably shaky on his feet. He took a few steps toward Amber, hesitated when Rosek began to tear up, then very carefully took her and pressed her to his shoulder. He patted her back, mimicking Amber's swaying motions, and did not appear to breathe at all until Rosek sniffled herself quiet.

"This has been," said Zhuqa, "your final forgiveness." He hung his sword back on his belt. "I suggest you go someplace private and meditate on that until you come to some lasting conclusion. Go."

Dkorm went. Xzem twitched as if to rise and follow, but Zhuqa's pointing hand defeated her. She settled back down, staring after Rosek with haunted eyes.

"Are you coming to watch the sale?" asked Hruuzk.

"No. My Eshiqi is upset and wants to go home."

Hruuzk grunted and patted Amber on the head when she came close enough. "You know I'd never presume to give you advice—"

"Never," Zhuqa agreed thinly, watching Dkorm disappear in the crowd.

"—but why haven't you just given the sprat to Eshiqi to raise up?"

"For the same reason I haven't given it to you."

Hruuzk's broken spines flared. "I could do it," he said, sounding wounded. "Half the bodies under my hand are sprats, you think I don't know how to raise one?"

"I think," said Zhuqa, softening enough now that Dkorm was out of the room to give his slave-master a friendly tap to the arm. "I think you have enough to do. My Eshiqi has too much to learn right now. A child would be a distraction. Perhaps when it's weaned and not so needful, eh?" He glanced back at Xzem, smiling. "It will need a mother when Xzem is gone."

Xzem ducked her head and nuzzled at the infant that suckled her.

"I've never seen a slave so quick to take to a sprat," Hruuzk agreed. "Must have lost one of her own. Sure you won't come? I expect good coin for Gold-Eyes here."

"I can trust you, can't I?"

Hruuzk widened his good eye and pushed his broken spines forward. "Yes," he said gravely. "Trustworthy as the wind and tides, sir. Why, my sire was turned out from Fol Mgesh for an excess of trustiness and to his great pride it was a trait I took on."

"To it, then," said Zhuqa, hunkering down to watch his child at Xzem's breast. "We'll settle tomorrow."

"To his trust, men say of me," Hruuzk loudly muttered, leading his slaves out into the packed hall. "And they'll sing it at my pyre, I'm sure. All right then. Quiet up, you pack of animals! Quiet up and clear a path! If I can't reach the bidding block, I'll buy these dips myself and you can all poke each other!"

The door shut behind the last lizardlady, muting much of the noise, which then slowly receded as the men making it followed Hruuzk to wherever it was they went to auction slaves. At length, there was quiet. Even the children, as keyed up as they were, stayed in the back room and did their work without their usual chatter while Zhuqa was there.

"How is it, Xzem?" Zhuqa asked finally, gazing grimly down at the drowsing infant. "Say truth. Is it strong?"

Xzem hesitated.

"Truth," he said again, his voice hard.

"It is not ill, my lord," she told him.

"But...?"

"But it was a difficult birth and the mother...suffered. What weakens the womb, weakens the child."

Zhuqa grunted, expressionless.

"It has a good appetite and a strong grip. If it can be kept warm and dry and allowed to rest, it can grow strong."

"Do you say it will live?"

Xzem bent her head even lower. "I say it can live, my lord."

Zhuqa grunted again and stood. "There is a difference, isn't there? All right. I'm pleased. Is there anything you require?"

"No, my lord."

"You have enough to eat? And Rosek? She's comfortable?"

"We are both kept very well, my lord."

"Good. Eshiqi, come."

The hall outside the workpit was empty now, but Amber could still hear the crowd somewhere in the labyrinth of the ruins, jeering and hooting as Hruuzk called out bids. Zhuqa tipped his head to listen, but took her to the stair and down into the dark.

"You're very quiet," he said, when they'd passed the last set of guards and were alone in the long corridor leading to his private room.

"I don't have anything to say to you."

"Again?"

She glanced at him, but he just kept walking with the same distracted look about him. "I don't have anything to say."

He grunted thoughtfully.

They walked.

"You're quiet too," she said.

"I'm a quiet man."

Her feet rooted so suddenly that she stumbled. He caught her—he was so damned fast—and waited for her to steady herself before he continued on. He was smiling, just a little.

Lucky guess. It had to be. Meoraq had picked up English fast, but not that fast. All the same, she was glad she'd kept the bitchy out of her mouth for a change.

He unlocked his door and held it for her. His lamp was already lit inside. There was food on the table—tachuqi and roots and what looked like a short stack of pancakes. Zhuqa had to tap her shoulder to get her attention again. "Take off your clothes."

She did and he took them, feeling out every fold before tossing the robe carelessly over a crate.

"Now you," he said, and put his hands on her.

She waited, staring fixedly at the wall while he satisfied himself that she had no weapons socketed away, and when he was done, before he could give an order, she moved in close and touched her cheek briefly to his chest.

His spines flared. "My Eshiqi," he said, rubbing her back. "When Hruuzk called to you, you didn't know he saw me coming, did you? You thought he meant to put you on the block with the other slaves." And he smiled, like it was funny.

Amber didn't smile. She didn't swear at him either, or call him names or make any of the sarcastic comments she might have made if it wasn't for the little matter of how much English he might or might not understand...and if he wasn't right.

"Come to my table," he ordered, moving ahead of her to take his seat—still the only seat—and giving his thigh an inviting pat. When she sat, he pinched off a large bite of tachuqi meat and offered it up. "Hruuzk tells me you've been a good worker. You may think Hruuzk praises all the women who have played Zhuqa's House with me, but he doesn't. You have been my loyal woman...and a good mother to my child." He watched her eat. "Did you lose one?"

"No," she said, but thought of Nicci. "Never had one."

"I've lost five so far. I try not to see omens in piss anymore, but...this is my sixth." He took a bite for himself and chewed, gazing up at the ceiling as if he could see through it to Xzem and the baby, far above them. When he swallowed, he looked at her again. "A child needs a mother."

"A child needs not to grow up in a place like this even more."

"As the Word says, a father is God upon the living world," said Zhuqa, giving her another bite of meat. "The only God my son is likely to know. I can train a son. I can take him on hunts and raids. I can teach him blades and spears and grappling. I can be proud of him. I can even be fond of him, from a distance. But even a warlord's son needs a mother to hold him."

"I guess you're not always a dirty girl, are you? Sometimes you're a real sweetie. A prince among thieves. Or a princess."

He grunted, rubbed her thigh, fed her another bite.

"What if it's a girl?" asked Amber. "What happens to all your fatherly affection and pride then? Do you sell her?"

"Eh?"

She put her hands together in the teardrop-shape, but he continued to look blank. Amber made rocking motions with her arms, then realized she'd never seen Xzem rock a baby that way. For that matter, she'd never seen a human rock a baby that way, either. Awkwardly, she cupped her arms as if holding a baby upright at her breast and rocked back and forth instead. This put unpleasant pressure on her sex, but after she'd again made a teardrop-shape and repeated the baby-rocking, his light bulb finally came on.

"You think it will open up female?"

"You've got a fifty-fifty chance, don't you?"

Zhuqa grunted and stroked his throat, studying her through narrow eyes. "Zhuqa the Warlord has only one use for daughters," he said after a long silence. "But in Zhuqa's House, all children are prized. If I gave her to you, would you be grateful?"

"That depends. So far, all of your promises have only been good for a year."

He grunted, but in a thoughtful way that made her wonder again how much of what she said he was starting to understand. It didn't help when he said, "This place will never be better than a raider's nest to anyone who has ever known a true home, but you might be surprised how long a child can be happy here, if it's cared for."

"That's a horrible thought," said Amber, taking the piece of tachuqi he offered her.

"To a child who is not...well, you get Iziz." Zhuqa gestured broadly and helped himself to a root. "Who, I think, would never imagine that he has been mistreated in his life, but who was surely bought and buggered six times for every finger and toe on his body before the last of his scales went black. Raider-sprats like Iziz or Xzem...they're not unhappy just because they take a poke ten years too early. That's only hell to people who know better. So I ask you again—" He held up another piece of meat and cocked his head. "If I gave her to you, if I let you be the God in her living world, if I let you decide how much hurt is normal and how much is never visited...will you be grateful?"

"How grateful do you need me to be?"

"I'm giving you a chance to have a family," he said quietly. "But I won't let you raise my child to hate me. If you want it, you will have to decide whether you want to be my loyal woman or my fierce little slave."

She didn't answer, not out of defiance, but simply because, for one terrible moment, she wasn't entirely sure what her answer would be.

Zhuqa's eyes stabbed into her, deeper and deeper. At last, he leaned back in his chair and gave her another bite of meat. "But I won't ask you to choose tonight. For now, I am content as long as you play the game, Eshiqi. You don't have to mean it, but you have to play the game."

She closed her eyes, took a few breaths, then looked at him and forced a smile.

"I suppose you think it's silly," Zhuqa mused, tracing the shape of her lips with his fingertips. "And I suppose you would be right. But what else do I have here, eh? They taught us about evil when I was a boy, and about God's love and the promise of His forgiveness. I believed it. I believed that I knew where I fit in the world. I believed that I would serve Him someday and if it was His will, I would return with honor to be steward of my father's House. I believed I would have children in a place where it was not expected and acceptable for the first one to die. Now these things, the very idea of them, are nothing but pieces in a silly game." His eyes sparked. "Why shouldn't I want to play it?"

Amber did not answer. After a few seconds, he grunted and shifted her off his knee. "It's dark in here," he said.

Amber looked around, then went to the nearest lamp and pulled the wick up a little. The flame lengthened, but guttered. The pitcher of xuseth oil he kept in his room was nowhere obvious. While she looked for it, he went to the wall where he kept his awful drink in a new waterskin, poured himself half a cup, thought about it, then poured the other half. By the time she'd found the oil (on the shelf where it belonged, and God alone knew what it was doing there), he was back in his chair with his feet propped up on the table, drinking.

"Do you want to know what I did?" Zhuqa asked suddenly. His voice was mild; his scales, dark. His eyes, half in and out of shadow, had all the expression of cigarette burns. "Would you like to know what great unforgivable act cut me from my father's name and put me here? Would you like to know why I am so unfit to keep his House, why my children, if any of them survive, will never have the name I was born under? Eh? Do you?"

She ducked her head and fussed with the lamp, hoping that if she stayed quiet, he'd change the subject.

He took his boots off the table and brought his chair crashing back onto all four feet. She jumped; he watched her, calmly picking through the bowl of roots for one to eat. "Two years before my ascension, the training master I was brunt to broke his leg. They replaced him with someone new, someone from outside. He took an interest in me. Used to keep me extra hours, teaching me advanced fighting forms, but didn't work me too bad afterwards. We spent a lot of nights just sitting up together, chatting while I cleaned his boots or put an edge on his blades. I liked him," Zhuqa said, twisting the words like a knife. He laughed once, shortly, and drank again.

"So. So one night, after hours, as we were chatting, he brought out a flask of wine and offered me a swallow. The Word forbids all things which cloud the mind and corrupt clay, but this man, my master, my friend, told me that only applied if you did it to excess. And he would know, wouldn't he? He had been a Sheulteb once. He was a Sword and a true son of God. He gave me a swallow and he gave me a few more, and when I was warmed up nicely, he brought out a few leaves of phesok and gave me some of that. I don't remember falling asleep. I just remember waking up...when he was in me."

Amber ran out of things to do to the lamp. She got up, feeling his stare on her like a physical weight, and went over to the cupboard. She straightened the pillows, shook out the furs, brushed grit off the mattress.

"To this day, that baffles me," said Zhuqa. "Just outside the masters' gate, not a hundred walking strides from where he stood when he fucked me, slept one or two hundred women desperate for the healing fires of a son of Sheul. He didn't need to make a boy drunk to get a poke in unless he wanted to. Suppose I should feel flattered." He drank, eyed the empty cup, then got up to pour the last of the wine. "I don't. Come and take this, Eshiqi."

She went, but she took the empty flask, not the cup he tried to give her. There was a moment when he thought about forcing it on her—she could see it glittering in his eye as he watched her hang the flask upside down to dry—but in the end, he let it go and sipped at it himself.

"In the morning, I told my blademaster. They called a tribunal. I had to tell the story to a room filled with men and boys I knew. The man, my master, denied everything. He went on to say that he had caught me rubbing my cock and this was the act of a boy who feared to have it made known. And since neither of us would recant, it went to trial. He stood for himself. My father sent a Sheulteb. He wouldn't...He wouldn't stand for me himself. And this man, this lying man, this man who gave me drink and gave me phesok and bent my sleeping body over the back of a bench, this man won that trial."

In spite of everything, Amber turned around. "And they threw you out?"

"No," said Zhuqa. He was looking right at her with his face now full in the light, but his eyes were still cigarette burns. "It's not unforgivable to fuck your fist or to tell lies to a tribunal. They held me in a cell and whipped me at fourth- and tenth-bell for a full brace in the public courtyard and then they gave me back to him. I went to lessons every morning. He had me every night. Without drink or phesok." He shrugged his spines stiffly. "Too hard to come by in the city. Anyway, I managed with the help of the one boy I still trusted to send a message to my father. He came in person the next day."

Zhuqa was quiet for a time, just holding his cup and staring at some point in space between the two of them. At last, he shrugged again and drank off the last of it. "He dragged me out of lessons to the first empty room and beat me until I went black. Then he went home. My master took me out of the infirmary a few days later and fucked me three times. Making up for time lost, he said. He couldn't manage the last go, so he used the hilt of a practice sword. It was bigger than he was. I bled. He told me to clean it. I killed him with it," said Zhuqa, tossing the empty cup on the table. "He wasn't sleeping. His back wasn't turned. I took him on in the full sight of the God that let him fuck me and let him lie about it and let me be whipped for the lie and I killed him with a wooden toy of a sword. Then I gave myself over and they turned me out. Not for the murder, although they did call it that. No, they turned me out for blasphemous and malicious lies, because I said that he had fucked me when God had proven that he had not. There I stood, with my own blood and his stinking grease still inside me..."

He trailed off, then gave the empty cup on the table a morose flick with two fingers and stood up. "A man named Chuaan hunted me down later that year and fed me to his men for a catch-cock. Shouldn't have bothered me—not much did by that time—but I saw fire as soon as the first hand was on me. I killed six of them, they tell me, and so the legend of the mighty Zhuqa who has never been poked was born. I let them think so. I am—" He smiled, thin and hard as razors. "—such a liar. Come here, Eshiqi."

She went. He slung his arm around her shoulders and she held him steady all the way to the cupboard. She took his boots off, helped him out of his harness and picked his legs up for him when he dropped back onto the mattress. "Say something," he said, staring at the top of the cupboard.

"This man you hate so much," said Amber. "You turned into him."

She said it in English, but he said, "I know," and turned his dead gaze on her with a smile. "Would you call that proof of God, eh? Is it keeping balance in the world, in His great, unknowable design?"

"I call it proof that people can be horrible without God's help."

She could tell he didn't get much of that, if anything, but he didn't let it bother him. He plucked at her arm, pulled her in with him and shut the cupboard door.

"I'm too drunk to fuck," he muttered, rubbing at his face. "Use your hand."

She did. It took longer than usual. She wiped him off with the edge of a blanket when it was over and lay down beside him.

"Your Sheulek," he said, so thickly now that he could scarcely be understood. "The one you think is coming...if he really believes all the piss he was taught, he'll never take you back. And if he doesn't...he won't come for you at all." His hand brushed at her hair, then slipped down to cup her hip and pull her back against him. "You've gone to Gann, Eshiqi, just like me. If God Himself would not forgive you, why would he?"

She didn't answer. Eventually, he fell asleep.

She lay awake.

10

Amber was surprised to see the new slaves back in the workpit the next day, although after some thought, she supposed it was as good a place as any to put them. Some of them were dressed now. Some of them had been given names. All of them had the same distant stare, even when they looked right at her. But when Hruuzk gave them instructions, they listened and did what they were told. Not as smoothly or as well as the long-time slaves who shared the workpit, but that would surely come in time.

After getting everyone started, Hruuzk gathered up the kids and a few of the women and took them away, saying something about work 'up top' that needed doing. He was gone a long time and came back alone, carrying a huge sack over his shoulder and a small chest under one arm.

"Here to me!" he called. "Yllgami! Ena! Eshiqi! The rest of you, keep on with what you're about. All right." He thumped sack and chest both on a table and opened them. The sack was stuffed with a confusing jumble of rope; the chest, with hundreds of small fish hooks.

"Mud's thawing and snow on the mountain's melting, so we'll have aamyr washing in from the lake any day. Yllgami, you sort out the nets. Ena, you mend them. Eshiqi—" Hruuzk produced a mending kit that had been tucked into his belt and held it out to her. "—sew on the hooks. Yllgami will show you where and how."

Amber slowly took the kit from him and turned it around. It was Meoraq's.

"I want the first of them ready for the water this evening and the last of them in the water by tomorrow night. Show me those clever hands, eh? Good girl."

Hruuzk gave her head a pat. She looked at him, thinking of the night she'd first held this kit, and Meoraq beside her as she made new soles for the boots Zhuqa had taken away. Someone else in this camp was wearing them. Someone else had the white thuoch hides which would never be her coat. Someone had stolen the clothes she'd spent all winter making.

Someone had stolen her.

"Get to it," Hruuzk ordered, already on his way out. If he'd seen anything different in her eyes, he hadn't thought it worth mentioning. And why should he? An unhappy slave in the workpit? No, really?

Yllgami was brushing at Amber's sleeve with the very tip of her knuckles and making mewing sounds scarcely loud enough to hear. Reluctant to put Meoraq's mending kit aside, Amber tucked it underneath her arm, but gave Yllgami her full attention. Life went on. Mothers died, ships crashed, people left you, people stole you...but life went on.

It helped to think of the nets like Christmas lights. First, they had to be untangled, and while it was obvious that whoever had packed them away had made an effort to bundle each one separately, they'd all knotted together. As soon as the first one was free, Ena had it and a spare coil of rope and was using what looked like a giant wooden barrette to patch holes in the loose weave. As Amber continued to help Yllgami, Dkorm and Xzem arrived.

He kicked some sacks into a heap and sat down, tucking Rosek under his arm with an expression of profound dislike. She was restless, wriggly, and already making those breathy barking noises that meant a crying fit wasn't far off.

Amber hesitated, picking at her net, then pushed it back and headed over.

"Take the fucking thing," Dkorm groaned, but instead, Amber rummaged in the crates and bags around him for the scraps of clothing left over from her mending of a few days' ago. With rags in various colors and a little thread from Meoraq's kit, Amber threw a crude doll together. She wasn't good at domestic shit like this, but good enough for Rosek, who gawped at the gift like it was the first she'd ever seen...which it probably was. She took it, chewed it, shook it, and let out a shrill squeal and began to beat it vigorously against the side of a crate.

"How is that better?" Dkorm demanded, spines flat.

Amber went back to the nets. Ena had finished her repairs and Yllgami was waiting anxiously next to the box of hooks. Amber watched without interest while Yllgami deftly and wordlessly sewed about a dozen fish hooks into the weave, not too closely spaced and all pointed in the same direction, then took the needle when it was offered and got to work.

She immediately stabbed herself with a fish hook. The hooks were barbed; pulling it out tore the little wound even wider. It bled enough to draw a thin red line from the tip of her finger to the crease of her first knuckle, but that was all. 'Just lick it,' she thought in Meoraq's terse, irritated voice, and did. It tasted bitter.

The fish hook was a swoop of metal lying in her palm, reflecting nothing but the lamp light. 'Meoraq could kill a man with this stupid thing,' she thought sourly. But what did that prove? Meoraq could kill a man with a beach ball.

Breath on her shoulder. She stiffened, but didn't turn around. She didn't try to hide the hook either, knowing it had already been seen. She simply picked up a needle and started tying it onto the net.

Dkorm snorted at her back. "It amazes me that you can work all those fingers without getting them confused," he remarked and started to turn away. He paused. He turned back, jogging Rosek higher onto his shoulder so that he could reach out and play with Amber's hair. "Does Zhuqa know how clever you are with your many fingers, Eshiqi?"

"Fuck off. I'm working."

"Zhuqa told me I couldn't have a poke." He leaned in to lick at her. The waxy nub of his tongue, dry and repulsive, swept back and forth over her shoulder while she fought and failed not to squirm. "As far as I know, everything else is just fine."

"If you believe that, you're even dumber than you look." Amber shrugged hard enough to hit him in the jaw and followed that glancing blow with a glare while he rubbed his snout and looked thinly amused. "And you're not scaring me with any of this macho shit, so just back off and let me work."

"You talk too much." He moved to the other shoulder and licked it, too. Tiny hands caught at her wrap as he worked his way methodically to her neck; the baby, Rosek, trying to wriggle out from between them. "Fucking sprat," she heard him mutter and he leaned away.

Her hand tightened on the needle before she could make herself relax. It wasn't much of a gesture. He should have missed it if he'd been looking anywhere but right at her hand.

But he snorted again. "With that thing?" he asked derisively. "Go on, then."

She made another knot, furious and silent.

"You don't think I mean it." He caught her wrist, turned her roughly around and shoved her against the table. Her ass hit the corner just right and she toppled back, catching herself in the split-second before she took a painful sprawl across the hook-studded net. She had the needle raised in a fist before she knew it.

Dkorm stepped up invitingly, the baby in one arm and the other open wide, displaying the whole of his scaly chest for her sliver of baked bone to pierce. "Go on. You killed a man, they say, so you must have some arm in you, no matter how you look. You could even hurt me if you sink it in my eye, but I warn you, you might hit the sprat." He jogged Rosek again and she squealed happily and waved her new doll over her head.

Amber put the needle down and gave it a push out of her easy reach.

Dkorm grunted and fingered her hair, then wrapped a hank of it around his wrist and pried her head slowly back, further and further, until her shaking arm couldn't brace her anymore. She fell with a weak, angry cry, anticipating a dozen barbed hooks in her back, but the hand that pulled her down also held her up. She waited, suspended over the net with her eyes squeezed shut, for him to work out what he wanted to do.

After a tense silence, Dkorm rasped out another lizard-laugh and backed up, tossing her by her hair to her knees on the floor. "You are the ugliest Gann-damned thing I have ever seen," he announced, handing her the baby as he beckoned to Yllgami. "I honestly don't know what it is about you that makes me want to fuck."

"Of course you want to fuck, you're nothing but a giant dick," Amber said, and was glad he didn't know English enough to know how shaky and frightened she sounded. Behind her, she could hear as Dkorm bent his slave over the table. He was loud—grunting, slapping, hissing; Yllgami never made a sound.

Rosek, larger and stronger than Zhuqa's baby, struggled to get away from the smooth-skinned, hairy monster now enveloping her, and finally Xzem crept forward and snatched her away. Amber rubbed at her empty arms and watched Xzem nuzzle Rosek while nursing the smaller infant. Dkorm's violent sex went on and on.

"Look at you...pretending...not to care," he panted, finally shoving the lizardlady away and wiping his cock clean on her skirts. "Look at you staring me down like I couldn't stand you up and put it to you so hard, you'd be coughing on my cum before the end."

His boots tromped heavily around until he stood in front of her, over her. He didn't move to take the baby back, either of them. He just stood there while Amber glared at the floor and made herself keep quiet. Then, with a curt laugh, he caught her by the hair and yanked her head up. Looking at him meant looking past the cudgel of his erection, already weeping fresh beads of oil in readiness. "I can see murder in your eyes. When are you going to learn that you are a slave now?" he wondered, giving her hair a shake. "You can be as fierce as you want, Eshiqi, but all it will get you is killed."

He was right. Thoughts of the needle and the fish hooks taunted her, but the real bitterness was that she'd come to think of them as any kind of weapon at all. Even if she could get the needle through his thick hide, how much damage could she do? She remembered the kipwe all too well and how its quills—the smallest of them twice the size of her needle—hadn't slowed Meoraq down in battle. He'd actually been able to sleep through their removal. She also remembered the way his scales had sealed up over the wounds as she pulled them out, so even if she got in a good hit, she'd never do any real damage. Maybe she could stab him in the slit, where his scales were thinnest and didn't overlap, but if that was the best she could do, what was the point?

"Zhuqa seems to think that you're smart," Dkorm was saying, running his thumb idly up and down along his shaft as he toyed with her hair. "But you're not smart enough to know that making me happy is much better for you in the long term than showing me how fierce you can be."

All this with his dick right in front of her. Amber felt a moment's nostalgia for the days of Crandall and subtle innuendo. She started to twist her face away from the hook-tipped thing Dkorm kept aimed at her, but then flinched a little and stared right at it.

"I wish you would take a stab at me, Eshiqi," he said, and let her go again to grip his cock, squeezing once wistfully before pushing it back, grimacing with effort, into his slit. "There's not a scale on me you could poke through with that toy you had, but if you at least tried, maybe Zhuqa would give me one hour to poke b—"

Amber reached out and caught him by the narrowing tip of his cock before he could force it all the way out of sight. He let go with a startled hiss and out it came, thrusting through her fist in oiled urgency until the knot at its base bumped her hand.

And there it was.

Meoraq could kill a man with this stupid thing, she'd thought, looking at the fish hook, but she hadn't meant it, not really. Not even Meoraq could magically make that insignificant bit of metal into a murder weapon when every part of a lizardman's body was armored and every vein protected.

Every vein...but this one. That thick, black, throbbing vein that crawled along the surface of the bulging knot at the base of his cock.

"Get off me," Dkorm warned, glancing over his shoulder at the workpit door, but he didn't try to pry her off. Zhuqa could walk in at any moment, and if he found her here with her hand on this man's dick, he'd probably do all the killing she could ever want for her, but it wasn't Dkorm she wanted dead.

'I could do it,' she thought, stunned. 'Even with a fish hook.'

"Get off me, I said!"

Amber looked up past the slick head of his cock to his strained, somewhat dazed face. His spines were low, but not flat, and the color was coming in at his throat. If she gave him a stroke, she had no doubt that would be the end of his objections.

'Because he's sick,' she thought, staring. 'Once his neck lights up, it all about sex...or killing...and all they want to do is more of it. It's only, what? Seventeen years of training that keeps Meoraq more or less under control—'

Training that Zhuqa shared. Training that just might give him that one moment's pause to think, 'Hang on, this is suspicious.' And then he'd kill her.

And how was she going to smuggle a fish hook out of the workpit anyway? More importantly, how was she going to smuggle it into Zhuqa's room? He'd strip her as soon as he got her home and as soon as he saw a weapon, even if it was a silly little finger-length fish hook, he'd kill her.

And even if he didn't, even if by some miracle she killed him, there was no way out except up ten flights of stairs, past ten pairs of guards and then past all the rest of them living in the ruins on the surface before running out into the wildlands to get lost and die anyway.

'So stay,' she thought in the voice of her dead mother. She looked at her hand on Dkorm's dick and it was Bo Peep's hand. It was Bo Peep's heart inside her feeling nothing but hopelessness and hate, feeling it so completely that it was almost comforting. 'Stay and be Zhuqa's Eshiqi. Be a mother to his kids. Help train the new slaves he brings home for his men to fuck. Suck it up or blow it out, little girl. There's no such thing as a fate worse than death.'

In the stillness of that moment, she was tempted.

"Fuck you," Amber whispered, appalled. She let go of Dkorm and wiped her hand on her shift.

He socked her in the ear. Probably not as hard as he could have, but hard enough. Whether he hit her for grabbing his cock or letting go, she didn't know and he didn't explain. He just knocked her aside and pulled Yllgami back to finish him off. Less than a minute later, he was back on his throne of crates and sacks, swearing at Rosek and drinking.

Amber sat on the floor. The other women worked around her. She watched them; they did not watch her.

Meoraq was looking for her. She still believed that, but every time she woke up beside Zhuqa, it was getting harder to believe he'd find her. And if God told him to get on with his life—if he saw a funny shape in the clouds or if the fire burned a weird way or if any one of a thousand random things happened—he'd do it.

Maybe he'd already done it. With Bo Peep sitting so close beside her, it was easy to imagine him coming back to camp and praying instead of looking for her. She could see him kneeling beside the dead raider all night and then leaving him to rot on the ground in the morning. Why burn him? He'd gone to Gann. He was corrupted beyond all forgiveness. And so, perhaps, was she.

'No one is going to save you, little girl.'

"Fuck you," Amber said again.

Bo Peep shrugged inside her head, smiling her mean, drunken smile. 'Sometimes you have to say the bad stuff. Hope is nothing but pretty lies, like those storybooks they gave you in state-care, where the dragon always dies in the end and the prince climbs the tower and carries the prisoner away to be a princess forever and forever. Bullshit, baby. In the real world, nobody saves you. In the real world, it's live in Zhuqa's House...or die there.'

Amber opened her mouth to tell her mother's fake ghost to fuck herself for a third time, but couldn't. Bo Peep was right. And since the only part of Bo Peep that was still around was a figment of Amber's own imagination, she guessed she knew what she was going to do.

She was going to escape.

* * *

They finished three nets by the end of the day, with little enough for Amber to do that she also learned how to repair them. She needed the distraction, badly. With nothing to think about except the hook—not even the hook, but the possibility, the *potential*, of the hook—she had become tense enough to make her neck and back ache. Aching muscles needed to be stretched. Walking helped the stretching, but made the other lizardladies distinctly nervous. So she picked up a pair of the odd wooden tools Ena was using and watched until she figured out how to fix a hole in a fishing net.

She kept at it long after the rest of them were gone. Hook and pull, wrap and knot, wrap and hook. It made the time pass.

Zhuqa came. Amber put Meoraq's needles back in Meoraq's mending kit and set it carefully on the table where she had been working. Then she turned around to face him, tipping back her head in case he wanted a nuzzle. He did. She stood very still until it was over and then followed him out into the hall.

Alone in his room, Amber took the initiative, stripping away her clothes before he gave the order and standing patiently by while he searched her. She could feel the plan throbbing behind her eyes like a headache, until she could not bear to meet his gaze and had to look away.

"You should know," he murmured, stroking at her throat, "I find coyness deeply arousing. Come and greet your man, Eshiqi, before we share our meal."

Amber stepped close, still staring at the table to keep her thoughts, her plan, away from his too-piercing stare. She pressed her cheek perfunctorily to his chest and her hand to his groin, thoughts racing. She loosened his belt to work her hand beneath his metal loin-plate and kneaded at him, seeking the hidden hardness of his cock beneath his skin.

"Enough of that," said Zhuqa, chuckling as he patted her hip. "Food first. Then we play."

"Believe me, I'm not playing," said Amber, resisting his nudge toward the table and moving her hand instead to his slit.

He caught her wrist, the hard edges of his belly-scales flexing shut around her fingertip. He didn't look amused anymore. She glared, because she knew he expected to see it, even as she felt her heart pounding at her ribs...and her ribs pressed too goddamn close to his.

His eyes narrowed. Deliberately, he cocked his head—a warning.

“Please,” she said in lizardish. Nerves made her voice shake and that was good, as long as she sounded broken and not like her head was burning up with secrets.

“You want something?” Suspicion dimmed, but didn’t die. “What do you want?”

What, it wasn’t enough that she was trying to ingratiate herself? She had to have a reason?

“Take me out,” she said. “Just for a little while.”

“Eh?”

Fuck this stupid impossible goddamn tonal language. “Out,” she said, or tried to. “Craoo. Trooo. Sky.”

“You what...?” His head slowly tipped back. “You want to see the sky.”

“That’s right,” she said, gratefully falling into English again. She kneaded at his slit some more and gradually he relaxed enough to let her finger penetrate, although he kept his hold on her wrist. “I want to see the sky. You said Zhuqa’s woman doesn’t need to be locked up. I’ve been good, haven’t I? I want to see the sky.”

“What exactly do you think you have to barter with that I do not already own?” he inquired. His spines were coming up, away from flat suspicion to cautious enjoyment.

Amber found his sa’ad, gave it a stroke, then looked into his eyes and knelt.

He had to be able to see the plan in her eyes. He had to. Because she could see as clear as the sun back in Earth’s sky his memory of how she’d licked the meaty juices off his fingers the other night. His slit bulged with the sudden prodding of his erection; the scent of cloves and musk welled, cloying in its closeness.

Amber held the stare. Her lips parted, She breathed on the crown of his slit where her thumb pierced him, then looked at his hand on her wrist.

He grunted and tightened his grip. “The game is ‘Zhuqa’s House,’ woman,” he said. “Not ‘Eshiqi’s bargain. I did not ask for this. Up.”

But his cock was a dark gleam between the widening folds of his slit, and she could feel the tension in his muscles as he fought to hold it in. He told her to get up, sure he did, but he didn’t pull her to her feet and he could have.

She rubbed the ball of her thumb over his sa’ad in two slow revolutions, then put her other hand up to pry the top of his slit open so she could see it—a dark, pointing gnarl that resembled either the world’s largest clitoris or the tiniest penis, visibly twitching in time with his pulse. ‘Meoraq has one of these and I never knew it,’ she thought suddenly and had to bite down on a giggle because it really was funny, wasn’t it, to think that she could be that unadventurous about having sex with her alien lizardman.

She caressed Zhuqa’s sa’ad, still in that light-headed, dangerously amused mood, now thinking of it less as a blowjob and more of a lesbian experience. Her very first. She leaned close, exhaled.

His cock lurched out maybe halfway and pulled back out of sight.

“Please,” said Amber, in case he’d forgotten why she was doing this.

“I did not trust you before,” he said tightly. “I trust you damned less n—”

She licked his slit.

His last word swept into a lizardish snarl and his hips jerked forward, impaling the air with the sudden stabbing bar of his fully extruded, cum-spitting cock. He jerked her trapped wrist up over her head even as his other hand came clawing down at her shoulder.

Amber pried his slit open (much easier to do with his cock out) and licked it again, sweeping her tongue back and forth like she was licking an ice-cream cone into shape. The taste was strong in ways she couldn’t identify (but not of cloves, oddly) and not as unpleasant as she’d been braced for, except for the little matter of whose clit she was licking at all. Each wet swirl of her tongue beat another convulsion of some sort out of Zhuqa—a cough, a curse, a staggering step or a clenching fist—until he let go of her hand and she was free to use it on his cock.

The instant she closed her fist around him, she pursed her lips around his clit and sucked it into her mouth. Sucked hard.

"Fuck Gann!" roared Zhuqa and then grey light burst over the left side of her head and suddenly Amber was sprawling over the floor.

He looked almost as surprised to see her there as she was.

Amber put a hand cautiously up to rub at the hot throb of her left ear, but it wasn't bleeding, of course, just slapped really good. She looked at him, and then she bounded to her feet, shouting, "What was that for?"

He glared at her, breathing hard but silently, and then pointed at the ground between his feet.

"No!" she snapped, then said it again in his language.

He was fast. He was so scary fast. He had her by the neck while the word was still hot in her mouth and choked it off, half-spoken. He started to speak, then paused and looked away to take a few more silent breaths. His cock moved slowly up and down, keeping time. He looked at her again. His grip eased, then opened.

"I did not mean to hit you," he said. "You startled me. I won't do it again. Use your mouth on me, Eshiqi, and I will take you to see the sky."

She gave her left ear a sullen rub, glaring at him, thinking, 'There it is and that didn't take long at all, did it? I can do this. I really think I can.'

Zhuqa nudged at her head, but gently now.

Amber shifted his breeches, glared some more, and then knelt down again and stilled the flexing of his cock with her touch. She stroked the shaft, licked once at his sa'ad, and then turned her head and sucked lightly at the slick side of his cock.

"Fuck Gann," he breathed, sagging back against the door.

Back and forth, from clit to cock, licking, sucking, squeezing, flicking. She rolled his sa'ad between her lips, bathed every side of his shaft, licked all the way up his slit and down again in one slow sweep, pursed her lips around the blunt hook at the tip of his cock and suckled it, then latched her mouth around the base and let the tip of her tongue trace the many valleys between the rubbery spikes that grew along the knot, feeling it fill with fresh cum as he hissed and groaned and screamed obscenities.

And with it all so close to her face, she could not help but also see the thick, black vein pulsing just where the soft inner meat of his slit hardened into the base of his cock. Amber stared, feeling nothing, tasting nothing, seeing fish hooks in her mind.

His knot was swelling already. Time to bring the curtain down.

Amber took the full length of his cock in both her fists, working him in milking motions as she sucked at the hook and flicked the opening eye with her tongue to drink away the first drops. And when he started to cum, she was quick to suck the whole head into her mouth, bobbing as deep as she could manage, letting him feel her swallow each hot, oily stream that burst across her tongue.

She knew when he finally looked down and saw her doing it because both his hands came down to clench in her hair and he spent the last few seconds of his climax fucking furiously at her throat and calling out some of the most filthily creative things Amber had ever heard and never could have imagined, ending with, "Fuck Gann fucking God fucking *me*!" before he finally staggered back and slid down to join her on the floor.

Amber waited, just in case he had it in him to keep going, but once he had his breathing slowed, Zhuqa pulled his cock in and closed his breeches. He grimaced at her.

"You promised," said Amber.

"I hear you." He reached out and rubbed a finger along the corner of her lips, then showed her the smear of semen on his fingertip.

She thought about it, then licked it off.

He shuddered. "That is the most profane thing I have ever seen," he told her. The front of his loin-plate was bulging.

"Please," said Amber.

"You never should have bartered with me, little one." Zhuqa got to his feet and pulled her up beside him, grimacing his lizard-grin at the world. "Because now you are going to have to buy everything."

But he took her out, up ten flights of stairs, past dozens of saluting, well-armed guards. He did it without any suspicion. He did it with a smile on his face. He did it without ever thinking in any way that she could sense how vulnerable that one little vein might be and how readily he'd put her on her knees before it and then closed his eyes. He just took her out.

It was hard to be outside. She hadn't thought about how it would be to actually see the sky again, feel the wind, taste the freshness after the deep, stale air of the underground ruins. It had just been something to ask for, something she'd known he would believe. She thought she'd be able to take a few deep breaths, maybe gaze intently into the clouds, and her only concern had been how she was going to make that look convincing when she didn't really care.

But the wind was cool and wet with the promise of clean rain. There was a greenness to it, some springtime flavor that she caught on her tongue when she breathed, and for a while she forgot about Zhuqa entirely, even as he stood watching her.

She did all the same things she'd planned to do after all, although she didn't think about that until later. She took those deep, shaky breaths. She tipped her head back and stared at the grey smudge that marked a full moon's light behind the ever-rolling clouds. She didn't speak and didn't move until Zhuqa put his hand on her shoulder and said, with that hateful gentleness he so often had, "Enough, little one. You're shivering. Come inside."

Then she began to cry, sort of. There were no sobs, no ugliness, no lump in her throat that needed choking out. There were just tears, pouring out of her one after another, so quiet and easy that if it weren't for the heat of them, she might not have known she was making them. She looked at Zhuqa and he reached up to wipe at her cheek with the back of his hand. She realized that she'd made up her mind already, that the fish hook was not a possibility, but a plan. Tomorrow's plan.

"Ah, Eshiqi, hush," he said, brushing at her other cheek as the first trickled more tears. "Zhuqa's woman does not stay forever in his lair. One day, all the world will be your House."

"You said the same thing to Zru'itak," she said and turned toward the stair.

"And I would have kept my promise," he said evenly, "if she had remained loyal to me." He studied her as she stared at him, then smiled very slightly. "That was a good guess, I think," he remarked to himself. "But I'm not guessing at every word, believe that. You are losing your secrets, Eshiqi, a little more each day. One day very soon, you will have to be honest."

She heard herself laugh without feeling it. "Not today, I hope. And not tomorrow."

He frowned, capturing each word as it left her mouth for further study. He waited a long time after her last word, as if to be sure she was done talking, but when her gaze wandered back to the sky, he grunted and took gentle hold of her arm. "We have a meal waiting for us," he said, leading her in their descent. "It will be cold now, but you will sit on my knee and hold my cup and show me your gratitude, and tomorrow, perhaps, you will see the sky again."

And the tears kept coming, because Amber knew she was never going to make it that far out, and she'd already had her last look at the sky.

11

Sixteen spans, the boy had said. Meoraq had always felt he had a good grasp of distance, even in the wildlands. Years of travel and Master Darr's notorious book of maps burned into his brain combined to keep a subconscious tally wherever he went. It was not infallible—all things mortal succumbed at times to deception or delusion—but it had served him well and he had every reason to put his faith in it as much as God. He began his hunt for ruins at an estimate of fourteen spans and when he reached eighteen without finding them, he stopped, turned back alongside his trail, and sought them further south.

Back and forth he went in this fashion, waking before dawn to make use of each second that God gave him light. He stopped at every stream to scout for boot-prints among the animal tracks. He knuckled through the gnawed leavings of each carcass for signs of butchery. He searched each promising thicket or valley deep enough to hide a nest, climbed each hill that might show him a better vantage.

He found everything—muddy tracks, blade-marked bones, discarded scraps of cured leather, broken sleds, ashpits—but none of it was fresh and in finding everything, he found nothing. As for ruins, he knew the signs well enough in Yroq, but in this land of hills and valleys and chokes of trees, anywhere he aimed his eyes showed him signs. And yet he found no ruins.

He told himself he would finish out one more day southward and then turn around. He would run through the night back to his first trail, roughly, and begin a northerly search in the morning.

Good. Sound. Sensible.

But when night fell on the fifth day of futility, Meoraq camped. He didn't really know why. He hadn't found anything (two separate heaps of half-burnt branches, a rotted harness, a dead man tied to a hsul tree and left to be eaten alive a brace or so ago: nothing) and his last glimpse of the landscape before the sun fell showed him nothing worth exploring further, but he camped all the same. He lit no fire, just sat in the dark, trying to meditate while his nerves gnawed at him.

When he slept, he dreamed in confusing tangles of his father returning from Kuaq, of silver shards in the shape of a ship flying through broken tiles, of thunder and rain and the stormway tunnel collapsing around him. He did not dream of Amber.

He woke just at dawn feeling that scant minutes had passed since he'd shut his eyes, and yet he felt...not invigorated, really, but awake. Like the stinging sensation that comes to a numbed arm or leg when it is first moved, it was not a pleasant feeling, but ominous, a sign of something greater still to come.

He prayed at least an hour, largely without words, as the morning moved on ahead of him. At the end of his prayers, he started walking south again.

He had always had a good sense of time as well as distance. Today, although painfully aware of direction (and it was pain; he could feel Praxas like a fish hook in his flesh, tied to a line that threatened with every step to snap), he had no grip at all on the hour. The sun moved overhead and if it were not for the fact that he could see it (not the sun, but the light of the sun, and there was another fish hook), he would have no sense of time at all. To judge by that light, it was near eighth-hour—almost the whole day walked away—when he came to the top of the hill that had the tree.

It was the only tree left on the hill, of some kind unknown to him. Its body was very tall and straight, burnt black by some misfortune in the far past. Its single surviving branch had broken close to the trunk, half-fallen, but sprouted new life at its tip, so that the whole thing took on the appearance of a fish hook, and why in the two names of God and Gann was he so obsessed with fish hooks? He didn't think he'd ever in his life seen one except in shops or pictures. But there it was, this ruin of a tree, this monument to all fish hooks of the world, an obvious landmark for even a boy to find and follow, and so Meoraq put down his pack and climbed it.

At the top, just where the branch hung down, Meoraq looked out over the furthest ridge and saw dark shapes too perfectly squared to be natural, set in patterns only men could design.

Ruins.

'And it's nineteen spans from Praxas if it's a damned step,' he thought. The boy was no better at gauging distance than he was putting a choke on a man.

Not even for a moment did he question whether these were the ruins where his Amber had been taken. Neither did he stop to wonder how many raiders were nesting in its belly. Some things were manifestly obvious. Some things didn't matter. He knew.

* * *

She stole the fish hook. She meant to wait until the end of the day, the last possible minute, so the chances of being caught with it were at their lowest, but as much sense as that made, she was only able to stand touching them, sewing with them, staring at them, for so long before she just had to take one. And the opportunity, when it came, was too golden and glorious to overlook: Hruuzk, out of the room; all the slaves, occupied with work; the children, who were the most wildly unpredictable variable, up top with Hruuzk; and into this almost-perfect scenario, Rosek suddenly peed on Dkorm. Swearing, he scooped her up and stomped into the next room where there was water to get cleaned up.

Amber didn't watch him go, didn't hesitate, didn't think. She stopped sewing on one hook, reached into the box, and hooked another on the inside of her sleeve where it was out of sight and could still plausibly have gotten there by accident. Then she went back to sewing. She attempted a few deep breaths—a slow-count of six, as Meoraq would say—but only made it as far as three before her nerve buckled and she looked around to see if she'd been caught.

Dkorm was still in the other room, scrubbing at himself with a rag and hissing at the baby. The slaves were right where they ought to be, necks bent, silent. Xzem—

Xzem was looking at her. She ducked her head when their eyes met, rocking Zhuqa's baby and trying to coax him back onto her breast, but she had definitely been looking. What had she seen? What would she say?

She didn't have long to agonize over it. Dkorm came storming back into the room while Amber was still sewing on the same hook, her hands too weak and fluttery-feeling to manage the simple knots. He shoved Rosek roughly into a crate and threw himself down, still wiping at his chest and muttering. His mood infected the other lizardladies with enough anxiety that her own went unnoticed.

The fish hook pulled at her sleeve, a thousand-pound piece of metal smaller than her thumb. Everything was relative.

Somehow the day passed. She sewed mindlessly on the same net for most of it, forced to go back over the same places again and again when she consistently put hooks in upside down or sewed folds of the net together. When she was finally finished, it looked worse than the very first net she'd done, but at least it was finished and she could go clutch at Zhuqa's baby and calm herself down.

Xzem sat very still beside her and did not look at her.

The baby purred, its tiny hand squeezing Amber's goliath finger. It slept and

Amber cupped its small, warm head and stared into its snouted face and thought, 'I'm going to get you out of this, baby. It's you and me, all the way to the top.'

When it woke and began to bite sleepily at her breast, Amber gave it reluctantly back to Xzem and returned to her work-table. Ena had another net waiting, the last net. Amber got to work.

She had nearly finished when Hruuzk came at the end of the day to gather up his slaves. He took Meoraq's mending kit and tucked it back into his belt. She protested. Stupid of her, but she wanted to finish the net and she was at least three lengths of sinew from done.

"Eh, it's good enough," Hruuzk told her, inspecting the net. "I'll talk to Zhuqa about putting you in the kitchen. Shame to waste your energy doing sprat-work like this."

He patted her on the head and gave her his usual, "Good girl," and ambled away with his ladies all in a slumped, silent line. Dkorm left, taking Xzem and the babies. Amber sat down with a pitcher of xuseth oil tightly gripped in both hands and waited for Zhuqa. If he found the hook caught in her sleeve here in the workpit, she might still be okay. Maybe.

Hours, each one ticking away at its own elastic pace. She could hear herself breathing. She didn't think she'd ever heard herself breathe in this room before.

Zhuqa came. He smiled at her, filling the doorway. "Where is my greeting?"

Amber took one step toward him and froze. The hand she usually put on his chest was attached to the arm wrapped in the sleeve *with a fish hook in it*. If she raised it up as high as his heart, he would be looking right down the fucking thing, wide as the Lincoln Tunnel, with the lamp on the table blasting light right on it. If she used her other hand, would he notice?

'He's noticing this pause, little girl,' the ghost of Bo Peep drawled. 'That's what he's noticing. Get the stick out and do something.'

Her next step was something of a lurch, but it was movement and it took her to him. She put her arms around him (the hookless arm considerably tighter than the other) and pressed her cheek to his chest instead.

"You must want something," Zhuqa remarked, patting her back. "As it happens, so do I. Come, Eshiqi. We'll take our game below."

He took her out into the hall, keeping her at his side all the way to the stair. Her arm, the one with the hook, hung between them, threatening at each step to snag on his scales when he brushed against her. Amber began to feel distinctly light-headed. Was she even breathing? No, she was not. God.

At the stair, he went ahead of her, but there were guards at every landing, their faces all pointed up at him, at her. When he stepped off into the hallway, he stayed ahead of her, but there were guards at every crossway, standing at attention, showing their salutes. When he came to his door, he stopped to take out his squarish keys, and it was there, in the two short seconds it took him to unlock the door, that Amber pulled the hook out of her sleeve and put it in her mouth. She heard fabric tear even over the sound of the key turning in its lock, but Zhuqa never glanced back. The hook felt enormous clenched between her teeth, as if it were stretching out her whole face into a Halloween mask, but Zhuqa only smiled and beckoned for her to precede him.

"Zhuqa has come home," he said.

She walked in and began undressing without waiting for his order. Surely it was her imagination that made her think he looked at her for a heartbeat longer than usual before he took her shift, her imagination that made her think he was more meticulous than usual when he felt his way through it. He tossed it aside the same as ever, that she was sure of, and then his hands were on her.

'God, don't let him feel my heart pounding,' she thought. Prayed. No atheists in foxholes, wasn't that the saying? Well, there were no atheists in Zhuqa's room with fish hooks in their mouths, waiting for him to finish checking them for weapons either. In that moment, for as long as it lasted, Amber Bierce was a True Believer.

Zhuqa finished feeling between her thighs and stood up. He checked her armpits—*sweating so much he has to notice that why is he pretending not to goddamn sadistic lizard*—then moved on to lift her breasts in his hands, slipping his thumbs between them like always just in case she had a—*fish hook*—weapon stowed away beneath one of them.

And there he stopped.

For one illogical instant, Amber thought he'd found something. Her mouth tried to drop open in a gape; she clenched it shut and then had to relax her jaw so it didn't look like she was clenching it. She stared at him, fighting not to stare, knowing she had to be either white as a sheet or blushing to the roots of her hair, or heck, both.

Still cupping her breasts, with absolutely no sign on his lizardish face that anything at all was amiss, Zhuqa bent down and nuzzled at her throat.

Oh Jesus, really? The giggles came streaming out of her around the fish hook. She pressed her lips tightly together and stared at the ceiling while Zhuqa finished that side and moved his snout tenderly to the other side of her throat. The hand covering her left breast lightly squeezed, experimenting with her.

"I guess you remember yesterday," she said, because silence was never golden with this man for very long and if she had to talk, she wanted to do it when he had his face buried in her hair and not when he was looking right at her. Hopefully—*please god no atheists here tonight nothing here but us chickens please god*—he didn't know English so well that he could tell her teeth were clamped together.

He grunted softly against her skin, moved his hand from her right breast to her hip and tugged her lightly against him. "You are a terrible distraction to me, Eshiqi," he told her, and if there were more chilling words he could have said, she honestly didn't know what they were. Zhuqa the Warlord could not afford distractions. "My mind has been with you all day. Tell me..." He caught her hand, licked the palm, and then put it on his loin-plate. "Would you like to see the sky tonight?"

She smiled and started to kneel.

He stopped her. "Not here," he said, still apparently unaware of anything amiss as she struggled not to stare at him or show the racing of her heart. He pointed back at the table, where their meal had already been set aside in anticipation of the evening's festivities. In its place, an extra lamp burned brightly. "This time, I want to watch you."

* * *

In the first creeping hour after dark, when the last of the light was gone from the sky and any thinking man might know that it was time to seek shelter from the night's preying beasts, Meoraq came at last to the ruins and found them lit in welcome. His first foolish urge was to draw his blades and charge ahead. He mastered it and instead hunkered low in the grass, watching and praying in silence.

He saw men—or what might be called men, if one knew no better—moving below the lamps that hung at the open doorways of the ruins. When the wind was with him, he could even hear them, however dimly, laughing and calling to one another as any men might do at the close of their day. There were not many, not at this first accounting, but even then Meoraq noted that the ruins were in a most carefully kept state of workable disrepair. The high towers had fallen in, yes, and the wildlands had reclaimed much, but here where the lamps were lit, the remnants of the Ancient roads were remarkably cleaned of loose debris. Whole fields had been laid within the roofless shells of great buildings, ready for the season's first crop. There were indeed canals, not dug in the age of the Ancients, but relatively fresh; brackish water ran in a swift current, caught from some unseen waterway and turned through these ruins as expertly as any irrigation system he had seen in the cities. He could see hooked nets at every landing, set to catch whatever swam in its muddy flow, but while the water was not clean, neither did it reek of waste. There was a hint of that on the wind when it turned, but only a hint; they kept their fleshing vats covered and regularly cleaned, and their compost freshly-turned.

The more he saw, heard, smelled, the more Meoraq understood that this was not a den of raiders like any he had come across in the past. This was no winter-camp just waking from the cold. This was a settlement, with many years of success rooted beneath it. The eleven men he could see moving about in the lamplight could not possibly account for the work that had gone into making this camp, or sustaining it. There might be fifty men waiting in the foundations below. And whoever led them was not only strong enough to hold the loyalty of such deadly men, but clever enough to have built all this.

He thought of Szadt, the Raider-Lord, who had stabbed his way into Kuaq and held it for three days with the aid of Gann's weapons. Whoever nested in these ruins might well have such weapons also. Explosive fires that burned the flesh off a man's bones in moments. Lights that cut like swords. Thunder in a man's hand that could crush another's brain right there in his unbroken skull. All this, and Sheul alone knew what other forms of undefendable death were there to be found in Gann's world.

But Szadt had been killed. Meoraq's own father had climbed the bloodied wall of Kuaq and hurled the Raider-Lord's headless body to the ground in spite of all the weapons Gann had given him. A man might armor himself in wickedness and arm himself with machines, but he would always be a man, born of clay, and all men trembled before Sheul's might.

A ghost of memory in Amber's voice, uninvited: *If you're stupid enough to jump off a cliff, God doesn't catch you.*

It pierced him, but not as the warning she had meant it to be on its first speaking. His Amber. His outrageously audacious and uncouth Amber. He could see no slave-pens, which only increased his surety that the true nest was below ground, out of sight and far better defended. His Amber was there, unseen, suffering as she had suffered every hour of these past seven days, and if Gann himself rose up, still Meoraq would have her back. His throat still ached where the boy had choked him and his body was worn to the very edge of exhaustion after this run, but Sheul was with him and that was all that mattered.

He could all but hear the smacking sound of her little hand against her smooth forehead, all but feel the puff of her breath as she sighed.

Meoraq drew the knife of his fathers from its sheath and touched the smooth knob of Rasozul's thigh bone to his heart. "See me now, O father of my flesh," he whispered, and glanced upwards. "See me always, O Father of my eternal soul. Be with me now, both of you, and be with my wife. If it is Your will, O Sheul, I will hold her in my living arms again. And if it is Your will, my beloved Father, I will hold her in Your halls. Wherever I do come to hold her, I thank You for bringing her once more within my reach."

The wind blew, whispering its own refrain. Meoraq tapped the knife twice to his chest and sheathed it. He drew his kzung instead, the blade for the killing of beasts, and began to crawl. He felt no fear, but his heart still hammered. His limbs carried him without shaking. His mind was clear, painfully so, like the coldest winds of winter that seem to crush the throat that breathes them in. He crawled without questioning what might become of him when this hour ended. He was not Uyane Meoraq any longer, but the Sword in God's hand, and when he reached the first of the raiders—a man strolling out alone into the grass, opening his breeches with one hand; the other was nothing but a raw-looking stump, fresh enough to show scabbing along the stitched end—he cut without hesitation, without emotion, without design.

There was no moon behind the clouds, no flash across his blade, only a hiss and a spray of heat and the wind blowing to hide the sound of a body falling in the grass. He did not stop to drag the corpse away or try in any way to hide it. His eyes, Sheul's eyes now, were already moving on to the next man. He breathed deep and slow, a master of his clay and of his killing hand, and went with God's blessing burning in his heart to get his wife back.

* * *

Zhuqa leaned back on the table, a lamp burning to either side of him, black scales flickering with reflected light—a demon in repose. He watched, hissing softly with pleasure, as she nuzzled at his slit and tried desperately to think of how the hell she was going to either take the fish hook out of her mouth without him seeing it or give him the blowjob with it in, options which sure as hell seemed to mark the opposite ends of a whole spectrum of failure. So far, he was showing phenomenal restraint and a willingness to let the moment draw itself out, as demonstrated by the fact that he was still tucked away despite the spicy-sweet oils bedewing his slit, but any second now, he was going to lose his patience with this kittenish crap and expect her to lick something. And one of the many sad realities of life was that it was impossible to lick while holding something clenched in your teeth.

She supposed she could move it into the fold of her cheek...where, the way her luck was going, it would hook itself in and stay.

The image of half a fish hook protruding through the soft side of her face was pretty bad. The image that replaced it—same image, really, only with the addition of Zhuqa beating her to death—was worse.

Amber brought both her hands up, kneading firmly at his loins as she breathed over his slit, and watching through her hair for him to close his eyes.

He saw her watching. His head cocked.

Oh fuck Gann.

He reached out and brushed the hair out of her eyes, then gathered most of it up and held it for her, resting his hand comfortably atop her head. "Better?"

If her hands hadn't been full of lizard-dick, she'd have hit herself on the forehead.

"So much better," she muttered and stared without a lot of hope at his gleaming slit.

Well, what the hell. He could only kill her once.

'Yeah, but I bet he can make it seem like more,' she thought.

Never mind. Whatever happened, happened. It was all in God's hands.

Amber slipped her thumb upwards along his slit and in, teasing at his sa'ad. The edges of his slit relaxed at once, letting his cock extrude. She gripped it in her fist—*here goes nothing*—and bent low, sweeping her free hand down over his belly as she opened her mouth—*i'm actually going to die with a dick in my hand life is full of the weirdest surprises*—and slipped the fish hook against the cup of her palm a fraction of a second before sucking the nub of his clit into her mouth.

She waited, tonguing the alphabet over and around the stiff little knot between her lips, but she didn't die. The fish hook was a huge, obvious secret tucked between her thumb and her palm. She'd cut herself already. She was bleeding on him. He had to see the blood, even if he couldn't smell it or feel it. Damn it, how long was he going to make her wait before he stabbed her in the ear?

She raised her head and looked.

His eyes snapped open at once, burning like two more points of lamplight, as he gave her hair a vicious yank. "*Don't you fucking dare stop*!" he hissed, yellow popping out in vibrant stripes on both sides of his neck. In the next breath, he visibly fought himself to a calmer place, relaxing his hand and even brushing at her cheek. "I won't hurt you, Eshiqi. I won't hurt you. But be careful how you play with me." His eyes, clearer now, shifted to the tip of his cock and back to her. He let go of her hair and gripped himself at the base of his shaft. "Do that again...with your mouth."

She couldn't believe she actually had the hook in her hand—

—and now he was covering the vein.

* * *

Meoraq circled the ruins several times, as much as the crumbling buildings and overgrowth allowed, trusting darkness for cover, the wind for sound, and Sheul for everything else. No raiders who lived in such a well-organized nest could be entirely careless and these had many sentries set high on the fallen walls and patrolling through the grass. The urge to stab himself into the heart of the camp and find his woman was a live coal in his gut, but he did not succumb. He was Sheulek, a master of his impulses, and so he circled as a Sheulek would do, killing them one by one where killing would go unnoticed, tightening his grip on an enemy that remained unaware of his predation even as his heart beat out the very throbs of Amber's human name. But eventually he was there, one hand resting on the stone wall of the ruins themselves, his boots just at the golden line of light that came from the first of the hanging lamps, looking at six men and the end of silence.

No fear. No thought. No plan.

He leapt. The techniques he used had names. At another hour, he would have known them. For now, he had only the vaguest sense of balance and motion, obstruction and momentum, hot blood and cold wind. They shouted, some of them. Some fought. Some ran. He dared not stop to do real battle, but cut where the cutting was easy and ingloriously effective—opening bellies if they faced him and hamstringing from behind—until they were all down and the attention for a killing blow could be afforded. None of the six had escaped him, although one had managed to flee as far as one of the phesok fields and tried to hide there, holding his bowels in both hands, too dazed to scream even when Meoraq found and finished him. But they had made enough noise in their dying to stir up the nest and he could hear the rest of them through the dark openings of the ruins, calling up from the deep places, wary.

So. Meoraq—without thought, without design, but with the flames burning in his chest and his brain—cut the head from a dead man with five or six hard strokes and hurled it through an open door. He listened to it smack into a wall and tumble in its clumsy way down what sounded to be at least four flights of stairs. He lost count of the men who shouted out as it passed them, but there were many.

The first of them, the foolish ones, erupted from the dark in the next moment, stolen blades in hand and challenge in their throats. Meoraq met them, burning brighter at every jarring clash and spray of blood, reeling from one lamplit door to another in a storm of severed limbs and screams until his boots were skidding in mud gone black with gore and all he could smell was spilled shit and death.

It did not end with six men this time. It did not seem to have an end at all. Swords and fists and hissing faces, they came and kept coming. He clung to the discipline of his training, but he could feel his throat throbbing hotter and hotter with every passing moment, until the blood that splashed back into his face seemed cool. He fought and he killed them and it was carnage on every side as the skill and the finesse he had practiced all the years of his life first strained, then cracked, then crumbled. They kept coming and he finally knew—without fear but with a terrible swelling rage—that there were just too many. He was not his father and he could not win this fight.

They would kill him. They would keep his Amber, use her until her soft body broke, and then they would kill her too.

This echoed in him for the briefest moment, trapped in the stillness between one beat of his heart and the next. And suddenly the fires surged and took him.

There was a moment, endless, lost in the blackness of that inner space where Meoraq could still dimly hear his own breathing, deep and slow and even. Then he heard, even dimmer, a roar like something from a nightmare—a monstrous demon sound that surely could not issue from any dumaq throat, except that he could feel it humming somewhere in his clay, which meant that it was his roar, his own.

'No,' he thought, his last conscious thought. 'It is Sheul's. He has taken me.'

Then, nothing.

* * *

The hardest part of the fight to supplant Zhuqa's hand with her own lay in not letting him know it was a fight. Which was not to say that everything else was easy—not even holding onto him was easy anymore—only that if there was an axis point to the battle, that was it.

For someone who'd never had a blowjob before yesterday, he was full of advice on how she should be doing it. Each time she tried to ease her hand around his shaft and bully his out of the way, he wanted it somewhere else. "My sa'ad!" he'd be panting, or, "Get underneath and push—harder!" or, "All along my slit, Eshiqi, fast now, faster," and the whole time, his hand was working away, just like cock-rubber wasn't a curse.

When he finally did relinquish his grip, it happened fast, as he rocked back onto his elbows looking for the necessary leverage to pump up into her mouth. He wasn't sure how to do it and was too far gone to stop and puzzle it out, so he simply hooked his leg around her, dug his toes into her back, and lunged at her in a rapid-fire series of what she believed the yogas called the bridge pose. This had two results: the first and most obvious was that he came for, she thought, the sixth time, although by now this meant little more than an extra-hard jerk and a few bitter drops of whatever it was he had in him after his cum was gone. The second thing was that, between the abrupt kicking motion of his leg, his foot unexpectedly clutching at her, and having a hot, scaly bar suddenly banging away at the back of her throat, Amber dropped the fish hook.

She heard it hit the table with pindrop clarity in spite of Zhuqa's draconian roars. Gagging, she slapped frantically at the tabletop, searching for the hook. She found it, or rather, felt it stab into the center of her palm, and choked out a howl around the enormous muzzle of his cock.

"Sorry," groaned Zhuqa, letting up on her a little. "Don't stop. Close your mouth again, just close your—yes! Ah, fuck Gann!"

Amber shrugged his leg off, tonguing madly at the hooked tip of his cock, and he dropped flat on the table, spreading his legs wide open around her—Zhuqa the dirty girl—grabbing her head between his hands like it was a zit he wanted to pop. And there it was and this was it and even he couldn't go all night, so Amber reared back with a gasp, bit the hook from the meat of her hand, plucked it back from between her lips, and slashed.

If it took as much as one whole second, it would have surprised her.

He still almost kicked her away in time.

His feet were on her shoulders hard the same instant she had the hook in her hand and she went flying. Her cut went wild, but she got something because she felt him ripping all the way up her arm to her shoulder and the heat of the blood spraying over her hand. Then her back hit the wall and her ass hit the ground and Zhuqa was on his feet with one hand clapped to his gushing slit and a knife in the other. He took two running steps, roaring as he came, and went down on his face hard enough that she heard the crunch of his jaw breaking on the stone floor. Blood spat out between his teeth. He sucked in a breath, spat out some more, and lay writhing just a little.

She got up, staggering some on her bad hip, ready for him to leap up and take her down. He might have tried. His legs shifted, dragging through what she now saw was an amazing lake of blood for just a few seconds' worth of bleeding, but that was it. His eyes alone moved, watching her inch closer so that she could first kick the knife out of his hand and then pick it up. He said something too mangled to make out when she did it, then spat out a bit of ropy blood and said, with startling clarity, "Fierce little thing."

And then he was dead.

It wasn't a big moment. There was no sudden sagging of his body, no death rattle at the end of some hoarse exhalation, no nothing. He was seeing her one second, and the next, he wasn't.

"Yeah," said Amber shakily, circling around him. "Yeah, I've seen this movie. Fuck you."

She dropped onto his back—the death rattle finally came out with a gurgle between his broken teeth—yanked his chin up—it came easily—and cut his knife across his throat. She felt the knife's blade scraping over his spine and his open eyes just kept staring. Amber scrambled back, rubbing at her mouth until she realized she was rubbing his blood onto her lips. She spit it out, gagged, then went ahead and threw up so she'd get it over and done with and could get on with the escaping.

"Okay," she whispered once that was done. "It's all over. Time to get up—"

The door banged open. "*Get up*!" bellowed Iziz. "*Ghelip*—ah," he said with remarkable mildness as he skidded to a stop in Zhuqa's blood. He looked down at his boots, his brow-ridges creased with confusion, and then over at Amber. At Zhuqa's body. At the knife in Amber's hand. At Zhuqa.

His spines flicked once and lay flat.

His throat filled in with color.

His chest began to heave.

And then he yanked out his hooked sword and came at her, screaming.

Amber threw herself back and rolled under the table. The sword hit the floor twice and then the table—*chink chink chunk*—before he came diving in after her. She kicked him in the face; he caught her by the ankle and yanked her out beside him—*shhhhoop*!—in a single pull, sliding easily over Zhuqa's blood and her own puke. She still had Zhuqa's knife in her hand. She realized that only after she saw her hand on the hilt that was buried in his back.

He let out a howl that was more angry than hurt, slapping at her in a storm of inarticulate snarls. She flung her arms up, but he knocked them aside without trying, maybe without even noticing. Through the dark blur of his hand hammering at her, she could see the colors at his throat actually shimmering with the force of his rage, but as soon as he remembered that he had a sword—

'Sex and killing,' she thought, as suddenly and as calmly as if it were a separate person whispering in her ear. With a cry, she abandoned her feeble efforts at defense and instead thrust her hands between them to loosen his loin-plate.

Iziz reared back without hesitation to battle it all the way open and let his cock out. It didn't take long. Just long enough for her to yank the knife out of his back and slam it home in his head.

It hit hard, numbing her hand, and suddenly Iziz was two hundred pounds of lizard on top of her, oomphing his last breath into her face. She heaved him off without really being aware of doing so and then stood over him, brandishing her knife for maybe half a minute before realizing there was no blade in it anymore.

It had broken off.

In his head, she thought, looking down in horror at the remarkably small, bloody gash in the center of Iziz's flat skull. There wasn't anything sticking out. It must be all the way in there. In his brains.

grey

'You absolutely will not faint!' she thundered at herself, and like thunder, it had to roll a long way to meet her. She climbed up onto the table and there she sat, her eyes going from one raider to the other, waiting for them to move...rise...maybe get their cocks out and come finish what they'd started...

The only thing moving was the blood out of Iziz's head and it was a slow, small trickle at that.

"Okay," said Amber.

No one answered.

"Okay," she said again and slid off the table onto her aching hip.

Still no answer. The door still stood wide open. Zhuqa and Iziz were still dead.

Amber started to bend over, but it made that faint feeling come back, so she knelt instead, tugging the sword out of Iziz's slack grip. His hand, emptied, curled slowly into a loose fist.

"Okay," said Amber, and to her surprise, it came out almost exactly the way the old Amber would have said it: tough and strong and able to handle things. It didn't even sound like the voice of a stranger. "Come on, little girl," she said, liking that voice more and more. "They say it ain't over 'till the fat lady sings and I've lost too much weight for the bitch to be me. Let's see how far we can get."

There was no one in the corridor, no one on the stairs. This she found so unbelievable that her feet kept backing up on her, wanting to retreat to the false security of Zhuqa's room where being ravished by two zombie-lizards was infinitely preferable to being ambushed and ravished by all the live ones. She had to keep reminding herself of the way that Iziz had torn into the room. Surely he'd been raising the alarm all the way down; anyone who had been here had simply gone up to fight. She could hear commotion of some kind on the surface—people running, screaming, fighting—and she had no idea how she was going to get past it, but never mind that for now. Xzem might know of a back door, but whether she did or not, Amber had to get the baby.

She knew the floor where the slaves were quartered, not because she'd been going there every day, but because there was a dead lizardlady lying on the landing, hacked almost in half.

Gripping her sword in both hands, fear churning like molten lead in her belly, Amber ran down the hall, opening every door she found.

Empty. Empty. All empty.

She could hear whatever was happening on the surface working its way down into the stairwell. When she cast a terrified glance over her shoulder, she was just in time to see a headless body drop down the shaft. 'It's a raid,' she thought. 'It's a raid from this Ghelip person and they've already taken the girls. Run. Just run.'

She did run, but she kept stopping, cursing herself for the futility of it each time she flung a new door open on an empty room.

They were all empty. Every last one.

"Oh please, God, no," she babbled, backing out of the last one—the one where Zru'itak had given birth—knowing there was nowhere else to look.

wait

A roar of rage and defiance on the stairs maybe only two or three flights up became a wet, gargling sound and a short, heavy tumble. Boots thundered down the corridor just over her head, running toward the stair.

Not away.

listen

Toward the stair...from the barracks?

Welcome to the next year of your life...Xzem lives with you now...

The baby wouldn't be in the slave pens. It was living with Dkorm in the barracks.

Amber let out a scream of embarrassed frustration every bit as mindlessly as an angry lizard, slapping herself in the forehead. Then she turned around and ran for the stairs.

Three lizardmen came charging out of the corridor right as she reached the landing, but either didn't see the sword in her hand or were too far gone to care. The one in the lead shoved her to one side and they all went furiously by, roaring as they threw themselves at the enemy bearing down on them. She was close enough now to hear the crash of their weapons.

Never mind. Get the baby. Get the baby, get Xzem, get out.

Amber started opening doors again.

Empty. Empty.

On the fifth try, a raider lunged out, knocking her to the ground as he sprinted down the hall, away from the stairs, and vanished around a corner, leaving a bloody trail behind him. Then empty. Empty.

She might have run right past the room where she finally found the baby if she'd stopped to think about it. From a purely logical frame of mind, the room wasn't worth checking. The door hung open. It was quiet. Surely, it must be empty too.

But Amber was beyond reason by that time. She checked behind the door not because she hoped to find the baby anymore, but because she'd fallen into a routine of panic in which finding the next door and flinging it open was all she could do. So she opened that one.

And, looking right at the lizardlady kneeling beside the cupboard, turned around and bolted blindly for the next door. She made two running steps and staggered (just like Zhuqa, a part of her piped up) as what she'd seen belatedly processed. She turned around, uncertain, listening, and heard a very faint breathy sound—Xzem's nearly silent tears.

The door was still open. A lamp inside was still burning, spilling a pleasant golden glow over Xzem's thin, shaking frame as she curled herself around the limp body of the baby.

"Oh," said Amber. (*Ah, said Iziz.*)

Xzem raised her head, still stroking and rubbing at the small dome of the baby's head, its narrow chest. Tears continued to run out of her eyes even though her breaths were slow and deep and virtually soundless. She looked back down at the baby in her hands, rocked twice more, and finally sighed. She pointed.

Amber's neck turned, turned, and ultimately dragged her eyes off Xzem. She stared instead at a thin, stained mat tossed up against the wall, a threadbare cushion, a rough blanket. And the leather-wrapped swaddle of Zhuqa's baby, sleeping with its tiny fists tucked up by its snout.

Amber started forward, then stopped again and turned back to Xzem. To Rosek, who, so limp and quiet, had seemed as small in Amber's eyes as a six-day old infant. She limped closer, touched Xzem's shivering shoulder, and only then noticed the baby was still breathing. She opened her mouth—

—and closed it again. The baby's head under Xzem's gentle hand was round, much rounder than it should be. Amber looked at the room again and saw the rumpled bedding in the cupboard, the mat where Zhuqa's baby slept, the open door. She looked and could almost imagine Dkorm drowsing in his bed with Rosek; someone, Iziz maybe, bursting in to raise the alarm; Dkorm dropping the baby to run. Not setting her aside, dropping her. Throwing her.

"I'm sorry," said Amber.

Xzem rocked and stilled, rocked and stilled. The tears, soundless, kept falling. The crash and roar of combat got closer, not above them anymore, but right on the landing. Xzem showed no sign that she heard it. She held her baby and watched it breathe and sometimes tried to rock it.

Amber touched her arm. "We have to go," she said, not knowing if Xzem would understand her clumsy lizardish or not.

Xzem sighed and looked at her.

"Please. We have to get out while we still can."

"I wanted one," said Xzem. Her voice was soft, but steady. "Just one to keep. After I have lost so many..." She looked down at Rosek and tried with trembling hands to arrange the baby's arms over its chest, but the little limbs slipped off and dangled, lifeless. It breathed.

"Please!" Amber couldn't bring herself to shake her, but she tightened her hand where it gripped Xzem's arm. "We have to go now!"

Xzem looked at her. And then past her. Her expression did not change, but she brought the baby to her chest in a futile, shielding motion and closed her eyes.

Amber turned around.

For an instant, she thought it was Meoraq. From the moment that Iziz had burst in through Zhuqa's door, that possibility, far-fetched as it was, had been shivering at the back of her mind. Even as she heard the carnage above her and knew it was more than one man, even her man, could make, she'd hoped...but it was still a shock to see him.

Except that the gore-splattered lizardman filling the doorway looked back at her without any recognition and she realized it was a stranger, this Ghelip person or some other raider like him. He roared, raised his swords, then focused in on Xzem. Something in his eyes sparked. He sprang at her, but it wasn't until she saw the badly-braided loop of her own hair around his arm that Amber realized it was Meoraq after all.

And he was entirely out of his mind.

She screamed his name, flinging out her arms and legs like a screen in front of silent Xzem, but she couldn't even begin to form the word 'Stop' before he hit her. His fist, wrapped around the hilt of his sword, hit her in the shoulder, spinning her hard and smacking her up against Dkorm's cupboard door. She stumbled back, stunned, as Meoraq gave his hand an equally dazed glance and threw his sword aside. It hit the wall above Xzem's mat, shocking Amber back to life. She leapt for the baby, but Meoraq snatched her out of the air and threw her. She crashed through a short stack of crates, her heels going madly up and dragging her over in a backwards somersault—*ass over teakettle you know i've heard that all my life and never knew just what it meant*—that ended with her sprawled, legs wide open, over a heap of dirty clothes, broken pottery, and the other detritus of Dkorm's life.

Meoraq froze. His burning, blank gaze dropped.

"Oh God," said Amber. She snapped her legs together. "Meoraq, it's m—"

And he was on her.

The broken crates fell on top of him as he grappled with her. He stopped to beat them back, roaring and bashing indiscriminately with fists and sword, completely oblivious to her as she scrambled out from beneath him, but as soon as the crates were 'dead', he was looking for her again.

"Meoraq, it's me! It's Amb—"

He lunged, caught her by the same ankle Iziz had, and dragged her screaming back to him as he tore his loin-plate loose. He didn't bother to fight with her. He didn't have to. He was so much stronger that her struggles were completely beneath his notice as he alternately pulled and twisted at her legs, already pumping furiously at her hip and her stomach and her side until he found her opening and was in her.

She screamed his name, screamed her own, and then just screamed, groping behind her as best she could in the twisted position in which he'd bent her to slap and scratch and try in any way to make him see her. He came and just fucked harder, clawing at her stomach and kicking at the tiles to try and shove himself further and further inside her. His every breath was a snarling, hissing, slobbering grunt that spat hot, animal drool out in ropes over her skin. He didn't know her, didn't hear her, didn't even want to fuck her. He was gone. And when he finally came out of it, he was going to find himself lying on top of a corpse, maybe still sunk in a hole in the back of her head like the mummies back at the ruined lab in Yroq.

Panic took her, and for however long it lasted, she was just as lost as he was, but hers at least faded out and left her rocking under the hammer of his body, her face rubbing painfully against the tiles in a slick of blood and tears. She reached back for him, groaning, but when her fingers met his scaled hide, he erupted in such a storm of slapping, punching, snarling fury that all she could do was cover her head and wait for the sex to eclipse the battery. It did, but the fucking was more violent and he stayed bent over her, his sharp teeth snarling too damned close to her naked neck.

"Meoraq," she moaned. "Please! This isn't you!"

He grabbed her shoulder and shoved her into the floor, grappling himself into a new position without ever breaking rhythm.

"You're a Sword and a true son of God!" she cried in desperation. "A Sword of Sheul is a master of his clay!"

Frustrated with the obstacle of her legs, he reared back and pinned them together on one side before plunging back in. His hand on her bad hip was a brand of pure hell; it was only a matter of time before he broke it and she knew he still wouldn't stop.

Somewhere in the room, Zhuqa's baby woke up and started crying.

Meoraq stiffened, his head whipping around to aim at the sound. He hissed, let go of her—

Amber lunged and grabbed him. He fought until he remembered his cock was still inside her and then resumed fucking.

But he'd heard the baby. He'd heard the baby so he could hear her.

Amber put her arms around him. He spat like a cat and tried to thrash free of her, but she held on, hiding from his blows against his chest until he lost himself in the sex again.

"You are a master of your clay," she told him.

He hissed at her.

"You are a faithful servant of God and you keep His laws! You—" She broke off with a wail of pain as he pitched himself savagely against her hip, and for the first time, that seemed to get through.

He looked directly at her, his eyes narrowed to slits of unfocused rage.

"You wouldn't kill me," whispered Amber.

He roared, hot breath blasting at her face.

And out of nowhere, she suddenly found herself remembering that day he'd first caught her with Scott's stupid little space-scout knife. He'd been ready to kill her then and he was going to kill her now. The only difference was he wasn't sorry about it anymore and he wasn't going to give her any last words.

Do you wish to pray? She could still hear his voice and the terrible emotion that had hoarsened it. *I have no mercy to give you...I am sorry...Do you wish to pray*?

"Our Father who art in heaven," said Amber. It was the only prayer she knew.

Meoraq's head ticced, not quite tipping to one side. He flared his mouth open, displaying his teeth in the silent gape of a crocodile, then recoiled slightly, frowning. He looked at her, looked down, flared his teeth again and threw a few rapid, rough thrusts into her before faltering. He panted, glaring without focus at the knotted place their bodies met.

"Our Father who art...who lives in heaven," Amber said again, louder. He'd heard her and some part of what he'd heard had reached him, but its hold was weak. She couldn't afford to confuse him now with words he didn't know. "Hallowed...or...Holy be your name."

He reared back and grabbed her throat, hissing, but although his grip was painful, he didn't crush her. And he could have.

"Your kingdom has come," wheezed Amber. "Your kingdom...is here. You...You have built Your House so that we can live in it. Let...Let Your will be done...on Gann as it is in heaven!"

His hand, an iron collar at her neck, shook. He looked away again, his throat arching so that she could see the yellow streaks across those scales flash and throb.

"You feed us," she said. "You have set our table and filled our cup—"

Meoraq's spines flicked hard. He looked at her.

"And You forgive us our sins—"

He saw his sword, lunged out and snatched it up to raise over her, snarling.

"—as we forgive those who sin against us!" Amber shouted. "For Yours is the only vengeance!"

Meoraq recoiled again. He reared back, pulling free of her as painfully as he'd ever stabbed himself in, and stood over her with the sword high and an awful look of confusion bleeding into his crazed eyes.

"And that is the grace and the glory of God!" cried Amber, reaching out to catch at him. "And you know it, Meoraq! You are the master of your clay and you know I am not your enemy! I'm your wife! I'm the woman you were born into this world to find, remember?" She grabbed a handful of her own hair and shook it.

He hissed, but shakily, then turned his head and looked at the braid that wrapped his bicep. He flinched, spat dazedly in the direction of the crying baby, then looked at Amber again. One hand rose, hovered in the air, and dropped again. He rubbed distractedly at his cock, not masturbating, but only an exhausted man kneading at a deep, overused ache. She reached out to tug his loin-plate loose and he watched, frowning, as he retracted.

"You are not your clay," she told him, lifting her hand toward his face. He flinched back twice before he let her touch him. "You are Uyane Meoraq and you would never hurt me."

He opened his mouth and hissed silently through his teeth, through her fingers.

"Take six breaths," she said. "Count them off with me. One. For the Prophet."

He inhaled in hitches.

"Two for his brunt. Breathe with me, Meoraq. Three for Uyane."

He grunted.

"Four for...for..." God, he'd been counting all winter long, why didn't she *know* these? "Mykrm!" she blurted, praying she was right. "Five is for Oyan—"

"Ash," he said, in a voice like char itself. "Stained. Leaf."

"Six is for...is for..."

"Thaliszr."

Recognition came like dawn behind the clouds of this world: dim and colorless, but steadily growing until its light was complete. He stood up, and it was Meoraq who did it, the real Meoraq. He looked around, seeing this place, seeing her at his feet. The yellow stripes stayed high and bright on his throat, but he sheathed his sword and held out his hand.

"Please be okay now," Amber whispered, and took it.

"I'm burning," Meoraq said curtly, pulling her to her feet and releasing her at once. "But I see you. I think...I'm here." He looked back at the baby again, then at Xzem, who had not moved in all this time, and finally at his other sword. It seemed to surprise him to see it lying on the floor. He had to check his belt and see that it wasn't there before he went over to pick it up again. "Stay close behind me," he ordered, and headed for the door.

"Wait!"

Meoraq watched her limp across the room with distracted concern, but it wasn't until she bent down and picked up the baby that he seemed to realize what she was doing.

"No," he said.

"I have to." Amber hugged the baby closer and pointed at Xzem. "Tell her she can come with us!"

"I will not." Meoraq glanced swiftly down both sides of the hall and came back in, reaching out his hand to her. "There is no time for this! The enemy is all around us! Now come!"

Amber bit back her first impulsive words on the subject of how much time he'd had on his hands when the issue at stake was sex. That wasn't his fault and they sure didn't have the time to fight about it. She said, "I'm not leaving without this baby."

"I did not come here to liberate the whole of this camp!"

"Are you sure?"

His hand lowered.

"God doesn't give you what you want," said Amber. "You tell me that all the time. God sends you where you need to be."

"If we try to save them all, we will surely be taken," he said, not arguing, but only stating a fact. "We must leave them. Come. They will not harm their own."

Amber stalked over to Xzem and put her hand on her shoulder. After a tense, shivering silence, Xzem sighed and loosened her shielding arms enough to show him Rosek.

Meoraq looked at that for a long time. Then he looked at her. And at the ceiling, not in his exasperated are-you-seeing-this-too way, but in an uncertain frown. He stayed that way for a while, probably praying. "So be it," he said at the end. He beckoned to Xzem and she rose, her neck bent and silent tears still falling, to follow him.

"Wait," Amber said. "I think there's another way out."

Meoraq glanced in the direction of the stairwell, which was suspiciously quiet, then followed her pointing finger to the ground, where dots of blood marked the path taken by the panicked raider she'd passed on the way in. He took a few steps in that direction, keeping his sword at the ready as he searched the darkness. "Do you know where it leads?"

"To the well-room," Xzem said softly.

They both looked at her.

"There is a second stair," she told them, stroking Rosek's swollen head. "But the door is always locked and only Zhuqa and his most trusted hold the key."

"I'll go get it," said Amber, and turned to flee.

Meoraq caught angrily at her arm, but looked at the baby and released her, unsure.

"I'll be all right," Amber promised, not at all certain this was true, but knowing she could get to Zhuqa's room and back faster than grieving Xzem could be coaxed to follow. "Stay with her! I'll be right back!"

His spines flattened. He took the baby and shifted it to one arm, gripping his kzung tightly. "Run, then."

She tried, galloping through a haze of pain much faster than her hip wanted to hold her, and conscious of every second as it slipped by. There were two bodies on the landing, two more sprawled over the stairs, but no one was waiting there to cut her into pieces. They all knew better than to fight in the cramped, dark shaft, she supposed. And just the fact that it was this dark meant that they'd shut the access door. It couldn't be blocked from the outside, so if they'd shut it, it was to keep Meoraq blind to how many men were waiting for him on the other side.

'It could be worse,' thought Amber, forcing herself down the stairs as noisily, in her own mind at least, as a rhinoceros. 'They could be getting ready to drop a bomb down the shaft.'

She ran faster.

Zhuqa's door was yawning open just as she'd left it. She bulled through and limped around him to the heap of his clothes, and thank God he'd actually undressed for his little game tonight, because he'd never done that before and she'd been so badly beaten up between one thing and another that she honestly didn't think she could have rolled him over to get the keys. Amber got them, looked around, and then—what the hell—limped over to get her shift because it was bound to be cold and rainy outside and there was no point escaping from raiders just to freeze—

Amber froze.

She thought, 'I didn't see that.'

She thought, 'No, I did see that and I just think I didn't.'

She thought, 'Please, let me have seen that.'

She turned around.

On the floor between her and the table, Zhuqa lay naked in a thick, black clot of blood with his eyes open and a few splinters of what were probably his teeth strewn loosely in front of his mouth.

The floor directly next to the table was empty.

Well, not entirely empty. She could see the hilt of Zhuqa's knife lying where she'd dropped it. And she could see, a little ways away from it, the broken blade that she sure thought she'd left buried in Iziz's head.

It wasn't even all that bloody. Just a little smear at the very tip. There wasn't anything at all on the flat end, where she reasoned he would have had to grab it to pull it out, if...if she'd really hit him.

"I hit him," she whispered, staring wildly all around her at the stubbornly empty room. "I know I hit him."

And she had hit him. She'd hit him so hard, her hand had gone numb. So hard, the blade had broken. So hard—

—she'd knocked him out.

Oh God.

She'd only stabbed him through the scales. She'd hit the bone of his skull and broke the knife. She hadn't killed him. She might not have even hurt him all that much.

Iziz was still alive.

'Well, by all means stand around,' Bo Peep invited. 'You can apologize when he comes back.'

She shuddered once, hugely, as if physically shaking free of the hold that empty patch of tiled floor had on her. The first step was still hard. After that, she turned and bolted down the hall like her hip had never been hurt at all. It had been and it let her know it, but by God it didn't slow her down.

She tore up the stairs, her bare feet banging out echoes they must surely be able to hear wherever they were waiting to ambush them. Meoraq ran to meet her, hugging the baby under his arm like a football, so that her first words on reaching him weren't anything to do with Iziz at all but a shrill, "Oh for Christ's sake, lizardman, what's *wrong* with you?!" She gave him the keys, took the baby, and smacked him in the side of the head, all in the same half-panicked movement.

His arm swung hard enough to make the air howl, but he caught the blow before it hit her. They both stared at his fist, cocked and shaking in the air—he, with glazed eyes and yellow flashes at his throat; she, in open-mouthed astonishment. He recovered first. Without a word, he turned around and ran the other way.

Xzem was waiting at the end of the long hall, next to the fresh body of a raider. It might have been the same one she'd passed earlier; she couldn't tell when he was lying face-down like that and didn't want to look. Meoraq worked the keys and tucked it into his belt immediately, freeing his hand for his samr. The stairwell on the other side of the door was dark and silent, catching every sound and throwing it back in echoes. Meoraq listened, then closed the door to hiss, "If it goes badly, run and I will find you. If I don't find you...go on to Xi'Matezh. God will send you on."

Knowing there wasn't time for words of comfort, even if she could have thought of something to say, Amber reached out and touched his arm.

And felt him stiffen. Shudder. And pull out of her grip. He started up the stairs without looking at her.

Suddenly, Amber's hip hurt more. She let Xzem go ahead of her, watching Meoraq climb around the corner and out of sight without ever once glancing her way. The baby snuffled against her chest and reached out its tiny hand to pinch at her. She hugged it closer, dragging herself up one stair at a time, thinking, 'That shouldn't be much of a shock either, little girl.'

And the worst of it was, it really wasn't.

The stairwell was capped, like the other stair, with an access door that opened into a covered building. This one had the look of a stable, long and not too narrow, with stall-like partitions indicated by wooden poles and plenty of harnesses and lengths of chain hanging on the walls.

It was a stable, built for raiders' cattle, the two-legged kind. The only other door was at the far wall, where Hruuzk was yoking slaves together in a double line. He didn't bother to look around when he grunted, "This is all there were in the pens. I didn't stop to hunt up the rest of them. Where do you want me?"

Meoraq attacked. He did it without asking for prayers, without any warning at all. His boots struck three times against the planks before he leapt, and by then Hruuzk had already shoved the team of slaves away and was turning to meet him.

They crashed together, four swords and two bodies in a terrible riot of screaming women and spraying blood. Amber thrust the baby into Xzem's listless embrace and darted forward, snatching up the first thing she saw that even looked like a weapon: a short length of chain attached to a heavy collar. She didn't try to swing it—couldn't have, not without hitting Meoraq, a slave, or Xzem and the babies—but she jumped on Hruuzk's mammoth back the very instant he offered it to her and bashed him on the head as hard as she could. If she could knock Iziz out with a knife-tip, she reasoned, she could surely take Hruuzk out with an iron ring, or whatever the metal was.

Hruuzk did stagger. He also reached back and plucked her off him, swinging her on a short, violent arc over his shoulder to strike up against his chest with his sword suddenly at her throat. "Drop it or she dies!" he bellowed.

Meoraq lunged without expression, stabbing his samr under Amber's arm and into the slave-master's heart. She felt and heard the splintering of bone when Meoraq twisted and then wrenched the blade free. He knotted a fist in her shift and yanked her to him as the slave-master collapsed. She could feel the hot gush of his heart's blood on her back, not quite shocking enough to distract her from the equally hot tickle of blood on her front, streaming from the little nick on her throat where Hruuzk's sword had cut her.

She stared at him.

"Quiet that...Quiet the child." He let go of her and moved on to the outer door, pulling Zhuqa's keys from his belt.

The baby was screaming, tiny fists balled and hammering at the scaled arm that held it. Xzem gave it up wordlessly and stroked at Rosek's swollen snout. She was still crying. Amber was dangerously close to joining her.

Meoraq cracked the door open and looked tensely out, threw the captive women an assessing stare, and finally gestured to Amber. She joined him at the door, not so numb that she failed to notice the perfectly chilling glance he sent at the baby now purring resentfully against her breast. But he moved aside, careful not to touch her, and let her look.

She didn't try to count them. The distance and the dark would have made that difficult even if there weren't so many or if they were holding still instead of prowling impatiently around the building where they thought Meoraq had to emerge. She could hear shouting, but couldn't make out the words. Moving torches throughout the ruins told her they were making a search of the other structures, and sooner or later, they'd come here.

"For the moment, they still believe they are attacked by a band of men," Meoraq told her, grimly watching the torches. "And they have not yet fully rallied. Once they do, or once they learn it is only one warrior who stands against them, it is done. Be silent, all of you!" Meoraq snapped, and the white-noise whimpering of the captives dialed itself down into sniffles. To Amber, brusquely, he said, "We will go out, that way, around the wall. When it is at our back, we run. Be aware, the wind will cover only so much sound."

"It'll be quiet now," said Amber, holding the baby securely against her body.

He grunted, checked outside, and looked back at the women. "We will go as far as we can as fast as we are able, but it is three days running to Praxas."

She didn't think she had much of a run left in her, but didn't dare to say so.

He grunted and moved away to unlock the women. Amber stayed at the door and watched the torches track slowly back and forth across the camp, listening to chains clink behind her as Meoraq gave everyone their orders. Amber's hip ached. She shifted her weight onto her other leg and listened to the baby purr until Meoraq rejoined her at the door, brushing her aside to peer out. His body was hard as marble. He didn't say anything to her. He waited, coiled and ready, then pushed the door open and moved out, sword in hand. The women followed, as tight in their formation as if they were still yoked together. Then Xzem, her head down and tears shimmering over her scales. Last of all, Amber, straining to limp at any kind of speed and praying the baby wouldn't protest this treatment as long as it was her doing the jostling. By the time she got around the side of the stable, the only one she could see at all was Xzem, and only for a few more seconds.

She ran anyway, blind in the night, following the smudge of moonlight behind the churning clouds, even though it showed her nothing but the ghost of her own body. When Meoraq at last came lunging out of this impenetrable black, it was only her breathless exhaustion that kept her from screaming surprise.

He caught her arm as she staggered, and let her go again as soon as she had her feet solidly under her. He looked at the baby and his flat spines quivered against his skull.

"I'm not leaving it!" she hissed. "So don't you even ask me!"

"You can barely carry yourself, woman!"

"Then leave *me*!" Tears of horror sparked, as if she somehow hadn't known she was going to say it even with the words in her own mouth. She shook her head, her arms tightening around the baby until it squeaked in annoyance. "Leave us both!"

Meoraq looked at her for a long time.

And then he turned around.

As Amber pulled in the shaky breath that would have become her first wail of despair, he dropped to one knee and made a gesture like throwing something over his shoulder. He did not speak. His back was very stiff and straight.

"Are you...praying?" she ventured.

"No!" he snapped back, and made the gesture again. "Hold on to me. Hurry!"

She couldn't wrap her legs around his hips without a moan, and that moan became a wrenching cry when he seized her thighs and hupped her up higher. She dug one arm around his neck, kept the other tight around the baby, now riding squeezed between them and not very happy about it, and Meoraq began to run.

Even burdened as he was with her weight, he caught up to the others in just a few minutes and soon was running at their head again. Amber bumped along in agony on his back, clenching her jaws to mute the screams she could not stop herself from making, and just waited for it to end.

12

He could not run them all night, although he tried. Their pace slowed and slowed and finally, he was forced to cast it all in Sheul's hands and set them down in a camp. He allowed them no fire. They had no food. He gave Amber the swallows that were left in his waterskin and she annoyed him immediately by passing it off to the slave-mother, who drank it all without thanks and resumed her silent vigil over her dying child.

The wind gave way to rain. The women huddled together to defend against it as best they could, miserable and making little secret of it. Amber sat apart from the rest of them and held the infant close to her heart. Meoraq knew she was watching him, but he could not make himself go and sit beside her yet. He made endless patrols in the dark, waiting for an enemy that never showed itself, and caught himself several times rubbing restlessly at his loin-plate. He had burned longer and deeper this night than he had ever even imagined, but the flames were still close. He wanted to find raiders in pursuit of them, wanted to give that blessed heat possession of his hands and heart and mind. Failing that, he wanted to lie with his woman, but not in front of an audience of six witnessing slaves.

And their children.

The baby bothered him. Not the slave-mother's yearling, which was already dead in every way save that of its clay, but the other baby. The one that Amber refused to leave behind even at the risk of her own life. He did not know precisely what she would say to him if he told her that the creature she was cuddling only looked like a baby with a soul, but was in truth no more than Gann's clay given the seeming of life by the abominable sin of its conception...no, he didn't know what she would say to that, but he was reasonably certain it would come in shouts and perhaps with her fist bouncing off his hide.

Meoraq grunted to himself, glancing back into the darkness where he knew his wife to be, even if he could not see her. Sheul's urges again flared, but he walked on and gradually the fires became coals. Once he was rid of the slaves, he would show Sheul a proper thanks for the return of his Amber, but for now, the enemy was surely close.

And the enemy's clay-born spawn, even closer.

It looked like a baby. It sounded like one. Its tiny fingers gripped at Amber's soft breast like the fingers of any true baby he had seen. Not that his interest in watching such things had ever been strong, he had to admit that, which meant that if there were some subtle clue proving the child's innate sin, he could only assume he'd missed it.

The child's sin needed no proving. All his life, the priests had made it clear that if the corruption of Gann was in either parent, the corruption was in the child. What was bred into the clay could not be smoothed out, even by the Father's hands. This was truth.

And it was truth that the thing that looked like a baby had surely been sired by one of the raiders—men who freely indulged the urges of the clay until Sheul Himself closed His eyes to them. Men who poisoned their minds and bodies with strong drink and phesok. Men who carried bladed weapons and who used them to do wrongful murder upon other men. Men who made trade of female flesh for their sexual pleasure, and of male flesh also, if no females could be procured. The women who lay in union with such men had either been born to them, sired of their sin, or had been exiled from their cities for sins of their own. Either way, they were also lost to Sheul and therefore it followed that all children born to them—all, regardless of what innocent mask the offspring might don—belonged to Gann.

The sun was rising. Through the rain, he could see faint threads of grey in the east, a reminder of the pilgrimage he was supposed to be taking. How could he go there now, with Gann's corrupted own in his keeping?

"Sheul, my Father, You have been with me and led me well to this moment," Meoraq said, searching the skies through eye-stinging rain. "I pray You guide me now. What am I supposed to do? Where am I meant to be?"

"Meoraq?"

Amber's voice, low and hesitant upon the wind. Truly, the sun was rising, because it only took a few moments of searching before he could make out the pale shape of her a short distance away. She could not see him as well, it seemed; she was not quite facing him and did not stop squinting into the black until he was nearly close enough to lay his hand on her.

She startled, but didn't cry out. She knew the enemy might be close as well. Which meant she wouldn't have risked calling out his name without a reason.

"What is it?" he asked.

"I...Can you come back to camp? Xzem's baby is...I need you to talk to her."

He could have nothing comforting to say to the mother of a clay-born child, but grief was raw in Amber's voice and the other infant was there in her arms. With an uneasy glance heavenward, too aware of Sheul's watching eye, Meoraq went back to camp with his woman silent at his side.

Gann's child was dead. Its mother knelt, still holding it, still gazing into its empty face. Amber had called the slave a name, but in a human mouth, the sound could be anything. Meoraq paced unnecessarily around the other women, deeply uncomfortable with what he was about to do, but finally went to stand before and speak directly to a slave.

"How are you called?" he asked tersely.

Amber stared at him, her soft mouth opening a little.

"Xzem, sir." The slave looked up at him, heaved a tearful sigh, and raised the dead clay in her hands for him to take.

Meoraq did not want to touch it, but Amber was watching, so he did.

It felt like a real baby, too.

"Can we..." Amber came a small step forward, interrupting his uneasy inspection of the thing. The infant-shaped creature she held yawned and scratched contentedly at its snout, too sleepy to open its eyes. The slave-woman at his feet shifted her eyes from her dead child to the living one and then looked down at her empty arms. "Is there any way at all to have a fire?"

"A fire?" Meoraq echoed, alarmed. "You mean...for a funeral?"

The slave looked up.

"Please," said Amber softly.

He reached out and took her sleeve, meaning to pull her aside and explain that if Gann's children received any funeral at all, it was to be returned to the clay that had spawned them, but as soon as he actually touched her and felt her warmth beneath his hand, all reason left him. His loin-plate restrained him, but if it weren't for that, he would be extruded, he knew. He would be on her and she beneath him...and whether Gann's or Sheul's, he had a dead child in his arms.

In that moment of sickened confusion, a hand touched at his boot. Meoraq looked down, first at the body in his hands and then at the slave who had mothered it.

She did not ask. She shivered on her knees, her eyes like open wounds, and did not dare to ask.

The weight of the lifeless clay dragged at him, far heavier than it had been. 'It only looks like a baby,' he reminded himself and, as if in answer, suddenly found himself thinking that Amber looked nothing like a woman and yet he had believed that at once.

The children born of Gann's corruption were soulless. They were abominations of living flesh. They were sins incarnate and Sheul did not see them. They were clay.

They were clay...and this one's mother had carried it all through the night knowing it could only die in her arms.

"I...need to pray," said Meoraq. He turned away and realized only after he had done so that he still held the child's clay in his arms. He could not think of a good way to turn around and pass it back, so he carried it with him into the trees and set it before him where he ultimately knelt.

He was not quick to speak Sheul's name or to invite His eye. Meoraq knew the word of Sheul and it was absolute. The child before him, however pitiable in its seeming, was a child born of Gann. To give it a funeral as if it were a true dumaq—

He would have given Amber one once, he recalled, again without conscious deliberation. When she lay in her stupor and her treacherous people could not be troubled to care for her, he had been ready to give her a gentle end and see her to Sheul's halls. She had not been his woman then. She hadn't even been dead. And if he would be honest, he would have to admit that when he thought of her fellow humans at all, he thought of them as animals. They might walk as dumaqs. They might have speech and wit and reason. They might have in every way the look of people, but they were no more than animals, and a venomous, brutal breed at that.

Yet Amber had a soul and her soul was hammered at Sheul's forge just the same as Meoraq's own. Her clay was Meoraq's clay, shaped upon Sheul's wheel. Her light was the light of any dumaq, shining from Sheul's lamp. And where it was true of her, surely it must be—

Meoraq put a hand to his brows and rubbed the rest of that thought away before it could come to some sacrilegious ending. Sheul's word was absolute. The children born of Gann's corruption had no soul to find welcome in Sheul's halls. A funeral would be blasphemous.

It looked like a baby.

Its looks were a lie.

The blood that stained its thin scales looked like the blood of any dumaq.

Its blood was the blood of Gann.

Its mother grieved for it.

The grief was a lie. Its mother was as soulless as her spawn and had no true heart.

Then why did she carry it so far?

Meoraq hissed as the futile circle closed itself around the same arguments. He didn't know why he was tormenting himself like this in the first place. A funeral fire was out of the question. The raiders were surely in pursuit. He could give an honest answer to his wife that they could not risk such a thing being seen. He would offer to bury it, since he knew that what distressed Amber the most was the thought of abandoning it to be scavenged by beasts, and even that was surely more than its mother expected.

It occurred to him—not all at once, but slowly, like the light of dawn even now revealing the empty world to him—that there was nothing in the Word that expressly forbade funeral fires for Gann's children. Priests had, yes, but not the Prophet.

It was an uneasy thought, but now his eye was moving over the newly-illuminated plains, seeing the thick copse close on his sunward side where a fire could be better hidden as well as fueled. The wind would thin the smoke and perhaps even carry it away from the raiders so that it could not be seen at all. It would mean holding to this camp all day, but he'd been considering that already, hadn't he?

Meoraq tried to shake the thought away, but it stayed, growing until he could see just how the fire would be laid. So now it was not a thought at all, but a plan. And perhaps a sin.

He reached out to tap the back of one finger against the misshapen head. It felt like skin, soft as only a yearling's could be, sticky where its blood had dried and been wetted again by the rain. There was no avoiding it.

"Sheul, O my Father," he said heavily. "See me now, I pray. Before me, there is one of Gann's getting and I mean to give it Your final rites. I know it is a terrible thing I do and I must answer for it when I stand before You, but it is too much like a true child, Father, and that is surely how my woman sees it. I will not ask Your blessing, only Your forgiveness, and if there be a sin in what I am about to do, let it all be mine, great Sheul, because my woman knows no better, but I do." He gathered up the limp body and held it. "And I mean to do it anyway."

Sheul had no answer for him, which only seemed fitting as he'd asked no questions, but the rains slackened. By the time he'd returned to his camp with the child, it had stopped entirely. Amber watched him come from where she knelt on the ground with her arms around the slave-mother, comforting her. Xzem stared at the ground, her hands clutching at one another and every muscle tensed.

"There will be a fire," Meoraq said, fully aware that those five words might well have damned him. "We will go to that thicket and there remain until—"

That touch on his boot again. Meoraq felt his spines twitch, but did not allow them to flatten. He looked down, ready to be as patient and sensitive as a man could be while ordering a slave to stop grabbing at him, and found her with both hands on either side of him, palms to heaven. The touch he felt was the top of her head as she pressed it to his mud-caked boot and silently wept.

"Thank you," Amber said, hugging the other infant even closer. Her shift, overlarge, slipped down at the subtle movement to expose her bare shoulder and the mark of his teeth. Thoughts entirely inappropriate to this moment briefly clouded even the unpleasant sensation of the slave sobbing on his foot. His spines did flatten then, and there was nothing he could do about it. He turned his face away.

Xzem raised her head as Amber stepped back. "Her name was Nali," she said tremulously. "But I never told her so. Will she...know it? When you pray for her, sir? Must you call her Rosek even then?"

The order to stop touching him burned hot in his throat, and his belly, but it did not touch his voice. "Sheul knows His children."

The frantic light in her eyes did not dim. "But will He know mine?"

There were no magical answers to that and he could see his troubled silence crippling her with every passing moment, until finally, and for no reason at all, he looked at Amber.

Seeing her, the will of Sheul became vast beyond the imagining of any man. To say that it could be captured in anything so finite as written words suddenly seemed fantastically arrogant. Even the Prophet's own great work must pale beside His will.

"We were all lost to Gann once," he said. The words did not come easily, but they felt like truth. "What is lost can be found."

She searched his eyes, her own bleeding despair and hope so long damaged she didn't even seem to know it was there. "Swear it, sir," she whispered finally. "Please, swear it and it is true."

"No man speaks for Sheul," said Meoraq. "But I will observe that the child lived through a long night to die here, where it...where Nali was not a slave."

Xzem stared at him, trying to believe him as the tears spilled endlessly from her eyes, but he had no more comfort to give her and Amber was too close, so he turned away and walked fast into the cooling wind.

At the heart of the thicket where he took the baby was a clearing, abutted by a fallen tree, long dead and well-seasoned and protected enough by the living to be mostly dry. He built the pyre and lay her down. He still didn't know what she was or how much sin adhered to him for the speaking of these rites, but when the hour came to make the prayers, he made them. And he made certain to call her by her name.

13

He took them to Praxas. He could have given a number of reasons if asked to do so (he was not). He had scant provisions and too many mouths. The raiders had every advantage in the wildlands if they ever decided to pursue. The...infant was far too young to travel indefinitely. And he had to take them somewhere, didn't he? Surely Amber didn't expect to keep them?

He would have liked to ask her, but he was afraid of starting a fight. Not because of her moods, but because of his. To say truth, he couldn't even claim to know just what her moods were, his own were so demanding. Gann's corruption emanated from the slaves like smoke—invisible, odorless, but choking in his throat whenever he was among them. He kept his distance as much as he could, patrolling while the women rested, but as soon as he was among them, the fires began to burn in his belly and the blackness came creeping in at his mind. And Amber was always there trying to talk to him, touch him, come and sit beside him, unaware that it was Gann's animal lust that lived in him now, Gann's honeyed words that whispered in his ear to take her, revel in her, *rut* with her.

When Amber tried to lie down with him at night, he got up and left. When he had to speak to her, he did it facing away, feeling her wounded eyes on his back like live coals. She was hurting and he did not dare embrace her. He could hear her crying softly at night, but the creeping blackness that took his words would not let him explain. She needed comfort, but until he was away from these women and cleansed of Gann's taint, he could not give it.

So Meoraq went back to Praxas for the very simple reason that he wanted to be rid of the slaves as soon as possible. The little time he'd spent in that city (not even the city, but at most ten paces down its Southgate tunnel) had given him the impression of an evil place, largely inhabited by men he was ashamed to call brothers under the Blade, but that wasn't his problem. His entire intent had been to find and reclaim his wife. He had surrendered to Amber's insistence that the raiders' slaves had also been set in his path to be rescued solely because there wasn't time to argue with her. Perhaps it had been Sheul's will and so perhaps the slaves could be redeemed and brought back into the light of His lamp, but that was for the priests of Praxas to decide. Meoraq's interests began and ended with Amber.

At first light following the funeral for the...for Nali, Meoraq started them moving. It took too long, owing to the weakened and generally useless condition of the slaves, time which Meoraq spent as far away from them as possible while still keeping them in the shadow of his protection. With Sheul's guidance, they reached their destination in four days and broke free of the woods surrounding the city close to dusk.

Again, he met no sentries, but this time, it was not for lack of them. He saw one almost immediately after leaving the treeline, but rather than come forward and challenge his party, or at least hide until he had reinforcements enough to make that seem like a good idea, the sentry took off at a run.

Well, all right. Not a commendable act, but perhaps an understandable one. Praxas had sent away a single man and now came eight figures. The obvious conclusion? A raiding party, coming to find out who they had to thank for the visit from a Sheulek.

Before long, the braziers were lit on the wall. In the growing dark, this sign of alarm only illuminated how much of the wall had been too heavily damaged to allow access to a brazier. Meoraq was not intimidated, but he was careful to begin hails at the soonest opportunity and to persist even when he was not answered. Their silence disturbed him far more than the lit braziers, yet they must have recognized him. No one fired upon them anyway, although he could see figures moving on the roof and behind the sealed gate. The Word forbade the use of all weapons which delivered death 'not requiring the blow of a man's hand,' as the Prophet had written, but priests had ruled long ago that a man's hand could deliver blows in a number of lawful ways—the cut of a sword, the throw of a spear...the tipping of a barrel. In defense of their cities, warriors of the walls kept flammable oils and acids or other volatile substances, not to mention hot coals in the braziers themselves, to repel attack. A city like Praxas, which commerced with raiders, might have anything...but they let him come.

He continued to hail and they continued to ignore him. A body's length from the gate, Meoraq halted his herd of women and went the last few steps alone. He would be calm. Threading his arms through the bars, Meoraq clasped his hands and leaned on the gate which Praxas boldly shut against him. He looked at each man who had perhaps come to fight him off. The only one who held his stare was Onahi.

"I have not released this city," Meoraq said at length.

Onahi raised his spines slightly in acknowledgement. He did not answer.

"Praxas stands in the shadow of Uyane," Meoraq said. "Open to me."

"I am barracks-ward here, sir," Onahi told him. "I no longer hold a key."

Barracks...ward? Meoraq had never seen that title held by a boy older than sixteen. "What is happening here?" he asked bluntly.

"They've gone to fetch the governor. It won't be long. He's been boarding here since you left us, sir. I turn his sheets," Onahi added caustically. He glanced behind his shoulder and stepped aside as Warden Myselo lumbered into sight.

"Open this gate," ordered Meoraq in what he felt was an admirably patient voice.

Warden Myselo drew himself up importantly and raised a hand in salute, not to Meoraq, but to one of the two men coming up the tunnel behind him. "Governor Rsstha Tolmar of House Rsstha, a son of Lonagra, who was son of—"

"I've never heard of you," interrupted Meoraq, and knew at once which was Rsstha by the flattening of his spines.

"—a son of Posh'ar, who—"

"I am Uyane Meoraq," said Meoraq, lowering his own spines with deliberate insolence. "Son of Uyane Rasozul, steward of House Uyane which is champion to the city of Xeqor in Yroq. Have you heard of me?"

"—who is Praxas in the sight of Sheul," Myselo finished, flustered.

Governor Rsstha gave the warden a tap of release that did not quite reach the man's actual shoulder. "I have," he said. His voice was ridiculously deep and full coming from such a reedy, workless body. "Praxas welcomes you, Sheulek."

Meoraq leaned back to run his gaze over the bars of the gate. "Such is Praxas' welcome, eh?"

"We are happy to make provision for you on your journey. House Rsstha itself shall board you for however long you desire to rest within my walls, but before I open to your conquest, I will hear your intentions."

How easy it would be to argue. Meoraq had never once been given so audacious an order in all his years of service and he thought no tribunal in the world would so much as call him for query if he cut Rsstha down for making it. He yearned to say this aloud...

Ah, but even valid arguments turned easily to insults, which had a way of building to a surge of temper when Meoraq was tired, even when he hadn't been four days keeping a herd of unwanted women ahead of the murderous raiders who may be in pursuit. So instead of parrying the governor's demand, Meoraq simply said, "I do not intend to stay. I will speak with the high judge here. Afterwards, I have a short list of needs for your provisioner and as soon as they are met, I will release your city and go. Open the gate."

"You will go," the governor repeated. "You and your...party?"

Meoraq's temper, none too secure already, slipped. "Take the sneer out of your tone when you speak of them," he said, and Myselo took a broad step back, bumping into his watchmen. "These women come from this city, *your* city, and it was here just days ago that their own fathers conspired to place them in Gann's hands for coin."

"You have proof of this accusation?"

His temper slipped again. "I am proof!" he snapped. "Are you involved in this commerce?"

"Certainly not!" The governor's indignation did not appear to be feigned. "Neither have I any reason to question the judgments executed at my tribunals! These women were exiled according to the laws we are all sworn before God to uphold!"

"These women were not exiled, they were *sold*! That crime is unforgiveable and will be rooted out at its source and if those roots go as deep as the Governor's Seat, so be it!" Meoraq bared his samr and stabbed it suddenly through the bars, restraining himself with less than a finger's breadth between his blade and Rsstha's neck. "Open this gate or here do I swear in the sight of Sheul that I will come through it."

The governor hissed at Myselo and retreated to an ignoble distance with his aide. The nervous jangling of the warden's keys could not quite cover the sound of their voices, but Meoraq did not care enough to listen. He returned to his herd with an itch under his scales and paced among them, coming to stand at last beside his wife. Predictably, the women shrank away, leaving a wide space around him.

And Amber.

Activity at the gate ceased. Rsstha came a few steps forward, staring, then retreated again. More hissing.

Warden Myselo opened the gate and raised a salute. "Honored one, the governor wishes to speak."

"Is everything okay?" Amber whispered.

He glanced at her, wondering blackly how close he'd come to being able to just do what he'd come to do and walk away. He shouldn't have pulled a sword on the governor. A Sheulek was supposed to be the master of his emotions at all times and this was probably why. Fuck.

"Stay here," he said and went to see what the piss-licker wanted.

"The barracks-ward here will take your list of needs to be filled," Rsstha said with a wave at Onahi. "And to arrange your meeting with the high judge. Until that matter is settled, I must insist the women be confined under arms. Regardless of the sins of their fathers, they still stand convicted of criminal acts and have by your own acknowledgement been exposed to further corruption in the grip of Gann."

"Insist," Meoraq said. His hand flexed on the hilt of his samr. "Go on."

"The human." Rsstha tucked his hands into his sleeves, oblivious to all danger. "My guards will take it now, honored one."

"I'll split the man who so much as..." Meoraq's hiss died in his throat. His head cocked. "What did you just call her?"

"Human." Rsstha flared his mouth and hissed delicately through his teeth. "It is the word for their monstrous kind."

"It is." Meoraq tipped his head further. "How did you come to hear it?"

Rsstha's answer took few words. Meoraq stared at him, at Myselo, at the ceiling of the tunnel (which had several disturbing cracks). He took six deep breaths and six again. At length, he released the grip on his sword. He brought his eyes down and his spines up. He looked at Onahi.

"Do you have a room where these women can be held?" he asked. Calmly.

"Yes, sir."

"And defended, if need be?"

Governor Rsstha bristled. Meoraq ignored him.

"Yes, sir."

"Gather your men, then. See that the women of my party are provided food and fresh clothing. A bath, if one can be managed. And hold that door until you are given my word to open, do you mark me?"

"Yes, sir."

Meoraq released Onahi, who left the tunnel at a soldierly run, and turned to Myselo. He leaned in very close, taking up every step that the warden tried to put between them, until there was a wall at the man's back and Meoraq full in his face. "You know my father," he said.

"I, eh, I've heard of him, sir."

"You've heard of how he climbed the wall at Kuaq."

"Yes, sir."

"Killed one hundred and eleven men, alone. Killed the Raider-Lord Szadt."

"Yes, sir."

"Who am I, warden?"

"Sheulek, sir."

"Who am I?"

Myselo's throat worked weakly as he cast his eyes about for aid. "Uyane?"

"I am Uyane. I am my father's son. I am the Sword and the Striding Foot of Sheul. I am—" Meoraq caught the warden's broad face and forced him to look at him. "—the man who comes to you now from the ruins where your Raider-Lord Zhuqa laired and who killed his way in and out to bring you these women. I did not count them," he admitted. "I will not say that I have bettered my father's tally at Kuaq, but I will tell you this, warden." He yanked Myselo's snout down so that he could lean even closer. "I can climb this wall."

Myselo had no answer other than his rapid breath and the metallic stink of fear that rode it. Meoraq released him and went through the gate back to his women.

"A room is being prepared," he told them. "You will rest there until permanent arrangements can be made. I want you with them for now," he said to Amber.

"Where are you going?"

He didn't know how to answer that. "Not far," was the best he could think of.

She took a small step toward him. "I want to go with you."

"No."

"But—"

"No. Get back!" He held up his hand and looked aside until she stepped away again. His throat felt hot. He rubbed it, breathing until he had lost some of the blackness that clouded his brain. Some. Not all. Rsstha's words—those few, simple words—scratched bloody furrows in his head. Damn him. Damn *them.*

Onahi was back, waiting at the mouth of the tunnel with several armed watchmen. Meoraq put his women in a line with Amber at its tail and took them into Praxas. "To my word," he reminded Onahi, "and no other."

Onahi saluted. His men echoed him. They closed their small ranks around the women and marched them into darkness. Meoraq watched the cracks in the ceiling of the tunnel until they were gone.

"Take me to them," he said, and felt his heart begin again to burn in spite of all his deep, calming breaths. "Now."

* * *

Myselo lumbered off ahead of them, ostensibly to find a boy and a cart, but the governor's carriage was waiting at the inner road, and over the governor's outraged exclamations, Meoraq tore the standards off and took it for his own. Rsstha kept a bitter half-silence all the way to the Temple District, which was to say that he glared at Meoraq with his mouth shut tight while his aide made polite objections at regular intervals.

Meoraq ignored them both, meditating with his eyes open and his arms folded. He was quiet, but he was not calm.

There was no one at the gate of Xi'Praxas when they reached it. Meoraq had to bang on the bars with the hilt of his samr for several minutes before a swearing abbot finally let them in.

The inner halls were dark and empty. The abbot brought them a lamp and took himself back to his rooms, muttering loudly and in no uncertain terms about his cold dinner and certain slit-lickers who abused their powers of authority. Meoraq amused himself during much of the next walk debating whether it were himself or Rsstha who had been the slit-licker in question. His tendency to toy with the hilt of one blade or another as he waged this mental argument kept Rsstha and his aide very quiet.

He was led to the Temple's infirmary, past several unattended watch-points, and at the end of the hall in the wing reserved for the needs of the oracles and the high judge, propped up against the wall with his arms folded and his chin tucked against his chest, was a watchman. He appeared to be asleep, but at least he was at his post. He roused himself at their footsteps to say, "Fifty rounds for a dip, five hundred goes an hour, next hour opens at—" He opened his eyes to check the time and saw them. His hands flinched to his sword-belt as his eyes darted to the door, but he drew nothing, and after a tense, considering silence, Meoraq saw him surrender.

Meoraq no longer knew what to expect behind the door, but he was suddenly intensely glad he had not brought Amber with him.

"What is the meaning of this?" Governor Rsstha demanded and his aide went scurrying forward, demanding that the door be opened and didn't the watchman see that this was House Rsstha before him and who was his commander, what was his name, stand and answer.

The watchman dropped his arms to his sides, away from the hilt of his sword. He didn't answer, didn't even salute. His eyes were for Meoraq alone. "I wish to pray," he said simply.

Meoraq drew his samr. "Do so."

The watchman bent his brow to the ground and made his prayers in silence while Rsstha tried to take control of what he obviously perceived as an embarrassing breach of security which Meoraq had no right to judge. He was ignored, and after several minutes, the watchman rose, took the key from his belt and walked to the door.

"Hold where you stand! Honored one, I assure you, we will pursue this matter," Rsstha said stiffly. "But I think it is not your place to—"

"My place," said Meoraq calmly, pensively, and the governor fell silent at once. "My place is to enforce the law of Sheul. That is my place and I know it well. Your place is to run this city in accordance with those laws, and if you believe that doing so allows you to challenge me—" Meoraq's eye at last broke from that of the silent man before him to slide back and stab at Rsstha. "—judgment shall be passed."

The governor made a few flustered gestures, but couldn't seem to think of anything to say.

Meoraq stared at him for a while, then glanced at the watchman. "Open the door and await the will of Sheul."

"Outrageous," the governor said again, but very quietly this time. He stalked away a short distance and came back, then had to do it again because the guard's hands were shaking too much to work the key. For a time, the only sounds to be heard were the key rattling at the lock and the governor's angry footsteps.

Until the door opened.

It was another guard, by the look of him, one still meant to be at his post somewhere in the city. The sound of his armored leg-plates striking against the bars of the cage rang out in discord against the weak cries of his prisoner.

This had not long been a prison. Meoraq could see that by the lightness of the mortar where the bars had been set, and the bars themselves were neither straight, nor smooth, but crude as it was, the cage was more than sufficient to hold the humans. The cage ran the length of the far wall, but was no deeper than a man's arm could reach. There was nothing inside but the prisoners themselves, not even a pail to piss in or dried grass to soak it up. Grooves in the floor were clearly meant to carry wastes away, but they weren't over-careful about using it; they were sitting in filth even now, just watching him. He saw recognition in no one's eye, not even Scott's.

"What the hell is this?" Rsstha demanded in a high, almost comical shriek.

The man at the cage bucked, startled into an early climax. He looked back at them, already furiously snarling out something about that not being anything like a full hour, but then really saw them. He froze, panting, wide-eyed, then shoved himself away from the bars, letting the body he'd been deep inside fall carelessly to the ground as he buckled his loin-plate hurriedly back in place. The girl in the cage rolled onto her side, reaching down between her legs to wipe his semen away.

For one terrible moment, even knowing she was safe under Onahi's honest eye, he thought it was Amber. Then he saw it was Nicci, and he wondered if it made him an evil man that he felt even a moment's relief. He would pray on that later. For now...

He counted ten men, and though he should have known them all, Scott was the only one of them he recognized straight away and only because his face was so hateful to Meoraq's eye, even now as it was, bruised and smeared with unmentionable grime. Ten men and Nicci. Of forty-seven human lives, ten men survived. And Nicci.

"Is this all there are?" Meoraq asked.

Rsstha stammered for a second or two, then swung on the watchman, screaming, "How long has this been going on? How dare you? How long have you been selling time to these...these deviants? Answer me at once, you—"

Without turning, Meoraq slapped him across the snout, knocking the governor of Praxas sprawling across the floor. "Is this all of them?" he asked again, just as calmly.

"These are all that remain," said the watchman.

"I assure you, I had no knowledge of this!" Rsstha said, scrambling to his feet. He shoved his aide away and aimed an accusing hand at the guard standing silent by Nicci's cage. "This...this...bestiality shall be punished!"

Meoraq's head cocked at a dangerous angle. "It is no sin for Sheul to urge a man to lie with humans," he said. "We are all His children."

Rsstha blinked rapidly for several seconds before, perhaps, visibly recalling Amber and the scar on her shoulder.

"It is no sin to feel that urge. The sin," said Meoraq, "lies with selling it."

The watchman took a deep breath and did his best to let it out slow. He raised his chin and closed his eyes. "My name is Seelat Vin."

"Seelat Vin, you have broken the Fifth Law. You have made trade of flesh and so acted against the Word of Sheul. You have broken your faith with Him and as His Sword, I deem you unforgiveable. Stand and be judged."

The nerve which had steadied the watchman until this point crumbled. He cried out for his father, flinching back from the cut that swept across his throat, but it was already over by then and the flinch only opened the fresh gap between head and neck that much wider. He staggered as blood poured in a dark flood across his chest and then fell, his last breath turning to froth under his sagging chin.

The humans in their cage at last showed some reaction, recoiling with even more force than the governor and his aide, who found themselves splattered with blood. And then one of them—he really should know the name—surged forward to seize the bars, saying, "Holy shit, that's Meoraq!"

Meoraq paid the death a proper witness and then, with great effort, turned away. "Get out," he said to the other guard. The humans set up an immediate clamor, beating on the bars and calling his name in their mangled way, but he ignored them for now and turned to Governor Rsstha. "Release them. Do you have a tablet?" he asked the aide.

"Release...? What?"

"Yes, sir," said the aide, producing one from his deep sleeve, along with a stylus.

"I require..." He eyed the humans, blackly considering. "Four tents. Each human is to have a pack, two sets of clothing and a blanket. I will also have four travel-flasks and four bricks of cuuvash. You will take everything to Southgate immediately."

"Honored one, you cannot take these creatures!" the governor stammered. "Sheul gave them to Praxas for study. They are mine!"

Meoraq turned on him fast and hissed, "If you claim possession, then you have broken the Fifth Law yourself! All of you! All who have penned these people as cattle, who force bestial behavior upon them against the Word of Sheul, have broken faith with Him! Do you submit to my judgment then or do you release them?"

Rsstha rather visibly groped for his wits, ultimately falling back into the habits of his office. "I will call for a tribunal—"

"It will be your own!" Meoraq leveled his bloody samr at the guard, still standing silent beside the cage where Nicci huddled, looking back at him without expression. "Get out, I said!"

The guard still did not immediately move, which was understandable since there was no way out of the room save through the door where Meoraq was standing, but when Meoraq looked at him, he eased forward, hesitated again, and then fled.

Rsstha hissed to his aide, who sprinted down the hall, snatching up his robes around his knees. Then he turned a haughty eye on Meoraq and said, "Honored one, you overstep yourself."

Fire burst in Meoraq's brain and before he could stop himself, he'd seized a ruling governor by his fine robes and slapped him across the snout. And again. And again. "*I hold this piss-gully in my fucking shadow*!" he roared, still slapping. "I would not be overstepping by a fucking scale if I ran a sword up your slit and out your mouth! *Open that fucking door*!"

With that, he turned and hurled the man across the room and into the bars of the cage with force enough to bend them. Meoraq clapped both hands over his eyes and breathed in the dark, listening to Rsstha fumble with his keys and babble out all the ways in which it was obvious that humans were in no way people and that Sheul could not condemn their use in any fashion any more than he condemned the use of cattle for hides Meoraq himself wore. Then the door was open and Scott came spilling out to catch at Meoraq's arm, saying, "Jesus Christ, am I glad to see you!"

Meoraq shook him off. "Gather your men. N'ki, come!"

Nicci rose, but slowly. Surely she knew him—by Scott's words if by no other reason—but her gaze remained dull and lifeless. She moved out of the cage and toward him without making any effort to cover herself, and Meoraq sent a second prayer of thanks to Sheul that Amber was not here, but it was a heavy gratitude, for he knew his wife would have to see what her blood-kin had become soon enough.

"I told you he'd find us, didn't I?" Scott was saying, standing tall at Meoraq's side as Nicci hobbled her vacant way across the room. “I told you he wouldn’t stop looking!”

“I had not started looking, human,” Meoraq spat. “Nor was I inclined to start. It is Sheul who apparently wishes you spared and I can only think He does so to teach me humility.” And because no one was making a damned move in that direction, Meoraq stalked furiously over and picked Nicci up himself, tossing her across his shoulder where she hung like a sack of grain, half-emptied. “And I tell you right now that He had best make His will very damned clear if He wishes me to move you even one damned step away from this city, because I would just as soon see you all rot in its ruins!”

“Are you mad at us?” Scott asked. He sounded surprised.

Meoraq walked away, letting the humans scramble after and Governor Rsstha stand alone in the mouth of an empty cell. The feel of Nicci swaying with the force of his stride was extremely unpleasant; her hand smacked against his thigh now and then, lifeless as a corpse.

“You *are* mad,” said Scott, now angry as well as surprised. “Just what the hell do you have to be mad about? You abandoned us, remember?”

Meoraq swung around so fast that Nicci’s limp hand struck the wall behind him. “*Lies*! You did the leaving, human!”

“She was dying! What were we supposed to do, stand around and watch?”

Meoraq cocked his head warningly and took a few soul-soothing breaths. When he was calm once more, he said, “If you had, you would have been there to see that she did not die.”

They all stared at him, all these flat and ugly faces he had almost forgotten, simply amazed.

“She didn’t?” Scott said finally.

“No.”

“Not then or not ever?”

Meoraq leaned back a little and gave him a hard, dangerous stare.

“Well, I mean...where is she?”

“With me,” said Meoraq and started walking again, reminded by these words that she was not, for the moment.

The humans followed. He could hear them whispering amongst themselves. If any of them were pleased to learn that Amber lived, they showed no sign. He expected no better of them.

‘And so do I stand again among them, O my Father,’ he thought crossly, jogging Nicci’s dead weight higher up upon his shoulder. ‘If this is the price You would have me pay that I receive my woman once more, I will even thank You as I pay it, but of all humans You have chosen to spare, why Scott?’

Sheul had no answer.

The governor’s carriage was too small to fit all the humans. Meoraq ordered a cart and loaded them into the back like sacks of grain. The driver, who had obviously never seen or imagined anything like the humans he was now pulling, got them back to Southgate in half the time it had taken the carriage to make the same trip, a feat even more impressive considering how often he’d been staring back into the cart instead of directing his blindfolded bulls.

Meoraq did not speak to his humans. They did not speak to him.

At the gate, Meoraq again hupped Nicci onto his shoulder and demanded to be taken to Onahi. He and his humans were led into the barracks, to a sealed door guarded by five watchmen and Onahi himself, armed and armored.

“Is there something you require, honored one?” he asked respectfully. He did not so much as glance at the humans, not even the one on Meoraq’s shoulder.

“I am leaving as soon as my provisions arrive. I am taking the women with me.”

Onahi frowned. "The high judge would not receive them?"

"I didn't meet with him. It is my judgment that Gann holds this city in his shadow. I say the eye of Sheul is upon Praxas and His eye burns with wrath. I am certain He has not directed me to lead these people from death into damnation, therefore I...damn it, I must be meant to lead them on."

Onahi gazed at him for a short time in perfect stillness. Then he turned and made a gesture of his own, and while his men opened the door and passed out of sight, presumably to gather the refugees sequestered somewhere within, looked back at Meoraq and calmly said, "Is it for you to know if the wrath of Sheul is upon me as well, sir?"

Meoraq gave him a second, more thoughtful stare. "And if it were?"

"I serve Sheul in faith. If it is His will that I die here, I am ready and go to His judgment without fear. Yet if it is not, for my own will, I would live."

Meoraq listened past the chatter of his humans, and while he heard no specific word from Sheul to approve this suggestion, he heard no word against it either. He began to give a cautious assent and then said instead, for no reason he could fathom, "Have you a family?"

"I am of the House Xaik, sir," Onahi replied, showing no sign he thought the question an odd one. "Descended low by their champion, but born under his blade."

Which was to say, he was a bastard, the son of a Sheulteb and one of his House's servants.

"Have you a woman? Sons?"

"No," said the guard.

Meoraq pondered the matter while Onahi patiently stood by, but could discern no reason for asking such things. And so perhaps Sheul had spoken after all.

So be it.

"Gather those of your men you trust and whatever gear you can readily manage. We leave as soon as my provisions arrive. Fuck," he finished, glaring as Amber came through the door. He looked at Nicci's upturned ass on his shoulder, fought and mastered the urge to hurl her violently to the floor, and instead shrugged her upright and set her carefully down.

"Oh my God," said Amber in a voice so unlike hers that if he were not looking at her, he never would have believed she'd said it, human words or no. She staggered forward, gripped the restraining arms of Onahi's men and shoved them aside. "Oh my God. Nicci!"

And then she was flying forward to seize her unmoving blood-kin and embrace her, and there were tears streaming from her eyes and happy sounds like screams pouring from her throat, and it was joy and relief and wonder in volume too great for any mortal heart to bear, and so Meoraq turned his back on it and stared instead at Scott, whom he hated. He thought there must be a lesson in that somewhere, but his brain was full of that terrible, black fire and he couldn't think past it to what it must be.

BOOK VIII

Xi'MATEZH

They left the city. Amber couldn't really say they were run out, since Meoraq was in charge of the leaving, and because of the way he was doing it, she couldn't even say they were sneaking away, but she felt like they were doing both. Walking down that long, dark tunnel with dozens and dozens of lizardmen standing on either side watching them go was about the worst way to leave a place as anything Amber knew, and that included standing in the rain waiting to board the ship that was about to crash.

She didn't ask where they were going. She didn't ask who all these lizardmen were who'd joined them. She stayed at the back of the line with Nicci and didn't say a word. Even in the cloud-covered moonlight, Meoraq's throat was bright, bright yellow.

They didn't go all night. After taking them back across the open grass and into the woods and hiking for maybe two hours up and down the hilly wilderness that was this part of the world, Meoraq brought them to a fairly level place and camped them. The lizardmen had some of the same sort of leather walls that Zhuqa had used, and after tying them up around the trees, they formed a pretty good shelter. It wasn't as good as a tent, but it pushed back some of the wind and held in some of the heat and some, Amber was coming to find, was better than nothing.

Tents went up. Packs were opened and cuuvash produced, but the guard took a long time looking it over...scraping at it with his fingers...sniffing...and finally calling Meoraq over to do the same thing. There was some low talk and at the end of it, all the cuuvash was pulled out and dropped in the fire. They sat in groups to watch it burn—lizardmen, lizardladies, and humans, with Amber and Meoraq forming the blurred place between the beginning and end of their circle.

The baby cried. So did Nicci. Amber, torn, sat with her sister and watched Xzem stroke at the tiny back. After a while, one of the guards—Onahi—moved from where he sat with his men to the place right beside Xzem. He leaned in close as Xzem shrank fearfully back and ducked her head, then turned a grim eye on Meoraq. "It is hard travel for a fresh mother," he said. "But with an empty belly besides is harder than it has to be. Have I your will to hunt, honored one?"

Meoraq thought about it as he gazed over the leather walls at the sky. "If it is God's will to provide game, I will not protest it, but we are very close to a city where evil men show no love for God's laws. We may be followed even now. Those who hesitate to invade this camp surely will not when it comes to striking at a hunter upon the plains."

"I walk in God's sight," said Onahi, rising. "And if I meet Him before the night is ended, I will not be ashamed to tell Him the reason. Be easy, mother," he added to Xzem, bending his neck politely and showing no sign that he saw the way she cringed around the baby. When he left, two of his men left with him.

Meoraq watched them go, his restlessness betrayed by the tightening of his jaw and throat muscles. Amber reached out a hand, but he flinched away before she could touch him and stood up. “I will make a patrol,” he said to Onahi’s remaining guards, refusing to look at her. “Until I return, no one is to leave the camp.”

They all saluted in near-perfect unison, all with the same troubled sidelong glance at the humans clustered at one side of the walls. Meoraq took that in, grunted, and said, “If you must force their obedience, do so carefully. These are people, not animals, and they are people under the protection of House Uyane. Mark me.”

They saluted again, now sending their nervous eyes toward the lizardladies.

Meoraq grunted again. “You may know these women as criminals and exiles, but I am Uyane Meoraq, a Sword and a true son of Sheul, and I judge them innocent of crime and innocent of corruption.”

Some of the slaves looked up.

“Hear me and mark well: I take them from their fathers. I take them from the city of Praxas under Gann. I take them into House Uyane and I forgive them all their past. I say they are daughters of Sheul and they stand in His sight.” Meoraq drew his samr and took one long step forward, standing between the lizardladies and the lizardmen, and cocked his head. “I say they stand under *my* protection. You watch them. You do not touch them. If you feel the fires in your belly, think of it as a test of your will...because I will think of it as an assault upon my House.”

A clumsy scattering of salutes apparently satisfied Meoraq that he was still a menacing badass when he wanted to be. He turned around, and for a moment, he and Amber were unavoidably faced off.

The color at his throat visibly brightened. He turned his head, stared at the wall beyond her for a long, long time in silence while his scales faded to black. Then he left.

Only after he was gone, as the guards began to mutter and the humans whisper, did Amber realize what Meoraq had entirely forgotten.

“Hey,” she said.

The lizardmen all looked at her.

“Do any of you understand English?” she asked.

Three pairs of eyes stared blankly back at her. One of them looked at another. “Is that thing talking?” he asked.

“What are you telling them?” Scott demanded.

“Nothing. We’re going to be incommunicado for a while, that’s all.” Amber gestured at the lizards, all of whom looked alarmed to find themselves at the end of even a casual wave, all but Xzem, who actually eased a little closer to Amber’s arm. When Amber looked at her in surprise, Xzem ducked her head and offered up the crying baby.

Scott recoiled violently when Amber took it. “Jesus Christ, is that thing yours?”

Heat flared in her cheeks. She didn’t let that stop her from tucking the baby down into her wrap where it immediately quieted against her breasts. “No, of course not,” she snapped.

“Where’d you get it, if it’s not yours?”

“Stop saying ‘if’ like you think you’re going to catch me in a lie. It’s not mine!”

“You’re being awfully sensitive about it,” Scott said and Crandall muttered, “Hormones, man. She just had a baby.”

“Stop it!” Nicci hissed, so suddenly and with such violence that they all looked at her, even Amber. Nicci still had tears on her face, a firelit shine that made her anger look a lot like hate...and hate made her look like their mother. “We haven’t even been out of the cage one whole day and here you all are, cutting into her again!”

Some of them looked away. Only some. Crandall just looked back at her and Scott’s eyes turned, if possible, even colder and more contemptuous.

After a long, ugly silence during which Amber was only too aware of the watching lizardmen, she finally cleared her throat and said, "There were these people. Exiles. Bandits. That sort of thing. The baby was their leader's. I couldn't leave it."

"What were you doing there?" Scott asked.

She stared at him for a moment, utterly dumbfounded by the tone of undisguised suspicion he was throwing at her. "I was captured," she said slowly. "What the fuck do you think I was doing there? Selling Space-Scout cookies?"

"I don't know...maybe Meoraq sold you to them. He sure acts like a raider. For all I know, he's one of them. Maybe even their king."

Amber had just enough time to think clearly (very clearly, that alone should have been a clue) that nothing Everly Scott said was ever worth a damn and she needed to be a big girl and let it go. Then she was on her feet with the baby pressed to her body with one arm, clocking Scott right in his big, fat mouth.

Scott staggered. Crandall started to hop up only to sit down again very fast, so that his legs kicked comically out in front of him. No one else moved and the reason no one else moved, Amber discovered upon a backwards glance, was because the guards had all drawn weapons. They might not speak English, but clearly they knew whose camp they were in and who put the scars on her shoulder.

"Call them off," said Eric at last, in a strained let's-be-reasonable voice.

Now Amber gaped at him. "Did I fall through a hole in time?" she demanded. "These are still not my trained alligators!" And just to make the moment complete, she turned to the guards and made settling motions with her hand, doing her best to say, "Easy...down...please," in lizardish while pissed off right to the red line. As they slowly sheathed their swords, she swung back on Scott and said, "If you want to stay here, you better have a goddamn good apology for me in the next five seconds. One—"

"Jesus fucking Christ, sorry!"

"Two!" shouted Amber, and the baby added its own furious, if muffled, howl.

Scott put his hands up like a man being mugged. "I'm *sorry*, Bierce! Goddamn! I just got out of a fucking cage! Pardon me all to hell if I'm not in love with the fucking lizards!"

The word *three* hovered on her lips, but in the end, she swallowed it. "Fine," she said, patting at the baby through her wrap until it settled. "You're on edge. I'm on edge. We'll put it behind us."

"Jesus!"

"But you better believe that was your only free pass." Amber glared at him. "Your days of throwing your attitude in my face are all over. You're in *my* camp now and if I don't like the way you talk, *commander*, I will leave *your* ass behind!"

He opened his mouth angrily...worked it for a bit...and finally closed it again, brick-red and actually shaking a little. He got up and moved as far away from her as he could go while still being within the boundary of the leather walls. Crandall went with him. After a moment, Dag and Eric joined him. Then they were all over there, all but Nicci, muttering at each other under the wind and looking at her with mistrustful eyes.

"What do you think that was about?" one of the guards asked quietly.

"I know it was bad," another replied, letting his hand rest on the hilt of his sword. "And I know it's getting worse by the moment."

It was. And it was her fault as much as Scott's. She only had to look at them, what was left of them, to know they'd been through hell and the first day out of it was way too soon to expect them to shake it off. Amber took a deep breath (*one for the prophet*) and let it out slow. She sat down.

Nicci came to sit with her, warm and alive and so much older than Amber remembered. It was like looking into her mother's face, that last day, and knowing it was Death you were looking at. Knowing it was looking back at you.

"I'm sorry," Amber said.

Nicci nodded without looking at her.

"This isn't how I wanted this to go. You don't know how I've dreamed of this moment…and I've already fucked it up."

Nicci shrugged.

The baby in her arms began to purr.

"Was there…" Did she really want to know this? "Was there really a cage?"

"Yes."

"How long…I mean…"

"I don't know. You couldn't count the days in there. Or maybe you could. I didn't try." Nicci stared at the fire some more, then shrugged again. "There was still snow on the ground, though. How long ago was that?"

"I don't know," Amber admitted. "Meoraq made us stop for the winter. We only just crossed the mountains when I got caught. That must be the official welcome in Gedai."

"Must be."

The quiet was not an easy one. The lizards watched them. So did Scott.

Nicci sighed. She bent her head—an eerily lizard-like gesture—and said, "We were walking along in this tunnel, you know? Only it wasn't just a tunnel. It was a…like, a pipe. A sewer pipe. A storm drain, really. And I remember thinking how stupid that was, because of how much it had been raining. But it was mostly empty that day, and Commander Scott said it would be dry and there wouldn't be any animals and it had to be safe because the bots were going in and out. We didn't want to, but he kind of went off on it, you know how he does. So we went in anyway. And I knew it was stupid."

The baby bit her, whimpered, and bit again. Amber brought it out, wrapped it regretfully in its smooth hide, and gave it back to Xzem. Nicci waited for the end of this process without watching it, then went on in the same dull, inflectionless voice.

"When it flooded, it happened all at once. And I know how that sounds, but it's true. There wasn't any warning. It wasn't like it was raining and the water rose up. It had been raining for days and the water was still pretty much just around our feet, and then suddenly there was this wall of water coming at us. It hit and we all went away, all mashed together, and that was pretty bad," said Nicci in a vague, thoughtful tone. "The lights all went out. It was pitch black and so loud. Everyone was grabbing at everyone else and all you could hear was the water and the bubbly sound people make…you know…when they drown."

Amber didn't want to hear any more, but she didn't try to stop Nicci from talking. Sometimes you had to say the bad stuff. She put her arm around her sister's shoulder and watched the baby nurse at Xzem's breast.

"Then the tunnel dropped away and there was this grate or something across the whole floor. It was rusty and there was a big hole through it, but some of us managed to catch it and climb out to where there was a kind of ledge. Not all of us. Just…some. We all held hands on the ledge until the water went down and we could find our way out. I didn't think we would, but we did. After that, we kind of camped there for a few days. I guess we were waiting, you know, for you and Meoraq. But it kept raining and there were these storms…storms like I never knew could happen. The buildings we were next to fell down and then the street dropped out from under it and all this water started bubbling up and it was still raining, so what were we supposed to do?"

The wind died down, as if in sympathy, and Scott's voice was right there in an urgent whisper: "—need to think about what's best for *us*!" Then silence and the weight of their stares.

"We turned south," said Nicci, "because Commander Scott said it would be warmer."

"Now wait just a goddamned minute!"

"That's a logical assumption," said Amber, as indifferently as she could.

"And we took a vote! We all agreed it was our best chance!"

"The men took a vote," said Nicci. "You were right about that, too."

Scott started forward. Lizards drew swords. Scott retreated to slap furiously at the leather wall, looking like nothing so much as an angry ape.

"That thing gets just one more of those," said one of the guards, pointing his sword at Scott, "and then I kill it. I am not waiting for it to come at me."

Scott hunkered down, muttering and swiping at his hair.

"So we turned south, but it didn't get warmer. It started snowing. And then it started freezing. And it was so cold..." Nicci trailed off. Her head cocked—again, like a lizardman expressing interest and reluctant humor. "There wasn't any water, unless it was coming down in sheets and freezing on our bodies, and there wasn't any food, unless it was chasing us down and trying to eat us. And six more people died, and Commander Scott said we should cross the mountains after all—"

"Hey!"

"—because the skyport was our only hope."

"We all agreed, goddammit!"

The lizardman who still had his sword drawn came suddenly, swiftly forward and dropped to one knee before Amber. He bent his head, clearly unsure of the protocol, then gave her a hard stare and said, "If you understand me, keep it quiet."

"Scott..."

"She's misrepresenting the facts!"

"Not by much," said Eric quietly. "Sit down, man." And to Nicci, just as quietly, he said, "You really are a two-faced little whore, you know that? Acting like it's such a conspiracy that you girls didn't get to vote. Did you even try? Hell, no. You just sat there like a bunch of dummies waiting for us to make the decisions. When it came right down to it, you wanted us to take care of you. We did, so shut up about it."

The lizardman kneeling in the grass before Amber hadn't moved, although he had shifted the focus of his uneasy stare.

"We went into the mountains," said Nicci. "There wasn't a road or anything, so we just went where Commander Scott said our chances were best. The snow was over our boots the first day and over our knees the second day and by the third day we were trying to walk on it because we couldn't go through it anymore. We should have gone back," she said, turning her dull eyes on the rest of them. "We all knew it. We should have gone back but we followed him anyway."

"That's enough," said Eric, still without raising his voice.

"Sabrina froze to death," said Nicci. "Only she didn't just freeze. First, her fingers turned black. Commander Scott tried to rub them to warm them up and they broke off. Sabrina's fingers broke off in his hand like..." Nicci's head cocked the other way, thinking hard. "Like icicles breaking off the bannister back when we were kids, remember how we'd do that? Snap snap snap, all in a row. While Sabrina was watching. They fell into the snow at her own feet. And I remember how Commander Scott started to bend down, like he was going to pick them up, you know? Like he was going to *hand* them to her. And then he just walked away like he hadn't seen it happen."

Amber tried to say something. Anything. All she could do was breathe. She looked back at Scott and for once, for maybe even the first time since she'd met the prick, she looked at him without any anger in her at all, only a heartsick throb of horror that was, for a change, *for* him and not aimed against him.

She didn't know what he read in her eyes, but it wasn't sympathy. His face turned ugly. He looked at the lizardman kneeling before her and turned away.

"Then her feet turned black and she couldn't walk anymore. We were all standing around waiting for her to die so we could keep moving. And she did, but by then, there were others. We had to keep walking, but everyone was dying. Mr. Yao—remember him?—fell down dead. I didn't know people could really do that. We were walking and he just fell down dead. And we kept on walking. Like we didn't even see it. But we all saw it. We all walked right by him."

Amber couldn't stop herself. She reached down and plucked the sleeping baby off Xzem's breast, cuddling him back to her own. It woke up, bewildered, then recognized her and snuggled down, purring itself back to sleep. Xzem shifted her wrap up over her nipple and waited to be needed again, watching Amber's face anxiously.

"Every day, there was someone else dead. Every single day. But we still followed him."

"We made it out," said one of the Manifestors and the others muttered agreement. "We didn't lie down and die like you would have done, lizard-bait. We made it out because of him."

"We did," Nicci agreed. "All fifteen of us. But Lani died the next morning. I don't know whether it was cold or hunger by that point. I guess it could have been either one. And Mr. Briggs died two days later. He just walked out into the snow to go to the bathroom and didn't come back. We never found him. I don't know whether he got lost or got eaten...or just kept walking. And then there was Maria." Nicci looked at Eric, politely inquisitive. "Would you like to tell her about Maria, Mr. Lassiter?"

"Go to hell, you scalie-fucking cum dumpster," said Eric gently.

"Maria got pregnant," said Nicci, unmoved. She went back to staring into the fire. "Which was what I seem to recall our role was by that time. Their most precious resource, remember, Amber? We were their wombs. Only now that one of those wombs was full, suddenly our leader was saying...well, pretty much what you said when he called you a womb. Suddenly having babies was right down there with...what did you say? Building a community theater and casting for *Miss Saigon*?"

"I don't remember," said Amber numbly, thinking *The King and I* over and over, like the tolling of a funeral bell.

"So they took another vote. It was very democratic. And after the vote, they caught Maria and while she was screaming and pleading for them to stop, Mr. Lassiter and Commander Scott took turns punching her in the stomach."

Silence. The fire hummed and the baby purred.

After a while, Nicci said, "It worked. Eventually."

More silence. Scott swiped at his hair. The lizardmen watched him. The lizardladies huddled together and tried not to look at anybody.

"But she kept bleeding—"

"Oh, shut her up, for Christ's sake!" Scott exploded.

The lizardman stood up. Amber touched his wrist. He shut his eyes and hissed, then shot her a very Meoraq-like look of annoyance and knelt down again.

"She kept bleeding—"

"It's enough, Nicci," said Amber. "Come on. Stop."

Nicci considered, gazing into the fire. "She kept bleeding," she said at last, decisively. "And she got really sick. And in the morning, Commander Scott and Mr. Lassiter said she was dead and we kept going, but we all knew she wasn't dead—"

"Nicci."

"We could all hear her under the wind—"

"Nicci, please."

"—crying—"

Amber pressed her face to the baby, as if its sleeping purrs could drive every other sound away.

"—begging us to come back." Nicci thought about it while Amber enveloped herself in the peaceful song of a small life that knew only how deeply it was loved. "And we left her there anyway," said Nicci. "We all walked away and pretended we didn't see those big weasel-things at all, didn't we? We pretended we never heard her screaming."

"I swear I'm going to hit her if she doesn't shut up," said Eric in his soft way.

"I'm not sure she can shut up," Amber answered wearily. "Let her say it all. Who can it hurt now?"

"When we saw that place, Commander Scott said it was the temple, even though Meoraq told us to look for the ends of the world and we all knew we weren't there. But we followed him. And the place got bigger and bigger and we knew it was wrong, but we all kept going. They sent someone out to look at us or something, and Commander Scott sent Abdullah to go meet him, only I guess it freaked him out to see Abdullah coming right at him like that because he..." Nicci shrugged again. "Commander Scott knelt down in the snow, so we all knelt down in the snow with him. So they took us away. And they cut us up and they did a lot of things...but they fed us and they kept us warm, so...and this is actually kind of ironic...being captured like that probably saved our lives."

And that, mercifully, seemed to be the end. Nicci watched the baby doze against Amber's chest, the scantest hint of emotion wrinkling at her brow, although Amber couldn't say quite what that emotion was. She only knew that it was better—not much, maybe, but better—than the total lack of life that her sister had exhibited throughout her awful recital.

"So are you happy now?" Scott asked bitterly.

Amber looked at him, helpless to do anything but shake her head.

"You sure? Not even one I-told-you-so? One If-only? One steaming Bierce-knows-best pile of bullshit we can warm ourselves by as we gather around your campfire?"

"Go to sleep, Scott," said Amber. "It's over, all right?" She had to chew her next words a long time before she could keep them down, but in the end she was able to say, "You did the best you could," and mean it.

Scott stared at her for a long time and then dropped his eyes. He looked at the fire and said, in a strained, distant sort of voice, "You know...that first night after we left...that very first night, when we were alone and we all thought, you know, that you were dead..."

The fire snapped. The baby shifted, purred for a few seconds, then slipped easily back into sleep. The lizardmen watched from the far wall, hands on swords, restless.

Scott looked up, his lips pulled back from his teeth in a hideous imitation of the charismatic smile she remembered. "That was the night I fucked your sister," he said. "She said she didn't want to, she even pretended to struggle, but she came. And she wasn't even a virgin, so yeah, Bierce, you really dropped the ball somewhere along the line, but that's okay. I'm sure you *did the best you could*. You want to know something? Huh? You ruined everything, Bierce."

"Yeah, and I broke your flashlight, too."

"Fuck you!" he spat, and didn't flinch even when every lizardman in camp whipped out a sword. "You! Ruined! *Everything*! We'd have been just *fine* if you'd only *died*! We'd be *home* by now if it wasn't for you! *You*!"

And then he lay down with his back to her and pretended to be asleep.

Amber closed her eyes and concentrated on the baby's little purrs, its small hand so warm against her breast, its living, loving reality. Gradually, the hot knot in her stomach loosened, although the bitter taste in her mouth remained. When she finally opened her eyes, Nicci was looking at her with those dead eyes and Bo Peep's own bitter smile. "Aren't you glad you found us?" she asked.

* * *

Meoraq found the soldiers sent to assassinate him without difficulty. There were nine in all—two groups of four and a lone man wearing the governor's colors. He killed them swiftly, tied the corpses to trees with their own belts, and left them to be found. Perhaps they were, for there were no more assassins that night. As his last empty patrol along their back-trail came to an end, Meoraq met with Onahi and his men, and with them took a rogue kipwe they found sleeping in the trees.

It was another hour before they returned to camp, bearing what they could upon two hastily constructed litters. Amber had a grimace of some unhappy sort for him, but did not stir herself from the fireside. The watchmen, however, came at once to make their unsettling report of angry words and blows struck and Meoraq knew even before they pointed him out who had been at the root of it all.

"Honored one, you have said these creatures dwell in the sight of Sheul," Onahi murmured, frowning now at Scott. "And you have proven that it is His will you have their care, but it would seem a far simpler matter to care for them were they kept bound and hobbled."

Meoraq flared his spines reprovingly, but spoke no censure. His heart was in the right place. And honestly, Onahi just wanted Scott hobbled. Meoraq wanted him dead. And buried.

He left the preparation of the first skewers to Onahi and made a quick count of his camp. All were present—watchmen, slaves, humans, and his Amber. She had the infant in her arms again, he saw. It slept too deeply to sing, even when she stroked a careful hand across its little back. 'Someday it will be my child at that breast,' Meoraq thought, but he did not disturb her or the child to say so.

The meat roasted and the humans clustered close to watch it. Meoraq tried not to resent this. They had endured a terrible captivity and they were doubtless hungry. All the same, his days of tending to them like cattle were done.

And so when Scott deemed the meat done enough for his taste and reached to have the first skewer out, Meoraq caught him unhurriedly by the wrist and pushed him back. "This is my camp," he said. "And you are not my welcome guest. You have what I give you, human, when I choose to give it, and you will receive it gratefully or it will be the last thing you ever take from my hand."

Scott's face puckered and colored in that way Meoraq so well remembered. "We're starving," he insisted.

Meoraq flattened his spines in disgust. He let go of Scott's wrist to seize the edge of his loose tunic and pull it up, revealing the man's pink body, which was not an abundant one, but certainly was not emaciated. "No, you aren't," he said, and covered the man curtly up again. "Sit and wait for your share or go hungry."

"Does it understand you?" Onahi asked, watching Scott limp sullenly away.

Meoraq grunted a caustic affirmation as he tested the skewers himself and decided one of them at least was indeed ready. He took a token piece for himself and gave the rest to Amber. She offered it at once to Nicci.

"She'll have her own," he said testily, very much aware of the men watching him. "That is yours."

Amber's little brows twitched together. She put her arm around Nicci's shoulders and would not look at him. Nicci did, her eyes glinting like light on the edge of a blade as she ate his wife's first meal in days.

The color throbbed in his throat. He turned his back on her and breathed.

The sun dropped further behind the clouds. On the distant walls of Praxas, the braziers were lit, tended by far more men than were needed for the chore. They were watching, Meoraq knew, but he did not think they would dare to come for him. Which was almost a pity, as he was right in the mood to deal with them.

What in Gann's grey hell was he going to do with all these people? It was not a new thought, but it was one he hadn't had to consider for some time and he'd never had an answer even when the matter had been pressing. Now here it was again, grossly compounded. There would always be room in the barracks for Onahi and his watchmen, as they were born under the Blade and shared some of the rights of entitlement all of Sheul's favored had been blessed with, but what to do with these fatherless, mateless women? Meoraq could demand they be taken in, but he had no illusions; as soon as he had left again, some corruption would be found in them and they would be turned quietly back out into the wilds. So what was he supposed to do with them? Go on to Xi'Matezh with this...this caravan like nothing had happened? And after that, take them all back to Xeqor? His was the championing House of all that great city, its bloodline unstained and renown unspoiled back to the very day of its founding. He could not fill its halls with raider-slaves and remain its steward.

Meoraq hissed and rubbed at his throat, which felt disturbingly warm already. 'Patience, Uyane. Patience is not a word to a warrior, but a way of life. Honor Him and show patience.' "How well do you know this land?" he asked.

Onahi tipped his head toward him without taking his eye from Scott. "I have been all my life within those walls, sir, save for one summer spent with my mother's people in Chalh."

Meoraq grunted morosely, poked at the fire...and then looked around with a frown. "Chalh?"

"To the south, sir, and eastward. Just out of the shadow of the mountains, in the lie of the road that leads out of Yroq."

There was a question, scarcely hinted at, in those last words. Meoraq supposed he had an accent. "We didn't come by road," he said. "You have kin in Chalh?"

"My mother's kin. In service to House Ylsathoc."

"Ylsathoc," he echoed. The name was oddly familiar to him...and then he placed it. "I knew an exarch of that name. Exarch Ylsathoc...ah...Hi-something. Hilesh?"

The watchman of Praxas betrayed dumaq emotion at last with a snort, taking his eyes off Scott just long enough to roll them. "Hirut. Exarch, is he?"

"You know him?"

"I knew a swaggering little sprat who seemed to think the wind itself would stop blowing if he didn't point it in the right direction. How did he turn out?"

"He's taller."

Onahi snorted again.

"Would you know the way to Chalh well enough to guide a man?" asked Meoraq.

"There's little enough to know, sir. Three days of brisk travel would take us to the Prophet's Crossways. From there, the southward road will lead us directly to the gate. It should be in fair repair," he added. "There's a shrine at the Crossways, popular with the priests and blade-born pilgrims."

"But no road from Praxas."

Onahi grunted and flexed his spines in a shrug. "The city of my father gave its love to Gann long ago. I always had a mind to make the journey to Chalh, but never won release from the warden."

Small marvel, that. Warden Myselo would not be quick to let another man free to speak of what he may have seen, certainly not to the sort of city that birthed exarchs.

"You never stood a watch without the walls?"

"Many times."

"You could have left."

"I suppose so."

"You never wished to?"

Onahi grunted and spared him half a glance before Scott redrew his attention. "It never felt like the right thing to do."

"You left tonight."

"Tonight, it did."

"Sheul's hand is ever upon the hammer," Meoraq mused, looking around at his Amber, safe again within his keeping, and at her Nicci, safe again beneath her arm.

Onahi acknowledged this politely and quiet passed between them for a time. At length, it was the other man who broke it, raising a hand first in salute. "Forgive me, honored one, for my boldness. Is it your will to travel on to Chalh?"

"It would appear to be Sheul's will," Meoraq answered, taking another skewer off the coals. "How does that find you?"

"I obey Him in all things." He paused. "It will be a relief to settle there, sir. Chalh is a good place." He paused again, his eye drifting from Scott to the fire, and to the slave who crouched there at Amber's side, suckling Gann's child. "A good place for a family."

"Perhaps you will have one someday," Meoraq said, as if this were not an absurd suggestion to make of a Sheulteb's bastard. He liked the man.

Meoraq took the skewers off the fire and, ignoring the immediate outstretched arms of Scott and his humans, gave them out to his brothers under the Blade.

Onahi watched Scott stomp and swear his way back over to the edge of camp while his skewer cooled, but when the human finally quieted, his attention drifted. He took a small bite, swallowed quickly, then stood up.

Meoraq prepared more kipwe to roast, watching without seeming to watch as Onahi crossed around the fire and went to one knee before Xzem. "Mother," he said, respectful as a man at prayer. "It is Onahi Chasa before you."

The slave ducked her head and rocked the child of Gann, giving Amber short sidelong glances until she realized who it was the man addressed. Her next wary glance was to Meoraq, but he kept his own eyes on the roasting meat and let whatever was happening here happen without him.

Onahi waited. Patience was not a word to him. Meoraq felt a little envy stinging through his grim amusement as he let this scene play itself out. He did like the man. He was a bit of a fool, but a good man, and after the unpleasantness of this day, even a foolish sort of goodness was a soothing thing to see.

It was obvious Onahi had no experience with servants, let alone with slaves. One did not directly address them unless one were giving orders. The slave knew this even if Onahi did not. If he had simply dropped the skewer in her lap and walked on, she would be eating now, not cringing in confusion under the weight of his gentle gaze. But this was no proper household, no more than it was a raiding nest, and it seemed neither of them knew the rules of conduct.

The slave ultimately seemed to realize that the man before her would not leave until he had an answer of some sort. Short spines shivering, her neck bent so far that her chin touched her chest, Xzem finally managed a wordless mewl of feminine inquiry. The little sound cracked in her mouth, uncertain.

"It is Onahi Chasa," he said again. And when the slave continued to shrink away, he looked back at Meoraq.

'O my Father, why are You including me in this?' he thought. Aloud, he grunted only, "Xzem," as he fussed determinedly with the meat.

"Xzem," the slave whispered and rocked the baby a little faster, as if she feared a beating to go along with the introductions. Not an unreasonable fear, all things considered.

Onahi relaxed, believing himself to be on firmer ground, rather than further out in the mire. "Mother," he said, offering the skewer of his hunter's portion of kipwe to a Gann-born raider's slave. "Take and be fed."

Xzem hesitated, but only for a moment. She gave Amber the baby. Without a word, she rose and moved to the wall of the windbreak, gripped a post, and bent. She stood her legs well apart; the wind flattened the folds of her worn shift to her body so that she might as well be naked there, and every man's eye was on her. She waited.

Onahi stared, as all the watchmen of Praxas stared, at the rounded curve of her hip and the shallow valley beneath her shift where her sex must be (and worn well open, all things considered). Meoraq had seen many women bend for him this way and even he stared for a short time before running his brooding and distracted eye over Amber. She still wouldn't look at him. Which was just as well, he supposed. The fires of Sheul were burning—they had not cooled completely since he'd found and reclaimed his wife—but there were twenty other people in this camp now. Meoraq was not ashamed of Amber, but he hated the thought of other people listening in while he had sex.

'Not tonight, Uyane,' he thought bitterly, turning the skewers. 'Not while she sits there with her damned Nicci under her arm. Not unless you want the whining little pest in the tent with you.'

Onahi stood. He went to Xzem and, just as Meoraq was reluctantly opening his mouth to order him back, he took her arm and stood her gently up. He placed the skewer in her puzzled hand and released her. "Take and be fed, mother," he said.

The other watchmen of Praxas exchanged glances. One of them picked at the remaining portion of his own meal and looked at one of the slaves.

Onahi turned around and came back to the other side of the fire. He knelt. His fingers brushed at the buckle of his loin-plate, testing, before he set his hands on the ground. He closed his eyes and prayed in grim-faced silence.

One by one, the watchmen of Praxas offered food to the slaves. Thanks were spoken by some, softly, uncertain of propriety. Meoraq let them be, even when one of the watchmen sat boldly at a slave's side and ate with her. He didn't care if they ate together, scandalous as that was. He didn't care if they spoke to one another. At the moment, he didn't care if they all stripped to their scales and formed a dip-ring. His battle-wounds were a constant ache in every part of his body, like the anger and resentment throbbing in his throat or the heat of Sheul's fires churning in his belly, and he cared about nothing and no one else.

And he was tired. All at once, the sleep he had not caught in the past several days seemed to drop into his bones. He doubted he had the strength to do what the fires demanded. He didn't even have the strength to pray. So he gave the next set of skewers to the humans, including another for his wife and one for Nicci (who did not, he noticed, share it out with Amber), and ordered the rest cooked and held until morning. "I want to leave at dawn," he said, addressing all of them together, but Onahi most of all. "Keep a strong watch and let no one enter or leave this camp unless they do so under my eye."

"I hear you, sir," Onahi said, his brow still pressed to the ground in prayer.

Meoraq grunted and stood up.

Amber lifted her arm from her blood-kin's shoulders and began awkwardly to rise without disturbing the sleeping baby at her breast.

Meoraq's selfishness let her gather her feet beneath her, but he was only so much a selfish man. She would be tired and sore as much as he. He knew he would not be able to lie beside her without taking her and he could not take her gently, not yet. So Meoraq stopped her with a raised hand before Amber could stand. "Not tonight," he said sourly, and went into his tent before he could change his mind.

2

Amber slept on the ground by the fire. She didn't have to and she knew it. They had plenty of tents—one for the lizardmen, one for the lizardladies, one for the humans...and the one where she knew she wasn't welcome.

So after Xaom took the baby and went into her tent with the other ladies, she just lay down where she was. She felt awful. Not just sad, but sick, as if his rejection were a poison she could swallow over and over the longer she lay there. She didn't think she'd sleep, but eventually she did, and dreamed of Zhuqa, who was sometimes with her on the *Pioneer* or in the ruins of that lizardman city with the metal spiders scuttling forever on their empty web, and even her mother's squalid little apartment back on Earth. "This is Zhuqa's House," he kept telling her, through all the confusion of that nightmare. "And once you enter Zhuqa's House, you never really leave."

She woke up crying, which was bad enough, and rolled over to discover one of the strange lizardmen just staring at her, which made it humiliating as well. She sat up, using the excuse of looking for Nicci in the empty place beside her to wipe at her cheeks, and felt her stomach flip ominously over. It didn't surprise her, as miserable as she'd been, but she'd only rolled onto her knees when that small warning became irrelevant and she puked right into the ashes of the fire. Her empty stomach had nothing to give up but a little bilious slime, but it kept trying until she could feel herself trying to pass out as well as throw up. Not her usual post-trauma puke-session, but it did ease up eventually, thank God. By then, she only had enough strength to heave herself onto her side instead of dropping face-down in the stinking mess of it.

The lizardman got up and walked away, leaving her to gasp and spit weakly where she was. After a moment, footsteps returned.

"Are you dying?" Nicci's voice, not very interested.

"I kind of want to," Amber muttered and then had to make her aching stomach force out a laugh because it sounded so true.

More footsteps, several sets. A scaly hand gripped her shoulder—Meoraq's hand, she knew it even before he rolled her over and she could see his frowning face—as somewhere in the world, Scott said, "Do you have to do this now, Bierce?"

"Hit him," said Meoraq curtly, and someone did. "Show me your eyes, woman."

She looked at him and saw his spines flat with annoyance and not forward with concern. She scooted back out of his grip and sat up, fixing her burning eyes on her knees as she brushed them off. "I'm fine."

"She's fine," said Nicci. "It's just something she does when she gets upset."

Meoraq looked back and forth between them, then at the other lizardmen, and then over the windbreak at the wall of the city. He stood up. "Break the camp."

Lizardmen moved at once to obey. Meoraq took two steps toward his tent and paused. He looked back. Then he turned around and came back, passing Amber and Nicci without a glance to seize Scott by the hair. He dragged him over to the tent where the humans had slept (Eric and the others got out of his way and the lizardmen didn't even look at them) and threw Scott into the side of it. "If you want to sleep in it," Meoraq hissed, "you pick it up and carry it! No one in my camp serves you, S'kot!"

"Jesus, fine!"

Meoraq's head tipped. "You speak to Uyane Meoraq, a Sword of Sheul, and you had better do it with more respect than that if you want to walk away from this."

"He's in a mood," Nicci remarked.

Amber did not reply.

"Thanks for the tent," said Scott, flushed and scowling.

Meoraq grunted and took Scott by the wrist. He lifted Scott's hand, hissed to make him stop struggling, and forced it into a fist. "This is a salute," he said, thumping that fist against Scott's chest. "And when you speak to me, you salute."

Scott was about as close to openly gaping as she thought he'd ever been.

Meoraq released his wrist and got a fisthold in his hair again, pushing Scott's head down and holding it there. "When I speak to you," he said, "you bend your neck in respect."

Scott still said nothing, but he was breathing pretty hard.

Meoraq released him and stepped back. "We will practice once, because this is new to you. Break your tent and make the other humans ready to travel."

Scott kept his head down and lifted his fist slowly to his chest.

"Fair for a first effort. Now hear me, S'kot. These men are born under the Blade as well and you owe them the same respect. You do not speak to them unless they address you first or unless you have something damned important to say. Am I heard?"

"Yes," said Scott, glaring at the ground. He touched his chest again.

"You do not walk in the shadow of my House, human. You are a burden I endure. Do not interrupt me for any reason. Do not give orders in my camp to anyone. Do not take what you are not offered. Do not offend me, S'kot. You have none of my forgiveness. Do you mark?"

"Yes."

"Good. So. To be clear. When you speak to me, you speak with respect. When you speak to my brothers under the Blade, you speak with respect. And when you speak to her—" Meoraq pointed at Amber without looking at her, shoving his snout kissing-close to Scott's face. "—I cut your fucking head off."

How horrible did a person have to be when hearing something like that made her feel a fluttering of hope? Amber rubbed her eyes and looked at her knees some more.

Scott must have saluted even though he didn't say anything because Meoraq said, "Good. This is the last time we have this conversation, human. Get moving. We eat as we walk."

And that was all. Meoraq crossed the camp and took his own tent down. Eric and Dag went over to help Scott, who didn't seem to know what to do. Crandall took Nicci by the arm and led her a little ways off to whisper at her. The other humans huddled up and just tried to stay out of everyone's way, the same as the lizardladies were doing on the other side of their dead fire.

Amber sat, alternately rubbing her stomach and her eyes, and finally got up. She headed for Xzem, because she couldn't think of anyone but the baby who'd want to be with her after that, but she'd only taken a few steps when Nicci caught at her.

"Come on," she said, turning Amber around and taking her by the hand. "Let's go pee while we still can."

Meoraq glared at them as he dismantled his tent poles, then used one of them to point. "No further than the ravine. Go and come back."

Nicci showed him a salute. After a moment, so did Amber.

Meoraq, bending to pick up another pole, straightened up to give her a second look. "Don't do that," he said and went back to work.

They walked to the ravine, hand in hand. The wind was warm and light. It was about as sunny as it ever got on this planet, which meant that it was visible as a smudgy disc behind the clouds. A nice day.

They peed, then climbed back to the top of the ravine and sat down. "Funny how girls can never go to the bathroom alone," said Nicci, plucking absently at blades of grass.

"What did Crandall want you to tell me?"
"He wanted to know if you were pregnant."
"Oh for God's sake."
"Are you?"
"Is that supposed to be a joke?"
Nicci shrugged and tossed some grass away. There wasn't enough wind to carry it far. Most of it landed on her leg.
"It isn't funny," said Amber.
"I told him you throw up a lot when you get upset. At least you used to."
It was Amber's turn to pick at the grass. "I didn't know you knew that. Why didn't you ever say anything?"
"You don't like it when people think you have...you know."
"Problems?" Amber offered with a listless smile.
"Feelings."
That was ugly. The wind stayed warm.
"I used to figure that if you were bulimic, you'd be losing weight," Nicci said after a little time had stretched itself out to the snapping point. "But you weren't, so I figured you were fine. And then, at the end, when you *were* losing weight...I just didn't care that much. Sorry."
"It's okay." She wasn't sure it was.
The walls of the windbreak were coming down. Nicci twisted around to watch, plucking more grass. "Mom used to get morning-sick," she said.
"Yeah, I know." Most of the time, it was how she knew to go to the aborters.
"So did I."
Amber closed her eyes and pressed at them.
"Want to see where they took it out?"
She didn't, but Nicci leaned back and opened up her tunic to show the raised pink dash of the scar over her belly. It was surprisingly neat.
"They had something so I didn't feel it," Nicci said, rubbing at it. "And it kept me pretty high afterwards, too. It was nice, while it lasted. I don't know how they knew I was pregnant. I wasn't showing. But I guess they were doing these exams almost every day...and they're not, you know, cavemen. They know what they're doing. It's amazing, really, what they can do without a real hospital. But when you stop and think about it...scalpels and needles and things...none of those are machines. Anyway, I guess they might have heard the heartbeat or something. I don't know."
"I'm so sorry, Nicci."
"I'm not. I didn't want it. It was one of them."
Amber watched her little sister close her tunic and tie up her belt again, trying to make that make some kind of sense. "What do you mean?" she asked at last. "That...That it would turn out like...like Scott?"
"That would be pretty bad, too," Nicci agreed with another careless shrug. "But I mean it was one of them. One of the dumaqs."
"That's impossible."
"Whatever. I saw it come out of me. I know what it was."
"But...But they're aliens!"
Nicci picked some more grass and dropped it.
"It's not possible!" Amber said, louder.
"Commander Scott said it was probably the Vaccine."
"What?"
"It mutates, remember? So that we don't catch any alien viruses. We just sat there in the Sleeper for God knows how many years, soaking in that Vaccine, letting it change...whatever it felt like changing. You know the only thing that stops us from

catching pregnant from any old...you know? Stuff? It's that our bodies don't know what it is, so it doesn't take. Everything has to match up, you know? All these, I don't know, millions and millions of connections."

"But—"

"But we had the Vaccine," said Nicci in a thoughtful way, "and here's what I think. You know how regular vaccines work, right? They're little teeny tiny pieces of the virus that makes you sick, just enough so that you make the, I don't know, the anti-virus. But our Vaccine works on all of them. How is that possible, Amber? You went to the seminars. You remember all this. How can one shot be made up of billions and billions of different diseases, even alien ones?"

"Because it...it changes," said Amber. "It finds the bug and it copies it so we can make our own cure before we ever get sick."

"Right," said Nicci, nodding. "It finds the bug. And it copies it. It takes our cells, with our DNA, and it changes them."

Amber stared at her.

"Well...every new drug has unexpected side-effects, right? Headaches. Dizziness. Insomnia." Nicci looked back into the sky to watch the sun climb higher. "Ours just may cause lizard-babies."

Zhuqa. Zhuqa, over and over. It was impossible and she didn't believe it and she didn't care what Nicci thought or what she said she'd seen, but oh God, not with Zhuqa.

She looked back and saw Meoraq standing at the edge of camp with his arms folded, watching them while all the other lizardmen rolled the windbreak into bundles and shouldered supplies. Her heart ached once, as sharply as a stabbing, and then bled down into her belly.

'He is never going to want to touch me again,' thought Amber, almost calmly.

Then she bent over without warning and threw up again.

"Yeah," said Nicci, watching her. "You're just upset. That's what I told Mr. Crandall. Come on. We'd better go."

* * *

They walked the day out undisturbed either by men from Praxas or from Gann, not that there was much of a distinction. They had a stream to keep their flasks filled and good stony ground that would not show their tracks and always the cover of trees around them, so if that made a day good, it was a good day, but they made miserable distance.

Onahi's men marched in pairs around the rest, relieving Meoraq's burden considerably as he watched for the ambush that never came. The women were slow, still fearful of the open wilds and unused to so much walking, but they were obedient and not difficult to manage even so. The humans, now. Oh, the humans...

They walked as if they had only just learned how that morning, constantly staggering and catching at one another, constantly out of breath, constantly whining at his back. Meoraq wasn't completely insensitive to their condition. He knew they had been penned all winter, ill-fed and ill-used. He knew they were trying. He let them rest an hour for nearly every hour walked and never said a word against it. Some muttered thanks, but not many. Some clustered around Scott and whispered, but not all. It did his bitter heart good to see that the polish was finally dimming on that gilded lump of ghet-shit, but he could still feel color itching in his throat all that interminable day.

So he halted them in the early evening after traveling less than two spans—less a call for camp than a cry of surrender—with plenty of good hours left in the day to hunt or patrol or just pray before night truly fell. The walls went up. Fires were lit. The women went to work brewing tea and heating cold kipwe, all but Xzem, who knelt with

Amber in the mouth of a tent with the infant singing in her arms and Nicci close by to watch. Most of the humans rested by their fool abbot, but Eric went out to gather deadfall for the fires and Dag actually helped the women with the cooking.

Around the small camp, Onahi's men—now men under Uyane, he supposed—kept watch. Their quiet talk eased him; not their words, which were exactly the sort of low garrison-talk one would expect, but just their speech. Dumaqi in male voices, relaxed and uncomplicated, with meanings he didn't have to guess at. He didn't think he was lonely and wouldn't have believed it if someone told him he was, but the pleasure that came just to listen was almost enough to take even the ugliness of Praxas from his heart. How much better would it be, he wondered, to be home again in Xoqor, to hear not only familiar words but familiar voices? See his brothers' faces? Sleep in his own bed?

He was ready, he realized. The fate that had been so damning when he first confronted it now seemed to him as welcome as Sheul's own Halls. Home. Family. Rest.

Amber.

And there his gaze lay for some time, upon his wife and the infant she held to her heart. She sensed it, looked up. Their eyes met and Sheul's fires, cooled but never entirely gone, surged at once to greater life.

Meoraq turned away and beckoned Onahi to him. He had to do it twice; the other man's attention had been fixed and somewhat glazed upon Xzem. "Call your sentries in," he ordered. "I want a private hour with my woman. No one is to leave this camp for any reason until my return."

"I mark." Onahi's eyes traveled the camp, counting his men...but came back to Xzem. And lingered.

"These are women of my House," Meoraq reminded him, trying not to sound as if he were also warning him.

"I will not dishonor your camp, sir."

Meoraq grunted, now studying Onahi instead of Amber. The fires were insistent, but a Sheulek was the master of every impulse, even that one. "Have you seen women before?" he asked bluntly.

"At a distance." Onahi managed with effort to look at Meoraq. "But no mother...apart from my own." He hesitated, clearly battling the urge to speak further, and ultimately defeated by it. "I have gone to Gann, sir. I submit myself to your judgment."

Meoraq's spines snapped up. "Eh?"

"I have gone to Gann," Onahi said again, his words all but bleeding in the air. "I have tried to pray. I have begged our Father's forgiveness all this day and all last night, but I..."

Meoraq waited, beginning to feel restless now that the first astonishment of this incredible confession was fading. The fires in his belly burned and Amber was watching him. "You?" he prompted impatiently.

"It is unforgiveable to lie with a milking mother," Onahi said and seemed to break. Without moving, his strained body became soft as clay. "It is unforgiveable. The taint of my city is on me. I must submit to your sword."

Meoraq took a moment to puzzle this out. "You want a woman," he said at last.

Onahi closed his eyes.

So did Meoraq, before someone could see him rolling them. He rubbed at his brow-ridges, took six breaths (without sighing and that was nearly an ordeal in itself), and said, "I do not see Gann's hand on you, watchman. It is the fires of our Father you feel. Take a woman."

"It is unforgiveable—"

"Take another woman." Meoraq beckoned to his own and started to turn away. Sheul's hand fell on him at once; he turned back and yes, Onahi was staring at Xzem.

There was something in this, he was certain, something he was meant to see...but whatever it was, it would have to wait. Intellectually, he knew no man had ever died of lust, but his belly felt as if it were filled with molten lead and his thoughts had begun to slip toward the same killing black that took him in the arena. If he did not take his woman soon, he thought it very likely that Sheul would take her in his stead. As for Onahi—

"Go to my tent," Meoraq ordered. "Make your prayers and be prepared to submit to my judgment upon my return."

Onahi saluted and went without question as Amber came near, looking back over her shoulder either at the baby or at Nicci. "I'm really worried—" she began.

"Come with me," he said and left the camp.

Onahi's watchmen raised their fists as he passed by, but he was beyond acknowledging them. He strode swiftly out between the walls and as soon as Amber had joined him, he took her roughly by the arm and walked as far as he could stand to go. He refused to rut with his woman on the ground where anyone could hear them. He could see a sturdy-looking tree twenty paces away, maybe thirty; it may as well be a thousand.

"Wait," said Amber, pulling at him.

He grunted and kept going, dragging her with him, seeing nothing but that tree.

"I have to talk to you! Damn it!" And with a mighty yank, her hand was gone from his grip. "This is important!"

He turned on her, hearing the hiss that spat out of his throat, but unable to feel even a spark of shame for it. She was his woman, his wife! Why could she not give him her obedience for one fucking day?

Blackness took him for a heartbeat, no longer, but when it faded, he had his hand on her throat and his face biting-close to hers. Confusion swelled, overshadowing rage but not killing it. He shut his mouth, leaned back, and finally released her.

She stared at him, trembling and furious even with tears welling in her eyes. It made him think of Nicci, which made him think of the watchman in Praxas fucking her through the cage, which made him think of the tree he may not reach tonight. He had to turn around, facing into the chill spring wind, and took several minutes to breathe himself calm. One for the Prophet...two for his Brunt...three for Uyane...

He was Uyane.

"Speak," he said at last.

"Aren't you going to look at me?"

"No."

There was quiet at his back. He did not hear her crying, not until she spoke again. The tears were in her voice and they cut at him, but he did not look at her.

"You have to get the baby out of here. This is taking too long and it's getting weaker."

"The humans are at their limits. They can go no faster."

"Then you have to leave us behind."

Us, she said.

"It's too cold," Amber said. "We barely got anywhere today and I know it's our fault—"

Our.

"—but I can't make us go any faster and you can take that baby to Chalh."

"No."

"I heard those other guys talking. Even they know it's going to die if...It's just a baby!" she burst out. He could hear her slapping at her face, punishing the eyes that betrayed her with tears. "How can you not care about that? You said you forgave everyone! Didn't you mean it?"

He glanced at her, but his troubled thoughts turned to flame and he faced back into the wind at once. "It is not for me to forgive the children born to Gann."

"I don't care whose it is!" she sobbed. "It's just a baby! You can't let it die because it's Zhuqa's! That's not its fault! God, Meoraq, look around you! How can you even think of letting it die? In a world where so many of you have died, you should be doing everything you can to save it just because it's alive!"

The words stabbed him twice—once for their edge alone and once because she believed them. It didn't matter to her that the child was sired of her enemy by a slave. She saw only an innocent life, and where the right was hers to end it out of vengeance, she wept because she could not save it.

'Yes, my Father,' thought Meoraq, once more in the tribune hall at Tothax with the daughter of Lord Saluuk weeping at his feet. 'I hear you.'

And he was ashamed.

"I will send it and the others on with Onahi in the morning," he said at last, but the words were ash in his throat. Onahi may yet have kin in Chalh, but the gates would never open to a man who had ended his time at Praxas as barracks-ward, a man who came with a procession of fatherless women, unhooded, unveiled. It would be a Sheulek's command alone that could open those gates and win welcome.

Her hand stole in to touch him—that fearless hand—weakly gripping at his arm just below his sabk. "Please look at me."

He tried, but her tearful face inspired only greater heat and furious urgency in his belly, and that was obscene to feel when he knew a life waited on his judgment. He stepped away from her, clapping a hand to his throat to try and cool the color rising there. "I can't," he said. "Leave me. I have to pray."

She did not. She stood silent at his back as he forced himself to kneel and, as he was taking only the second of his first six breaths, suddenly her hand came out of the wind and slapped him in the head.

"Are you breaking up with me?" she shouted, sobbing so explosively that she could hardly breathe. "Because if that's wuh-what this is, I can tuh-take it! But don't you may-ake me fucking wuh-wuh-*wait* for it!"

"What are you talking about? What's broken? What—"

And then he thought he understood.

"Do you think I'm putting you aside?" he asked incredulously while his belly groaned and his loin-plate strained. "Why would you even think that, woman?"

"Gee, I don't know," she said, trying to sneer through her tears and succeeding only in sounding more pathetic. "You won't touch me. You won't look at me. You barely even talk to me and you're always angry when you do!"

"I'm not angry." His hand stole down to check the fit of his loin plate. He coughed out a bitter laugh, muttering, "I'm the furthest thing there is from angry," but it didn't feel true. The idea that Gann's loathsome hand was on him came creeping in, as it had so often during these last days and burning nights—that he had breathed it in like a sickness somewhere in the raider's camp or that it had rubbed off from the flesh of all these damned women...but not from Amber. Never from his Amber. Sheul could not give her back to him only to see her and him both tainted beyond redeeming.

"I'm not angry," he said again, gazing into the darkening sky. "I just need time."

"Time for what? Is it...Is it because I was one of them?"

That made no sense to him no matter how many times he turned over her odd human words. "One of what?" he asked cautiously.

She glared at him, flushed and trembling and miserable, and suddenly shouted, "A slave! Because I was their slave—*his* slave—and you've got a lot of goddamned nerve breaking up with me for that, you scaly son of a bitch!" The last words degenerated into fresh tears. She clapped her hands over her face and choked on them.

"You were never a slave. You were always mine! You are still mine!" He caught her wrists and forced them down, forced her to look at him through the wet shine of her tears. "Sheul Himself gave you to me and what He has bound, *nothing breaks*! How do you mark me, woman?"

She sobbed, if possible, harder.

"I will have an answer," said Meoraq, beginning to be alarmed.

"You don't mean it!"

"Stop telling me what I mean!" he snapped. "You're always doing that and it's infuriating!"

"You don't!" she shouted. "You told everyone out there you forgave them! You told me there was no sin in conquest, but that's still what you see when you look at them! That's what you see when you look at *me*!"

He recoiled. "I do not," he said, but it was only a half-truth and the Sheulek in him knew it.

"Then tell me that baby deserves to live! Tell me it doesn't matter who its father was! Tell me you think Xzem is a good mother!"

He looked at her, and just as her eyes welled up with fresh anguish, he said, "Truth."

She blinked, knocking tears loose, but not sobbing them out. "Huh?"

"Truth," he said again, now frowning.

They stared at each other as the wind blew between them.

"You don't believe it," she said again, but timidly now.

"I don't have to. I hear your words. I judge them truth. If I struggle with acceptance, that is my failing. I will have to pray about that." He braced himself and gave her a tap, just the backs of his knuckles to the side of her arm, and still almost more than he could stand. "But you are still mine. I never questioned that."

She looked away. "It won't ever be the same."

"As what?" Meoraq asked. "As life before my father's death? Before you sailed your ship? I don't want the same life, damn it, I want this one!"

She sniffled and rubbed her face. He couldn't think of anything better to convince her and couldn't keep looking at her, so he faced into the wind again.

"Are you mad at me?" she asked in a small voice.

"A little," he admitted, and rubbed hard at the end of his snout. "Do you want to be broken from me? Is that what this is about? Because you don't get that!"

"No!"

"Is it because I left you? Because I wasn't there and you were...taken..."

"We can't be together all the time. No, Meoraq, that was just..." She paused and uttered a short, tearful laugh. "I was going to say dumb luck, but you don't believe in that. I guess you'd say it was God's will."

Meoraq thought about that.

"Perhaps it was," he said slowly. "For Xzem's sake. For Nali's. For Onahi and his men. For N'ki. Even...for S'kot. I hadn't thought of it that way..."

But he did now, thinking of all the wooded hills of Gedai and how easily he might have walked through them and on to Xi'Matezh, never suspecting the city of Praxas with its caged humans even existed. He had been meant to find them, to save them. No matter his personal feelings, God had given them a new chance at life.

Meoraq rubbed at his snout again. "Xzem...does seem to be a good mother."

"She is. She really is." Amber sighed. "And I want her to have the baby. I know she can take care of it better than me, okay, I know that. I just...worry about who's going to take care of her, you know? But I've seen Onahi with her and if they're not shacking up yet, they will be by the time you get to Chalh."

Meoraq grunted, now thinking of Onahi meditating in his tent, patiently awaiting death at a Sheulek's hand for his perceived corruption. And who was Meoraq to say it was not so? However good the man might seem, it *was* unforgiveable to lie with a milking mother. Was it a greater sin to end the man now, while he still had some chance of finding peace in Sheul's Halls, or to wait until the unforgiveable act had occurred? The temptations of Gann were no easy ordeal (his constrained cock throbbed abysmally, sunk in fire, bruising the edges of his slit, and he was never going to have Amber against that fucking tree).

But wait...

It was unforgiveable to lie with a milking mother...unless the man had married her.

And suddenly Meoraq realized what had been before his damned eyes since leaving Praxas: There were six women in his care, five and Xzem, and six watchmen, five and Onahi.

"That's it," he said.

"Huh?"

"I'll marry them."

"Who?"

"Onahi and Xzem. I'll marry them. I'll marry all of them!"

Amber stared at him, not in awe, but in horror. "You can't do that!"

"Of course I can. And why are you looking at me like that?" he asked testily. "If I presented them at the gates of Chalh as fatherless women, they'd never be admitted. I will give them husbands and I will name those men soldiers under Uyane. There has to be a House Uyane in Chalh and its steward will *have* to take them in when I command it as Uyane of Xeqor."

"Meoraq, you can't! You're just...passing them out. You're not even discussing it with them first. It's like they're not even people to you, just..."

"Problems," said Meoraq.

"I was going to say 'things'." She looked at him and just as swiftly looked away. "Are we all that way to you? Just problems you need to solve?"

"In the wildlands," said Meoraq bluntly. "Yes."

"Even me?"

"You?" He snorted again and rubbed at his brow-ridges. "No. There is no solving you, Soft-Skin. You are my problem forever." And before she could turn away, he said, "I am yours. And you will never solve me either, but at least you are trying. I will take the baby to Chalh."

She scrubbed her arm across her face, erasing the last trace of her tears. "Tonight?"

The wind gusted. He looked up to watch the high branches come together and sway apart. "Yes. Come with me," he said hopelessly.

"I can't leave my sister," she said. He could have said it with her if only his mouth could make the words. "And I can't leave those idiots to fend for themselves. They've been prisoners so long...If anything happened, they'd be helpless."

If anything happened...

She saw his face, read his eyes. "Yeah, I know. But I can take care of my people. And you can take care of yours." She seemed to grope for something more comforting to tell him, but in the end, all she had was, "We'll be waiting right here."

"In easy distance of Praxas. And there are uncounted raiders left in the wildlands! How shall I stand before Sheul and tell Him I left you unguarded when He has only just given you back?"

"You can tell him I begged you. I'm begging you, Meoraq."

He looked away.

"I'll be all right," said Amber.

"You cannot know that."

"Some things you have to just take on faith." She hesitated, then said, "Do you have to pray about it?"

He glanced up at the grey heavens where Sheul watched him, then bent his neck. "No. So be it. Don't," he said as she reached for him. "I can let you go, Soft-Skin, but only if I do not hold you first. Go. Please."

She took one step away and there watched him while he took six breaths and six more. Then, finally, she left him.

Meoraq fought through three more slow-counts, keeping the Prophet's name and Sheul's holy Word close against his heart until the fires subsided. The rotten-tooth ache remained; he just knew he was bruising something down there. Cooled, if not at peace, he returned to his camp. He took Onahi, visibly braced for death, out of his tent and bound him to Xzem with a few terse words. He left the two of them staring at each other and went swiftly through the rest of them, matching man to wife without really looking at either of them and especially without looking at Amber. Then, before he could change his mind, he struck two of the tents, packed a portion of the kipwe, and loaded one of the litters. As the humans were beginning their first alarmed outcries, he gave the order that moved them on to Chalh.

Amber followed him as far as the walls, but no further. He left her there without a word (his throat was tight as Gann's fist), but managed only six steps before he halted.

He turned around.

He walked back to her, seized her by the chin, pressed his unfeeling mouth to hers and then scraped the end of his snout hard along her throat, filling his aching head with her scent, her taste, her soul.

She unclipped the kzung from his belt and held it in her hand, searching his eyes. She didn't speak either.

He stepped back, turned away. He took a breath (one for the Prophet) and walked on.

3

Unencumbered by humans, the journey to Chalh lasted only six days, the latter half on a good road. They were first hailed easily five spans from the city and escorted the rest of the way by three sentries in gilded uniforms. If that were not warning enough of Chalh's nature, the walls of the city were trimmed in gold, or at least, gold paint, and a statue of the Prophet had been positioned over the gate, hands outstretched in benediction. The sleeves, Meoraq noted, were hollowed out, so as to pour hot oils or acids should any raider be fool enough to assault the first founding city of the Prophet.

"Where are the other five?" Meoraq asked, making half a joke in an attempt to appear patient while the gatekeeper meticulously checked his book of Houses.

The gatekeeper, having no sense of humor, replied, "Each has their own gate, sir. If you wish to be admitted through Gate Uyane, I can make those arrangements."

Meoraq rolled his eyes discreetly. "That won't be necessary."

The gatekeeper continued his inspection with the same excruciating attention to detail, came to the conclusion that Meoraq was in truth who he claimed to be, and snapped his book shut. "It is Uyane before me," he announced. "If it is your intention to seize the city of Chalh, you will have to wait in the arena hold for the Sheulek in residence to meet with you."

"I am here to see my kin. My conquest shall be limited to that House."

"Do you wish me to send for one of Uyane's carriages?"

"Just a public carriage will do." Meoraq tapped pointedly at the gate.

"Do you prefer to go under your House's standard?"

"I would prefer to be behind walls before the damned year is out!"

The gatekeeper bowed and unlocked the gate. "If I can be of service—"

"Carriages for myself and my party, and an usher to take us immediately to House Uyane," interrupted Meoraq, waving his people inside.

"It may take some time to locate a veiled carriage suitable to transport your, ah, women. Perhaps you would like to take the rooftop while you wait? The barracks of Lashraq's Gate has an excellent meditation garden."

"I must seem tense," Meoraq remarked, but Amber wasn't there to tell him he was, in fact, acting like a scaly son of a bitch and no one else was about to argue or, worse, agree. "Any carriage will do," he said, looking back out into the open wilds, thinking of Amber. "Just fetch a few blankets and we'll cover the windows."

"My apologies, honored one, we have no blankets in Uyane's colors."

"Cover them in grain-sacks then! I don't care! Great Sheul, O my Father, give me patience! And you, just give me a damned carriage!"

The gatekeeper bowed and locked the door before wandering unhurriedly away. And really, what could Meoraq do about it? It wasn't as if he could just march all these unveiled women across the city on foot.

So he waited. The carriages eventually came, along with drivers and ushers and window covers emblazoned with the standard of the city. Meoraq put the women in one, the soldiers in the other, and himself alone in the last. The boy who held the carriage door passed him a bottle of cool tea before closing it. The driver leaned in through the window as Meoraq plucked idly at the cap and passed him a flask of hot nai.

"Keep it," the driver grunted as Meoraq took his first swallow. "I see you've not got one, and it's a hard lack on a long journey."

Meoraq lowered the flask, staring.

The driver shut the window and snapped the tethers. Bulls bellowed. The carriage rolled on.

He knew what the days of hard travel had done to his appearance, let alone the battle at the raider's nest, the mountain crossing, and all the days that had gone before. Meoraq had been fully prepared to recite his lineage, show his signet, and perhaps even battle their champion to prove his kinship, but he did not expect the gates of Uyane to open on the steward himself.

Meoraq knew at first sighting this was no toy-lord, no high-born diplomat with a stable of Sheulteb to do his fighting for him, but a Sheulek in his retirement. He dressed not in lordly robes, but in plain leather breeches with a warrior's harness snug over his open tunic, displaying his scarred chest and hard belly with careless indifference. The bone hilt that cased the ancient blade hanging around his neck stood out like lightning over his scales, polished by use and yellowed with age.

They eyed each other, and then Meoraq took the first step forward and boldly raised his hand. "I come to you as kin and conqueror," he began. "Your House stands in the shadow of—"

Lord Uyane let out a rude, barking laugh. "By Gann's crooked cock, you even sound like him."

And before Meoraq had could even think of how to react, the steward stood aside, already beckoning to a small crowd of sleepy-eyed boys. Onahi and the other men of Praxas, along with their nervous women, were led away to be billeted and Meoraq was taken to the warden's office to sign them all over into Uyane-Chalh's garrison. As swiftly as this was accomplished, however, an usher from the governor still managed to be waiting before they were through, and Meoraq spent the next two hours reporting to Chalh's leaders.

It should not have taken so long, but Praxas had sent a messenger to warn against the ravings of the wildland-maddened Sheulek and even if they had not, Meoraq's tale of men who sold their daughters to raiders and who kept scaleless people in cages was too fantastic to be believed. Meoraq answered their questions without embellishment, but when they began to repeat themselves, and worse, to ask if he were sure he had seen this or if he could clearly recall that, his temper began to fray. Ultimately, he was compelled to challenge them all for the truth, and after some muttered discussion, the governor sent down not one but all three of his Sheulteb to meet him. Meoraq was burning almost as soon as he crossed the threshold into the arena, and although he knew none of it, he supposed Sheul must have made an impressive showing in the battle that followed because the first thing he heard as he came slowly out of the black was the governor's reedy voice ordering Praxas to be struck from the roster of cities under Sheul and all their people to be turned back from this hour onward as children of Gann. So that was done. Meoraq refused the girl the governor presented and left the arena hold at once, still spattered with the blood of three good men.

But it had been many days of travel, a battle, a mountain crossing, and it caught up to him at last. His desire to see Amber safely within his reach once more could not take the weight from his weary clay and when Uyane's usher met him at the governor's gates to escort him back to that House, he went.

The boy brought Meoraq to the vacant room of the steward's own eldest son, where a warrior's meal of cold meat and fat-toasted bread awaited him. As he struggled to stay awake long enough to eat it, a knock sounded.

It was Lord Uyane, accompanied by two servants, both carrying steaming ewers. Meoraq's first impulse was to turn them all away, but remembering that he would be sleeping in another man's cupboard and it might be a kind gesture not to cake it in the grime of an old trek through the wildlands and a fresh fight in the arena, Meoraq gave humble thanks and stood aside.

The servants brought a bath out from a closet and filled it, then bared their faces, demurely averting their eyes as they awaited his selection.

"Understand that I am not in the habit of offering mere servants to the Sheulek I am honored to receive," Lord Uyane remarked, watching Meoraq pointedly resume his meal. "But as we share blood, any kin of mine is kin of yours."

"Understood and forgiven."

"I suppose I should offer my wife," the steward continued, casually folding his arms and laying his fingertips across the hilts of his sabks. "But she's not feeling well tonight."

"My prayers for her recovery," said Meoraq.

The steward watched him eat. The servants glanced at one another. One of them fidgeted briefly with her sleeve.

"How long have you been traveling?" the steward asked suddenly.

The question caught him by surprise. He had to think about it. "I left the walls of Tothax mid-autumn...after the gruu harvest," he said, recalling the last judgment he'd made there. Lord Arug and his curse of daughters. And Shuiv, another good man with a blade broken under Meoraq's heel. "Not long after the night of the burning tower, if you heard of that here."

"We heard. I admit I heard it for a child's knee-time tale, but I believe it better than I believe a man could walk away a quarter of the year and not want a woman."

Meoraq glanced at the servants. They dipped their necks in unison and let out twin mewls. He had to suppress a shudder as he turned back to his meal. "I thank you for your consideration, steward, but I would make poor company tonight."

Lord Uyane's spines twitched forward. He looked at the servants and then at Meoraq again. "Company?" he echoed. "If it's company you'd rather have, I could set out a game of Crown-Me or read the Word with you, but unless you make it a Sheulek's command, I'll be damned if I bathe you."

It wasn't worth the explanation. "You, then," said Meoraq, waving at the girl on the left.

At Lord Uyane's nod, the other girl hooded herself and took Meoraq's boots away with her to be cleaned. The steward remained, unabashedly watching as Meoraq unbuckled his harness. "Have you any other requests of me, honored one?" he asked, and immediately snorted and muttered, "Honored one. To think I've lived so long as to give Razi's sprat my obedience. You are the very image of him, you know."

"How did you know him?" Meoraq asked, allowing the servant to finish undressing him.

"He came crawling over the mountains in his first striding years and stayed the winter with us. New Sheulek, eh? They want to see the sun rise over the edge of the world and drink the waters that come washing in from whatever lies beyond. Never understood that," he added. "The sun is the sun no matter where it rises and that water tastes like fish fuck in it. You look a little old for that nonsense, yourself. Pilgrimage?"

"Yes."

"To Xi'Matezh? What else is out here?" he asked wryly at Meoraq's startled glance. "They tell me Gedai used to be the center of the world in the age before the Fall. Ha. Nothing out here now but rock and ruins. And the ocean, I suppose. Where the fish fuck. I could tell you the way to the temple easily enough," he went on. "There's no road as roads are reckoned, but there's a broad enough footpath most of the way and a few underlodges for pilgrims to take a night's ease. I try to make the walk myself once a year. Usually try to time it with the Festival of the Fifth Light so I don't have to listen to all those fucking bells."

"Have you ever seen the doors?"

"You mean, have I seen them open? Not for me and not for your father, but I know they do. Happened right in front of me once."

Meoraq's spines swept forward and he sat up fast, splashing water over the sides of the bath.

The steward glanced down, scratching his toes through the spreading puddle on his tiles. "I don't like to think of it, but it's truth. I'd been there most of the day and I'd have sworn to our true Father's face that I was alone the whole time, for I never heard a sound inside, but then the doors opened. A man came out. Sheulek. I didn't know him. He looked..." The steward's gaze shifted to the servant, who was trying very hard to be invisible as she went about her duties despite what must be very exciting talk to one of her kind. "He looked like a dead man," he said finally. "And he looked at me like I was a dead man."

Meoraq felt the servant shiver a little as she scrubbed his back.

"I was burning a candle there. Nothing fancy, just a sign to the Six. Most do. He looked at it and he looked at me. Then he started walking. He took his blades off—his sabks, I mean—and he broke one and stabbed the other through the Prophet's mark without ever breaking stride. He walked through the doors and out of the shrine and then he walked himself right off the edge of the world. There's a drop, you know, and the rocks where the ocean rolls in. He never said a word, never took a breath to brace himself. He went over like it was what Sheul told him to do."

Amber's voice, like a chill breeze through a warm room: *If you jump off a cliff, God doesn't catch you.*

"Never said a word," the steward said again, rubbing at the side of his throat with one rough thumb. "To say truth, that was the last time I went in as far as God's doors, but I keep going back. How long will you be staying with us, honored one?"

"Just the night."

"I'll freshen your pack then. Have you any special requests of my provisioner?"

"No...Wait. A set of women's clothing. Her size is near enough," he said, gesturing up at the servant.

Lord Uyane's spines twitched again, but, "Have you a preference as to color?" was all he said.

Meoraq didn't, but before he could say so, he found himself thinking of Amber's eyes. "Something green. With slippers. Eh, best make it boots. And..." What else did women like? "A girdle. Something...pretty."

"It shall be do—" He broke off with a sigh and rubbed his brow-ridges, then slapped his thigh and said, "I can't pretend I'm not intrigued. You've got a woman with you? Ha! Wouldn't that have made some long walks shorter back in my striding days?"

"My wife," said Meoraq, feeling as though he ought to say something in Amber's defense.

"Well send her in, for our Father's sake! My Nraqi would love to see a fresh face, if only for the night. She's not fevered or anything catching, just thin-blooded and slow to come out of winter's grip."

"She stayed behind with her people so that I could travel more quickly. There was an infant among my camp and she was concerned that it should come out of the wildlands as soon as possible."

The steward's spines flicked as he smiled. "Fine woman. I'll let Nraqi pick a few things out for her. She knows more about pretty things than I do. Sylseth, make yourself available for sizing when the Sheulek is done with you."

"Yes, lord."

The steward left them alone at last and Meoraq leaned back and let the girl bathe him. It was his first real bath since Tothax, and he enjoyed it but did not prolong it even for his pleasure. The girl was pleasing also, but mewled and bowed and proved herself so, well, grotesquely feminine that what arousal she inspired in him soon withered. It was Amber he wanted...and Amber was worth waiting for. Cleaned, dried and oiled, he dismissed her untouched and put himself to bed.

* * *

He slept like a stone, yet woke far too early, so that when the boy came trotting in to ring the daylight bells in House Uyane's foyer, Meoraq was there to see it. He had been waiting as deferentially as was possible when lurking in a relative's foyer, but as soon as dawn's hour had been rung, he put a blunt end to courtesy and sent the boy to find him an usher out of the city.

Shortly afterward, as Meoraq stared broodingly at the tilework on the ceiling in an effort not to pace, Lord Uyane himself arrived to see him off. He brought with him a few servants to manage Meoraq's provisions and a veiled woman walking slow at his side. She averted her eyes and mewled as her husband made the necessary introductions, then raised her open hands and called him kin and made all the proper obedience a wife was expected to show to the conqueror of her husband's holdings, and then she reached right out and caught at Meoraq's sleeve. "My Lord says I mustn't ask," she began, dipping her head prettily even as Uyane rolled his eyes and strolled away to inspect the bell-house. "But if you have no will in the matter, perhaps your wife might stay with me a small time while you make what remains of your journey? It is not so very far to Xi'Matezh, I know, but women do not measure distance or hardship as men do. We are very weak and silly things, sir, and a small time here among her kin would be a pretty present to grant her before she makes the terrible journey to Xeqor."

"Wife," murmured Uyane.

"I do not say that Xeqor is terrible," she hastened to assure Meoraq. "Even here in sacred Chalh, Xeqor is known as one of Sheul's brightest lamps, but even one hour in the wildlands is a terrible thing to a woman. Oh, please send her to me, sir! She shall be my daughter while she is here and have a mother's love once more, if only for a few days. How find you?"

Flustered, Meoraq looked at Lord Uyane, but he was no help at all, deep in the study of the bells so that he would not have to notice his wife's scandalous behavior.

Which was certainly far less scandalous than spear-hunting or wearing pants or calling her man a scaly son of a bitch or any of the myriad scandalous things that Amber did. All at once, Meoraq felt a momentary divide of sight: he saw the woman clinging on his sleeve and looking at him with those shy, earnest eyes the way he would have seen her a year ago, as a grossly unmannered embarrassment, and he saw her as she surely was, a lonely woman bored with lying around and convalescing, who would risk even her husband's displeasure for a chance to see a new face and hear talk of the greater world beyond these walls. Just a lonely woman, who didn't mind mewling at a stranger or calling herself weak and silly if it meant that, believing it, he might grant her just a few short days of fresh company. Amber's company, even.

'Perhaps they could go hunting,' Meoraq thought, and laughed aloud.

Lord Uyane's eyes were on him at once, narrow as a knife's edge.

Meoraq put his hand over hers until she, with a sigh of defeat, removed it from his sleeve. He said, still smiling, "I do have a will in this matter, kinswife, and it is my will that the fierce woman who has dared as much as I to make this journey stand at my side when the doors of Xi'Matezh open. Yours is a kind offer, but I do decline."

The woman gave obedience and retreated a few steps, enough to pick at one of the bundles carried by a stone-faced servant. "I set some things aside for her, although I had to guess at the fit," she said, not quite pouting but near enough to it that her man sent her a censuring glance. "They're all my own and not new, but in very good repair. I haven't fit in this in ages," she sighed, lifting out a richly embroidered girdle for a last wistful look. "And this...this is the cloak I myself wore when I came to Chalh to be married...and the crownet that went with it!" she exclaimed, holding it up to be admired. It was an uncommonly fine thing—a long strip of golden mesh meant to fit around a woman's spine-ridge, with a clip on the end to keep a hood in place—although he doubted Amber would ever have any use for it. He thanked her anyway.

"Perhaps you will stop again on your return," she said hopefully. "I could have more garments set aside and even have them altered for a better—oh! Oh, we could order a tailor in! Jaza!" She clasped her hands and sent a wide-eyed stare at her husband, her short spines quivering at their highest point.

He went back to looking at the bells, the coward.

"I haven't had a gowning party since my little Semrrqi was a child," the woman told Meoraq.

"She was twenty-two," Lord Uyane remarked, scratching at the top frame of the bell-house and examining his fingertip.

"And a child."

"The gown in question was for the wedding feast."

"It was deep red all over," the woman sighed. "With a white underdress and blackweave girdle and sleeves, all gilt with gold, and a hood to match. It took all day to make and we sat by the window for hours and ate little blue cakes." She was quiet for a moment, her gaze far-off even as it rested on the crownet in her hands. "They were horrible cakes," she said at last, dreamily. "I should very much like to have a gowning party again."

"Wife," Lord Uyane murmured again, just as indulgently as he had before.

"It isn't the same when it's just for me!" she insisted, then gave Meoraq an imploring stare. "Won't you come to stay on your return, sir?"

"We may," Meoraq said, because he could see no other way out of this house within the hour save to appear to consider. And knowing that Amber may indeed be amenable to a night or three out of the wildlands, he grudgingly added, "She will not be what you expect."

"Oh yes, someone told me she didn't have a proper face," she said, waving one hand dismissively. At a sharp glance from her husband, she vaguely added, "I don't recall who. Certainly none of the servants of this House would ever engage in gossip, but one...one hears things, you know. Through the wind-ways. One hears such dreadful gossip through the wind-ways. They let anyone at all wander out in the streets."

Lord Uyane grunted and glared at her while she packed Amber's things fastidiously away again and pretended not to notice.

"We may stop in," Meoraq said, and this time, he meant it. "But now I will demand the gates open to me."

"I have a carriage to take you as far as the Prophet's Gate," Lord Uyane said, opening the inner doors himself. "I'll make you the offer of my table before you go, but I know you'll refuse so I put a hot bit of something in your pack, there."

Meoraq acknowledged this with a grunt, taking his pack and the second, holding Amber's things. "Thank you."

"Never heard thanks from a Sheulek before," Uyane remarked, nodding at the watchmen outside who ran ahead to open the gates. "I'll tell you something, son, which you'd find out on your own soon enough anyway. Women are like handfuls of sand. They all rub up under your scales now and then, but the finest ones do put a polish on a man. That's far enough," he said once they'd reached the other gate, and to the watchmen posted there—one of them, none other than Onahi—he brusquely added, "Leave us."

Meoraq waited restlessly by the gate as the reception courtyard was cleared. Lord Uyane shut the inner doors, held his open hand on the latchplate a moment more, then turned around and faced him.

"I don't listen at wind-ways," he said. "I went to the governor's seat and asked my questions there. Am I to understand that your woman is one of these...humans?"

"Yes."

Uyane grunted and rubbed at his throat, inspecting the lamp that hung over Meoraq's shoulder. "I saw a lot of things in my striding years that no other man would believe, and I think that may be the only reason I can believe what they told me you said about the creatures you brought with you out of Praxas. And it is speaking to you as the Sheulek I was that I ask you now to tell me His truth." Uyane looked directly at him and leaned close. "If you do not, I will judge you for it."

"I hear you," Meoraq said mildly.

Uyane sent a swift, brooding glance over his shoulder at the sealed doors of his House...and above it at the vented wind-way. He took Meoraq by the shoulder, moved him right up against the gate and leaned in so close it put Meoraq uncomfortably in mind of humans kissing. In a low voice, low enough that a man could not overhear it if he were hanging out the nearest wind-way by his ankles, Uyane calmly said, "Are there others?"

It was not the question he expected. With the word 'creatures' spoken and the city of Praxas named, Meoraq had been preparing himself to make a defense of the humans as a true race of people and as children of Sheul, not this.

"There are a few," he said, shrugging. "I'll not call them untroublesome, but I know them and they are, for the moment, grateful so I can keep them easily in hand."

"You do not mark me. You told the tribunal that these creatures came on a ship from another land. You may be able to keep your handful penned up and well-behaved all the rest of their lives, but I ask again, will there be more?"

"They didn't intend to come here. That was Sheul's will and if it is His will, there will be other ships."

The steward of Uyane-Chalh uttered a caustic laugh and leaned back. "You'd best pray there are not, son. By your account, there are twelve of these things, these humans, and still the tribunal set three Sheulteb against you. If there were a thousand—ha! If there were even only fifty, you would see no end to battle, and while our Father moved in you in the arena, I do believe the tribunal's men would be putting their blades in human necks just as fast as they could."

"You don't believe this."

"Don't I, eh?" Uyane eyed him, thinly smiling. "When even the true and natural children of Sheul are capable of such evil as you and I have seen, you can't present the world with a real, breathing monster and expect it to be embraced."

"They are people."

"They may well be, but with no face, no scales, fur in thatches all over and Gann alone knows what else, they are *monstrous* people." Uyane looked at him, head canted but spines all the way forward. "And you married one. Why?"

"I had to," Meoraq said.

Lord Uyane snorted. "There had to be other ways to prove these things were children of Sheul. You're a young man. You have the fame of your bloodline, the favor of God and the face of your father. Why bind yourself to a...a creature?"

"I had to," Meoraq said again. "We were married before I even met her. We were married before I was ever born."

Uyane took the tilt out of his stare and leaned back a little. The sense of judgment was again very strong, stronger even than it had been in the arena.

At the end of it, Uyane reached out and pressed his palm to Meoraq's chest.

Meoraq returned the touch. Their hearts came into rhythm.

"You're a bit of a fool, but I'm proud to call you kin," said Uyane, dropping his arm. "Bring her by, son. My Nraqi will probably chatter a hole in her scale-less head, but love her all the same. She hasn't had anyone to coddle over in eight years. So." He opened the gate and stood aside. The carriage was just without, two masked bulls harnessed and pecking at the street, the young boy who drove them waiting by the open door. "Go in the sight of Sheul and serve him well."

"I release you, steward. Await my return and be ready to receive my wife."

"It won't be this easy when it's your own House," Uyane called as Meoraq boarded. "I hope you know that."

"Then our Father has prepared me well," Meoraq replied as the carriage lurched forward. "Nothing is ever easy with that woman, but the worst is behind us now."

Rash words, but perhaps he could be forgiven for them. He was Sheulek. Not a prophet.

4

It was harder than she thought it would be, being left behind. Even at the worst of times, before they'd ever been physical, Meoraq had been an anchor to a sense of stability she found nowhere else on this world. Without him, weird noises in the night belonged to creatures without names and any plant she saw might be poisonous. Suddenly, Amber was lost again.

She wished Meoraq would get back or at least that she had some idea of when to expect him. She didn't even have anything to do while she waited. Oh, there were always fires to tend and water to carry, but it still left her with a lot of time to sit with Nicci and pretend she didn't care what Scott was muttering about on his side of the fire.

She let him talk. Not everyone was in his corner, but she was still outnumbered and Meoraq wasn't here to scare them off. Basic mathematics, as Crandall would say. One loud-mouthed dick plus five or six true believers minus one badass lizardman equaled a very quiet Amber Bierce. She made some of Meoraq's tea whenever anyone asked. She let them help themselves to the meat that was supposed to last until he got back. She shared everything except Meoraq's tent and his sword, and because they were so obviously his, no one but Scott even asked.

Too cold, not enough tents, Scott passing out the food. It was all the same old shit on a smaller scale, with the added fun of Praxas perched on the horizon like a tombstone and the threat of raiders in every shadow at night. And just to put the frosting on the shit-cake, Amber didn't feel well—tired and oddly disoriented, as if she were running a low fever, heavy and achy and oh yes, nauseous.

She couldn't be sick and she refused to be pregnant, but she felt like shit all the same. It was purely psychological. She knew that. She'd undergone a traumatic event—hell, a whole chain of traumatic events—and the only thing she was suffering from was survivor's shock. She'd suck it up, life would go on, and everyone would know Amber Bierce was the tough one.

So tough she threw up almost every morning. So tough she cried nearly every night after Meoraq didn't come back. So tough she hid in Meoraq's tent whenever Scott started in with one of his speeches and sometimes fell asleep, taking naps in the middle of the day like an old lady.

Like now.

Amber woke up, thought about it for several minutes, and decided she had successfully slept away the vague nausea that had plagued her all morning only to replace it with a headache. She was probably dehydrated. As soon as she'd dredged up the energy, she'd go out there and make tea. Maybe even brew the stuff Meoraq called nai, just because he liked it, even though Amber herself thought it tasted exactly like burnt roots in a cup. And if today was the day he came back and he found a hot cup of nai waiting for him...

"Please come home," she whispered. "Please."

No answer, not even from her mother's drunk ghost.

She got up, crawling stiffly out of the tent into the stark grey light of another alien afternoon. The first thing she noticed, when she had it in her to notice anything, was the quiet. Nicci sat by the fire, drawing in the ashes with the blackened end of a stick. Crandall was stretched out nearby, one arm crooked over his eyes. Apart from them, the camp was clearly empty.

This was not alarming, not at first. Amber hadn't been awake long enough to feel very strongly about anything, except maybe how much she wanted Meoraq back.

"Where is everyone?" she mumbled, trying to rub some life into her body face-first.

"Out," Nicci replied.

"How helpful. Where'd they go? We're really not supposed to wander around."

"Doesn't bother you when you want to sneak off for a skinny-dip in the middle of the night," Crandall remarked without raising his arm.

Irritation woke her up a little more. "I forgot my swimsuit. And how the hell would you know what I was doing last night? Were you spying on me?"

"I was taking a piss when you barged in and got naked. So technically, you were the rude one."

"Did you watch, you perv?"

"And whacked off," he agreed, raising his arm to give her a friendly leer. "Twice. You look pretty good, you know. In spite of...all that."

Amber managed not to say anything for maybe a whole three seconds. Then, gritting her teeth in self-disgust, she said, "In spite of what?"

He shrugged and dropped his arm over his eyes again. "It ain't an easy life, that's all I'm saying. You're a bit banged up."

She looked away.

"But you still look pretty damn good to me. Toned, you know? I think muscles can look hot on a chick if she doesn't overdo it. You're walking that line, but you're walking it well."

"You have no idea how many nights I lay awake worrying about that."

"Don't be a bitch, Bierce. I'm trying to pay you a compliment. Like, you've always had pretty good tits, but now they really stand out. Best tits on the planet."

"Fuck you," said Nicci, scratching out her drawing and beginning a new one.

"Okay, look, I don't even care. Back to the original question: Where is everyone?"

"Out," said Nicci again.

"They went hunting. I'm protecting the women," Crandall added.

"Hunting?" Amber looked over at the mound of kipwe meat Meoraq had left them, but it didn't appear to have gone anywhere. "What for? And with what?" she asked, ducking back into the tent to make sure Meoraq's kzung was still where she'd left it. It wasn't.

"That son of a bitch!" she exploded, and burst back out.

"Don't get your panties in a knot. He'll bring it right back."

"What the hell does he think he's doing? He can't walk up and stab something!"

"Chill out, would you? He made spears too." Crandall pointed without stirring himself, and sure enough, there was a spear stabbed ingloriously into the center of a pile of shavings over by the rock where Scott held court.

Amber went over and pulled it out. It was light in her hand, way too light. "Out of *this*?"

"Oh let it go, Bierce," sighed Crandall, at last sitting up. "He's bored, that's all. Let him break a couple sticks and run off some steam so people see him being all commanding and forget what he looked like sitting naked in a cage."

Amber knocked the spear against the ground a few times, not trying to break it, but unable to help hearing the dull sound of dead, brittle wood. She shook her head and turned on Crandall. "How long do we wait?" she demanded.

"He'll be back. I'm sure he hasn't gone far. He's not a complete idiot."

"Yes, he is! Damn it, does someone have to die before it's enough to stop him? Is that what it's going to take?"

"People already have died," remarked Nicci, utterly absorbed in her drawings.

"But they still follow him."

"If they find anything out there, it's going to go bad. And honestly, the very best scenario is them getting gored to death by an animal because the most likely thing to bump into is a raider or someone from Praxas. I had a spear," Amber said furiously. "I had a damned good spear and I knew how to use it and they took me like *that*."

"Nothing's going to happen to them," said Crandall, but he wasn't smiling anymore.

"Because everything's gone so well up till now," murmured Nicci.

Crandall heaved a sigh and got to his feet. "If you're going to freak out, let's just go find them. But I want it on record that you're acting like a "

And then, reedy as a birdcall behind the ever-present wind, the scream.

Amber froze. After all that tough talk, after all that stomping around and swearing and what Scott would surely call her Bierce-knows-best bullshit, Amber froze. It was Crandall who jumped up, Crandall who started running, and if that was all he'd done, things might have gone very differently, but Crandall was there to 'protect the women' and so his parting words as he bolted around the leather wall were, "Stay here."

What toughness failed to provoke, defiance finally did: Clutching the spear, she ran after him, but Crandall ran ahead of her the whole way and he'd been in a cage all winter so what did that say? She'd recognized that it was a human scream, a man's scream, even if she couldn't tell who'd made it. The fact that it was not repeated only made things worse. Something had found them. Something had maybe taken them. And was she really going to let herself be taken too? For *Scott*?

'Just go back,' Bo Peep suggested. 'Nicci needs you, right? Nicci always needs you. You can say it was for Nicci while you hide.'

Shame became anger and anger, as it so often did, became strength. "God damn it," she snarled, running faster, passing Crandall at last. It became her mantra: "God damn it, God damn it, God fucking *damn* it!"

She reached the bottom of a rocky hill just as the first Manifestors spilled over the top. They didn't see her, didn't see each other, didn't see the trees. When two of them inevitably collided and went sprawling, the others trampled right over them. It was Dag, badly out of breath, who lurched over to help them up.

"Run!" he shouted. Gasped, really. "It's coming!"

Eric appeared, pulling Scott along with him. "I think we lost it," Scott was babbling, hugging onto Meoraq's sword with both hands. His eyes were eating up his face. "I really think we did. I don't think it's still—hey! That's mine!"

Amber had snatched the kzung out of his grip and now shook it at him. "It's not yours, it's Meoraq's! And if he caught you with it, he'd kill you!" But the rest of that promising fight was forgotten when the kipwe came crashing through the trees.

It was a big one, a male in its prime, and it was breathing almost as hard as Dag after its run. There were a few broken spears still stuck in its side, quivering along with the rest of its quills as it raked a paw over the ground, tearing up roots and winter-hard earth with ridiculous ease. It stared them down and in its eyes, she could see the ponderous weight of its animal thought: People running was one thing. People standing, challenging...that was something else.

Amber's instinct was to run, but she made herself stand her ground. This wasn't a hungry predator, just a big, mean animal that handled being startled and stabbed at badly. It was dangerous, yes; it would chase whatever ran and kill whatever it could, but it wouldn't die trying. If the odds weren't in its favor, it would go.

"Get up," said Amber, moving closer to Dag and the Manifestors. "Everybody, come together. Don't r—"

"Run!" Scott shouted and the two Manifestors with Dag immediately bolted for camp.

The kipwe roared and charged them.

There wasn't time to think about it and if there had been time, she'd have only thought what a stupid thing she was about to do. She dropped the useless spear and ran to meet it, screaming in perfectly mingled fear and frustration as she swung the heavy kzung and hit the kipwe square in the throat. Her moment of surprised triumph was damned short; the blade skated harmlessly over the creature's quills and drove itself in somewhere in the chest. Suddenly the hilt in her hands was shoving back at her. Amber flew back, hit the ground, caught a glimpse of half a kzung with two tons of kipwe behind it coming right at her, and rolled. The hilt hit the ground where she'd been and the rest of the blade vanished into the beast's body. The kipwe bellowed, backed up, then saw her on the ground. Amber lunged out to grab the spear, which she knew damned well was nothing but a pointed piece of dead wood. She scrambled up, turned around right as the kipwe stood up on its hind legs, and stabbed as it swung.

She missed its eye, missed its nose, even missed the gaping open target of its mouth, but the stick went in somewhere. She felt it puncture flesh in the split-second before its paw connected with her side. There was no sense of flying, only the second, immediate-seeming impact as she hit the ground and slid across it. Damp earth sluiced up over her arms and into her face, clogging her nose, filling her mouth with the taste of the grave she wouldn't even get. She rolled over, spitting and swiping at herself with one hand and digging frantically for another weapon—a stick, a rock, one of the Ancients' plasma cannons, anything!—before climbing to her feet again. She had nothing but her bare hands, but she ran at it again, because it was just a kipwe for God's sake, and maybe it would turn around if she charged it, maybe it would run.

The kipwe reared again...then listed, swatted drunkenly at its face. It bellowed, shook its head hard, grunted, and then toppled over.

Amber slowed her run to a stagger and then to a stop. The beast stayed down. It did not appear to be breathing. She stared at it for a while, still breathing hard, alert enough that she knew she was winded, not so much that she knew she was hurt, and finally took the last three steps and gave it a cautious kick.

It did not move.

"No way I killed it," she said to herself in a remarkably calm and conversational tone.

The kipwe did not reply. It was very dead.

Amber started to bend over for a better look, but pain washed out from her side enough to prevent that. She clapped a hand over the hurt (wet hurt, not a great indicator of things to come) and knelt instead, prodding at the beast's body.

She found fragments of her spear imbedded harmlessly in its cheek, beneath the spiky tuft of its hilarious muttonchops where it had done no good at all. It took a little longer to find the kzung, buried to its hilt in the thick, prickly quills. Getting it out meant tugging, shaking, and finally planting a foot on its head and heaving back in spite of the hell in her side. The kipwe's wound wheezed at her, blowing a foul slip of air in her face with a wet, farting sound. Swimmer's air, they called that. She'd stabbed the kipwe through the lung.

And it had still taken it *that* long to die.

"Jesus," said Crandall behind her.

She turned around, holding Meoraq's sword limply in one hand, trying to think of what to do next. People saved, check. Dead kipwe, double check. Moving on.

"I'm going to need your help cutting it up," she announced. "There's no reason it should go to waste, you know? Oh. And I may have a few splinters." She held a hand up and sure enough, there were half a dozen kipwe quills sticking out of her arm at various points. "So if you think you can grow up just long enough to take them out without masturbating all over me...”

The rest of that bitchy comment lost itself in Crandall’s silence. He was still staring, not at the kipwe, but at her.

Amber looked down, past another half-dozen broken quills all down her side to her left hip. “Goodness, that’s a lot of blood,” she remarked, watching it stream down over her thigh.

And then the world turned white.

* * *

She came around slowly, not to the pain, which was tremendous, but to the relatively innocuous sound of laughter. She’d been tucked beneath a blanket, which was hot and scratchy and unbelievably heavy on her right side, where the pain lived. Her skin felt far too tight over the swollen, throbbing hell of her side, threatening to split whatever bandage had been tied over her. It hurt to breathe, it hurt not to breathe, and she was reasonably certain it would hurt to open her eyes, so she just lay there and concentrated on not embarrassing herself with a lot of loud moaning. The laughter came and went, curiously high-pitched for a camp mostly filled with men...and slightly crazed.

Actually, a lot crazed. Less laughter than full-on lunatic gibbering. She wasn’t the only one who seemed to be concerned; she could hear Scott holding court close by in a tone of deep concern. He was using all his old familiar catch-phrases, too. Explore our options. Make decisions. Take command. The only thing he didn’t do was tell the people laughing at him to shut up and she kind of wished he would.

‘No one’s laughing, little girl,’ Bo Peep told her.

Beneath the heavy blanket and the heavier pain, Amber pulled the scattered pieces of her brain together and listened.

That sound...that high, chattering, lunatic sound.

Her eyes heaved themselves open. She tried to bolt upright and managed only a slightly deeper, choking breath. Her cry of, “Those are ghets!” came out as little more than a hoarse gasp and a rusty groan. The world went briefly grey on her and came very slowly back.

“She’s awake,” Crandall said in the distance.

A blurry shadow grew over her—Scott, looking down. “I don’t think so,” he said after a moment’s study.

Amber tried again to speak and again could only push air around. She was beginning to think she might be seriously hurt this time.

A second blur appeared, bringing with it a cool hand that wiped the sweaty hair out of Amber’s face. A woman’s hand, although not a soft one. Her mother’s hand, she thought, and it was her mother’s face leaning over her now, looking haggard and bitter and way too solid for a dead lady. “Amber?”

Nicci? Impossible. Nicci was half this woman’s age. But no, it was Nicci, and as soon as she realized it, much of the woman’s hard edges seemed to soften until she could see her baby sister above her instead of their mother’s ghost.

“You look like Mama,” Amber tried to say, but of course, all that made it into the world was a whispered, “...mama.”

“She’s delirious,” Scott declared, sounding annoyed and she couldn’t really blame him. He hated it when his speeches were interrupted.

“Guys?” That was Dag, looking back over his shoulder at the leather walls that surrounded the camp, beyond which the ghet-song had suddenly degenerated into snarling and screaming.

“They’ll be back,” Scott said grimly as the sounds receded. He folded his arms.

One of them was distorted, stretched long and broken at odd angles; he had Meoraq's kzung in one hand like a scepter. "And they're coming right in here...unless we can give them a reason not to."

All around the camp, Scott's surviving Manifestors looked at Amber.

'Oh please,' she thought at them irritably. 'What do you want me to do about it? I can't even move!'

...oh.

Amber put all her strength into sitting up and managed to lift her head a few trembling centimeters before it dropped meatily back onto her mat. Had she ever thought waking up from her snake-bite or whatever that had been was the weakest a living person could feel? At least she'd been able to hold her head up! This...This was really bad.

And Meoraq wasn't here this time.

"You can't, man," said Eric, coming out of the shadows to stand between her and Scott. "Whatever you're thinking, you just can't."

"I'll tell you what I'm thinking, Mr. Lassiter. Look at her! She's dying! It's a miracle she's lasted this long, she can't possibly live out the night! All she's doing is stinking like blood and telling every predator in miles to come and get us! Now we can rally around her and get everyone killed or..."

"You're not leaving her again!" Nicci leapt up to stand at Eric's side, her hands balled into fists.

Scott stepped right up to meet her, putting his face too close to hers and cocking his head to one side. He'd picked up some dumaqi habits, it seemed, living in that cage. "I made a command decision," he said tightly. "We couldn't take her with us and we couldn't wait around for her to get better or die, so yeah, I made that call. You want to stand here now and tell me I did the wrong thing, you go ahead because you are absolutely right. If I'd done what I *should* have done and she'd died like *she* should have done, we'd have had the lizard with us the whole time. How would that have changed things, huh?" Scott swung around, raising both arms over his head and shouting out to his Manifestors like they were a cheering throng that filled a stadium instead of a handful of men a few meters away. "He stayed with *her* when he should have been with *us*! Instead of blaming me for everything that went wrong, put the credit where it's due! On Amber-fucking-Bierce!"

Murmurs.

Amber tried and again failed to make any kind of useful contribution to her own defense and the effort left her so wiped out that she had to close her eyes and rest.

"If we'd had a guide, we'd have reached the mountains long before the snow. We never would have gotten stuck up there for so long and we never would have come down so close to that city! We'd have had food the whole time! And water! And fire! No one would have gotten hurt, no one would have gotten killed, and you, Nicci, you wouldn't have spent so many nights with a scaly cock shoved up your trap, now would you?"

"I wouldn't have had yours either!" Nicci hissed. "And believe me, that's the one I regret the most. This is not Amber's fault! It never was and you know it, you and all your ignorant fucking sheep!"

Scott slapped her. His Manifestors murmured some more, angry now, but they were angry at Nicci. On the ground, her eyes still too heavy to open, Amber made a loose fist and grunted.

"Come on, both of you." And that was Eric, doing his let's-be-reasonable thing. She couldn't see him, but she could picture him clearly enough: both hands raised, eyes moving cautiously back and forth between the main opponents, and well out of range just in case the punches started flying. "Nicci, just give us some space for a sec. And let's think about what you're saying here, okay? She saved our lives."

"I had everything under control until she charged that giant porcupine and got herself torn open. What she's doing right now is *endangering* our lives, just like she did before. Don't you see that? Don't you realize? This is all about keeping us away from the skyport! If it hadn't been for her, we'd be on the ship right now, all of us, and on our way home! The way I see it, Amber Bierce is directly responsible for the deaths of thirty-six people and that makes her an enemy of the state! Why are you defending her?"

That didn't sound good. Amber pulled her eyelids up in time to see the blurry smudge that was Scott raise Meoraq's kzung—not in a menacing way, but more like a young Arthur who had just pulled it from the stone as proof of his right to rule. "What do we do with enemies?" he called to his Manifestors. "What do we do with tumors? Do we give them a comfortable place to sit and grow, to infect the rest of the body? Or do we cut them out?"

"I'll kill you if you try it!" Nicci shouted. "Do you hear me? I'll kill—"

Scott pointed Meoraq's sword at her, silencing her so suddenly that Amber thought he'd stabbed her until she backed up. "I'm going to put it to a vote," he announced, turning back to his Manifestors. "All in favor, say aye."

A solid wall of ayes went up.

"In favor of what?" Crandall asked coolly. "If you're so damn sure it's the right thing to do, why don't you want to say out loud what it is?"

"And if you're so opposed to it, why don't you say nay, Mr. Crandall?" Scott countered. "Say it so we all know where you stand. Say it or shut the hell up."

Amber sucked in a painfully deep breath and croaked, "...nay."

One by one, they all looked at her.

Amber pressed her noodle-weak arms to the mat and forced herself up a mountainous few centimeters. A light, chill sweat broke out all over her body, washing her briefly back into winter. She glared as best as she was able while gasping and shaking. "Nay," she panted and for good measure, added, "Mother...fucker."

Scott cocked his head at her in that eerily lizardish way. "You don't get a vote, Miss Bierce. You are not a member of this colony. Your rights as a colonist and a citizen are revoked." He turned that same stare on Eric. "Get out of my way."

Nicci clutched at Eric's arm. "Don't," she begged.

Eric looked at her, then back at Dag and Crandall. Neither of them moved to join him. He looked at Scott again. The wind flapping lightly at the leather walls that surrounded the camp and the gentle crackling of the fire were the only sounds...until Meoraq's, "What in Gann's unholy name goes on here?"

People who had been sitting sprang up. People who had been standing jumped back. Scott dropped the sword and hid his empty hands behind him, trying to look in all directions at once.

Meoraq came out from the shadowed opening between two overlapping walls and stood over his kzung where it lay in the trampled grass. He looked at it without expression as his throat slowly lit up. He took six breaths in the absolute silence and then said, "You had my sword in your hand, S'kot. In your naked hand."

Amber licked her lips several times, braced herself for another deep breath, and rasped, "Meoraq, don't."

He pointed at her to shut her up without taking his eyes off Scott. "Var'li S'kot," he said, making each word distinct, "son of Var'li Reshar, you have broken the Third Law and taken up a bladed weapon. The law of my caste requires that I ask, but to say truth—" He bent down and plucked the kzung out of the grass, straightening up with a smile and a hiss. "—I don't give a clay fuck if you pray or not."

Amber gripped at the ground and tried to sit up further, but her arms collapsed.

She hit the mat and an elephant stomped on her stomach and she let out a scratchy scream that, weak as it was, finally got Meoraq's full attention. He crossed the camp in just three long strides, shoving Eric and Nicci out of his way before he dropped to his knees at Amber's side. He stabbed the kzung into the ground and put his hand roughly on her forehead, pressing her flat; the other carefully peeled back the bandage on her belly.

His spines came slowly forward in a silent, oddly graceful flare above his? otherwise expressionless face. "Oh my fearless Soft-Skin," he said after a moment, without readable emotion. "I could just slap you."

"It's not what it looks like," Scott said quickly.

"I do not hear you. Await the sword of Sheul's judgment."

"It's not," Amber said. "It was a kipwe."

"I see that. I say stand where you are, S'kot," Meoraq added, no louder and without seeming to have even noticed Scott's silent attempt to disappear behind his Manifestors. He bent further over her, peering into her eyes and then prying her mouth open, of all things, before looking under the bandage again.

"It didn't look that bad to me," said Crandall, watching him. "Once we got the bleeding stopped, I mean."

Meoraq didn't answer, which was about the worst response he could have given. At length, he replaced the bandage and covered her over with the blanket. He put his hands on his thighs. He bent his neck. He took six breaths. Then he brushed the backs of his knuckles across Amber's brow and said, "I forgive you, Soft-Skin. Rest now. You are in our Father's sight."

The little comfort this gave her lasted just until Meoraq gripped the hilt of his kzung and stood up, ripping it from the wet ground and spattering Amber lightly with grass and mud. "I'll try not to enjoy this," he said, seizing Scott as he bolted for escape. "But you haven't made that easy."

"Meoraq, don't!"

"I am not Uyane Meoraq but the Sword in His hand," Meoraq replied, calmly towing Scott toward an opening in the walls. "Rest. This will not take long."

"Let him go," said Amber. The words were bitter as ash.

Meoraq stopped walking. He stood silent, staring straight ahead at the leather wall while Scott gasped for air at the end of his fist. The color striping his throat throbbed in time with his pulse. But for that and the heaving of his chest as he breathed, he did not move.

"Please let him go," said Amber, hating herself for feeling the mean hope that he would ignore her and kill Scott anyway.

He turned and came back to her, dragging Scott with him, perhaps entirely forgotten. The color was bright enough almost to seem to be glowing in the firelight and his eyes were starting to glaze. "He broke his faith with God, if he ever had it, and as His Sword, I have no mercy to show him and would not even if I did! If I could not spare you, why in Gann's name would I spare him?"

"Because we're all that's left. That...has to matter."

"More than the Word?" Meoraq demanded. He struggled visibly with his temper, then lost it, roaring, "More than *your life*? What do you think he meant to do with my sword, fool woman? If I had slept tonight, if I had stopped even once to rest, you would be dead now! Dead and...and buried!"

She stretched out her hand toward his boot, palm up, trembling.

He looked down at that as everyone watched and Scott twisted and gasped in his unmoving fist. At last, Meoraq's neck bent. His burning eyes shut and opened again, calm. He studied Scott for a while in silence, then released him and let him drop in the muddy grass. "I am not Uyane Meoraq but the Sword in His hand," he said as Scott scrambled back, clutching at his neck. "I am a true son of Sheul, by whose laws you are judged unforgiveable. You are welcome no more among men. However, exile is permitted as a lawful alternative to execution and so I offer it. Shall you stand and submit to my sword, Var'li S'kot? It is a far easier death and, for my wife's sake, I will even burn you when it is done. Gann will give you no such mercy."

Scott retreated another step, still breathing hard, then suddenly snatched up a rolled tent and held it before him like a shield.

Meoraq spat contemptuously and picked up one of the travel-sized waterskins, shoving it hard against Scott's chest. "Take it and go, then. You and all your cattle. Go and let the Dark Father who shat you out, take you in."

"Come on, men," Scott rasped, gathering up supplies with shaking hands. "I've spent...enough time...with lizards...and their...whores!"

Meoraq's head cocked. He looked at Nicci. "What does that word mean?"

"It means he's leaving," Nicci said.

"And you're not...coming with me!" Scott declared, pointing at her. He waited, perhaps expecting some tearful plea to reconsider, but when Nicci only sat there, he finally sneered and turned around. He left, staggering as he went, either from the lasting effects of his throttling or under the weight of the many waterskins he'd taken with him. After a long silence spent eyeing the supplies remaining to them, the last of the Manifestors scratched up some food, some blankets and another tent and hurried after him. The rest—Eric and Dag and Crandall, his one-time loyal lieutenants—stayed.

Meoraq looked at them. The stripes on his throat were still bright, bright yellow. "Get out."

"For what it's worth," said Eric, "and I know it's not worth much, we never should have left her."

Dag grunted, a disturbingly lizardlike sound, and Crandall, looking back over his shoulder at Scott's retreating colony, agreed, "He was a fucking loon. What do you say, Bierce? No hard feelings?"

Amber smiled weakly. "Yeah, okay. We're good."

Meoraq stepped up and shoved Crandall so hard and so unexpectedly that Crandall lost his feet and nearly fell in the fire. "This is not her camp!" he spat, this time shoving Dag, who only staggered. Eric stepped back on his own. "It is mine and I forgive you *nothing*! You, who acknowledge you should not have abandoned her to die in the open plains—not apologize, but acknowledge—have nothing to say about the fact that you stood and watched S'kot raise a blade over my wife?"

Eric kept his wary distance, but didn't flinch. "I tried to stop him."

"He did," said Amber. "Please, Meoraq."

"No! I give you your blood-kin. The rest of them can go to Gann. Out!"

"Hey, he had a sword!" Crandall shrugged off Dag's helping hands and bounded to his feet. "What was I supposed to do, take it away from him? Huh? So you could come back and find *me* holding it? Who the hell do you think carried her back here and bandaged her up? Isn't that worth anything?"

"We made a mistake," Eric added. "We made a lot of them, okay? We just want the chance to make it right."

"It's okay," Amber tried to say and this time, Meoraq rounded on her.

"Stop telling them that!" he hissed. "You have no power to forgive them!"

"You do."

He recoiled, spines flaring and flattening with a brittle snap. "But I won't!"

"Please."

"No!"

"I'm begging."

"I don't care!"

"Meoraq—"

"*They don't like you*!" he bellowed, pointing at Crandall and the others with the sword. "This isn't *liking* you, damn it! This is groveling for their worthless lives! Nothing has changed!"

"I don't care if they like me," she said, just like she'd used to say it to herself so long ago. Somewhere along the way, it had turned into the truth, but it didn't make her feel tough or hard or strong, only tired. "But if I let them walk out there and die just because I don't like them, then something's changed, all right. Please."

They all looked at Meoraq.

He did not say anything for a long, long time.

At last, he sheathed his sword and turned his head just enough to look at Eric and the others. "I am Uyane Meoraq, son of Rasozul," he said tonelessly, "who was son of Ta'sed, who was son of Kuuri, who was the forty-third son of the line descended of the Prophet's Uyane Xaima. I am a Sword and a true son of Sheul...and I forgive you all your pasts. But I do not take you in," he added in a hiss. "You are not Uyane under me. You are not welcome in my House. *We* are not *good*."

Crandall started to speak, but Eric stopped him with a warning glance. No one said anything.

Meoraq turned his back on them and knelt again next to Amber. "For you," he said simply. "Hold on to me now. This will hurt."

He lifted her. He did it slowly and even gently in spite of the color that was still so strong at his throat, but it did hurt and in spite of her determination to suck it up, she had to cry a little. But she got an arm around his neck and kept it there, anchoring herself to him while the rest of the world lurched and spun.

"I'm sorry," she said as he took her into his tent. "This is a hell of a thing to come back to."

He coughed up a humorless laugh and lay her down on his mat. "I asked God to bring me back to you. I left the details entirely to His whim. There is a lesson in that. Now rest. Tomorrow will be a difficult day."

"You'll have to remind me...when were the easy ones?"

It was a rhetorical question. Meoraq had never been good at recognizing those. "All things are relative," he told her. "There are no easy days in the wildlands, but tomorrow...tomorrow will be difficult."

5

Meoraq had run all night on nothing but a few bites of cuuvash, praying at every step that Sheul would keep his camp shrouded from the eyes of his enemies and tormented by visions of what he would find if He did not. He would have thought he had imagined every possible scenario. A kipwe attack—which he could not help but think of as roughly on a level with a mimut or a saoq attack—had never crossed his mind. It was the sort of thing he would have found laughable had he seen it in a play or a book—a tragedy on the indistinct edge of comedy—until it was his Amber lying there, as pale as a yearling...and as weak.

But she would not rest. Meoraq understood that she had not seen him in many days and that she wanted to know that Xzem and the infant had reached Chalh in good health. He understood also that the mood within his small camp was a dark one following Scott's exile and she wanted to lighten it. And he understood best of all that she was hurt and hurts have a way of growing when there is nothing else to do except think about them. A Sheulek learned early to embrace pain, to own it and sleep in spite of it, but Amber was not Sheulek.

In the end, Meoraq brewed her a strong cup of tea with a few leaves of healershand, chewed some more leaves and packed her wound with the pulp, then set the humans on watch—ha—and went out with his lamp to pray. Sheul brought him to a hive of soldier beetles; Meoraq caught twenty and wrapped them awkwardly in a fold of his tunic.

He returned to find Amber, as he'd hoped, deeply asleep. So was Nicci and the other humans, who had, he saw, helped themselves to the rest of the tea. Just as well. He moved Nicci to the humans' tent (as he knelt to set her on her mat, she mumbled and caught at his harness as if to pull him down with her. It took some effort to get away with waking her and even more effort to do it without hissing), left the rest of them where they lay and directed himself to Amber without distraction.

The medicine had done its work well by that time and the wound was bloodless when he pulled the bandage away. He washed the wound to clear it of clinging pulp. Amber murmured, but that was all, even when he pressed the severed edges of her flesh closed and hunted out the first beetle, holding it carefully by its shiny shell. Already deeply aggravated, it needed no encouragement to bite. Its massive mandibles punctured both sides of her torn muscle, squeezing them tight together, and at once, Meoraq pinched off its head. Its insect will was greater than death; it would hold its grip until its shell crumbled away.

Beetle by beetle, he closed her wounds and sealed it with a paste of healershand and honey. He examined every part of her for kipwe quills the humans had missed and licked every scratch. He changed out her bandages for clean cloth taken from his provisions seized in Chalh. After that, there was nothing he could do except sit and brood over the many wounds he'd seen sour in spite of the best surgeons and those that had healed cleanly with no care at all.

"She rests in Your sight, O my Father," he muttered, rubbing at last at his brow ridges, and this was true, but she also rested in the wildlands. Between the threat of revenging raiders and hungry beasts (he counted Scott somewhere along this line) were too many dangers to defend against. The nearest city—well, the next nearest, as Praxas would be no shelter to him—was Chalh again, four running days at best, and in light of Lord Uyane's last words to him, he was hesitant to take her there. If she was to have any chance at all of recovery, it would have to be somewhere else.

They must be ready to move on at first light.

So decided, Meoraq again took his lamp and went out into the darkness, this time to build a sled. He was so tired by now that he watched his hands cut and trim poles as if they were the hands of another man, feeling nothing of what he did. He didn't know how he was going to walk all day, let alone carry Amber. The humans would be no help to him in that regard; their treatment in Praxas had not left them able to bear weight for great distances even if they could be made willing.

Anger rose in him, bitter as bile. He swallowed it, but the taste remained.

When he returned to camp, the fire had burned itself down to lightless red glints. He built it up again and when he could make out one human from another, he woke Eric (with a none too gentle nudge of his boot). "Take the watch," he said, noting even as he gave the order the groggy glaze of healershand tea in the human's eyes.

But Eric nodded and sat himself up, rubbing at his flat, ugly face.

"Wake me at first light or if Scott should return. Do not—" He pointed the whole of his hand into Eric's face and immediately won the man's full, frowning attention. "—speak with him. He has gone to Gann and so too have those who treat with him. How do you mark me?"

Eric yawned and showed his fist, saying, "He won't be back. He knows you'll kill him. Hey. Is she going to be okay?"

Meoraq glanced behind him, but of course saw only his tent. "I cannot answer, but that isn't what you truly want to ask, is it?"

"I don't know what you—"

"If she dies, I will turn you out." Meoraq glanced around and caught a shadow of dark thought in Eric's eye before his human face closed. "There was a time I thought almost well of you," Meoraq said with a thin smile. "But you have grown to like the taste of the poison S'kot fed you. Now you talk out of two mouths, the same as he. I have no use for you. If my wife insists on it, there will be a place for you in Xeqor. If she doesn't—" His spines flicked. "—there won't."

"You have no idea what we've been through." Eric's jaw clenched, but his voice did not rise and he bent his neck before he spoke. If his time in Praxas had taught him nothing else, it had taught him manners. "I don't even think you *can* understand it. I don't think there's one thing in your privileged life that allows you to know what it's been like for us since we crashed on this planet. Even Amber knows we did the best we could."

Tired as he was, Meoraq smiled an honest smile. "She said that, didn't she? I can almost hear her say it. And if I had been there to see it, I would have seen no lie in her eyes and do you know why? Because she wants so much to believe it. Like S'kot and his fever-dream ship. She believes it because she has done the best she could every step of this road. Yes. Now. Look into my eyes, human, and tell me you have done the same."

"Why should I? I already know you think it's a lie."

"I do know it's a lie," Meoraq agreed. "I want to know if you do. So speak, human. We'll judge your words together."

"I think I'll wait," said Eric after a moment, "until you've slept."

"Is my sense of judgment in doubt?" Meoraq asked, blackly amused. "Is that what you're telling me? Is that what you're saying to the Sword and the Striding Foot of God?"

"I'm saying when I'm tired, I'm not always as objective as I could be."

"Spoken like a priest. It's easy to tell who had the keeping of you." And that really was spiteful. Meoraq made himself stop talking, even if he couldn't quite make himself apologize. A Sheulek was not required to be civil so long as he was honest.

Eric made no reply, but his eyes in the firelight burned.

"At first light," Meoraq said again and was answered with a silent salute. He went into his tent where the scent of human blood was strong and lay down as far from his wife as he could. Her breaths in the dark were loud and not even; her face, if he could see it, would be strained. He listened, thinking he should pray for her once more so that those were the last words Sheul heard from his heart tonight and not the ones he'd given Eric, and so thinking, he closed his eyes and was deeply asleep at once.

* * *

His dreams were tangled things, impossible to put in meaningful order. It seemed to him it began in Tothax, because his cousin Nkosa was there and the two of them spent some measureless time together on the rooftop before the edges blurred away and he was walking with Amber across the plains of Yroq. She was limping, falling behind, and when he finally turned around in a senseless kind of dreaming rage to yell at her, it was not Amber any longer but Nicci instead. Her shoulder was bleeding, fresh blood in the shape of toothmarks, and he knew with all the certainty of dreams that her father had bitten her, to force Meoraq to take her in. She held out her arms to him, her face cold, mewling at him after the manner of a dumaqi woman and hating him with her eyes. Then he was somewhere deep in ruins, slaughtering raiders as they came for him, slaughtering their slave-women as they cowered and ran, slaughtering their screaming children. He thought he must be looking for Amber, to save her, but when she came out of the darkness, his sword went before him and the roar that tore from him as she fell was not grief, but rage. He turned around, surrounded on every side by blood and death, and found himself trapped behind a wall of glass and there were Ancients on the other side, standing over their unknowable machines, watching him. One of them came down from the dais and reached out to him, reached right through the glass that Meoraq beat his fists raw against, and put his hand on Meoraq's shoulder.

Meoraq awoke with a violent start, seeing first the figure from his dream looming over him and then Scott and finally, truthfully, Eric.

"You said dawn," the human reminded him, withdrawing. "I made some tea."

"Stay out of my tea box," Meoraq muttered uncharitably and rolled over to have a look at Amber's wound in the dim morning light.

She came awake with a high cry as he lifted her blanket, then slumped back and stared at him blearily from deep in her sunken sockets. "What is it about the second day that makes everything hurt worse?"

"Swelling," he replied, peeling away her poultice. The flesh beneath was deep red and swollen, but not so badly as he feared. Blood stained her bandages, but not pus. Not yet. He grunted, then carefully pressed it down again. "How do you feel?"

"Like I have a fever."

He moved closer and lay his chin briefly over her brow. "You don't," he said, relieved. "But you have lost a great deal of blood. It must be—"

Her arms slipped around his neck and weakly held him. He shut his eyes, feeling only her trembling embrace, and wished with all his bitter heart that they had never come to Gedai.

"I want you to drink a little tea," he murmured at last, gently pulling away. "And then we have to go."

"Oh, Meoraq, I don't think I can."

"I've made a sled to carry you."

Her face twisted, dismayed, even as she tried to laugh. "It's one slice of shit-cake after another with me, isn't it? Why did you marry me?"

"God gave you to me."

"Did you keep the receipt?"

He didn't know what that meant, although he knew it wasn't worth a response. He lifted her, ignoring her sounds of pain and the obvious strain of not giving them full voice. Shouldering his way out of the tent, he found Nicci and the other humans by the fire, warming up cold meat for the morning meal. "Leave that," he ordered. "You can eat as we walk. N'kl, fill the flask and pack the food. The rest of you, take down the tents and the walls."

"Please," called Amber, white-faced with pain.

"You don't say please to servants," he said crossly, setting her on the sled.

"Yeah, I know what you people do with servants. Leave them alone." Her brows furrowed in an expression something like embarrassment. "Feels like I'm bleeding again."

He checked. She was. He didn't have much healershand left—it was surprising enough that the provisioner in Chalh had thought to give him any—but he chewed half of what he had and painted it onto her wound, careful not to crush the beetle heads.

"You want to hear something funny?" Amber asked in a muffled voice. She'd shut her eyes as soon as he'd lifted her bandages and now had her hands firmly pressed over her face, as if to stop herself peeking.

"Not really, but go on."

"This would be no big deal where I'm from. I could just go to the clinic on the corner and get patched up. They'd give me back all the blood I lost, slap on some syntheskin and send me home with some pain pills and if it had happened on a Friday, I'd be back to work on Monday. Do you believe that?"

He grunted, re-affixing her compress. "I believe you are not lying. I have no idea what you're saying. You can look now."

She lowered her hands—they trembled—and opened her eyes—they were glassy. "When are you going to tell me that this is what I deserve for doing such a stupid thing in the first place?"

"I'm not," he said, bringing out the first of the binding straps and passing it beneath her legs. "I know you acted only to save the lives of your..." He paused to let a few unspoken adjectives blow away in the wind, then finished, "people."

"Yeah, but not getting yelled at is making me think I'm a whole lot more hurt than I thought I was. Level with me, lizardman." She grabbed at his arm, missed, and finally caught him. "How bad is this?"

"Lesser wounds have killed," he said. "Greater wounds have healed."

He could tell that wasn't much comfort to her. Truth, it wasn't much comfort to him either.

He fetched what tea was left in his stewing pouch after the humans had been at it and poured it into his new metal flask, then brought it back for her to drink. She managed only a few sips, grimacing at the taste, which was a perfectly good winterleaf blend. "For now, know that you are in His sight."

"Like I was when He let me get on the ship?"

"The ship that brought you to me, yes." He grazed the backs of his knuckles gently across her brow. "He set you on this path, Soft-Skin. Have faith that He will see you reach this journey's end."

She looked up at him with her weary, pain-dull eyes and said, matter-of-factly, "He doesn't love me like He loves you, Meoraq."

It hurt his heart.

"Even if that were true, and I say it is not..." He knelt down beside the sled and lay his hand over hers. The only warmth in it came from the flask she held. "If He loves me, He will never let you die."

"And nobody believed me when I said they were doing it," Crandall remarked, helping Dag roll up one of the walls. "That shit's just embarrassing."

Meoraq grunted, still looking only at Amber, who offered him a crooked sort of smile. "You're not going to let me hit him, are you?"

"You really shouldn't."

"Opinions differ." He tapped the flask in her hands meaningfully and left her to help his humans finish breaking camp. As he passed Crandall, he glanced back and, seeing Amber's eyes shut tight against the taste of the tea, delivered a swift slap to the back of the human's hairy head.

* * *

They made terrible distance that day, but Meoraq comforted himself with the knowledge that every span gained was another he put between them and Praxas and that, at least, was something. And it wasn't as bad as it could have been because in spite of his sour prediction, the humans did volunteer themselves to carry the back end of Amber's sled when the terrain made pulling impossible, which was often. There was far less complaining than there had been herding them across Yroq (he could not remember much of their nature in the few days he'd had them after Praxas. Truth, all his memories from the moment Sheul had taken him in the raider's nest until his arrival at Chalh were stained dark and remained largely beyond recall) and they kept quietly to themselves whenever he stopped them for rest. It could never be a good day, given the circumstances, but it was tolerable.

Yet as the hours wore on, Amber visibly weakened. She remained cool to his questing touch and her wound did not worsen, but the unavoidable rocking of the sled caused her such pain that she could not bear to travel more than a quarter-span at a stretch. He urged tea on her until the single waterskin S'kot had left to them was dry, trusting to Sheul to fill them, but the only water they met with on their travels was the rain, which was just heavy enough to soften the ground, not enough to fill their flasks.

The sun had scarcely begun its descent when Meoraq ordered the walls up and while his humans made his camp for him, he ran on ahead to scout this inhospitable land. He found no free water, but in a murky fen half a span away, he did find an abundance of wild healershand just out of the bud, as well as some iseqash herb, which would help her to sleep. Meoraq knelt in the mud and gave thanks, took what Sheul had given him, and ran with it back to his camp, arriving just after nightfall to find Amber and Nicci asleep in his tent, the rest of them asleep in the other tent, and a small pack of ghets making an easy meal of their provisions.

Meoraq's roars brought the humans out of their tents (except for Amber, although by the sound of it, she tried) and chased off the scavenging beasts, but the damage was done. The mouths of ghets were the mouths of Gann himself; every scrap of meat they'd touched must be presumed to be poison now.

Meoraq sat up through the late hours to burn it, counting six breaths whenever he felt the color coming to his throat and giving God thanks at each one that the ghets had fed out of his packs and not the tent where Amber lay helpless. He had most of a brick of cuuvash left from that given him in Chalh and it would have to last.

It was the first of seven days' travel, but each was essentially the same, trapping him in one endless hour for as long as the sun shone behind the clouds. He led them well around Chalh—not without misgivings—and picked up the thin trail of the Crossways in the east, following it through the hilly forests of Gedai and along the crumbling streambanks where they drew their bitter water. He did not seek for Scott and his cattle in their shadow. He tended only Amber, spoke to no one but God.

On the seventh day, as his cuuvash was down to its final bites and Amber's swollen wound had begun to show the yellow crust of infection at last, the road brought them to the open mouth of an underlodge—old, but not too long empty or at least not overgrown. Uyane's steward in Chalh had mentioned there were many of these along the way to Xi'Matezh. Heartened, Meoraq called a halt and pried open the door to investigate.

The short stair opened on a large round room, equipped with a fair-sized hearth and separate smoke-room, various pots and basins, a table and chairs, even a proper cupboard to sleep in. It would hold all his humans comfortably and provide them sturdy shelter against both the beasts of Gedai and the weather while Amber recovered.

When he went back to the surface and told the humans of his decision, they all looked at Amber and then gave Meoraq the same unquiet glance.

"What?" he snapped, glaring at Eric, who seemed to have made himself their leader in Scott's absence.

"Nothing."

"Then take the gear and get below."

They took him at his word, each man carrying the sheets and poles of the windbreak into the store-house and then going down into the underlodge, where they stayed. Only Nicci lingered beside the sled, although that was most likely to avoid having to carry provisions, since she made no move to help Amber up. Meoraq unloaded alone, dropping blankets, packs and bundled tents down the opening (and perhaps on some lazy human's head, he thought peevishly), before unfastening Amber from the sled and gathering her into his arms. She slung her arm around his neck to help support her weight, but she did not open her eyes. Seven days of rest in a moving sled in the wildlands was no rest at all; she looked even paler and more strained now than when he'd first seen her and her only response to his nuzzling was a weary pucker of pain.

"Is she going to be all right?" Nicci asked.

He didn't know and his uncertainty sparked at once to anger. "Why are you asking me?" he snapped at her. "I am not Sheul, to close wounds and purify flesh! I end life, I don't make it."

In his arms, Amber frowned. "Should I be worried that you seem to think making life is going to be necessary?"

"Hush," he told her.

They went down into the darkness, which was not as dark as it could have been, since Eric had done him the astounding service of rifling through his pack to light his lamp. Dag had brought out what remained of Meoraq's wrapped cuuvash and the little pot of honey he'd been using to sweeten Amber's tea, and Crandall was even now pouring himself a drink from Meoraq's flask into Amber's cup.

"What—" Meoraq began, almost conversationally, then changed his mind. "Get back, you parasites!" he roared, and they all scattered to the walls.

"Six breaths," Amber murmured in his arms.

"I'm calm. A Sheulek is always calm." He sat her carefully at the table and gave her her cup. Grumbling, he hauled his mat to the simple cupboard and opened it violently enough to pull its neglected door off its runner. It took some time to shove it back into place, but soon enough he had it on and the interior slapped clean of beetle-husks and grit. "Great Father, give me healing for my woman's wound," he hissed, as he unrolled his mat and made up his bed within. "And if You cannot give me that, give me the strength not to kill the rest of her people in front of her."

"You're in such a cheerful mood," Amber remarked.

"Lies."

"All right, you're being a bitch."

"I told you to hush."

He put her in the cupboard and set a blanket over her. The humans watched him warily as he unpacked the rest of his gear and put the lodge in order. It didn't take long; he didn't have many things. "We stay here until I give the order to move on," he announced, snatching up the empty waterskin to sling around his shoulder. "My kills are not yours. Hunt for yourselves or go hungry. My woman is resting. Do not disturb her."

He ascended and passed out of the overhanging hut, but stopped there to take a deep breath of Sheul's air and let the wind cool his temper. He could hear their voices muttering, and although he knew he should rejoice in the sound and celebrate the miracle of their survival, he could not help cursing Praxas in his heart, not for the terrible crimes they had committed against those humans, but for harboring them at all.

"What the fuck was that?" Crandall demanded below. "Now I've got to ask the lizard's permission every time I use a fucking cup? What am I supposed to do, drink off the fucking floor?"

Eric answered, too low to be heard, followed by Nicci: "I told you he'd get mad."

"Shut the fuck up, lizard-bait."

"Leave her alone." Amber.

"You can shut up too, *woman*. Lie there and bleed or something. The big boys are talking."

Meoraq breathed. One for the Prophet...

"Come on, man," Eric said. "Lay off her. She's hurt."

"Oh yeah, she's hurt. I'd completely forgotten, seeing as she's spent the whole damn day bitching and moaning about it." Crandall's voice skewed up into a shrill mewling, grotesque to hear. "'Please, Meoraq, put me down! Oh, please stop, I can't stand it!' Like you had such a hard day when we were the ones hauling your fat ass around."

"It's not fat," said Amber, her irritation clear even though the cupboard door.

"Whatever, *woman*, I saw you naked. You're putting the belly back on you."

Saw her naked? Meoraq put a hand on the hilt of his kzung and closed his eyes, trying to come up with just one reason not to go right back down those stairs, haul Crandall out into the rain and cut his ugly head off. Amber had reasons, or thought she did, but Amber's reasons were not, in this moment, good enough.

"Stop trying to shut me up!" Crandall shouted suddenly, breaking Eric's low murmurs. "I'm not his fucking dog and I'm sure as hell not yours! Hey, woman!" A rapping of a human hand on wood. "Am I *disturbing* you? Why don't you cry some more? You've gotten awfully good at that, Miss I-Don't-Need-My-Hand-Held, Miss I-Don't-Need-A-Man. Let me tell you something, I'm not spending the rest of my life getting slapped around by your scaly dickman! You and your scale-bait sister ought to remember that not everyone can fuck their way to the lap of luxury on this planet and show a little goddamn respect to the guys who are picking up your slack!"

Enough. Meoraq swept his samr from its sheath and turned around, but he had only just put his foot on the first descending stair before the scrape of the cupboard door silenced the human below. It was Amber's voice that rang out next, slurred but strong and filled with fire: "You want to thank your God and his that I am a girl, Crandall, because it's my girlie squeamishness at seeing a man sliced up the middle that's keeping you alive right now. You don't like it? Feel free to go back where we found you! Otherwise, shut the fiddling fuck up, and if you say one more word about my sex life, I will knock every tooth out of your ungrateful mouth, so help me, God. There's only one person who calls me 'woman' and gets away with it and buddy, you aren't it."

Silence. Not even mutters. The cupboard door scraped shut again.

'She doesn't like them,' Meoraq thought sullenly, tapping one finger along the hilt of his sword. 'Why does she want them with us?'

For answer, the memory of her exhausted, broken voice: *We're all that's left. Please. That has to matter.*

It did. Of course it did. Did the Prophet love all those he brought into Sheul's light in the days after the Fall? No, no more than the Ancients deserved to be saved from the wrath their great sin had brought upon them, but the Prophet understood what apparently Uyane Meoraq only gave voice to: Life is the most precious of God's gifts. When so few of the Ancients survived the Fall, Prophet Lashraq did not judge this or that one unlikeable and therefore unworthy to seek God's forgiveness. No. He forgave them all their past and welcomed them, every one.

Meoraq glanced upward through the rough roof of the lodge's storeroom, properly chastened, and sheathed his blade. "I hear you, Father," he said. "Not so clearly as my wife, but I hear You and I am humble to Your will."

Sheul's hand touched his shoulder as below him, Crandall muttered something uncouth and kicked the walls of the underlodge that sheltered them in the wildlands where Gann ruled. Meoraq sighed, feeling the bitterness and anger in his mortal heart until he had mastered them and could set them aside. Then he turned away from the humans in his keeping and went out into Gann's world to hunt.

6

It did not take much work to make the underlodge habitable for a lengthy stay. Cleaning, of course. The crafting of various tools. The mantle shelf needed repairs, which Meoraq could manage, and half the cookware he was able to find had been broken, but the ways of working clay were unknown to him and they would just have to make do without. The one metal pot he'd found and his own stewing pouch were more than enough for his needs. If his woman were well and at his side to help him, the lodge would have been fit and comfortable by the second day. As it was, he had four lazy humans who seemed to think the job of improving their camp to be a show he enacted for their pleasure each day, and Amber, who would be only too willing to help and tear open her wound in the effort. So it all fell to him.

Nevertheless, it gave him something to do and so Meoraq worked. He fixed the shelf. He manufactured a simple grass sweep to get what had already come in out again. He found a way to turn one of the leather walls of his unneeded windbreak into a curtain so that the humans had 'their' half of the lodge and he didn't have to look at them as much. They were all much happier with that arrangement.

To further keep himself out of slapping distance, Meoraq took lengthy patrols, familiarizing himself with this land of hills and forests. He hunted when he had to, but one mimut each day was more than enough to sustain his small party, even after he relented and allowed the other humans to share his meals. He searched daily for medicinal herbs, but found no more healershand, only a little iseqash, and a small patch of wild phesok. He stared at this last discovery three days, meditated three nights, and then went back and took it, for despite the plant's dangers, he knew Amber would need it.

She had showed many encouraging signs of recovery in the first days. She drank as often as he gave the order, and although she required his help to make her way up the stairs and out to pass her waters, she did that often as well. She could not stand very long and had twice collapsed from the effort of climbing out of the cupboard (against his orders), but she rested well when sleeping and seemed alert when awake.

And all these things were very good, but Meoraq cleaned her wound at the start and close of each day, and he could see the infection growing in her. At first, it was only that yellowish crust around the edges of her wound, easily wiped away. Then the viscous pools of pus welling up around the beetle heads. Her skin swelled and grew hot. She needed more iseqash in her tea to sleep at night and began to ask for it during the day. As the pus thickened and took on a greenish tinge, her lethargy and confusion grew until she did little more than lie in the cupboard and stare into the fathoms. Then came the night he woke to her moans, struck a light and found her shined with sweat and insensible beside him, impossible to wake. When he opened her bandages, he could smell rot.

So be it.

Meoraq put his palm over her burning brow and bent close, his mouth against her flushed cheek. "Sheul has been with you, Soft-Skin," he told her quietly. "Believe that He is with you now. And so am I."

She moaned.

He covered her over with his blanket and left the cupboard, closing it gently behind him. It was early, well before dawn. The curtain that halved the living space was closed and the only sounds to be heard beyond it were the growling breaths Amber called snores. Moving quietly, so as not to disturb them (and Amber said he wasn't 'nice'), Meoraq cut the sleeve off one of their spare tunics (if the owner didn't want it cut, he shouldn't have left it on the floor), tied a knot in one end to form a crude sort of bag, then went up the stairs and out into the forest.

"O my Father, guide me now," he said, but he did not need Sheul to find what he was seeking. He had laid the bait for this most particular prey himself.

Near to the stream where he had brought his mimuts to be butchered lay a small, reeking heap—wet flaps of skin cut from the belly where winter's fat was thickest, tailbones and the sagging pouch of the anus, intestines, feet, ears. It was too cold in these early hours for the carrion-beetles to crawl droning over his offering, but he could hear their countless bodies grinding together deep in the rotting flesh.

Meoraq knelt and brought out his makeshift pouch. He lifted a rancid coil of intestine, unleashing a plume of steam and fresh stink into the air. The beetles burrowed deeper, leaving their offspring to squirm together, exposed to morning's chill.

Nauseating. He did not hesitate. He ran his open hand along the rumpled surface of rotting offal, taking exquisite care not to crush the larvae. He could not feel them in his hand, but seeing them there was bad enough. No matter. He shook them gently onto the sleeve and reached down for more. It took some effort to target only the larvae and not the mess they were feeding upon, but he had all he needed in just a few more passes and soon returned to the underlodge with the churning mess of them unpleasantly secured in the sleeve.

Amber had not moved, save to throw off her blanket. He let her alone for now while he arranged a fresh compress and bandage for her. Last of all, he took a dried leaf of phesok from the pot by the hearth and put it in his mouth. The taste was golden, surprisingly sweet, not at all what he'd expected. He chewed resolutely as he returned to his wife's side and cleaned away the old, soured dressings.

She moaned, but turned toward him when he put his hand on her cheek. He spat juice into her mouth. She sputtered, swallowed, panted, all without opening her eyes.

Meoraq watched her for a time, then grunted and brought out his carrion-beetle larvae. He shook out half of them and waited for them to burrow into her heat, spitting juice for her to drink when it overfilled his own mouth, then shook out the rest and covered them loosely with the compress. He was beginning to feel light-headed. Never mind. A Sheulek must be above the distractions of his flesh. Most distractions.

He sat in the cupboard with his woman, chewing and sometimes spitting, and ultimately beginning to sway just a little. Amber's face seemed to soften, blurring into new lines only to throb itself back into sharp focus. His Soft-Skin. His good woman. His wife. She was so unbelievably ugly.

He started to laugh, choked on a mouthful of juice, swallowed it, then laughed again because that was such a stupid thing to do. But a Sheulek does not make mistakes. Sheul is always with him. So there. He spat some juice into Amber and swallowed another mouthful (deliberately, this time), humming to himself as the colors began to shift around in the air, but humming quietly because the other humans were sleeping and he was so nice. Amber would be proud of him. His ugly, ugly Amber.

"I love your ugly face," he told her, then bent down to move his mouth parts against hers. Horrible, unsanitary thing to do, and it left her bleeding a little besides. Never mind.

"I love your ugly fur," he said, taking up many long, damp strands and spilling them through his fingers. It seemed that they kept on spilling for a very, very long time. The phesok was almost out of juice; he swallowed what there was and chewed harder.

Amber shifted below him in the bed, pushing more of the blanket away so that her bare chest was exposed. The sight attracted his staring eye and then his hand. "I love your ugly teats," he mused, stroking at them. His hand moved up. "And I love your beautiful shoulders."

Such beautiful shoulders. Smooth and pale as sculpted stone, perfectly rounded, perfectly sloping upwards into her scrawny neck and downwards into her skinny arms. Even the gross distortions on her chest seemed flawlessly balanced beneath those amazing shoulders.

He sucked hard on the pulp in his mouth, held it a moment, then bent reluctantly and spat it into Amber. She mewled a protest, but swallowed it. Her soft mouth, very lightly bleeding, parted for her panting breath. He could see the pink glisten of her tongue. Without warning, sexual urges swept over him, more dizzying than even the phesok in its strength. Meoraq loosened his belt, but his organ would not extrude. The urge died, leaving him with a confused re-discovery of her fevered face and the dressings at her side. It was unforgiveable, even to a Sheulek, for a man to lie with a woman on her sickbed; Sheul, in his wisdom, had prevented it. He spoke a shamed thanks, but already his eye was moving on, becoming fixed on the oddly graceful whorls and ridges that ringed her ear. He sucked on the phesok pulp again, but it had no more juice to give him. He spat it into his palm instead, shook it off into the other room, then closed the cupboard door and lay down beside his woman. He supposed he ought to pray, but couldn't quite focus on what words to say.

Meoraq pulled the blanket up around Amber's beautiful shoulders, then dropped a careful arm around her chest where it could not hurt her. 'I am cuddling,' he thought, pleased with himself. Then the dreams started, dreams of Amber beside him at Xi'Matezh reaching out to hold his hand when the doors hushed open, Amber sitting with him on the rooftop garden at home with the first of his many sons in her arms, Amber holding Nicci's hand as they waited in a long line of white-garbed people before a great glass-walled shrine. Always it was Amber, sometimes with him and sometimes with her blood-kin, now creased with age and now half-grown, fighting and laughing and weeping and in every way alive. The dreams were glorious and it was a very long time before Meoraq, reluctantly, closed his eyes and slept.

* * *

Amber woke up first to the sounds of people talking none too damn quietly in the main room. Not even really talking, but actually hollering up the stairs to other people outside, just like it wasn't first thing in the friggin' morning, which it had to be because Meoraq was still sound asleep beside her.

Her annoyance was the first thing she was really conscious of. The second was a tickling sort of sensation in her side. She started to scratch at it, but was smart enough to stop herself as soon as her fingers touched the bandage. She really did not want to tear herself a brand new gash now that it was finally starting to heal up. And it must be healing up because that's what things did when they healed, right? They itched? And even though this was more of a tickle, it tickled like six bitches in a bitch-boat, so it better be healing.

Ah, it was great to feel like herself again.

Amber smiled to herself without bothering to open her eyes. She sensed she could open her eyes if she wanted to, however, which was better than she'd felt all night. In fact, the last three days had been like trying to cross quicksand—sinking further and further the more she moved. Yesterday, she'd been absolutely certain she was going to die. The stench coming from her side had been so bad, she was amazed Meoraq could stand to touch her, but he didn't even mention it.

And maybe he knew something she didn't, because she felt worlds better this morning. Apart from a headache and an absolutely epic case of morning-mouth, but if that was what it took to wake up free of the fever that had been chasing her down, she'd learn to love it.

But the tickling...

Amber squirmed, as if shifting her weight could actually help. It didn't.

Out in the main room, Dag was stomping around and bitching about having to go all the way out to the stream for water when it was raining.

"Coming down hard enough," Crandall commented. "Could probably just stand outside with your mouth open and drink just fine."

"Give it another hour and you could probably drown that way," Eric added. "Sheesh, did the lizard die in there? What is keeping him?"

"Keep your voice down," Nicci said. "They're sleeping."

"Sleeping, hell," Crandall muttered. "They're probably screwing."

Amber frowned, then caught herself reaching to scratch again. Dammit, this was going to drive her crazy!

He'd put some sort of plant in there that first day. She didn't recall it itching—the pain had pretty much occupied all her nerve-endings at the time—but maybe that was the trouble now. He probably wouldn't like it if she just opened up her own bandage and took his leaves out, especially since they might be working, but she couldn't stand this and anyway, he was asleep and therefore did not get a vote.

Casting furtive glances at the alien snuggled up beside her, Amber began to extract herself from his uncharacteristically clingy grip. He slept on, oblivious, even when she picked his arm up and put it down again on her thigh. Next to go was the sweaty (and now smelly) blanket. She could see the bandage now. It wasn't even tied on. Maybe it tickled because it was loose. Felt like a bigger tickle than that, though. God, it was all she could do not to get in there with both hands and just go to town.

She pulled the bandage off, already reaching with her other hand to gingerly pick away whatever voodoo he'd packed in there. For a moment, she thought it was rice.

For a moment.

Her breath caught, but she sucked it in and shrieked anyway, tearing up her throat like her screams were made of fishhooks. Meoraq bolted up, banged his head, and dropped back down with a snarl of sound she could not begin to process, much less translate. If she hadn't been frozen by horror, she might have dug the maggots out then, but the split-second it took for her to act was all the time he needed to recover. When she did slap wildly at the boiling mass of their pearly little bodies, he caught her.

"The hell is going on in there?"

"Getthemoffmegetthemoffme*getthemoffme!*"

"What is wrong with you, woman?! Lie still!"

She fought, but there was no fighting, not before he straddled her thighs and bore down on her from above, and certainly not after. Kicking was futile under the blanket. Bucking dislodged some of the maggots, but only so they could rain their repulsive little bodies down over her stomach and her hip and oh God what if one bounced high enough to land in her mouth?!

Screaming for release, screaming for help...just screaming. It was all she knew, all she was capable of. *There were maggots in her*!

Then the cupboard door flew open and there was her baby sister's half-glimpsed face, staring at the lizard atop her in open-mouthed shock. And then she screamed.

Meoraq looked around, startled, because even an alien had to know that wasn't a human scream of fear, but of rage. Little Nicci dove at him, clawing for his eyes, so that Meoraq was forced to release one of Amber's twisting arms to shove her back. Amber immediately went for the maggots. He caught her again, swearing vigorously, and pushed her arms together, wrists-to-elbows. Now able to restrain them one-handed, he reared back and whipped his belt off. He used it to bind Amber's arms together so that she was unable to scratch anything but her own arms, which she did in helpless panic.

The next time Nicci came for him, he was ready. He caught her in one hand and dragged her with him as he flipped athletically from the cupboard onto the floor, and from there across the room to the water bucket, where he dunked her head repeatedly.

Nicci's screams turned to sputters. Amber's went on, but they were dying in spite of her, torn to hoarse shreds by their own violence. No one else was making a sound.

Meoraq turned in a full circle, hauling Nicci with him, to face off against the rest of them. "Are you all mad or is it just your women?"

"Hey, do what you want with them," said Crandall, holding up both hands as Amber howled for help.

Meoraq tossed Nicci in a heap by the hearth where she curled herself up small, sobbing, and returned to the cupboard. He studied Amber while she struggled in her bondage, then reached out and laid his hand over her mouth.

She stared up at him in weepy dismay, unable to believe he could be so calm when there were bugs eating her.

"I have Gann's own headache," he informed her after a moment's meditation. "So I am going to ask just once what is wrong with you and you are going to answer quietly. Now. What is wrong with you?"

He removed his hand.

"I'm rotting," she whispered, and felt tears drop hotly out of her even though she couldn't blink. "I'm rotting! There's maggots in me!"

Behind him, the others recoiled and immediately began to mutter at one another. None of them looked very upset, only a little wary and a lot disgusted.

Meoraq, on the other hand, just kept staring at her. After a while, he closed his eyes and went someplace private with his God. He was gone a long time. His eyes opened. His head cocked, demonstrating resignation and some small amount of humor. He took a deep breath and said, "I know there are maggots in you, insufferable woman. I put them there."

And as Amber still reeled from that, he bent down and began to put them back.

The panic was gone and the adrenaline with it. She could do nothing but sob out wailing, incoherent pleas as he scraped up all the disturbed maggots and placed them carefully back in the wound. He put the compress back on. He loosely tied the bandage. Then, in that same calm, deliberate, God-alone-knows-how-hard-it-is-not-to-slap-you-woman voice, he said, "The maggots eat only dead flesh. They will clean your wound and at day's end, I will wash them away."

Amber cried harder.

"They will eat the beetles as well, but—"

"*Beetles*?!"

"—but you have had many good days of healing, and—"

"You put *beetles* in me too?!"

"—and I think the wound will not reopen if you are careful." He gave the bandage a final light tug and glared at her. "Being careful means you will lie still. Agreed?"

Still weeping, she made herself nod.

He unbound her arms. She had to keep clutching her elbows to stop herself from immediately grabbing at her side. She could feel him looking at her, his stare almost as physical a thing as his irritation.

His thumb brushed at her cheek. That was all for a while.

"Get out," he said, adding crossly, "Not you," when she tried to sit up. "The rest of you. Get out."

"It's raining."

Meoraq clamped both hands suddenly to his brow-ridges and bellowed, "*I don't care*!"

Dag wisely shut his mouth and backed away.

After a minute and several deep breaths, Meoraq began to speak in the tight, rapid way of the kind of anger he usually reserved for dealing with Amber herself: "God has given me the strength thus far not to knock the head off your skinny neck but don't try His patience, human, because *mine is gone*!" he finished at a shout and had to stop for some more deep breathing. "I suffer your presence as a gift to my woman's gentle heart and for no other reason, so get up and leave my camp one damned hour or be turned out for all time at the point of my blade! Don't whine at me! *Go*!"

A shuffle of feet and murmurs marked their obedience, but sniffling told her Nicci, at least, had stayed.

Meoraq let her. He sat down on the edge of the bed, prodded broodingly once at his brow-ridges, and then put his hand on Amber's thigh and waited.

What was she supposed to tell him? Knowing intellectually that the maggots served a useful and even necessary purpose meant nothing compared to the feel of them crawling and writhing inside her own body. Inside her own meat! It wasn't just a bunch of maggots, it was a premonition of her own mortality in a universe without a God—a playful sampling of an afterlife in which she was nothing but food for the lowest forms of mindless life—and Meoraq could never begin to comprehend that. Oh no, he rode around in God's back pocket all the damn time!

"I dreamed of you," he said suddenly, softly. He continued to gaze out into the main room and not at her, but his hand again brushed back, this time along her shoulder. "I dreamed much. Awake and asleep."

Amber pressed her palms over her eyes and made herself take deep, slow breaths until she finally quit leaking. The maggots rolled and wriggled and dug themselves around under the compress; knowing what they were, she could no longer feel them as anything so benign as a tickle. She'd probably never feel a real tickle again quite the same way, either. She had god-fucking-damn larvae crawling around inside her and he was talking about his dreams!

"They're in me, Meoraq," she said shakily. "They're eating me like I'm already dead."

He sighed. "I know. And I suppose it is terrible. Yet you live, Soft-Skin. You live and will be well."

"For how long? God! Why are you trying so hard to save me?"

She meant her outburst for him, but he apparently took it for a prayer, because after a respectful silence, he grunted and said, "What does He tell you?"

"He? What, you mean God?" Momentarily unpinned, Amber erupted into giggles just as fantastically inappropriate as her hysterics had been. "He tells me I'm going to need saving for the rest of my stupid life, that's what He tells me!"

And Meoraq nodded, either oblivious to her sarcasm or pretending to be. "Then I will always be there to save you."

"Oh for—Leave me alone, lizardman! Let me die already! I've done nothing but get hurt from the moment we got here. This isn't fair!" she burst out, once more on the brink of hateful tears. "I don't get hurt! I'm the strong one!"

"Yes," he said, with no trace of irony.

The dam was good and broken now. It all came flooding out of her—not tears, but words—in a hot sluice of emotion as bitter as bile: "I hate this! I hate lying here day after goddamn day staring at the top of this goddamn cupboard! I hate riding around in your stupid sled and watching you have to carry me! I hate that every single fucking creature on this planet wants to eat me and half of them have tried! And I hate you telling me it's all God's will!"

"His will is great, Soft-Skin. There is room for all things in His eye."

"If God actually wants me to lie here with maggots in my guts, I want no part of him. I hate your God!"

It was the worst thing she could think of to say to him—the most vicious, blasphemous, mean thing to say—and she did it half-hoping he would walk out and give the tears struggling inside her an easy way out. Instead, he snorted, as if she'd told a joke that was perhaps in poor taste but still very funny.

She stared at his back for a long time as anger was replaced by exhaustion. The itch in her side just grew and grew with every passing helpless second.

"And I hate you," she whispered.

"Lies."

"What can I say?" Amber asked at last, her voice raw and shaking. "What can I say to make you leave me?"

"Try insulting my father," he suggested.

"Stop making fun of me! I can't do this, Meoraq! I can't spend the rest of my life being your God-given burden!"

"Your trials are mine, Soft-Skin. As you learn from them, so do I."

"Bullshit."

"Truth."

"What are you learning right this second?" she demanded.

"Patience." He glanced upwards. "I learn that a lot when I'm with you."

Amber clapped her hands over her face again. "You're a zealot."

"And you hate me," he prompted.

Again, he waited. She did not reply, but her hand went to the bandage at her side, wanting to scratch but tortured by the image of crushing their disgusting little bodies into slurry right inside her.

He did not look at her, but must have been able to track her hand regardless, because he said, "It will heal."

"But there'll always be something else. Something worse."

"Such is life."

"I don't want to live like this." Her hand went to her side again, rubbing sickly at the skin around the bandage since she didn't dare touch the actual site. Her stomach cramped; she might survive the maggots, but honesty had turned toxic and there was nothing she could do but keep on puking it up. "And don't feed me that what-doesn't-kill-you-makes-you-stronger bullshit! What doesn't kill me just makes me *worse*! I don't want to be *ugly* like this!" She scratched miserably at the places that didn't itch, scratched until she felt blood wet beneath her fingernails, until he reached back his hand and stopped her.

"No warrior should be ashamed of the scars he carries. Each one is proof of courage. Even this one." He touched the pink marks of his teeth he'd left her with on the night they'd first been together. "Perhaps particularly this one." His eyes shifted to meet hers. "You are mine."

"Because God gave me to you." She tried to say it in her old tough-Amber voice, but it came out in a lost crybaby-girlie way instead, all the sarcasm lost in a quaver. "Thanks a lot, huh?"

He grunted, gazed at her for a long moment of silent thought, and just when she thought he was about to speak, he bent down and kissed her.

His rough mouth scoured across her lips as gently as she supposed he could do it, considering he couldn't feel what he was doing. His breath, warm and dry and tasting faintly stale, blew in to mingle with hers. His tongue, hard and smooth as wax, nudged into her, inviting at first and then demanding.

She felt nothing at all for a second or two, and then something inside her seemed to erupt and she was kissing him back the way a drowning woman drinks air. Her hands dug at the back of his neck, pulling him closer even as their mouths mashed painfully together, and closer was never close enough. She sucked and bit and ground at him, making all the semi-mute, unlovely sounds of carnal desperation, and for God's sake, Nicci was still sitting right over there, but as soon as his hand skimmed beneath the blanket to grip her bare breast, she didn't care and wouldn't have cared if they'd been center-stage in front of thirty thousand people.

"You are my—" He snapped his bone-hilted knife out of its sheath and stabbed it down over the head of the bed. "—insufferable—" His mouth scraped at hers, licked away a bead of blood, and came back for another kiss. "—senseless—" The hand at her breast rasped over her skin in a sudden, urgent journey to delve between her ready thighs. "—faithful wife."

"Don't!" she moaned, even as she bucked up against his questing hand. "I wasn't! You know I wasn't and you don't want me anymore!"

"Shall I swear it before God?" His hand moved, stroking steadily and with embarrassing ease in and out. He looked down at it, his eyes smoked and hungry. "Upon this altar, all vows are surely made sacred. Let Him hear me. Let you hear me."

She cried, clutching at him.

"You are always for me, Soft-Skin. Though your nearness and infirmity are a terrible trial upon my years of discipline, I will stand fast with the aid of God against my natural lusts. And when you are whole again, I will fill you. Between those hours, and for every other hour from now until the end of Time, *you are for me.*" He paused to watch with grimacing, lizard-like satisfaction as she came to a swift, violent climax. His hand stilled, but stayed where it was, cupping and not quite caressing her. "This day will end," he said, softly. "You and I will go on."

She caught his hand as he withdrew it, clutching it in both of hers and holding it to her heaving chest. He waited, but she couldn't find the words to fit the storm of thoughts howling through her, and at last he pulled from her grip.

"Rest now, Soft-Skin," he told her, standing up and away from the cupboard. The first thing he did was to cinch his belt even tighter, which she guessed meant he was concerned about protruding. The thought made her smile, and he ducked back inside to claim that smile with another of his harsh kisses. "When you wake, I will have tea for you. It will be bitter and unpleasant and you will drink it all."

"Meoraq—"

He put his hand over her mouth, his eyes sternly narrowed. "And you will drink it all, woman. Give me your obedience."

She rolled her eyes and raised her fist.

He tipped his head and gave her a warning hiss, then removed his hand.

"Yeah, fine. I'll drink it all." She sighed and lay back in the cupboard, rubbing at her side.

He glanced at her hand, then stepped away. He didn't tell her not to remove her bandages. He didn't have to. The maggots itched and ate at her every bit as much as they had before, but she guessed she could handle it. She hated it...but she could handle it.

He dressed, muttering to himself as he strapped on weapons and buckled things. The words she caught were enough to tell her it was one of his many prayers, this one on her behalf. When he was done, he came back to tap her shoulder briefly in a parting salute, and then he left. Her man, off about his manly business.

Amber pulled her blanket up with a sigh and tried to get comfortable. Her side itched. Her stomach still hurt from all the emotional craziness. She had a huge pot of bitter tea to look forward to and plenty of cupboard ceiling to stare at until then. It was going to be a long day.

'Yeah, but the day will end,' she thought, and smiled.

"I thought he was hurting you."

Oh yeah. Nicci was still here. Amber felt herself blush a little, but only a little. Mostly, she just felt sexy and quiet and tired and good.

"No," she said. "I'm sorry. I flipped out completely." Yeah. Flipped out. Right before she made out. Could you still call it making out when someone rubbed you into cumming from your toenails? Probably not. Sheesh, what a sleazeball she'd turned into.

"He's different with you," Nicci said.

"Is he?" She really didn't think so, but upon reflection, she decided it might seem that way. He was himself with her. He was different with the others.

"You're different with him."

"Am I?" That was less surprising. She'd been different since she first set foot on this planet. Nicci just wasn't used to the whiny, weepy, hysterical Amber yet.

Nicci got up and came over to the cupboard, looking down at her with an expression that was disturbingly lifeless. "I want to go home."

Amber stared up at her, more than a little thrown by this statement. What did she honestly expect her to do about it?

"Do you?" Nicci asked.

She still had no answer.

"If we get to this temple and there's a ship there and someone can fly it and we can go back to Earth, are you coming with me?"

Amber's mouth moved. No sound came out.

"If there isn't a ship," said Nicci, "are you going to take care of me?"

"Nicci—"

"Or do you think you've done enough? After you brought me here, after you made me come with you, are you just going to wash your hands and say you've done enough? You got your man who loves you and will take care of you and save you forever, so maybe you don't care anymore, but I'm still here, Amber. I still need you."

"I'm here," said Amber, reaching out to touch her arm. There was no answering touch, not even a glance in that direction. It was like touching a corpse. "And I'll always be here for you, Nicci. We're sisters. Nothing's going to change that. Look, I know it's hard, but you can do it. I'm sure I'll have plenty of time to sit around. I can teach you how to make hides and clothes and stuff."

"You said you'd always take care of me."

"I am."

"Not like you used to."

Amber nodded, accepting this, then shook her head, and then just sat there and stared at the cupboard ceiling. "I don't think I did either of us any favors hovering over you like that back home," she said at last. "Mama wasn't much of a mother...and neither was I. I love you, Nicci, I do..." She sighed and rubbed her eyes, then made herself turn around and face her expressionless sister without flinching. "...but I'm not going to carry you for the rest of your life. The ship crashed and I'm sorry...but it's time to move on."

Nicci said nothing, did nothing, just let the minutes tick out. At last, she reached out and gently closed the cupboard door, leaving Amber in the dark to listen as her baby sister walked away.

* * *

The remainder of the day passed in relative peace, although given the chaos surrounding his awakening, anything short of a direct attack could be considered relative peace. The humans kept their distance, wisely. Meoraq's headache had lost its sharp edges over the course of the day, but it still sat heavy behind his eyes. He had drunk four pots of tea and his throat still felt scratchy and tasted like a long lick up Gann's slit. He was aware that all these things made a light penance for the sin of chewing phesok, but it still made for a deeply unpleasant day.

He meditated as much of it away as possible, rousing only to attend his or his woman's most basic bodily needs. When he wasn't meditating, he sat at the table and stared at his humans, making a game of herding them from one wall to the other by his looks alone. He made no patrols, no hunts. When he decided he was hungry enough, he ate half of the previous day's stew, cold. If Amber had asked, he would have stirred himself to heat the rest for her, but she claimed a weak belly and took nothing but tea all day. As for the other humans, they could eat cold stew or starve for all that Meoraq cared.

All days end, as he had reminded his wife that morning. In the last quiet hour before dark, his day's idleness bit back at him in an entirely foreseeable manner: He was not in the least tired.

His humans were already settling in for the night, sharing out the remains of the stew and throwing sullen glances at him. That cheered him somewhat, but it really was a poor show of his true character and he ought to pray about it. In the meantime, however, there was Amber.

Although she had been dozing most of the day, she did not share his restlessness now. She was sleeping soundly when he woke her to tend her wound. The maggots had done their work well; the flesh looked pink and had a strong knit going where the beetle heads had been placed. He washed the wound twice with tea and licked it thoroughly, ignoring Amber's informative mutterings as to how 'gross' he was.

But with this done and the wound wrapped again, he had nothing else to do. If he were in the city, Meoraq could simply light a lamp and read the Word or take the rooftop or find some other way to entertain himself, but he was loathe to waste what little lamp oil he'd brought with him out of Chalh. In their winter's camp, when he had spent days on end confined to a cave, he'd always had the option of rigorous sex to exhaust himself before bed. He didn't know what he was going to do with himself tonight.

"Are you tired?" he asked, without much hope.

"Yeah. Why? What's up?" She visibly rallied herself to appear alert. A good woman was always thinking of how to lessen her man's burdens and see to his needs. Meoraq's selfish heart burned a little, but not enough to keep him from undressing and crawling into the cupboard with her.

"We going to fool around?" she whispered when the door was shut. Her hands were brazen on his back. Her little teeth nipped at his shoulder.

"No," he said. "That would be unforgiveable."

"Oh." She drew away and nestled herself into the bedding. "Good. Because in all honesty, I had maggots in me all day and I'm feeling about the most unsexy I've ever felt in my life. Want to talk?"

He did, but she was so obviously weary and he didn't have anything to say anyway. "Just sleep."

She did—the only command he'd ever given that she'd followed without question—and he lay with her in the cupboard for a time, resting in the hopes that he might sleep as well, but it was not to be. He could hear the humans bedding down, their low chat giving way to grunts and shuffling, and then to the growling breaths of heavy sleep. Meoraq tried to meditate, but his mind was as restless as his clay and in the end, he rose and pulled his breeches on, then climbed to the surface where he couldn't disturb anyone.

The night was warm and windy, but dry yet. He basked a short while in the pleasant sensation of standing against the wind and what a fierce, masculine picture it must make, and then heard the clumsy tread of a human footfall on the stair behind him. Nicci, he saw. He reminded himself to be polite.

"How is she?" Nicci asked quietly.

"She rests in Sheul's sight," he replied, moving aside in case she wished to go past him and out to the fleshing pit to urinate.

She joined him at the doorway, but that was all. Her eyes went to the horizon, to the distant black line before the mountains that was Praxas. She gazed on it in silence and without expression.

Meoraq groped for something to say as the moment stretched itself indefinitely outward. "What do you want?" he asked at last.

"Nothing. I can't sleep."

He grunted, thinking she might manage a better effort were she lying down with her eyes closed. Of course, so could he.

"I'm sorry I, um, attacked you. Earlier."

He glanced at her, then back into the trees. "I forgive you."

He waited for her to leave. She didn't.

"Am I bothering you?" she asked.

Meoraq tipped a brooding eye upwards at the heavens where Sheul sat in judgment over every lie and told one anyway. "No."

"Can I stand with you?"

He grunted again.

She moved a little closer to him. There was no polite way to step back, so he stood there and did his best to ignore her. After a very long, suffocating silence, she said, "You saved our lives. All of us. I thought I was going to die in that cage."

He was uncomfortable responding to this in any way—to agree was to take the credit for Sheul's hand upon him, to deny seemed to dismiss her suffering in that place—and so he said, "Sheul's judgment shall fall upon Praxas in His own time," and tried to leave it at that.

"I know."

There was an answer he had never anticipated. "Do you?"

"If He hadn't been with me, I never would have survived at all," she told him, and watched his face closely.

He turned into the wind, aware that he was frowning, unsure exactly why. It had certainly been a good answer...but he could not shake the feeling that it had not been an honest one.

"Will you take a walk with me?" she asked after another grueling silence.

"Why?"

"I'm restless and I don't want to go anywhere alone."

Sensible answer. He did not want to agree, but this was Amber's blood-kin, and if blood ran true in no other manner, doubtless it would do so now and she would stride out into the wild without him upon his refusal.

"A short walk," he said, and set a course for the stream.

She followed obediently, beside and a little behind him, with head bent and hands meekly clasped before her. It was deeply disturbing to him, and after a moment's thought, he knew why: It was the respectful walk of a well-bred dumaq woman at the side of her man. Realizing that, he tried to put some distance between them. She reached out and caught his hand. It took all his will not to pull out of that flimsy human grip, but only to walk, staring straight ahead and leaving his hand limp and unfeeling in hers.

It had never been so long a distance to the water. He had actually begun to think he had somehow lost his way when he heard it ahead of him in the same place it had always been. He checked for tracks out of habit, but no sooner had he hunkered beside the muddy bank than she was kneeling next to him, resting her hand upon his thigh. A light touch, surely. A thoughtless touch, perhaps. He could think of no good way to throw it off and so he stared fixedly into the ground with his damned thigh on fire under her unwelcome hand and wished he knew what the hell she was on about.

Of all his wishes, that was the one Sheul chose to grant.

Nicci kept her hand where it was, then turned toward him and placed the other with deliberate intent into his breeches and beneath his loin-plate. The tip of her wind-chilled finger slipped along his slit, seeking entry, but only for a moment. The world crashed back into focus; Meoraq shoved her violently away, slapping one hand to his groin and actually rubbing, as if her touch came with some polluted grease. Such was his horror in that moment that if she'd come at him again, he would have drawn and stabbed her.

But she didn't. She sprawled across the bank of the stream and began to run water out of her eyes. "It's okay," she wept, trying to smile at him. "It's okay. I won't tell. I know you want to. It's fine."

He took two swift backwards steps, well out of her reach. "I don't want this! I don't want you!"

"I'm just the same as she is!" she pleaded, wiping mud onto her face with every swipe of her hand. "We look the same! We sound the same! You can do anything you want to me and you can...you can take care of me!"

And there it was. Shock died at once, crushed by the weight of his sudden disgust. "Take care of you."

She crawled toward him in the muck, fumbling at her clothes, the shadows of her face in the moonlight such that it seemed a skull leered at him and it took every measure of his will not to draw his father's blade and ram it through her throat. "I can be good," she was saying. She might have been weeping or laughing as she said it, he could not tell which. "You can do everything you like that you'd never ask Amber. You can hurt me if you want to. You can—"

"*Get away from me*!" he roared, and that at last stopped her. She huddled at his feet, poised upon her knees with her bare chest exposed to him, motionless and watchful while he paced the urge to slap out of his body. When he wheeled abruptly and came back to her, she did not cringe, only lifted her head a little higher and reached out her hands.

He caught her by the wrists before she could touch him and pulled her roughly up before shoving her back. He eyed the growths on her chest with disgust and turned away. "Cover yourself."

She did, silent and small.

"She is my wife and your blood-kin," he said tightly, facing furiously into the wind. "This is incest! Blasphemy before Sheul!"

She uttered a high, shivery sound. He was fairly certain it was a laugh, but a laugh such as the damned must use, once death and eternity had driven them mad.

"Do you think you're any different from them?" she asked, scorn like knives in her querulous words. "Do you really? God makes it happen, remember? It's not a sin because God made them want me, right? So if it's God's will, what are you afraid of?" She came toward him, her mouth a black and ghastly crescent of a smile, to put her hands on him again. "What does *Sheul* want you to do with me?"

"Kill you."

She flinched back, her smile lost at once. The wind smeared water across her cheeks. "I'm just the same as she is," she said in her fragile voice.

"No," said Meoraq. "You are not. And if you ever touch me again, I will see you judged for it. Hear me, N'ki, and mark the word of a Sheulek. It is for her sake alone that I do not cut you down right here. When she hears of this—"

"Don't tell," she whispered. "Please, don't. She'll hate me."

"She should!" Meoraq spat, but then took a slow count of six and cleared his heart of Gann's grip. "This once. Because she is weakened...and so happy to be with you again," he added in a bitter rush. He breathed some more. "Go."

She slipped away like a shadow on the grass. Meoraq did not watch her. He took six breaths and six more and then knelt on the wet bank to pray until peace found him. He stood, breathed, and knelt again, this time to ask for healing for his good woman and the strength and patience to tend the humans with whose care he had been charged. He stood, breathed, and knelt a final time, wetting his fingers with mud and painting his naked chest. He prayed, and in that silent prayer were thoughts of black gratitude that Sheul had held him fast against Nicci's hand, because for a moment...

He stood, brushed the dried flakes of mud from his scales, then returned to the underlodge alone. He did not look for Nicci among the sleeping humans at the wall. He went to his cupboard. His woman roused halfway to raise the bedding and let him come beneath, then snuggled close and began to growl softly in her sleeping breaths, the way she claimed not to do. He held her, loving her, hating Nicci—Gann and Sheul each with a hand on his heart—and lay awake for hours.

7

Being hurt sucked.

It wasn't the pain. The pain was extremely present, but Amber could handle pain. What she couldn't handle, at least not with any good grace, was the boredom.

Amber knew how it felt to recover from whatever had bitten her that day back in the prairie. She remembered the weakness—needing to be carried, to be fed, to be tended like some...some sick person. But she also knew that it hadn't lasted long. She'd been pretty out of it for a while, but once the fever broke, she was on her feet and walking in just five more days. Maybe not at her full speed, but walking.

But five days after Meoraq washed the maggots out of her side, Amber felt no better. She wasn't walking, full speed or any speed; she still needed help just getting upstairs to pee. The pain gradually subsided, but she was always cold, always dizzy, always tired. She wasn't getting better.

"Nothing's happening!" she moaned as Meoraq carried her outside on Day Eighteen. "What's wrong with me?"

"You lost a lot of blood," he replied. "Sheul can heal your flesh, but blood takes time to renew."

"It's taking too long."

"Stop whining. Try to see this as a time of leisure. Enjoy it."

Enjoy it. Amber's experience in the cave in the mountains should have prepared her for a lot of lying around doing nothing, but what she'd failed to consider was that, in the mountains, she'd hadn't done much nothing at all. She and Meoraq had managed to keep busy most days, and on those rare occasions when they'd run out of busywork, there was always sex. These days, sex was as far out of the question as walking up the stairs.

All she could do was lie there.

Meoraq kept busy, because he was sadistic like that, but he refused to let her out of the cupboard. He got to bustle around the underlodge doing minor repairs and arranging things in their limited space until it was almost homey. He got to do all the cooking and cleaning and hunting. He got to scrounge up pieces of wood and carve them into various utensils, which he did in a yellow-striped state of high piss-off and which he would not allow her to do for him, even though there was no good reason why not, unless he thought she was going to maim herself some more. She told him as much in one of her surlier moods. He shut the cupboard door on her.

And that was how the time passed. Meoraq hunted, gathered, patrolled, prayed, built, repaired, replaced. Eric and Dag and Crandall had occasional spasms of productivity, doing whatever small tasks Meoraq assigned them without complaining, or at least complaining in a laughing way. Even Nicci, who did little and said less, wandered in and out whenever her odd moods took her. Amber lay in the cupboard and grew blood.

Meoraq washed and licked her wounds twice each day, and while he often told her she was healing well, he never said she was going to be as good as new. The kipwe's claws had left three broad furrows in her side, which Meoraq's bug-based first-aid had twisted into a godawful mess. The baby-new skin growing there was pink and shiny and unbelievably sensitive; the scar tissue knotted up in it, thick and white and dead. Sunk in the middle of this was a narrow depression, slightly askew, like a second, drunken belly-button.

She hated to look at herself under the blanket, so much so that every time Meoraq left the underlodge, she snuck out and put her tunic on. For Meoraq, wearing clothes in bed made about as much sense as wearing them in the bathtub—something which was not merely unnecessary but a little bit crazy. He'd come home and take them off her. She'd sneak out and put them on. After a few days of this, he made some ridiculously mild remark she couldn't even remember now and she'd burst into tears and cried until she got a headache. He immediately handed over her clothes, which made her cry harder.

And that was something else, the emotional stuff. Like a playground seesaw with tears on one end and throwing up on the other, as her bouts of unplanned puking slacked off, the equally sudden crying jags picked up. She felt like a crazy person and she had no one to talk to about it.

"You're pregnant," said Nicci, the one time she'd tried to bring it up.

"Oh bullshit."

"When was your last period?"

"I don't know." But she knew it had been in the cave where she and Meoraq had spent the winter. And she knew she'd finished not too terribly long before they'd left.

"When were you supposed to get it?"

"I don't know! Quit talking like that!"

Nicci did, but now the thought was there, itching under her scales, as Meoraq would say. It had been thirty-two days already by that time. She knew because the interior walls of the cupboard were made of bricks, cut from some sort of chalky stone, aged to a dark grey, but which left nice white lines when chipped at with the sharp tip of Meoraq's kzung. Thirty-two days and change since Crandall had watched her bathing and decided she was 'putting the belly back on'. Thirty-two days and change plus however long she'd been with Zhuqa, plus the six days it had taken to climb down out of the mountains, plus however many days it had been since she'd finished her period. And that was way too long.

Never mind. It didn't mean anything. She'd get it when it was time to get it and she sure as hell wasn't in any hurry for that to happen before she could at least walk herself out to clean up.

She waited. That was it. That was all she could do.

So she did it.

* * *

Amber woke up to the cupboard door sliding open. She kept her eyes shut until she heard the familiar sound of his strikers scraping together, but after he got the lamp lit, she raised her head to watch Meoraq go through his usual morning stretches with her usual morning depression. He caught her looking, paused mid-flex, then abruptly stopped and got dressed.

"Are you awake?" he asked, meaning, 'Are you going back to sleep or do I have to carry you upstairs now?'

"Yeah, probably. You go ahead, though."

He grunted and left without a goodbye or a backwards glance.

Amber reached out and groped until she found Meoraq's sword-belt hanging on the cupboard door. She unclipped his kzung and made the day's mark.

"Do you guys have to talk so much?" Crandall muttered behind the curtain.

"What do you want us to do, pass each other notes?" Amber replaced the kzung and rolled onto her back, staring at the familiar and hated sight of the cupboard ceiling.

She could hear Eric muttering, probably telling Crandall not to be such a dick first thing in the morning, because the next thing she heard was an angry sigh and

Crandall saying, "How you feeling, Bierce?"

"Got a stitch in my side," she replied flatly. She said that every time someone asked her that. One of these days, it was going to be funny.

"See? She's fine."

Now it was Dag muttering, but it was Eric who got up. He pulled back the curtain to open up the room, folded his blanket, packed his pack—a Fleetman still, after all this time—and came over to the cupboard. "Let me see it," he said.

Amber's hand clenched on the blanket over her side. "Fuck you! Why?"

"Because it's making you miserable to keep it a secret. Let me see."

Amber stared at the ceiling for a few more seconds, hoping he'd go away, not enough to actually tell him to go away, then finally threw back the blanket and lifted her tunic to the waist.

"Wow." Eric's eyebrows rose appreciatively. "That's pretty gruesome."

She felt herself relax without ever feeling herself tighten up. She'd been so sure she was about to hear him tell her all the ways it wasn't so bad when it plainly was. "Yeah," she said and looked at it herself. It was just as ugly as it had been yesterday, but for some reason, with Eric standing there, it also looked rounder. Her stomach clenched; the scars buckled.

"Does it hurt?"

"Not anymore. Sometimes, if I move just right, it kinda stretches and feels tight, you know? And sometimes the new skin hurts if you touch it." She prodded at the dimple, resisting the urge to shudder. It felt firm, if alien and horrible. She was not getting fat. "Feels like wax."

Eric touched her stomach. She could feel the heat of his hand, but not the texture. Looking at her scars, Eric said, "I don't think anyone's said this yet, but you really showed your stuff out there."

She frowned, ready to be offended if that was the insult it sounded like. "Is that a joke?"

"I don't mean just the porcupine-thing. I mean how you went after it. For us. After everything..." He looked her in the eye at last, his hand heavy over her unfeeling scars. "You even stood up for Scott and I know you don't like him. I guess...I guess you deserve to hear someone say thanks."

She hadn't realized how completely she'd given up on that until she felt how shocked she was to finally hear it. Her mouth was actually open. She was gaping.

"I'd really like it if we could start over," said Eric. "I realize that's asking a lot, but...Do you remember when I told you how friends matter?"

"Yeah."

"I was trying to tell you how important it was for you to get along with us." Eric smiled crookedly. "We really should have been making more of an effort to get along with you. It's not too late, is it?"

Eric's direct stare was getting hard to meet. Amber looked away and, like a ghost in a bad movie, Meoraq's head was there, floating in the shadows just over Eric's left shoulder.

Eric saw something in her face. He turned around and promptly tried to jump back, banging his shoulders into the cupboard frame and his hand into the door in his hurry to take it off her. "Oh, you're back. That was quick," he said, trying to laugh.

Meoraq did not respond, unless you counted a very slight tilting of his head.

Obviously, Eric knew what that meant now. "We were just talking," he said, holding up his hands.

Meoraq didn't answer, even with a grunt. He also didn't step back, forcing Eric to retreat by sidling along the cupboard door until he had enough room to make a dive for the stairs. Meoraq watched him go, then glanced back at the others.

Dag and Nicci got up immediately and left the underlodge. Crandall followed at his own deliberate pace, laughing.

When they were gone, Meoraq unexpectedly flared his mouth open in a lizardish grin and coughed laughter of his own.

"Tell me you didn't scare the crap of him just because you could," Amber said.

"He put his hand on you," Meoraq replied with a casual shrug. He went to light a fire in the hearth. "How did it feel?"

"His hand? What kind of question—"

"His words. His..." Meoraq snorted with extra-special sarcasm. "...gratitude."

"Don't say it like that," said Amber, annoyed. "At least he's making an effort."

"He certainly is," Meoraq murmured, smiling.

"What the hell is that supposed to mean?"

Meoraq set the heat stones in the fire to warm up, filled his stewing pouch with water and hung the half-emptied flask back on the wall. He was still smiling.

At last, exasperated beyond belief, she got it. "You think he was coming on to me, don't you?"

"I suspect that is just what I think."

Amber slammed the cupboard door on him.

He opened it and leaned inside, spines relaxed, smirking. "How long would you say we've been here?"

Amber moved the blanket and checked her notches. "Fifty-three days," she said and heard, like a ghost of a ghost, Nicci whisper, *When was your last period*? She shivered.

Meoraq didn't notice. His spines were at full attention as he leaned into the cupboard to look at her calendar. "Why are you defacing my bed?"

"It's how prisoners keep track of time where I'm from," she told him, making sure there was an extra emphasis on 'prisoners'. "Don't change the subject."

"I don't have a subject. I merely observe that a man doesn't take fifty-three days to say things he feels strongly about. He had another motive."

"You don't believe that," said Amber, watching him withdraw to his chair at the table.

"You sound very sure."

"He still has the hand he put on me."

"Ha! But I don't need to defend my woman from his conquest," he added. "She defends herself."

It was praise and she knew it, but all the same, she felt that phantom tug of resistance as the fish hook tore through flesh, felt the sting where Zhuqa's heat splashed over her eyes, tasted blood and cum in her mouth. She defended herself all right. Fierce little thing that she was.

She couldn't hide that shiver. Meoraq noticed, but obviously didn't know what to make of it. "Are you angry?" he asked cautiously, flaring his spines to suggest that, if she were, he was prepared to insist he was not at fault until she agreed with him.

"No. I'm not, I just...hate lying here!" she finished in a sudden illogical rush of fury. She shoved the door over as far as it could go and swung her legs out, sitting up. When Meoraq only twitched his spines, she stood. After another pause to assess him, she walked over to the table and stood in front of him.

"How do you feel?" he asked.

"Fine."

He raised his chin, his eyes narrowing.

"A little shaky," she admitted and sat with relief on the table.

"Truth," he declared, leaning out to put the first heat stone in the water.

"But that's only because you never let me get up."

"Evil Uyane," he agreed and hissed to himself, heaping embers over the remaining stones. "Vindictive brunt, who in his cruelty, would not allow his wife to tear open her soft skin."

"My skin has been all sealed up for days."

"Only in seeming."

"I'm better now," she insisted.

"Truth, but 'better' is not 'healed'."

"When are we leaving?" she asked.

"When leaving will not kill you." He slid a pointed glance her way. "I feel I've said that before. No matter. Your clay requires time to strengthen. Shall we say—"

"Six days?" she guessed.

"How well my wife knows her man's mind."

"And then we go on to Xi'Matezh?"

"Xi'Matezh," he agreed, or maybe he was correcting her pronunciation. "We aren't far."

"Half a brace, right?" she said, rolling her eyes. "You've been saying that since the mountains."

"Less than that. Perhaps even less than half that."

"So...You could have been there and back, like, three times by now."

"No arguments, woman. This is not a discussion. We go to Him together." He looked past her, loudly flattening his spines. "I have not invited you back."

"It's raining," Eric said on the stair.

"Excellent. Keep me informed. Get out." Meoraq continued to stare until Eric and the others turned around and tromped back upstairs. "Raining," he muttered, and prodded at the heat stones.

"How long are you going to keep them outside?" Amber asked.

"They aren't 'out' anywhere. They're in the foreroom. Listen." Meoraq looked up at the ceiling, scowling at the sound of footsteps pacing above them. "I ought to make them stay up there until we move on. I'm sick of having humans underfoot."

She looked at him.

He noticed and predictably misunderstood. He scowled back at her, saying, "I'll call them down once I've had my bath. Enough. I am still the master of this camp and I am not a harsh one." His spines lifted in an overture of peace. "An hour, eh? A private hour, you and I, and all the world outside."

For Nicci's sake, not to mention the other three, Amber knew she really ought to do some of the standing up that Eric found so praiseworthy, but the idea of privacy was a powerful temptation. "So," she said, beginning to smile. "Did you have any ideas on how to pass the time until the water heats up?"

He changed out the stone in the pouch for a hotter one. "We can walk down to the stream, if you're feeling strong enough. We're going to need more water if you want a bath too."

The sight of her words going over his head made whooshing sounds in Amber's mind. She waited a second or two, then stood, moved the stewing pouch out of his reach and sat down on his thigh.

"What are you doing?" he asked, by all appearances with genuine surprise.

Amber wordlessly took his favorite bone-handled knife out of its sheath and stabbed it meaningfully into the back of his chair, above his head.

He looked at it. "Ah."

She caught him by the jaw and aimed his face back at her so that she could kiss his rough mouth. He allowed it, but certainly did not encourage it, and when she was done, he said simply, "It is an unforgiveable sin to lie with a woman in her sickbed."

"I don't appear to be in it at the moment." She loosened her tunic and slid it off one shoulder so he could see his bite-marks. "You made me certain promises, lizardman."

He eyed the scars with distinct pride, only to glare at her. "Your humans are right above us."

"We'll be quiet," she promised.

"I don't like being quiet." He paused, frowning as he watched her unbuckle his belt. "And I don't think you can be."

"Then we'll be noisy, but we'll be quick and finish up before they come down to investigate," said Amber, now at work on his breeches-ties.

"My desires come from God. They should not be hurried."

"Then they shouldn't be denied, either," she said piously, and slipped her hand beneath his loin-plate.

"You may have a point," he said after a moment's meditation. "Are you sure you're strong enough?"

She kissed him again. This time, he kissed back at her, his broad, dry tongue nudging at her lips and into her mouth to taste her. His hands caught at her thighs, kneading lightly before moving up to wrap her waist. He didn't try to undress her; he'd probably never heard of doing it in a chair, she thought, remembering Zhuqa.

She broke the kiss with a shudder and looked away, waiting to feel arousal curdle into shame, but it didn't happen. Meoraq, oblivious, saw the sudden exposure of her throat as an invitation and leaned forward to nuzzle at it, reaching beneath her wrap to cup her breast. He was never quite sure what to do with it once he had it in his hand, but at least he tried.

She looked down at him, faintly smiling, watching his spines flex and quiver with restraint as he fit his teeth into the impression of his scar, nuzzled, fit them again.

He was never going to be Zhuqa, no more than Zhuqa could have ever been Meoraq. It didn't matter what he did, what he said, how he looked. Zhuqa had tried to be her lover as part of his little game, but his gentlest touch was loathsome. He didn't deserve the hold he had on her memories now.

Amber brushed the back of her hand over Meoraq's brow. He grunted pleasantly without opening his eyes, lost in her shoulder. Nothing they did together could ever be ugly, she thought. Nothing they did together belonged to Zhuqa.

She knelt down.

He started to move out of the chair and join her on the floor, but stopped, puzzled, at her silent insistence. When she started in again at loosening his loin-plate, he tried to help.

"Let me do this," she said, pushing his hands firmly away. "I want to please my man."

"It does not please me to see my woman on her knees."

She looked at him, crookedly smiling. "I want to please my man. Whether I'm on my knees or on my feet or standing on my head." 'And I want to take every ugly thing he did away from him,' she thought, but didn't say that. It was bad enough that she could still see Zhuqa with them in this moment; she didn't want Meoraq to see him too.

"This is a human mating technique, is it?" Meoraq asked uncertainly, watching her peel away his loin-plate. "Do I take my boots off or do you remove them for me?"

She leaned back to look at them, then up at him.

"Humans take their boots off for formal matings," he explained, looking very mildly embarrassed. "This is a formal mating, isn't it?"

"Do I dare ask why you were watching humans have sex?"

He mumbled something, scratching at his snout, then shook his head and snapped, "I am not to be blamed if humans insist on mating in the open wilds where anyone can see them! Do you want the boots off or not?"

"Take them off," she said decisively. "Take everything off. Let's do this right."

Muttering under his breath, Meoraq stood up and shucked out of his clothes. Amber did the same, still giggling now and then, even though she honestly didn't know what struck her so funny about the whole thing. It wasn't the concept of Meoraq as a Peeping Tom, which was pretty ludicrous all on its own, as much as it was the idea of human mating techniques (*step one remove boots step two insert penis*), formal and otherwise.

"And now?" Meoraq asked, standing naked and proud above her with his hands on his hips and his best glare on.

"Now sit down again."

"Sit?" He looked at the chair and back at her. "In the chair?"

She nodded, trying to hide her grin under her hand.

"I thought we were going to have sex."

"We are. Sort of." A sudden sobering thought occurred as he gingerly lowered himself into the chair. "Is it, um, against God's laws to do things that can't, strictly speaking, produce babies?"

"Things?" He frowned. "How strict do you mean?"

She put her hands lightly on his thighs and leaned between them to lick all along the tight crease of his slit, penetrating at the crown to tongue at his sa'ad.

He watched her very closely. Apart from the immediate and forceful extrusion of his slick cock, he did not move and did not make a sound until she leaned back to look at him again. "I have to pray about this," he said seriously.

"I'll wait."

He tipped his head back and closed his eyes.

A few minutes ticked by. She changed out the stones in the stewing pouch. Meoraq breathed.

His eyes opened. "You are mine," he told her. "And I am yours. Nothing we take as our pleasure together offends the eye of God."

"Really?"

"He was quite clear." He looked upwards, thoughtful. "Unusually clear, one might say."

She cupped the hot swell at the base of his cock and bent again, this time sucking the nub of his sa'ad between her tight lips to flick it with her tongue. His taste was strong, yes, and sweet and intoxicating and entirely his own.

A pair of heavy feet came across the ceiling and started down the stairs.

"If no one has been killed," Meoraq called, "someone is about to be."

The feet stopped, turned, galumphed away.

Amber giggled around his clit, which made the muscles in both his thighs jump.

"Ease off a moment," he ordered, resting both hands on her shoulders. "Just a moment. This is...this is very different."

"Do you need to pray again?"

He tried to glower at her, but was too obviously flustered to be effective. His eyes closed. His breath deepened and slowed. He appeared to fall asleep.

Amber rolled off her knees and sat cross-legged. The floor was very cold on her ass. She dragged her discarded wrap over and sat on that instead. She traded out the stones again and waited.

Meoraq's eyes opened. "Proceed."

"Everything's still all right with God?"

"Yes."

She weighed the pros and cons of her next nagging doubt while she stroked his shaft gently in her fist, but in the end, felt she just had to ask. She wasn't sure how...but she really felt she had to.

And then she remembered Meoraq's 'anatomy lesson' the first night they'd made love. *This is my masculine member...it will go here...*

A smile tugged at her lips. She rubbed his cock in one hand and pointed at it with the other. "I would like to suck this."

His spines came forward.

"And lick it all over until you cum in my mouth."

His cock twitched in her grip. He frowned.

"I just want to be sure that's okay." *...the most profane thing I have ever seen...* "Especially if I swallow it."

She watched his face closely, where 'Yes, do it now,' fought a visible war against 'Sex is for procreation only' and finally he passed his hand over his eyes and looked at her through his fingers. "Give me a moment."

"Take all the time you need."

He did some muttering, but closed his eyes and that was all for a long time.

She found herself watching the way the light played along the wet shine of his oiled cock—red light and black shadow, stark and smooth and beautiful. She wanted to feel it in her hands again. She wanted to kiss it, taste it, not to kill a ghost or prove a point, but just to hear Meoraq's hiss and feel his hands clench in her hair. She imagined that penultimate spasm, the flood of his heat across her tongue, the roughness of his scales under her hands as she held him close to drink...

Amber shivered. She wasn't cold.

"Tell me why you want to do this," Meoraq said without opening his eyes.

"God wants to know?"

"I suspect He already knows." He sounded very faintly annoyed. "Yet I am compelled to ask anyway. Answer."

"Because you're mine and I want to make you happy in every possible way."

"I have always been happy without this act," he said, but it was a grudging admission.

"I still want to share it with you."

"And if I say it is an offense?"

"Then I won't ask you again."

His brows knitted heavily over his closed eyes. "So you don't really want to do it."

"Right this instant, it's probably the thing I want most to do in the world, but I'm not going to do it if it offends your god."

His eyes slid open just to slits. "You don't believe in God."

"You do."

"You have tried often enough to convince me otherwise, but you will not do so now with your human mating rituals?"

"Whether or not I believe in your god is irrelevant. I'm trying to make love with you. It can't be making love if you think it's corrupting you."

Meoraq tipped his head back and gazed, not at the ceiling where human feet were once again loudly tromping, but through it and straight on to heaven. Looking God in the eye, perhaps.

And if so...she found herself wondering if this was the strangest prayer He'd ever been asked to mediate.

"Yes," said Meoraq.

Amber started. "What?"

He looked at her, gestured at his cock. "The will I receive has not changed. No pleasure we find in one another offends the eye of God. You may do as you wish."

She stared at him for a while, then up at the ceiling and back at him.

He grimaced at her, an expression which was never going to grace the covers of one of those sultry bodice-rippers her mom had like to read (and which was far more likely, come to think of it, to be found on the splash page of a horror comic), but something in it made that not-cold shiver come right back, even harder than before. Amber rolled onto her knees and arched up to kiss him, to feel his dry tongue prod at hers and his fingers comb carefully through her hair, and it was beautiful, like the heat and pulse of his cock when she gripped it, like the musky sweet taste that coated his sa'ad, like the orgasm that swept through her when she brushed her lips across the head of him and heard his rich, full groan. She did not drink him in with the pleasure she'd imagined, but with joy beyond *all* imagining, right up until he fell out of the chair.

Footsteps on the ceiling. Meoraq panting on the floor. Amber watched him, giggling now and then when the happiness threatened to split her in half, and finally draped herself across his chest and thighs where she could both snuggle platonically and fondle him at the same time.

"Say something," she said at last.

"God is in His heaven," said Meoraq in a distant voice. "And loves me."

Zhuqa had said something like that once. This time, it was beautiful.

8

They were a frustrating six days that followed. Meoraq's limited healing lore had always served him well in the past, or at least, that part of the past which did not include his Amber. It was not the alien workings of her body that concerned him now—that, he was content to leave to Sheul and He seemed to have mended it. No, what he did not know how to manage was his woman's spirit, and in particular, her will to leap from her sickbed and be immediately whole.

Amber's long lying-in had left her weakened and restless. Six days was not enough to restore her to her fullest, but it was all she would allow.

He had sympathy. Some. No one liked to lie around and be tended, and certainly no one enjoyed being reminded that they were any less than what they had been, what they should be. His Amber's fierce will chafed at inactivity. It was no less than a punishment to her and Meoraq understood that feeling. He also understood, as his wife apparently did not, that overworking weakened flesh only slowed one's recovery and that the mistakes made while in that state could cripple his woman for life.

He explained this. She claimed to accept it. And then she refused out of hand his suggestion of meditation and stretches, even for one day, and instead began a regime of climbing the stairs over and over. Before the day was out, she had set the goal of walking all the way to the stream and back, and achieved it despite his warnings. Was he surprised? He was not, not even the next morning, when she wanted to hunt.

Meoraq had only a few moments to think that over without arousing her suspicion, but the facts were simple enough. Point: If he denied her request and left without her, she would likely begin again with her own idea of how best to recover. Point the second: She was equally likely to go hunting without him. Point the third (and most significant): At least one and perhaps all three of the human males in his camp had eyes on her. Meoraq did not believe any of them would dare to attempt conquest and he did not doubt Amber's ability, however weakened, to put a scar on them if they did, but it was a point and worth the consideration.

So he took her hunting. All that day and all the days that followed, he led his woman on long walks, well away from any game trails or spoor, and let her believe herself hunting. He lost hours to her stubbornness that could have been spent packing his lodge back onto the sled, but then again, even when there were no animals to track, there were plenty of trees to lean up against.

Exercise was exercise.

On the seventh morning following Amber's emergence from her sickbed, Meoraq woke early with too much to do. He nuzzled his wife all the way awake, since there was no hope of escaping the cupboard without disturbing her anyway, and told her to be ready to leave within the hour.

"Got it," she mumbled, rolling over to spread herself out over the bed as he left it. "Gonna sleep a little bit, be right up, okay?"

He grunted assent, patting her fluffy head, and shut the door quietly. After a few short stretches and his morning prayer—*my thanks Sheul, O my Father, for the shelter of this lodge and its civilized cupboard which is half the size of mine at home, and my thanks Sheul, O my Father, for the woman who shares it with me and has not failed once in fifty-nine nights by her own reckoning to hup her bony knee into my groin*—he went upstairs.

The foreroom of the underlodge was empty at the moment, although someone had moved the sled on which he had half-heartedly packed their provisions. Leaning close to straighten them, Meoraq smelled the unmistakable tang of sex. Damned humans. Now every time he put the walls up, he was going to think about that.

He opened the door and pulled the sled outside, facing into the wind to clear his scent cavities. It was not quite dawn, although the sky was greying in the east. A fine morning, dry and cool. A good day for travel.

He was not alone.

Meoraq stiffened, fighting the urge to hiss. He did not turn to look at her, did not hear her little footfall or catch more than the usual smoky scent in the breeze, but he knew who it was with him and he saw no reason to pretend otherwise. "What do you want, N'ki?"

"You told Amber you wanted to leave."

"In an hour. Wait below."

"Can't I help?"

"Don't insult me. You wouldn't lift your hand to help if it were resting on live coals. What do you want? Speak plainly."

"What are you going to do with me?"

"Nothing." Meoraq busied himself with the sled, re-stacking things that did not require adjustment and tightening straps he was going to have to untie and fasten again when the rest of the gear was loaded. Anything to keep his hands busy so they would not be tempted to strike.

"When this is over, I mean. You can't—" Her hand caught at his sleeve.

He slapped it off. Hard. But at least he only struck her hand.

"You can't leave me," she said in her shaking voice. Her eyes filled with water. "Please, Meoraq."

"Don't say my name like that and don't you dare cry at me," he added, pointing the whole of his hand right into her flat, ugly face. "I am not my wife, to be caught and reined by the little water you run out of your eyes."

She did not answer, but her eyes dried in the wind and did not tear up again.

"You sicken me," he spat, yanking at the sled's ties. "But you are my wife's blood-kin and so I will take you into my House."

"Thank y—"

"Thank *her*, not that you ever would. I can only pray that one day she will see you for what you are, but until then, know that *my* eyes are open. You'll come to my House, yes, and I'll shut you behind as many doors as I can and if God shows favor, neither she nor I will ever see your face or hear your whining voice again!"

"Perhaps you can find a cage to put me in."

"Don't you dare hook that at me!" he hissed. "You'll have a room, human. You'll have your meals brought and baths at your pleasure and all manner of comforts, ha, and you won't even have to ply a man's slit to get them."

It was, in truth, a low thing for any man to say, and despicable in the throat of a Sheulek. Still, he did not expect the slap. It caught him right across the snout with a flat, undramatic sound, and although it didn't sting much, it briefly whitened his vision on that side.

He recoiled to stare at her. She neither excused herself nor asked forgiveness—would that have made a difference?—but just stared back at him, her chin raised, defiant. And why shouldn't she be defiant? She knew he wouldn't strike her back. Because of Amber.

"Go below," he said at last. He could feel the color throbbing in his neck, but his voice was calm. "I am done with you."

She made a sniffing sound, jerking her head as she turned so that her hair snapped a bit, as in a short gust of wind. The sight, the sound, sparked a flare of such rage that his hand went to his waist, gripping at the air where the hilt of his kzung should be, if only he were wearing it. His head cleared after a few slow breaths, but while it lasted, the killing urge was bitterly welcome.

'Patience,' he told himself, and made his empty hands go back to work. 'Great Sheul, O my Father, help me to remember that my wife loves the useless little poke.'

And if she had the power to hear those thoughts, they would have been as good as a knife in her belly. He remembered only too well the look on Amber's face when she had seen her Nicci again, and he knew he had done nothing since to keep the fire of that first joy lit. Even now, knowing all that his wife had suffered and all that it would mean to her to see him at least trying to show her blood kin some small friendship, the only kindness he could muster was to stay where he was instead of chasing after her and slapping an apology out of her whining mouth.

He hated Nicci. Even before she'd put her hand on him in that evil way, he'd hated her. She was no worse than any other human he endured with far better grace. Indeed, she was quieter than most, which should have made her far more tolerable. She wasn't. He hated her.

Footsteps on the stair, uneven in gait but familiar. Meoraq raised his head and flared his spines, grunting a wordless greeting. Amber yawned back at him and sat down on the sled. "Morning," she said.

He glanced at the sun, still touching the horizon. "Almost."

"You okay?"

"Yes."

"You look pissed."

He grunted.

"Hey. Come here."

He eyed the bundled leather walls she patted so invitingly, leather that some other human had already perfumed with...fluids...and straightened up. "You come to me," he ordered, slapping lightly at his chest.

She did, rolling her eyes but smiling as she slipped her arms around him. "It's almost over," she murmured.

He acknowledged this, rubbing at her back and gazing meditatively into the distance, into the east. The shrine was there, so close. He had more fingers than days left in this journey. Sheul awaited him. Sheul, manifest as flesh.

"I could hunt," he said, already feeling the futility seep into the air. "One good hunt to leave here. You and I could go on together. The humans could wait here for us."

Amber frowned, but did seem to think it over.

"If that's what you want to do—" she began at last. Meoraq finished it with her, each in their own tongue, "—I'll wait here with them. No," he said at the end and hissed under his breath.

She said nothing for a time, only held him. At length, softly, she said, "Do you want me to talk to them about something?"

"No."

"Do you want to put off leaving for another day?"

"No."

He felt her fingers drumming against his scales as she thought.

"Want to fool around before we go?"

He drew back far enough to see if she was serious. She was. And even though that changed absolutely nothing, his mood immediately lightened from the choking black it had been to, oh, a dull sort of grey. "Yes," he said, releasing her. "Go get the flask. We'll fill it on the way back."

"And they say men can't multitask." She stood up on her toe-tips and pressed her mouthparts to his snout. "It's almost over," she said again. "Try to remember that, okay?"

He grunted and watched her go back downstairs, trying for her sake to find some hidden reserve of patience and goodwill. It was almost over, that was truth, and he shared responsibility for how it ended. When he overheard Amber telling his children the tale of this pilgrimage, he did not want to hear the words, "...and your father acted like a bitch the whole way back."

Someday, he really had to find out what that meant, exactly.

He could hear Amber coming back already, talking over her shoulder in a gratifyingly terse tone. He met her at the door of the underlodge, caught her by Lady Uyane's fine green girdle and pulled her to him, pushing his snout hard against her skin all the way up her throat and down again. He kept her there, just for a moment, not thinking but only breathing her in. When he released her, it was with a hiss and a sigh of surrender.

"I am the master of this camp," he told her. "And I could be a better one. We'll move on, Soft-Skin. All of us."

Her furry brows arched. "Does that mean we're not fooling around?"

"It does not." He took the flask away from her and started walking. "Come."

"That's the goal, lizardman."

"Eh?"

"Nothing." She caught his hand and held it as she walked beside him, inexplicably grinning. "It's so nice to know that no matter what else happens, I'll always have moments like this...when you don't have the slightest idea what I'm saying."

"This makes you happy?"

"Yeah, a bit."

Meoraq thought that over and shrugged his spines. "If it makes you any happier, I have at least one of those moments nearly every day."

Her smile widened. "Guess that means we're married, huh?"

The last of his dark mood blew away like smoke in Sheul's good, cleansing wind. He put his arm around her. "I suppose it does."

* * *

The land which would eventually be known as the Ruined Reach had once been among the greatest lands of Gann. Images preserved from that time showed its cities, like pools of glittering light, reaching north as far as the ice deserts and south into the Green Sea. The Prophet wrote much of life in that land, of its loss and of the sins which had made that loss so necessary, and of the poison that had so permeated its soil after the Fall that he warned no man should seek it. Long after the Prophet's death, one of the Advocates had decreed that the land had healed enough that those seeking pilgrimage in that land had liberty to do so, but in keeping with the spirit of the Prophet's warning, no road had ever been built that led into the Reach, not even to Xi'Matezh, mere days out of holy Chalh.

Yet with Lord Uyane's directions and fair weather, the remainder of the journey passed without difficulty. Meoraq's humans were inclined to be obedient, or at least unobtrusive, and easily managed. Nicci shared his tent and there was nothing he could do about that, but a tent wasn't much privacy anyway. And it was only for a few more days. He had already decided to demand another tent on his return visit to Chalh and give it to Nicci. Also a bedroll, blanket and even a cushion. Anything to keep her from robbing Amber of her comforts.

Patience, Uyane. Patience for another day. The doors of Xi'Matezh would open and he must not pass them with anger in his heart.

Days passed. He did not count them, although he meditated each night on a new horizon and felt the soil softening beneath his boots. He tasted salt on the wind and felt the damp of the ocean long before he saw it. And when he saw it...

It had been there before him most of that last day, but the glimpses of greyish green he could see through the branches were not worth the inevitable stumble as his feet caught in the clutter of Gedai's trees. He knew it was the ocean, the end of his journey. He knew it was a marvelous sight, utterly unknown in the city of his birth. He also knew it wasn't going anywhere.

So when Nicci lost her footing and spilled herself down a sandy slope onto a fallen log, Meoraq called camp, meaning to stay through the night even though the afternoon had scarcely started. He felt no great sense of time lost in doing this—what was another day, more or less?—but considered it a test of his resolve to show patience. In that mind, he sent Amber away with the empty flask and knelt to inspect the injury, ha, of Nicci's scuffed knee and bruised arm.

Amber returned in mere moments, the flask just as empty. She let it drop. "Come and see this."

The three human males and Amber's own Nicci sat around her, but Amber said this only to him.

Meoraq went and through the trees, not twenty paces from his camp, the forest broke and the ground dropped away. They stood at the top of a cliff, nearly sheer, six times the height of any city wall, plummeting down onto a deadly mash of rock and steel and ruin, sloping away over a wide swath of rust-colored sand, and there was the ocean at the end of it.

He had seen pictures. He had thought that would prepare him, that he could see the ocean and somehow still know how he fit beside it. But there it was and it was as deep as sight would go, so vast that it became the horizon, so entire that he could see the very curve of the world along its skin.

He did not think to look for the temple in that first moment. He did not think at all. Uyane Meoraq beheld the naked body of Gann—its breathing lung, its beating heart, its pregnant belly—and forgot his own entirely until Amber took his hand.

He looked at it, anchored suddenly into his own clay's dimensions, and then at her. She did not meet his eye. She, too, was lost in the sea.

He looked back into the ocean and was at once dizzied. The way it moved restlessly toward him...it felt as though he were falling and there was nothing to grab at, no hope of rescue. He felt that he could fall along that undulating skin forever until he slipped up into the sky. He looked and saw Gann pressed to Sheul's heaven with nothing between them, no difference at all.

"Is it...beautiful?" he asked uncertainly.

"I don't know." She hesitated and shifted a little closer. "I don't like it. It's too high. And everything down there...looks dead. I don't know," she said again. "I've never been to the beach before. This wasn't what I imagined."

"Hell, no," Crandall announced.

They both turned, and just why he should be surprised to see the others, Meoraq truly did not know, but he was, as much as if he were seeing them for the first time.

Crandall crossed his arms back and forth in front of his chest, shaking his head for emphasis. "*Hell*, no," he repeated. "The joy ride ends here. I am not climbing down that. Bull-*shit*."

Meoraq looked again at the cliff, but not for long. The height, the eroded fingers of the ruins pointing out of the sand, the constant swallowing sound of the sea—the single glance that Meoraq took found its way to his belly and knotted there.

"You and the lizard can do what you want," Crandall was saying. "I ain't killing myself so he can plant a tree in Israel or whatever the fuck he thinks he's doing."

"Relax, man. There has to be another way down."

"Says who? Don't you ever watch the travel shows? Since when do they ever put temples where any old asshole can walk in?"

"Hey, Bierce." Eric reached toward Amber, visibly thought better of it when Meoraq looked at him, then settled for pointing. "What's that look like to you?"

Meoraq looked along the top of the cliff, since that was where Eric seemed to be pointing, but saw nothing except the same thick forest they had been struggling through for days. Yet Amber actually gasped, her hand clenching where she still held his. So Meoraq looked again, at the treeline this time and then the treetops and finally at Amber, who was looking back at him with wide, disbelieving eyes.

"You don't see it, do you?" she said.

He looked a third time, squinting as if through smoke and darkness and driving rain, but saw only the same close growth of trees, too tall and thin for Meoraq's comfort, almost black against the grey sky. With a little imagination, he could see a thousand, thousand crooked fingers, pointing in defiance at the God that had judged this land and found it wanting, but he could not see a temple.

Even when she pointed, he saw nothing but another tree, a little taller than the rest, but no more or less remarkable than any other. But where the others were wrapped in years of parasitic growth, dripping creepers and grasses that would have had no chance at life on the sunless forest floor, this tree stood naked, branchless, burnt black. A dead tree then, and yet he could see by Amber's face that it was more.

"I cry," he said. "What is it?"

"I...It...I don't know."

"Well, I don't know either," said Eric, shading his eyes in an effort to see the thing better. "But it sure looks like a transmission tower to me. Sheesh. Wouldn't that just chap Scott's ass?"

* * *

The walls that surrounded Xi'Matezh had been raised, it was said, by the Prophet's own Oracle Mykrm, and his mark was said to have been carved on the very last stone to be set. Meoraq looked for it as they circled around in search of entry, but with only half an eye. There was so much else to see. The curious color of the stone—nearly black, mottled through with grey and green—made it all but impossible to see through the thick trees. Meoraq had never made a formal study of stone, but all the rock he saw beneath his feet was of that pale, flaking kind; this stone had been quarried elsewhere, brought for the singular purpose of enclosing this sacred place, and the sight of it did his weary clay great good.

They were beautiful walls, deceptively plain, perfectly molded. At one time, there must have been gates, but the damp corrosive air had claimed them and they had not been replaced. It gave him a twinge of disappointment, seeing that anyone could walk in, and he had to stop there in the opening with his neck bent until he had reminded himself that Sheul's house was open to all His children. The inner doors, those were the true test.

"Are we going in or are we standing here all day?"

"Dude, just give him his space. This is a big deal for him."

"Yeah, yeah. Lizardman's gotta get right with the Big Liz. Meanwhile, I'm freezing my nuts off."

Six breaths, deep and slow. One for the Prophet, who had been the first to enter these ruins and hear the true voice of God within. Two for his Brunt, who had surrendered everything, even his own name, to serve others in faithfulness and humility. Three for Uyane, the first Sword, father of his own line. Four for Mykrm, the hammer, who had raised the first true cities under Sheul and taught men to rule them fairly. Five for Oyan, who carried seedlings across the ruin of the Fallen world and brought life out of the poisoned earth. Six for Thaliszr, priest and healer, who had brought the man Lashraq out of death and restored him as Sheul's own Prophet.

Meoraq raised his head and crossed through the gateless portal into Xi'Matezh.

He saw the ruins at once, ruins he had every reason to expect to see, ruins he had no right to resent now that they were before him. There were several buildings within the walls, much eroded by the ocean air, windowless, doorless, lifeless. He saw the thing the humans called a transmission tower—weathered, but still standing, still humming beneath his hand when he reached out to touch it. He saw no machines, but the courtyard was too well-kept to think none were here, even here.

The next thing he saw was the ocean, which he could see only because of the huge, tumbled hole in that beautiful wall. Not just one or two missing bricks, but a whole length of them, loosened by the constant pounding of the waves on the cliffs or eroded by the wet wind that had pitted so many of these other buildings. If he and his humans all joined hands, they still couldn't make a line long enough to touch both sides. This fine wall, the life's work of who knew how many master masons, carried block by block to be raised here under Oracle Mykrm's own living eye...This beautiful wall was falling.

But beside the hole, Meoraq saw the only thing that really mattered: a dark stone dome enclosing the true shrine and the heavy doors that sealed it. The doors were made of qil, the same as his sabks—a lost metal, from a lost age. Perhaps Oracle Uyane had made the knives from the scraps left after the doors were cast. Perhaps he had always carried a piece of Xi'Matezh with him and never knew it.

"Wife," said Meoraq, and when she was with him, he began to walk.

"God, there better be wall-to-wall booze and burgers in there," Crandall said, falling into step at his side.

Meoraq halted. He turned, his head cocked, and thrust his snout into the human's flat face. "You," he hissed, raking his gaze across the rest of them as well. "All of you. You wait here. This place is sacred."

"Oh what the hell, man!" Crandall looked back at his people, then at Meoraq, and finally at Amber. "What, we're not good enough to see God? We've come just as fucking far, haven't we? Maybe I got some questions too!"

"Stay here," Meoraq said again and snorted, blowing back the dirty hair from Crandall's brow. "Look for your abbot's ship. Wife, come."

Crandall faced him down for a second or two, but did turn away in the end, pucker-faced and full of color. "Fucking lizard's pet. Come on, guys. I ain't standing out in the wind."

Amber had a special look for him when Meoraq turned back to her, but he didn't care. He went on ahead to open the outer doors of Xi'Matezh. The hinges were stiff, but they opened, blowing the dank, waxy-scented breath of the temple back at him.

The doors were too heavy to hold indefinitely. Meoraq gave his wife a not-so-subtle nudge with the toe of his boot and let go of them. They immediately began to swing shut, ponderous as doors in a dream, and closed with no more than a muffled whump, trapping them in black.

Meoraq took his pack off and found his lamp and strikers. He waited until his hands steadied before he made a light, and it was all there, just as he'd imagined: a thousand half-burnt candles like a second wall all around him, melted together, stacked one atop the other, like a city made of wax; the Prophet's mark painted on the wall, renewed by countless pilgrims over the years; the building, not ruined but maintained, a relic outside of time, and the doors, marked with the names of those who had passed through. Meoraq raised the lamp and approached, his hand skimming the air just over the doors until he found one name he knew: Tsazr Dyuun.

"Your teacher?" Amber asked, watching him.

He grunted, his eyes tracing each line of each letter. They were not even, which surprised him some. He remembered Master Tsazr as such a meticulous man, but then making letters was a very different thing from teaching boys to beat one another senseless. Still...

"Are you sure you want to do this?"

He looked at her, his spines flexing forward. In the close air of this place, he could actually hear them flexing, which was so unnerving that he reached up to rub at them. "Why would you say that? I've walked across the world, woman!"

She averted her eyes, rolling her shoulders as she hugged herself. "This doesn't look like much of a temple, is all. It kind of looks like a bunker."

"Whatever it may have been before the Fall, it became a temple when God entered." His eye wandered back to Master Tsazr's name on the wall. "All things change when He enters, Soft-Skin."

"I don't want you to be disappointed."

"How can I be? Look there." He nudged at her arm and pointed to the wall. "The mark of the Prophet. Prophet Lashraq made that mark."

Amber studied it with a singularly dubious expression. "It looks awfully fresh."

"It's been repainted, I'm sure, but he made it first. He was here, Soft-Skin. Here, where I stand." He dropped his arm and turned to her, holding his lamp before him like a candle-ward. The flame underlit her odd face in unflattering ways; he leaned close and nuzzled at her chin. "Will you stand with me, wife? One more hour?"

"Meoraq...what if—"

He pushed his mouthparts against hers and rubbed them lightly together until she pushed him away, laughing. "Will you stand with me?" he asked again.

"I think my lips are bleeding."

"Will you?"

"Oh for Christ's sake, I have to say it?" She sighed, wiped her mouth, then suddenly raised both arms and dropped them loudly to her side. "I'm with you," she said. "I'm always with you. So...open up that door, Meoraq. Let's do this."

He smiled, nuzzling her one more time, and put his palm to the lock-plate.

It warmed, clicked twice and began to hum. Lights came slowly to life all around the door, soft white and palest blue. Another click, and then the voice, echoing off the rounded shell of the dome so that it seemed to be speaking directly in Meoraq's head: "Warning. This is a secure area. All access restricted. Warning. Lethal force authorized."

"Nuu Sukaga."

The humming changed pitch. Small vents opened to either side of the door. "Defense imminent. Present mnabed. This is your final warning."

Amber took a large step back, catching at his arm, but Meoraq was not moved. "Nuu Sukaga," he said again.

The vents closed. The door opened.

Deep in the darkened room beyond, Sheul the All-Father stood, the sword of war sheathed and the light of wisdom burning in His hand.

9

Amber never doubted for a moment that she would see a big, empty room and that was just what she saw. But she knew what Meoraq was expecting too, and so she knew what was going to happen next. And oh God, it hurt to see it.

"Father," he said, and with a flicker and a whine, lights all around the room came wearily to life. As they strengthened, the huge monitor on the far wall lost some of its mirror-like shine, but still Meoraq took two steps toward it before he realized what it was. He stopped, blinking rapidly as he stared first at his reflection and then at hers and then at the rest of the room. There really wasn't much to see. It was nothing but a reception area, reduced by military design to six angled walls, several banks of computer consoles, one horseshoe-shaped desk with a single chair aimed at the door they'd come in through, two other doors, and of course, the enormous display monitor behind the desk in which the yellow light of Meoraq's lamp still sparked a ghost-like echo.

He took it all in, plainly puzzled but showing no doubt, no real concern. When Amber hesitated a touch on his arm, he gave her an inquiring glance, but shrugged off her silent sympathy and instead marched over to one of the other doors and nudged the lockplate. It blatted at him but didn't open. "Nuu Sukaga," he said, and the door behind Amber hissed shut.

"Locks engaged. Timeout to systems restart. Doors will open in ten and ninety. Present mnabed to override." The lockplates lit up helpfully, but no one had anything to offer any of them.

Meoraq backed away from the door, looking frustrated but not alarmed, not really. He turned around again, all the way in a circle, as if checking to make sure God hadn't materialized behind him while he was distracted by the door. He ended up facing Amber and the two of them just looked at each other for a while.

"I don't understand," he said.

"I know."

"Everyone hears Him!" he insisted, just as if she'd argued. "Everyone! He has to be here! It has to be...some kind of test!" He swung away, holding up his lamp and searching each shadowed, empty corner. "Father?"

The lights pulsed as if in answer and grew that much stronger. The big monitor flickered. Smaller ones evenly spaced around the otherwise featureless walls snapped on, one after the other, showing first a clean black screen and slowly spilling out lines of silent code. Somewhere, speakers thumped on at an ear-splitting level and hummed their way down to something subaudible. "Operational drive activated," said a lizardish voice. "Systems override. Searching for file. Please wait."

"There's no one here," she said softly.

"He's here! He has to be here! Maybe..." He turned back, still not panicked, still with that awful bafflement. "Will you pray with me? Maybe we have to pray."

The big monitor flickered again and pulled up a very obvious load-bar. As it crept toward completion, that cool, androgynous voice came back with, "File recovery in process. Please wait."

"I'll pray with you," said Amber. "Tell me how."

But he didn't, not right away. He just looked at her, standing alone in the center of that empty room with the big screen firing up behind him. The lamp in his hand trembled. He looked at her. He did not speak.

Amber gently took the lamp and set it down on the edge of the console nearest to her. He let it go, his eyes fixed to the little flame, but otherwise, he didn't move, not even when she came back and tried to put her arms around him.

"He didn't lie to me."

"Who?"

"Master Tsazi." Meoraq pulled out of her reach and paced back to the door, pushing at the lockplate twice before going on to the next door. "I saw him. I saw his face! He heard God's voice! That is truth! It..." His long stride slowed. He looked at her again, lost between one door and the next. "It's me."

"No."

Meoraq's spines lowered until they were shivering close against his skull, but his back stayed straight and his shoulders squared. His eyes drifted from one computer to another, beginning and ending with the big screen and the nearly-there load-bar. "He doesn't want to talk to me," he said, and staggered without ever taking a step.

"Meoraq, don't. Please, don't." She caught his face, made him look at her, but it was a long time before he saw her. "It's not you, I swear it's not." And wildly, because anything was better than this...this awful dead confusion in his eyes, she said, "Maybe it's me, okay? Maybe women aren't supposed to come here. You did everything right, Meoraq, you know you did."

His brows furrowed, the knobby ridges cutting shadows down his lizardish cheeks. "I don't...know what I did wrong..."

"Recovery complete," said the voice. The monitor went black and then came to sudden life. It showed a room—this room, she realized. The camera was aimed down at the desk, where a lizardman in a grey and black uniform crouched. He wasn't sitting, wasn't standing. There was a chair, but he wasn't using it. He was just...hunched there, holding onto the desk like it was keeping him on the ground. There was no sound, but lights were going wild all around him in that/this room, making madhouse colors dance across his scales. His mouth was open; his eyes were hell. Slowly, his head turned until he was staring directly at the camera, directly at them.

Meoraq's hand twitched toward the hilt of his kzung, but he stood his ground. "This is a recording!" he said, and turned in a sudden, curt circle, shouting, "I know the difference! This is just an image! This is not Sheul!"

The picture on the monitor died.

Meoraq glared at it, his mouth flared open, hissing through his teeth. "I am not deceived! I am Uyane Meoraq, a Sword and a true son of—"

The picture came back. The same room. The same man. He was sitting now, his eyes staring and glazed. "I want to say that I didn't know," he said, and it was the voice that did it. Recognition like a hammer slammed down into Amber's brain and she suddenly knew him, knew this room, knew that voice. The kiosk in the ruins; Scott and Nicci and everyone standing around to listen while the man in the recording—this man—told them to come to Matezh, that they had to come together, that there was still hope.

Now that man clapped a hand to his brows and clenched it there, shaking his head over and over before suddenly slapping at the desk. "How can I say that?" he cried. "How can any of us say that? After we spent years in development to make sure we got it as virulent and as violent as the science allowed, how can anyone pretend they didn't know it would end the world?"

Something in the recording sounded a tone. The man looked around at the wall behind him as one of the green lights turned yellow. "Ghedov is gone," he said, running out to tap at that computer. "I guess Daophith and Jezaana will be next. Saiakr is still sending me the numbers—that's Technician Raaq Saiakr at Culvsh—and everything is working just the way we planned. I can't..." He trailed off, staring at the screens, then shook his head again. "I can't," he said simply, and switched the recording off.

Amber looked at Meoraq, but he was still frowning at the screen. His spines were flat, but in spite of his obvious confusion and frustration, his neck was still dark.

The image flickered and came back. The same man at the same computer leaned back in the same chair. He was barefooted and naked to the waist, but was still wearing his uniform pants. Behind him, the wall of lights was entirely yellow.

"It's all over," he said. "So I guess I should talk about it. For posterity." He snorted without much humor and bent out of frame, coming back with a bottle. He drank, then rubbed his brows and put the bottle on the desk next to his computer. "For all the people," he said dryly, "who are going to see this and want to know what happened. So. What happened is, making war makes money. I wish we had a better reason. I wish we had enemies at least, a war that we were making the stuff for...but it was just something we were making. Just our job."

He drank again, leaning back to put his feet up on the side of the desk, one leg crossed over the other. He looked at the camera, then at the bottle, then snorted again. "Water," he said. "Enhanced, though. Something else we were working on. Everything the body needs in one bottle. We were all the way into development when that contract was canceled—feeding our soldiers just isn't as profitable as killing them—so there's a whole storage cell full of the stuff down below. It's not bad. Tastes a little like ykara." He drank some more, then set the bottle aside.

"So what happened?" he asked. "How did all these nice, sane people who designed the annihilation of the world let it get out? It wasn't on purpose. It wasn't even by accident. It was just one of those things, as my daughter would say. Just one of those things. Who knew? Wait."

He got up and walked out of frame, then came back with a small, black disc-shaped object. He held it up for the camera, then sat it down and tapped it. A second image sprang up, flickering so madly that only the most general outlines could be made out. He tapped through a few different shapes before he stopped and held the disc up. "This is Bsaia," he said. "She's thirteen. And if everything happened the way it was supposed to, she died eleven days ago, in the first two hours after the cloud hit. She and her mother—" He tapped back two images. "—Ylati, and our two sons—" Forward one tap. "—Tivon and Uluraq, went to the safe-room of our house as soon as the alarm went out, not knowing that the safe-room's air circulator is not rated for a Class 5 contaminant. So. Two hours after the cloud hit, one of two things happened. Either our neighbors broke in or Tivon and Uluraq did it themselves, but my wife and my daughter were raped to death, and my sons either killed each other or were killed by one of our neighbors. I honestly don't know what to hope for." He looked at the images once more, then switched them off and looked at the camera.

"I keep talking about the cloud like you know what it is. So. Each of our development stations is powered by a geothermic fission system. Safest and most reliable form of power in the world. Cheap, too. Once the fixtures are in place, the generator runs itself, all the way down to the automated maintenance system. The surplus power it puts out pays for its installation before the first year is done, so naturally, only the military knows about it." The man started to say something else, then laughed curtly and waved it away. "Never mind. I'm sure I'll come back to that at some point. I've got all the time in the world to talk now...there's just no one left to listen to me."

The man leaned over his desk and covered his face for several long, brutally indifferent minutes of silent recording before he finally switched the camera off.

Meoraq turned around and went to the door. He hit the lockplate twice. Both times, the door clicked and counted down the minutes for him until the locks would open. He stood rigid, staring into the closed face of the door until, with a curt motion, he looked at her. He didn't say anything.

Neither did she.

The monitor flickered. Meoraq turned his head a little more, enough to watch the man in the recording lean back in his chair. The bottle was still there beside him. He said, "Safest and most reliable power in the world. I'm sure there's been a few close calls that I'm not aware of, but there's never been an accident. The system maintains itself. Under optimum conditions, they say it can run without dumaq intervention for a thousand years. Maybe more. So. The military uses it for all its most sensitive installations. Because it's so safe. And no one wants these things to get out, remember. No one built them to actually be used. That would just be crazy, right?

"Kunati exploded," he went on without any change in his tone or expression. "Saiakr says they were working on three major projects, but the Wrath was the only one that seems to have gotten out. I guess the others were incinerated in the blast. I don't know. I only know no one's bleeding out their eyes or having their bones turn to jelly while they're being fucked to death, so it's not as bad as it could have been.

"Kunati was in a relatively unpopulated area. Protected. No one wanted this stuff to get out." He snorted, uncapped the bottle, but then capped it again without drinking and just held it restlessly between his hands. "But the virus was designed to be delivered through explosive payload, so when Kunati blew, it did just...just what we built it to do. It turned to vapor and the wind took it away."

The man gestured back at the wall of yellow lights without looking at it. "Saiakr says, when the virus hit, you could actually see it happen in the way people started fighting. If you were close enough, you could hear it...the roaring...coming in like the tide. He said, in the cities, the fires were opening up like flowers. Blooming. Isn't that a pretty way to describe the end of the world?"

"Blooms," said Meoraq, impassive. "I call it, 'Blooms'." He looked at the lockplate, pressed it, punched it.

"All of us were locked down by then, of course. Watching the blooms. For the first two days, we were told that it was temporary and we'd all go home as soon as the risk of contamination had dropped to acceptable levels. Like there were acceptable levels. Like none of us knew what the damn thing had been designed to do. And on the third day, a few hours before the cloud reached the capitol, the word came down that we needed to start incinerating the viruses. And firing the bombs. Because—and this was actually what they said—we couldn't allow Tirazez to fall when the rest of the world still stood. So. So." He dragged in a deep, shaking breath and looked right at the camera. "So, knowing that billions of people were dead and millions more would be dead by the next day, someone out there loaded up the rest of God's Wrath and fired it. The whole world...bloomed."

He looked at the camera stonily for a few more seconds, then switched it off.

"It's just a recording," said Amber softly.

Meoraq pressed his palm to the lockplate and rested the top of his head on the door. "I know."

"It's awful, but it'll be all right."

He glanced at her.

The recording came back on. The man was back. This time, he was entirely naked except for some lizardish underwear. To see him wearing something as flimsy as fabric there instead of a metal loin-plate was a little shocking. "It's day sixty-three," he said, dropping into the chair. "It's late. I was exploring the administration levels today and found some koa, so I'm drunk as fuck. Celebrating," he added, and raised his empty hand in a salute. "I saw a fire today. Which means someone's still alive to set one. I lit the outer lamps, but no one's come yet. I'm still hopeful." He snorted, muttered, "So hopeful," under his breath, and laughed.

"Saiakr killed himself this morning," he said at the end of it, and raised his imaginary cup again. "Or as good as. He's been talking about it for a while, although he doesn't call it that. He doesn't have any enhanced nutrition water at his base, just what comes out of the purifiers, so he's been eating out of the officers' lounge all this time. This morning, he brought out the last of it. Then he called me up to say goodbye. Said he was going to eat all he wanted and then take a transport from the garage and start driving. Said he could be here in three days. He said...Contaminant levels are still at ninety-nine percent," he said suddenly. "But I still saw that fire and thought..."

He bent over, rubbing at his brows, and abruptly laughed. "If he makes it, I'm letting him in," he announced. "I don't care if he's infected or not. Even if he's fucking me to death, it's still a living touch, you know? It's still another person. And it's still sixty-three days gone and I'm the only one left and I thought, for posterity, I ought to maybe explain how that happened.

"I'm a technician. I maintain the equipment that built the viruses. There are three other technicians that work here, so there's always one of us on site, but we're not soldiers. We're not military. We're not scientists." He snorted. "Thank God for the cleaners or we wouldn't have anyone to bully around. Of course, the cleaners don't have to have someone on site at all times. Or the scientists. When Kunati blew and the base locked down, we were on dead shift. Ironic, eh? Six soldiers and me. And they were all down in the garage, playing High Six. Technicians not invited. So I was locked in when the cloud went up. And they were locked out."

He was quiet for a moment, staring impassively into space, and then he said, "There were cameras down there. There's cameras everywhere. And I could see them banging on the door trying to get back in, but I couldn't override the system. I did try. Eventually. When the cloud was coming. But I couldn't. The cloud hit and they...I shut off the monitor, so I'm not sure exactly what happened. I know there was one of them left alive, because I'd turn on the monitor sometimes and see him still...on them. But he wandered off eventually. I don't know where. Maybe out to the base housing, eh? Maybe he was the one who found Ylati...and Bsaia...and the boys. I suppose it doesn't matter, really. Saiakr had a full shift on at his base, though. All their people were safely locked in just like they should have been. One hundred and fifteen people, he said.

"But the word came down, like the word always does. The viruses were incinerated. Then the scientists were killed. Then the officers were told to kill the low-ranking soldiers, so they did, and I guess the commanding officer took out the officers. Saiakr was a technician, I don't remember if I told you. Our job is to crawl around inside tiny tubes and under machines and behind panels. Nobody knows how to hide like we do. He worked his way up through the air system until he was in the floor under the commander's office. That's where he was when the base commander came back and shot himself. One hundred and fifteen people were saved from the cloud. One hundred and fourteen of them killed each other anyway. Because those were their orders. He told me that," said the man, rubbing at his brows, "and what can I say? We called the stuff God's Wrath, did I tell you? We called the stuff God's Wrath...and maybe it was."

He shut the camera off. The monitor flickered while Meoraq leaned on the door and took deep breaths and then the picture came back. The man was there, fully dressed, haggard, with a device in his hand that could only be a gun.

"I can't believe I'm down here again," he said and looked at the gun. "So. Fuck it. It's day one-eighty-eight. Saiakr isn't coming. No one is. I've been transmitting non-stop over every channel every day, but no one comes. I've got enough nutrition water to last a hundred people a hundred years, but there's just me...and I'm tired. So." He hefted the gun briefly. "So this is it. I just wanted to say, just in case there's someone out there after all, that I'm sorry. If you find me...fuck, I don't know. Burn me, I guess.

I shouldn't be infected, but burn me anyway. Just in case. I'll understand if you want to piss on me first."

He lifted his head and looked directly at the camera. "My name is Nuu Sukaga and I helped to kill the world." He raised the gun and fired. The shot was silent, producing nothing but a pulse of light that briefly rippled across his scales. The sound of his skull bursting open and his brains hitting the back of the chair behind him was wet and loud. The body slumped over and out of frame. The camera kept recording.

Meoraq watched for a short time, then pushed himself slowly off the door. He walked out into the room and looked behind the desk.

"Is he there?" Amber asked uneasily.

"No."

"Are you...Are you all right?"

He glanced at her, then at the monitor. "Apparently not. You understood more of that, I think, than I did. And you were not surprised." He turned around to face her. "How long have you known?"

"I..."

"Since the niyowah in the ruins, the night of the storm," he mused, looking away. "I think you tried to tell me. You had a word for it. I remember that."

"Meoraq—"

"Tell me the word. I can't say it. I want to hear it again."

She felt her shoulders falling without ever realizing how tensely she'd been holding them. "Biological warfare," she said softly.

"This means fighting? With...blooms?"

"With disease," she said.

He looked at her, then at the monitor again. A cleanerbot had come silently into the room. She could just see the top of its rounded head as it hovered beside the chair, moving minutely back and forth as, presumably, it cleaned the corpse. "You built them?" he asked. "Like machines? You could actually make...madness? And hurl it, like a spear?"

The monitor went abruptly black. He looked at it, frowning, as a new image snapped on. The same room, now with several lizardmen standing around the desk. The nearest of them stepped back, his head cocked at a critical angle, and said, "There it is."

"Is it working?"

"Says it is." The man's spines flared forward and snapped back in a terse shrug. "The only way to check is to turn it off."

"Check."

"Mkole!" one of the others groaned, but the first man, although plainly irritated, stepped forward again and the screen went briefly black.

"God, that's awful," said Amber, watching. "How long...I mean...Do you think that's Saiakr?"

Meoraq grunted one of his I-don't-know grunts, frowning.

The image came back in the middle of Mkole's waspish, "—only to find out it was never recording!"

"Leave him alone, Brunt," said the first man, his spines now completely flat. "Let's just do this. My name is Oyan Ichazul."

Meoraq startled. After a moment, Amber realized the name was familiar to her as well. Oracle Oyan was one of the Six. It could be a coincidence—who knew how many Bierces there were back on Earth?—but no sooner had this thought ventured itself into her brain than the others added themselves to the roster.

"My name is Uyane Xaima."

"I am Surgeon Thaliszr Mkole."

"Shev. Mykrm Shevas."

"I was Amagar Silq. They call me the Brunt now."

"And I am Lashraq Zhan," finished Zhan. "It is now 3046, what some people are calling Year Seventeen after the Fall. Sometime in the spring, I think."

Shev snorted. "Not that anyone can tell. The U'uskirs dropped their whole fucking array when they got hit by the cloud. They didn't even aim the fucking thing, just fired whatever they had at whatever it all happened to be pointed at. Over seven thousand disruptors going off at once. Irradiated the whole fucking planet, and you can't hear it from in here, but the storm it kicked up when it happened is still going on. I haven't seen the sun once in seventeen years."

"I'm sure we'll be seeing the casualties for some time," Mkole added anxiously, "but we seem to have stabilized for now. Death by direct exposure to radiation seems to have receded to nominal levels and the risk of related complications appears to be dropping as well. Along the eastern seaboard of Tirazez, anyway."

"Ah fuck me, here we go," muttered Xaima, rubbing at his brow-ridges. "Zhan, shut him down or tie me up. I can't listen to this again."

"Breathe, Xaima. Breathe and let him talk. This is part of why we came here."

"What is this?" Meoraq asked. His spines were flat, his eyes wide, betraying a terrible tension and fear that had not been present even during Technician Nuu's short series of narratives. "Who are these people? What are they saying?"

She put her hand on his arm and he looked at her wildly. "It's all right, Meoraq."

"Those are not priests!"

"Just listen."

Mkole concluded his rather rambling summary of the post-apocalyptic health hazards he'd seen with the optimistic note that, "We've estimated that life expectancy has risen almost six months in the past seven years and although female fertility remains dangerously low, from all reports, one out of every thirty pregnancies is now being carried to term with no marked increase in infant defect or mortality."

"That's enough."

"But this could be important!" Mkole protested, looking wounded. "Statistics like these are absolutely vital in the process of—"

"Enough for now then," said Zhan, but gently. "Just for now. Thank you, surgeon."

"We need to make records," Mkole insisted, retreating with the help of the burly Brunt to sit in the chair where Nuu had blown his brains out. He wiped at his eyes. "It's important! We have to tell them about...about how it all ended!"

"It's not over yet," the Brunt rumbled, patting him, and Xaima, scowling at them with his arms folded and looking so much like Meoraq that Amber had to check and see that it wasn't just his reflection in the video screen, flicked his spines and muttered, "It may as well be."

"No! Listen! We have seen..." Mkole's words faltered. For a moment, he merely stared at the camera, his eyes flicking back and forth like an actor reading his next troubling lines. It took Lashraq's hand on his shoulder before he seemed to pull himself out of it, first with a shaky breath and then the continuation of his even, almost unemotional recital. "We have seen what is unquestionably only the beginning of a devastating wave of extinctions. You...You simply can't imagine how quickly it happens. The collapse is..."

Mkole lapsed again into blank-faced silence.

"We still have some livestock in the middle districts," Lashraq said, frowning. "Mostly ilqi. But I don't think they'll last much longer."

"It turns out that cattle need feed," Shev pointed out wryly. "And feed needs to be planted, grown, harvested and processed."

"Oh, it's got nothing to do with feeding them," said the Brunt, looking very mildly surprised. "Ilqi, tuk-tuks, woolyvibs, and every other kind of cattle we keep, I promise you, even the so-called natural-grown ones—most of them are surgically altered to keep them from fucking and the rest probably couldn't figure out how."

"All the animals are dying," Ichazul said suddenly. "Wild and domestic. It's not the Wrath and it can't all be the weather—"

"The weather's part of it," Lashraq muttered, glancing up as if he could see through the roof to the storm howling behind it.

"Of course, it's part of it!" Ichazul snapped. "There's no direct sunlight anymore, the fucking rain never stops until it freezes, and the ice storms never stop until they turn back into rain! But it's only part of it. The real problem is the plants. Nothing grows like it used to. There's something, some kind of chemical wash in the rain or maybe a parasite or a virus, but whatever it is, it's killing everything."

"Untrue," the Brunt said. "Thorns and rockweed are growing. They'll grow right up your boots if you stand still."

Ichazul rolled his eyes and gave his spines an irritable flick. "Fine, it's killing all the crops. By which I mean the stuff we need to eat."

"By which you mean," the Brunt corrected, smiling, "the stuff we've made dependent upon us. Think about it. Artificial pollination, climate control, nutrient-enriched soil...koitaan and pialhfruit were never meant to grow in Gedai. Are you really surprised it's all dying? Everything that was already in the ground grew wild after the Wrath fell," he added, looking directly into the computer's camera. "But it takes men to grow crops these days and all the men were busy killing each other. So it all died."

"I have tried on six separate occasions to grow riak," Ichazul countered. Faint lines of color were becoming visible along his throat. "Riak! And I know what I'm doing, damn it! I'm telling you, it's more than that! There's something wrong, something in the soil or the rain or...something!"

"Who knows what we shot at each other?" Xaima asked, showing very little concern. "I don't see any reason why you can't both be right. It wouldn't take much of a contaminant to kill off a grove of koitaan in Gedai, or for animals to eat all the crops and seed that were left. Because for a while there were animals everywhere. Not just the vermin, like you'd think, but everything. All the people were dead and the animals simply exploded to fill all that empty space. We were hip-deep in ponucs that first year and then they all dropped dead and the uzayas and ebii were everywhere until they dropped dead. You'd think all our pet apas would just go feral and be all right, but they were all gone by the third year." He stopped there, his spines slowly lowering, and finally said, "I still can't really believe that. I've had an apa underfoot all my life. But they're gone. Everywhere. They just..."

"Collapsed," said Mkole.

"And he's right, it's probably just the beginning," Lashraq agreed quietly. "I don't know if anything will be left at the end, but there's always hope. We still have some ilqis and if we can take care of them, they'll make it. There will always be yifu, I suppose, and the ghets seem to be doing all right."

"Naturally," muttered Xaima, rubbing at the side of his snout. "All the apas are dead, but we have ghets."

"They're little and furry. Maybe we can make pets out of them instead," suggested the Brunt. "You've still got your apa's collar, don't you?"

"Fuck a fist," Xaima snapped.

The Brunt's spines flared lazily forward. "Is that an offer?"

"So we've lost most of our domestic animals and about half the native wildlife," said Lashraq as his men visibly defused themselves, edging away from one another and taking slow breaths. "But several conservation parks seemed to have opened their doors in the first days of God's Wrath and while most of the animals have died off, some of them actually seem to be thriving."

"There are saoqs all over central Yroq," Shev inserted with a laugh. "I mean it. They're everywhere."

"And corrokis," grunted the Brunt. "Wild corrokis. In herds."

"Right. The apas die. The woolyvibs die. The oshe? I haven't seen even a track in the mud in more than ten years." Shev leaned forward into the camera's eye, spreading his arms and flaring his spines fully forward to make himself as impressively sincere as possible. "But there are corrokis all over Yroq. Chew on that for a while. Right this moment, there are probably five, six corrokis eating the shrubs off the Prime Chancellor's lawn."

"They'll die out," said Lashraq with finality, proving that whatever else he might be, he was no prophet. "Nothing that size could possibly survive now, but other animals might. And as long as we have something to feed on and something else to clean up after us, we have some hope of restoring and maintaining a natural balance."

"Natural," snorted the Brunt.

"I believe the world will survive. In our arrogance, we may have thought we could destroy it, but the world is more resilient than any weapon our mortal minds could dream up. All we can do is kill each other," Lashraq said.

"But we are damned good at that," agreed the Brunt, striking his chest with feigned pride. Shev and Ichazul laughed.

Zhan stared at his boots until they quieted. At last, he raised his hand and indicated the group as a whole. "Hard to believe this started out as a supply raid."

Meoraq started again. "Raid?"

"I'm from Daophith, originally. After the cloud hit, somehow a fire got started and the whole city burned to the ground, along with Jezaana and Zethoze and half the northern states. Best thing, really. The cities were no good after the Fall, nothing but killing grounds for God's Wrath. I ended up outside Ynanje with Shev and Ichi here, living in an old waystation. By the time the cold season came along, we were all six together and Shev made two fairly sky-shaking observations. The first was that God Himself couldn't have arranged a better group to survive the annihilation of all life as we know it: soldier, mechanic, surgeon, historian, technician and botanist. The second was that we had no women."

"And you all were starting to look pretty damn good to me," Xaima remarked.

"So with the lofty goal in mind of acquiring, in no particular order, food, water, supplies and sex," said Zhan archly, "we set out from our cozy waystation to see what was left of the world. Somehow, that turned into a two-year trek across the fucking country, stopping in at every house with a lit window along the way."

"Got dipped once in a while, didn't we?" Shev grunted.

Zhan acknowledged this with a shrug of his spines. "So. The Brunt back there pointed out that we were probably the first people to really get a good look at the world beyond the one little piece we inhabited after the Fall and we had what he called a divinely-ordained obligation to record our findings."

"Fuck you, O noble leader," said the Brunt, amused.

"Records are important," Mkole whispered, and the Brunt patted his shoulder.

"Records are important," Zhan agreed, his spines lowering. "Because when we sat down to really talk about it, we realized we'd actually learned something pretty damn amazing. I think it was...I think it was you who noticed."

"In Reqann, yes." Xaima stepped up as Zhan moved back, eyeing the camera with an expression of rueful humor and contempt. "By that time, we'd been to a few of these military outposts and finally found out just what the fuck had happened. Most of them had some kind of survivor's journal left for us to find, like the one this poor pisser made, but with the exception of that crazy woman with all the dolls, they were dead. We couldn't ask any questions and if we didn't have Ichi along, we could never have run the damn videos in the first place."

"Almost every one of them were technicians," Ichazul remarked, "and not one thought to put their video on automatic playback. Sure, the recording will last until the end of Time or until their roof caves in, but in fifty years, everyone who knows which buttons to push is going to be dead."

"So here we are," said Zhan and snorted. "And I don't know how happy you're going to be when you hear what we have to say, but if you're standing there to hear it at all, then our plan probably worked. Just remember that." He glanced at the other men, grunted to himself, and looked back at the camera. "If we did our job right, you may have heard that we came here to meet with Great Sheul and that we heard His words and wrote His laws," he said. "But honestly...we're going to make it all up."

* * *

Amber and Meoraq listened. There were plenty of words she didn't know, but she was able to work most of them out by context; there must have been just as many words he didn't know, and set down in ways just as foreign to him, but Meoraq asked no questions. Her awareness of him faded as the men on the screen talked about the virus Nuu had called God's Wrath with the kind of clinical callousness that came so easily to survivors. They didn't pace, rarely gestured, and had a habit of looking right at the camera even when they weren't talking so that it began to feel uneasily like they were alive—that they were here in this room, in this very moment—so much so that Amber found herself nodding now and then to show them she was listening.

Beside her, Meoraq remained motionless. He listened and did not react at all.

"The virus had absolute communicability in its first stage, the cloud stage," Xaima said, gesturing vaguely towards the consoles surrounding them. "And if Ichi really knows how to read these machines and isn't just lying us along for the dips and the good times—"

"Oh fuck me, my secret is out," said Ichazul dryly.

"—then it's still at ninety-six, seventeen fucking years after the Fall. The shit is in everything now. The air, the ground, the water...everything. So I guess it's safe to assume that everyone has it. Why isn't everyone dead?" He paused. "I have it. I woke up alone in the streets of South Thuure covered in blood. Caked in it. And I don't know what I'd been fucking, but I'd scraped half the scales off my dick doing it and what was left was also caked in blood. I found a—" He stopped himself there, rubbing restlessly at his throat, which was still safely black. At last, he tipped his head slightly and went on.

"So. God's Wrath is finite. Eventually, no matter how deep in you are, you run out of things to kill and things to fuck. You calm down. Of course, you're ready to rage again the instant Mkole starts talking or, hell, even if you get a little too deep into a nice, tight woman, but if you feel it coming on, you can sometimes get clear of it. It's not like being crazy, at least not all the time. You're aware when you start to burn. You can stop it if you try. The problem is what the problem's been with us dumaqs all along: Trying is hard and we don't want to do it."

"Burning is easy," added Shev. "Especially when we can all tell each other that it's the virus and how impossible it is to stop once you've let go. We're not in control. It's all the virus."

"But there is a scale," Ichazul put in. "Some of us let go slow and come out of it fairly quick. And some of us go completely fucking out of their scaly skin and stay there for days. So far, we haven't found anyone who's actually immune, but there's obviously some kind of resistance. And since we're starting to see the first generation after the Fall coming into their maturity, it seems like it might be genetic."

"Right," said Xaima, flaring his spines with irritation, although the interruption itself hadn't appeared to have bothered him. "Now I'm going to talk about a place called Nishi, which used to be some holy site two or three thousand years ago—I guess it still was—but for the most part, it was a city like pretty much every other city except for the eastern edge of town, which was occupied by the Sheulists."

Amber glanced at Meoraq. He seemed calm enough, but only if one didn't look at his eyes.

"When the cloud hit Nishi, it went down exactly like every other city we've visited...except along the eastern edge. There were over a thousand people living there after the Fall, and just in case you don't understand how significant that is, I don't think we've come across a thousand more people anywhere else in the world, even if we lumped them all together. When we first found them, we didn't know what to think except that maybe they were somehow immune or maybe they'd all been underground or maybe they'd been transmitting their location to survivors and most of them were refugees, but no. The only difference between eastern Nishi and the rest of the world was the Sheulists, and the biggest thing about the Sheulists is not just that they believe in their god, but they believe that their god is in control. These people work, and I mean *work*, for hours every day, systematically reinforcing the idea that nothing a man does has any lasting effect and any perception to the contrary is only part of God's plan."

"We're not in control," said Shev, in exactly the same tone he'd used before and with only the slightest arch twist to his expression. "It's all God's will."

"That shit is maddening," Xaima commented, glancing that way. "I had to be tied down for eight days because of the rage those fools put in me with that."

"I didn't handle it too well at first either," Shev admitted. "But it was hard to ignore a thousand people in one place where everywhere else, you couldn't count fifty. I'm sure Mkole can fill up a few hours talking about the altered mind states of meditation or how it suppresses this chemical or excites that gland or what the fuck ever it does. It worked, that's the important thing."

"Right up until their high priest decided they should all go to Sheul's Halls together," Ichazul said with a snort. "Crazy fucking zealots drank deathweed. Brewed it up with honey, lined up and drank it. Like they were drinking tea."

"Yes, but they were calm when they did it," said the Brunt. "And when we moved on from there to Maiaq, Zhan told the leader of those refugees that if he gave himself to Sheul, the Wrath couldn't take him. Maybe it helped that none of them had ever been a Sheulist themselves or knew much more than whatever you pick up listening to some idiot pray up a transport dock. Zhan told them—correct me if I exaggerate, noble leader—the most outrageous packet of lies ever emitted by the mouth of a man."

Zhan didn't correct him. He just stood there, arms folded, brooding on his boots.

"And they bought it," Xaima said, flinging out his arms. "They bought every fucking word. In a single day, this man reinvented both a caste system and a working model of a fucking theocracy and hammered them together, and by the very next morning, forty-two people were out in the fucking rain, praying. These were people who would have laughed at the very idea of god-worship just seventeen short years ago."

"Gets harder to laugh at the idea of a vengeful god after the world comes to a burning end," Zhan remarked.

"I guess." Xaima gave his head a shake. "We spent the whole cold season there, the six of us wedged in with forty-two other people in a warehouse no bigger than this room, and no one died. He had them praying every morning, meditating every night, and preaching Sheul's grace and Sheul's justice and Sheul's hammer and Sheul's fires farting out Sheul's ass until we almost had to tie Ichi up again."

Ichazul snorted. "No crying. I was that close."

"But no one let go. Not one of them raged. So suddenly, he's Prophet Lashraq and we're his holy oracles. And we're not chasing after slit and free food any more, we're preaching about Sheul's burning hand and the caste of the Hammer or the Sword and the sacred number of creation."

"And being handed slit and free food," said Shev.

"Never got so much dipping in my life as I did after I turned holy," added the Brunt in a reflective manner.

Still nothing from Meoraq.

"And it seems to work everywhere we go," Xaima went on, "but what good does that do, really? The cloud will be around a hundred years at least. The virus will be in everyone's fucking *blood*. We'll all be dead, but the rage goes on, and already we're finding people pretending to be priests of Sheul and adding their lies to our lies for their own unscrupulous purposes."

"Like chasing slit and getting free food," said the Brunt.

"So Zhan says we need a holy writ, something people can read, something that will last," Xaima concluded. "We found a printing shop in what's left of Pholcha and Ichi says he can get it running and bind us up some books. All we have to do is come up with some sufficiently holy-sounding way to keep people from letting go to rage. Zhan studied this piss for who knows how many years, so we'll let him do all the wording, but for posterity's sake, here's what we've come up with so far. First, limit the fucking."

"No," said Zhan quietly. "First, Sheul's word alone is law. There are no other gods and no men with authority to alter or interpret his word. His law is absolute as written. There is no other truth."

"Whatever," said Xaima, rolling his eyes. "Second is to limit the fucking. God's Wrath doesn't just make a man mad. It hits him in the part of his brain where all us civilized dumaqs keep our most basic impulses."

Mkole raised his head, blinking as if he'd heard his name. "It attacks the hypothalamus, primarily, and through it, the adrenal system. Females have been, ah, depressed and males, stimulated. Rage is essentially an overdose of male sexual hormones, ah, which dominate our aggressive response and...and...hyper-sensitivity to female pheromones."

"That's what I said," Xaima snapped, looking annoyed. "If he gets a whiff of a woman, he'll fuck her. If he gets caught up fucking, he'll eventually go into rage. The longer he's in rage, the more he'll want to fuck, and while his brain is burning up, he's killing and fucking everything that moves. So lock up the women and limit the fucking."

"Be very careful when you write that one up," Shev added. "You'll have them castrating themselves or killing their daughters."

"Right. Sex is fine—"

"Sex is great," said the Brunt, with feeling.

"But limit it. We've been saying no more than twice a dip—"

"Because three is the sacred number of creation," agreed Shev and threw Zhan a grimace of admiration. "I honestly don't know where he comes up with this stuff."

"—because two seems to get a man past that first desperate stage, even if he hasn't had a righteous poke in a year, but two doesn't wear him down so much that the burn just takes over. But the challenge is going to be limiting the killing. If we did this right, you probably don't have any idea what kind of killing is going on out here," Xaima said in a low, suddenly somber tone. "You'd think, in a world where so many people have died so senselessly, that we would do anything to preserve another dumaq life, but let me tell you, it is not so. We are killing each other over water, food, medicine, women, blankets, shelters, books, boots, who won the fucking Cenuqa tournament in 3013, whether or not corrokis can look up—"

"They can *not*," Shev interrupted, sending a black glare at the Brunt, who calmly replied, "Of course they can, they just choose not to."

"Anything and everything," Xaima concluded with a sigh, rubbing at his throat again. "Not because we're sick, not because of the virus, but just...because. And we're doing it more than ever before, because now there's no one around to tell us not to."

"Yet," said Zhan.

"I don't know how the hell he thinks he's going to scare us so bad we stop fighting overnight, but if I have the broad strokes right, it comes down to three things: Take away the knives. If they don't see or smell blood, apparently, they won't think about it. Like there aren't a hundred other ways to kill a man, Zhan."

"Have to start somewhere."

"Here's an idea, start with the fucking *guns*!"

"I will. That kind of technology will be part of Gann's corruption. We'll make it a sin to work machines."

"The piss you say!"

"You can't mean it, Zhan. What are we supposed to do, live in caves and wear animal skins?"

"Who's Gann?"

"We'll destroy whatever we can, of course, but all we really have to do is convince them that the cities carry Gann's taint and can corrupt anyone who enters."

"But why?"

"Because they can," Zhan said quietly. "They did."

"That is shit and you know it," spat Xaima. "Zhan, there have to be a thousand people, *good* people, trying to make lives in those cities, trying to build them up again and make them safe. They're not going to leave just because you offer them a god! You give this ridiculous fucking cult of yours ten years and your Sheulists will kill those people for no reason! For *God*!"

"I know."

"And you don't care!"

"I can't, Xaima. I have to care about what else they were making when they dropped God's Wrath and who might be looking for it. There may be a thousand good people in those cities, but there have to be ten thousand weapons and they're all just lying around. There's no way we can pick everything up ourselves. We have to make them all *want* to just...not look."

"What are we supposed to do without cities?" Shev demanded.

"Build new ones." Zhan looked up as a faint rumble heralded a particularly vicious peal of thunder in whatever storm beat on their walls in the past. "Stronger ones. The old cities aren't safe anyway. Not anymore. Even this place will fall down if we don't protect it."

"Right, so let me see if I have your plan. We herd everyone out of their shelters, tell them technology is bad and give them a pointed stick and a fucking spoon to build a new home with, and then we take the most violent people we can find, the ones with the absolute least resistance to the virus, and, instead of just killing them—"

"We can't just kill them, Xaima," Zhan said patiently. "If we turn it into a fight, they'll win it. They'll rage first, they'll rage longer, and they'll rip us apart."

"Whatever. We tell them the reason they're so violent is because God has blessed them, have I got that right?"

"Yes."

"We make them members of the highest caste instead. We give them the knives no one else gets to play with and we tell them they're holy warriors instead of the psychotic murder machines they really are."

Amber looked at Meoraq again. His spines were flat and shivering slightly against his skull, but other than that, he looked only very mildly interested.

"When they believe it, they'll pray," said Zhan. "When they pray, they'll calm down."

"We give them all the women they want—"

"Provided they respect the sacred number of creation—"

"He said it with a straight face," murmured the Brunt.

"—and raise any children they make as members of their caste."

"What the hell good does that do?" Xaima burst out. The patches along his throat began to pale ominously. "Why the fuck would you go out of your way to find the worst fucking strain of the virus and breed *more* carriers?"

"Calm down, Xaima."

"*It makes no sense*!"

"Xaima. Breathe."

Xaima clapped both hands to his snout and bent himself in half, choking in air and hissing it out while the others watched warily. Gradually, very gradually, his scales faded back to black.

"The idea," said Zhan, "is not to breed carriers, but to isolate them. We start them praying as soon as they can talk and keep them at it all their lives. We let them fight each other away from the public eye and we make them kill each other when they do. We give them women so they don't have an excuse to riot through people's homes and take them. We take the children away and start them praying and on it goes. If we do this long enough, with any luck, we'll breed whatever quality it is that makes some of us so predisposed to the virus into the smallest percent of the population, which will then kill itself off."

"Never work," said Shev.

"Probably not, or at least not for a long time. But it will keep them under control. Look," said Zhan, his own scales lightening although his tone never changed, "if you throw a man in a cage, he will spend the rest of his life fighting to escape. But if you tell him no one else in the world gets the cage but him, dress it up and throw in a few pillows, then he'll walk in on his own."

One breath. That was all Meoraq did. Just took one breath a little harder than the rest. Amber took his hand impulsively. He looked at it, then at her, and then up at the screen again, all without expression.

"What a shining flood of ghet-shit!" Xaima was exclaiming.

"They'll believe me," said Zhan, not looking up from his boots. His scales were already returning to their normal color. "They want desperately to believe in something, anything, and there is nothing else left. Yes, it's a lie. But the lie will be glorious. If it's the one lamp left burning in the whole world...everyone will come to see it."

The doors clicked. The androgynous lizardly voice informed them that the timeout had ended, the locks were released.

Meoraq turned around.

Amber started after him, but he stopped her with the cut of one upraised hand.

"Stay," he said in a hoarse voice that strove for calm. "Stay and hear them. I need to...I need to think."

He walked away. Amber watched the doors groan open and shut as Zhan kept talking, outlining the principles of a gospel Meoraq could probably recite in its polished form from the first invocation to the final amen. His glorious lie.

10

It couldn't have been much more than an hour before the recording finally finished, but if someone had told her that it had been three hours or even six, Amber would have believed it. She felt older, right down to her bones.

She didn't want to move, but she didn't linger. The lights were already fading, the room powering down, and she did not want to be trapped in here when the doors died. Human voices weren't the same as a dumaq's. She wasn't at all sure 'Nuu Sukaga was going to work for her.

But the lockplate took her tap and the doors hissed open and there was Meoraq, sitting just outside, his knees drawn up and his chin resting on his arms, staring at the mark of the Prophet on the wall. He'd lit some of the candles. He'd stomped on a few too, but at the moment, he was just sitting there.

"Hey," she said.

He did not reply, not even to look at her.

"Do you want to hear any of it?" she asked, because she felt she ought to offer, even though she knew damned well he didn't.

No response.

She went over and stood next to him, fidgeting unhappily with the front of her tunic. She felt awful, too awful to cry, too awful to even throw up. She touched his shoulder—it was stone wrapped in leather—and then petted at the top of his head. His flat spines flicked hard, throwing off her hand. She took it back and kept it to herself, clutching at her girdle. "Please talk to me," she said.

Silence.

"Can I talk to you?"

His faceless stare wavered and finally shifted up at her. He still didn't answer, not even to grunt, but he watched as she moved around and sat down in front of him.

"There's this saying I used to hear a lot," said Amber. "It goes, 'The road to Hell is paved with good intentions.' I used to think it was total horseshit, to tell you the truth. I mean, intentions matter, so if someone tries to do something good, I mean really *tries*, that ought to count for something."

Meoraq remained immobile, silent.

"I can only imagine what you're feeling," she said. "And I don't think I can imagine it very well. But...he had good intentions, Meoraq. People were killing each other. The last people on the whole planet, the very last ones, were still killing each other. He stopped it the only way he knew how."

"He lied."

The words were wounds in Meoraq's throat. She could hear them bleeding.

"Why?" he asked suddenly. "Why did he have to leave a message? Why couldn't he just do it and let us have the lie if we needed it so much?"

"Maybe because...he wanted to believe you wouldn't always need it. He was a teacher once. He knew the value of preserving the past for the future. And he—Listen to me, Meoraq!" She caught his arm and refused to be shaken off. "He thought he was doing the right thing. And maybe he was. If people could change on their own, don't you think they would have in the seventeen years before this guy Lashraq came to Xi'Matezh?"

"Don't call it that," Meoraq said harshly. "This is no shrine."

"Yes, it is. It may not be the one you thought it was, but it is a shrine. When it would have been so easy to make sure no one ever heard any of that, Lashraq wanted it heard. He wanted people to know what he did and why he did it. Meoraq—" Amber moved her hand from his shoulder to touch the heaving plates over his heart. "He wanted people to know the truth."

"Truth? What is the truth, eh? Yesterday, I was the Sword in His hand! Today, I am sick! Today, God's hand on my heart is a poison in my fucking brain! Today, I have murdered *hundreds of people*!" He slapped a hand hard over his snout and shut his eyes, taking several deep breaths before he spoke again. "Stop trying to comfort me. I have been well-trained by their lies. A Sheulek is always calm."

"You told me once that truth isn't always just what someone says," said Amber after a moment. "But what something *is*. What it means."

"This place means nothing. Sheul's Word means *nothing*."

"So God didn't open up the door and shake their hands and say things out loud while Lashraq wrote it all down, but so what? When God talks to you, do you hear it with your ears? It's...hard to believe in God, but if there is one, I can believe He brought them here. I saw that whole tape and I can believe it because I believe it was the only thing that could have helped your people save themselves and maybe God knew it too."

"There is no God!" hissed Meoraq. The stripes along his throat brightened visibly in surges, throbbing with his pulse. "There's *nothing* here! He lied! They all lied and I can live with that, but right now, damn it, just shut up! There is no God and you knew it all along, so just let me be!"

She did, but she kept looking at him, watching the yellow bloom and die on his scales, and eventually, he looked back at her. "Can I tell you something?" she asked quietly. "Something I really have known all along. Something that is one hundred percent true. Something...Something I could have built my own shrine on."

He didn't answer, but he didn't say no.

"You're an alien," she told him. "Or I am. One of us is, at any rate."

He sighed and rubbed at his brow-ridges.

"Our worlds are billions of miles apart. We come from two entirely different evolutionary trees. You have scales, I have hair. We have different skeletons, different organs, different everything, right down to the number of fingers and toes. We are one hundred percent incompatible. The only thing we have in common is a carbon base."

"So?" he said wearily.

"So I'm pregnant," said Amber, and was amazed at how matter-of-fact she sounded, saying it for the first time. "What the hell do you call that if it isn't God?"

He raised his head from his hand and stared at her.

"You told me once that I was good at seeing evidence and, boy, did it piss me off because this is something that I really did not want to see. But men can only push themselves so far, Meoraq, and men with faith can only push so much further. All the evidence is telling me...there's something else out there, pulling from the other side. I don't like it," said Amber bluntly. "I'm not at peace with it. I sure as hell don't take comfort in it...but I'm glad you do."

He frowned, tried to look away, but Amber caught his snout and turned him back.

"Because all the things God isn't for me," she said, "you are. Because of you, I see Him every day. So start talking, lizardman, but I warn you, you've got a hard talk ahead of you if you're going to convince me there's no God after He gave you to me."

She waited, but he didn't say anything. He took a few deep breaths, then reached up and brushed the back of his hand along her cheek. His eyes closed. He bent and let her guide his head to rest on her shoulder. He put his arms around her. He did not rage.

He wept.

* * *

He cried off and on for a long time. Even after he was done, he held on to her, so heavy and so quiet that she thought he'd fallen asleep. Amber stroked his back and stared into space and after an eternity of this, was startled when he thickly said, "What are you thinking?"

"Huh?"

He lifted his head off her shoulder and shifted around until he was sitting at her side, facing the same blank stretch of wall. "You were very quiet."

"So were you."

"But I know my thoughts. What were yours?"

"I was thinking of the day my mother died," Amber admitted. "Sorry."

"Why are you sorry?"

"I don't know," she said uncomfortably. "I should have been thinking about you or something. You know. So you could ask me what I was thinking while you were at the lowest point of your life and I could say, 'How much I love you,' and you'd feel better."

He smiled faintly. "I feel better."

"Because I was thinking of my mother?" she asked, surprised.

"Because you told me the truth, even when you thought it was something I did not want to hear. That is how I know how much you love me. I do not need to be told." He brushed the back of his knuckles across her brow, then dropped his hand to his lap again and stared at the wall. "What happened the day your mother died?"

"You don't really want to know."

"You always sound so certain about the things I want."

"Fine," she said, rolling her eyes. "Nothing happened, really. I mean, we were there, but they didn't let us in to see her. We were just sitting in the room outside, me and Nicci, and I was holding her kind of like this. Waiting for the world to end."

He grunted.

"But it didn't. End, I mean. Life went on." She heard herself utter a surprisingly sincere little laugh without knowing she was going to. "Look how far it went on."

He said nothing.

"What were you thinking?" she asked.

"That I'm glad you're here with me." He said it without emotion, without looking at her. "Master Tsazr had to hear that message and walk all the way back to Xeqor alone. I couldn't do that."

"He probably thought that too, until he did it."

"I *couldn't*," he insisted. "My life ended when I heard those words. I may have looked and sounded like a living man, but I was clay, soulless *clay*...until you spoke to me again. One word changes all the others. Truth." He shut his eyes and rubbed his brow-ridges. "I am so thankful that you are here...and I have no one to thank."

Amber held him while the silence grew heavier and heavier, and when she couldn't stand it anymore, even knowing she couldn't make it any better, she said, "What are you afraid of the most?"

He was quiet. Neck bent, he opened and closed his mouth several times before finally whispering, "Being alone."

She put her arm around him again.

"I know I should be more worried about my soul," he said in a quick, almost embarrassed way. "But I think I have one and I don't think I'll care if I'm wrong when I'm dead. What frightens me is knowing I'm alone now. When it matters."

She nodded, gently rubbing at his bicep, right above his sabk, and feeling his scales scrape at her palm. "I know that nothing I say is going to fix what you're feeling right now, but listen to me, Meoraq, please. If there is no God, then you've been making all the decisions up until now and you've done just fine."

He made a sound of lackluster agreement, not looking at her.

"And if there is a God, He'll be there, the way He's always been there," said Amber. She hesitated and then softly said, "If there is a God, He's with you now."

Meoraq flinched a little. He looked up, searching the sooty ceiling as his spines slowly came all the way forward. He wiped at his eyes, glanced at his damp fingers, and stood up. "Let's go."

"Are you going to be all right?" she asked, following him to the door.

"I don't know," he said. "But at least I have the comfort of knowing nothing worse can possibly happen."

And with that, he pushed open the heavy door and stepped out into a pool of blood. He looked down; the hilt of a kzung came whistling down and cracked against the top of his head. Hands seized her, pulling her roughly out into the light over Meoraq's crumpling body, and the first thing she saw—perhaps not unsurprisingly—was neither the raiders nor their captive nor even the dead man at their feet, but Nicci in their leader's grip.

Amber let out a cry and lunged, but all this accomplished was to catch the leader's eye. He looked at her, cocked his head, looked more closely at Nicci, and then tossed her carelessly aside for one of his men to catch. He smiled.

"Hello, Eshiqi," said Iziz.

11

Nicci didn't cry. She didn't fight, either. She only stood in the bruising grip of the raider who held her, looking back at Amber with their mother's eyes. There was as much of Bo Peep's aimless, haggard accusation in that silent stare as there was pain, but there was no confusion. She didn't ask who these men were or what they wanted. She didn't ask Amber to make them go away. She just stood there.

"It'll be all right, Nicci," Amber told her, just as if she weren't also in the unbreakable grip of a lizardman, just as if Meoraq weren't lying on the ground being tied up while he was still unconscious. Just as if there were some chance it might be true.

"It will *not* be all right, Nicci!" Iziz snapped. He did not falter over her name and why should he? He had been born into Gann's world. Creation was not sacred to him; nothing was. "No matter what happens, it will not go well for you!"

Nicci did not shiver, did not even look at him. She turned her face away from Amber and watched the waves roll in from the sea.

Iziz spared this emotionless response a glance, but no more than that. Whatever he was looking for, he wanted it from Amber. "You look good, Eshiqi," he said, with surprising mildness following the venom of his other words. "I mean that. I didn't think you would. You are so fucking ugly and I hate you so fucking much, I am truly astonished by how glad I am to see you. So often, the things you look forward to the most are just sparks, eh? A flash, a little heat, and nothing but ash for the rest of your life. But you look good. Come here. Let her go," he said to the raider holding her. "She won't run. Come here, Eshiqi. Right to me."

The hands gripping her arms loosened and finally fell away. Amber walked on legs like water past Meoraq and Nicci both to stand before Iziz, close enough for him to hit her if he wanted to. She didn't think he'd kill her yet, but hitting was definitely an option. Her heart was pounding worse than it had ever done on the Candyman's humming little injections a lifetime ago, punching at her ribs from the inside so hard she couldn't believe that he couldn't hear it too.

But if he heard it, he ignored it. He gazed into her eyes like a lover—smiling, marveling, savoring. Then he reached one hand into the pocket of his sword belt and held up an insignificant slip of bent metal. He pulled a bit of mganz-wood off one sharply-pointed end and there it was: a fish hook.

Iziz looked at it. He started to speak, then just stopped and sighed instead. He looked at her.

Where was he going to use that? On her neck, on the vein that had to be throbbing there in this panicked pulse as thick as a subway tube? In her eye, or even both eyes, before the real fun began? Or would he try to use it like she'd used it on Zhuqa, and how much damage could he do down there, ripping at her insides in search of a vein she didn't even know if he'd find?

"He was my friend," said Iziz. It was not an easy admission for him and he made it like they were the only ones there to hear it. "He was our leader, but he was my friend. How many of those do you think I have, Eshiqi?"

Behind her, Meoraq groaned against the ground. Amber strained in vain to see him through the raiders and it was only because she did that she finally saw the body and recognized it as Crandall.

"Little piss-licker took a jump at me," Iziz remarked, watching her reaction.

"Friend of yours?"

"He did?"

"Seemed to think he'd have help." Iziz ran his eyes over the few remaining humans, ably held by his men. "And if he'd had it, maybe they could have had me. Not all of us, but me for certain. But they let him jump alone."

She looked for and found Eric and Dag with the raiders. They wouldn't look at her.

"I didn't kill him right away," Iziz was saying. He turned around so that he could stand at Amber's side, see what she saw and think his own thoughts. "I told him he could live if he'd raise a fist to me. You may be ugly, but you can still be useful. So I gave him the choice: Keep my camp, carry the tack, catch a few cocks or show me he can fight them off, and who knows? Maybe someday he could have a sword on his belt and a slave for his own. It's the sort of thing Zhuqa would have done," he added meditatively. "So for his sake, I offered. He told me to fuck myself. But the rest of your men put their fists right in the air when I slit his throat, didn't they...what's your name? Nicci?"

Nicci did not respond. She and the ocean were in their own world.

"I thought she was you until you came out," said Iziz, studying the two of them, first Nicci, then Amber. "I thought she was you and that maybe we'd killed you after all. They say the dead can walk again if they aren't burned and Gann won't have them. She looks like you," he mused, eyeing Nicci slowly up and down. "But she bent her neck for me and you never would. Or would you?"

Behind them, a sudden scuffling as Meoraq tried groggily to rise and was beaten back down to the ground. It took a lot of beating. Iziz watched. Amber didn't dare to, no more than she dared to look at Nicci. Iziz still had the fish hook in his hand; he was just looking for the best place to stick it in.

"What would you do, Eshiqi?" Iziz asked. His voice was low and too close to her left ear. She could see the dim dazzle of cloud-covered sun on the fish hook on her right. "If I told you I would let him go, would you raise your fist to me?"

"No."

"Why not?"

"Because you'd be lying."

He grunted, a soft paff of air against her neck, and combed through a few strands of her hair with the hook. "I suppose I would be. Get him out of here. And don't get stupid with him. That's a Sword of Sheul you're handling. Tie him up, keep both eyes open, and leave him the fuck alone until I say different. Go on."

Two of them went, dragging Meoraq between them. He let himself be taken without resistance, but his eyes were open and they were not defeated.

She knew better than to ask. She knew and she asked anyway.

"What are you going to do to him?"

"Do you expect me to answer honestly?"

"Zhuqa would."

His glance was ice on the edge of a knife. "He probably would. But he's dead. And his killer is talking at me like that's a safe or even a sane thing to do. Do you really want to know what I plan to do? Do you really think that will somehow help while you wait for it to happen?"

His throat was still black. She risked another question. "Did you burn him?"

He leaned back. "Who?" he asked, but his eyes told her he knew who.

"Zhuqa. Did you burn him at the funeral?"

Some of the raiders close enough to hear exchanged glances and murmured to others further back.

"What makes you think he even had a funeral?" Iziz asked finally.

"Because you were his friend and he would have wanted one."

He stared at her. No one else moved. No one else spoke.

"That was a damned good hit," Iziz said at last. "I mean it, Eshiqi. You aim for the gut like a fucking tachuqi. Yes, we burned him. You want to know how long it took or how it smelled?" His voice was rising, but she didn't need it. The yellow was coming in at his throat now and coming in strong. "You'd think it would smell like meat cooking, wouldn't you? But it doesn't. It smelled fucking awful. Gann's *breath* could not be more rank than the smoke from my only friend's funeral. Why would you even ask..." He trailed off, his head tilting by degrees, like the head of a clockwork toy. "You want to make me angry, is that it? You think if I'm angry I'll just spit up everything I'm going to do to you and you can make a plan. What do you need to plan for, eh? Do you think I'm going to kill you?"

"Eventually."

"Oh, that's a good word. Eventually." He circled back to where he could stand and face her, folding his arms to tap the point of the hook against his own arm. "You haven't asked how I know your language."

That startled her. She hadn't thought about it. With everything else there was to see and hear and wait for, the little matter of a lost language barrier had not even begun to send up its alarms. Iziz raised a hand and gestured without taking his eyes from Amber. He watched her while she looked and saw raiders drag a slumped, limping human unwillingly out into view.

He was naked, except for leather strips wrapping his feet and the metal band around his neck to which a chain might be attached if the need arose. His arms had the washed out color of a man who used to get a lot of sun before being stranded on this sunless world. The rest of him was a grub-pale pinkish-white, where he wasn't bruised or scraped or just plain filthy. He stood where they made him stand and put his hands over his groin and stared at the ground.

"We call him Druud," said Iziz. "He's been very helpful."

"Are you all right, Scott?" Amber asked finally, knowing perfectly well that he was not. They weren't starving him. He had no scars, no branding burns, no obviously broken bones to show for his time in captivity, but he was not all right.

Iziz waited with her for an answer that never came, then took two easy strides forward and slapped Scott hard across the face, knocking him back into the chest of another raider, who had to catch him before he fell to the ground. "Eshiqi asked you a question," he said.

"I'm fine," said Scott. He didn't look at Amber.

"Eh. He's a liar." Iziz gripped Scott's chin to make him face this way and that before shoving him away again. "At his best, he's never even close to fine. What would you say, Geozh?"

The raider holding Scott uttered a considering grunt. "He's a hot grip when the urge comes on. That's fine enough for me, sir."

Scott flushed and stared fixedly at the ground.

"Zhuqa once said you were like a slow fuck into God, Eshiqi. I confess, I was expecting better, but Geozh is right. This one's nothing but a little soft meat and a squeeze. He doesn't even squirm anymore." Iziz gave Amber a long, assessing glance, but did not seem to find what he was looking for. He grunted and stepped back, rubbing at his throat and frowning as he studied her. "I suppose you cast him out for a reason," he said at last. "What did he do?"

Amber didn't answer, not out of any planned defiance, but simply because she didn't know what to say. There was no satisfaction in seeing Scott the prisoner of these horrible people, only the same sick horror she had felt in their grip herself. She'd survived it and he could survive it too, assuming any of them walked away from this...but she'd had Meoraq to take her in, to tell her she was his, to make her believe it. Scott had nothing and she had nothing to give him except silence when Iziz might be asking for a reason to hurt him.

Iziz grunted mildly after a suitable span of time had bled itself out, then turned around and walked over to Dag and Eric. "What did he do?"

"He tried to kill her," said Dag.

Iziz flared his spines forward. "Truth?" he asked, almost but not quite laughing. "And all you did was exile him? You didn't stab him in the head first?"

"She couldn't," Dag told him. "She was, um, hurt."

"Hurt?" Iziz came back to her, his head still cocked, still smiling. "You didn't look very hurt the last time I saw you. Did Zhuqa get a cut in after all? Did I? Tell me you bled for me, Eshiqi."

"It was a—"

Iziz turned back in the same easy, friendly manner, drew his sword and hit Dag in the face with the hilt. The sound of bone crunching was somehow louder than Dag's scream, and the spattering of blood and teeth falling over the ground was even louder than that. "When I talk to you, I'll look at you," Iziz said, and looked back at Amber. "How bad were you hurt when Druud tried to kill you? I'm curious. Wait." He glanced behind him to the raiders standing over Dag, who was still screaming even as he tried to fit his shattered jaw back into place, and said, "Shut that thing up or get rid of it."

The nearest raider helpfully kicked Dag in the side, then smacked him in the head with the pommel of his knife a few times, and finally grabbed him by the hair and started hauling him toward the hole in the shrine's crumbling wall. Nicci moved out of the way.

"Stop it!" Amber shouted. "He's hurt, for God's sake! He can't help it!"

Iziz swung toward her, moved in close, but did not hit her. "Pick someone to take his place," he said, staring hard into her eyes. "I'll let him go. I'll even patch him up first. Druud, fetch me the humans and put them in a line. Pick someone to go over, Eshiqi."

Amber couldn't stop herself from looking as Scott assembled the last of his Manifestors—naked, shivering, mutilated, and still following him—but when they were all there, she clamped her jaws shut tight and stared back into Iziz's eyes.

He waited, his spines ticking out the seconds. "Not even you?" he asked softly. "It'd be quick, at least. Quicker than all the *eventual* ways I had time to think on while I stirred Zhuqa's burning bones."

She closed her mouth.

"Please yourself. Geozh!"

Dag's mushy pleas and promises to be quiet turned into screams, turned into receding shrieks, turned into nothing. Amber didn't watch. She looked at Iziz looking back at her and said, "What do you want?"

"From you?"

"Yes."

He seemed to consider the question fairly. It seemed to be the truth when he finally said, "I don't know yet. But for right now, I want to know how bad you were hurt when Druud tried to kill you."

For answer, since answers had become inevitable, Amber loosened her girdle and opened her tunic to show him the scar left by the kipwe's attack. Iziz's spines flared again as she undressed to this small degree. Faint smudges of yellow lightened his throat as he looked down at her chest, then her belly, and finally at the scar.

"Fuck Gann," he said mildly. "Or fuck a kipwe, anyway. They used to have kipwe shows in the camp when I was young. I may have mentioned that once. Druud, get over here."

Scott came, his head bent and jaw tightly clenched.

"Did she fight back?" Iziz asked, prodding at the worst of the scars with his fingertip.

"No," Scott said sullenly.

"Could she? Or was she just lying there in a pool of her own fucking blood?"

"She wasn't bleeding."

"She wasn't bleeding," Iziz echoed, again in that almost-laughing way. "That bled, Druud. Tell me it didn't again and I'll tear your squirming little tongue out and feed it to you. You've seen me do it before. Dare me not to now."

"She was bandaged up when...She was bandaged by then."

"I see. You really are a shining drop of poison shit, aren't you?" Iziz asked, almost admiringly. He fingered the edge of the scar for a moment more, plucked at it just once with the rough scale that acted as a fingernail, and then moved his hand unhurriedly lower, wedging it beneath her breeches with a grunt of effort to grip at her sex. He had to hook at her girdle to hold her from her instinctive flinch, but he wasn't bothered by it. His expression remained serene if distracted as he felt between her legs for her opening and forced a finger inside.

Not a sound from him. Not a sound from anyone, unless the low mutters and speculative grunts from the watching raiders counted. Iziz worked a second finger in and rubbed them slowly back and forth, watching her watch the sky. At last, he wrenched the fishhook out of her girdle and cupped the back of her head instead, more or less making her face him.

"I'm going to fuck you," he told her grimly. "I don't think I'll enjoy it much, but I'm going to do it. After that...well, I promised my men a fresh poke if we ever found you. So. Here's what's going to happen, Eshiqi, if you want to start making your plan. You're going to catch every cock in my camp all the way down to little Thirqa unless you pick someone to take your place."

Amber pressed her lips together and glared at him.

His spines flicked. "You don't mean that."

That felt horribly like the truth, but she shook her head and glared at him anyway.

"Point your finger for me, Eshiqi," Iziz said, working his own a little deeper into her. "I promise not to kill them if you give them to me freely."

She shivered, but kept silent.

Iziz waited, running his gaze over Eric and Nicci, and then the rest of his huddled human slaves, keeping his hand at work the whole time. When his eyes finally came back to her, he pulled his hand out of her breeches and wiped it on Scott's chest. "Not a damn one of them would do the same for you," he told her seriously. "You know that, don't you?"

She said nothing.

"When I told Druud to pick one of his for mine to play with, he did it. He would have sold them if I'd offered him coin. He promised me you before I even knew he knew you." He smiled with his head cocked and the yellow throbbing on his neck. "I'll make it easy for you, just tonight. I'll let you choose Druud."

Scott made a cawing sound, but she didn't look at him.

"It's not the fresh poke I promised, but then again, it's nothing new to Druud either," Iziz said. "Point him out to me and I'll even let you sit with your man tonight where you don't have to watch. No?" The tilt came out of Iziz's neck. He leaned very close, his breath hot and bitter on her lips. "Say it, then. Tell me no. Say it like the fierce little thing Zhuqa always said you were."

Amber did not answer. Her jaws ached from keeping them clenched. Her palms hurt where her fingernails dug at them in fists. Her heart hurt, but it kept beating.

Iziz turned his head slightly while keeping his eyes on Amber. "Nicci!" he called.

"You stay the fuck away from her!" Amber shouted, and she must have lunged too because there were hands all over her all at once, yanking her back and holding her tight. "Leave her alone! I'll kill you, motherfucker! I'll kill—"

Iziz slapped her. He didn't let her see it coming like Zhuqa would have done. She scarcely saw him move at all. There was a black blur and a white light and then she was sagging back in a raider's grip, staring dazedly at the sky while her face swelled with heat.

"You had the first choice," Iziz spat. "You threw it away to score points off me. How many points was it worth, eh? Nicci!"

Nicci came. No one brought her. She just came. Her neck was bent, like a lizardlady's, to a subservient angle. "Can I pick someone else?" she asked.

Iziz, one hand on the buckle of his belt, paused. His spines flicked, then flared curiously. "Who?"

Nicci looked at Amber.

But of course that didn't happen. Of course it didn't. They were sisters. They were all each other had. Amber had taken care of Nicci all her life. She'd tucked her in at night, got her up in the morning, walked her to school, done everything their mother was too strung out to care about. Amber was the one hiding with her in the bathroom when Bo Peep brought her bad dates home. Amber was the one stealing fruit cups and milk cartons off the lunch line so Nicci would have something to eat that night. Amber had fought off big kids and alley dogs and their mom's drunken punches and every other goddamn thing the world had thrown at them and they loved each other, they were sisters, and this was not happening!

"Take her," said Nicci. "She's the one who deserves it. Not me. So you take her. You make her *feel* it."

"You don't mean that," Amber heard herself say. Heard someone say, at any rate. It sounded more like their mother, when she was stoned and half-asleep.

"She looks like she means it," Iziz remarked. "But I'm not bargaining with you, Nicci. Not tonight. On your belly."

"Don't hurt her!" Amber lunged again, but she was held fast. "Please! You can take me, just please let her go!"

Iziz finally looked at her, but he never had a chance to answer.

"Go?" said Nicci. "Go where? Look where we are! You...You *made* me come here!" Nicci shook her head in an incredulous, angry series of jerks. "How could you do that? How could you do that? You were supposed to take care of me!" she screamed suddenly, throwing open her arms. "Me! And you picked him! So fuck you, Amber! You hear me? Fuck you! I hope you choke on their fucking cum and die!"

"You don't mean that!"

"Let's find out." Iziz offered the fish hook.

Nicci looked at it, then snatched it from his hand and stepped up, holding it in her shaking fist.

The hands pinning Amber to this moment tightened, but she wasn't struggling. She couldn't move, couldn't even feel the air in her lungs. This wasn't happening. It just...just wasn't.

"I hate you," said Nicci. "I want you to see this. I want you to know that this happened because of you."

She swung. But not at Amber, motionless, stunned.

The curved edge of the fish hook sank as easily into Nicci's throat as it had into the soft inner meat of Zhuqa's body. She screamed again and ripped, grunting with the effort to make the hook move. A hot, heavy gush struck Amber in the eyes. She slapped at them, screaming and tasting her sister's blood—swallowing it—and still somehow heard Iziz's quiet, "Ah," just exactly the way he'd said it over Zhuqa's corpse.

The fury of Nicci's features slackened, twisting into something merely bewildered in the moment before she staggered. Amber lunged to catch her, punching at the lizardman who tried to restrain her, but Nicci's weight was too much to hold and her hands were slippery. They went down together in a hot, wet heap with Amber on top, trying desperately to push the blood back in through the open gash in her baby sister's neck. It didn't last long; she could have counted the seconds by the slowing spews of fresh gore if she could have counted anything at all, but there weren't many. Nicci clutched once at her arm and once at her hair. Her lips moved, but there was no sound, no way to say for sure just what she would have said. It looked like 'help'. Or 'hate'. Then she was dead—warm clay in the shape of Nichole Sarah Bierce and nothing was left to move her blood except gravity.

"That was even better than I hoped for," said Iziz, but so far away and through so many muffling layers of cotton that she could barely understand him. "Stand her up."

Someone must have tried because it seemed to Amber that she fell upwards for a moment, then downwards, then both at once and then she was gone too.

* * *

The lights came on, vast bright lights with no particular source, whiting out the world to a clean, featureless blank in which Amber stood alone. After a while, it occurred to her that she was standing in a line, and sure enough, there was a string of people in front of and behind her. They were all in white, like the lights, like the walls and floor and ceiling. She was in the Manifestors' skyport, she realized, and there it was, the *Pioneer*, not in space at all but sitting right there on the tarmac, waiting to board.

She looked to her left and there was Nicci, hugging her duffel bag and crying because she didn't want to go. She looked down and by God, she was fat again, her belly straining at the stiff fabric of her brand new colonist's shirt.

None of it had happened yet. She could stop now, walk away. There'd be fines to pay, but she could figure something out. Get another job. Lose the weight (again). Hell, she could leave the city and watch on the tiny television above the bar where she worked just down the road from the trailer where she and Nicci lived as the whole world wondered what had happened to the *Pioneer*, and on the other side of the universe, Meoraq would go to Xi'Matezh without her.

Scott was waiting to scan her thumb, only she didn't know he was Scott yet. She didn't ever have to know. She could still walk away.

And Meoraq would walk home from Xi'Matezh alone.

"Let him."

She turned to her right and there was her mother, somewhere between Bo Peep and Mary Bierce, wearing a white t-shirt and no makeup, smoking a cigarette. She smiled with half her mouth, not mean but just tired, the look of a woman who knows. "You can't save everyone, little girl."

Maybe it was the dream that made her do it, although none of this felt like a dream yet. Maybe it was her bitchy nature. Maybe it was just because it was Mama saying it, but Amber suddenly had to argue.

"I could save them," she said. "I could shout the place up right now, tell them the ship's going to crash, tell them everyone who goes is going to die."

"Go ahead," said her mother. She tossed her hair back and looked at the ship, her eye lingering over all those people going in. She looked...sad. Honestly sad, not angry or self-pitying or bitter but just...sad. "They'll drag you out of here and launch anyway."

"So what if they do? If I could just delay them five minutes, maybe five minutes is all it would take."

"For...?"

"For the ship. You know, for whatever happened out there to miss us."

"You think so?"

"Maybe," said Amber defensively, but now her mother's sad eyes were staring into hers and she remembered all at once that there had been four more days of boarding after this. Five minutes, give or take, just didn't mean that much in the end. "Maybe," she said again, but she didn't believe it.

"A butterfly flaps its wings in Japan and it rains in New York."

"Huh?"

"A butterfly flaps its wings in Japan," said her mother, "which blows pollen into the nose of a cow, which sneezes, which startles the rest of the herd into running, which changes the air currents by just a tiny fraction of a degree, which picks up momentum and instability as it travels across the ocean until it becomes a storm front, and it rains in New York." She paused for a puff. Her eye sparked red with reflected light from the cherry. Meoraq's eye. "Is that what you were thinking, little girl?"

"That sounds like total horseshit," Amber admitted.

"That's because it is. It relies on the idea that while all these little things are happening, the rest of the world is holding still to let them happen and that simply isn't the way the world works. The reality is, it would have rained in New York anyway. The reality is, a butterfly flaps its wings in Japan and a fence gets broken, but that just doesn't have as much punch."

Amber hadn't moved in all this time, hadn't taken a single step, but she found herself at the head of the line. Scott was waiting in his clean red uniform, one of thousands of brand-new crewmen, a cog in the machine that was about to blow up.

"So you're saying it doesn't matter what we do?" Amber asked uncertainly.

"Of course it matters," said her mother, now gazing at the big television monitors where the Director was giving his uplifting speeches over and over...like Nuu Sukaga inviting all the post-Wrath survivors to come to Matezh hundreds of years too late to matter anymore. "But you can't always stop it."

"Because...it's supposed to happen?"

Her mother looked at her, still not in a mean way, but with such bizarre force that Amber had to drop her eyes and even squirm a little.

"Are you asking if this was God's plan?" her mother asked quietly, and suddenly the skyport was gone, replaced by the screaming wind and wasteland of Meoraq's world. She could see the *Pioneer*, there at the end of the long, black scar it had left in the crash. She could see thousands of moaning, weeping, terrified people staggering around in the wreckage, illuminated by a sky filled with fire. "Do you really think this was part of anyone's *plan*?"

Amber couldn't answer. She could see herself down there, dragging Nicci through the crowds with her duffel bag firmly over her shoulder, heading for Scott and that other man (*he was going to need someone to roll around with he said and then he apologized but not because he didn't mean it and his name was john something french i think and if he'd only come with us we'd have rolled around plenty and how different things could have been maybe better maybe worse but oh so different*).

"People make their own choices," said her mother, now walking away behind her. "And God has to let them live with the consequences."

Amber turned around to follow and staggered in the sudden silence. The wreck of the *Pioneer* was gone; she was in the courtyard at Xi'Matezh. The cliff was cold and muddy. That crumbling wall surrounded her, blocking out all but a little piece of the ocean. Her mother was already leaning up against the broken wall, smoking and watching the tide come in. Amber hesitated, then turned away and tried to open the outer doors of the shrine. Meoraq was in there. He was watching the video without her and she had to get to him before he came out. But her hands slipped weirdly over their surface without finding a gripping place; the more she struggled with them, the taller and heavier they seemed to get, until they towered over the whole enclosure, threatening to fall.

She gave up, stumbling back in their shadow, and turning at last to discover a lizardman standing where her mother had been. He was strangely hard to see. The sun was coming up over the ocean, stinging at her eyes like tears, blurring him in and out of recognition. She thought it was Meoraq at first, then Zhuqa, then some stranger in a white hood, but when she got closer, he looked back at her and she realized he was Lashraq. He still had her mother's cigarette in his hand. He waited for her to join him at the hole in the wall and then took an impossible drag through his inflexible lizard-lips and turned back to watch the ocean.

The Ruined Reach as she'd last seen it was gone. The flotsam of a million bloated bodies bobbed on the tide, stretching out north to south as far as she could see, interrupted only by the carnage of a ruined port the land hadn't yet reclaimed. There were no seagulls to scream over this feast, no crabs or sharks to pick it over from below. Everything was dead: the people, the animals, the ocean. She couldn't smell it, which was the first she knew—cigarette-smoking lizardman and all—that this wasn't real.

"Am I dead?" she asked warily.

"Does it matter?"

"It matters to me!"

"Only if you're not dead."

That...made a certain amount of sense. If she was dead, she had a feeling not much would matter at all anymore. So since it did matter, was that proof she was alive? But if she was alive, she had to be dreaming, and if this was a dream, it wasn't proof of anything.

"Are you supposed to be God?"

He snorted and glanced at her. "You sound skeptical."

Amber groped for and found an irrefutable argument. "God doesn't smoke!"

His spines shrugged. "You'd know, I guess." Lashraq stubbed out his cigarette on the back of his hand and tossed it into the wind, leaning out over the broken bricks to watch it fall. "Want to know why I called it Gann?"

"Huh?"

"This world." He gestured. "Clay. The evils of men. And all the other things it means. Want to know why I called it Gann? Would that prove something to you?"

"It's the name of this planet, isn't it?"

"Before the Fall, we called the planet I'az. It's an old, old word that means, eh, foundation. The stuff beneath your feet."

"Earth," whispered Amber.

Lashraq shrugged again and turned back to the sea. "More or less. I called it Gann in the Word, though. That is, I said that Sheul called it Gann. I thought it sounded more otherworldly, you know, that God had a secret name for all things, that He had knowledge beyond ours. And I picked Gann specifically because my youngest brother was born with a mild deformation of the throat and until they fixed him, he couldn't talk right. He couldn't say Zhan." He glanced at her, smiling. "He called me Gann."

"You named the devil after you? As a joke?"

"Not the best joke in the world, but I laughed now and then."

"This doesn't prove anything," Amber insisted. "This is nothing but...but subconscious crap! You're not my mother! You're not the ghost of Lashraq Zhan! And you're for damn sure not...not..."

He waited.

Amber shook her head and went back to the doors of the shrine. They loomed, blacking out the sky, holding the whole world in its shadow, impossible to touch. The part of her that believed this was a dream insisted Meoraq was in there, that he needed her. But if it was a dream, she'd have to wake up. Meoraq needed her there, too.

"Can you help him?" she asked awkwardly. "If I...believe in you or...do things for you?"

"That isn't how it works."

"Well then how *does* it work, goddammit?!" She swung around, her hands in fists, but Lashraq didn't flinch. "You don't plan things, you don't help people, you sure as fuck don't care when people die, what *do* you do?"

"I talk," Lashraq said quietly. "But I can't make you listen."

"All you're telling me is you can't help! What good are you? You...You son of a bitch, look at me!" she exploded. "Don't you know what we've been through? And you just stand there and talk about fucking butterflies when we've come all this way and lived through so much and now *this* is how it ends? It's not fair!"

"Suck it up," he replied and lit another cigarette.

She cried until she could make herself stop and then she took a few deep breaths. Six of them. She looked at him. He watched the tide come in.

"Who are you?" she whispered. "Who are you, really?"

"Me?" Lashraq shrugged his spines and shoulders at the same time. "I'm the warning."

And as she tried to wrap her head around that, he reached out and clasped her shoulder. His grip was strong; his eyes were kind.

"But there will be a boat," he told her. "And a helicopter. So hold on, Amber. Watch for them. And take the chance when you see it, because I can only give you one."

He tipped his head back, grunting thoughtfully in the back of his throat. "Looks like the storm is clearing," he said.

She looked up. The sun behind the clouds turned the whole sky a blinding white. For a moment, she was back in the skyport again, and then she was nowhere at all.

* * *

Amber came around in a lamp-lit tent to the sound of lizardish laughter and the ocean. She was not alone. She rolled over with difficulty and at first tried to see Meoraq beside her, but the face was all wrong, and so were the scars and the clothes. It was Iziz, just sitting there with his knees drawn up and his hands clasped around them, staring at the side of the tent. He said, "You ever been to the mountains, Eshiqi?"

It wasn't another dream. She didn't wake up.

"We lived there a few years when I was very young. I spent a lot of time alone, up in the rocks. One day, I found a thuoch den with two pups and no parent. I tried to raise them, because I was a sprat and sprats are stupid like that."

Nicci. Nicci was dead. They might all be dead by now, although it stood to reason that someone had to be alive to make the raiders all roar and laugh like that. It wasn't any fun to torture someone who was already dead.

"I stole away every day to look in on them and fed them what I could of my own meals. God and Gann alone might know what I would have done with them if that had worked, but it didn't. I crawled down into the den one morning to find the big one eating the little one while the little one whined and shivered in its own guts. I ran screaming down the side of the mountain until I fell and went the rest of the way down on my belly. My mother found me, fixed me up, and while she was doing that, someone tracked up the mountain to see what scared me. They brought me back the big pup, all warm and wriggling. I hugged it all night, crying while it licked my face and loved me in its dumb pup way. In the morning, I killed it with a rock."

Amber turned back onto her side.

"My mother told me it was pointless to hate the pup. All animals kill each other when they have to, she said. We all eat each other to survive. Thuochs, dumaqs, humans. My mother was the worst fuck in that camp," he added in a pensive tone, "but she had her moments."

Amber did not answer. She tried to pretend she didn't even hear.

"I don't think I've ever told that story before," said Iziz. "Unless I got drunk and maybe told Zhuqa and then forgot. Which is possible. But you remind me of that pup. The little one, I mean, getting your guts gnawed open by your littermate and just writhing while she did it. I wouldn't have thought it of you."

"What are you going to do with me?" Amber asked dully.

"Patience, Eshiqi. Patience is more than a word. Zhuqa used to say that. Made me just spitting mad, but that doesn't mean there's nothing to it. I'd never heard of this place," he remarked, looking around at the walls of his tent as though he could see right through them to the shrine. "Doesn't look like the sort of place God would spend much time. Kind of a piss-gully, if you ask me. Druud seemed to think there'd be something big here. If I understood him right, he thought there'd be some kind of flying machine. We've been here for days and we've been looking, but we couldn't find it. Did you?"

"No."

Iziz glanced at her, then grunted and shrugged his spines. "None of that old shit works right anyway. If it did, we wouldn't be scratching out nests in the ground like beetles. Zhuqa gave us as much of a city as we'll ever know." He gave her a longer, more assessing stare. "You ever live in a city?"

"Yes."

"A real one?"

"A human one."

He grunted, looking thoughtful and curious. "Describe it."

She closed her eyes, not to help her visualize, but just to shut the sight of him away. He let her and did not interrupt during the long silence she took to put her thoughts in some kind of order. Nicci was in every one of them. At last, she gave up and simply said, "Have you ever seen pictures of your Ancients in their cities?"

"Some, sure."

"They looked like that. Tall, narrow buildings. No walls. Lots of machines." She rolled onto her back and opened her eyes, staring at the ceiling of the tent and only vaguely aware of Iziz beside her. "It stank. Especially when it rained. Hot tar in the summer, wet gutters in the winter, just a constant nasty stink. Even the good smells, the food places and all that, reeked of hot grease and garbage if you went around the back. And our place, that was all rancid booze, pot and piss. And dead cats, that one summer."

He put his hand on her stomach. It was neither a menacing touch nor a lascivious one, just the absent-minded touch of a man's rough hand, there between her navel and her pubis. He gazed straight ahead at the wall. "Druud talks about your Earth-place a lot. We encourage it. We don't have much to entertain ourselves with these days. You took all the fresh dips and Ghelip took the rest. What have I got, eh? Druud. Druud and his piss-talk of Earth. What color was the sky?"

"Blue."

He grunted and rubbed at her belly. "That's what Druud said. I cut off one of his toes for lying to me. Guess I owe the little piss-licker an apology."

A gust of wordless hoots and laughter erupted outside. She thought she heard Eric in the middle of them, but couldn't make out what he was saying, just that it was hoarse and hurt.

"You have me now," said Amber, going through the motions without hope, without feeling of any kind. "You can let the others go."

"I could," Iziz agreed. "I certainly could."

"Do you want me to beg?"

"For Druud?"

"For Scott," she said. "For Eric. For anyone else that's left."

"There's a few. Not many. Humans break easy." He gazed at the tent wall, his spines flexing now and then as he thought, and finally he said, "All right. Beg and let's see what happens."

She started to roll over onto her knees, but his hand on her stomach turned hard and pressed her flat where she lay, so she just reached out her hands instead. She held them up, palms empty, but he wouldn't look at them. She let them drop. They both stared, each into their own wall, and then she said, "Please."

He grunted.

"Please let them go."

"Go on. I'm listening."

"I won't fight you."

"Mm."

"I'll do whatever you want."

His fingers drummed over her stomach.

"I'll be good." It was the only thing she could think to say.

"What will you do for me, Eshiqi? Just for me."

She thought.

"I'll cry," she said.

He looked at her.

Outside, raiders laughed and cursed, ate and drank. The waves rolled in and out, in and out. The wind blew.

"That was good," said Iziz, and turned back to the wall. "I was tempted. I didn't think I would be. I'm keeping them, Eshiqi. I'm keeping them and I will personally see to it that they are starved and worked and whipped and fucked right up to the last hour of their lives, and do you know why?"

"Because you can."

"What a spiteful thing to say. I can do a lot of things that I don't do, Eshiqi, and let me tell you, torturing humans without killing them means far, far more work for me than any fun I'll ever get back out of them. A man has to have a reason to put up that kind of coin, so why don't you think? Think hard and tell me why I'm doing it."

"Because I killed Zhuqa."

"No. That's the reason I'm killing your man. Think harder."

"I don't know."

"You don't?" Color grew along the side of his neck. "You don't know. You can't think of anything else you might have done."

"I..." Her thoughts seemed to sink away from her grasp. She shook her head, but couldn't shake them any clearer. "I took...your women."

"You took his *baby*." His spines lowered. His head cocked. He did not look at her. "Did you tell him what you were going to do before he died, Eshiqi? Is that how you twisted the knife?"

"No."

"But you took it. Druud says you sent it on to Chalh with Xzem and the other dips, and since I don't see any of them out there, I guess it's true. Why did you do that? Why did you take his baby if you didn't even want it?"

"I wanted it," Amber said. Strange, how she couldn't lie to him, almost as strange as him asking her these things in the first place. His pain and hers filled this small space, choking out all other feeling, even hate. "But it was more important that it have a real home, even if it wasn't with me."

"A home." Yellow flared on the side of his throat. "It had a home, Eshiqi. It had a *fine* home."

"It deserved a better life."

"Shit on that. Do you really think that worn-out catch-cock cared about Zhuqa's sprat as much as he did? Do you?"

"If Zhuqa could have given it a home inside the city walls, he would have."

That, Iziz did not answer. She lay beside him, watching the color fade out of his scales without any sense of relief, sunk in grief. He watched the wall of his tent. Time passed, unnoticed, unfelt.

His hand moved suddenly. It slipped between the wrapped edges of her tunic to rest on her bare belly, just below her navel, just above the top of her breeches. Iziz turned his head toward her, but kept his eyes on the wall. "Is this what I think it is?"

Nicci's voice, like a hook in the back of her mind, tearing open her heart and bleeding a memory: *Want to see where they cut it out?*

She couldn't answer. Silence could be deadly here, but she simply couldn't speak.

Now he looked at her. His hand flexed; the muscles of her stomach tightened.

"Is it his?" he asked. His voice was low, but strained.

It was Meoraq's, it had to be. Too soon to show a bump if it was Zhuqa's. Too soon to show Iziz anything that could have made him suspect this. No, she didn't know that for a fact, but facts weren't everything. For some things, faith was stronger.

"It's mine," said Amber. "That's whose it is. Mine."

"I guess that makes it mine, then," Iziz mused. "Never had a sprat before, not that I knew of. Never even had a thuoch pup."

"You did until you killed it."

"At least mine died loving me."

'You getting out of this, little girl?' Bo Peep wondered. Her mental voice was quiet but not slurred, not just doing the mommy-thing while she nodded off. 'Seems like you came an awful long way just to give up now.'

"Fuck you," said Amber.

Iziz's spines flicked forward.

"Not you. I'm sitting up now."

He took his hand off her. She pushed herself up, feeling the drag of her body in ways she never had even when she'd weighed two hundred pounds. She wiped at her eyes, but they were dry. She wasn't crying. That didn't seem fair.

"What did you do with my sister's body?" she asked.

"Threw it off the edge," he replied, without venom.

"Zhuqa would have made me eat her."

"Maybe. He might have burned her. You never knew for certain. He had moods. But one thing I can promise you: He would have killed your Sheulek and he would have made you watch."

She nodded listlessly. "Is that what you're going to do?"

"Oh yes," Iziz said. "And he's going to die hard. Before I'm done, you won't be able to put your hand on him without bloodying your fingers. He may not scream much," he remarked, scratching restlessly at his throat, where the color was starting to come back. "I never saw Zhuqa give up better than a hiss in all the years I knew him. Made no difference how hard he was bleeding. Want to know what he used to say?"

"I am not my clay," said Amber.

Iziz looked at her, head cocked and smiling, both at the same time. "Just so. But that's fine. I don't care how much he feels it. It's really you I want to hurt."

"For how long?"

"As long as I can. I'm going to make you live, Eshiqi. I'm going to kill your man and take your sprat and I'm going to make you live."

"I'll kill you if I can," she said. It wasn't a threat, wasn't a warning. She didn't know what she meant by it, only that it needed to be said.

"You killed Zhuqa," he acknowledged. "He got careless. I won't. He liked you." Iziz looked at her, neither sneering nor smiling. "I don't."

12

He raped her three times in grim-faced silence, braced high above her on stiff arms, moving hard, scarcely touching her. She didn't resist, didn't cry, didn't even close her eyes. She stared at the ceiling of the tent; he stared at the wall. When it was over, they put their clothes right and then he tied her comfortably yet securely at wrists and ankles and left her there.

Alone, with the rest of the world covered up, time had a way of melting into strange new shapes. She sat for a while, then lay down and rolled onto her side, then struggled until she could sit up again. Her mind worked, mechanically filling up the empty places where minutes ought to be. She thought of Nicci, just seven years old, holding her hand on the way to school, and Amber looking both ways all the way across the street because sometimes the cars didn't stop. She thought of the boy Iziz had been growing up to become the man who had burned his only friend's body. She thought of Nuu Sukaga, that poor son of a bitch, standing by the window in his underwear for a hundred and eighty-eight days, waiting for Saiakr to drive up. She thought of Meoraq, but no matter how she tried to think of him, it all faded into black.

The sun went down. The tent got dark, lit on one wall by the fire outside. Dumaq shadows, huge and indistinct, passed back and forth as raiders settled. It was a quiet night, peaceful in its way. The irony did not escape her.

When Iziz came back, he untied her ankles and took her out, but she couldn't see anyone she knew—not Scott or Eric, and not Meoraq. He didn't watch her pee, didn't speak to her, didn't offer her a bite of his stolen food when he took her back into the tent. He just tied her up again, lay down with his back to her and slept.

She slept too. She didn't think she would, but she was just so tired and it was the only possible escape. She had no dreams.

In the morning, he raped her again. Only once this time, and she didn't think he came. It wasn't really sex for him, just another weapon. He knew he wasn't killing her with it, but he wanted to keep it sharp. When he finished, he took her out for her morning pee, then brought her over to the fire and gave her a bit of cold meat and some tea in her own cup. She dropped them both on the ground and he threw her down beside them and made her pick them up and eat, mud and all.

"Don't do that again, Eshiqi," Iziz said, standing over her while she took the last shaky swallow from her cup. "You won't make me mad enough to kill you, but I will trim you down some. Remember Zru'itak and mind your fucking manners. Geozh!"

"Sir?"

"Get the slaves in a line and load them up. The rest of you, break camp. We're moving on."

"No!"

Scott ran forward, caught a cuff from Geozh, and went sprawling on his face in the mud to the general amusement of the raiders. Undaunted, he got back on his feet, alternately wiping at his face and finger-combing through his hair. Now and then, his hand twitched down toward his hip, wanting to straighten a jacket he was no longer wearing. "Not yet. No. Absolutely unacceptable."

"You have something to say, Druud?" Iziz asked, turning all the way around to look at him.

"We haven't found it," Scott said. "We had an agreement."

Iziz leaned back a little, his spines flaring forward, but he raised his hand to stop

Geozh when he cocked a fist.

"I brought you here," Scott was saying. "I agreed to allow my people to...to serve in...in certain capacities and I brought you here and I said...I said you could have *that bitch*!" he shouted suddenly, pointing at Amber. "That lying bitch! This is all your fault! This is all your—" He stopped and smoothed down his hair some more. The mud was drying to his scalp like the plastic hair of a cheap doll. "But there is a transmission tower," he said calmly. "And that proves there's a ship. So. We need to find it."

"Eshiqi says there is no ship," Iziz said.

Scott laughed scornfully. "Of course she does! She wants us to be afraid! She came here," he declared, coming at Amber with his hand raised, pointing, "for the sole purpose of undermining the colony's efforts! Of course she says there's no ship, but there is a transmission tower, we're all looking right at it, Miss Bierce, so *fuck you*!" he screamed. "Fuck you! I was right and you were wrong! You threw away all the concrete and you stole my flashlight and broke it and you fucked the lizard and turned him against us but you're not taking the ship so where is it? Where is it, huh? Where—"

Iziz reached out without hurry and gave Scott a tap on the underside of his chin. Scott's jaws clopped shut. He grabbed at his face and looked at Iziz, all wounded eyes and stiff shoulders. Then he turned around and walked with silent dignity back to Geozh.

Iziz folded his arms, watching impassively as Scott directed his people out of their cluster and into a line. Through the wind and the tide, Amber could hear snatches of his speech: true pioneers rose above adversity, the good of the colony came before personal feeling, and Amber Bierce was a bitch.

"Sometimes I think he really believes that if we found a ship, I'd let him sail away on it," Iziz remarked. "The first night we were here, picking the place over, he must have had a thousand chances to run, but he never did. Little piss-licker came to get me five times, trying to work the doors open. You believe that?"

"Yes."

"Came to get me. But the doors wouldn't open. Druud wanted me to pry them open. Old places like this... sometimes the doors burn you. I told him. He wouldn't hear it. So I gave him a sword." Iziz glanced at Amber. "You'd have stuck it in me. But Druud passed it off to one of his pokes and he stabbed it right in the door, just because Druud told him to, when he'd heard me say what could happen."

Amber didn't ask.

"There was a light," said Iziz, as if she had. "And then there was a hole through him. I could have put my hand through it. Thirqa could have put his *head* through it. No smoke. No blood. The meat didn't even look that burnt, but the fur on his chest was charred. He didn't die right away. He looked down first and he let go of the sword. I was watching to see if he'd put his hand through the hole, and I really think he might have but he didn't have time. He dropped. And Druud said, 'Maybe he loosened it.' I think he would have set another of his pokes on the door if I'd let him." Iziz thought about it and snorted. "I think the poke would have done it if he'd asked."

Raiders were breaking down the camp, stacking tents and packs indiscriminately on the sleds. She still couldn't see Meoraq.

"But you got the doors open." Iziz gave the domed shrine a meaningful glance. "What was in there?"

"Nothing you could steal."

He looked at her, snorted. "I can steal anything, Eshiqi. If you haven't swallowed enough of that yet, I can serve up some more."

Amber shut her stupid mouth and stood silent.

Iziz gave her a second, harder stare. "No apology?"

"I'm sorry."

He slapped her, not hard, just enough to sting. "No, you're not. Don't lie to me again or I'll carve your man, Eshiqi. I'll carve him and make you eat the pieces I cut off." He eyed her, his head cocked. "Beg me not to hurt him."

Did that mean he was still alive? The words spilled out of her in a breathy rush: "Please don't hurt him!"

He slapped her again, rocking her a little this time. "Slaves do not give orders in my camp! Beg my forgiveness!"

"Please—"

This slap smashed her lips into her teeth, filling her mouth with the taste of her own bitter blood. "Get on your knees and beg like a slave!"

Amber dropped to her hands and pushed them both palms up on either side of his boot. Somewhere in the world, Scott laughed.

Iziz twitched in his whole body at once. He looked around, blinking, color coming in strong at his throat. "Who was that?"

"Druud," said Geozh, rolling his eyes. "Who is it always?"

Iziz cursed and turned, ready to walk away, to go deal with Scott and his petty nonsense until the day was gone and they were moving and where was Meoraq? Amber lunged out in a froggish hop to slap her hands down in the mud again, this time pressing her head to Iziz's boot, just the way she'd seen Xzem do to Meoraq once.

He stopped. She could hear him breathing, feel him looking down at her.

The waves kept coming. The ocean never cares.

"Get up," Iziz said finally. "I know what you want. Get up and we'll go see your Sheulek. Druud, you're coming too, but I hear one more sound out of you and I'll sew your mouth shut. The rest of you, keep working."

And with that, he started walking, leaving Amber and Scott to come together in his wake and follow.

Inside one of the many ruined structures of Matezh was Meoraq. Impossible to say just what it had been, once upon a time—a garage, maybe, a workshop, something that needed this wide open floor. If there had ever been anything inside, it had been picked clean over the years and now there was nothing left, nothing to distract her from the sight of Meoraq dangling from the rusted girders with his feet just off the floor. There was a crack in the ceiling where two panels had fallen away from each other enough to let in a little light and a steady trickle of windswept spray that had collected on the roof. Naturally, Meoraq was positioned just below this. He was naked. They'd wrapped a scrap of filthy cloth around his head to mask him and the cloth did not appear to be moving with his breath.

Iziz let her look as long as she wanted, but at her first step forward, his hand dropped over her shoulder and forced her back onto her knees. "He's alive," he said. His voice echoed; Meoraq did not move. "Say something, Sheulek. Your woman is here."

Silence. The water dripped and spattered.

Iziz walked calmly over, drew Meoraq's bone-handled knife from his belt and stuck it in Meoraq's thigh. Meoraq jerked violently—a fish on a line—and hissed through his hood.

"See? He's fine. We're going to play a game," said Iziz, coming back to Amber. "Zhuqa liked games. Most of us do. A raider's life is more boring than people realize. My game is called, 'God and Gann.' Wait here and don't move. You don't get to speak to him, Eshiqi. Remember Druud is watching."

Iziz left them.

After his last footstep faded, Scott whispered, "You may as well talk, Bierce, because I'm going to tell him you did anyway." And grinned.

The hood shifted. Meoraq said, "S'kot."

Scott flinched and stared around.

A second hiss, longer and quieter than before. "Bastard son of Gann and a she-ghet, so you have found your pack. Now hear the words of Uyane and mark well: I will not die here."

"No. No, you probably won't." Scott backed up, trying to laugh, but it came out in such a high, unnatural patter that if Amber weren't looking at him, she might not have recognized the sound. "They have plans for you, lizardman. You're not going to die anywhere close to here, but they will kill you."

"But they won't," said Meoraq, "burn me. And so I will be free to follow you all the days of your treacherous life. I will hold your face in my heart at the very moment of my murder and when I am made mad by unending death, I will still know you, human, and I will gnaw your living bones."

"Is that a real threat?" Scott asked, but he kept backing up. "That's the stupidest thing I've ever heard!"

"You shouldn't laugh, Druud. I've seen men die for no reason." Iziz returned, his boots clomping heavily across the floor. He had one of the sleds, helping him to carry the odd assortment of things he brought with him. When he reached Amber, he began to unpack, laying everything out in a neat line. "I've heard things on the wind myself. My mother called them the howls of hungry ghosts, the voices of men who'd forgotten how to speak. So. Are you calling my mother stupid?"

Scott shot Amber several sidelong glances and suddenly pointed. "She talked."

Iziz sent Amber a narrow stare, still arranging things, then straightened up, caught Scott by the hair and slapped him hard and fast, forwards and backhand, on his face, throat, chest and any other part of Scott's screaming, struggling body he could reach. "Don't you ever lie to me again," he said at the end of it, dropping Scott carelessly on the floor and stepping over him. "Come here, Eshiqi. It's time to play."

Amber eased forward into striking range, but he merely folded his arms and watched as she examined the three distinct selections he'd set out for her. Meoraq's clothes—his neatly folded tunic and breeches, his travel-harness, everything but his boots, which Iziz was wearing. One of the large travel-flasks, filled, by itself. Six or seven small vertebrae, cut from whatever animal the raiders had been roasting the night before, with shreds of greasy meat and stringy tendons still clinging to them.

"Choose," said Iziz when she finally looked up. "Each one is a blessing. Each one brings pain. God and Gann. That's the game and if you don't play with me, he goes right over the edge."

Amber looked at her choices with new eyes. The bones seemed the most ominous, although she couldn't say exactly how. There wasn't much meat on them, but what there was might be poisoned or maybe Iziz meant to force Meoraq to swallow them whole. That left his clothes or the flask. She couldn't see how clothes could hurt, unless they were ratted up and used to throttle him. On the other hand, Meoraq wasn't as susceptible to cold as Amber and walking naked might not be too hard on him. What about the flask? He might be able to live without clothes for a day, but not water. But she was assuming there was water in the flask, which was not at all certain. It could be poison. Acid. Anything.

"One," said Iziz quietly. "Two. Three. Four—"

Her arm felt so much heavier than it should be. Raising it to point made her entire right side cramp.

Iziz grunted and picked up Meoraq's tunic and breeches, revealing the coiled leather belt hiding beneath them. He handed her the clothes, wrapped the belt around his fist so that the buckle dangled, and walked forward.

"Oh no!" Amber dropped to her knees, palms up, crawling after him. "Please, no!"

The belt howled. It hit like a fist dead center of Meoraq's back. He jerked, swinging wildly by his bonds, but Iziz had no trouble at all hitting him again. He swung the same way he'd slapped Scott: quick, brutal, roundhouse blows that hit anywhere, everywhere. He never spoke. His throat stayed black and cool. He ignored Amber until she grabbed at the belt, then stopped just long enough to push her to the ground and step on her before resuming the attack.

When it finally ended, Amber was crying too hard to tell. She knew only when he took his boot off her back and dropped the belt on the floor in front of her. Iziz, only slightly coarse of breath, crouched down beside her and knotted his fist in her hair, raising her head, forcing her to see the damage: what seemed to her eye hundreds of mottled, irregular blotches all over where his scales had been beaten out of pattern and a few bloody trickles making their way down his limp body to drip onto the wet floor.

Iziz stood up, dragging her with him, and held her on her feet until she steadied. "You can talk to him now if you want to," he told her. "But for every word you say, he gets one more stroke."

Amber's hands rose in shaking flutters to press over her mouth.

"You sure? He's Sheulek. I'm sure he could take it. And just imagine how much it would mean to him now to hear his woman's words of comfort."

She shook her head, too numb even to hate him while Meoraq hung there, silent.

"Please yourself. Bring him down and get him dressed, Druud," Iziz ordered, and took a long drink from the flask. "Make sure you get his harness on tight. Doesn't look like he'll be walking much, so we'll need to drag him. He slips his tether and I'll whip you both together. Let's go, Eshiqi."

Iziz started for the door and Amber followed, walking backwards, unable to keep from staring at the horror she had helped to happen. Scott watched her for a second, then went ahead and untied one of Meoraq's wrists. The sound of his body hitting the floor stung at Amber's eyes, but she didn't make a sound. "Looks bad," Scott called after her, his brow furrowed with exaggerated concern. "You know, he probably has broken ribs. He could have a broken rib right now sticking into his l—"

Meoraq drew up one leg and slammed his foot square in Scott's stomach. Scott flew back, hit the wall first and the floor second, bent over and threw up between his splayed legs.

Iziz paused in the doorway. "Druud, for fuck's sake," he began, and that was when the lights came on.

Iziz looked up, frowning, then down as the floor shuddered. The wall panel where Scott had impacted, now slightly bent, dropped away to reveal the ancient control panel beneath. It sparked twice and emitted a high-pitched whining sound, echoed as a bone-humming groan beneath them. Cracks appeared right down the center of the floor—four of them, exactly the same length with exactly the same space between them, in perfectly straight alignment. They widened as the wall squealed and the floor shook.

There were doors in the floor. The doors were opening. One, two, three—all empty holes with rising platforms that slowly sealed them off again.

Up through the fourth came a dust-dull wedge-shaped ship.

* * *

The swaddles of his crude hood kept air suffocatingly close. Meoraq could smell nothing but his own unwashed hide and blood-tinged breath. Before the beating, sounds had been muffled; afterwards, pain dulled everything to a grey groan. He was aware that something had happened, but didn't care what, beyond the thought that the raiders might all be standing around Scott's caved-in corpse and paying it an apprehensive witness.

That hope died with Scott's sudden, shrieking, "*Haaaaa*!"

"Leave it, Druud. You have work to do."

'Yes,' thought Meoraq, flexing his bound hands. 'Come and dress me, S'kot.'

He had no illusions. His blades were taken. He had been roughed some and hung for hours, denied food and water, and now whipped with his own belt. To judge by what speech he'd caught, the leader of the raiders meant to keep him alive as some torment to Amber, but raiders were not a patient breed. Meoraq thought it very likely he would be dead within three days.

For the first time in all his life, Meoraq did not know what that meant. Would he see the Halls of Sheul growing from the clear light of heaven, his father and mother come to meet him? Would he wander the lightless reaches of Gann forever, losing all his mind and memory until he had become as empty as the deadlands he traveled? Or would he simply end?

No matter. He would know the truth soon enough, but before then, he would kill Scott.

But Scott did not obey his master. Instead of coming to harness Meoraq, he ran to another part of the room and seemed to circle, calling to his men. And they came. Meoraq could hear them crying out like madmen, some laughing, some weeping—reactions the raiders found greatly entertaining.

Meoraq knew his best chance of killing even a man like Scott depended on lying still and feigning helplessness (which did not require much feigning), but he simply had to see what was going on. With effort, he rolled onto his side and rubbed his snout on the floor until he'd pulled his hood loose enough to work it down over one eye.

He saw Amber first. She saw him. He didn't know how he looked to her, but he thought she was beautiful. There in the open doorway with the light of day behind her, turning her hair to a haze of white and gold, wearing one of his tunics and the green girdle given by the lady of House Uyane. Frightened, but standing, because she would know no other way than to survive for as long as she had breath. He looked at her and from where he lay with all this empty room between them, he could still feel her arms around him.

And then he noticed the ship.

Surprise took him, but not for long and what it left after its fading was the same sort of baffled exasperation he so often had when trying to understand human motives. What were they so excited about? If the thing were nothing but a husk, a crate in the shape of a ship, still it would be scarcely the height of a man, again as wide and perhaps twice that in length. Room enough for the humans—barely—but only if there were no mechanics to move the ship and no supplies necessary to sustain them on their journey. And that was assuming the ship could move. Dust, not even dust in so thick a coat as this, did not always mean a thing was broken, but the strange metal of its hide was obviously pitted with corrode and its windows remained dull even when Scott wiped at them. An idiot could see the ship was dead. But Scott had a long way to go before he could be considered so well as an idiot.

"Druud, leave it. It's old, but it can still bite if you tease it. Leave it alone. All of you, back to work."

The humans stayed where they were, whining protests. Scott actually put his arms around the ship, hugging it like a child with a toy that might at any moment be unfairly stripped away. Surprisingly, some of the raiders protested as well, more and more of them coming to watch Scott's men make fools of themselves over a broken machine.

Meoraq lay quiet and counted them. Sixteen. There might be others out in the courtyard, but sixteen was not an insurmountable number, if he had his swords.

Or if he could use them. Meoraq tested his clay and found it heavy, thick with hurt. A Sheulek could endure pain, but his flesh was swelled and he could feel blood pooling under his scales and those were simply facts. If he'd cracked a few bones, as seemed likely, six might well be beyond him, much less sixteen.

Yet he may only have to kill a few to make the rest run. If he could gain his feet, gain his weapon, seize just one short second of surprise, with God's favor—

But he didn't have God's favor. He had the strength the sickness gave him...and that might not be enough.

Scott was still whining for his ship, so Meoraq looked that way, because if his journey was to end here, at least it would end with Scott dead and he meant to watch. If there was no God, there was no sin in spiteful pleasures. But the sword—Meoraq's own sword—never left the belt where it hung.

"Let them play," a raider said, ducking his head deferentially as his leader threw a cold glance his way. "We take them away now, they'll sour. Let them break their toy first. What's another day?"

Their leader hissed and rubbed at his throat, his head tipped back, eyes shut. "All right, all right. Fucking little pests. One more day. Druud, if you want to play with your toy, you do your work first. If I have to tell you to get away from it one more time, I'll strap you to the top of it and set it on fire! Slaves, out! Eshiqi, go wait in my tent."

She went. Meoraq watched her for as long as he could see her, then dropped his head back onto the ground and closed his eyes. The hollow dark closed in around him once more. The cold took away his heart. He could hear the sound of boots, striding heavy and insolently slow, coming closer. He listened and did not count his breaths.

"Zhuqa had her," the raider said finally, after he had stood over Meoraq for some time. "Did you know? Did she tell you she had been his slave?"

The words passed over and through him and were gone.

"I saw her once, sitting naked on his thigh with his fingers inside her, holding his cup. She didn't fight."

Beyond this little room, the rain fell lightly on the roof. The trees of Gedai whispered in the wind. The ocean rolled and groaned.

"Do you know what he told me, Sheulek? Eh?" Leather creaked as the raider hunkered down, not quite within reach. "He told me she oils up when she cums."

The rain. The wind. The sea.

"She hasn't cum for me yet," the raider said. "The day she does, I'll let you know. But she's not fighting me. That, you should know right now."

Meoraq grunted and said, without opening his eyes, "All this time, I thought I killed your Zhuqa, but I didn't, did I? She did. You'll have to tell me how she did that someday, eh? Tell me how bravely he died, your raider-lord. Did he piss himself and beg for his life like all the rest of your pack?"

A long silence, broken only by the weather and by Scott, shifting on his feet nearby. Meoraq waited, bracing himself for the blow. The first kick caught him in the gut, turning his breath to bile and his belly to lead. The second and third hit wherever he could not defend against them, but he scarcely felt them against the backdrop of so much pain. He retched and had to lie in it, gasping and light-headed, feeling himself roughly jostled as he was dressed and bound and finally hoisted into the air again.

The raider's leader hadn't even stayed to watch him suffer. Two of his men lingered in the doorway, hands on weapons, but they were looking out into the courtyard, overseeing humans. The only one left to see him in defeat was Scott himself, standing before him now with a look of smirking satisfaction on his flat face. Meoraq hissed wetly through his teeth and let his heavy head drop to his chest.

"I'm going home," Scott whispered. "I'm going to save those people and I'm going to be a hero, and you and your fat whorebitch Bierce are going to die right here. Yeah. So there's just one thing I want to say, lizard, and there's one more thing I want to do and then I'll leave you here to think about how it could have gone if you'd shown me some respect. Okay? Here it is." Scott circled around to Meoraq's back before easing closer, close enough that Meoraq could feel the heat of his breath. "I was right," whispered Scott, "and you were wrong."

Scott patted his shoulder and crept the rest of the way around him until he was in front of him again. He grimaced hugely, showing all his teeth, and then he swung his arm with an animal howl and slapped Meoraq in the snout. Coming as it did from Scott, the blow hurt his straining shoulders more than his face. Meoraq dangled, silent, swaying gradually to a stop, his eyes fixed on the enemy and his throat throbbing.

"I was right," Scott said again, backing toward the door and the two sentries who were now watching him with amused contempt. "I found a transmission tower and a ship and a skyport and what did you find, lizardman? Huh? Nothing! There's no God here! There never was!"

The words slapped harder than Scott's freakish little hand, but even so, it was a slap, not a stab. He looked at the machine and the machine was a dead thing, just another decaying piece of the past. Scott could call it what he wanted, but he was still only pissing out of his mouth. Perhaps Meoraq had not heard Sheul's true voice, but Scott hadn't found a ship either, so there was still justice in the world, even if there was no God.

No God. The slap of those words struck even harder and so Meoraq brought them back and stared them down. The holiest shrine of all the world was empty. The Prophet Lashraq had been the leader of a band of foul-mouthed raiders. The Great Word was a book of lies and the fires of Sheul were a symptom of sickness.

Truth. All truth.

But did it really mean there was no God? If a blind man says the sky is grey—

Except that the sky wasn't grey. Meoraq raised his head and looked up through the hole in the warped panels of the roof, at the little piece of the world that existed for him beyond this room. The clouds were grey, but he had seen the clouds open, however briefly. The clouds were grey, but the sky was green, and all the blind men in the world did not change that.

Scott left him, laughing, reveling in whatever suffering he imagined he had caused. Left alone, quietly and futilely hating him, Meoraq suddenly realized that somewhere along the winding road that had led to this moment, he had come to believe in Earth. He believed in this other world, this impossible blasphemous thing, and he believed that Scott and Amber and every other human, seen and unseen by him, had traveled through the sky between their two worlds in a ship. He believed the tower of fire he had mistaken for the very arm of Sheul was indeed the fire of that burning ship. He believed in all these things.

But he still could not believe that ship had come here by accident.

It was not the faith he'd had in his life before entering Xi'Matezh. It did not come with the name of Sheul or the certainty that he was seen by some greater eye as he hung here in Scott's power, but it was still a comfort. His clay would perish, yet he had a soul and that, somehow, would go on.

Meoraq closed his eyes and stretched his toes toward the ground to take some of the weight off his screaming shoulders. He took deep breaths. He did not count them.

He waited in the dark to die.

13

They passed the day at Xi'Matezh and it was, for many, a good day. Scott had his moment of triumph, complete with a ship to show to his surviving men as proof of his superior leadership. The raiders encouraged his speeches and even called for a few when things threatened to get quiet; the delirious joy of the humans for what must seem to them just another relic in the ruins made it a day of rare entertainment. For Amber, it was a day in Purgatory. Not Hell itself, but only its cold grey antechamber—the waiting room where there was no time and no relief from the awful weight of anticipation.

Iziz kept her close, kept her servile, but did not allow her to work. The other humans hauled wood and water, and answered whatever need any raider had, whether it was for tea or stew or sex, with plenty of time to stand around their ship and daydream. Amber could only kneel with her hands below Iziz's boot, aching with the strain of staying small and quiet, feeling his stare cold on the back of her head. She had nothing to do except think and when she wasn't relentlessly playing out every possibility that began with getting a weapon away from Iziz (and ended with going through the broken wall and over the cliff more often than not), her mind brought her back to the same questions:

What was that thing in the garage where Meoraq hung? What was that thing that Scott and his Manifestors were all but praying to? Was it a ship? Was it really?

Or was it a boat?

She thought it was. She really did. And worse, she sometimes found herself thinking of it as proof that the helicopter was coming too, a thought that grew less and less comforting the longer she had to listen to Scott. He still hadn't figured out how to open the door (as far as Amber knew, he hadn't even identified which panel was the door), but he was completely confident that he could fly it home. Funny, how faith could look like crazy when she saw it on someone else.

She could try to fight. Iziz had plenty of weapons on him. Unfortunately, the only one she had any hope of getting at down here was the dagger in his boot, whereas he was in the perfect position to lop her head off.

'He won't do it,' Bo Peep said sleepily. 'He wants the baby.'

But he could still kill Meoraq.

'He's going to do that anyway. If you make him mad, at least he'll kill Meoraq quickly.'

Nicci had died quickly. That didn't make it easy.

'If you do nothing, he'll definitely die hard.'

But if she waited, she'd have more time to plan and maybe stumble into a better opportunity to take one of his swords.

'Or lose it,' said Bo Peep's ghost. 'If you see the chance, little girl, you take it. Maybe there is a God and maybe there isn't. Maybe He helped Scott cross the wires that raised that boat and maybe He didn't. Maybe this and maybe that, but you know damn well He isn't going to drop out of the sky and put a gun in your hand, so you forget all about good opportunities and better ones. If you see the chance, you take it.'

Fuck it. Amber made a grab for the dagger in Iziz's boot.

Iziz yanked his foot up and then slammed it forward, catching her in the chest and sending her skidding backwards through the mud until she collided with one of the Manifestors. He kicked her too, and Iziz leapt up and slapped him. "You touch my

Eshiqi again and I'll whip you bloody! Geozh!"

"I've got him. Urgath, get over here, what's wrong with you?"

Amber spat mud, raised her head to catch a glimpse of metal—the shine of a buckle on the side of Iziz's boot—and dropped it again, knowing it was all over now. Meoraq was dead; she'd helped to kill him.

Iziz stood over her a long time without speaking. "Get up," he said at last.

"Fuck you," Amber replied. The enormity of her risk and the self-disgust behind her failure combined to make her feel a little drunk. "Kill me on the ground, motherfucker."

Several raiders hooted, hearing this. Several more wandered over to watch.

"Get up," said Iziz again. Over his shoulder, he added, "Bring me the Sheulek."

It was on the tip of her tongue to tell him to fuck off again, but she knew this might be the last time she saw Meoraq, the last time he saw her. She didn't want to be lying in the mud for that.

She climbed to her feet as they dragged Meoraq into the courtyard. He did not appear to be conscious, but they took no chances; his wrists were bound behind his back and then tied to his belt.

"That's far enough," said Iziz, and the raiders holding him let him drop. He collapsed face-down, but proved he was at least alive by rolling slowly onto his side and spitting out a mouthful of mud.

Iziz let her stare, but at her first hesitant step forward, he caught her by the arm and pulled her back. He studied the ground, gauging the distance between them and Meoraq, and took her with him all the way to the outer doors of the shrine. "He looks dry," Iziz remarked, keeping his grip on her arm. "Lkonu, give the Sheulek a drink."

With a snort, one of the raiders beckoned to the human acting as a serving slave.

"No," said Iziz. "He looks very dry. Make sure he gets a long drink."

Lkonu got up and took one of the big travel flasks from a sled. He needed the help of two others to stand Meoraq up and pry his mouth open. While they held him, Lkonu stuck the neck of the flask all the way into Meoraq's mouth and began to pour.

The first few swallows must have been good, but they kept coming. Meoraq choked, tried to turn away; they held his head and kept pouring. He began to struggle, violently enough that they had to put him on the ground, but Lkonu stayed with him the whole time and kept pouring. How much did those flasks hold? Two gallons? Three? Amber saw his chest heave, water spewing from around the neck of the flask. She heard the sound that Nicci had spoken of—that bubbly shout that people make when they're drowning.

At last, Lkonu came to the end of it, holding the flask up by its bottom and shaking to get the last drops. Then he took it away and the raiders pinning Meoraq to the ground let him go.

He kicked once, feebly. His mouth yawned. His head swiveled slowly side to side and then, in near-perfect silence, a great torrent of water erupted out of him. Most of it went spilling back into him and then came out again as foam. The raiders found this uproarious.

"God and Gann," said Iziz, watching her, only her. "They come together out here. Understand that...and pick a sword."

She looked at him, tears and mud drying stiff on her face, frozen to her heart. "Are you going to make me kill him?"

"I can't make you do anything," he replied evenly. "We all have a choice. My mother told me that. Didn't yours?"

"No. Wasn't really her style." She looked at Meoraq again, lying on his back and choking on the froth of his own watery vomit, still too weak to roll over. "She was always a victim."

"Sword, Eshiqi." Iziz spread his arms, inviting her to take her choice—all of Meoraq's and his own besides. "You wanted it enough to risk his life and yours, so don't flinch now. Take it and swallow the consequences."

Everyone was watching now. Raiders, Manifestors, even Eric, the newest slave of the bunch if you didn't count Amber herself. Everyone except Meoraq, who didn't do anything but breathe, and couldn't do that very well.

The wind and the salt in the spray stung her eyes. She pointed at Meoraq's samr, because she'd practiced with it before and because it was the heaviest and had the best chance of taking someone's head off clean if...if that was where this was going.

Iziz drew it from the sheath strapped to his back and handed it to her. "All right," he said, unclipping both kzungs and holding them, one in each hand, relaxed. "We're going to play a game. You see your man there? If you can reach him—" The kzungs in his hands twirled in the careless manner of a trick played too many times to be considered showboating anymore. "—you can have him."

"You lie."

He shrugged. "I never said you could keep him, but I'll give you one hour's liberty. That's fair, isn't it?"

Raiders consulted one another and, after much serious talk and dramatic gestures, unanimously agreed. Very fair.

"One hour to do what you will with him. If you want to run or leap into the sea or just give him one last poke, that's up to you. But you have to put your hand right on him, you mark?"

"And if you reach him first?"

"Probably won't be pleasant. Just remember, it doesn't end until you have him or until you cry surrender. If you cry, the game is over." His head cocked. He smiled. "But if I reach him first, Eshiqi, you don't get to cry anymore. You just get to watch. So really, the wisest thing for you to do is cry right now, before we get started."

But she would never get another chance. Amber gripped her sword in both hands, holding it the way she'd trained during all those long, boring winter days.

Iziz snorted and slapped at his chest. "Let's have it, then. Make me bleed."

She stabbed. His sword smacked down on hers hard enough to sting her palms and numb her elbows. He could have disarmed her. He could have cut her throat on the backswing if he wanted to. He just stood there, his arms relaxed at his sides, his throat black and cool, waiting.

Amber stepped back, suddenly feinted left and swung from the right. He knocked her sword aside and slapped her with the flat of his blade.

The raiders cheered.

They stared at each other. Amber reached up shakily and rubbed at her cheek. She wasn't even cut.

"Ease up," suggested Iziz. "Your arms are too stiff and they're telling me what you mean to do. A relaxed stance keeps secrets."

She lunged, coming in low and slashing sharply up, but he was there to knock her sword uselessly aside and slap her other cheek. His men cheered again.

"You really are a fierce little thing, aren't you?" Iziz murmured.

Amber feinted again, stabbing for his heart and then thrusting down with all her weight, hoping to nail his boot to the ground. His playful swat became a hasty leap backwards and she darted forward, slashing and stabbing and skidding in the mud. He let her come four, maybe five steps, and then he stopped parrying.

And started attacking.

Even as she scrambled to defend herself against the steady rain of blows, she knew he wasn't trying to kill her. He was just thinning her nerves and wearing her out. And it was working. As she began to slow, so did he, until they were just standing and staring at each other once more.

"I can see your arms trembling," said Iziz.

She stabbed. He knocked her sword aside and took a step forward. Amber backed away with her sword raised and yes, it was shaking. He took up every step she put between them until her back bumped against the outer doors of the shrine.

"So." Iziz looked around, his spines relaxed and throat black, calm. "You began the game with fifty paces to claim and now have, what? Seventy-five? Do you cry, Eshiqi? You have to say the words."

'Say it,' said Bo Peep. 'You don't have to mean it.'

True. She might even get that fabled better chance, but she had the sword in her hand right now and that might never happen again.

Amber screamed and lunged at him. All around them, raiders hissed and stomped, calling encouragement to her as she drove the smirking Iziz back. As he parried with one sword, the other played, flicking at her hair and cutting at the fastens of her girdle until it popped open and fell off. Her tunic gaped; the sight of her naked human breasts set the raiders to roaring, even louder after she shrugged out of the useless, flapping tunic and threw it to the ground. Bare-chested, she pressed the attack and Iziz agreeably backed up until he was maybe three meters from the place where Meoraq lay. There he stopped, content to parry her increasingly ragged thrusts and slashes until, with a snort of disdain, he clipped one of the kzungs back on his belt and gave her a shove.

She staggered, flailing wildly to keep her balance. She kept her feet, but lost her momentum. Panting, her arms like hot lead hanging off her shoulders, she could only look past him to Meoraq, but he gave her nothing to draw strength from. He lay in the mud without moving, unconscious or...no, he had to be unconscious.

"On your knees, Eshiqi," Iziz warned her. "Cry to me."

Everyone was watching, listening. Beneath their expectant silence, she could clearly hear Scott picking his stupid ship apart in the garage, actually bashing his way into it with the reassurance that they could fix that later, just keep going, keep at it, grab that panel there and *pull*. She could feel the waves hitting the cliffs, feel each wet slap vibrating up through her naked feet to shiver in her bones. The wind blew saltspray in her eyes like tears; Amber had none left of her own.

She stabbed the samr down into the mud—not a calculated expression of defeat but only to brace herself against—and dropped beside it on her knees. She did not look at Iziz. She didn't look at anyone, not even Meoraq. Now and then, she could feel her head shaking slowly back and forth, but she felt none of the disbelief the gesture confessed. She felt tired. Not angry, not defiant, not even grieving and sick and scared anymore, but just...just tired. God did not live at Xi'Matezh and He wasn't sending a helicopter. There was only her and she'd tried and failed, so what else was there to say?

"I cry," said Amber.

Iziz cocked his head and put one foot forward. He waited.

Amber bent over, palms up to either side of his scuffed boot, and the very instant that her sweaty brow touched leather, Scott's ship in the garage exploded.

She was not immediately conscious of the noise—it hit her ears like a ton of cotton, deafening her before she knew what it meant—but only of an intense heat lashing up her back, so that her first thought, when she could think, was that someone in the crowd had whipped her.

She cried out and fell flat, twisting around to see her unwhipped back, and when that finished making no sense to her, she finally raised her eyes and saw three raiders lying dead in the mud. And not just dead, she realized, not just that, but decapitated. She saw the smoke next, the smoke that was not only pouring out through the open doorway of the garage in a greasy, black fog, but also sprouting straight up in the air through the much bigger hole in the roof and sort of...folding under. Roaring. She could hear almost nothing, but the smoke was roaring.

Amber looked up at Iziz. He did not look down at her. All his attention seemed fixed on his hand, which he had apparently been holding up, perhaps in some sign to his men that she hadn't seen because she'd been bent over his boot, but anyway, he was looking at that hand with a deep, frowning confusion because it was now missing all its fingers. The strip of blackened, shiny-burnt metal that had sheared through three necks to cut them off was now lodged in another raider's chest. That man was still standing. Except for the thing jutting out of his tunic, he didn't even seem all that hurt.

She had enough time to see all this, not quite enough to know what it all meant, and then the ship blew up again. The ground heaved up beneath her, as impossible as that should be, actually seeming to smack her in the chest even as she had both hands in the mud. Then she and Iziz and Meoraq were all sprawled together and the ship just kept exploding, ripping the garage apart from the top down. In the curious quiet, she could see chunks of metal and broken bricks hurtling through the smoke, see them soundlessly punch through fleeing men, taking them apart piece by piece until there was nothing left to keep running. Through it all, the fire kept rising, vomiting up through the smoke, pushing a flat, burnt panel on the very top, tumbling it playfully over and over, like a paper sailboat caught in a fountain.

It couldn't have lasted long and when it was over, the courtyard was empty except for the mud and the mess and the bodies, and there was a quiet like nothing Amber had ever known.

Then that piece of paneling which had ridden the explosion so high came down out of the black, blown into a shape something like a flower, a daisy, so that it spun as it fell, chopping at the air, whup-whup-whup...

'Like a helicopter,' thought Amber, watching it cut right through two legs of that long-suffering transmission tower before crashing into the outer doors of the shrine of Xi'Matezh.

Amber pushed herself up on her hands. Beneath her, Iziz also stirred and sat up on his elbows. They looked at each other. He opened his mouth and emitted a godawful yowling that seemed to shake at her very bones— but no, he did not do that at all. He opened his mouth and the yowling was all she could hear of the scream of tortured metal as the tower that had sent out uncounted years of unheard hope for Nuu Sukaga buckled slowly over and smashed down into the dome of the shrine. It collapsed and then the building beside it collapsed, along with a large chunk of the wall, and suddenly, the whole courtyard of Matezh shuddered and dropped about twenty centimeters.

Amber and Iziz looked at each other again. Then he grabbed for the sword on his belt and she grabbed for Meoraq's knife tucked into his waist and he was still so much faster but he grabbed with the hand that had no fingers and while he was staring at that in astonishment, Amber's fist closed tight around the bone hilt of Meoraq's ancestral knife and yanked it free.

They stared at each other a third time, motionless, as mud began ominously to flow toward the fast-crumbling wall. Then Iziz closed his eyes.

"Do it right this time, you murdering cunt," he said dully.

She stabbed him in the neck and cut, stopped to spit out his blood and rest her watery arms, then cut twice more just to be sure. He jerked under her a few times, but that was all. He was dead at the end of it, nothing but weight she had to shift to get at Meoraq, who had not moved once in all this time.

He groaned when she rolled him over, but it was hard to hear him. He may have told her to leave him. He may have told her to run. Amber paid him absolutely no attention. She sheathed his bone-handled knife, stuck it down the back of her breeches, and got a good grip on his harness. She pulled. She did not allow his screams or the limp silence that eventually followed them to slow her down. All that mattered right now was that they had to go. God had sent a boat and a helicopter; the rest was up to her, so Amber pulled. When she bumped into one of the sleds, she put him on it and kept going. The runners moved through the mud much easier than the drag of a body, and even with the extra weight, Amber was able to run the last length and out through the gateless archway just before the ground heaved up for the second time and threw her down. Her ears, still numbed, gave her nothing—it would be three days before she could hear anything that didn't sound like it came from underwater and a room away—but she didn't need them.

Matezh fell.

But when Amber raised her head in the stillness and looked, the sled was there and Meoraq was on it. She lifted her head a little higher and there was the archway, with just a few broken bricks on either side of it to prove there had ever been walls, framing a small portrait of a monstrous, green sea.

Meoraq's hand brushed her arm. His mouth opened when she looked at him, but if he was talking, she couldn't hear it. He made a few weak gestures, then groped until he got a hand behind her neck and pulled her close. His rough mouth scraped against hers and in that moment, she thought she could have carried him all the way back to the mountains and over them.

She didn't, of course. But she made it as far as the underlodge where she had spent fifty-three days shut up in a cupboard to recuperate. She couldn't lift Meoraq up into it, and he, weakened by days of fever, could do nothing to help her, so they were there on the floor—he, gasping and raving; she, rubbing palmfuls of water over him in a desperate effort to cool him down—when Uyane Jazuun, lord-steward of the bloodline in Chalh, stopped in on his yearly pilgrimage to escape the ever-ringing bells of the Festival of Fifth Light and found them.

14

They camped only once on a four-day journey, in another underlodge very much like the one they'd just left. They ran whenever they had strength to run. They walked the rest of the time, passing flasks between them and sharing cuuvash on their feet. Meoraq took nothing. Every few hours, Jazuun would stop and bend Meoraq forward, pounding on his back until Meoraq woke enough to cough. It helped, but not enough. His breath had taken on the soggy, snotty sound of someone trying to breathe through a bowl of soup. He was delirious by the end of the first night, silent by dawn on the third day.

Dying. He was dying.

She cried once, just once, the night they camped. Lying in the cupboard, trying not to touch the man Amber still sometimes feared might be the ghost of Meoraq's dead father, listening to the gasp and burble of creeping death, she put both hands on her belly—on the only part of Meoraq she could reach—and cried. Jazuun didn't budge until she was done, but as she drowsed unhappily toward sleep, he said, "He rests in God's sight, woman, and if he sees our Father's face tonight, know that he sees it with joy."

He meant it well, she knew, but it only set her off again, weeping until she had no tears, only the stuffy ache of their lack. When she finished for the second time and lay shivering and wiping convulsively at her face, Jazuun rolled over with an air of grim determination and gave her shoulder a clumsy pat. "I know who you are," he told her. "If he goes to the Halls, I will keep you as kin. You'll have a good man to marry and I'll see your sons raised under the Blade."

She rolled onto her stomach and brayed into the musty bedding. He stopped trying to comfort her.

It was the last real rest they took. Shortly after dawn, they were moving again, and this time, Jazuun did not stop until they broke out of the woods into open plains. In the distance, the lone monument in this vast, green patch of nothing, stood the black walls of Chalh. Jazuun checked on Meoraq, took a long swig from his flask, then gave Amber a hard stare.

She knew what he was thinking. "Go," she said in lizardish. "I'll stay here."

"Fuck that in the fist," he replied, and then rather visibly recalled he was speaking to a woman. "You couldn't hide anywhere in sight of Chalh that our sentries couldn't find you, and if they do...I'm going to run you in," he said decisively. "I don't think they'll challenge me if they don't see you."

"How the hell do you think you're going to hide me?" Amber asked, stunned.

"You know I don't speak that gabble!" he snapped back at her.

"How?" she asked, this time in his language.

"Well, we don't have time to be clever, so we'll have to be bold." He loosened some of the belts holding Meoraq to the sled, pounded him distractedly on his back and then whisked the blanket covering him away. "Get on."

"Can you pull us both? Damn it." Amber concentrated and tried again in lizardish. "Can you carry us together? That far?"

"Great Sheul, O my Father..." Jazuun pounded Meoraq on the back some more. When he straightened up, he had his head cocked. "Do as I say. No, I don't know it will work, but it's the only plan we have time for, so just do it."

She got on the sled, reluctantly straddling Meoraq and trying her best to keep her weight off him. To her utter astonishment, Meoraq raised one arm and placed it on her back—the first voluntary movement he'd made in two days. "You're going to be fine," she told him, just in case he could hear her. "We're almost there. Hang on, okay? Just hang on."

No response, but hope remained as long as he had his arm around her.

Jazuun threw the blanket over the top of her and cinched it down with belts. "Can you breathe?" he asked.

"Yes." The air was stuffy and smelled of sweaty human and dying dumaq, but she could breathe it. "Go!"

The sled lurched. She had a certain amount of experience with riding on sleds, but there was a huge difference between lying on one and perching backwards like this, an even bigger difference between a walk and a run. Despite her best effort, Amber lost her balance immediately and fell into him. Meoraq's groan of pain broke into racking coughs, then to a strengthless, "I see it. Like an arm rising...It's mine, 'Kosa. It's for me," and then his arm fell limply away from her.

She'd seen the walls. She knew how fast they were going, how long it would be before they reached the city. She knew everything and still it was endless, in the dark. She was lost until she heard Jazuun say, "Here they come. If it goes bad, I'll kill them. I shouldn't be challenged over it, but do not come out no matter what you hear."

"Yes," she told him, which was not quite the right answer, but which was all she could manage being bounced around like this.

"Stay low," he hissed. "Stay quiet."

Amber gripped the blanket tighter and pressed her cheek to Meoraq's chest.

"Stand where you are!" someone called, someone new. "Stand and be—"

"I am Uyane Jazuun, steward of my House, named fourth of the governing Houses of Chalh. This man is Sheulek, kin to me and badly injured. You, run for a cart, and you, get healers and a surgeon to House Uyane! Go now!"

There was no answer. The sled rolled and bounced and jerked. The struggling of Meoraq's lungs under the heavy blanket was so much louder than his heart beating.

"Open!" Jazuun shouted, and was answered by metallic clanks and groaning.

The sled heaved and suddenly the rear end was up in the air and the sound of boots drumming hard in a stone hall was all around her.

"Cart's at the end of the gate, sir," a new voice said. "Should have it emptied when we reach it. What is that?"

"It's mine is what it is and I'll kill the one who challenges me over it now, when this man lies in the shadow of Gann! Do you hear him, eh? Do you? This is Uyane Meoraq, son of Rasozul, who was champion of Xeqor in Yroq. *That* Rasozul, sprat, and his son is who this is, and if he dies, by God and Gann, so will every man I hold even a shard responsible!"

There were no other questions, nothing at all but running feet until Jazuun's, "Easy with him now."

They swooped up and then down, thumping into the bed of a cart on top of rough bags of seed or sand or God knew what. Meoraq groaned at the impact, then clutched at her through the blanket, and how blind could these people be? How could she help but look like a whole other person crouching in this litter with him?

"To Uyane!" Jazuun called, as boots leapt up into the cart and his heavy hand rested briefly on Amber's head.

"Sir, the temple surgery—"

"I say Uyane! Mark me and pull, you gutter-sons!"

The cart lurched forward to the deafening hail of hooves on stone. Here, blinded, the speed felt dizzying, unreal, faster than a subway car, faster than the shuttle that had taken them into space. They did not drive out into the city, but were fired into it—a rabble of voices, a thousand smells, unseen people on every side, and Meoraq groaning beneath her.

In the dark, with the sound of his heartbeat obliterated by the chaos around her, it took hours. She knew they were there only when the cart stopped, pitching her off the litter so that she had to climb back on, and someone had to have seen that, surely, but Jazuun just bellowed for someone to open the gate and someone else to come and carry. Then it was running again, with her clinging to Meoraq like a baby monkey, until suddenly they were set down, the belts loosened and the blanket whisked away.

Light blinded her. She raised her hand against it, squinting, and heard a lizardish scream. Jazuun was an immediate blur, leaping across this wide, startlingly elegant room in an instant to swat the lizardlady responsible on the snout. "Keep your fucking head or I'll spin it around for you," he hissed.

The lizardlady, gripping her snout in both hands, bowed herself over at the waist and stayed that way. It wasn't until she did it that Amber noticed the second lizardlady standing beside her. She didn't scream. But of course, she'd seen Amber before.

"Xzem?" she stammered.

"Eshiqi!" Xzem set the armload of linens she'd been holding on the nearest surface and rushed forward to clasp Amber's hands.

"Get her out of here," Jazuun ordered, throwing the blanket back over her. "Take her to my wife's chamber, and you, take this silly dip someplace with a lock on it. No one knows about this until I give the word."

"I mark, sir."

"Then go. All of you, go."

"I'm not going anywhere!" Amber pushed the blanket back defiantly and grabbed Meoraq's hand. His fingers clenched; he groaned.

Jazuun came back in just a few long strides, his hand darting out to grip her by the chin. Up close, the family resemblance was next to nothing. "The surgeon will be here any moment and if he sees you, he will lose his wit and his hands, and he needs them both to save your man."

He released her and gestured. Xzem brought the blanket back and hooded her. This time, Amber bent, swearing, and made sure her face was covered.

"You'll have the first word after me," Jazuun said, but he was already moving away. "Go. Now."

Xzem's rough hand tapped at hers. She offered her sleeve and Amber took it. They left, keeping low and close to the wall, passing a small group of running lizardmen in the hall just outside. Meoraq's doctors. Amber lingered until the door had shut them away, but then there was nothing else to wait for, nothing else to see. She let Xzem take her away.

She didn't count the turns they made or the doors they passed. This wasn't like Zhuqa's camp; it wasn't someplace to escape. It wasn't home, either. It was a waiting room, that was all.

Xzem came to a door, guarded on either side by lizardmen in highly-polished boots, which were all that Amber could see with the blanket pulled so low. "The Sheulek-kin of my lord is returned," Xzem said softly, bowing. "My lord commands his wife receive the wife of Uyane Meoraq."

The boots moved aside. With a dull clank, the door opened to reveal another door right on the other side. One of the lizardmen, maybe Xzem herself, knocked twice, but the sound of running feet over tiles told her the knock was unnecessary. The second door rattled impatiently on its hinges and whooshed open.

"My lady, my lord commands—"

A kitten bawled. And even knowing she was untold lightyears away from all the kittens that ever were, that was still what Amber heard—the sickly, ear-piercing mew of a newborn cat. Before she could react, she felt herself seized by the shoulders and towed over the threshold.

Xzem followed, patiently continuing her introduction half-heard beneath an urgent chorus of kittens, and shut the door. The guards on the other side shut theirs, and whoever was impersonating the cat grabbed Amber's blanket and pushed it back.

Maybe it was just because of the sounds she made, but she actually looked like a cat...at least as much as a lizard ever could. Her eyes were wide and curiously slanted. Her cheekbones were rather broad and her snout exceptionally pointed. But most of it was due to the odd ornament she wore over her hood, which capped her short spines and then arced off to either side of her head in twin points of glittering metal and beads. The edges of her hood were even trimmed in wispy bits of fringe like whiskers.

"Oh." The lizardlady's left hand rose to tap delicately at her breast. The right went even higher, cupping the end of her narrow snout. "Oh," she said again, her dark eyes brimming with sympathy. "The poor deformed creature."

"Lady, she knows our speech," Xzem murmured respectfully.

"I don't imagine it's any secret to her that she's deformed. It would be more impolite to pretend otherwise, I think. I am Nraqi, little creature." Nraqi reached to take Amber's hands and bring them to her heart. She made another weird animal sound, wordless and mushy, like a knife right to the ear, before adding, "Your mother in Chalh."

"I don't need a mother," said Amber and pulled her hands back.

"Does it have a name?" Nraqi whispered.

"Eshiqi," said Xzem, bowing.

"It's Amber, actually."

"Eshiqi." Nraqi leaned back, cupping Amber's face gently between her hands and smiling. "Such a pretty name for...well...such a pretty name!"

Amber detached herself as gently as she could and went back to the door, straining to hear through it—and the ten or twelve walls that stood between her and Meoraq. She couldn't even hear the two guards she knew were just outside. She couldn't hear anything except her own breath bouncing off the door into the suffocating echo-chamber of this stupid blanket.

Amber yanked it all the way down around her neck and then, in a sudden illogical fury, she took the whole damn thing off and threw it in a heap on the floor, going as far away as the room allowed, to the only window. The glass was stained a deep red and had a weirdly bubbled and streaked appearance. 'Like blood,' she thought.

Bo Peep's reflection floated in the window, slack-faced, loveless. Then it was Nicci's face, the eyes sunken and accusing. She didn't see herself, and never would, she realized. The last time she'd seen a mirror had been in the Manifestor's compound the day of the flight, just a sidelong glance as she climbed out of the shower, the memory stained with resentment because it would be right across from the shower and how many people really looked their best naked first thing in the morning? The old Amber. The tough Amber. The Amber who could be a bitch and a bully, but who by-God got the job done, who took care of things, who had been born old and was nobody's little girl, where was she now? Who was this scrawny, useless person with her eyes brimming with blood? Who had God, ha, picked to be the last human left alive on this whole planet?

The last...

The thought had been creeping in on her for days, but with Meoraq to look after, she'd always been able to push it away. Now it crawled up her spine and bit in deep. Fifty thousand people, winnowed down just that easily to only one, only her.

She was alone. And if Meoraq...left her...she'd be lost.

"Eshiqi?" Nraqi's reflection fretted with her sleeves and then said decisively, "Tea, I think. Tea and cakes. Poor thing hasn't eaten and everything seems worse on an empty belly. Xzem!"

"Yes, my lady."

Hungry? Tea and *cakes*? "No!" said Amber in choked lizardish. She wasn't sure which 'no' she used, but she used it loud enough to halt Xzem in her tracks. Covering her stinging eyes, Amber turned back to the window.

"Just the tea, then," Nraqi said after a moment.

"No."

"Water."

"Lady, I know you're trying," said Amber in dull English, "but if you don't leave me alone, I think I'm going to lose my mind."

Xzem slipped quietly out through a side-door. Gone to fetch drinks, no doubt. Which Amber would have to choke politely down while the friendliest cat-lizard in the universe chatted her up and Meoraq died somewhere in this God-forsaken house.

Amber squeezed her eyes shut until they quit leaking and opened them again to stare out the blood-red window at an empty world.

Quiet footsteps heralded Xzem's return, but instead of the clinking glasses she expected, Amber heard a muffled purr—the sleeping song of Zhuqa's baby. She turned around and there it was, wrapped in a clean, plush blanket. She supposed it had outgrown its need for smooth skin, but it woke when Xzem passed it into her arms and snuggled up to her the same as it had always done. Its tiny fist punched once at Amber's breast, then found a gripping place on her tunic. It sang.

How long Amber stared into its tiny, pale face, she couldn't know, but when she raised her eyes at last, there was Xzem.

"I never had the chance to thank you," said Xzem, reaching out to brush her fingertips along the tiny ridge on the top of its skull where someday, spines would grow. "Or to show your lord my gratitude. Now that I have that chance, I cannot find the words. Your lord raised me out of darkness and put me in the sight of Sheul. He placed my Nali in God's hands and placed this one in mine. He made me a mother, after all this time...after so many lost and left behind me. He made me a wife. He made me a good woman—" Her voice broke. After some short time, she went on. "—to a good man. This child, when it is grown, it will be a good woman or a good man, and it may never know there was another way to be."

Amber could only look at her. A part of her knew what Xzem was saying and another part even vaguely knew what her own response should be, but both of these were only whispers beneath the silent screams of *i don't* care *lady i don't care it isn't equal it isn't fair god gives and god takes and maybe he thinks that's a fair trade but it's* not! In the end, she only gave the baby back, her throat too tight to let her speak anyway, and turned back to the window. The baby woke and fussed a little, but its mother soothed it back to sleep and soon it had forgotten Amber again.

"It's all right," she heard Nraqi say behind her. She heard Xzem's footfalls retreating. For a while, there was nothing, and then a soft, four-fingered hand brushed at her back. Amber tried to shrug it off, but the hand did not go.

"Come with me," Nraqi said. She wasn't a cat anymore.

Amber resisted, but the stiffness of her body beneath that gentle touch felt petty, a child's tantrum. She turned around, away from the window and the lie of its reflection, and followed Nraqi through a heavy curtain, down a narrow, unlit hall, past banks of doors standing open on empty rooms, to a winding, rising stair.

It led up into the open air of a high-walled garden, long and oddly wedge-shaped, like a polite slice of cheesecake, with benches along the sides and a light at the pointy end. Two lights, really: a tall brazier of open coals below a hanging lamp with an opaque glass cover, both burning in full daylight. Over the walls, wisps of smoke and all the sounds and smells of the city reminded Amber of the world outside her own personal hell.

"This is my chapel," said Nraqi. Her gaze trailed along the tops of the walls and all the way around. "The one below...a plaything for the House priests. I let them see me there at times, the way I let the linen girls see me at my wardrobe and the serving girls see me at tea. But I have worn the same three gowns every day for sixteen years and I hate the taste of frosted cakes. Here is my true chapel. Here is where I stand that I know..." Her head tipped back. The delicate fringe at the side of her hood fluttered in the breeze. "...I know God sees me."

"I can't," said Amber, shaking her head in tight, hurtful jerks. "I'm sorry, lady. I know you mean well, but I can't listen to that right now."

"I had never felt His eye upon me before," said Nraqi, still serenely watching the clouds roll by. "Not all my childhood years in my father's House, not with all the prayers I learned to sing or in all the hours I learned to kneel so still and just...just think of nicer things. I never saw God when they took me out from Gelsik and across the mountains to this place. I did not see Him in my lord-husband's face on the night I was given to him, conquered by him. I was, I think, eleven years gone in this House before I ever knew God as more than a word in the mouths of old men, and it was here. My little one, my Varis...three times, I carried her and three times, Gann snatched her back and those wicked old men wouldn't even let me sit with her after she was gone, so I was here. And Jazuun brought her to me. And we sat together. It is such a quiet thing, Eshiqi—" Nraqi reached back and took Amber's hand, lightly squeezing. "—when God speaks."

"I don't want to hear Him telling me there's nothing He can do," said Amber hoarsely. "I don't want to hear Him tell me to suck it up! I don't want to be saved if it means watching him die anyway!" She fought with it, lost, and burst out, "I can't lose *everything*, damn it! He can't *do* that to me! It isn't right!"

There was more, but even that much was too garbled by tears to understand and no one up here spoke English except her anyway. Nraqi tried to put her arms around her. Amber stumbled back, but Nraqi wouldn't let go and after the run she'd just had, Amber didn't have it in her to struggle for long. At the end of it, exhausted, she simply slid down on her knees with her hands folded limply in her lap, leaned her forehead into Nraqi's hip, and bawled.

"God does not always give us what we ask for," Nraqi said, wrapping her in folds of her robe to shelter her from the wind. "But after all my years, I have come to believe He gives us what He can. So pray, even if all He can do is sit beside you. I know that doesn't seem like much, but sometimes, I tell you, it is everything."

* * *

Meoraq had not known he was dying, but he knew the very moment he was dead. He knew not because he was standing and not because he was no longer in pain, although both these things should have been clues, but because he was at home. He was in Xeqor, standing in his father's rooftop garden, where the breeze was impossibly sweet and the sky, filled with lights. Stars, Amber had called them. The sky was filled with stars and so Meoraq knew he was dead.

He went to a bench. He would have liked to have at least staggered there, but this body was fit and strong, and his mind filled with rest. So he just walked. And sat.

Meoraq waited. He'd heard about things like this—for as long as there had been death, he supposed there had been men who had gone only to the threshold and come back to tell of it—and he already knew it wasn't going right. There was no dark tunnel, no pure white light, no Sheul to reach out His arms in welcome, only this familiar and disturbingly silent setting and an alien, glittering sky.

He was not alone, although he appeared to be. He could feel eyes on him...but that wasn't right. What he felt was not a sense of being watched as much as companionship. He found himself looking around quite often, trying to see whoever it was with him, but although the rooftop of the city burned with hundreds of fires, he saw no one. The world of the dead, it seemed, was as empty as the world of the living.

Perhaps this was Hell, he thought. And it was not the endless walk across the grey wastes of Gann after all, but only this glimpse of what might have been paradise, and himself, alone.

No sooner had this bleak thought occurred than it was disproven.

Rasozul appeared on the bench beside him—a much younger man than Meoraq had known, but it *was* Rasozul and not just a familiar face for someone else, some Other, to wear.

Meoraq leaned sidelong into him at once, not like a grown man at all, but like a boy. His chest ached, thick with unhappiness, but he could not cry here. It was impossible to cry here. Because he was dead.

His father did not ask questions. Explanations were unnecessary. Understanding moved between them, unspoken, more complete than anything words could accomplish anyway. His father knew all about Amber, the way he heard and accepted Meoraq's apology for all the years of thoughtless disdain he'd shown Yecedi, who had always loved him anyway.

"What happens now?" Meoraq asked at last, because that was the only thing unclear to him. It felt like forever in every second. Amber might have been alone out in the world for years already.

"I can't answer that, son."

"You mean you don't know?"

Rasozul smiled and slipped his arm around him like he'd done it all his life and not for the first time. "I mean I can't answer for you. If you wanted to know, you'd already be moving on."

"Moving...? Isn't this it?"

"Not quite."

"I don't understand," said Meoraq.

Rasozul acknowledged this with a smile, but made no attempt to explain.

"There's either more or there isn't! How can this be 'not quite' all there is?"

"It would depend."

"On what?" Meoraq demanded, as frustrated as he could bring himself to be in this perfect place.

But Rasozul's smile was just the same. "On where it is you think we are now," he said patiently. "And why you need to be there."

Meoraq looked around at the rooftop, the stars, the empty wilds beyond Xeqor's walls. "Am I making this up?" he asked uncertainly.

"Not exactly."

"Are there...Halls? Is there..." Meoraq clapped a hand to his eyes, but there was no way to hide shame anymore. He wished there was, and that was shameful too. "Is there a God?" he whispered brokenly. "Are there Halls where He resides? I'm not asking for welcome, I just need to know!"

"Ah, my son..." Rasozul pulled Meoraq against his broad, unscarred chest and rubbed his back. "Why would you not be welcome?"

And he couldn't cry in this place, not with these eyes, but there could still be pain and it came splintering out of him: years of murder, of death within the arena and without, from the very first—that brunt in Tilev and the feel of his bones breaking—to the last raider in the ruins; every theft taken as a Sheulek's due from men who did not dare to refuse him; every woman bent and used and mostly forgotten, and like the murders he had done, they were not uncounted anymore, not here. He saw them all, each one a stone in his heart until the weight was more than he could carry and he covered his face again and cried out, "*Father, I have done such terrible things*!"

Rasozul held him, rocked him. "No one is beyond forgiveness."

"Whose forgiveness?" Meoraq asked, even as he pressed his eyes tighter into his shielding hands. "Is there a God? Does He know me?"

"I can't answer, son."

"Why not?"

Rasozul's hand rubbed gently up and down over his bent back. "Because you have to ask. Ah, boy, look up. Look around you. Can't you see?"

Meoraq slowly lowered his hands and raised his eyes. He saw the stars, shining out even brighter and more numerous than before. Their beauty had a sound, like a memory of music he could no longer hear with his ears but could still, however faintly, recall.

Meoraq looked away, at the braziers glittering over the rooftop of Xeqor. "It is nice," he mumbled, rubbing at his snout.

Rasozul sighed. "It is," he agreed.

They sat.

"How long do I have to wait here?" Meoraq asked.

"I can't answer that, son." Rasozul bent his neck and rubbed at his own snout. Patience colored all his thoughts and feelings. "We'll move on when you're ready."

"Where are we going?" Meoraq looked out into the darkened wilds beyond Xeqor's walls and, for a moment, thought he caught the suggestion of mountains to the east, the ghost-glow of golden light filling the barren washes between them, but then it was only blackness. "Is it far?" he asked uncertainly. He didn't want to go any further from Amber than he had to.

Rasozul sighed again and patted Meoraq's knee. "Only as far as you make it, son."

"Do I have to go right now?" Meoraq asked. "Can't I wait for her? I want to be here when she comes. She'll be frightened."

The stars began to wink out, one by one. The breeze, so sweet and soft all this time, gusted suddenly. His chest cramped. Oddly, pain was something he could feel in death.

"What—" Meoraq bent, one hand scratching over his chest, dumbly seeking some physical cause for this sudden assault. "What's happening?"

"Just look at me." Rasozul cupped Meoraq's face between his hands and leaned close. "Son, look at me. You're all right."

"Is this a punishment? I'm not leaving her!" he declared, shaking off his father's touch to shout into the darkening sky. "You can take me this far, but no further! Do you hear me? I...am not going...anywhere!"

Pain slammed like a hammer right into his heart, knocking whatever air filled his dead lungs out of this body. Meoraq fell back into Rasozul's gentle hands and writhed there as that hammer struck and struck and struck.

"Oh, my son," Rasozul said somewhere above him. He sounded as if he might be smiling, in a weary and resigned sort of way. "You don't have to fight."

Meoraq roared, kicking and slapping at the wind as it gusted, battering its way inside him. "No!" he spat, twisting his head violently back and forth until the wind went away. "Not! Leaving!"

"Meoraq."

It was a woman's voice, a woman's hands that brushed along the sides of his face, cupping him and making him quiet as the hammer rose and fell, rose and fell. He opened his eyes and saw his mother, fresh as on her wedding day, bending over him with loving exasperation shining down out of her eyes. Her eyes were golden brown and warm as tea; he'd forgotten.

The wind slackened. A few stars flickered and grew. In the east, the mountains he thought he saw flickered as well; Rasozul glanced that way and then at Yecedi.

"I know," she said, as if he had spoken. Perhaps he had, in that way of silent understanding which Meoraq had so briefly shared and which the pain had utterly taken from him. "But he's not ready. And he doesn't have to be. Meoraq," she said again, bending even lower to touch her brow to his. "Trust me. Do you trust me? I know you are very tired, but you must trust me."

He groped for her hand and found it, weakly squeezing, trying to fill that touch with all the years' worth of love he'd denied her for all his arrogant, stupid reasons, but he could feel her withdrawing from him. He could still see her and she was still smiling, but she was holding herself separate from him and she was doing it deliberately. It hurt and as he withdrew himself in confusion, that hammer suddenly smashed into him again.

"Breathe," his mother said, stroking his face. "Don't fight. Trust me, Meoraq, and relax."

He tried, but at the slightest loosening of his will, the pain took his whole body, burrowing into his throat like a living thing and swelling through his chest.

"Breathe it in," his mother said, and although she was still holding him, he could scarcely see her. The stars were going out in sheets now, all the world filling up with black, and ah, he hurt, he hurt, there was nothing left to feel but hurt.

"We'll wait for you," his father said. "Remember that and let go."

Let go. He'd said that to Amber once, in the ruins the night of the storm, and although he couldn't bring that night fully into focus through this terrible pain, he thought she'd done it. Because she'd trusted him to hold her. Meoraq battled his eyes open, but there was nothing of his mother left but her hands like shadows to either side of his face, nothing of his father but a voice beneath the killing wind telling him to breathe. The hammer struck; Meoraq opened his mouth to scream and the pain clawed at once down his throat.

He breathed it in.

* * *

Meoraq was awake long before he was able to do anything about it. Awareness was a live coal in his chest, a thick pool of pain much wider than the dimensions of his body. His arms and legs, of no significance, floated elsewhere. He drowsed in the thoughtless black, listening to low speech and shuffling bodies without the ability to make words of what he heard. And that was fine.

Gradually, the pain grew sharper and as it sharpened, it shrank. With the shrinking came a better sense of the rest of his clay until, all at once, he had an arm with a hand attached at the end of it, and within that hand, another hand. A soft hand. With many slender fingers.

He knew it was Amber before he knew he was Meoraq. Smiling, he squeezed the hand that held him. She squeezed back.

"Where is the knife of my fathers?" he asked. His voice was a whisper, a ghost in his throat.

She lifted his hand and laid it over the smooth bone hilt.

He smiled in the darkness. "Draw it with me, wife."

Someone coughed. Not Amber. Someone else.

Meoraq opened his eyes. He lay in a sickbed—a raised mat, open all around to allow ease of tending—and a rather large blurry man stood at the foot of it with a scattering of other blurs around him. People. Damn it. "Leave us," said Meoraq.

"That's not His fire in your belly, son," said a familiar voice, not moving. "That's wetlung."

Meoraq saw no reason it couldn't be both, but the act of opening his eyes had forced daylight into the whole of his body. Now he could see that the sickbed in which he lay was in a room, which was in a House, which was in the city of Chalh. He started to sit up, but his brain threatened to leave if he insisted, so he settled back into the bedding under Amber's guiding hands. "It is Uyane before me," he said, fitting a name to the man just now coming into focus at the heel of his sickbed. "Lord of his House under my descent and steward of his bloodline in Chalh."

"Keeper of the armory keys, warden over the Holy Fire of Gedai, guardian of the Oracle's Fourth Order, and too damned old to care," Uyane agreed. "But it's just Jazuun when I stand with kin. Or are you holding my House in your shadow?"

"Not from your sickroom, I'm not." He looked around again. "How did I get here? Wait..."

Meoraq thought.

He remembered.

He looked up at his wife. "You saved my life."

One corner of her mouth ticced up in her crooked, human smile. "Feels awful, doesn't it?"

"Yes." He thought some more—it was disturbingly difficult, a physical strain—and looked at Lord Uyane...Jazuun. "You found us? How?"

"Tripped over you on my way to Xi'Matezh."

"What were you doing there?"

Jazuun snorted and shrugged his spines. "Said I went there for Fifth Light, didn't I? All those fucking bells...I think a better question is, what were *you* doing there? It's been a brace and more! I thought you'd gone home."

"We were delayed." Meoraq tried again to sit up and again abandoned the effort. He put a hand on his chest, feeling at the pains within as if it could tell him something. "I don't remember this," he muttered and looked up. "How do the surgeons say?"

"They say rest for half a brace or so and if Sheul shows you favor, you'll be whole as you ever were. You've lost some juice and cracked some bones, but none of that was too serious apart from the strain it put on you. It was the wetlung that nearly killed you, boy, so you're to be resting on your feet as much as possible."

"And you?" Meoraq tried to raise the hand that did not grip Amber's to touch her heart, but his clay was heavy. He could manage only to rest his palm on her belly, which he supposed was just as appropriate. "Were you injured?"

"No, for a change. I'm fine. Or...we're fine, I guess." She laughed a little. Her laughter, even self-conscious as it was, was beautiful. "I'm still getting used to that."

"Then all is well." Meoraq closed his eyes to think some more. The darkness helped. "Are they feeding you?" he mumbled. It seemed very important in that moment.

"Oh boy, are they feeding me. The lady of the house here has been stuffing cake into me with both hands practically since I got here."

"At least it isn't marrow, eh?"

"Marrow would actually be a nice change. I could really go for a steaming heap of marrow right now."

He smiled. "You don't mean that."

"Not yet, but I'm getting there."

With effort, Meoraq turned his attention back to Lord Uyane, who had been watching this one-sided exchange with undisguised curiosity. "How long have I been here?"

"Six days, in and out. You've muttered some before this, but this is the first I've seen you give sensible speech. If you want to move to a decent bed, I'll let you, but your woman stays with mine. No arguments," he added, cocking his head at Amber, who did indeed have an argument gleaming in her eye. "You can see him in my company, but then you let him rest. How in the hell do you get this she-Sword to obey you, boy? It's like putting a tether on the wind."

"It is," Meoraq agreed, petting Amber's hand. "A fine, fierce wind." He dozed, fitting himself back in his flesh as if his body were an old pair of refurbished boots—familiar, but stiff and a bit too tight.

Boots...

"Where are my boots?" he asked, rousing.

"Up Gann's ass and around the kidney," Lord Uyane replied with a snort.

"I didn't have time to look for anything," Amber added. "We only have what was already on the sled when I put you on it, and we left a lot of that behind so we could get here faster. We still have a few things, I guess. Mostly stupid little stuff...your tea box...my mug. But..." She took a deep, bracing breath, dropping her eyes. "But you lost your knives. Or I lost them. Iziz took them and I didn't think...anyway, they're gone."

Meoraq glanced at the knife of his fathers resting on his chest, then at his arm, naked but for the cord of her hair. His sabks...? His *sabks*! Handed down from the firstborn son of Uyane Xaima himself, perhaps the oldest set of honor-knives in all the world, blades that had never known defeat, and now they were gone.

He pulled in breath and hissed it out, pulled in another and just let it go. He reached out and stroked once at his wife's brow, doing what he could to wipe away the guilt and shame she carried there. "So they are gone," he told her. "Uyane Xaima was only a man. His sabks were only metal. And what does it matter now, eh? The Age of the Warrior is ended. It is only right that they end with it, there...where it all began."

He had managed somehow to forget they were not alone in this room until Lord Uyane said, "Ended."

They both looked at him and then beyond him to all those other watching, listening, invisible servants. Alarm flared in Meoraq's chest as hot as fever, but Jazuun didn't seem all that upset. Or even surprised.

"I knew it just by looking at you. Even at your worst, I could see it on you...on both of you." Jazuun looked them over—first Meoraq, then Amber—and raised his chin like a true Sword in judgment. "You opened the doors at Xi'Matezh, didn't you? You entered before it fell."

Alarm flared again, which was twice too often for his ill-used clay. Meoraq put a hand over his heart to steady it and kept his spines still. "You don't blame me for that, surely."

"Blame you?" Jazuun tipped his head back in mock puzzlement. "It was God who held the shrine up all these ages. How is it that you dropped it? Although if any man could...If you can walk," he said suddenly, "there's something I want to show you."

A strange sort of knowing entered Amber's face. She looked at Jazuun and then at Meoraq, biting at her soft lip, and finally shook her head. "Come and see," she said, holding out her hand.

Meoraq consulted his clay, which had used the little time since his awakening to decide it was not dying after all, but which had not yet decided whether or not it was glad to hear that. He sat up, clasped Amber's little wrist in one hand and Lord Uyane's considerably more helpful one in the other, and heaved himself over the side of the sickbed and onto his feet. Standing was bad enough; walking, where every step jostled the broken shards of hell occupying his lungs, was worse; the worst, what Amber would call the frosting on the shit-cake, came when Lord Uyane opened the door and Meoraq found the hall simply choked with people, startling him into an unplanned, "Fuck Gann!" for all of them to witness.

His voice rolled out in a fine, firm thunder, silencing all the mutters, coughs and shuffling that large crowds produce, and as one body, all turned to stare at him.

And there he stood in nothing but a loin-plate—an adolescent nightmare come to horrifying life.

"Motherless pack of ghets," Jazuun said, but he said it under his breath and when he stepped forward to clear a path, he did it without slapping or swearing. The crowd, a faceless mass of rich robes and garish jewelry, gave ground with great reluctance and no small amount of posturing. These were not servants, scribes, messengers or any other breed of man Meoraq was accustomed to see collected in another man's halls. These were priests, landholders, judges, lords—the wealthiest and best-bred that Chalh had to offer. He saw, by God, the standard and flashes of the governor, jostling and being jostled by those of the Great Houses, the Temple, the Tribune and—

Meoraq cocked his head, then raised his arm off Amber's shoulders and aimed it like a spear into the crowd, trapping one man in frozen horror at the end of his pointing hand. "Ylsathoc Hirut!"

Like the cursed virgin in that old knee-time tale, hearing his name freed Exarch Ylsathoc from his paralysis. "I knew I knew that name," he whispered, backing clumsily away. "I *knew* I knew that name!"

Lord Uyane was waiting beside the open door to a stairwell, so Meoraq moved on, but he was loathe to let his prey escape unscathed. "Keep him close," he told Jazuun at the door. "I'm going to need provisions."

Jazuun eyed him curiously, then shrugged his spines and signaled a guard. The unfortunate exarch was escorted from the hall, gesticulating wildly and making vague, incoherent allusions to all the places and people who were at this moment expecting him, including his infirm father.

"You really are a scaly son of a bitch sometimes," Amber said, leading him onto the stairs.

Meoraq grunted agreement, still smiling. His body ached in every bone, but he felt so much better just knowing that pompous little fool would be waiting in mortal terror of him the rest of the day. "It has its uses," he told Amber. "Perhaps now the rest of them will leave."

"You couldn't disperse that lot with flaming oil, son," Jazuun snorted. "There will be twice this number and twice again once word slips out that you're awake."

"Me?"

Jazuun gave him a dry sidelong glance. "Who else would they be here to see?"

Meoraq looked at Amber.

"Well, yeah," she admitted. "I've had some of that, but believe me, it's always as your little monster."

"Why?" asked Meoraq, genuinely baffled. "What did I do?"

Lord Uyane laughed, clapped him once on the shoulder and bounded on ahead to open the rooftop door.

Light flooded the stair at once, blindingly bright. Meoraq's vision swam. He raised a hand to shield his eyes and left it there, his neck bent, seeing nothing but the stairs under his bootless feet until he reached the top. And so he was looking down when he stepped out under the open sky and saw the shadow of the stairwell hatch sprout long beneath him, as stark and black as if it had been painted there. Then he stepped around the stairwell hatch and suddenly the sun was in his eyes—not the light of the sun, but the sun itself—dazzling white, burning ghosts of pink and yellow in his eyes. The clouds that had been endless all his life had swept themselves into no more than a handful of high, wispy smudges. The sky beneath was green, as it had always been green, whether anyone knew it or not.

He had no idea how long he stared. He did not notice whether he found the stairwell wall and let it guide him to the ground or whether he simply collapsed. He did not see the others who shared the rooftop with him, not even Amber, whose hand remained clasped with his the whole time. It was not Sheul's lamp or the glow of His forgiveness, but it was the sun and the sun was still a miracle.

When at last Meoraq came back to himself, there was Amber, sitting beside him on the rooftop, her hair turned to white gold around her face. Her mouthparts were smiling, but her eyes were watchful and unsure.

"When?" he asked her.

"Same day we got here." One corner of her mouth crooked up a little higher. "I saw it happen, actually. I was right here on the roof. Praying."

Jazuun waited for her to stop talking and then gave Meoraq a light tap to catch his attention. "The Oracles have been in sequester for days, but the only thing they've decided is that you'll be able to explain it."

Meoraq could feel his throat working, but could not hear any words. Amber squeezed his hand. He looked at it, at her, at the sun, at Lord Uyane.

"I don't envy you, son." Jazuun braced a hand on Meoraq's shoulder and eased himself down with a grimace and a curse. Then he leaned back, rubbing at his knee and watching the few clouds drift in the wind. "But it isn't really you they care about. Oh, you'll go home with the kind of fame fools dream of and twenty years from now, your sprat will be taking six breaths and counting them slow every time some piss-licking gatekeeper holds him out in the rain to say, 'Uyane? A son of *Meoraq*?'"

Meoraq coughed out a laugh and clapped a hand to the end of his snout, rubbing hard.

"But that's his problem," Jazuun finished. "All you have to do tonight is tell them what happened in Xi'Matezh. Let them decide what it means."

Gentle words. They pierced him like a sword, pierced and twisted.

Meoraq shut his eyes against the sun and let his head drop. Lord Uyane let him be. Perhaps he thought he was praying. He wasn't. He was trying to think, just think, and the thought that kept coming back to him was that of Lashraq, no Prophet but only a man, who had nevertheless raised Sheul's lamp for the whole world to see, and of Master Tsazr, who had once told his awe-struck brunt how he had passed the doors at the holiest shrine the world ever knew and heard the voice of God and how Meoraq had judged him honest.

He gave himself a slow-count of six, this time with faces to put to the names he had chanted since boyhood, and when he was done, when he was decided, for good or evil and for all time, he raised his head and said, "I stood before the doors in Xi'Matezh and Sheul our Father brought me in. He spoke to me."

Amber reached up and stroked the back of her hand across his brow. He closed his eyes and felt her warmth, together with the warmth of the true sun.

"His words were not a comfort," Meoraq said. He caught her hand, pressed it over his eyes and kept it there until he knew he would not show tears, then released her and stared boldly into the face of Lord Uyane Jazuun. "How do you judge me?"

Jazuun held his gaze a long, long time before it finally wavered. He looked at Amber, then at the sky and the other braziers lighting along the rooftop and finally back at Meoraq. He frowned. "Truth."

"Truth," Meoraq echoed. He nodded—a human gesture—and rubbed at his snout some more. "The Word which was given to Lashraq was for an age which has ended. Some things...must change. We must learn to judge with wisdom and not with blades. We have become too eager to see Gann's taint where there is none. We must learn to show mercy. We must try to forgive."

Jazuun breathed in deep and let it out slow, looking out over the city as if all the sins and wisdoms of its uncounted masses could be seen and weighed in a glance. "You have a great deal of faith in men," he said at last.

"More than I had at the start of this journey, but it is Sheul whose faith in men burns brightest. We believe that only He can save us. He believes that we can save ourselves."

"And do you?"

Meoraq watched the clouds drift.

"I don't know," he said at last. "But I hope so."

Jazuun grunted and labored himself back onto his feet. "I'll start arranging audiences, I suppose. I'll hold as many of them off as long as I can, but you'll be seeing the first of them tonight, that's as good as a promise, and you may never see the last."

"I mark. You may as well begin with the exarch I had you confine for me," Meoraq added. "He and I have unfinished business."

Jazuun acknowledged this and retreated, leaving them alone together on the rooftop.

"What are you going to do to him?" Amber asked.

"I'm going to demand my oaths of office," he replied distractedly, still gazing at the sky. "And I'll probably make him my personal scribe for all my future dealings with the Oracles, at least until I've finished rewriting the Word, which should keep me occupied while I finish coughing out my wetlung and you and Uyane's wife have more gowning parties."

She bore up under that news well. "And then?"

"Then we go home. Where we would have gone even if the doors had opened on God Himself...or if they had never opened at all. We will go home. With God's..." He trailed off, waiting to feel that hollow loss and feeling instead the sun's warmth on his face and Amber's hand twining with his. "With God's favor and fair weather, we will be in Xeqor before the hottest days of the season come."

"Are you sure that's what you want to do?"

"Yes," he said. "Truth, all the reasons I had for coming here were answered long before now. I know I could stay here if I asked and I know the Oracles will probably push for it, but I want to go home. I want to see my child born behind the walls where I was born. I want to see my wife lying in my bed. I want to see my brothers again, even if it means I have to fight them a few times first. I want to go *home*, Amber, and I want to stay home when I get there."

She leaned against his side in sympathy, then startled and gave him a sharp, wondering stare.

He noticed and shrugged his spines. "If there is no God, it doesn't matter. If there is, surely He would want me to call my wife by her beautiful name. Amber." He pinched her chin and leaned in to nuzzle at her. "My Amber. Come home with me."

She cupped his face and kissed him back. "You know I will."

"Do I?"

"Meoraq, if there had been a starship waiting there all fueled up and freshly-waxed just the way Scott wanted, I'd still be going home with you. Didn't you know that by now?"

"Yes," he said and nipped at her shoulder. "But I like to hear you say it."

She stood up, hugging herself as she watched the sun sink over the mountains, setting the sky around it on fire. The first timekeepers began to ring the bells of tenth-hour and the rest quickly joined in. Kitchen smells began to ride the wisps of smoke leaking from the wind-ways. Somewhere on a neighboring section of the roof, music began to play: a celebration of life, a song of praise before God. "I really am sorry about your little knives," Amber said.

"Eh, you saved me, didn't you? Besides—" He patted her braid on his arm. "—I still have this to wear. And I have your cup."

"And your tea box."

"Then life is good. Help me."

She took his arm and together they managed to get him on his feet. He took a moment to adjust to his weight and the way the world wanted to pull at it and then just looked at her.

"Life is good," he said again, not without some weary surprise. "Isn't it?"

She thought it over, her soft brow furrowed, frowning. "Yeah," she said at last, and even huffed out a little laughter. "Yeah, I really think it is."

He put out his hand. She took it and together, they left the roof. The sun slipped away, but the clouds kept burning, outlined in shocking shades of pink and blue. The clanging bells died and the music played on. The last hour of Gann ended, the hour of Uyane began, and in the east, the first star of evening came out.

THE END

Also by R. LEE SMITH:

Heat

The Lords of Arcadia Series:
The Care and Feeding of Griffins
The Wizard in the Woods
The Roads of Taryn MacTavish
The Army of Mab

Olivia

The Scholomance

Cottonwood

Keep reading for a sneak peek of R. Lee Smith's next book

LAND OF THE BEAUTIFUL DEAD

CHAPTER ONE

The ferryman had six more fares in the back of his van and a long way yet to drive, so he didn't stop at town. He just rolled up to the docking gate, opened up the hatch and told her to get out.

Lan got out, moving carefully along the van's armored roof and trying not to look at the Eaters clambering below her. They hadn't seen many on the drive, but there were always Eaters at the towns and this one was pretty big, as towns went these days.

There were kids up on the wall, taking shots at Eaters and smoking. They had bows and buckets of smouldering pitch beside them, but it had rained most of the morning and the dead were too wet to burn, so they were using guns instead, showing off the wealth of a town that could afford to waste bullets on Eaters. When they saw her, one of the kids dropped a ladder and steadied it for her while another jotted down the name painted on the side of the ferry beneath the picture of the red-haired siren with her sword raised high over a heap of decapitated corpses. *The Boudicca*, it said, which Lan only knew because the ferryman had bragged it up all the way from Morrow-up-Marsh where he'd taken her on.

"Bloody Irish," said the kid, now turning to her, tapping his stub of a pencil so she'd notice him writing and be impressed. "Welcome to New Aylesbury. What do you want?"

"Just passing."

"Well, first night's free if it's just you, but it'll be a 'slip a night for a longer stay, plus the cost of the bed. If you're set on paying for a bed," he added. He didn't look at her when he said it, but she could feel the unspoken invitation hovering between them.

Lan said, "I'm just passing," again and left it at that. She had no coin, but she had plenty of barter in her rucksack and in any case, he was too young for her. A girl on her own couldn't afford many scruples, but Lan was not going to be some wall-rat's first brag just for the price of a bed in some mudlump of a town.

If the kid was disappointed, it didn't show. He just moved on to the next question. "Where from?"

"Norwood."

He looked up from his book, smiling beneath puzzled eyes. "Where's that?"

"Near Lancaster." She shrugged. "Nearish."

"And you?"

"Lan."

The kid rolled his eyes and wrote it down. "Yeah, okay, *Lan* from *Lan*caster."

"Lan," said Lan in a soft, stony voice. Her mother's voice. "From Norwood."

"Whatever you say," said the kid, not believing her and not caring if she knew it. He made a point of drawing a line through the letters in his book and writing new ones in. This done, he nodded to his friend, who in turn signaled the ferryman below. The kids pulled the ladder up as the ferry drove away, bumping over Eaters and leaving smears of old blood and rotting flesh in its wake. "So, Lan from Norwood," said the kid, putting his book and pencil away. "What can we do for you?"

"I need another ferry. They come through regular?"

"Yeah, we got a few in, although they're not leaving until morning. Hey, Jakes!" he called, leaning out from the docking tower. "Got a fare for ya!" He pointed Lan toward one of the kids looking curiously up from a corral of armored ferry-vans and went back to the wall, leaving her to climb down alone. The kids all had vans with pictures of scantily-clad ladies on the side, either posed to do in an Eater or just posed.

The one with the kid called Jakes working on it had the stamps of a dozen towns or more painted on the side, underneath the naked lady hacking open Eaters with the machetes she carried in each dainty hand.

"This here's Big Bertha," the kid said proudly, wiping a greasy hand on his shirt so she could shake it. "Fastest, meanest bitch on four wheels. Where bound, luv?"

She told him.

He laughed. All the ferrymen laughed. "Not in my ferry. This may not be much of a world, but I'm not leaving it that way."

"I pay good."

"You could pay in clean cunny and pure meth, but you'll still be paying someone else."

She didn't argue with him. There wouldn't be any more ferries this late, so instead she asked him the way to the hostel.

Like all hostels these days, it did double duty as the prison and as the emergency shelter, should the town walls ever fall. Lan took her key and locked herself in the first available cell. A guard came by every so often with boiled water; everything else had a price (although the currency was negotiable, he said, reaching through the bars to stroke at her arm). She had food in her rucksack, but she didn't want anyone in this strange town to know she had it. She could have used a bath, but knew she'd be watched while she took one. All Lan wanted was to sleep until the next ferryman came through, but she didn't believe hers was the only key to this cell, so she sat on the lumpy mattress that was her bed and looked out the narrow window at the unnatural mess that was the only sky Lan had ever known. Although no one could seem to agree on exactly how long it had been since Azrael's ascension, Lan had never known any world but this one. Her mother used to say she remembered, but she'd been a kid—six or seven or maybe only five—when Azrael came.

No one knew who Azrael was or even what. Demon was the popular theory. Azrael never denied it. Neither did he deny sorcerer, Satan, alien, or mutated man. But whatever else he was, Lan's mother would say, he was Death. As the master of that domain, he had torn his first companions from their rightful rest and set them at his side under new names, without memory, without humanity. Perhaps he expected Mankind to meekly surrender their world to him, to accept his rule without question and worship him without resentment.

"We fought back," Lan's mother would always say, should this part of the story come around. 'We,' she said, and she said it with pride, she who had been that child of maybe seven, maybe only five. "He raised his so-called children and before the sun had set, we killed them again. Most of them."

Lan knew how that had gone. Norwood's sheriff had saved pictures, but even if she hadn't, plenty of people still talked about it, whether or not they were old enough to remember. They were proud of it, proud of the troops who had broken down the doors of Azrael's first home, slaughtering the newly-raised corpses where they stood unresisting, until Azrael fell on them. Before the sun had set, Lan's mother would say, and before that same sun had risen again, Azrael and his three remaining Children had fled, but not far. He was back soon enough, bringing with him the fires and the poison rain and the skies that were still lit up with that sick color that had no earthly name. All of that, yes, and the Eaters.

There had been other names for them in the beginning, back when people thought they knew what the Eaters were, back when people thought they could be stopped with something as simple as a bullet to the brain. No. This was Azrael's world and nothing died save by his word of release. You could break them, burn them, or just wait them out until they had rotted away to bones and could no longer come after you, but even then, whatever remained of them still retained some kind of horrible life. Lan could remember her mother pulling the teeth from a charred skull after a neighbor's death and showing them to her, how the teeth had trembled in her mother's hand, trying to come together and bite. There was no hope then, only the diminishing living, the growing ranks of the dead, and less and less unpoisoned land to share between them.

Surrender was inevitable, no matter how bitterly Lan's mother spoke of it now, but surrender had not ended the war. Azrael had accepted the leaders of that broken world for his unending retribution, but he did not forgive the people who gave them up. In the years since his ascension, Azrael had harrowed his great army to a whisper of its former magnitude, but even a handful of Revenants was enough to wipe out whole villages when all they had to do was break down one wall, let the Eaters in, and wait. Everything else they did—the burning, the dismemberments, the impaling poles—served purely as a warning of the fate that awaited all those who took such unwise pride in defiance.

And really, what did Azrael have to fear from them? The world which had once groaned under Man's weight was quiet now. Cities made to harbor millions had been empty for decades, fallen in and grown over. The last dams had long since burst, the last bridges collapsed. Deer grazed on the old roads, Revenants patrolled the new ones, and folk mostly stayed home these days. So long as they did, Azrael seemed content to tolerate the living even here, provided they stayed well away from his city, his Haven, the land of the beautiful dead.

She was close now, so close. This fool's journey, begun when Lan walked away from her mother's smoky pyre two months ago, was now only a day from over, if only she could find someone to finish it for her.

Lan dragged her eyes open without any conscious memory of closing them. She was falling asleep and sleep was never safe in a strange town. She got up and dragged her mattress over to the cell door, propping it against the sliding panel so that she could not help but be jostled awake should someone try to come in with her in the night. Then she lay down, pillowing her head on her lumpy, uncomfortable rucksack, and went to sleep.

Made in the USA
Middletown, DE
09 December 2019

80306928R00384